70 A.D.

WARS OF THE JEWS SERIES

70 A.D.

A WAR OF THE JEWS

PETER J. FAST

authorHOUSE®

AuthorHouse™
1663 Liberty Drive
Bloomington, IN 47403
www.authorhouse.com
Phone: 1 (800) 839-8640

Cover, spine, and back illustration by Jonathan Fast
Cover, spine, and back design by Jonathan Fast
Photo of coin used with permission by Gemini Auctions and www.wildwinds.com

Map illustrations by Peter J. Fast
Map graphic design by Jeannette Van Der Merwe

This book is based on a factual historical account retold by the author with an interwoven, fictional, element. The names, characters, and incidents portrayed in it, while many are fiction, remain widely based on historical places, geographical locations, languages, customs, military methods, and religious expression. However, much of the book remains as an element of fiction which is the work of the author's imagination based on extensive research.

Visit author's website: www.peterjfast.com

Published by AuthorHouse   01/12/2015

ISBN: 978-1-4772-6585-7 (sc)
ISBN: 978-1-4772-6584-0 (hc)
ISBN: 978-1-4772-6586-4 (e)

Library of Congress Control Number: 2012920731

To my wife, Deanna Renae. You have always inspired me to reach the heights of heaven with my writing. I love you.

To my loving parents, James and Elizabeth, and my Nana, Ruth.
Your steadfast encouragement and support has been the pinnacle of my writing.

Acknowledgments

I would like to start by saying that this work, which has taken over four years of intense research and writing, would not have been possible without my wife, Deanna. I want to thank her for spending many hours brainstorming with me, hearing my thoughts, reading and editing my work, and keeping the creative juices churning. It has meant the world to me to see her steadfast dedication and encouragement in journeying with me to see this book published. I love you with all my heart.

I also want to deeply thank my parents, James and Elizabeth, for inspiring me to pursue writing, to always imagine and create new worlds, and for instilling in me a love for reading, literature, and history. They have walked with me through these years, read my drafts, and sent their love to me, even across to the other side of the world. I am also honoured to extend my love and thanks to my in-laws, Harvey and Gail, for their place in my heart through these years of marriage to their daughter. They have always given encouragement to publish my works and have paid an attentive ear to my ideas, even at times if those ideas seemed off the wall.

It is also a great honour to extend my love and praise to my Nana, Ruth, who has inspired me to be a writer and who read portions of my writings. Even in times where my writing was still developing and held the tone of inexperience, she would always encourage and push me to continue and not give up. She will always have a special place in my heart.

I want to thank those who have acted as readers, proofers, and individuals who have walked with me through the inspirations, early writings, drafts, and changes. I want to thank my "Israeli parents," Barry and Beth, for opening their door to Deanna and I, and loving us as parents would while living overseas. They have grappled with this book and their advice, comments, praises, and criticism will always be important to me. I also thank my friends: Greg, Theuno, and Taryn for the time they set aside to read portions of the book and the advice they offered. In this spirit, I also thank my friend Andrew for the pleasure he brings me through our Writers Guild, and for the inspiration he gives me as a fellow artist.

In closing, my sincere gratitude goes out to two individuals who have worked hard in aspects with the final product of this novel. The time my brother, Jonathan, put into designing the book cover and spine was a delight. His creative eye and mind was an enormous aid in this trek, and it was a pleasure to bounce ideas off of him which led to the creation of art that is the door to this novel. The second person is Jeannette, whose talent for graphic design and her experience has helped me publish the four maps in this book and to give the professional touch they needed to stand by themselves. I thank you both.

- Peter J. Fast
December 2012

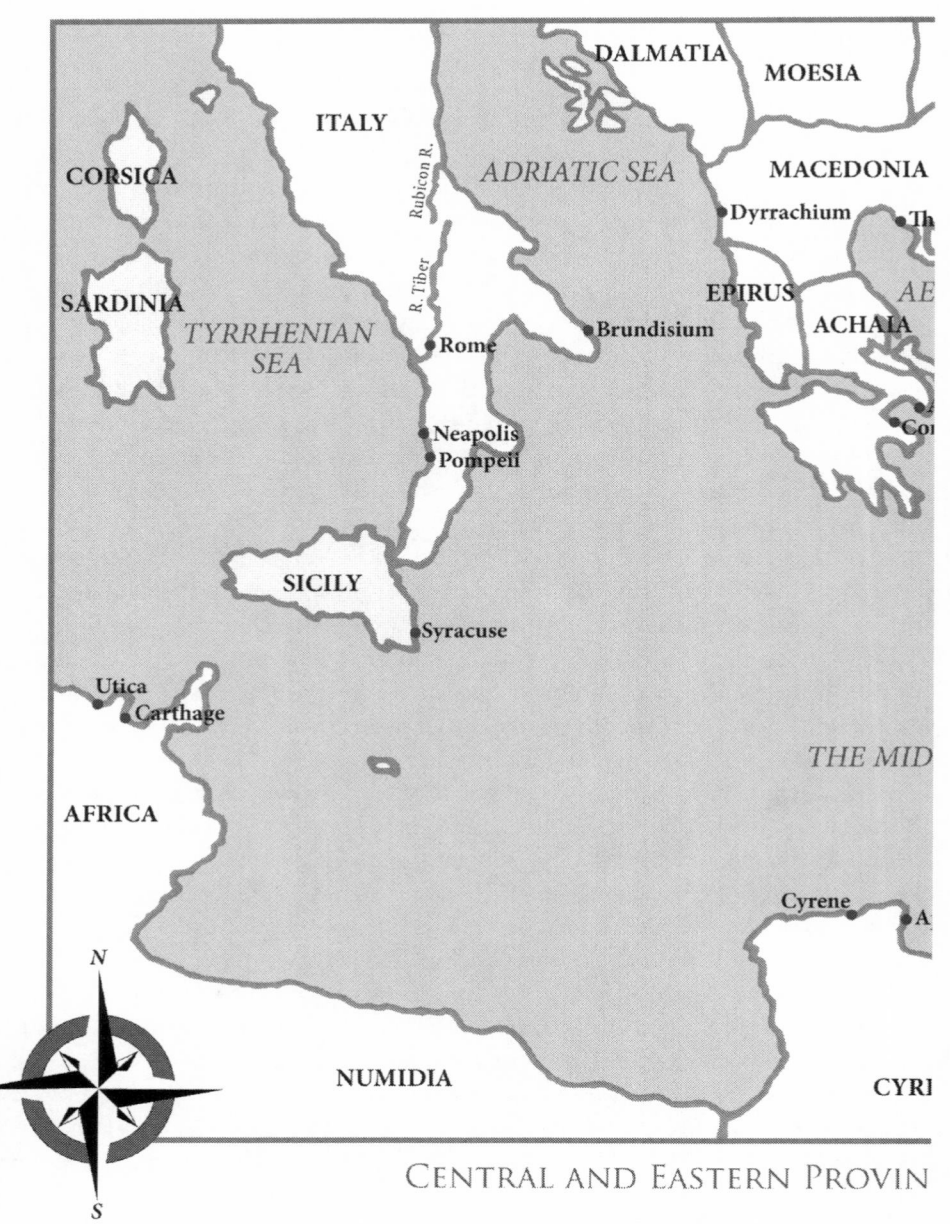

CENTRAL AND EASTERN PROVIN

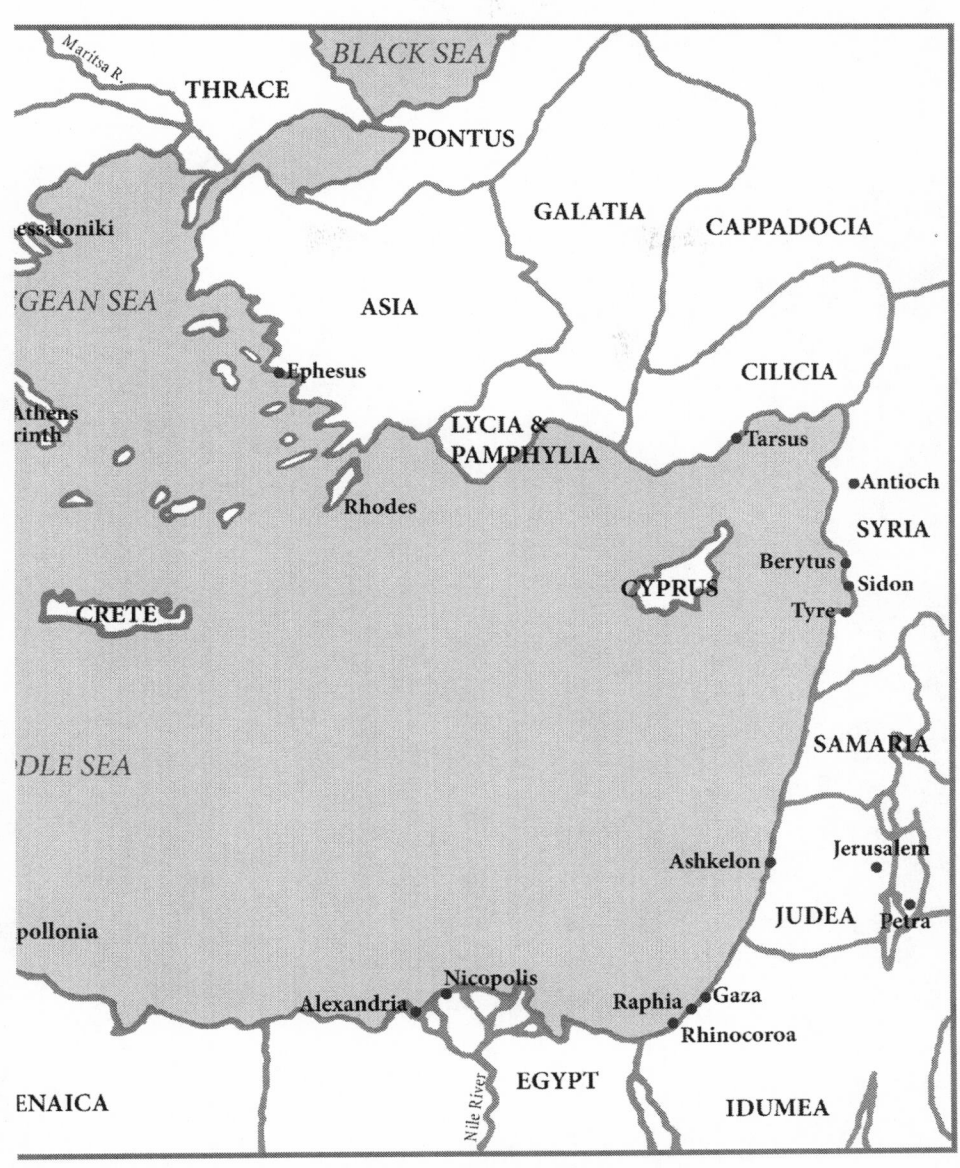

Maritsa R.

THRACE

BLACK SEA

PONTUS

GALATIA

CAPPADOCIA

essaloniki

'GEAN SEA

ASIA

•Ephesus

CILICIA

thens
rinth

LYCIA &
PAMPHYLIA

•Tarsus

•Antioch

SYRIA

Rhodes

CYPRUS

Berytus •
•Sidon

CRETE

Tyre •

DLE SEA

SAMARIA

Ashkelon •

•Jerusalem

pollonia

JUDEA

•Petra

Nicopolis

Alexandria •

Raphia • •Gaza

Rhinocoroa

ENAICA

Nile River

EGYPT

IDUMEA

CES OF THE ROMAN EMPIRE 69 A.D.

ROMAN JUDEA AND SURROUNDING PROVINCES, 69 A.D.

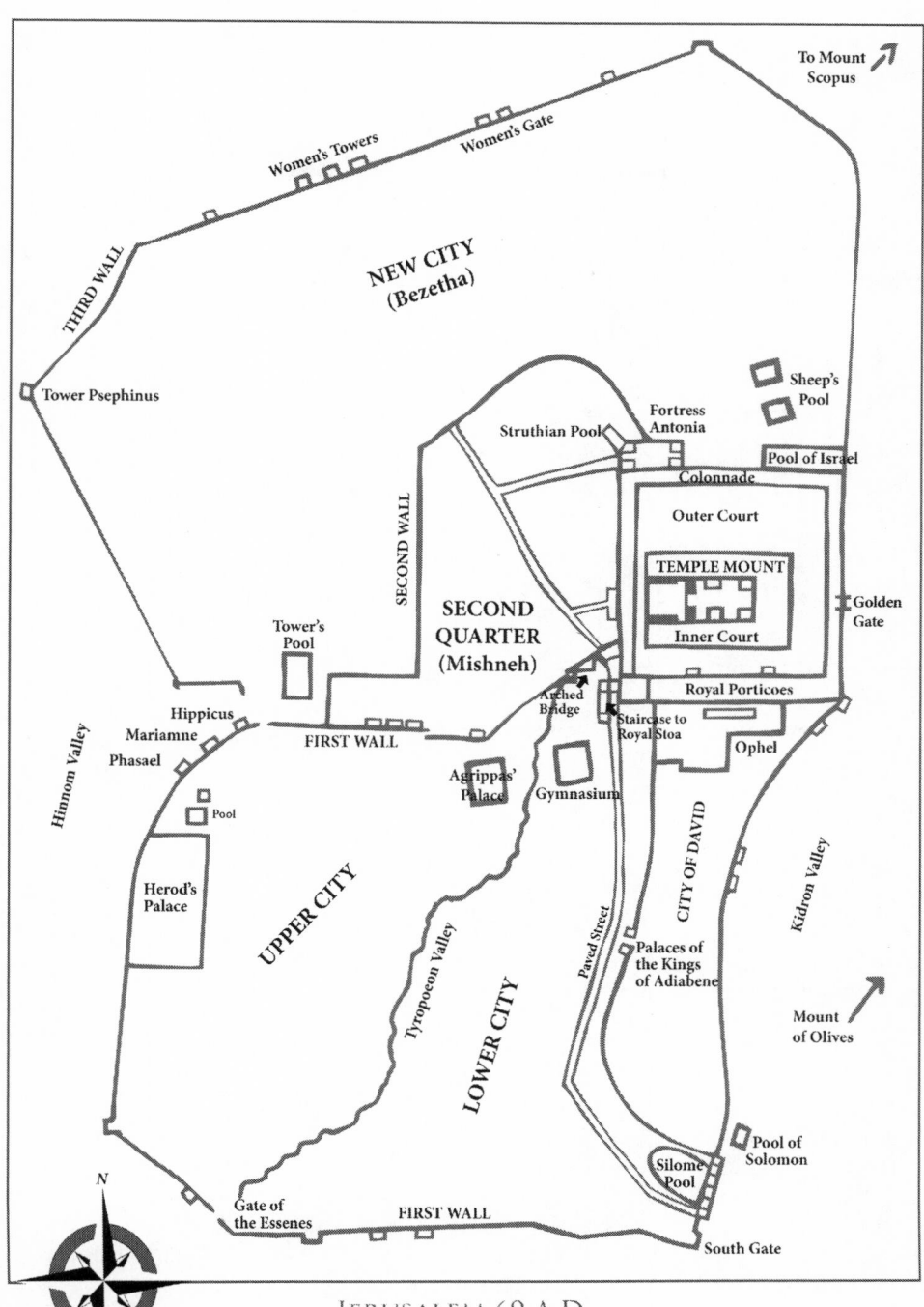

JERUSALEM 69 A.D.

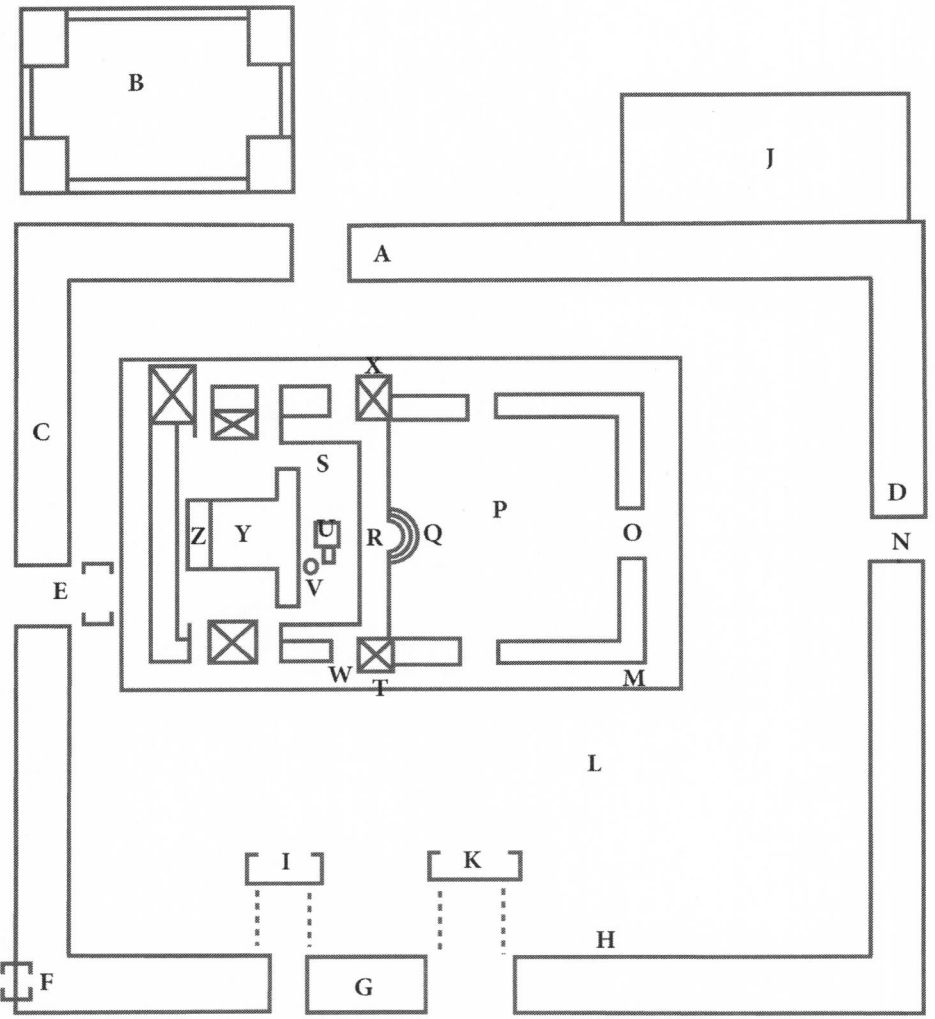

A. Northern Colonnades
B. Fortress Antonia
C. West Colonnades
D. Solomon's Colonnades
E. Kiponus' Gate
F. Staircase of Royal Stoa
G. Royal Stoa
H. Southern Porticoes
I. Hulda Gates

J. Israel Pool
K. Triple Gates
L. Outer Court
M. Balustrade
N. Golden Gate
O. Eastern Gate
P. Court of the Women
Q. Nicanor Gate
R. Court of the Israelites

S. Court of the Priests
T. Chamber of Hewn Stone
U. Burnt Altar
V. Laver
W. Water Gate
X. Gate of the Flame Singers
Y. Temple Sanctuary
Z. Holy of Holies

"Silent enim leges inter arma"
"Laws are silent in times of war"
~ Marcus Tullius Cicero, 106-43 B.C. ~

"And the fourth kingdom shall be as strong as iron,
inasmuch as iron breaks in pieces and shatters everything;
and like iron that crushes, that kingdom will break in pieces
and crush all the others."
~The Book of Daniel 2:40 ~

PROLOGUE

May 16th, 66AD / 6th of Sivan, 3826
Roman Province of Judea
Jerusalem

The Roman *Procurator* stood by his chair staring at the anxious faces before him. Complete control lined the edges of his lips and eyes, yet stirring rage burned within. "Jewish whores," he whispered under his breath as he felt a trickle of sweat run down his neck. He glanced at the long silk curtains that swayed gently from the breeze which struggled to cool down the palace. He had taken sanctuary the previous day after he had unleashed a small detachment of his troops to pillage the upper city of Jerusalem. It had all been the fault of pompous priests and royal nobodies, thinking they knew best.

Gessius Florus turned slowly and walked around his chair, his hands clasped behind him in complete confidence with a smug, comical expression upon his face. He could have heard a pin drop upon the stone floor due to the nervous silence of the Sanhedrin, who quaked before the power and intimidation his presence commanded. There was nothing to debate. Florus knew they hated him, but he grinned because he hated them more.

He glanced at them swiftly to see their reaction and many of the Jewish elite shifted uneasily, unbeknownst of what was coming their way. Florus stopped in front of his chair, straightened his purple sash edged in gold, then slowly sat down, attempting neither to disrupt his toga or the sash. He mumbled to a slave nearby to fetch him wine and then slid his hands down the arm rests. Florus glanced for a brief moment at his filed finger nails, inspecting the work of the groomer and then exhaled loudly as if bored. Straightening one of the many jeweled rings upon his plump fingers, he began to drum the ivory gilded edges of the chair.

The slave was nervous as she brought a copper jug towards her master. A silver goblet was passed to Florus, who waited impatiently as it was filled with wine. Without even looking at the slave, Florus motioned her away with a flick of his hand. He proceeded to drink, meanwhile eyeing the members of the Sanhedrin with a piercing gaze. Once he finished his drink, he dropped the goblet upon the ground as if it were a worthless clay vessel and sneered through clenched teeth. "Is anyone... going to say... a damn thing?"

Anyone with a sense of observation could have seen all the members of the Jewish elite swallow nervously as if large rocks had been lodged in their throats. A second of hesitation crept by and slowly a man stepped out nodding towards Florus. "I am Ananus ben Ananus, High Priest of Jerusalem, my Procurator, and the voice of this council." Florus nodded and rolled his eyes, so Ananus continued, "We ask as a council, what is it that the procurator wants to know having already sacked the upper city before a decision or court ruling was made?"

Florus exploded to his feet shouting with anger, "You dare play stupid with me, you sack of swine, you holy, fringed, catamite, bastard!" Two guards behind Florus half drew their *gladii* as the Procurator seethed. "You all know what I want! The names are what I want! Nobody makes a fool of me in my own city! You remember Caesarea, you impotent cow! I am Procurator of Rome and I serve the ruler of the world. I pray by the powers of Jupiter that I will get what I want!" His chest heaved up and down beneath his breastplate, richly decorated in wreaths and faces of gods. He stared around the room wild-eyed daring anyone to oppose him.

The problem had arisen weeks earlier when Florus had demanded seventeen talents of gold from the Temple treasury, coining the phrase sent by the envoys, "for Caesars needs." However, when he had arrived to collect the money, Jewish youths had openly mocked him with bowls of collected pennies from the citizens throughout the city of Jerusalem. Florus had been so insulted by this display that he had set loose his cavalry on the Upper City to profit from whatever they could lay their hands on. A high number of crucifixions had decorated the streets outside the city as Florus had extended his brutal hand to include men of equestrian rank to suffer upon the crosses as an example. Florus had watched them nailed in contorted positions, with spikes driven through arms and feet, screaming terribly. After awhile of amusement at the spectacle, he had finally sought refuge in the royal palace where he had summoned the Sanhedrin.

Ananus collected himself from the sudden outburst of this madman. *Convincingly similar to Nero*, Ananus thought, staying silent for a moment longer as he sought a strategy in which to try and reason. It was more like attempting to befriend a stone then trying to exchange a logical conversation with this man who had turned an entire country against him. Yet, Ananus still feared Florus for he knew the man's unpredictable temper and had witnessed the extent of his brutality.

Ananus found his right hand feeling for the fringes of his robe as he silently prayed for the right words, desiring to avoid another disaster. When he found his voice he said, "Your excellency, we as a council do not pretend that what happened wasn't wrong. The offenders were merely a group of hotheaded youths, young and stupid for trying to lash out at you in petty ways. But we have consulted many and as a council, we also agree that what happened was a terrible mark upon us as the nations Jewish representatives to Roman rule. We wish you to know that we are in your debt and we gravely apologize for everything that has occurred."

Ananus paused, watching Florus slowly sit back down with a dark look cast upon his tense face. Ananus swallowed. "We ask for the sake of our nation and for the safety of the city, for both inhabitants and your troops, to forgive the guilty few rather than seek them out and punish a large number of innocent people." Ananus took a step back and it was as if time ceased to exist as the room drew completely silent.

Florus suddenly grinned and shook his head. He raised his hand and beckoned a hard looking centurion over to him. The soldier halted abruptly before Florus' judgment seat and saluted as he struck his leather breastplate. "Capito, they do not wish to give me the names of the guilty." Florus tapped the edges of his fingers together in a pondering motion and slowly stood. "Listen to my judgment. If you will not tell me the names of the guilty, then all are guilty." Florus nodded to Capito and the centurion grinned and quickly exited the hall.

Ananus' eyes grew wide and he outstretched his arms in a pleading gesture, calling out, "What shall his excellency do? Use violence? We must talk, we must…"

"Silence yourself, Ananus, or I will nail you to a cross! You've seen me do it before. Equestrian, patrician, you will all face the same fate. You all scream the same way, you virgin boys! First you piss yourself then you beg for your mothers! Take your circumcised foulness out from here or you will all die! Guards!" Florus shouted, turning as he addressed a dozen legionaries. "Escort these priests out of here now. If they resist, kill them all." Florus faced the shocked, grieving council and smiled bowing. "For all are guilty."

* * *

"Judah, Judah, you are as strong as ever." Miriam smiled teasingly at her betrothed as he loaded three grain bags into a small cart hitched to a whining donkey. Judah grinned proudly under the weight of the sack as he admired his future bride.

Her deep blue linen garment accented her petite frame as her auburn curls flowed down her back with a scent of jasmine. Miriam had soft olive skin and defined features. She was the epitome of beauty. Despite glances from men and the offers of marriage dowries, she had chosen Judah, and for that he would love her endlessly.

"You are so strong," she said, mimicking him. "Your strength, no doubt, is why my *abba* accepted your dowry."

"I might just have to rethink whether I am doing the right thing, girl." Judah heaved the last sack onto the cart and wiped his hands upon his cloak. The sun was hot, but that never failed to empty the upper market and chase people into the shade. This was life in Jerusalem and everyone was a part of it, rich or poor. "Where are *Abba* and *Ima*?"

"Your parents? Last I saw them they were arguing over the price for some hens." Miriam glanced around the bustle of people, jumped down from the edge of the cart, and playfully slapped the donkey's backside. "They must have come into some money, perhaps your Abba is an aristocrat now."

"Always playing games." Judah grinned as Miriam laughed aloud.

Judah approached the donkey and checked the strength of the harness. "We must go now."

"And your parents?" Miriam asked shielding her eyes from the burning sun.

Judah smiled. "They will meet us along the way. We move slower than them with this." He gestured to the cart and donkey and stooped to grab the lead rope from the drooping animal's head.

Suddenly, abnormal shouting arose from the vendors and booths filling the market. Judah squinted and shifted his head-covering to the side as he tried to find out what was going on. He noticed a number of men and women who held baskets, staring towards one of the wider streets that converged on the marketplace. A man tugging on the reins of a camel was yelled at to move his beast and that only encouraged the angry driver to shout profanities and tug on the rope harder as the camel brayed loudly.

"Miriam, where are you?" Judah said to himself without turning to find her.

Miriam ignored Judah, moving between a woman and child, and climbed upon a small fountain nearby to gaze over the throng. She felt a strange sensation come over the market as the shouting continued with vendors talking fast and moving animated hands in the direction of the street. "Judah, what is happening?" she asked bleakly, her attention fixed on the stirring commotion.

"Romans!" someone shouted in a panic. "They're coming! Florus has sent them on us!" A man desperately pushed through the crowd which was beginning to take notice of him. "God, stop them!" The man's footing gave way and he slipped on the slick stones. A robed Pharisee tried to help the man and that was when the women began screaming.

The first sign of the legionaries was a bright splash of blood that erupted from a man's throat. Centurion Capito's blade had easily cut through cloth and flesh, the steel severing the man's spine. Capito urged his men on as they poured from the mouth of the street charging into the market. They gave a shout of triumph and the killing began as they used their *scuta* to knock people over and stab them with their short swords.

Judah instantly reacted shouting Miriam's name as he swung around, expecting her to be standing behind him. His eyes darted back and forth desperately as suddenly everyone in the market begin stampeding in all directions trying to escape the thirsty blades of the legionaries. "Miriam!" Judah bellowed as the legionaries threw their *pila* into women, men, and children in a horrific display of barbarity to those trying to escape the onslaught.

Near the wall of shields that closed in on the tightly packed people, the ground was slick with sheets of blood. The legionaries lunged, thrusting their blades into people's chests and backs as they attempted to flee. Blood sprayed upon scaled armour and washed upon shields. Those nearest to the slaughter slipped on the smeared crimson stones and struggled for their lives as blades came down upon them dealing death with precise blows. This was the wrath of Rome the Jews had known all too well.

"Kill them all and take what you want!" Capito thundered, hacking off a limb from a screaming boy. "No mercy, Florus' orders!" Capito waved his men forward and stepped over the body of a woman outstretched and reaching for her mutilated baby. A soldier knelt next to the dead woman, rummaging through her clothing and Capito grabbed the man by his plated armour and shoved him along. "Not until all the whores are dead!"

Judah spotted Miriam on the edge of the fountain transfixed with shock. Expressions of terror filled the eyes of everyone. Judah watched helplessly as a few people fell, only to be trampled to death by the panic stricken people. "I'll come to you!" Judah shouted, fighting his way through the surging mob.

Judah pushed a man aside and squeezed between a small boy and a woman who ran past him. "Out of my way!" he roared. Suddenly a warm spray struck his face, momentarily blinding him as he stumbled sideways. He wiped his hands across his face, and for a moment his mind could not interpret why they were red. He took the edge of his garment and buried his face in it and when he examined the cloth it was dark crimson. He turned to a scream and saw a Pharisee nearly get cleaved in two as he fell to the weight of sword blades cutting into him. Two legionaries withdrew their dripping blades, stared wild-eyed at Judah, and then charged him.

Judah ducked the swift thrust of the lead Roman's blade as it seared past his face. Judah was unarmed, and so he lunged forward with a thunderous shout using his weight as a weapon. Judah's strong frame crashed into the chest of the legionary and the man grunted with the impact as he pitched backward. With lightening hands, Judah snatched the soldier's dagger and plunged it into the neck of the other legionary.

The blade easily pierced the soldier's throat, underneath the cheek plates of his helmet and the man made a gurgling noise. As Judah fell with the dying soldier, suddenly more civilians pushed past him, followed by the Romans. Judah rolled off the dead man he had killed expecting to defend himself and then realized there was nobody immediately around him. A number of merchant booths belched black smoke as they burned. The ground was a mass graveyard of bodies. Judah tried to stand but slipped on the blood that covered the stones. He quickly crawled over the bodies until he made it to the fountain and then sat for a moment recovering his wits.

The air reeked of blood, urine, and human excrement; bodies everywhere lay in contorted positions along with limbs and entrails. Judah tried to stand, but his knees trembled and so he used the stone of the fountain for support. He saw his grain cart overturned and the donkey lying dead next to it. Nothing moved in the marketplace except for the legionaries who were now pillaging through bodies and houses at the far end of the market. For the time they did not know he was there, but Judah knew they would find him soon enough.

He turned and stared into the fountain, all care in the world fleeing from his presence. Judah gazed into the dark red water at the bodies, some lying face down and pushed towards the bottom while others floated peacefully as if asleep. One body in particular mattered more than all the rest and that was a woman pierced through the back with a spear. Judah leaned over, gripped Miriam by the foot, and slowly pulled her towards the edge. Gently, with a delicate touch, as if she were merely sleeping, he rolled the body over so he could look into her face. Her eyes were tightly shut and although a line of blood ran from her parted lips, she otherwise looked at peace. The impact of the spear had sent her crashing into the water and had likely punched a deep hole through her lung. Judah touched her face and sniffed, stiffening his upper lip. Her slender body was under his right arm and his left hand held her head out of the water as her long brown hair hung wet and heavy. She still smelled of the perfume she always loved to wear, a scent which he would sometimes dream of lying beside. Now she was dead and everything had changed.

He quickly looked around the vacant marketplace, emptied of all living things apart from the Romans who seemed to be drinking themselves drunk, despite a few who stood casually around scanning the area. One of them noticed him and spoke something to a Centurion who turned and gazed at Judah. Judah shuddered as he let Miriam slip back into the pool.

Capito wanted this land cleansed of filth, which he naturally interpreted as the Jews. He had no real reason to hate them, but all his time around Gessius Florus had influenced him so. Besides, he could always count on the plunder and women which came flooding his way as a result of following Florus. Capito knew not all Romans felt this way. He knew a number of soldiers who would rather live in peace with the Jews than fight them, which is why he had not called on those soldiers to carry out this service for Florus. However, Capito believed it was easier to kill Jews then to live with them and so he did what he did with justification and a twisted conviction.

However, this Jew now seemed to challenge him from across the marketplace which had become vacant of living souls. *Defiance is their only weapon*, Capito thought to himself. *Yet, should I kill this one?* Capito grinned at the man and muttered to the legionary who had pointed the Jew out, "Better let this one live to stir up their anger against us. Florus seems to want them to rebel against Rome, that way we can clean this place out. I don't know what the procurator's issue with them is, but better for us."

"You mean the Temple riches and the plunder?" the soldier asked, leaning on his bloodied spear.

"And reward." Capito turned to the man. "When we carve up this province and kill them, there will be plenty of land for us all. Besides, I am mustering out in a few years; I have kind of gotten used to this place. Maybe a nice palace along the northern wall would do me well, or perhaps I'll make the Temple my home and their Holy of

Holies is where I will bed my women." The legionary chuckled. Capito spit on the ground. "Better let this one live."

Judah saw the centurion turn his back to him and he realized they would not come. His mind was numb, and filled with so many confusing thoughts. But one thing remained clear: he now hated Rome more than ever. He wished to see every Roman dead and laying before his feet, starting with the arrogant Gessius Florus and the centurion. Judah turned and made his way to the Roman he had killed. He bent down and picked up the *gladius* lying next to him. It was a simple sword but had a razor-sharp blade. The wood pommel had been oiled and cared for and the steel's edge was finely sharpened. Along with the sword, he removed the dead legionary's belt which contained the scabbard. He slowly sheathed the gladius, taking one last glance at the drunken Romans. Then Judah ben Yosef fled the marketplace, vowing revenge, even if it killed him.

*   *   *

"For who is so worthless or indolent as not to wish to know by what means and under what system of polity the Romans in less than fifty-three years have succeeded in subjecting nearly the whole inhabited world to their sole government — a thing unique in history? Or who again is there so passionately devoted to other spectacles or studies as to regard anything as of greater moment than the acquisition of this knowledge?"

~Polybius, 200-118 B.C. 'The Histories'~

CHAPTER I

5th Day before the Ides of July
Anno Domini 69

"Hail *Imperator*! Hail Imperator!" The thunder of voices rose up in unison from the walled camp causing horses penned inside a corral to toss their heads and back up uneasily. One such horse, a stallion, had heard the shouts of war before. This horse was accustomed to hardened years in the field and the chaos of battle. Standing sixteen hands high with muscular flanks, he had been bred in the hills of Spain to carry the iron fist of Rome to Germania, Britannia, and now the ancient land of the Jews. Adrenalin raced madly through his veins with the image of a solid legionary charge clear within his mind's eye. The wall of red scuta would slam home, as the chopping sound of gladii, biting into flesh, would mix with the din of fighting men. These were common sights and sounds for the stallion, as war was all it had ever known.

The horse snorted loudly and turned around in its pen swishing his black tail at the flies. As his ears twitched, a stable boy grabbed the halter and soothed the stallion by rubbing his forehead and whispering quietly. The war equestrian thumped his hooves upon the earth, breathing heavily and then was calmed by the boy's warm voice as he whispered in Hebrew, "You want to charge into battle, ol' boy? Hey, Prometheus, what do you think?"

The boy glanced around as he listened to the voices which continued shouting beyond the canvas army tents around him. A Roman sentry on patrol slowly walked by with his *scutum* firmly pulled up against his left side; the shield bore golden lightning bolts of the Twelfth Legion which were emblazed upon the stretched linen cover. His pila rested against his scaled armour and his steel helmet concealed much of his face with the cheek guards firmly tied under his whiskery chin. The stable boy watched the guard halt between two tents, slowly turn, and stare at the horse, then at the young, tanned boy.

"Hear that, lad?" The soldier beckoned to the shouting by jerking his head in the general direction. "He's earned it. The old man has earned it. Perhaps we'll see this through and go home." The man looked weary as he slowly turned and trudged on, disappearing behind the tents.

The boy slowly exhaled and stared back at the stallion which had calmed down despite the chanting. "Home? What is home?"

* * *

~ 1 ~

Primus Pilus Centurion Gaius Cornelius Antony led a detail squad past rows of tents towards the stables. Much of the camp had been emptied in great anticipation of Vespasian's speech. They passed a legionary guard standing post, as their hobnailed sandals pounded the earth and shook the metal joints of their bulky chest armour. Gaius, however, did not wear the *lorica segmentata* armour that the regular legionaries wore, and he was thankful for that. Since he was a centurion of senior status, and a veteran of the First Cohort of the Twelfth Legion, he wore a fine, oiled cuirass strapped over his standard Roman tunic.

Covering his cuirass was a leather harness held by large brass rings. It was his harness which supported his decorations, *phalerae*, and torques. These had been awarded to him through the campaigns he had served under Vespasian long before his deployment to the *Fulminata* prior to the outbreak of the Jewish war. After the disastrous defeat of the Twelfth at Jerusalem in the first months of the rebellion, Gaius had been attached to the Fifteenth for a number of years as a centurion with veteran experience.

It had been during this time that he had received another *dona* for organizing a cohort of troops who had been ambushed in the town of Gamla in the Galilee region. They would surely have suffered higher casualties had not Gaius come to their aid by slaying three *Sicarii* which had given enough time for the retreating soldiers to stumble past him. Vespasian had commended him in front of his senior staff, calling Gaius by his clan name, Cornelius. It made the Gaius proud to serve under him, even after he was sent back to Antioch for the rebuilding of the Twelfth to prepare for the final stages of the war. Since popularity of Vespasian had grown with the political rumblings in Rome, the Twelfth had received its marching orders to meet up with the Judean Army and bask in the glory of electing a new emperor.

This was a momentous day and Gaius had been called to run a simple errand which would be the making of a man-now-turned-god in the minds of his troops. Vespasian would sit atop his powerful war horse arrayed in splendour, like the triumph of Gaius Julius Caesar from the Temple of Jupiter, and accept the men's title that they bestowed upon him. And why should he not accept the title Imperator?

The *Prefect* of Egypt, Tiberius Julius Alexander, had hailed Vespasian as Emperor, compelling the legions of Africa to do the same. Gaius Licinius Mucianus as Governor of Syria had also pledged loyalty and a life of service to Vespasian, as would the troops on the Danube as soon as they caught wind of what was happening. Everyone wanted change and the last year had been particularly testing for the empire. It had left everyone speechless and tense at the labour pains of an empire stricken with civil war and reckless murder. All could count the names of the year's emperors upon the fingers of a single hand: Nero, Galba, Otho, and now Vitellius. Yet, the tide would turn to Vespasian, who alone the troops believed could end the inner chaos, restore the empire from the scoundrel Vitellius, and sit proudly upon her throne.

The soldiers knew one or two more battles would be all that it would take to usurp the throne from Vitellius and see him brought low. Yet it was in the omens and oracles of Carmel and Delphi which pointed to the Flavian line and her time to rule. Another rumour had circulated the legions, spoken of by a captured Jewish general, who was considered to be a prophet by many Romans. The man had declared over a year ago that Vespasian would become emperor, and now it looked as if his prophecy would come to pass. Finally, the time had come. With the troops of Judea in support, nobody could stop Vespasian now, for there lay the real power in the emperor of Rome: the flexing of the military arm.

Gaius moved with perfect military parade skills as his hobnailed sandals rapped upon the streets that ran throughout the standard Roman camp. He could not count the amount of times he had supervised setting up or breaking camp as they all seemed to blend together. However, the methodology was all the same and every man knew his part. Whenever a legion first approached the spot to set up camp, there waving in the wind would be the white consular flag dictating to everyone where the camp was to be. Gaius would oversee his *centuria* hard at work as men dispersed to set the defences, erect the blocks of tents and lay the streets.

The troops knew by heart where the quarters of the commander, legionary tribunes, and officers would be. The location of the stables, blacksmith forge, and hospital were always in the same place. The soldiers own personal quarters, shared with eight to ten men from their centuria, were always mapped out in the exact format from their last camp. It was this proficient military system that caused the Romans to rise above everyone else in the world as the single dominant power to reckon with. The Romans were meticulous, efficient, professional and deadly. All this could be observed by the way they applied themselves to the dedication of the campsite.

"There he is." Gaius scowled at the stable boy and exhaled loudly. "Marcus, inform the boy!" Vespasian's war horse snorted and then whinnied with anticipation at the sight of the soldiers standing before him. Gaius glanced casually at the trooper named Marcus as he approached the boy. "I trust this won't take long." Gaius scratched his chin and looked up at the sky.

The sun was at its zenith and it was heating up, yet the sea breeze always seemed to cool the sweat upon his neck, a relief he thanked the gods for. Gaius removed his helmet and one of the soldiers behind him stepped forward and took it. Titus the younger, Vespasian's son and second-in-command of the Judean campaign, had personally called on Gaius to fetch Prometheus and make the horse ready for his father's speech. Carrying the standards of Rome, he would approach the backside of Vespasian's tent so the general could mount his war horse and be presented to his troops who had gathered in the front.

"Do as I say!" Marcus shoved the boy against the horse pen and raised his hand, intending to slap him. "We don't have all day, slave, and I will teach you Roman manners if you do not listen." The boy's eyes were wide with fear and he quickly shook his head indicating he did not understand the soldier. Marcus swiftly swung his hand and struck the boy's face with a loud stinging smack. The slave yelped, flew backwards, and crashed upon the straw-covered ground with a whimper.

"The lad obviously doesn't understand you, Marcus, so help him with saddling Prometheus and he will soon catch on." Gaius sighed, rolling his eyes as Marcus straightened and stared at his officer in frustration at being ordered to do a slave's job. "Hurry it up, Marcus, you fool, or else you will feel the sting of a whip, I promise you."

Marcus snapped out of his temporary stupor, swore quietly to himself, bent over, grabbed the boy by his filthy brown tunic, and hoisted him to his feet. He clutched the sobbing slave's throat and pointed a sharp finger into the boy's face. "Now look what you did, pig shit. Come and help me."

A few of the soldiers behind Gaius chuckled as Marcus and the red-faced slave saddled the stallion, tightened the straps, fixed the bridle, and quickly combed the horse's mane and swishing tail. The reins were made of red-dyed leather and were studded with gold rivets. The saddle's pommel was decorated with ivory and small gems; its quality being the finest in the world. The blanket draped over Prometheus' back was deep purple, trimmed in silver, as Vespasian's family insignia was embroidered upon the rich cloth.

"Let's move. The standards and the eagle should be at Vespasian's quarters where the others are. Marcus, lead the horse and keep a tight formation, men. Let's show the general how professionals do it." Gaius stepped back as the gate to the pen was opened and Prometheus was paraded out tossing his head up in the air with anticipation. Gaius pointed sternly at the horse. "You have him, Marcus?"

"Yes, Centurion!" Marcus responded, wrapping the reins tightly around his hands and scratching the horse's chin.

Gaius nodded and then ordered, "Helmet!" The soldier who had waited patiently holding his officer's helmet carefully handed it over and then retrieved his own *pilum* from one of his other comrades. Gaius gave the steel helm a quick inspection to make sure it had not gotten dirty and that the blond, transverse, horse hair crest was still finely straight. Slipping the heavy war helmet upon his head, he tied the leather cords from the metal cheek straps under his chin, rested his left hand on the pommel of his gladius, and marched away as the detail squad, leading Prometheus, fell in step behind him.

*   *   *

"Cornelius is taking his time, my son. We can barely hold back the troops," Vespasian said comically. He carefully drew back the tent flap for a brief moment and caught sight of the hundreds of cheering soldiers which filled the grounds before his quarters. One legionary in the front of the great host thought he had seen the tent flap quiver, and he lifted his spear into the air and hollered Vespasian's family name with exultation as tears streamed down his face.

"He will be here, Father. I have never doubted Gaius." Titus stepped forward and shook his head in amazement. "They truly love you."

"They have fought admirably for me while losing many brothers, Titus. I will be forever in their debt." A moment of reflection crossed the aged general's face of fifty years, until he exhaled loudly and added, "I sometimes wonder if listening to Mucianus will get us all killed for treason." Vespasian chuckled to himself and let the flap go and walked to the centre of his tent.

"You believe something will happen?" Titus appeared slightly worried and glanced at the entry way to make sure none of the guards were listening. "Have there been threats?"

"My dear son, Titus. No threats, no wolves, and no bastard senators have said anything. We are quite safe. True power for our family lies outside," he said with a gesture towards the front of the tent. He then glanced upward at a hanging oil lamp coated in silver and burning with a low flame. "This is history in the making, my boy, and all we have done here has proven to me the validity of our calling in life. Mars has been with us from the beginning as have the oriental gods of Egypt. The omens haven't always been what we want, but that is how the gods play. The cost of goats and bulls is a trivial matter to ensure a successful campaign. Alas, it keeps the gods in their rightful place."

Titus nodded in agreement and replied, "The bribes to the priests are what cost the most, but I sometimes wonder if the gods have ever cared at all."

Vespasian shook his finger at Titus gently and smiled. "They don't care about us in the way of affection, but we do our duty to stifle any jealousy or rage they might impose on us. First, they give you confidence and then when you are on top, they love to topple your walls. That is why the priests say to honour them and they will eventually respect what we do here." He relieved an itch on his neck and hurriedly stated, "The gods have been quite good for Rome, my dear son. Continue to offer the regular sacrifices and pay the priests their due amount. I wonder sometimes how the gods truly feel about me."

"The Alexandrians seem to show their exultation to you, Father, and don't forget the omens of Serapis or the signs of the eagles, dog and ox." Titus lowered his voice and uttered, "You were like a god in the Hippodrome when they donned you with garlands and the boughs of one as victorious as you, and where they called you a Son of Amun Re. Your Prefect Alexander declared it in his speeches and so did the masses. You're blessed by the titles of the pharaohs and the wealth of the Ptolemies as past kings, Father. When I consulted the oracle at the shrine of Aphrodite at Paphos, both predictions pointed to you, my Father, as Caesar. Do you remember what the oracle of Carmel said?"

Vespasian nodded seriously and sighed, "That I would be the master of a mighty seat: possess vast properties and have an abundance of men." He rubbed his chin and looked up at his son. "At the shrine of Serapis I saw a radiant man who appeared to me named Basilides, Son of the Monarch. He presented to me palm branches, garlands, and cakes. I have done everything correctly and consulted astrologers concerning this future of mine. The gods seem to point down from the sky to me. Many a bull has spilled its blood as an offering; I must show the gods I am worthy and strong."

"Father, even upon your arrival in Egypt you must recall the priest of Amun Re at Montou and his response at the Temple of Peace." Vespasian nodded and Titus continued, "He offered you the fertile flood of the Nile and the quartz statue of his sixteen children. The gods of the orient are with you, and it even appears as if the Jewish God honours your destiny. Remember Yosef ben Matityahu or Rabbi Yohanan ben Zakkai? This shows heaven's support for you." Titus paused for a moment to collect his thoughts and then said with passion, "I swear to you now that when this is all done I shall observe the consecration rites to the Apis bull in Memphis. I will do this to honour you and honour the gods for seeing this campaign brought to a swift end."

Vespasian confidently took hold of a bronze pitcher and poured wine into two silver goblets. He suddenly cackled with laughter and said as he extended one goblet to Titus, "I don't usually do this now, do I? I mean, serving wine to my son, or anyone for that matter. I suppose I must look quite silly to you: a servant in the finest of armour."

Titus smiled and drank his wine. "Your servant did look confused when you sent him out and told him to busy himself with rubbish."

Vespasian grinned and sat down on a soft cushioned stool by his bed. "He had already suited up his general, so why should he stay? He is entertaining, though. A bit of a bore at times, but he is nonetheless entertaining. Perhaps I should find me a beautiful Jewess to look after me, now wouldn't that be nice?" Vespasian seemed to ponder for a moment and then started laughing before his son could respond to his rhetorical question, his plump cheeks growing red from the drink. "How do I look?"

"Vitellius would run away at the sight of you, Father, and beg the women of Gaul to come to his aide." Titus laughed and continued, growing sentimental, "You look like an epitome of Caesar himself and no doubt a different man then the one who sold mules from his village of Rieti." Titus was enjoying this time with his father, for he rarely saw him in high spirits. Most of the time, the image of his father was one of him bent over maps, studying landscapes, discussing strategies with legionary commanders, or pondering what his next move should be. It was the side of his father he had known for most of his life. However, once in awhile Vespasian would show a calm, attractive side, where people felt comfortable in his presence and not in the least bit threatened; this usually occurring at a feast where plenty of wine was available.

"A Sabine and Nero's man, no doubt!" Vespasian announced with a smile as he finished his wine and set the goblet down on a silver table.

"But truly, you have the appearance of a warrior and have been hailed by the men who call you Imperator," Titus said with flattery. "It is a show of power we must give them; you must surely wear your ceremonial sword and hold it high when they shout your name."

Titus was in full armour, as was his father, except men of their prestigious positions always kept a suit of armour for festivities or celebrations. Both wore gold plated greaves covering much of their legs and leather belts were bound upon their waists fixed with bronze scales. Brightly polished bronze and leather *cingulum* hung from their jewel-studded belts. Black breastplates bearing the faces of gods had been strapped to their chests and Vespasian had hung the pennant, given to him by Nero, around his neck. Three years ago, the pennant had been issued to Vespasian as a decree that he represented Rome and fought in the name of the Emperor Nero. However, in the last year Fortuna had been cleverly at work, for Nero had had committed suicide and the Roman world had changed forever.

Vespasian touched the pennant and thought to himself how ironic it was that he should find himself in a bid for power against an unruly emperor, when it had been an unruly emperor three years earlier who had commissioned him to quell the Jewish rebellion. Was Vitellius so different from Nero? In truth, Vitellius had never tried to condemn Vespasian to death as Nero had tried that day when Vespasian had fallen asleep during one of the emperor's dreary singing performances. However, Vespasian and Vitellius had long been political opponents and over the years Vespasian had grown to loathe the man.

Titus saw his father touch the pennant a second time and mistook the action for discomfort from his armour. "Is the breastplate too tight?"

Vespasian glanced at his son and shook his head. He stood and walked to his son and placed a hand on his shoulder. "Today is a momentous day that I never could have dreamed of. I want you by my side, Titus; I want everyone to see a strong father and son who will carry them to *Roma* in glory. You are my eldest son and heir to all I have. You and Domitian make me as proud as a father should be of his sons. You, Titus, will be emperor after I die. I know this for a fact. It has been confirmed by the gods who have predicted it. You must be strong in the coming years, particularly with the closing of this campaign yet before you."

"You talk of Jerusalem?"

"Yes, the holy city of the Jews and a fortress of such great size never before attacked by Romans in the way which we must engage it. There are other minor strongholds, yet mere flies on a horse's back compared to the Jews' holy city. Its walls are strong and the land is unfavourable for the legions.

"You will have to think ingeniously to complete this task. It will not be like Cestius Gallus, my son, for we cannot abandon this campaign until Jerusalem falls completely. Many will die and I pray we see the city crushed and this rebellion over. We cannot wait for the Jewish squabbling within Jerusalem's walls to be sorted out. Yes, it's weakened them, but their resolve remains."

"They will rally to fight us when we arrive on Scopus, for that I am sure of," Titus queried, pondering the reality. He looked at his father then said, "Did we miss an opportunity when Ananus ben Ananus controlled the city?"

Vespasian chuckled lightly. "If we had been more alert and better informed we may have had a powerful ally in Ananus, but, alas, the Zealots with the help of Idumeans from the south saw Ananus and his party destroyed, thus eliminating the sensible people which we could have reasoned with. Now it is just the rabble that controls the city." Vespasian sighed. "Who knows what the gods had in mind when they spared that dog Simon ben Giora and allowed him to gain power. We must not underestimate him; he is the most dangerous of the three."

"More than John of Gischala or Eleazar ben Simon?"

"Simon is cunning and I believe he lacks the capacity of affection for his own people. He is truly bloodthirsty and possesses no sense of ethical duty to his own brothers." Vespasian lowered his gaze for a moment. "John and Eleazar are Zealots who act and make decisions in a reckless manner; however, Simon is cold and calculated. He manipulates a situation and truly delights in causing pain and suffering. The stories of his devastation in Idumea sounded like the terror caused by the *Picti* upon Roman villages and settlements in Britannia when I was stationed there. It was only with a show of brutal force upon the Picti that the raids ceased and you could control them; it is the same with the Jews."

"We will defeat this Simon and see him brought low. He is only a man and we have the blessings of the gods and the might which is in our hands as Romans. Only the strong rule this world and *Roma* has seen nations pressed under her heel. The Jews will be another people reminded of the steel of our swords and the passion of our resolve." Titus had a fire in his eyes as he recalled the glorified stories of the past, from the battles with Carthage to Augustus.

Vespasian licked his dry lips and turned at the sound of three repeated knocks upon a post behind the tent, as this was the agreed upon password. He looked back into the eyes of Titus and nodded. "We go now, but we will meet in Berytus soon to discuss the steps of power and the end of this campaign."

Titus nodded and watched his father turn and walk to the back of the tent where a section was drawn aside letting in a flood of sunlight. He retrieved a beautiful gladius which hung near his bed. The sheath was of a dark, rich wood, plated in decorative gold with the imprint of Augustus and the eagle of Rome upon it. He quickly secured it to his belt and as he rested his hand upon the white pommel of the sword, he exited the tent.

Titus saw Gaius standing at attention before Vespasian as a stepping stool was brought so the Imperator could mount the tall stallion. Gaius quickly moved to his general's side to help and Vespasian nodded with appreciation. Titus observed the centurion lower his gaze in humbleness.

"I always had a love for horses, Cornelius. Prometheus has protected me for years." Vespasian patted the horse's neck as it seemed like he was drifting away to another age of fond memories. The moment was but a breath's time for he then stared at the tent and beckoned his son with a smile. "Come, Titus. Mount your horse and let's be presented to the men."

Titus stepped into the heat and cleared his throat as a legionary approached him holding the bridle of a black stallion named Achilles. When Titus saw the centurion's eyes dart over to him, the young prince nodded with respect. "Lead the way, Centurion, and reflect on the truth of today, that today is history. Someone will write about us and many will remember this moment."

Gaius struck his cuirass in the customary Roman salute and bowed his head slightly as he replied with a firm, "Yes, my lord."

Titus sat atop Achilles for a moment waiting beside his father as Gaius and the others moved in front of Vespasian. They held aloft the four golden eagles of the legions, with *SPQR* imprinted beneath each bird's perch atop of the three metre standards of gold plated wood. Along with the eagles, a legionary carried Vespasian's personal *signum* which contained bronze discs attached to the shaft of the standard bearing the emblems of the Flavian line.

The signum represented Vespasian's generalship as commander of the Judean forces and his emblem of governor of Syria after he had taken over from Cestius Gallus. It was also topped with a golden wreath coiled around the face of Mars, who was the war god of the Romans. Jeweled chains, woven together like rope, hung on either side of the mystical face.

Gaius led the men as they held the standards high above their heads for the entire assembly to see who was accepting this title of Imperator. He glanced back to make certain his soldiers were marching in perfect column, followed by Vespasian and Titus. Gaius thought to himself that this day seemed like something resurrected from the mind of Homer or another one of the great thinkers of history.

Vespasian became incredibly stoic, holding his chin slightly higher than normal as he looked down upon the faces of the cheering men when they emerged from behind the general's tent. A line of tribunes sat on their horses in perfect formation stretching outwards from the front of the tent and they drew their swords as they honoured Vespasian with their allegiance. Thousands of legionaries began chanting his name in unison as they shook their spears in the air and lifted their heavy *scutua* off the ground. The *signi* of cohorts rose above the ranks in a display of loyalty and many of the shields had Vespasian's name inscribed upon their faces.

Gaius was awed into silence by the spectacle. He wanted so very much to join in the chorus, but maintained his professional duty and demeanour. As rehearsed, Gaius marched his company detail along the line of cheering veterans who were reduced to tears of joy over the sight of their commander.

"Halt and form line here!" Gaius shouted to his men dictating exactly where they should stand at attention. "Do not lower the eagles or his lordship's signum throughout his entire speech." The men stood rigid but stared longingly with radiant faces as Vespasian edged Prometheus away from Titus and sat in his saddle basking in all the grandeur surrounding him.

Gaius could hear his own heart pounding within his chest. Never in all his days of service, would he have ever counted himself so lucky to witness the coronation of an emperor by his troops. Although it had been talked about in the last couple of months, nobody thought it would become a reality. Gaius noticed other banners waving among the assembly and realized that a delegation of King Marcus Agrippa was among them pledging loyalty and fidelity.

Vespasian slowly held up a plump hand glittering with large rings and a ghostly silence suddenly befell everyone. "My fellow countrymen, fellow Romans and comrades in arms…" With this last title of acknowledgment a large section of the troops let out another blast of enthusiasm. A smile flickered across Vespasian's face and then it was gone.

"This fifth day before the Ides of July is an omen come true. The gods have finally smiled upon us after all the hardships we have faced these last years. We have faced everything the gods have thrown at us: the House of Hades and the very breath of Pluto and we have succeeded. Soon we will triumph over this enemy who has no care even for their own people. We will show them the sword of *Roma* and the fire of the civilized world. My legionaries, born of wolves and lions, men of ferocious valor, you do declare me your Imperator?"

Every mouth that could open and every throat that could make a sound bellowed in approval as they waved their hands and weapons at Vespasian who leaned forward in his saddle and raised his hand. "I accept this title, and by the oracles given and the power of the gods of *Roma*, we will usher in a new dynasty, one which knows the bounds of law and mercy and one which can bring this world under a single Roman banner! I do declare before you all today that you will always be my men!" Men wept. "And my troops." Men cheered. "And your emperor will never forget you, for it is your loyalty that I can firmly trust!"

Vespasian paused and glanced back at his son and motioned him to come forward. Titus edged Achilles alongside Prometheus and bowed his head in respect. "We will see this campaign won and honour carried back to *Roma*. *Roma victa*!"

*　　*　　*

July 19th, 69 A.D. / 14th of Av, 3829
Ten miles north of Jerusalem

Absolute silence enveloped the area as Judah ben Yosef held his breath and listened for the approaching Roman patrol. With fingers stained with dry blood, he held the gladius firmly and glanced at the other fighters lying upon the ground who clutched spears, swords, and a handful of bows. Judah and his men were motionless, hidden behind a high cleft of rock topped with what remained of an olive grove. On the other side of the rock lay a road used by Roman patrols trying to link up with troops in Joppa and the lands to the south.

An abandoned peasant's farm house was nearly fifty metres to the east where they lay shielded by the rock, the owners of the home having fled when Judah and his band of marauders arrived. The group called themselves, 'The Lions' after they had nicknamed Judah after the Hebrew tribe which bore his name. There were forty of them, all heavily armed, but lightly packed so they could move anywhere at a moment notice.

Each man knew the landscape by memory, where every cave was to hide, farm to get supplies, orchards and vineyards to steal fruit from, and the best positions to attack from. They had been fighting in this area since the outbreak of the war, usually venturing in a five mile radius in order to forge from or gather news of Roman patrols. In all their engagements, the Lions had only suffered minimal losses which naturally attracted more fighters their way, since men wanted to follow a leader who would not rush carelessly into a fight, but valued lives enough to plan the perfect ambush.

The formation of the Lions had begun with Judah calling on a number of friends to join him after they heard of the massacre done by Florus' troops in the market place of Jerusalem. They did not need much convincing and each man had brought whatever weapons they owned or could steal. Over the next two and a half years, many more had filled their ranks, mostly displaced Galileans whose families had been killed, scattered, or enslaved by the Romans. Nobody questioned another's motives for joining to fight. They just lived with hate in their hearts for their common enemy and the belief that they were serving God who had delivered the Romans into their hands to be destroyed.

It was not always easy, however, to recruit fighters. Throughout the years of ambushing Roman patrols, and sacking small villages loyal to Rome, they had constantly come into contact with countrymen who wanted nothing to do with the war. Judah had heard the explanation time and time again; the people were poor and had practically nothing to give. They would argue the simple question, what quarrel could Rome have with such impoverished peasants? Only fighting against *them* would bring more death and suffering among an already suffering people. Jewish farmers in the Galilee had constantly refused to join the fighting, exclaiming that nothing could possibly be done to defeat the strongest military power in the world. They were only humble farmers, not experienced in war like the zealots. They had families to attend to and the harvest of their crops and orchards.

Judah had only once killed one of his own, and he had regretted it ever since. It had been over a year ago as fall had settled upon the land and still he felt like he needed to wash the unseen blood from his hands. Even though the man had been a farmer, he still was a Jew. The look on his face as he lay dying, and the cries of his family had never failed to leave Judah's memory.

A number of small, brown conies scurried among the olive trees lining the cliff, as they looked for rocks to sprawl upon and soak up the heat as the sun began to rise. Caleb made his way towards Judah as he moved along the line of men, clutching weapons, and listening to anything out of the ordinary. Caleb glanced up at the remaining olive trees littering the cliffs plateau and thought back to last night when he and three other fighters had slowly moved up the rock face to survey the road below on the other side. Prior to leaving, they had spent some time stripping the trees of branches for firewood and then had hastened back to the hideout to report to Judah that the patrol would be arriving in the early hours of dawn.

Caleb tried to steady his breathing as he settled in beside Judah and thought of the food awaiting him upon his return to camp. "They should be here soon."

Judah nodded without looking at Caleb and cleared his throat. A black beard covered Judah's chin while his eyes were mysterious and penetrating. His skin was darkened from the sun and his hair was unkept. However, despite Judah's shaggy facial appearance, he was a strong man who kept his sword belt strapped tightly overtop of his long, brown tunic and wore legionary hob-nailed sandals which he had stolen off a dead soldier months ago. Neither Judah nor any of his men wore Roman armour from the men they killed. Their only interest was to pillage the bodies for money, food, clothes, and weapons. The rest they would leave, the corpses strewn upon the ground, mutilated and unburied.

"Have you eaten?" Judah asked.

Caleb shook his head. "Not this morning. I had some water and that was it. I will eat after this."

"You're always so sure you will survive."

Caleb thought for a moment and nodded. "I know I won't die in the wilderness, God has assured me."

Judah stared strangely at his friend and rolled his eyes. "In all my years knowing you, Caleb, I have never heard you utter something as odd as what you have just said."

"I had a dream last week and a voice told me that I would not die in the hills, or in a valley or forest. I was shown a desert and the voice said that I would not die in the sand or the rocks. Then I was shown a city, I don't think it was Jerusalem, but I cannot be certain."

Judah shifted slightly, leaning on his elbow, and looked intensely at his friend, his sarcasm evaporating. "What did the voice say?"

"The voice said nothing. I heard nothing but the prayers of people."

Judah stared at his friend for a moment and then gazed down at the rocky ground he laid upon. He whispered quietly so none would hear, "Was it God, Caleb?"

"I thought you didn't care about God anymore since Miriam and your parents died in the massacre."

"I never said that, I just think God is punishing me. Perhaps I have sinned."

Caleb scratched his chin while watching his troubled friend. He finally shrugged and whispered just loud enough for Judah to hear, "I think it was God, but there is one thing I believe."

"What is that?"

"I believe I will die in this war."

Judah's eyes filled with compassion. "We will die together saying the *Shema*, my friend, and kill as many of those vile dogs as we can."

"Judah! Judah!" one of the Lions called out in a hoarse voice as he scrambled down the side of the rock, keeping low. The fighter held his sword and moved fast as he shouted, "A patrol of around thirty are approaching. A mounted officer leads them!"

"Around thirty?"

The fighter shrugged. "A hill blocked the bend in the road. I couldn't see if there was a vanguard or anyone trailing behind, but they are moving fast. I think it's your tribune." A dark grin flashed across the man's face.

Judah did not have time to contemplate what the next move would be. He had done this dozens of times, so much so that the Romans had a name for them, 'The Beasts of Hades'. Judah glanced left and right, then motioned for the group to advance. They moved quickly, staying low against the ground as they breached the top of the cliff.

Judah crawled a few metres ahead of his fighters, making sure none followed. He had positioned his bowmen on either flank whose sole job would be to inflict the first casualties and block their escape. Success depended upon speed and the ability to prevent the Romans from forming any kind of solid formation.

Judah could see the approaching column of mounted troops moving quickly upon the road.

They were riding two abreast with their oval, black cavalry shields protecting their sides. Perfect formation was maintained as they rode onward, the jingling of mail and the studded aprons they wore sounding above the beating hooves. The officer was a stern looking man and a warrior. He wore a brass cavalry helmet with a black plume crested upon the top along with his red *sagum* strapped to his cuirass. An expensive looking gladius hung at his side and he wore metal greaves. The other troopers wore light cavalry helmets made of leather with their cheek plates firmly tied under their chins as they carried the longer Roman spear preferred by the cavalry. Each man looked seasoned and experienced, and that was what Judah worried about. It was easy going up against raw recruits, as they had in the early stages of the war, but with each ambush the Romans were getting tougher and craftier.

"The Boars and their hog leader," Judah uttered softly with contempt. Jews everywhere had heard of the notorious band of Roman marauders who had been raiding, burning, and pillaging the countryside like a swarm of locust. They were the shock units Vespasian had unleashed upon the rebellious country and were a mighty tool to win the war for Rome.

The Boars had inherited their name from the lips of Vespasian himself who had praised them once at a feast comparing them to wild boars stamping over the country and staining their tusks red with blood. The name had stuck as the legions and other *alae* units had come to respect them and give them their space in the field. To the Zealots and other Jewish factions, they seemed an impossible force to annihilate since they were incredibly mobile and ferocious.

Over the years the Boars had become an obsession for Judah in which he tried over and over to slaughter them. In the last couple of months he had come to learn of the power and prestige the Boars' leader possessed. He was a tribune of nobility and a battle-hardened man, gaining the fear and terror of everyone circulating the countryside. The tribune had clearly become Vespasian's puppet, and Vespasian, as the puppet master, allowed no end of cruelty to be executed by the elite cavalry unit. Thus, Judah was convinced that if he could assassinate the tribune, it would deliver a devastating blow to their cavalry organization of the war.

*   *   *

Tribune Marcus Sulla Maximus had been ordered by Titus to travel lightly and with much haste to scout and gather information from the countryside surrounding Jerusalem. The tribune had been on dozens of these patrols in the last year of fighting and with the success of the Jewish bandits he had learned to take more men with him. The key was speed and pure military discipline which had saved their lives many times. Each man had served him faithfully and was a hardened fighter. It was the deadly speed with which his unit operated that made them a force to reckon with. Marcus was the perfect leader for the unit, handpicked by Vespasian. For with his promotion to the office of tribune, Marcus could utilize his vast array of experience from his posts stationed in Germania, Britannia, and now the ancient land of the Jews.

Since being dispatched to destroy the rebellious Jewish forces, the Boars had first skirmished against the Jewish general Yosef ben Matityahu's rabble in the early years of the rebellion. Since then, they had gone on to slaughter Jews in the fortresses of Jotapata, Tiberius, Mount Tabor, and the recent capture of Gischala.

Upon every engagement they fought in, the unit's strange signum was carried by Marcus' standard bearer, Publius. The signum was topped with the brass head of a tusked boar baring black eyes of fire and glaring straight ahead. Below the head of the boar was a bronze disc stamped with the unit's legionary number and then below that an iron plate, revealing an engraved hand, its fingers outstretched and palm out. Inscribed upon the palm was the Latin phrase, *"Alea iacta est,"* which had been the very words Gaius Julius Caesar had uttered before crossing the Rubicon to fight his civil war with Pompey Magnus. Marcus declared to all who inquired about the strange choice of words that his unit had fought in the most dangerous of missions, and had ventured deep into enemy territory. To Marcus they were always gambling with their lives.

Marcus had been decorated handsomely for his achievements and recognized throughout the army as Titus' man. The medallions hanging from his cuirass clearly revealed this, but nevertheless, Marcus always was a soldier's soldier. He shunned feasts and loathed senators. He rudely swore at officers and disrespected politicians whom he labeled as 'that filth which comes from the rectums of rats.' He was a brash man and one loved by women. Marcus had heard many rumours trickle down upon his ears from places of higher standing and they were all the same; that some Roman officers and senators were so jealous of him they wished him dead. Nothing would delight the aristocracy more than to hear that his life had been snatched away in his sleep by the bite of a viper, poisoned wine, or a cruel dagger to his throat. Yet first, any assassin would have to get past Marcus' men, and all knew they were fiercely loyal and loved him with all the passion and fighting spirit capable of possessing a man's soul.

The culminating events of Marcus Sulla Maximus' prestigious career were what had landed him the post of tribune in charge of reconnaissance and disrupting the rebel activity by sabotage, arson, and direct confrontation. Titus paid him well and Marcus' purse had never felt heavier. The Boars tribune ventured forth on a weekly basis, wiping out any resistance that should fall before him, and over time resistance seemed to slacken except for some rogue bands which remained. He would find them and kill them all, giving no quarter, even to those who surrendered.

* * *

"Bowmen, kill the officer and sergeants first. Pass it along!" Judah whispered to the nearest man on his right and left. Then he steadied his breathing and concentrated on the mission at hand. The Roman column approached closer and closer to the point where The Lions would spring their trap. Judah pushed up from the ground and nodded, drawing his sword simultaneously. The bowmen had been watching him carefully, for hardly a moment had passed before ten arrows flew down upon the Romans with deadly force and accuracy.

Marcus had been just about to relay an order to his standard bearer riding next to him when an arrow struck painfully into his upper thigh. The impact instantly sent a shooting force of pain through his body as blood streamed down his leg and pulsed around the quivering arrow shaft buried deep in his muscle. Marcus clenched his teeth in pain as his horse reared as if losing its mind from another dart which had driven into its hind flank. He tried to control the beast as the trooper next to him grunted with the impact of an arrow tearing through his mail. The man's eyes were wide with terror as blood oozed around the shaft of the bolt and with a whimpering sound he fell hard from his saddle as his horse stampeded away.

"Close the ranks!" Marcus bellowed as he drew his gladius with one smooth motion and held it aloft to rally his surprised troopers. His eyes darted left and right. Marcus did not yet know where the attack would come from, but if his men could meet the ambush in a solid formation, brute Roman discipline would win the day. His standard bearer hoisted the signum as the rallying point, and instinctively the troops nearest him closed ranks and leveled their spears.

Marcus could see one of his Sergeants at the rear of the column unhorsed and thrashing upon the ground in pain with two arrows buried deep into his gut and a third through his throat. The Sergeant tried to scream but a fountain of blood poured from his affixed, gaping mouth as he slowly drowned from the gore. The Sergeant reached out, clutching the ankle of a trooper who had dismounted to save him as an explosion of cheers with pounding feet echoed from the towering hills above the road. Instinctively, the trooper turned, shook away the dying Sergeant, and leveled his spear to meet the attack.

Within seconds the Jewish fighters were pouring down the short slope, attacking the Roman left flank before they could close their formation to meet the assault. Marcus watched the trooper, who had went to aid his Sergeant, get swarmed, knocked to the ground, and his throat slit which cast a jet of dark blood upon the dry earth. The Jews delivered a high pitched war cry and charged into the Roman line, hurling spears and rocks.

Eight Roman troopers upon the left wasted not a moment and hurled their spears with deadly accuracy into the onslaught. The balanced weight of the heavy spears easily soared through the air and found targets, as the Jewish fighters rarely wore any kind of armour. Five Jews pitched back in a bloodied mess, writhing on the ground in excruciating pain as the impaled javelins reached up to the heavens. The Romans charged with swords drawn and shields protecting their unguarded flanks. The horses pounded forward, hard and calculated, like black demons bent on insane rage.

A Jewish man with wild eyes and a black beard screamed a challenge at the Romans and led a frenzied charge directly into the mounted troopers. Beyond the natural instincts to survive, the Jew clutched his sword, closed in on the first horse, leaped to the side of the beast, and sprung for the trooper's exposed left side. The Roman panicked. His shield failed to block the Jew's thrust, and before his eyes the blade severed the muscle and sinew of his thigh, instantly drenching his leg in warm blood. The trooper screamed hideously as he was dragged from his saddle by the bear-like hands of the Jewish warrior as his horse reared in fear.

The Roman crashed upon the ground, knocking the wind from his lungs and losing his sword. A fire of pain tore through his leg and he clenched his teeth in agony. As he was rolled over, he found himself staring into the grim eyes of the Jew. To the trooper, the man was enormous and he fought back pathetically as the Jew grabbed his throat to choke him.

The Jew paused and the Roman gasped with pleading eyes as his enemy stared furiously at him. The black-bearded Jew suddenly straightened and surveyed what was happening around him. He smiled as he realized their victory over the Roman horse charge. Bodies of troopers lay strewn and mutilated upon the ground in great pools of blood which soaked the parched earth. The Jew raised his red sword in the air and shouted something in Hebrew at the Romans who were trying to escape. Then he slowly looked down and tore the helmet off the head of his captive.

"Please, don't do this!" the Roman sobbed as tears welled up in his eyes. "I surrender. I'll join you!" He was now kneeling in the dirt, his legs trembling from the pain as blood pulsed from the wound. His enemy seemed to take a moment, as if trying to understand what he was saying. "I'll convert, be circumcised like you!"

The eyes of the Jew glared at the pathetic Roman. He released his grip on his throat and slowly brought the blade of his sword under the soldier's chin. These men were the men who had brought suffering to his country and murdered his people. It had been men like these who had deprived him of a wife and family. The Jew's eyes burned with anger and he slowly said in his native tongue, "I am Judah the Lion and I take your life because of what you have done and that of Rome!"

*   *   *

Marcus parried the spear head aside just inches from his face and his warhorse surged forward like it had been trained to, catching a Jewish fighter off balance. The tribune dispatched him with two quick thrusts of his blade.

"Trumpeter, sound retreat!" Marcus shouted as he watched the Jews cut down his left flank and now turn in strength against the center of his line. He was an experienced soldier and seasoned enough to know that this was a futile engagement. The Boars would have their revenge, but it would be on their terms, not by this Jewish scum. "Sound retreat!" Marcus bellowed at the startled Roman trumpeter. The man raised the instrument and with a blast from pursed lips, sounded the tune above the shouting and clashing of weapons. Marcus raised his sword in the air and roared like thunder, "With me!" He then wildly turned his war horse away from the fighting and beckoned to his surviving men.

"Tribune, look!" One of the troopers pointed with his spear across the road, a ghastly expression upon the man's face.

Marcus saw one Jewish fighter standing near the back of the surging rabble who tried to pursue the retreating cavalry. The Jewish warrior was a hulking man, his arms drenched in blood, appearing like a beast from the Greek mythologies. A long, black beard filled the Jew's face, but it was what he held at his side which caused Marcus to glare with vengeance.

*　　*　　*

Judah slowly raised the decapitated head of the Roman in the air with victory. A trail of blood dripped from the severed neck and stained Judah's cloak. He held the head tightly by the scalp as an exhilarating force rushed through his veins. Then he tossed it in front of him and called off the attack with one command for the Romans had escaped them. Judah's goal had been to kill the tribune, but the swiftness with which the Romans had formed to meet the attack had been too quick to have completed the envelopment of the scouting party. It had not been a failure. The bodies of fifteen Romans attested to that. The capture of four horses and plunder would suit them perfectly, but the tribune's escape did not bode well for Judah. "Do not pursue them! Quickly, gather weapons and let's clear out of here. Caleb, take some men to fetch our dead." Judah glared at the retreating Romans and then turned away with a heavy sigh as he gave a final, disgusted glance down at the headless corpse at his feet.

The Lions stripped the Roman corpses and then shoved a few heads onto stakes which they drove into the ground. Whatever horses they could capture they used to carry their own casualties, as the Jewish band of warriors made for the hills with haste. They knew it would only be a matter of time before they were hunted by a larger contingent of cavalry led by the vengeful Tribune Marcus Sulla Maximus.

*　　*　　*

CHAPTER II

July 20th, 69 A.D. / 15th of Av, 3829
Berytus, Lebanon
Two hours after dusk

"What if I was a prophet? What would God have me do?" The middle aged Jewish man hung his head as he sat upon a small cushioned stool and sighed loudly. The mental stress upon his mind sometimes brought him to the climax of life's decisions, as if the weight of the world was upon his back like the pagan god Atlas. Although he was a Jew descended from priests, he had always pondered the image of the pagan god struggling with the world upon his muscled back. The Jewish man slowly brought up his weathered hands and rubbed the weariness from his heavy eyes. He felt he had neglected sleep, or sleep had neglected him. The weight of exhaustion clung to his eye sockets as if great stones hung from his lids suspended by chains. All he wanted to do was close them, curl up on his mat, and see the world float away into a dismal, indifferent form where Atlas' burden would only seem like a phantom to the harsh reality that threatened to overtake him.

Life had offered him a diamond. The predicament he had found himself in only months ago felt ages away in another lifetime. Now they *had* to offer him freedom. It should have been torture, shame, a public spectacle, and then death, but God had spared him. The captured Jewish general had been given a gift: the chance to make a prophecy. The prophecy predicted the choosing of an emperor, and he had to be recognized, he had to matter. The man licked his dry lips and stroked his bearded chin. The Gentiles had treated him well; they were known for barbarity among non-citizens, but his new life had completely changed his thinking. It was not like they had invited him to parties, but merely had provided him the necessities to get by, and a little Homer.

The Jewish man knew that many of the Roman officers wanted him dead. They still saw him as the rebel general who had led the Jewish forces against the Roman army two years ago. He had fortified cities, trained rabbles of brigands into something that resembled an army, and now had nothing to show for it. The prophecy had saved him from the Roman sword and his wits had saved him from his own people.

Who started this war? Jew or Gentile? The rebellion had already been glowing like white coals in the base of an oven when he had returned from Rome. Caesarea had been a mad house: Jews leaving in record numbers as the Greek youths pillaged and killed, hostilities naturally being encouraged by Gessius Florus. Florus would be known as the procurator who had started the entire mess in the first place. At least this was the way most people saw it, including King Marcus Agrippa in his speech to the people of Jerusalem. That day he had also decided to do nothing.

Agrippa had stated, '*Live under the rule of Florus and eventually he will be replaced. Nero will see reason and sort everything out.*' That had been the message Agrippa had pleaded with the Jews. Every Jew knew Agrippa's advice to be a suffocating death sentence and naturally the country had imploded on itself. But war with Rome? Who in their wildest dreams could have ever imagined such a sight as Roman legions thundering through the Galilee burning every Jewish village, town, and city that did not surrender.

Sepphoris had been one of the first to house a Roman garrison, and many from the rebellion had accused the Jewish general for not taking a harsher stand against the population of predominantly Greek citizens. But what was he supposed to do? The Peace Party of Jerusalem, a quasi new form of government elected from the aristocracy, both high born priests and Sanhedrin, were the ones who created rulings and had elected him to the office of General. Even he, as a patrician with friends in high places, could not make them see the insanity of fighting against Rome in the end. When Tiberias, Gamla, Tarichaeae, the west coast, and Joppa had fallen nobody saw the lunacy of their epic struggle. Even as the golden eagles were carried up to the gates of Jotapata, still they resisted. He remembered that night very well. It was so clear, like gazing into a mirror.

It all seemed so long ago and forgotten. The faces of the dead fading from memory. Had Titus thought he would get a reaction from the deposed General when he told him of the fall of Mount Tabor and Gischala? The son of the would-be emperor had been told by the Jewish captive that the struggle against Rome would utterly fail, and he knew it. The rebellion was an ideal, maybe a religious one, but definitely an ideal created by fanatics and savages.

One such savage he loathed was John ben Levi, also known as John of Gischala. It had been this man who had defied him, even attempting to murder him, but it had been intelligence, one thing John lacked, that had saved the general. The former Jewish General grinned to himself and shook his weary head. How many letters had been penned to the Peace Party? How many times had he pleaded with them to silence the ignorant ramblings of John?

Even as a Roman prisoner, he could still recall how disappointed he had been when he had received news of John and his party escaping the clutches of Titus at Gischala. The Zealot had used trickery and the sanctity of *Shabbat* to ensure his plan would work. Even in his chains the Jewish General had been looking forward to gazing into the eyes of the captured John, bound and beaten. Then he would softly say to John, "Where did you think this would get you? Now look at your brothers to the south. They too will die, for the Romans will not stop. They are confident and will march to Jerusalem, and you will be taken to Rome in chains, to be strangled in the Forum." However, this had now been delayed as John was in Jerusalem and there he would make his stand.

The Jewish man slowly stood, feeling an immense weight upon his shoulders, a burden fed by the image of his country burning in his mind's eye. He gazed at his mat upon the floor and then inspected the chains upon his wrists and feet. He was still a prisoner, even with the literature of Homer, and he wondered how this would end. He shuffled over to his mat and awkwardly laid down; the links of chain clinking together as he stretched out to get comfortable. He exhaled loudly and whispered, "Abba, what would you think of me now? Is this how you raised your son? Am I a traitor?"

Yosef ben Matityahu, closed his eyes and mumbled something inaudible, as the soft murmur escaped his lips and left the room. As he lay in the darkness of his quarters, sleep overtook him. He imagined the heat of fire radiating off his body, the smell of smoke, and the clash of steel. Great resounding crashes of stone cast up dust clouds that blinded men, causing them to choke. In the midst of death, the sound of wailing was heard as his memory drifted back in time.

*   *   *

"How many are here? How many have made it?" a voice whispered in the blackness of the cave.

"You shut your mouth, or we're all dead! They have breached the walls and will cut our throats!" another voice whispered back.

A dark form shook his head in the hiding place. "You all fled and they are being butchered. We should be out there fighting."

"And to what end, Amos? We must think of a way to escape."

"Where, Yosef? What did you have in mind? Shall we just pop our heads up and ask the Romans to forgive us for disturbing everything?"

"Don't mock me, Ezra, I am still in command." Yosef glared at the man despite knowing full well none could truly see him. Silence overtook the hiding place as everyone held their breath. Screams and the crashing of what sounded like timber made someone in the darkness start to softly weep.

"They will die quickly with no pain," Yosef mumbled the empty words as if trying to comfort himself as he spoke to nobody in particular. Despair filled his soul and he fought against the fear stirring within, fear of spikes driven through flesh as the Romans would crucify him and everyone who survived the sacking of Jotapata.

"We can't let them catch us," Ezra strained, his voice sounding hoarse.

"If we stay silent and still we will live," a new voice whispered. "Nobody saw us come down…"

"They will find us," Ezra interrupted. "The Romans know Yosef is here. They will pull apart every building, overturn every stone, and use prisoners to identify bodies. They will find us here. Yosef?"

Yosef nodded and swallowed. His throat was dry, like a desert. "What do you propose Ezra?"

Everyone could hear the heavy breathing of Ezra as he thought hard. The older Jewish officer, who had served Yosef ben Matityahu all this time, knew this was the end. He glanced around the darkness of the hiding place and counted the forms of thirty-nine men who had fled into the cave when the Romans had smashed through the walls. Trails of dirt every now and then dropped into his hair from the cave's ceiling due to the thundering of feet and the chaos of fighting.

Ezra knew exactly what they had to do. "They will find us. There is no doubt in my mind about that. Give them an hour, maybe two, but they will pull us from this hole, torture half of us, and slaughter the rest. Then Yosef will be flogged before the soldiers while we watch. We will be stripped naked and crucified; some may be used for spear practice while we hang from trees screaming like children. That is what will happen. No quick executions, no slavery, no freedom, just painful and prolonged deaths. I have seen it, we all have seen it, and we know this to be fact."

"We pray!" a pious fighter named Yakov said passionately.

"We act!" Ezra countered Yakov's command and continued. "We should kill ourselves and take the pleasure away from the Romans."

The cave was completely silent from Ezra's advice. "I am the general of the forces of the north," Yosef said standing. "I will go out and parley for your lives. The Romans are not animals, and Vespasian will listen."

"No," Ezra replied, rising quickly to face the darkened figure of his commander.

"They will listen! We should not give up and kill ourselves."

"No, Yosef! This is the only way!" Ezra took a step closer and faced Yosef with his hand on the pommel of his sword.

"If the Romans will spare anyone, it will be Yosef. We will all die if he goes up there, don't let him go up!" A young fighter named Benjamin stood and half drew his sword. "I cannot let you do this, General!"

Ezra nodded. "Benjamin speaks sense. We will all die without you, Yosef, and you cannot leave us. If we stay here, we will die anyway. We must end this ourselves and in our fashion!"

"And by 'your fashion' you mean by killing yourselves? How is that honourable? What do you think will happen when word gets to Jerusalem about what we've done? How will that instil hope in others to win this war?" Yosef gazed around the cave, sensing the situation turn dire.

"Silence everyone!" Yakov stood and gazed up at the black ceiling of the cave. "I hear nothing from above."

Ezra opened his mouth to mock Yakov about his religious zeal but then held his tongue and realized the screaming and fighting had ceased. The muffled sounds of trumpets could be heard and then the stamping of marching feet in unison. Voices shouted and orders were given, the city had been silenced and soon a search would be conducted for the general of the northern Jewish forces. "We have no time." Ezra slowly drew his sword and pointed the blade at Yosef.

"Do you expect me to resist, that I will fight the whole lot of you?" Yosef calmly looked around and slowly sat down in a nonthreatening manner, watching the shadow of Ezra lower his blade. "If suicide is the only way then let's conduct this affair and see it through." Everyone was silent. Benjamin and Yakov sat down leaving only Ezra standing as the sword shook in his trembling hand. "God will understand this decision for there is none other left to us."

"Is the Jewish General Yosef ben Matityahu, down there?" a foreign voice called out somewhere above the mouth of the cave. "The city has fallen and the population is subdued, but our Lord Vespasian offers you a pardon you cannot refuse. Although you deserve death for opposing your

Emperor Nero, his servant who is commanding the Roman legions and who has dashed your stronghold to pieces offers your life servus. You will be spared, you and your comrades, if you but surrender and lay down your arms."

"We end this now; do not listen to him, brothers. Vespasian will see us all killed." Ezra glanced around desperately, the fear inside him gripping his soul.

Yosef stood. "Let us do this the easiest way. Quick, light a fire." A small fire was made using a few scraps of wood and dried grass and it burned pathetically as the dim light faintly glowed throughout the cave. He stared around the silent hideout for a moment feeling the tension among the brave men. "We will draw lots, yes that will do." Yosef caught sight of an old clay jar lying upon the dirt floor. "Destroy that vessel and make your mark upon a shard, then we will pile them in the center. The first lot I draw will determine who will go first and then every third man will fall on their sword until the job is done." Yosef nodded at his men and few responded, but there were no objections.

One large warrior near the back of the group slowly walked over to the jar and with one swift motion, brought the pommel of his sword down upon the clay vessel, reducing it into dozens of shards scattered over the floor. Yosef nodded and a few men collected the pieces and calmly handed them out. They used whatever they had to inscribe their names, mostly scraping with the blades of knives until each name was inscribed and piled at the feet of Yosef.

"May Adonai bless Israel!" Yosef said above a whisper as he slowly bent down and picked up a piece among the pile. He held it close to his face to read the name in the dim light and slowly uttered in Hebrew, "Ezra. Shalom my brother."

Ezra looked stunned for a brief moment before raising his chin and clearing his throat to rally his confidence. He nodded at no one in particular and turned the blade inward so the point was touching the hair of his chest. He placed the pommel on the ground and shuffled back so he was hunched over the sword. Tears streamed down his cheeks and a line of spittle hung from his mouth. "Do your part, Matthias." His voice shuddered like a ghost as the man to his right slowly leaned over and supported the sword which Ezra held so it would not slip. "We had good times, General. Damn the Romans." Ezra fell on the blade in one transfixed motion which caused him to gasp as the blade tore through his back. A wash of blood flowed over the blade and its warmth was felt as it covered the hand of Matthias who still held the sword.

A few men began to sob quietly as Ezra's body slumped to the floor and lay motionless. Then one by one each man faithfully held the blade of the other as gasps and exhales were heard of the dying. Only one shrieked horridly for air as the blade punctured the lungs and broke ribs. The man laid upon the ground bleeding to death until Yosef dispatched him with a single stroke. All thirty eight died as brave as men in defiance against their victors who waited above.

"Hello down there? We know you are below in hiding. Come out or force will be used. His lordship is only so patient!" the foreign voice bellowed.

"Well, Yakov, it's just you and I. Shall it end this way?" Yosef gazed around at the bodies and then stared into the face of the only remaining survivor, a young priest who had fought with him for years. When Yakov dropped his sword and began sobbing uncontrollably, calling out the name of his mother, Yosef slowly stood and walked to the cave entrance and shouted in perfect Latin, "Will His Lordship Vespasian keep to his word?"

"That depends if it is Yosef ben Matityahu speaking!"

Yosef sighed and looked at Yakov, who whimpered as he lay upon the hard stone floor. He gazed at the entrance and replied, "It is I!"

*   *   *

The hallway was dark and quiet except for the flicker of a torch carried by a servant, who was closely followed by two soldiers carrying spears. The tapping of the hobnailed boots upon the tiled floor mixed with the jingling of keys from the servant's belt, echoing in the quiet palace. The walls were decorated in colourful tapestries, richly painted in blue and red. Miniature marble pillars stood throughout the hallway within small enclaves in the walls with the statues of gods and goddesses upon them, as the rustling of palace curtains could be subtly heard. The servant's eyes darted to the left as he passed an enormous floor vessel, painted in the Hellenic style and adorned with a large plant growing from within.

The soldiers followed the servant who turned down a small corridor of multi-coloured floor mosaics. They quickened their pace until they finally found themselves arriving outside of a heavy oak door guarded by a single palace sentry clothed in blue robes with a white turban upon his head. The man was of darker skin and held a great spear in his large hands. The guard nodded a warm greeting at the servant and then shot a fierce glare at the two legionaries.

"They are with me, Asaq. We have come for the prisoner, Yosef ben Matityahu." The servant swallowed the lump in his throat and continued, "I have a letter from Vespasian that might…"

The guard growled something under his breath and allowed the servant to approach. The legionaries seemed nervous as they heard the silent whispering pass between the servant and the palace guard. Finally the guard snorted and lumbered off down the hallway. The servant glanced back at the soldiers, grinned and then unlocked the heavy oak door with the set of iron keys he produced from his belt. The door creaked open and a blue haze of moonlight, shining through a tiny window in the corner of the room, revealed a wooden desk scattered with papers, a low burning oil lamp, a stool beside the desk, and the figure of a man asleep upon a mat.

The servant quietly approached the sleeping man while the guards remained near the door. Bending down next to the still form, with the burning torch held low in his hand, the servant gently touched the sleeping man's shoulder. "Yosef ben Matityahu, you must wake."

At first, Yosef had thought the voice was part of his dream, but when the servant shook him again, and repeated the greeting, he grunted and rolled over. When he opened his heavy eyes, Yosef found himself bathed in the warm light of a torch and glancing into the face of a black man. Yosef squinted and sat up, rubbing his weary eyes. "What have you come for?"

The servant smiled. "For you, Yosef. Vespasian has called you to his chamber. There are important men there as well, big deal for you." A smile of ivory teeth lit up the servant's face and Yosef stared at him questionably. "I, Himilco, will guide you!" He stood and quickly said, "You must gather your things, Yosef, and follow me."

Yosef glanced at the two soldiers standing by the door. "Are you sure this is a big deal for me?" He slowly stood and when he noticed Himilco thinking about how he could answer the question Yosef held up his hand and shook his head. "I have nothing to bring. Are you moving me?"

"No, not to my understanding. You are to look presentable and hail Vespasian as emperor."

"In these chains?" Yosef held out his hands. "Come, if I am to look like a guest of the emperor I can hardly do so in these."

Himilco looked at the captive awkwardly and then understood the Jewish General wished to groom himself. He glanced at the soldiers and indicated to them to remove the chains. "We must hurry. Not much time." The chains were removed and Himilco stepped back impatiently and let Yosef fix his garments and comb his beard. Himilco heard a murmur escape Yosef's lips and with a frown he asked, "Excuse me?"

Yosef turned around and realized Himilco had heard him. "I was praying, Himilco. Surely you pray?"

"I do so when it is needed. You pray to your Jewish God?"

"I am Jewish, Himilco, and yes I pray to God, who is the only God." Yosef turned and faced the men. "I am ready now."

Himilco gestured to the soldiers and the chains were returned to Yosef's wrists and feet. "Now we are ready. Follow me."

Yosef was led back through the halls and into a large room featuring complex mosaics covering the floors with animals from all over the world. Situated throughout the room were lounging chairs, couches, stools, and other pieces of furniture. *This must have been from the party two nights ago,* Yosef thought to himself. He had heard the voices late into the night and had even received a small portion of food for his evening meal from a partially drunk legionary.

Large curtains swished upon the floor as they covered the windows of open balconies as a gentle breeze caused them to move like ghosts. Himilco led them out of the chamber and into a small indoor garden. A fountain churned with water and then its sound faded as Yosef passed a pool surrounded by Corinthian pillars. This sight was a common reminder for Yosef of the days he had spent in Rome before the war, attending conservative bath houses where many of the aristocratic Jews gathered. Himilco interrupted his thoughts as he opened a door, leading the procession across a courtyard and into another wing of the palace.

"This is nothing of the palaces and villas of Rome," Himilco stated, trying to impress the captive. "Indoor plumbing, heating, bathhouses, pools, gardens, banquet halls, and gymnasiums. Vespasian had much of this expanded to accommodate his taste of fine life after you Jews started all this mess." Himilco glanced at Yosef to see if he would react, but the general just smiled. "Have you been to Rome?"

"I lived in Rome. I was a guest in the courts of Nero and was shown gratitude by the Empress Poppaea. I heard she had a portrait bust of me commissioned by her greatest sculptor. Alas, I never saw it with my eyes." Yosef smiled at the sudden shock upon Himilco's face and then the servant looked away, remaining quiet until they arrived at the entrance of Vespasian's chamber.

Himilco clasped his hands together for a moment as he thought and then he motioned to the two soldiers. "You are to wait until I announce you and then bring him inside."

"And what of his chains? Should they be removed?" asked one of the soldiers who motioned to retrieve his keys.

Himilco shook his head furiously. "Not unless his lordship commands it." He turned and placed his torch in an empty bracket on the wall. "Now wait for my invitation." Himilco took a deep breath and approached the guarded door which was opened to him and then closed.

"Did Poppaea really commission a bust of you?" asked the soldier holding the keys for the prisoner's chains. He grinned widely and waited for an answer as the other legionary stood nearby, pretending not to be interested.

Yosef slowly nodded sadly. "Yes, but that was so long ago."

The door opened and Himilco stood bathed in the warm light that flooded from the chamber. He waved them forward eagerly, stepping aside as Yosef and the guards entered.

The hall was enormous, almost as large as the lounging chamber Yosef had been led through. Furniture littered Vespasian's hall and a number of high ranking generals and tribunes stood around with goblets of wine as slaves stood nearby waiting to be called upon when cups became empty. Vespasian was at the far end of the room slouching on a large chair with a sleeping hound at his feet. White and red silk robes hung from his body and a green-leafed wreath sat upon his balding head. Yosef saw the Emperor gaze at him for a moment and then finish a piece of fruit. A slave retrieved the core of the eaten apple and then was motioned away by Titus. The Prince stood up from a stool next to his father and nodded at Himilco to bring the prisoner.

The low voices in the room suddenly hushed as the Roman nobles watched Yosef pass by, a few having looks of disgust upon their faces at the sight of the chained Jewish captive. Yosef noticed a number of consular badges upon the breastplates of the men in the room and wondered if this all had to do with him. Then he recognized the familiar face of King Marcus Agrippa and his sister Bernice as they stood talking candidly with another richly dressed darker looking man with gold jewelled rings covering his fingers. Agrippa gave Yosef a strange look and then turned away as he finished his conversation. Why had Vespasian called him to such a place at such a time? The look on Vespasian's face seemed to betray the reason for this meeting, and Yosef worried it might not look favourable in his position.

Yosef was left to stand before the throne-like chair where Vespasian sat as Titus dismissed Himilco and the two legionaries to the back of the room with a wave of his hand. A strange, colourful bird in a cage sang loudly and startled the hound at Vespasian's feet. The dog sat up, scratched its ears, and then trotted off to find comfort in one of the darker corners of the room. Yosef slowly bowed low to the floor and held the pose for a moment as he felt the stare of Vespasian upon him.

"Remove his chains," Vespasian slowly said. "Have a seat, please."

The soldier with the keys approached Yosef. With a quick snap, the chains were removed from his hands and feet and a padded stool was brought for his comfort. Yosef sat down and kept his gaze on the floor.

"Are you not the Jewish General who led rebel forces against my legions in the north? Are you not the man responsible for organizing the outlaws and brigands, training them to fight against *Roma*?" Vespasian paused and bit his lower lip. "You, Yosef ben Matityahu, sided against the late, Emperor Nero. You rallied men to your command who have all been enslaved or killed. Your cause is like a flickering flame about to be extinguished. What have you to say to this?"

The embarrassment and shame was mounted upon Yosef's shoulders like a great tower, with all his defiance having evaporated due to his current state. He simply nodded and replied, "Yes, my lord, what you say is true. It would only be just for you to condemn me to the fate of the rest of my people who were defeated in the Galilee."

"Just? What is justice to you, Yosef? What I have said is true, but here is a man before me with another talent, a connection to the God of his people. You're someone who knows the mind of his god and has the sense to see it. I see someone with a brain, which is hard to find in this place of dogs and beggars. It is by the power of the gods and the chance that they give to us to make something of our lives. The gods have been good to me and they have saved your life. The gods of *Roma* are powerful and will never succumb to destruction. They fight for Roman glory and power, and we honour them.

"I think your God is Roman, but just goes by another name. He is hard to understand. The way you people worship Him, I cannot see the sense. Yet, you're dedicated and serve Him faithfully, sometimes stupidly, but faithfully. I have seen it in the way your people fight. They are ferocious warriors and willing to die for their God. I have been in Britannia and Gaul and have seen all forms of fighting men, but you Jews we underestimate. Your valour is great and something I respect. Nevertheless, your people are my enemies and the enemies of *Roma*. Nero commissioned me to put an end to this rebellion after the disaster of Cestius and I aim to see this finished by the power of my hand." Vespasian spread apart his arms. "I am the embodiment of power distributed through me to see the enemies of *Roma* destroyed.

"The gods have favoured me, and as you know, your God has favoured me. When you see me you see the face of *Roma*. What I say is truth, for I am your god now and your life is in my hands. I know of your past with Nero and Poppaea, I know of your involvement in Galilee, and I especially know of your, let's just say, *predictions*. You're like a prophet of your people, are you not?"

"Just a humble *patrician*, my lord."

Vespasian grinned and rose from his seat. "I have you to thank, Yosef, not condemn. Your voice is honoured by your God and, in no doubt, all the other gods. You predicted the fall of Jotapata in forty-seven days, which has been confirmed by witnesses there. And furthermore, Yosef, do you remember what you stated to me the day we put you in chains? You declared that you would be released by the same man who would be Emperor. It appears as though that day is approaching. The oracles at Carmel and Delphi confirm this as did the ox which stumbled into my banquet hall on that day.

"Otho is dead, Mucianus will soon advance towards *Italia* to meet Primus and the Danubian Legions, which will force Vitellius into action and remove him from the throne. Vitellius is weak, as are his soldiers. It will soon be over." He paused and glanced at his son and then back at Yosef. "I will be going to Alexandria for a time and then to *Roma* to rule as emperor and your life will be spared and given into the service of my son, Titus. Let me remind you that if we are not successful against Vitellius in *Italia* you will face a very painful death."

"As will you, Father," Titus interrupted with a grin and Vespasian laughed loudly and took a long drink of wine.

"It looks like some form of treason will get the better of us all." Vespasian downed the rest of his wine and held the empty goblet for a moment. "Very well, once Vitellius is dead you will be reinstated and no longer declared *servus* to this court. You will, however, remain a prisoner for the time being, but a prisoner with privileges. We want to demonstrate to you and your people we are not here to destroy you all, merely to regain control and see the criminals all dead. This country's uprising must continue no more."

"What do you expect of me then, my lord?"

"That will be for Titus to decide; I think he will make good use of you." Vespasian descended from his chair and Yosef rose in respect. "Jerusalem is the spirit of your people as well as the mind of your faith. Jerusalem is a captured stronghold by your own rebellious factions: Simon ben Giora, John of Gischala, and Eleazar ben Simon. They oppose everything *Roma* stands for and are in direct violation of the *Pax Romana* which has been kept since the days of Augustus. Jerusalem cannot stand as a force shaming the Roman people; its defiance must cease. You know what that means, Yosef?"

Yosef nodded. "I understand. You talk of attacking the city."

"There is no other way. Will your people surrender when the legions arrive outside the city?"

Yosef shook his head. "It is the heartbeat of our people, and it has been for over a thousand years. Long before Roman legions set foot upon the shores of *Eretz Yisrael* and inside her borders, Jerusalem was our Holy City and her people, a nation serving God. They will fight, my lord."

"And will no doubt hate us for it." Vespasian eyed the Jewish General from head to toe and then sighed. "In another lifetime you might have made an excellent king of your people, like Herod. You're a man who truly thinks of them before yourself. Although it is said your people hated Herod, I still think he wished to serve them until the end." Vespasian smiled for a moment and then noticed the sullen look in Yosef's eyes. "You do not see it this way?"

"Many think of me as a traitor."

"You held onto your morals throughout war and have kept your allegiance to *Roma*. When I am emperor, you will be rewarded and your country restored." Vespasian nodded firmly and then walked away, exiting the room with his officers.

"Those are legionary officers of only a part of the army which will march on Jerusalem." Titus stood and motioned Yosef to follow him to a table nearby covered in delicacies. "Do you like cheese? Figs or dates?"

Yosef nodded and helped himself to the food in a reserved manner, understanding it was not kosher but careful not to touch both dairy and meat. Titus watched him closely misunderstanding his caution, and then chuckled shaking his head. "I know you are hungry and you won't offend me. Please eat and enjoy."

Titus picked up a handful of figs and glanced over his shoulder at a slave who stood next to a white column. "Fetch a goblet and bring wine. You may speak freely." This last statement was directed to Yosef who ignored the cheese and was currently eating from a shank of lamb. Yosef nodded courteously and Titus had another slave bring a tray of picked food to some lounging cushions surrounding a low table.

"This is how you people eat now, isn't it?" Titus gestured to the table and cushions. "That is one thing you have taken from us in your higher circles, to eat in comfort and ease. I remember the remarkable feasts I used to attend in *Roma*, all the food, wine, and dancers. Feasts would last sometimes all night. However, with Nero it could really drag on if he decided to entertain his guests with poetry or song."

"Was it at such a party that he poisoned your friend, my lord?" Yosef asked meekly, glancing at the young man of twenty-nine years of age.

"His name was Britannicus. I had known him most of my life. Nero had him poisoned and in despair I finished the wine which bore the poison." Titus looked at Yosef for a moment's hesitation and then continued, finishing his thought, "I nearly died, but I recovered and now Nero is in Hades for what he did. Many people loved Nero in the early years, but by the time he murdered Britannicus, he was a vile rat, cunning and paranoid of everyone."

They laid down upon the soft pillows and mats surrounding the table as the food and wine was served. Titus felt his guest's discomfort and smiled. "You're probably wondering what the son of the Emperor-to-be is doing dining with a lowly Jew?"

Yosef shook his head. "I was wondering what the son of the Emperor-to-be was doing dining with a prisoner."

"He did give you privileges and promised to reinstate you, now that must mean something." Titus reached out and took a strip of honey covered lamb and ate it eagerly, savouring the taste as juices from the tender meat ran down his chin

"It does mean something, my lord."

"Good." Titus dipped some bread into a bowl of lentil stew and devoured it in a single bite, washing it down with a gulp of wine. He skewered another piece of lamb with a fork, plopped it onto his plate and cut it into smaller pieces with a knife.

"My lord, I wish to know plainly what will happen to me," Yosef said after a moment of silent eating.

"You will be my advisor, Yosef. I want someone of their kindred who is educated, to be my envoy and herald. We have a lot of work to do and this cannot be seen purely as a Roman endeavour. Agrippa will be accompanying us as well as other client kings, and we believe there is a peace delegation of upper class priests and rulers in Jerusalem that support us. I need you to represent certain edicts to the people of Jerusalem and to be a symbol of how well we treat those who serve *Roma*." Titus continued to eat and Yosef's goblet was refilled by a slave.

"I have considered myself a faithful servant of *Roma*. Even when I was in the north commanding forces there I made no direct aggression against Romans or Greeks. I merely bided my time, defending villages and towns in order to survive."

"My Father knows this, Yosef. You must not feel the need to defend yourself."

"But I have always been against Roman aggression inflicted upon my people: the terrors that Florus brought and the unfair arrests in which Nero committed against men of high rank, Jews that were patricians and Roman citizens. This I do not support, my lord, yet many of my people in Jerusalem believe I do support those antics which have terrorized them for over a decade."

"I see," Titus slowly replied. "We only wish to see the rebellion stopped, not terrorize the population. The battles we fought in the north were against Jewish factions bearing arms. We didn't harm surrendering towns and villages. Only those who didn't surrender by the time the ram hit the wall were punished and enslaved. This has always been the Roman will of orchestrating warfare and it will continue.

"However, I do not wish to see Jerusalem destroyed or its population killed. That is where you come in, Yosef, and your skills of oratory. I do believe that once we have our army outside of Jerusalem's gates, the people have to see the insanity in standing up against us. They will surrender." Titus slowly placed a grape in his mouth and continued to eat as Yosef thought about his words and the weight they held.

* * *

War Council of Vespasian
One hour later

"Now, I extend my thanks to you all in attending this council on such short notice, but we have a lot to discuss and plan." Vespasian glanced around the room at the faces before him. All the officers were seasoned men of high ranking birth. They stood before the table wearing their finest armour and all had freshly shaven faces. Each commander had pledged loyalty to Vespasian and called him their emperor even though Vitellius still ruled in Italy. "We must look at two different issues at hand." A door opened behind the officers and Titus stepped into the room. Vespasian nodded to his son and motioned for him to come forward. "I trust the prisoner has been well fed and seen to his room?"

Titus nodded expertly and resumed proper formalities in front of the others in addressing his father. "The prisoner has been escorted back to his room, Imperator."

"Very well, then." Vespasian ushered with his hands for the legates, tribunes, and allied kings to gather around the table which boasted a large map of the surrounding provinces of: Galilee, Samaria, Judea, Perea, and the southern desert the Jews called the Negev or Idumea. "I will begin by informing you that we have both the support and troops of King Agrippa, King Sohaemus of Emeas, and Antiochus of Commagene in this upcoming campaign." The Roman officers noted this by nodding at the foreign allied rulers who stood among them.

Vespasian continued, "It will involve maximum infantry support and regular patrols by cavalry. We will concentrate all forces on Jerusalem and Titus will lead them. We will have to muster troops from Alexandria, march up the coast, possibly rally at Caesarea Maritima, and then embark for the journey inland to Jerusalem. It will require absolute control of your units and precise techniques in foraging and remaining active.

"All forces will make a swift approach and hem the Zealots into the city before they can spring an attack or escape. Tiberius Julius Alexander, prefect of Egypt, will be your number two, Titus." Vespasian glanced up at the older Tiberius who had traveled to Berytus for the war council. Tiberius nodded seriously as he stood staring at the map with folded arms over top of his polished brass chest armour. "Gaius Licinius Mucianus will be on the move into *Italia* soon but has provided much of the necessary siege equipment needed and this will be added to by Cestius Gallus and his forces at Antioch."

"My lord, hasn't Gallus had his chance and failed miserably? He should be left out of this," piped up Titus Frigius, commander of the *Apollonaris* Fifteenth Legion who stood near the back of the officers. A few other heads nodded and Titus continued, "Can't we assume control of Tiberius' siege engines in Egypt and not rely on Gallus?"

Vespasian shook his head. "Tiberius doesn't have the numbers in equipment and engines that we need, nor are they in the prime condition that Gallus' are in. Gallus has better engineers than Tiberius and we will be already attaching two thousand troops from his force to strengthen the weaker legions that have seen action in West Africa. I don't want to weaken Alexandria's forces any more than necessary. It would be unwise with the pockets of heavy rebel activity south of Jerusalem and bordering Egypt around the city of Gaza. No, Gallus will do just fine despite his past failures." Vespasian took a breath to gather his thoughts.

He had been relieved at the absence of Gallus who had duties in Syria. The shameful retreat three years ago by the Fulminata Twelfth Legion and other forces of Gallus' had left many in the army's ranks bitter and embarrassed, their humiliation complete when they lost their golden eagle. A new eagle had been commissioned, but the memory was never distant from the minds of men, and much of the blame had landed squarely on poor Gallus. Vespasian knew most of the officers resented Gallus, which was why he had made sure to put as little authority on him as possible for the upcoming campaign. Vespasian understood the necessity in his bid for power and what the support of Gallus could provide, and so the presence of the legate and his soldiers would do just fine, but nothing more.

"So, Tiberius' III *Cyrenaica Legio* and XXII *Deiotariana Legio* will be used to reinforce any units that we see fit. This will be looked at in greater detail by Titus, Tiberius, and I at a later time. We will be combining our forces into around twenty cohorts of troops and eight alae under control by Titus. This will be the equivalent of eight legions and around three thousand horses. Tribune Marcus Sulla Maximus and his Boars will lead as the scouting force and the cavalry units will remain under command of their local tribunes. I will leave it up to Titus to arrange and plan for marching order and the placement of units.

"Titus Frigius, you will have your XV; Larcius Lepidus, you and your X *Fretensis* will make up the veteran numbers."

"The best of men!" Larcius laughed and a few booed. "We will set up camp outside Jerusalem and wait for your slow, tired asses." He thumped the table with his knuckles and Frigius just shook his head and downed his wine.

Vespasian waited for the men to calm down and then continued, "Sextus Cerealis and the V *Macedonica* will be joining the party, and Tribune Marcus Tullius Octavian will lead the XII Fulminata, which shall be brought back up to strength, assembled, and given the chance to redeem themselves."

"Thunderer!" Octavian announced. "They are eager for the chance, Imperator!" He cheerfully raised his goblet at the thought of his new command and drank long and hard.

Vespasian nodded with a grin and continued, "More precise orders will come in the near future, but for now the gods have blessed us with the best soldiers in the empire to see this business done. We have a lot of work to do and I expect this to continue at an aggressive pace throughout our wintering in Alexandria."

"It's much warmer in Egypt. I think I shall join you, Tiberius. If but I beg a little, perhaps his Excellency would have mercy," Larcius called out and a number of the men chuckled lightly as they continued drinking their wine.

"Larcius, you will winter with your troops in Jericho." Larcius nodded with a grin and Vespasian glanced to the other side of the table. "Sextus, your men will be stationed in Emmaus. You will both await further instructions from me as to when we shall depart for Jerusalem. Now, the next order at hand regards me." Vespasian glanced at Mucianus who had been instrumental in all his work to ensure the Flavians held power.

Mucianus approached the table, sidling up against Vespasian's left, as he pointed to the map. "Five days ago I completed and secured the support of all the Syrian cities and the provinces of Asia Minor. All have been issued with orders and letters declaring support for our Lord Vespasian and his right to the seat of Emperor and Father of us all. The next order of business will fall upon a series of moves to secure power. It isn't enough to just attack Vitellius; we must cripple him and then destroy him. I will be joining Primus to move on *Italia* soon, but until then, there are things to see done." Mucianus smiled playfully at the men, then drew his finger in a circle around the province of Syria and continued, "We will be leaving the IV *Scythica* Legio in Syria to remain in support and see to matters here.

"Next, as you know, wintering will be in Alexandria; however, this will give the option for our Lordship Vespasian to march Egyptian legions, not used in the siege of Jerusalem, along the west coast." Mucianus glanced at Vespasian and then scanned the faces in the room. "Following a swift coastal march, our Imperator can join our faithful Calpetanus Valerius Festus in Africa to complete the blockade along with Alexandria. Grain is the key here. Alexandria is vital to hold, but Africa may be an important move, not yet agreed on, however."

"Has there been any word of the Moesian legions regarding their allegiances?" Agrippa asked.

"Any day now, for that I am sure of, your Majesty; it is merely a matter of time. Moving on now, shall we?" Mucianus turned slightly as one of his aides handed him another map in which he unbound the leather cords and spread it on the table. Sextus and Titus placed weights on the edges of the parchment so it would not roll up and Mucianus gave an appreciative nod. "A task force from the legions of the Orient are here," he pointed. "The VI *Ferrata* and thirteen thousand other legionaries and auxiliaries are being organized. They have precise orders that when the time comes they will pass through Anatolia and along the *Via Egnatia* through Thrace and Macedonia, to seize command of the Adriatic from the strong position of Dyrrachium."

Mucianus glanced up and saw a number of heads nod as they saw the ingenious significance of holding Dyrrachium. Mucianus was in his glory as he and Vespasian had planned this through hours of calculating arrangements, dispatching orders, writing letters, and scouring the Roman east for support. Mucianus puffed out his chest and declared, "Having troops in Dyrrachium will be a direct threat to Brundisium, Terentium, and to the entire heel and instep of *Italia*." He tapped the map firmly at the allotted place and said with vigour, "This will threaten to split the Vitellian forces and be our door to power."

The men clearly liked the plan and started talking at once as a few leaned over for a closer look, while others drank to victory. Titus stood across from his father with his arms folded across his breastplate, totally enthralled with the plan.

Vespasian held up a hand and silence filled the room. He nodded at Mucianus and said, "I am strong in cavalry and have support from legions across the empire. We have sent letters to legates and armies making the necessary promises to the restoration of former *Praetorian* Guardsmen and have secured allegiances with fleets in 'Our Sea' and the Black Sea. With the absence of Mucianus from Syria, I have re-elected and assigned an acting governorship of Syria over to Pompeius Collega, who will be leaving the IV *Scythica* as legate. Thus, this region will stay in our hands and be administered during all that is to come.

"As you are all aware, once Mucianus reaches Primus in *Italia* with the Danubian Legions, it will be a quick action to locate and destroy Vitellius. Once that is complete and the occasion is right, I will sail for *Roma*. For the time being, I will be in Alexandria with Titus and the wintering legions, where I can have full control of the grain supplies and send out envoys into *Italia*. I estimate in a matter of weeks Vitellius' popularity will be very ill among the people." A few of the officers grinned and exchanged whispers. "Soon, we will all march to Alexandria and see to our winter quarters where training for the siege must begin. Some of our forces along the way will detach in Caesarea Maritima to keep a firm presence in this territory and in the spring we will reconnect with them and push to Jerusalem."

"What of the letter of Otho, my lord? Is it true?" Sextus asked, leaning in slightly over the map.

Vespasian nodded briefly and sighed. The letter had existed, composed by one of his personal forgers, and it had worked wonderfully. He had needed the extra leverage. It had been Titus' idea from the beginning. *Compose a letter from Otho and everyone will rally around you and spit on the face of Vitellius,* Titus had said.

"This is personal for me," Vespasian began, lowering his gaze and staring at the map. "A letter arriving into my hands just days after Otho's forced suicide. The letter called on me to come and defend him from Vitellius. I had pledged loyalty to Otho and now with this barbarity of insolence and violation of justice I will see Vitellius brought low and slain in the Forum if that is what it takes." The room was silenced by Vespasian's passion and a few heads nodded solemnly in agreement.

"The people of *Roma* will have their eyes opened to the truth," Titus began. "We have all pledged our loyalty to my father, the true and rightful Emperor of *Roma.*"

"And our loyalty stands more firm than ever, my lord," Lepidus added.

"We have watched our men inscribe your name upon their shields and we have honoured you," Sextus stated striking his fist in salute across his breastplate.

Vespasian bowed his head in gratitude towards this display of loyalty. "I have never questioned any of your allegiances and you have all served me with steadfast faith and fidelity."

"We would follow you to Pluto's door, my lord." Tiberius grinned and a number of the men chuckled lightly.

Vespasian pounded the table in his old rhetoric fashion and said, "Then let's make haste in the coming days, for we must prepare for the siege of Jerusalem, my friends, which is upon us. We will offer a sacrifice at first dawn to commemorate the coming campaign. Let us hope the entrails of the pure, white goat provide us with a favourable omen, and do pray for speedy news arriving from *Italia*. May the gods bless Mucianus and Primus in the campaign before them!"

"And may Jupiter be with Vespasian!" Marcus Octavian announced loudly from his mildly drunken stupor. The men cheered and drank their wine. Meanwhile, as Marcus Sulla Maximus stood at the back with his broad arms crossed, he growled under his breath that to conduct business as such, Octavian might as well bed a drunken whore.

* * *

Chapter III

It was at dawn, as the sun began to bake the dry earth, when the Lions spotted the man. He had looked drunk with exhaustion as he had stumbled around the naked trees stripped of their branches and the ground littered with jagged rocks. It had been the scouts near the entrance to the group's hideout who had sounded the alarm and with swords drawn they had descended on the lone wanderer. The man had begged for mercy, dropping to his knees and sobbing horribly. He had sworn upon everything sacred that he was no spy; instead, he was an honest man who had fled the legions to desert to the side of the Jewish rebellion.

The man had vowed an oath to convert as the blade of a sword had touched his throat. The blisters upon his feet from his sandals were evidence enough that he had been wandering for days. The sores had formed until swollen, burst and then had been rubbed raw; the blood and pus caked around his toes. His red tunic was so sun bleached from exposure that it had now turned to a lighter shade of pink with great stains down the back and front from sweat. He was incredibly thirsty and hungry, and his facial features were bony with signs of at least a week's growth of beard sprouting from his chin.

Judah strapped on an iron-studded leather harness over top of his garments and cinched his richly crafted belt to his waist to support the gladius strapped at his side. He slipped on his head covering and then slowly drew his sword. He motioned for a group of armed men to follow him and then moved silently through the cool hallways of interlocking caves which formed their refuge. Until now, the refuge had stayed absolutely hidden from outsiders, yet somehow this legionary deserter had come dangerously close to finding their hideout, which greatly disturbed Judah.

The Lions had held up in the caves for nearly three years and had constructed ovens hewn from the rock with narrow holes for the smoke to escape. These were used almost constantly by a small group of women who had fled with some of their men from the north, the latter who were now Lion warriors. The women's duty to earn their place at the refuge was simple: look after the food and tend to any wounded individuals. In return, they would be protected and could stay with their husbands. Judah had made sure this code of conduct was closely kept, for any breach in the protocols could result in the deaths of the greater number.

Along with ovens, latrines had also been cut from the stone near the back where a small creek ran beneath the rock to carry the waste away. It was nothing compared to the elaborate latrines of the Romans, but it made due as an underground current helped conceal any human excrement. The Lions also understood the lifeline of water. Where water ceased to thrive, so did everything living. Thus, they had carved small cisterns out of the limestone which enabled them to survive without having to do too much foraging on the outside.

When Judah and his armed band entered one of the smaller caves they halted at the sight of the kneeling captive, his mouth gagged, hands bound by leather cords and eyes blindfolded. The man was still whimpering slightly but had ceased sobbing. He kept moving his head in the direction of every little sound he heard but finally just hung his head and waited. Judah left his men near the entrance and slowly approached the man. Judah's eyes did not miss a thing: the condition of the man's tunic, his feet, face, hair, the sunburns on his arms and legs, the dirt and sweat covering the back of his neck, even the small black inked tattoo on his right forearm which bore the distinct legionary mark, *SPQR* and below that the numeral XII.

Judah stopped in front of the man and slowly said in Latin, "*Senatus Populusque Romanus!*" Then he repeated it in Greek, "The Senate and the People of Rome." He sheathed his sword and crossed his large arms. "Cut his bonds, Simon," Judah uttered in Hebrew and glanced over his shoulder. "Caleb, Adam, watch him!"

As soon as the man's gag was removed, he coughed, spit a gob of saliva mixed with blood onto the cave floor, and looked up after having his blindfold removed. "You speak Latin? The tongue of the Roman people?" He squinted at the large, black bearded warrior standing before him with a darkened complexion and penetrating eyes. The man gulped up the stale air as his chest heaved and he shielded his eyes from the torchlight with his weak hands.

Judah shrugged and turned around to take a seat on a stone near the entrance. "I don't understand Latin; I have just heard that title said by your kind in the past. We can speak in Greek though, if you are fluent." The man nodded and Judah continued, "My family was middleclass and had a trade where *Koine* would come in use. I learned it well when I was young." Judah watched the man's eyes dart in a panic around the room as he stared at the other large beastly forms of the Jewish fighters. Judah noticed the man's fear and smiled. "They won't kill you, as long as I don't wish it. They don't understand Greek either, so you can talk plainly, and that you better start doing at once. Who are you? Why have you come this way alone?"

The man nodded and swallowed the lump in his throat. "My name is Quintus Fabius and I was a soldier with the Twelfth Legion as of a week ago when I fled. I was chosen that week to be a night guard of an overnight patrol detail sent out to keep training; they don't want us slacking. So, when I went forward as night guard of the second shift I fled my company. It was the fifth hour of night and most of the other members of my company were asleep. I told my comrade I had to piss and when I was far enough away I ran. I just ran."

"And you did this with no preparation? No thought of how you could obtain food or water? What of bandits like us? What did you expect would happen? You're of good fortune that my men didn't skewer you instead of sparing your life. Usually they can't bear to see the sight of a living Roman, or a dead one for that matter." Judah glanced over Quintus' shoulder at the six scouts who had captured him. "Maybe *my* men need a night patrol. They seem to be going soft on you Roman dogs."

Quintus winced in pain as he shifted his weight onto his right knee. The dark grim expressions from the scouts made him uncomfortable and he gazed back at the Jewish leader with pleading eyes. "What I say is the truth. I did have a small sack of food and a water skin hidden under my plate armour. Once I was far enough away I stripped down to my tunic and fled as fast as I could.

"You have never been in the Roman army; you don't know what they do to deserters! Flaying alive, clubbed to death, beheaded or driven into the wilderness with no food, sandals, or clothing. I had to get away fast; the harsh rules and life of the army has never been for me. I was a thief in Corinth, a nobody! I joined the legion out of desperation and was sent here to this land to fight for Vespasian. I don't want any part of it, so I got out. I told your scouts I will convert to your faith if that will make you believe me. I don't care anymore. I just wanted to escape Vespasian's army, and I reasoned with myself that if that meant joining your side, then so be it. There was nowhere else to go."

"You think we will win against Vespasian?"

Quintus nodded furiously. "He had success in the north against your ill equipped armies, but even your ill equipped armies killed hundreds, if not thousands of Roman legionaries. The word throughout the army is that Jerusalem will be impossible and a suicide mission. Some men, like me, have defected to your side or have tried fleeing the province altogether, heading for Alexandria or Corinth. They have money and can pay their way from this land, given they don't get caught. I have nothing, just a poor soldier I am. But I will fight for you if that means I can survive and live free from the yoke of legionary law."

"How did you hear of this place?" Judah chose his words carefully but had relaxed since beginning the conversation.

Quintus thought for a moment and shrugged. "I had only heard of your band, you are the Lions are you not?" The Jewish leader nodded slowly and Quintus continued, "I pretended to be a Jewish refugee fleeing from Tiberias, I hear many there speak Greek. Anyway, I came to a village not far from here and met a travelling priest who told me about some of the activity he had heard going on in this region. The ambushes of Roman patrols and the foraging of supplies was what he told me. The old priest, however, didn't know where you were hiding. I just thought I would poke about the caves near here, and I have done so for two days. I thought these would make for a good bandit hideout or at least I could find shelter and maybe some water." This last word was said with conviction and an overwhelming desire to quench his thirst.

Judah stared at Quintus for a moment considering everything he had just heard. He slowly stood and rested his hand on the pommel of his sword. Everyone and everything was silent except for the distant chirping of birds outside the caves. Judah slowly nodded towards the scouts standing behind Quintus and said just above a whisper, "Get him some water and circumcise him if he truly wants to stay."

As the scouts led Quintus to the nearest cistern, Caleb approached Judah cautiously and sighed exclaiming, "You really believe him?"

Judah shook his head and stared up at the ceiling of rock. "I don't know what to believe."

"We can't jeopardize our hideout, Judah! There are over sixty of us here."

Judah turned around and glared at Caleb. "You don't think I know that?" Judah shot a glance at the tall figure of Adam who remained standing near the entrance. "I want you to select two men, Adam, to take a constant watch of Quintus. We will only know his true colours when we see him kill his own kind." Judah looked back at Caleb with an apologetic look in his eyes for he knew he had hurt his friend. "I trust you, Caleb, above all, I do." He lowered his voice and rested a hand on Caleb's shoulder. "You're one of the only men who I would do anything for. But you must know this: I would rather give this Quintus a chance then murder him in cold blood."

"I have never known you to spare the life of a Roman. In three years I have never heard you say this. Why now?"

"Because there is something which tangles with my conscience, and I can't quite explain it. All the men I have killed have never given me satisfaction. There is only one man I truly wish to kill, Caleb, and he is far from my reach." Judah slowly turned and stood like a statue staring at the dirt floor. "I have told you of the man?"

"You mean the Centurion who killed Miriam?" Caleb's voice was filled with sympathy yet he did not understand the sudden change in Judah and this perplexed him.

Judah nodded. "I found out his name, Caleb. Have I told you?"

Caleb's mouth opened but nothing was said. For a moment the two stood in silence until he found his voice. "How did you find the name of this centurion?"

Judah took a deep breath and shuddered. He said in almost a whisper, "After the massacre in the Upper Market, I challenged a centurion who had led the detachment. I had seen him only once in the past, when Florus had ridden into the city the day before when the people had mocked him. Well, I recognized him that day when his sword was red with blood and his men were drunk. But the man wouldn't fight me."

Judah gazed up at the walls of the cave. He stared at them transfixed and obsessed as if he was in some sort of a dream. "I was so enraged I could hardly think. To see my Miriam floating in the fountain pool pierced through the back by a spear and slain before my eyes, tore me apart and I lost myself that day. I would no longer be a man to roam this world. I had traded my soul, Caleb, for something dark, something from *Gehenna*. I would join the king of Babylon in *Sheol*, like the prophet Isaiah wrote about. Except I would be the one shocking the ancient kings upon their thrones, not the king of Babylon brought low. I would even cause God to shudder with disgust."

"What did you do?" Caleb asked quietly, for he had never heard of this before. He glanced over his shoulder and realized Adam had left and it was only the two of them in the cave.

"I ran from the marketplace and followed two drunken soldiers, Florus' men." Judah wiped the sweat from his brow and a disturbing look covered his face as if he was reliving the events. "I crept up from behind and jumped the one to my left. I quickly slit his throat and spewed his blood all over his friend. The man shouted in alarm and knew he wouldn't have time to draw his sword, so he tried to run. I wasn't afraid of people seeing us. The air had been so full of screams and noise that everyone had fled.

"So I chased the man and caught him. I dragged him into a small alley and questioned him. He wouldn't tell me, so I cut three of his fingers off. When he finally gave me the name of the centurion who had led the assault I beat him near to the point of death. I then cut both his hands off and castrated him. I left him bleeding upon the stones, unconscious." Judah turned slowly and his gaze fell upon Caleb who was completely still. "But I did get the centurion's name and with that I will seek my revenge. I had days and weeks to think about what I did in the alley, and I have never committed something so vile since.

"When I looked into the eyes of Quintus, I saw the man I tortured in that alley. I can't send Quintus away for he knows our location and I will not execute him for I must show *HaShem* I am worthy. So, we will give this Roman a chance. If he tries anything we can kill him then, but not in cold blood and not without giving him the honour of trust." Judah patted Caleb's shoulder and moved past him to leave the room.

"What was the centurion's name, Judah?" Caleb asked, turning slowly.

Judah stopped abruptly. "Capito. His name is Capito."

*   *   *

July 24th, 69 A.D. / 19th of Av, 3829
Jerusalem
House of former High Priest Matthias ben Theophilus

"*Shalom*, my lord. King Simon ben Giora calls for your council."

Matthias glared at the servant and then shook his burly head. "Don't call him by that title, Moshe. That is absurd. What is it now? Does he wish for godly advice?"

The servant hesitated, unsure of what to say, and then shrugged while lowering his gaze. "I don't know, my lord. All I am told is that he wishes to see you." The servant slowly backed up a respectable distance and then left the peaceful sanctuary of his master.

Matthias took the fringe of his garment and ran it through his fingers as he sat alone in his garden. His breathing was deep and the fragrance of flowers filled his nostrils. The sun had already set and the expanse around him was lit by an eerie blue from the coming night sky. He listened intently as he heard the braying of a donkey somewhere in the city and the sound of excited voices outside in the streets. Shabbat was ending and so much was different in Jerusalem, so much had changed.

The former high priest could remember a time when the city would brace with excitement and religious fervour as the holy Shabbat approached. Meals would be prepared beforehand, psalms sung, and the *shofar* blown throughout the city. The scent of roasting meat would drift into the homes from the smoke wafting from sacrifices of the Temple as the priests worked without cessation and people would rush through the narrow streets to their homes to celebrate the day of rest. Lamps would be lit, hymns sung, and Jews everywhere would observe the day set aside since creation for the temporary end of labour. Shabbat was always something to look forward to in the midst of a busy week; however, treachery from John of Gischala against the government had changed all that, as well as the penning of a letter sent south into Idumea.

The letter had been a plea for help to the Idumeans claiming falsities against the government. Ananus ben Ananus became the scapegoat as John, who once had been trusted by the Senior Chief and head of the party, had claimed that Ananus had dispatched messengers to Vespasian to surrender the city.

Furthermore, the letter had stated that Ananus had planned on giving up Temple treasuries to pay for the entire Sanhedrin's safe passage to Rome where they would be granted large villas for ending the war. Matthias knew this to be a blatant lie, but the manipulating words of the letter had contained volumes of declarations against the government stating they were corrupt, Roman sympathizers, out of the will of God, blasphemers, whores of plunder, and murderers of patriots. The letter had been a genius move by John and Eleazar ben Simon, who at the time had been one united Zealot faction. Thus, the letter had been a death sentence for the Provisional Government.

The response by the Idumeans had been shocking with the arrival of a large army. Matthias could still recall Ananus shutting the gates of the city in the faces of the enemy and Yeshua ben Gamlas shouting out at the Idumeans from one of the towers, trying to parley with them. The Idumeans had believed they were on a quest from God and would not relent. They had also been enraged at having the gates shut, denying them the right of passage they had to the city as fellow Jews. Despite all the shouting from both sides, a storm had moved in and battered the land. This had caused the guards on the ramparts to seek shelter and the Idumean army to scramble for cover and sit angrily upon the ground under their shields.

That night as the storm raged, Zealot soldiers and sworn enemies of the Provisional Government had crept along the ramparts, slaughtered the sleeping guards, and opened the gates to the Idumean army to the blast of a horn. All sense of morality and ethics in battle had vanished as the combined coup, Idumean and Zealot, rampaged through the city and slaughtered the troops of the Provisional Government.

When dawn broke, thousands had been killed, their bodies scattered in piles around the Outer Court of the Temple and through the streets, blood staining the stones and running down the culverts. Ananus ben Ananus and Yeshua ben Gamlas were swiftly executed by the orders of John of Gischala, who had their throats slit and their bodies cast over the wall into the Kidron Valley. There would be no burial for them, their mutilated corpses exposed to the sun, bloated and swollen. Matthias' life, however had been spared. Later, he had been told his exoneration had something to do with the Zealots believing he had rejected Ananus as a leader, but Matthias had no idea where that story had come from. All he knew was that he had miraculously escaped certain death.

When the rage had subsided, it was to the dismay of the Idumeans that much of the letter, which ignited their bloodthirsty passion in the first place, was proven to be false. They had expressed grievances and shame over the travesty, and then justified it as a noble act by freeing over two thousand prisoners.

What followed next had been a gift to the Zealots, as the Idumeans marched out of the city with disdain, only a handful of them joining the Zealots who now ruled the city unopposed. Matthias had watched the departing Idumeans from the ramparts, the city now vacant of government soldiers and replaced with Zealots. It was as if darkness had descended over the city.

The supremacy of the Zealots had been terrible. John of Gischala, Eleazar ben Simon and their factions had terrorized, pillaged, and run the city like a mob of outlaws with many citizens fearing to go out day or night. This culmination of terror tactics finally turned into inner fighting among the Zealots themselves as John and Eleazar bickered between one another about who should rule the city. Matthias had been brought into the mess to bring order as High Priest, yet he had tried to remain neutral as many died attempting to choose sides. Finally it had ended with the creation of two Zealot factions, as they strove to drive one another from their footholds of power. All this was to change, however, with the threatening danger the Zealots saw to the south embodied in the army of Simon ben Giora, the exiled renegade from Jerusalem and friend of the Sicarii of Masada.

Matthias could remember hearing about the Zealot army routed in an attempt to crush the early roots of Simon ben Giora's seizure of power. The soldiers of John of Gischala had stumbled into the city, fewer than had been sent, as many bore bloody wounds, hacked and slashed open from knives and swords. Their eyes had been wide with terror. John had questioned many and found the news of Simon's strength to be one of a terrifying magnitude.

The Zealots could not stop the discipline of Simon's horde, even when it had surrounded the city of Jerusalem for a long siege. Simon had been incapable of waging a battle to storm the city, but his strength was vast and a testament to his victories over the Idumean armies and their strongholds. It still seemed like a dream to Matthias when he recalled the Idumean refugees in the city. These had been the men who had remained from the Idumean army that had ousted the Provisional Government, and now they approached the priest and begged for his council. Matthias remembered the panic on their faces as they had given the news of murdering over a dozen Zealots in a brawl and seizing much of the loot John of Gischala had stocked. When the Zealots had rushed to kill them, the Idumeans had surrounded the house of the High Priest and had begged him to do something.

Now, Matthias closed his eyes and prayed. Had he done the right thing? He looked around the quiet garden as a breeze disturbed some of the bushes and flowers and caused them to stir. What had he said to the Idumeans on that day? The statement still pounded in his ears, but he swore he had done the right thing. *"God is with us and has provided an army at our gates! We must decide between the lesser of evils. If you want an end to the tyranny of John and Eleazar then I shall go down and invite Simon inside our walls."* God had provided an army and the defence of the city was vital. Ananus was already dead and the Provisional Government was no more, so it was either count on Simon to run things or let the city die at the hands of brigands.

"My lord, are you going to see Simon?" said Moshe, as he returned holding a jug of wine.

Matthias gave his servant an apathetic look. "Do you remember what we once were when we gathered here with pride?"

Moshe glanced around the garden for a moment and then shook his head. "I am confused, my lord."

"The supper is what I meant. I was referring to the night of the dinner."

"There have been many suppers here, my lord, most recently with Simon and his men," Moshe replied innocently.

It was as if Moshe had said nothing since Matthias had an empty look in his eyes and his gaze fell upon the small stone pathway. "We had so much influence and power among the people, and it all changed. Ananus said we should think about what to do about the Romans but some wanted a disciplined army. There were so many opinions you lost count. What were we supposed to do? What was I to do? I survived the battle that ended the lives of so many of the government and then I had to pick a side. It was either choose or be thrown in prison or worse. I believe that somewhere in the madness of this all God wants us to win, like the Maccabees. We have been divided for so long."

"You thought Simon would solve that, my lord?" asked Moshe as he watched the face of Matthias turn to him. A bird began singing somewhere nearby as night closed in around the palace.

"You remember that night, Moshe? The night I called for an assembly of the few I trusted the most?" Matthias did not wait for an answer but continued sadly as he recalled the familiar faces long since dead or imprisoned. It was like a collision of worlds: one of regret and the other of apathy. The storm that raged in Matthias' mind seemed one of uncertainty in its outcome or path and bent only on gratuitous inner torment. The endless struggle was viewed in the mind of Matthias from two angles: one of a godsend of Simon's army, strong and disciplined to defend the city, and the other as a betrayal towards the government and a fear that God had left Jerusalem's fate to Rome.

Matthias had never spoken of it to anyone since the overthrow of the government and the containment of John of Gischala and Eleazar ben Simon's two Zealot factions. However, it had to surface; it was better to confess to someone as unimportant as a slave. Thus, it was at that time that Matthias finally beckoned Moshe to join him and ushered him to one of the stone benches. "Let me tell you of the night when Ananus and the others were brought to my garden for dinner. What I tell you is secret; you must swear an oath upon your life not to relinquish any details to anyone. If this was to get out, Moshe, Simon would see us both dead. Do you understand?"

Moshe nodded cautiously, knowing what night Matthias spoke of in particular. He should know as he had organized the food and drinks for that evening and also was the head chef in charge of the kitchen, making sure the other slaves did their jobs. However, he had not the slightest idea of what they had actually discussed. He could imagine what went on, but the events of that evening had remained wrapped in utter secrecy and most of its attendants were now dead. "I understand, my lord. I shall not say a thing. What of Simon though? He awaits your presence."

"Simon can wait for the time being. I will confide in a slave, Moshe, for you are probably the least I have to worry about in this city ripe for revenge and filled with fear. So pay attention and if anything is ever to happen to me and you find yourself in the presence of a literate priest, then tell him my story and tell him the truth: I didn't abandon the government and sell out the others."

Matthias paused for a brief moment pondering where to start first and then a twinkle of light flashed in his eyes. Leaning forward he continued, "Very well, we go back then nearly five months ago, I believe." Matthias began to relive the details of the most vital meeting the Provisional Government had ever had, and the last time they would ever meet again as a council in the presence of distinguished colleagues and friends.

*   *   *

"What is the password?"

"Don't be foolish, Moshe, and step aside. You know who it is."

Sunlight streamed through the doorway as the wealthy aristocrat and member of the Sanhedrin, Joshua ben Gamala, pushed open the door, shot the young servant boy a strange look and shook his head. As a member of the Jewish elite and a priest, he entered the home wearing expensive garments, adorned with a long head covering lined with a white stripe signifying his position as an elder council member. Joshua stared at the boy for a moment with small eyes seeming to hide under bushy eyebrows. His long beard would have given him the appearance of a wild prophet if it had not been so neatly groomed. Jerusalem had had its share of prophets. Some were sent by God, while others were more concerned with filling their coin purses. Only a few were disputed by the religious elders, both Pharisee and Sadducee who questioned their motives and authority as to what power gave them the clout to preach. The Jewish elders had come to loathe anyone calling themselves a prophet or Messiah, especially since the Galilean Rabbi had roused things up. The Roman authorities in the past had silenced many, seeing 'prophets' as an excuse to rebel with religious fanaticism. But Joshua ben Gamala was neither a prophet nor a rebel leader. He was a man who believed in three things: honouring God, keeping the Torah, and making sure sacred Jerusalem remained safe from heathen hands.

The long robes of the other members of council brushed lightly against the floor as one by one the distinguished and most powerful men of the United Provisional Government gathered. Eleazar ben Ananias arrived with a calm and patient look about him. Zechariah ben Baris and former high priest Yeshua ben Gamlas entered next discussing some topic of Isaiah and whether it was true or not if the ancient prophet's wife could have been a virgin and pregnant at the same time. Gorion ben Joseph and Simeon ben Gamaliel, great speakers and well known orators, arrived one after the other, walking in a distinguished manner, heads held high. A number of their students were left outside to wait until the meeting was adjourned. The young talmid chacham sat down under a small tree and continued debating the questions Gorion and Shimon had drilled them with earlier in the day. The last to arrive was the grey-bearded Shimeon ben Gamaliel, of a different family then Simeon. He was the eldest of the government and personal friend of Ananus ben Ananus, Senior Chief and head of the United Provisional Party.

The men were ushered into one of the large wings of the house which opened up into a small garden within, built as a relaxing retreat for the High Priest and a place where he could receive guests. Matthias ben Theophilus, the recently deposed high priest of Jerusalem, stood on a stone patio of mosaic murals constructed from tiny coloured tesserae stones. The patio had been built in the center of the garden where a low seated table had been set with cushions and pillows scattered around it. Ananus ben Ananus stood beside Matthias holding a goblet of wine as he closely studied a flower.

The garden was filled with wild flowers of many varieties, such as purple perennials that had been personally transported from the Sharon Valley and lilies from all families. Large groups of cacti sprouted fruit and could be seen throughout the precincts. Each cactus was surrounded by beautiful roses and other wild plants that were native to the area. A number of lemon, pomegranate, and apple trees grew from thick roots in the neatly gardened soil, giving off a favourable aroma. It was obvious Matthias loved his garden retreat and he smiled warmly at his guests. Those who had never been there glanced around, impressed at what they saw. Those who were familiar with the paths twisting throughout the garden took their seats, sprawling out comfortably with support from the pillows which surrounded the table.

Once seated, Matthias passed out leavened bread cakes from a basket in front of him and welcomed the guests to his table. As they all broke bread and dipped it into small bowls of honey, six servants emerged from the house carrying great trays of appetizers, including olives, bowls of almonds, pistachios, raisins, pomegranates, figs, dates, and sliced apples. To wash it all down, copper pitchers of dark red wine was served. Matthias had given strict instructions to keep the wine flowing steadily and had reserves in the kitchen, where more drink and food waited. The honey soaked goat, strips of lamb, and fowl were served with a bean stew filled with lentils, onions, garlic cloves, and bitter herbs.

The men thoroughly enjoyed the meal which was proven by the level of talk that ran about the table. Everything from temple taxes, the finishing touches done on the outer porticoes of the colonnades, to the unwanted activity by Eleazar ben Simon was discussed. This last topic was one of great discomfort, as many of the priests and leaders held very opinionated views, despising the sacrilege which had been committed for the last few years. Wishing for this choice of topic to dissipate rather than ruin the mood at the table, Matthias had a number of musicians enter and play a few choice songs from their flutes and lyres. Once this was done, Matthias ordered refills on the wine and then sent the servants away. He cleared his throat, indicating that he wished to discuss the matter at hand and everyone grew quiet; only Ananus continued eating from a small bowl of olives, leaving the pits on the table in front of him.

"I have called each one gathered here today because you are of the most trusted lot. We, the members of the government elected by our people to serve Jerusalem and this land throughout this struggle, are seeing trying times. I know this because of the voice of pessimism which seems to speak volumes louder than those who believe we can win this war. Fear is dangerous for us and can destroy our system here, so we must remain calm and keep our wits about us.

"We have no doubt tried to remain faithful by consulting God throughout this war, and the daily sacrifices have continued to this very moment, unhindered even by the rude presence of Eleazar ben Simon's Zealots who control the Temple Mount. We must trust in God and continue to do so, even with the loss of the north. However, we know the Romans are coming. Our sources say they are gathering and training even though they do not threaten us with any major action as of yet. The death of Nero was a blessing from Adonai and the year's disruptions have brought this godless tyrant called Rome to a halt in this land. We must look to the next year which is upon us with haste." Matthias gazed up at the sky solemnly for a brief moment and then slowly sat down while uttering a prayer.

All at the table were hushed, taking in the words of the High Priest and then Ananus stood. "The government is breathing its last breath. We have seen our effort in this land collapse upon us with suffering. With each and every day we have been defiant, that has been a day of freedom from Roman rule. However, they will come to this city and it will not be like Gallus and the narrow victory we had which, God be praised, developed into a full route for the Roman governor and his army.

"We have heard that Vespasian is making a bid for power, which will no doubt leave him out of the upcoming campaign which is sure to come. Thus, I cannot see Jerusalem, as important as it is for the Romans to crush, being left in the command of a lesser man than Titus. This is who Matthias *and I believe will conduct the attack on our city. Now I say to you, we must think rationally and buy our time. Three years ago when this started we were strong in mind and number. We have been seriously weakened by the loss of the Galilee; this summer's harvest has suffered greatly creating a food shortage and the city is overcrowded. Many think we have experienced the full fury of Rome but I say to you that what we have heard or seen is nothing compared to the force which will arrive outside our walls in due time.*

"With our hold over the greatest city in the east Vespasian cannot be emperor for long, especially with his hope for popularity and the trust of the Senate. It is no longer a matter of 'if' they will crush us, but when. Without a standing army organized and strong to protect Jerusalem, the outcome is inevitable. This war will end abruptly and be filled with suffering beyond our wildest dreams. It will be like the lack of shock a fly must feel when he is utterly squashed upon a stone without the slightest idea of what has become of him."

Ananus stared with piercing eyes at the other men as he watched them mull over in their minds their current status. He took a stab in the air with his finger and said firmly, "We must look to the concern of our people, the city, and our Holy Temple, the latter the Romans must never take. What would we have, Romans profaning our Holy Temple as they sack the city? I believe, with Matthias, that we must continue to observe the Romans and at the right time offer terms; this is the only way to save ourselves. I will no longer place my trust in empty platitudes. God has let the Galilee fall and the countryside is being pillaged by bands of our own people. Eleazar has turned the Temple grounds into a fortress and gangs are sprouting up everywhere. There is murder and theft constantly. We must look to our own survival, we the elite of this city and the learned minds, surely we know best."

If a pin had fallen upon the stones it would have filled the garden with its noise. The priests and members of the government sat unnerved by the speech for they were of the closest advisors to the Senior Chief. They all knew it was coming. City after city had been crushed despite resistance to the Romans, and now the door was wide open and nothing could stop them from advancing upon Jerusalem. A clammy silence filled the air and Ananus seated himself and whispered something to Matthias.

"We will hear any objections or thoughts," Matthias said and then sipped his wine.

Yeshua ben Gamlas cleared his throat and bowed his head with respect to the elders. "I support you, Matthias, and agree with your words, Ananus, but how will we take this to the others? The Zealots are powerful and will view us as traitors. We have all heard the rumours concerning what the Zealots do to their own kind when someone is suspected of treason. How will we stem the tide if they should charge down from their fortress, our Holy Temple, and try to kill us?"

Ananus' face was fiercely passionate and he addressed them with this same fire. "Gorion and Simeon can make speeches to the people as the time approaches. They are trusted individuals and have a large following. We have power in this city, unlike the violence from the Zealots and the Sicarii who keep people in fear. We must stand as one and confront them as the united government. We represent law and order and we must stand apart from the bloodthirsty brigands. If the people see us as a force, with their best interests in mind, they have to support us. The greater majority does not want war and certainly do not want the Romans laying siege to this city. If we symbolize God's will upon the city, then I dare anyone to stand against us. If they resist, we can organize and fight them if it comes to that. We have a lot of support."

"Shall we send a letter to Titus?" asked Zechariah ben Baris.

Ananus nodded. "That has been discussed and is most likely the wisest action to take once we are sure we can control the city. We have to watch both fronts: the Romans and Eleazar ben Simon."

"What of John ben Levi, or better known as John of Gischala? He is in the city and grows stronger daily," Simeon added.

"He must be approached and invited to join our party. If he is left to roam wild he could cause trouble," Eleazar ben Ananias said.

"He is a dangerous man and not to be trusted. He should be assassinated! Hire some knife men," Yeshua uttered, causing all eyes to look at him. "I have known of John since the beginning of this struggle. I first heard of him when I was High Priest and Yosef ben Matityahu was elected as general of the north. I know the father of Yosef and I have known nothing but deceit and scheming to come from John of Gischala. He tried to murder Yosef on a number of occasions and stirred up villages and towns against him. This in no way helped our cause; when it needed unity the most, all it got was dissention. He is a dangerous man and one to play sides. My heart is telling me we should be rid of him."

Matthias shook his head. "He curries support of many, and he is an experienced and able commander. I know of the delegation sent to relieve Yosef and that inquiry was disrupted and never examined. Many believe John would have done a better job. Anyway, that is the past and we are faced with few experienced allies in war."

"You would call John of Gischala an ally? He is just as dangerous as Eleazar. To even consider him a friend is preposterous. Have you forgotten how he and the Zealots deposed Matthias who was the legally chosen High Priest? Once they were rid of him they elected a nobody by a cast of lots! This Phanni ben Samuel has no connection to priestly descent and mocks God with his charades as he wears the ceremonial robes. He was elected by the Zealots and no council or proper authority under God ever gave him that title," Yeshua retorted.

"We know of Eleazar's involvement in that, not of John's," Ananus countered. "Besides, John is a pious man and desires to uphold the law. He is not like the others." Ananus glanced at Matthias as he saw the former High Priest lower his gaze as he recalled the humiliating, shameful day. The two had discussed John of Gischala prior to the meeting, and had come to the opinion that despite the Temple conundrums that had taken place, John may be their only hope of winning the strife within their walls. "John should be approached and offered a truce. We can hire him, even pay him, if we so wish. I believe John is an able commander who has fought faithfully for this government. The issues of the Galilee between John and Yosef should be laid to rest and not held as a weight to judge John by.

"What happened up north was tragic. Man's first instinct is to survive and John thought he could do a better job than Yosef, and perhaps he was right. Where did it get Yosef? Rumour has it the Romans captured him at Jotapata, but we can't confirm that. He will most likely die in some obscure arena. Would you stand in the place of God and judge John, Yeshua ben Gamlas?"

Yeshua rolled his eyes in frustration and spoke while shaking his hands in the air with annoyance, "Whether you think he was right or wrong, John should be treated with suspicion and not be trusted.

We need to stay strong as the elected government and not employ outsiders. The people know of John as a bully, like Eleazar. It would do us no good to include such a man, especially with his background. Judging him has nothing to do with it, Ananus. Only facts and the man's bloodthirsty nature will sentence him justly," Yeshua pleaded, shaking his head.

"John is not all wicked, Yeshua. You make him seem like Ba'al Zebub. We should have more faith in him. However, I do see the wisdom in at least questioning him and voting on the matter if we so wish him to join our government or represent us before his supporters," Shimeon ben Gamaliel said, adding his gruff voice to the council for the first time.

Matthias nodded gratefully at Shimeon and then swung his gaze to Yeshua. "Your opinion is noted, but we will ultimately see what is best for this government's survival. We will be careful with John, but we will not alienate him. That is all on that issue!"

The members at the table whispered amongst each other. One asked if the Sanhedrin should gather in its entirety to demand Eleazar ben Simon vacate the Temple Mount and that if he refused they should storm the compound in a surprise attack. A few men shouted the uselessness of this request and others shrugged, not seeing a clear answer.

"Even by offering him a truce and letting him leave, where will he go? No, he knows his life is forfeit if he leaves. His army would scatter and dissolve in the desert or worse; he has made many enemies. If we organize to attack, he will make the first move and we need to be ready," Joshua said, standing up to get attention. "I believe the best action is what Ananus proposed; keep a close watch on his movements and contain him on the Temple Mount."

"Thank you, Joshua." Ananus stood and nodded at his friend. "We can start by raising soldiers in our circles of trust; we have many whom we can turn to. With an army at our side, the Zealots cannot threaten us. Furthermore, we will not directly threaten the Temple. If we are able to get in contact with the Romans, Eleazar will be forced to lower his arms and surrender."

"Well, he won't starve. The Temple storehouses are packed with grains, vegetables, fruits and many more rooms of food. We'll be lying in our tombs before that man runs out of food for his small rabble." Zechariah cleared his throat and set an olive pit on the table. "It must be a show of force from either us or the Romans, but I don't believe they will ever surrender to the Romans, crazed men they are."

Ananus shook his head. "When Titus arrives and accepts our formal surrender, then Eleazar will become the coward he is."

"What if we were to have an army worthy of defending the city, Ananus?" Shimeon asked with a sleepy look upon his wrinkled face. "Have you considered that option? We are all traitors to Rome for fighting against her, and this government we have formed is punishable by crucifixion. Even meeting around this table in this fashion would be considered illegal. What if we assembled an army strong enough to fight back? What if Titus doesn't accept our surrender?"

All eyes were upon Ananus and he swallowed hard. Matthias, lounging on the cushions next to him, pondered that very question. What if they had an army? He knew no army existed at the present time but prayed silently that God would provide an army like from the ancient days that would destroy the Romans and cast them out forever. It would be like Joshua of old at Jericho or King David against the Philistines.

"No army exists!" Ananus suddenly blurted out angrily, startling Matthias and attracting all attention in the garden. "We can assemble enough men to defeat Eleazar and police the city, but to hold off fifty to sixty thousand trained legionaries, impossible without a miracle of God! As for Titus, with the Temple treasury overflowing with gold, I am sure he could be bought, especially being able to avoid a siege. His men would mutiny if he refused our offer. Anyway, this has not yet been the agreed method of diplomacy at this point. We have not contacted Titus in anyway, nor have we sent a delegation up north. The possibility of surrendering the city would have to be brought before the entire Sanhedrin and Provisional Government."

"What of Simon ben Giora to the south, Ananus? Will he ever come to Jerusalem?" Gorion asked glancing around the table and causing heads to nod concerning the serious weight of the question.

Simon ben Giora was the most dangerous of man in Ananus' opinion and he loathed him. The aging priest had driven Simon from the toparchy of Acrabatene, wrenching any rule in the administrative district from his hands because he had feared the man's popularity which had begun drawing strong forces of support from the peasantry. Simon was a charismatic man and an unpredictable one, which had been Ananus' justification to see him expelled from Jerusalem shortly after the beginning of the war. Rumour had spread that he had joined the Sicarii on the mountain fortress of Masada and that he was staying there, joining the knifemen on cattle raids and plundering insignificant villages. Simon would amount to nothing and Ananus dreamed of his death, skewered by some Roman spear. With Simon ben Giora on Masada and out of the picture, Ananus could concentrate his power and influence on securing the city.

Ananus looked sharply into the eyes of each member and then began speaking in a low voice, "He would not be welcome! He is a bandit and stands against the very morals of our people. He makes no move at the present moment and only wishes to convince the people of the south that he is some desert king!" Ananus pointed his finger in the air and continued, "We must have the support of the people and keep our gaze on Jerusalem which is all that matters. Eleazar must be contained and then we can bring it to the council and vote."

The plan seemed reasonable and possible. The delegates of the government nodded with affirmation and gave vocal support, only Shimeon ben Gamaliel sat quietly, one elbow on the table and his hand propping up his head. His eyes darted around from face to face observing the activity. The hinges of a door creaked from behind him as servants emerged carrying pitchers of wine to refill the cups. All the men seemed to be speaking at once with excited voices, but Shimeon's mind was troubled.

The discussion was left open and with no real plan, just words stacked upon words. The council seemed perfectly fine with waiting and seeing what would happen, when under their very noses the city was retching with labour pains and division. Ananus appeared confident, that with raising a number of amateur soldiers from the upper echelon of wealthy Jews, this would be enough to confine Eleazar. As if it was that simple. Eleazar may be mad, but he was not stupid. The committee seemed to believe that a simple delegation to the Romans would end the war. This may be true, Shimeon thought, at least with the struggle in Jerusalem, but if Eleazar stayed faithful to his convictions, then civil war would continue to divide them and pose a problem to those who wanted peace.

How could the Peace Party surrender the city to Titus with five thousand soldiers still bearing arms? If a lion was cornered, it would fight for its life. Was this not true of desperate men? What if Eleazar could not be contained? Surely the Romans would have a nightmare trying to clear the Temple Mount, and the possibility of the Temple's destruction could still occur. Every situation Shimeon analyzed he saw the same end. The only real chance they would have would be a complete assault on the Temple Mount. That would mean storming the Inner Court and hunting every Zealot down. Other than that, the Zealot problem could not be solved. However, these men seemed to know how all the puzzle pieces fit. The die had been cast in their minds and they could not lose, but they had underestimated one man who had the power to change everything, and that man was John of Gischala.

*   *   *

Matthias was quiet as he reflected on the words of his tale. "That will do, Moshe." The former High Priest stood, making sure his garments appeared fine and his tassels were untangled. Then he left the garden to meet Simon, unsure of what would become of Jerusalem, the City of Gold.

*   *   *

Chapter IV

July 25th, 69 A.D. / 20th of Av, 3829
Caves of the Lions
North of Jerusalem

The faceless woman screamed in pain as the iron spearhead tore through muscle and sinew, causing her body to fold over the shaft and pitch backwards. A dark cloud swirled around her body as it slowed in mid air and then stopped, as if she were held by invisible cords controlled by some indifferent force. The spear kept driving through her with brutal force as bright blood sprayed through the air and splattered upon stones. All voices were muffled around the woman as she screamed, arced her back, and then snapped forward in a thrashing motion.

Her hair slowly rose into the air from her suspended frame and her eyes suddenly burned like a demon. The strands of hair became black, as oil and pitch dripped upon the ground from its roots and then a ghostly wind stirred it until it was like rope. The woman's scream became one continuous sound as some invisible force sealed her mouth as if sewn together by cords. She shook her head in shock from the closing of her mouth and found her nostrils flowing with an unending stream of blood, slowly suffocating her. Suddenly, the ground under her body exploded into flames as smoke rose beneath her feet and her flesh began to sizzle and blacken. She struggled to breathe and clawed at her face desperately to tear open the unseen cords of flesh sealing her mouth. The flames rose from the ground burning her body and the spear drove deeper as blood flowed from the wound, but still she did not die.

Suddenly she fell upon the ground and everything was still. The fire, smoke, spear, oil, and pitch disappeared. Blood ceased to flow from her body and nostrils; her hair was washed and untangled. The cords of skin from her mouth snapped and she gasped for air. She tried to look around, but found her eye sockets empty, revealing a cavity filled with tears which fell upon stones stained with her blood. Then she died and the silent void was filled with the rush of fire and the echoing of a hammer upon iron.

*   *   *

Judah bolted upright from his bed and found himself sweating profusely, his chest heaving from lack of breath. Was it a dream? It took him a moment to recall the image, still a bit hazy in his mind, and then he realized it was Miriam who he dreamed of. He had been having this nightmare for months and still he could never see her face or explain the unforeseen torture she was under. The only two men he had confided in concerning the dream had been his friend Caleb, and his trusted captain Adam, a member of 'The Way', or what some had labeled as Christians in the city of Antioch years earlier.

Judah glanced around the expanse of the cave where he slept. All he heard were the snores of men as dawn was yet an hour away. He pulled his blanket off his body and fumbled in the dim light for a jug of water he had left nearby. After taking a long drink, he set it down and sighed, feeling the cool sensation as the water calmed his mind. Judah relieved an itch on his forearm and slowly stood as he decided to get an early start to the day by sharpening his sword. Later, he thought, would be a convenient time to pay a visit to Quintus Fabius, the Roman deserter and newly elected member of the Lions. No doubt he would be recovering from his recent circumcision as a recent convert to the Jewish faith, Judah pondered with a clever grin.

*　　*　　*

Adam stood steadying the ladle of water as he brought it to his thirsty lips and drank. He exhaled loudly with satisfaction and bent down for another scoop. Dawn was at the gates of the cave and he would soon relieve the guard watching the southeastern entrance and there stand at his post for the next four hours.

He belted his sword firmly to his waist and picked up a hefty spear. He trusted in the forged blade fitted onto the ash wood shaft almost as much as he trusted in the Galilean Messiah whom He followed. Some of the men had ridiculed him in the past for his messianic beliefs, but not anymore. As the fighting became more desperate, they had stopped hurling insults his way. Whether or not it was because of his current promotion as one of the Lion officers, Adam had the feeling that the insults had ceased because he firmly kept to his beliefs amidst the death that every so often touched the band.

Trudging through the cool tunnels of the cave, Adam made his way along, quietly passing by sleeping forms and smelling the familiar scent of baking bread which was a welcoming aroma for his nostrils. The women worked tirelessly to prepare breakfast for the band of warriors; his food would be brought to him within the hour.

"Abram, go to sleep. I am here," Adam spoke with a yawn as he neared the entrance. No one responded and not a sound escaped through the tunnel where Adam halted. *This is odd*, he thought as he held his breath listening. A whistle of wind lapped by the cave's entrance as the early sun lit the dirt floor like gold from the brown soil. A torch flickered upon the wall secured by an iron bracket and the caw of a raven suddenly caused Adam to lower his spear and stare with intense eyes beyond the barbed point. He could skewer a boar at thirty yards and this usually gave him confidence, but not on this morning.

"Abram, Abram," Adam whispered, lowering his voice as he edged his way along the dirt floor, the entrance of the southeastern doorway slowly coming into view. Sweat soaked his hands as he tightened his grip upon the spear shaft. Perspiration gleamed from his forehead and ran down the sides of his face as it dampened his beard. He shuffled forward in quick succession, trying to peer around the corner and possibly gain an advantage on anyone or anything waiting there.

The crow cawed loudly again and then Adam heard the pumping of large wings as it darted away, sensing his presence. He noticed something dark mixed in with the earth as it stretched like twisting veins from a circular blotch. Adam froze as he succumbed to the realization of a sweet, pungent smell wafting in the air, overpowering his senses. He feared the worst as his eyes beheld the crimson sight which stained the cave floor. Adam steadied his breathing, telling himself to calm down and make his attack with brutal force. Tightening his grip upon the spear shaft, Adam took a deep breath and surged forward, catapulting his two-hundred-pound frame behind the flashing spear point. He hardly was given a moment to jab the spear forward with a calculated strike before he lost all motivation. Shock, horror, and alarm filled his entire body at what he saw.

Lying upon the ground with his throat filleted like a fish was the dead body of Abram, strewn in a transfixed pose with mouth open and eyes agape. His throat had been peeled open by the edge of a wickedly sharp blade and blood had soaked into the soil around him. Once the blade had cut his throat, Abram would not even have felt a thing. As the pulsing blood spilled upon his chest, Abram would have already been slipping into an unconscious state as his body furiously pumped the living fluid from him.

Adam stood in a frozen stupor, his eyes fixed on the corpse and his spear lowered in trembling hands. Who could have done this? Had one of the Lions committed murder? Then the mental wall built up in his mind came crashing down as he considered Quintus Fabius, the deserter. All the Lions had been fighting together for months with no new recruits other than the Roman. Adam made a quick reconnaissance of the area and then his heart and soul fell at once. Approaching rapidly with a dust cloud behind them, was a formation of Roman cavalry hoisting a signum which bore the snarling head of a boar. Tribune Marcus Sulla Maximus had returned for blood.

Adam had little time to react as the charging cavalry were the least of his worries. Below where he stood, advancing fast, dismounted cavalry were cresting the top of the rock shelf near the entrance and were closing in on him with a deadly speed. An arrow tore past Adam's face smacking the wall behind him. Adam took a step back, turned slightly, and bellowed down the tunnel to warn the others. A shout of defiance came from Adam's front and the Jewish warrior turned to face the first Roman trooper charging forward. The man was armed with a long *spatha*, its blade glistening, and an oval shield protecting his left flank. Adam jabbed his spear at the man's face causing the Roman to raise his shield in an effort to protect his eyes. Adam used that moment to drive his shoulder into the heavy cavalry shield, thus throwing the man off balance and over the edge of the four-metre drop.

With wild eyes and a will to survive, Adam hefted his spear above his shoulder, picked his next target, and then hurled it with all the strength in his arms at a trooper to his left who had crested the rock. The javelin soared beautifully as if it had wings and found its target in the centre mass of the trooper. The point tore through the man's mail cuirass, crushing his rib cage, as the impact sent him hurling over the rock's ledge. Before the dead trooper had even hit the ground below, Adam had drawn his sword, anticipating the next attack as three more troopers breached the crest.

*   *   *

Judah had heard the roar of Adam's voice echoing through the tunnels and had instantly known something was dreadfully wrong. Raising the alarm with a blast from a ram's horn found nearby, Judah began shouting as men everywhere scrambled for their clothes and weapons.

"Judah! Judah! What is happening?" Caleb hollered, as he pressed through fighters with drawn swords and brandished spears who rushed to cover the other two cave entrances of the hideout.

Judah caught sight of his friend and while clutching his own sword, he pointed the blade towards the passageway which led to the southeastern side of the caves. "I think we're under attack!" Judah's eyes darted over to a group of warriors who had rallied to his side. "Keep your shields locked and press hard, men! Do not let up or we're dead! Follow me!" Judah leapt forward, plunging into the tunnels, followed by Caleb and his men.

The sounds of their pounding feet and heavy breathing filled the enclosed space as they pressed on illuminated by the few torches which still burned in their fixed iron brackets. As they neared the mouth of the cave, the air was filled with the clashing of steel.

When Judah rounded the final corner with sword in hand, he was greeted by the sight of two bloodied Romans sprawled upon the ground at Adam's feet, while the large Lion warrior was desperately trying to keep the blade of another trooper's spatha away from his throat as the two were locked together. The Roman clearly had not known of the arrival of the other Jewish fighters for only a second had passed before Judah's men reacted swiftly, plunging two spears and a sword into the struggling Roman. The trooper screamed painfully as a spearhead was driven into his groin, ripped out and then thrust into his gut. The man dropped his blade and fell writhing in pain as the Jews finished him off with a strike to the throat. Adam stumbled back revealing a deep gash across his left arm as skin and muscle were peeled back from the wound.

"Quintus! It was Quintus!" Adam shouted in pain, clutching his wound and watching the blood flow over his hand.

"Form up!" Judah suddenly hollered as his fighters pressed forward, locking shields to meet another attack as more Roman troopers crested the rock face and charged. The men grunted and the Jews pushed forward, thrusting spears at the stubborn Romans.

"What did you say?" said Judah running over to Adam who was leaning against the wall of the cave.

Adam shook his head and pointed to the corpse of Abram lying untouched on the dirt floor. "The deserter cut his throat, Judah! He led them here!" Adam's chest heaved up and down from exhaustion and stress. "Quintus must have led them here, how else?"

Judah wanted to scream in rage. How could he have been so blind? He should have killed the Roman where he had knelt in the cave during the interrogation. It had all been a setup from the beginning: the desertion, journey, conversion, everything. Quintus Fabius had brought the Boars to their door. "We have to get out of here," Judah frantically said as he contemplated their situation.

"Judah, what should we do?" Caleb shouted supporting Adam's weight as the man was growing weak from lack of blood.

Judah lowered his sword and glanced up at the stalled attack. A Jew lay on the ground bleeding out from a slice to the throat and groin, but another fighter had taken his place. For now they were holding the attacking Roman line. He saw more Romans cresting the rock and at least another sixty milling about at the bottom on horseback. Judah stepped forward shaking his head and said to Caleb, "We can't hold them much longer!"

"Judah!" another voice boomed from the mouth of the cave as a breathless fighter emerged covered in sweat and blood. "Judah they have broken through!"

"What? Where?" Judah scowled, instinctively raising his sword.

"The Romans are at all our entrances. Most of the men are dead and the rest are trying everything. We're done for! They have cavalry watching the perimeter; none of us can escape!" The man looked about ready to break into tears as he dropped to one knee trying to catch his breath.

Suddenly the shrieking of women wailed from within the cave and the clashing of swords rose along with the chopping sounds of metal into flesh. The Lions had been destroyed from a single deserter whom Judah had pitied, trusted, and spared. All that mattered now was survival.

"Right, can you support that man?" Judah spoke quickly addressing the fighter and pointing to Adam who had a crude tourniquet bound to his wounded arm. The frightened man stiffened and gave a sharp nod. "Caleb, let's make for Silome!" Judah turned and cupping his mouth shouted, "Silome!" This meant everything was lost and each man was responsible to save his own skin.

"Judah! Amos and I will hold them!" a large man shouted from the fighting line while he sent a Roman crashing backwards with a heave from his shield. It was obvious the troopers were not legionaries, but they put up a staunch attack that would not relent and the Lions were beginning to tire.

Judah gave the man a nod and then dove back into the tunnel followed by a number of fighters who scrambled after him. Led by the man named Amos, four large Jewish warriors were all that was needed to hold the Romans for another minute as they charged angrily, splintering shields with their sword strokes. Amos was armed with a heavy hammer which he swung, with a victorious shout, into the side of a Roman's helmet, crushing the ear piece into his brains and splitting his skull. The man flew backwards, knocking two other Romans aside as Amos stepped forward with a mighty roar, seeking vengeance on his vulnerable enemies. However, suddenly an arrow tore through his gullet causing a crimson spray to blind the man next to him and he gagged horribly. This was all it took for the Romans to gain the confidence they needed to drive forward and skewer the remaining Lions with a dozen spears.

"Move the bushels!" Judah screamed, looking back down the tunnel for the pursuing Romans who were sure to come. Amos and his men could not possibly hold them for long and time was running out. Judah wiped the sweat from his eyes as Caleb and another Lion shoved stored bushels of straw aside, throwing them to the floor. Judah paced nearby listening to the fighting which was growing closer all around them. He glanced behind him and saw one of his men sitting upon the ground at the far side of the room with his back up against the cave wall. A sheet of blood was splattered across his chest and the man took shallow breaths as Judah could make out a deep gash across his stomach, bubbling with blood.

"There it is! I can see it!" Caleb shouted with hopeful excitement as his eager hands grasped bushel after bushel and hurled them to the side. Beyond the stacked stores of food a secret tunnel was revealed.

It was the entrance to a water cistern with a hidden pathway to the wilderness. The Romans would not have the slightest idea about the escape route which had been carved out two years earlier when the Lions had built their rebel kingdom. In planning the hideout, Judah had taken every precaution never to be cornered. A proper means of escape always made the difference between life and death. Now all that stood between them and freedom was plummeting down into the narrow, damp passageway.

"They're breaking through! They're breaking..." the desperate shout was quickly silenced by the chopping sound of swords as a wave of Jewish fighters splattered in blood, sweat, and dirt, emerged into the main cavern where Judah and his men uncovered the tunnel.

"Judah, it's lost!" a fighter bellowed trying to rally a number of comrades to press into the Roman advance as it ploughed onward with locked shields and spears.

"Hold the lines!" Judah yelled and motioned for a number of his men to support them. His fighters were being crowded into the centre of the cave by the Romans who were pushing and hacking their way through the three interlocking tunnels. A massacre would soon ensue and Judah's mind swirled. Then his eyes fell upon a torch nearby. Judah grabbed one of his men and shoved him forward bellowing, "Grab the torch! Light the bushels! Burn them!"

The surviving Lions scrambled for the dry straw piles and hurled them into the tunnels setting them alight. The fire soon began roaring madly as the straw burned while smoke billowed around them, choking men and causing chaos. Both Roman and Jew fought madly and died brutally as they whimpered, called for their mothers, or wept while bleeding to death. With no other options before them, the Romans held up their shields against the flames and found themselves stumbling around in the suffocating haze, unable to see.

"Now, into the tunnel! Down to Silome!" Judah screamed as he parried a sword thrust and drove his own blade deep into the chest of a Roman. Judah turned and followed Caleb, Adam, and a few other men as they managed to plunge into the cistern. Soon the shouts of battle were left behind them, reduced to hearing only the pounding of their own hearts. With eyes wide with fear and an animal instinct to survive, they drove deeper into the cool tunnel, wondering if they would make it out alive.

The men came to the bottom and proceeded to wade through the dark water, a number of them pausing to take gulps to relieve their thirst. One man, who halted in the middle of the cistern, began to weep as he tried to wash the caked blood from his face. Judah turned, moved back through the water, grabbed the man by the wrist, and almost had to drag him to the other side as the man continued to sob. Once out of the pool, they rolled aside a small boulder. Dropping to their hands and knees, they crawled to freedom. Only Judah paused before entering the hole and listened for anything from above. There was only silence.

*   *   *

Tribune Marcus Sulla Maximus splashed water onto his face and sighed loudly as the cool liquid ran under his breastplate. He ran his fingers through his soaked hair, then was handed a cloth to dry his face. He stared around at the rebel hideout, expressionless at the sight of four of his men lying dead beneath the main entrance they had assaulted. The tribune tossed the towel to one of his troopers, retrieved his helmet, and nudged his horse along as he was followed by a procession of *decurianes*.

Soldiers began to emerge from the cave's entrance and a trumpet blast signaled the end of the fighting. A few troopers sat down upon the edge of the rock, dangling their feet over as they recovered from the exhausting fight. Officers shouted up at them to remain alert, cursing their undisciplined nature. Only a few soldiers responded, with a number pretending they had not heard the commands.

Marcus could not care less about some of the troops lack of discipline. They had fought bitterly in the caves against a desperate enemy. Many had been killed or wounded, but like always, his Boars sought revenge and had won the day. Marcus had been worried when he had seen smoke pour out of the caves mouth. When the report had come to him that the other two entrances were in the same state, he had nearly dismounted, tempted to lead the attack himself. Soon, however, a messenger had reported that the smoke was simply from a fire the Jews had lit and that it had been contained with minimal losses. Remaining unconvinced, Marcus had given orders for a detachment of his cavalry to circle the caves and kill anything in sight; no Lions would remain alive to ever embarrass him again.

"Tribune, we really caught them by surprise. By the power of Mars, I would have to say it has been a complete victory," a *decurion*, named Drusus Valerius Livian, stated with a smile as he rode alongside Marcus.

"Mars was busy under the skirts of Venus to pay any heed to us," Marcus muttered sarcastically, ignoring the young man as he stared intensely at the rocks, covering every crevice and gorge with his eyes.

"My lord, it was an excellent, calculated attack. The way our troops sprung upon them went exactly as planned," another officer named Varro piped up, wanting to be recognized.

Marcus glanced over his shoulder at the man and then shook his head and said to nobody in particular, "The Jews are excellent fighters and desperate men. Even in an ambush they rallied and fought better than us. Let that be a reminder to you all who wish never to get your hands dirty." The column of Romans quickly grew silent from the Tribune's words. Marcus spurred his horse away towards two dismounted soldiers and a group of alae archers searching the smaller boulders beyond the caves.

"Tribune!" The men saluted as the Boar's leader reined in his horse and stared down at them with weary eyes.

"Still alive?" Marcus asked, leaning forward in his four-horned saddle.

One of the men smiled. "Still alive, sir." The man lowered his bow and admired the large, black war horse and the richly decorated leather *chamfron* harnessed to its head for maximum protection.

"What is your name, archer?" Marcus queried inquisitively.

"Philip, Tribune."

"Where do you call home?"

The man stiffened at the question as he thought of his years in the service and then slowly said, "Macedonia, a village near Thessaloniki."

"Long way from home, are you not?" Marcus scanned the rocks for a brief moment and then sighed. "I grew up in Pompeii. Two different cities but a grand view of the sea, am I right?" The man nodded but remained silent noticing the officers beyond the Tribune waiting impatiently. "Although, now I call a small villa outside of *Roma* my home; it is everything I desire though it is missing a wife." Marcus grinned at the man. "So, do you think any of the Jews escaped?"

Philip shrugged, unsure of how to answer, and then nodded. "They're clever. It wouldn't surprise me, but we definitely destroyed their band."

Marcus gazed down at the archer for a moment and then turning his horse away he replied, "Thank you for your honesty. I believe you're right." He rode towards the rocks followed closely by his officers who grew annoyed at the brashness of their leader. Marcus dismounted and tossed the reins to his standard bearer, Publius.

"Tribune, where are you going?" called out a Decurion named Cato, as he watched the fearless Boars leader make his way up a narrow stone path towards the northwestern entrance.

Marcus slowly turned without saying a word. He slowly pointed above him with a single finger, shook his head, and continued his climb. The other officers just sat in their saddles scowling, once again appalled at the unpredictable nature of the Tribune.

When Marcus reached the entrance of the hideout, bodies of the Jewish dead were being sorted through and piled nearby. Blood soaked the ground and was streaked across the walls. Two dead Romans lay nearby, completely mangled with skin scraped from their legs as if dragged. Marcus knelt down next to one of the dead men and noticed claw-like markings upon his face and reddish blue bruises covering his neck. The soldiers were young, possibly some of his new recruits which had joined in the spring, now they were no more.

Marcus continually reminded himself that the lesson learned by all soldiers was that death was never far away. It was with this mentality that the few who survived became extraordinary troopers, both reliable and deadly. That had been Marcus' plan from the beginning: harness a lethal killing machine of seasoned veterans of the Roman military, unleash them on Rome's enemies to deal out judgment, and be praised by the gods.

"Tribune," a soldier said softly, standing a few metres away.

Marcus rose slowly and glanced at the man who was holding a water skin in his filthy hands. The man's face was streaked with dirt and crusted blood was caked across his chain mailed cuirass. The soldier's sword had been sheathed. His sheath revealed stains of blood and dust around the pommel, indicating that the soldier had failed to clean his blade prior to sheathing it. His face was pale, nostrils stained black, and eyes blotched-red from the smoke which had filled the caverns of the cave.

Marcus motioned to the water skin and replied, "Have you had some?" The man shook his head in a dazed expression. "Then take some, trooper. Sit down and rest." Marcus approached the soldier and patted his shoulder. "You have done well today." He strolled past the man and entered the cave.

Inside the cave the skeletons of straw bushels crackled and sparked from the recently doused fire. Smoke began to thin as it escaped through the tunnels outside and left a grey haze in the air around the working soldiers. A brute Sergeant was directing traffic. He had the Roman dead neatly piled against the east wall with the Jewish corpses counted and stacked apathetically in the middle. Weapons were collected and checked, while numerous soldiers were sent to explore some of the other corridors interconnecting with the main hall.

Marcus stepped over the bodies of a number of slain women, their chests revealing sword wounds and other mutilations. One body's clothes had been lightly burned revealing breasts and bloody legs which were partially smouldering. *She must have died and fallen in one of the burning piles of dried straw,* Marcus thought. The floor was black around the woman and a few metres away lay a dead man with outstretched arms, as if he had been trying to save this woman. His head was resting upon the floor with his chin tilted up and eyes frozen, gazing at her. A large spear shaft protruded from the man's back as he had been dispatched in quite a gruesome fashion. His back revealed repeated stab wounds and torn flesh as blood darkened his tunic, trailing off from the body along the stone floor.

Marcus shook his head and moved on. It was not the sight that troubled him, as he had seen it in the past, often participating in such forms of slaughter. It was just the intimate connection that seemed to elevate above the two bodies as it was obvious that they had cared for one another, perhaps husband and wife or maybe lovers.

"Might bit messy in here, my lord." The Sergeant scowled, shaking his head as he looked upon all the bodies. "The bastards just finally caved in on themselves, unable to fight from three sides. Sergeant Varro thinks some got away over there, crafty men these Jews are." The Sergeant lightly kicked an arm from one of the corpses nearby and then wrinkled his nose from the putrid stench that rose up from the body's spilled intestines upon the floor. "Poor buggers! Perhaps a few were lucky!" The man pointed over to where some troops were examining a small hole carved out of the wall. "That's Varro over there, Tribune. Just discovered that little surprise a short while ago."

"Has anyone gone in yet?" Marcus asked.

The Sergeant briskly shook his head, causing the loose metal cheek plates to pat against his whiskery chin. "None of the lads want to get sticked, if you know what I mean." The man thumped his spear butt upon the floor and chuckled. "No one knows if there is a Jew hiding in there with a spear or something just waitin' for one poor bastard to crawl in. Don't want another name to add to the ledger!" He made a mock thrust in the air with his spear, simulating the killer blow in which a concealed Jew could make upon an unforeseen Roman trooper crawling into the hole.

Marcus crossed his arms. "Well done here, sergeant. Make note of the number of enemy dead and report back to me later. It appears that their famous band of Lion outlaws have come to an end."

"Well, the rebels have paid in blood."

"They had got the better of us once before, remember that." Marcus would forever punish himself for that episode. He was better than that to get caught off guard, and he hated himself for it.

The Sergeant bowed his head with a nod and shrugged. "I'm afraid the Lions will never outsmart the Boars again, right Tribune?"

"Mars has given us victory today, no doubt, but at a cost. Casualties?"

"By the light of Apollo, I don't know for sure at this moment, sir, perhaps twenty or more. The filth put up a fight."

"Respect them, sergeant," Marcus interjected. "This was their land once. They fight with the same passion I would hope you would fight with if *Roma* was ever under attack."

The man shrugged in agreement. "By Helius' balls, my lord. I would give my life for *Roma!*"

"Then pay these men respect, Sergeant."

"I will indeed, my lord, and I will whip anyone who disagrees." The man smiled with pride at his commander, and then digging under his leather breastplate he produced a coin. "Found many of these, Tribune. You should take a look at it."

Marcus took the copper coin and inspected it carefully. An olive branch had been stamped into the metal beside a *menorah*. Turning it in his hand he studied the writing on it in silence. The Sergeant, who could not decipherer Hebrew, wrestled with the urge to ask if the Tribune knew what the statement meant. It was common for Romans to think of Hebrew as a crude language. It was viewed as distasteful to know the language of the common people, yet some did understand the tongue of the Jews, having been stationed in the land for years.

Marcus exhaled loudly and then translated aloud closing his fingers upon the coin, "Liberty for holy Jerusalem." He glanced at the Sergeant. "I have seen these before. You probably found more?" The Sergeant nodded and Marcus casually said, "Find me Quintus Fabius at once."

The Sergeant saluted, struck his breastplate firmly with a closed fist, and trotted off to do his Tribune's bidding. "Someone get down there and search it out," Marcus ordered to the soldiers standing around the suspicious fissure. They nervously gazed at their commander for a moment and then one volunteered, shedding off his breastplate and helmet. "See anything?" Marcus asked joining the men and gazing down the damp shaft.

"Nothing, Tribune!" answered the soldier who had volunteered to enter the hole as he drew his *pugio* and stood near the entrance. He grinned at his jealous comrades and reveled in the fact that they had missed the opportunity to crawl down the hole under the watchful eye of the Tribune. Perhaps there would be a small reward for the first to enter the deep, unknown shaft. It would either be the reward of a few extra *sesterces* into the purse of the trooper or else a spearhead in the face from a Jew hiding within. Either way there was no turning back now that the Tribune had ordered someone to explore the hole. Perhaps he would earn a dona to the envy of all the Boars for this feat.

"We can hear some tapping sounds from within, sir, most likely from a water source. It is dark, though, and possibly dangerous." The man grinned at his commanding officer and everyone understood what the man hinted at.

Marcus removed his purse from under his breastplate and jingled the cloth pouch in his hand. "Four *denarii* for your duty, soldier." Marcus walked over to a torch secured to the wall, snatched it out of its bracket and hurled it down the shaft, illuminating it with a glow. "Now in you go!"

The man smiled, bowed his head, and then crawled into the shaft head first as he disappeared, shuffling downwards through the damp hole. The men waited a few minutes, holding their breaths and straining their ears for any sound or shout from human vocal chords, but there was only silence. One soldier standing near Marcus, grew annoyed from the other sounds in the cave hall and shouted for everything to cease.

"What is his name?" Marcus asked.

"Piso, my lord," answered the soldier, leaning against his spear.

"Your friend?" Marcus queried and the man nodded. "You're Sergeant Varro, are you not?"

"That's right, Tribune. I am Varro of Ephesus, my lord."

Noticing the man's grey hairs, Marcus handed him a drachma and said, "You must have taught him some principles of the Roman character, Varro of Ephesus. Let this get you into some trouble with the whores."

A few of the men chuckled nearby and then a shout rose up from the mouth of the shaft. Varro leaned forward and hollered down, "Piso, what do you see?"

"Just an empty water cistern, nothing else. There is another route near the back; I will be a moment!"

The men looked at each other as some considered the likelihood that some of the Jews had escaped and a few swore under their breath. The ambush had been carefully planned and well executed, however it was clear that not all the exits had been blocked which did not sit favourably with the company's pride.

"Tribune, I present trooper Quintus Fabius!" The Sergeant, whom Marcus had spoken to earlier, bowed his head humbly and then marched off to oversee other duties.

"My lord." Quintus saluted and stood before his commander still donned in the same garments he had been graciously given by the Lions the night before. As a reasonably wealthy soldier, Quintus marveled at the fact that he had come out of this mission alive and now likely to be honoured by his Tribune. "Always a willing servant, sir."

Marcus glanced briefly at Quintus noticing how wandering for a day in the heat had taken its toll on the trooper, but it had all been crucial for the success of discovering the Lions hideout. The soldiers of his unit could always use more money and where similar plans in the past had failed, Marcus had been sure to pay attention to every detail. He had simply promised the young recruit a handsome reward if it proved successful and at least a minor dona to be attached to his rank; perhaps he would make a decent sergeant.

"Follow me, Quintus." Marcus led the soldier out of the tunnels and into the fresh air where they stood admiring the rocky landscape stretched out before them. "How are you keeping?"

Quintus smiled and nodded with a shrug. "I cannot complain, Tribune. As you can see, the mission succeeded and you have had a great victory."

"With some cost, perhaps." Marcus crossed his arms. "Tell me, did you meet their leader? The large man with the black beard?"

"Yes," Quintus replied in short. "Judah ben Yosef."

"What kind of a man is he?" Marcus gazed with hawkish eyes into the face of Quintus, causing the grin to vanish.

"Serious, he was very serious, Tribune. Like talking to a king or something, but he was someone with a past. I felt that he hated me."

"It is what you represent to him, Quintus. You represent *Roma* and with that he interprets it as oppression and slavery. These people have had it good in the past. This is not like Britannia with its dank weather, strange rituals and clans. No, the Jews had it good." Marcus was silent for a moment as he seemed lost in old thoughts. "It is important that *Roma* be known to all; it is like lighting an oil lamp in a dark room. The glory of *Roma* helps people see the mastery of man. It brings civilization to their shores and glory to the empire."

"Whether the Jews had it good or not, Tribune, I believe that has all changed for them now, hasn't it?" Quintus paused shaking his head. "His men wanted my head; I nearly was slain when they found me. It is by the power of Jupiter I am alive. By the wisdom of the gods they saw value in this mission and spared me. Helius must have clouded their thoughts. But this man you speak of, my lord, he was educated. He was not like the others who come across as a rabble." Quintus lowered his voice as a few soldiers moved past, giving a respectful distance from the Tribune.

"How do you know he was educated?"

"He knew Greek, and some of our tongue. He was in control every second and seemed to be bearing a lot on his shoulders. I thought he would give the command for my life to end, but he spared me."

"They peeled back your manhood, though, I suppose a decent ploy to save your life. Does it hurt?" Quintus gave an uncomfortable nod and Marcus chuckled, shaking his head. "So this Jew trusted you? Would you do it again?"

"No, Tribune." Quintus replied, recalling the terrifying ordeal in the caves when he had been at the mercy of the Lions. He swallowed hard as he thought of the moments of the early morning when he had crept to the mouth of the cave and sliced open the neck of Abram, the man who had given him the very garment he wore now.

Quintus had felt a tinge of regret from killing the young man, but it had been necessary before he had run for his life to alert the Boars. He would never forget the look his Tribune had given him when he had arrived at the doorway to his tent, faintish, chest heaving, and a thin trickle of blood running down the inside of his thigh from the circumcision. The Tribune had stood in the centre of his tent, while his servant made sure the straps were tight on his bronze greaves. Then Marcus had said with an expressionless, stern face, "The traitor returns!" Quintus had been paid handsomely, and then the Boars had ridden to seal the fate of the Lions.

"May the payment for your services find you pleasure, Quintus. That will be all. Report back to camp and restore your armour; you are mine now." The dismissed soldier saluted and quietly left the crevice.

"Tribune! Tribune, I have news, sir!"

Marcus turned and was greeted with a hasty salute upon the dusty breastplate of Sergeant Varro. "What is it?"

"It's Piso, Tribune. He found the end of the secret channel exiting the cistern and it leads south of here."

"To Jerusalem," Marcus growled shaking his head and biting his lower lip. He glanced annoyingly at the Sergeant. "What else?"

"Well, we know some escaped, Tribune. It can't be many, perhaps six or seven. But their leader, the man with the black beard who beheaded Sallust at the ambush days ago, well he isn't among the dead." Varro hung his head in shame not wanting to make eye contact with his disgruntled commander.

Marcus turned away from Varro and swore to himself as he smacked his fist into his open palm. It had already been well over an hour since the Romans had dispatched the last Jew, and he had no idea when Judah and the other fugitives had actually escaped. Marcus swung around and pointed at the Sergeant. "Rally thirty of the troops and make haste. Sweep the land and find them!"

Varro stumbled off through the caves shouting orders and Marcus gazed down at the junior officers who had begun to laugh upon hearing the commotion. Soon they realized Marcus was staring down at them like the thunder god, ready to smite them, and they quickly looked. Marcus moved with the agility of an ibex down the rocky path. He cursed the insolence of his officers as he mounted his black charger, and shouted for them to fall out in pursuit of the remaining Lions who were somewhere in the Judean hills which stretched out in the distance towards Jerusalem.

*   *   *

Two hours later

"Judah, Judah! We must have water! In the name of Abraham, Isaac and Jacob we must have water," Caleb pleaded as he turned to help Adam whose face was pale, as if death was at his gates.

"We don't stop, Caleb, not now! The Boars are a cavalry unit, which means horses! They will come for us!" Judah replied, wincing from the intense ball of fire burning high in the sky. His body stung with pain as it shot through his inflamed muscles as his mind screamed at him to collapse and rest.

"We have to rest, otherwise Adam will die!" Caleb yelled back as he ordered two of the other Lions to support the large man and his cleaved arm. Caleb exhaustingly ran to Judah's side with legs that felt weighed down by lead. "Judah, Judah, listen to me. If we rest for an hour and drink water that should be enough to set out again."

Judah stopped momentarily to get his bearings. His chest felt like it was ready to explode with fire and his throat was dry. He gave his friend a quick glance, noticing Caleb's split lips from the heat and his bloodshot eyes from the smoke. Judah gave a tired nod and pointed over to some boundary rocks marking the edge of a field piled nearby under the shade of a few spindly Carob trees.

The six men pushed themselves the remaining forty meters and collapsed with exhaustion upon the hard ground as they rested beneath the shallow canopy above them. After ten minutes had past, Judah pointed with his weary hand to the south. "Those are the hills of *Beit El;* beyond that is Jerusalem."

"Is that where we go?" replied one of the men who collected a number of hardened carobs and passed them around.

"Yes, Aviram, that is where we must go." Judah lowered his hand and accepted a carob and a small, half filled water skin from Caleb, the only nourishment the men had in the rising heat of the day. He bit hungrily into the sweet carob and chewed it, savouring the sugary taste.

Caleb rose slowly and glanced around. Nothing moved, apart from a single black raven flying in the blue sky above them. "Why Jerusalem?"

"Where else?" Judah replied.

"We haven't been there for awhile; we know not what is happening there," Caleb said and looked around the group.

"It still stands, Caleb; I have seen many pilgrims at the time of the feasts," Aviram added with a sore chuckle.

Caleb looked at the man distastefully and tried to ignore him. "Judah, we're Lions! We should regroup and recruit, continue our fight on the outside. I have heard nightmares of the struggle within the walls of Jerusalem."

Judah shook his head. "We will never survive on the outside. We must align ourselves with whoever controls the city."

"It is murderers who control the city! Remember Ananus?"

"I am not stupid, Caleb, I remember. There are some good men still in the city."

"John of Gischala, maybe?" Aviram said excitedly. "I hear he practically runs the place."

Caleb looked irritatingly at the young man with his dusty brown hair and sprouting beard. "You're misinformed. Simon runs the place; John and Eleazar are penned into a corner."

"I heard Eleazar was dead!" another one of the exhausted men added.

Judah rolled his eyes and slowly climbed to his feet. "Either way, it is our only chance for survival. Our only choice lies with John of Gischala; he will let us join his band. He is a Galilean and so are you all." Judah swept his hand over the other five men and nodded. "Yes, things will be better and then we can mobilize with John's men to fight the Romans when they arrive."

"Things are never that simple, Judah. If Simon is alive and controlling the city, we will be coming between something I would never invite." Caleb looked to the others for support but they clearly liked where Judah's head was at. He stared down at his hands which were still covered in dried blood and tried to clean them upon his cloak. "I can't believe what happened. Everyone is dead! It was the deserter, it had to be!"

"That pig shit Roman!" Aviram shook his head as all the memories flooded his mind. Until now the men had been desperately fleeing, trying to survive, but in the stillness of everything around them and far away from the edged steel of the Romans, his true emotions ran like a dried riverbed suddenly overflowing.

"I would like to see every last one dead!" said one of the men named Moshe. "Adam, what of you?"

Adam closed his eyes and softly replied, "I kill my enemy when he tries to kill me but as for all the rest of the Romans, I pity them."

"Pity them? How can you say such a thing?" Aviram asked, raising his voice. "Is this what your Nazarene rabbi would want?" Adam held up a hand in objection, but Aviram continued, his face flushed with anger. "Would he want Jewish blood spilled? Wasn't *he* Jewish like you and me, and look what the Romans did to him!"

"You are not yourself, Aviram," Adam responded, supporting his wounded arm. "You do not understand."

Before Aviram could lash back, Judah quickly stood and moved between the two. He silenced them with his very presence and looking among the men he said in a cold tone, "We have to go! We cannot linger here. The Romans will come when they have figured out we still live. They would have found the cistern, there was no concealing it."

"Judah is right, we must keep going." Caleb stood, urging the men to rise. So with heavy hearts, close to the point of exhaustion, they pressed on at a slow pace, climbing the hills of *Beit El*. Within a few hours, they soon encouraged by the sight of a distant funnel cloud of smoke drifting above the hills from the unseen mountain of Moriah, where the descendents of Aaron worked faithfully offering up their sacrifices to God from His holy Temple.

* * *

CHAPTER V

July 27th, 69 A.D. / 22nd of Av, 3829
Jerusalem
Ophel Quarter
Midday

A woman knelt upon the stones, weeping with long, deep sobs as she held the limp body of her son in her bloodied arms. Three arrows, lodged in the chest of the boy, were the lethal missiles that killed him. He had attempted to cross the street during one of the many skirmishes between the warring Jewish factions and had been slain without anyone taking notice.

The mother remembered screaming his name, as she had tried to stop him. The boy had panicked at the sight of a mortally wounded man stumbling through their door. The soldier had been one of Simon's men, and he had clutched his stomach covering a grisly wound. A distinct stench from the blood flowing freely had filled the home, and the boy's face had gone chalk white. The man had grunted and collapsed to the floor spilling his entrails while wheezing for air.

The mother's children had shrieked, her daughters hiding their faces and screaming. Her son had fled in terror, like a stampeding animal. He had charged out into the street, slick with blood and corpses. The sounds of battle and chaos had been ominous, yet had drowned out all her pleading and shouting for her little one to come back. It had been too late. Her son had become disoriented among the packed bodies of fighting men and then the volley from the high walls above had been unleashed with fury. Arrows and scorpion missiles had peppered the street spraying blood and hurling men aside like tatters of rags. His little body had been torn apart and lay among the stench and puddles of blood, his brown hair spattered with gore. She had run to him, almost blindly, without even heeding the cries of her other children. She loved them all, but he had always been special.

* * *

"You cross that street and attack the porticos from the outside with your men, or I will personally have your head to toss over the colonnade at John's bastards," Simon ben Giora threatened, poking the chest of a frightened Idumean officer, trying to muster the courage to lead the next attack. "Now, how hard can it be, Asher? I have given you an additional eighty men for the job. Get across the clearing, use your archers to scatter the men on the ramparts, and breach the walls. Once we're in, I will host a dinner in your honour and we shall drink wine out of the hollowed skull of ben Levi!"

Asher the Idumean wiped the sweat from his eyes and nodded. "What of the scorpions? They are slaughtering us, Simon!" He gestured with a trembling hand at the dismembered bodies of his fellow soldiers strewn upon the streets below the Royal Stoa of the southwestern tip of the Temple Mount.

"That is why you have eighty additional men, you coward! What, that should give you two hundred now, isn't that right?" Simon poked his head around the corner of a home. His eyes darted from the dozens of corpses laying everywhere, to the weeping woman holding the dead boy and then gazed up the high walls to the Zealots on the ramparts scrambling to cover all possible positions. "Now," he said turning back to Asher. "We need John's men cleared of that rampart, which is why you have nearly sixty archers at your disposal. We have gone over these plans time and time again." Simon turned his face away and shouted, sending spittle from his mouth, "Yohanan! Up front, now!"

The fearful face of Asher turned to watch a bear-of-a-man emerge from a group of soldiers. The soldiers were formed up in close order, filling the street which was concealed from the enemy. The man pushed a few of his fellow comrades aside and stepped forward carrying an enormously heavy javelin. His face revealed long deep scars that stretched over his jawbone. Little holes riddled both sides of the scar, evidence from an amateur doctor's attempt at stitching the wound closed. He stood before Simon glaring down at the Idumean officer, uttering a low growl under his breath as if he were an animal.

"That is Yohanan. You've seen him before?" Simon asked Asher and the Idumean nodded, recovering his posture and wiping his sweaty hands upon his garments. A thick leather breastplate, completely foreign to any Roman fashion, protected the officer's chest and a simple pointed helmet was strapped to his head. Simon smiled and continued, "Yohanan has eight kills to his name. That is eight of John's men who he has made squeal in pain with the jagged end of his spear. He even strangled one. Now, listen to me! You will lead this attack and Yohanan will accompany your men. Capture the wall or die trying! But if you fail and return alive, Yohanan will tear your arms from your body, then dangle you over a wall and squeeze the life right out of you." Simon locked eyes momentarily with Asher, and then stepped back.

Simon listened for a moment to the sobbing sounds of the woman amidst the bloodied flagstones and then rolled his eyes. "Is she still out there?" Asher glanced around the corner at the woman rocking back and forth while holding her dead son and then nodded. Simon shrugged and while fixing his hair he said, "Attack."

Asher exhaled loudly, waved his hand at the soldiers cramming the narrow street, and said a silent prayer. He glanced back and whispered harshly, "Foot men in front and archers follow from behind!" Yohanan stood a few feet behind Asher with his spear lowered and a look of sadistic joy in his eyes. Asher knew as soon as they emerged from the street and out into the open it would be another death trap, a massacre. All they had to do was make it to the wall and clear the attackers above on the ramparts. If they were able to force their way through the Hulda Gates, then they stood a chance of ending the bitter deadlock. It seemed simple, but this was the fourth attack of the day and so far each assault had left a bloodied trail of dead scattered everywhere. Asher held his shield firmly against his left side and took three quick breaths. He raised his sword, screamed and then leapt forward into the open followed by his howling troops.

*   *   *

John of Gischala's men had practiced the art of firing the Roman scorpions and catapults hundreds of times. In regards to the loading of the scorpion it was simple, but it required a professional to aim it. First, two men exerting themselves from the tension of the rope would crank the cord back on the horizontally mounted bow by using a wooden winch. A metal ratchet would click with each crank in and out of slots designed for securing each rotation so it would not snap forward prematurely and break the arms of both operators. Once the cord was at its zenith, they would clamp it in place, and load the projectile into the machine, which could either be an iron arrow or stone bullet. With the scorpion aimed at its desired target, it would be a quick release of the cord. The machine would snap back in awesome power, and death would soar down on anyone in its path.

The precision and marksmanship of John's artillery crews was all that kept them alive. Since the arrival of Simon ben Giora and the admittance into the city by the former High Priest, it had been a constant strive for power by the three factions. Simon's obsession to be the supreme ruler of Jerusalem was no secret, and he used his immense army to make sallies against John's forces almost daily as they probed for weaknesses to their southern and western fronts. The threat existing from the middle of John's position came with the presence of Eleazar's rabble holding the Inner Court of the Temple. Although the pressure they exerted upon John's army was nothing like the force of Simon.

With the expectation of a fifth assault from Simon's men, John rallied his troops, reinforced his positions and ordered them to load the deadly Roman war machines with much haste. Archers were scattered upon the ramparts of the colonnades and the scorpions were aimed with men standing at the ready, waiting to unleash another wave of iron missiles capable of slicing a man in half. The evidence of this was strewn below the walls as blood stained the streets and houses surrounding the suburban battlefield. So when the echoing war cry rang out from below, John drew his sword, stepped back from the edge of the ramparts, and made ready to defend himself once again.

*   *   *

Simon heard the audible recoil of the scorpions firing almost instantly as Asher charged into the open with over a hundred soldiers at his heels. The next image Simon observed was Asher's body splitting apart at the waist from the impact of the iron spear which hurled him into the air in two pieces spraying blood everywhere. Not a sound had been heard from the Idumean officer who was killed instantly, as the screams of two men behind Asher, impaled from the same spear, writhed in pathetic misery upon the stone street. The attack was briefly halted due to the blood of Asher which soaked the front rank, but then Yohanan spurred them on, shaking them from their shock by bellowing and charging forward as if he were invincible.

Simon screamed for his archers to fall into rank behind the foot troops, as they slipped upon the blood-stained streets, getting killed by a rein of arrows which fell upon them. The first volley from Simon's archers looked promising. Four of John's men pitched back with quivering arrow shafts protruding from their chests as one toppled from the rampart screaming the whole way down. The archer's victory, however, was short lived as three iron spears from the scorpions and a hail of stone bullets tore through their ranks spreading panic and death. The stone bullets crushed the chests of men, threw them aside like rag dolls, and even decapitated two soldiers as their headless forms sent a fountain of blood upon the men surrounding them.

"The ladders! Bring the ladders!" Yohanan shouted with thunder as he stood at the base of the colonnade. He was waving his spear wildly in the air, in a rage at the reluctance of his men. Suddenly two arrows shot from above, drove deeply into Yohanan's back and he staggered, shuddering from the blow. Then, as if unaffected from the pain, he continued shouting and even looked up to curse the Jews above.

Simon stood behind his men transfixed by what played out before him. Only a handful of archers remained. Many had fled or been wounded, and at least twenty lay dead upon the ground. The houses behind the slaughtered men, revealed gaping holes from the stone bullets which had crashed through the archers and into the buildings. He watched his men push forward again with a defiant shout, relief upon their faces at the lull in the deadly volleys of the battle. Simon's men hoisted four long ladders above them and surged onward with whatever shields they carried raised above their heads. A number of large stones poured down on them from above, and Simon watched as one man's shield shattered, his head twisting with a crack, and his body crumpling to the ground.

Desperate, wild eyes scanned the ramparts and Simon's mind swirled with sudden caution at the slacking rate of fire from John's troops. Before he could react, a stone door along the wall suddenly opened and out leapt a dozen archers who released their volley into Simon's men. A number of the soldiers dropped in agony, screaming and clawing at the street. Before the rest of his formation could react, sixty Zealots from John's force charged from the doorway in a precise assault, with barbed pikes, and hammered into the flank of Simon's men. Yohanan, barely given the time to confront the attack, roared in hysteria as four spear heads punched into his chest, knocking him to the ground. One of John's captains slashed his sword blade over the exposed throat of Yohanan, thereby finishing him off. At the sight of blood spewing from Yohanan's lifeless body, Simon's men turned and fled, dropping weapons and shields, anything that would encumber their retreat.

"No!" Simon shouted, pulling his hair. He jabbed a finger in the air at his archers and screamed, "Cover their retreat!" The archers response was instantaneous. What was left of them, sent a powerful volley into John's men, dropping three and wounding five others.

A horn blast echoed from the colonnade and the attack was called off. John's men withdrew, slipping back through the stone doorway, as reloaded catapults and scorpions sent another volley at Simon's position. John of Gischala grinned from the colonnades and shook his sword in the air to the exultation of his troops who cheered at yet another victory. The Zealots blasted horns from all over the ramparts and congratulated each other with pride as many hurled insults down upon their unwanted rivals. The day was far from over and men searched the streets for any sign of a renewed assault. However, nothing stirred and the only sound heard was one that carried with it a haunting melody as the weeping mother, who had miraculously survived the battle, picked up her dead son and stumbled away.

*   *   *

Near the town of Beit Ani
Outskirts of Jerusalem

The landscape around Jerusalem dipped and rose with rocky terrain scattered with olive groves. The sun baked everything as burnt grass, scorched from the summer heat, longed for water which was still months away.

However, it was the Judean sun which gave the city of Jerusalem its most magnificent feature, for the rays of light would reflect off the high walls of gold-coloured stone. The pinnacle of the white marble Temple upon Mount Moriah and its golden, crowned points would shimmer, like a ripple of fire suspended above the earth. Every Jew seemed to savour the newly renovated Herodian Temple, completed five years earlier, and believed by the children of Abraham to be the most sacred place of worship in the world. The Temple, in their minds, was the conscious soul of their faith. It was the reminder of God's covenant with them, since Abraham, Isaac and Jacob.

Jews all throughout the known world travelled up to Jerusalem. They came to dedicate their children to God in the Temple after the circumcision of Jewish male infants on the eighth day, to offer ritual animal sacrifices, and attend the feasts. The Temple of Jerusalem was one of the greatest spectacles on earth and an enormously profitable institution as Jews of the *diaspora* continually sent their money as tithes of support. Pilgrims from Ephesus, Thessaloniki, Corinth, Alexandria, Tyre, Athens, Antioch, Sardis, Carthage, Aleppo, and hundreds of other cities, even Rome, would fall to their knees in worship of their God to the sound of psalms, praises, and *shofar'ot* rising above the amazement.

Judah held up his hand and Caleb stopped the men. A circular stone well stood before them and next to it a beggar sat clutching a clay cup, which he shook for alms. The man's skin was like brown leather and his patchy, white beard was stained with sweat and dirt. The beggar's robes were filthy and he wore no sandals, revealing calloused, bruised feet. A simple staff lay on the ground next to the old man who every now and then outstretched his hand to make sure it still lay beside him. Then he would turn and bob the cup up and down, all the while making a humming sound to catch the attention of any generous travelers.

Judah and his comrades stared past the beggar down the Roman road, laid with perfectly shaped stones. It was the road which would lead them to Beit Ani and onward to Jerusalem where they would seek shelter, company, and survival. At the base of a large sycamore tree, a woman clothed in simple fabrics of the lower class slowly stood and picked up her clay water jug to approach the well. She spotted Judah and his men, and cautiously approached the well, making no eye contact.

Caleb wiped the sweat away from his forehead and exhaled loudly for all to hear. "Finally, some water." The men had scrounged on their journey, finding enough wells to extract the precious liquid from, but most of the wells had been dried up due to abandonment and lack of care.

"Wait here," Judah said. "Conceal your weapons." He gently pulled the robes of his cloak over the gladius strapped to his waist and then approached the woman, slowly raising his hands to show he was no threat. "Excuse me, woman." The woman glanced up, set her jug on the side of the well and plopped a coin into the beggar's cup who giggled with amusement at his fortune. She brushed a lock of hair from her face and tucked it within the shawl she wore draped over her head. She straightened and stared at Judah with her brown eyes. "My friends and I mean no harm." Judah turned pointing to them and looked back at the woman. "Could we have some water?"

The woman nodded and Judah waved his men to the well, who hardly took any convincing. They tried not to run, wanting to appear dignified, but soon found themselves kneeling on the ground, lapping up the cool water like thirsty dogs. Judah found a wooden bowl, reached down to dip it into the well, poured it down his throat, and spared some to dump upon his sweaty head. He breathed heavily as the water cooled his body and it was then that he noticed the woman was studying him.

Judah set the bowl down, took the woman's jug, slowly dipped it into the deep well and brought it up full. He set it on the side with a grin and crossed his arms. "Aren't you going to thank me?"

"You should thank me for the water you and your men have helped themselves to."

Judah smiled. "Is it your water to give or God's?"

"God has given it to my father. My father dug this well, he owns it too and the water in it. He also owns the sheep and goat herds to the east of Beit Ani."

Judah scowled. "If your father is such an important man, then why do you dress the way you do? Why are you fetching the water and not a slave?"

"Times have changed. Most of the slaves have run away and father doesn't trust most men." She gently pulled her cloak tight against her body and shrugged. "So I dress this way so I don't attract attention; a rich girl could find herself in a world of trouble."

"What has changed, woman?"

"Mira, my name is Mira."

Judah nodded graciously and sighed. "I'm Judah ben Yosef; this rabble is what is left of my band. That is Caleb, Adam, Aviram, Moshe, and Aaron."

"You're band? Are you Zealots? Sicarii? Or are you with Simon?" The woman backed up a couple of feet, suddenly fearful as she contemplated fleeing.

Judah held up a hand in restraint and shook his head. "We are neither; we see to our own needs. Now we make our way to Jerusalem to find shelter."

"You won't find shelter there, Judah ben Yosef. It is a place of death. Many suffer."

This perked the attention of the men who stopped talking and drinking as they stood around the well staring at the strange woman. In a moment of silence, they digested her words of caution. Finally Caleb sat on the edge of the well and stared to the southwest at the rising smoke from the Temple's Inner Court in Jerusalem, which was still hidden by Mount Scopus. Caleb looked at Mira and said, "What do you speak of, woman? Tell us!"

"It is a wild place," the shaky voice of the elderly beggar interrupted before Mira could answer. "You are all young, too young to know such things. Years have evaded you and now you find yourselves wondering what has happened to the city? Where have you been, for God's sake?" The man laughed turning his head and revealing cloudy eyes with a pasty film smeared over his retina. His grin showed a toothless mouth, then he shook his head and made a whimpering sound as if he were crying. "Ezra is my name, like the prophet of God sent to speak to his children. The city has changed, I say. Many suffer, says she."

"Speak plainly and not in riddles," Judah said as he stepped near the man and crouched down to look into his blind eyes. "Are the Roman's there? What is happening?"

Ezra looked up and stared with his dead eyes into the sky. With wrinkly hands he felt Judah's face and then nodded. "The Romans have not come yet, though they will. The city is divided: our brothers kill each other, many have fled, the Hinnom burns, and their bodies lay in the tombs of the Kidron." Ezra held up his cup and shook it next to Judah's face. "A penny for a man with nothing, bless you."

"I have nothing to give, Ezra." Judah glanced up at Mira and stood. "Who fights in the city if not the Romans?"

"The Roman garrison was massacred long ago, have you not heard?"

"We have been away; I was in the north."

Mira stepped closer. "Fighting with General Matityahu?"

"Not really."

Mira glanced at the other men and then scratched her neck. "John of Gischala is there. He holds some of the Temple and the Antonia. That horrid man Eleazar ben Simon is also there. They have been here for awhile. News of the defeat of the Galilean forces changed everything. My father says John is here to make Jerusalem rise up as a unified force to stand opposed to Rome. Eleazar wants to be the leader in charge, yet John despises him."

"What of Ananus and the council?" Adam asked.

Mira shook her head. "All killed, at least most of them perished with the arrival of the Idumeans, they were the Zealot's friends from the south. My father heard that the Zealots feared Ananus would turn the city over to Vespasian. Though this is not true, John saw Ananus as a coward. My father believes Ananus meant well, but was not a good leader in times of war. Once the Idumeans heard that a lie had led them to the city to destroy the government forces, they left. Most of them left, perhaps. It is hard to say. I saw them streaming from the gates in their formations, no more raised spears and defiant marching; they looked ashamed and returned to the south. Many in Beit Ani thought peace would soon come, but people who thought that were stupid. John and Eleazar's rabble ruled the city. They stole, killed, and paraded around keeping their respective distance from each other, sometimes fighting. That is until Simon's army arrived."

"Simon?" Moshe said.

"Simon ben Giora. He came from Masada, the fortress to the south by the Sea of Salt. He's from Gerasene. My father tells me Simon wishes to make Jerusalem a capital for his kingdom. He conquered the Idumeans and destroyed their strongholds and armies. My father says Simon is strong but mad and that Simon wishes to rule this land. The three hate each other: Simon, John, and Eleazar. That is the fighting poor Ezra speaks of. None can pry the other from his foothold and all are powerful. Simon is the strongest, though. My father tells me he commands fifteen thousand men."

"Your father tells you a lot," Judah replied. "How does he know?"

"He has many contacts in the city as he deals most with merchants and herdsmen. He also knew Ananus ben Ananus and Shimeon ben Gamaliel." Mira looked down at Ezra who was quiet and had laid his clay cup in his lap.

"Who is the High Priest if they are dead?" Caleb asked.

Mira shook her head. "Not all are dead. Word is Ananus and Joshua ben Gamala are dead. Some have been arrested and others escaped. Now, the Sanhedrin is run by Matthias ben Theophilus who used to be on the government council and was a chief priest until he was deposed by Eleazar's men; he has sought power through Simon. It was Matthias who opened the doors and let Simon into the city. I suppose he chose between a lesser of the evils which existed in their walls, but the populace demanded it from him and he went to Simon. My father says Simon rode into the city like a king."

"So the Idumeans killed Ananus and Joshua?" Judah softly asked. Mira half nodded but remained silent as Judah wrestled with the gravity of the situation. A soft breeze from the north blew at their backs and rustled the leaves of the sycamore tree. Judah raised his eyes to meet Mira's and slowly said, "You say John is in the city and holding out?" She nodded. "He holds the Temple?"

"Part of it, I think. There are battles almost daily. My father has heard the fighting and word travels fast. He says many have even fled Beit Ani afraid of the Romans who are sure to come in the spring."

Judah turned and looked at his men, his mind made up. "We must go to the Temple and join John. He is the man we can trust and he holds the Temple."

"You think we can trust him because he holds the Temple like a fortress? Judah, we should go another way," Caleb suggested. "Perhaps to Masada?"

"And rot away on some rock, Caleb? I think not. I have heard good things of John. He is an able leader and one to serve. We must go to the city; we cannot survive outside the walls as it is getting more perilous day by day." Fierce eyes of passion darted from man to man and then Judah said sternly, "Are we not Lions? Do we not still live? Our one purpose must lie in the protection of the holy sanctuary and our city. We must defend it from either Simon or Rome. I do believe John holds Jerusalem's best interests at heart and looks to raise its strength to fight Rome, but he can't with Simon and Eleazar."

"John is a Zealot, Judah. Perhaps cut from a different cloth then Eleazar but still a Zealot. He is as careless with life, as Simon is. We cannot expect him to be civil, especially when he kills civilians."

"John of Gischala may have done evil, but a necessary evil I am convinced of in order to hold his power in Jerusalem. He knows Jerusalem is the best form of defence against the legions and he cannot give it up. We must go there, Caleb, and aid him. Our duty as Jews must drive us there. I need you, Caleb, and we must do this together. We must go!"

"I am with you, Judah," stated Aviram with a grin as Moshe voiced the same support.

"My parents live there, so I can go nowhere else," Adam responded plainly, still favouring his wounded arm which had been crudely wrapped in rags.

"I fled the north to fight the Romans, and I will not flee now. If they are to advance on Jerusalem, I shall be there to stand in their way with my blade." Aaron tapped the pommel of his sheathed sword.

Caleb let out a grunt of frustration and shook his head. "Whatever, I will go with you, because I have never left your side." He walked up to Judah and stared him in the face. While lowering his voice, Caleb said, "Just tell me what this is really about? Is it about killing Romans? I will follow you into that city and fight by your side, but we must fight for something different than just to slay men."

"We fight to defend the Temple, our city, Caleb."

"Is it to forget Miriam? Do you think the more blood you spill will help you forget? Or is it Capito?" Caleb knew he tested the patience of his friend but in all his years of knowing Judah one thing was true, his friend was bull-headed and needed to hear the hard truth at times.

Without lowering his gaze Judah muttered, "I spill blood upon my hands, Caleb, because I hear the cries of my murdered parents and my betrothed ringing in my ears. Miriam is in my dreams, my friend, wailing in pain and dying from the blow of the spear. It is not the life I desired but is one given to me by force. I need you by my side, Caleb. You are the only one I trust in this world. I now know that everything I have lived for has been meaningless. God has changed my life and sent a dagger into my back. I live for nothing now except to see the ground I walk on drenched in the blood of Rome."

"God cannot be blamed, Judah, as it is just evil men." Caleb sighed and glanced up at the blue sky and watched a hawk soar by at ease. He then looked sternly at his friend. "Vengeance, Judah? That is what you want?"

Judah nodded. "That is exactly what I want."

"You won't get far, Judah, not with Simon's rabble milling about," Mira spoke up with confidence. "Simon's men have orders to search pilgrims and they control much of the walls apart from the colonnades and the eastern gate of the Temple. Simon has men in the valley too, and sometimes they walk upon the hills. Only twice has Simon come to Beit Ani and he does so to recruit. Some have gone with him, but a few he has murdered. He rapes married women and imprisons their husbands. My father hides me in the mill behind our home whenever Simon pays a visit." Mira saw the impact of her words. "If it is John you wish to see my father can arrange it. He can take you down into the valley near the garden and then to the pinnacle of the Temple. The Golden Gate is too risky as they may think you are a group of Simon's men and they watch it like hawks. You will have to go along the wall past the tombs. There is a door my father has used in the past which leads to a side entrance near the Hulda Gates. They will be guarded by John's men, because Simon is afraid of the great machines. John has slaughtered many of Simon's men near the Ophel with those machines."

Judah's spirits rose at this news and he nodded with satisfaction as Aviram and Aaron smiled. "Take us to your father, Mira."

*   *   *

CHAPTER VI

July 27th, 69 A.D. / 22nd of Av, 3829
Palace of Herod Antipas
Upper City, Jerusalem
Controlled Area of Simon ben Giora

"It is nearly an hour before Shabbat, Simon," Matthias ben Theophilus said, raising the point for the fifth time to the despot ruler who sat like a spoiled child upon a large throne-like chair. To Matthias, Simon's greed knew no bounds as he delighted in filling his halls with beautiful motifs, tapestries, vases, and furniture which he seized from the elite population of the city. Even Simon's close band of officers benefited greatly from his exploits. They were men who had followed him in his conquests of Idumea, and now they joined him in fattening themselves on the misfortunes of others; it trickled down throughout the army as many became enriched on loot and took what they wanted.

Matthias often regretted letting the warrior brigand into the city, but had felt he had little choice in the matter. The city had practically begged him to do something against John and Eleazar, and Simon had seemed the only logical option. Who could have foreseen this? Simon's cruelty equaled that of John and Eleazar, and now with the Zealot factions penned in on the Temple Mount and restricted to sections of the Lower City, it appeared that Simon was willing to go the next mile in evil-doing. One priest, who was exiled from the Temple Mount, had even compared Simon to Manasseh, the ancient king of Judah who had delved in child sacrifices in the Hinnom, paying homage to foreign gods such as *Moloch*, and had murdered the prophet Isaiah.

Simon was truly an unpredictable man. He was cunning towards people of all sorts; any form of conduct was proper in Simon's mind in order to get his way. He could be charming and debonair with a sense of propriety and then become like a wild man bent on destruction as a gleeful, sadistic sense of debauchery would consume him.

He regularly held feasts to entertain his officers and other supporters. These banquets would often include mountains of food, men singing in a drunken stupor, and foreign women who would be forced to dance seductively for the men. This typically resulted in the dancers clothes being torn from their bodies and women carried off to be raped in adjoining rooms. Before the pleasures of the male appetite could be quenched however, the men would have to observe Simon's reaction to the dancing girls. If there was one he fancied then all eyes would be diverted and she would summarily find herself in his bedchamber later that night for his amusement.

The officers had learned this lesson earlier at another banquet. There, Simon had bestowed particular interest for a certain dancer he had ended up throwing coins to. However, when one of the drunken men caught her, in an effort to strip her publically, Simon had leapt to his feet and killed the man by slashing his throat open with a dagger, spraying blood over the screaming girl. Simon had stared around the hall at the men lounging at low tables, challenging them with his eyes.

Not a man had moved or dared voice disapproval. The musicians had ceased their music, their lyres and flutes lowered with shocked expressions upon their faces. Simon's sober voice was all that had split the silence as he rebuked the men and warned them to never cross him again. Simon had ordered the body removed, the blood cleaned from the floor and the celebrations to continue. Simon's men soon learned their fearless leader's desire for women and none would ever challenge him again.

Thus, it was after the fifth skirmish of the day that Matthias found himself in the hall of the Palace of Herod Antipas. Having reminded Simon again of Shabbat, Matthias gazed across all the officers and soldiers who had gathered under orders following yet another defeat. Matthias shrunk away from the throne once Simon gave the former High Priest an unfavourable glance with dark eyes and a furrowed brow. Matthias sighed heavily and humbly stood in a corner of the hall wearing the elaborate clothes of the priesthood and holding a signet staff in his aging hands.

Simon glared again at the priest and shook his head. *Matthias only cares for the Law*, he thought. *But it will not be the Law which will see us triumph over John's men.* Simon knew that victory would only rest in the simple fact that his soldiers and officers needed to grow some balls and become men. He was sick of the disasters near the Temple Mount and in the Lower City. He sat upon the cushioned chair, growing angrier as he wrestled with humiliation endured at the cost of his army's incompetence since arriving at Jerusalem. He was frustrated and wanted to see John's men suffer and their position overrun. More importantly, Simon wanted supreme power. Finally he stood, brushed his long hair back from his eyes and cocked his head to the side, forcing a grin which seemed to silence the entire hall.

"Which of you were with me in Idumea?" None moved and Simon pointed a finger at the many faces. "Come, I won't bite. Raise your hand if you were with me in Idumea!" Slowly hands were raised throughout the hall from at least two-thirds of the men. Simon nodded as he collected his thoughts. "And who here standing before me has the slightest idea of how we can destroy John of Gischala?" The hands dropped and nobody moved.

Simon gazed around taking a moment; he even gave Matthias a glance and then just shook his head. "You are women! Are we to become the eunuchs of John ben Levi?" Simon shouted, his voice booming in the hall. He sat back down upon his throne with his chest heaving, wiped his brow and then calmly uttered, "We have attacked their positions five times today and gained no ground. We have attacked every possible point in John's line and he regroups his men perfectly to repel our assaults. He makes us look like a whore upon the ground begging for it and crying like a child.

"Is my officer's lack of competence wearing thin? You burned the strongholds of Idumea, butchered men in the thousands, and brought ruin to their crops and towns! We brought our fists to their gates and spoiled their wells with animal carcasses. We taught them the punishment of resistance by the cries of their women and the wails of their children! Where is Idumea? Where is Idumea?" Simon shouted spitting upon the floor, his face red with rage. "We ruled in the south, and the smoke from our fires filled the sky. God has given me a vision that the land would run with blood from the strokes of our swords and that we would carve a kingdom for ourselves.

"If we destroy the Zealot command, their soldiers will flood to our ranks. The people will join us and Rome will find herself facing such a formidable enemy unlike any she has faced before. Rome may control the Galilee, but with our numbers we will soon gain that back and liberate these lands. I will be king and you shall be richly rewarded. Now, how hard is that to grasp?" Simon leaned back and sighed as he saw the effects of his words impress themselves upon the men. "Now, I ask kindly, what is our strength?"

A tall man of rank, who had not flinched at Simon's words, stepped out from the men and bowed his head. He wore a dark cloak and the fringes of his *tzitzit* hung from the corners. A gladius was strapped to his waist, partially concealed from the outer garments he wore, and each of his broad arms bore bronze wristlets of the Roman kind. A short, black beard grew from his square chin and his mailed hood lay draped upon his back. "My lord Simon, I will report."

Simon nodded at Nathanial, who was one of his captains. "Your voice will be heard. Tell me what our strength is?"

"We still control the Upper City, most of the gates, and sections of the Lower City. We hold the valleys around Jerusalem, have men in Beit Ani, and we are gathering more support from the villages nearby, even to Beit Lechem. John and Eleazar lack the resources and manpower to do anything to us. They do, however, have plenty of food to last them for years from the stockpiles under the Temple. Water is the only thing I could anticipate them running low on in less time. Their accuracy of the Roman machines they possess is their greatest defence against our attacks. This is no secret. What we saw occur in the final assault today was calculated, timed perfectly, and executed well. We will continue to suffer high losses until we even the score with heavy siege equipment."

"What do you propose?" Simon asked, seeing where this was going.

"We should try and acquire siege engines. We could buy them from Parthia, or hire mercenary forces beyond our lands."

"Not in a thousand years! Simon, this is not possible," Matthias interrupted approaching the throne. "The city would rise up in revolt. An attack on the Temple with catapults with the aim to destroy its walls might unify the Zealot factions within. It would be devastating, as well as not favoured by God." Matthias pounded his staff upon the tiles dramatically, flustered from the proposition of Simon's captain.

"For once in an age you make sense, Matthias." Simon chuckled, pointing at the deposed High Priest. "Yes, using engines against the Temple could pose a problem in uniting the factions from within. Plus, hiring mercenaries or Parthian siege equipment takes time. We have sent our share of letters to Parthia requesting them to support our cause and they do not respond. If they were to send us equipment, that would certainly be an open challenge to Rome and they aren't ready for that. No, we must look to our own strength and plan the next attacks."

"We need proper weaponry to match theirs, my lord, or we stand the same fate as we have suffered before," Nathanial boasted glancing back at the officers and soldiers behind him. "My lord, we have nearly seventeen thousand troops at our disposal. John can't guard the entire colonnade or the Antonia properly as he would spread his men out too thin. Why not regroup and launch a full out attack on him? We can overrun the colonnades and butcher the dogs in the Outer Court."

"Let me remind you we also control an entire city, Nathanial. To launch such an attack would take maximum numbers from all our centers of control and we wouldn't be guaranteeing victory." Simon stood again and stepped down from his throne. He placed his arms behind his back and strolled over to an open terrace and stared outside. "We must regroup and plan for another battle after Shabbat. Leave me at once."

Nathanial was the first to exit the hall and with that everyone slowly shuffled out carrying their weapons and talking in hushed voices. The great doors were opened and sunlight streamed in as the men parted to their respectable positions or homes in the city to rest for Shabbat. Only one of the officers was left standing near the back and that was a short, fat man with curly hair and a stubby beard.

The man had an enormously round face with a squat reddened nose, blotchy skin, and the signs of a knife wound across his cheek which had claimed an eye. He now wore a black patch covering the empty socket and to add to his ugliness he possessed only four teeth remaining in his calloused gums. The form of his great belly protruded from his cloak and jiggled as the man strolled across the floor shaking his head and giggling to himself. The man's name was Yehoram and he was possibly the only man in Simon's army who truly enjoyed the suffering of others and rivaled the conniving mind of Simon ben Giora himself. Yehoram could never be a leader, in fact he was not even an officer, but nobody stood up to him, as Simon, in a bizarre fashion, favoured the man.

"My lord Simon," Yehoram said with a chuckle. "Have I got something for you."

Simon turned and stepped back inside from the terrace and glanced at Yehoram, his interest piqued. "What have you been up to this day, Yehoram?"

Yehoram glanced at Matthias who gave him a disgusted look as he loathed the vile man. He smiled and said allowing the priest to hear, "I have a young girl outside, of marriageable age. I think you would fancy her."

Simon scoffed at Yehoram loudly and shook his head amused. "Is that what you think of me, you swine? You think Simon is lonely and wishes to marry?"

"Oh, but this one is already engaged, my lord. I thought you might find her entertaining before you sit down to take part in the Shabbat meal. She is young, like I mentioned, and very beautiful."

Simon turned. "Engaged? To whom?"

"Oh, a young wealthy swine, my lord. A boy lover and a sympathizer to Caesar, no doubt; he doesn't matter. Her parents are dead. They were murdered by Eleazar's men before we got here, but not before they had accepted the dowry from the betrothed. They are to wed, oh, such a blessed thing." Yehoram clasped his hands together and laughed. "I had two men kick her door down and bring her here. Let me tell you something. I have seen her on a number of occasions and thought to myself, my master would like a taste of this young, virgin flesh. So I go, ask a few questions, pay a few people off and find that she is an Alexandrian Jewess. Her parents lived there and moved to Jerusalem years ago before the sacrifice was suspended. Now they are dead, their house looted, and she is outside awaiting you."

Simon stood motionless for a moment, his eyes drifting over to Matthias who had taken a step forward in disapproval to Yehoram's story. "How old is she?"

"I think fifteen, maybe." Yehoram smiled and licked his lips playfully.

"You dog! You wretched beast!" Matthias shouted at Yehoram, startling the portly man, and then looked to Simon pleadingly. "My lord, you cannot do this. We are waging a fight here and do not need God's wrath upon us. Do not break the Law and ruin her purity. And what of the betrothed's honour? She is to be wed and it is nearly Shabbat."

"Silence yourself, Matthias. It is but an hour to Shabbat. I have time." Simon smirked.

"You dare bring sacrilege upon this city I should…"

"You forget yourself, Matthias!" Simon interrupted. "Remember, your purpose here is as my guest. Your voice carries not the authority it once did, that authority I hear passed to Phanni ben Samuel a long time ago." Simon saw the effects of his words cause sting in Matthias' proud eyes and he smiled. "Your life lies in my hands." Simon glanced at Yehoram casually. "This woman better be as beautiful as you say, Yehoram. Bring her to my chamber and make sure her skin is scented with the finest perfume. Arrest her betrothed and throw the useless man in prison. I will see to him later." Simon picked up the corners of his long robe and before departing he looked the priest in the eye and whispered, "Offer a brace of pigeons on my behalf, priest, and send it to the Temple with much haste." Simon took notice of the anger and shame on Matthias' face, and while smiling in a sly manner he softly said, "It was you who let me into the city, Matthias. My guilt can be upon your shoulders."

*　*　*

July 29th, 69 A.D. / 24th of Av, 3829
Jerusalem
Eastern side of the Temple Mount

The lanky figure of a young boy, not more than nine years old, made his way along under the shadow of the high walls of the ancient city. Jerusalem at this hour seemed asleep, somber, predictable and passive, which was a stark difference compared to the months of inner fighting between the factions. The boy had listened many times to the shouts and clashing of weapons from the safety of his home in the Lower City. The loud sounds of crumbling stone and mortar, or the high pitched screeching of catapult missiles soaring through the air were all too familiar. His father had joined the ranks of Simon ben Giora's army, hoping for an opportunity to put food in the bellies of his family. However, it had been five weeks since the boy had seen his father, and the looks of starvation were settling into the eyes of his mother and two sisters. As a result, he had grown accustomed to scrounging outside the walls at night, looking for anything edible. Sometimes he was fortunate enough to find some stale bread or dried meat cast over the walls from the guards above, but often nothing would turn up and his family would go hungry for another day.

He stopped abruptly, clutching his narrow frame as if cold, and stared up at the dark walls. The battlements, illuminated in glowing torchlight, revealed nothing at the moment. A breath of wind could be heard sailing overhead and the sound of a dog barking within the city echoed over the porticos. A shadow of a sentry glancing downwards cascaded across the stone and the boy hurriedly pressed onwards, gazing to his left at the darkness that swelled the expanse of the rocky Kidron Valley below. He was all alone and felt like sobbing. The boy sniffed and whimpered softly as he stumbled along using the stones of the wall as support.

Suddenly, he heard some movement behind him and he spun around holding his breath from the fear that clutched his soul. Shadows moved towards him, the shadows of men wishing to stay hidden, and this did not sit well with the boy who scurried out of the way and dived behind a boulder.

The boy's tired, red eyes watched the shapes of seven men shuffle past him without a word, clothed in long cloaks and faces wrapped in dark cloth, appearing like lepers. The leader, at the front of the group, halted twice, silently raising a hand and would stare up at the battlements above as if afraid of any movement or unwanted eyes. Then the leader would shake his head, beckon them forward with a wave of his hand, and they would continue on.

The boy felt an impulse to reveal himself and beg for money or food, but it was only an impulse, possibly a dangerous one. He had heard of such impulses that brought death to other children similar to him living in his neighbourhood, so he just watched the shadows of the men disappear in the darkness as they hurried on. The boy, overcome by grief due to his predicament, curled up in a ball and cried himself to sleep.

David ben Asher held up his weathered, aged hand and stopped the men behind him. He leaned out slightly from the wall examining the terrain before him and then glanced back the way they had come. With a smug grin he asked, "So, Judah ben Yosef, what do you think of my daughter?"

Judah scowled. Had he heard the old man correctly? "What?"

David held back laughter and shook his head. "What do you think of Mira? Surely she piqued your interest."

"Is this the time or place to discuss such things?"

David nodded and reached back and patted Judah's shoulder. "Many men want to marry such a daughter as mine. I threaten their lives and send them on their way. No man is worthy of my daughter or ever will be. She is smart and has learned to be cunning, like her abba, no doubt."

"Sir, I am not looking to take your daughter as my wife. I only met her days ago at your well."

"Ah, and she brought you and your men to my house. We fed you, clothed you, and certainly enjoyed your company." David's ivory teeth glistened in the darkness from the wide smile he gave Judah.

"My men and I are eternally grateful for the shelter and food."

David shrugged and nodded. "What do you think of Beit Ani? Certainly not a bustling city as this one we are creeping into, but a quiet village, yes, and one of opportunity. If you were to consider staying and helping an old man in his business, I may consider turning a lovely daughter such as Mira over to such a leader as Judah ben Yosef to be his wife."

Judah warmly bowed his head in appreciation at the invitation, so as not to offend the old man. "I thought the daughter of the house of Asher was unworthy for any man. Were not those the words of her abba?"

David was still for a moment and then a large smile filled his round face and he slapped Judah on the shoulder and controlled his laughter to a deep chuckle. "You are right there, my son. You are witty and blessed from above with a sense of humour I pray never leaves you." David cleared his throat and with all seriousness restored to his great frame said, "Will you consider the matter?"

Judah gently shook his head thinking of Miriam, his parents, Capito whom he hated, the slaughter of his men in the caves, and now his desire to join the ranks of Gischala. It was as if his life had flashed before his eyes in a torrent of the blood he had spilled and the pain which gripped his heart. He would never be the same, nor could he ever see himself successful in life and giving love to another woman. His life had been pointed in one direction, and that was vengeance upon Rome. When Judah looked into the eyes of the old man, for a second he thought he saw his father. The lined edges of his strong jaw bone, the length of his beard and his dark eyes. Then the image vanished and all Judah could do was whisper as the wind chilled his back, "I must go into the city, David. Forget you ever knew me and find a man worthy of your daughter's hand. I do thank God our paths have crossed, and I will always know of your kindness."

David was taken aback by the callus look in Judah's eyes and the level of pain which could be seen in the young man's face. He nodded and while touching Judah's hand briefly he uttered, "Very well, Judah, very well, as you wish. Come. Follow me!"

The men hunched over and stayed as close to the wall as possible as they moved along, steadying the swords belted about their waists David led them as promised, to a small door bolted from the inside underneath the pinnacle of the Temple.

Upon their final night in Beit Ani, when they had crowded around the Asher table, David had informed the Lions of their entrance into the city. He had warned them of breaking silence so that Simon's men would not spot them, and then had spoken of an old door which he used on numerous occasions to gain access to Gischala's position on the Temple Mount. *"The door will lead first into the Ophel, and then to the Triple and Hulda Gates. Yet you will be taken through the Hulda Gates to the Temple plateau. If you should get that far then Heaven may smile upon you and take you to meet John face to face. But first, before all that, expect to be searched and questioned."* David had made this statement with a mouthful of honey-soaked bread and then had downed his goblet of wine.

It all seemed like a distant memory the moment David pounded on the door and waited for an answer. The Lions listened intensely, their sweaty hands feeling underneath their cloaks for the security of their swords.

"Who is it?" a muffled voice croaked through the wood door.

"David son of Asher!"

"What do you want?"

"I seek John of Gischala."

"At this hour, old man?"

"Yes, indeed, and may the Lord bless and keep old John as protector of the Holy City."

"That is a damn fool thing to say. You wish to curry favour?"

David paused for a moment and smiled at Judah in the darkness. "What favour? I am already a friend of ben Levi."

"And who accompanies you David ben Asher?"

"Only the humblest of men. I have six of the Lions with me, tell that to John. Tell him I have brought men desiring to fight alongside those loyal to John."

"The Lions?"

"Yes, you have heard of such men? Or beasts maybe?" David smiled again. "I have Judah ben Yosef by my side."

There was a pause from within. "Are they armed?"

"Would that matter?" David replied.

"Only if you were lying, you old bastard. What if they were of Simon's crew instead and had come to assassinate John. See my point?"

"Clearly I do. They are equipped with swords and are warriors worthy of songs. It would be in good nature for John to welcome these men and I leave them in your keeping. Search them for weapons if need be and send my regards to John. It is always nice to do business." David turned from the door and whispered, "Do as they say, Judah, and everything should be fine. Say a prayer for old David in the Temple, would you?"

"You're not coming with us?" Judah said, stepping in front of David as the old man tried to pass.

David shook his head and took the young warrior's hands in his and replied, "May God bless you and your men and whatever mission He has you on. I can go no further, you don't need me anymore, and for God's sake, Judah, consider my proposition to you and your men. I would find you a worthy husband of my daughter." David smiled, planted a kiss on either cheek, said farewell to the other Lions, and vanished into the darkness, making his way down into the Kidron and back towards Beit Ani.

The grinding sound of a bolt slid back and the door became ajar revealing a flood of light into the darkness and the sliver of a man's burly face. "Swords, damn it! Let me see them." The man had lowered a spear point near the opening in the door and four other men stood with swords drawn firmly behind him.

"Do as he says," Judah simply said and the Lions complied slowly by opening their cloaks and revealing the blades strapped to their waists.

The gatekeeper seemed unconvinced by the open display of cooperation. As long as strange, armed men stood outside his gate wanting admittance, he could become like a charging, wild bull and skewer anyone he thought posed a threat. He stabbed the air with the point of his spear towards Judah, who he figured was the ring leader of the band, and ordered in a stern voice for them to remove their swords and lay them on the ground. This command was received with complete willingness while the gatekeeper kept a sharp eye on the men as they bent down and set their blades upon the hard, stone ground.

The door opened and a young boy darted out hurriedly to collect the swords. Judah noticed three more guards standing beyond the men with drawn swords, and these soldiers held bows loaded with sharp, barbed arrows, cords drawn to the ear.

Once the boy had slipped back inside the gate holding the bundle of sheathed swords, the door opened completely and the gatekeeper raised his spear, beckoning them inside with a nod. The archers dared not lower their bows as Judah and his men entered through the gate. The door was firmly shut behind them and bolted as the Lions found themselves standing within a large room lit by torches.

"Welcome to Jerusalem," the gatekeeper said in his gruff voice. "If you but move, I will impale you where you stand." This last statement was said to Aviram who had been glaring at the burly, fat man. The gatekeeper nodded at one of the guards standing watch and the man left. "He goes to get more spears." The gatekeeper grinned and waited patiently.

When the guard finally returned, another twelve men were with him armed with all sorts of weapons and lightly fitted in armour, some Roman and some eastern. Numerous soldiers wore helmets of different shapes and styles. One man even wore an old Greek-styled helmet covering his jaw and neck but the common choice was Roman, most likely seized from the Jerusalem garrison that had been slaughtered years ago.

"Search them!" the gatekeeper bellowed, lowering his spear and watching the six men get frisked thoroughly by the newly arrived guards.

"Malchus, they are clean," the tallest of the guards stated, folding his arms.

The gatekeeper Malchus handed off his spear to one of his comrades and stepped forward to begin his interrogation. "Who is your leader?"

Judah turned and nodded to identify himself. "I am."

"And your mysterious friend, David ben Asher, who has conveniently left you, stated that you're Judah ben Yosef of the Lion band. Is this true?"

"It is."

Malchus folded his broad arms before him and bit his lower lip. "Identify your men, Judah ben Yosef."

"That is Caleb, Aviram, Moshe, Aaron, and Adam."

"And how did you come to know David ben Asher?"

"I met his daughter, Mira, outside Beit Ani two days ago. She gave us water and her father took us in, fed us, and gave us shelter."

"Why were you at Beit Ani? Are you not brigands of the north? The illustrious band of Lions? Now there are six of you?" Malchus glanced over his shoulder at the other guards standing by.

Judah cleared his throat. "We were at Beit Ani because my band has been slaughtered, we six standing before you are all that are left."

Malchus watched Judah with shifty eyes and lowered his gaze. "And how did that happen?"

"Many moons ago we ambushed a contingent of Roman cavalry. You may have heard of the Boars?" Malchus nodded and Judah continued, "We attacked them at dawn, killing around ten. We suffered minimal losses and they retreated. Our aim was to disrupt Roman scouting parties and cavalry patrols, but my desire was to kill the Tribune of the Boars, Marcus Sulla Maximus. He got away with his remaining troopers and we returned to our hideout.

"Following this, my men found a deserter named Quintus Fabius. His story was believable and he converted to our faith, only to betray us in the night and lead the Boars right to our hideout. My men were massacred. Myself and these men here were all that survived. We escaped through a cistern, made our way to Beit Ani and then received the help of David ben Asher who brought us here."

"And why are you here?" Malchus asked simply.

"To fight with John of Gischala. We have nothing left and nowhere to go. We considered Masada, but the Romans are sure to come here first and Jerusalem will need swords to defend her." Judah was silent and held the gaze of Malchus who seemed to be considering what to do.

"The Romans are coming here? How can you be so sure?"

"They are sweeping close to the city. Their patrols burn villages and kill anyone who resists. The Galilee has already fallen and I hear they are training in their winter quarters and preparing for the siege which is sure to come. By the spring they will be here."

Malchus licked his lips and shrugged. "How can I be so sure you are not Romans posing as Jewish fighters and wanting into our city to betray it? What do you say to that?"

"The woman I was to marry was slaughtered in this very city in the upper market massacre along with my parents before the war. She died before my eyes by the edge of a spear and was cast into a fountain to drown. I found her there, floating amidst the dead, her blood darkening the water. I sought my first vengeance that day, and killed my first Roman. I have slain many and cast their bodies upon the ground, my hands drenched in their blood. I still carry the sword of the first soldier I sent to Sheol.

"I then was driven into the wilderness where many men rallied to my side to fight against the power of Rome. They named me "The Lion" and the name bore the very force of the Jewish fighters I led. I have spent three years killing Romans and leading men with the same desire. Now, they have all been killed, all but these men who stand before you today. We have suffered, starved, bled, and died for the cause of sparing holy Jerusalem from the unclean hands of the Romans. I live for one reason and that is to seek my revenge on Rome. I swear this to God. And if you stand in my way, may the plagues of Egypt follow you and find you no matter where you hide. Now, you will take me to see John."

Malchus stood before Judah, his glare having vanished and a look of complete empathy upon his face. The gatekeeper thought to himself for a brief moment and then said, "Come with me."

Judah and his men filed in behind Malchus as the old man led them from the small gatehouse. They emerged into a large opening with high-rising steps before them and the looming Triple and Hulda Gates set against the high walls of the Royal Stoa dimly lit in torchlight. A dozen soldiers from the guard house accompanied them, and while ascending the steps, Malchus raised his spear in the air and shouted a greeting to the guards on the stairwell platform to stand aside and allow them admittance.

Judah and his men were led through the Hulda Gates into the coolness of the tunnel. Large columns of granite and marble held up the extreme weight of the roof as the gates gave access to the Temple Mount from beneath. The glowing haze of torchlight from within the courts could be seen casting an orange hue through the tunnel. Malchus led them past a row of pillars as they climbed a staircase, finally to emerge onto the grounds of the Temple with the Royal Portico at their back. Walls rose all around them from the colonnades as endless columns and arcades stretched the entire length of the southern end of the plateau.

The marble pillars were enormous as they held up a massive, decorated ceiling, on top of which rested battlement walkways patrolled by Zealot fighters. The shadows cast from the pillars stretched out across the Outer Court. Beyond that, Judah and his men could see the silhouetted outline of the Temple reaching up into the night sky.

Judah held his breath, wanting to fall to his knees and kiss the ground. He heard Caleb mutter a prayer of the Psalms and felt a light air mill about his body as if he could sense the beating heart of the Jewish people before him. The edifice and grandeur of the Temple was remarkable. Even in the dead of night its white marble stones and gold capped roof glowed from the city lights as if it's very stones burned with a magnificent divine fire from heaven.

The face of the Temple was cast in shadows and flickering light, as fire burned from the great candelabras within. Voices could be heard rising up from the din inside the Inner Court as priests worked steadily in the slaughter of animals and the recitation of prayers. A coil of smoke twisted up from the concealed Burnt Altar which sent a pleasing aroma wafting on the air. Malchus slowed his pace, as a number of white-robed priests passed by. Judah watched the men of Levitical descent move across the expanse of tiled stone in the direction of the Temple while singing psalms. Their simple garments gleamed in the torchlight as they were the relief for the priests who had been at their duties for hours.

Malchus halted abruptly and looked over his shoulder at Judah. Seeing the awe and amazement upon the young man's face he said, "If John doesn't believe your story, ben Yosef, you will all die as spies. I hope that isn't a problem." He laughed and continued on across the Outer Court.

Judah could make out a force of at least sixty men milling about in full battle gear, carrying swords, spears, axes, and bows. Despite them being in the proximity of such a holy place, nobody objected to the display of arms. They were all very strong-looking men resembling some of the most experienced Jewish fighters in the region. Most of them had long beards, and a few pious ones openly revealed the fringes of their prayer garments which hung from the edges of their cloaks. Some wore leather breastplates and others wore the plated Roman chest armour. These were the crack troops of John of Gischala's force and they had gathered to see what the legendary Judah ben Yosef looked like.

"Those are John's finest; you don't want to mess with them. You'll find yourself without a head." Malchus chuckled to himself, amused at the dark, grim looks the soldiers gave the newcomers. "You should have seen them in action days ago when Simon's pathetic force charged those very gates you just entered through. The poor bastards were cut down without a chance. When John gave the order to preserve arrows, these dogs here opened the gates in full view of Simon's force, and launched a full attack right down the steps, killing men with every metre gained. The steps are still streaked in blood; you just can't see it during the night."

Malchus seemed to be enjoying himself as he told tales of the zealot fighters in the Outer Court. Every once in awhile he would glance back at Judah and his men and either smile or wink, but the stories continued as they passed by more Zealots, following the porticos. Malchus directed the men to the far right and approached a high tower-like structure built into the southeastern corner where the walls met. Light poured out of the windows in the building and Malchus pointed and said, turning his head slightly, "That is where John is. He will be expecting you, Judah."

"He only wants to see me?" Judah replied, looking at Caleb sheepishly.

"The rest of you will wait outside. It appears you, Judah, are all he cares about." Malchus chuckled, wiped his nose, than rapped on the door with his spear. He waited for an answer, stared up at the high walls and then impatiently pounded upon the door.

"Malchus?" a muffled voice asked within.

"I have the man," Malchus replied with a grin. A dead bolt was slid out of its lock and the door suddenly opened bathing the men in light.

"You're late Malchus. Do you think John wishes to stay up all night while you parade around?" A short man stood in the doorway dressed in the garments of a priest. He stepped aside and gestured with his hand for Judah to enter. "My name is Zechariah and I am John's personal aide, among other things. Now come, we haven't got all night."

Judah only had time to give Caleb an awkward look, unsure of what was to happen next and then he entered, standing next to Zechariah as the door was firmly shut. His eyes darted around the chamber they were standing in and he noticed the simplicity of it all. There was no luxurious furniture, tables of food, men partying, or wealth to be seen.

Zechariah followed Judah's gaze around the chamber and gathered what the young Jewish man was pondering. "No riches here, young man, just a humble tower where John conducts much of his business." Judah gave the old man an inquisitive look and Zechariah nodded continuing his rant, "I mean, it's not like John needs all the riches in the world, some to help fund what he is doing here, but then again I am only babbling." Zechariah took Judah tenderly by the elbow, like a grandfather would a grandson, and led him to another door.

"Are you a priest?" Judah asked eyeing the old man.

"When my services in the Temple are not required I find them much useful here. I am literate, you see, and can write extensively, almost as well as the Essenes. I suppose John finds a use for me despite my age. Now, come!"

Zechariah opened the heavy door and led Judah up a long winding flight of stairs that seemed to twist like a snake up the heart of the citadel. With every turn, Judah would pass a window revealing a dark Kidron Valley below with a few lights flickering in the darkness from the Mount of Olives which rose above the valley on the other side. Zechariah ascended the steps quickly, not saying a word and never looking back to check where Judah was. His whole attention was given to proper breathing as the climb was always stressful on his body. However, he never let anyone notice the sweat forming at his temple or the redness upon his face.

When Zechariah reached the top, there was a ledge with another door. Torches hung on either side of the door and upon its stained wood was mounted a heavy brass ring. "Now, he is in a sour mood today, trying to figure out complicated issues concerning Eleazar and Simon. It's been quite the week."

"Eleazar ben Simon?"

Zechariah ignored the question and took the brass ring in his hands. "He is waiting for you, Judah. Just mind yourself." Zechariah heaved the door with a push and it opened. "Off you go now. I wait here."

Judah hesitated for a moment. Zechariah gave a convincing nod and stepped back giving the obvious hint that this was no time for questions. Judah took a deep breath, his heart beating like a pounding drum, and entered the room. The door shut with a resounding thud behind him and his body was bathed in warm light.

The long chamber of the citadel was lit by torches and completely absent of any décor or fine furniture. An oddly shaped table stood against one of the walls with narrow legs and an oblong top made from olive wood, its surface scattered with scrolls and jugs that contained wine. A simple, cushioned stool, captured from the Antonia when the Roman garrison fell, had been placed along the wall to the right of the high table. The felt on the cushion was worn down and one of the legs appeared to have sustained a little damage to the molding, perhaps when it had been ousted from the Antonia and relocated. A robust looking table with a touch of Hellenistic taste dominated the center of the room. Discarded goblets and sheets of leather animal skins lay upon it with a number of sharpened quills upon the hides, their tips crusted over with dried ink. The table top was lit by numerous clay oil lamps which burned brightly, their wicks cut short as not to spark or drip upon the leather hides. A hanging, wrought iron candelabra of eastern design hung from the high stone ceiling above the table with only half of the lamps burning low from lack of oil. The room was inviting, yet obviously a chamber to conduct business in.

The figure of a tall man stood at the end of the hall. He was dressed in the clothes of common men, freed from hindering armour, and was holding a fine looking golden goblet in his massive, bear-like hand. He slowly turned to the sound of moving feet, grinned at Judah, and then gave him a nod. The visage of John ben Levi was instantly alluring to the eyes and inspiring to any solider who had ever walked the earth. He stood over two metres tall, had shoulders as thick as the Cedars of Lebanon, and had a beard like the mane of a lion. His dark eyes bore a strange light which was appealing, yet his demeanour proved he could be a man of instant action and vengeful fury. His chin was squared like his chest and his powerful arms were larger than any Judah had ever seen. He wore leather boots, obviously stolen from a centurion of high status, and about his waist was an iron studded leather belt. A Roman pugio hung from his side, the dagger's hilt bearing the eagle of Rome and numerals representing the detachment it had been a part of. John's giant frame was a symbol of Jewish resistance to the iron fist of Rome, and merely looking at the man had the power to recruit simple farmers into the life of the Zealot cause.

"I trust Malchus retained his manners and Zechariah's company was pleasant?" John's voice was dark and rich, with the accent of the Galileans.

Judah bowed his head. "They were, my lord."

John laughed with a rolling chuckle that instantly made Judah smile. He covered the distance between them within a second as he took Judah in his arms and planted a kiss on either cheek. "I am John to you, Judah ben Yosef. Neither lord nor master here, my brother. We are all fellow Jews in this heavenly struggle to rid us of Roman filth. You never have to bow your head to me, am I clear?"

"Yes, my lord, I mean, John."

John's face was like a bright beacon and he slapped Judah's shoulder in appreciation and then walked him to where he had been previously standing and pointed out the window to the lights of the Temple flickering in the night. "Have you been to Jerusalem, Judah? Have you seen the Temple?"

"I used to live in Beit Lechem, John. My family and I would attend the feasts; I particularly enjoyed *Pesach* and the winter festival. I was dedicated in the Temple and heard the teachings of many rabbis." Judah's eyes took in the entire magnificence of the Temple as he could hear the singing of priests and the braying of sheep.

"You are quite a Jew then. A man of the Scriptures? Were you ever a disciple?" John inquired.

Judah shook his head. "My father was more dedicated to the Law and proper observance than I was. He wanted me to study in Jerusalem under a Rabbi Amos ben Zakkai, an old friend of my father's and a Pharisee, but that never came to anything."

"But you know Greek and are educated, yes?" Judah glanced up at John with surprise and the Galilean smiled. "I have heard much of you, Judah the Lion."

"I was educated here in the city in the *yeshiva*, and was tutored in Greek. I excelled among my classmates. My father was in the trade business through Joppa and he wanted me to take over when I was older. He would tell me that Greek was essential because it connected the world; then I could deal with foreigners and increase the business."

John nodded. "Gischala is where I grew up, and it is no more. Titus destroyed it." A moment of silence grew between the two men and then John turned to him. "Your band of Lions has been defeated and the Boars still terrorize our people?"

"Yes, but how did you hear of my men?"

"I have connections and people who trust me, Judah. I run an enterprise here and fight for control of this city so I can harness its potential and prepare it for war. Rome is coming, for that I am sure of. This squabbling with the emperors has just bought us time. I have been praying someone might knife Vespasian and throw the entire gamble in an uproar. It appears Vespasian might overthrow this Vitellius dog who cowers in the capital. We have the fall and winter to prepare; Rome will come in the spring." John strolled over to the table and his attention fell upon the leather hides, studying the ones which bore lines of Hebrew etched into the material.

"What of the Boars? Will they just be left to their own free will?"

"There is nothing that can be done now. We possess no cavalry and cannot afford to leave our hold on the Temple. Have you any idea of what is going on here?"

Judah shrugged. "I have heard some, mainly from an old beggar and a woman in Beit Ani."

John jabbed a finger in the direction of the Upper City beyond the porticoes of the Temple plateau. "Simon ben Giora, that devil embodied in a man, controls the entire city, upper and lower, except for the Temple Court and the Antonia which are under my sway. Simon has support from the Idumean refugees commanded by James ben Sosias, only God knows why, since it was Simon who murdered the Idumeans by the thousands in the south."

John glanced at the floor for a moment and then added, "Simon also has the notorious Ananus ben Bagdatus who will crush the life out of anyone Simon orders him to, woman or child. Rumour is that Bastard Bagdatus strangled two of five children from a family that Simon suspected of hiding food; that is Simon's agenda."

John shook his head and observed the shocked expression on Judah's face. "The Ophel and the Kidron are neutral; nobody really controls it. Eleazar ben Simon is hemmed up inside the Inner Court like a madman, accompanied by Judas ben Chelcias, Simon ben Ezron, and Hezekiah ben Chobari." John shook his head and swore silently. "Eleazar has turned the Court of the Women and Israelites into a bloody fortress. He does, however, allow the priests to attend their daily duties and worshippers to gather, yet all are under watchful eyes. They obviously don't mess with the Court of the Priests. They still fear God, to some extent, those dogs, but they control the entire place with such paranoia that the odd man still gets beaten or killed due to Eleazar's fear that I am sending men in to secretly oust him. That is on the agenda, but I haven't put anything together at this point."

"I have heard of fighting, of many suffering among the inhabitants. Is this true?"

John stared long and hard at Judah and then nodded. "I will admit, no one has clean hands in this city, Simon least of all. I have tried to stem the reckless violence, Judah, but it is difficult when you're completely surrounded and hemmed in. If it wasn't for all the weaponry the Romans left behind, I am afraid we would have been overrun. Simon wishes to control the city and set himself up as king. I seek only to defend Jerusalem from the Romans who wish to profane its holiness.

"Matthias ben Theophilus is responsible for letting in the madman. Eleazar and I ran this city, and were making preparations to see it ready for battle against Vespasian; we had an uneasy truce, you see. I don't trust Eleazar. He is weak and has the mind of an ass." John licked his lips and shook his head. "Simon arrived outside the city and surrounded it with his army. He demanded admittance, and Matthias let him in as he felt he could play God and replace us with a madman. We were pushed back to this position. All the stockpiled plunder I had amassed with the intention of enticing Parthia to support our cause fell into Simon's hands and he has been trying to overwhelm our positions since. Eleazar broke the truce he held with me and has been trying to contact Simon to arrange an alliance. If this succeeds, then Jerusalem will fall when the Romans arrive."

"What of Ananus ben Ananus and the government? I heard they are no more. Was it Simon?"

John raised his eyes and momentarily held his breath. The events of that desperate night came flooding back into his mind. He could still see the gaping, bulging eyes of Ananus and hear his raspy, drowning inhale for air as blood had spilled from his mutilated throat, his bowels giving way to soil the stones beneath him. After days of hunting down Ananus and Joshua ben Gamala, they had been found hiding in a sewer and had been dispatched gruesomely and thrown from the walls. John, recovering his wits, swallowed the lump in his throat and shrugged. "After I had arrived from Gischala with the fall of the north under the incompetent Yosef ben Matityahu, I was elected to the side of Ananus to work with the government on destroying the Zealots under Eleazar.

"The government had already gained control of the city and had a strong force, raised from the citizenry, to guard the Temple courts and keep a watchful eye on Eleazar. However, Ananus had plans of surrendering the city to the Romans, and so I sent information to the Zealots and met with them. I encouraged them to seek the help of the Idumeans to the south and they responded with an army of twenty thousand.

"When they arrived at the city, Ananus wouldn't let them in and Joshua tried to make a truce with them. A great storm arose and the guards from the battlements sought shelter, and in that time I sent word to Eleazar to launch an attack and open the gates to the Idumeans. The plan worked and the government soldiers were massacred, yet the Idumeans proved to be unstable and uncontrollable. It was them who finally caught Ananus and murdered him along with Joshua, only to cast their bodies from the walls.

"Finally the Idumeans got tired of the city and decided to retreat back to the south to their strongholds. Still, a large force of Idumeans decided to stay and over the next while we became worried of Simon's activity in the south. He was gaining enormous support. He had put together an army of brigands and had begun attacking Idumean strongholds, towns, and cities, slaughtering people by the thousands. There were a number of pitched battles at Nain and Olurus, but slowly the Idumean power began to dwindle. We even dispatched an army to stop him and met little success against his hardened veterans. We tried ambushing them in the mountain passes and even captured his wife and brought her back to Jerusalem.

"We hoped it would bring him to the negotiation table and it did indeed bring him to Jerusalem. He left behind dozens of burning villages and in a rage, started killing everyone outside the city walls. He would cut off their hands and send them back in. It was the first time I felt my power directly threatened as the city was near open revolt. We simply handed Simon back his wife and he left. He went south again to pillage more and see the Idumeans destroyed. He made Idumea a desert, a place of corpses, with so much to offer the ravens; they dined from great feasts and became fattened. The stories of refugees were heard everywhere as they swelled our city. My men stayed loyal, but everyone feared Simon."

John relieved an itch on his neck. "Simon arrived here sometime later and surrounded the city and camped near its walls, fully content to do nothing but wait. Eleazar rewarded his men with allowing them to do anything they so pleased, as a demonstration of thanks to their loyalty. I couldn't stop them. They looted homes, murdered people who resisted, and raped women. Many of my own men joined in such despicable acts, but I couldn't control them. It was like all their fear from the past months was spilling forth in an untameable, relentless rage at everything which had happened. I do say, I am not proud of what my men did.

"Fear began to grip the city and countless times I was dragged into councils of the Sanhedrin who demanded that Eleazar harness control over his men to regain law and order. Eleazar wouldn't listen to any sense and carried on promoting himself as some ruler and then broke the truce he had made, ending peace between us. I managed to control my men and mobilized them into battling squads where we clashed forces with Eleazar's Zealots in the streets, where we tried to destroy him and crush all resistance, but this became impossible.

"Before I could produce any results, it was a group of Idumean refugees that turned on a number of my men this past Nisan. They murdered many, then drove them into the royal palace, where I had been staying, and plundered it. My men retreated back to the Temple and I organized a counterattack from the Outer Court while the bastard Idumeans plundered my residence. They must have caught wind of the war party I was amassing, for they assembled the chief priests and demanded that Matthias ben Theophilus do something. Later, I questioned the priests that had been present, and they told me that Matthias had merely offered them the solutions available. They must choose either blood-thirsty Simon to rule or me. The Idumeans chose Simon and Matthias got down on all fours like a shit-covered dog and crawled to the feet of that bastard and opened the doors to him like he was the Messiah. Now we have this predicament that we find ourselves entwined in."

The room was silent. Judah mauled over the story and shook his head. "It is a wonder Ananus could even have conceived such a notion as to surrender the city. After all we had fought for against Cestius Gallus and the many battles of the north."

"Ananus was a coward and a traitor to our people. Although I didn't wish his death, or that of Joshua, it was God's judgment on them for working with the Romans." John glanced back down at the figures and information written upon the leather hides. "I command six thousand men, Eleazar has something around the number of two thousand, and Simon must have at least fifteen thousand." John shook his head trying to make sense of the numbers and then crossed his arms. "What I could do with that many troops, only God knows!"

"Well, John, if it pleases you, my men and I would be honoured to join your ranks and help defend the Temple."

John smiled. "How many?"

"Five."

"Any Galileans?"

"Two."

"From where?"

"Tiberius and Capernaum."

John chuckled. "A city and a village. On the edge of the water." He rubbed his chin and cracked his giant knuckles. "With a properly organized army we could have given Vespasian hell. General Matityahu didn't do so badly at the start, but his heart was not in it. I think he cared more for his life and his wealth than defending our lands. He had everything to lose, that and his fat reputation. Damn patricians and sympathizers. He betrayed us and let the Romans destroy everything."

John's eyes burned like a great smelting oven, fed with so much fuel that its coals glowed white. Then the exasperated look vanished and John smacked a tight fist into the palm of his left hand and grinned. "Welcome, Judah ben Yosef. It would honour me to have a Lion among the ranks of this motley crew."

* * *

CHAPTER VII

August 5th, 69.AD / 1st of Elul, 3829
Caesarea Maritima
Military Drill Grounds
Legio XII Fulminata

The heat seemed unbearable. The breeze cast off of the sea gave little relief, as every man was expected to drill in full battle gear. This consisted of an army-issued wool tunic and *lorica segmentata* scale armour strapped overtop for ultimate chest protection. A heavy leather cingulum, studded with bronze, hung down to the knees to protect the waist, thighs, and groin of each legionary. All wore the standard issued hobnailed sandals and the heavy Gallic-styled Roman battle helmet, with hinged cheek guards tied firmly in place, and the wide neck guard extending from the back. Every man carried the modified Spanish gladius strapped to their waist, a large scutum shield bearing their company's insignia upon the leather hide, and a two metre pilum with its deadly pointed iron head. The entire outfit was heavy and could be awkward for an amateur soldier, but for the men of the Twelfth Legion, they were battle hardened veterans, accustomed to the fit and feel of the polished, greased armour.

The officers, on the other hand, who stamped their feet angrily upon the ground and shouted orders, were in full regalia consisting of polished iron helmets and transverse plumes of different colours according to their rank. A white or blonde transverse plume identified a centurion by status, whereas a red or black lengthways plume was kept for the junior officer or tribune. They all wore bronze greaves upon their legs and some even were fitted in expensive boots.

The Twelfth Legion was a proud legion with an elaborate history that had taken them into some of the most grueling and unforgiving regions of the empire. All ten cohorts of the Twelfth were experienced men; they were the cream of the crop of Vespasian's army and the legion which would march boldly to the walls of Jerusalem, hoisting their signi for every Jew to see that the wrath of Rome was upon them.

After the humiliating withdrawal from the city of Jerusalem three and a half years ago, and the near total destruction of Cestius Gallus' army, the Twelfth Legion had refused to remain in dishonour, appealing for active service by crushing the Jewish rebellion. For nearly three years Vespasian had ignored them as they had waited miserably in the lands of Syria, biding their time and praying to Mars to give them another chance as Vespasian's legions triumphed in the north. However, finally orders had been issued, a commander put in place, and the Twelfth had marched proudly to join Vespasian's army knowing full well that their destiny lay enshrined in the coming siege of Jerusalem. The men could see glory before them and taste the sweet wine of victory which would wash away all shame. Soon, they would be put back into action on the right wing of the advance, their honoured placement, and this time they would not be defeated.

Orders for the morning had brought all five centuries of the First Cohort to the parade grounds outside of their camp. Training of the day would consist of *testudo* siege formations, flanking manoeuvres, and storming battlements from mock siege towers for close quarter combat. Orders were handed out to commanders stating that all training was to be solely dedicated to bringing the legionaries to a level of perfection in order to take the city of Jerusalem. Rumours circulated the camp that a storm of the city and an all out sacking of its buildings were highly unlikely. Most of the men slept under the illusion that with the destruction of the north and the arrival of the legions, the enemy would capitulate, give in to Titus' demands to vacate the city, surrender all arms, and have the leadership bound in chains.

"Halt! Centuria commanders of the Wolf! Shift your men to the right and look smart. I will not take this *cohors* to battle unless I see some damned professionalism!" Gaius Cornelius Antony, a Primus Pilus centurion and *Primi Ordines* of the First Cohort, glared at the formations of men before him and shook his head as the soldiers shuffled to the right by the aide of their *optiones*. Once in proper formation, they stood at attention with their scuta resting upon the ground and spears pulled tightly against their sides. Gaius held his head high as he marched down the front of the each century's formation, inspecting their equipment, weapons, and discipline. The *torques* and decorations hanging from the leather harness he wore upon his cuirass glistened in the sun as beads of sweat trickled down his cheeks under the weight of his helmet. He gave a stern nod and then grinned towards a fellow centurion, impressed with the appearance of his commanding century.

"We continue with drills today and after your allotted break at noon, we will commence on a field march of five miles! I want battle formations and proper discipline. Maintain your order and may the gods preserve *Roma* and our Imperator Vespasian! May the fortune of our unit's history go before us and may all who oppose us be destroyed!" The men replied with a resounding three shout cheer and then were silent again. "Centuria dismissed and cycle your units according to the week's procedures."

The officers in the front ranks saluted and then instantly started shouting, leading their units away to the sound of company trumpets and drums from the rear. Two tribunes mounted upon horses, reined in their mounts to a grinding halt, and the senior of the two pointed a finger at the flexibility of one of the centuries as it wheeled left in a tight column and then suddenly changed shape into a battle formation at the command of the centurions who kept a close eye on the troops. The legionaries locked shields, forming a solid wall of scuta facing an imagined enemy, with pila lowered and at the ready. The officers restrained their men from cheering and kept them on a tight line of discipline. The mounted tribunes watched the century silently march thirty paces and then come to an abrupt halt where stacks of hay had been piled before them in great mounds, and beyond that stood over a hundred posts with sacks of straw tied to each simulating the form of a man.

The century was silent for a moment as the optiones in the rear checked the ranks, giving a numerous legionary's a slight shove every once in a while with their *hastile* staffs to make sure they maintained a perfect rectangular formation. A whistle was blown and the legionaries suddenly shifted forward five paces, halted and hurled their pilum in a deadly hail storm of flying iron missiles which plunged into the piles of hay. Almost immediately the sound of scraping metal reverberated across the drill grounds as one hundred and sixty blades were drawn. With another blast from the whistle, the century broke their silence with a bellow and surged forward like an avalanche of Roman fury. They quickly overcame the straw piles, flooding onward as the ground thundered from their attack. With fury bellowing from their lungs, the legionaries closed in upon the personified posts and hacked them to pieces with quick successive thrusts, and slashes. After the successful attack, the century filed back into column and continued their march as if the sudden rage upon straw and wood had been part of an everyday normality. Servants rushed onto the drill grounds to retrieve the scattered pila while the two tribunes clapped and whistled at the impressive display of the departing infantry.

Gaius sighed and squinted up at the burning sun as if its very intent was to melt the earth of all moisture. His body ached from his lack of sleep the last couple of nights. With so much demand in the preparation for the siege and a constant stream of orders from the upper echelon, he felt weighted down and plagued. It was not like Gaius had not felt the sting of duty and the sweat of hard work before in the service for the emperor, it was just this time it seemed different. Ever since the fifth day to the Ides of July everything had seemed tense. The omens had continued to show the gods favour upon the troops through the interpretive signs found in the entrails of goats and rams. The change, however, was the mood of the men. Not a single man wanted to let Vespasian down, and every man knew where their loyalty and honour lay. When the campaign had begun, the north had been a series of countless obstacles to overcome; every town and fortified city was something to reckon with. The relentless attacks the Jews had made on the army were proven by the billeting of the men every night when they returned to camp. The numbers showed the losses they had suffered fighting in the north, as many tents were now spacious with the lack of soldiers to fill them, and some tents had even been packed up completely. But now Vespasian had been crowned 'Imperator,' and that was the basic fundamental reality that changed everything.

The men drilled differently, with an intensity rarely seen among centurions. Gaius understood this as a pride among the men, but also a determination not to let their emperor down, an emperor whose eyes watched them daily. A serious nature had descended upon them, one which sometimes started brawls or arguments, and one which pushed them to the limits in their training. Gaius could clearly see the effects. In the past he would have to blast his whistle countless times and sometimes use physical force to drive the men and bring them under the brutal discipline of the Roman army. Now, however, the men would assemble early, drill hard, and march with meaning. Gaius only feared that with such determination within the hearts of his soldiers, they could be devastated if they should fail. Everything seemed to ride on one principle: men should trust their leaders and be of good morale, but men should never be overconfident. That was what Gaius feared the most, that when the men were in the thick of the fight and the eyes of Titus were upon them, they would weaken and be destroyed.

A loud chorus of trumpet blasts and cymbals rose above the din of the grueling training going on throughout the drill grounds. Gaius turned and was joined by a young optio and a *signifer* from one of the centuries carrying the unit's signum, which boasted a muscular arm gripping a lightning bolt on one of the bronze discs. The optio was a young man with about two days growth of whiskers on his stubby chin and with mellow eyes of a gentle nature. When he was within a metre of the senior centurion, he halted abruptly and struck his mailed chest. The short sleeves of a freshly laundered white tunic were exposed beneath the man's mail cuirass. Light brown leather straps outlined in gold thread hung from his shoulders and he wore the Gallic helmet, which was brightly polished, topped with a lengthways white and black upward striped plume.

"Primus Pilus, sir, I have news for you!" the young optio declared, lowering his gaze in the customary fashion of submitting to a senior officer with twenty years experience and a Primi Ordines of impressive prestige.

Gaius faced the two men, resting his hand on the pommel of his sword, as he noticed how the standard bearer remained a pace behind the eager Optio. "It took the two of you to bring me news? It must be important, Optio. Speak now!"

"His Excellency Titus Vespasianus the Younger will be touring the grounds of the Fulminata today and wishes proper demonstrations of the testudo and siege tower manoeuvres." The Optio regained his confidence and enthusiastically pointed across the field to where the mock siege towers were being set up by a horde of men, soon to begin their routine drills.

"Who informed you of this?"

"His Excellency Titus did, Primus Pilus. I was given strict instructions to deliver this message at once. You are to select one centuria for the testudo and two for the siege tower operations. They will be setting up over there!" The young man pointed to where a small veranda with overhead shade was being set up as couches and stools were carted out to it in a wagon.

"When?" Gaius exhaled loudly, shaking his head. He hated surprises, especially drills of this kind.

"In the hour, Centurion."

"Then you have an hour to shave and look smart; your toga looks it, not your face," Gaius made the jab remark with a frustrated tone. "Inform the centuria under the *hastatus* that they can give the siege tower a run before the eyes of royalty and the centuria of the *princeps posterior* can run the testudo."

"And what of the second centuria for the siege tower, Centurion?"

"That will be my own." Gaius paused for a moment and then added, "Please inform His Excellency to enjoy the performance. And Optio?"

"Yes, Centurion?"

"What centuria are you under?"

"The Serpent, under the *hastatus posterior*, sir." The Optio glanced back at the Signifer, unsure of what was to come next.

"Let that dog Centurion Rufus know that twenty of his men are up for cleaning duty in the baths, praetorium, and latrine."

The Optio grinned relaxing, as he understood the joke and with a firm salute, made off with the standard bearer to spread the orders.

*   *   *

"Sire, they will be ready shortly. The other cohortes need to move their drills to other parts of the field," Tribune Marcus Tullius Octavian said with a slight bow of his head and then covered his mouth as he yawned, stretching beneath the canopy of his litter.

Titus glanced at the legionary tribune, elected general of the Twelfth Fulminata, then drew back the red linen curtains. He would have preferred to ride Achilles onto the drill grounds to the ovation of the troops, but his father, Vespasian, had been trying to encourage his son to show some royalty at times for he knew the troops would be expecting it from the young prince-to-be, for Vitellius was not yet dead.

Titus rolled a grape between his fingers, studying its texture, and then tossed it into this mouth. "How are your men, Marcus?"

"As fine as men can be who were born as whelps into this miserable world, sire." Marcus chuckled to himself and then looked annoyed as his litter shifted uncomfortably from the eight slaves that carried it. "Careful now. Remember you're carrying a general." Marcus glanced at Titus and caught a flash of a smile from the prince, then he roared with laughter and helped himself to a small block of cheese.

Titus sat up and steadied himself from the motion of the litter carried by his slaves. He observed the veranda fifty paces away and the men who were draping the roof with long palm fronds to provide shade. "There better be wine," he mumbled aloud.

"It has been fetched, sire. There shall be plenty of wine and food for the afternoon's events. Perhaps gladiators tonight? Make a few of the northern scum fight it out again!" Marcus spit out an olive pit, aiming for the back of one of the slave's head, and when he missed, he reclined in disappointment. "A pity," he said with a sour expression and then shoved another olive into his awaiting mouth, eager to try his luck a second time.

"Marcus!" Titus said. "My father will not be watching today's drills. Pass the word to Centurion Antony when we arrive that I want the best. Do not disappoint me this day. We have a lot ahead of us and your men will be in the thick of it."

Marcus graciously bowed his head. "The Fulminata is always at the service of *Roma* and ready to do the will of Mars. You shall not be disappointed in our lads this time, not like with Gallus or its mucky history in Parthia, sire." Marcus rolled over in his litter and caught the attention of one of his squires. The young man ran to the side of his master and lowered his gaze in submission. "Send word to Centurion Antony to make damn sure his men do nothing short of perfection in this drill."

"Yes, my General," the squire whispered softly.

"And make sure you bring my hat when I climb out of this cumbersome thing."

"Yes, my General."

"And make sure there are fresh olives at the veranda and cheese. Tell that fellow, Lucius, to have fresh cheese." Marcus jabbed a chubby finger, with a large jeweled ring, in the face of the servant.

"Yes, General, as you wish."

"Good, now go." Marcus turned, ushering the man away from his litter with a wave of the hand. *Gaius better be in top shape with his men*, he prayed to the gods. In front of the emperor's son he did not desire to be made a fool.

When the litters arrived before the veranda, a table had been set up, a carpet spread upon the ground, and a number of couches scattered with plush cushions. The litters were gently set upon the ground, each before a stepping stool, and the curtains were secured to the side by golden ropes. The slaves, all shirtless with oiled chests and defined muscles, stood motionless as Titus and Marcus stepped down from their litters, surveying the scene. Marcus' servant handed his master a finely woven straw hat, followed by a silver goblet of wine. Titus was given his consulship rod of power from his personal steward, and then was offered wine, which he accepted, and a foot massage, which he declined.

"How could I have my feet pampered when my men have been slogging in this bloody heat for the last two hours?" Titus replied with a sarcastic scoff. He squinted up at the burning sun, took a long drink of wine and then striding over to the veranda, entered the cool shade and made himself at home upon one of the couches. "Marcus, with that hat you look like the image of a freed man, who tills the ground impetuously." Titus chuckled. "Where in the name of the gods did you find that?"

Marcus removed his hat and studied the tedious hours of craftsmanship that had gone into the construction of the hat. "I found it in the marketplace of Tiberias. Fixed a good price for it! I merely had to announce that I was the commander of the

Twelfth Legion and everyone seemed to shit themselves and hand out free hats. Two of my tribunes each received one."

"Truly, you are not serious?" Titus replied shaking his head.

Marcus shrugged with a grin and entered the shade of the palm branches above. "Would I lie to the man who will be emperor one day when Vespasian has left us?" Marcus sat upon a couch across from Titus and having finished his wine waited while it was refilled.

Titus nodded and smiled. "Well, you look as ridiculous as a catamite in love with a girl."

Marcus laughed, letting the impolite comment roll past him unhindered. It was Titus' form of amusement, and most of the higher ranking officers had grown accustomed to it.

Titus' scribe, who was a large, elderly man in his early sixties named Albinus, leaned in and whispered next to his ear to alert him. "Sire, Gaius Cornelius Antony approaches."

Titus nodded. "Thank you, Albinus." He sat up and watched his father's favourite officer of the legions approach the veranda accompanied by an entourage of centurions involved in the demonstration.

They were all proud men and Primi Ordines of the First Cohort, the honourable and most elite cohort of a legion. They had all earned their ranks through bravery, disciplined work, and grueling service for the glory of Rome. Each man was a battle hardened leader from years in the field, and all had had their lives threatened countless times. They would lead men into battle at the front of their formations, and would be the first into the fray. Gaius, however, was different.

It was no coincidence that Vespasian called the centurion by his clan name, Cornelius, in a tender and respectful voice. Gaius had saved countless legionaries from certain death, and had turned many hopeless situations into victory by the edge of his blade and his beast-like ability to valiantly inspire his men in the worst combative scenarios. The torques and dona hanging over his cuirass spoke volumes of the kind of man he was, and the weight of his purse was handsomely heavy from the rewards he had reaped from his service. The scars on his body attested to the price he had paid to obtain such a high status, as he was given authority over all the cohorts of the Twelfth, and as a Primus Pilus, Gaius was senior commander of the First Cohort.

Gaius saluted striking his chest and bowed in the presence of Titus and his commanding general. "Sire, if you will allow us to proceed with this afternoon's demonstration, we will be underway."

"Proceed!"

Gaius took a step back, turned swiftly, and marched away with his fellow officers. Princeps Posterior Cicero Vindacian, charged with demonstrating the testudo for Titus, halted before his men as his standard bearer came alongside him. Cicero shouted something to Gaius, and then turned as trumpets blasted across the grounds from the legionary *cornucen* musicians as they stood off to the right of Cicero's century sounding the high brass call to arms from their long, curved trumpets.

Cicero pointed his staff before him and then barked orders to each optio who responded mechanically with great speed, assembling the men into formation. Drums beat steadily from the flanks of the century as it closed into a rectangle, and waited while the optio checked the wings and front for perfection with the phalanx-styled battle manoeuvre that was to take place.

The princeps posterior turned and bellowed towards the veranda, "May his Excellency observe the testudo in siege formation of the Lion Centuria under the command of I, Cicero Vindacian Princeps Posterior, of the Fulminata." Titus gave a nod and Cicero turned to face his motionless legionaries. "Strength and honour!" Cicero shouted and then raised his whistle and placed it between his lips. He jogged to the rear of the formation followed by his standard bearer. Upon another number from the musicians, he sounded his whistle and the company's banners were hoisted in the air and held firmly, despite the sea breeze that lapped at the heavy, red fabric.

The optio in the rear shouted a muffled command and to Titus' pleasure the century suddenly sprung into action collapsing in on itself with a low din of pounding feet and jingling iron-studded cingulum which each man wore. The formation now faced Titus in a compact square before the veranda, as if the shelter was a dreaded Parthian stronghold or besieged by the war elephants of Hannibal descending upon them. Another order was given, followed by a blast from Cicero's whistle, and the shields of the century snapped up into place. A wall of scuta from the front rank faced the veranda as the remaining three ranks in the rear of the formation raised their shields above their heads, forming an overlapping roof.

Titus shifted in his seat and glanced at Marcus. "Now the hard part," he muttered while sipping his wine.

The formation was motionless, resembling the great body of a tortoise. The optio glanced back for approval from his commanding officer and when it was given, he took a step forward and sounded a high pitched whistle for the signal to advance. The formation slowly shifted and then began to move, almost glide, as it seemed to hover across the drill grounds, bearing down on Titus and Marcus. The interlocking shields above the men's heads were held intact as the scuta in the front row and upon the sides were pulled in tight to create and impenetrable wall. A low rhythm of grunts rose up from the testudo, as the men timed it with their steps. It grew louder with the formation's movements, but the shield wall did not break or shift. Another whistle blast brought the testudo to a halt. Then a signal and a shout from the optio caused the formation to slowly shift and wheel to the right before they continued marching.

"Impressed yet, sire?" Marcus asked, watching the troops.

"I will be when they march before the walls of Jerusalem while under attack," Titus replied.

"Well, you won't be disappointed. You're looking at the best of the army. I would volunteer them for anything, my lord."

"I will keep that in mind. I should send you to the walls first, Marcus. Then you could lead them by your example." Titus grinned.

"Whatever must be done for victory. Our eagles will take the city." Marcus graciously did a swoop with his hand and gently bowed his head. He chuckled and watched the testudo reverse its direction and wheel left to make a pass by the veranda. "The rumour is strong among the men that there won't be anything left of Jerusalem by the time we get there."

"You speak of the factions and their civil war?" Titus inquired, extending his empty goblet to be refilled. A servant holding a copper pitcher gracefully approached the couch and filled the cup without spilling a drop.

Marcus shrugged and stuffed a number of grapes into his mouth. "Simon is in the city, sire. He'll crush the other two soon if he has any competence. That's what scouts report after crucifying a number of slaves who finally talked, or more like cried like whelps for mercy." Marcus chuckled and helped himself to some of the goat cheese. "Well, if Simon wins, at least we only have to deal with him and not the other two bastards."

"John of Gischala is the only capable man in that city and the only one who can unite them under a strong banner. I trust they will surrender when they see our legions march up to the city, but I am not so certain of that."

"Why?"

"Have they ever surrendered, Marcus?"

Marcus sighed and raised his goblet. "Till the ram touches the wall!"

Titus met the toast, drank half of his cup and then handed it to a slave. "Bring me some fruit." He bit into a juicy apple and savoured the sweet taste. The testudo had turned and now was stamping past the veranda as the optio shouted for the men to give three cheers for Titus. This brought a smile upon the Prince's face and he nodded with appreciation. "I do like the Twelfth, Marcus, despite its past. They will learn to crave steel and the rush of battle. They are not spoiled; they were just poorly led when Cestius was at the helm. I am satisfied with your drills. Excellent form with the men, and they respond impeccably to commands. Very satisfactory. I am pleased."

Marcus was stunned for a moment and then beamed with pleasure at the gracious words from the prince. He bowed his head in a groveling nature as he softly replied, "My lord is most kind." Titus nodded in recognition and Marcus leaned back, sprawled upon the cushions. "My lord, how goes it with the campaign against Vitellius?"

"Pieces are being moved into place. Our forces on the Balkans are moving, Primus is putting pressure on our foe, and the Danube is strong, including men on the Rhine. Mucianus is almost ready to move out; he has gathered much force and will link up with Primus. We hope in a couple of months to be rulers of this empire, the way it should be. *Roma* needs to wake up and realize her power, like the need to stand up and crush this rebellion in this land."

"And the rumblings in Germania and Britannia, I might add, not to mention the damned Dacians and Sarmatians," Marcus replied.

Titus nodded and glanced away as Cicero Vindacian, called his company to halt. "We must not be seen as a weak empire. This last year has been testing on the nerves of our people. First there was Nero, then Galba, Otho, Vitellius, and soon my father. Vespasian and the gods of *Roma* are the only things that can save us." Titus slipped an olive into his mouth and spit the pit out. "This must never happen again. It's going to cost us a fortune to restore order."

"What of the other rebel strongholds beyond Jerusalem, like Herodian, Machaerus, and Masada?"

Titus slowly turned as trumpets blasted to signal the end of the demonstration. "They will all be crushed. None can remain to be seen as a thorn in our side."

"You will destroy Jerusalem? The magnificent Temple?"

"It is up to them if I can spare the Temple. I sometimes ponder to myself whether or not if I should just destroy that building."

"Then every Jew in the empire will be knocking at our doors, my lord. It is the center of their faith and their one God," Marcus said the last words with spite as Cicero's men broke their testudo and rallied into the standard rectangular battle formation.

Titus shrugged. "It will depend on how things go. I will not have my army destroyed in the process of this upcoming siege. I will offer mercy and clemency, but my mercy has limits and when it runs out I will slaughter them in the thousands." He sat up as Cicero approached the veranda and then the Prince looked at Marcus. "They have to surrender, Marcus. It is hopeless for them to continue."

Cicero Vindacian halted abruptly in his military demeanour and saluted outstretching his arm in the Roman custom. "I trust my lord has found this afternoon's demonstration entertaining."

"Almost as entertaining as a gladiatorial fight, my dear Cicero. Your father spoke very highly of you when you were granted this promotion. He is a friend of my father's and a fellow Sabine like my family. It will be a comfort knowing you lead a centuria of the First Cohorts. Your men are superb and maintain perfect form. You may dismiss your troops."

Cicero saluted with pride and stamped off shouting for the optio to assemble the men to fall out and observe the siege demonstration from the sidelines where the other two centuries had waited patiently.

"Did you hear about the Christians of Jerusalem?" Marcus suddenly piped up enthusiastically, waving his hands in the air. Titus turned and glanced at the general who continued, "They all left, just packed up and left for the city of Pella."

"Is not Pella in Perea?" Titus retorted with a scoffing tone towards the idea of the Messianic Jews fleeing. "Strange new cult! Why did they leave? Are they radical?"

"Our scouts report they are harmless. Just another messianic mob which *Roma* must contend with! They think the end has come and their God will return to set us on fire and destroy *Roma*. Or is it they believe the city is doomed? I say, you can't keep track of the prophets, self proclaimed kings, and the noisy rabble that we have to squelch in these parts."

"Are these Christians treasonous?"

Marcus shrugged. "This new cult has come from the Jewish faith. In fact, many are Jews themselves, but they also accept Gentiles who believe in their divine messiah saviour." Marcus noticed Titus was interested and leaned forward as he spoke, making sweeping gestures with his hands. "Many still celebrate the Jewish feasts and continue to gather in the synagogues I am told. The Gentile believers refuse to worship Roman gods of course, or eat meat from our temples like the Pharisees warn the people about. The Christians also claim that their messiah has fulfilled their sacred Scriptures. They are unanimous in their belief that their God will return...and you know where He is supposed to come back? Jerusalem. I was told a great teacher of theirs, who brought this message to our provinces around the sea, was executed under Nero's reign. Apparently he was a Pharisee and a Roman citizen...quite well educated and a traveller."

"A Pharisee?"

Marcus nodded. "His Roman name was Paulus, at least that is what I have been told. He found many eager people around our empire to sway with his message and now they have sprouted up everywhere. A bloody nuisance but their harmless if you ask me. Anyway, as for the Nazarene Christians of Judea, they refuse to take up arms and join the Zealots, the Sicarii or Simon's forces. If you wish for my opinion, it's less people for the Twelfth to kill. It's a pity."

Titus shook his head. "They refuse to worship images of our people, like their Jewish brethren? Perhaps more will follow these ones?"

"Not in the desert or in the wilderness. Remember Pella is a Greek city, so most religious Jews would never go there. We Gentiles are unclean to them," Marcus said shaking his head. "But, the Christians have been more sympathetic. The one big problem for any Jew remains to be our many gods." Marcus grinned and gave a sarcastic snort, shaking his head. "Nonsense and foolish the whole lot of them.

"Well if they are considered a sect of the Jewish faith, then of course they would have a problem with our gods," Titus murmured. "We always had problems with the Jews in this region and their religion. It was a nightmare at times, and men such as Herod, Caligula, Pilate, and Florus did not help."

"They are intriguing though," Marcus replied. "I heard about Paulus' defense in Caesarea Maritima you know, at the theater before Felix and Agrippa. Quite a staunch show, almost as good as a chariot race. These Christians, Jew or Gentile, share many things in common with their Jewish brethren, especially the Pharisees, perhaps that is how Paulus ended up believing in the first place. The Christians of Judea, go to the Temple and observe the feasts, it's just that they're a different crop when it comes to issues of their Christ and something of a Kingdom of Heaven. They are not so much about armed resistance as they preach the end of the world and anticipate their coming messiah, kind of like the sect to the south, the Essenes."

"An end of the world theory has been preached in this region for a hundred years, Marcus. This is no different than before. You know what it usually means? A lot of talk about getting rid of Roman rule so the Jews can set up a kingdom of their own. I am quite familiar with this rabble." Titus helped himself to some fruit as he pondered over the level of conversation. "You know a lot about these Christians, don't you?"

Marcus picked up a large apple. "We have a Christian as a slave in my villa. We bought him from this land years ago. I would question him regularly of the bizarre beliefs they hold. I suppose it is no stranger than an orgy for Dionysius, but bizarre in that they believe their God came to earth as a man called Yeshua of Nazareth, a Son of God, was nailed to a cross like a common criminal, and then rose from the dead." He took a bite from the apple and nodded in favour of the luscious taste. "Let's hope that none of these zealots we kill get into the habit of rising from the dead!" Marcus roared with laughter until he was red in the face and then dabbed his watery eyes with the edge of his sleeve.

"Sounds like the visitations of our gods with men," Titus remarked.

"Except they believe He physically walked this land, died, and was brought back to life."

"How did this man, this slave of yours, come to believe? Was he a Jew?"

"The man was so much in debt he was sold as a slave. He was a poor Jew from Migdal, not far from Tiberias. He told me some man claiming to have known this God-man from the Galilee had seen him rise from the dead and was telling people. I suppose with a lot of talk about Kingdom of Heaven and such, this Jewish slave was convinced. Then one of my stewards from *Roma* purchased him in an overseas deal and I ended up with the man. Now he trims the hedges on the grounds of my villa. The man was a gardener by trade and experienced so I set him to use."

"What do the Jews say of these people, the Christians?"

"The Sanhedrin and Sadducees outright hate them and see them as trouble makers. The Pharisees, on the other hand, are divided on the issue and remain suspicious of the messianics. I think the rest of the populace just makes them out to be another strange messianic sect. The Christians keep to themselves. They are kind of secretive and I don't care for secrets." Marcus set his apple on the cushion next to him and bit into a fresh date, chewing it with quick successions.

"You have your secrets, Marcus, we all do, and besides, every god we worship practically has their elite members and their closed doors. It costs money to see beyond those doors and it is mostly intoxicated naked women, burning incense, and hearing the recantations of a couple of priests over the bleating of sheep, goats, and the odd bull. I wouldn't suppose the Christians would have any of that now would they? Anyway, Nero never cared for them. A great time of persecution was ushered in during his reign; the poor wretches used to light his gardens at night as human torches, and then got blamed for the great fire."

"Well if they started the fire, they are enemies of the empire, my Prince, and thus it was proper justice to punish them. They conceal much from the eyes of the throne," Marcus replied.

"Simply unproven rumours, Marcus. Nero was mad to blame them. I sometimes have a mind to think he torched *Roma* himself. He was a man with few scruples to fill the air in his head," Titus stated and then turned to a trumpet blast.

Gaius Cornelius Antony, having assembled his century in perfect order alongside the century of Hastatus Quintus Cassius Aemilius, approached the veranda and saluted. Gaius glanced at his legionary commander for permission to continue and Marcus gave him a steady nod while praying to the gods.

"I present the Hydra Herculean century of the First Cohors Fulminata under command of I, Primus Pilus Gaius Cornelius Antony." Gaius turned and glanced at Quintus to continue the formal introduction. "Hastatus Quintus Cassius Aemilius, commanding his Wolf centuria of the First Cohors Fulminata, will be accompanying me in a siege demonstration of troops assaulting the battlements of a fortified wall from an engineered siege tower." Gaius took a breath and continued. "Men of the two centuria will advance under protection of a two level cart, representing a standard twenty metre siege tower. This drill is to increase the reality of being under fire from a protected and concealed enemy from above.

"The Hydra Herculean and Wolf will advance in battle formation until the cart is in place next to the three metre wall over there, representing a fully manned wall fitted with battlements. Under orders, the men of both centuria will file into the cart, ascend the two levels, and when the bridge is lowered, will assault the tower by dropping down and taking an offensive position against any attackers on the other side." Gaius half turned and pointed his finger to a lone wall erected upon the grounds, constructed of large wooden beams reaching three metres high and eight metres long. On the other side of the wall were numerous posts which depicted men with bags of sand hanging from the cross beams. Gaius turned back to face the prince and waited while sweat ran down the sides of his face.

"Proceed, Centurion." Titus said with a nod and Gaius saluted marching away with Quintus. "By the gods sense of humour, don't tell me that's the tower?" Titus glanced at Marcus and shook his head.

A man carrying a switch directed a team of oxen which pulled the teetering tower onto the drilling grounds. The tower was mounted on wheels of wood and stood five metres tall. The face of the tower was compiled of slates of wood fixed with iron spikes and fitted with a secured drawbridge held tight by ropes from within.

The tower swayed from the wind and its wheels squeaked above the low moans of the oxen. As it was drawn up into position, the rear of the tower revealed an open two-story structure fitted with ladders between the levels. The cart tower was neither intimidating nor impressive, it just appeared to be some idiotic, two level fort which served no purpose whatsoever.

"Well, my lord, this is just for training purposes. I assure you the towers that we build to attack the walls of Jerusalem will be much more beastly." Marcus glanced from Titus to the tower and then back to Titus.

"Let's hope so. It is so pathetic looking. I can use my imagination, Octavian, but this will be a stretch." Titus laughed and leaned back in his seat. "More wine!"

Across the field Gaius gathered with Quintus while the tower was set up and positioned. A number of impatient engineers were shouting and directing the setup phase as a few troops were sent to aid them. The engineers unhooked the oxen, brought them around the tower, and then fed ropes through two pulleys planted at the base of the wall. The ropes were then attached to the tower through iron rings hanging from the sides. Once secure, the ropes were looped through the rings and then tied to the harnesses of the oxen so they could be led away from the tower while pulling the cart forward.

Quintus seemed nervous as Gaius spoke, clear and deliberate. "I will lead my men to the second level with the rest waiting below. When I sound the call the bridge will drop and we will file through. We will leap down, assault the posts, and take up a battle formation upon the top. My optio will run the men through and you come up from behind and follow suit. We will clear the area and make room for your deployment on the walls. Once the breach is clear, have your men release a missile volley, draw blades and we will advance beyond the posts as if engaging more enemy. Questions?"

"Just have your men clear the ramp and not linger. We will follow behind and bring the standards. How far should we charge from the breach?" Quintus asked, staring past Gaius at the tower.

"Twenty paces, no more."

When the tower was ready all the workers scattered except the oxen driver who readied his switch and swatted a fly above his head. Another trumpet blast signaled the beginning of the drill, and a drum beat reverberated from the grounds, synced to the jingling of the legionaries marching steadily past the veranda in column formation. The colours were held high and the company's signi hoisted. Each optio held his hastile firmly, calling out orders and commands for the men to hear and respond to as the three hundred and twenty men of the two centuries swung wide in a wheeling manoeuvre. They approached the rear of the tower and the oxen bellowed with nervousness at the sudden appearance of the troops filing past.

Gaius glanced to his left and right making sure his men were in perfect step as he drew his sword and shouted, "Battle column!" The formation tightened as shields were tucked against their bodies and spears were angled forward. The silence that filled the ranks was replaced by the pounding of feet as they approached the back of the tower and halted. Gaius turned, inspected the column for a moment, raised his whistle to his lips, and blasted a high pitched call. The oxen grunted and tossed their heads briefly as the driver snapped the switch before their eyes. The sweaty beasts dug their hooves into the dirt and tugged on the ropes. The tower creaked forward and the Roman soldiers followed their centurion as they approached the mock wall under the cover of the tower.

"I can't believe they have us running this drill, on this day and in this heat!" a legionary in the front ranks mumbled shaking his head. "I have to take a piss and I'm expected to jump from the wall! Mad, if you tell me."

"I will have you branded and drinking piss if you so as open your mouth again soldier!" Gaius replied without looking back. "We do this drill so one day after you have taken a piss in comfort, you will look back and thank the gods you were out here in the heat, made to jump from a wall of wood and fight posts so you can then jump from a wall of stone and shed blood and live! So shut your mouth and do as you're told! Then you can go to the latrine and piss!"

A number of the troops chuckled quietly from the ranks at Gaius' rebuke for it was stern, instructive, and meant to humour them, all at the same time. When the tower was before the wall Gaius shouted for the column to halt, stepped up into the cart, and then called out in a booming voice, "Number one rank follow at the step! Optio watch the rear! Forward!" Gaius moved to the ladder and started to climb as men scrambled into the base and began to mill at the bottom as one by one they hastily climbed to the second level. By the time Gaius was before the bridge door, the level was full with troops and he turned to them. "You there, take the lever for the bridge!"

"Yes, Centurion!" a soldier responded, firmly gripping a long wooden lever extending from the floor.

"Now upon release, no pushing, mind your step, and move as one! You are to follow my lead! Step forward, approach the edge, watch your footing, and then leap down and bend your knees to break your fall! If you break your ankle, no one will be there to help you! We are assaulting a breach, soldiers! The eyes of Titus watch us. Do not disappoint me and let's show them what the best centuria of the First Cohors can do!"

His heart was racing now, despite it being a drill. Gaius had trained for this his whole life. Everything he had done was to perfect his military career and survive in the theater of battle. His eyes narrowed with concentration and his breath steadied as the air about him was humid and smelled of sweat. "Mars will grant us strength and honour! We will be the first to set foot in Jerusalem and our swords will become red with *victrix*! Onward!" he shouted, and with that the lever was pulled and the bridge came crashing down upon the top of the wall, creating an extended platform, which Gaius leapt upon as if there was fighting all around him.

Encouraged by their fearless leader, the troops of the Hydra Herculean followed Gaius out onto the platform, protecting him with locked shields. Then like a roaring endless current of water pouring over a cliff, they sprung from the platform and dropped to the earth below with grunts and shouts. Recovering from their fall, each man instantly was driven forward as they thrust their spears into the sand bags of the posts and overtook the positions. The pounding of feet could be heard as more men thundered across the platform, leapt from the bridge, attacked the posts, only to join their comrades and form an impenetrable battle line. Gaius shouted at them and checked their stance as his eyes darted up at the bridge as Quintus jumped off followed by dozens of his troops. One solider screamed as his ankle shattered on the ground and he winced in pain as he dragged himself to the base of the wall for protection from the falling men around him. He swore loudly at his insolence and then stood and hobbled to the rear of the ranks forming up.

When all the legionaries had cleared the bridge, assembling into a tight battle formation, Quintus gave the signal and his Wolf Century unleashed a volley of pila which sailed through the air and struck the ground with force. Gaius then had his own century deliver an equally deadly volley, which would have caused extreme carnage, destroying any enemy foolish enough to confront them.

"Draw blades!" Gaius shouted as one hundred and sixty men of his century grabbed the hilts of their gladii and scraped them from their sheathes. With faces of steel, each man peered over the golden-rimmed edge of his red scutum, with lightning bolts jabbing outwards from the silver boss in the centre and the numerals "XII" emblazoned beneath. At his command, Quintus' men also drew their swords and with great anticipation, the two centuries surged forward with a resonating shout.

Titus clapped his hands and nodded with satisfaction. "I will use you greatly at Jerusalem, Marcus. Your men are well beyond that of the other *cohortes* I have seen from among the legions. We have all winter to train and drill, but your men are superb."

"I thank you, my lord. Will we be training in Caesarea Maritima for the winter?"

"About half the army will march to Alexandria once winter approaches. The Fifth will go to Emmaus and the Tenth to Jericho to keep the central region under watch. Caesarea Maritima will be the rallying point when we return in the spring to meet the auxiliaries before we march to Jerusalem. All the auxiliary forces will meet here: Agrippa, Sohaemus, everyone. The Fifth and Tenth will make their approach separately to Jerusalem to complete its envelopment. It will be vast and terrible!" Titus finished his wine as the two charging centuries were halted to recover their formation for the completion of the siege tactic. A small host of servants scattered in the porcupine-like field to recover the spent spears and pile them in carts.

Gaius and Quintus made their way over to the veranda with the sound of trumpets and halted before the pleased prince. Both centurions saluted, catching their breath, and then gave an official report to Titus that the drill had ended.

"Tell me of the name of your centuria, Centurion Antony?" Titus asked as he stood up and walked out from the veranda. He squinted from the sun, and a slave holding an umbrella, attempted to follow him, but he waved the man away.

"You know the story of the Hydra, my lord?" Gaius politely replied, removing his helmet.

"The Lernaean, yes! The ancient Greeks taught it. Yes, I am familiar with that story." A tray of goblets filled with water were brought out and Titus gave one to Gaius and the other to Quintus. "It was mighty Hercules who slew the foul, nine-headed viper. His friend Iolaus cauterized the wounds as Hercules cut the heads off to prevent more from growing back. It was to be Hercules, son of Zeus' second labour, and he used the poison of the Hydra to wrought great pain upon his enemies. Alas, it would be the end of many of his friends like Chiron and indirectly his own life. So, why this name then for your centuria?"

Gaius paused for a moment to collect his thoughts. "The Hydra was the deadliest viper in the world, unable to be defeated but by Hercules himself, and even then, to be buried and still remain alive below the great rock piled on top of him. It was Hercules who would take the poison to bring desolation to his enemies, and it was Hercules who completed his labours in immense strength and agility. We take the strengths of both the Hydra and Hercules and seek to achieve them all as an elite unit of the First Cohors."

Titus glanced back at Marcus and the *legatus* stood at the visual acknowledgement of his prince. "Marcus, your men are phenomenal. I want training like this to become routine. Every man must be ready for the road ahead."

"Yes, sire, we will do as you say." Marcus stepped out from the veranda and nodded to Gaius and Quintus.

"The Primi Ordines are invited to feasting tonight at the Sea Palace. We would greatly welcome such noble centurions of yours, Marcus, if you would be so kind." Titus glanced at the legatus and then back at the stunned centurions. He smiled, nodded, and then strolled back to his litter where a stepping stool was positioned next to it for his comfort. Titus ignored the stool, climbed in, tapped the side with a ringed finger, and was slowly carried from the field.

"You heard your prince. You men are to appear groomed and in clean clothes. I will not have my best centurions looking like a pack of dogs. Clean the dust from your faces and arms, scent yourselves with anything, and I will see you tonight. Inform the other officers; I'm counting on you." The centurions saluted their general and in mid-stride Marcus stopped, glanced back at them and said, "Tonight you dine with your Emperor. Let that sit well with you."

Quintus waited till Marcus was out of earshot and then shook his head. "By the power of the gods, I swore we were perfect! Gaius, we may indeed survive the fight to come." He slipped his helmet back on his head and exhaled loudly with relief.

"Well, there is a difference from fighting posts with sand bags to getting a spear head driven through your chest by a man who loathes your existence. The training is vital, but nothing compared to Jerusalem," replied Gaius.

"Always an idealist, are you not, Gaius?" Quintus smiled and shrugged. "Anyway, Vespasian the Younger has thought this through. We're in good hands."

Gaius nodded and the two men turned and made their way back to the formed ranks of their centuries. "I just have seen too many times where something seems grand and then turns to total chaos. We can't underestimate them."

"I'm not underestimating them, Gaius. We will have the largest army ever fielded since the days of Pompey and we have them hemmed in. It's just a matter of time, if you ask me. Don't worry, your skills and quality will hone in when you need them."

"Pray to the gods and hope the omens are trustworthy!" Gaius poked back and then became serious as he shot a fierce look at the ranks of eyes watching him. "That's enough for today! Good work and steady drilling, men! Centuria dismissed!" Then Gaius marched off to find the other centurions of the First Cohort to inform them of the party where dignitaries, generals, foreign kings, and ambassadors would assemble to drink all night and feast till early morning.

$$* \quad * \quad *$$

Herod's Sea Palace
Caesarea Maritima
Evening

Vespasian was donned with a green, laurel wreath placed upon his head. Garlands and strings of flowers hung from his chair, given to him by the Egyptian supporters attending the feast and by the Greek aristocrats of the city. Men of different skin colours mingled around, some of Persian origin, but most from the coastal cities of Africa who had come to give their allegiance and pay handsome amounts of money into Vespasian's personal coffers. A chained hyena cackled by a pillar and then was distracted by a bone with scraps of meat upon it, thrown upon the floor to calm the beast.

Legates and tribunes walked around drinking wine and helping themselves to food which was served by scantily clad, female servants. Some of the officers would stop midsentence for the chance to grab a handful of a woman's behind or gawk at their beauty, for every female's face had been prepared for such an occasion as this. "A fine, firm behind, if I don't say!" laughed one of the tribunes. The man made a donkey's whine, clearly showing to the other guests his drunken stupor, but to his laughing comrades, no one seemed to care.

Only one man in the room, standing off in a dark corner, shook his head in disgust at the incompetent behaviour of the drunken officers. Marcus Sulla Maximus hated the wealthy and snobbery of senators and ranking officers. He only wished to rid the world of them all and relieve himself on their corpses. It was this attitude that made him a lonely man among feasts, alienated from the other officers, for none desired to be merry with such a sour tribune as Marcus.

The eyes of Marcus darted around the room, from the processional of delegates standing before Vespasian, to his son, Titus, engaged in a hot debate with Agrippa and Gessius Florus who reclined at a table, helping themselves to the food. Torches burned brightly and silk curtains, blowing from the sea breeze, covered the spaces between looming columns. The floor was an expanse of black and white checkered tiles, magnificent in design and luxurious in cost. Mingling in the room, Marcus spotted the Primi Ordines of the First Cohort, which included Gaius Antony, who was a man held in great respect by the cavalry tribune. The others he could care less for, but Gaius was a married man who did not whore himself around with other women, nor become intoxicated beyond any natural state. Most of all, Marcus knew Gaius to be a man who could not be bought with bribes. To Marcus, Centurion Antony reminded him of himself: an honourable soldier willing to take life for the empire, but a man with the sense to see all senators as a filth-infested, political cesspool of boy-lovers and forked-tongued vipers.

"Gaius Cornelius, drink with me," Marcus casually offered, taking a sip.

Gaius saw the Tribune wink at him over the rim of his goblet and he nodded with a grin. "Tribune, so good to see you. I heard you were successful in destroying the bandits north of Jerusalem."

"Only half successful," Marcus sullenly stated.

"Tribune?"

Marcus shook his head and held out his hand. "I will be Marcus Sulla to you, Primus Pilus Gaius Antony. Shall we save the titles for the field?"

Gaius nodded and outstretched his hand as both men clasped each other's wrists in greeting. "How was it half successful, Marcus Sulla?"

"Their leader and a handful escaped. My cavalry could not find them. I'm afraid Jerusalem may have a few more rebels for us to tangle with." Marcus chuckled at the thought and both men drank in silence for a moment taking in the revelries around them.

When the silence had grown slightly awkward for the pair, Marcus said, "I heard you completed an excellent demonstration for Titus today?"

"Yes, it went well."

"Did your heart pound in your chest? Mine does when I lead my men, even if it is a drill. The rush of battle overtakes you as you fight and fear for your life. It is when you conquer that fear, Gaius, that you truly become a beast. I have fought against many in my days, but that Jew they call the Lion, is a beast. That is the ultimate, dangerous foe to have: one who can think and be collective during a fight.

"I watched him once cut the head off of one of my men who was kneeling before him, begging for mercy. The Lion, a tall man with a blackish beard, beheaded him with a primal roar. He screamed at us holding the head in the air. I cannot get the image out of my mind. It was something to behold, Gaius, truly it was. I was angry and bitter. The Jews, you see, had ambushed a small company of mine, while we hunted them. I was enraged at that. Did you know I have never been ambushed before?"

"Really?"

Marcus nodded. "I could taste the desire to kill him. It was so strong in my being, but I was too far away. Later that night, I sort of came to admire the man. I thought to myself, what would I do if someone tried to kill my family? Or take my land? How would I respond? I am a warrior. I have spent my life with the sword; we are married, steel and flesh. How would you respond, Gaius, if your wife and children were killed before you?"

Gaius was silent for a moment and then softly said, "I would butcher everyone in the world until I felt my cup had been filled with vengeance."

Marcus nodded. "Good answer. We old soldiers always have the right answer. Hate the enemy and cause him as much suffering as he has caused us."

"What went through your mind, Marcus, when you realized the Lion had escaped your trap?"

"I smiled inside and said, *go to Hades and dine without me, I will meet you there soon.* He is honourable and responds swiftly and meticulously, as I would if I wore his sandals." Marcus took a long gulp of wine. "We will meet in the city, I am sure of it, and if he should be captured by my men in combat, I will make sure he dies swiftly." Marcus snapped his fingers at a slave and had his cup refilled. "Here, I want to show you something." He retrieved a small coin purse attached to his belt and tossed it to Gaius. "Open it, look and see."

Gaius handed his empty goblet to a slave, then untied the leather cord and poured out a number of coins into the palm of his hand. "Sesterces minted in Jerusalem."

"A patrol of my men caught three bastards the other day on horseback. We cut off one's manhood, and nailed another to a tree before the third spoke, sobbing like a little whore. They said they were from Jerusalem carrying a message, destined for the east."

"Parthia? That would be ill-favoured if they got involved."

Marcus nodded. "Parthia's ass is shaped for a throne. They wouldn't get off it to challenge us. It is true they've got the better of the legions in the past with old Crassus, but they have learned to stay in their dunes of sand and keep out of our way."

"And the Jews you captured were going to Parthia? I wonder how many messages they have already got through."

Marcus shook his head confidently and motioned to the coins Gaius held. "Bastards are trying to gain favour with those Persians, only we got to them first.

They tossed the message when we sighted them. It took us awhile to find it, but we did. The Jews are growing desperate, Gaius, and the gods stir the pot of Jerusalem. The Jews are killing themselves in their civil war for control. There are three factions I am told: Eleazar ben Simon, Simon ben Giora, and of course the bastard of Gischala, John ben Levi. He was the one who escaped our clutches when Titus honoured their Sabbath."

"I heard of that, slipped away in the night with all his men and women, only in the end he had to leave the women because they were too slow." Gaius flipped the coins over and studied the engravings on the back. "Holy Jerusalem and Liberator!" He read and glanced up at the tribune. "I have seen coins such as these before. The Jews think their messiah will come."

"He may, but not soon enough! That's all the Jews talk about is this messiah, and look at where it has got them? Every time they bring it up, some Roman governor is ramming a sword into their guts. They might as well leave that business for their holy men and their holy books. Anyway, that doesn't matter now, does it? As soon as this business with Vitellius is wrapped up, we march. Mucianus is leaving soon and Primus is already controlling much of *Italia*. Vespasian will go to *Roma*, and we shall march to Jerusalem in the spring."

"Maybe after we will be disbanded."

"Not likely. We're more likely to be stationed somewhere far away. Of course the veterans will be discharged, but as for the rest of us, it will be other fields of glory, my dear Centurion! So many people to kill in this world of ours, until *Elysium*, I suppose."

Gaius mulled over Marcus' words and then said, "I am coming to the end of my service in two years."

"Surely you have seen enough battles to be discharged, perhaps after Jerusalem smoulders."

"The money is good in the Primi Ordines and it serves for a better life when I shall leave."

Marcus scowled as another donkey impersonation erupted from the junior officer who interrupted the party, and then Vespasian's annoyance could no longer be contained as he ordered the man to be tossed out. Marcus snickered, shaking his head, and glanced back to Gaius. "What will you do when you're finished in the army? Farming can't be that exciting when compared to storming a breach at the head of your men."

"I own a small villa in the hills outside *Roma*. There my wife awaits me with my three daughters. I haven't seen them in almost five years." A dreamy look filled Gaius' eyes. "My wife, Livia, is a hard worker, even though she doesn't need to be. She always enjoyed the garden. I miss the scents of that region, so distinct and favourable."

"Well, return to Livia and have a son. May the gods spare you at Jerusalem. The Jews have never surrendered in the past. I am sure they won't welcome us as guests when we arrive at the city with our eagles."

Gaius grinned. "An orderly told me that three hundred unblemished goats and sheep are accompanying the army."

"The priests will be busy then, fully intending to gain Mars' attention, and invent stories no doubt to keep morale up."

Gaius shrugged. "It will be nice just to silence the creatures; I can hear them from my quarters at night. I trust the entrails will be pure on a daily basis and then Jupiter will go ahead of us and vanquish the enemy."

Marcus raised his glass and smiled. "I can drink to that, my dear friend."

*   *   *

Chapter VIII

November 3rd, 69 A.D. / 3rd of Kislev, 3830
Yavneh, Roman Province of Judea
Camp of Vespasian

Darkness had finally descended on the scattered Roman camps littering the borders of the small Jewish village of Yavneh. The thousands of flickering torchlight's from the encampments dwarfed the insignificant village with the presence of a mobile city of troops and slaves surrounding it. After a long grueling march, having left Caesarea Maritima three days ago, Vespasian had pushed past Joppa and onto Yavneh with the intentions of resting the men for a day, on route to their winter quarters in Alexandria. Only two legions would not be accompanying them across the wilderness into Egypt. That had already been arranged with the legionary generals for the coming campaign which would resume in the spring. The Fifth Legion would march in the morning for its winter quarters in Emmaus, and the Tenth Legion, avoiding Jerusalem, would set up quarters by the city of Jericho. The plan had been carefully thought out and would provide both legions the ability to close in on Jerusalem like pincers while the rest of the army descended upon the city from the north. With nowhere to go, the Jewish city would be crushed.

The camp preparations were finished within three hours as thousands of troops had been ordered out of their marching columns to be dispersed for work. Their orders were always the same after a day's march: dig trenches, create fortifying rock walls surrounding each camp's perimeter, and set up the strict Roman layout for the campsite. The camp contained officers' quarters, stables, latrines, hospitals, and legionary housing, consisting of row upon row of canvassed tents with roads intertwining between each unit.

Observing legionaries conduct the setup of their camp was an awe-inspiring thing. Wherever the Roman eagles were taken abroad, they seemed to be absorbed into the land as if they possessed a sense of ownership. The Roman military camp was of this very nature. It was built strong with defences in order to protect those from within and keep the desertion rate to a minimal. The camp echoed the might of Rome, intimidated enemies, and gave comfort to those being protected.

However, on this day, desiring to make for Alexandria with haste, Vespasian had ordered minimal defences, having sent out squadrons of cavalry to scout the land. Once with the cavalry returned, having discovered no threats, night patrols of soldiers were stationed, passwords were agreed upon and the men of the Judean army slept.

One large tent stood out from all the rest, Vespasian's. Guards had been posted outside, large men standing behind their scuta and gripping the hilts of their swords. They were part of an elite bodyguard, similar to the praetorian of Rome, but handpicked by Vespasian as his most trusted men. They were on a two hour cycle throughout the night so they could maintain sharp senses and a clear focus as the hours passed and dawn approached. Deep within the tent, Vespasian slept upon a bed warmed by thick blankets and sheets of silk. A single oil lamp burned upon a table with scrolls piled high and an empty goblet that had once contained wine. On the edge of the table was a small, dark wooden cabinet with locked doors edged in silver.

As a private nightly ritual, Vespasian would light one of the dark incense roots he carried with him. While muttering prayers, he would unlock the cabinet doors and be greeted by a number of small sculptured images. First, he would say his prayers to Mars for victory over his current struggle against the Jews and the distant campaign against Vitellius. Next, Vespasian would cradle the images of Venus and Minerva. He would pray to Venus because of her connection to Mars for the sake of his wife, and to Minerva, for desired wisdom. Then he would study the feminine face of Isis, yearning to gain power and approval from the most powerful of the Egyptian deities.

For years, Vespasian had held a deep interest in the gods and goddesses of Egypt and this had conceived a desire to look into his future. He had connected himself deeply to the deities that truly mattered in such an unpredictable world. He prayed that through their guidance he would become victorious and supreme on earth, and in this way he honoured them.

Vespasian would then conclude the ritual by taking the image of Flora, his wife's favourite goddess, praying that the flowers in his villa would continue to bloom and that she would watch over his family. Having consulted the gods and goddesses directly, Vespasian would offer a prayer to any power he may have missed, kiss the marble images representing his family, then close the doors and lock them.

Climbing under his blankets for yet another night on the march, Vespasian had finally fallen asleep with his mind clouded by the ever impending obsessions of his recent life: anticipating the time of Vitellius' fall and the threat of Jerusalem which would pass to his son. In the darkness, Vespasian tossed and turned. Beads of sweat broke out upon his body and he fought to wake, but a dream held his mind captive. He groaned and shuddered, clenching both hands in anguish. As his eyes suddenly snapped open he gasped loudly and shrieked, "Basilides!"

Outside, the guards heard the shout. In alarm, they burst into the tent drawing their swords.. One of them yanked back the veil of Vespasian's private sleeping chamber and there sat their General on the edge of his bed, his face buried in his hands.

The eyes of the guards darted around the room and one quickly said, lowering his blade, "My lord, are you well? Shall I fetch a doctor?"

Vespasian glanced up at the men and shook his head. "It was a dream, that is all." The guards sheathed their blades and sighed. "Go get my son and send for more wine."

"Yes, Imperator." The men saluted and left immediately.

"Basilides, who are you really?" Vespasian whispered to himself. He wiped the sweat from his brow, stared up at the ceiling of his tent, and watched the shadows dancing upon the canvas from the flickering light of the lamp.

By the time Titus arrived, Vespasian was finishing his second glass of wine as he remained seated upon the edge of his bed wearing a white garment of linen. "Father, are you all right?" Titus wiped the sleep from his eyes, crossed the room, and knelt at his father's side.

Vespasian nodded warmly and turning to face his eldest son, he laid both hands on Titus' shoulders. "Remember my vision in Alexandria years ago? When I was at the temple to the venerated oracle Serapis?"

Titus nodded. "Vaguely. You said you saw a man during the ceremony."

"Yes, his name was Basilides. It was dim in the temple and with all the incense burning and smoke from the altars it was difficult to make him out, but he was there. He gave me garlands, a palm branch, and cakes. I ate the cakes and he told me his name."

"What about him?"

Vespasian shook his head. "He came to me in my dream just now, but it was like he was here with me in the room. The 'Son of the Monarch' crossed the floor, glowing with radiance, his hair touching the ground. It was a terrible and mighty power he had; he held me to my bed with his very presence. I was unable to move and my sheets became soaked with my sweat. He said to me that one had fallen and I would rise, that a mother would grow strong again. When he opened his mouth an eagle with talons as sharp as any sword burst forth from his lips. It came from his throat and it nearly killed him. I could only watch as the bird fell as if dead and then suddenly extended its wings and flew from my tent. Then he said his name to me over and over as I was in a trance, unable to move. He said that my son would become like his name, and then he vanished."

Titus was silent for a moment, dreadfully silent, choosing his words with precision. "Son of the Monarch," he whispered to himself shaking his head. "That can only mean one thing, Father. I am your son...the eldest, above Domitian. I will inherit as Imperator when you die; this must be what Basilides meant. The one who must fall could only be Vitellius, the mother. *Roma* will grow strong, as seen in the image of the eagle. Consult the priests, Father, but this must be the meaning. Praise Jupiter!"

Vespasian slowly stood, causing the light from the lamp to flicker gently. He scratched his bald head as he quietly walked across the floor and over to the table piled with scrolls. He stared for a moment at the cabinet and Titus stood, tempted to follow. "I don't understand why this dream came to me now, but this must be as you say. I should offer a sacrifice to the gods so through blood they may see that I honour them and that I am willing to seek their council."

"Father, we must pray and honour Basilides. He is among us and must favour this expedition to rid this land of rebels and restore the empire after Vitellius is done away with. We must look to Basilides and tread lightly. I will be in prayer and offer the proper signs of petition to curry favour."

"We stay the course, do what is necessary, and watch our backs, my son. We are not fully clear of the dreams interpretation. We must be prudent in our actions and consult priests and oracles for the meaning." Vespasian looked years older as he sighed and scratched his chin. "This campaign has taken much strength from me. It will be a pleasure to return to *Roma*. I have been in this forsaken land too long. I look to pass the responsibility off to you; may the gods bless you as they have blessed me."

"My lord, will you allow admittance to a messenger?" echoed a stern voice from outside.

Titus eyed his father for a moment with an inquisitive yearning to understand what the dream truly meant, and then silently left the room to see what was going on. Vespasian poured himself another goblet of dark wine and changed into a clean tunic while wrapping a purple cloak about his shoulders.

"Imperator, are you decent?" Titus asked from outside.

"Enter!" replied Vespasian as he crossed his broad arms.

A curtain was drawn back and Titus entered, followed by a thin man dressed in armour and clutching a wooden rod sealed with a gold lid. One of Vespasian's guards lingered behind with a firm grip on the hilt of his gladius as he watched the stranger carefully with intense eyes beneath the brim of his helmet.

"Who are you?" Vespasian demanded.

The man bowed low and then spoke with a perfect Latin accent, revealing to all that the man had clearly been educated. "I am Cato. I landed earlier this evening in Joppa, my Imperator, and I bear victorious news from *Roma* that concerns you. The journey has been long and I have been as swift as I could, but this news comes from Mucianus who linked up with the Danubian Legions and Antonius Primus. Ten days ago the combined forces loyal to you, my lord, destroyed the armies of Vitellius at Cremona!"

Silence filled the room. Cato outstretched his hand with the rod and Vespasian took it without speaking a word. He unscrewed the gold lid and removed a scroll sealed by a mass of red wax, imprinted with Mucianus' seal. As Vespasian broke the seal and read, Cato continued, "Vitellius has retreated back to *Roma*, leaving behind thousands of captured prisoners. His army was utterly destroyed, over fifty thousand dead."

"Victrix!" Titus declared gazing at his father with excitement. "Vitellius still lives but it is a matter of time before his life is over! Mucianus and Primus will deal with the prisoners and their own wounded and march on *Roma* to wrest it from the clutches of Vitellius' gluttony. They could be at the gates of *Roma* as we speak!"

Vespasian read the letter over a second time and handed it to his son. "What is the condition of our forces after the battle?"

"It was a one sided victory, Imperator. Vitellius is no general and was soundly crushed. I don't have exact numbers but our casualties were low. Primus has more than enough provisions for the push to *Roma* and it is only a matter of time before complete victory." Cato glanced at Titus as the Prince shook his head with a grin, grateful for receiving the news.

"Jupiter be praised!" Titus lowered the parchment. "Cremona was the very place where Vitellius defeated Otho last April. Now Vitellius shall get a taste of vengeance dealt to him by the power of the gods who see our cause as greater for the empire."

Vespasian, still retaining an element of seriousness despite his son's joy, looked directly at Cato and asked, "What of the city of Cremona? Its condition?"

"The city was sacked, I am not sure by whom at this moment, but many were killed and parts lain to waste."

Vespasian nodded. "You were there?"

Cato nodded. "Yes, my lord. I was with the ranks of Primus after the battle. Mucianus arrived, had a bull slaughtered, and then penned this letter."

"Who sacked Cremona, in your opinion?" Vespasian asked cautiously.

"My lord, I do not feel as if my opinion is of any value in your presence," Cato stammered, diverting his eyes from the noble Flavian man standing before him with an expression of inquiry. Cato was simply fortunate to be alive and to have been chosen to deliver such a message of joy and rebirth for the Roman people as the stage was set for a new emperor of the Imperial Empire.

"Don't hesitate or waste time. Speak plainly, Cato; you were there by the side of Mucianus. Who sacked Cremona? Was it us or them?" Vespasian replied with an edge of annoyance.

"Primus' troops, I think!" Cato blurted, his face reddening with embarrassment. "Cremona was a Vitellian city with much political support. That is the opinion of those who heard of the destruction which was brought to its gates."

"Do you have any other news from the regions, Cato?" Titus asked as he handed the letter back to his father.

The young messenger nodded, catching his breath. "There is one more thing that will interest you. I heard it from Consul Mucianus who told me to inform you of the activity on the Black Sea. The former commander of the Pontic Fleet, a man named Anicetus of five years service, led a rebellion in Vitellius' name and massacred a Pontic cohort at an ambush in Trapezus. Afterward, he formed a pirate fleet, small in number, to raid anyone loyal to your name, my lord. Anicetus was caught by a legionary detachment sent against him and his entire fleet was burned and he was killed." Cato glanced from Vespasian to Titus as the two men listened attentively.

"Order has been restored to that region and they are now fiercely loyal to you. Your forces on the Upper Danube and in the Balkans remain at your side, and *Italia* now lays wide open with not a single force large enough to confront Primus and Mucianus."

Vespasian turned deep in thought and approached the table. Staring down, he studied a map of the Roman world and all its provinces including some stretches of territory such as Africa and the lands controlled by Parthia. He traced his finger over the Black Sea, then to Sicily, and upwards into Italy. He tapped the map where it outlined the River Tiber and Rome. "You are dismissed, Cato. I thank you for your speed in delivering this message. You are to tell no one at this point regarding this news." Vespasian dismissed Cato with a wave of his hand and shook his head, deep in thought, as a dark frown descended upon his face.

Cato bowed humbly and backed away without Vespasian watching him leave. The guard escorted Cato from the tent and all who remained was Titus and his father. Titus licked his dry lips and could feel the pounding of his heart within his chest. His mind was swirling with the wondrous news of Cremona and the reality of the situation that his father was within arm's reach of being declared 'Father of his Country' and Emperor by the Senate and the people of Rome.

"Shall I send news for the consuls of the legions to come here at once?" Titus asked meekly.

"Do you know the four chief attributes of a Roman general, my son?" Vespasian questioned just above a whisper. "Have I ever taught you them?"

Titus raised his chin slightly and shook his head. "You have taught me many things, Father. I have followed you on many battlefields and led units into combat, but I have only studied the attributes of a Roman man, not a general. What are they?"

Vespasian turned. "*Scientam rei militaries*, that is the first chief attribute. It is incredibly vital in any campaign for you to have proper knowledge of your enemy and to understand them. I believe this is true with the Jews here in this land, but with Jerusalem approaching, you will need to evaluate every possible solution, and those which seem impossible. Choose wisely, my son, and sacrifice regularly.

"The second is *virtutem*. Have courage and stand up for what is right as a Roman general. When I give to you the powers of consulship, to conduct the siege and oversee over forty thousand men, that is when you will need courage. Be merciful when you must, but always be ready to bear your sword of wrath and fury lest the Jews believe you are weak.

"The third chief attribute of a Roman general is *auctoritatem*. You will be my eyes and ears; you represent *Roma* and you are a Prince of *Roma*. You will carry my banner which is the authority of the glory of *Roma* and may it cause those to tremble who stand in its way. Be the general the troops need. They love you, Titus, my son, and I do not doubt that they would follow you into Hades. Learn from your mistakes, but never admit them; possess total authority and keep a sharp eye for those who will hate you for it and wish your demise, whether Jewish or Roman.

"The last attribute, Titus, my son, is *felicitatem*." Titus smiled and Vespasian nodded. "Never profane the gods and keep the rituals and rites proper. They will reward you with victory."

Titus bowed his head. "Very wise, Father. I will remember all you have told me. What will you do about Cremona? What about Primus?"

Vespasian turned back to his maps. "Nothing! I have given strict instructions to destroy all allegiances of Vitellius and for those who resist. Primus is a warrior and a damn good general. It is unfortunate about Cremona but a necessity, regardless of the cost of life. Vitellius must be destroyed and all his allies. As for Antonius Primus, I have made secret arrangements that once *Roma* is occupied by him and Mucianus, and Vitellius is dead, I will publically rebuke him and then allow him to live out his years in a villa arranged for his comfort. I am indebted to his services, and Mucianus' as well, but I have other needs for Mucianus. I have instructed him to stay out of the brawl which is coming to the gates of *Roma*. The public must see it as Primus' men getting out of hand, but not directly from him and certainly not from me. There are certain ways the wheel must turn, and things are set in motion that cannot be undone."

"Shall I notify the consuls of the news of our victory?" Titus asked.

Vespasian shook his head. "We shall do so in the morning. I must get some sleep, and may Basilides leave me alone for the rest of the night." He took a long drink of wine from his goblet and then poured the remaining onto the floor. He gazed up at the canvas ceiling and shook his head at the memory of the gods and the radiant face of Basilides.

*   *   *

November 15th, 69 A.D. / 15th of Kislev, 3830
Temple Mount
Jerusalem

The winter wind dropped into the Outer Court of the Temple, stirring the burning cooking fires of the Zealots. The bleating of sheep from the Temple sanctuary rose above the wind followed by prayers and the blasting of shofar'ot to signal the approaching Shabbat. The last few days had provoked little activity between the three bands of fighters who had been squabbling for months at each other's throats, looking for that golden opportunity to overthrow the other in a death match which dragged the entire city to its knees.

People everywhere mourned the loss of loved ones and forged for food in desperation with grief-withered forms. Disease was rampant and struck down entire households as people struggled to continue to abide by the proper laws of cleanliness according to the Law of Moses. One man in particular had even been chased out of the Court of the Women as he had declared with a thundering voice that he was a prophet and that the Cohens and men of the Kathros families were profaning the name of God. The unfortunate man had fled for his life out of the Dung Gate followed closely by hurled stones and curses from Pharisaic mouths.

Time and time again John had met every attack from Simon's men with a calculated and swift response, so much so that now the attacks greatly dwindled. The madman called ben Giora, seemed content to be held up in his palaces throughout the city entertaining his men and taking the wives of nobles to be his own. Rumours of murdered and imprisoned husbands flowed throughout the city. Even the odd suicide would bring looks of apathy and indifference from Simon and his hierarchy of elected officers as they struggled to stay afloat on an ocean of misery, death, and suffering. Simon was loved and hated, envied and loathed. His madness seemed to know no bounds and Ananus ben Bagdatus' arm of tyranny was allowed to extend throughout all regions of the city controlled by Simon, the despot king.

Bagdatus, known as 'Bastard Bagdatus' by the populace, was someone to avoid at all costs. All would relinquish whatever Bagdatus and his militia gang demanded, that is unless one did not value his or her life. Many had been murdered by the gang as Simon allowed them to operate against whoever he considered an enemy and a threat. People hated Bagdatus, that was clear enough, but overall they feared Simon more, for he was the man who held the rope tied to the neck of the roaring lion, and it was he who even managed to be feared by someone as violent as Bagdatus.

For these countless crimes, John detested Simon more than life itself. It was more likely that he would rather befriend a leper than be associated with the 'pestilence from the south', which he sometimes referred to Simon as.

John of Gischala had worked tirelessly at keeping his army united, trained, and healthy. It was routine now for his soldiers to patrol, gather intelligence, forage for food, or loot supply depots throughout the city that belonged to Simon. This drove the 'Sicarii King', as Simon sometimes called himself, into endless fits of rage as he would rant, overturn tables, throw things at people, and spew out all his venomous hatred for John ben Levi.

From dawn until evening, anger would seethe from the palace in which Simon called his headquarters. At every feast and banquet held for his men, Simon would demand for John's head to be brought in on a platter. Pledges of great bounty and reward would fall from mad lips upon the ears of drunken men who would all voice their outrage towards Gischala as a sign of appeasement for their king. When this did little to appease him, Simon's bouts of anger would break into a maddening tantrum. During these nights, Simon would fill his chamber with the cries of naked women as he beat them relentlessly during his sessions of rape, only to banish them from the city after he was through with them. Then he would repent for his profaning of women, and justify his actions by laying the blame squarely on John for his miseries. But this was to no avail as the cycle was only doomed to repeat itself, as a platter containing the head of John was never delivered. Therefore, every renewed assault by Simon ended with John's men outsmarting the Sicarii King's army, making it pay dearly for every attempt to storm the Temple Mount.

Although being a warrior, John was respected by many of the religious members of the Jewish elite. They saw him as a fighting holy man, one who attended worship with his fellow Jews and tried not to spill the blood of men upon the stones of the Temple grounds. He would often speak about the Scriptures with a fervent love of his ancestry and honour to God, and would invite the teachers of Torah in small groups to encourage his men and teach them the ways in which God desired them to live. The sacredness of the Scriptures was infused in many and all believed the time of reckoning was at hand. God would soon lift the veil from the ground and show them a might beyond any of their imaginations, a might which would crush the evil of Rome.

Every Shabbat John would attend worship and sing with his brothers, often shouting, *"Eretz Israel"* and other slogans as they would talk of liberty and freedom. They yearned for a land where they could unite all Jews under the Temple Law and return to the roots of their faith, unimpeded by Hellenism, which they interpreted as following the ways of the Gentile pagan world. John would often speak long into the night, lounging around a table, honouring the day where work would cease. On that day the entire city would shut down and nobody thought of surprise attacks or worried of treachery. All Jews observed the command to honour the Lord and honour the Shabbat which was essential in keeping the Torah.

John, loved to share his passion of the future and how he saw their part as God's instruments, restoring heaven on earth, like what Messiah would do. Anybody at John's table would soak up his energy like a sponge. It was impossible not to feel a connection with the great warrior, who had arms like stone and a frame like the largest cedar ever dreamed of. Whenever John spoke of the future, his eyes would soften, his face would relax, as a childlike longing filled his soul. It caused men to hold their breath, imagining a time without oppression and without Rome. One such man was Judah ben Yosef.

Judah had grown to admire John and learn from him. The warrior leader was true to his word, a defender of his people, and had grown accustomed to taking Judah aside countless times to instruct him in the virtues of a leader and what God expected of men. They often would stroll on top of the colonnades, pointing out the weaknesses of Simon's forces, and how to adapt to new situations in order to soundly defeat each attempt made by him. Soon, John rewarded Judah with a commission as a captain among his soldiers, and counted Judah as an equal.

Judah had demonstrated through each skirmish against Simon's forces that he was a capable leader, cared for his men, was daring in the face of all obstacles, and able to see through an impossible situation, reacting every time with a ferocious speed. It was from following the example of John, and the spell he seemed to cast upon people, that Judah pledged allegiance to him, even unto death. It was out of respect that Judah followed John, for to him the man from Gischala was the embodiment of the Jewish warrior who dared not to let his hands become tainted with uncleanliness.

"To defeat Rome would usher in a new time, one where we are free to worship God and be the strong nation we once were under King David," John said breaking a piece of bread and dipping it into his stew. "David was a man after God's own heart and a man of principle. He was a true military leader who led his forces against many enemies and understood honour. The Philistines quaked under the wrath of David and it was his sword and God's blessing which made a mighty nation of our people. Would you not agree, Judah?"

Judah set his wine down and nodded. "Solomon could live in peace and build the Temple; he could rule a country where peace had been carved out. Yes, John, I believe David, with the power of God, created the nation Israel was destined to be, but look at the son of Solomon, such waste and neglect. Rehoboam did not take heed of his magistrates' advice or that of his councilmen. I believe this demonstrates our need to look to God and not to man."

John smiled. "Or less we divide among ourselves. At least he should have trusted in God to direct his men and make the right decision, yes?"

"Perhaps, but it was the waywardness and transgressions of his father who started the decent into ungodliness," Judah replied glancing around the Shabbat table. He noticed Caleb grin at him warmly and Judah blushed. He was not apt to discussing things related to Scripture, not since the murder of Miriam and his parents.

"Tell us, Rabbi, of the transgressions of Solomon!" John laughed sarcastically.

Judah sighed and cleared his throat, feeling embarrassed. "Solomon clearly broke the Law; he took foreign wives, honoured their gods, erected idols, and paid homage to them along with the God of Israel. Solomon broke the commands not to have graven images. With the idols, pagans moved into the lands and brought unclean foods, foods of forbidden animals, offering them to their gods from high places."

"He brought about Rehoboam's imminent fall you would say?" John asked.

Judah slowly nodded. "I did not live in those days, but as the Scriptures teach and what the rabbis say, 'Solomon's sin became Rehoboam's burden and collapse.' It was the sins of his father which destroyed the son and plagued the land. God instructed Abraham concerning the blessings, and this must have been the result, I dare say, unless someone learned shall disagree."

"I disagree," Aviram, one of Judah's Lions, intervened. "One man's evil of another generation cannot condemn a nation or cause it to fall, it must be the collective! Someone must have carried it onward to appease the majority."

"Think of David, Aviram. Was he not cursed with his relationship with Bathsheba? What of his murder of Yuriah the Hittite?" Caleb added. He swallowed a morsel of bread and washed it down with wine. "The generations of his bloodline who suffered from his choice, which was against God, can only be explained because he was cursed. Solomon was the only son who sought God's will, but even he fell away.

It is true that he repented before his death, but his failure to uphold the Law gave way to Rehoboam's ungodly decision which was the result of the curse, it is plain and clear. Look at Manasseh. He burned our sons in the Hinnom to Moloch and slew the prophet Isaiah. Judgment befell him, even despite his repentance, but it grew long ago in the minds of men to finally culminate in his demise and the sacking of Jerusalem by the Babylonians."

"Good debate allows for a more restful sleep!" John added, clapping his hands as more wine was served. "Teacher Zechariah, you have been silent, my dear friend. You are educated and well versed. Tell us please; answer this question so that I may sleep better tonight. Was Rehoboam cursed? Was it inevitable that he would do evil because of his father?"

The old priest, who was a common face at John's side, was slouched over at the table with bags under his drowsy eyes. When John had spoken his name the old man burped, glanced up, and quietly scanned the table at the bearded men enjoying their food. "The one who is right? Now that is a question to ask, is it not? Was King David a man of God? Yes, I believe he was as is written in his poetry and the example of his life in the writings and annals of the kings. Did he do wrong? Yes, I believe he did as he was of mortal flesh, and the prophet Nathan received a word from God concerning his sin against the Lord. David was not God, as no man is. Do we do wrong? Yes. But did the fall of our mighty nation begin with David? No, it began in the beginning when we were cursed and broke the word of God and violated his command. I hear it said differently, that mankind fell from God in the Scriptures at the beginning of it all when he chose to serve himself rather, and not the One, Blessed be His Name, whom Moses met in the wilderness and gave His Torah on Mount Horeb.

"We were and are a chosen people, but we did not have faith to possess the land under Joshua, not until later were we strong to face giants and wild men. We still suffer to this day and have paid dearly. We Jews struggle in an ungodly world, one that does not know God, but we say we do. Do we live it? That is a question Rehoboam should have asked himself. I believe if he had asked himself that very question and lived it, Israel would never have split. Was there a curse? Yes. Judah is right in saying that his father's transgressions sealed his fate in that the way we raise our sons and daughters reflects the godliness of the next generation. As Moses taught, Torah is vitally important to pass down to our children and their children's children. As it is written, *meditate on the law day and night.* We are to live and serve one God, as the Scriptures attest to, *Hear oh Israel, the Lord is our God, the Lord is one.* It is our light in a dark world and a guide for our souls. It is complete truth. If this were to cease, God help us. Ultimately, we need the promised Messiah, whenever he may come, though he not tarry." Zechariah slowly stood up, bowed and exited the room.

The men were all silent as they digested the priest's words, even Aviram, commonly one to make a jab at the old man, held his tongue and wrestled with the wisdom which had rolled from the lips of the priest at the command of the *Shema*. John finally raised his glass and said. "*Baruch atta Adonai, Elohenu Melech ha'olam, boray pree hageffen, Amen!*"

The men recited 'amen' in unison and then drank solemnly until John broke the silence and said, "You have all heard that the Romans have reached Alexandria, their winter quarters. The legions are coming, men, and there is no one I would rather have by my side than those who sit at my table on this night. It is good to discuss such things, but never forget who you are and what we do here. We guard the sanctuary and protect the house of Almighty God from unclean hands who wish to profane it. Like the Maccabees of old and the fall of Antiochus, that man who claimed to be a god, we will one day purify this land and reinstate the age of David where the world will know who God is."

"Will we make an alliance with Simon?" Caleb asked. "We will need a united front to meet such a force as the Romans are sure to bring against us."

A burly captain named Isaac spoke up in a gruff voice, "It has to come to that. Simon and Eleazar must recognize our strength and we must fight as one."

John was still for a moment and then shook his head. "I cannot see a union with Eleazar being anything but dangerous. His mind is warped and jealously fills his heart. He is unpredictable and an incompetent leader. He must not have a say in anything! We will have to deal with him soon."

"Simon is just as dangerous, John!" retorted Isaac.

"Simon is too powerful. If we overtake Eleazar and defeat him, we can gain his forces under our banner and even the odds between us and Simon. That is our only chance of success. We must look ahead, not just at the present. We have to think of defeating the Romans and restoring this land. We cannot do so with men like Eleazar on the loose. We must play Eleazar and at the right time topple him if we are to gain control. It was Eleazar's fault that Simon was invited into this city in the first place, that and the bastard Matthias ben Theophilus. When we are strong we can take on Simon and the city will join us. They suffer under Simon's rule; there is no good in it. What do you say, Judah?"

"I'm with you, John. Eleazar is the closest to us and it is no secret he wishes to join Simon and destroy us. We must act soon, with haste, especially with spring not far away." Judah saw the disappointment on Caleb's face but continued, "Eleazar should be killed. He cannot be allowed to live. Once we overtake the Inner Court he must be killed."

John nodded. "Eleazar will be suspicious of an attack during the winter months; his men are always on guard and keep a close eye on the pilgrims as they worship. We will wait for the right time. Meanwhile, we will see to our defences, store up food, and train." John glanced around the table making sure his men understood the importance of preparation and dedication.

"I heard that Simon's men finished the building of the Third Wall," Isaac said as he ate some stew.

John shrugged. "The walls are strong, no doubt, but the Romans are crafty and we must use our heads. We will need to consider tunneling as an option, and fire teams."

"Yosef ben Matityahu is with the Romans. Perhaps he will come to the city with Vespasian?" Aviram asked, piping up.

John glared at Aviram for a moment. "Who told you that?"

Aviram glanced around, slightly uncomfortable. "A traveler near the Hulda Gates told me. He said he had come from Joppa where he had watched the legions marching and he had been questioned by Roman cavalry. He said that one of the soldiers had threatened to crucify him because they thought he was a spy. The man pleaded with them finally convincing them that he was a humble pilgrim and nothing more. The Romans said he reminded them of Titus' whelp, Yosef ben Matityahu, and that it hurt their eyes to watch such a great prince as Titus, letting a dog like Yosef live because he had been with the provisional government. That is all I know, John."

The room was silent as all eyes stared at John and the dark cloud that seemed to gather around the illustrious fighter. "May God curse that man," John mumbled under his breath.

"And what of Ananus ben Bagdatus, John? He terrorizes all in this city and they suffer," Adam said, breaking his silence with a concerned expression.

"It is regrettable, but one we cannot change. We have no control over those parts of the city nor when Bastard Bagdatus leaves and who he meets with." John could see how his words personally affected the large man. "Leave it, Adam, it will do no good."

"John, would you permit my voice at your table?" Adam waited a second until John nodded slowly and then continued, "I have not seen my family in three years, but I know they live, yet they are under much fear. They live in a small home in the Lower City and have little food." Adam pushed his stew bowl away and painfully continued, "Bagdatus beat my father because food was discovered hidden in his home. I hear that Simon has decreed a law that none are to hide food and all are to offer half of their household's provisions. If this is true, my parents will soon die for they are old."

A stunned silence filled the room. Every man's eyes dropped to the floor in a solemn moment, as minds drifted to their loved ones and families. Judah's mouth parted but nothing came out. Anger swelled within him at the news and pity flushed through his being as Adam caught his gaze and wiped away a tear which clung to his left eye.

"There is nothing to be done; I am sorry for your pain. We have all lost so much." As if personally responsible for Bagdatus' actions, John emptied his wine goblet, rose from the table overcome by grief, and left silently for his private quarters.

Caleb watched a look of hopelessness enter Adam's eyes as the large Jewish man thought hard about John's words and then returned to finishing his meal, with a look of complete misery set into his great frame. Caleb leaned over and whispered in Judah's ear, "I pray to God the Romans forget us and sail back to Italy." Judah gave his friend a scowl and Caleb shrugged. "Why judge me with that look when I state the obvious. It would be a blessing if they would simply sail away, then we wouldn't have to face our enemies as far as the eye can see."

"My sword will cut out their eyes, Caleb. They will wish they never came here."

Caleb nodded. "Maybe...or maybe we will all die. Have you ever considered that? If they defeat us that will mean our city will be destroyed, just like in the time of the Babylonians."

"Then you and I will have to pray for strength like Samson," Judah replied.

"So we can carry away their siege towers like Samson carried away the gate of Gaza? I don't think so." Caleb chuckled. "How are your dreams?"

Judah stiffened and he stared at his friend. "Why do you do that? Why do you ask me questions like that?"

"Because you are my friend and I wish to drive you mad." Caleb smiled. "Pray to God, Judah. Seek him and He will bless you."

"I can't, Caleb. God has looked away. I have unfinished work and God cannot watch."

"He knows your heart. He knows all, Judah."

Judah nodded with conviction. "And that is why He will not extend His gaze to me. He knows what I will do and I cannot seek anything from Him but forgiveness when it is completed."

"You speak of your revenge against Capito?"

Judah shook his head as a few of the men laughed at something Aviram said. Judah leaned over and whispered to Caleb, "Do not call it revenge, Caleb. It makes me sound so low. It is more than revenge. I must do this for Miriam so I can clear my conscience and lift the curse from my head. Her blood howls out from the ground, and I must listen."

"You surely go to your death, my friend. I will be there to bury you, but I pray it doesn't come to that."

Judah's eyes grew cold. "Pray it comes to that, for then I will have killed the man I hate the most and will go to the grave in peace. I cannot die until Capito has come under the blade of my sword, which is an oath I swore before God. For if I shall enter the grave and Capito still lives, cover up the spirit window of my tomb, so that my soul may never find peace and will wander to the end of time."

*   *   *

CHAPTER IX

November 18th, 69 A.D. / 18th of Kislev, 3830
Roman Region of Arabia Petraea
Midday

The dust cloud from hundreds of hooves could be seen for miles as it rose into the blue sky against the sun. Winter had come to the desert. Few rains had touched the barren lands stretching for an eternity before the eyes of the squadron of heavy cavalry who carried banners and the image of a boar's head. Men's lips were caked in dust, their mouths longed for water, and their mounts tossed their heads in the air as they sensed an oasis some distance in front of them. The oasis had been spotted over a week ago by the passing legions and it had been well marked on maps and charts for a viable place to rest during future military endeavours.

The Boars made for the oasis with great speed, monitoring their flanks and keeping a watchful eye on the cliffs, the thousands of crevices, and the many caves which dotted the region. The only life which existed in this part of the world was the odd hawk in the sky or ibex among the rocks. The long-horned, small, deer-like animals would dart away, ascending cliffs or hiding in the caverns of the wilderness, afraid of the thundering horses and the column of dust-covered armour made ready for war.

Orders had been simple for Tribune Marcus Sulla Maximus as he led his men deeper into unfriendly territory. His orders seemed to blend together like a thousand other orders in the past, all bearing the same directive: seek out valuable information and kill the enemy. Marcus had served Vespasian faithfully over the years, and the soon-to-be-emperor had always known who he could trust. Yet, the need to guard the coastal highway was always something vital to their survival and important to keep lines of communication open with Agrippa, Sohaemus, and the other allies of the north. Having fitted enough provisions for a week, Marcus had led his force of one hundred and twenty Boars from the camps of Alexandria two days ago. The company had crossed the Nile by ferry and then had followed the coastal road refitting at Roman outposts and fortified stations along the way. There, they could rest their mounts and maintain a swift pace towards Gaza. Then they would ride inland and survey the regions around the Jewish occupied stronghold of Masada.

Marcus slowed down the column as they encountered unstable and treacherous rocky ground and shook his head as he cursed the nature of the place. He often told his men that this was what Hades must look like: dry, dead, nothing noteworthy, and no attractive women. He would get roars of laughter and applause from the common troopers who loved his dry sense of humour, but he would be looked at with disdain by his junior officers who loathed him. However, on this day in the sweaty, unforgiving terrain of the wilderness, Marcus was not far from their thoughts as they cursed him to the gods.

"Bleeding dog!" Varro winced as his thighs chaffed the sides of his saddle, while blisters formed. He bit his lower lip in pain as he was forced to draw on the reins and slow down to an awkward trot because of the rocky ground. "Bastard and unholy sow!"

"What is your matter, Varro?" an officer named Titus asked, slowing his horse in beside his friend. "Is it your boyish thighs?"

"Damn you, Titus," seethed Varro shaking his head. "The man has gone mad. What is the purpose?"

"What, of this? It's orders, Varro. You should know orders from Vespasian rarely make any sense or contain purpose. We patrol the highway and kill anybody we come across." Titus took a long drink from a water skin he carried and offered it to his friend.

"What about if we came across the Tribune?" Varro replied, taking the water eagerly.

"Watch it now. You don't want to bring any of that to your door," Titus warned.

Varro shrugged and wiped the sweat away from his reddened, sunburned face. "Just a wish, don't you worry about anything. My thought is that the Tribune will get it soon on such a ride as this. There are bandits all over these hills."

"What are you two talking about?" Drusus Valerius Livian called out as he drew his horse onto Varro's left side. The three men were lower ranking decurianes in the cavalry unit of the Boars and had been so for three years. All wanted to rise in rank and accomplish great things, but all knew that to be impossible with such a man as Marcus in charge. It had been Marcus who reminded them regularly that until they left their 'soft boy-loving demeanour at home', none would ever outrank him or feel the comfort of a legate's seat. For this, none hated him more than Drusus.

Titus hesitated to say something to Drusus, for he knew the man's limits of jealously could get out of hand at times, but it was Varro who jumped at the opportunity, speaking his mind. "We were just having us a discussion about Marcus and his desire to see us all die of thirst and saddle sores on this perilous journey. I told dear Titus here that there are many bandits in these hills and we should keep our eyes open so no harm would befall our mighty Tribune."

Drusus looked over his shoulder at the long column of weary faces and shook his head. "He is mad, an idiot." Drusus gazed forward at Marcus riding further up the line with his mounted signifier, always at his side. He imagined his sword blade cutting clean through his Tribune's neck and ridding the world of the arrogance of Marcus Sulla Maximus. "It could work you know. We would plan carefully, but it could work."

"What do you speak of?" Titus replied before a look of horror spread across his face. "You cannot be serious? If we were caught or unsuccessful it would be a traitor's death, the humiliation! We could be scourged or worse. I cannot condone this, even against Marcus. He is still our Tribune!"

"It would be the only way to ever get out of this unit or become something greater. You will never rise through the ranks as long as Marcus Sulla commands this unit! It would be carefully planned; you risk little, Titus," Drusus added and then shook his head from the cowardly, pale face of Titus. Drusus turned to seek approval from Varro. "Varro, I know you want more in life. You're unhappy with the fortune that has been given to you. Trust me when I say this will work."

Varro looked straight ahead and rubbed the stubble on his chin, mulling over the new turn of possibilities laid out before him. "Let me think on it."

Drusus was silent for a moment and then slowly said looking at Titus' uncomfortable demeanour, "You won't say a thing, right, Titus?" Titus swallowed the lump in his throat, licked his dry lips and nodded sickly. Drusus eyed his fellow officer suspiciously. "We're comrades, right?"

Titus nodded. "Comrades, Drusus."

A trumpet blast brought the cavalry to a gradual halt as horses snorted, pounding the ground in frustration and discomfort from the heat. Across the sand, rocks and jagged cliffs laid the oasis of fresh water, palms, and a number of colourful tents with kneeling camels in a cluster nearby. Marcus leaned forward in his saddle, rested his hand on the pommel of his sword, and squinted in the sun while sweat beaded down his temple, causing streaks of dirt upon his face. A grunt beside him revealed his signifier kindly holding a water skin out to his Tribune. Marcus sighed and shook his head.

"Thank you, Publius, but not before my men. These beasts behind me need a drink, the horses maybe even more." Marcus rubbed his nose and carefully scanned the tents taking note of them. "Four in total, around fifteen camels, and no people. Strange, its unlike like merchants not to keep an eye on whatever riches they transport."

"There is a man to the far left, Tribune, see there! He squats in the dirt." Publius pointed to one of the great tents with bright red stripes on the canvas and said, "Arab caravan most likely."

Marcus nodded. "They're probably resting or eating within. They will come out as we approach. Pass the word along to be on guard, but nobody draws swords unless these men are more than just merchants."

Publius nodded and relayed Marcus' orders to a man a few metres back. A hawk screeched loudly from the sky above them and then flew away with the breeze which was gently coming from the distant coast. Marcus observed the distant squatting man rise and stare their direction for a few moments before running to the nearest tent shouting.

"Forward!" Marcus bellowed. He dug his heels into the flanks of his horse and catapulted ahead like an arrow being released. The thunder of the hooves beating the earth pounded behind him and the troopers prepared themselves for anything as they straightened their ranks, suspiciously eyeing the caravan tents and the braying camels as Arabs began to emerge under the high palms.

The gap between the Boars and the Arab merchants was closed within seconds as the column of horses snaked between two rising cliffs of sand and stone. The merchants, shouting at each other in a language foreign to the Romans, tried to calm their startled camels which were trying to stand despite having their front legs tied.

A man, decorated in elaborate robes with a great white turban upon his head, emerged from the largest of the four tents and stood his ground under a canopy. He watched with distaste as the Roman cavalry drew up into a double-lined battle formation facing the tents, having disrupted the calmness of the afternoon. A well built, dark-skinned Nubian warrior stood behind the man holding a great boar spear in his large hands. His master, the man in the turban, faced the Romans boldly and stroked his finely oiled, groomed black beard which had been curled with precision and scented with fragrances from India.

The man was the owner of a vast merchant enterprise, possessing fingers bearing jewelled rings, a wristlet of golden snakes coiled upon his left arm, and garments comprised of silks from the Orient. At his waist was strapped a curved knife in a jeweled hilt, and upon his feet he wore expensive red leather boots, personally made from the Greek lands of Thrace. He was responsible for a fleet of twelve ships in the Mediterranean that sailed the waves, docking at the most prominent ports of the sea, from Corinth to Rhodes, Alexandria, Syracuse, and Joppa. He had twelve hundred men operating thirty caravans throughout the Roman Empire, and was one of the main providers of gladiators and animals for the Roman games in the lands beyond the great city of Petra. He had amassed a fortune, and was known by the name of Pepi, or his personal favourite, 'the Tiger of Carthage' for his fascination with both animal and the ancient enemy of Rome.

"How can I be of service my Roman masters?" Pepi announced in fluent Greek, bowing in the shade of his tent and extending his arms outward in humble submission. The cavalry was finally still as a single man of high rank edged his horse forward and stared him down not knowing whether he was a threat or not. "What do you seek on this hot, dusty day? Is it merely the desire to stretch the legs of your horses? There is no danger here, nor do we seek trouble. We are just honest merchants trying to make a living in this divided country ruled by Vespasian." Pepi smiled and admired the view of motionless Roman troopers suffering under the blistering sun. "Do you seek water? Come. Use it to nourish your mounts and gain your strength. I have food within and wine that would make Dionysius' blood run with jealousy."

Marcus tapped his horse's flanks gently with his heels and rode forward, followed by Varro, Titus, and Drusus who kept a respectable distance behind their Tribune.

Marcus brought his large, sweaty, dusty horse within a metre of the Arab merchant and then reined in the charger which pounded the hard earth with an impatient hoof. "Who are you?" Marcus asked, paying attention to the black man with the spear who stood behind what appeared to be his master.

"My name is Pepi, Tribune. I am but a humble merchant and one who is blessed by your company," replied the clever Arab trader.

Marcus shifted in his saddle, pointed to the Nubian man and said with a boorish tone, "Is that your bodyguard?"

Pepi glanced behind him and chuckled. "Who? That man? Nonsense, he is but a poor man I have hired to help me from place to place. He hails from a savage tribe. Turns out he made some enemies and had his tongue steadily removed."

"What is your business here?" Marcus asked pointedly, ignoring the merchants attempt at humour and sarcasm.

Pepi bowed his head and squinted from the sun. "Would it please you, Tribune, to discuss such matters inside my humble abode while your men can water their horses and rest? I have grapes, wine, cheese, and meats of all kinds."

"You would attempt to bribe a Roman officer? Do you not know who I am and what orders I bring?"

Pepi bowed again. "I am not trying to bribe, merely offering the hospitality that my father would have offered and the honour of my family." Pepi glanced up with a slight grin upon his face.

Marcus was still for a moment, then slowly dismounted, surveying the tents and many faces of the other merchants who looked on him with interest. He turned and nodded to his other officers who gladly dismounted, willing to leave the discomfort of their saddles for a chance to stretch their legs. Marcus removed his heavy helmet, instantly feeling relief as a breeze stirred the curls of his hair and cooled his sweaty neck.

"Come inside, please," Pepi said excitedly. "My men will see to your horses that they are watered, fed, and rubbed down." Pepi took a step back and let the Nubian pass him as a handful of Arabs emerged from the tent.

"Titus, order the men to stand down and rest. See to it that the horses are watered and every man refills their skins," Marcus ordered and then signaled to Varro and Drusus to follow him inside the luxurious tent of Pepi, the Tiger of Carthage.

The tent was more than luxurious, it was ornate. Mats and rugs of every colour imagined decorated the floor. Brass and copper lanterns hung from the ceiling giving light to the room while a few pieces of furniture had been set up to support a banquet of foods. Platters of grapes, apples and other fruits decorated the room's furniture and a number of baskets bore breads, fresh meats, and figs. Pillows and plush cushions were piled upon the floor where men had recently been seated, and a small monkey, dressed with a turban upon its head, sat perched upon a locked chest surrounded by jars made from alabaster and Roman glass. Behind the monkey, hung a giant curtain separating another room from the main dining area. The enormous piece of fabric was made up of rich colours and strange designs embroidered into the material, while its bottom revealed small silver bells of intricate beauty.

"Welcome to my humble home." Pepi smiled at the curiosity upon the faces of the Roman officers as they gazed around at the culturally foreign dwelling before them. "I assure you, the food is as good as you Romans enjoy it and better. Come, sit if you will."

"Why are you here?" Marcus asked, skipping formalities. Drusus and Varro watched the question catch the Arab merchant off guard and the Nubian slave holding the spear in the doorway, frowned at the tone of Marcus' voice.

"We are merchants. I sell goods to the local cities and export them from Alexandria or Joppa."

"You wouldn't be taking anything to Jerusalem would you?"

"No."

"What of Herodium or Masada?" Marcus asked turning slightly, uncomfortable with the presence of the Nubian at his back.

"I would not dream of it. They are all places which house the enemies of Rome. Rome has filled my purse with much gold; I would never deal with such people." Pepi was silent for a moment. "We are bringing a load of grain, jasmine, linen, and papyrus to the port of Joppa. This cargo is sailing for Corinth ten days from now. I tell you the truth."

"I have orders to clear this road from any unwanted trouble, and I intend to do just that." Marcus held his helmet under his left arm. "What is beyond that curtain?"

Pepi turned and shrugged. "A group of donkeys brought in from the sun, they carry my furniture and most of what you see here. Through the other side over there is my sleeping chamber." Pepi pointed to where the monkey sat.

"Drusus, Varro, have a look," Marcus said.

The two officers did not hesitate and pushed past the merchant gripping the hilts of their swords as a number of Arabs in the tent scattered. The Nubian took a step forward and Pepi held up his hand in protest and the man halted.

"Should I be wary of that man?" Marcus asked.

Pepi shook his head. "He does not understand what is going on. That man has been by my side for nearly twenty years and will cause no harm to anyone."

Marcus glanced at the Nubian, taking note of his chiseled frame, bare chest, and defined muscles as his fingers tightened around the shaft of the spear in anger. Marcus turned when he heard the return of Varro and Drusus. Both men shook their heads.

"It is as he said so. I believe he tells the truth, Tribune," Drusus stated.

Marcus nodded at the report and glanced at Pepi. "What is in the chest?" He pointed to where the monkey sat and the little animal made a high pitched shriek and then chewed on the shell of a nut.

"Scrolls containing the goods of what I carry in this caravan. It is important to my business that I keep records of where the goods were purchased, weight, amount, and my destination." Pepi paused for a moment and then added, "There is also money for my expenses." Pepi glanced at the other Roman officers and then bowed his head.

Marcus eyed the merchant suspiciously for a moment and then said, "Have I seen you somewhere?"

Pepi was still like a statue. "I see no reason to believe we have met. I did follow the army two years ago when Vespasian was fighting in the north of the Galilee. Perhaps it was there."

"You followed the army?"

"It's a great business following an army, Tribune. Very profitable. Let's just say I offer more than just slaves and grain." Pepi smiled and nodded. "Women provide a two way benefit; they keep your troops entertained and their morale high and put money in my purse. I own some of the most beautiful women in the region and they are always at the service of good paying legionaries." He paused for a moment and then glancing at Marcus he said rubbing his hands together, "I have two women with me, perhaps they might pique your interest? They would be free of charge. They would be most willing to do whatever you ask of them."

"Perhaps another time," Marcus grumbled. "We will be on our way."

Drusus watched Marcus leave the tent and hesitated a moment, thinking about how nice it would be to have his way with a woman on this day. It had been months since he had enjoyed the naked body of a woman and with the stress of past duty fleeing his mind he suddenly felt a craving to satisfy a deep desire which stirred within him. He glanced at Pepi and asked directly, "Are the women here?"

Pepi nodded. "Yes, but you will have to pay, my offer was only for the Tribune."

"How much?"

"Two denarii."

Drusus scowled at the Arab. "That is too much. We will be leaving soon."

Pepi walked over to Drusus and clasped his hands together. "Ah, but when you see them your eyes will behold heaven on earth. They are young and vigorous, my dear Roman, not yet spoiled by the many hands of men. They are virgins." Pepi glanced at the other officer seeing a chance to make some money. "And you? What say you?"

Varro shrugged and glanced at the tent entrance where Marcus had disappeared through. "Make it quick," he said producing two silver coins and tossing them to the Arab who smiled, picking them up off the floor.

"Very well, as you wish." Pepi clapped his hands and two men entered from a side chamber. "Bring our guests the entertainment and hurry." He turned to the officers and continued, "There is a smaller servant quarters adjacent to my sleeping chamber. You can do your business in there."

Drusus paid Pepi his due and accepted a drink of cold water from the Arab merchant as the women were quietly brought into the tent through the room with the donkeys. The women were beautiful as Pepi had said, and native to the land. Their hair was dark, their skin an olive hue, and their clothes styled after the people dwelling in the lands of Perea. They seemed surprised to see two handsome looking Roman officers staring at them and one of them rubbed the bruises upon her wrists from being bound.

"I see you keep your best tied up, Pepi," Drusus said with a grin. "They are lovely; Venus came down and shaped these young beauties." Drusus approached one and reached out a hand and touched her face. The woman whimpered slightly, stiffening at his touch, but was held firmly by one of the servants. "I think she is smitten for me." Drusus smiled as the brushed the back of his hand sensually down her neck. "I want this one," he said just above a whisper and slowly took a step back without lifting his gaze from her tiny frame.

"Worth every penny, I might add." The Arab laughed and then glancing at the servants standing quietly behind the women he said, "Take them into the back to the servant quarters and make sure they smell nice."

The women were taken away without uttering a word and Drusus tossed Pepi another coin as he said with a loud sigh, "I will enjoy this."

Outside, Marcus retrieved his horse and proceeded to feed it a handful of dried corn as he glanced around at his men sitting under whatever shade they could find. Around thirty of his troopers had commandeered the shade from the merchant tents and had chased off any presence of the Arab traders. They laid or sat upon the ground, enjoying stale water and eating whatever food they had brought. Forty men remained in the shallows of the oasis pool dunking their sweaty, grimy heads under the surface, laughing from the relief of the hot sun as their horses helped themselves to the coolness of the water.

Marcus made his way on foot beyond the merchant tents and climbed a steep cliff of shale where four of his men were posted as a temporary lookout. The soldiers noticed their Tribune and saluted, turning in their saddles.

"All is quiet, Tribune," one man said, opening his water skin.

"How long are we staying, my lord?" another soldier asked.

"Not long, it is too quiet here. I would rather be moving," Marcus replied. He crossed his arms and stared off into the distance as the sun seemed to cook the very ground he walked on. Marcus could feel the heat of the stones through the leather of his boots and he gently pushed a small rock away with his foot.

"I wouldn't expect anything in these lands, Tribune. The army passed through here weeks ago," said one of the men. "Perhaps they work as a deterrent." He pointed down the other side of the cliff at a number of boulders near the bottom with the remains of prisoners tied to them.

The blackened corpses had become like leather in the heat. These men had been captured by Vespasian's legions weeks earlier for banditry and sentenced to death, by being left to die of thirst. It was considered just, by the cruelty of Roman law, to be left as a meal for vultures, which would strip every bone of flesh. It was the second favoured form of torture by the hands of Rome, crucifixion being number one.

Marcus shook his head. "We are always being watched. This land crawls with brigands and war parties. You just don't see them." His eyes searched the surrounding cliffs for any sign of life, but all he spotted was a bird soaring high in the cloudless sky.

"But nothing could live out here; it is barren."

"If we're out here, they're out here." Marcus turned and pointed to the merchant tents. "We must see to our ranks and join formation." He turned and made his way back down the steep slope as pieces of shale slid ahead of him.

"Titus! Where are Drusus and Varro?" Marcus shouted in his commander's tone when he found the incompetent man sitting alone next to the water under the shade of a palm.

Titus promptly turned, nearly dropping a chunk of bread he was eating. "I am not sure, tribune," he stammered looking around and feeling nervous, unsure of Marcus' intentions.

Marcus crossed his broad arms. "Make ready, we leave soon." He hesitated and then his attention snapped to Pepi's tent. A low growl escaped Marcus' throat and he stomped off towards the bright coloured tent leaving Titus confused, unsure of where he should go or what he should do.

*   *   *

Drusus had finished early and was drinking wine as he stared at the naked woman huddled in the corner of the room nursing a large bruise upon her face with a damp cloth. He glanced down at his scratched arm and smiled shaking his head. "You're not a very nice girl. I thought I should marry you." He laughed at the moans coming from the other side of the curtain which separated the two men for privacy and raised his goblet in the air. "Varro, you dog! She is cooperating." Nothing but heavy breathing and panting was the response and Drusus shook his head.

The girl lowered her cloth and started crying softly as she tried to cover her nakedness, sheepishly glancing at her torn garments which lay on the floor next to the cruel Roman's feet. Drusus rolled his eyes and shrugged. "You wouldn't take them off. Besides, Pepi will mend them for you. It would have been a whole lot easier, girl, if you had just acted the part as the whore you are instead of struggling and crying." Drusus raised the cup to his lips and then heard muffled shouting outside followed by a loud smack and then a thud. By the time Drusus had risen to his feet, the curtain was batted aside and Marcus stood in the doorway with clenched fists and five of his troopers at his back with drawn swords. The Nubian slave lay on the ground behind him, blood flowing from his nose and his eyes shut tight in his unconscious state as Pepi stood mortified, unable to say anything.

"What the hell is this?" Marcus shouted as the moaning on the other side of the veil behind Drusus suddenly stopped. "You do not whore yourselves out while on duty!" Marcus stepped past Drusus and with a single yank tore down the veil exposing Varro on all fours between the legs of an unconscious woman. With not a moment of hesitation, Marcus descended upon Varro, and with a stern kick in the ribs, he sent the officer sprawling to the ground with a yelp of pain. "Get dressed and report outside immediately! We will discuss this later!" Marcus stared at the naked woman for a moment, bent down, retrieved a blanket, and covered her. "Bastards," was all he uttered as he stormed from the tent shoving Pepi aside as he was followed by his troopers who sheathed their blades.

Drusus' face was flushed with rage as he dropped his cup and collected his helmet from the floor. He turned to a whimper of pain from Varro who was attempting to get dressed. "He will pay dearly for this, I swear to the gods."

Varro glanced up at Drusus with red eyes of humiliation and struggled to pull down his toga and fix his greaves. "We're officers! He just can't treat us this way! They were only whores and we paid! It's not the first time we've had a bit of fun. We are entitled to the bodies of prostitutes as long as we honour their masters and pay the acquired sum. By the gods I hate that man." Varro shook his head and struggled as he straightened his chest armour. "He's only a tribune, not a damn consul or legate!" Varro complained, wincing in pain from his bruised side.

Drusus clenched his hands into a tight fist and seething he said, "We have to be rid of him, Varro. We have to be rid of him."

*   *   *

December 4th, 69 A.D. / 4th of Tevet, 3830
Jerusalem
Temple Mount
Solomon's Colonnade near the East Gate

Judah passed the flickering torchlight upon the battlements surrounding the Temple Mount as he conducted a routine inspection of the guards of the second watch. The walls were enormous and inspiring, as they had been built from golden stones forged from the quarries of the land. Each stone told a story. They revealed the painstaking hours of masons chiseling and bearing them into the shapes required to bulk up the defence and grandeur of the porticoes lining the mountains plateau, never to be moved, standing as a beacon of Jewish virility and strength.

From Solomon to Herod, the Temple had undergone glory and destruction, rebirth and advancement. It was considered for all, Jew or Gentile, to be a wonder of the world, and it was a place of serene holiness and wealth due to the Temple stores beneath the edifice that housed the taxes and tribute paid by Jews worldwide.

Singing ascended upon the air and lifted from the Inner Court as priests continued their rituals, unmoved by the bleating of sheep echoing from the walls as one by one they were slaughtered for the daily sacrifice commanded in the Law of Moses. Judah pressed onward with purpose, not allowing himself to be distracted by the worship going on from below as he passed armed guards facing outwards toward the Mount of Olives. Resting his hand upon the pommel of his sword, Judah moved with determination, for as a captain elected by John, he was chief of the watch and charged with making sure the colonnade was under discipline at all times.

Men stepped aside for Judah, nodding with grins while others looked on with thoughts of jealousy and contempt for the loved Lion commander who had John's attention. Judah was given stay in the officers' quarters and dined on the best food available, always accompanied by his Lions and many of the other commanders, including John. The zealots had fashioned themselves over the months into a formidable fighting force and had honed their military skills to such an extent that Simon ben Giora's attacks had become like wisps of smoke. The zealots, housed up inside the Temple Courts, continued to trust nobody and suspect everything as Eleazar grew desperate, constantly trying to make contact with Simon for a truce.

Judah halted abruptly and dropped his gaze to a guard slumped over, with his back against the wall of the rampart. The man was wrapped in a cloak as if asleep, and rested his spear upright against his shoulder; all was concealed from the cloak but his sandals. Judah frowned and approached the man. "You there! Guard, why are you not on your feet keeping watch?"

A head rose from the mound of cloak revealing a dark, messy crop of hair and a long beard with cold eyes staring into the night sky. "I still see their faces, Judah, trapped and suffocating from the smoke. Their screams fill the tunnels as they die, and no matter the number of Romans I slay, I cannot clear my conscience."

Judah was taken back. "Adam?"

Adam nodded and glanced up at his friend. "When I sleep, I still see Abraham's body lying upon the sand, his slit throat peeled back, and his blood soaking the earth."

"That was not your fault; we were betrayed." Judah approached his friend and slowly sat down beside him. "I pray to God that Quintus Fabius may be among the legions marching here in the spring, then, perhaps, one of us surviving Lions may kill him and hang the dog from these walls."

Adam shook his head as he closed his eyes. "I try to love my enemies, Judah; they are lost."

Judah scowled and glanced at Adam with a confused expression. He slowly said with shock, "You love your enemies? You wish to love the Romans?"

"I do not ignore the fact they are evil and have wronged us, Judah. But they are God's creation and He created them. Who is without evil? Who is without transgression and a corrupt mind which seeks its own desires? I try to love them and see them as people, lost and in need of the truth. I will defend this city against

Rome's armies, but they need the truth which alone has the power to save humans from corruptness."

"And you think you can give them the truth? They are wicked and set themselves as gods! They care nothing for other people and enslave the world to the pleasures and godless riches of Rome. We *can* teach them the truth, the truth found by the edge of our swords and our resolve not to be governed…that is all!" Judah looked away from Adam in disbelief at what he was hearing. Silence fell between them for a few moments as Judah tried to clear his mind before he turned to Adam and said, "What is this truth you speak of? What do you possess that can save them?"

"You mock me, Judah."

Judah shook his head. "No, tell me."

Adam turned to his old commander and shrugged. "The rabbi from Nazareth, Yeshua. He is the truth. He alone can save a man."

Judah sighed. "You really believe He was *the* anointed one? The one the prophets spoke of? *Meshiach*? Adam, this rabbi may have talked some sense, but if you listen to what many of the other rabbis say and teach, they say this Yeshua was not Meshiach for He never delivered us. He died, and we are still here, fighting for our lives. If He was Meshiach, why are the Romans still here? Where is David's restored kingdom? When I was young, a rabbi who was close with my father told us that the Meshiach would redeem the world and bring mankind back to Eden. Why do we scrape our bodies in the gutter if Yeshua was the one we look for? Yeshua left and was murdered by the Romans. Clearly this unjust act should motivate you to see the truth that Rome must leave here. Rome must be destroyed!"

"You sound like John of Gischala."

Judah nodded. "He has taught me a lot about the darkness which has befallen our people. Rome only wishes to make us slaves and pollute the minds of our children. Have you learned nothing in the years we have fought against them? They have always wanted more from us and many innocent people have been murdered at the sake of Rome's thirst for blood and power, including Miriam!"

"And what if they win? What if it is God's wish that we serve Rome?"

"To utter such things is blasphemy, my friend. God would not wish it."

"You dare say you know the mind of God?"

"God is not with me, Adam, for that you cannot understand. But God is for His people and will use our swords to protect His holy Temple." Judah looked away with conviction and with a sense that someone was listening. A number of soldiers nearby quietly walked away along the battlements while a shofar was sounded from the Outer Court signaling the final hour for the second watch.

Adam stretched his legs and exhaled loudly. "I heard something disturbing from a fellow brother two years ago, before he went to Pella." Judah made a guttural noise of anger at the reminder of the Jewish members of 'The Way', abandoning Jerusalem for Perea, but Adam ignored the insinuation. "He said that Yeshua made a prophecy once when his disciples were admiring the Temple and its stones."

Judah turned, annoyed at Adam's pause and said with interest, "What did he say?"

"He said with great sadness in his voice, 'Not a single stone will remain one on top of each other.'"

*　　*　　*

December 5th, 69 A.D. / 5th of Tevet, 3830
Roman station at Alexandria, Egypt

Vespasian had a habit of rising early, prior to the daily morning sacrifice, in order to wander the boundaries of the camps in search of inspiration from the gods that they would bless the upcoming siege of Jerusalem entrusted to his son. He would pass by the barracks which housed sleeping troops and continue on towards the white flags of consuls and legionary banners outside officers' quarters. The smell of horse shod and manure was always a favourable scent for the elder Vespasian, as the smell fondly reminded him of the life he had grown to embrace, the life of the campaign. That familiar smell would linger near the stables and mix with the smoke from crackling wood fires burning where guards would take turns huddling around them for warmth before continuing their rounds.

The camps were large and detailed, much different from the marching camps. The Roman camps stationed in Alexandria enjoyed maximum protection, as their perimeters were enclosed by three metre high walls and fitted with sharpened stakes on the top. Meanwhile, the dykes and ditches, circumventing the base of the stone walls, were fixed with angled wooden spikes. Alexandria possessed a stationary force dispatched to guard the city and rule the province. It was home to the legions of the III Cyrenaica and XXII Deiotariana overseen by the powerful prefect of Egypt, Tiberius Julius Alexander.

Tiberius enjoyed a palace in the city and constantly hosted guests at parties. He was widely known for his personal selection of gladiators, hiring the best *Lanisticius* to train and prepare them for matches throughout the empire. Tiberius was an older man who had dedicated his life to the empire and was a committed soldier. However, he possessed a fierce passion and unbound loyalty to Vespasian and had personally seen to it that the emperor would never bore during his stay in the city. Despite many offers to settle in Tiberius' palace, Vespasian still felt compelled to be seen regularly among the legions to keep morale high. Yet, he never ceased his habit of early morning walks around the perimeter of the camps spread out in the plains before Alexandria.

Vespasian filled his lungs with fresh morning air and sighed with a smile. It was a crisp morning and the sun had just begun to warm his face as the dew dried upon the ground. A thick bank of steam drifted lazily out of the city from the Roman baths which were being tended to and he thought to himself that an early dip in the cold water of the baths, followed by a massage, would do him fine. He adored the splendour of the city and the wealth of history which seemed to breathe from its very buildings.

The last few days, Tiberius had taken it upon himself to be a tour guide as an array of delegates had led Vespasian, Titus, and a number of legionary officers throughout the colonnades of the city. They had visited such sights as the Serapium, the Temple of Poseidon, and the Timonium, built decades earlier by the illustrious Marc Antonius. Tiberius had even led them beneath the earth into the catacombs of the city and then towards the Great Harbour where they finished the day with some light theatre. A banquet had concluded the evening, fitted with dancing Nubian women and a display of hyenas captured from the African plains to the south. Tiberius had also declared to Vespasian and Titus that they should visit the Temple of Saturnus and the Great Library. However, as Vespasian strolled in the coolness of the morning, they had yet to arrange the time needed for a visit to these landmarks of genius, human endeavours.

"My Imperator, it does me well to see you in good health, no doubt a gift from the gods." Tiberius said, joining Vespasian's side as the two men continued their stroll. "I saw you leave this morning as you do every morning and I thought to myself, *Come, Tiberius, drag your unfortunate, wretched self out of bed and let's walk with an emperor on this fine day blessed by Jupiter.*" Tiberius humbly bowed his head, and then stole a glance back at the six guards who accompanied Vespasian on his walks. "I do pray I am not infringing on anything?"

"Not at all, my dear Tiberius. I merely stretch my legs," Vespasian replied.

"Then I shall stretch mine alongside yours."

"Have the men been selected from your legions?" Vespasian said getting right to business.

Tiberius nodded brushing aside a blonde curl of hair which dangled before his eyes. "The process is underway. I wish to give you the best so that Titus may simply stomp the city out of existence."

"Woe to them if it shall come to that. I do pray they see sense."

"The Zealots see sense? That would alter the world, no doubt," replied Tiberius with a sarcastic chuckle. "I do think that when the day comes when Zealots see sense, Venus shall become celibate."

"Not all the fighters are of the Zealot band: many are priests, common men, and refugees from the north. It is no secret the leaders and the core of their troops consist of this type of rabble, but if the populace could be convinced of their utter demise which creeps upon them, I do hope they will fling open the gates to the city and let our legions in." Vespasian rubbed his hands together from the cool of the winter morning.

Tiberius noticed Vespasian's reaction from the cold and took it that the emperor was ready to retire from his walk. He halted abruptly and glancing back to the six body guards he said, "Shall I send for your litter, my Imperator? These mornings in the winter can be quite cool."

Vespasian shook his head and yawned. "That won't be necessary. I have been through worse. It is a plight of the gods to cause a man to age; it is the mortality of us all that becomes our great foe. I am not what I used to be as I climb in years."

"But in wisdom, my lord, there is none better." Tiberius smiled as he continued walking.

"You seek council is it now? One old man to another?" Vespasian laughed and then dug his hands beneath the heavy cloak he wore as a sharp, cold wind picked up blowing from the coast, stung his balding head.

The sounds of hooves beat the ground behind the two men and they turned along with the guards who held their javelins in bear-like hands. Titus was seen directing his stead, Achilles, as he rode his mount at a gallop. He waved at his father, making sure he knew who approached, and then pulled in the reins to a slow canter until Achilles halted before them. Titus tossed the reins to one of the guards and leapt excitedly from his horses back.

"It appears news has arrived," Vespasian said softly.

"Father, I bear word from the harbour that was just brought to my ears moments ago, and I could not wait for you to return from your walk." Titus closed the gap between him and his father within seconds and then paused to catch his breath. He nodded towards Tiberius in greeting and then continued, "A messenger from our loyal forces has just brought word of Vitellius' condition."

Vespasian bit his lower lip in anticipation and then blurted out, "Will he surrender?"

Titus shook his head. "He has retreated with his forces into *Roma* and barricaded the city. Cremona is forgotten and Primus advances swiftly while Mucianus is cleaning up the countryside of all those who oppose you. It appears Vitellius is witnessing his final days. Word is that he hosts great banquets and orgies where everyone is drunk and all hope is lost. He calls upon the gods to save him but then laments of how his house is ending. The man is an utter disaster and the people fear him. The praetorian are afraid of what is to come and many have tried to stir him into action to face Primus outside the city. Now Primus controls the region and has the city in sight. His forces are deployed and will strike any day now."

"By the gods, it is almost over," uttered Tiberius.

Vespasian was silent for a moment and noticed that a few of the guards standing behind Titus had removed their helmets in adoration and joy at the news they heard. One soldier even wiped tears away from his eyes as he believed he was witnessing in his heart the coronation of an emperor, mighty and just, terrible and powerful in every way.

"Primus will move with much speed and seize *Roma*. It has been arranged what will happen next. Vitellius will be killed, he and all who remain loyal to him." Vespasian nodded as his forehead wrinkled in concentration and his cheeks reddened from the breeze.

"The praetorian must swear allegiance, as well as the Senate. If they do not, they can be replaced at once." Titus paused for a moment considering the options before them. "Support for the Flavian line must not waver in any way. Strength must rule. We should send messengers immediately to Primus with instructions on how to deal with the Senate, as they hold the voice of the people and must recognize our legitimate right to rule."

"The Senate can be swayed," Vespasian muttered. "Like they announced Vitellius as Emperor, they too will see my strength. Jerusalem is the key; we must destroy all resistance and appear to the people to be in control. We cannot allow one ounce of rebellion to exist." Vespasian looked at Tiberius and then back to his son. "When the time comes, you will march swiftly and descend upon that city."

"I will speed up the process of my legionary forces that will be joining the upcoming siege, my lord," Tiberius said. "I will also pen letters to the allied kings of the north and rally support where it is needed."

Vespasian nodded. "Tiberius, go at once to the city and secure messengers to deliver letters to Agrippa and Sohaemus to prepare for an early spring departure to Caesarea Maritima where our forces will meet." Tiberius saluted and then left at once.

Vespasian glanced at Titus and smiled. "Fortune has favoured the bold indeed, my son. Ride to the city and dispatch a messenger to Primus concerning the Senate and Praetorian Guard. Then sacrifice a bull in the Temple of Saturnus to ensure that the harvests grow abundant this spring so we shall have corn and feed for the coming battle that lies before us. Then pay the priests to commence the morning sacrifice and I shall meet you there among the assembled men. We shall not break word of this until we hear of Vitellius' demise."

Titus nodded eagerly, fetched his horse, mounted Achilles, and saluted with a clenched fist upon his breastplate. "I will see you soon, Father."

Vespasian watched Titus gallop away and then turned his face to the sky and whispered upon the breeze, "Basilides, you have given me the inheritance that is mine. Now, let the great eagles of *Roma* descend and snatch the life out of her enemies." With that, Vespasian had his litter fetched and wondered what the oracle's message would be this morning, when the goat was sacrificed and its entrails inspected.

* * *

CHAPTER X

December 28th, 69 A.D. / 28th of Tevet, 3830
Alexandria, Egypt

Gaius Antony sat upon a simple wooden bench under the cover of his tent with the remains of breakfast upon a plate in front of him. Quintus Cassius Aemilius, Hastatus of the Wolf Century and Rufus Garus, who was the Hastatus Posterior of the Serpent Century, dined with their senior commander of the First Cohort of the Fulminata XII Legion. The men were close comrades, a friendship fashioned by hard years of fighting throughout the Roman world, and were now all highly experienced officers who were vital to the functioning arm of Marcus Octavian's formidable fighting legion.

Gaius' squire entered the tent quietly, refilled the cups of each man, and then left to polish his master's armour and sword. Gaius raised his cup high in the air and with a noble nod of respect and gratitude said, "This is to my closest comrades in arms, and their fine ability at making me appear like a god in the eyes of Vespasian and Titus. I thank you, and my rank thanks you."

The men chuckled while raising their goblets, consumed the wine, and then slammed the cups upon the table with a roar of laughter. Rufus took a cold slice of meat from the scraps of food which remained upon the platter in the middle of the table, and shoved the entire thing in his mouth. Chewing with content, he stuck a finger in the air and called out, "Primus Pilus, we will continue to always make you shine and hail you as a man with no brains due to the fact that you have placed men such as us in charge!"

"You tread upon sinking sand, my dear Rufus," Gaius responded shaking his head with a grin.

"He teases like the dog he is, Gaius. Never mind the antics of a worm." Quintus clapped his hands and then slapped Rufus hard on the shoulder in fun. "I do believe things are going to look up for us, maybe in the way of promotions after this ill business concerning Vitellius is complete."

Gaius nodded. All the legionary commanders had tried to control their joy upon hearing of Vitellius impending doom which appeared only days away. Vespasian had gathered all his officers together in one large meeting, dispatching the news to them in a wave of emotion as every man saw a glorious future unraveling before them, full of victory and wealth. Vespasian had done well to promise them all an increase in pay as a tribute of thanksgiving for remaining loyal to him. With the upcoming defeat and removal of Vitellius, it all seemed to be a swiftly approaching reality that would change the lives of the Judean armies of Rome forever.

"The old man will rule well," Gaius said using the title the officers had given Vespasian with much affection over the last years on campaign. "He is direct and has handled things brilliantly. *Roma* has recognized his power and Vitellius has become incredibly unpopular due to the grain shortages and the presence of Primus. The criminal can't hold out much longer, I dare say."

"What a year it has been and one which has brought us rank and admiration. Vespasian will never forget his Fulminata, nor the Hydra, Wolf, and Serpent or the men who lead them." Rufus nodded and then rapped his fist upon the table. "This spring we march with Titus and glory awaits us there, my friends."

The tent was silent as each man considered this news and then Quintus softly said, "It will be like nothing we have ever faced before. There will be cohorts of the legions completely annihilated, I wager. Mark my words, friends. We must use extreme prudence, fight like beasts, and pray to the gods that we are victorious."

Rufus wiped his mouth with a cloth and then took another sip of wine. "I heard a rumour that some spirit god favours Vespasian, a god or spirit he saw in a temple."

"Everyone knows he consulted oracles and has respected the power of Egypt's gods, Rufus, this is no secret." Gaius sighed and inspected the ring he wore on his index finger, than relieved an itch on his neck.

"Listen here," Rufus leaned forward, catching their attention. "This has nothing to do with the oracles or the reports of dogs, eagles, bulls, or some prophecy of a rabbi or Jewish General. This concerns visions that the old man had in the Egyptian temples, where he saw a man appear to him giving him power and blessing for the upcoming attack of Jerusalem."

Quintus was still for a second. "If that is true, then I dare say music may play in my ears. If Vespasian has a god appearing to him, then my heart can rest. Jerusalem will be ours."

"Rumours can change, never forget that. We all have known about how the gods can alter their opinions of what we do here," Gaius reminded the centurions with a stern but low voice. "The gods favour the strong and look down on the weak. We must concentrate on our units, our training, and our instinct. That will win the day and keep you all alive to see this completed." Gaius finished his wine and held the cup in his hands as he peered at the men over its brim. "I trust more in my blade and my ability to sniff out an ambush then a rumour of a god in a vision."

"My lord, Antony, commotion fills the camp!" his squire shouted as he burst into the chamber where the men ate.

Gaius rose with concern, dropping his cup. "What is the matter?"

The squire shook his head searching for the right words and finally blurted out, "Men are running everywhere. It's as if they're all mad!"

Gaius glanced at Rufus and Quintus, then without saying another word, he pushed past his squire, followed by the other centurions. When he exited his quarters, he was confronted by a startling sight as men of the Twelfth Legion, by the hundreds, ran by with exultation upon their faces and no regard for rank. Small camp fires were stamped out in the excitement and large vessels were overturned as men fought hard to pass their comrades. Some of the troops were half dressed in their battle gear and others wore nothing but their togas. The thunderous booming of officers shouting at the men to maintain discipline was to no avail. They bellowed in utter frustration with the camp seemingly oblivious to standard Roman conduct.

Baffled shock filled Gaius' eyes as he stepped out from his tent watching the mayhem. He deduced that an attack was impossible, due to the excitement and joyous expressions on most faces, but the confusion was beginning to agitate him. He needed answers.

Gaius only had but an instant as he suddenly saw the tripping legionary in his peripheral. Gaius leapt backwards, rather than be trampled, as the man tumbled into him. Gaius grabbed the man by his segmented armour and hoisted him to his feet. Staring with eyes of fury at the surprised soldier, Gaius shouted into his face sending bits of spittle into the man's eyes, "I demand to know what is going on! What is happening?"

On an ordinary day the legionary would have begged to be spared a savage beating, but on this morning the man, eyes lit with victory and praise, shouted above the din, "Vespasian is Emperor! Vitellius is dead! Vitellius is dead!"

Gaius slowly turned away in shock while still retaining a firm hold on the soldier. For a moment, colour seemed to drain from his face as he stared at Rufus and Quintus who appeared suspended in a frozen state of utter disbelief at the news. Gaius suddenly felt his mouth go completely dry and then emotion welled up in his eyes. He gazed back upon the soldier and slowly said, "Vitellius is dead?" The tone of his voice sounded muffled and suppressed, as if his head had been dunked underwater. Yet the soldier was there before him as good as life to convince him he was not dreaming.

"We just heard the news, Centurion. A messenger from the harbour was making his way to Vespasian when he was confronted by a group of men from the Fifteenth who suspected it to be news from *Roma*. They demanded to know what was happening and the messenger gave in. Vitellius was killed eight days ago and the Senate declared Vespasian Emperor the following day. Now, there is only rejoicing among the legions."

"But where do you go?" Gaius asked.

"To our Emperor Vespasian, of course! Where else would I go? He has heard the news and word has spread rapidly. He has assembled the priests and is sacrificing a bull before the men in honour of Mars, Basilides, and the gods."

Gaius let the man go feeling overcome with emotion. Rufus stepped over to his friend shaking his head. He watched the soldier, whom Gaius had questioned, stare at the officers for a moment and then rejoin the swelling mass of excited troops as they streamed past them.

"Shall we follow?" Rufus asked.

Gaius ran his fingers through his hair in disbelief and squatted upon the ground as his eyes beheld the mayhem swarming about them. Quintus now stood by Rufus as the two of considered joining the mob roaring about in the camp. They finally turned together and gave Gaius a look of concern as their senior commander's face seemed drained of colour and disturbed.

"Gaius, shall we follow and see for ourselves?" Quintus asked. "What is wrong with him?" he asked, turning to Rufus.

Gaius felt like a dream had descended upon the land for everything appeared as a blur; even Rufus' response to Quintus' query was inaudible and distant. His mind pounded like a drum. Suddenly everything became clear as if Gaius could see the long lines of Romans marching towards the Jewish capital. With Vitellius dead and Vespasian as Emperor, the remaining weeks of winter would quicken, for the departure of the legions was inevitable. Vespasian had put the Judean campaign on hold as he had focused on his bid for power. Now with Rome taken, with no more obstacles set before him, it would be Titus who would rise up as Supreme Consul. The eagles would be carried to Jerusalem's gates and the fray before its walls would consume thousands. The legions had trained for months to fight this battle, but all the strategy and drills seemed to be an indifferent force, beckoning with false assurance despite the grim path that lay ahead.

"Gaius, are you well?" Rufus asked, bending down and gently touching his friend's shoulder.

Gaius' eyes met Rufus' and he shook his head, snapping out of his deep thoughts. He slowly stood with a nod and rubbed his hands together to revive the circulation. "We should be present before our Emperor."

Rufus nodded. "Should we see to our dress?"

"There is no time," Gaius responded softly and stepping forward, he was joined by his friends as they plunged into the mass of troops converging on the consular tents of the camp where a pillar of smoke rose and a nervous bull awaited.

*　　*　　*

Vespasian was dressed in red and purple robes as he waited, a wreath of interlocking olive branches sat upon his head and a look of stone was embedded into his eyes. The white-cloaked priests sang their incantations, brought the bull before a large altar and halted as a sea of faces silently watched the ceremony. Guards held burning torches as they surrounded the wooden platform where Vespasian stood upon, appearing like a statue. A tambourine rattled from a junior priest who wore a white skull cap upon his shaved head. The man shook the tambourine every couple of seconds as the bull was inspected by the Chief Priest, who was armed with an ornate staff, fitted at the end with long, white horse hairs.

When the animal was declared unblemished and a proper sacrifice to the gods, the Chief Priest turned with a wail, flicking the horse hair staff to his left and right. The tambourine rattled rapidly towards this sign, than the Chief Priest grew silent and outstretched a thin, bony arm before the assembly. "Blood is a sign to the gods of our submission before their judgment. Blood is craved by Mars as an honourable sacrifice, and he is seen wanting, for his eyes are upon us now. Mars is the god of war and bloodshed, and he consumes the enemies of *Roma* in fury and destruction. Flesh goes to ruin, to fill Jupiter's cup and the eyes of *Roma* are upon us." The priest extended his other hand and pointed the staff to the sky. He gazed upward, inspecting the clouds as if searching for a sign, and then shouted, "Jupiter be with us as the gates of your temple may stay open. From the earth we look to you, god of gods and great ruler. Mars, son of Juno and Jupiter, triumph with our Emperor Titus Flavius Vespasianus and go before our legions with wrath and war. We shed blood to grant honour and return to the earth that which pleases you!"

The tambourine rattled incessantly as a young apprentice approached Vespasian with a small, opened sack which he held out before him with a bowed head. Vespasian rolled up his sleeve, than lifted his hand in the air to reveal his ring of power and office. Thousands of eyes watched him as he reached into the bag with his left hand and then drew forth a handful of dirt. The soil was cool in Vespasian's hand as he walked past the apprentice and approached the sacred bull. The large animal snorted and stomped a hoof upon the platform as fearful eyes tried to anticipate what was happening. Garlands and ribbons of all colours were wrapped around the animal's neck, a golden ring was skewered through its nose, and its horns were painted red.

"This earth which is about to be poured upon the head of the offering is of *Roma*. It is filled with power and is an honourable gift to Mars; we pray that it may be accepted graciously. *Martia Victrix!*" The Chief Priest paused for a moment as his eyes scanned the men before him. "Blood may fill his cup and look favourably upon the throne of Titus Flavius Vespasianus, our father and lord."

A jeweled knife was handed to Vespasian who took it firmly and showed it to his troops by raising it in the air. "With the blood of this offering, I dare go forth in triumph to lead *Roma* to future glory." He raised his left hand above the bull's head and poured the dirt upon its black forehead. Then, without hesitation, he suddenly slipped the knife under the bull's neck and slashed open its throat as a spray of blood doused his garments.

The bull groaned, its legs trembled and then buckled, as it dropped to its knees with a thud, a fountain of scarlet crimson spilling upon the floor boards of the platform, soaking Vespasian's bare feet. A couple of priests quickly rushed to the expiring animal's side, pushed it over and began their expert work with knives as they opened the bull, digging their hands inside of the beast to remove the necessary organs. After a few moments of hushed silence from the soldiers, the job was completed as a number of silver platters and bowls were brought over for the heart, liver, and kidney which were placed in the dishes, with the intestines coiled on the platter. One by one the Chief Priest inspected them, poking the organs with his staff and picking through the intestines with his fingers. Finally he allowed Vespasian to approach. After showing the bloody organs to the Emperor, the Chief Priest tipped the bowls before the altar and watched as each organ tumbled into the hot, cast iron cauldron. Next were the intestines, which the priest cast onto the altar as they hissed and sizzled from the heat of the fire burning beneath.

"Blood is the food of the gods!" shouted the Chief Priest, and then while turning he raised a blood-stained hand in the air and bellowed, "Hail Imperator and *Rex* Titus Flavius Caesar Vespasianus Augustus, *Pontifex Maximus* and Father of *Roma*! All *Imperium Maius* is upon him as our Augustus and Caesar with all the empires *auctoritas* due him!"

Thousands of troops exploded into a chorus of cheering as they raised their hands, spears, and shields into the air, in response to the energy that had been building throughout the cultic ceremony. The camp reverberated with chanting as the cohorts began shouting their Emperor's name and men broke down, weeping everywhere as there seemed no end to the elation.

Titus, who was standing a ways behind his father, approached him and as he raised his father's arm in the air, he shouted, "Hail Caesar Vespasianus! *Roma Victa!*"

Vespasian had never felt so young in his life. He had strived for power and had fought countless battles throughout his years to get to where he now stood. His trek had taken him from Rome to Britannia to the far eastern provinces. He had seen the demise of four emperors before him, and now he was sole ruler of the world. Primus had sacked Rome and occupied it as Mucianus backed off and crushed any remaining resistance. Soon, Vespasian would sail for the city and claim his destiny. The Senate had already declared him as Emperor, and with Primus' troops murdering Vitellius, nothing was left undone. The pieces had fallen into place and the gods favoured him above all else. He would lead Rome into a new era. As the head of the world, he would make Rome great again, as the gods justly expected it. Amidst the cheering legions soaking up the contagious atmosphere and chanting his name, Vespasian saw Gaius Cornelius Antony standing in the front ranks with an outstretched arm, hailing his new title. Vespasian made eye contact and smiled at him for he would need his best Centurion for the road ahead, and that road led to Jerusalem.

∗　∗　∗

January 12th, 70 A.D. / 12th of Sh'vat, 3830
Jerusalem
Fortress Antonia
Headquarters of John of Gischala

The column of men climbed the dank stairwell within the Antonia Fortress at the northwestern tip of the colonnades surrounding the Temple Mount. The fortress had once housed the Roman garrison, but since the city's capture by the Zealots, it had been under the control of John's men and used as the dominant factor in defending the northern colonnades from Simon's forces.

Once being a place of Roman judicial judgment and legionary billeting, the stronghold had become John's preferred place for hosting guests and assemblies for the elite ranks of his small army. Furthermore, the Antonia was highly regarded as a military structure, strategically built in the place of what would be an exceedingly vulnerable corner of the Temple Mount. John had realized this immediately upon arriving in the city and from that day onward he had stationed troops upon the four enormous towers rising from the corners of the square-shaped castle. As well he positioned catapult and scorpion batteries adding to its defence.

The towers gave protection to the Temple grounds behind them to the south, and provided the ability to monitor the *Mishneh*, a suburban cluster of homes which stretched out beyond its thick, stone walls. Herod the Great had perfected the fortress into a masterpiece and its might spoke volumes of the achievements of mankind in the field of structural fortitude and human determination. The Antonia's walls rose much higher than the colonnades of the Temple Mount to the south of it, and was connected to the Temple enclosure by two colonnades of its own spanning around two hundred metres further north, with a narrow space between them. Despite the distance between the Antonia and the Temple Mount, the enormous citadel was easily defendable due to its ramparts, battlements and towers as John viewed it as the key to protecting the Temple.

Now deep within the bastion, Zealot officers of John's army ascended a stairwell, having been summoned for a secret meeting. The stairwell had been climbed by most before, always led by the aging priest Zechariah, and was always dimly lit by torches mounted upon the walls with the odd window letting in light from the bright sun. The vastness of the sprawling city could be seen from the windows, stretching out as it covered the Tyropoeon Valley, enclosed by a wall known as the Second Wall.

This wall began from the northeastern corner of the Antonia and ran outward as it followed the natural shape of the plateau which enclosed much of the city past the Fish Gate. Then it turned south for nearly a half of a mile until it hooked to the west where it connected with the Phasael Tower, continuing on until it met the exterior walls of the Hinnom Valley. To the north of this separation was a vast area known as *Bezetha*, which contained a smaller population of the city, and was enclosed by a great wall on Jerusalem's northernmost border, constructed decades earlier by Herod Agrippa I.

Slightly further south of the Second Wall, another wall stood dividing the Upper City from a part of the suburbs known as the Mishneh, which populated the area of the Tyropoeon to the Fish Gate. This wall, known as the First Wall, occupied the two western towers of the Antonia and divided the Upper City from the Mishneh, running east from Herod's Towers to the great colossal bridge that met the high Temple porticoes. These walls provided a maximum fallback position from within in case the city's outer walls should be breached. They also had provided excellent protection years earlier against the forces of Cestius Gallus. It had been these very walls, which John had so regularly spoken of, that would come down to life and death during the inevitable Roman assault. Jerusalem's walls would be a stalling factor to frustrate the legionaries and inflict heavy casualties.

Within the Antonia, every man was tired, having been awoken by messages delivered for an early morning council, and now they all grumbled due to the emptiness in their stomachs. Among the officers filing up the stairwell was Judah, Caleb, and Adam, all called to attend the urgent council which was shrouded in mystery.

"This must be important, for John has called everyone," Caleb said, glancing over his shoulder at the tired forms of the men behind him.

"Definitely strange," Adam added as he tried not to constrict Caleb who climbed the steps beside him.

The line slowed as men breached the top and passed through an open door filling the chamber above. Judah rubbed his eyes and yawned as he waited his turn. Isaac, one of John's captains, looked back and then grinned at the Lion Captain. "Perfect time for Simon to attack, if he knew of this meeting with all the officers emptied of the courtyard."

"The man might be a stark raving lunatic, but he knows better than to tangle with us," Judah replied.

"Does he? The possibility of spies among our ranks doesn't concern you?" Isaac shrugged, giving away a hint to the nature of this called gathering. Isaac laughed at the surprised expression on Judah's face as he passed through the door.

There had been much talk of spies lately, spies for the Romans and spies for the other factions in the city that sought their own interests and tried to disrupt things. *But spies among the officer ranks of John ben Levi? Impossible*, Judah thought. *Nobody could exist this long as a spy and remain alive. With all the soldiers scattered about the Outer Court and the trust that ensues between them, somebody would have talked.*

Judah entered through the doorway and was greeted by a packed chamber. Men stood milling about in close quarters before John and a number of high ranking Zealot officers. A hooded man, lying upon the floor bound with cords, was the topic of discussion as men whispered and pointed towards the hostage. John stood to the side, clothed in battle gear with his sword strapped to his waist. His arms were crossed before him and a grim expression was plastered upon his face. Caleb and Adam followed Judah as he pressed through the crowd yearning to get a better view and to discover the identity of the man who lay upon the floor motionless but still breathing in quick recessions as he was obviously frightened.

"Quiet yourselves!" shouted one of the Zealot officers next to John, his face overtaken by a large curly beard. "Silence!" he bellowed again until all voices were hushed.

John allowed a few seconds of stillness to descend upon the men, then took a step forward, relaxing his arms at his side, and began pacing back and forth, watching them all with intense, dark eyes. "I have summoned you all here so that you can witness justice today. I have been chosen by God to lead this army and I have seen many years of battle before me and have lost many brothers in our struggle. We fought in the Galilee against the legions and then when the time was right and God had it this way, he led us through the hills into the plains to this city so that by His power we might occupy it and make preparations for war.

"We have struggled to survive here and have fought off countless attempts by the wicked Simon ben Giora to desecrate this holy place and slay us all. We have put up a strong front against Eleazar and his rabble that still hold the Temple hostage and profane it with their existence. We have shed the blood of our corrupt brethren upon the Temple steps and throughout this city in the last months.

"There is nothing new under the sun. Over two hundred years ago we fought against pagans who wished to destroy our faith, our people and drag us into the pits of *Gehenna* along with them. They demanded we sacrifice swine to their gods, and they tortured our people and defiled our women. They outlawed our worship of the one true God and brought abomination to our Temple. However, with the strength of lions and blessings upon us as the people of God and the sons of Abraham, Isaac and Jacob, we fought back and destroyed the Greek Syrians, winning back our right to govern. Who would have ever dreamed of that day? We cleansed the Temple and still celebrate that event in the winter months.

"You have served me faithfully, and have led your troops in brave raids and attacks to stem the frothing tide of Simon's men. We fought against Gallus' legions years back, and now we prepare for the onslaught which is sure to come this spring. We have heard of Vitellius and his death in Rome. Vespasian who has been waiting patiently, will soon be coming to deal with us." John suddenly shouted, pointing at the assembly before him, "So I now say, with the arrival of the legions almost at our doorstep, why do you betray me? Why do you betray God who is the ruler of us all? Do you dare betray your brothers? This Holy City?"

The room was so utterly silent a coin dropping upon the stone floor would have echoed. Men held their breath in shock and stood perplexed at the display before them. Then as silence eluded the scene, a few voices, and then many, began rising above the crowd as men declared their innocence and loyalty to John. Within seconds everyone seemed to be disagreeing with the charge of betrayal made against them and John stood motionless while listening to the defence by his fellow Zealots.

Judah had not the slightest idea of what to say when he heard John's accusation nor had he any clue of where it had come from. Isaac had mentioned something about spies and that pricked his mind into thinking that anything might be possible. Then John threw his hands up in the air and shouted, "There are spies among us! Men who have betrayed you and me! What are we to do with these traitors?"

The response was a collective agreement, as everyone shouted back in anger, "Kill them!"

John slowly turned and nodded as one of his bearded officers dragged the bound man to his feet and removed the hood. The prisoner squinted in the light of the chamber and his face revealed bruises and swollen eyes as the man had succumbed to torture. His mouth was gagged and his nose was broken as dried blood could be seen staining his upper lip. The prisoner whimpered as John approached him while shaking his head, and the man flinched as a hand was raised as if intending to strike him, but no blow came.

"Here is the spy, caught leaving the East Gate at night, bearing a message for the Romans. The message bore information of where they should attack and what walls are the weakest." John produced a letter and held it high above his head. "It also states that there are many more people in my army who will try to arrange a time when they can open the gates to the legions and let them in. I dare say that if this is true, then I condemn their souls to the darkest realms of hell and that God has turned His back on them."

Shouts of anger burst from the mouths of the officers in the room as many condemned the man to death. A number of Zealots hollered out that the man should be thoroughly questioned to discover who the other traitors are but John just shrugged and pointed to the prisoner's bruised face as a testament to the savage interrogation he had received.

"This is a capital offense and one which must be paid in blood," John bellowed, throwing the letter to the floor and stepping on it.

"Let the man speak, John!" a man shouted from the front of the crowd. "Let him defend himself to see if these charges are true."

"What do you think I have been doing since we caught this man? Entertaining him at my table? We have questioned him fully and found him guilty!" John raised his fist in the air.

"Then why have you not spoken of this? This is the first time we have heard of such things, I cannot believe it unless I see the letter and hear from this man concerning his involvement!" the man replied sternly. "He should be brought before a proper court, the Sanhedrin could judge him. Does High Priest Phanni know of this?"

"And why should the prisoner be allowed to speak? So he can spread lies and deny what is obvious?" John lashed back. "Why do you defend him? Perhaps you are one of these spies?"

The man looked aghast as he shook his head and flung his hands in the air in a dastardly manner. "That is absurd! I have been among your ranks for over a year. I merely try to remind you that we are not animals. We are under God, who alone is the Judge! We must judge this man fairly."

The crowd was beginning to quiet as they witnessed the argument. A number of the Zealots hollered for the man to shut his mouth as others beckoned for John to carry on with the condemnation of the prisoner, but the determined man kept shouting, declaring that the prisoner must be tried fairly.

Judah was beside himself with how things were playing out. He had been in the company of John for the last two nights and had not heard an ounce of discussion concerning anything about spies, so he was confused more than ever to find this unfolding before him. Caleb and Adam tried to peer through the crowd to discover the identity of the prisoner but the man was not permitted to speak and his face was so badly swollen that it was impossible to recognize him.

"Arrest him and take him away!" John finally bellowed in order to silence the rebel rouser.

A majority of the crowd voiced approval at this order as some people shouted against it, but not a single man stopped the Zealots from taking the trouble maker away who struggled and swore at John that he would incur the wrath of God for shedding innocent blood. Once the man had been forcibly dragged from the chamber all eyes turned to John in anticipation for the judgment upon the prisoner.

"They can't kill him here," Caleb said in disbelief. "John must put the man on trial."

"They won't kill him here and if he is a spy he deserves no trial," Judah replied.

"And how will we find out if he is a spy to begin with since he is gagged and not permitted to speak? What if he is innocent and John is wrong?"

Judah glanced at Caleb pondering the wisdom from his friend's lips. "It appears John has questioned the man and found him guilty. There may not be time for a trial and an example might be the only way to get the message across if traitors are among us. It is out of our hands, Caleb."

John silenced the crowd by raising his hands. "We cannot let this stand, and the stench of betrayal could have cost us all our lives had the prisoner's message successfully reached Titus." He slowly drew his sword, holding it in his bear-like hands with the blade pointed downward. "A traitor must be made an example of." The prisoner ceased whimpering as he stared at the blade in the hands of John.

"Judah, someone should stop this!" Caleb said turning to his friend. "Say something, he respects you and will listen!"

However, before Judah had time to protest, John raised the blade, turned, and with lightening reflexes, drove his blade through the chest of the prisoner. The man's eyes bugged out, his face contorted with pain and a strained, muffled scream exited the prisoner's gagged mouth. A gush of blood erupted from the man's back as the blade tore through his spine and punched out the other side cascading gore over the floor tiles. Blood streamed down the man's chest as he dropped to his knees, his body now a withering form, crossing into the realm of death. John tugged on the blade with a grimace and a grunt, than pulled the sword out of the man's body. The prisoner fell on his side as a dark pool formed around his chest, spreading through the cracks of the tiled floor. A slight whimper escaped the man's mouth, then he was still and lifeless, his eyelids half open.

The chamber was spell bound and silent. John wiped his blade off on the prisoner's garments and then sheathed it with a loud scraping of steel. He crossed his broad arms, glared at his men, and said, "Let this be reason enough never to cross me. All traitors and spies will receive the same judgment alike; they will be refused a burial and cast from the walls to rot in the Kidron. If anyone opposes me for what I did and thinks they can do a better job, than let that man come forward at once so that all may recognize him." John looked at his men and when nobody moved, he smiled. "You are dismissed to your stations. Spread the word of what happens when you choose to spy for Rome."

*   *   *

CHAPTER XI

March 2nd, 70 A.D. / 3rd of Adar, 3830
Alexandria, Egypt
War Council of the Judean Army

The faces of the officers displayed the utmost sincerity in the low light from the oil lamps burning upon the table. Each man wore his best armour, taking the time to have their swords, sheaths, greaves, breastplates, and helmets polished so they shone like fire. Their togas had been freshly laundered as the men had bathed and scented their bodies, in order to present themselves as professional commanders of the Roman army before their Prince and General, Titus Flavius Vespasianus the Younger. Now they stood rigid and stiff, like pillars encircling a table. Each man supported his helmet under his right arm, and rested his free hand on the pommel of his sword.

Titus stood before his generals and glanced down at the enormous, unfurled map before him. He leaned forward, supporting his weight by planting his clenched fists upon the table, and looked from man to man silently. It was a small group of men, but all of them were vitally important for the coming months of fighting. Of the men, Tiberius Alexander, the Prefect and Governor of Egypt, was present and dressed in his finest. Cestius Gallus, the Legate of Syria, also stood among them followed by the troublemaker Gessius Florus, the one who, in Titus' opinion, had started this whole mess. Also present was Gaius Cornelius Antony, who Vespasian had encouraged Titus to include in the council despite only being a Centurion, though highly esteemed.

The last week had washed by Titus like a whirlwind and it had brought about dozens of letters bearing the seals of governors and nobles throughout the Roman world pledging allegiance to Vespasian. Titus had waited for this moment for so long. He was now a true Prince and inheritor to the seat of Rome. Months had passed him by one after the other, with each day reminding him that if his father's bid for power failed, they would die a traitor's death, forever shaming the annals of history. Now, those tables had been turned, and with Vitellius dead, the world was theirs and Basilides, the Son of the Monarch, had kept his promise.

"We now look to Jerusalem," Titus said, breaking the silence of the room. "Everything thus far has been to propel my Father as Emperor, and now that Vitellius has been removed and Primus and Mucianus have found victory, we look to Jerusalem." Titus outstretched his finger and tapped the map in two places. "We have sent letters to Emmaus and Jericho and they know what to do. When we arrive at Jerusalem, Sextus Cerealis and the Fifth Legion will descend from the west and Larcius Lepidus and the Tenth Legion will move out from Jericho, marching south to arrive at the city. We will have the Tenth make camp near the mountain they call Scopus, and the Fifth shall enforce the western side of the city and the aqueduct route across from the *praetorium* and Herod's Palace.

"Tiberius Alexander will be assuming control as second-in-command of the campaign and will bear the rod of consular power. He will carry my name with him upon the field and will receive total and complete cooperation. Peducaeus Colonus has been assigned as acting Governor of Egypt to replace Tiberius during this campaign and will see to our necessary supplies as we conduct the siege." Titus glanced at Tiberius, who was next to him, and motioned for him to speak.

"Two thousand troops from the III *Cyrenaica* and XXII *Deiotariana* have already been assigned under Aeternius Fronto to replace those dispatched to Mucianus' forces in *Italia*, so this shall increase the strength of those legions who have suffered heavy casualties in the last years." Tiberius briefly pointed to one of the new officers standing in the room and the man slightly bowed.

"In all, we will be moving upon Jerusalem with one of the largest armies fielded in decades," Titus intervened. "We will be leading four legions brought up to strength, eight squadrons of cavalry, including squadrons of Syrian and royal contingents much larger than we possessed in the Galilee campaign. These will be led by King Marcus Agrippa, King Sohaemus of Emesa, and Antiochus of Commagene and his Nabateans. We have been reinforced with an additional three thousand men from the Euphrates region as well as nearly twenty-five hundred men from Zeugma. We will rally in Caesarea Maritima where we will be united with an additional twenty auxiliary infantry cohorts. In all, the army will comprise of nearly sixty thousand troops." Titus let this figure sink into each man's mind as they imagined the vast horde which would descend upon Jerusalem in all its fury.

Titus traced his finger upon the map as he spoke, "We will depart from here in three days and pass through Nicopolis where we will board galleys and sail down the Nile through the district of Mendes; this will save us some time.

"Next, we march for the city of Thmuis where we will continue by land until we reach Tanis. There we shall set up a fortified camp for each legion. The following day, we shall make for Heracleopolis and then on to Pelusiun where I intend to rest the army for at least two days."

"My Prince, what is the pace you wish us to press the troops at?" General Octavian asked, working out the distance in his head as he looked up and down the sketched coastline.

"Sixteen miles a day. We must move swiftly and have everything in order. We will not tarry for anything," replied Titus. "Following the rest in Pelusiun, we shall ford the estuary and march through the desert where we will reach the temple of Casian Jupiter. There we will make camp. Next, we march for Rhinocorora through the city of Ostrakine, and I hope to make that in two or three days.

"After that, we march for Raphia along the Judean border and then onto Gaza where we must see to it that we set up another fortified camp. We have to expect the possibilities of brigands along this route or anyone who might try and disrupt things. Always keep the baggage train closely in check and our marching columns alert and ready.

"From Gaza, we break camp and march on to Ashkelon, Yavneh, Joppa, and finally Caesarea Maritima. From there I wish to rally the army and regroup our forces with the arrival of our allies. This will take a number of days, but I want the men kept fresh and active." Heads nodded in the room and Titus continued, "Once we break from our base in Caesarea, speed is the word. We make for Jerusalem through Antipatris, Thamna, Gophna, and finally Beit El. We shall arrive at the northernmost point of the city on Mount Scopus. From there we can navigate our position and scout out the proper campsites for the rest of the legions and allied units. I will be based near the Tower of Psephinus before the far exterior wall of the city. We will place camps on the Mount of Olives, Scopus, and along the backside of the city to completely circumvent it. Nothing goes in or out. Once the siege equipment is unpacked, the engineers will see to the placements of where the ramparts should be located and what else needs to be conducted. We will convene at a later date when we arrive at the city and then can review a more precise method in which to take her." Titus took a deep breath, than crossed his arms. "Any questions?"

"Where would you like my Boars during the march, sire?" Marcus Sulla asked.

"Where it is needed most, no doubt, at the front of the column and stationed at the vanguard. I will not have this army made a fool of because our baggage gets robbed or disrupted. We must maintain complete discipline and maximum focus. Your squadron will divide and watch the flanks and venture away from our lines to keep eyes all around us. Much of our cavalry units await us in Emmaus, Jericho, and from the allied kings. For now, we will make do with what we have."

"What if the rebels should engage us when we advance upon Scopus, General?" asked Titus Frigius. "What if they lay an ambush before us? Should we pursue them to the city if we get the chance?"

"By the fury of Mars, I pray not. We do not pursue the enemy to the city until all our force is collected at Jerusalem and deployed. If we are ambushed, kill the damn Zealots, but we do not engage them openly or pick a fight." Titus looked around the room making sure everyone understood. Florus stood a metre behind Cestius with an aggravating grin upon his face. Desiring to make an example of the man, Titus pointed at him. "Do you wish to add something to this council, Gessius? Perhaps your voice should be heard?"

The grin vanished from Florus' face and he shook his head. "I pray, my Prince, my voice is not pure enough for this council. I have nothing to add."

Titus scowled slightly. "What is your opinion of the Jews of Jerusalem? You were stationed there once, were you not?"

"Again, my Prince, I have nothing to say. It was long ago that I held power in that city." Florus bowed slightly.

"That bastard condemned the men of the Gallica from his arrogant actions. The poor lads were slaughtered to a man," Marcus Sulla whispered in Gaius' direction, catching the Centurion's attention.

"What do you mean?" Gaius asked.

"The garrison stationed at Jerusalem, is what I mean, all killed because of that shit."

Florus heard the whisper escape Marcus Sulla's lips, but unable to make out what was said, he just glared with seething eyes at the Tribune. He watched the Tribune glance back at him, hold his gaze for a moment, and then turn away shaking his head. "My Prince," Florus spoke up, ignoring the egotistical cavalry officer. "The Jews are dogs, not fit to piss by a Roman, I dare say. They are barbaric, heathen, and are secretive. They plot behind our back and demonstrate a vileness which should be cast from this world. I say, not an ounce of goodness towards *Roma* lies in their hearts, including the one you keep by your side, my General."

The room was silenced by Florus' words. Every man present had been involved some way or another with conducting warfare against the Jewish rebels, but none seemed to harbour such dark sentiment concerning the entire Semitic race as did the former procurator of Judea. The Roman Empire was such a mixed basket of cultures that rarely did someone demonstrate such hatred towards a people group as Gessius Florus now revealed.

Titus stood his ground and rubbed his hands together, pausing for a moment to collect his thoughts. Then he said in a captivating, dark tone, "I pray to Jupiter, Gessius Florus that you're past actions and reckless leadership qualities do not condemn the lives of more legionaries then necessary. The wives of the men slaughtered in Jerusalem's garrison still wail at night. Their blood cries from the stones they were cast upon. You will not be one to delegate at Jerusalem, and you are damn lucky my Father didn't feed you to his hounds when Nero killed himself. You are by my mercy and grace allowed to live unpunished and unscathed concerning your history. You are never to speak so brash with me again or I will see to it you are shamed and sent back to *Roma* to cower in the sewers, you swine. You no longer deal with a General here; you face the Prince of *Roma*."

Marcus Sulla gripped the pommel of his sword and half drew it as he glared at Florus in fury at his incompetence and disrespect for his Prince. Had it not been for the hand of Titus which stayed him, he would have drawn his blade with a smile and severed Florus' windpipe and spinal column. But the Prince shot him a quick look, motioned for him to stand down, and the tension dissolved into an awkward silence.

"Am I clear, Gessius Florus?" Titus asked.

Florus, realizing the jeopardy he was in, bowed his head humbly. "My Prince, forgive me and my regrettable rudeness. I will do as you ask and follow your orders as your humble servant. If you see fit, I shall retire and not take part in this campaign."

"That is not necessary. Just remember, Gessius, that what a man does is how he is judged. He may redeem himself, but if his past is marred by much regret, it may cost him that much more to clear his name." Titus ignored the disappointment on Marcus Sulla's face at reinstating Florus, but sometimes Titus had to think about what someone could bring to the table as an offering rather than his ugly qualities as a man. "Very well, I consider this resolved." Titus glanced at the men. "You are dismissed to your quarters. We begin preparations for leaving at first light. May Jupiter be with the legions and the upcoming battle which lies ahead."

* * *

March 7th, 70 A.D. / 8th of Adar, 3830
Near the Temple Mount
Jerusalem
Noon

"You bastards, still suckling milk from your mothers?" Ananus ben Bagdatus spat upon the stones of the courtyard and then pointed up at the high walls. "Cowards and men of filth! I call on you to recognize strength when you see it. I have the strength of a thousand bulls and not a whelp or little shit like yourselves can stand up to me! You are dogs and swine! Men with no fathers and whores for mothers! Your sisters and daughters warm my bed and moan like cattle when I rip the clothes from their bodies to spoil their flesh! But they don't mind; old Bagdatus knows best and makes them into real women!" He laughed, slapping his knee as he made a grunting noise and licked his lips hungrily, drooling upon the curls of his own beard. "I spit on your family names and piss on your dignity!" Bagdatus then hiked up his garments, revealing his ankles, as he strutted around imitating a chicken, being mindful to keep out of range from John's archers who angrily fixed barbed arrows onto their bowstrings, praying the imbecile would stray too close.

"Come, you women way up there! Come fight me! I won't even use a weapon, you young virgins!" Bagdatus scoffed as he threw his hands up into the air. "Come, see!" He unstrapped his sword and cast it upon the stones. "I am unarmed!" he roared and the other large men that made up his gang of cutthroats and murderers howled with laughter as they stood by.

"I swear by all that is holy, I would gladly kill that man and put his head upon a pike," Isaac, a captain of John's army, muttered under his breath as he stared down from the battlements. "He is a murderer and an abomination to this city."

Judah glanced at Isaac, the Captain's bitter words driving deep within his soul. For five days, Bastard Bagdatus, as John's men called him, would approach the northern defences of the Antonia and scoff at the men upon the ramparts, jeering up at them and calling them out to fight. It had successfully worked only one time, where one young Zealot named Eli, overcome by anger towards the insults and suspicious that Bagdatus had raped his sister, charged down from the ramparts and burst from the fortified doors to do battle. However, the poor man had died swiftly under a concealed dagger Bagdatus had kept within his garments, after declaring he was unarmed.

"You there, is that old man Isaac? The bastard pretending to lead a rabble of dirt, who call themselves soldiers?" Bagdatus pointed up at the high ramparts. "You think your fit to be a Captain? You're an old man who has seen too many years. You're too old to know how to fight, and useless, I would say! Throw down your toy weapons and I will teach you what it is to be a man!" He laughed at the hatred that fell upon Isaac's face like a dark curtain shutting out all light.

"I will go down with you if you're thinking it, Isaac," said Aviram, one of Judah's Lions.

"No sense in wasting one's life, boy, there are too many of them. Besides, can you trust him? The man has no honour and is only a loud voice filled with air, nothing else." Isaac looked sternly at Aviram and then took a step back so Bagdatus could not see him.

"Running to hide, Isaac?" Bagdatus called up squinting in the sun. The walls of the Antonia loomed before him and there was nothing he could do but rant in the fashion he knew best. Simon had instructed him to proceed with the mocking calls, in an attempt to demoralize John's men and probe them for weaknesses. Simon understood the power Ananus' presence held, for everyone had heard the tales of what he had done.

"With a well aimed shot, it is possible to hit him from here, Isaac. What if we tried?" Judah asked looking back at Isaac.

"And miss? If we missed they would mock us more, we will not give them anything. Let them try and come up here, we will slay them all," Isaac retorted and rubbed his nose. "We will do nothing. Those are John's orders when it comes to this nonsense."

Judah sighed and stared back over the ramparts to the men below in all their pomp. Each day when Ananus showed up sauntering around at the base of their walls and bellowing up at them, the ramparts would become a cluster of armed troops expecting an assault. John had grown too accustomed to the attempts at distractions from Simon's men who tried to keep their attention in one place while they scurried around and attacked from another angle. His tricks had come close to victory too many times, and now John treated every stunt as if it were a decoy for something bigger. With the presence of Bagdatus and his gang, John had doubled the guard on the Antonia and resupplied the ammunition for the catapults and scorpions upon the towers.

Judah held his shield firmly and scratched his neck. His other men stood on either side of him observing the fiasco, silent like everyone else upon the battlements. Judah naturally was concerned for Adam, as numerous times in the past, he believed the hulking man wished to hurl himself from the twenty-metre walls and charge Bagdatus like a berserker filled with blood lust. Adam's eyes would narrow and his face would become overwrought as his hands tightened upon the shaft of his spear causing blisters. Adam's dark face always appeared as if burning and his long black beard would only fuel his beast-like image with primal rage.

It was known among many of John's other men that Adam's family had suffered under the routine visits Bagdatus paid them. That is what Judah feared, that by feeling overcome with desperation and wrath, Adam might try and avenge his family, only to end up like the decomposing body of Eli laying a ways from the fortress. However, with the Upper and Lower City under Simon's control, there was nothing in the world anybody could do but hope and pray that God would strike Bastard Bagdatus with a pestilence to make his flesh rot and worms burrow into his skull.

"Some more people approach beyond the street!" Caleb called out standing on Judah's right. "It is a delegation of some kind. Isaac, come!"

Beyond where Ananus ben Bagdatus heckled and terrorized John's soldiers, appeared a column of troops arrayed in the garments of the Idumeans, who carried oval shields and spears. Among them was an elderly man dressed as a priest, who walked alongside a richly decorated litter carried by eight men. The column moved slowly but with perfect form and rhythm as the soldiers pounded their feet upon the ground with every step. They were silent in their approach, as nobody shouted or no instruments were sounded. The delegation was noticed by Bagdatus' men who stepped aside and cleared the area before the Antonia. Finally, Bagdatus closed his mouth, and like a little boy responding to his father's harsh discipline, he bowed his head, backed up a few paces, then stood with his men, silent and grim.

"Matthias ben Theophilus is among them," Caleb said as he pointed to the elderly man escorting the litter. Noticing Matthias' staff of identification, Caleb lowered his voice and leaned over to Aaron, one of his fellow Lions who stood beside him. "I haven't seen him in the flesh, just heard of John and Eleazar stripping him of his title."

"And rightly so, Caleb. The old priest supported the Romans and then opened the gates for Simon," replied Aaron.

Caleb glanced at Aaron and shrugged. "Well, when the title of High Priest was given to Phanni, Matthias hadn't let Simon into the city yet, and nobody really knows even if he was a Roman sympathizer. He is still here in the city, is he not?"

Not a soul moved among Bagdatus' men as the litter was gently set upon the ground. Matthias approached a drawn veil which concealed the traveler inside and whispered something through the curtain. Everyone upon the ramparts watched with interest. Some wondered if a deal might have been made with Agrippa, who had been allowed back into the city to try and parlay with the Zealots, but the mysterious traveller remained hidden from view.

"That must be Simon," said Moshe, one of Judah's Lions, breaking the hush among John's men.

"Has Simon ever done something like this before?" called out a Zealot, shaking his head.

"That must be Simon, it wouldn't be anyone else. What is he doing here? And he comes to us as a king? What arrogant filth!" Moshe bitterly spit over the wall and snarled. "We should charge from the walls in force and cut them down."

Isaac furled his bushy eyebrows in confusion and scratched his temple. "If he saw us leave the walls they would know something is up. If that is Simon, what in hell does he want?" Isaac bit his lower lip, and then turning he shouted at one of his soldiers to send word to John.

The curtain of the litter was drawn back and all eyes watched the illustrious, self-proclaimed king finish a goblet of wine and then sit up from the many scattered cushions. Simon yawned, scratched his arm, then shook his head as if this tedious business was making his cranium split and he had better things to do with his time. He slightly leaned forward, squinted up at the high walls, and then groaned dramatically as he awkwardly climbed out of the litter. Simon smoothed his garments so that they flowed properly, fixed his hair, and then waved up at the faces peering down at him in a mock gesture. "I want to speak to John now, so fetch him!" Simon bellowed in a condescending tone of snobbery. "I will wait here for the meantime, but a word to the wise, do not test me. Bring John to me."

"You think you have power from down there? Come up here so we can talk?" called out one of the Zealots.

"No, you buffoon!" Simon replied in exasperation. "John can speak to me from the walls, can he not? Then your leader will be safe from my hand." Simon held up his hand and showed off the large jeweled rings he wore.

"Where did you get those? From the houses you plundered and the families your pet Bagdatus killed?" shouted a Zealot with disgust.

Isaac hushed the man and Simon laughed, tossing his head back as he clapped his hands together. Then he sat down and proceeded to wait while a fan and an umbrella were brought to him by two women.

"The man has no shame. He thinks he is the king," Adam said in disdain.

"Keep silent!" Isaac scolded them looking back and forth down the line of troops. "He has come to parlay. Nobody lifts a weapon to harm him." He glared back at a man standing a few metres away and harshly growled, "Where is John?"

"A messenger has been sent, Captain, he will be here soon."

"John is coming!" Isaac hollered from the walls, as he watched Simon shrug and begin to eat olives.

It took nearly fifteen minutes until John emerged from one of the tower doors. He was followed by a number of his officers and they made their way along the crowded ramparts in full battle gear with stern glares emblazoned on their faces.

Isaac turned with relief at the sight of John and pointed over the wall. "It's Simon down there, John. It seems he wishes to offer terms."

"Has he said anything?" John asked.

Isaac shook his burly head. "Nothing. He just arrived, asked for you, and is now sitting in his litter eating olives. He has a party with him: Bagdatus and his men are down there and Matthias accompanies Simon."

John halted abruptly, before revealing himself to Simon, and shot a curious look at Isaac. "Do you think he wishes to join forces because of the Romans?"

"Bastard doesn't deserve our protection. I wouldn't trust him to keep any deal or truce. He should be fed to the Romans, I say." Isaac glanced at Judah and many of the other soldiers, then stepped closer to his commander for privacy. "I say let him fend for himself."

"I disagree, Isaac, and I say to you that it would be dangerous for us all and the city. You truly believe we, Simon, and Eleazar can function as three separate parties when the rams touch our walls?" John paused and then planted a firm hand of assurance on Isaac's shoulder. "Trust me when I say that God will protect us. HaShem will convict Simon of the reality that we must unify if we are to have victory." John nodded at Isaac, moved past him, resting his hands upon the battlements as he gazed down at the deceitful, conniving king.

"John, it really is you!" Simon called out leaping to his feet as if he and John had been the closest of friends, separated for years. "It is so good to see you."

John cleared his throat as he carefully studied the men gathered with Simon. He identified a few familiar faces out of the party and motioned towards them with a pointed finger. "I see you still have that fat Yehoram on your leash! Do you keep him close by so he doesn't bite, Simon?"

Simon glanced at the fat, ugly man who scrunched up his blotched face at John's harsh words. Simon chuckled and shook his head. "Yehoram is a faithful servant of mine, but one who must be restrained from time to time."

"And greetings to Simon ben Cathas," John said ignoring the jest from the Sicarii King. "Have you truly betrayed the memory of your brothers who fell under the blade of Simon ben Giora to the south? Their blood still wets the sands, yet you stand by his side? Has it cost you your honour, Simon son of Cathas?" John glared at the Idumean officer standing a few feet behind Simon and the man lowered his gaze. "And what of you, James ben Soras? Have you not thrown in your lot to follow the slayer of your people? A man who purports himself as a king?"

Simon ben Giora glared up at the walls, trying to control the rage that seethed within his soul as John's men could be heard laughing upon the ramparts. Simon looked to James ben Soras, one of his Idumean officers who had liberated the city over a year ago from the clutches of John and Eleazar, and said, "Do not say anything to provoke him. I will handle this." Simon squinted up at John and replied, "We have all been forced to rethink things, John. The world is a strange, frightful place, and we now find ourselves standing before you, our enemy, but we are setting aside differences in order to do this now, are we not?"

"What is your purpose here, Simon?"

Simon outstretched his arms in fake gratitude. "To be your servant, of course, and discuss things with a likeminded brother-in-arms."

"I am not like you, Simon. You have pillaged the city, killed many, desecrated what is sacred, and violated the purity of women. You are reckless and dangerous."

Simon looked hurt but then smiled and shook his head. "John, John, come now. Is that anyway to talk to a fellow Jew? We are on the same side, you and I. We both want this city restored and the enemy defeated and cast from this world."

"Does that enemy include the innocent people of this city who suffer under your rule?"

"The people suffer no more under me than they did while you and Eleazar ran things. Don't confuse the facts, John. I have come as their saviour and king, like Herod. I will be good to them and they can prosper under me. I but ask for their allegiance and that is all." Simon gazed up at the walls and one of the women holding the umbrella moved closer to shelter his eyes from the sun.

"You wish to become king?" John asked, dodging the accusation that he and Eleazar had caused suffering in the city under their temporary rule. He noticed Judah give him a questionable look but he brushed it away as foolish. "Only God is king in this city and we wish to restore it to its proper place, unhindered by the Romans."

"Glorious again like in the age of the Maccabees? Or the Hasmonean Dynasty? Or what about David and Solomon? These fantasies will exist only in your dreams if you do not heed my voice. John, I come to you despite our differences with an urgent message I wish you to consider," Simon spoke seriously. "The Romans are on the march. John, you know that. Titus will bring his legions to our walls."

"And you think I haven't considered that? You have tried to overrun the Temple and slaughter us all. You have attacked my men and looted my possessions! You conspire with Eleazar to unite and turn against me. I have repelled wave after wave that you have sent and every attack has been sent back like the receding waters of the Kinneret, but drenched in the blood of your men. I would fight and die for my men while you would send yours to their doom! Why should I trust you?" John shouted as the men upon the ramparts cheered their leader and shook their spears in the air.

Simon was silent as he tried to control his anger. Rolling his eyes, Simon motioned Matthias to come to his side and when the aging priest was close, Simon turned and whispered, "I can't control him nor make him see reason. Speak to him, Matthias, tell him what we know."

Matthias slowly nodded and gazed up at the walls. He grunted to clear his throat and struggled to make his voice loud as he tapped the end of his staff upon the stones and prayed for strength. "John ben Levi, hear my voice and take the wisdom which comes from it. We cannot look into the past or at the terrible things that have occurred. We only have one Jerusalem and one Temple which is the beating heart of our people and stands for what was given to Moses on Sinai. We have a common enemy, and he approaches the walls with haste, to slay us all and enslave our children and women. We have all suffered from Rome and have fought so long against the legions. Surely you, even above myself, know of the sufferings, I speak of, from your battles in the north." Matthias paused as he watched John's face reveal a tinge of emotion at the memory of the sacking of Gischala, and the retreat south to Jerusalem.

"Continue, Matthias, I am listening," John said.

Matthias raised his staff in the air and bowed his head briefly. "I am old in my years but wise in experience. I can look past the wrongdoings where your men disregarded the priestly ritual of selection and cast me from the Temple, but I have dedicated my life in service to God, and that does not end with the removal of a title, for which you have deprived me of. I still serve God, this city, and our people. You must realize that Titus will lead an army to this city to burn it and destroy everything we take as sacred. It has been confirmed by brothers from Masada that the Romans have left Alexandria and have crossed the Nile. Word from the north bears the report that the allied kings are emptying their lands of troops to join Vespasian. They will march for the port city of Caesarea Maritima. That gives us only weeks to prepare, for when they arrive upon these hills and mountains surrounding us, it will be too late.

"So, my lord Simon offers you a truce, to consider his offer of alliance." Matthias glanced back at Simon and for the first time since Simon's arrival in the city, the man looked pleased with the priest.

"Hear his words, John, and consider it. I ask for an alliance which will not offer up the points we control in this city, for that we can settle peacefully later. I only offer that we work together, share information, and unite our troops against concentrated attacks where need be. I will dispatch a messenger tonight to offer you a declaration of my word, and one which I ask you to provide to Eleazar so that we may meet together. That is all." Simon slowly turned and returned to his litter. He climbed inside, made himself comfortable upon the cushions, then taking one more glance upward, he nodded and the litter was picked up and carried away.

John watched Bagdatus and his men follow the litter as the moaning of the wind raced between the towers. All eyes seemed to fall on him as each man considered the words of Simon and Matthias. No matter how one looked at it, or how much one hated Simon and what he stood for, everyone knew that the three men: Simon, John and Eleazar, needed to face the Romans as an equal front or risk losing the city.

When Isaac felt that the silence was too much he became uncomfortable and shouted, "No more gawking here. Back to your stations and make ready until the changing of the guard."

"Isaac, Judah, come here," John finally spoke, swallowing the lump in his throat. "Matthias is right, we do have to think about an alliance."

"I don't trust him, John. It would be just like him to greedily storm the Outer Court the first moment we open the gates to his men thinking we're all friends. His men will not soon forget the casualties we caused them these last months, and Simon is one to loathe our very existence for the successes we have had." Judah looked to Isaac for support and received it with an eager nod from the Captain.

"I agree with you." John sighed and gazed up at the clouds spreading across the sky. "Once I have Simon's official declaration, I will deliver it to Eleazar, and await his response. If we can arrange a meeting, I will demand that Simon's men are not allowed admittance beyond the porticos of the Outer Court unless I allow it. We can station guards to keep an eye on things and trust that once the Romans do attack, Simon will be too caught up in defending the far northern walls from the enemy than to care about us. Once those siege towers and ramps are built, which the Romans are sure to construct, Simon will come crawling to us for our catapults and scorpions."

"Right." Isaac grinned nodding. "We can let the mongrel of a king know that it is we who hold the power in this city to cause hell for the Romans, and it is we who know how to operate the engines, not Simon. The man will be indebted to us and must realize that."

John rubbed his hands together. "Very well, look out for the message which Simon promised to deliver, and then alert me as soon as you have it in your hands. But do keep a wary eye on things; Simon has been known to be a man of smooth words and a desecrator of oaths." With that John departed taking a contingent of troops. Meanwhile, Isaac and Judah were left upon the ramparts to wait until dusk when the declaration of peace would be delivered to unify the city in a collective display of defiance against a world power that marched towards them from the deserts of Africa.

*   *   *

March 18th, 70 A.D. / 19th of Adar, 3830
Five miles southwest of Raphia
Near the Judean Border

Gaius waited for his troops to get the screaming prisoner under control as he stood in the heat of the day with a hammer lowered at his side. The man tried to lift himself from the wooden crossbeam, but the iron nail held firm, which had been driven through his wrist just below the hand and between the bone crushing the veins and arteries. Blood seeped from the wound and bubbled around the head of the nail as the man howled in pain and shook his head, spittle spraying from his mouth. His eyes filled with agony and he shouted in a language not understood by the soldiers who laughed, slapped the man in the face, and then overcame the prisoner's fury and held his outstretched arm firmly against the wood.

Gaius stepped over the crossbeam and knelt by the man's unscathed arm as the prisoner was trying to brace himself for the next shock of pain that would split through his naked body. He started sobbing horribly as he felt the nail's spike touch his sensitive skin. Soon it would be driven through him into the wood beneath by a succession of hard pounding blows. Gaius held the nail upright, moved the hammer above it, counted to three in his head, and brought it down with a crushing speed as it pierced the skin and slammed its way through the bone. With another heavy delivery the nail split through the other end and had broken the wood. After two more steady pounds upon the nail's head, it was firmly embedded. Saliva ran from the corners of the unconscious man's mouth as his body shuddered from the shock of pain that raced in tremors through his body.

The legionaries cheered Gaius for the quick delivery but the Centurion shrugged it off. He shook his head as he took a step back, dropped the hammer into the dust, and motioned for the troops to raise the beam upon the top of a tall two-metre stump which had been dumped upright into a hole and then filled with dirt. The business was quick; the two soldiers on each side picked up the beam with another holding the dangling legs of the prisoner. Then quickly, they passed the beam up to another soldier upon a ladder leaning against the pole. With a grunt, the legionary manoeuvred the beam into a chiseled gap on the top of the stump. With an extra long iron spike, the man on the ladder pounded the nail through the cross beam and into the stump, thus securing the beam to the pole for a traditional Roman-style crucifixion. While the top nail was hammered in place, the soldiers on the ground who held the prisoner's legs, twisted them sideways, and turned them inwards at an awkward angle, too low for the condemned man to breathe properly.

Next, another long spike was brought to drive through the man's ankles. This was done with precise blows upon the iron head as the nail shattered the bone and sprayed blood upon the executioners. The final spike was driven as deep as it would go and then the job was done. The legionaries congratulated themselves on a job well done while the prisoner, now slowly waking up, was condemned to a slow death in constant agony. With every strained breath, the man would be forced to lift his body upward upon the iron nails. The legionaries knew that eventually the man would grow too weak to continue breathing, which required the painful shift of weight. He might last two days, maybe three, but it always resulted in the victim's eventual suffocation.

Gaius sighed and looked around at the other four prisoners being hoisted up by their crossbeams to the waiting posts behind them. They all struggled and wailed for mercy but the more they sounded their agony, the more the soldiers laughed and mocked them. Gaius spotted Titus sitting upon his horse, Achilles, watching the spectacle. The prisoners had all been brigands, believed to be spies from Masada or Jerusalem, trailing the army and sending back valuable information. Without mercy, Titus had listened to the captured prisoner's defence, and then had condemned them to die upon the crosses using whatever wood could be gathered. It was the Roman method of warning everyone who traveled this road that those who took up arms against the Roman Empire would be shown no quarter and would surely die a painful death: rotting upon the crosses from which they hung.

Titus noticed Gaius' stare and gave a firm nod before turning Achilles and galloping off to rejoin the legions which marched by in successive order. The long column of troops stretched for miles as cavalry patrols constantly skirted their flanks and drove out into the wilderness in search of mischief, while baggage trains of donkeys, oxen, and camels carried and pulled supplies. Soon, the order of priests passed, clothed in their white robes and accompanied by carts containing sheep and goats for future sacrifices. Junior apprentices kept a sharp eye on the braying animals as a number had tried to leap to freedom near Tanis, one even drowning while they boarded the galleys on the Nile from Nicopolis.

"Finish quickly here and let's move on!" Gaius barked the order, retrieving his helmet from one of his men standing nearby. The First Cohort had disappeared from sight through the winding desert hills of rock and sand, but Gaius knew he would rejoin them when they set up camp. Titus had pushed them hard and they had averaged nearly sixteen miles a day with few water breaks to recuperate. It was rumoured among the ranks that despite the urging of his officers against marching the men to exhaustion, Titus believed it necessary to impress the enemy with the legion's speed and to clear the enemy territory swiftly in order to reach Gaza where the presence of resistance thinned.

The night camping around the temple of the Casian Jupiter had been one of the coolest and had brought relief to the cohorts throughout the two legions of over ten thousand men. The temple had been an inspiring and sacred sight to behold, but strict military discipline had prevailed as the soldiers and a majority of the officers had been forbidden to even approach it. The local priests had put up with the presence of the soldiers but had warmly catered to Titus and his senior staff. They allowed the Prince to make payments for sacrifices as a ceremony ensued in honour of the passing legions so that the gods may grant them the necessary strength to crush Jerusalem.

The night at the Casian Jupiter, Gaius had spent within the confinements of his personal quarters involved in a competitive game of dice with Quintus, Cicero, Marius, and Rufus, all trusted brothers-in-arms. They drank wine and talked long into the night. Finally, in the early hours of the morning, they had departed, feeling like scholars of the world, as they made for their tents in order to catch a few hours of sleep before another long day's march.

Now, only a few miles from Raphia, Gaius took a long drink from his water skin, slung it over his arm and held his head high as he carried his rod of office. He led his execution detail silently back upon the road for Raphia while a dust cloud drifted above the earth engulfing the snake-like column of troops, arrayed in armour as each man carried his supplies upon his spear balanced on a shoulder of steel plates.

Once upon the road, Gaius noticed a strange man riding a mare and wearing expensive, long cloaks of linen and silk coloured with priceless dyes from the orient. The man had a long beard, tanned face, and wore a simple, knitted flat head covering which only concealed a small section of the top of his head. He had long curly locks flowing over his ears and had a distinguished, educated dignity about him as he seemed completely unaware of the column of troops marching next to him. The only significant gesture he gave, which betrayed any awareness of the troops, was an annoyed wave of his hand every once and awhile at the dust lingering in the air from the thousands of marching hobnailed sandals.

Not recognizing the man, realizing he was neither of Italian decent nor from the nobility of allied kings, Gaius quickened his pace until he was within earshot of the man and called out to him raising a hand. Yosef ben Matityahu, who had graciously been loaned a horse by Titus, heard the beckon immediately and glanced over his shoulder to see a Centurion signaling him to hold up. He reined in the stubborn mount and turning, smiled at the approaching officer.

The Centurion looked middle aged to Yosef and appeared to be one of Titus' battle hardened soldiers with vast experience due to the torques which hung upon his cuirass overtop his breastplate. The sight of this Centurion was unique compared to the smooth faced, young, junior officers he had witnessed on the drill grounds outside of Rome before the war. As the Centurion drew closer, he gazed up with puzzled eyes and Yosef bowed his head respectfully, saying in Greek, "What can a humble man do for such an officer as yourself?"

"Who are you? I have never seen you before." Gaius came to a halt and motioned for his men to continue ahead of him.

"I am Yosef ben Matityahu, former General of the northern forces that were driven into the dust by your Emperor Vespasian."

Gaius licked his dry lips and lowered his rod of office as he felt a bead of sweat run down the side of his face. "I have heard of you, the Jewish General who was captured at Jotapata. Why are you with the army?"

"My order is to accompany Titus as an interpreter."

"You go to the city?" Gaius asked perplexed. "They will do everything they can to capture you, you understand? Then what a frightful way to meet your end."

"Maybe better than your crucifixions, I might add," Yosef said, gesturing to the distant crosses.

Gaius pointed his rod ahead of him and said, "Come, let us continue moving."

"Begging your permission, Centurion, but who might you be? You're obviously one of high importance to whatever legion you hail from." Yosef studied the decorations upon Gaius' chest for a moment, then noticing an image of a lightning bolt upon one of the torques, he said, "Fulminata, you're with the XII. Let me guess, judging by your class you're a Primi Ordines of the First Cohort, maybe the Primus Pilus of that centuria." Yosef smiled at the impressed look on the Centurion's face. He pointed to one of the medals, which signified bravery, and then to another which stood for being the first man over a walled city. "I conclude that you're Gaius Cornelius Antony, am I right?"

Gaius' face could not hold his surprise and Yosef chuckled merrily at the shock upon the officer's face. He looked up at the strange man and nodded. "A sharp eye, I might say, and one who knows the meaning of Roman military medals. How did you know my name?"

"Ah, well Titus and I have conversed on a number of occasions. He brags about you, but never tell him I said so. It is you who should be riding this horse, not I."

Gaius shook his head. "I march with my troops."

"And you're content with that?"

Gaius shrugged. "I'm a Centurion, it is my duty. It's a soldier's life, the life I chose."

"And it leads you through a hot desert on the way to lay siege to a vast city of world renown. You may find comfort in the life of a soldier, but that life I could never have asked for."

Gaius scowled and squinted as he looked up. "But you led forces against the legions in the north. You fortified towns and trained your men to bear weapons against us."

"Yes, I did, but it was not the life I desired. The government had elected me as a General to organize the resistance of the north. I did not choose it. Yes, I organized armies and armed cities, but only in preparations for defence. I never led a full scale assault against the legions and when I had no other choice in Jotapata, alas I had to surrender. I am a priest by birth, and a scholar. I spent much time in Rome. I learned many things from your customs and discipline. Your military training and drills fascinated me, but it would never be the life I would crave."

"I do not crave military glory. I merely serve Rome and do this to keep my family fed. It is the only life I have known. I went through the schooling to get where I am now. My family was of high birth, and I never had to serve in the ranks with a pilum. I rose through the class of the Centurions and was elected to the First Cohort late in the first year of the rebellion, well after Cestius Gallus' defeat."

Yosef was silent for a moment and then looked down. "How did you receive promotion after that defeat? Was not your legion the one operating in that withdrawal?"

"What a polite way of putting it, Yosef ben Matityahu. We never operated in the withdrawal from Jerusalem. We were routed and butchered on account of our leading

Consul and Governor Gallus; he himself had not the balls to take the city, and we lost an eagle." Gaius momentarily hung his head in shame. "I shall never know why he fled the Upper City while we prepared to sack your Temple, but he did and my men died for it. I was one of the few who covered the breach as the legionaries filed out. I met a Zealot ambush head on and even after my men were slain, I kept fighting until near exhaustion. My right thigh was sliced open, my left arm broken, and my helmet was partially crushed into my skull. I was carried away leaving behind eight dead Jews upon the ground and I was still holding my sword." Gaius touched the round pommel of his gladius and Yosef noticed a small silver plaque screwed into the polished wood.

"It says '*Victrix Judeo*'," Gaius did not bother translating as he knew Yosef would understand the meaning. Gaius saw a flash of sting against Yosef's pride at the meaning of the Latin phrase and he quickly said, "Cestius Gallus had it commissioned for me when I took charge of the Fulminata the day it was assigned by Vespasian for the Judean campaign. I wear it to honour my Imperator and his gracefulness he has shown me."

"You need not defend yourself, Gaius Antony," Yosef said. "You only fought against your enemy and did so because it was your duty and will to survive."

Gaius solemnly nodded. "I have killed many men in many different campaigns throughout the empire. You Jews have been some of the toughest warriors I have ever come across. However, despite all the men I have killed, and those who have fallen beneath the feet of the legions, it never gave me satisfaction like it may give some."

"Then why do it?"

"For the glory of our empire and to protect her borders," Gaius replied.

"There is no end, is there, Centurion?"

"What do you mean?"

"Our Holy Scriptures outline many empires like Rome who were once mighty and bathed in glory, only to be crushed and erased from the annals of history. God allowed a time for the Egyptians, Philistines, Hittites, Assyrians, Babylonians, Greeks, and the empires of Alexander's generals, and they all came to an end, including our Maccabean era." Yosef paused for a moment to retrieve his water and then slowly said, "I dare ask you, Centurion, when will Rome's time come?"

"When the gods see fit not to use us anymore in the world, I would suppose. Rome was built out of strength, and as long as the gods see that power they will look favourably upon us. The reason why those other empires fell was because they lacked the strength to lead. Rome has conquered the earth and therefore possesses the power of the gods as Romulus must have felt."

"*Shema Yisrael Adonai Elihenu, Adonai Echad.*" Yosef watched Gaius glance up at him with a puzzled expression and the Jewish General leaned forward, gently pointing at Gaius like a tutor instructing his student. "God is one, and there is no other God but the God of my people."

"I almost forgot, your people only worship one god and have one Temple," Gaius sarcastically replied, shaking his head. "I will never understand you people. Your eating customs are strange, you cling to your books and scrolls, you become like sloths one day of the week, your people wear strange boxes on their foreheads, and they dress in funny garments with strings hanging from them. However, I will say," Gaius pointed his finger in the air. "The strangest to me is your stubborn worship of the 'one *true* God'. You even refuse to have an icon! Your invisible God. Why believe in such a thing?"

Yosef shook his head and gestured to the desert around him as he spoke, "Because God chose Abraham and revealed to him that all other deities were false. God chose a people, the people of Israel, and saved them. He proved to them through our history that all the other gods of the world were foolish. The God of my people gave us His Law to be written upon our hearts and a godly set of dictates to live a life of purpose, one that was pleasing to Him. We are called to be holy and upright, to preserve His Torah, and to keep His precepts. We are to honour God, observe the Shabbat, and love our neighbour, which was and is the essence of Torah, Moses' revelation at Sinai."

"I will never understand that about your people. In a world such as ours, it seems beyond my sensibilities how you can believe in such a thought as 'one true God'. It is strange indeed, since there has been a belief in many gods for thousands of years. We honour them and they give us what we need so they don't interfere with our lives. You can never quite trust them, but it is our duty as rulers of this world to acknowledge their existence and pay homage to them."

"God alone is the ruler of the world, not Jupiter or the many others you trust in." Yosef chuckled lightly to himself. "May I speak plainly?" Gaius nodded and Yosef continued, "Perhaps it would save you all from so much wasteful rituals to these gods of yours if you would only believe in one God. Now who sounds strange if a man worships a god he cannot trust so that the god will only leave him alone and not torment him? It is but figments from the minds of men, myths intended to control and keep men in fear."

Gaius shook his head and looked up at Yosef. "It does sound strange when you state it such as you have. However, I have always honoured them and my ancestors, and they have watched over my family for years. Besides, if they do not exist, or are foolish figments of the imaginations of men as you say, than what power gives strength to our armies? Would the Jewish God allow Rome to oppress *His* people? This Jewish God appears to have left you to the wolves."

"Who knows the mind of God? Our God has never forsaken us to utter destruction, but according to the Scriptures, He promised Moses and the Children of Israel that as long as we followed His guidance we would be blessed; when we did not, we would be judged." Yosef stabbed the air passionately and declared, "I dare not say I know the mind of God. Perhaps it is a judgment we must pass through and

Rome is that judge for the time being, or perhaps this is the burden we must bear as the people chosen by God to be His nation. I believe God will one day cause the earth to tremble to awake the nations from a slumber so that the whole world will realize the power of God."

"Then if this is true, and the nations must awake from a slumber as you call it, then I dare say, 'Woe to Rome' if this God of the Jews shall unveil His power as we march to destroy the capital of His people. I will leave that to the power of Jupiter and your God to decide who should unveil power and when."

Yosef looked down and grimaced at the heathen statement. He shook his head and hastily said, "Such a saying should be used with great caution, for something just like it was declared long ago, Centurion Antony. From the mouths of the priests of Baal, they mocked the prophet Elijah, until from heaven there poured fire, it consumed an altar of wood and water, and four hundred and fifty priests of Baal were put to the sword."

* * *

CHAPTER XII

April 12th, 70 A.D. / 15th of Nisan, 3830
Southern side of the Temple Mount
The Great Arched Bridge
Jerusalem

The colossal bridge of stone, so often crowded by pilgrims, had been forcibly cleared at noon. Soldiers from Simon's army within the city had emptied the plaza and shops upon the streets, which caused uproar from the merchants who cursed them and complained concerning the money they would lose. The money changers and regular handlers of sacrificial animals were ushered away with much shouting and protest. Under the strict orders of Simon ben Giora, his soldiers showed no sympathy and were determined in their yelling and shoving for the people to leave with promises that they could return in two hours time. John of Gischala had been equally charged with a task that called for maximum security, as his Zealots made sure the Royal Stoa was secured and all unnecessary soldiers were vacant from the colonnades of the porticoes looming above the Great Arched Bridge and steps below them.

The typical day's business was disrupted for the second time in years of inner strife and civil war, as the three factionary commanders agreed to hold another meeting regarding the defence of Jerusalem. Being able to temporarily set aside their differences, John of Gischala, Simon ben Giora, and Eleazar ben Simon gathered to meet at the bridge on the southwestern side of the Temple Mount, a well-known place where all three commanders could keep an eye on each other.

Representing each of the three factions, twenty soldiers had been agreed upon to accompany each commander. They stood behind their respected leaders exchanging glares of loathing aversion. Thus, upon a beautiful spring day, the base of the arch was bristling with twenty armed guards of Simon's force. John's troops were stationed at the top of the bridge and Eleazar's men allowed upon the colonnades above. Besides the selected troops accompanying each warlord, officers of each faction stood at the helm of their troops, anticipating the moment when the three commanders would partake in their council concerning the imminent arrival of the legions.

Simon stood at the base of the stairs among his men and motioned for them to remain. All his officers were present, James ben Soras and Simon ben Cathas being the most experienced and influential of the force. However, Simon ben Giora had given specific instructions that it was to be him solely who would ascend the stairs and meet with John and Eleazar. With much dispute over the matter, Simon had silenced the men with vicious threats. Then he had climbed the stairwell, dressed in elaborate garments, with a grim smile upon his face.

John stood at the top of the arch, arms crossed and a look of disdain within his eyes as he glanced at the hulking form of Eleazar at his side. Since the birth of Simon's power in Jerusalem, John had hated Eleazar, but on this day, and with pressure from Simon, Eleazar had been allowed to gather for another meeting which would decide the fate of the city. Eleazar gave John a questionable glance, shook his burly head and then scratched the deep scar upon his cheek which always irritated him. John sighed, troubled by Eleazar and annoyed at the competitive Zealot commander.

"Wait here, I'll be back," John said turning slightly, looking back at Judah and Isaac. Next to John's two most trusted men stood three of Eleazar's officers: Simon ben Ezron, Judas ben Chelcias, and Hezekiah ben Chobari. All the men were hardened fighters, and had proven to be ruthless and unforgiving in the midst of fortifying the Inner Court of the Temple which had become their stronghold. John sensed a foreboding edginess in Judah and furrowed his brow in question. He glanced at Isaac for a moment and then cleared his throat. "Is something wrong, Judah?"

Judah felt foolish and shook his head. He watched John give him a strange look and then he turned away. This was the second meeting the three commanders had staged in the last number of weeks since the visit by Simon at the base of the Antonia. A lot of measures had been taken to ensure trust between the men as messengers had delivered letters declaring honour and temporary peace. John had boasted to his officers the importance of the union. It was imperative for them to overlook the wrongs that had been committed in the past as the time had come to set aside differences and look to the future. Although, John had seemed optimistic towards the union, the first meeting had proven to be a tense time due to the fact that on two occasions the guards had nearly erupted into a fight over heated words.

Saying nothing, John and Eleazar quietly strolled out from the shade of the colonnades and descended the stone staircase to a large landing. The meeting place held strategic significance for it was in the open and neither side would be able to spring an ambush to violate the alliance. John and Eleazar halted when they reached the landing and the air about them was hushed because the streets below had been cleared of vendors and merchants. John approached the edge of the landing and glanced down upon the homes stretching beyond the high walls of the arch. The rooftops were vacant of all life as the inhabitants possessed more sense than to emerge and witness the meeting of the three feared warrior leaders.

When Simon appeared at the crest of the steps, he slowed his pace and let go of the hems of his robes. He smiled, politely bowed, clapped his hands together once and said with a laugh, "How fitting it is that we should gather here under the shadow of the Temple walls." He paused for a moment and then continued, "Eleazar, have you anything to say?"

Eleazar gave a low guttural sound of displeasure as he glared at Simon, and John quickly spoke up, not giving the man a chance to say something offensive, "We have gathered here to discuss the terms for defending this city."

"Why, yes we have," Simon smugly replied.

"First, there is a matter to settle. We have been fighting among ourselves for many months now and have tried to preserve our own interests. With the arrival of the legions, we must be able to effectively mobilize and shift positions to counter assaults. There needs to be freedom to move our forces in and out of our controlled positions."

"You speak of letting Simon's men into the Inner Court?" Eleazar retorted, shooting a hateful look at John and shaking his head.

"No, Simon's men would have no reason to enter your held ground unless it was for reasons of worship. I merely point to my forces having the need to move through the upper or lower parts of the city and Simon's men needing admittance into the Temple courts," John replied.

"You speak only of reinforcing positions, am I correct?" Simon asked.

John nodded. "Yes, it must be allowed and our men must not be harassed."

Eleazar grunted to himself and crossed his arms. "This should be cleared with us, or through our ranks. I trust no man who would enter the sanctuary suspiciously. I let one man in and they all could come."

"You speak of the sanctuary as if it were your own, Eleazar," Simon said, which resulted in another guttural grunt from the displeased Zealot commander. "I agree, in circumstances that warrant reinforcing or designated patrols cleared by us or our higher ranks, men should be granted access to different areas of the city. Apart from that, we defend our own corridors and share information. The Romans will surround the entire city and seek to shut us in."

"We must look to food storage," John stated as he rested his hand on the pommel of his sword.

"We would have been in a better state had not you two burned many stores of harvested grain," Simon added shaking his head.

"The same could be said to you, Simon!" Eleazar countered, raising his voice. "You parade like a king and steal our due wealth."

"Are you and John on speaking terms now, Eleazar, that you must become his voice?" Simon replied back.

"Silence!" John said, holding up his hands. "We cannot do this. Once Titus arrives, we will have nearly fifty thousand Romans at our gates. We cannot stay divided." John paused for a moment and continued when he had both men's attention. "Eleazar, you have vast food stores in your possession that can be distributed, we can gather more in the city and forage outside the walls. Declare rations for your troops and we should make due."

"Very well. So, it is agreed, no mixing of units and soldiers unless it is authorized or needed for reinforcing points of our defences that come under extreme pressure." Simon glanced from Eleazar to John. The men nodded and Simon continued, "It has been weeks since they departed Egypt, and we know they left the northern coast some days ago. Reports from the countryside state this as fact. When the legions arrive we must understand that it will be near impossible to access proper information beyond our walls, at least information we can rely on. The Romans will hunt out spies and anyone connected with us, not to mention farms and towns surrounding Jerusalem will be sacked and burned."

"They will no doubt be bringing siege equipment and will do what Romans do best, build. That will require timber for ramps and earth for their works. While we wait behind our high walls, the Romans will dig and work continuously. This will give us an advantage over them to ambush." The first grin since the meeting's opening spread across John's face. "There are many gates and doors from this city, some known by the Romans, some not, and we can use that to our advantage in order to spring quick and calculated ambushes upon them. This could lower their morale and cause them to abandon their effort. We have something they do not possess, the resolve never to give up. We will sell our lives willingly for the protection of this city. The Romans will be overwhelmed and brought to their knees. We shall orchestrate precise attacks, use trickery and fight them with everything we've got."

Suddenly a commotion grew from the men above the colonnades as they shouted and pointed towards the northeast, arguing among one another. Others stood in shock holding their spears close to their bodies and unsure of what to do. The three commanders, who had been engrossed in their complicated debate, now abandoned their discussion and stared blankly as a single soldier quickly trotted down the stairs. The man's eyes were filled with worry as sweat beaded his face. A look of utmost urgency was woven into his expression as he halted before the commanders and said, "Titus has arrived!"

John opened his mouth, but nothing escaped. He stood, dumbfounded at the report, as if he had never expected to hear it. A cool breeze quickly picked up and tugged at the loose garments hanging from his body. John tightened his grip on his sword and narrowed his gaze. As if captured in a daze, he bit his lower lip and softly said, "Where?"

The man nervously swallowed hard and took a deep gulp of fresh air. "They have crested the peak on Mount Scopus. They are still a fair distance away, but Titus' banner can be seen as well as that of cavalry contingents."

John hesitated a moment and then said, "Has anyone been alerted to this?"

The man nodded. "The guards posted saw the first glimpse; I heard them shout and ran to see for myself. By now the news will have spread."

For the first time in either Eleazar or John's recollection, Simon was completely serious as he took a step forward. Staring at John, he said, "We must go have a look and deploy our men to the walls. Keep a watch in the city, for we don't need the citizenry getting out of hand."

John nodded at Simon and glanced at Eleazar. "Come, let's look."

Simon turned and gave a wave to his men to follow and then the three commanders climbed the stairway and passed beneath the colonnade of the Royal Portico as they entered the Temple Mount. Men everywhere seemed to be immersed in chaos as they ran to and fro donning their armour, gathering weapons and loading catapults upon the walls. When they saw John emerge into the Outer Court accompanied by Eleazar and Simon, a sense of order was restored. With shouts from officers, the bustling soldiers tried to organize their defendable positions upon the ramparts which stretched the entire perimeter of the Temple plateau as trumpets blared above the commotion.

"Isaac, go send word to the Antonia to maintain maximum force above the walls and towers. I want a show for the Romans and for Titus to see the force which stands before him," John shouted to his captain who then ran towards the fortress.

"Bastards," Eleazar grumbled aloud. "So we will finally see the buggers we have all been waiting for."

John gave Eleazar a puzzled look and pushed the comment out of his mind. He watched the colonnades about the Outer Court bristle with spears as men manned the walls. The three commanders made it to the pillars of the eastern wall and passed beneath the portico roof. They ascended a set of stairs which led to the ramparts above and John shouted for the ramp to be cleared as he pushed his way through the throng of men. Eleazar and Simon followed closely along the walls above the Eastern Gate, as they glanced nervously out across the rising mountains. John looked over his shoulder and caught Judah's eye. The young Lion officer stared back as if he wished to say something, but his mind was a whirlwind, dealing with the harsh reality that now stood before him.

When John reached the edge of the rampart wall, he called for the men to step aside and to make way for him and the other commanders. The entire rampart became silent when John halted at the wall and stared out over the Kidron Valley and beyond at the hills connecting to the Mount of Olives to where Scopus lay. For the first time in his life, he felt his heart sink as the breeze stung his face. John fought to muster the strength he needed to show his men, but for a second he could not help but wonder about the road that lay ahead of him. Far in the distance and breaching the crest of Mount Scopus, he saw a dark mass of men slowly making their way down the slope into the saddle to climb the steep heights of the mountain known as Olives. Banners, flags, and standards could be seen hoisted above the ranks and carried proudly.

A formation of Roman cavalry broke off from the cohorts of troops and rode towards the west. When they crested the hill, they rallied into a large square formation among the rocks and olive groves littering the landscape. John squinted, sheltering his eyes from the sun as he saw a single Roman manoeuvre his horse a few metres ahead of the halted formation. The man sat atop a large black war horse, wearing a breastplate of gold and a silver helmet. He raised a baton-like rod high above his head and John anticipated the man shouting something inspirational to his troops. The man lowered the baton, remaining motionless as he gazed at the city which lay before him, the massive Temple rising up above the walls. John imagined the Roman taking in the grandeur of the city, considering the enormous endeavour entrusted to him, to take Jerusalem and crush it without mercy. John straightened, and while pointing towards the man on the black horse, he motioned to Judah to come to his side. "See that man there, Judah?" Judah nodded anxiously and John softly said, "That's Titus, and he has come to kill us."

*   *   *

CHAPTER XIII

April 12th, 70 A.D. / 15th of Nisan, 3830
Mount Scopus
Outskirts of Jerusalem

"My Prince Titus, Jerusalem's walls stand before you. What shall you do?"
Tiberius Alexander, the second-in-command of the legions of Judea, leaned forward
in his saddle. He pointed to the distant city walls beyond the rocky valley below him
which was filled with obliquely situated gardens, groves of olive trees, hedges, and
boulders scattered about.

Titus raised his chin slightly and gently tapped his heels into the flanks of Achilles
and his horse cantered forward from the formation of Roman cavalry. He navigated
around a large rock surrounded by olive trees with thick trunks as his men remained
drawn up behind him, with all eyes on their prince. Titus saw the entire city before
him, as if it had risen out of the ground like a mighty titan released from the depths.
The enormous walls stood defiant, and the glistening white marble of the Temple
shone in the sunlight. His eyes scanned the walls beyond the Eastern Gate, as they
wound down into the City of David below. The battlements were high and sturdy, the
ground at its base unforgiving and rough. All gates were barred, and Titus watched as
hundreds of people appeared on the ramparts to observe the arrival of his legions.

Glancing to the far right, Titus traced the walls as they followed the plateau of
hills and then turned west as they stretched as far as the eye could see. The view
appeared to ripple like the sea due to the heat which beat upon the land. In the
distance, and rising up like a beacon from the earth, loomed the Psephinus Tower, a
thirty-metre-high, octagonal structure defending the northwest corner of the Third
Wall. Beyond the looming white face of the Temple, he could also make out the
shapes of the three sister towers: Hippicus, Phasael, and Miriamne, with Hippicus
being the tallest at thirty four metres.

Jerusalem was massive; it was a city of walls and narrow streets, of obstacles
undeniably immense, like the four-towered Antonia, and it was filled with a population
which hated the very existence of Rome. These were the last great defenders of
the Jewish cause. Titus felt the weight of the task, appointed to him, rest heavily
upon his shoulders. He knew that the city had three main bastions of walls defending
different corridors, and the Temples colonnades made the holy sanctuary of the Jews
a fortress in itself. As well as being a fortified city, it also contained beauty, not to be
compared with Rome, but nonetheless filled with palaces, gymnasiums, baths, pools,
high archways and bridges of stone.

Jerusalem was divided into five sections and Titus had thoroughly studied them all: the City of David to the south of the Temple, the Lower City below that, the Upper City to the northwest. Beyond a high divisional wall lay the Second Quarter or the Mishneh, and to the north was the recently developed 'Bezetha' or New City. Titus knew every corridor housed endless possibilities for the Jewish rebels to ambush his troops and rain fire down upon their heads, and every street would cost many lives as they would drive deeper and deeper, strangling the city slowly until it would be out of breath. Titus knew the demise of the city would not be taken by a simple siege, but by grim determination, accepting the fact that many of his troops would perish.

Titus glanced to his far left and observed a number of the alae accompanying him as they ascended the heights of the Mount of Olives. Their ranks were neat and assembled with perfection. Although they did not march like legionaries, nor draw the same attention, they were still an impressive force. Banners and standards could be seen hoisted above the ranks, along with a mass of Syrian and Palmyrene bowmen, winding through the hills like a serpent, accompanied by nearly six hundred mounted cavalry.

Titus turned in his saddle, looking to the north, as he observed the solid advance of Legio XV led by Titus Frigius, and Legio XII commanded by Marcus Octavian. Both legions marched in column upon the road stretching into the far distance as hundreds of pack animals hauled artillery pieces and provisions. A separate army, of a much smaller scale compared to a legion, was made up of priests, servants, and slaves, who trailed in the rear, shadowed by a vanguard of cavalry.

Titus could make out each proud signifier throughout the ranks as they carried the signum of each century with the sun reflecting from the metal emblems upon the poles, which were topped by hands with the palms facing outwards. Along with the military standards, men bearing *vexilla* in the front ranks stood out from all the rest as they paraded the brilliant red and purple banners of fringed cloth with legionary designations upon them.

At the extreme head of each legionary column rode a delegation of officers supported by the *imaginifer* carrying the *imagio* of Emperor Vespasian and the *aquilifer* who hoisted the eagle at the head of each First Cohort. The eagles were the pride of the five thousand men strong, and any one of them would sell their lives dearly in the protection of the eagle's preservation, rather than see their legion shamed by losing it in combat. That had been the case with Legio XII in the first year of the rebellion and Titus knew it would be fresh in all their minds. This would be the place to cleanse their name from the disgrace of history which had befallen them.

A thunderous blast of the *cornu* sounded, reverberating from the mountains as the legions made a declaration of their presence and a display of their power. Each aquilifer, hoisting the legionary eagle, raised them higher to the pounding drums as they paraded the symbol of Rome. The jingling of the men's studded iron straps hanging from each cingulum added to the inspiring dread of the troops as they beat the road with their *caligae* in quick time with drums and trumpets sounding from the military bands.

The previous night Titus had reviewed all plans and expectations with his senior command, then had passed the same message in person to all centurions gathered before his tent at Beit El. It was clear what Titus wished to relay to the Jewish rebels of the city, that to make a stand against the power of Rome was futile and they would be treated as traitors and criminals of the empire. There were to be no mistakes, no mishaps, and no engaging of the Zealots of Jerusalem on this day. Everyone looked to a tense standoff as the equivalent of four legions of alae and two Roman legions would dig trenches around the perimeters of their camps and pile the stones high to ensure effective protection.

The allied kings and the cavalry accompanying Titus would set up camp upon Scopus and in the gap before the Mount of Olives. Fulminata XII and Apollinaris XV would secure Scopus until the other legions arrived. After this, they would pack up and move to a new location, three hundred and seventy metres to the north of Psephinus Tower, which was to be Titus' base camp. During the next day, with the arrival of Macedonica V from Emmaus and Fretensis X from Jericho, the final two legions would dig in deep. Legio V would be across from the Hippicus Tower on the western side of the city and Legio X would hold the Mount of Olives. If the Jews thought the sight of the alae and two legions was frightening, then Titus dared them to face the hopelessness of their future with a grand display of might as another ten thousand legionaries would appear, spewing over the mountains the following day.

"There moves Agrippa's units and bowmen, my Prince. Sohaemus is behind him, and Antiochus moves his troops around to the west as planned," Tiberius said, swatting a fly away from his face and shifting uncomfortably upon the back of his mount. "We shall have the Twelfth and Fifteenth follow suit to their respected positions, securing this mountain and enforcing your camp. Word is that the legions of Emmaus and Jericho will be on time for your show tomorrow."

"Very good, Tiberius," Titus replied, wiping the sweat from his brow. He felt emboldened and godlike atop Mount Scopus wearing his finest armour, despite the other mounted officers who wished to escape the heat under the shade of their tents. He lowered his gaze to the rod of office clutched firmly in his hand and stared like a visionary at the bronze eagle attached to its end.

"Sire, you should address the men," Tiberius said, letting out a sigh. A short breeze cooled his tanned thighs, uncovered from the tunic he wore under his armour. Greaves of silver and bronze were strapped to his shins as a sticky sensation could be felt beneath them from the sweat that collected.

Titus swung Achilles around and faced his troopers. A look of passion and fire filled his eyes as he cleared his throat and shouted, "We stand now at the gates of destiny. Look before you! Behold a city of rebels dwell there, defiant and mocking the power of *Roma*. We are sons of Mars and inheritors of the will of the gods. We are strong and have marched across the world. We now see the face of our future, wrapped in glory and bathed in immortality.

"You men are the finest of *Roma*. I would not go to war with anyone else. Mars has given us his will to conquer and crush all those who oppose him. He is the god of war and blood, and he is the god of our ancestors. Do not fear the Jews. They only worship one God, but we have many, and they are with us today! Men, you are Romans, you represent the face of Caesar! *Roma* has come to the gates of Jerusalem; may the city quake under its foot. May their men feel pain and their wives and children taste slavery for the treason they have committed. Do not be faint of heart beneath the shadow of Jerusalem's walls. We shall destroy them and watch as the towers and stone crash upon the ground. May the populace moan in misery when the ram touches the wall and may the city weep." Titus raised his rod of office high above his head and shouted, "Hail, Caesar, Father of us all!"

The troopers replied with a bellow as they raised spears and the officers outstretched their hands. Tiberius Alexander rode forward and drew his horse up alongside Titus. "So, how do you want to do this? There are still some civilities we must abide by."

"You liked my speech?" Titus replied with a clever smile.

Tiberius shrugged. "It was necessary. We definitely need to inspire these men for the coming weeks ahead."

"They are wolves, they shall do just fine."

Tiberius nodded solemnly. "Shall we send Yosef down to them or wait for the legions to arrive tomorrow?"

"Yosef is a weapon I intend to use, but not this early. I wish to let the fate of those people confront them personally with the arrival of the rest of the army. As for now, I wish to ride forward and inspect Psephinus Tower and test the city." Titus noticed Tiberius' shock, removed his helmet and tossed it at a servant who came running over.

"My Prince, I strongly advise against that. We do not have an accurate measure of their potency at this point and we have not gathered our full strength."

"My dear General, we go forward not to engage them, just to get a closer look at the one who stands in our way." Titus swung his leg over the saddle and hopped down upon the ground. With a jerk of his neck he directed the servant to remove his breastplate. "We shall descend this mountain and ride past the large gate upon the length of the wall which the scouts reported to me earlier this morning. We will detour away from the gate and along the wall until we can have a closer look at the tower. Have the auxiliary shadow our unit and form up the Boars. Marcus Sulla shall ride with us." The servant finished stripping the Prince of his breastplate and Titus shooed him away.

"My lord, you go without armour?" Tiberius worriedly asked.

"I do, it's bloody hot out. Anyway, I have what I need," he tapped his sword upon his side and leapt onto Achilles' back. "Now, I want Marcus to accompany me with his men."

"Yes, my Prince, as you wish."

"I do wish it, Tiberius," Titus responded with a grin.

Tiberius struck his breastplate in salute and then swung his mount around and shouted to the company of troopers as a single, loud trumpet blast echoed from the rocks and trees about them. Titus pointed his rod ahead of him as Marcus Sulla Maximus came to his side followed by a contingent of his Boars. Like a bolt of lightning suddenly shattering the ground, Titus led the way with a shout and Achilles lunged forward into a gallop.

* * *

"John, they're on the move! Titus leads his men!" shouted a soldier to the left standing upon the battlements to get a clearer view. "They ride west!"

John pushed past a number of soldiers followed by Judah, Caleb, and the other officers upon the ramparts. Both Eleazar and Simon had not moved as they watched the distant enemy cavalry pouring down the slopes of Scopus and into the valley. John did not waste a moment waiting for the other factionary commanders for he was worried what Titus was doing. It had not taken long for them to realize the distant mass of troops upon the slopes were not Roman legions but allied contingents aiding in the siege of Jerusalem. A banner of Agrippa had been sighted among the small army and that had sent the men upon the wall into an uproar. They had shouted and hurled curses to the distant army, but that had come to nothing as the troops most likely could not hear a thing above the marching ranks and the pounding of hooves.

Now, John seemed spooked as he pushed men aside and found a spot along the wall where he could make out Titus and his cavalry much clearer. He squinted and shielded his eyes from the sun as he strained to make sense of the sudden manoeuvre. He ignored Simon's annoying proclamation that with a hundred mounted horses, Titus was a harmless threat and was most likely scouting the city for himself, but John would have none of it.

"The Boars! Caleb! It's the Boars!" Judah said suddenly with intensity.

John turned swiftly, glaring at the two men standing behind him and then a look of question filled his eyes. "You know them?"

"I would recognize their banner any day, John. Look, see the standard they carry. Mounted on top is the boar head. They are a horse unit that we fought against. That is Marcus Sulla Maximus riding with Titus; the bastard massacred all my men." Judah clutched the hilt of his sword as vengeance seethed through his veins.

"We nearly killed him on two occasions," Caleb added, shaking his head and seeing his old rival near the bottom of Scopus. The uneven ground had slowed Titus' advance but the highly trained horses seemed to shrug off the treacherous rocks and pass by them as if they were nothing.

"John," Judah glanced at Caleb for a moment and then back at the bear-like man standing before him. "Let us use the far gate, the one along the wall. If we are quick enough, we can dash out and perhaps catch them off guard."

"And if we miss? We look like fools," John retorted.

"We have to take that chance. That's Titus down there, if we could kill him we…" Judah paused and glanced at Caleb for support.

"Yes," John thought to himself. "We would need a strong force."

"Use my men," Simon shouted joining the group. "I have at least five hundred men in that corridor." Simon pointed to Judah and said, "He could lead them; you seem like this is personal."

Judah nodded entertaining the idea. "Say the word, John! Caleb and I will kill them. We can reach the gate shortly."

John looked to Simon for a split instant and then gave a hurried nod. "Go, and fight hard."

A grin spread across Judah's face. This was the most alive he had felt in weeks and the adrenalin raced through his body. Retrieving a shield from one of the guards nearby, he sprinted off along the colonnade ramparts, followed closely at the heels by Caleb and Adam.

*   *   *

Achilles broke into a full gallop when he reached the bottom of the mountain, thundering upon the hard earth, and darting easily between gardens and trees. Titus slowed Achilles to a canter as the Boars accompanying him tried to keep up amidst the obstacles. The sun was at its height, but Achilles felt exhilarated as the trumpet call still sounded in his ears. Feeling the motion of his rider upon his back, Achilles tossed his head up in excitement and snorted as the wind rippled his mane and dried the glistening sweat upon his muscular flanks. Achilles responded to every motion of the reins, yielding to his rider who directed him to the left or right. The high walls of the city seemingly rose up into the clouds. The mass of horses behind him naturally chose the easier route across the ground in a rolling wave of thunder as if the very earth shook and threatened to split apart.

Titus leaned forward in his saddle and holding his rod out before him steered to the right as they approached the gate. He glanced left and squinted up at the high walls of gold coloured stones, massive in size, with distant faces upon its walls watching him. The column of smoke spiraling up into the heavens from the Inner Court of the Temple darkened the sky and the air smelled of a sweet burning aroma. The city was enormous and Titus imagined its walls being built by giants or the Cyclops of Homer's tales. It was so different than Rome, but still the fashion and architecture of the Italian artisans were emulated in its designs. Titus could see aqueducts in the distance and knew of the forum built within the city and the Antonia which had garrisoned the troops long ago. Still, the landscape was decorated with evidence that this was neither Italy nor a Roman city. Gone were the Italian hills and lush fields of green, instead they were replaced by tombs, gardens plots, olive groves, vineyards, shepherds and herds of sheep which dotted the countryside. The land of Judea was beautiful in a different way, but so foreign to the lands of his youth.

Titus glanced to his side, his musings interrupted as Marcus Sulla drew back on his reins like a crazed demon, flashing the blade of his sword in a sudden motion as he shouted, "To arms!"

Before Titus could react, Achilles suddenly reared, nearly throwing the Prince, as a barbed javelin narrowly missed his horse's throat. With a quick reaction, Titus drew his sword and while swinging Achilles around was confronted by a horde of Jewish fighters. Behind him, Marcus bellowed such a vicious and primal shout that some of the horses milling about reared in fear. Pointing his blade ahead of him, Marcus suddenly spurred his horse into the fray, knocking aside three Jewish fighters.

*   *   *

Judah had rallied Simon's troops quickly and had assembled them at the gate with the booming authority of his voice. Brandishing spears and swords, they had waited while a guard from the battlements above them had given the signal. The gate had opened with a mournful creaking sound swallowed oblivion as the Jewish soldiers surged from the gate like an unstoppable tidal wave. Around five hundred had been rallied in the muster, and now they charged across the ground closing the distance between them and the arrogant Romans who had been oblivious to this possibility. Titus and his Romans had thought of themselves as invincible, but as the hurled javelin had nearly killed the Prince's horse, he now learned firsthand what it was going to be like to attack the city of Jerusalem.

At first, it seemed like all five hundred soldiers had tunnel vision as they, in a wedge-like formation, made for Titus with echoing war cries. However, once the Roman cavalry had recovered from its surprise, they were able to present a partially solid formation and with a weak charge they slammed into the flank of the Jewish sortie. Despite the counter attack from the Romans, they were sorely outnumbered which began to show quickly as Jewish blades went to work stabbing the legs of the troopers, cutting their horses, or trying to pull the riders from their saddles. One horse darting out from the skirmish revealed its rider slumped over in the saddle, impaled by a spear as a loud ovation from the men on the battlements of the city broke out. The horse galloped away in fear, finally managing to spill its baggage as the body fell upon the rocky valley floor to be a meal for ravens later that day.

Judah narrowly dodged the thrust of a blade as it grazed by his face and then was retracted for another attempt by its wielder. Judah dodged around the Roman's mount staying out of the way from the horse's angry hooves. Finally, he was able to deliver a quick slash from his sword across the Roman's exposed thigh. The man wailed in pain and pulled back on his reins. Judah seized the opportunity, leapt forward, slashing the horse's chest open and causing the terrified animal to rear. The Roman tumbled from the saddle, shattering his arm upon the rocky ground and his shield was knocked away by Judah who then rammed the blade of his sword between the chinks of mail the man wore. The Roman screamed, horribly clawing at the ground in agony as he began to choke on his own blood while Judah drove the blade deeper. When the sword was withdrawn from the man's body, the trooper lay dead as the blade dripped with scarlet.

Judah glanced up and surveyed the scene. A number of Romans lay dead while a few others retreated with injured mounts. The ground also revealed numerous Jewish dead who lay between rocks and thistles, impaled by lances or cut apart by swords. Titus was still alive and had managed to retreat to the rear, his leg was covered in blood, yet Judah could not make out if he had been wounded.

Judah looked everywhere for Marcus but could not see the Tribune as a trumpet sounded and the Romans were recalled. The Jewish attack was dwindling down at this point as men were exhausted or had more sense than to attack the formed Roman cavalry with lowered spears at the ready. While men were still fighting in isolated numbers, the main group on both sides seemed to be giving way. Then Judah saw him, the large Tribune brandishing his blood-stained gladius with gore splattered upon his greaves and breastplate. The man seemed to be daring the Jews to attempt another charge. Every so often when a few did, Marcus would ride out alone and scare them away with a valiant shout. Titus could be seen behind the Tribune waving his hands about and yelling at nobody in particular. Enraged that this had even occurred, Titus appeared to be trying to organize some kind of action as he hotly discussed something with another officer who kept pointing back to Mount Scopus.

"That's him!" Caleb said, lowering his sword by Judah's side. "Adam couldn't get to him. He threw his spear but it was as if the Tribune expected it."

"Where is Adam now?" Judah replied, trying to catch his breath, his cloak soaked in sweat and stained in blood.

"Rallying the men on the flanks. Shall we fall back?"

Judah shook his head. "We can't let the city see us retreat first. Form up the men. We will charge them head on. They will break for sure and it will be good for morale."

Caleb turned, shouted, and waved his sword in the air above his head. Judah kept staring at Marcus as the Tribune rode up and down the formation of his exhausted men. It appeared that Titus was not in favour of another attack for he had broken through the ranks and was now talking with the hotheaded Tribune. Judah watched Marcus shake his head and turn away. It was then that Judah knew Marcus had locked eyes with him. For a moment, Judah wondered if the Tribune would even recognize him. Suddenly the Tribune, known for being ruthless, loving women, and hating his fellow officers, lifted his blade and bowed his head with a grin plastered across a blood speckled face. He gave a shout acknowledging Judah, then turned his horse and rode away accompanied by Titus and the remaining troopers. With the sight of the retreating enemy, the men upon the walls of Jerusalem cheered for their first victory had been secured over the godless, Roman pagans.

*   *   *

Pure joy and exultation seemed ripe within the walls of Jerusalem. Civilians and soldiers alike celebrated at the news that Titus had nearly been killed by a Jewish onslaught and had fled leaving behind many dead. The weapons and armour brought back from the dead attested to this fact as Simon's Idumeans and John's Zealots cheered and paraded the helmets and segmented chest armour through the streets on poles. Men waved sword blades in the air and others hoisted shields and spears. The captured plunder would be put to vital use when the waves of legionaries attacked the walls. For the time being however, men, women, and children tried to ignore the impending danger that loomed beyond the walls as they celebrated.

Others were not as eager to celebrate as men lined the walls and ramparts staring out at the two legions cresting Scopus and slowly marching west where a contingent of horse troops had gathered by a white flag beyond Psephinus Tower. The allied formations had begun to prepare defences and everyone was left to worry about the reality of what their future would hold.

When word spread that two legions had arrived and that thousands of allied troops could be seen, many civilians tried to climb the walls to observe, but had been chased away by Jewish soldiers by order of John and Simon. With no access to the walls, civilians had opened gates, snuck into towers or stood on tall buildings in order to get a glimpse of the army in the distance. Some of the populace had begun to complain about their current status, but most stared in silence as they watched the Roman soldiers digging ditches and setting up walls under the direction of qualified surveyors. It seemed to many as if the entire northern landscape stretching beyond Jerusalem had suddenly come alive as thousands of soldiers dispersed to erect their camps. Anyone with a properly trained eye and experience in battle pointed out to their comrades, that while the soldiers set up their camps, there were also over a thousand men from each legion standing guard.

It was through this combination of feelings, both elated and cautious, that Judah, Caleb, and Adam were recalled from the streets of the Bezetha to a council in the Antonia where John, Eleazar, Simon and much of the command structure from these factions were gathering.

"You must clean, Judah. All of you must clean. You are filthy," Zechariah the priest stated shaking his head as he handed each man a clean towel and guided them to a basin of water. "I have never been one to celebrate in the destruction of others, but on this day, God has blessed us. The Romans were cast from our walls and fled with their tails between their legs. Perhaps Titus got a glimpse of Jewish resolve?" Zechariah smiled as he clasped his hands together and watched the men immerse their hands and faces into the water.

"We were close, Zechariah, Titus was so close." Adam glanced at the others and then buried his face into the towel. When he was finished cleaning, he looked back into the basin and grimaced at the pink tinge.

"You go now, we can talk later." Zechariah took the towels and ushered them into the main hall of the fortress where Roman soldiers had once stood guard. "I remember when this was the place where the priests assembled to stand before the Roman governor. We always trembled and wondered what awaited us from the foul lips of those arrogant men. We do not wonder anymore."

"Because we are the masters of this city now, Zechariah," Judah replied.

"For the time being, and I pray for all time, I do. But now I wonder how long we will be masters of this city?" Zechariah led them through a long corridor and up some stairs.

Judah felt annoyed at the bluntness of the priest and he looked at Caleb who just offered a shrug, not wishing to get caught up in the discussion. "We drove the young dog prince away from our walls by the steel of our swords, Zechariah."

"Yes, you did," the old priest replied.

"And we will do it again so long as this is God's city."

"It will always be God's city," Zechariah glanced back as he hobbled along.

Judah felt puzzled. "Then why the uncertainty?"

"I am a skeptic, Judah, and a priest. When I read the Scriptures, I can't help but look at them in both lights. I study them to increase my knowledge and understand how to lives its message. But the skeptic side of me has to wonder about the tests and judgments we, Israel, have experienced, if they will repeat again and if this is such a time. Forgive me for this natural inclination. I am but a humble priest and one who serves this city. I do pray God will vanquish the enemy before our gates, but as the psalmist wept for his people, so do I if this be a time of judgment." Zechariah stopped by a door and opened it revealing a crowded room of the Jewish elite.

"You should be careful with your skepticism, Zechariah, as it could get you into trouble," Judah warned as he passed by the old man.

"If you are threatening me, my dear Lion warrior, John already knows my doubts."

"And?" Judah said stopping.

"He tries to ignore me but I know he ponders over my doubts and immerses himself in prayer regularly at worship where he wraps himself in the cloth. His *tzitz'ot* are nearly worn through with all his petitioning. He is a good man, but a troubled one." Zechariah motioned for Judah to enter as the old man stepped into the dimly lit room and closed the door behind him.

All eyes fell upon the three Lion warriors as they stood in the large council chamber. The room had been designed for Roman delegation meetings as a long table stood in the center and many pieces of furniture were scattered throughout the hall. At the far end stood a large throne-like chair used by past governors and benches lined the walls upon a tiled mosaic floor of wealthy appeal. Well over thirty men crowded the room, sitting upon the benches or around the table as many held goblets of wine or torn chunks of bread. The officers and delegates known to Judah and his comrades included: the chief captain of John's men, Isaac, High Priest Phanni ben Samuel, Eleazar ben Gion, Zacharias ben Phalek, the notorious Yeshua ben Sapphias from Taricheae, and numerous others. Simeon ben Gamaliel, one of the few men alive from the provisional government and a close friend of John, stood next to Matthias ben Theophilus, who stared at Judah with an inquisitive and captivating look. He silently nodded Judah's way and then whispered something into the aged Gamaliel's ear.

Also in the hall stood the officers of Eleazar ben Simon who were given glaring and foreboding looks by many of the men. They stood completely oblivious as Simon ben Ezron, Judas ben Chelcias, and Hezekiah ben Chobari remained near the back with their fearless leader, helping themselves to a number of wine jugs. Along the east side of the room stood a number of Simon ben Giora's officers: James ben Soras and his son Jacob, Simon ben Cathas, and the fat Yehoram stationed off in a corner. John had specifically requested that Bastard Bagdatus and his men be denied access to the council due to the fact that too many men hated the man, and Simon had graciously respected the request by giving Bagdatus orders to protect Herod's Palace from any intrusion.

John and Simon stood at the front of the room and it was John who smiled first, extended his hands outward and said above the hush, "Judah, your Lions are welcome here. You all fought well. Adam, is your hand tired yet from the Romans you slew before our walls? Caleb, had you not been so caught up in killing the guards of Titus, you may have slain the Prince himself!" John laughed and clapped his hands together as he waved for them to approach.

Judah nodded, took a step forward, and walked to John's side where the warrior from Gischala embraced him firmly and then did the same to Adam and Caleb. Judah blushed from the gesture and glanced around the table as everyone watched the intimacy John demonstrated towards the three men.

"These are the men to inspire you. They rushed from the gates leading an army and drove Titus away. Sadly, I wish you could have had your other Lions to fight by your side, but other duties kept them away. Yet, Judah, they are here among us." John gestured to Aaron, Aviram, and Moshe who stood on Simon's left, impressed at the spectacle given to their legendary band.

"We, Simon, Eleazar, and I, have assembled this council of officers and nobles to discuss the matter at hand," John said glancing annoyingly at Eleazar who lowered his wine goblet and glared back. "What we witnessed today was a test, perhaps an arrogant one, but a test nonetheless. Titus wished to get a closer look at our city, and he left twenty of his men dead upon the ground. We showed him our resolve, and our fierceness which goes hand in hand. Now, we see their faces. Finally, after all these months the legions have arrived. They set up their camps as we speak, before our walls and in the open." John looked around the room with eyes of ardour. "We have sighted only two eagles, there will be more."

A groan escaped the lips of the men in the room. Hezekiah ben Chobari lifted his hand to question and asked, "How do you know this?"

"Because Sicarii from the south told us of four legions, and this has been confirmed from men in the north," John replied.

"Then where are the other two?" Hezekiah asked.

"Emmaus and Jericho, at least we believe that is where they reside. If Titus only brings his allies and two eagles, the other two won't be far behind. We should expect them for sure in the next day or two." John glanced around the room and saw the effects of his words. He knew that despite the minor victory of today and the celebration in the streets, these men were well aware of the fury that awaited them. "We have to show them our strength, and we must fight as one. You may see only numbers before our city, but I see an army of Rome, like the ones we fought against in the north. I swear to you they will be so ruined and discouraged that it will be the end of Vespasian. I pray, that for him to try and take this city will be the death of his army. If we halt this army here, Vespasian will not last long. We need to hold out and prevent this army from succeeding."

"Will Parthia come to our aid?" James ben Soras interrupted, unmoved by John's passion.

A number of the men shouted in agreement with the question as they shook their heads. John motioned for silence and when it did not come, Simon shouted, "Are you that weak, James, that you look to Parthia? What John says is true! We saw how the bid for power among the Romans can corrupt and cause havoc. Vespasian couldn't even continue his campaign, and it was too much. If we can stall this army, we can win."

The room quieted down and Simon looked at John to continue with the agreed plan. John gave Simon a respectful nod and said, "The current arrival of the legions and allied units are stationed to our north. Emmaus is to the west and Jericho in the north. Simon, Eleazar, and I believe the Emmaus legion will camp on the west and the legion from Jericho will set camp somewhere to our east. Titus will have to surround this city if he wishes to contain us; he can't leave anything unchecked. The allied troops will likely monitor the south and that is how it must be done.

"We must maintain a presence on the walls at all times. When the others arrive, we need to look strong and unified. Orders will be given out regularly and we do not act on impulse, unless it is cleared by command. We will not have wasted attempts made which result in deaths due to the fact that a group of renegade troops see an opportunity. We need strict discipline and regular troop rotations at the watch.

"Now, for the arrival of the two legions to follow, we desire to hit them where it hurts. We will keep a watchful eye on their movements when they arrive, but I want two mustered forces of our best troops at the Hippicus and Outer Court to be ready for anything." John crossed his arms and stared down at a crudely drawn map of the city and the region.

"What will these forces be mustered for?" asked James glancing down at the map.

"We need to be ready to spring a trap at any moment. What these Romans are not used to is quick and calculated ambushes. That is how we will win this fight. We will attack them constantly and deny them the chance to reinforce a position or defend themselves. It will be sporadic and impossible to predict." John let that sink into everyone's mind. He tapped the map where the Mount of Olives was located and said, "We shall attack the Jericho legion with deadly speed while they set up camp. There are many exits out of the city on the eastern side, and the valley will be quick to cross. By the time the legionaries know what is happening we will fall upon them and cut them to pieces. Let us test the arrogance of the Romans firsthand." John drove his fist into the open palm of his hand as men nodded in agreement. He knew he had their loyalty and trust.

*　　*　　*

Mount Scopus
Titus' Camp
Before midnight

"It wasn't a disaster, Tiberius, we tested them," Titus said, stripped of his armour and donned in a comfortable toga with gold bands about his wrists.

"And you were nearly killed, my Prince! Can you imagine what that would have done to the army had that happened? My Prince, begging your pardon, and with your permission, we must be more wary of the Jews. They defend their holy city and the Temple will unite them. They are no longer the divided factions we once knew." Tiberius took a breath as he wiped the sweat from his forehead. "I beg you to be more prudent in how you wish to scout the city, and take a larger force next time. May the gods forgive me if I shall be the one to bear the news to your father that you have fallen."

Titus shook his head, rested his arms on his hips and countered, "I cannot lead men from the rear; I will not. Today was a test to show them *Roma* fears nothing."

"And *Roma* fled like a school boy from a rabble, my Prince," Tiberius replied rolling his eyes exhaustingly.

Titus grimaced for an instant and then sighed. "You are a lucky man, Tiberius. You are the only man I would ever allow to be that honest and plain spoken with me. But I value your opinion and recognize your capability; relish in that fact." Titus chuckled and shook his head at Tiberius' shocked expression.

"You fought well, my Prince, but please, hear me when I say you must seek to preserve your life, not to ride forth like a champion of the Greeks, dragging Hector around the city by the speed of your chariot."

Titus threw his head back and laughed pleasantly. "There you are again, my dear Tiberius, the honest man."

"But..." Tiberius started.

"Yes, yes, I will seek to put your mind at ease and not appear so reckless." Titus snapped his fingers loudly, a slave entered the tent and filled the empty cups of the generals with dark wine. "But I do say, my good man, the speed at which those Jews responded was impressive, and gave us something to think about."

"And what would that be, my dear Prince?" Tiberius replied taking a drink.

"That the Jews are not the dogs we thought they were. They are organized and good fighters."

"They were decent in the north as well, if I am not mistaken. I read the reports."

Titus lowered the cup away from his mouth and sighed. "My dear Tiberius, the Jewish forces in the north gave way under the pressure of our legions. Yes, some fought well, but most crumbled with little resistance. What I saw today was an organized attack with very aggressive fighters, which will give me caution in the coming weeks. Jerusalem has many gates and this will have to be something we watch for, but we must be equally ruthless."

"Were the deaths of eighteen men necessary for us to gather that information, my Prince?" Tiberius asked.

For a moment Titus appeared as though he would suddenly shout in anger as his face tightened. Then he exhaled and calmly said, "Regrettable, but necessary, my dear Tiberius. I will have little Yosef adjust the figures in his histories; not everyone needs to know of today. It is the way of war, my dear Tiberius. You of all people should know that. The legions will hear of the attack and know what to expect. I pray they arrive on time, and then we move to our spot near that large prick of a tower! Nearly as long as mine, hey?" Titus laughed out loud, his belly shaking, as he grunted and coughed, giving Tiberius a chance to roll his eyes. "Don't worry; I will never do such a thing again. From now on, no chances, strictly business."

A scribe named Sabinus, silently drew back the tent flap and stepped into the lit room which had been unpacked hours ago. A small army of servants had seen to it that Titus' furnishings were placed the way he liked them. It was imperative that his bed was made properly with the veil hung, and that his wooden desk was placed near the back with enough sharpened quills, sheets of papyrus and bottles of ink to last him a year. A number of statues, depicting the gods Titus honoured and prayed to, had also been set along the edges of the tent. Each had been formed by expert craftsmen around the empire bearing the likeness of the deities the Romans knew them by. Minerva and Mars were among the larger of the images as well the Apis bull, which Titus had sworn to his father he would sacrifice to when the campaign was done. A section of his quarters had also been laid out as a sanctuary where Titus could seek solitude, pray to his ancestors, and entertain a woman if he chose to. The tent was colourful, full of lustre and wealth beyond most men's wildest dreams as the scribe, who was the personal assistant to the Prince, felt immense pride to be a part of.

"Yes, Sabinus, what is it?" Titus asked in a low tone.

The scribe bowed and without hesitating said, "They have arrived."

Titus gave a nod and Sabinus left just as suddenly as he had appeared. Tiberius grunted as he cleared his throat and said just above a whisper, "Will you give out your orders for the Kings and Generals?"

"Yes, that is my plan," Titus replied as the tent flap was drawn back by a soldier standing guard and Agrippa, Sohaemus, Titus Frigius, Marcus Octavian, and Marcus Sulla Maximus entered. "Welcome Kings and Generals," Titus said warmly, snapping his finger for a slave to serve wine. "You're all settled in then, I presume? King Agrippa, I see we are not blessed this time with the presence of your lovely sister. How do you find your quarters?"

Agrippa humbly bowed his head and then swatted a fly that had followed him in. "I'm as comfortable as I can be. It is strange to be back to this city, and to camp outside the walls when I am so used to the pleasantries within. I dare say I heard some of the cursing from the city walls, they must have recognized my banner."

"Barbarians indeed," Sohaemus retorted shaking his head.

Wine was served as bowls of figs and olives were passed around so the dignitaries could help themselves. Titus begged for a report from Frigius and Octavian at the progress on Scopus and the men simply stated that the ground was hard to dig up for the water-piping and plumbing. The earth was made up of clay and rock which caused the ditchers grief. Olive groves had been stripped for wood to build fires and supplies for the upcoming siege. However, the Generals concluded that dykes had been cleared, walls erected, animals penned, wood workers set to repairing carts and damaged artillery from the march, and finally all tents had been erected giving each *contubernium* a place to rest their heads. The main concern seemed to lie in the precious commodity of lumber for the siege and flat ground to fight on so that the cohorts could maintain formation and be effective.

Titus was pleased with the report from his legionary generals. He praised them for their excellent timing in setting up the camps and for their expert watch on the city so that no more sorties could be launched against the working soldiers. Titus noticed Marcus Sulla still had yet to clean the blood and dirt from his armour and face and shook his head bowing gracefully. "I see the only true soldier is one who still remains soiled by the day's struggle, comrades. Tribune Marcus performed handsomely, despite my foolish acts of curiosity which landed us in peril. I do believe Marcus would agree otherwise that the horse troops performed with a perfect counter measure and excellent swordsmanship."

Marcus nodded and grimaced at the other nobles in the tent. He was uncomfortable amidst the elite of men, and could feel their glances of disgust at the fact he had delayed in cleaning himself. "My apologies for arriving unclean, General, I but had to see to the wounded and my own mount which received a slight wound above the hind flank."

"Nonsense, Marcus. If you had not the time to bathe then I commend you, you think of others above yourself and seek not to win my favour with petty things. I do ask, how does your horse fair? I trust it won't put that beautiful beast off the field too long?" A look of concern filled Titus' eyes as he stared at the embarrassed Tribune, ignoring the others.

Marcus Sulla nodded. "He has been stitched up with little blood loss."

"Excellent," Titus pointed, glancing at his other legionary generals. "This man and his cavalry will save us, I tell you the truth. Truly, we must maintain a maximum advantage by keeping the horse troops active and the auxiliary units. Make the notes, men, and always be ready to improvise and expect new orders." Titus beckoned the small group of men across the room to a large, leather mural map hanging from the ceiling. The map bore the inspiration of an artist's impression of Jerusalem, the gorges and hills that surrounded the city. The map had been expertly drawn and labeled, providing the best means to coordinate attacks and dispatch units.

Sohaemus outstretched a ringed finger to the map and said, "Antiochus entrenches his men to the south, my Prince; he was unable to make this council."

"My dear Sohaemus, Antiochus' horse troops will patrol wonderfully along this ridge and can link up frequently with the camps which will be stationed on the Mount of Olives to the east and the Hippicus side to the west. Once the Fifth and Tenth arrive, we shall circumvent the city and then make preparations to attack. A council will be called later once I have all my legionary generals, and I would like to ask that centurions of each First Cohort of the legions be present." Titus glanced at the two kings, rubbing his hands together. "Any high ranking officers that should be present from the alae I will leave to you, Agrippa and Sohaemus." The kings nodded and quietly whispered to each other as Titus stared up at the large map.

"How will we maintain control over pilgrims, my Prince?" Frigius asked shaking his head. "They continue to gain access to the city, and we are unsure who are Zealots and who are not. A number were beaten earlier by sentries, but they keep coming and my troops grow anxious."

"Pesach approaches, the Feast of Unleavened Bread. It is one of the holiest holidays of the year and the city always swells in numbers. Pilgrims are inevitable and will come in the thousands," Agrippa added receiving a worried look from the General of the Fifteenth Legion.

Titus retrieved his sword and using the blade as a pointer he tapped it upon the leather at the popular points of entry. "When we move to our new location tomorrow and set up camp, things will be easier to control, I promise you. We shall not stay upon this rock for long." Titus glanced at the kings and shrugged. "Set up checkpoints at all gates to the south. I doubt pilgrims will attempt at the eastern side once the Tenth is camped there." He sighed and shook his head. "The fools wish to still attend worship in the Temple, even when we besiege the city?" Titus turned to his generals. "We must search them all, wagons, carts, even the women and children. I will have no weapons or food smuggled in. If the pilgrims wish access to the city, so be it, but they shall not take food or weapons inside."

"What of the men in families caught with weapons?" Marcus Octavian asked.

Titus was silent for a moment as he mulled over the question and then staring up at the map he said, "We crucify the men as collaborators and enslave their families. Let it be known that no aide be given to the rebels. Have the men make signs in Greek and offer a warning for Jews foolish enough to try and profane my will. As for the genuine pilgrims, let them through and do not molest them. I will not have their God despise me for interfering with a holy feast."

"As you wish, General," Frigius replied.

"I thought you would like to know, my Prince, that I had scouts reconnoiter the city and only one place looks possible for an effective approach," Marcus Sulla said, gaining the attention of the generals and kings.

"Please continue," Titus stated, intrigued.

Marcus Sulla pointed to the map and tapped the western side of the city. "You plan to camp the Fifth here, right? Well, just further to the north, out of the way from Hippicus following this road here, the wall is weaker and unfinished." Marcus traced his finger past the markings of the triple towers and the wall. "The ground is rocky, but it would be easier to level and also provide enough space for a full attack. We gather this section of the city is controlled by Simon's rabble and they have no long range artillery."

The room was silent. Titus looked from Marcus Sulla to one of his best advisors around the table for a matter such as this. "Agrippa, is this true?"

The King nodded. "Yes, it is. I financed the strengthening of that wall years ago, but it was never finished due to Roman sanctions, money, and Jewish opposition that was heating up at the time." He leaned over, sweeping his hand across the northwestern parts of the city neatly displayed upon the leather, and said with confidence, "If you attack from this side and breach the walls, it will give you access to the city. You will have control over the entire Bezetha, the Upper City, and will clear the way to the Antonia. This is the strategic heart of the city. If these sections fall the Temple will be exposed. I see no reason to doubt that once this is a reality, the Jews will surrender."

"Enough room for ramps and legions, Marcus?" Titus asked staring at the cavalry Tribune.

"Enough room, my Prince."

"Very well," Titus grinned, staring at the map for a second longer. "You are all dismissed and we shall speak later, but you, Octavian, to you I must have a word." Titus set his goblet down on a small table decorated in coloured squares of wood from Syria. The two kings bowed humbly and Titus Frigius along with Marcus Sulla offered up the typical Roman salutes as the four men exited the tent. Marcus Tullius Octavian, accepted a refill of wine from a servant and then made himself at home upon a cushioned sofa at Titus' invitation.

The young Prince, taking a cluster of grapes from a silver bowl, walked across the carpeted ground and sat upon a chaise as he devoured the grapes in silence. Marcus allowed his eyes to wander and then pointed to a hanging mosaic above Titus' bed, offering his pleasure and compliments on the perfection of the masterpiece. It was of the sea god Neptune clutching his trident and riding the waters in a chariot pulled by two horses with fish tails. The flickering lamp light in the tent cast an aura of warmth upon the border of the mural shaped in a zigzag design of gold and yellow hues. The water upon which Neptune's chariot rode was an emerald green with blue stones.

"I had that done in Alexandria before we marched. It took the mosaicist a month to complete. It had to be perfect and I had the picture sketched in drafts prior to its official creation." Titus spit a grape seed upon the floor and then snapped his finger. His slave appeared obediently and Titus ordered, "Fetch the gift from the priests of the Nile." He turned to Marcus with a look of excitement. "You must see this. Before I left, I attended prayer at the Temple of Saturnus and when I was done I was approached by a priest of the Nile who gave me this." Titus watched as his slave returned carrying an object enclosed in white linen. He took it from the slave and a small table was brought over and set between the couches so Titus could reveal the gift to Marcus.

When the Prince unwrapped the linen, a strange image of a hand chiseled from stone was placed on the table. Out of the knuckle of the small finger was the head of a viper and upon the thumb was an acorn seedling. On the open palm of the hand was an engraved image of a ram and below that a scarab with the Egyptian image of eternal power.

"What does it mean?" Marcus asked while leaning forward for a closer look.

"The aged priest said the viper was to strike out and conquer, the acorn seedling was for our future to implant itself in the world. The ram was to be our way into the city and to be revered in sacrifice. The scarab was placed as a charm against the spirits that should muddle our ways and the eternal symbol to be recognized by Basilides should he show himself again." Titus sipped his wine and gently leaned back upon the chaise.

"Has he returned since your father's last dream?" Marcus asked.

Titus shook his head. "I have heard nothing. He eludes us, but we feel not yet abandoned." Titus was silent for a moment as he stared at the hand contemplating its meaning. Then he snapped his fingers again and the slave arrived. "Take the image to the quarters of my tent, place it near the images of my ancestors, and be most careful." When the hand was removed, Titus finished his wine and set the goblet upon the ground. "I wish to ask you something about Gaius Cornelius."

"What do you wish to know?"

"How long has he been Primus Pilus of your First Cohors?"

Marcus shrugged. "Since the beginning of the rebellion, I would presume."

"And you have not promoted him? He has shown admirable qualities, has he not?" Titus pressed as he leaned upon his left elbow.

Marcus nodded. "He has, my Prince, very much. He is my best. Much has happened; I thought a promotion would come perhaps at the end of this siege."

"And miss the opportunity to instill more courage in the man? Nonsense, he must be recognized and used. I want you to make him *Praefectus Castrorum.*"

Marcus was still for a moment. "Praefectus Castrorum?"

Titus nodded. "That is exactly what I want you to do. Normally men are promoted to this office much sooner, are they not? Gaius has served his legion well, and kept its honour, despite the legion's shaky past."

"What Cestius Gallus did at the beginning will not stain its image in this fight, I can promise you that," Marcus said.

"Granted, the Twelfth will have time to prove itself, and I do not doubt its future exploits. Cestius Gallus is still here with the army, as well as Gessius Florus and I need more men I can count on. Promote Gaius and he has a voice among the council. Without promotion the Generals will not count him as an equal nor respect him as my father does."

"Your Father loves, Gaius. He is an extraordinary soldier, but I fear your father's love distances him from the other centurions."

Titus gave Marcus a sideways glance and then shook his head with a smile. "My Father loves him as a son, and I respect that. Gaius is loved by his troops and envied by generals and officers alike who are jealous of the man's accomplishments. Yet, I have seen Tribune Marcus Sulla by Gaius' side, and I dare say as long as those two are comrades, nobody will say anything to cross Gaius."

"Interesting you should mention people not crossing Marcus Sulla. I have heard complaints from Marcus' own decurianes concerning treatment of his own fellow officers, especially Drusus and Varro. Something should be said, I might add," Marcus suggested finishing his wine.

Titus tossed his head back and laughed. "What? I should scold Marcus because of that man's tongue? Why, are his decurianes offended? Does Marcus insult their powdered noses? I dare say that man will save us all! His junior officers are the ass ends of swine compared to that man. I say everyone should strive to be like Marcus and acquire some balls when confronting danger. Did you see his decurianes flee the battlefield and leave me? Marcus stood his ground and fought the bastards until they bled the ground. Tribune Marcus saved my life, truly."

Marcus Octavian shrugged again and rubbed his weary eyes. "Very well, my Prince, I shall promote Gaius the day after tomorrow and give him the dona of Praefectus Castrorum. I will swear him in before the troops and have the men recite the *sacramentum* following the ceremony."

"And sacrifice a bull in Gaius' honour," Titus added.

"Very well, in Gaius' honour, my Prince."

*   *   *

CHAPTER XIV

April 13th, 70 A.D. / 16th of Nisan, 3830
Mount of Olives
East of Jerusalem

Larcius Lepidus rode ahead of the Tenth Legion as they stamped their feet upon the road which took them up to the heights overlooking the city. A steady beat of drums accompanied the men to the deep groans from a host of *tubicen* horn blowers who played the *lituus* as they marched within the heart of the legion. Among the other musicians were cornucen trumpeters adorned with wolf skin helmet covers who blasted high notes on their cornu and *buccina* which were welcoming sounds of the arriving legion, arrayed in full battle gear and guided by their golden eagle. Larcius guided his mount away from the columns of troops as they passed by, century after century, cohort after cohort, maintaining formation under the direction of centurions and optiones who led them down the slopes to a designated spot where the camp was to be situated.

A number of tribunes rode up alongside Larcius and the General turned in his saddle before the men had a chance to relax and said, "I want the *imaginifer* to stand in the center of where our camp will be and hoist the imagio of the Emperor high. Surround him with the trumpets and drums and carry on. We can't let Sextus and the Fifth get all the attention on the other side of the city. I want this to be a show to the Jews of what is coming their way. Hurry now and report to me later."

The nearest tribune saluted and the officers left Larcius' side immediately as they galloped to the front ranks. Larcius scanned the city walls on the other side of the valley and took a deep breath of the crisp morning air. The sun was rising quickly and the heat was coming, but for this day, he did not expect anything out of the ordinary. He had made the necessary arrangements for the attached horse units of his legion to skirt around the Mount of Olives.

Orders had been direct and were handed to him as he had marched south from Jericho. He was to set up a fortified base camp, keeping his distance from the city. The camp was to be entrenched upon the Mount of Olives with complete defences including: towers, walls, ditches, dykes, and all the other necessities for nearly five thousand troops for a long siege. Sextus Cerealis on the other hand, advanced from Emmaus to the west, and would camp within sight of Titus' headquarters, yet within striking distance of the Hippicus Tower and the entire western defences of the city. Even now, Larcius could hear the distant trumpet calls from the Fifth Legion as they moved into position and he sighed as he let his mind wander to all the work which lay ahead of him.

He looked to his left as the column of legionaries began to break formation as cartloads of shovels, picks, and hammers were brought up by a group of mules. Centurions blasted whistles within the ranks, shouting for the men to stack their weapons to the side and grab tools. Engineers and surveyors skirted in and out among the soldiers who began working aggressively as rocks were moved and earth was dug up. Thousands of Romans laboured with sweating bodies as they leveled the ground and piled the stone, all under the constant oversight of the supervising officers.

Larcius dug his heels into the flanks of his mount and tugged on the reins as he swung to the left following a goat path down the slopes to where the legion was hard at work. He waved his hand at one of his centurions who immediately lowered the short staff he had been using to direct his men and jogged over to his General. He halted before his commander and struck his breastplate with a closed fist.

Larcius ignored the man for an instant as he listened to the din of tools striking earth and stone. The sun was getting hotter by the minute and he wanted this work completed swiftly. He glanced around the centuries spread over the slopes and shook his head, not liking what he saw. Larcius glanced down at the awaiting officer and pointed a finger towards a group of men hauling away stones and dirt upon their backs. "Why is there no guard drawn up?"

The Centurion stiffened to attention looking briefly over his shoulder at the busy soldiers. "Tribune Publius passed out the order for everyone to set camp; he wanted it done with no time wasted."

Larcius leaned forward in his saddle and said, "We are still under the watching eyes of the city, Centurion. I will not risk an ambush. We watch our flanks and get the work done. Have a guard drawn up. I want three cohorts on watch and tell Publius to gather the auxiliary and have them scout the ridge above. Keep the music playing so the men will work harder."

"Yes, General." The Centurion saluted, turned, and shouted to his optio to rally his cohort to arms and pass the order to officers from cohorts four and five to form up.

Larcius looked behind him as the baggage train was cresting Mount Scopus and shook his head in annoyance as a wheel from the head cart broke. He watched as a man was thrown from the side with a yelp and heard the low moans of the oxen as they yanked back, splitting the yoke. The fat quartermaster stood beside the driver shouting and cursing as a number of servants rushed to the moaning beasts as they continued to drag the damaged cart. By the time they had grabbed the harnesses of the animals and surveyed the broken wheel, the entire train had come to a halt.

The echoing sounds of mules, oxen, and donkeys reverberated across the hills to the shouting of frustrated men.

*   *   *

The ramparts of the city had been filled to capacity with the arrival of the Tenth Legion which had now dispersed to set up camp. Most of the Jewish fighters said nothing as everyone watched the hardworking legionaries battle the unforgiving ground while they slowly developed the immense camp. Stone walls rose up from the earth as the distant troops piled rocks of measurable size upon each other, and the sounds of hammers thumping and whacking became constant as soldiers and wood workers began constructing small towers.

Earlier in the morning before the arrival of the Tenth Legion, the blasts from rams' horns had wakened John. Once he emerged upon the ramparts he witnessed the distant legionaries of the Twelfth and Fifteenth breaking camp upon the slopes of Mount Scopus. The Jews had laughed and joked that the Romans were afraid and packing to go home, but John knew better than that. After two long hours, the laughter had died down as everyone watched the legionaries march to the west with their baggage trains and cavalry squadrons, to begin setting up a massive camp around a white consular flag directly opposite of the Psephinus Tower. With the arrival of the other legions, it was clear Jerusalem was being surrounded.

The Tenth had appeared in all their pomp and splendour. Blasts of trumpets and the thunder of drums had been heard for nearly an hour before the eagle had crested the plateau of Scopus. Word spread throughout the city that the Fifth Legion had also arrived from Emmaus and now had set up camp on the western side.

A small uproar had arisen within the streets of Bezetha with the arrival of two more legions as panic stricken civilians had demanded to be allowed to leave the doomed city with their belongings. They shouted at Simon and John who confronted them with three hundred soldiers, and appealed to the warlord's sense of decency to open the gates and allow them, with their families, to vacate the city and seek mercy from Titus. John scoffed at the people, most of whom were from the wealthy class, and ordered spears lowered to their bellies, daring them to leave. This action served him with the desired result. The riot dispersed within minutes and the people returned to their homes grumbling. Once order had been restored to the Upper City, John and Simon returned to the ramparts of the Outer Court to watch their enemies hard at work.

John waited impatiently for Judah and his men to arrive. They had been summoned from the Antonia to make haste and be suited for battle. He turned away from the Romans and looked at Simon who was resting his hands upon the battlements with an unsettled look, grimness filling the lines of his face. "Are you worried this won't work?"

Simon shot John a glare of annoyance as he rubbed his bearded chin. "I have led battles before, my dear John. This is not my first lesson."

John sighed shaking his burly head as he stared at the thin man. "I only sense your reluctance, Simon. You are not yourself."

"I just foresee the Romans regrouping to meet our attack to slaughter my men."

"Since when have you ever cared how many of your men die?" John lashed back in anger.

"Don't test me, John. We may be working together, but you push me the wrong way and I will sweep through this place and slaughter you where you stand." Simon narrowed his eyes with vengeance and shot a hateful glare at John's Captain, Isaac, who stood with cold eyes and an eager hand upon the pommel of his sword.

"Don't threaten me, you scum. Look out there!" John gestured to the mountains stretching beyond the valley. "The Romans have no guard stationed and they work with their heads down. We must pounce on this chance. Do you have men in the lower parts of the city?" Simon nodded and John continued, "Send them from the southern gates after we charge out of the Eastern Gate. We can feed more men into the fight as it progresses, and with God on our side we can prevail in destroying their camp. That is the Tenth. If we can beat them now, we could deliver a huge blow to Titus early on; we have already sent him reeling once."

"That was only a hundred Roman horses, John. Out there are five thousand of the world's toughest soldiers," Simon responded, hissing the words through his gritted teeth.

"And we can match their numbers in an instant." John turned to the sound of beating feet and a smile spread across his face as Judah and his men arrived. "We shall send a force of seven hundred men right at them, and if you match that, we can reinforce them swiftly before Titus gets word of our assault. Have two waves of troops ready. I will station equal numbers of men and we attack in sequence."

Simon nodded reluctantly and backed away from the wall. "Very well, I will give orders for my men to attack when the first wave reaches the valley's bottom." He turned, gave a signal to his officers, and descended the battlements, crossing the Outer Court for the Royal Porticoes with much haste as he hurried for the City of David stretching beyond.

John glanced at his Captain and said, "Isaac, rally the men to the Eastern Gate." He watched Isaac depart, then looked Judah up and down. Judah carried a round shield and rested his free hand upon his gladius which hung at his side. A leather breastplate was strapped to his chest and he wore a Roman styled helmet upon his head with the cheek plates firmly tied under his bearded chin. Adam and Caleb were also dressed in similar fashion, with Adam gripping the shaft of a long javelin and fitted with a Persian styled helmet. The men's beards had been groomed and all had shed their cumbersome outer garments. Moshe, Aaron, and Aviram stood behind Adam armed with an assortment of weapons and donned in captured armour.

John gave the group a nod and pointing outwards said, "You men will lead the first charge. Pray that God gives you speed and courage. Apart from a handful of sentries, the Romans have foolishly neglected to post a strong guard. Cross the valley and attack them head on. An equal sized force will advance from the southern gates and support your attack by hitting their flanks. Judging by your success, we have another fourteen hundred men who can reinforce you at a moment's notice."

Judah looked at Caleb and said, "Let's get on with this."

"I will be watching from above the gate; fight hard and drive them from the slopes. Now, go and wait for my signal," John said.

Judah led his men down from the ramparts and joined a mass of Zealots forming on the grounds of the Outer Court before the Eastern Gate which loomed ahead of them. They were John's best men, and all were feared as they clutched spears, swords, axes, clubs, and shields. Some wore armour and appeared as bearded legionaries, while others stood among them in their cloaks. Anything that was of no use for the coming battle was shed and discarded upon the stones. A number of women ran to the mass of men and embraced their husbands or lovers as they said farewell. When the women were finally pulled from the armed men, they wept and called out waving their hands in the air or collapsing upon the ground in grief.

"Refrain from shouting your war cries until you are upon them, we need to gain as much ground as possible!" Isaac bellowed at the men as he walked down the line holding his sword.

Judah and Caleb stood at the front, in complete silence, trying to make sense of what was about to happen. They held their swords with nervous hands as the sun reflected off the steel. Neither man could look at the other. A dreaded silence began to filter throughout the seven hundred as they waited.

Judah held his breath and heard Adam nervously exhale behind him as he muttered a prayer. He turned and looked at Caleb and Adam. "Fight well, my brothers. It has been a long road to this point."

Caleb swallowed hard. He felt a rush of blood flow through his body as a breeze cooled his form. "We will not die, not today." He glanced at Judah. "You think Capito is here?"

Judah nodded. "I am sure of it, and I shall think of Miriam as I kill those men."

"Lord, forgive us for what we are about to do," Adam whispered, noticing the strange look Judah gave him.

The gates were opened just enough for eight men to charge through abreast. The mass of Jewish fighters surged forward and funneled through the entrance into the bright sunlight. Many of the soldiers tried to kiss the *mezuzah* on the inside of the gate, but Isaac pushed them back into line as men with spears stood guard on either side making sure the formation did not falter or slow.

Judah led the charge maintaining a fast pace as he pressed for the bottom of the valley with the pounding of feet behind him. He could hear panting and grunts as the men poured down the slopes like a giant wave of water overtaking everything in its path. Swords and spear-heads bristled with intensity as the formation reached the rocky bottom of the valley and catapulted forward with a shout to climb the quickly rising ground before them. Judah saw a look of utter shock fill the faces of the sentries posted on the outskirts of the developing Roman camp. They stood for a moment frozen and dazed as the mighty force rolled towards them. Then in total panic, the guards turned and fled shouting, attempting to raise the alarm. Most of the Romans were oblivious to the approaching threat, as the hammering and hacking at the ground drowned out the approaching mass Judah saw a number of men carrying rocks upon their backs, turn to the shouting of the sentries, drop their loads and scramble like madmen through the workers for their weapons.

A cohort of Roman infantry, which had already begun to assemble further up the slope, reacted quickly when they noticed the sentries fleeing before the tumultuous tide of Jews bearing down on them. The cohort's Centurion blew his whistle as loud as his lungs would have him, and ran forward followed by only half his men while the other portion were still equipping themselves. The Centurion led his men into the fray only to find his force outnumbered and exhausted due to the day of marching and setting up camp.

Judah was the first to reach the Romans, as his blade eagerly severed the exposed throat of the Centurion who was looking back and attempting at rallying his men. A fountain of blood erupted from the man's throat as he stumbled forward, crashing upon the ground with a silenced scream. The Jewish force suddenly delivered a terrible shout as they drove into the Romans with deadly speed, slaughtering any who tried to fight and pouncing upon the exposed backs of those who tried to flee. Screams and cries echoed above the clanging steel. Men were butchered and skewered by spears. Others were beaten to death and crushed by the very stones they had been carrying, their broken bodies only to be trampled and ravaged.

Soon, like the ripple effect made from a stone cast into water, the entire Roman force reeled. Men everywhere panicked and fled, dropping tools and anything which would impede their flight. Tribunes mounted upon horses looked in shock and disbelief as another formation of Jewish fighters of equal density crossed the valley floor from the south and charged up the slopes. One Tribune waved his drawn sword in the air and shouted valiantly as he spurred his horse forward only to have a hurled spear graze his helmet. The officer slid from the saddle stunned by the blow, and by the time he recovered and was able to stand, a ferocious Idumean with a sword decapitated him with one deadly blow.

Judah screamed until his throat was hoarse and raw. He brought up his shield just in time to feel the impact of a pilum delivered by expert hands as it punched through the layered wood. Judah carried the shield for a few steps, then nearly tripping over the protruding spear, he cast his shattered shield aside. He leapt across the partial ditch which the legionaries had dug and then climbed the outer stone wall of the camp as his men poured over it. A dozen arrows flicked by Judah's face and he heard screams of pain wailing from the rear, as a number of Jews collapsed in agony from the Roman darts which had found their mark. Judah's lungs now burned and sweat soaked his garments. His arms felt like fire while his muscles flared with agonizing thrusts as he swung his sword at men and soon became red with blood.

"Judah, they are trying to make a stand!" Caleb shouted from the left as he finished a Roman off who had been crawling upon the ground.

Judah watched a number of signi further up the slopes hoisted above the heads of about three hundred Roman troops organizing a square at the desperate orders of centurions and scrambling optiones clutching their hastile staffs. To the right, Simon's men had pressed through the Roman auxiliary, slaughtering them upon their horses, and now joined the main assault with lowered spears dripping with blood. Behind the Jewish attack, another two waves could be seen erupting from the city gates with confidence. Seeing this support, Judah raised his sword high, let out a blood curdling scream, and charged forward as he was followed by the howling mob at his back.

However menacing the Jewish onslaught appeared, the discipline of the Romans was impeccable. Two cohorts that had managed to form a battle line, now stood behind their red *scutua*, emblazoned with the bull at the top, the war ship near the bottom, the horizontal spear and two dolphins splitting across the center. Just above the metal boss was the numeral X. Centurions paced down the lines shouting for them to calm as the legionaries braced themselves for the enormous attack rolling their way. Suddenly a trumpet blasted and in unison the cohorts hurled their pila in a deadly volley. The Jewish assault faltered temporarily as dozens of men pitched backwards with spears imbedded in their chests while others writhed on the ground in agony, wounded and unable to carry on.

For a moment the Romans thought the attack would dissolve from the demoralizing blow of the missile volley, but then, with primal rage, the Jews exploded with a new found energy. The earth shook from the thunder of their feet. The legionaries, at the commands of their centurions, drew their swords, hefted their shields, and stepped forward simultaneously to meet the onslaught.

Judah narrowly dodged the first thrust as a Roman blade cut his left arm and found its target in Aaron who tried to press past Judah. Aaron crumpled over the blade as his blood gushed upon the ground. Judah drove his body into the Roman's scutum and brought his sword blade down upon the man's exposed arm as the legionary was trying to retract his gladius from Aaron, who wheezed in pain upon the ground. The man's arm shattered with a spray of blood under the weight of the blow. The Roman dropped his sword and wheeled backwards in horrible anguish as another legionary lunged forward, filling the gap with his blade flashing through the air. Judah howled in a deep rage and met the attack, clashing steel upon steel. The horde of fighters behind him pressed into the Roman line, driving many to their knees under brutal crushing blows from swords and spears.

The Roman line shuddered, suddenly turning against the pressure of the onslaught. A victorious shout of pure exultation rose up from the Jewish fighters as they trampled across the ground and struck the backs of fleeing Romans. They slaughtered them in droves and for a moment it seemed as if the Tenth would be driven from the mountain, never to return.

*   *   *

"My Prince Titus! General!" shouted a sentry standing guard at the mouth of Titus' tent. When the soldier heard nothing from within he took the liberty to slide the canvas flap aside with his spear and bellow again, this time much louder as if it sprang forth from a lion.

Titus jolted upright from his bed, his chest slick with oil from the massage he had received earlier. He had decided to rest for an hour following the strenuous early morning relocation to the north of Psephinus Tower. Leaping to his feet, he pulled on his tunic and ran for the entrance as a bright ray of sunlight suddenly lit up the room followed by the booming voice again. His guard saw him and holding back the tent flap shouted, "Sire, the Tenth is under attack!"

Titus burst from his tent and felt the sweltering heat of the day hit him like the heat of the *caldarium* from the baths. He squinted in the sudden light, sheltered his eyes, and was able to catch two large formations of Jewish fighters surging up the distant slopes of the Mount of Olives as they poured out of the valley below. He watched in horror as the working legionaries were cut into like a swath blade cutting down rows of barley. Titus saw Romans scrambling all over, some trying to flee while others attempted to reach their weapons and defend themselves. In a moment of utter desperation, Titus reacted quickly shouting, "Bring me my sword and helmet!" He turned wildly to the guard and shouted sending a stream of spittle at the man, "Go alert Tribune Marcus Sulla and his cavalry; I need them all!"

Titus' servant appeared from the tent holding a sword and helmet which he quickly handed to the Prince and then fled to fetch Achilles from the stables nearby. Titus belted his scabbard overtop of his toga and firmly planted his helmet upon his head as he turned to the sounds of beating hooves. He ran to Achilles and leaping high, swung into the saddle by gripping the black mane of the stallion. Titus drew his sword and with a voice of thunder shouted at some centurions who had emerged from their tents to the commotion, "Double the guard in the camp now!"

The centurions saluted and ran throughout the camp blasting whistles and rallying the soldiers who began to burst from their tents, some half suited in their armour. Soon a massive dust cloud could be seen rising against the sky as news of the attack brought the Boars to the camp of the Fulminata. Titus turned in his saddle as his standard bearer and a few other officers joined him on horseback. They rode from the camp at a steady gallop towards the dust cloud.

Marcus Sulla watched the young Prince gallop from the eastern entrance of the camp followed closely by his staff and signifer. Marcus waved the formation of five hundred horse troops forward to meet the Prince. He thanked the gods under his breath that they had already been mounted as they had been returning from a reconnaissance of the city. The cavalry had been divided into three separate groups for patrols, but the blasts of trumpets had summoned them swiftly once word had been given to Marcus concerning the peril of Larcius Lepidus' troops.

"My Prince, should you be dressed?" Decurion Drusus called out from beside Marcus as Titus drew back on the reins of Achilles and halted before them.

"There is no time. Marcus, draw up your troops into battle formation; we ride to save a legio! Come!" Titus raised his sword in the air, and while swinging Achilles around, he leaned forward in the saddle as the black stallion bolted ahead followed closely by the Boars.

The pounding of hooves shook the earth as the Boars' signum led the hundreds of troopers with drawn swords and black oval shields. They moved as one as they quickly drew up into a wedge formation at full gallop. The muscles of each horse rippled with intensity as they beat the ground, and with nostrils flaring the horses were guided up the slopes of Scopus where they pushed along, guided by Titus.

When they reached the summit of Scopus, the legionaries of the Tenth were in full flight. Titus had just enough time to watch a small square formation of defiant soldiers break by the Jewish pressure which roared over them. "Attack the flanks! Trumpeter, sound the charge!" Titus screamed and launched Achilles forward to the glorious brass tones of the call. The Boars covered the distance swiftly and poured over the Mount of Olives with deadly precision.

The next moments were like a dream of Roman glory for Titus and a nightmare for the Jewish soldiers unfortunate enough to be in the way. The Roman cavalry ploughed into the Jewish flanks, completely halting their attack and trampling men under the sharp hooves of the horses. The Jews, caught by surprise at the counterattack, recoiled in a grim determination to protect themselves. A number of missiles hurled from the Jewish ranks found their targets, but for the most part new screams of death were added to the fray of battle as men's bodies were hacked apart, crushed by the weight of the war horses, or impaled by lances.

As sudden as the charge had been, it slowed as the Boars began the tedious business of killing men. Swords descended and retracted, sheeted in blood, as the fighting intensified. A number of desperate Zealots took to attacking the horses themselves as they sliced them open and drove spears into their muscular flanks. Many mounts collapsed amidst the carnage, letting out terribly high pitched wails as their riders fell, shattering legs and arms upon the rocks, only to be greeted by spearheads from enraged Zealots. However, as fierce as the Jewish onslaught had been, it soon began to dissolve as they realized their predicament. The last straw which destroyed the Jewish resolve to capture the Mount of Olives came finally with the reformed ranks of the Tenth infantry which now returned to crush the Zealots in revenge. Reflecting the sunlight, the eagle of the Tenth stood high above the thick Roman ranks as they charged into the front of the Jewish attack. As sudden as the Jews had swept across the valley and up the slopes, they now fled for their lives.

"My Prince, shall we pursue?" Marcus shouted, pointing his sword at the Jewish ranks flooding back into the valley below.

"To the city!" Titus hollered. "Push them to the city!"

"Advance in close formation!" Marcus bellowed leading his men forward, engulfed by over a thousand legionaries of the Tenth who sought vengeance on the heels of the Jewish retreat.

"My Prince! My Prince!"

Titus turned in his saddle to see Larcius Lepidus draw in his horse alongside him. "This is an outrage, Lepidus!" Titus shouted, flushed with anger. "Your legio has been disgraced! The army has been trampled on! We give power to the Jewish rebels who see legionaries fleeing with their tails between their legs! They acted like damned *Picts*! And the Tenth? This is absurd! What happened?" Titus asked, shaking his head and watching the fight spill into the Kidron as cavalry units clashed with groups of Jews forming up to cover the main retreat.

Larcius' voice was shaky and rattled with nerves as he fought to find the right words which ended up tumbling out in a torrent. "Forgive me, General! The responsibility rests on my shoulders; the gods have cursed me!"

"You're damn wrong, Lepidus. Why did you not obey my orders? You had no guard posted? Your entire focus was on fortifying your camp with no stationed guards? This is not your fashion of command, I dare say. Speak up now!" Titus' anger had cooled but he still remained on edge watching the Jewish forces attempt to reinforce their attack at the valley's base of blood-stained rocks and piles of crushed bodies.

"We were digging in as directed, sire. I noticed that the guard had been neglected and I inquired as to why. Tribune Publius had ordered against the guard, defying my strict orders, but before I could move the guard to the front, the Jews attacked. Most of the men didn't even see them coming. They must have used the gates." Larcius held his sword at his side, his face pale from humiliation.

"Is it possible you mistook my orders?" Titus queried furrowing his brow.

Larcius took a deep breath and shook his head. "Orders were exactly relayed as you commanded. The legionary logs shall bear witness to that, sire. In no way did I seek to judge those orders incorrectly. The neglect of the guard was due to my arrogant tribunes and my oversight." Larcius paused for a moment watching Titus shake his head again in frustration. "I directed from the rear. We were trying to make a stand on the crest, but the pressure was constant. I owe you my life and command, my Prince."

Titus shook his head. "No, I would just prefer the life of Publius. Isn't his father a senator of *Roma*?"

Larcius shrugged and offered Titus his wine skin. "Yes, and his father is now without a son. Publius is dead so you won't have problems with him from now on." Titus raised an eyebrow and Larcius nodded. "He was killed moments into the fighting as he tried to organize an auxiliary counterattack."

Titus took a long drink from the wine skin and handed it back. He watched the Jews scrambling up the other side of the slopes beneath the walls and with one massive shower of arrows at the Romans from above the Roman attack was brought to a halt. Nobody was ready or prepared to assault the city, and the Jewish fighters who had survived the retreat, gathered at the base of the walls hurling insults.

"I shall never understand their tenacity for as long as I shall live." Titus licked his lips and sighed as he felt the adrenalin and excitement of battle leave him.

"You don't understand them, sire? Why, they fight like you! They fight without mercy and they hate us. If you were one of them, I would think you would fight the same. We all would," Larcius replied.

Titus nodded. "They aren't idiots. Look how they taunt our troops. They know they have the superior position: we would have to fight uphill, across uneven ground, all the while under a hail storm of arrows and missiles. Come, let us ride down to them and sort this out. I don't want the men being lured in, we have already lost too much today." Titus glanced around for a moment at the hundreds of bodies littering the ground about them. Disemboweled horses and dismembered men lay together, the low sorrowful moans of the wounded drifting upwards as they bled to death. Both spears and swords stood upright from dead victims, and the smell of blood and urine was foul in their nostrils.

Titus and Larcius rode down into the Kidron guiding their horses around rocks and the dead bodies of men. Behind him, nearly a hundred slaves had already been dispatched with empty carts to collect the Roman wounded. Scattered numbers of allied troops also scoured the hillside dispatching the Jewish wounded with quick strokes of their swords, and without mercy.

At the base of the valley, Prince Titus and Larcius were greeted by Marcus Sulla and his three decurianes: Varro, Drusus, and Titus. All the men were filthy from the dust as blood caked their armour, hands, and faces, yet the three junior officers seemed relieved the fighting had come to a standstill. Marcus, on the other hand, was in a sour mood as he cleaned the blade of his sword using his tunic and sheathed it loudly with annoyance.

"The Jews have reinforced their numbers and have drawn up at the base of the wall. They called my mother a whore, can you believe that?" he commented sarcastically. "Bunch of little shits!"

"Have some allied cavalry units brought down; retire a third of your men, Marcus. The fighting for today should be done." Titus glanced at Larcius. "Thin out the line and stretch them out, send the majority of your men back to collect our dead, clean up, and continue camp construction. We need that completed before nightfall."

"Bloody mess," Larcius commented watching a wounded legionary limp by in shock, his face slashed open by a sword blade, as a sheet of blood covered his neck and chest.

The officers watched the man hobble by as if drunk. Marcus spit upon the ground and swore as he stared at a number of horses from the Boars squadron, run by in panic, their saddles emptied of men. "What is the bloody time?" Marcus asked, scratching some dried blood from his forearm.

"I believe noon approaches, Tribune," Varro replied.

Marcus sighed and looked away from Varro at the sullen expression cast upon Titus' handsome face. "What would you have me do, sire?"

"Well, let us remain here for a while longer, and then we can retire for some lunch," Titus responded. He licked his dust-caked lips, rolled his eyes in exasperation and shifted in his saddle. "Larcius, have one of your men bring us some cold water. My throat is quite parched, I say indeed."

* * *

"Eleazar, keep watch!" John shouted squinting up at the high ramparts from the armed throng amassed in the Outer Court. "Where is Titus?"

Eleazar ben Simon strained his eyes as he gazed over the walls at the long skirmish formation that the Romans had formed as they took the insults shouted at them in silence. Behind their ranks the cavalry could be seen riding up and down the lines of legionaries, scanning the Jewish fighters at the base of the walls for any sign of aggression. Eleazar shrugged, stepped back from the walls, and called down to John, "Titus remains in the center and it appears he has assembled his officers. The Romans seem content in holding their position, nothing more."

John growled under his breath and watched as Judah entered through the Eastern Gate which had been left slightly ajar. The Lion warrior was drenched in sweat, his breastplate and sword stained with blood, a look of wildness in his eyes. John greeted him quickly and pointing upwards he said, "Eleazar has archers covering the walls. The legionaries can't advance unless they risk a hail from above. We have them in a perfect position, a standstill for the time being. Your attack was perfect. God has used us this day to strike down hundreds of the enemy. I knew we would triumph over them. We can still ruin their morale with our relentless attacks."

Judah hunched over slightly as he tried to catch his breath, than wiped the sweat from his eyes. "Well, there are many of them and they organize quickly. We were nearly slaughtered when the cavalry charged. We didn't see them arrive. Many brothers fell upon the slopes. I saw one of my men, Aaron, die." Judah was silent for a moment and then said, "Anyway, they can't stay there all day. They will need water in this sun and need to finish their camp before nightfall. We can charge them when they try to withdraw, perhaps, and damage them more."

John nodded as he took Judah aside. "Word is that Isaac is dead." Judah was still and John thumped his chest pleasantly. "You are my new captain, Judah. You keep watch. I will have Eleazar give us the signal if the Romans fall back."

"Only if they are not reinforced or maintain a loose order should we attack, John. If they meet our attack in solid formation, they hold the higher ground and can strengthen their numbers just as quick as we can."

"Leave the worrying to me, my friend." John patted Judah's shoulder. "It does me good to see you well." Then he ran to the ramparts near the Eastern Gate.

Eleazar met John at the top of the steps, trying to remain inconspicuous amidst the hundreds of Romans watching them, he pointed to the enemy lines and said, "They can't approach the walls, John. They are not prepared to attack the city now."

"I know that. I will pass the word to Simon's forces in the south to keep watch. If the Romans head back or deplete their numbers, let me know." John glanced at the bowmen upon the battlements stretching before him and felt his soul lift.

"What will you do if the Romans thin their ranks?" Eleazar asked.

A dark smile appeared upon the bearded man's face. John replied without a second's hesitation, "Avenge my village of Gischala and kill the Roman Prince."

*   *   *

Drusus walked his mount down the line of infantry. He cursed the gods for the heat, the Jews, and the fact that he could have been receiving a massage rather than listening to the shouts and curses springing up from the Jewish formation massed along the base of the city walls. Why they could not organize a controlled withdrawal back up the slopes and finish their camp was beyond Drusus' comprehension. He cursed the young Prince under his breath and killed a fly that had landed on his thigh. He glanced to his left at the backs of the legionaries standing three rows deep and wished he was back in Rome attending the theater with his friends, or admiring the temple prostitutes.

He liked the adventure of the legions, but without the responsibilities of work. Looking at the foot troops, he shuddered at the thought of himself as a grunt soldier of any legion at that, which was why he had used his money to purchase the equestrian office he now had. When he had first drilled with the Boars and had been accepted into the cavalry auxiliaries of the east, he had met the challenge with great anticipation, seeking glory and rank, but so far both had eluded him and he blamed Marcus Sulla Maximus for his woes.

"Drusus, wait up!" Varro called as he rode with his fellow decurion, Titus.

Drusus drew back on the reins, shook his head, and looked up to the sky. "Would it not hurt the gods to send us rain to cool our bodies? This is a damn nuisance."

"The Prince will be sending men back to return to camp duties," Varro replied, ignoring Drusus' complaining. "I was told by Marcus to inform you that you are to take charge of the auxiliary and hold the far left."

"I piss on Marcus, and you should too, Varro! He has us tromping around here like monkeys. This is absurd and an embarrassment," Drusus retorted. "The damn man thinks himself a god! Why, if I was a *consul* I would have him chained to the oar of a galley before the sun would set on this day."

Varro shrugged. "I feel the same, Drusus, but we are under the watch of Prince Titus. Nothing we can do now."

"Are you not embarrassed? We save the worthless hides of the Tenth and are left out here to bake in this damn heat. We should be retiring to our tents as heroes." Drusus glared at the Prince for a moment and then glanced at Varro who was delaying. "So when do we do it?"

"Not here," Varro lowered his voice. "It isn't safe."

"What isn't safe? What are you two talking about?" Titus, the younger decurion of the men, asked.

"Shut your pathetic face, Titus. You know of what we speak of." Drusus smiled and motioned discretely to Marcus who was some distance away, staring at the three officers.

Titus felt fidgety and nervous as he quickly busied himself, scanning the lines of legionaries making sure none had heard. "We can't touch him. We will get promoted when this is done. Things will be better."

"You live in a fantasy, Titus. Things can never be better until we kill the bastard Tribune. I have told you that before," Varro scolded his friend. A whistle suddenly sounded followed by a trumpet and nearly half of the troops, formed in the skirmish line, hoisted their shields, turned, and started trekking back up the slopes, heads hung in exhaustion.

Drusus watched the departing legionaries pass by and making sure none heard him he leaned forward and said, "Look, next patrol we're on, where it's just us and Marcus, we jump him and kill him. We can say that it was Jewish rebels, and nobody will know any better."

"What if someone sees?" Varro questioned.

Drusus shrugged. "Pay them, kill them, I don't care. We have to deal with him. This can't go on any longer."

"Decurianes!" a man shouted as he rode up behind the three congregating officers. "You are ordered to the centre by the Tribune."

Drusus sat upright and glared at the rider. "We will be there momentarily."

"Now, decurion!" the man replied, raising his voice.

"And who are *you* to talk to me that way?" Drusus lashed back.

The man smiled bowing his head. "My name is Pedanius, and the Tribune said to take things up with our Prince if you had any grievances." Pedanius swung his horse around and galloped back, his mount kicking up clumps of earth and dust.

Drusus glared at the arrogant Pedanius as he rode away. He shot Varro a look of anger. "Have you heard of that man before? What is he, alae?"

"His behaviour should be reported?" Varro suggested. "Insubordination if you ask me."

"And what good would reporting do? Who would we report to? It was Marcus who sent him," Drusus vented and shook his head. He caught the end of Titus mumbling something and turned, his rage threatening to boil over at the young officer, but his eyes suddenly saw a flash of fire shoot high into the air above the city walls. By the time Drusus interpreted the meaning of the fire to be a signal for attack, it was too late. He watched the gates of the city suddenly open and from within came a wave of howling Jewish fighters driving like a spear head for the center of the thin column of infantry.

The mere presence of the Jewish attack was all it took. With raw intimidation, and overwhelming numbers amidst the Jewish horde, the legionaries scattered like terrified sheep. Turning, they discarded their shields and spears and fled up the slopes to where work had continued on the camp. Those men already tired from the day's events and worn down from the heavy armour they wore, were slaughtered where they stood. The Jewish onslaught soared onward, pursuing the broken lines that scrambled up the hill. When the camp was alerted to the renewed surprise attack, hundreds more legionaries working with tools and carrying stones dropped everything and fled to the crest of the mountain.

Nobody had predicted the second attack. Prince Titus had given orders for half of the soldiers to return to camp after an hour of standstill. Now he found himself and whatever mounted troopers he could gather, surrounded and cut off from support. Reacting quickly with blind rage, Titus drew his sword. While leading a weak charge, he crashed into the Jewish ranks as they surged by, obsessed with the sight of the fleeing legionaries more than they were with the routed Roman hierarchy. Titus brought his sword down again and again as with each delivery flesh was peeled apart to the sounds of screams as blood soaked his feet and legs. His arms, with beastlike momentum, plunged the steel of his sword into anyone threatening him. He heard the powerful shouts and curses of Marcus as the Boars Tribune pushed forward, trampling men and striving to get to Titus' side to protect the Prince, but the Jewish attack was too thick and dense to move.

Titus saw Larcius' horse rear in fright as the legionary general clenched his teeth in wild wrath. Like in the tales of ancient Greek heroes, Larcius regained control of his horse, lunged forward in the saddle with his sword, and severed the arm of a Jew who had cut his leg badly with a barbed spear. The Jewish man clutched the bloody stump which had once been his arm, fell backwards, and rolled upon the ground screaming as more Zealots closed in upon Larcius to finish him off. Suddenly a high pitched trumpet blast seemed to shake the ranks loose and the Jews turned and fled in a stampede back to the gates as three organized cohorts of legionaries thundered down upon them making piecemeal of the Jewish flanks.

Titus watched as Jews poured back into the city. He lowered his sword and breathed a sigh of relief as the cohorts drove past him and formed up near the walls, covering themselves with locked shields from the rain of arrows falling upon them. Titus surveyed the fresh bodies lying about. Miraculously none of his officers with him had been killed, but nearly all of them had received sword wounds as Larcius examined the deep slash across his thigh and winced from the pain.

"Centurion!" Titus shouted to an officer nearby. "Secure the lines and pull your men back to a safe distance." The centurion saluted and bellowed at his men to retreat while maintaining their battle formation. Titus rode to Marcus and then scowled when he glanced around for the absent decurianes. "Where are your officers? We need to reform and shadow this ridge."

Marcus scanned the ground about him, than shrugged. "It appears they fled with the soldiers. Anyway, I will assemble my unit in full force."

"Send a man to the top of the ridge to gather some crack troops, at least four hundred men, and have them posted to the south."

"Yes, my Prince. What shall I tell the alae below the lower part of the city?" Marcus asked.

Titus sheathed his gladius and squinted at the city walls as the Jews erupted into cheers despite their frantic retreat. "Inform them of this fighting if they don't know it already for themselves. I want a show of arms from the camps. The Fifth is to keep an eye on the west, the same for everyone else. This cannot happen again!" Titus drove his fist into the palm of his hand, than turned to the sounds of galloping hooves and Marcus swearing aloud.

Pedanius, the alae trooper who Marcus had sent to inquire as to what his decurianes had been up to earlier, arrived dragging one of the Zealots by the ankle. The man was limp and had been silenced by the brutal chastisement he had received. The captives face was a bloody pulp while his arms were bruised and torn up from the sharp rocky ground. Pedanius, however, did not seem to care as he grinned and drew on the reins of his horse. He let go of the unconscious Jew's ankle and bowing in his saddle said, "My Prince, I bear a gift for you."

Titus dismounted and walked over to the beaten and broken body of the fighter lying upon the ground barely breathing. He looked into the man's face without mercy and with dark brooding eyes. Titus stepped back and crossed his arms. "An impressive catch. You deliver the enemy to me? To my very feet? How did you capture this man?"

Pedanius glanced at the other officers, but Larcius seemed to be the most interested. He exhaled loudly and replied, "I chased him to the south. I wanted him alive, and as I rode up beside him I just thumped him on the head with the pommel of my sword. Then I simply took him by the ankle and dragged him through the valley bottom to deliver the gift."

Titus turned to his signifer who stood holding Achilles reins and said, "Priscus, remind me to send a reward to this man."

"Yes, sire, I will," replied the tall soldier who steadied the bobbing head of Achilles.

"Marcus and Larcius, will you accompany me back to camp? There are things we must go over." Titus walked back to Achilles and with some help from Priscus, he mounted the tall warhorse.

"What do you wish me to do with him?" Pedanius asked pointing to the dying prisoner.

Titus glanced at the city seeing all the eyes gazing his way and without emotion, he said, "Crucify him before the walls, and any others who are worth the spectacle."

*   *   *

CHAPTER XV

April 14th, 70 A.D. / 17th of Nisan, 3830
Camp of the XII Legion

All the centuries of the First Cohort had been instructed to gather before the tent of the *principia* in full military regalia with signum deployed and banners flapping in the morning breeze. Each century was positioned in regular order as the legionaries stood at attention with their scuta resting upon the ground. The Serpent Century, led by Rufus Garus, was stationed to the left of the enormous principia quarters of Marcus Octavian and was followed by in successive order: Quintus Cassius Aemilius' Wolf Century, Cicero Vindacian's Lion Century, Marius Junias Livianus' *Fortis* Century, and Gaius Cornelius Antony's Hydra Herculean Century. Each respected Primi Ordines stood out from the ranks, the filed men behind them appearing like statues, waiting for their General to emerge from the tent and recognize them on this early morning.

Each Centurion had dressed in their finest, displaying their phalerae and torque awards which hung from each man's cuirass overtop highly polished chain mail. The officers fitted their legs with bronze greaves, cleaned their tunics, and made sure to shave for the ceremony.

Long before the ceremonial announcement had been delivered to Gaius Antony, the men of the First Cohort had wondered about the condition of the X Fretensis after the ravaging the legion had taken upon the slopes of the Mount of Olives. Word had spread like wild fire throughout the ranks of the XII, and they had been deployed to the walls and towers of their camp against the possibility of another Jewish attack. Men everywhere had talked and shared what little news came back, despite the constant reminders from the centurions to cease all gossip and keep watch. The soldiers had only the returning columns of horse troops as evidence that some Romans had survived the fight as they filed by, heads hung low and exhausted from the battle.

Legionaries closest to the cavalry units called out to them wondering if the X Legio had ceased to exist or whether the Romans had managed to bring the fight to the city. Getting accurate news, however, seemed impossible as each man willing to talk about the battle told their own opinion of what had happened. The stories had consisted of the Tenth Legion having been wiped out, Titus being captured, Marcus Sulla's Boars gaining access to the Temple and fighting off thousands of Zealots. Whatever images they had conjured up in their minds of the utter destruction of their fellow brothers-in-arms, had been dashed to pieces when the sun rose revealing to the sentries of the XII the hundreds of cooking fires of the Fretensis upon the distant mountain slopes.

Gaius glanced to his right, filled with a sense of pride. He had been informed that this morning he would be promoted as camp prefect, thus thrusting him to third-in-command of the entire legion. The news had certainly caught him by surprise, but he had celebrated nonetheless with his fellow officers. They now stood before the quarters of Marcus Tullius Octavian with their centuries drawn up in strict formation behind them awaiting the religious and sacred ceremonial Roman military custom.

A number of priests stood off to the right dressed in cloaks of white and wearing their usual skullcaps. A junior priest, with strange pale skin, held the rope of a young bull, adorned in garlands and its horns painted red to honour the god Mars. The animal moaned with frustration as it tried to pull away stomping its feet, but the priest held his grip.

"Company, attention!" shouted an optio who emerged from the tent followed by Marcus Octavian. The General wore elaborate, expensive armour with a brass and silver helmet crested by a crossways red plume. He also wore polished brown riding boots, gold plated greaves, and a red tunic under his armour. A signifer holding Marcus' signum followed a few feet behind the General as he held the pole high declaring to all the badges and symbols of family lineage and power. Another standard bearer also followed raising the *vexillum* of the legion which hung from a crossbar. Both soldiers wore polished tunics of mail and had the fur of wolves covering their shoulders and helmets and tied about their necks in front. Marcus halted before the cohort and scanned from left to right, noting the impressive display from his Primi Ordines as they all saluted while the ranks of soldiers pulled their pila against their bodies in formal military recognition.

Marcus turned slightly and nodded at the priests who led the bull quietly before the troops. One priest began chanting a song as he struck a brass bell he held with a small iron rod. Following the priest with the bell was another priest who shook a rattle and joined in the incantation lifting his voice up high above the ranks of soldiers. Finally, a very tall, thin priest drew up behind the man with the rattle holding a large oil lamp made from silver which vetted out a black, sweet smelling smoke, the fragrance of the Apis bull and the lingering reminder of Minerva's wisdom.

When the priests had circumvented the cohort, the music and singing ceased and the men drew up behind Marcus. A large brass bowl was brought forward and placed on legs of iron as a fire was built underneath and stoked so it glowed red. When the priests were ready, Marcus cleared his throat and said, "Men of the First *Cohor*, and of the Thunderbolt Legio. Your ranks have been assembled here today to witness the finger of *Roma* pointing upon one of the Primi Ordines to honour his service and reward him this day. An altar shall be built outside the camp and dedicated to *Jupiter Optimus Maximus* marking this occasion." Marcus pointed sharply at Gaius and straining to be heard shouted, "Primus Pilus Gaius Cornelius Antony, step forward and recite after me."

Without hesitation Gaius approached Marcus and then bowed his head and saluted striking his chest. He could not believe it was finally happening. He had been a high ranking officer of the First Cohort for three years and had served as a centurion in other cohorts for nearly twenty-four. All the battles he had fought in and all the thousands of miles he had marched seemed to suddenly melt away as he looked back upon his life. Now, he would become a prefect and have his voice accepted in the council of Titus. In the past he had felt out of place at councils, yet it was with Vespasian's personal request that placed him in the tents of dignitaries and kings. However, that would all change. He would be given the dona of camp prefect and be equipped with his own signifer and standard bearing the image of both Marcus Octavian and Titus Flavius Vespasianus.

"It has been a long time to get you here, Gaius," Marcus said just above a whisper. "The gods favour you and so does Titus. Now, recite what I say to you and pledge it." Gaius nodded and Marcus continued, "I, Gaius Cornelius Antony, do swear on the memory of the ancestors of my line."

"I, Gaius Cornelius Antony, do swear on the memory of the ancestors of my line."

"And the gods I pray to," Marcus said raising his voice for the legionaries to hear.

"And the gods I pray to."

"That I will be a servant to *Roma* and a steward to almighty Caesar."

"That I will be a servant to *Roma* and a steward to almighty Caesar," Gaius responded.

"On my life I pledge to serve well and defend the glory of *Roma*."

Gaius took a deep breath and repeated the line feeling immense pride as the words rolled off his tongue. Marcus continued stoutly with the sacramentum committed to memory, "I will serve my legio faithfully and willingly surrender my civil rights," Marcus waited for Gaius to repeat the line and then he continued, "to be bound to the anvil of Roman judicial power which is guided by the father of us all, Augustus." He paused listening to Gaius and then said, "I will never abandon my cohorts; I shall never forsake my men; and I shall always lead them to victory or death as the gods see it." Marcus waited patiently to the echoing reply of Gaius and recited, "I will uphold all military oaths and expectations and will not fail to sacrifice life when needed, should it be my own or that of my men."

"I will uphold all military oaths and expectations and will not fail to sacrifice life when needed, should it be my own or that of my men," Gaius declared loudly as he listened to the cohort vexillum flapping in the wind behind him.

"I swear to act without question when I am called upon, and go where I am sent." Marcus took a breath and raised his chin as Gaius finished repeating the sentence. "As a faithful soldier of *Roma*, I pledge to serve and honour the gods of

Roma which go ahead of us. As Praefectus Castrorum I do swear!" As Gaius finished the sacramentum, Marcus signalled to the priests with a nod. He then lifted his hands in the air as Gaius finished the oath and all the centuries of legionaries before him responded in a resounding chorus, *"Idem in me!"*

A knife was brought to the bull's throat as the summons to the gods began from the mouths of the priests and a tambourine was violently shaken. Gaius watched motionless as the blade cut through the beast's flesh, spurting blood in a surge upon the steel of the knife and the hide of the animal. The crimson blood poured upon the dirt causing it to darken as the bull groaned and collapsed. The priests removed the organs, and after Marcus checked their level of purity, they were dumped into the bronze bowl to complete the sacrifice. Then with a trumpet blast Marcus shouted, "I give to thee, Praefectus Castrorum Gaius Cornelius Antony, to lead my cohortes into battle. May the gods preserve his life and bring him victory."

Eight hundred men, which until now had remained silent, suddenly raised their spears in the air and with a unified cheer they hailed Gaius' promotion. Marcus approached Gaius with a gold medallion hung from a thick woven cord of red. Gaius removed his helmet, bowed his head and received the dona which was the emblem of his title of power.

"Congratulations, Gaius. This doesn't happen often," Marcus said with a grin and a firm nod. "I pray to Mars he will use you mightily in the coming weeks. This promotion comes directly from Titus. He wishes he could be here, but other matters were pressing. I believe he sees quite the influential use for you. I do pray you survive to see further glory bestowed upon your shoulders."

"Thank you, General. I am at the disposal of Prince Titus and anything *Roma* requires," Gaius replied, feeling the words jostle about uncomfortably from his mouth. Something pricked at his conscience that he could not identify, and he suddenly felt a sting of cold fill his being.

Marcus humbly nodded and then while ushering Gaius to turn, said, "Now, face your men and be recognized, Praefectus Castrorum."

*　　*　　*

Upper City of Jerusalem
Early Morning

Judah stood motionless, his eyes fixated on a dried-up fountain that had the appearance of years of neglect as dust and dried animal dung were caked inside the basin and the edges of the marble mouldings were chipped and cracked. A decorated Corinthian-styled spout rose up from the middle of the once beautiful fountain, and it to bore the marks of disregard as the top had been broken and never repaired. The fountain, to many people who could remember the erection of the project, had been commissioned and paid for by Herod the Great in an attempt to appease the local people and provide a glimpse of luxury. To Judah however, the fountain was only a grim reminder of the past which sealed itself deep within his soul and closed the iron-spiked doors of his heart and mind.

He exhaled calmly as his eyes surveyed the inner bowl of the basin. Studying the marble carefully, Judah approached. The fountain had obviously been cleaned long ago of any blood, but the image of Miriam floating in the water was still vivid as if he was staring at her lifeless body at that very moment. His body shuddered and he stiffened against the emotion welling up within him as he quietly turned, hesitating, whether or not he should leave. Adam and Caleb stood a few meters away, a look of puzzlement upon their faces wondering what had suddenly come over Judah. It had started as a routine patrol, but as they neared the market place, Judah had strayed off down a street as if in a daze and ended up in the vast courtyard which once held hundreds of kiosks of venders and merchants.

"Judah? There is no one here," Caleb said glancing at the fountain and then back at his friend. "What is it?"

"Nothing," Judah replied shaking his head. He gave the fountain one more longing gaze and then slowly outstretched his hand and touched the stone. Despite it being hot from the sun which hung in the sky, it felt ice cold to Judah who reluctantly swallowed the lump in his throat. For a moment he swore he could smell the fragrance of Miriam's hair and see her brown eyes, but then in a fleeting torrent the image and sense vanished from his mind like a robber snatching a man's money purse. Judah pulled back his trembling hand and rubbed it, shaking his head, disturbed at the grief he felt.

A gust of wind found its way into the courtyard, stirred some dry, dead leaves in circles and then skirted away leaving the debris scattered about. Caleb gave Adam a shrugging glance and then motioned for the large man to stand his ground. He walked up to Judah's side and silently gazed into the basin, resting his hand on the pommel of his sword. He glanced at Judah, observing the emotion as it washed across his friends face. He had only seen grief such as this at times when Judah regaled to Caleb the tales of Miriam and that fateful day. Realizing his insensitive words spoken earlier, Caleb swallowed his pride and remorsefully asked, "Is this where she died?"

Judah nodded. "I miss her, Caleb. We were to wed in a month, my parents were so proud of me. Miriam and I grew up together. She was perfect and I had grown to love her." Sorrow edged his broken voice as Judah stared off into the sky for a moment fighting back tears. Then a dark look filled the worn lines of his face, like the brewing of a storm which shakes the earth, and he vehemently said spitting forth the words, "The bastard still lives!"

"He will not live for long, my friend," Caleb replied.

Judah turned and faced his friend with salty tears clinging to the rims of his eyes which were reddened and grey. "My heart is filled with hate, my friend. I desire not only to kill Capito, but to cause him to suffer, so he may know my suffering."

Caleb listened carefully and then glancing back to Adam for support he said, "When the time is right, my friend, if it is God's will that this centurion be judged under the steel of your sword, then so be it. I will not stand in your way." He paused for a moment and then whispered, "My heart weeps with yours, Judah. I will help you avenge the blood of your parents and that of your love. Like the story of Cain and Abel, the blood of those slain cries out from the earth."

Judah was motionless, as if he had turned to stone. Then he slowly nodded and said, "Peace be upon you, Caleb, but when the time is before me, I shall snatch the life from Capito alone. Only through his death, shall I have satisfaction."

A scream interrupted the stillness of the courtyard as it echoed from a street nearby. All three men near the fountain reacted quickly, turning in the direction of the sudden eruption of terror that had filled their ears. Adam lowered his spear and furrowing his dark eyebrows looked out past the pointed bronze tip. "Those are Idumeans," he said.

Down a neighbouring street that branched off from the marketplace a number of soldiers could be seen emerging from the doorway of a house boisterous with laughter. Three of the Idumean soldiers stood in the street wearing long robes, armed with swords, spears, and shields. A fourth man, who remained in the doorway of the house, kept shouting and shaking his hands with an excited and animated display as he clearly was entertained by another one of his comrades within the dwelling. The Idumeans in the street continued laughing as they approached the house, peering through the door and windows at the spectacle inside. The sounds of a woman's pleading sobs wailed aloud, followed by a loud smack which silenced her.

"Bastards!" Judah vented, seething within as he drew his gladius. With grim strides, he made his way from the fountain towards the Idumeans.

"Judah? What do you intend to do? Those are Simon's men!" Caleb called out as Adam, with spear lowered and fingers tightening around the wood shaft, jogged over to his captain's side as they crossed the courtyard.

The Idumeans standing in the street had been so involved in watching their comrade tear the clothing from the woman within the home that they had not even heard the approach of Judah and Adam. The man in the doorway gazing inside the house grinned with pleasure as he watched his fellow soldier start to howl like a dog, drawing apart the woman's legs for a better view. He suddenly burst out laughing and then stood to disrobe. The Idumean tossed his belt upon the floor and then turned, shouting at his gawking friend to close the door for some privacy. "We can all share her!" he laughed gazing down at the sobbing woman with licentious eyes as he licked his lips.

"Stop this at once!" Judah bellowed with fury as Caleb ran to his side and drew his sword at the startled Idumeans who had swung around to meet the confrontation. The three Idumeans closest to them reeked of alcohol. The middle one staggered slightly and then smiled in a friendly gesture.

"You want the woman? You may go before my turn." The Idumean bowed graciously and would have toppled over had it not been for his friends who reached out and caught his arms.

"You have no business here. Leave now or you will fall where you stand!" Judah pointed his blade at the Idumean across from him.

The man in the doorway stepped down slowly. He studied the three Jews and shrugged. "What, you three will do something? You're Gischalan pieces of shit! You actually think you three with your toys can do anything to us? We have been ordered by Simon to search these houses for food. Do you know who we are?"

"Do you know who *we* are?" Adam said jabbing his spear in the direction of the man. "Make one move I don't like and I might use you for spear practice. The steel pierces deep and no mail or armour can stop its thunder." Adam grinned darkly at the men.

The Idumean laughed as he took a step forward and shook his head. "Come now, are you really going to threaten fellow brothers who have a common enemy as you do?"

"You're no brothers of mine," Judah said glaring at the man. "What you do is dishonourable. Leave at once!"

"Or what will you do, Judah the Lion?" said another man emerging from the home and tightening the belt about his waist. He was slightly taller than Judah, had a short cropped beard and piercing eyes. He wore no armour like his other compatriots, but was armed with a sword and a long dagger. "Ephraim is my name." He crossed his broad arms and snickered. "You had all better scamper back to John, or we shall take matters into our own hands. We are under direct orders of Simon; you don't really wish to interrupt those orders, now do you, Judah?"

Judah lowered his gaze at the man, wishing him to be struck down by fire from heaven. "I know who you are too, Ephraim. You were there that day Bagdatus cursed us at the Antonia, and Simon arrived to offer terms." The tall man bowed humbly with a grin and Judah spat upon the ground in disgust. "You throw in your lot with him? Well then, these are interesting circumstances. You shame us all and this city you claim to defend."

"Careful or I shall have to tame the Lion with steel," Ephraim uttered, lowering his voice and tapping the pommel of his sword.

"You are a spoiler of women, and you profane this city." Judah pointed his blade at the Idumean who narrowed his gaze and suddenly half drew his sword. Judah braced himself for the attack which was sure to come. He gripped the hilt of his gladius and made sure his stance was widened as Ephraim seemed to be contemplating whether or not he wished to provoke this wild man before him. Judah slowly lowered his blade, locked eyes with Ephraim and said, "Come, Ephraim, let us see who God chooses."

Ephraim's eyes dilated as his face paled. Suddenly with a great cry of rage, he drew his sword, charged forward and pushed through his comrades, slashing the blade at Judah's gut. Ephraim shouted again as he missed and then jabbed again, cutting the air with a deadly slice, the blade flashing near Judah's throat. After the second miss, Ephraim lunged again, hacking forward with the blade as it met resistance upon the edge of Judah's gladius. The steel impact echoed in the narrow street and Ephraim's arms shook from the blunt force. He stepped back in panic as Judah countered with a massive blow from above. Ephraim watched the steel descend as it cut the cloth of his cloak, sending him stumbling back into his comrades.

"Ephraim, no!" shouted one of the Idumeans who tried to restrain his friend. The danger was imminent and all seemed to realize it with the expert, professional sword strokes Judah delivered. Blow after blow rattled Ephraim's frame. However, Ephraim was lost in a world of rage as he leapt forward swinging his blade, finding nothing but air.

"Fight me!" Ephraim shouted seeing Judah step back and lower his sword.

"To come to me, Ephraim, is to die," Judah muttered.

"I shall send you to hell, coward." Ephraim charged forward and with a mighty slash, aimed for his enemy's throat. He watched as the blade singed through Judah's beard, but with no greeting of spraying blood, Ephraim realized he had missed again. However, in one cataclysmic moment of dread, unable to change his imminent doom, Ephraim knew he was exposed. Judah's blade slashed brightly through the air where it met the soft tissue of Ephraim's neck. The steel edge tore through arteries and sinew right to his spinal column in one ghastly display of gore.

A rush of blood flowed over Ephraim's chest as he gasped, then collapsed to his knees and dropped his sword. He tried to reach up to the wound but then a strange hiss escaped his lips. As his eyes rolled back into their sockets he fell upon his left side dead. The Idumeans watched in horror as blood continued to seep and bubble from the wound and surround Ephraim's still frame. They quickly looked at Judah who had recovered from the lethal blow and was now pointing his blade at them. Adam and Caleb joined Judah's side holding their weapons with grim determination and a steady resolve.

"Take him and leave. Tell Simon he has no right to do whatever he wishes to people. This is not his city." Judah took a step back and glanced down at his blade which dripped with blood. The Idumeans slowly bent down, took Ephraim by the arms and began to drag him prudently across the stones. When they were a safe distance from the Lion warriors, Judah watched two of them carefully pick up the body and carry it away, disappearing down one of the side streets that led through the Upper City.

"I can't believe you killed him, Judah. This could damage the treaty," Caleb said, referring to the agreement the three warring factions had made.

"The man deserved his fate. God sealed it, Caleb. There is nothing more to be said. John will understand and will consult with Simon." Adam stared at the pool of blood upon the stones and the smeared trail that stretched out before them.

Judah squatted upon the stones and stared at the blood. He had been driven by rage and anger at what the Idumeans had done, but he could not wrestle from his mind the look of shock upon Ephraim's face. It had been a painless blow; Ephraim would not have felt a thing. Yet, by the time he realized what had happened, he would have been drifting into a sleepy death as his body pumped his life blood out from the gaping wound. "Have peace, my brother," Judah silently whispered. He cleaned his blade on the edge of his garment as the blood soaked into the cloth, then stood only to realize a timid set of eyes was watching him from the doorway of the house.

The woman looked frightened, trying to maintain her composure despite her torn and ruined clothing. Judah sheathed his sword and slowly approached the house with his hands open in a nonthreatening gesture.

"That is far enough," the woman said, breaking the silence.

"Are you hurt?" Judah asked.

"The man was to rape me." She touched a bruise on the side of her face and winced from the pain.

"You're safe now," Judah said. "How old are you?"

"Seventeen," she replied dryly.

"And where is your husband?"

She shrugged and lowered her gaze. "Died of sickness two years ago. We had only been married a short while."

"And your parents? Who protects you? Who provides for you?" Judah queried, gazing at her delicate features.

"My father died in the fighting. My brothers were captured in the north and have been taken as slaves to the mines of Corinth. I look after my mother as she is sick." The woman, who had been shielding part of her body behind the door frame, now stepped out to show herself to the man who had saved her.

"What is your name?" Judah asked.

"Hadassah. My father was Shmuel. He was a sandal maker and leather worker. This is my home; I was born here." Hadassah's face was dirty and swollen from the beating and her hair was messy. Her fingers were thin and dirt had been smeared into the lines. She wore no makeup and was clothed in a simple garment dyed blue and black. However, Judah could see beyond the edges of pain ingrained into her face that she was a beautiful woman masked by misery and sadness. A light flickered in her eyes as Judah took a step forward and this intrigued him as she glanced awkwardly back at the other two men who waited.

Judah noticed her nervous curiosity at his men and he said, "Hadassah, this is Adam and Caleb. I am Judah." She nodded and he continued, "Do you have food?"

"Food is hard to come by. Those men claimed to be looking for some, same with others such as that vile Bagdatus."

"Don't you worry about him."

"I hide whenever he walks these streets. I think he believes the only one who lives here is an old widow, my mother." Hadassah clasped her hands in front of her and sighed.

Judah turned and signalling Adam said, "Give me your bread." Adam reluctantly surrendered the food and Judah handed it to her. "Here, take it and I will pray for the recovery of your mother."

"I don't know what to say." Hadassah held the dry bread in shock as tears welled up in her eyes. "My lord, you have saved the life of my mother and me. What right do I have to take your bread?"

"You have every right to live free of bondage, whether it shall come in the face of a Roman or Idumean. We shall watch this house, Hadassah. All who live here will be protected by my sword and the swords of my men. I am a captain for John of Gischala, and I shall spread the news of what has happened here so Simon's men leave you alone." Judah turned to leave and whispered, "Go in shalom, Hadassah."

"And peace be upon you, my lord."

*　　*　　*

CHAPTER XVI

Roman Camp of Titus
North of Psephinus Tower
Noon

Titus bit into the cheese hungrily as he reached for his wine to wash it down. Roasted pork and freshly baked bread had been placed on the table to his delight, followed by olives, nuts, fresh dates, and grapes. A jug of wine was always kept at the ready as a slave stood a few metres away while the famished Prince devoured the food with pleasure at the succulent taste of the dripping meat. A small silver bowl sat next to his plate where he disposed of the grape seeds and olive pits along with any bones that he had stripped clean of meat. He leaned back in his chaise and snapping a finger he was greeted by the slave who refilled his goblet. The Prince exhaled loudly, belched with satisfaction, and began popping dates into his mouth, one after the other.

The tent flap was drawn back and a legionary bowed humbly as he said, "My Prince, Tribune Marcus Sulla Maximus is here to see you. He says it's urgent."

"Are you blind, soldier? Can't you see I am involved?" Titus replied with annoyance.

The solider hesitated for a moment and then bowing said, "I am sorry, your Majesty. I shall inform him to wait until your meal is complete."

"No, no, wait." Titus sighed as he wiped his mouth with a towel. "What kind of a Prince would I be if I didn't have time for urgent news brought by my esteemed Tribune? Tell him I will see him immediately."

The soldier saluted and left the tent. A slight murmur was heard outside and then the flap was drawn back again. Marcus Sulla strode into the dim light to a welcoming smile emulating from Titus' face.

"What can I do for you, Marcus? Have you no Zealots to kill today?" Titus laughed sarcastically and held his hand out to motion for the Tribune to seat himself. "Bring this man wine!" Titus ordered the slave and then pushed the bowl of dates across the table awkwardly and said, "You must try these, fresh this morning and elegant. Do please help yourself, Tribune. There are no barbarians in these quarters."

"Thank you, sire," Marcus replied as he collected a handful of the dates and then sat upon a plush couch a few feet from the table. He nodded at the rich taste of the first date and Titus laughed as a cup of wine was offered to the Tribune.

"That wine is aged well. It comes from vineyards to the north, in the regions around the Galilee. They say it is pressed ever so carefully and then they have a system to remove the pits and any seeds still present. Then they then trap the juices and store them away. It is a secret ingredient I believe, that gives it such lustre and taste. It is just, how shall I say, remarkably Roman. I shall threaten the next winemaker I find from the north and demand he give me their fermentation method," Titus said almost as an afterthought. "Well, I suppose that is what gives it such allure, isn't that right, Tribune? The fact that it is kept a secret."

"Yes, my Prince."

Titus lifted his cup in a toast and finished what remained. "Now, I find myself disturbed at my table while eating my lunch. Who disturbs me? Why it is you, Tribune, and the *why* evades me, yes it does. What can the reason be that you would pay your Prince such a private visit? It can't be fighting, nothing happens as we speak. No officers have soured your mood, and the camps have been completed. Maybe some minor issues but we are finally back on schedule." Titus cringed at a thought and then shrugged. "I dare to think it might have something to do with yesterday but in the end we carried the victory to their walls."

"It is nothing to do with orders, camps, or the fighting yesterday, sire." Marcus leaned back in the couch and shot the slave a glare.

"Leave us." Titus waved his hand annoyingly at the slave and the servant departed quietly. "So why have you come to me? Or am I keen to guess."

Marcus shrugged and raised his glass. "It is nothing his Majesty has said which reveals the nature of my visit, although you came close when you mentioned officers souring my mood."

Titus laughed. "I do like the riddles we seem to play. You speak your mind, Marcus, and for that I respect you. You are not from the stock of aristocracy who plays me for a fool. Senators of *Roma* are notorious for that. Most of them are fat, boy-loving whelps that come to me and my father for advice. They have names, my dear Marcus, but in their case, their titles are what they throw at me, that and their precious balls which seem to enlarge, visit by visit so I don't forget how important they are to our war effort. Legates, consuls, generals, prefects, tribunes, decurianes, centurions, optiones, however you put it, it is possible for me to be surrounded by incompetent and impotent idiots. Now, I do posses in my arsenal irreplaceable men, men who will serve me at a whim and with passionate loyalty and virtue. These men bear the legends that make up the ideal Roman man, virtues that can't be bought. These men have graced our past, such as Pompey, Caesar, Augustus, or the infamous Marc Antony, who bedded Cleopatra and suckled upon the tit of the east. I look through our ranks now and see Titus Frigius, Sextus Cerealis, Tiberius Alexander, Gaius Antony, and so far you, my dear Tribune." Titus chuckled and grabbed a handful of nuts.

"I am honoured to be on that list, sire." Marcus humbly bowed his head, set his cup upon the couch and leaned forward.

Titus briefly nodded then raised his chin in question. "So, now that you have heard me state this, you still feel it necessary to speak to me?"

"I do."

"I see, and the nature of your visit has to do with sour tasting officers?" Titus said playfully.

Marcus nodded firmly and sighed. "It does."

Titus chuckled to himself as he mulled over a play on words in his mind and then came out with it, "Sour tasting officers? You're not resorting to cannibalistic tendencies, my dear Marcus?"

Marcus smiled and shook his head. "No, my Prince."

"Tell me, what news of your decurianes?" Titus replied getting straight to the point.

"You know of them?" Marcus asked caught off guard.

"Marcus Octavian warned me, before he made Gaius Antony Praefectus Castrorum. He offered the suggestion that there are officers who despise you and have grievances." Titus leaned back upon his lounging couch and rubbed his hands together. "What do you say to that, Marcus?"

"They do despise me, I know. It is because they are soft and not fit as decurianes. You know this yourself, Majesty; you watched their backsides gallop away twice yesterday."

Titus nodded slowly and then cracked his knuckles. "You mustn't feel you have to defend yourself, Marcus, or your good name. I know you for who you are and I know them to be cowards not fit to wear a toga, but this is a delicate matter and I do not need this while I conduct a siege. One decurion causing a stir can be dealt with easily, but group a few together, they can cause problems. They circulate enough among the alae to worry about what might be said there. You could have enemies at your back that you know nothing of." He paused for a moment and then said slowly, "What news do you bring me?"

Marcus scratched his chin then casually replied, "They wish me dead, Majesty. In fact, they wish to do the killing. They conspire to assassinate me and most definitely will try."

Titus was motionless for a moment, his smile vanished and his demeanour froze, as he fixated on the chiselled frame of the warrior Tribune staring silently at him. "You can prove this?"

"Yes, I have an inside voice to this plot." Marcus sighed and massaged his left arm briefly which bore a long, snake-like scar from past battles.

"Who is your man?" Titus asked bluntly.

"Well, it is decurion Titus, the son of Brutus, a magistrate of Syracuse. He approached me this morning. He was shaking and trembling, I knew right away this was serious and so I questioned his presence. It does not surprise me, but the man broke down in shame right before my eyes. He told me the other decurianes, Varro and Drusus, wish me dead and conspire to run me through with a blade. They would cover up the murder to appear as if I had been jumped by rebels.

"Decurion Titus said the officers felt this was the only way they could advance in title of office." Marcus paused and then shrugged. "It comes as no surprise. The decurianes have been plotting for some time; I have sensed it. After we ambushed the Lions to the north, I caught Varro and Drusus with a number of whores at a desert oasis, and since then they have had it out for me. I believe they fled the ambush at Psephinus Tower and the attack on the skirmish lines yesterday hoping I would be slain." Marcus chose his words carefully as he slowly said, "To their misfortune I survived and now I know about their dirty, little secret."

Titus sat forward and dangled his legs from the edge of the couch. He stared at the Tribune over the scraps of leftover food covering the table and asked, "His word can be trusted?"

"Varro and Drusus are comrades; the three have been like brothers since we came from Syria years ago. Decurion Titus only wishes to save his worthless skin rather than face the punishment which naturally would be handed out. That may be the only intelligent thing this man is capable of." Marcus finished his wine and set the goblet on the floor.

The Prince was silent for a moment as he considered a method of diffusing the situation. "What do you wish to do? The penalty for this is certain disgrace and death."

Marcus raised an eyebrow. "You don't need something like this affecting the ranks. Just think what it might do if it should ripple through the officer ranks that two high level junior officers are plotting to assassinate me. These two are dangerous and capable of anything. Leave it to me, Majesty. I can silence the two shits quickly and without an audience. Then you can continue as planned and move forward with no disruptions."

"Agreed. Just make it look like an ambush from rebellious Zealots who slipped through the cracks. Be sure to strip them of any wealth and hide it, keep it, I don't care. It will appear as mischief and logged in the company ledgers as such. I will leave it to you; handle this quickly and in your style. You need not tell me your plans. I just wish to hear the end result: that they are dead and the problem is resolved." Titus sighed and sat back. "What of the third man?"

"Harmless, my Prince. I only heard his tale and sent the man away swearing to him his secret was safe and he was in no danger. When he hears about the deaths of his two comrades, that will be enough to gain loyalty from him. He will piece the puzzle together. He is a coward and will not cross me." Marcus stood silently and bowed. "That is all, my lord."

"Very good, Marcus. I look to you to see this through. I have a use for you in the coming weeks, one that will be vital. I believe the gods have smiled upon you. The gods have a sense of propriety to the strong, my friend. They will preserve us so long as we give them due honour and respect." He covered his mouth as he yawned and then smiled. "May the gods preserve *Roma* and that of your fighting spirit, Marcus.

Now, you may go, but can you inform Yosef that I will see him now. He should be waiting outside. Oh, and tell that useless slave of mine to bring in more wine. My cup is empty."

Marcus snapped to attention and saluted. "I thank you, sire, and I shall send you an official report concerning the fate of Varro and Drusus." He bowed and exited the tent leaving Titus alone for a moment as the young Prince pondered the interesting set of events that he and Marcus had discussed. *If the decuriones could be silently disposed of then the outcome could actually send a message throughout the ranks that unity is the key and these lands are unforgiving, even if they are held by the equivalent of eight legions,* Titus thought.

He sat upright when a flash of light filled the quarters and Yosef ben Matityahu stood quietly before him. A smile appeared on the princely face as Titus stood and waved the Jewish general forward. "Sit, Yosef. Please take a seat and put up your weary feet. Are you thirsty? Hungry?"

"I am impartial, my Prince," Yosef replied diligently in Greek, his thick eastern accent masked by the smooth sounding syllables of the common language.

Titus grinned and sat as the slave reappeared with a pitcher filled with wine. "Fill his cup and then I will have some." Titus offered Yosef some of the food and the middle aged Jewish man eagerly helped himself to the bread and olives. "Yesterday was interesting, my friend. Your people fight with such tenacity it is impossible to predict. Will they continue to fight like this when we approach the walls?"

Yosef nodded without hesitation. "Certainly and with little doubt. They will fight with a ferocious mentality. They will see your soldiers killed at the walls and praise God for every Roman casualty. It is imminent, sire, expect your ranks to thin with every attack."

"And they cannot be bought?" Titus asked.

"With money? Certainly not! Nothing can be paid for in gold, certainly not how these Jews think of the city and its greatest treasure, the Temple. They are messianic: they long for messiah and diligently study the holy books of our Scriptures," Yosef retorted and leaned forward. "You underestimate their resolve, my Prince. You have brought your legions to their holy city. It is the conscience and spirit of my people. Jerusalem is not just a city. The Temple sits atop Mount Moriah, which emanates from our Scriptures and is the very beginning of our faith since Abraham." Yosef drank the wine and then pointed in the air to make an important statement, "The Temple will be the hardest to take, near impossible, I say."

"Why is that? We will build towers, ramps, and have artillery that can hurl heavy stone balls to crush rooftops and slaughter people." Titus jabbed the air to make his own point and Yosef shrugged.

"As a Jew and a priest, I have been within the inner courts. The Temple compound is a fortress in itself, as strong as the Antonia, except much larger and more complicated. Tens of thousands of fighters can be crammed within and the colonnades give height advantage to reign down fire on the heads of your troops." Yosef shuddered at the thought and said, "I pray it does not come to that."

"I have no desire to destroy the Temple or attack it, but I will reduce it to a quarry of rubble if they should press me. I would rather not see that outcome either, Yosef, but these people must see reason. I can crumble their walls and burn their city. I have been given power by my father to enslave everyone. I can line the Mount of Olives with so many crucifixes that the land will be stripped of every tree. I do not wish that outcome, but I posses the power to do it. The gods favour the strong, and despite your disbelief in the gods of *Roma*, I know that the power of my ancestors and Basilides are with this army. Your people must see that." Titus finished his wine and set the empty goblet upon the table. "So, having said this, I desire to tarry in my actions at conducting this siege, but only for a few days. I want to use you, Yosef."

Yosef slowly lowered his goblet and swallowed what food was in his mouth. "Me? What does *Roma* want with a lowly prisoner?"

"Not a prisoner, Yosef. When this is over I will reinstate you and reward your efforts and your faithful allegiance to *Roma*. I know you wish to compile annals of what occurs here. You have already begun preparation and I will see to it that you get to question captured Zealots. Your research and my seal will bear your masterpiece into a published form for the empire to read. Whatever you dictate, will be preserved and commissioned, for that I give you my word. As for a reward, well that is simple. How does tracts of land, title, and a villa in *Roma*, sound? Whatever I can give, as long as it is in my power to give, it is yours.

"As for now, however, I need you to reason with your people. You shall become my mouthpiece and orator. I will have you approach the city, under guard, and call out to them in the next hour. I want you to relay a message I will give you to John, Simon, and Eleazar. I want you to tell them resistance is futile but there is still a choice to be made. Your Passover Feast begins tonight, does it not?" Yosef gave a suspicious nod and Titus continued, "Seek to reason to their religious nature, give them the option to surrender before such a holy feast and that if they do, their God will bless them. I will even let them celebrate the feast in peace before the formal surrender afterwards."

"You would have me parlay with the Zealots? John despises me and hates my very name, as do many of the others. I would only represent *Roma* in their eyes. My use in this matter is something which will not benefit you at all, my Prince." Yosef watched Titus hide a twitch upon his face as the man turned away and pondered.

Titus cleared his throat and said, "I will have mercy on them, Yosef, to you I swear that. I will spare the city and spare them so long as they swear allegiance to *Roma* and my father as their emperor. If they do this, as well as start the daily sacrifice in the Temple again to the emperor then I will have mercy on them."

Yosef leaned forward and replied, "You would spare the lives of John and his officers? Men who killed your soldiers and fought against them in the north? Men who still defy you?"

Titus nodded. "I spared you, did I not? You fought against *Roma* along with them."

"But I had always been an advocate of *Roma* and what they had done for my people. John loathes *Roma*. It is intertwined in his being, just like muscle and flesh is a part of him." Yosef pressed with passion in his voice. "He will not bend the knee to any emperor. You will have to kill him."

"Nevertheless, Yosef, there are certain customs and standards that we must abide by as a civilized people and for this, I must give them chance to surrender and more chances if necessary. I have never wished for this siege to be conducted. Frankly, I hoped for the surrender of the city when the north fell or the terror that was brought with the arrival of the legions, but still they defy me. The next step is one of conducting political business. I must use you to speak with them and call to the people to abandon their rebellious ways and open the gates of the city. As to John and my promise to spare him, I would send him and his whole family into exile as a sign of my mercy. It has limits, Yosef, and I dare not wish them to test me. For when the ram touches the wall, the city will shudder under the thunder of my legions. I can roar the loudest above all other lions."

*   *   *

A small detachment of legionaries slowly descended the rocky slope of the Mount of Olives keeping a tight formation with spears raised, revealing to the hundreds of Jews gathered upon the walls that they were not a threat. A single signum and vexillum stood hoisted above the ranks with pride as the soldiers moved as one entity at the direction of a centurion and optio guiding them. Upon the satin cloth of the vexillum was the legionary Roman numeral of ten and below that in gold threaded letters the legionary title of Fretensis.

The men held their scuta against their bodies and with a resolve of steel they reached the bottom of the Kidron and proceeded forward, keeping a safe distance from the walls. The cautious eyes of the Centurion leading the small *vexilliatio* darted along the high ramparts as many Jews lowered weapons and leaned forward with curiosity to see what would unfold. Many of the fighters had wrapped their faces in scarves and only their dark eyes watched the movements of the Roman detachment as they navigated around rocks then finally came to an abrupt halt at a shout from their commander. A silence filled the ramparts as a gust of wind rolled through the valley and then dissipated before reaching the legionaries.

The Centurion strained his eyes as he gazed up at the ramparts dotted with fighters, then stepped out from his men. He turned his back on the city walls and exposed a white cloth from under his armour which he held aloft for a moment as the wind picked up, as if the natural force sought to steal it from the man's firm grasp. A murmur rose up among the Jewish fighters as they watched the Roman centurion let the white cloth go. The swatch of silk fluttered away as it sailed upon the wind, and before it touched the ground, a lone rider dressed in an elaborate cloak of blue and purple emerged from the main entrance of the Fretensis camp upon a white horse.

To the left of the Tenth legionary camp a column of mounted officers had gathered. Their purpose, under strict orders, was to observe the protocols of the Roman army and the 'civilized policies' which they felt compelled to make before the fury of the legions would be unleashed. Titus was among them along with much of his ranking staff as he sat rigidly in his saddle, the halter of Achilles firmly held by a servant boy straining to see the parlay play out before his eyes. Larcius had joked all morning concerning the futility of such charades, but after numerous glares from the Roman prince, the legionary General had learned to bite his tongue.

Deep within Titus' heart he wished the Jews would come to their senses and see the hopelessness of their current state of affairs. He hoped to assist the Jews in this decision by using a powerful weapon he knew would test their resolve and spread doubt in their minds. That weapon could be stronger than a siege tower or the iron head of a ram; it could be as intimidating as a cohort of legionaries bearing down with fury, and that weapon now rode a horse towards the city walls, dressed in fine garments to demonstrate Rome's generosity.

Yosef ben Matityahu tapped his heels into the flanks of his mount and pushed forward as he reached the valley's bottom. Nervous eyes watched the Centurion who had signalled him, give a sharp nod and then rejoin the legionary unit who stood like a cluster of statues in defiance before the thousands of hate-filled faces looking down from the high walls of the Temple Mount. Yosef felt a bead of sweat trickle down the side of his face and he shifted uncomfortably in his saddle. He had spent over an hour within his tent as a skilled slave had groomed his beard, combed his hair, and had even scented his skin with ointment and perfume, though Yosef had no reason to see how smelling pleasantly would woo the Jewish fighters to his side.

Titus had sent Yosef the largest gold ring he could find and had also provided a small chest of gold jewellery which the former Jewish General was to wear. This symbol and picture of individual wealth, as Titus had announced, *"Will show the enemy that Roma is good to those who obey her, and even better to those who cast down their arms and submit to her will which seeks the better for all humanity. Roma does not seek to punish, but to unite all men in order to show them potential and power."* Yosef had been instructed by Titus to deliver a speech on behalf of Vespasian and to try to persuade the Zealots to abandon the fight and surrender the city. Yosef felt the conditions of surrender were fair and well intended: full quarter for all fighters and their families who surrendered and a comfortable exile for the ringleaders. He did not doubt the Romans would uphold their end of the bargain, but he also knew who he faced on this day. John of Gischala, along with his men, were the ones who had gathered upon the walls and they would not hear reason, and for this, Yosef felt his heart sink low.

He guided the white Arabian, which had been loaned to him, over to the Roman unit as arranged. A single soldier stepped out of the formation and took the halter of the horse as Yosef swung his leg over the saddle and landed comfortably upon the ground. A chuckle rose up from sections of the ramparts as Jewish fighters began to notice who it was while others cursed him and shook their heads. Yosef ignored both insults, and while taking a deep breath, he strode forward to deliver his declaration and listen to the city rebuke him.

"Men of Jerusalem, I beseech you. Hear my voice and listen to reason! I come before you not as a collaborator as some may think, but as a fellow Jew! I am of the line of priests and a noble. I am a patrician of high birth, one who has worshipped in the Temple of our God. I have been taught from birth the statutes of our people, and the Law given at Sinai, delivered by Moses. I have followed these principles and teachings my entire life. I joined in arms with your brothers and was elected by the government, which is no more, whose bodies have long rotted away.

"I was given the title of General, in the company of those chosen I was elected by vote of the Sanhedrin and government. I prepared the north for war; I trained thousands of troops and defended towns and cities. I fought to reconcile Sepphoris and the differences at Tiberias. I kept back hordes of enemy auxiliaries and then faced Vespasian himself when he descended through the Golan.

"I found myself penned in at the great battle of Jotapata. Some of you may have been there. We defended its walls, fought from towers, and our resolve was mighty. At the sound of the shofar we fought off palisades and survived missiles hurled at our walls till they were reduced to rubble. When a breach had been made and the eagles brought through, we still fought them, house to house, alley by alley, until we were no more. The survivors were sent to Corinth to work in mines, sold as slaves because of our resistance. In the darkness I was captured and held prisoner. What should be my fate? I pondered this and felt as if my days would come to an end. But I tell you, Rome has seen reason; Rome has understood our oppression and heard our wail of misery. Vespasian is not Nero who ignored us, nor is Titus like Gessius Florus who persecuted us and murdered our mothers and children. I tell you now that Rome has felt mercy and pity for us and wishes to extend this to you now. I have never sold my brothers into slavery, nor aided in the destruction of a city. I have pleaded on your behalf and now I plead with you.

"Men of Jerusalem, young and old, you have taken all measures to protect the holy city and I commend you. You defeated the army of Cestius Gallus and drove him away. You have honoured your forefathers and fought valiantly like the Maccabees. The sanctuary is most holy and the God of Abraham, of Isaac, and of Jacob has not forsaken you, even now. But, I dare say He has allowed for our cause to crumble before the legions which have never stopped. All the strongholds have fallen except for this city and three others to the south. Once we had control of our lands, but only for awhile. The time of Rome has not ceased and they beckon you to halt this rebellion and see the benefit of her leadership. Rome has patience, but she has limits; she is merciful, but can become wrathful. I pray, do not test her any longer. She has come before you in power!

"Look, your walls are surrounded, your friends have been crushed throughout the land, and your people have been brought low. Pestilence and misery fill the land spread before you. Villages and towns that supported you now smoulder. I pray, as a fellow Jew, cease what you call rebellion and save yourselves, save the city and save the Temple. I not only come as a messenger, but one of you. See for yourself of Rome's generosity." Yosef held up his hand and revealed the ring. "I was once an enemy of Rome, like you, but they pardoned me and now have granted me title and a ring. I attend the legions not as a prisoner but as a member of council who seeks to turn the fury of Rome away from this holy city. I have seen the legions in war; it is not as you think. You men have not witnessed the full power of a Roman army, but you will if you tarry in your decision to surrender. Titus Vespasianus seeks not to destroy what we call holy, nor see the people of this city fall by the sword and experience the many calamities that follow war. But this will come about, should you rebuke me.

"Think of your wives, daughters, sons, and parents! Will your daughters fire an arrow? Will your mothers storm a cohort? Will old men hurl a javelin or young children man a catapult? This is but the fantasy that clouds your rationale. See logic, see reason. Do you dare bring wrath and death upon this city? Do you wish for its palaces, pools, markets and homes to burn? What of the Temple? Do you dare provoke a lion to attack? King Agrippa pleaded with you years ago, at the beginning, to abandon this futile effort and seek peace, but you drove *him* from the city. You slaughtered the Roman garrison and have murdered your own brothers; even after this Rome will show mercy. It is the eve of the Passover, the holiest day when we remember being set free and spared by the clutches of Pharaoh. Do not taint this feast by causing more suffering, set yourselves free. Rome wishes not to be a master, just a friend. Abandon madness and open the gates!"

Yosef stood silently for a moment as a breeze picked up and tugged at his garments. The city was silent and not a person stirred upon the ramparts above him. For a second Yosef felt that his words may have had the desired impact he hoped for. Then he saw a man stir among the ranks, and boosting himself up upon the battlements so that he could be seen in plain view, Yosef found himself staring at John of Gischala.

John crossed his broad arms and glared down at the traitor as anger filled his heart, feeling as if it would burst from his chest like an uncontrolled beast. His eyes darkened and he ignored everyone as if it were just him and Yosef to square off and fight to the death. John controlled his breathing to steady himself, pointed a finger at Yosef and hollered, "You bed with Rome, Yosef, and have forgotten *who* you are or *where* you come from. You *whore* yourself to her riches and *clamour* for her breasts as she suckles you like a bastard child. Your beard is stained with milk and your eyes are watery from the sight of her orgies. You have betrayed your people and sided with Rome and all her filth. She tramps around in our land, raping our women, enslaving our men, violating our customs, and blaspheming our God. She carries her idols forth and plants them in the soil, *our soil!* Now you accompany her? Does she promise you offspring? Do you wish to reverse your circumcision?

"You stand before these walls calling us to recognize the mercy of Rome, trying to scare us with the sight of legions, but I tell you, Yosef, we have all seen legions before and they bleed like all other men. However, there is one thing you have forgotten and it is essential: it is us who defend this holy city and her high walls. Has your Titus seen the Antonia? Has your Titus met the steel of our blades? Twice we have nearly killed the Prince of Rome but we shall not fail a third time. We slaughtered legionaries upon the Olives before they could even erect their camp and we spit upon their bodies. We fight for something which can't be bought; we are united. No more are there factions here; we are one common force which has the power to keep the legions of Rome here for years. I swear to you this oath, that it will be the end of Titus to take this city, and before it is done I will gladly see your head upon a pike."

Yosef shook his head dramatically and raised his arms, beseeching his absurdity. "John, you cannot speak for the city. You condemn them to certain death. Let the city meet and come to a decision. Titus is willing to wait. This cannot be about me or what you think has happened. This must be about reality and what lies before you. Set aside your differences with me and realize that there is no victory in those who oppose Rome. Do you expect to entice Parthia to your cause? Nobody stands with you anymore, John."

"I do not need anyone else by my side, Yosef. I have the best fighters in the country defending these walls and I have kept my honour, which is more than I can say for you. Away with you now, Yosef, depart from here so that Rome will be drawn to this city to be destroyed," John shouted back.

"You are a fool, John!" Yosef retorted shaking his head.

"A fool in good company and one who has made excellent preparations," John replied laughing. Then he clenched his hands into tight fists and raised his arms. "This is the city of Jerusalem, the city which is built high and solid. I fear not, and mock the very sight of Titus and his pathetic army!"

A single arrow shot with incredible speed from the walls and Yosef ducked as it sailed overhead and struck the hard earth behind him. A ripple of laughter rose up from the walls as Yosef recovered his balance and shouted back at them shaking his fist as he demanded an audience with the other city leaders. A small man leapt upon the battlements by John's side and pulled out a sling from under his garments. He placed a smooth stone in the leather binding and swinging it above his head, let it go with such a ferocious speed that Yosef barely leapt out of the way as the bullet passed by his head. The Zealots shouted in victory and suddenly a volley of arrows and stones were hurled at Yosef and the Roman detachment who began slowly backing up to protect themselves.

A legionary broke out from his unit at a fast jog and ran to Yosef's side, holding up his shield to block a number of small stones and an arrow which thudded into the hard layers of oak wood. Yosef recoiled backwards falling over, but was grateful for the shelter of the legionary's shield as the soldier shuffled back and tried to help him up under the hail of missiles. All the while laughter, curses, and insults rose up from the walls as the Jews spit at Yosef, calling out to the Romans to approach the city and test their resiliency.

"Are you hurt?" the legionary asked reaching out to Yosef while kneeling behind the shelter of his shield. "They can't hit us with anything larger then pebbles and arrows."

Yosef shook his head and took the soldier's eager hand and helped himself up. "Are you optimistic that your shield will protect us both?"

The soldier grinned and shrugged. "It has served us well so far. Now come, let us retreat back to camp." A number of trumpet blasts from the Tenth Legions camp sounded high and loud and the soldier gazed up the slopes before him. "Something is happening and we should go back." He turned slightly as Yosef huddled under the cover of the raised scutum and watched as his detachment, already a safe distance from the city walls, manoeuvred by wheeling right, then stamped boldly back up the rocky slopes to the sound of a succession of trumpets. A number of centuries filed out from the camp in organized columns of three men deep. They were led at a quickened pace by optiones who had them form up defensive positions under the watchful eye of Larcius Lepidus who rode down from Titus' side.

The Jews howled with laughter and shouted profanity at the Roman withdrawal. Many upon the ramparts cursed the lost opportunity to kill Yosef as slingers and archers alike argued about who had been the closest marksmen. It seemed as if the words of Yosef ben Matityahu had little or no effect upon the mindset of the fighters as they regaled themselves with the day's events and considered what sort of an impact it would have once the legions advanced upon the city. A number of men raised their concerns that with John's harsh response they may have missed an opportunity to negotiate with the Romans, but these men were quickly silenced by a roar of shouting.

Other fighters upon the walls stood silently amidst the activity wondering if the rebuking of Yosef had been the right thing to do. Many of the Zealots who had fled the north had experienced the bitter confrontation with the Romans and knew what the legions were capable of. It was Yosef's words that rang out like thunder in their minds as the former Jewish General had declared that they had never known such a fury as the one that would descend upon them in due time. With these thoughts, some of the Zealots left the ramparts and went to find their wives or friends while others groaned and covered their faces in despair. Whatever the emotions were that filtered through the packed ramparts, John of Gischala was at the center of it all as he continued to shout slogans of defiance and rally those closest to him.

*　　*　　*

Jerusalem
The Antonia Fortress

Night had fallen upon the land as thousands of burning torches could be seen illuminating the Roman camps surrounding the city. Despite the odd barking dog or beggar's cane rapping upon the stones of the city streets, Jerusalem had grown utterly silent like a cemetery. It was the eve of Passover, the Feast of Unleavened Bread, and besides the worship within the Temple courts performed by priests, people stayed out of the streets and kept to their homes. Light filled the eerie streets and cascaded upon nearby vacant homes now filled by pilgrims who had journeyed from around the country to celebrate the children of Israel's exodus from Pharaoh's Egypt long ago. Houses had long since been cleaned and inspected so as not to possess a speck of yeast as Jewish families and guests carried out the traditional purification ceremonies. Outside beyond the areas controlled by John, clusters of soldiers loyal to Simon patrolled the streets and shouted out curses to anyone foolish enough to be out. They banged on doors with the butt ends of their spears, only to laugh at the panic it created from the inhabitants within.

Upon the colonnades of the Temple Mount, John had stationed hundreds of guards to watch the deserted and blackened streets of the city stretching beyond their lines. He had ordered all scorpions and *ballista* machines loaded and at the ready in case an attack came from within. The three factionary warlords had not associated with each other all day. Frequent clashes had erupted with many fatalities, the wounded flooding the safe houses of each side, seeking whatever treatment available.

John sent threatening messages to Simon and Eleazar and the two leaders had responded with their own vows of revenge as a bloodied sheep carcass had been hurled up at the Royal Porticos by one of Simon's men. All three warlords spat and cursed each other through a protective screen of soldiers as they conveyed their grievances, threatening to storm each other's positions with a desire to slaughter the other in a melee of anger. However, by the time the sun had set, the reports of the two incidents that had occurred during the day, leading to the spark which had ignited the feud, seemed like a distant memory as John considered them in the presence of his fellow officers crowding the council chamber of the Antonia.

The two clashes had occurred earlier in the day, before Yosef's useless attempt to reason with the Zealots. First, while John had been occupied in the Antonia planning what to do with Titus' new camp north of Psephinus Tower, the report had come that his men were trying to force open the gates of the Court of the Women because

⌁ 246 ⌁

of the insults from Eleazar's Zealots above them on the walls. The men had started a yelling match, spears were hurled, arrows fired, and men filled the base of the high gates, pounding upon them in a fury with the pommels of their swords. John had dispatched his upper command to quell the riot and within the hour both sides had pulled back a respectable distance all the while exchanging heated glares.

The second report bore the news of a number of Idumeans plundering homes in the Upper City. They had been confronted by Gischalan fighters who apparently believed the woman inside to be a rape victim. Overcome by anger, with emotions ruled by vengeance on behalf of the molested woman, the Gischala fighters had broken up the raiding party, and had killed an Idumean officer. Simon had approached the walls of the Antonia, demanding the identity of the murderer while displaying the body of the dead Idumean. John had watched this display without a shred of mercy in his eyes and then had gone below to reconsider strategies that he had been working out with his senior staff. In a fit of rage, Simon spit upon the ground and had departed in frustration shouting loudly that John had crossed him for the last time.

"Now, I may not know who killed the Idumean even though he may stand before me, but we have bigger problems and it has nothing to do with Yosef's rant." John crossed his large arms and stared at the officers in his court who were crowded around the table waiting for their commander to continue. "Today we witnessed renewed hostilities from Eleazar's men. We have become divided again and we will not survive long if we remain this way. Simon has bulked up his guards along our borders and continues to terrorize civilians by plundering their homes. But my eye has been drawn to the inner courts of the Temple, my friends. We cannot let Eleazar hold up there much longer. Everyday his men look down on us is a risk we take of getting ambushed once the Romans approach the wall. Are we in agreement?"

Heads nodded as one man snickered and thumped the table with his fist. "We should have killed him long ago, John."

"And how can we? The man has turned the Temple into a fortress," retorted another officer angrily.

"We should burn the gates down!" Another man suggested.

"And risk destroying the Temple? You ask too much!" Caleb replied shaking his head as Judah nodded in agreement next to him.

"Are you thinking of a palisade, John?" Judah asked glancing at the other men who seemed divided on the issue.

John was completely still for a moment, as he stared at each man, as if weighing their consciences. He looked down at the table, leafed through a number of leather animal hides with maps drawn upon them, found the one he was looking for, and slid it out for all to behold. A detailed diagram of the Temple compound had been etched into the leather by the quill of a sharpened pen as the ink had stained the tan hide forever. The map displayed the colonnades and porticoes, the Court of the Gentiles, Court of the Women, Court of the Israelites, and the Court of the Priests with the Temple edifice within. John tapped the map with his index finger and said, "Tonight is the eve of the Passover. Tomorrow, as the custom requires, worshippers are allowed access for prayers. Tonight there will be sacrifices going on, but it will not be as crowded once morning breaks. When the gates are opened during the services, we slip in, disguised as pilgrims. Once in, we draw swords and slaughter them. Eleazar will surrender once he realizes he has been compromised and overrun."

The room was deathly silent. All the men seemed to weigh the heaviness of John's words against their spiritual convictions. A lamp upon the table flickered with the smell of burning oil present in their nostrils.

"What of Eleazar?" Judah asked solemnly as he watched the burning eyes of the massive Zealot warrior fix upon him. "What if he calls for mercy?"

"He can be spared, but only if he submits himself to my rule. Any of his men willing to join our forces will capitulate to my command. All who refuse, die." John leaned forward, both fists clenched, supporting his great weight upon the table. "That is my wish and only order. This inner fighting must cease if we are to face the Romans as a united front. Today's actions show that Eleazar still wishes to seek power, we cannot allow that. Eleazar must be dealt with, and this is how. Who is with me?"

Judah glanced at Caleb for a brief second. His friend caught his gaze and slowly shook his head trying to dissuade Judah. "I am sorry," Judah whispered into Caleb's ear and then clearing his throat said loudly, "I am with you John, I see no other way."

Following vocal support from most of the other officers, John licked his dry lips, glanced down at the map and said, "We will move at dawn. I will need at least one hundred men in long cloaks to conceal weapons. Judah," John glanced up, "You will lead the party along with any of your Lions who choose. Once you're through the gates, speed is the key. Kill the guards, cover your heads, and rush for the Court of the Israelites which Eleazar is sure to fall back on. Once you have taken that, he will flee into the chambers beneath the precincts as that is his only escape. Pursue him hotly and slay any who oppose you. I will follow in behind with a stronger force to reinforce the attack. With the blessings of Almighty God, we will take the tunnels and courts and secure the entire Temple Mount. With Eleazar defeated, Simon will have to make a truce so we can focus on the Romans."

"She has become like a widow who was *once* great among the nations! She who was a princess among the provinces has become a forced labourer!" All heads of the council turned in surprise as they saw an old man hobble across the stone floor, shaking his head, with tears running down his cheeks, and a bony finger pointing at them as he continued, "She weeps bitterly in the night and her tears are on her cheeks; she has none to comfort her among all her lovers. All her friends have dealt treacherously with her; they have become her enemies. Judah has gone into exile under affliction and under harsh servitude; she dwells among the nations, but she has found no rest; all her pursuers have overtaken her in the midst of distress." The old man halted and lowered his trembling hand as his reddened eyes gazed upon the men pleadingly. "The roads of Zion are in mourning because no one comes to the appointed feasts. All her gates are desolate; her priests are groaning, her virgins are afflicted, and she herself is bitter."

"Rabbi Gamaliel, is that you?" John asked as he stared at the old man in shock.

"Her adversaries have become her masters, her enemies prosper; for the Lord has caused her grief because of the multitude of her transgressions; her little ones have gone away as captives before the adversary." Shimon nodded at John and as his tears wet his beard and the stone at his feet he extended his hands upwards and said, "You, son of Levi, you make plans to attack the House of the Lord?"

The shock which had been plastered upon John's face quickly faded as he raised his chin and gave a sharp nod. "It is the only way, Shimon. We go not to destroy the Temple, but to cleanse it."

"You go to slay your brothers," Shimon lashed back suddenly as his shaky voice quivered.

John closed his mouth abruptly as he seemed caught off guard. Some of the officers hung their heads in shame while others either stared at the old priest or looked to John to end this outrageous interruption of their council. John, however, remained where he stood awash in stubbornness and pride. He slowly said gritting his teeth, "Shimon, we slay men who have not chosen the path we are on. You do not know things of this nature. Eleazar must be uprooted and the poison cast upon the road to be trampled by men."

"You risk all, John. I have known you since you were a boy; your father also possessed pride I have seen in few men. You must listen to reason. The Romans approach soon and killing your brothers will not make amends." Shimon wiped the tears away trying to gain his composure.

"This is not the government you were once a part of, Shimon. I am neither Ananus ben Ananus nor Matthias ben Theophilus. I am John of Gischala and I do what is best for my people, even if some must be sacrificed. Your age must be clouding your memory, to think that I am weak and will back down. God sent the angel of death to the homes of Egypt to remind Pharaoh he was not god and to divinely spare our people. It was a necessary cleansing of evil men who defied God. I see Rome and Eleazar as men such as in Egypt of old. Now, I go forth, like Moses, to lead my people, but this time they are divided. They must be brought into submission. I will spare whoever cries out for mercy, but for those who seek folly, they shall fall by the sword. I must lead them, and there can be no victory unless we stand as one." John paused for a moment seeing the effects his words had on the aging priest. "Do not stand in my way. Too many have died and I dare not wish you to be among them."

Shimon's face slowly broke out into a sad smile and he shook his head. "You cannot scare me, John ben Levi. I am old and ready to die if God wills my life. But remember this, if you shed human blood within the courts of the Temple, then it shall never cease and one day yours shall be shed far away in distant lands." Shimon sternly gazed at the man from Gischala who seemed unsettled and suddenly timid from the prophetic outburst which had sprung from the old priest's lips. The other officers awkwardly diverted their eyes from their leader and gazed down at the maps scattered on the table, feeling restless in the silence which enveloped the hall.

John wanted to respond. Anger welled up inside him as he glared at the aging priest whom he had known since he was a young boy in the hills of the Galilee beyond his town of Gischala. The priest had been a family friend, and a respected elder among the Jews populating the area. Whenever drought decimated the crops or orchards of local families, it was always Shimon ben Gamaliel's soothing voice which reminded everyone that God was in control and would restore their lost fortunes. However, all the memories of the a caring man vanished before John's vision as his heart was filled with embarrassment and rage at the priest's harsh words spoken so directly in front of his officers.

"John, what should we do?" one of the men asked, interrupting the warlord's thoughts.

"The rabbi should be arrested for such talk," another officer grumbled, jabbing a long finger in the priest's direction.

"Don't be ridiculous, he is a priest and is on our side," Caleb said scowling at the officer.

Shimon clapped his weak hands together jolting the men from their accusations and demands. "I am no threat, just the voice of reason in your head you should take heed to." Shimon shook his fist at the men, than exhaled loudly as he lowered his gaze and mumbled something.

"Caleb is right," John agreed with a sly grin as he glanced over to the priest who looked up. "Shimon is weak and is not a threat. We would do well to ignore him. The man has seen too many days and I fear he still holds to the old paranoia of the government that was formed here years ago. We must look ahead to the morning." John glanced at Judah and said, "I want you to put together a force of the toughest and most trusted men."

"Yes, John." Judah nodded firmly and rested his hand on the pommel of his gladius.

"Assemble them at dawn here at the Antonia, than we will move out. No shields or spears, just swords, and make sure their blades are honed and sharp." John crossed his broad arms and continued, "Friends, tomorrow we shall capture the Temple."

As the officers cheered and roared for more wine to be brought to the hall, Judah and Caleb slipped quietly from the room and descended a flight of stone steps which glowed from the torchlight of the lower level. Once outside, they left behind them the looming blackness of the Antonia's walls and walked along a row of high pillars in silence, the excitement from the hall fading into oblivion against the darkness which swallowed everything. As they walked, distant chants began to rise from the Temple sanctuary accompanied by the bleating of sheep. The priests worked endlessly reciting prayers, inspecting the lambs brought to them by pilgrims, than attending to the slaughter as the sheep were killed and returned to their owners for the Passover meal.

Judah and Caleb could smell the scent of blood and roasting meat as sacrifices burned upon the brazen altar. The two men passed beneath high arches of stone to find themselves among the colonnades of the Outer Court.

Judah looked troubled, and it showed upon his face. Caleb caught the dreary expression and steered his friend beneath the shadow of a pillar. He glanced around him, making sure they were alone and then asked seriously with a lowered voice, "What is wrong, Judah?"

Judah shook his head and exhaled loudly. "I am wondering if some of what Yosef said earlier may be right. I think of the people who will suffer once the fighting begins."

"People such as Adam's parents or Hadassah?" Caleb replied.

Judah nodded. "We cannot bow to Rome, for that I stand with John. But the innocent, the old and weak, should they not be removed from the city?"

"The Romans would never care for the weak while we stayed to fight them, Judah, you know that. If we were to send them out, the hillside would become scattered with crosses, Titus would see no value in making slaves from widows and the infirmed. It is either all out war or nothing; there can be no middle ground in this." Caleb thought for a moment and then said, "Titus has brought the legions to this city to seek victory at whatever cost. You heard Yosef command us to open the gates and lay our weapons down, that is Rome's resolve. John will never do so, nor will most of his fighters."

"I do not believe in surrender, Caleb. With Rome there can be no fair terms, unless they were to leave us forever. I merely worry about the civilians; they suffer as it is, let alone when the siege begins. Their calamities have not even begun." Judah appeared grieved as he stared at the ground. Then a look of passion flared within his eyes and he glanced up at Caleb, clenching his fists. "You have heard how Simon ben Giora plunders the city for food, have you not? Plague is rampant and many flee, but still more pilgrims swell the city for the Passover. There is not enough food to go around and when it comes down to it, food will be reserved for those who fight and contribute to the cause."

"I understand you, but there is nothing to be done now. This is John and Simon's city," Caleb shrugged. "Soon, as you and I know, Eleazar's power will come to an end. Things are changing quickly and looking grim. I do not doubt the city's defence, but I wonder if we are ready to repel tens of thousands of trained and disciplined legionaries? I don't know. This is nothing compared to the fighting we have seen, Judah. We battled small units of Roman cavalry and patrols, nothing of this magnitude."

"But this is different. We now stand behind the high walls of Jerusalem and are finally united against a common enemy." Judah pointed out across the courtyards of the Temple grounds and the colonnades surrounding them which were filled with soldiers. "The Romans will break upon our walls and we will find victory here. Titus has never faced such an obstacle, nor have the legions which he leads. It will break their spirits and demoralize them to the last man. We came so close to destroying them upon the Mount of Olives, and soon we will get our chance to see that task complete."

"They won't attempt to breach our walls until they complete their ramps and earthworks. Then they are sure to use towers and rams. If and when they do attempt a breach, I pray to God we remain upon the walls to repel them," Caleb replied slightly nervous at the thought. "What of Eleazar ben Simon? We plan this trickery tomorrow, flushing him and his men from the inner sanctuary, but why? To kill them? So that John can have more power?"

"It is necessary. Eleazar seeks not what is good for this city or its protection. The man has not once supported us, but only strives to undermine John and steal control. Eleazar holds the Temple hostage and he and his brute force desecrate it every day."

"And we won't desecrate it by plundering it and killing them?" Caleb retorted.

"We go not to kill and plunder, Caleb, but to flex our power and push them to surrender. Eleazar will see the sense in this and will be spared."

"You believe he will be spared? There is no way John would let him live after a raid on the sanctuary, not with the past so fresh in both their minds." Caleb countered.

"You couldn't be more wrong, my friend. John has assured me of this and I believe him."

"This is the man who killed a prisoner before our very eyes that night. John did not seek a trial for him nor reveal evidence to convict him. John interprets the law to be what he says it is and for that I am suspicious of what his business truly is with Eleazar. Sure we are to be his puppets and do his dirty work tomorrow, but for what end?" Caleb shook his head and crossed his arms.

Judah scowled. "You must be careful, Caleb. Look, you don't know John like I do. The man can be cruel, but his method of justice is be different than yours. He is a strong leader, one to be trusted. Eleazar schemes and has tried countless times to band with Simon to see us killed. He is a man who would not hesitate to run a sword through your gut and then spit on your writhing body. John sees the clear danger in this and must act, there is no other motive."

Caleb sighed and rubbed his neck. "I pray there is nothing else lurking behind the shadows."

Judah smiled gently. "Pray hard, my friend, for John seeks to solve the divisions within this city swiftly so as to unite the forces and face what lies before us. Don't doubt the strength of the Zealots or the mastery of John. It would do us all well to trust him. We will survive the initial assaults to see the Romans pay with their lives for attacking such a city as this, and we will praise God with every Gentile body that is slain and cast down from our walls. For that, I swear to you."

* * *

CHAPTER XVII

April 15th, 70 A.D. / 18th of Nisan, 3830
Feast of Unleavened Bread
Temple Mount
Jerusalem

Judah made sure the hood of his cloak covered enough of his face so none of the soldiers recognized him. He added a limp to his shuffle and bent slightly over to give the appearance of an aging man who had come to add his prayers to God amidst the throng of worshippers. As Judah hobbled along, from above the Beautiful Gate and within the Women's courtyard of the Temple, suspicious eyes from guards loyal to Eleazar watched him. Judah stole a glance at one bear-like soldier who held a broad spear in his massive hands. The Zealot saw Judah, shook his head and made an obscene gesture to what he thought was a senile, old man. Relieved that the sentry had been deceived as to his identity, Judah slowly glanced to his right as he slipped an unseen hand within his cloak and touched the pommel of his sword.

Like the deafening sound of thunder rolling over mountains, a chorus of rams' horns and silver trumpets suddenly filled the air. A wail of voices arose from the Court of Priests as Levites clothed in white robes sang out the *Shema* and *Hallel*. The priests continued to work around and upon the altar of unhewn stone which stood before the enormous edifice of the Temple. The massive five metre high altar belched a towering coil of smoke into the sky from the unblemished lamb sacrifices that fed the flames. The courtyard was filled with an aroma of roasting meat, a rusty iron scent of blood, and sweat from the packed male worshippers who filed through the glistening Nicanor Gate. The large gates were made from Corinthian bronze and were so heavy that twenty men had to open the massive doors to make the Court of the Israelites accessible to the ritually pure Jewish men.

Pilgrim men everywhere who had entered the Court of Women began shouting in frustrated tones, clearly annoyed at the delay which kept them from entering the Court of the Israelites. Hundreds of women, whose husbands demanded to be let through, gathered on the sides to drop tithes into the jars along the edges of the colonnades and then made their way up to balconies above to observe the ceremonies. Many of the women began singing and shouting out prayers towards the Temple, some raising their hands in the air while others covered their faces. Zealots from Eleazar's band hollered back while shaking their fists and arguing with one another as none seemed to know what to do. Eleazar's men had been given strict instructions to monitor the horde of pilgrims and keep the peace which was now deteriorating before their eyes.

Many of the worshippers stood up on their toes to see over the heads of those in front, smelling the burning oil from the *menor'ot* mixed with the sweet roasting scent of meat upon the altar. They shouted furiously as Eleazar's men refused to let them in.

Judah turned slightly and caught the cautious glances from at least a dozen men similarly dressed, all concealing weapons of their choice. There were at least one hundred of them. John had placed the entire command of the raid into Judah's lap. Judah had selected all the men. They had been specifically chosen because of their reputation for being swift, strong and not well known among Eleazar's soldiers. The remaining men of Judah's band of Lions certainly accompanied the party, and all had been instructed to leave behind armour and large weapons such as spears or bows.

The group of Gischalan fighters were organized during the night. They had managed to slip out from the Outer Courts unnoticed into the quiet streets of the city where they had connections within the population who housed them till morning. It was vital for the success of the raid that Eleazar's men suspect nothing suspicious about the pilgrims streaming through the gates of the Outer Court. For John's plan to be successful, trying to sneak men into the pilgrim lines in broad daylight would certainly run the risk of them being discovered by Eleazar's men. The shrewd eyes of the soldiers standing guard upon the walls of the Women's Court would only witness a mass of people pouring in from the city and would have no clue how to judge who was a genuine pilgrim and who was not. It worked brilliantly.

Judah received casual nods from many of his men as he singled them out from among the host of pilgrims. He sought to coordinate where they all were and that they were stationed in the correct places for the trap to be sprung. Judah could hear his own advice ringing loud and clear in his mind. *'Once inside the gates we wait until we have filled the court and then strike down all the guards swiftly causing a panic. Eleazar will have the majority of those on watch inside the Court of the Israelites and that is where we drive the pilgrims to. It will be impossible for him to organize a counter attack and the people will divide his men, causing panic. We can deal with those who challenge us, but most, I presume, will flee. Then we can expect John's reinforcements to follow. Once we have secured both courts there is nowhere Eleazar can go but below the Temple, which is to certain death or surrender. Speed is vital to this ambush. We fight in pairs. This will all be over soon. Before Simon knows it, Eleazar's force will be no more.'*

Without drawing attention, Judah signaled Aviram and Adam to the left to deal with the large guard who held the spear, having the appearance of a bear. Judah's two men returned the nods and pushed through the crowd of people. Ahead of him, were two more large men guarding the packed Nicanor Gate which led into the Court of the Israelites, each man armed with a spear and round shield. A shofar blew from the ramparts of white stone and a Zealot dressed in fine armour above the gate shouted down at the guards. Judah watched the guards respond quickly and then stepped out of the way as pilgrims were allowed to file past, finally alleviating the tension within the packed space. Judah squinted from the sun reflecting off the gold capped pillars holding up the heavy white marble rooftops of the terraces which were littered with guards. He saw his chance and knew the time was upon them as he pressed through the pilgrims for the two guards and motioned for more of John's fighters to follow.

The first man to die was the enormous guard who appeared like a bear with his curly beard and hefty shoulders. The man cast his spear aside, reaching for his blade when he spotted the pair of swords suddenly flashing from their hiding places within the cloaks of two men. Caught in the awkward stance of trying to avoid the edges of steel as he fumbled with his sword, the burly man let out a holler as his throat was peeled open by the first strike. At the same instant the guard's chest was pierced by Aviram who powerfully drove his blade deep through the man's leather armour. The guard's eyes bugged out in shock, then he fell backwards collapsing hard upon the stones with a deep gurgle.

Adam hesitated for a moment taking in the body upon the ground and the sheets of blood fanning out upon the white marble to the left of where the man had been standing. However, in an instant, Adam and Aviram recovered and simultaneously faced another guard who was charging towards them only to be slashed across his chest, sending a gush of crimson blood upon the marble pillar behind him.

"Cast your cloaks off! Cast your cloaks off!" Judah shouted cupping a hand around his mouth. "Secure the court!" Judah tore at his cloak flipping it quickly over his head as he drew his sword and spun around watching the entire raiding party respond to his command. Already a band of fighters had gained access to the ramparts above them and were charging with a ferocious wolf-like tenacity. The mere sight of the Gischalan Zealots descending upon Eleazar's men caused numerous soldiers to drop their weapons in surrender while others turned and fled, leaping down onto the floor of the court only to shatter their ankles. Judah dodged around pilgrims everywhere who streamed past him in a panicked stampede to evade the men with swords. Some people shouted, "Sicarii!", while others hollered that it was Romans in disguise. Whatever people thought it was, at least they kept their distance whenever they saw a man clutching a drawn sword.

Judah led the main force of Gischalan fighters straight at the Nicanor Gate which stood boldly at the top of a staircase of fifteen curved steps of marble leading to the Court of the Israelites. Only three guards remained, two holding their ground in the entrance of the gate and one standing above. A barrage of emotions flickered upon the men's faces as they stood in the path of certain doom. Each feeling horror at what was unfolding before them, helplessly watching Eleazar's reign of power swiftly coming to an end. The men felt anger as they knew they had been abandoned by Eleazar and the greater host of his army who remained in the priestly chambers below the Temple, unaware of the death above that would soon seal their own fate.

The man above the gate, an officer under Eleazar, shouted at the two men below and then drew his sword. Judah halted as he watched the two guards cautiously move towards him with lowered pikes as sweat stung their eyes and fear gripped their souls.

"Come, surrender!" Judah called out as thirty men of his raiding party amassed behind him, clutching daggers, clubs, and swords.

The two guards halted and one dropped his spear and raised his hands in the air to show he was no threat. The other guard spit upon his friend in disgust and then shouting aloud charged Judah, but it was to no avail. As swiftly as the guard had sprung his attack, it was countered by an equal speed as over a dozen Gischalan Zealots leapt out from behind Judah like a pack of hungry, starving dogs. There was no real danger for the odds were clearly against Eleazar's man. The head of the spear was simply knocked away, the shaft broken in two, and with three sword thrusts and a solid heavy stroke to the face from a war club, the soldier was silenced. The officer above the gate winced in horror as the guard's nose and jaw shattered into bloody ribbons of broken teeth and shards of bone. At this sight, the other guard collapsed to his knees, hunched over, and started wailing, begging for mercy. Without acknowledging the weeping guard, Judah led his troops past the man and through the undefended gate into the Court of the Israelites.

Judah knew they had to act quickly. His force overcame what little resistance they ran into as they spilled the blood of eight more men and captured thirty who fell upon their faces in surrender and called out for mercy professing that they would join John's war band. "Where is Eleazar?" Judah mumbled to himself as he caught his breath. His chest was soaked with sweat and adrenalin raced through his body. He had counted on heavy casualties in taking the courts. Eleazar ben Simon had not suspected a thing.

"Judah! Judah!" shouted a Gischalan fighter waving his sword while standing on the other side of the court.

Judah directed a few soldiers to keep an eye on the Court of the Priests, but not to enter. He trotted over to the man and glanced down at a body outstretched upon the flagstones, his lower stomach slashed open and entrails piled in a pool of blood that stretched out a metre from the corpse. "Who is it?"

"Don't you recognize him? That is Simon ben Ezron, one of Eleazar's ranking men." The soldier gently pushed the body with his foot and there was no response. "Poor bastard, he could have been nice to have around," the soldier muttered shaking his head.

Judah cocked his head to the side and leaned over for a closer look. He stared at the dead eyes of Simon's face, opened as if in alarm but appearing like glass, lost and strangely at peace. The corpse's arms were outstretched, as if reaching desperately for his sword which lay a metre away. A line of blood trailed out from Simon's mouth and twisted between the stones. A gentle breeze flicked the curls of his hair and his body looked cold and stiff. The last time he had seen Simon ben Ezron was when he had attended the council of the three factions. The man had said nothing that day and now lay in a pile of his own gore, never to speak again. Judah straightened giving a solemn nod and glanced at the soldier. "Did you kill him?"

"No, one of the other men did. I saw Simon cut down one of our men over there." The soldier pointed to another body. Just metres away lay a young man, lying face down in a dark pool of blood, arms pulled in as if cradling a baby and motionless. "When Simon dropped him, another fighter did this to him. He should have just surrendered."

Judah slowly walked over to the other body and knelt down beside it. His eyes became watery and tears of salt wet his dry cheeks flowing into his beard. Judah reached out and gently touched the still body and shook his head as he shuddered. Aviram, young in life and a beard barely sprouting from his chin, now looked asleep. His head was tucked in and eyes closed. The amount of blood upon the stones of the court attested to the severity of the killer blow that had snatched the life from this young man. *The pain would have been over quickly,* Judah thought as he sat back and stared for a moment at the body. It was not supposed to be like this. Aviram had waited for years to face the Romans in open battle. He had been so eager, hotheaded, and possessed a fury few could ever attain, and now he lay dead, killed at the hands of a fellow kinsmen.

Judah slowly stood and with a whisper said, "Farewell." He simply nodded and took a step back.

"Judah! Eleazar is underground in the chambers!" shouted another fighter who stood in the doorway of one of the buildings built under the terraces held up by tall gold capped pillars.

Judah glanced up at the enormous Temple looming before him with its doors of plated gold, four massive marble columns built into the high walls of the edifice capped with golden vines and pyramidal gold spikes. It was a glorious sight to behold, and one Judah had not seen since he was a boy. For a moment he stared dumbfounded at the beauty and majesty of the structure, but then the soldier shouted again and the sounds of swords clashing together jolted his attention to the present situation. "Forgive me, Adonai," he whispered as deep within his heart he wondered if he was slowly losing his soul because of what he was taking part in.

The fighting carried on down a steep flight of stone stairs which were packed by over three hundred fighters of Eleazar's band, desperately trying to regain their lost courts above. They all knew that if they did not drive the Gischalan men back, then all would be lost. Somewhere in the depths Eleazar's voice of thunder could be heard echoing through the chambers and rising up into the midst of the battle. Men screamed and shoved one another as Gischalan fighters poured down the stairs into the fray trying to gain access, while Eleazar's men struggled to hold them. Crashes sounded as men slipped on blood-soaked stones, their terror rising up in shrieks while they were beaten, stabbed, or strangled to death.

Judah could not get access to the battle. The entrance was plugged with soldiers from his raiding party who were standing around, waiting for the Zealots of Eleazar deep within the chamber to give up. Once that happened, a chase would ensue. A man emerged from the stairwell, squeezing through the sweaty bodies of fighting men. Judah ran over to speak with the soldier. When the exhausted man saw him he just shook his head at the blood stained blade he carried. "Eleazar is putting up a stiff resistance."

"What does it look like?" Judah asked.

The man shrugged. "They are packed in there like rats, all backed up through the tunnels. It will take days."

Judah turned as the sound of feet tramping upon the stone ground echoed loudly within the courts. Suddenly a wave of a couple hundred Zealots armed with spears and shields flowed into the Court of the Israelites lead by John himself. The tall warlord glanced around at the carnage, smiled at Judah and clapped his hands.

"I like what I see, well done! Leave it to a Lion to win the day."

Judah shrugged. "They still fight, John. There has to be over a thousand still below in the chambers. The stairwell is too tight. We're able to hold them but only for the moment."

John glanced past Judah to the mouth of the stairs where his men fought to gain access to. Another Zealot pushed his way back out of the stairwell, his face and chest sheeted with blood and his left arm limp from a deep wound. He collapsed upon the flagstones wheezing and John ran to him with a skin of water which he poured down the man's parched throat. Judah and a number of other soldiers gathered behind John as he knelt and asked the man what was happening.

"Eleazar shouted at them to fight to the last. None of us have seen him, but he is there. Men everywhere are dead. The space reeks of blood. We have killed many of them, but we are getting ripped apart. The bastards have spears and can reach over the heads of those in front, slashing and cutting those high up on the steps." The man gasped for air and then took another drink of water. "We can't hold them much longer."

"That is why I have brought help," John whispered with a grin and patted the man's leg congratulating him.

"What should we do? This could take all day," Judah asked shaking his head.

John stood and glanced around for a moment. "Bring me stones, heavy ones, stones that two or three men must carry."

"Where do we get such stones?" a soldier asked.

"There is a pile near the western side left over from the masons of the Gentile Court. Bring them quickly! Go!" John shouted at the mass of formed troops. "I need fifty of you to relieve the men in the stairwell!"

More than two thirds of the Zealots were organized by lower ranking officers who instructed them to drop their weapons and hurry to retrieve the slabs of stone. John stood with his arms crossed, as if he enjoyed this day of fighting. He watched a few dozen fighters emerge from the stairwell, relieved by fresh recruits, only to collapse upon the ground from exhaustion. They were covered in dirt, blood, vomit, and sweat.

Many of them gasped for air or drank water which was brought to them. Others, overcome by fear, retched upon the stones and covered their faces in embarrassment from the urine that stained their garments. All, however, were grateful to be alive. It was as if the very sight of John of Gischala had the power to restore their ill fortunes for many praised him and smiled despite their close encounter with death.

Soon pairs of fighters began to appear carrying large slabs of granite and marble. At least a hundred groups entered the court equipped with the heavy stones as they were directed to the stairwell entrance by John who ushered them as close as they could get to the fighting. Then with lungs filled with air John shouted, "Pull back!" His Zealots cramming the stairwell thought they had heard wrong, but when he shouted a second time they shoved back whatever soldiers of Eleazar's force they could and scrambled like madmen back up the narrow passage. As the last Gischalan fighter leapt from the stairwell pursued by the screaming mob of Eleazar's men, John shouted at the nearest pair holding a stone. "Throw it down! Crush them!"

The pair of soldiers did not need to be told twice. With wild eyes of rage, and bodies resembling that of demons, Eleazar's men howled up the stairs in a charge, drenched in blood and sweat. Out of terror at what was pounding towards them, the first pair suddenly heaved the stone with all their strength. The slab of stone soared about three metres and crashed into the first three soldiers of Eleazar's men whose bones were crushed with cries of agony. The stone rolled over top the bodies of the men and struck more beyond them as it toppled end over end knocking men aside. Soon another stone was sent down the stairwell to the same effect as men below pleaded with excruciating pain as legs, chests and skulls were crushed under the avalanche of stones.

After the dust cleared from the tenth stone, a glance down the stairwell revealed its brutal work. Nearly a hundred men lay in heaps, appearing like scattered mounds of straw. Bodies were entangled and strewn about, overlapping one another as the smell of blood festered in the air. Sounds of pleading and weeping filled the chambers as the wounded asked to be freed from their torment. Others lay paralyzed and bleeding to death.

"Bring me Eleazar alive, if possible!" John bellowed raising a fist in the air. "Chase them down and force them to surrender, kill all who resist." He saw Judah give him a surprised expression and John laughed. "God has given us this day, Judah! The enemy is broken and the Temple is reclaimed. We will purify it without haste once this mess is cleaned up." John gestured to the blood-stained flagstones and the motionless bodies about the courtyard.

Nearly three hundred Gischalan fighters raised up a war cry with swords drawn as they poured into the stairwell and trampled to death any unfortunate wounded lying upon the broken steps of granite. The war cry was carried deep below the Mount as hundreds of fighters searched the chambers and rooms, their shouts echoing among the corridors like jackals. Eleazar's men, disarrayed with their spirits broken, fled in desperation. Some were reduced to that of frightened children as they screamed and wept with terror, looking for a place to hide. However, for many there was nothing they could do, for surrender still invited the hungry blades of John's men as they slaughtered hundreds in the chambers of the priests. Finally, with blood dripping from blades of steel and eyes piercing the dreary light, John's Zealots discovered Eleazar demoralized, shamed, and cowering in a corner trying to hide among sheaves of barley.

Outside in the court, John ignored the ghastly expressions of horror by priests staring at him from the burnt altar. A tall priest, holding the incense of fragrance, stepped out from the altar and glared at John from the safety of the Court of the Priests. He stood, clothed in the Robe of the Ephod, its fringe lined with small golden bells in the shape of pomegranates.

The Robe of Ephod was donned overtop a white tunic of fine linen with the sleeves exposed. Overtop the blue robe, the priest wore the elaborate Ephod, embroidered with blue, purple, scarlet and gold. About the priest's waist was a girdle of expensive taste, the sash reaching down to his knees.

Upon his chest he wore the Breastplate of Judgment which glistened with twelve, rectangular, small inset jewels. This was the prized symbol of the twelve tribes represented by the weight of the stones which consisted of: sardius, topaz, carbuncle, emerald, sapphire, diamond, ligure, agate, amethyst, beryl, onyx and jasper. The breastplate was fastened by blue lace to golden rings about the Ephod, and secured by two clasps upon his shoulders which were inset by larger onyx stones, each inscribed with six names of the tribes of Israel. The priest stood barefoot, clutching a golden chain with a bowl on the end as it wafted with smoke from burning incense.

His face held a dark, foreboding glare as his black beard gave him a fierce look. Upon his forehead was the brilliant white *mitznefet* designating him as the High Priest of the Temple, and over top of the linen on his forehead was a gold plate in Hebrew stating, "Holiness unto YHVH". Filled with anger, he pointed his finger at John and shouted, "You profane the Lord's house! This is holy ground! Be gone, vile one!"

"Silence, Phanni ben Samuel, we do this for Adonai and so your duties are not spoiled!" John exclaimed shaking his head with annoyance.

"Silence yourself, man of insolence! I am the Chief Priest and this is erev Pesach! Should you not be preparing the *shulchan aruch* for your men to partake of? The *Seder* draws nigh and you do this? Have you even cleaned your quarters of *chametz*? Who shall sing the *Ma Nishtana* on this night? Our children have been killed and terrorized, what is left? This is a holy place! You spoil our service with your presence! How must we conduct our sacrifices of the lamb, when the blood of your brothers has been spilled? Adonai does not need more filth upon his steps! Where you stand is for ritually pure men only! You have defiled yourself and this sanctuary!"

"Don't tempt me to come to you, Phanni! You speak unwise words!" John threatened.

"You would cross through? You're not a priest! Or are you? Are you of the proper line of ancestry? Have you have immersed yourself in a mikveh? One of blood, I would understand, not of water! Tonight, many will taste the *maror* and remember not of bondage and tears in Egypt, but of the great suffering from John ben Levi!" Phanni clenched his fists as the smoke of incense floated around him.

"I would cross through if I did not fear God! Watch yourself, Phanni. I am a man who has a long memory! The Zealots made you and we can remove you! I am sure Matthias ben Theophilus would like his place back, am I not mistaken? Guard yourself." John turned with a heated glare that suddenly melted away as dozens of his soldiers emerged from the stairwell carrying the body of Eleazar ben Simon whose chest had been slashed open multiple times and left arm hacked from his body. John cringed slightly at the grotesque display of his rival.

He had known this time would come and Eleazar must have known it to. Somebody had to give, and John had always known it would be the weakening of the Zealots in the Temple. He had also known that Eleazar could never have stood the embarrassment of capture, which was why the warlord had fought to the bitter end. John approached the body as his men laid it upon the flagstones. He bent down and peered into the shocked expression etched into the lines of Eleazar's face, with mouth wide open and tongue slightly hanging out. Blood dampened his scalp and stained the ground under his skull where he had obviously received a harsh blow to the head in his final moments. "Goodbye, old friend," John whispered, closing the eyes of the corpse. He stood and signaled his men to carry the body away and with a grin he muttered, "The Temple is mine now."

*   *   *

April 18th, 70 A.D. / 21st of Nisan, 3830
Mount of Olives

The air was filled with a steady clamour of sound upon the Mount of Olives as hundreds of iron picks broke apart stones. Slabs of rock were pried from the earth by crowbars as shovels tilled the soil and packed it down where the land was uneven. The sight of thousands of legionaries and auxiliary troops scattered upon the rocky slopes gave the commanders a sense of accomplishment and purpose.

Preparations for the siege had been strict. The main focus and concentration of the army was to be devoted solely on leveling the earth and removing stones to create an even battlefield so the legions could be masters of the upcoming conflict. The camps had all been completed and soldiers were stationed upon its towers around the clock as they surveyed the city for any sign of suspicious activity. Stone walls two metres high had been built surrounding the camps as trails of smoke wafted upwards from cooking fires and smithies. The clanging of hammers upon metal seemed endless as blacksmiths fixed equipment, created nails, bands of iron for siege towers, and honed the edges of gladii for paying customers. The stables were just as active as men exercised their mounts and kept them active within a training field beyond the camp to the north east.

The day's duties had been announced and posted which included: cleaning of the latrines, hospitals stocked, ditches and drainages dug and walled properly to flush out the filth from both man and beast, as well as food preparation by a small army of cooks.

On the northwestern side of the city, just out of catapult range, hundreds of labourers had been added at midday committed to erecting siege ramps. Engineers and surveyors took to the heat from the comfort of their tents, working ceaselessly with their gauge instruments. They guided troops carrying loads of stone and dirt to the right places and instructed them on how to pack it down, counting on the weight of rams and siege engines. Battlefield experts had met in the early morning as they sketched out plans for the best possible places to construct siege ramps and the order of materials needed.

The list seemed endless: two thousand hatchets, three thousand shovels, eight hundred hammers, nine hundred crowbars, lumber in great portions, sacks of packed earth by the tons, iron spikes in the tens of thousands, hides of animals for fire protection, vessels of water and pitch, oil, rope by the miles, pulleys and on and on. Vast tracts of land began to be cleared for the constructing of three sieges ramps north of the sister towers along with Roman siege engines which, when assembled, would reach a staggering twenty-one metres in height. Supplies, however, were always an issue that required a separate army to maintain in its performance to keep consistent with the labouring legionaries. Supplies had to be brought up by hundreds of carts and soon the sounds of braying donkeys and grumbling oxen became something of a chaotic musical number amidst a thick dust cloud that lifted from the dry land.

In the early morning hours, Prince Titus' chief engineer, Porcius Gracchus, had sent men forward toting long lines of rope with lead weights tied to the ends. When they were within range they hurled the ropes towards the walls, unmolested from the curious onlookers who watched from the Hippicus Tower. It took a number of tosses for the Romans to get the preferred distance, but when this was gauged and marked down on a ledger, they dragged them back, coiled them up, then calmly walked back to camp.

Titus had called on Yosef just after midday to accompany him for a leisurely ride to inspect the progress and attempt to boost the morale of the troops with his presence. Titus still felt proud of himself for hefting the first stone of the morning to the ovation of his troops. He had completed the act as a symbol of Roman virility and masculinity, a sign that they were here for good and the Jews could watch their approaching doom, stone by stone. "Their days in that city are numbered," Titus had announced, receiving a cheer. He had hurled a stone at the city calling down Jupiter and then had mounted his horse, riding away to the sound of whistles blasting from the lips of centurions, announcing to all that work was to proceed for the next four hours before the changing of shifts.

Titus enjoyed Yosef's company. He was a man who was honest, spoke his mind, and more importantly, Yosef was safe to confide in. "You take charge of your mount, Yosef," Titus cheerfully said as they rode together. "I have known some men to be terrible riders, not an ounce of horsemanship in any of them, mostly senators and fat aristocrats, I might add." Titus chuckled and guided Achilles around a boulder that was being rolled to the side by a pair of Thracian alae.

"I grew used to riding when I was commanding forces in the north, my Prince," Yosef replied watching the Thracian men grunt and sweat on account of the stone.

"You organized cavalry units, did you not?" Titus asked, drawing on the reins. Achilles tossed his head at the command which restrained him from picking up speed.

"I trained them as well, with help from other Jewish officers who made the recruiting easier." Yosef swatted at a fly in front of his face and scratched his chin. "We raised squadrons of horse troops mostly from men who had never ridden in their lives."

"Where did your inspiration come from to train these troopers? You were not a military man before that, were you?" Titus questioned, squinting from the sun and wishing he had brought a slave to carry a canopy.

"I studied in *Roma* for two years. I was not a learned man in warfare such as yourself, your Majesty. I was from a priestly line, a patrician, yes, but not a military man. Remember, it was the government that elected me to serve in the north. I simply applied what I had learned watching legions in training or the praetorian on the Palatine." Yosef was silent for a moment as he thought back to all the notes he had taken and the drills he had witnessed as an observer. He had learned so much about Roman military discipline, but it had not been enough to prepare the north for the real thing. The education had been one thing, but to train men who had been farmers and wine makers their whole lives to be professional soldiers to face the legions? Impossible! When the eagles had come at the head of waves of legionaries, their thunder had trampled the earth and their appetite had consumed cities.

"I must say, Jotapata was well built up. That was one of the hardest sieges my father committed to," Titus commented relieving an itch on his nose. "Your culture is different in the area of warfare, far different than other tribes or armies in the north of the Danube or in Britannia.

"That is something Cestius had never anticipated, he thought you Jews hated one another and would ally with the Romans against opposing factions. But you didn't. The mere presence of *Roma* united you all and Cestius was caught bent over with his toga flung up and his ass burned from the sun." Titus laughed and shook his head. Then he pointed at Yosef and scolded him with three shakes. "You Jews fight each other when you have no enemy but then become one when we show up. It has worked for you in the past, but not this time. Your luck can only go so far and your God must tire of which side He should be on. That is a weakness of you Jews. *Roma* has been powerful because of unity in its past and will now continue in that direction as the gods see fit. These last two years were almost the death of her. The wars with Carthage, Germania, or against treacherous rebels, such as the Pompeian forces, have proven that through unity the spoils of war are lapped up by hungry tongues."

Yosef watched Titus gaze towards Jerusalem's walls for a moment and then shake his head. "Except, my lord, Pompey Magnus wasn't so much the rebel as the one he opposed who would not relinquish power and was a man declared to have committed treason against the Senate, Gaius Julius Caesar."

"We're not all perfect, Yosef. The Flavians come close." Titus chuckled tossing his head back. "I'm sure we will become gods in our own time, though, and then achieve perfection in *Elysium*."

Yosef ignored the blasphemous comment and leaned forward in his saddle. "Would my Prince take an interest in the history of my people?" Titus turned in his saddle surprised by Yosef's boldness and then nodded. "When we came to this land over a thousand years ago, we took it conquering by the sword. The armies of Israel marched throughout this land by the command of Joshua ben Nun, and we destroyed cities with high walls and armies vast and numerous. Under three kings, Shaul, David, and Solomon, we knew what kingdom meant. David was the greatest, conquering the lands around us and receiving tribute from those such as Sidon, Tyre, and the kings of Arabia. Solomon perfected this kingdom into a golden age where his throne was known throughout the world. The Queen of Sheba travelled from the lands of Ethiopia to pay tribute to such a man as wise as Solomon. She fell in love with him with a passion far beyond any I have known."

"Ah, *Eros*. The god Cupido struck both their hearts with his sharpest dart," Titus said laughing at the picture of the Roman god of erotic love and affection.

Yosef frowned respectfully at the usage of the Greek term. "It went deeper than erotic, sensual love, my Prince. Many say they truly loved each other. Solomon was the wisest man who ever lived. He was given this wisdom by God who had asked Solomon what he wanted most in life."

Titus drew on the reins of Achilles and halted. He leaned forward in his saddle, deep in thought, and then cleared his throat and said, "Solomon asked for wisdom? Nothing else?"

"He was given one request, and he asked for wisdom. Not just wisdom, but greater wisdom than Socrates, Plato, Pythagoras, Aristotle, or all the orators and philosophers of history. His wisdom led to poetry superior to Homer's Iliad or Virgil's Aeneid. Not a man in Italy, Greece, or throughout the Aegean can be found to ever match the Proverbs and Psalms of the great king Solomon who was in his splendour.

"However, being humble as he was, God gave him riches, land, a kingdom, and allowed him to build our Temple. He floated mighty cedars from Lebanon down the coast and brought them to the ports of Joppa. He sent thousands to work in quarries and taxed the population strictly to pay for such an enterprise as the Temple to our God." Yosef licked his lips, pausing in thought and then added, pointing to the sky, "But Solomon's wisdom was still human, not comparable to God, and he brought the wrath of God upon Israel's future by taking many foreign wives and building idols upon the mountains. It was his son, Rehoboam, who unjustly taxed the nation and caused the split between our people, Israel to the north and Judah to the south. Many years later it would be the Assyrians who would sack, plunder, and enslave the north, and the Babylonians would do the same to Judah, meanwhile burning Solomon's Temple to the ground."

Titus shrugged and shook his head. "The man loved women. I have something in common with this Solomon of your people's history. A seducer of queens and a well endowed lover. Once again I do not see the sense in your God punishing him for recognizing other gods, but then again, your God is strange to me. Come Yosef, tell me of this David."

"Well, Solomon's father King David, was a man anointed by the prophet Samuel to replace King Shaul who had become corrupt and wicked," Yosef said.

"So David was a great man, and Shaul was not? A clash of two titans, hey?" Titus asked.

"David was a great man, but there was a time he served King Shaul with a steadfast loyalty and a humble passion. He fought against the king's enemies and slew them with his sword. He even slaughtered a giant of the Philistines who was a champion, like the fight between Achilles and Hector. This Philistine was taller than any man you have ever seen, like the Cyclops of Homer or the Colossus of Rhodes. He was a brute of a beast, vast in strength like Hercules, and it took one man to heft his shield and another to carry his sword and javelin. The Philistine was from the coastal city of Gath, among the five coastal fortresses of the cruel Philistines, and his name was Goliath. Not a man among the Israelite armies could be found who could defeat him, save for David.

"The account is recorded in our Scriptures and oral records. David knocked the giant down with a stone from his sling and then beheaded the man for all to see. Thus, the armies of Israel drove the Philistines from the field. Sometime after, King Shaul grew jealous of David, but his corruption had long since begun years earlier."

"How did King Shaul become corrupt?" Titus asked as he genuinely pondered the story.

"King Shaul violated the role of the prophet Samuel and did not punish his men when they ate carcasses with blood in them, which is strictly forbidden in our dietary laws. He consulted a witch for his oracle of the future and grew jealous of David as he became a champion in his army. Shaul even tried to murder David with a spear as David played his harp. Once a shepherd boy from Beit Lechem and the youngest of his father Jesse's sons, David was known to be an amazing musician. Shaul then pursued David for many years trying to kill him, but again and again David spared his life, such as at the oasis in Ein Gedi to the south.

"Shaul had a son though, Yonatan, and he and David became like brothers until the end." Yosef paused as he saw Titus' interest piqued from the tale. "King Shaul and Yonatan battled the Philistine army, a great enemy of Israel, and they fought in the north, near the city of Scythopolis, as you Romans know of it as. However, when King Shaul found his army beaten, he felt God had abandoned him and so Shaul killed himself; his son was also slain in the battle.

"After this, David rose to power, fought against the Philistines and broke their armies over and over. He also conquered land, punished people, and became great. Yet, even in his greatness, David still committed murder, took another man's wife, and then repented. He was known as a man who talked with God and a man of action. King David was a master with the pen, and wrote many hundreds of songs and poems which are still known to this day."

Titus grunted with agreement and rubbed his shaven chin. "So, David was a great warrior, but a man of passion. He was a man who committed treacherous acts, but still was humble to his God?" Titus gazed out at all the workers and grinned to himself. "I like this David, a warrior, lover, philosopher, and one who speaks with a god." Titus glanced at Yosef, "Was he royalty from the beginning?"

Yosef shook his head. "He was a shepherd, a simple man, but was filled with great zeal."

Titus laughed. "A humble man, I like it." He sighed and raised his eyebrows in delight. "Your people's history is colourful; it pains me to wonder if your people had followed their God correctly, they might have been as powerful as *Roma*. It could have been you wearing my sandals and sitting upon my horse, and me, cowering in the city of *Roma*, surrounded by legions of Jewish soldiers." Titus pondered the image deep within the confines of his mind for a second and then laughed. "Your God is strange. He doesn't expect you to strive to be strong and intimidate, but instead to humble yourselves, serve Him, and appear weak."

"You are wrong, my Prince. Our God calls for genuine service of the heart, not in careless action or apathetic gesture. He wants us to keep His Holy Word and the Law. In doing that, we become great, not of ourselves, but because we serve the one and only God of our forefathers." Yosef nodded and sighed. "When God spoke to Moses, He told us that as long as we served Him we would be blessed, but judgment would descend upon our heads when we served Him not."

"Your God is strange indeed, Yosef." Titus rolled his eyes and picked up his reins. "You don't even call Him by a specific name like we call our gods. How can you know He is who He says He is? I cry out to Jupiter and can see his image which I am familiar with."

"An image of dead stone, your Excellency? Does Jupiter ever speak back? We Jews follow our God because He is active in our history has given us the Law to abide by and speaks through His words, the Holy Scriptures, which we study without cessation." Yosef pointed to the Temple glistening from the rays of the sun. "Even now they serve Him, and the future is in His hands. We have faced exile, displacement, and slaughter, but we cling to His Word. We know He will remember and keep His covenants with us. Israel is His beloved."

Titus mulled over Yosef's words for a moment and then turned to him. "I will call on you more to speak to the city; they must see reason. Do you hate them for trying to kill you? They are your people."

Yosef shook his head briefly. "The Zealots may share the same blood as I do, but they are not *my* people. I pity them sometimes, but John, Simon, and Eleazar have polluted their minds and turned the people against me and what is good. The priesthood is tainted and all that is good is constrained. I am happy many of the patricians and men of the equestrian orders have escaped, but there are many who suffer within her walls. I pray that all of this is over soon, and the city may be spared, for that I leave to God."

Titus shrugged. "You leave it to your God and I leave it to the Zealots."

$$*\quad*\quad*$$

An hour before midnight

The ramparts were vacant except for Judah who stood wrapped in a wool cloak and grasping a spear. He steadied his breathing and shielded his face from the wind which came up from the Kidron Valley. The flames of torches flickered upon the walls above the Eastern Gate. He had sent a number of guards away to catch some sleep and now stared with heavy eyes at the active Roman camps upon the slopes of the Mount of Olives. Music, composed of a Persian nature, seemed to take form as it drifted across the dark slopes of the valley. Fires burned by the hundreds further up the mountain side above the Fretensis camp, as caravan tents of Arab traders had been erected to attract naïve Roman soldiers who wished to purchase souvenirs or bed young prostitutes.

The harlots of the traveling caravans were always crafty women. Some of their masters taught them to steal from men they entertained while others were allowed more money if they would perform wildly for their patrons. Some prostitutes had become so experienced that they could usually handle a legionary within a half an hour, making room for many paying customers throughout the night.

The most money however to be made in the business of pleasure, was in young girls and boys who had reached the middle ground of puberty. They sometimes would be displayed in front of large tents with prices hanging around their necks. If they made lots of money and performed well, they could have their own personal quarters with a small sign carved in stone and propped outside their tent. Upon the sign it could read, "Come within, I wait," or, "Jason's Trunk," which usually would appear along with an image of a young man with an erect penis protruding from the stone. These sex slaves of the merchants were coveted and sought out in markets for it was their future services that would rack up the sesterces, catering more to the ranking officers than the regular grunts of the army.

To the northwest of the Roman festivities, the sky was dimly aglow from the fires of Titus' camp. Towards the east, the ridges of Scopus and beyond were ringed with thin trails of torchlight as columns of auxiliary cavalry moved among the olive groves, collecting timber to the sound of hatchets thudding in deep successions throughout the night.

It was a night such as this that Judah could easily grow lost in the deep realms of his mind. He mostly daydreamed of Miriam, trying to recall the things they had done together and the Shabbat meals he had shared at her family's table. The chilling thing that seemed to disturb him the most with memory of Miriam was the absence of facial recognition. Since the day she had been murdered, Judah had dreamt of her continuously, but her face was always hidden. He could sometimes smell her hair, or recall the touch of her skin, but the memory of her eye colour or the shape of her chin and lips fled his mind. It was obvious he felt tormented and bound by invisible chains which constantly reminded him of that day in the Upper Market. Yet the reminders were fleeting and sought to cheat him of any sense of peace and closure.

Judah gently closed his eyes and thought hard. He told himself that her hair had been dark brown and that she had loved the smell of jasmine. She had been short compared to his height, her forehead barely reaching his chin. Judah tightened his eye lids, trying to trap all darkness within as if any hint of light would spoil the fond memory he was trying to formulate. He focused and held his breath.

Judah saw her for a moment. He traced the strength of her legs up to the curves of her hips and then basked in the sight of her long hair which hung down the small of her back. She had been beautiful. Miriam had been old enough for the signs of a woman to show in the contour of her breasts and the gaze in her eyes, but young enough for her innocence to emanate from the soft, radiant touch of her skin and the glisten of her hair. Yet, what had her face looked like?

Judah concentrated hard, tightening his body almost to the point of perspiration, but any picture of Miriam's face eluded him. He suddenly exhaled and bowed his head in misery. Against the steady wind which picked up he whispered to himself, "Miriam, my love, how can I ever express to you my grief? You have left me here, where I sometimes wish to seek death." He stiffened his frame as he slowly glanced up to face the sky and said, "Death will find me soon, and when it does, please come to me so I can feel peace again."

A shadow seemed to move beyond the walls in the darkness and the thought of Miriam fled Judah's mind as he strained to see who it was. He could make out a single man, but the man did not appear to be dressed in Roman fashion as he quietly moved along the length of the city, tracing the Kidron. He was just out of bow range but Judah had no interest in killing him or raising an alarm; his interest was purely in the identity of the man who seemed to be more out on a leisurely stroll than spying on the city. Judah glanced behind him at the stillness of the Outer Court. A number of fires flickered as they were surrounded by sleeping forms of Zealots. The snoring of other men leaning up against columns or laying upon the flagstones of the court sounded like a strange song mixed with the crackling of sparks in the air. A few shadows stirred within the sanctuary of the Temple as a number of priests moved about, yet despite this the air was silent and uneventful.

Judah looked around the ramparts as far as he could see, only making out a handful of sentries standing guard. All of the guards looked out into the blackness of night, none seeming to have noticed the mysterious man on the edge of the city's perimeter. Suddenly, Judah felt an ounce of curiosity fill his being as to the identity of the man. For some reason Judah felt he may be able to talk with him and learn something of the Romans. With this thought prevailing through his mind, he silently left his post and descended the ramparts, slipping through a side door in the wall near the Eastern Gate.

*   *   *

Yosef tripped over a stone and cursed silently as his toe throbbed from the pain. He halted with annoyance, hoisted up his cloak so it did not hinder his walk, and then continued on. Yosef had not felt the need to inform anyone of his night wanderings. In fact, this had been the third consecutive night he had felt the desire to skirt around much of the city where he would sort things out in his mind. He liked the stillness of night. Something about its refusal to reveal anything beyond a hundred yards was soothing to him. It was a time of reflection and peace; reminding him of days before the war when he had lived in Jerusalem as an important man. Now he was still important, just not in the eyes of his own people.

Yosef took a deep breath of cool air and pulled his cloak tighter against his body to shut out any presence of the wind. He gazed to his right up the high slopes of the Mount of Olives and studied the outlines of Roman sentries patrolling upon high towers. Every once in a while he would catch a flash of steel from their segmented armour reflecting from the torchlight, then it would disappear only to outline the shape of a hulking man holding a shield and javelin.

The sweet scent of burning ropes and heated pine wafted in the air. Soldiers in the camps used scrap pieces of dried rope to start fires in order to boil the resin sap used as glue to repair almost anything as well as coating uncured hides to cover a ram or wicker hurdles to protect archers and ground troops, thus acting as a fire retardant. The scent was distinct and unique to the legions, but was a common smell when a Roman army was conducting a siege.

Beyond the camp, the fires burned brightly from the tents of the Arab merchants who had set up their tiny city market an hour before dusk. Titus had asked Yosef if he would attend to the Prince's side to keep him company and Yosef had agreed, unable to refuse. However, after two hours of seeing topless women shaking their breasts and pushy merchants, Yosef had retired from the commotion with the graces of Titus to seek peace and solitude.

Yosef turned away and stumbled again as another curse slipped from his lips. As he regained his balance he suddenly saw another man standing before him, almost completely cloaked by the night. Yosef froze immediately in shock and stared at the man. The stranger cautiously moved forward and held up his hands to prove he was unarmed. Yosef took a step backward, tempted to flee and then heard the man whisper, "I have no weapons and mean no harm. I am from the city. I was on guard and saw you."

Yosef's mind was a swirl of confusion, but he held his ground. He knew many people in Jerusalem wanted him dead, and he would not give this man another second if he showed sign of aggression. He slowly felt for the long dagger he carried concealed among his garments, and the touch of the cold handle gave him a calming effect. "Are you an Idumean, Zealot, or Sicarii?"

The unknown black outline of the man shook his head and whispered, "No, I am none of those."

"You are one of John's men?" Yosef asked.

The man nodded. "Yes, but not a Zealot. I joined him to defend the city, not take part in murder and theft as the others did."

Yosef held his breath for a moment and cocked his head partially to the side in question. "Did? What do you mean, the others did? What has happened?"

"Three days ago John's men raided the Inner Courts. Eleazar is dead and many of his men were slaughtered. Simon still controls much of the city." There was a moment of silence and then the man asked, "You are Yosef ben Matityahu, are you not?"

Yosef held his tongue, unsure if he should answer the question, yet his silence provoked a chuckle from the intruder who had surprised him on his night walk. "You can answer the question; I will not lift a hand against you. That is not why I have come." The man was silent for a moment and said, "I know you are Yosef, whether you admit it or not, you are he. I am Judah ben Yosef and I would like to talk with you if you would allow me."

"How do I know you're not lying, Judah ben Yosef? When I spoke to the city it seemed clear that John's men wished me dead," Yosef replied, testing the waters.

Judah shrugged and shook his head. "It is true they want you dead, but not everyone. The truth is, Yosef, that you can trust me. I have followed you since the Eastern Gate, which is at least fifty metres; I could have killed you anytime then. I only chose to expose myself when you noticed me."

Yosef was completely still, realizing his foolishness and ignorance for coming out this night. He had thought he was hidden from the eyes of the city, but if this Jew spotted him, and had followed him as he had claimed, then oddly Yosef felt a bond of trust. "Did anyone see you?"

"You actually think I would risk that if eyes could have spotted me?" Judah retorted in a harsh whisper. "I am skilled at not being seen, you must not worry."

Yosef glanced around, making sure everything appeared safe and then he stepped forward and asked, "Why do you wish to speak to me?"

"I have something grave to tell you and I seek news from a fellow Jew," Judah replied.

Yosef shook his head vigorously. "I cannot divulge any information concerning the Romans, it would be too dangerous. I'm not even supposed to be out walking."

Judah snickered in the night and rubbed his eyes. "I seek no news that would jeopardize your standing in the courts of Titus, for that I swear on the Law of Moses. Let us go someplace secret. Can we talk?"

Yosef stood motionless for a moment and then answered back, "Yes, do you know of a place?"

Judah slowly turned and began walking as Yosef followed through the darkness. The steady wind continued to howl through the valley as it rustled leaves and shook branches from what few trees remained standing. In his mind, Yosef could not believe he was actually placing his trust in this unknown man. Judah may as well have been a phantom for all Yosef could tell, as he followed the dark shape through the night. He had never heard of Judah ben Yosef before, but why should he have? The man had introduced himself as if his name had meant something, but what?

Yosef swallowed the lump in his throat like a giant stone sinking through a thick sludge. Had he become mad? Could it be possible he had lost his mind? For as long as Yosef could recall throughout his life, he would never have found himself trusting a man he had never known before. Judah could even desire to cut his throat, meanwhile leading him to an unknown and reclusive place to *talk*. Yosef grumbled silently at this thought and how foolish he felt. Yet, somehow and for some reason, Yosef wanted to trust the man, and that kept him going.

Judah led Yosef past the entrance in the wall which led to the Hulda Gates and then down a steep rocky slope where he whispered to Yosef to watch his step from the loose rock. Once at the bottom, Judah bent low and entered a cave-like mouth in the ground, descending some steps until he stood waiting at the bottom. Yosef halted abruptly at the entrance of the strange cave and hesitated, clearly battling whether or not he could trust Judah.

Yosef glanced back, contemplating fleeing rather than speaking with the Jewish fighter, but then Judah made a sweeping gesture to their surroundings and said, "It is a cistern. We are safe here and none can hear anything we say." Judah dropped his hands to his side and shrugged opening his cloak. "I am unarmed, come down here before you are seen."

Yosef took a deep breath and slowly ducked into the cave. He walked down the steps, keeping his hand near the hilt of his concealed dagger. He closely watched Judah's mannerisms for any hint or sign of danger. He gazed at Judah's dark figure with an intense stare as the fighter bent down near the back of the cistern. Yosef was about to object towards the suspicious behaviour, but then he heard the familiar sound of two flint rocks striking each other and within seconds a small oil lamp burned giving light to the cave. Judah chuckled, crossed his arms and stepped back. "You won't need your dagger, don't worry. I really didn't bring any weapons, and I don't intend to kill you, Yosef ben Matityahu."

Yosef moved his hand away from the dagger and tried to relax by taking a giant gulp of stagnant air. The cistern was cool and dry as it sheltered the men from the wind, but the howling breeze became like a moan as it raced past the mouth of the cistern. Yosef gave a sharp nod of thanks as Judah gave him space, taking a seat in a cleft of the rock wall.

Both men stared at each other for a moment and then Yosef cleared his throat and shook his head, "So why have you risked your life, Judah? What is it you wish to speak of?"

Judah rubbed the sleep from his eyes and sighed, choosing his words carefully. "I need to know if a certain Roman is among the legions."

A puzzled look came over the bearded face of the patrician as Yosef thought of the nature of this direct statement. "Why would you ever want such information from me? Who is this Roman? You wish to kill him? What does he mean to you?"

Silence crept into the cistern filling it as if it were a face with dark threatening eyes. It was as if a storm was forming within the limestone hewn chamber with its walls of peeling and stained plaster. Judah held his cold gaze upon Yosef for a lingering moment, saying nothing at first and then with a whisper asked, "What do you care?"

Yosef straightened his stance into something that embodied the last shred of nobility he felt he had maintained and clasping his hands in front of him he said, "You arranged this meeting, Judah. I care a lot concerning such a request for I could be seen as a conspirator just for being here with you, which could have me killed. Then, for me to give you information about the legions, why, that would be doubly worse for me. I would be flogged to death or crucified. So, I am allowed to care, and unless you give me something to change my mind then this conversation is through." Yosef took a step backwards, as if to leave, and glared at the arrogant Jew who remained seated.

"Once, I was not an enemy of Rome," Judah suddenly blurted out and Yosef considered the words and stepped forward. "My father was a tradesman. I studied under a rabbi in Jerusalem and learned Greek so I could help manage my father's business. I was engaged to wed. Miriam was her name.

"Then, one day in the Upper Market, a cohort of Roman infantry slaughtered everyone. They were sent by Gessius Florus and they took no heed of women or children. Bodies covered the ground, their blood ran like streams and women moaned as they were raped over and over, as they were passed from soldier to soldier. In the massacre, I killed my first man. I was fortunate, to say the least. Most Jews fell by swords and spears." Judah paused for a moment as darkness descended upon him. "I found my Miriam, slain by a spear and cast into a fountain of water where she died. I held her for a moment, close to my face, praying to God for her to open her eyes, but she did not. Then I heard laughter. In all the pain and death strewn about, I heard laughter.

"I looked up and saw the drunken legionaries as they plundered the market. Then I saw him. I saw a single Centurion of high rank standing amidst a group of soldiers. He was the only officer I saw that day and he was carrying on in his pleasure over what they had done. I retrieved a sword from one of the dead men I had managed to kill and stood challenging the Centurion silently, glaring at the man as hatred filled my soul. I remember the Romans noticed me; they pointed me out to the Centurion and then they laughed at me. I could not believe it. I was covered in blood, a ruin of a man, terrorized by the death of my loved ones, and the bastard laughed at me. If that was not shameful enough, the coward turned his back on me and refused to fight."

"What did you do then?" Yosef asked, stricken with shock from the tale. He had heard of the slaughter, but only when he had reached the seaport of Caesarea Maritima after leaving Rome.

"I ran. I could do nothing else. But I found two drunken soldiers in an alley and killed them both in my rage, but not before I got the Centurion's name." Judah glanced up and wiped away bitter tears. "His name is Capito."

Yosef was still as he digested the name and then rubbed his chin. "Is that all you know?"

Judah scowled and gave a nod. "Yes, why?"

"It could be helpful to know his full name, or what rank he was or the clan his family came from." Yosef grunted and then shrugged. "It is helpful that you know he was a centurion though, and that he served with Gessius Florus, that might help. But, now my question to you is, why should I help you find this man's whereabouts? I mean, I could still be executed for this if I was to even approach Titus and tell him I was speaking with the enemy. Titus might never trust me again."

There was so much Judah wanted to say in regards to Yosef and Titus but he bit his tongue and cast the barrage of thoughts from his mind. He simply leaned back and said, "If you go to Titus with this, tell him to recall when the Tenth Legion was nearly wiped out upon the Mount of Olives, or the two times we nearly killed the Prince of Rome. Tell your Titus that, and then inform him that many more attacks such as these are planned and will occur. The devastating blow to his troops and their morale will never be forgotten. Word will quickly spread among the camps and his army will mutiny rather than march against our city with its high walls. Tell him that, and then say to your Titus that there is a Jew in the city who can inform him of ambushes such as these. All I ask is that I want to know if Capito is with the army." A puzzled expression spread across Judah's face. "Is Florus with the legions?" Yosef nodded slowly and Judah bit his bottom lip. "Then Capito most definitely is."

"You just wish to know if he is here? Among the legions?" Yosef asked.

Judah stood and pointed at Yosef. "That is not good enough for me. I need Titus to swear before whatever gods he worships, that Capito is among them. I need physical proof."

Yosef suddenly felt cramped in the cistern as Judah's presence dominated the space. He took a prudent step back towards the mouth of the cistern and whispered, "How can Titus get you physical proof of Capito without your own brethren in the city finding out your arrangement? Titus can't send you a message, it would be too risky."

Judah shook his head and lowered his voice saying, "Tell your Titus that tomorrow at noon he is to sound a trumpet blast twice which will be the signal to change the work detail's upon the slopes. Then he is to sound the same trumpet one single blast to let me know that it is Capito who leads the next work contingent. Make sure Capito wears his helmet with his identifying colours, then I shall have no problem seeing him and I will honour my side of the bargain."

Yosef frowned. "You would give us credible information concerning ambushes if we just show you Capito from afar?" Judah nodded and Yosef said, "I thought you hated Rome? Why will you work with her against your people?"

"I hate Capito more than Rome. As for my other reasons, they are for me and nobody else." Judah watched Yosef scowl at this statement, unsure of whether he was trustworthy. "Tell your Titus all I have said, and he will remember the hundreds of troops he has lost at the swiftness of our attacks. Tell him of the trumpet blasts, remember, two to change the work party, one to identify Capito. I will watch for him and if Titus is true to his word, then take a walk around the city again at night and I will find you." With that, Judah pushed past Yosef, climbed the stairs of the cistern, and disappeared into the night leaving the former Jewish General dumbfounded, considering all that had been said.

*   *   *

Titus sat on the edge of his bed with a goblet of wine in hand and a stupor expression upon his face from the heavy drinking only hours ago. Yosef stood before him silently having given his report and Titus just shook his head and rubbed his temple from the splitting headache that tormented him. Earlier, he had hosted a feast with numerous generals and delegates, including Agrippa, Antiochus, and Sohaemus. The feast had been splendid, the tables overloaded with food and wine, leading to many of the men plunging into a drunken state upon their couches. The Roman nobility had filled the camp with a chorus of laughter upon the tune of jokes Titus told them and his impressions of women making love. Agrippa and Sohaemus remained reserved among the partiers as Titus had called out to them numerous times to relax and carry on in the feasting.

Afterwards, when the last man had been carried back to his tent, Titus had toppled into his bed, having vomited twice and refilled his stomach with more wine and food. He had slept in an agitated state for five hours only to be awoken by his fat scribe, an unfortunate looking man who could not grow facial hair and whose voice rang out in a womanly shrill when he grew excited. It was this homely looking scribe who reported to the annoyed Prince that Yosef the Jew was asking for admittance to the royal quarters. Titus had dodged the question and had asked his own, alluding to what hour it was, meanwhile rubbing the sleep out of his eyes. The scribe had grown nervous, bowed slightly in respect, and when the answer came that it was just before dawn, Titus had attempted to kick the fleeing man in the buttocks, provoking him to squawk like a goose as he leapt out of the way. Titus had shouted at the fat man to let Yosef in and then had cursed the gods, demanding more wine.

Now, with plenty of wine to last him through the early hours of dawn, Titus leaned back and exhaled loudly staring at Yosef. He burped and closed his eyes for a moment waiting for the splitting pain in his head to subside. "You should never have left camp. You are favoured by some god of ill repute who did not have the sense to tell you to stay put. If you had been seen by anyone among the low rank, I would have had no choice but to put you to death for committing treason. You understand what would await you if I had to do such a thing?" Titus was so exhausted that he could feel no anger over Yosef's foolish wanderings, but this news had certainly done itself well to pique his interest. "You say this Jew will help us?"

"Yes, my Prince. He says he will inform us of ambushes which will surely occur once your troops attack the walls." Yosef paused for a moment and then added, "I will not leave the camp again, and I ask for your forgiveness, my Prince."

Titus shook his head and waved his hand, annoyed at Yosef's groveling. "Why should I even care what this Jew says? I can handle the Zealots." Titus sniffed and then wiped his nose to relieve an itch as he refilled his goblet with dark wine.

"He said to remind you of the north, and to inform you that your soldiers will become so demoralized against the sudden attacks and that hundreds will perish. He also said to remind you it was he and the Zealots who hold the city of Jerusalem with its high walls." Yosef was silent for a moment and then said, "He wanted you to recall the two times you were nearly killed or the great battle that day the Tenth was almost overrun."

"He has balls like the sack on Apis," Titus replied with an exasperated tone. "You believe him?"

Yosef nodded. "It sounds genuine. The man sought me out and I have no doubt in my mind he spared my life and could have killed me. He was like a ghost; he came out of the night, like darkness was a part of him. Judah led me to a cistern so we were concealed," Yosef stopped abruptly as Titus started to chuckle.

"I just can't believe you followed the man and took his word." Titus cleared his throat and tried to contain his amusement. "Especially in light of what happened when you tried to speak to the city. They tried to kill you, and then you follow this man into a cistern at night?" He shook his head and continued, "I am still trying to figure out if I am still drunk or you are mad."

Yosef did not acknowledge the humiliation, and persisted saying, "He identified himself as *a Jew who could inform us of ambushes* so they can be stopped. I believe him because of the motive."

"And what is that? The death of his betrothed and family?" Titus watched Yosef awkwardly attempt to respond and then he closed his mouth trying to think. "You feel his pain?"

"Would not any man who was sane, my Prince?" Yosef replied.

Titus nodded. "Yes, I suppose. The slaughter of all those people and his betrothal's death could get in the way of thinking with a clear mind for this Jew. Consider his promise to deliver information. If this man seeks revenge this could fall apart. It could simply be blind rage, Yosef," Titus retorted.

Yosef shook his head. "I didn't see that in this man; rage yes, but blind rage, not a shred. This man is clear in his anger and hate and through it he must help us to get what he wants."

"So he is a sympathizer, and he just hates this Centurion?" Titus asked.

"I worry he will use us to get this man and that is all. Deep down I believe he wishes not to help us." Yosef glanced at the floor for a moment in contemplation and suddenly his attention snapped up as Titus clapped once and laughed.

"Yes, but he doesn't really want anything? You said he wished to know if this Centurion is in the army, am I right?" Yosef nodded and Titus exclaimed happily, "Then we show him this Capito and in return we get information, as long as it is valid we can continue to count on this Jew. When do you meet with him again?"

"He said to walk around the city and he would find me, I don't know when," Yosef replied.

"Well, this man needs to be shown we are men of our word and can be trusted." Titus clapped his hands twice and the fat scribe waddled into the room and bowed. "Find the ledgers for the centurions of the Fretensis immediately. I want to know if there is a Capito among the rank who used to serve with Florus the whelp." Titus grinned as he saw a flash of amusement upon Yosef's face which the Jewish General tried to hide.

The scribe bowed and disappeared into the adjoining quarters next to where Titus slept. The sound of scrolls being rustled was evidence that the scribe knew the general vicinity of where the logs were kept for the Tenth Legion, but locating the correct ledgers was another thing as the man mumbled to himself incessantly. Eventually a call of success echoed from the quarters and the fat man came hustling back to Titus' side clutching in his pudgy hand a rolled up scroll of papyrus.

The scribe glanced at Titus, and the Prince nodded so he unfurled it in a professional manner. While scanning the names, he finally came to one and announced in perfect Latin, "Capito Vorenus Bibalus: Centurion of the Third Cohort and commanding *Hastatus Prior* of his century. Says here he was transferred from Gessius Florus' Jerusalem garrison the 9th day of *Junius* before the *Nonae*, during the reign of Emperor Nero Claudius Caesar Augustus Germanicus in his twelfth year as Emperor. Medical examination results: good eye sight, five foot nine inches, brown hair, stout. He oversaw training at the gymnasium in Caesarea Maritima for two months and was transferred to Gessius Florus at the Jerusalem garrison."

The scribe scowled and scratched his head. "That is strange, there is no date." He shrugged and cleared his throat with a grunt. "He advanced through rank for skills related to: patrol, gathering information, some minor engagements with rebels, and became a personal attaché of Gessius Florus. Oh, and here is a note that he was transferred, due to his seniority as a centurion and his experience in the field with the natives of Judea, to the Fretensis as they were in need of raising the strength of their *centurionate*."

Titus glanced at Yosef. "So *he* is among the Tenth." Titus looked to his scribe and dictated quickly, "Compose a letter for General Lepidus of the Tenth. Give him orders by my authority and place my seal upon it. Dictate the letter with precise instructions for Lepidus to place Centurion Capito out at the work detail at noon. Say he is to announce the shift change by sounding a trumpet twice and then sounding another trumpet with a single blast when Capito leads his force down the hill to continue working. Inform Lepidus, Capito is to be in full armour and wearing his colours as Hastatus Prior. That is all."

Titus looked away from the scribe as he hurried off. "You see…if that is all this Jew wants then I shall show him Capito in return for information concerning planned attacks. There is no harm in it and Capito is kept from harm's way. The man won't even know what has been arranged." Titus nodded, feeling good about the outcome and then shook a steady finger at Yosef. "When you go to see this Jew again you are to bring with you Primus Pilus Gaius Cornelius Antony to be our Roman representative. You have met him?" Yosef nodded and Titus continued, "We shall see what this Jew really wants. There must be something more than just to see a centurion supervising his men tilling the earth."

Yosef was about to speak and then bit his tongue. He had an idea why Judah had requested the information. First he had to identify his enemy and once that was done, Yosef was sure what the next request would be. Titus, however, did not seem to put the two together and was just happy to feel as if he was getting the better end of the deal. "Whatever Judah wants, once Capito is sent out tomorrow then I will inform Gaius. We will have to go out the first night and see if we can make contact."

Titus nodded. "Remind Gaius to wear a cloak, I don't think he is that stupid, but one can never be too careful." Titus smiled and then rubbed his chin in question for a moment. "What is this Judah's full name?"

"Judah ben Yosef, my Prince," Yosef replied.

Titus scowled slightly as he muttered the name to himself quietly. "That name is familiar; I just can't remember where I have heard it before." The Prince of Rome looked troubled for a brief moment and then shrugged.

"I know nothing more about his history then what I have told you, apart from the fact he does not call himself a Zealot but he fights with John." Yosef observed another snicker escape the Prince's mouth and then continued, "But I will say this, he is a man with a deep seeded anger towards this Centurion and *Roma*, and whatever motive he has, despite his cooperation, we should tread carefully."

Titus glanced at Yosef with a pondering gaze. "You like him though, this Judah?"

"I admire him, yes," Yosef replied choosing his words carefully.

"And you trust his word?" Titus slowly asked.

Yosef was still for a moment and then nodded cautiously. "I think I do, despite the anger that was present. The man seemed to hold his head high with valour and honour. He spoke of himself in a plain sense, but I feel he is much more than that."

"So you are not sure if this man has another motive? Well, I can tell you this, my dear General, that we all have other motives. No man is like a mirror. You look in a mirror and the image is clear of what looks back, but men are more like a dark cave, you look into it and you can never be sure of what will occur, of what lies beneath. This Judah may be a man of honour, he may be trustworthy to a point, but he still serves John of Gischala. We will tread carefully, but you must see that war also makes sound men into desperate animals. The mind can be like a trapped beast, trying to break free from its snares. You must report everything to me and are never to approach this man without Gaius. He can never be fully trusted so long as he fights against us, but he can be used, and for that I am willing to comply."

"It just seems strange for a fighter of Jerusalem to want to help us so eagerly in return for such a strange request," Yosef said.

Titus rolled his eyes and set his cup down. "We have eyes and ears in the city already, but none in John's circle of friends. Simon's army was easy to plant spies, it's large and disorderly. The man is a pathetic *merda*, stupid and incapable of running an army, let alone defending a city with many gates. But to infiltrate the Zealots, now that is doubly difficult. We can just thank the gods John doesn't run the whole city and control its armed people.

"Now, to infiltrate the Sicarii, well, simply impossible. They are like a pack of hungry dogs, sniffing the ass of any dog they come across hoping its female so they can mount it. They question everyone, keep their circle of assassins close to them and despise any newcomers, instantly judging them to be spies and informers. We have lost six spies in the last year to those bastards. You send a man in, even if he is a Jew and you pay him well, and he is discovered within a week and sent back to you in pieces. Truly, I tell you the truth, Yosef. I received a basket once with a pair of ears and our man's circumcised dick and *colei*. They must have smelled him out. I shall never know how they found that one. He was one of them, a Jew from the north. We convinced him to go in disguised as a *Sicarii* who had travelled from Masada to join the fight in Jerusalem. We paid him a lot of money, that and we gave him our word his family wouldn't go to the auction block. Then I receive this basket two days ago. Revolting, I tell you, simply revolting and barbaric.

"It could do us well to know what he knows. Be good to this Jew and give him what he wants so long as he doesn't request the Judean army to pack up and march away." Titus raised his eyebrows slightly and shrugged. "One can deal out wrath for a time, but soon, we will govern these people again and they will have to know us for our merciful side. This war has seen the worse. Yes, it has helped bring down the price per head for a slave in the common market of *Roma*, but a people scattered abroad will only happen if they push me that direction. Remember Jotapata and how we left it in ruins? Well, if my legions enter that city with drawn swords, then you shall witness the annihilation and enslavement of half a million people. They taunt me with a stick thinking I am a dog. Well, I am the smartest dog and the most agile. I will jump at them, forgetting about the stick and sink my teeth into their soft throats and they will be no more. Mark my words, if it must come to that. However, there is another way, Yosef. Minerva has been kind to me despite my stupor which earns praises from Dionysius.

"This Judah ben Yosef might be our only hope of getting into the mind of John and ruining his chances of lashing out at Roman troops. Foil his attempts for a day and he becomes unpopular, do it for a week and his men start to curse him, do it for a month and they will gut him like a fish and cast him from the walls. Then the city gates will open and Jerusalem will be spared. I see the future, Yosef. Basilides has shown it to my father and I, and we consulted oracles and have the favour of Serapis. Your God can rest his head under the palm as we march past at the feet of Jupiter to declare victory over another city."

* * *

CHAPTER XVIII

April 19th, 70 A.D. / 22nd of Nisan, 3830
Mount of Olives
Noon

"Don't stand there like a bunch of vestal virgins squatting on the ground, you bastards. Spread out and get to work!" Capito shouted angrily as he shook his head and descended the slope. Rocks had been cleared, the ground tilled, and now work was to continue near the valley's bottom. The columns of troops carrying tools, twisted down the slope as soldiers from the previous shift climbed wearily past them. Numerous shouts rose up from the columns as the retiring soldiers jeered at the raw workers, calling out to them to enjoy the hottest time of the day. Capito glared at the passing men, taking the liberty to wack a soldier in the thigh with his wooden switch. The man yelped in pain and Capito roared with laughter, shouting at the useless legionary to return to his tent in silence or he would return with no teeth.

The day had begun sour for the Centurion as he had cursed the gods upon reading the strange orders for his work detail. The orders had come from General Larcius Lepidus of the Fretensis, and had simply stated that Hastatus Prior Capito would be leading the second work detail at noon and was to be in full armour with helmet and colours of rank. Capito had shredded the orders with a curse and then had thrown a goblet across his tent, spraying wine upon the canvas. He had watched in disgust as his slave cleaned up the wine, all the while spewing forth a rambling of vulgar words at the uselessness of wearing all his armour, medals, and helmet. He had shaken his head as he pissed in the corner of his tent, having no care to use the latrine, and then had ordered the slave to dress him.

Now standing upon the slopes of the Mount of Olives with the sun's blistering heat cooking him in his armour, Capito shouted up the hill for a drink of something cool. His slave was fetched and ran quickly with a skin of water as a sudden blast of trumpets bellowed twice with deep drones reverberating down the mountainside. Capito sighed and crossed his arms, wincing from the heat radiating from his breastplate. The water was soon brought and he took a long drink, pouring the rest down his neck to cool his chest. He caught a jealous grimace from a number of legionaries nearby who were moving a boulder and he spit at the men shouting, "What in the name of Mars' dick are you looking at? By the tits of Venus, keep digging in the dirt, you rats!" The men looked away with dark expressions. Capito shook his head and shifted the medals upon his cuirass to a more comfortable position. Another trumpet blast sounded which seemed odd as he stared up the slopes wondering what a single note from the brass tubas even meant. Capito moved his belt awkwardly to scratch his groin and then glanced down at the trails of sweat running down his dusty legs as it soiled his skin beneath his greaves. "By the might of Nemesis I pray that Lepidus will get his due pay for this," Capito prayed as he took a deep breath and then hollered for the men to pick up the pace.

*   *   *

Judah rested his arms upon the walls of the city and stared out at the Mount of Olives. The twin blasts from the trumpets had sounded to mark the change in work details and now he awaited the single blast to alert him of Capito. He watched the distant columns of Roman legionaries in their red tunics twist like snakes down the slopes of the hillside as the ground became more level from the days of steady work.

To the north of the city word had spread that piles of lumber were being collected and stock piled as John believed this was where Titus would concentrate his attack. The walls of Jerusalem were not as high to the north and the ground before them dangerously flat. The exterior wall had been repaired months ago, and although strengthened by towers and ramparts, it remained the most vulnerable place. However, John had tried to keep up rigorous activity upon the ramparts of the Temple Mount and had declared numerous times, "Plenty of room to cram the legions into, and more room for us to butcher the bastards." Despite trying to appear as though he was not nervous, John had quickly sent word to Simon that the exterior walls should be doubly manned and the strength increased within the towers of Psephinus, Hippicus, Phasael, and Miriamne.

Caleb came alongside Judah followed accompanied by Adam and Moshe. They clustered around their commander, elected Captain of John's forces, and watched the activity upon the Mount of Olives. Adam hugged the shaft of his spear and shaking his head said, "I still can't believe it has come to this. Sometimes I wonder if I will wake up from a dream and there will be no Romans left."

"You're not scared, are you?" Moshe asked scowling.

Adam glared at his friend and looked away. "No more than you. This is real. I fear not to fight them, but I do wonder how I will die."

Silence ensued upon the ramparts for a moment as the men contemplated their future. Moshe finally groaned and rolling his eyes said, "Well, we were quite good defeating Eleazar's men. Finally the city feels united and under one banner."

"At what cost?" Adam suddenly said pointing a finger at Moshe. "Have you forgotten your dead brother? Aviram was not yet twenty! What of those men who were crushed to death by the weight of stones? They died believing the same as you do: liberty and freedom for all Jews, the arrival of Meshiach to break the chains of Rome!"

"I'm no Zealot!" Moshe countered angrily.

⌐ 281 ⌐

"Are you not? We all are. We have all thrown our lot in with these men and the blood stinks. I thought I would fight against Rome, now I fight against my brothers and it stains my hands." Adam faced Moshe staring him down and then turned acknowledging the Romans. "They work together at least, and I can't say the same for us. It is madness. We have fought against Simon and Eleazar and we are still where we started."

"But Eleazar's power is broken. The man wanted us dead," Moshe shouted back.

"Silence!" Caleb suddenly bellowed, stepping between the men. "This does no good. It was a terrible thing with Eleazar's men, I do not deny it. I still can feel the weight of their bodies as I helped carry the dead out, all crushed and mutilated." Caleb was still for a moment and then glared at Moshe. "We don't discuss Eleazar anymore. What's done is done and nobody is proud of it. When the Romans come, what is left of us will have to fight from the walls and charge out from the city. We will all need to be thinking of that time, and not what happened in the corridors with Eleazar's men."

"Caleb is right," Judah abruptly said turning to face them. "John of Gischala bears the responsibility for the battle in the Inner Courts. The blood has been cleaned and the bodies removed. The priests have purified the courts and the sacrifice continues. What has happened must be left behind. Aviram's death is mourned, there is nothing else." Judah gently patted Adam's shoulder in comfort, gave the brute man a tearful nod and turned away to stare at the Roman activity upon the distant slopes. "You obeyed my orders, and the lives you took are upon my hands. You did no wrong."

A single trumpet echoed from the slopes beyond the Kidron and Judah gazed out to see the distant form of a centurion wearing his dona and helmet. A blonde, transverse plume topped the officer's helmet and the stick he carried was ever eager to strike at fellow legionaries whom he assumed were slacking. Judah watched the man drink from a water skin and then patrol around the working lines of sweating troops hauling earth away or prying up rocks to be split. The man seemed confident as he strolled along. Wearing fine armour, decorated by medals for bravery and combat, he assumed the stature of a high ranking centurion. An ornate gladius was strapped to his side and a slave followed behind him like a dog to its master.

Judah glanced up at the sun in all its glory, heating the earth without mercy as the Romans toiled at the ground with clanging sounds of picks and shovels. The lines of dusty troops preparing the battlefield in which they would soon march upon seemed like a dream. A cohort of armed soldiers stood silently nearby, drawn up into three long columns, miserable in the heat and donned in full equipment. Their task, to guard the work procession against any Jewish sorties.

Judah had pledged before Yosef to aid Rome. Yosef had suspected something else, but Judah hoped that Titus would be blind to any hidden plot and would only see Judah as a Roman sympathizer. He trusted that his tale of misery had struck a chord of grief in Yosef's heart so that the voice of Rome would sympathize and trust him.

The willingness to sound the trumpets and to place his enemy upon the slopes in broad sight was proof enough Yosef had delivered. It was clear he had believed Judah and now Titus was on his side, which helped immensely. Judah knew he had to arrange another meeting in order to ask for the second favour. To convince them more, he knew he would have to bring them information concerning attacks. However, he had to be certain they would trust him. Judah would never sell out the city to the Romans, nor give information leading to enormous casualties, but to relay the plans of a couple of ambushes seemed a fair price to pay to get what he really wanted.

It was no secret John was paranoid of possible Roman spies in the city, sympathizers to Rome willing to see the city burn and Jews slaughtered. Judah was not among that crew, but he knew that John would never see it that way. If his dealings with Yosef were to become known, Yosef could only imagine what would happen to him and then even his imagination could not stretch that far.

He had not told a soul about his meeting, even Adam and Caleb would not discover his plot. However, he toyed with the idea. They would only need to know if the situation became dire. They were the only men he could trust. He smirked at the thought of being in a city so packed with his fellow people and only being able to trust two of them.

Judah watched the Romans at work, keeping his eye on the Centurion. He heard Moshe curse the legionaries under his breath and pray to God that the sun would burn them all alive. As Moshe finished his prayer, Judah added one himself, as he knew beyond a shadow of a doubt that he was finally facing the murderer of Miriam. After nearly four years of hatred, bitterness, nightmares, and struggling to survive, he had finally found Capito. Judah would kill him and smile.

* * *

April 21st, 70 A.D. / 24th of Nisan, 3830
Mount Scopus

Drusus glared at the back of Tribune Marcus Sulla as he rode ahead of them. He glanced back at Varro and shook his head. He wondered at the nature of such a foolhardy patrol under the heat of the Judean sun and swore. Since the two decurianes had received word of the patrol, Drusus had been complaining and suspicious. Marcus had arrived at the tent of the two junior officers, arrayed in his armour, and had ordered them to prepare their mounts and be ready within half an hour for a routine patrol around Scopus. Varro had shrugged, responding to Drusus' incessant tetchy attitude claiming they had no choice. Thus, the two men met Marcus as ordered at the front entrance of the camp.

Marcus led them up to the bluff of Scopus where he drank from his water skin to quench his thirst. He grinned at the two sour looking officers, seeing their unsettled expressions divert from his gaze. Marcus pointed to the earthworks north of Jerusalem, made a half-hearted comment at the progress creeping closer to the walls, than continued on steering his mount away. Drusus and Varro followed reluctantly as neither one knew the purpose for such a patrol, suspicion rife within their minds.

"It doesn't add up," Varro whispered, spurring his horse to Drusus' side. He watched Marcus pull further ahead, as if the Tribune did not care for them to keep up. Varro liked the comfortable distance and leaned over. "Two decurianes and a Tribune? Strange. A regular patrol would have at least a handful of troopers and a standard bearer, but he has left Publius behind."

Drusus shot a dark look at Varro and said, "We should kill him up here. There is nobody around." Drusus glanced back down the slope at the Roman camps and then smiled. "We could."

"We have to plan for this, Drusus. We don't know if there are other patrols we cannot see." Varro shifted uncomfortably in his saddle and his face paled as Marcus glanced back at them briefly.

"If we ride down on the other side of the ridge and there are no patrols, I say we make our move. There are two of us and one of him. We can do it, Varro," Drusus replied without turning his head as Marcus glanced back again. "Are you with me?" No answer escaped Varro's lips as the decurion appeared as if he would be sick.

Marcus suddenly drew on the reins and his horse halted. He sat in the saddle for a moment and then dismounted. The two decurianes cautiously halted their mounts, unsure what was to happen next. Marcus tied his horse to a withered, old tree and then faced the men with his hand relaxed on the pommel of his sword. He waved to them and called out, "Dismount! We will check the ridge on the other side by foot."

Varro glanced nervously at Drusus and then back to the Tribune. "My lord? Why not ride down?"

Marcus wiped the sweat from his face and replied, "There have been reports of suspicious activity on this side of the mountain. If we ride, they may see us. Now, dismount and let's move." Marcus took a couple of steps away from his horse and then turned impatiently to face the two officers.

"Be on your guard," Drusus whispered to Varro. "This doesn't add up; something is wrong."

Varro sat rigid in his saddle, fear gripping his soul as he watched Drusus dismount. "We should flee."

"Get off your horse, you fool. We have no choice," Drusus hissed feeling the gaze of Marcus upon his back.

Varro whimpered silently as he climbed down from his horse, feeling his knees wobble from the lack of strength that suddenly left his body. Nevertheless, he managed to secure his horse to a dry shrub and look dignified as if he feared nothing. Drusus was at his side, trying to maintain composure, despite being hesitant of whether or not the Tribune was up to something.

"What sort of suspicious activity has been seen around here, my lord?" Drusus called out glancing to his left and right.

"You know, people treasonous to Roman rule," Marcus replied directly as he watched the two decurianes slowly approach him. He noticed Drusus scowl questionably and Marcus snapped, "Come now, move!" The two men were jolted by the sudden shout as they quickened their step and within seconds stood before Marcus.

Marcus gently bit his lower lip and took a deep breath. Only Titus knew of this day as it had been kept from the ears of everyone else. Marcus had always suspected some of his junior officers being capable of assassination, but an informant had turned his suspicion into a reality, shedding light on a plot that needed to be dealt with. This day's patrol had been thoroughly planned and he had been as wise as a serpent. "You two move ahead. Keep an eye out for anything."

Drusus faced his Tribune, weighing out the implications of this command. Could he turn his back on Marcus? He wrestled with the thought and then forced himself to see the truth: he was a decurion of the Roman army and an important man. As much as Marcus may feel threatened, the hands of the Tribune would be tied. Marcus could not do a thing. Drusus had also prepared a letter to Rome which would be the insurance that would keep him alive. If Marcus was to try anything, Drusus could inform him of the letter. A testament had been prepared by his scribe who was sworn to secrecy and the parchment bore the names of powerful men in the Senate. It could be mailed at any moment should Drusus feel threatened. He had explored every avenue to insure protection, until he and Varro would be ready to kill Marcus themselves.

"As you wish," Drusus said bowing slightly with a grin. He noticed Marcus give him a puzzled look and he fought back a smile for he knew the obsessive Tribune was powerless to do anything. Drusus turned and walked on as he descended the ridge, pretending to search for treasonous people, as Marcus had coined it. He halted a ways from the Tribune, unable to control the smile that came upon his face, for he knew what the Tribune had been planning. This would definitely give comfort to Varro and the two decurianes could focus on their own plot to remove Marcus' tyrannical command.

"I don't think we will find anyone out here, Tribune. I rightly think we are wasting our time!" Drusus shouted turning slightly as he shook his head and stared down the quiet slopes of the backside of Scopus.

A slight gurgle sounded behind Drusus, but was almost swallowed up by the gentle breeze. Had it not been for the brief moment of silence between Drusus' words, he would have missed it altogether, but he clearly heard the odd sound. He turned to watch Marcus let go of Varro's convulsing body as the Tribune had covered his mouth from screaming. The blade of his pugio shone bright scarlet as it was pulled from the back of Varro's throat. The body crumpled to the ground face first, gave a violent shiver, and twitched as blood seeped from the wound. Almost instantly, Marcus discarded the dagger and drew his gladius as he closed the gap between him and Drusus with much speed.

For a moment Drusus was transfixed in shock. The alarm within his head pounded for him to draw his sword, but his hands went numb and his body stiffened. It was too late. Within a second, Marcus was standing before the frightened decurion with the double edged blade of his gladius touching his throat. Drusus slowly raised his hands in surrender and fought back the impulse to beg for mercy. Staring at the fierce look in Marcus' eyes he said, "You should know something..."

"What? About the letter you had your scribe write for the senators? Think about that one, Drusus," Marcus said through gritted teeth. "Your scribe is poisoned and your letter is destroyed. You have nothing."

A sudden vengeful thought of Decurion Titus flashed in Drusus' mind and he cursed his comrade's betrayal. Then it dawned on him that he no longer had any leverage. Varro was dead and now Marcus sought his own life. "Please, I could serve you! I will serve you!" Drusus pleaded, trembling at his apparent fate as he stared at the length of cold steel. "I will do anything. Demote me. Send me away."

Marcus shook his head slowly. "It can't be that easy, I am sorry." He watched Drusus' face drain to the colour of ash. "You should kneel," Marcus said pressing the razor sharp blade against the throat of the decurion.

Drusus' eyes suddenly welled up with tears and his legs shook. He attempted to say something, but nothing came out. His throat became dry and sweat streamed down the sides of his face. "Please have mercy," he muttered like a child as he slowly knelt upon the ground. "Oh..." Drusus groaned as urine trickled down his leg. "Have mercy, Marcus."

"I am having mercy, Drusus," Marcus said in an odd, soothing voice, like a father would to a son who had done wrong. "I am ending your life out here, with the stroke of my sword, rather than have you face execution in the camp for treason. Your honour is still intact. Find peace, Drusus, in the halls of your ancestors."

"You dare send me to the land of the dead? To *Orcus*?" Drusus wept bitterly as he felt his dignity shredded from him, all sense of Roman virtue and masculinity gone.

Marcus leaned close to the terrified decurion and tenderly whispered, "I will scatter your ashes in the wind, Drusus, but not before I place a *sestertius* in your mouth to pay your toll across the river Styx."

"Not a single *obol*, Marcus? The boatman Charon will be pleased with a sestertius," Drusus somberly nodded feeling sick.

"I swear to you, your body will be collected, with Varro, and they will burn brightly upon a pyre." Marcus watched the young man nod gently with a sniff.

Drusus glanced up with hardened eyes. "You will send my effects home to my father? Promise me, Tribune," his voice wavered with fear.

Marcus tipped Drusus' chin up with the edge of his sword and looked into the pale face of the Decurion. "Your father will hear of your death fighting the enemy."

Marcus slid the blade forward as the steel and hilt became washed with blood. Drusus' eyes widened in horror for a moment and then rolled back into their sockets. The blood was like a fountain as it spilled upon Drusus' breastplate and soaked the ground where he knelt. When the blade was retracted, Marcus gently laid the body down and stood over his work. He shook his head and then proceeded to remove Drusus' valuables, as to give the appearance of a robbery. When he was finished with both bodies, Marcus buried the loot and returned to the horses. He freed Varro and Drusus' mounts and curiously watched them wander. Marcus retrieved his pugio, mounted his horse, and returned to camp to report to Prince Titus that two decurianes of the Boars had been murdered by thieves upon the northern slopes of Scopus.

*   *   *

April 24th, 70 A.D. / 27th of Nisan, 3830
Near the walls of Jerusalem
Midnight

"This is dangerous. We can't keep coming out at night like this, Yosef." Gaius pulled the cloak further over his face to conceal it from the torchlight that burned brightly from the Fretensis camp high upon the slopes. "This is the fourth time we have blindly stumbled around in this forsaken valley and this Jew has yet to turn up. Perhaps he lied? He could very well have been discovered, and then he would be dead." Gaius watched the dark shape of Yosef turn slightly as he considered this possibility, and then the Jewish General continued walking through the darkness of the Kidron.

"He swore to me," Yosef whispered loudly. "He can be trusted. The more I think of him I know he can be trusted."

Gaius hurried to catch up. "You really believe him to be a sympathizer to Rome?"

"Titus believes him, does he not?" Yosef replied.

"Yes, but what do you believe? You met the Zealot in the cistern," Gaius said shaking his head.

"He is not a Zealot, at least he claimed not to be one," Yosef said correcting Gaius.

"Yet, he fights with John. I can't see him being anything else but a Zealot. If he has thrown in his lot with that man, he must be as blood thirsty and wild as John." Gaius paused for a moment and then said, "I could see it no other way."

"You are free to believe what you must. As for me, I see Judah as an embittered man, not knowing how to channel his rage and frustration." Yosef halted abruptly and faced the Centurion. "His spirit was wounded deeply, Gaius. He lost everything."

"And you think, now that he has seen his enemy, Judah will help us?" Gaius retorted in a loud whisper. "He wants Capito's head, I can guarantee you that."

"What is the price of one centurion? This could end the ambushes and deaths of many of your men. Which sounds like a fair bargain?"

Gaius was silent as he considered the weight of Yosef's words and then continued to follow the dark shape through the dead of night. "Nothing is fair in war," he mumbled, shaking his head. "Should we head to the cistern?"

"He said for me to go for a walk and he would find me." Yosef stopped and squinted as he tried to differentiate between real shapes and his imagination. "If we wait in the cistern, he may miss us."

Gaius was tempted to complain or announce his retirement for the night but he held his tongue. Great torches burned brightly upon Jerusalem's walls, providing light for the guards above as they wearily patrolled. The fires glowed and cast flickering shadows upon the golden stones of the massive fortress walls as they rose up like great colossal mountains in the night. The two men stood silently for a moment, Gaius clutching the hilt of his gladius with a nervous hand, fighting against the urge within his mind to make every shadow or sound a threat.

Just as Gaius was about to order Yosef back to camp, the two men saw a dark form suddenly arise, a shadow silhouetted against the base of the city walls. The man had obviously meant to reveal his presence, yet before either Gaius or Yosef could say anything, the dark shape descended rapidly. The figure was slightly hunched over and was blatantly trying to stay hidden from the Jewish sentries atop of the wall.

Instinctively, Gaius partially drew his gladius and widened his stance before the mysterious visitor as Yosef stumbled behind the Centurion for protection. Gaius narrowed his eyes and gritted his teeth, weighing his options and wondering if this man had come to attack them. He wanted to look at Yosef to confirm if this was their man or not, but he had been trained his whole life never to take one's eyes off the enemy.

"Judah? Is that you? Call out!" Yosef whispered straining his voice to be heard behind the hulking mass of the Centurion.

Judah halted abruptly, realizing there were two men standing before him. He recognized Yosef's voice but was nervous with the appearance of the other man who clearly was a Roman due to the glisten of the half drawn gladius strapped to his waist. Not knowing if he could trust Yosef anymore, Judah took a hesitant step back and cursed loudly within his mind at his foolishness for not bringing a weapon. He had decided, in a good gesture, to travel without a weapon to appease Yosef, yet now he found himself caught in the darkness before a large Roman man who wanted blood.

"Judah? Answer me?" Yosef said quickly seeing the dark shadow of the man step backward. "You can trust me. I have brought a man with me sent by Titus, and he means you no harm."

"Who is he?" Judah said softly in Greek, but with command in his voice.

"A representative of Rome, he only wishes to speak with you. There is no trap here." Yosef cleared his throat quietly and waited for an answer.

"Does he speak Hebrew?" Judah said in his native tongue.

"No!" Yosef replied in Hebrew. "You wish to speak in Hebrew?"

"Can I trust him?" Judah asked, continuing in the ancient language of his people. "He is a Roman."

Yosef nodded in the darkness. "He is an honest man, you can trust him. Did we not show you Capito?" Yosef saw Gaius' head turn slightly as he picked up the name of the Centurion.

"You delivered him to appease my sight," Judah said. "If this man can be trusted, instruct him to sheath his sword, unbuckle it and place it in your keeping."

Yosef took a deep breath and then whispered in Latin to Gaius, "He wants you to show your trust by sheathing your sword and giving it to me."

"That would be a mistake, Yosef," Gaius replied keeping his piercing eyes upon Judah. "This man cannot be fully trusted."

"Does a man who desires trust enter into discussion carrying weapons?" Judah said interrupting Yosef and the stranger who were talking in hushed voices. "Do men who declare to be trustworthy whisper quietly?"

"No, wait!" Yosef begged in Hebrew, beckoning Judah to give him a moment. When he was assured Judah would be patient, Yosef quickly said to Gaius, "You must do this. This man will not bring harm to you or I. You must understand, he did not expect your company."

Gaius groaned, not favouring the idea of giving into the enemy's demands or being unarmed, but he knew Yosef had a point. Gaius nodded reluctantly and whispered to Yosef, "You had better be right on this one." He carefully sheathed his sword, unbuckled the heavy leather belt studded with iron rivets, and gently wrapped it around the scabbard. He held it straight out in front of him to show Judah what he was doing and then handed it to Yosef slowly. "There, I hope you are happy, *Zealot*," Gaius spoke the words with a flavour of anger coated by flawless Koine Greek, but suddenly regretted them as he may have muddled their chance for negotiations.

Judah stepped forward, sized up the man, glanced at Yosef without expression, and then said, "Follow me. We have a ways to go."

Judah led Gaius and Yosef back along the rocky bottom of the valley as all three remained quiet. The sounds of a lone dog barking echoed from the city followed by a strange insect which made a chirping noise. A lizard, unseen by any of them sped out of their way and a large raven, which clung to a withered olive shoot nearby, suddenly lifted off, delivering a deep throated caw as it disappeared in the night.

Finally, the three men arrived at the dried up cistern and Judah led the party down into the coolness of the rock cellar. He walked to the back of the cave and retrieving dried grass and wood from his cloak, stuffed it into a small nook and then produced his flint rocks. Judah held the rocks near the dried grass and after two strikes a small fire began to burn. When he turned around, Judah glanced at Yosef who was dressed in expensive garments with his beard trimmed and groomed to perfection. Judah watched Yosef step to the side to let the Roman enter and he was slightly unnerved by the boldness in the Gentile's eyes.

The man removed his hood, which shielded part of his face, and stared at Judah. He was taller than Judah, which was not the norm for most legionaries as they tended to be shorter built men. He had a clean shaven face, square chin, dark hair, and broad arms. He was ruggedly handsome, but had softness in his eyes. His frame spoke of a man who was battle hardened, had marched to the ends of the earth, was glorified, decorated as an officer who possessed both title and respect. He was the embodiment of the Roman image that was carved and shaped in the Greco statues that littered the country's palaces, villas, and baths. He stood with power and command within the dank coolness of the cistern, and that irritated Judah.

"You are a senator?" Judah asked in ignorance of the title and position.

Gaius shook his head and folded his large forearms. A ring glistened upon his finger and the bronze wristlets he wore reflected the low flame which burned behind Judah. He cleared his throat and in perfect Koine Greek said, "I am Gaius Cornelius Antony, Praefectus Castrorum of the Fulminata Twelfth Legion and I serve Prince Titus Flavius Vespasianus. I have been sent here as a delegate and representative of Rome, empowered by Emperor Vespasianus, and a mouthpiece of the Judean Legions which surround your city.

"I have been informed of your relationship with Yosef ben Matityahu, and I wish to oversee this unique agreement that you two have made. I speak for Prince Titus. May I remind you that although I represent Rome, I am a Centurion and commander in the First Cohort. This meeting and any in the future will remain secret, but will not stop me from carrying out orders or leading attacks against the city. I am also here to secure your trust as a possible ally of Rome, whether this is a figment or not. I cannot guarantee sparing your life or that of anyone else unless you prove otherwise, that is to say, if you do at all prove to be genuine in your faith and good service to Rome as a steward. Can Rome count on you to verify what you say is true?"

Judah was stunned by Gaius' speech which sounded rehearsed. He sensed the Centurion must have made that speech before, or something like it, but for the moment he was frozen into silence. The fire burned dimly behind him and Yosef gave Judah a strange look, almost as if he sought to ask him if he had understood a single word the officer had spoken.

"Did you not understand me?" Gaius asked. "You do know Greek don't you? Yosef tells me you are educated."

Judah gave a slight nod. "I understood you."

Gaius extended his hands slightly in a receiving gesture. "So, can Rome count on your word to bear truth?"

Judah scowled and found himself grasping the fringe of his garment in his hands. "What I want is of no purpose and service to Rome. I am not a steward of Rome, nor one to sell out the city. I will not be a puppet for your Prince's amusement nor will I regale myself with stories of your gods. I will not defile myself." Judah locked eyes with Yosef for a moment and then continued, "However, we, Rome and I, both seek a common interest and goal. I want something and Rome wants something.

"Your Titus wishes to destroy this holy city, burn our Temple, and slaughter its people. Despite what Yosef says before our walls the city is unified and will fight as a common body against every attempt the legions make to breach our walls. We are not to be mistaken as a city of peasants. There are thousands of us who have fought for years against Rome.

"Simon's army fought in the south and has history as an army. John's forces fought the legions in the north, and survived your sieges and battles. We are prepared and ready. We have weapons and armour, compliments from the Jerusalem garrison and legionaries we have killed. When you attack the city, it is not one wall you must overcome, but many. There are towers, fortresses, and battlements packed with Jewish soldiers eager to spill your blood in trade for liberty and freedom. They will stop at nothing to see the legions break upon our walls like water against rocks, and if you shall muster your forces against the Temple, you will only indwell each fighter with a heavenly strength in which to fight you off.

"So this is where your Titus finds himself. He can deny it once, or twice, but he has seen it with his own eyes and will face it again. I speak of ambush, sudden attack and slaughter where we dash out and slay Romans wherever we tread. You know what I speak of, Centurion Gaius, for your eyes have beheld such images. I need not pledge my trust or honour on my stake with Rome." Judah shook his head. "I do not, and you know why? It is because Rome will need me whether you like it or not and I do not have to defile my honour by making a pact with you. I am your best voice in the affairs of stopping ambushes; I am a soldier under John of Gischala. I know Titus will have no other voice as credible as mine. I will give you details as they come to prevent three ambushes and thus save the lives of many of your men, but in return I need something and for that I request a pledge of honour from you."

Gaius glared at Judah. "You refuse to pledge loyalty to Rome, yet you ask for a pact from me? This is absurd. There may be truth to what you speak, but hear me, Zealot. There are sixty thousand crack troops at your gates. The blood of your countrymen will never be cleaned from our blades when we are done, for it will be too much. Jerusalem will kneel before Titus, whether it is voluntary or forced, and it will be humbled by fire. You, a petty savage, make such claims? You think you know our plans and determination? I tell you that although your ambushes have worked, you will become suffocated and so closed in that you will be unable to move."

Gaius turned to storm out of the cistern, but Yosef suddenly said, "What is it that you want, Judah? You said there were two things: what you want and what Rome wants. What is it you want in exchange for information?" Gaius stopped, scowled at Yosef and then looked back at Judah.

Judah crossed his arms and appeared to be deep in thought for a brief moment until he slowly said, "All I ask for is the life of Capito. You found him for me, Yosef; I may be indebted to you for that. However, that is not enough, but I had to be sure he was here."

"You are mad to think Titus would give up a Roman to the slaughter to crave your appetite," Gaius said nearly spitting the words.

"Titus will give me Capito, I know he will and in return I will tell you about three planned attacks before they occur." Judah suddenly looked at peace as he thought about revenge. "What is his whole name?"

Yosef glanced at Gaius for permission, and when the Centurion nodded, the Jewish General replied, "His full name is Capito Vorenus Bibalus. He is a Hastatus Prior in the Fretensis. That is all I can tell you at this point. You can know more depending on what Prince Titus says."

"Madness," Gaius uttered, dumbfounded and shaking his head.

Judah ignored the remark and said to Yosef, "The life of Capito in exchange for the Roman lives that will be spared on the information I give you. Three surprise attacks planned by Gischala himself. That is all I ask."

Gaius was still for a moment as he glared with a deep foreboding grimace. Experience told him to have nothing to do with such a man. However, his conscience and conviction told him that if the roles had been reversed he would have suggested such a plan in order to gain revenge. *Maybe we are not so different*, Gaius thought to himself. He sighed heavily and said, "I will take this to Titus, as maddening as it seems. I will tell him your proposal. It will be left to him to decide on what must be done. I will not promise anything. If I were you, I would not get my hopes up and I would also surrender and beg for mercy." He paused for a moment and then said with puzzlement, "Why did you not want a pledge of honour from Rome? Why would you disdain such an offer?"

Judah shook his head, "No, not on my life would I trust the word of Rome. But I do see you as a man of honour and respect. From you I know I will be able to trust a pledge of your word that Capito will fall under my blade and the blood he spilled so long ago shall be avenged and paid for."

* * *

CHAPTER XIX

April 25th, 70 A.D. / 28th of Nisan, 3830
Agrippa's Palace
The Mishneh
Jerusalem

Simon ben Giora leaned forward and hurled his empty wine goblet at the officers standing before him. The throw was not very accurate as the cup bounced and clanged off the stone floor, but it got the desired message across. "You're all so weak!" he shouted like an angry child. Simon adjusted the silk robes he wore and sat back pouting, furrowing his eyebrows with annoyance. He played with one of the large golden rings he wore and then shook his head. "I am King Simon. I do not need John or his play things to entertain me, nor swell the ranks of my army. Eleazar may be enshrouded in a tomb somewhere with John picking up the scraps of power, but I will not seek peace with him. We have a current understanding at this point, but there can be no true peace so long as he holds the Temple Mount."

One of the officers sighed, then raised his hands in an animated fashion and declared for all to hear, "My King, we must look beyond this to the security of the city! Unifying with John does not have to seal a contract of peace between you and him, but it should stand for something so we can have freedom to move our troops around to confront the Romans wherever they attack. Ramps are being built on our west, and we will need John's scorpions and his experienced crews. We will need the reinforcements when the time comes, and John's men are good soldiers."

"My King, truth comes from our lips. The Romans draw ever closer to our walls and are nearly within shot of an arrow," another officer said loudly. "Their fortifications are deep and already the beginnings of three ramps can be identified. They guard themselves well and we will need to direct our attention to sporadic assaults to halt the works. This will cost lives."

"Lives are what I can spare on such attacks. We have a large army, many who are doing nothing but guard duty." Simon glanced to his left at Yehoram, whose fat belly shook with laughter. Matthias ben Theophilus, who had once been the High Priest, gave Simon a dark look and lowered his head in shame. Simon smiled and replied, "Once the Romans get closer, we will attack with such a fury that they will go mad. However, I wish to test their resolve with trickery."

"My King, should we not resolve the matter of peace with Gischala?" queried the confused officer who had last spoken.

Simon laughed out loud and stood, making sure his robes fell upon the ground properly. He enjoyed the wealth of the kingdom he had carved out for himself, but deep inside he knew that John of Gischala must be dealt with until he could enjoy complete power and rule. "This matter of John is over. I will not discuss such petty things and I forbid you to talk of such nonsense anymore. We must look to our own defences. Now, we all know Titus watches throughout the day as his troops work. His eyes have been on the approaching earthworks more and more. So, I will need at least two hundred volunteers to go outside the walls and surrender."

The silence that ensued was deafening and Simon suddenly burst out laughing. "They will not really surrender, fools, but I wish for the Romans to think so. I want this group to exit from the Women's Gate and huddle by the walls in sight of his camp while we have men on top pelting them with stones and cursing them. Have these men on the walls dressed as common folk; there are to be no weapons. Have one or two priests among them if you can. Now, once the Romans approach, which they are sure to do, we will have troop reserves behind the wall that can rush out and attack, joined by the decoy which will secretly be armed. Have men with torches stationed behind them ready. Perhaps we can drive the Romans back, wrap around the wall and scuttle the ramps before they gain more height."

Numerous nods could be seen among the council of officers as many saw the genius in the plan. A few senior Idumeans did not look so easily convinced and they shook their heads, unsure if this was too early for an attack on the northern works. Simon saw these looks and approached the men with a foreboding aura as he sought to stir fear within them. Some of the Idumeans glared back at Simon in challenge, yet most backed down and stepped aside.

"You think this is a poor plan?" Simon blatantly asked while eyeing the cluster of Idumeans.

A senior officer of the group stepped forward and bowed humbly. "We are just worried, dear King, that this might be too early for an attack north of the wall. There is much ground to cover. The Romans are concentrated in the area with two cohorts before the walls, and watchmen this morning reported artillery being organized at the camps."

"That is why we should join John as his men have plenty of scorpions," mumbled a man a metre away, but loud enough for Simon to hear.

"What did you say? You swine and whore!" Simon suddenly shouted, making the room shake. All the officers swallowed in fear as their faces became pale. "I should have you scourged for your insolence! John is a pig! We do not need him, and we do not want him! Can't you all see?" Simon said pleading. "If we join him we will never have power. You are my men whom I forged in the south through the fires of war! I made sure that booty was never far from your reach, that you always had a naked whore beside you, and now you dare say to me I should make peace? Look what he did to the men of Eleazar. They were crushed in the corridors of the Temple and died in the darkness. John has destroyed Eleazar and gained power, but he is not strong enough to come down from his perch." Simon's eyes were alight like a glowing furnace. "The Romans we can handle. I have made truces with John in the past and they have not been upheld. Now, you will keep to your borders and follow my command as King." Simon glanced back at Yehoram and shook his head. "The men who serve me faithfully are few, while too many question my orders. You elected me as King and I have brought glory upon your heads." Simon walked back to his throne and sat down.

"We do as the King commands," Yehoram shouted with a nod.

Simon rolled his eyes and sighed heavily. "The Romans will come to our walls soon and we must complicate their every move. Titus watches the city constantly. He will buy into this deception and more Romans shall wet the ground with their blood." Simon leaned forward and said while glaring at the Idumeans, "Am I clear?"

The senior Idumean officer nodded slowly and bowed his head. "We will serve and carry out your orders."

"Good," Simon replied sitting back. "Get out of my sight, all of you." The war council turned to leave and Simon suddenly shot out a hand and pointed at Matthias and said, "Not you, Theophilus. I seek a word with you."

Matthias obeyed as he stopped and watched the officers file out of the palace court in silence. He could not help but think they were right. An alliance of trust with John would be the only way to defeat the legions, but Simon's sway over his men was powerful. He had watched daily as the earth rose higher west of the wall and as hundreds of engineers and labourers worked around the clock; the ramps approached the city metre by metre.

Once the room was clear, Simon said, "My eyes have been upon you, Matthias."

"Upon me, my lord?" the priest responded, shocked.

Simon gave a brief nod. "Yes, upon you. You are so quiet all the time. You slither here and there and lurk in the shadows."

"I am a priest, and that I remain. You may never take that title from me for it is in my blood. I seek only to carry out the duties as required by Torah as a priest," Matthias replied in defense, feeling smothered by the discomfort which filled the room.

"You are banished from the Temple Mount. What duties do you speak of? Could they be for Rome?" Simon asked cleverly.

Matthias' face became flushed with anger. "I speak of study of Torah, ritual bathing, giving to the poor, and encouraging my brethren in their sacrificial duties!" Matthias replied, slightly raising his voice. "If you have a charge against me, my lord, then let me be taken away in chains. If not, let us abandon this absurd accusation."

"Is it absurd, Matthias?" Simon said coldly.

"I let you into the city, I have served the government of the past, and now I serve you. I do not cower and hide, but attend council. I have been humiliated and shamed; an embarrassment against God and a scorning against my people. Yet, I have held my head high and have served. For you to imply that I would jeopardize the city and my people to spy for Rome is ludicrous and speaks of madness."

"Is this claim implied or truth?" Simon asked as he grinned, unmoved to anger from Matthias' outburst.

Matthias suddenly grew calm and while staring Simon directly in the face he said, "Do you have evidence to convict me of such claims?" Simon shook his head and Matthias continued, "Then I will leave you unless there is anything else."

"Know that I am watching you and suspect everything." Simon held up his hand. "Your life and the lives of your three sons are in the palm of my hand."

Matthias stepped back, appalled at the threat and outstretched his arms. His beard was wet with bitter tears that fell from his eyes. "You would execute my sons? They fight for you and despite their defilement from killing, I, as their father, still love them. A priest is called never to kill, yet they have been zealous to your cause. But you, Simon, threaten my offspring? Deal harshly with me if you have reason to think I am a spy, but let them live. Upon the name of the One of heaven and earth, I beg you to cast your eyes from them."

Simon crossed his arms, scanning Matthias from top to bottom. "Remember the charter you gave to me and the names upon it? A charter trying to order me around and take my seat of power? Tell them there will be no action taken, that you were wrong, and that you will no longer lead such a group. Tell the Idumeans this, Matthias, and your family lives." Simon was still for a moment and then smiled as shame and remorse filled the lines of the aged priest's face. "Leave me, Matthias. Go bathe in the *mikvah* and cleanse yourself from your tears. I will be watching you and your sons. Let me not find reason to deal harshly with your family." Simon grinned as he watched Matthias back away, than leave the court.

Matthias had faced Simon days ago with a charter, signed from a group of Idumeans declaring Simon to dismantle Bagdatus' band of brigands or else Simon would lose hold of his army. Simon had shrugged the charge off and had sent Matthias from the room by the point of a spear. Now, Simon had regained his power over the priest's influence by threatening the lives of his family. For that leverage, he knew he could control the priest and thus continue orchestrating the brutalities by Bagdatus' men in their hunt to discover traitors.

Since the forced removal of Eleazar from the Temple by the army of John, Simon had become increasingly paranoid and suspicious of what he interpreted as treasonous activity. Already in the last week he had three men accused of being spies for John and the Romans. Two of them had been locked away in the dungeons and the third beheaded. The warning had to be severe and stern, for if people were to spy for the enemy, they would be found and dealt with.

* * *

Upper Market
Near the Ophel

"Will you not come in? I can give you fresh water to drink," Hadassah asked sheepishly as she saw slight embarrassment spread across the face of Judah.

Judah hesitated at the step of her house, not knowing whether it would be proper for him to accept the invitation. "Your bruises have healed," he stammered, trying to change the subject.

A bright smile lit her face and she took a step back holding the door open. "If you come in, you must be quiet. My mother is sleeping."

"She remains ill?" Judah asked peering into the home.

Hadassah gave a simple nod and stepped aside as Judah reluctantly entered and touched the mezuzah and then kissed his finger. "Do I make you uncomfortable?" she asked pointedly.

Judah was caught off guard by the question. He gave her a stunned look and unable to reply he just shook his head. He gazed around the simple three roomed house made from stone and mortar. It was cool inside and a faded curtain covered a single window in front of the home. A few pieces of furniture littered the space. A small room in the back, joined to the eating area, revealed a bed and the curled up form of a woman wheezing gently as she slept.

"She is not well." Hadassah shook her head and walked over to a small kitchen where a few jugs stood in carved notches in the wall. One was copper and the other was clay. She took the clay jug and taking a wooden cup beside it, poured Judah some water. Numerous clay bowls littered the top of a narrow counter and inside them were dried dates, olives, nuts, and some pieces of stale flat bread. A small table stood nearby Judah with two oil lamps burning, as the scent of oil lingered in the air.

Hadassah followed Judah's gaze from the oil lamps to the simple state of her home. "It is not much, but it is our home." She placed the jug back in the wall and handed him the water.

"Thank you," Judah replied, accepting it generously. "You are kind."

"I am poor, but at least I have my mother." She looked at Judah for a moment and then gently smiled. "I have a small amount of cheese, if you would like some."

"How long have you had it?" Judah asked.

"A week." Hadassah bent down near the counter and pushed a dusty, hanging blanket. She reached in and brought out a small block wrapped in strips of linen. She unfurled the cloth and showed Judah the moist cheese. "It is cool down there, which is how it lasts so long. I know an elderly man who has sold my family cheese for years in the market."

"Yes, but cheese must be hard to get now. The city crawls with soldiers and they are all looking for food it seems," Judah said eyeing the cheese with a hungry appetite.

"You won't tell, will you?" Hadassah asked.

Judah shook his head. "They have plenty of food. You can keep your cheese." He grinned as he watched her retrieve a thin knife and cut two slices. "From what animal does this come from?"

"Goat. It is soft and full of flavour. Here, try." She handed him a thin slice and he ate it. For a second there was nothing upon his face, and then he nodded and smiled. "You like?" Hadassah asked.

"Very much so." Judah watched her wrap the cheese and put it back in its secret place. She ate a slice of the goat cheese herself and then gestured to the door. "Would you like to go for a walk?"

Judah took another drink of water and stared at the floor for a moment. His thoughts were interrupted as Hadassah's mother coughed violently, groaned, and then was silent. "I do not know if it is safe, Hadassah."

"We can go to the market. It is empty since you and your men killed that Idumean. We don't have anyone come here anymore. They have forgotten about us, because of you." She smiled and stepped forward gazing into Judah's eyes. "Your hair is unkept," Hadassah said softly with a light in her eyes.

Judah grunted and looking to his left and right he stalled, not knowing what to say. He touched his curly hair and tried briefly to flatten it and then gave up and readjusted his covering. "I have not much need to stay tidy. We have been preparing for the Romans and keeping an eye on Simon's men."

"When the Romans amass for battle, you must come here and let me wash your clothes, clean your face, and comb your hair." Hadassah looked into Judah's eyes longingly and then said, "You must let me."

Judah gazed at the beautiful woman for a moment, wanting to reach up and touch her face with all his heart, but he could not for he felt reminded of Miriam. "I will," he replied shortly.

"Let us walk," she softly said and Judah nodded, setting the cup by the oil lamps.

The two stepped from the home and into the heat of the day. Judah kept one step ahead of Hadassah as she respectfully knew her place as a widow next to an unmarried man. However, they walked slowly, Hadassah enjoying Judah's company and Judah plagued with unknown certainties. They approached the broken fountain in the middle of the quiet marketplace and Hadassah sat down in the shade of the shadow it cast. Judah stood nearby, unsure of what to make of the picture before him. To Hadassah it was an old fountain which used to be filled with life and a center of bustling activity, yet for Judah it only held a memory of pain and anguish.

"If my mother dies, I shall not know what to do," Hadassah whispered just loud enough so Judah could hear.

He rested his hand on the pommel of his sword and squinted at her as the sun was in his eyes. "I will protect you."

Hadassah glanced up confused at the warrior before her. "You would risk your life for me?" When he nodded she looked away. "I have nothing of value to give you in return for such protection." She held her breath for a moment and said closing her eyes, "I could only give you one thing."

"I would never ask for such a thing," Judah replied, understanding what she implied. "I killed that man to protect your dignity. How then could I take it?"

Hadassah shuddered as a gentle flow of tears ran down her cheek and she quickly wiped them away with the sleeve of her gown. "You are a good man, Judah ben Yosef."

"I do not see it the way you do," Judah replied.

"But I do, Judah. You are a good man." Hadassah paused. "Will you fight here to the end?"

Judah nodded. "I have given my word. I could not abandon the city now."

"And you believe we will win? That the enemy will be vanquished before Jerusalem's walls, as the Zealots believe?" Hadassah watched his face fall for a moment and then he shook his head and shrugged. "You think the city will fall?" she quietly asked.

"I do not wish it. It is in the hands of God." Judah saw she did not like that answer, but he was a loss for words. He walked over to the fountain and stared into the dried basin. For a moment his mind journeyed back in time to the sound of fire burning, the wail of the dying, and the body of Miriam floating within the blood stained water. "Many say we do not deserve to win, that God has turned His face from this place. They say this on account of the Jewish blood we have shed.

"Many say the leadership is corrupt and seeks only personal gain, and that the Romans will be used to punish us." Judah shook his head and sighed. "I pray this is not the truth. Simon is a wicked man. John, well, I believe he wishes to do good, but he has committed wrong in the past. But should this be the doom of us all? John is pious and serves God. He desires to remove Simon and unite the city."

Hadassah scowled slightly and stood next to Judah. "Yet, it was John and Eleazar who killed Ananus ben Ananus and Joshua ben Gamala." Judah looked at her as though he had no clue of what she spoke of. "It was John who had their throats slit and their bodies cast from the walls."

Judah shook his head. "Impossible! John has sworn against it, it was all Eleazar," he retorted trying to defend his commander's honour. "John's forces committed atrocities, but not under the guidance of their leader. John has told me he tried to hold them back but couldn't stop the killings."

"I saw him, Judah. On that day the Zealots ran throughout our city causing much grief. I was terrified, but my father had gone missing and his absence was driving my mother insane. So I disguised myself as a man, slipped from my home, and wandered the alleys in search of my father. The screams were endless and some homes burned with fire. I saw the dead lying in the street and heard the shattering of pottery and dishes upon the stones as Zealots plundered peoples' homes.

"I approached the Ophel and when I could see the Hulda Gates I heard shouting, screaming, and curses. I remember looking up above the gates at the top of the walls and there upon them was a great host of men. Among them I could make out John of Gischala. There were two others who were forced to kneel upon the wall. I can't remember everything John said. Amidst the fighting that went on in the city with the Idumeans finishing off the government forces, John declared Ananus and Joshua as traitors. I watched him slit their throats with his own hand and cast them from the walls. I shrieked and turned away before they struck the ground. I fled back to my home lamenting the entire way. I felt as if the city had come to an end. Ananus was the leader of the government, and with him dead it was as if Jerusalem would be swallowed up into the ground."

Judah held a look of utter shock and disgust. He turned away and stared into the dried fountain with both hands clenched into tight fists. He knew what she said was true, but Judah did not want to believe it. He did not want to believe he had joined the army of a murderer. The fact he had admired John brought shame upon his head as he had never questioned John's side of the story.

The tales of the warlord from Gischala had filled the spirits of thousands of men throughout the country. He was known as a man who had defied the Romans and led battles against them. People admired him and sought to emulate his actions. Yet, Judah had never known the dark side of John. True, he had witnessed the execution of the prisoner in the Antonia and witnessed the glee upon John's face as Eleazar's men were crushed by stones, but to know he had purposely deceived the government and then murdered them was unheard of. Nobody was without innocent blood upon their hands, yet the realization that his hands might be as stained as John's appeared as a great weight crushing his body.

Seeing the grief upon Judah's face, Hadassah gently touched his hand and received a startled look of misery within the deep recesses of his eyes. "What gives you pain? You wear your torment before me like a great cloak. In front of the others you try and hide it, but I see through you."

Judah thought back to the two visits he had made with Adam and Caleb to deliver food. Even after John and Simon had severed ties, Judah was allowed to descend unhindered beyond the Ophel to the home of Hadassah, and Bastard Bagdatus stayed away. "You said I was a good man, and I denied it." He took a deep breath, not believing he was about to divulge his secret.

"Before the war, I was to marry. I lived in Beit Lechem during my childhood, and a close friend of our family was a man named Moshe; he had a daughter, Miriam. They lived in a village not far from Beit Lechem, and I was to marry her. It was not like your typical arranged marriage. Although it was to be that way, I had loved her since I was young. I was five years older than her when I was pledged to wed. We took the oath before a rabbi friend of my father's and we feasted that night. Then one day in this very market, Florus dispatched a cohort of legionaries to slaughter everyone. My parents and Miriam died." Judah looked at Hadassah and saw the effect of his words upon her face. She wiped away tears and remained silent, wishing him to continue. "I killed my first man that day. I took the slain man's sword...this one," Judah tapped the pommel of his gladius. "I faced a Centurion from this very spot who was plundering the merchant booths over there." He pointed across the courtyard. "One of his soldiers must have told the Centurion of my presence for he turned and faced me. I remember tightening my grip upon the sword and begging him in my mind to attack me. I wished to kill him, but more deeply within my mind I wished to die fighting as to end the pain in my heart. Yet, that is not how it happened. The Centurion smiled at me and turned away.

"I was ashamed. My betrothed had fallen before me and then when I tried to regain my honour this man denied it of me. I hated him right then, and I hate him now. I turned and fled. While running down an alley I found two drunken soldiers. I fell upon them and killed one. I dragged the other into a darkened street where I tortured him for the name of the Centurion. When he told me, I made sure the man would perish in agony and I left him.

"I was tormented by what I had done, and I could not pray or even read Torah for a long time after. When I would attend worship on the odd occasion, I would sit among the gathering, my *talit* covering my head, and I would softly weep. One man who had seen me once thought I was pious, I now know I was only a coward, beleaguered by the cruelty of my hand upon another. That day the portion read was when Cain slaughtered his brother Abel, and I felt as though the blood of the mutilated cried forth from the ground. My fellow Jews would tell me not to fret, as the man was a Gentile, but a priest once told me my guilt would never leave me for I had desecrated a creation of HaShem through murder.

"Then years ago, I killed a man in the north. The band of men I led was known as the Lions. We ambushed Roman patrols and lived off the land. We did what we could to interrupt Roman operations." Judah shook his head amazed. "When I look back, we really didn't do that much. Anyway, one day when we were foraging for food, we came upon a small farm. This man came out of his house and cursed us. He called us worse than the Romans, swine, and madmen. I became so enraged and filled with anger that I couldn't think. As he yelled in my face, I drew my sword and killed him upon the step of his own home. I shed his blood upon the mantel of his door and shed it upon his steps under the watching eyes of his wife and children. The moans of weeping and mourning still echo in my mind. The children's faces were like ash having watched a fellow Jew slay their father. I looked up at them slowly, feeling the warmth of the man's blood upon my hands. He had died quickly, with little pain, but the looks in the eyes of those children haunt me still. We left swiftly after that. I was praised by my men as a hero and one who had punished an unpatriotic Jew. Only Adam and Caleb thought of me foolish." Judah hung his head in shame and rubbed his watery eyes. "I have never forgiven myself for what I did."

Judah thought for a moment and then continued, "The worst of it is that I could do nothing that day in the market. I was totally powerless to act against the wall of shields that trampled over everyone. Women and babies fell under the sword; the legionaries spared none. I carry this weight with me and I search for shalom between myself and Miriam. I failed to protect her that day she died in the market, and since then I am haunted by dreams of her. I see her in agony, with a spear in her back, and fire beneath her. She screams but is unable to breathe. Her hair becomes like rope and I smell oil upon her head. I hear the sound of a hammer and she fights as she dies." Judah swallowed hard, his eyes red and face overcome by sadness. "I can never see her face, and I have realized *that* is the horror I experience daily. I cannot remember her and for that I must find a way towards inner peace."

"I remember that day in the marketplace," Hadassah said. "I remember more of the wailing the next day as loved ones collected the fallen. I heard the number was as high as three thousand dead. I was only eleven. My father had protected us inside, bolting the door of our home, but we heard everything." Hadassah paused and then said with a puzzled expression, "What will you do to find this peace you seek after?"

Judah looked at her, a cold glaze over his eyes and he gave an abrupt nod. "I will use the Romans in any way feasible to complete the mission set before me."

"Which is?" Hadassah asked.

"To kill Capito, the Centurion," Judah replied and then gazed back into the broken fountain.

* * *

April 26th, 70 A.D. / 29th of Nisan, 3830
Base of Mount Scopus

"Yosef ben Matityahu?"

Yosef turned in his saddle upon his horse and scowled, clearly annoyed from being disturbed. A legionary stood a few metres away, resting his shield upon the ground and holding a pilum close to his side. The man was in full armour and irritated at being the one selected to deliver the message. He had walked from the shaded veranda Titus sat under all the way to the base of the mountain called Scopus to locate the wandering Jewish General who insisted for permission to document the entire siege. Titus had granted the writing, declaring that he would personally publish it for Yosef, and since then, the prisoner would mingle with the troops, survey the construction, and interview officers. On this day, however, the legionary's mood was soured from the thirst that gripped his throat and the weight of his equipment.

Yosef lowered his parchment and pen. He stared at the soldier for a moment as he considered ignoring the fellow and returning to his work. "Yes, I am he," he finally said rolling his eyes.

"The Prince will see you north of the wall. You are to go at once." The soldier pointed behind him and stared back up at the finely dressed Jewish General.

"What does he want me for?" Yosef asked.

"In the bleeding name of Mars, how would I know!" retorted the soldier who was clearly exasperated and uncomfortable. "I am ordered to fetch you across this damned field and that is what I have done."

Yosef watched the man turn abruptly to leave and called out to the soldier, "Would you like some water? It is still cool."

The Roman halted and looked back, obviously taken by the idea. He hesitated for a moment, thinking over the offer. Finally it was the heat of the sun which won him over as he marched to Yosef's side and accepted the water skin. He took a long drink with eyes closed and felt as if he wore a fresh linen toga and was lying by a pool. A look of relief followed the drink as he surrendered the skin back to Yosef and giving a nod he said, "Thank you." Then the soldier turned and marched away to rejoin his cohort posted near Psephinus Tower.

Yosef rolled up his parchment and tucked it inside his cloak. Then digging his heels into the flanks of his mount, he leaned forward and galloped towards the veranda which had been built a hundred metres in front of the massive legionry camp. Titus' signum stood erect near the shelter, accompanied by a standard with the imagio upon it, another one boasting a golden eagle, and finally the banners of the legions taking part in the siege.

A troop stood guarding the veranda, surrounding it like a fortress. Titus was under the shade standing over a table and eyeing a map. He was joined by Tiberius Julius Alexander, Marcus Octavian, Sextus Cerealis, and Titus Frigius.

Marcus Sulla Maximus sat upon a cushioned chair, as if oblivious to the heated discussion among the commanders concerning the proper tactics in taking the city. He held a small bowl of grapes and was devouring one after the other while watching the distant legionaries working upon the ramps at the western side of the city beyond the octagonal Psephinus Tower. He watched silently as hundreds of soldiers hauled up dirt, emptied their burdens on top and then slowly walked back down to replenish their loads. The sounds of hammers and shovels filled the air as orders continued to be shouted aloud and men cursed the heat.

A team of engineers and surveyors stood atop the nearest ramp shielded by wicker hurdles to discourage any archers on the city walls. The engineers seemed to be involved in a heated debate as one pointed to the city and the other shook his hands in the air, yelling at a poor young man who stood behind them with his head hung low. An array of measuring instruments accompanied the group involving poles, lengths of rope, and sticks with etched numbers and dashes struck into them. Half a dozen soldiers held the surveying equipment as they waited for the argument to subside. It was not until a line of labourers piled up behind them that finally the argument was settled and the engineers stepped to the side to allow the soldiers to pass by carrying loads of earth, timber, and stone.

Yosef approached the veranda and dismounted. He was unsure of what to do with the horse until one of the guards approached him and silently took the reins. Yosef nodded with thanks, strolled through the armed men, and climbed the steps to the platform. The shade instantly felt wonderful as a breeze stirred the thin canvas above him. The generals were in a deep discussion as the Prince stood, hunched over a table with his gaze affixed to a map. The four other commanders, Tiberius, Sextus, Titus and Marcus continued talking as they rearranged small blocks with flags sticking out of them to different parts of the map. Upon the tiny flags were legionary numbers. Yosef quickly guessed that each block represented a legion and the planned military manoeuvres they intended to make once the official fighting commenced.

"You will not make sense of their ramblings," Marcus Sulla said nearby as he extended the bowl of grapes to the awkward Jewish General. Yosef took one with a smile and remained standing, awaiting Titus to recognize him. Marcus snickered to himself quietly and said, "You should sit. When they go at it like this, it could be awhile."

Yosef felt awkward that the Tribune was being so candid with him. He was reluctant to sit until Marcus Sulla snapped his fingers to a nearby slave and had a stool brought over. "Eat and drink," he said raising his cup. "Need not have manners here; you leave those in the palace. Out here is where a man is tested and can drink in peace."

Yosef wondered if the Tribune was drunk, but he dared not ask. He accepted a cup of wine and some more grapes as he sat awkwardly upon the stool. Finally, after what seemed like an uncomfortable eternity for Yosef, Prince Titus turned around with a smile and said, "Yosef, it is good of you to join us."

"I was sent for, my Prince," Yosef replied reminding Titus as to why he had come.

Titus shrugged. "I find it hard to keep up with the fine details at times. I believe you were sent for concerning our secret." Titus turned and took his wine goblet from the table. "We shall go for a stroll to stretch our legs." He glanced at his legionary generals and gave them a sharp nod. "We will continue this later." Then to Marcus Sulla he said, "You can come with us, you old drunk." The Boar Tribune gave a cackle of laughter and stood to join them.

"We need no guard," Titus called out as some soldiers moved to escort him. Then in a tender voice Titus asked Yosef, "Tell me how your research is going?"

Yosef looked flattered and bowed slightly as the men descended the veranda. "I have been recording the preparations for the siege, my Prince. I have finished writing about the city itself, from what I could remember and the people I could interview. The use of your maps has helped."

Titus nodded. "They are as accurate as I can gather. Some of them were from Cestius' campaign four years ago, and Agrippa lent me another. They are quite detailed. I am uncertain with some of the streets and scale of the Bezetha but that will come in time."

Titus finished his wine and stared at Yosef. "We will begin soon, you must know that. The ramps are nearing completion. We are using the hurdles because we are within range of their bows. I am pleased with one thing, though. You know what that is?" Yosef shook his head and Titus pointed to the city. "We have been within range of their scorpions and catapults for over a week, yet not one single shot has descended upon the working troops. You know why?" Yosef shook his head again and Titus raised his finger to make a point. "They are fighting each other again. John and Simon are at each other's throats, and that is good for us.

"A spy from the city informed me of Eleazar's demise and that John and Simon have fallen into discord. That is true by the fact that not a single stone missile has been fired at us. John's men were the ones who captured the garrison of the city and it is his army which holds all the artillery. And where is the idiot? On the Temple Mount! We can work unhindered and without fear of a hailstorm. Just look at the ground we have covered in the last ten days." Titus gazed over the ramps edging closer to the city and the trails of smoke that coiled upwards into the air.

The clanging of iron rang aloud as steel spikes were driven into timber which secured the foundations of the ramps as they climbed higher. Buckets of spikes were carried up as lengths of timber piled in wagons rolled by led by oxen and donkeys. Titus held out both his hands, directing them to the hundreds of working soldiers and said with pride, "This is *Roma* at its best. We can work and create anything. Soon, we will have towers and rams and the city will shudder." Titus looked at Marcus and said, "The banners of our legions will be planted upon the roof of the Temple if they should force our hand." He glanced back at Yosef and asked seriously, "They have to surrender and see reason. Their country still smoulders and their city will too, if they test me."

"I pray John and Simon will surrender, my lord," Yosef replied in almost a whisper.

The three men neared the ramps and halted, keeping a safe distance from the looming Psephinus Tower on the north western corner of the city. Titus gazed at the three massive earth ramps that stretched before him like great monsters rising up from the ground. Two cohorts of armed soldiers from the Fulminata stood by in rectangular formations as they faced the city under the flapping of their vexillum in the wind. The only words that escaped his lips were of personal reflection as he muttered, "It is an awesome sight." Then there was silence among the three men for a few moments as the work parties continued upon the three ramps. "Tell me," Titus said abruptly. "Yosef, what kind of a man is this Judah?"

"You have asked me this before, my Prince," Yosef replied. Titus gave the Jewish General a scowl and Yosef said, "A man of pride and torment. He is a man of principle and honour. I can see that in him."

"Like your King David you told me about," Titus said. "What are his principles?"

"To defend the city and regain his honour, which I think is peace with himself from what happened. I feel that Judah desires not to be associated with the Zealots. Although he fights with them, he seeks not to be branded as such men." Yosef stared at the Roman Prince, not knowing where he was going with this.

"And he wants the life of one of my centurions?" Titus gave Yosef a sideways glance and then shook his head. "That, I cannot do. This Capito is a senior officer with years of experience with the Jews. He served Florus, and now he's in the Tenth and has been there since its ranks were replenished. I can offer this Judah money, position, but I cannot give him what he asks for. I am sorry."

"So what is to be done? If we cannot meet his demands we risk ambush," Yosef said being very brash.

Titus picked up on the attitude and gave the Jewish General a stern look. "You think I haven't considered that. We will just have to offer something else."

"He will not take anything else, my Prince," Yosef countered quickly.

"And you are sure of what Judah wants?" Titus said snapping and glaring at Yosef. "I can offer the whelp the world if I but flick my fingers in the air, and you say he won't accept that? I tell you, Yosef ben Matityahu, you are not so different then Judah. You both fought against *Roma* and through the right circumstances you can both be spared. When it comes down to it, a man desires to live above all. I can offer him that and much more." Suddenly a shout echoed from one of the great earthen mounds followed by a blast upon a whistle. Titus stared past Yosef and scowled. "What is going on?" he murmured as Marcus Sulla moved beside him with alarm.

An array of Jewish civilians could be seen filling the ramparts above the high walls of the northern defences. Women and priests stood among the throng of people lining the battlements and all of them began jeering as a set of enormous timber and steel gates slowly opened with groans from the grinding hinges. Then, a host of soldiers armed with spears and clubs drove a smaller mob of unarmed men from the gates who were shouting back at the soldiers. The Jews moved along the wall to the west and then halted underneath the shadow of the octagonal tower behind them. The Roman cohorts, stationed away from the walls to the left of the ramps, suddenly spread their ranks, convinced a Jewish sortie was about to occur. Centurions on the flanks quickly drew their swords and optiones assembled the men using their hastiles. The air grew tense around the centuries as they stood like walls of steel and wood as the Roman infantry waited nervously watching the Jewish mob.

However, what happened next caught everyone off guard. The smaller unarmed group of Jews were forced out from the safety of the walls, belittled with curses hurled their way as the greater host of Zealots, with spears lowered, marched back into the city and closed the gates with a great thud.

Rotten food and other objects were hurled from the walls upon the heads of the unarmed Jewish men. A few tried to call up to the people upon the walls in mercy, but they were only beat down as they resorted to covering themselves. The group of men, which numbered close to two hundred, seemed nervous as they shuffled away from the walls to escape the hurled food. A number of men in the front ranks fell to their knees and held up their hands in mercy towards a cohort of legionaries who cautiously moved to face them, yet abruptly halted, standing in a solid rectangular formation of emblazoned red shields with palm fronds painted upon the surfaces. The second cohort slowly moved up to join their comrades and suddenly neither formation knew what to do or how to react.

A few men burst out with jeers towards the Jews but were threatened with a lashing from the optiones if silence would not ensue among the ranks. The centurions looked around aimlessly for answers, and some jogged a ways from their men to see if they could not recognize a higher ranking officer to give them guidance. A few troopers on horseback, galloped across the fields in the distance, but none seemed interested in what was happening at the city.

Titus thought about sending Marcus Sulla to fetch his horse. Then he thought of running back himself for his armour and to rally more troops. With each day's work, a sixth of the troops from the Apollinaris and Fulminata were put to use upon the three massive ramps. The Fifth Macedonica legion also worked on numerous projects that had their attention. They had been set to the task over a week ago to build dikes surrounding artillery positions south of the city directly in front of Hippicus and further on. Across from Herod's Palace, the Fifth had also constructed feint siege ramps built in the same manner as those to the north. These would never be used but would help scatter the Jewish forces. Among the Macedonica, were Titus' most skilled master builders who assembled siege towers, testudo battering rams, and other engines vital to the upcoming frontal assaults, which meant that their forces were scattered all over the place and impossible to assemble swiftly.

A quarter of the legionaries of the Tenth had also been set to work clearing the ground on the opposite side of the city at the base of the Mount of Olives. The rest of the legion would either be resting within their camp, participating in drills upon Scopus, or maintaining military discipline by forced marches to keep them from boredom. These troops would be a fair distance from the city and completely useless to call upon. Even the alae were predisposed to foraging for supplies, guarding the southern side of the city, and monitoring all the surrounding villages. Thus, all that Titus could draw upon were around nine hundred and fifty armed legionaries, including nearly fifteen hundred unarmed infantry working upon the ramps which would take time to fetch their weapons and armour to join the battle. To organize more cohorts of the Twelfth or the Fifteenth, would mean drumming them out of camp and assembling their ranks, which for a force that size could take two hours. However, the immediate problem Titus also saw remained in the fact that the soldiers working upon the ramps had already been active for three hours and would be tired.

Titus cursed the sky silently as he clenched his fists and battled in his mind what to do should the Jews attack. One thing he had quickly learned since arriving at

Jerusalem was never to take the Zealots for granted. Titus watched an optio from the nearest cohort take notice of him and leave his unit.

The man ran towards Titus and when he was within earshot he slowed his pace to catch his breath and called out, "My Prince! We think they are surrendering!" The optio saluted abruptly and humbly bowed his head as he wiped the sweat from his eyes.

Titus strained to see the city walls more clearly and then shook his head, staring at the man with wild eyes. "They are what?"

"Surrendering, my Prince. The unarmed mob at the wall looks as if they are trying to surrender. Centurion Qurinius of my centuria said he thinks they are the war party." The optio glanced back for a moment and then leaned on his hastile for relief.

"Is John or Simon among them?" Titus asked suspiciously.

The junior officer shrugged and shook his head. "None of us know what either of them look like, my Prince." He watched Titus glare at him unhappily and then the man quickly said, "But they look like Zealots. They are all large men and the people upon the walls are cursing them. We even saw some women waving our direction." The optio looked back and then muttered something with shock as a golden eagle upon a pole was lifted above the wall by two Jewish men.

"By the bones of the gods," Titus mumbled. "That is one of Cestius' eagles!" He watched a number of Jewish women place garlands upon the pole and call out with excited voices, meanwhile waving at the cohorts, inviting them to approach. Titus felt compelled to believe the Jews were genuine with this symbol of offering and tribute, yet suspicion still clouded his judgment. Then he watched as a number of children appeared on the battlements gripping small stones which they began to pelt at the men huddled at the base of the wall.

A second man, this time a regular legionary trotted up to Titus and saluted as he said, "Prince Titus, Centurion Qurinius has told me to say that he can hear declarations of peace from the walls. He says the Jews are saying that once the troublemakers are in chains they will open up the city." The soldier pointed to the closed gates with his spear and then squinted at the Prince, waiting for an answer.

Suddenly cheering arose from the cohorts and Romans upon the ramps, as soldiers began hugging each other and patting one another upon the shoulders. A signum was raised in celebration from the cohort stationed to the far right as men loosened their ranks and smiled, overcome by relief to the surrender of the city. As the Romans cheered, more Jewish civilians took to the walls and waved at them or danced. The sound of horse hooves beat upon the ground and the legionary generals from the veranda approached leading Achilles among them.

"The bastards have surrendered without a brawl," Frigius called out to Titus as the Prince took his horse.

"It appears as though the peace party is upon the walls." Titus mounted slowly, refusing to take his eyes off the huddled mass of frightened Jewish men. He sat boldly upon his horse for a moment and then looked at Yosef. "Approach the walls and hear their demands, Yosef. I wish for you to relay to them that *Roma* will uphold the promise of peace and the city will be spared." He glanced at the optio as relief began to wash over him and he said, "The cohorts are to advance slowly to within twenty metres of the prisoners. Wait until Yosef says his piece and then order them to slowly approach. You are to encircle them, bind them in chains, and hold them outside the Fulminata. We will sort them out later this afternoon. Leaders will be executed tonight and the rest can be held to be used as gladiators at our victory feast."

Yosef scowled slightly at Titus, knowing the Prince had lied about past promises concerning the fate of the prisoners. The generals cheered with broad smiles and Titus never saw Yosef's look of anger as the Prince of Rome felt emboldened and filled with pride. If this was really it, then the rebellion was practically over and all that remained were the scattered strongholds to the south which would fall swiftly. The Prince's father would be proud and could sail to Rome crowned emperor of the world.

The optio wasted no time as he and the legionary ran back to their cohort to inform the ranking centurions of Titus' orders. Yosef slightly picked up his robes, rather than let them drag in the dust, and silently crossed the ground, past the mounds of earth and wicker hurdles, to the high walls of northern Jerusalem. By the time he reached the cohorts they were already reorganizing into rank. With spears resting upon shoulders of segmented armour, the legionaries advanced in solid blocks of formation to the steady counting of the centurions who held their sword blades pointing to the ground.

Yosef kept a few paces ahead of the marching legionaries as he rehearsed in his mind everything he would say. He noticed that the shouts, curses, and abuse which rained down upon the heads of the unarmed war party so steadily before, had suddenly stopped. People grew quiet upon the walls as they recognized him and all faces watched with anticipation amidst the eerie silence.

Yosef searched the crowd of men before the gate for that one familiar face he knew he would never forget, John ben Levi. However, he did not recognize a single man. The more he strained to pick them apart, the less he was convinced this was a genuine expulsion of the war party. He cleared his throat to speak and then felt his voice melt away into thin air as he noticed all the men in the group were dressed in the colourful cloaks of the Idumeans. Their dark beards and mustaches only solidified in Yosef's mind that not a single man of John of Gischala's force stood outside the city walls. The war party was a trap as hostile eyes glared at him and Yosef stood blankly in the open, completely vulnerable.

Suddenly the mob of Jewish men opened and an enormous man dressed in scarlet robes pushed through gripping a heavy spear in his right hand. He had a long black beard that was braided at the ends and his eyes narrowed beneath the pointed helmet he wore. Drawing the long javelin back, he lunged forward and hurled the missile with a loud grunt. Yosef abandoned his strong stance and flung himself to the ground as the iron tipped spear sliced the air, narrowly missing his head as it drove into the ground behind him. The Idumean shouted in defiance and opened his robes to reveal a sword strapped to his waist. The behemoth of a man drew the blade and delivered a great bellow which shook the ground. A sudden jeer exploded upon the walls as a shower of stones, arrows and spears were released from warriors who had remained hidden until now. Yosef scrambled to flee the onslaught but yelped in pain as a small stone, hurled from the leather pouch of a slinger, struck his upper arm. He stumbled, collapsing upon the ground, and then picking himself up with desperate feet he ran cradling his injured arm.

"Shields up!" screamed a Centurion from the nearest cohort as he quickly raised his gladius. Like crazed demons the group of clustered Jewish men suddenly became valiant warriors of tales long ago. Nearly two hundred of them drew concealed blades of all sorts as the gate behind them opened allowing hundreds more to pour through with spears, clubs, and axes. The Centurion knew right away the odds were against him and he braced himself. "No retreat!" he shouted. "Spread ranks by the metre! Prepare for volley!" His desperate eyes darted to his left as the other cohort mimicked the same command as it readied for the attack.

The horde of Idumeans and Zealots surged forward with an earth-trembling shout as they thundered across the small expanse of ground closing the gap with incredible speed. The fury of their charge was chilling as the legionaries locked their bodies and held their shields with sweating hands. The order was given by the blast of a whistle and for a moment the Jewish attack was checked as a hailstorm of pila descended upon the onslaught, strewing corpses all about, spilling blood everywhere. Idumeans collapsed in piles, as spears protruded from chests and legs. Men wailed in agony as they fell, and the wounded tried to turn back towards the city despite the pounding of feet around them. At the blast of another whistle, the cohorts drew their blades, stepping forward to the orders of their centurions and optiones. However, within an instant, the Jewish attack gained a new source of strength as they poured forth and smashed into the locked shields of the legionaries.

Both sides grinded to a complete halt as men gritted teeth and cursed, slashing at faces, arms, and legs. The legionaries, with quick thrusts of their blades, found encumbered victims in the struggle and one by one men fell upon the ground with their stomachs slashed open or arteries severed as they bled to death. A deep roar went up from the Jewish fighters despite their losses and with a great heave they suddenly catapulted forward knocking legionaries over as men stumbled backwards. Shrieks and wails lifted up as Jews stabbed at the fallen Romans who were quickly cut to pieces. Some of the wounded legionaries tried to crawl back to their lines in an effort to escape the bloody fray, yet they soon became eager targets for clubs and spears.

A call went up from the centurions commanding their men to stand firm. Already the ground was littered with bodies and among them three centurions lay dead, faces stained with blood and eyes agape. The Jews sensed the victory and pushed forward as more reinforcements came from the city to the eager cheers of Simon ben Giora upon the walls.

"Fight them!" shouted Centurion Qurinius as he parried a sword thrust and drove his gladius into his attacker's chest. The man struggled amidst the penetrating blade and Qurinius simply retracted the steel and struck the man's head clean from his shoulders. A wash of blood showered the Jews behind their decapitated comrade and they stepped back, temporarily blinded. Qurinius saw the Jewish reinforcements pouring from the city and for a split moment he glanced down at the Roman dead strewn upon the ground. He looked at his century, seeing the fear in their eyes and how many of them were fighting with wounds. Some even continued using their swords despite missing fingers. He heard a legionary shout that they were doomed and had been abandoned by their legion, left to die. "Not on my watch!" Qurinius bellowed turning slightly to bolster the spirits of his men. Then a barbed arrow pierced his neck just below his cheek guard and he crumpled to the ground with a choked gurgle.

"Retreat!" an optio screamed as he covered his left eye with a blood stained hand. "Fall back to the ramps!" The Roman cohorts needed no third command to escape the fray about them. Like terrified civilians who had never known war, they turned and ran. The Jewish ranks cheered as if all chains of fear, that might have been holding them back, had been cut. They surged ahead, striking at the backs of panicked legionaries who were abandoning their shields and weapons. Neither cohort maintained order or formation, they simply fled as dozens were slain exposing their backs to the eager blades of the Idumean and Zealot forces.

As the first spear had been hurled at Yosef, Titus, who watched from the saddle of Achilles, started screaming at the legionaries working upon the ramps. With thunder and power behind his voice, Titus called them to arms to support the soldiers who were getting massacred before his very eyes. He used every curse he knew in three languages as he watched the unarmed legionaries scramble for their weapons stacked along the edges of the ramps. Titus galloped to the ramps, followed by his generals and Marcus Sulla who cursed the gods that he did not have his Boars at his side.

As the two cohorts suddenly broke in a panic and fled, Titus managed to assemble another two cohorts from the workers on the ramps. Organized in loose order, they still posed a threat to the Jewish attack. With mounted men behind the ranks, and more legionaries forming up behind these, the Jewish horde slowed its pace and eventually came to a halt between two of the ramps. They shouted, raised their weapons, and called the Romans cowards as some even held up the helmets from the Roman dead, mocking the men of the Fulminata and Apollinaris who stood before them.

"Drive them back, centurions!" Titus shouted, feeling his blood boil within his veins.

One thousand Roman legionaries, fresh from the fight but weary from the heavy labour they had endured upon the ramps, tried to summon the strength needed. Embarrassed and filled with a sense to avenge their fallen comrades, the cohorts grimaced at the Jewish mass before them, waiting for the call which would send them forward. At the blast of a deep brass horn the signum was raised. Under the units vexillum the legionaries locked their shields, lowered spears and charged. The cohorts closed in upon the Jews at an increasing speed of fury followed by the wild eyes of Titus.

The enormous Idumean wearing the scarlet robes shouted in Aramaic, and with a sense of organization, the mob of Jewish fighters turned and ran back to the gates. The Romans watched the Zealots retreat and some became so angry they tried to break from their ranks, hoping to catch up and strike at the backs of the Jews, yet it was to no avail. The Jewish forces, being much lighter in weight, easily outran them and poured back into the city with the heavy gates closing behind them.

Centurions sounded their whistles and called the companies to halt as Jewish archers took to the ramparts, hoping some legionaries would not heed the orders of their superiors. Titus stared up at the walls, glaring for a moment at the sound of jeering insults. "Bastards," he whispered vehemently under his breath. "Centurions, reform ranks and fall back to the ramps and secure them. We will resume work tomorrow. Have men collect our dead." Titus looked at the many legionaries strewn upon the ground in piles among the Jewish dead. He backed Achilles up a few metres and shook his head as he squinted up at the high walls. "They are tricky bastards."

"My Prince?" asked Sextus.

Titus looked to the General and sheathed his sword. His chest was still heaving from adrenalin which raced through his body. "They knew we would take the bait. We cannot appear desperate." He shook his head again. "I want an extra cohors from your legio, Sextus. Also, send word to Lepidus to get another cohors here on the double." Titus dug his heels into Achilles flanks and galloped away leaving a cloud of dust behind him. He noticed a man sitting upon the ground beyond the ramps and headed that direction. Titus saw the man look up and stand with wobbling legs as he nursed a wounded arm.

Yosef winced in pain as he watched Titus pull on the reins and halt the warhorse. The Jewish General bowed and then slowly looked up to say something, but no words found his tongue.

Titus glared down at him in apathetic silence. Then his demeanour was temporarily restored as he asked, "Your arm?" Yosef nodded and Titus sighed. "My surgeon will look at your wound." The Prince paused, deep in thought. "Your man, this Judah ben Yosef, you will speak to him again, but just once more. Then this matter is turned to Gaius Antony." Achilles tossed his head, snorted, and stepped to the side. Titus controlled the horse with the reins and drew closer to Yosef. "Tell Judah that the voice of *Roma* says if he can stop that from happening again," he pointed back to the dead beyond the ramps and continued, "I will give him Capito! I swear this upon my ancestors and to Jupiter. I will give him Capito." Titus glared down at Yosef, his face red while fighting back the embarrassment of what had happened. "Judah is to give us information to stop three such attacks as this, and if they are successful, I will offer him the life of Capito." Titus turned Achilles away to leave and then called back, "If you are to write of this in your histories, remember the first pair of eyes to look upon it will be mine. Speak favourably of me." Then he rode away.

*　*　*

CHAPTER XX

April 27th, 70 A.D. / 30th of Nisan, 3830
Temple Mount
Jerusalem

Judah shed his outer garment and draped it over the wall. Even after dark the heat of day still emanated from the stone causing perspiration to glisten from his forehead. He loosened his grip upon the shaft of his spear, glancing to his left at the guards upon the colonnades overlooking the darkness of the Kidron valley and the lights burning upon the Mount of Olives. The Romans did not bother to be modest and the sounds of their feasting and laughter drifted through the blackness of night.

"The bastards think that this is a party," grumbled a guard somewhere upon the rampart and then silence ensued upon the company like a spell.

Judah yawned and grunted, clearing phlegm from his throat. Guard duty could be long, uneventful, and boring. He knew that would soon change with the enemy siege ramps approaching the city from the north and the west. Once the Romans started the attacks on the city, things would become desperate and paranoia would set into the spirits of men, especially on nights as black as these. Every shadow or sound would be taken as an enemy cohort creeping up to the walls with ladders, to scale them silently and slit the throats of drowsy guards.

Judah had discussed this very thing with John numerous times, requesting the commander to implement more shift changes so the men would remain alert. John always responded with his usual grimness as he would state that since he and Simon were in poor standings, the maximum use of guards was needed to cover the colonnades, towers, Antonia, and the Hulda Gates.

John had become increasingly annoyed and irritable as the days stretched on. Some of the men said it was because he itched badly for a fight and wanted to face the Romans in battle. Others thought it more likely that John was frustrated at Simon's lack of cooperation. On numerous occasions, John had sent letters to Simon asking the egotistical king for permission to bring up his scorpions and ballista to the northern wall with the intent of raining fire down upon the heads of the Roman workers on the ramps. Each time, however, the letters would be sent back ripped to shreds and John would proceed to overturn tables and throw goblets of wine across the room in anger at the foolish, demented man. "*Is the man mad?*" John would roar. "*Can't he see the Romans are getting closer and closer to his walls? What is he going to do when siege towers roll up the ramps? Throw pebbles at them?*" However, despite the rumours that circulated among

John's men as to what aggravated the commander, Judah knew what really plagued the mind of the warlord from Gischala. The fear of spies.

Earlier in the day a man had been caught leaving the city in a most suspicious way. This man, to Judah's knowledge, was a genuine spy, not like the suspected accusations John had purported at earlier times. The man had been caught dangling over the wall by a rope with a map of the city and a piece of parchment containing information about troop numbers, artillery positions, and food storages. The man had been brought before John instantly and after a cruel beating had confessed everything with deep sobs. John had roared like a terrible beast filled with rage. With his own two massive hands, the Gischalan warlord had strangled the man to death while the spy's arms and legs had been held by four Zealots. The man shook with convulsions, drooled everywhere, and then had soiled himself. John had tightened his grip and within seconds he had squeezed the life from the man. He then gave orders for his body to be hurled from the walls, left to be eaten by dogs.

Not a soldier alive questioned John's actions, and deep within Judah's mind he knew that execution was justified. The man had been caught, obviously attempting to communicate with the enemy, and he had paid for it. The execution though, had unnerved Judah a bit as he contemplated his own recent actions with the Romans. He found himself constantly justifying his reasons over and over within his head, telling himself that he was not giving information that could damage the city's defences or result in mass casualties. He was doing this for revenge, in order to kill a high ranking centurion, and that seemed right within his mind.

Judah pushed the invading thought of strangulation from his mind and tried to remain calm, but the sight of the body lying at the base of the wall was a constant reminder of what happened to spies caught in John's service.

A tiny pebble suddenly struck the wall below Judah's position followed by silence. Judah crept forward, tightening his grip upon his spear. Another rock smacked the wall and he carefully looked over trying not to draw attention to himself. The light of a torch upon the wall just two metres away did not help much as it cast a glare, but as his eyes grew accustomed to the dark Judah saw a small shape of a boy at the base of the wall. The boy pointed to his left and quickly backed away into the darkness where he disappeared.

Judah glanced back at the guards, thinking about what the boy could mean. "I'm going to eat something," Judah called out as he slipped his outer cloak back on. The nearest guard turned, shrugged, and continued walking without care.

He descended the rampart quickly using a narrow staircase of stone along the wall which brought him to the plateau of the Outer Court. Small cooking fires burned within the space as the dark shapes of men clustered around them, silhouetted against the flames. A song drifted up within the court as a number of other voices soon added to the melody. Judah stared for a moment at the Temple edifice which glowed from the camp fires. It was oddly quiet within its courts as priests worked through the night and Judah thought this strange. However, he shrugged it off and ducked into the shadows of the columns which held up the ramparts above him.

Choosing to stay in the darkness and remain unnoticed was Judah's intention. He moved quickly under the dark rooftop of the stone ceiling and eventually found himself near a small door that was unmanned. He looked to his right at the opening of the massive tunnel entrance to the Hulda Gates not far from where he stood and could see a number of guards milling about. Judah had a strange recollection of when he and his Lions had first come to the city and how they had entered the Temple courtyard through those very gates. He remembered his first impression and how wonderful and exciting everything had seemed. Now, the air felt tense and his future unknown.

As quietly as possible Judah opened the door and stepped out into the cool night. He closed the door behind him, making sure he could reopen it when he returned, and then stood for a moment allowing his eyes to adjust. As Judah contemplated what to do next, suddenly a figure stirred from behind a gangly shrub nearby. With a lightening reaction, Judah lowered his spear, pointed the tip at the shrub and stood his ground narrowing his gaze. "Who goes there?" he loudly whispered feeling uneasy. "Show yourself or die!"

The shrub quit moving for a moment and then with one last rustle a boy crawled out from under it. He stood, dusted himself off, and then took four slow steps towards Judah with his hands raised to show he was not a threat. "I am Yehoshua. I signaled you from the wall."

"Who are you?" Judah tensely asked, not thinking about the fact that the boy had just made his introduction.

"Yehoshua," the boy replied again with a puzzled look and then gently took a bow. "My lord, would you be Judah ben Yosef?" The boy saw the man nod and then said with an excited whisper, "I have been sent to you with a message from Centurion Gaius Antony. You know him?"

Judah raised the spear understanding what was happening. He leaned on the shaft for a moment sizing the boy up, and then gave a stern nod. "I know Antony. So, what message do you bring?"

"He says he and the Jew are in the cistern where you met. I don't know which one, there are many, but he said you would know." Yehoshua stepped closer to get a better look at Judah.

"That is all?" Judah replied giving the young boy a hesitant sideways glance.

"That is all they told me, my lord. They wouldn't trust me with anything else. They paid me an obol though, for my services of course." Yehoshua was still for a moment and then pointed to the spear, "Were you going to stick me with that?"

"These are unfriendly times," Judah answered stepping forward. "Where do you live?"

Yehoshua shrugged and gazed at the warrior with bright eyes. "I don't really have a home, I work for the Romans. I have a special job."

"And what is that?"

He gave a boyish grin revealing ivory teeth. "I look after Prince Titus' horse, Achilles. Large black warhorse, that one, but as tame as a lamb when I am around. I used to care for the Emperor's mount, but he is no longer with the army."

Judah looked puzzled for a moment and then softly said, "You are a Jew though, am I right?"

"Yes."

Judah scowled at Yehoshua who could not have been any older then eleven. "Where were you born?"

"Joppa, by the sea."

"And how did you come to work for Titus?" Judah said.

Yehoshua was still, his pride vanishing, as if he had lost his voice. He felt a surge of tears well up from within and then he quelled them, mustering the strength needed. "I don't remember," he lied. "I better leave now." He turned and trotted off into the darkness leaving Judah by himself.

A gentle breeze tugged at Judah's garments for a moment as he thought about the boy. *Most likely a slave for Titus with his parents dead,* Judah thought. He shook the sorrowful thought from his mind and glanced around for a moment to get his bearings as to where the cistern lay.

* * *

"He will come," Yosef said with confidence as Gaius rolled his eyes. "This will be our third meeting with him, well, second for you and third for me. Anyway, I would guess the man is showing trust which we could give him in return."

"I will never trust this man," Gaius said coldly. "He has another motive that goes beyond this Capito." Gaius shook his head and leaned against the cool stone wall of the cistern. He stared for a moment at the oil lamp which burned. "I can't believe Titus will sell this man's life to a Zealot. Capito may have done a terrible thing, but there are not many men whose hands are clean of blood."

"And you, Praefectus Castrorum, are your hands clean? Truly there must be a difference between killing in battle and murder. This Capito slaughtered many innocent people; his fate is deserved if Judah should kill him." Yosef watched the Centurion glare at him for a moment and then look away. "Would we not all seek such revenge?"

"I suppose," Gaius grumbled. "You can cease with your philosophies, Yosef, you bore me."

"These are not philosophies, Centurion, but affect life and morality and one must…"

"Duly noted, but you can stop," Gaius interrupted.

Yosef was silent for a moment and then crossed his arms with annoyance and sat down in a niche in the wall. A few minutes crept by of uneasy silence between the two, and when Yosef was about to say something, a shuffling sound was heard from the entrance to the cistern. Both men turned to the mouth of the cave and watched as Judah appeared, slowly walking down the steps into the orange haze of the lamp light.

Gaius' eyes immediately went to the spear in Judah's hands and he quickly pushed away from the stone wall, gripping the pommel of his gladius. "Lay the spear down," Gaius ordered in a challenge as Judah checked his advance.

Yosef glanced at Gaius, shocked by the command. "Judah means no harm. He has come from guarding the wall."

"Either way, I am not discussing anything while he is armed. Lay the spear down." Gaius half drew his blade and glared at Judah with eyes of steel.

Without a word of complaint or protest, Judah bent over and laid the spear upon the ground. Then he opened his cloak, unbuckled his sword belt and laid it next to the spear. He watched Gaius give him a nod of gratitude and then the large Roman pushed his sword back into its sheath and leaned back against the wall of the cistern.

"It is good to see you, Judah," Yosef began. "We have news for you. But first, I take it the boy Yehoshua was able to give you the message from us?"

"Yes, I did receive the message from him. Who is he?" Judah asked calmly sitting upon the floor.

"That does not concern you. He is a slave." Gaius peered suspiciously at Judah and watched the Jew give him a sour look. "He was made servus."

Yosef could sense the strained tension between the two men and was quick to intervene by changing the subject. "After the ambush two days ago, Prince Titus changed his mind regarding Capito. When I had first given him the message concerning your request, the Prince had summarily turned it down. Yet, after another ambush involving Simon's men, who concocted a fictitious surrender outside the walls, Titus changed his mind.

"He has declared that if you surrender information to us which foils three attempts by Jews to attack Roman positions then he will in turn give you the life of Capito." Yosef watched the news sink into Judah's face as he stared at the floor for a moment and rubbed his chin. "Do you understand? You must aid us with valid information so we can halt three attacks."

"How does he plan to give up Capito?" Judah asked.

"He has not yet informed me or…" Yosef glanced at Gaius and the Centurion shook his head. "Either way, the Prince is a man of his word, and he will grant you this request."

"Like I said at our last meeting, I cannot trust the word of Rome. I have seen the evidence of Rome's word time and time again, and it is not a favourable record. I will only trust the two of you." Judah looked at Gaius with stern eyes. "I want your word, your oath, that this is true and will be given to me."

Gaius stared back at the Jewish warrior for a moment and then calmly reached into a leather pouch that hung from his belt. He pulled out a small clay trinket and when he held it up in the light Judah could see it was a molded image of a woman. "This is the imagio of my wife, Livia. This reminds me of her and the children that we have." Gaius tossed it to Judah, who caught it. "I swear upon the lives of my family that I will give you this oath. Capito will be given to you, I swear this."

Judah looked down at the image of the woman. He noticed small intricate eyes had been etched, the presence of hair scraped into the top, and breasts protruded forth from the hardened clay which had been darkened in a kiln by fire. One of the feet was missing, as it had been chipped off and Judah could make out small painted toe nails on the one that remained. He glanced up to Gaius and as he held it in his hands he replied, "I will take this as a sufficient oath. I will give it back to you when Capito's blood wets the ground."

Gaius leaned against the wall and gave a sharp nod. "It is precious to me, so please take care of it."

Judah looked at the image again and then tucked it inside his cloak where it would be safe. He knew it was a pagan item of prayer, and that if a priest or rabbi had known he had accepted the item they would have cried out that Judah had become defiled. However, he would respect Gaius and keep the image hidden so nobody would find it.

"Do you have anything we can take back to Prince Titus?" Yosef asked, hoping Judah would have something favourable.

Judah nodded heavily, committing himself fully. "A day ago a meeting was held in the quarters of John, within the Antonia. I was present, as were a majority of the officers. Plans were laid out for a night attack which will happen two days from now. It will be another attack against the Fretensis. John hopes to continue the pressure on this legion so the men will be demoralized and afraid.

"The attack will be led by Simon ben Ari, who serves John like a puppet. I expect the attack to be composed of at least four to five hundred men. They will be lightly armed as usual and will attack the camp itself. John hopes to overrun the sentries, burn the towers of the camp, and spread panic throughout the legion, convincing them that the attack is larger than it is."

"Why doesn't John send more men to completely overrun the camp?" Gaius asked leaning forward.

"Because Simon and John are divided. John cannot spare more men for a large attacking force without weakening his own defences inside to repel anything Simon might launch. The city is ripe with fear and John is holding onto whatever power he may still have." Judah closed his mouth, feeling a wave of shame flood over his body.

He fought against showing it and stood abruptly. "I will go now." He bent down and collected his weapons.

Gaius watched Judah and interpreted the sudden discomfort as being an attempt to salvage dignity and honour. Judah had finally opened his mouth and told them credible information which would lead to stopping an attack and the deaths of his countrymen. As much as Gaius felt for Judah, he also understood that because of guilt Judah may inform John about his deception. "Can we be sure that this information you have given us will stay credible?"

Judah's face was flushed with anger at himself for betraying the Zealots, but his hate for Capito ran deeper and for that he pushed the shame aside and nodded at Gaius. "John will not know of anything different. Remember, night attack on the Fretensis." Judah turned and ducked out of the cistern, leaving the Roman and the Jewish General who would take the news to Titus, thereby informing the Prince that Judah ben Yosef would cooperate.

*   *   *

Camp of the Titus
Just before midnight

"You will wait here," the guard said to Gaius and Yosef as they stood outside the praetorium in the midst of a circle of burning torches attached to iron stakes.

Gaius shed the long cloak he had worn in the cistern and now thanked the gods he had done so, for the heat from the fires was intense. He stood next to Yosef perspiring under the weight of his helmet. The torques which hung by bronze rings upon his cuirass reflected the glow of light in a sporadic dance.

One disc of bronze hanging among the medals revealed the face of a man with a great moustache and flowing hair. It had been finely crafted and doubled the weight of any other torque Gaius wore. He noticed Yosef eyeing the medal with a curious glance and tapped it proudly saying, "I was awarded this by Nero for recovering the loss of his baggage train years ago upon the Appian. Clever bastards the thieves were. Disguised themselves as sheep herders and slaughtered the servants and two guards manning the baggage. Then they made off with the belongings into the tracts of farmland stretching beyond. I was on leave at the time with my family outside of *Roma* on our villa. We had been given a week furlough before shipping out to Judea and I was among a vexillatio from the legio. You see, Cestius was raising his army to strength and I was being transferred with numerous veterans to deal with the early signs of rebellion in this province.

Gaius grinned at Yosef. "Somehow, and not to my understanding, my name was given to Nero to lead a centuria of soldiers to recover the lost items. The praetorian had their hands full with squelching riots and couldn't help in the time Nero wished, so I came into the picture.

"We tracked the filth down, slaughtered them all, and crucified two of them in the very spot they had sprung their ambush. Needless to say, Nero was ecstatic about the return of his treasures. I was awarded this medal, forged by the best craftsman in *Roma*. Nero had it designed after Ulysses from Homer's tales. Nero said I was dastardly clever and shrewd, like Ulysses. With him being obsessed with Greek tales, I believe this was a fitting gift from such a man as Nero." Gaius chuckled as he stared at the medal.

"It is magnificently crafted," Yosef commented.

Gaius nodded. "You know what was in the stolen treasures of Nero?" Yosef shook his head and Gaius whispered, "Stacks of writ for plays and songs: Euripides and much more. At that point in his life, Nero sought rather to bless the theatres and halls with his time then run the empire. He thought his voice was a gift from the gods. He saw his will to write poetry and song as a gift from a cherub. He destined that the empire should hear his wonders and be whisked off to sleep by the fairy tales of goddesses."

Yosef smiled. "Well in the end, the Jews could find no favour in him in the least bit."

"Neither the Romans or other allies for that matter," Gaius added. "Nero was hated and loved throughout his whole life, right down to the moment he drove his dagger through his own throat."

A call to salute sounded outside the circle of torches and Titus entered the circle. He was followed by his personal signifer who planted the signum firmly into the ground and stood back a few metres from the Roman Prince. Gaius snapped to attention, striking his chest, and Yosef gave an honourable bow.

Titus wore a very expensive evening garment that had been woven from soft cotton in Egypt, its edges hemmed with a delicate, golden thread. His hair had been styled and his body scented with the aroma of lavender and spice from the orient.

"You two have been busy, have you not?" Titus asked delighting in the bit of humour to the rhetorical question. He glanced down for a moment at his filed finger nails and sighed. The hot oiled massage and the three goblets of wine had suited his fancy. The feast had ended early as Titus had sent the officers and kings packing. Now all that was on his mind was ending the formalities of this evening with Gaius and Yosef so he could return to his quarters and bed two young Syrian women that the Arab trader Pepi had sent over.

"What have you to say concerning Judah ben Yosef?" Titus asked getting straight to the point.

Without giving Yosef a glance, Gaius relaxed slightly and reported in a serious tone, "The Jew will comply with our wishes and has agreed to surrender the plans of three attacks as your Majesty requested. He has indeed already told us of one such attack."

For a moment Titus forgot about the vixens awaiting him in his quarters and he took a step closer and lowered his voice, "What attack? Tell me?"

"The attack will be in two days time, the night of the half moon," Gaius relayed to him. "It is organized by John of Gischala, yet will be led by Simon ben Ari who is now serving under the rebel leader, but he is not important to us. John wishes to spring a night attack against the front of the Fretensis camp. He intends to kill the sentries quietly and spread panic by plundering the tents. Judah said the attacking force will consist of four to five hundred strong."

"No more," Titus asked with a look of deep concentration etched into the lines upon his forehead.

Gaius shook his head. "Judah says the rebels are worried about reprisals from Simon's forces in other parts of the city. John is both smart and scared. He wishes to spring an attack on us where we would least expect it, yet at the same time he is terrified of his own comrades."

Titus was motionless. He turned and quietly walked away to the edge of the torches where he gave the *signfier* an awkward glance. The standard bearer did not even see the look for his face appeared like stone as he stood motionless attending to his one duty, holding the standard and appearing invisible until called upon. "This is valid information?" Titus asked clasping his hands behind his back.

"Yes, my Prince," Gaius responded staring at the back of Titus who remained deep in thought.

"And you believe the Zealot?"

Gaius nodded without hesitation. "He is sincere and determined to seek vengeance. I believe he understands that without us, getting to Capito is impossible."

Titus turned and stared for a moment at the camp prefect. "He trusts us?"

"He trusts me, he said so himself." Gaius watched Titus' face twitch slightly and then the Prince was motionless waiting for him to elaborate. Gaius took a deep breath and continued, "He said, my lord, that he could never trust the word of *Roma*, because he had seen what *Roma* had done to his life. However, he said he could trust me because I was a…" Gaius' voice trailed off as he searched for the right word.

Titus smiled. "A man of honour and prestige, am I right?" A look of embarrassment flashed across Gaius' face and Titus stepped forward. "You are indeed a man of honour, Centurion Gaius. My father saw that in you. Did you ever wonder why he was the only man who ever called you Cornelius? He respected you. You are a man of the legion, a true Roman for others to emulate." Titus stared directly into Gaius' eyes and whispered, "Never forget that." He relaxed and gave a brief shrug. "This Jew sees this in you. You are a man of your word and he understood that as a sure sign. He is our enemy, Gaius. I do not expect him to trust us at this instant. Yet, will he become an ally of *Roma*? In time, yes, that is what I want. We need men of high regard among the Jews to realize their feeble attempts and surrender. That is what will fragment their cause."

"Yes, my lord."

Titus scowled for a moment. "Did he ask you for your word? Did you swear an oath?"

Gaius nodded. "I had to show him that *Roma* was trustworthy. I proved this to him by swearing upon the image of my wife. The Jew will return it when Capito is dead."

Titus cocked his head slightly to the side and grinned. "A most noble oath given indeed. And the Jew will return the image and not destroy it?"

"I have reason to believe he will return it, my lord." Gaius watched Titus nod with a bob of the head and then cross his arms.

"Well, I applaud you both. Gaius, you will continue further contact with this Judah when necessary. Yosef, you are finished with your night wanderings. I am serious, no more." Titus gave a sharp glare Yosef's direction and watched him bow humbly. "Now, you can leave and I bid you a good night." Titus nodded as Yosef bowed again and then turned, quietly leaving the circle of light. "Fetch Tribune Maximus from his quarters and tell him to hurry," Titus ordered the signifer firmly as he grew annoyed concerning his absence from the young women who would be getting bored by this point.

Gaius watched the signifer leave quickly and then everything was silent except for the roaring of the torches. Titus appeared tempted to say something but then in a quirky manner just looked away with a grin upon his face. Gaius' curiosity was peaked about what the Prince could be pondering, but he dared not ask. A few more moments crept by as the two men stood within the ring of fire. Just when it was beginning to feel uncomfortable for Gaius, the light jingling of chain mail could be heard approaching the torches.

The hulking form of Marcus Sulla Maximus appeared abruptly. He stepped out from among a line of tents and crossed before the praetorium using one of the camp's many roads which interlocked among the tent city. He wore his toga and had a long cloak draped about his shoulders which hung down his back, nearly reaching the ground. It was clasped around his neck by a golden pin and its heavy wool was dyed red. Marcus nearly tripped as he entered the circle. Swearing loudly, he regained his posture and saluted coming to a halt before Titus.

"The wine has still hours to wear off, Marcus?" Titus asked smiling and clapping the man on the shoulder in a rough fashion.

"Always ready to fight, my lord," Marcus replied and tapped the sword which hung from his waist.

"Well, there will be plenty of that to come. With the ramps near completion, we will begin our attack in five days time. The towers will be paraded before the walls to pique their curiosity." Titus used his hands to animate his thought pattern as Gaius and Marcus watched his charades. "I will dispatch a large force of labourers to build these. I intend to build three rams and towers to be used upon this northern wall. The Macedonica will use two towers and a ram to keep the rebels busy on the western side. Our bowmen and archers from the alae will support our attacks providing excellent cover. I want units of the Fretensis to scatter about in the valley Kidron, and I will have allied horse units riding back and forth from the south to the east. I want the Jews terrified and scattered about. I will use Yosef once more to call to them, and then I will unleash the fires of Hades upon this city.

"Now, to other business that I know you will find most entertaining, my dear Tribune." Titus smiled warmly at Marcus. "I have been informed by Gaius that a certain Jew, who is cooperating with us under the command of Gischala, has told us that a night attack awaits the lads of the Fretensis in two days time. I want you two to command a counter attack." Titus watched the two officers make brief eye contact at the news. "I will give you a force that matches the enemy, four hundred men. I cannot spare more because you will be most uncomfortable and none of you can be seen. Over half of your force will be archers, the Palmyrene bowmen from King Agrippa's force. You will conceal yourselves with dark tunics and slip out after dark and hide in the foremost ditches of the Fretensis' defences. That should give you all a nice trench of at least a metre and a half wide, plenty of room to squeeze your Latin asses inside." Titus grinned, feeling a sense of ecstasy as his plan evolved.

"I will give orders for Larcius to cut his numbers of posted sentries in half and to pull them back. I want them to look disorderly and poorly conducted. When the Zealots see this as they approach the camp, their eyes will see nothing more than the prize before them. It will be their doom. Have a man next to you keep watch as the Jewish sortie approaches. He will need to be a man whose patience is larger than the balls of Mars for you should wait until the Jews are breathing down your necks. Then, when the time is right, the archers can unleash a hail of steel at their hairy colei from ten metres out and then you and your men will spring upon them. Victory will most assuredly be yours." Titus rubbed his hands together seeing his plan come to life and without having the sense to ask for questions, he turned and scampered off to his quarters to the sound of giggling women.

* * *

CHAPTER XXI

April 29th, 70 A.D. / 2nd Iyyar, 3830
One hour till midnight
East side of Jerusalem

John silently pushed through the mass of cloaked warriors. Not a single spear was brandished or shield hefted. This attack was intended to retain utmost silence, secrecy, and draw no attention from the Roman sentries until the Jews were past the first set of ditches surrounding the Fretensis camp. All Zealots had been instructed to conceal swords beneath their cloaks and to smear mud and soot upon their faces to blend into the darkness of night. With great beards and fierce eyes, the Zealots looked like monsters more than men.

The silence was surprising as over four hundred men stood before the gate waiting for the night to wear on and for assurance that the Roman camp had settled down from their normal state of evening feasts. John had declared to the Zealots hours earlier, that they should pray and hope that Titus had set his men free into the stores of wine. Every man had understood John's intended meaning for they believed all legionaries were notorious drinkers and would be twice as vulnerable to attack if they let their guard down by becoming intoxicated.

John found Simon ben Ari standing near the front of the horde. He was leaning against a broad spear which had its point covered by a black cloth. John stared at the weapon for a moment considering saying something, and then held his tongue for Simon was an awkward and sour man. Simon caught John's stare and glared at him. "What do you want?" he said bluntly, unhappy about the attack since he had been opposed to it.

John scowled back and shook his head. "You can move out shortly. Make sure you're quick and don't stop for anything."

Simon chuckled and whispered, "This is not my first tangle with Romans, John. I was one of the big bastards who chased Cestius' army from here, before I went north."

John crossed his broad arms and stared at the wild man with little regard. "I understand, Simon. I speak not to you, but for your men. It has been sometime since you went on a raid."

Simon ben Ari shrugged and replied, "But I am not out of practice. Killing Romans is a simple matter: you just grit your teeth and the bastards piss themselves." A few men near him chuckled. The big warrior Zealot nodded to the men and then looked back to John. "We will creep up on the whelps and before they know it the sentries will have their throats slit and guts ripped out. We shall be plundering their tents and killing men in their sleep." A wide grin spread across Simon's face and his teeth flashed in the night. No torches burned upon the walls surrounding the Zealot army as the space was dark and somber.

John stared for a moment at Simon, unsure of whether to trust his optimistic outlook on the attack. They had already charged the Fretensis on two occasions, and he did not know if they would be so fortunate a third time. On this occasion, John had not favoured the night attack. Night assaults could be disorderly, confusing, and often times resulted in men accidentally killing their own comrades. But with pressure from his officers to make a frontal assault, in the end they had won the day and John could do nothing.

"Just be quick, strike hard and fall back if the Romans reform. We cannot push a full assault with them. I cannot reinforce you even if you are successful in plundering their camp. I have reports that Giora has doubled his guard facing our western border and I cannot weaken our force." John paused for a moment staring up at the dark sky. "Just do as much damage as possible. Perhaps we will put so much fear into them they will move camp."

"No sport if they move," Simon commented smiling. Then he gave a sharp nod and John left. The big man turned raising his spear in the air to get everyone's attention, and said in a raspy whisper, "Stay with me. We form a spearhead. Spread out in a line when we hit the bottom of the valley and drive straight for them. The Roman ditch will be dark and so we can slow, but it will be at least a two metre leap. Don't anyone be a bastard and fall in for nobody shall carry you back. After that, another ditch will be a couple metres and that piss hole will be filled with wooden spikes."

Simon chuckled. "Anyone fall in that and you're dead. From there we weave through the spike field up to the wall. Kill the sentries and men on the flanks, climb the towers, and deal with the guards. The rest of you go into the camp and kill anything that moves." He pointed his spear at the mob and continued, "I personally will thump anyone who stops to plunder. Remember what John said, we've got no reinforcements coming. We only plunder if the Romans turn and run, if that buys us time, take what you can carry and we fall back in order. Do I have men here who will fire the towers?" A few men volunteered and Simon nodded firmly. "Let's go!"

*   *   *

Gaius lay in the ditch as flat as his body could be against the cool dirt. All around him he could hear the soft breathing of men. Every so often a man would slightly groan and shift his position as a leg or arm started to cramp or numb. They had not been sure when the Jews would spring their attack. The only information that had been given, compliments of Judah ben Yosef, had consisted of a night attack. With that being the only information the Romans had to act on, Titus had deployed the hidden force into the ditch before the Fretensis camp shortly after dark. The men had been assembled from the Fulminata Legio to prepare for battle in their own camp so any Jews upon the walls scanning the camp of the Tenth would see no unusual activity.

Orders had been strict in the area of concealment. No armour of any kind with steel or brass upon it was to be left uncovered for fear of reflection from the torches burning in the camp which would be situated to their rear once in position. To prepare for this, it had taken nearly three hours. Gaius and Marcus had wanted their men suited in battle gear to cut down on casualties, and so this had meant covering their plated chest armour, helmets, and greaves in dark strips of cloth. Overtop of this, each man was to wear a dark cloak and blacken their scabbards with mud or ash. Some men had also smeared clay upon their faces while others did not bother and with a short ceremonial sacrifice by the priests, the squad of legionaries and archers had set out.

Gaius and Marcus had led the vexillatio north of the Fulminata camp accompanied by a deployment of oxen and carts which wound up the slopes of Mount Scopus disappearing over the summit. The hope was that any curious eyes gazing from the city would be unable to make out anything suspicious about the carts and oxen. For the Jewish guards, they would merely dismiss it as a foraging expedition, meanwhile not realizing that five hundred soldiers were among them in plain sight. In this case, it would be distance which would protect the Roman force.

Once above the crest of Scopus, Gaius and Marcus had broken away from the lines of carts and groaning oxen, leading the soldiers at a quick pace as they traced the far edge of the mountain down into a valley and up to the Mount of Olives. By the time they had reached this, darkness was descending upon the land. With a gruff command from Marcus, the men had increased their pace to a light jog. Eventually, they had crept down the slopes of the mountain, circled around the camp of the Tenth Legion, and had filed silently into the foremost set of ditches. Their mission was simple: fill the ditch facing the city, get as low as one could, and wait for the expected attack.

Gaius pushed himself up by clawing at the earth, made sure the three spotters along the line were doing their job, and then slid back down. He heard a grunt from beside him and turned to see Marcus shake his head. "Is there something wrong?" Gaius asked innocently.

Marcus shrugged in the dark and put a strange root in his mouth which he began to chew. "I just say, don't worry about them. They will see the bastards when the time is right."

"I just want them to be ready. When this starts, it will be mayhem." Gaius thought for a moment and then swore to himself and scratched his chin. "I hate night attacks, something always goes wrong. It is impossible to lead the men perfectly."

"Does it ever go perfectly?" Marcus replied.

Gaius grinned and gave a nod. "I forget so easily in my long years."

"Not a problem, we always wish it to go right." Marcus shifted onto his left side and sniffed. He quietly drew his gladius and carefully hid it under his cloak. He gave an unknown wink to Gaius and said, "Just want to be right. I feel naked if steel is not in my hands."

Gaius ignored Marcus for a moment as he studied the line of archers behind the legionaries. The men were awkwardly bent as low to the ground as it would permit. Each one clutched a bow in one hand and a quiver in the other. Sacks of black stained cloth covered the white feathers of the arrows and every man had been relieved of their armour. Gaius had stated to the Palmyrenes that they would not be expected to fight hand-to-hand, but would have to maintain absolute agility and speed. When the Jewish attack would draw close, it would be them who would first scramble to their feet and deliver three volleys into the horde of Zealots at close range. With this short gap, none of the bowmen expected to miss their targets and the arrows would penetrate any type of armour. Once the archers had sent their hailstorm of carnage upon the Jewish attack, it would be the legionaries turn. With deadly speed they would rise suddenly like a tidal wave and with thrusts of pointed steel they would deal out death.

Gaius turned away from the ranks of bowmen and looked at Marcus. "Are you a family man, Tribune?"

Marcus would have died with laughter had they not been lying in a ditch with the sole purpose of maintaining complete silence. He did chuckle with tears in his eyes for awhile and then shaking his head he said, "Me, a family man? Not at all, my dear Praefectus Castrorum. I wouldn't know where to start."

"With a wife and home perhaps," Gaius replied matching Marcus' sarcasm as the Tribune nearly lost it, his body shaking with laughter. "I was serious, but I see you're in no mood." Gaius' tone was slightly exasperated as he rolled his eyes.

Marcus caught the hint and quieted down. He thought for a moment and said, "I never met the right woman I wished to marry. They either wanted me for my pay, which I have no clue why because it's a sour, rotten mess. My fortunes, if you can call it that, are nothing compared to that of a consul or legate. But I suppose it is enough to attract certain ladies." He paused for a moment and said, "I hate snobbery, Gaius, which is why I hate most officers and practically all senators. Politicians only wish to fill their purse with gold and their bed with other men's wives. If you have a pair of tits and you're around a senator, you will find yourself on your back in no time." He spit the root out of his mouth and shook his head. "I only trust whores. You know why? They only want your money once you're through with them. You don't lose your villa to a prostitute."

Gaius considered Marcus' words for a moment and frowned. "I have been married for twenty-two years, Marcus. I took Livia as my own in my third year of service, during leave. It was proper through our family relations that we wed, but there was more. I love my wife, and have never lain with another woman than her. So, you are telling me you have never known…"

"Love?" Marcus interrupted finishing Gaius' sentence. "Once, but that was long ago, my friend."

Gaius glanced at one of the spotters and when the man did not move he looked back at Marcus. "What happened?"

A sadness silently filled Marcus' eyes as he seemed to stare into nothingness, then he said in a hoarse voice, "She died."

Before Gaius could speak a legionary touched his shoulder and whispered, "My lord, they approach forty metres out and quickly."

Gaius looked to Marcus, gave a stern nod, and crawled forward to peer over the edge. He squinted in the darkness and then saw the Zealots. It was their pounding feet he heard first before catching sight of the formation. Slowly, Gaius began to make out the outlines of hundreds of men climbing the slopes at a rapid pace.

"We will be attacking downhill; we will have the advantage," Gaius whispered to himself trying to muster the assurance he should feel. For an unknown reason he felt uneasy about the attack. Perhaps it was because it was night, or perhaps there was doubt in his mind about the possibility of being misinformed. What if the Jewish number of Zealots was double to what Judah had said? What if Judah had laid a trap for the Romans and the Jews knew of their plot? Either way, it was too late and Gaius would have to find peace in the fact that his men had done this most of their lives. They would survive this night.

"Archers, ready," Gaius whispered as the order was quickly relayed down the line with hushed voices. Gaius fought against the temptation to stand, to show his men where their leader was and to inspire them, but he had to wait until the archers had stalled the attack. Upon his right arm was a scarlet ribbon of cloth tied in a firm knot. Marcus had one to, similar to Gaius', and they were the only symbol both men wore marking them as officers for their plumes had been removed and their helmets concealed.

Gaius watched as the Jewish force suddenly slowed their pace to a fast walk. He told himself that he expected this. The Jews would be familiar with the Roman defence system surrounding the camp and especially at night, they would not wish to risk broken bones by falling or tumbling into the ditches unaware. He watched them draw closer. Some seemed to hesitate, and so a large bear-like man with a great beard and carrying a spear gestured with his hand for them to move. Gaius judged the distance from the Zealots to be around twenty-five metres and he glanced back at his archers and raised his hand.

As the command was relayed down the line, the archers slowly removed the black sacks which covered their quivers, thereby revealing bright white fletchings. Each Palmyrene bowman selected an arrow and notched it upon the cord of the deadly weapon as they waited for the command to unleash hell. A few archers squinted in the darkness, examining the goose feathers of each fletching while others inspected with their fingers, making sure their first notched arrow would be a good one.

Gaius counted to five in his head and peered again as the Zealots were nearly upon them. He could hear their panting and even a few whispers among the group. With sudden electricity racing through his veins, he lowered himself, waved his hand at the archers, and held his breath. The Palmyrenes were professional and experienced. They suddenly came to life as they stood, and for the briefest of moments the Jews would have seen them. It was like a dream for Gaius as he watched the bowmen. In one smooth motion the Palmyrenes drew the cords back to their ears and by a single command they loosed the long arrows with a snap of two hundred bow strings. A white streak flicked through the blackness above Gaius' head as the arrows soared in complete silence, yet with incredible force.

The arrows were like a great scythe as nearly the entire front formation of Zealots reeled in terrible shrieks as men doubled over or pitched backwards. The volley had been delivered at point blank range and the effects were catastrophic for the Jewish attack that was fumbling as men tripped over the maimed and dead upon the ground. Total chaos and confusion quickly replaced all confidence. Men stumbled in the darkness calling out and shouting with panic. The Palmyrenes quickly fitted their bows a second time and loosed another mass of concentrated, barbed steel heads into the disorderly, thinning ranks of Zealots who quickly piled up into a great host of men.

Zealots everywhere screamed in agony as the arrows struck their chests, legs, and tore open throats. Scarlet ribbons of blood spewed as men fell upon the hard ground. Bodies lay strewn about, their blood quenching the dusty earth. Some Zealots, realizing their doom, begged for mercy with flowing tears staining their cheeks as others dragged themselves back towards the distant city, hopelessly weak from their wounds as the steel driven into their muscle and flesh was agonizingly painful.

Simon ben Ari was transfixed into shock. The hiss of the second volley of arrows had done nothing to bring him back to the urgency of the ruin that unfolded before his eyes. One moment he was leading an attacking force of four hundred prime Jewish warriors, and the next moment his ranks were reduced to dying men and blood everywhere. The smell of urine was suddenly strong in his nostrils as a man grabbed the hem of Simon's robe. He reacted in fright and jumped away as the man called out to his commander with deep sobs. The man's face was sheeted in blood and his fingers scratched the ground in pain, tearing his nails away as his eyes were wide with desperation and terror. Simon looked at the man for a moment until he heard a deep trumpet blast and then a new cry of terror rose up in volumes from his men as they watched a formation of legionaries arise from the ditch The wall of shields closed in upon the frantic Jews with a menacing speed and soon the air was filled with the deep sounds of splitting flesh and crushing bone as men recoiled in fear, dropped their weapons, and fled back to the city.

Simon watched his men get butchered in droves. He did not even witness a single Zealot even attempting to attack the Romans. His men simply struggled to avoid the eager Roman blades, even at the expense of pushing a fellow comrade in the way of a striking gladius. A sickness welled up within the proud Zealot commander as Simon stumbled backwards in shock. He tripped over a body and crashed to the ground, dropping his spear. Rolling over he groaned and then grimaced as his hands became sticky with the warm blood that soaked the ground. He was lost for a moment in a trance as all around him was chaos. Simon flipped over as he watched the legionaries begin to spread out and deal with wounded Jewish fighters in their helpless state. A tall Roman with his face stained black, suddenly pointed at him, shouted something, and stepped over a body as he raised his sword. Simon quickly found strength in his weak legs, and scrambling to his feet he fled.

The Roman shouted angrily at him but Simon did not dare look back. His long legs pumped hard as he ran leaping over rocks and piles of earth. Soon his muscles burned from the strain, but he hardly even felt it. Saliva and mucus stained his beard and his eyes began to dry as they refused to blink. His chest heaved and his lungs seemed to be lit on fire as sweat drenched his body, but he would not slow down. Simon reached the bottom of the rocky valley and scurried up the steep slope as he neared the city with its glowing torchlight upon the walls. He caught a glimpse of a hobbling man he passed, bleeding from the chest and legs, but Simon did not even offer to help him. The only thing on his mind was getting back to the safety of the city and behind closed gates. He felt the pounding of his heart pulsing in his head as the large city gates opened and men armed with spears and carrying torches stepped out in shock.

Simon burst past the guards, not heeding their calls, and collapsed inside the gate on all fours, retching upon the ground in heaves as he choked, gagging on the vile taste. "The bast…the bast…" he gasped trying to speak to no one in particular. He rolled over onto his back and covered his face, trying to shut out the shrieks of the arriving wounded.

John burst through the Hulda Gates followed by a mass of men carrying torches and brandishing spears. He quickly descended the steps and moved through the Ophel. They arrived to the scene where the last remnants of the foiled attack were gathering. John watched in disbelief as men streamed through the open gates, many splattered in blood while others were carried through by their comrades, barely living and exhausted. Some men, who had collapsed in sight of the walls, were fetched by Zealots carrying makeshift stretchers as they wailed and moaned in pain from their wounds.

John walked among the wounded in disgust and anger. He stared down at a man with a broken shaft of an arrow protruding from his shoulder. The man groaned, rocking back and forth as blood bubbled around the blackish wound. John knelt by the man and when he touched him the fighter shrieked painfully, and then collapsed unconscious. "Carry this one away," John commanded to some of the guards behind him. "See to the wounded and take them below the Temple." His eyes wandered around the ghastly scene for a moment longer and then he shook his head and shouted, "Have the women see to the wounded!"

"John, there is Simon!" One of the guards clutching a torch pointed through the piles of men scattered upon the stones, some lying down, others sitting, and few standing.

John saw the once great and proud man curled up in a ball upon the street, motionless as if dead. He watched him for a moment, unable to tell if Simon was alive and then he saw the man's chest expand for a breath and roll over onto his side. John signaled to a few of the guards to follow him. He crossed the crowded space, taking care to avoid stepping on the wounded, and came to a halt near Simon who was lying pathetically upon the dirty stones.

"Are you wounded, Simon?" John asked, waiting for an answer. When none came, John slowly knelt and touched the man's shoulder. "Can you hear me? Are you hurt?"

"The bastards knew we were coming. They were hiding in the ditch," Simon replied in a defeated, broken tone, refusing to face John.

"I know, I saw some of the fighting from the wall," John responded.

Simon suddenly sat up and swung around as he grabbed John's shoulders and shook him in a rage. "There was no fighting; we were butchered!" John grabbed Simon's hands but did not pull them away. He stared into the eyes of the Zealot and searched for sanity, but all he saw was a shamed man, humiliated and distraught. Some of John's men had half drawn their swords when the big Zealot had grabbed their commander, but nothing from John's face told them to come to his aid and so they backed off.

"Tell me what happened?" John asked, his fingers tightening around the large man's wrists. John watched Simon's eyes close as tears ran down his red cheeks and fell into his beard. The large Zealot's hands clenched the cloth of John's cloak until his knuckles were white and the weight of his grieving body nearly cast John off balance. "Those were our men who fell out there, Simon. Tell me what happened?"

Simon ben Ari groaned and sniffed. He raised his great head and slowly opened his bloodshot eyes. He stared for a moment at John and then said, "There had to have been over one hundred and fifty archers. They murdered us with two volleys, point blank. There was no avoiding it. I couldn't say a thing. The men never saw it coming. We clustered into a mass, nobody knowing what to do. I felt my voice snatched from my throat, and I couldn't speak." He shook his head. "Then out of the ditch they arose. I saw legionaries who wore armour, but they were disguised, kind of like us. They had their faces darkened, helmets covered, chest armour blackened; even the scabbards for their swords were dark. They were like ghosts, demons. I saw a flash of steel as they drew their swords and with raised shields they plowed into us.

"The distance from us to the ditch could not have been more than a stone's throw. We had no chance. None of us had shields, armour, or spears. We were slaughtered." More tears flowed down Simon's face and he hung his head in shame. "I said nothing. I fled after falling upon the ground and was scared for my life, something I haven't felt in years. I felt as though nothing would stop the killing and we would all be swallowed up."

John was motionless, his face pale at the words he heard. What he saw before him was the image of a man brought from the heights of patriotic pride and fervour to the depths of despair and darkness. Simon's spirit had been crushed and his eyes spoke of terror. He would never be the same. John slowly pulled the great man's hands from his shoulder and backed away. Simon seemed drunk as he watched John stand up and stare down at him. A line of spittle clung to his lips as his eyes were sunken and burdened.

"You have a spy, John. You have a spy in your ranks. How else could the Roman's have known?" Simon angrily shouted, and then his mind seemed to swim. Feeling overcome by dizziness he collapsed, smacking his head upon the stone ground. He groaned briefly and then mumbled, "Check your officers, you have a spy. We met in secret for this attack, there were but thirty men. You have a…you…spy." Simon was silent as he passed out with a moan and the eyes of John stared down at him.

"Pick him up and carry him to my quarters. He is to be cared for. When he wakes, let me know." John stood aside as a group of four men approached Simon then awkwardly lifted the enormous body and were escorted away by a man holding a torch.

"What happened?" a familiar voice asked.

John turned shaking his head and crossed his arms. He stared at Judah for a moment and then shrugged. "They were ambushed on the outskirts of the Roman camp. We still have no numbers confirmed of those slain, but I expect them to be high." John glanced at the wounded being carried away.

"Ambushed? How is that possible?" Judah replied acting shocked.

John shrugged, his face tense and mind pondering over all who had been present at the war council two days ago. Having no such luck at recalling the names, he finally said, "How is the western colonnade?"

"No movement. Shortly after Simon ben Ari was supposed to make his attack we saw a column of Giora's troops move quickly by. I had archers at the ready and the scorpion crews wanted to release a volley, but I ordered them to stand down. After a few moments, the streets below the walls were silent and nothing else has stirred all night."

Although it had been Judah's information to the Romans that had assisted in foiling the attack, he felt a tinge of guilt at the report of high casualties. *Only two more and then Capito will be mine*, Judah thought longing for that day.

John sighed thinking there may be a connection between what Judah had told him and the massacre among Simon ben Ari's attack. "Could Giora have a spy in our ranks? Perhaps he sent word to the Romans? Would he?" John groaned as if he felt he was going mad and then looked at Judah with fierce eyes. "Get me a list of all the names who attended the war council. I want to see if there are any men who may have been with Giora at an earlier time." He hesitated for a moment and then said, "I want you to raise a group of a dozen men, Judah. They are to be my most trusted advisors and men you have complete faith in. They must be loyal to our cause."

"What is the purpose of such a trusted group, John?" Judah asked.

"You will be keeping a watch for spies. Someone is giving information to the enemy and we must find out who it is." John clenched his fists and stared at the ground for a moment. "Return to your post. We will speak of this again soon." He gave Judah a prolonged look of suspicion and then marched away towards the Hulda Gates feeling utterly vulnerable for the first time in his reign as warlord of the Zealot forces.

*   *   *

CHAPTER XXII

April 30th, 70 A.D. / 3rd of Iyyar 3839
Camp of the Tenth Legion
Three Hours after Dawn

Gaius and Marcus walked among the dead strewn upon the rocky ground. The exhausted legionaries had discarded all cloths used to conceal the glare of their armour, and washed their faces from the dry, caked clay. After the fight, a reinforced guard had been posted around the ditches relieving the majority of the vexillatio that had fought so they could retire and rest. Now, many of them were awake as they examined the effectiveness of their work from the night before.

Gaius pushed aside all sympathy from his mind as he stared down at the mutilated bodies. Limbs and scraps of flesh lay discarded like rubbish as hundreds of arrows protruded out of the ground and corpses seemed like the back of a porcupine. The thick smell of blood, urine, and other bodily fluids was strong in the air as the wind refused to blow, leaving the heavy stench in Gaius' nostrils. Already insects were beginning to explore the cleaved bodies as ravens and vultures cried out in their typical eager excitement at the sight of the battlefield.

Blood settled in long, dark trails as the ground refused to soak it up. The mouths of the dead were agape, their eyes appearing like glass as limbs were contorted in all sorts of positions. Intestines lay strewn about, as chests, torn open by the edge of the sword, reached up to the heavens baring rib cages of white bone and dried blood. A raven clung to one such rib as the victim lay in a pool of scarlet. The bird cawed loudly, peering into the open chest cavity of the man and then pecked at a strip of flesh clinging to the bone. A legionary standing nearby groaned with disgust and shooed the bird away. He then quickly approached the body, picked up a discarded cloak, and turned his face as he flung the garment over the corpse.

The bludgeoning had been sudden and vicious, as a lamb led to slaughter. None of the Jews had worn armour or carried shields. Gaius could only guess at their intentions. The Jews were notorious for lightly equipped attacking parties, darting out from their strongholds to charge into oblivious legionaries to spread panic and disorder. Gaius had seen it time and time again since Vespasian had invaded the north. The Jews excelled with the shock charge. The sudden terror they were able to instill upon their enemies was horrific, and the Romans had learned of this firsthand after many thousands of dead.

"Almost takes the pride of victory out of it," Marcus said, examining the body of a young man. "How old do you think this one is?" He gazed up at Gaius who in turn gave the Tribune an uninterested look. Marcus glanced down at the corpse, touched the dead man's chin, and turned the cold face away. "It was like he was staring right at my soul," Marcus uttered as he stood. He gave a deep sigh and pointed past the camp of the Tenth. "More crosses to show off Titus' artwork."

Without a word, Gaius turned and looked up the steep slopes of the Mount of Olives. Six new crosses were being erected at the summit with the screams and pounding of nails ringing out. "Prisoners?" he said slowly. Marcus nodded in agreement and Gaius sniffed. He shook his head and rested his hand on the pommel of his gladius. "We did well," he said with a blank expression.

"Yes, we did." Marcus turned as he watched a group of his Boars descend the hill; his own horse among the group led by Publius, his standard bearer. The colours of Marcus' marauding band were displayed and the grim head of the boar seemed to glare at the city as it sat atop its signum. "It would appear as though I am needed elsewhere."

Gaius nodded as he watched the cavalry come to a halt as the large horses kicked up dust. The armour of the troopers was blackened and all wore shirts of mail with long capes fastened to their shoulders. Their equipment was polished and cared for and the hides of their mounts gleamed from the rising sun. Despite the men's care for looks, Gaius saw in their faces the hardened men they were. These were the veterans of the horse troops Titus possessed, the best in the army and some said the empire.

Gaius watched Marcus lift himself up into the saddle and get comfortable as he took the reins. Publius said a few quick words and then the Tribune gave a sharp nod and gazed down at the weary-looking Centurion.

"Well, it appears I am needed. Word is that the siege equipment will be shown to the city today, compliments of the baggage train." Marcus smiled and took a deep breath as he gazed over the quiet valley. Then he looked to the north as the Roman work crews approached the earth ramps for another day of tedious labour. "It will be complete soon, Gaius." Marcus stared down at his friend with a sentimental look in his eyes. "When the ramps are done the rams and towers will move up. I would say with the success of your career, and with today's work, Titus will want to use you often. Get used to it." Marcus chuckled lightly and leaned over. "You led your men perfectly last night; it couldn't have been better."

"Not a single casualty," Gaius replied.

"And your man Judah's help paid off. Perhaps he is a sympathizer?"

Gaius shrugged. "I wouldn't count on that."

"Yet he helps *Roma*? He condemns his own kindred to die by our swords. The man must have higher expectations than fighting us in that squalor of a city." Marcus watched as some Jewish fighters gathered on the walls and he shook his head wearily. "I hear some men say they wish the Jews would just open the gates and surrender."

"What do you say?" Gaius asked.

"I say leave them shut!" Marcus glanced at Gaius with excitement. "More victory for us if we storm a city, am I right?"

"I would rather avoid storming Jerusalem. With all the pilgrims, there must be over four hundred thousand people in there. Can you imagine such a mess? If we storm the city, it would take months. Remember Jotapata or Gamla?"

"Mere children's forts compared to this, yes, I know. Jotapata was made of twigs when placed alongside the Antonia. But it is for the sport, my dear Gaius. Men will either become lions or fallow deer; it is up to you to decide." Marcus roared with laughter.

"Venus blesses the soil and Flora shows colour through her blooms everywhere in the empire, but here, what do you make of that, Marcus?" Gaius rubbed his chin and removed his stifling helmet.

"What do you imply? You say we are cursed, is it?" Marcus shook his head. "The oracles made claims, the bull, the eagles, your Jew Yosef, and the power of Basilides! How can the absence of flowers contend with the power of the Son of the Monarch?"

"The visions and dreams of Basilides should be met with suspicion, dear Marcus. We do not know clearly whose side the god is on," Gaius replied lifting his eyes to the sky.

Marcus was still for a moment. "Do not confound them, Gaius, especially Basilides. Although I am inclined to think little of the gods and the affairs of man, Vespasian saw him and Titus has heard the voice. He is a presence among us and I shall sacrifice a calf in his honour. Just guard your tongue. Our Prince Titus is quite fond of the idea of a god laying out the future before us."

"Do stars confirm this or Titus' paid priests?" asked Gaius lowering his voice so only Marcus could hear.

"Speak plainly, Gaius."

Gaius stepped over to Marcus' side and gazed up at the proud Tribune. "I am here to serve and do what the Prince commands; it is not a question about loyalty or service. I just want to see this dealt rightly, the rebellion crushed, those responsible punished, and order restored. Not open war and not a Jerusalem that burns."

"I see. I respect that of you, Gaius, I do. The rebels will pay, indeed they will. But see clearly, I do urge you. The rebels have never yielded ground; they are not about to do so here as well." Marcus stared for a moment at the city. "Jerusalem will burn, Gaius. The rebels will never give it to us intact. But if Jerusalem should be spared, how many of your men will it cost? What is the butcher's bill?"

Marcus watched Gaius' gaze fall with discouragement and the Tribune leaned forward and planted a firm grasp on the Centurion's shoulder. "You must ask that of yourself, my friend, and be prepared for the worst." Marcus firmly nodded and then lifting the reins in his hands he said, "What we have seen so far is nothing at all compared to what awaits us inside. We will no longer be men when this engagement is decided."

Gaius only saw sincerity in Marcus' eyes. Without uttering another syllable, the Tribune rode off towards Titus' camp at the head of his Boars as the dew began to dry and the sun heated the land.

*   *   *

Noon

"One hundred and twelve dead, ninety-five wounded, and six crucified!" John shouted with a sudden burst of hysteria. A line of spittle clung to the edge of his lip as he gazed around the table with wild eyes. The officers were startled, but kept their silence with downtrodden faces. Simon ben Ari sat upon a cushioned stool, slumped in the corner of the Antonia council room with a blank look upon his face, red swollen cheeks, and filthy hair. "Someone talked!" John pounded his fists heavily upon the table. "Someone damned talked!" He pounded three more times until a goblet toppled over, rolled to the edge and fell with a clang upon the stone floor. "It had to be someone, maybe one of you!" John pointed an accusing finger at the forty blank faces staring back at him.

A sudden murmur rose up from the doors at the back of the hall as Judah appeared with Adam and Caleb. The men walked swiftly across the floor and Judah held up a rolled scroll in his hand. "A letter from Simon, John. It was sent by a runner from the western colonnades."

John regained his composure as he gave one last hateful look at the officers. "At least there is one man with honour among us, and he is here now." John walked around the table as the officers parted. "When did this arrive?" John asked, taking the scroll.

"Just now John as we stood guard. A boy approached clutching this in his hand and claimed it was from Simon." Judah glanced at the ashen expressions upon the faces of the officers and he knew John had been delving into more accusations concerning spies among his ranks.

Considering the ill fate of Simon ben Ari's men and the Roman victory, Judah would have to be careful. He knew that his survival depended on absolute secrecy concerning his part with the Romans remaining concealed from John, while fulfilling his promise to Titus in order to get his revenge.

John hurriedly broke the wax seal and unfurled the parchment. His eyes narrowed for a moment as he scanned the letter reading the Aramaic script. His face relaxed and then a look of shock struck him. John lowered the letter in silence gazing about the room and softly said, "Simon wishes to renew the alliance." A gasp of surprise rose from the officers as many began whispering among each other. John laid the parchment on the table and scratched his head.

"Is it the genuine seal of Simon ben Giora? The pomegranate and the palm frond crossed behind it?" asked one of the officers.

John nodded and crossed his arms. "Giora will launch two attacks tomorrow against the ramp workers north of the city. He will have torches to burn the artillery which has been brought up. It says he hopes to get to the rear of the stationed baggage train which the Romans are using to unload the siege equipment."

"He wants peace?" Judah asked quietly.

"He declares it at the end," John picked up the letter and read aloud, "To my brothers on the mountain we all revere as holy, let us fight the Gentiles as one and let us triumph." John was speechless and then said, "We will match his valour by launching another attack to be sequenced to Simon ben Giora's assault. We shall move out in force at the Tenth camp, burn their towers and capture as much food as possible. Should Simon's attacks be successful, we can reverse this siege and spread misery into the minds of our enemy."

The officers cheered, relieved that John had abandoned the spy hunt for the moment, and exhilarated by the news of the renewed alliance. All of the men had been itching to relocate their scorpions to the northern walls to begin pummeling the workers, and up until now that had been impossible. With the renewed alliance would come more effective ways to strike at the Romans beyond their walls, and that put smiles upon their faces.

Orders were handed out and a collection of eight officers were organized to assemble an assaulting party of six hundred fighters to spring out of the eastern gate at the same time that Simon ben Giora would make his own attack.

Simon ben Ari continued sulking upon the stool as men made plans for battle and spoke of glorious visions of Romans fleeing beyond the hills with the Jews slaughtering them in the thousands. The atmosphere had changed with Simon pathetically watching with red eyes and shame etched into the lines of the old warrior's face.

"Judah, I must speak with you," John called out as he stepped back from the table desiring some privacy.

"What is it, John?"

He signaled Judah with a gesture to follow him away from the table and into a dimly lit section of the Antonia hall. Once the two men were away from the jabbering Zealot officers John grew serious and said, "Have you or your men found anyone who could have talked? Anyone who could be passing information like the bastard I found over the wall?"

Judah shook his head choosing his words carefully. "Nothing, John. I have men keeping watch and listening in on what the soldiers speak of, but so far nothing suspicious."

John shook his head. "Someone is talking. Someone is passing those damn Romans information. Ari's men were slaughtered. The Romans were waiting for them. Have you ever heard of Romans in ditches? Waiting in bloody ditches? Simon said they even had archers in there. The bastards had mud on their faces and their armour was blackened. They were bleeding organized and we walked right into a trap, a trap that could only have been planned by precisely what they were told. It came from in here, Judah, from in here." John's eyes were lit as if on fire. He scratched his dark beard and shook his head. "I feel like I have ants on my skin. To know someone you trust, someone you would call *brother* is a damned forked viper is more then I can imagine."

Judah shrugged trying not to show the sickness and guilt he suddenly felt. He buried the emotion and narrowed his eyes as he gazed back at John with fury. "We will find them and strike them down by the blades of our swords. Then they will hang from our walls."

John responded with a shudder. He gave a heavy nod and laid a gentle hand upon Judah's shoulder, looking him square in the eyes. "You are a captain of captains, Judah ben Yosef. Had your father been alive he would have hailed you as the best man in this city, as I do. You are a man I entrust my life to and God has blessed. I feel, with men like you, we will truly win this war and the Romans will be defeated. When that time comes, Jerusalem will need a prince. If this nation is to be under God, and proud again like the age of the Hasmoneans, then she will need heirs and protectors who fear God. You are he, and thus, I shall adopt you as my son when the time draws near. It will take you and I to bring this nation back to its rightful place to await the arrival of Meshiach."

Judah was stared into the dark eyes of the Zealot commander and saw a man he could respect, despite all the atrocities he may or may not have committed. This was not the man Hadassah had spoken of. Could he have slit the throat of Ananus ben Ananus and Joshua ben Gamala? Judah could not see him commit such murder, but Hadassah had sworn it was him. "I am unworthy of such a proclamation, John."

"We are all men of unworthiness, Judah. Our hands are stained with blood and our eyes have beheld the suffering of innocence." John's voice changed as he suddenly sounded like the teachers of the Torah Judah had heard so many times, yet his voice maintained a soothing authority. "The Scriptures say King David was a man after God's own heart. However, he was withheld from power above to build the House of God, our Temple, for his hands were the hands of a man of war and were stained with the blood of men. His hands were like ours, Judah. Yet, King David had a son, who was noble and upright in the eyes of God, and he was chosen to build this House and fulfill the promise given to the House of David. Solomon had his faults, and incurred the wrath of God in his later years, but he was noble and loved, and men like him will come after us, when men like us have killed the enemies of God. It is up to us to see this through and one day, I swear, there will be peace and the enemy vanquished."

Judah stiffly nodded. "I do pray for that day, John, I do." Then he quietly left knowing what he must do next. Again he would have to separate guilt from what he understood to be the vital pursuit to finding inner peace, and that alone rested in a particular man's blood upon his hands.

*   *   *

Evening

Everything was set. The day had rewarded Titus' sight with three long ramps of earth and timber nearing completion and the sounds of hammering behind the Macedonica camp as towers and rams were assembled. He counted down the days in his head, two more, he guessed, until the attacks could begin. Of course he would send Yosef to the walls in another attempt to demand surrender, but all of Titus' officers saw the folly in these escapades as none believed the Zealots would give in.

"Maybe when the western wall is reduced to rubble and the New City smoulders from flames will the insolent bastards give way to reason," had been the comment of Titus Frigius. The other legionary generals had toasted that statement and the Prince had calmly rolled his eyes, reminding them that Rome would not stoop to a barbaric level. Negotiations were important, and protocol must be obeyed. The men had grumbled in agreement, but Frigius had spoken the truth and the Prince knew it.

Now, Titus stood outside his camp, his hands clasped behind his back, watching the flames of the torches flicker upon the boarders of the ramps. A heavy guard was stationed from the camp of the Macedonica past the earthen mounds to his own base camp to discourage Jewish sallies and he had taken every precaution to foil every attempt. With this in mind, he thought of the successful information Judah had provided in the trap they had been able to set for Simon ben Ari. Gaius' men had combed the battlefield for Simon's corpse which had failed to turn up as prisoners had been unable to identify it, yet the blow had been serious for the Jews and another victory for the Romans.

Finally things appear to be under control, Titus thought as he grinned. The Jewish problem of surprise attacks had always made him cringe and remain slightly nervous as they seemed so successful at hitting them right where they least expected it. But now, with a man on the inside, Titus could finally sleep comfortably at night, at least when he was not in the company of a woman. The Roman Prince smiled thinking of his last duel between the female gender and he mauled over the possibility in his mind if he was in the mood for another evening of pleasurable entertainment.

"My Prince, men approach!" a sentry called out standing three metres away, squinting through the dusk. The soldier picked up his shield and stepped toward the

⌐ 341 ⌐

Prince, tightening the grip on his spear. When he realized the forms moving towards him were Roman, he relaxed and blew a sigh of relief.

Titus scowled as a party of soldiers slowed their pace and halted before the Prince. An optio adorned with the skin of a leopard which covered his helmet, snapped to attention striking his breastplate and planted his hastile firmly upon the ground. The cluster of legionaries behind him parted and brought forth three women, an elderly man, and four children.

It was clear the captives were all Jews from the city of Jerusalem. It was also clear that none of them were Zealots, most likely pilgrims or members of the poorer sect of the Lower City. Titus crossed his arms as a humorous look spread across his face, and he instantly examined the women to see if there was any real physical attraction. One may have passed a test of beauty, but the others were common looking and scared of the great Prince standing before them.

"My lord and Prince." The optio bowed his head and then signaled to the legionaries to bring the captives forward into plain view. "These ones were found lurking near ramp two."

Titus scowled. "Lurking?"

The optio nodded. "Larcius here was posted on the right of the ramp and spotted them coming into the light with hands lifted and speaking their tongue. They simply surrendered."

"Any of them speak Greek?" Titus asked.

The optio turned and said to the group, "Koine? Koine?" He glanced sheepishly back at Titus and shrugged.

"They are of the lower class. They smell," Titus said with a look of discomfort. He stared unsympathetically at the children and shook his head. "A waste of time if these ones come to surrender looking for a better life, what am I to do?" He sighed. "We look for patricians, aristocrats, nobles and learned people. We need civilized people if we are to end this and rebuild the land."

"Well, they aren't spies!" called out a soldier sarcastically and a few chuckled.

The elderly Jewish man seemed to sense their ill favour by the look on the Prince's face and he suddenly started talking quickly as he pointed back to the city. Titus cringed at the dialect which evaded him. After listening for a few moments he rolled his eyes and let loose an exasperated groan. "Silence the fool, please."

"As you wish, my lord," replied a gruff legionary who stepped forward leaving his shield with a comrade and thumped the elderly man in the gut with the butt of his spear. The old man retched forward with a gasp followed by a painful groan as he collapsed to his knees. The soldier laughed aloud at the fear in the children's eyes and the sudden begging for mercy from the women. "Shall I thump them too for you, my lord?"

"Better to nail them up," replied another soldier.

The optio glanced at the Prince not knowing what to do next and said, "My lord?"

Titus suddenly held up a hand. "Be quiet!" The old man had said something that had caught his ear. He heard it again and quickly approached the old man and bending low said, "What did you say?"

The old man looked up clutching his gut and winced. Then with a shaky voice he responded saying, "Judah ben Yosef."

Titus was still for a moment, as if he had seen a ghost. He slowly stood and without taking his eyes from the man shouted, "Bring Yosef ben Matityahu here right now!"

It only took a split second for the fun to be washed away from the faces of the legionaries as they had hoped for a bit of amusement with the Jewish women and a quick crucifixion. The look on Titus' face confused them all but the optio did not hesitate to send runners in search for the Jewish General.

When Yosef finally showed up, he was running ahead of the legionaries who had fetched him. Yosef instantly caught sight of the Prince and then immediately slowed his pace when he noticed the Jewish captives standing near an old, white bearded man kneeling on the ground. Titus faced Yosef and sternly asked, "What is he saying?"

A look of surprise filled Yosef's face when he heard the name the elderly man was mumbling. He quickly ran to his side and knelt beside the aging Jew. Yosef touched the man's bearded face and the man opened his tearful eyes. "How do you know Judah ben Yosef?" Yosef asked in Hebrew. The man replied, then pointed first to the city and then to the children and women. Finally he looked up at Titus and gave a nod.

"What did he say?" Titus queried.

Yosef rose. "My Prince, you will not wish to harm this man. He says that this is his family, and that Judah went to them when darkness fell and told them he knew a way out of the city. He told them to find you, and that Simon ben Giora will attack tomorrow in the morning with two war parties. Simon will attack the workers of the ramps and try to burn them." The old man began speaking again and finished. Yosef nodded to the man, thanked him, and then looked back at the Prince. "He says, John will come from the East Gate and attack the camp on the olive mountain. He says Judah ben Yosef wishes to remind you that this will be a total of three attacks he has told us about." Yosef listened some more to the elderly man speak and then translated for the Prince. "He begs for his life and the lives of his family."

Titus was still for a moment and then hesitantly replied, "You are sure of this?"

"That is what the man says, two attacks from the north and one from the east tomorrow morning." Yosef slowly stood and looked at the shocked optio.

"If this is true, then John and Simon have formed an alliance." Titus cringed slightly at the thought. "Optio, take these people, have them bathed, groomed, fed and give them a tent for the night. Tomorrow, have two soldiers and one of my scribes go by cart to the village of Beit Ani, the family can go where ever they want from there."

"Yes, my Prince."

"Also, let the soldiers be aware," Titus said continuing, "That I trust my scribe; whoever you pick will report to me every detail. If those legionaries so much as lift their togas and show off their pricks to those women, I will have them scourged and shamed."

The optio swallowed hard and gave a brief bow. "Yes, my lord."

"Go, take them and show care." Titus watched the optio signal some of the soldiers to help and as Yosef informed the Jews in Hebrew the elderly man began crying and the women bowed many times as they gave their thanks.

Titus watched the family regain their composure and quietly get escorted away. He looked at Yosef for a moment and softly said, "So, this will be your man's third aid in foiling the Zealot attacks? I will have to think of how I will uphold my end of the bargain. You still consider Judah reliable?"

"With all my heart, my lord, I do."

"Good, then I have much to do. I bid you a pleasant night, Yosef." Titus kindly smiled and then strolled away humming a song he had heard months ago while wintering in Alexandria.

* * *

CHAPTER XXIII

May 1st, 70 A.D. / 4th of Iyyar, 3830
Temple Mount

"No!" John roared in disbelief as he covered half his face, staring in a state of horror and anger. When the attack had been launched, his Zealots charged out of the East Gate in mass against a few hundred Roman workers leveling ground near the bottom of the Mount of Olives. However, once the Jewish attack had been fully committed, suddenly the Roman labourers had cast off their cloaks, producing an assortment of bows and drawn swords. At the same time two cohorts of legionaries had poured out of the Fretensis camp with utmost speed as their centurions led them like rolling thunder down the slopes. John could only watch in dismay as his Zealots split their formation in a desperate effort to dodge a volley of arrows and then scrambled back towards the city with the cohorts hot on their heels.

Men watching upon the eastern colonnades had sensed something treacherous about the whole escapade. Despite them cursing the Romans from the few Zealots who collapsed dead upon the ground, with black arrows protruding from their backs, every man upon the wall knew a traitor was among them. John gripped the edge of the stone battlements and gazed below at his frantic men dashing back through the opened gates. He summoned his own archers to the wall to hold back the Roman tide and prayed for them to come near.

The image of bowmen suddenly crowding the ramparts seemed to be enough of a reminder to the Romans that although they may have foiled another Zealot attack, they would not survive coming within twenty metres of the high walls. The cohorts halted and clustered into a mass of steel, their red shields adding a bright flash of colour to the barren landscape. Just out of range from the bowmen, centurions sounded blasts from their whistles and with steady counting in Latin the legionaries obediently formed into their uniformed and symmetrical rectangular regiments. Then like one giant body, they wheeled left to the beat of a steady drum and retired in good order back to their camp singing like victors.

John did not move. He could hear shouts from the courtyard below and men calling for water and attention, but he dared not move. His eyes narrowed and he felt completely lost and betrayed, not knowing what he should do. John stared down at six bodies strewn upon the ground, the victorious product of yet another Roman counterattack that could not have come about unless someone amidst his ranks was passing information. He turned and watched the lines of archers lower their bows and stare at the cohorts of legionaries marching back up the hill. A few glanced to John with expressions of doubt and fear, while some looked on with a foreboding grimace that blamed him.

Without saying a word, John quickly descended the ramparts and strolled into the courtyard as he took in the sight of his exhausted men. Some were lying around, although most wandered aimlessly. A large officer approached John, shook his head, lowered his sword, and angrily tossed his shield away.

"What is going on, John?" the officer snarled. "We can't fight this!" He threw his sword upon the ground and spit upon the flagstones. "I will gut the pig that pisses in the enemies' cup!"

John was speechless for a moment as his mind raced. He glanced past the officer noticing that other soldiers were watching the scene. Then mustering up his courage he swallowed heavily and said through barred teeth, "This will get sorted out, now pick up your sword and go disband your men."

The officer shook his head with a sarcastic smile. "Sorted out? Sorted out!" he shouted. "How in God's name will this get sorted out?"

"Don't blaspheme upon this ground, friend!" John warned. "Now, pick up your sword and disband your men."

The officer widened his stance and lifting a hand he stroked his beard in a comical way. "Maybe you're the bastard talking to the Romans, hey? Big man from Gischala wants to cut a deal?"

The officer had hardly finished speaking when the back of John's heavy hand cut the air and struck the man across the face so hard a string of blood sprayed from his mouth. The officer stumbled back completely in shock and unsure of his footing. He shook his ringing head as he opened and closed his eyes and touched his jaw as spittle, blood, and mucus covered his beard.

The officer dropped to one knee grunting loudly. He spit a stream of red saliva upon the stones and then looked up. "You bastard! I will…"

John did not let him finish. Moving quickly, the enormous man from Gischala curled his fingers into a fist and rammed it into the officer's nose, feeling the cartilage and bone crack under his force. A hollow pop echoed from the pillars of the colonnade as the nose shattered and broke. The officer yelped in pain as his body was flung back from the blow causing his head to smack with a thud upon the stone. John rubbed his fist and examined it. Then making sure his Zealots were watching, he walked up to the officer and planted his foot on the man's throat.

"You should cry out so that I don't crush the life out of you! Why should I hesitate to erase such a putrid life as yours? It should have been you to die out there and not those men who have fallen so that we can go on fighting! You are a disgrace in God's eyes, in the presence of His Holy Temple, and in the sight of Jews who stand against the enemies of God. What do you say to that?" John stared down at the helpless man who did not have the strength to resist. He only stared up at the calm warlord, barely able to breathe from his shattered nose and the pressure upon his throat. John held his breath for a moment and then gazed up at the Zealots who clustered around. "You there, what is your name?" John pointed at a strongly built man.

"Eli, my lord," the man responded awkwardly.

John lifted his foot off the officer's throat, bent down, picked up the man's sword, and tossed it to Eli. "You are now a captain of my army. This man is in disgrace." John shouted, "I am the commander of this army, and will not tolerate anarchy! This man I will spare, but only once! He has used up the only patience I have left! If anyone does as much as cross me, they will die! We shall beat the Romans, and we must do so through unity, not division." He said these last words staring down at the bleeding man. "Take him away and out of my sight."

Eli gave a sharp nod and signaling a number of men to help him they grabbed the officer and dragged him away as he whimpered pathetically. The rest of the soldiers quickly dispersed and John suddenly noticed Judah running toward him from the western colonnades.

"John, John!" Judah glanced for a puzzled moment at the bleeding officer's face as he was dragged passed and then shrugged it off quickly. "Simon's attacks have failed! They were repulsed by organized Roman infantry. They fought hard but were turned over and fled."

"What?" John retorted his face growing pale.

Judah nodded and shook his head. "A runner brought the message to me. He said Simon's forces have broken and many are dead. The ramps lay untouched and the legionaries massed precisely to meet the twin assault."

"How can this be?" John replied shocked and covering his mouth. "Both attacks?"

"Men of the Fifth were the legionaries involved in the ambush and I was told they had captured numerous Idumeans who they are preparing for crucifixion as we speak." Judah's face was downcast as he was plagued by guilt, shame, and sorrow for the dead. He knew his message had been received by Titus, and that his word was trusted among the Romans, for in the morning he had seen no new crosses lining the hills. Thus, he knew Titus had spared the family he had managed to smuggle out at the risk of his own neck, but the thought of the Idumeans suffering on account of his relationship with the Romans grieved him.

John saw the despair in Judah's face and interpreted it as anger and resentment over the foiled attacks. He stared with fierce eyes at the Lion warrior and speaking in a low voice said, "We need to see Simon now! Come with me!"

The two men crossed the expanse of the vast grounds which surrounded the Temple and passed beneath the high pillars of the Royal Porticoes at the southwestern corner. Neither acknowledged the guards standing near the gates as they descended the staircase where the three rebel commanders had met months ago during the initial stages of the peace process. John was eager to reach the bottom and quickened his pace. Judah fell into step behind the warlord as the sun burned from the sky upon the rooftops of the houses which stretched beyond them into the city suburbs.

John led Judah past the abandoned gymnasium in disrepair and away from the long plaza of shops along the length of the high walls of the Temple plateau. Beyond that was the fortified castle of the Antonia and then the Pools of Bethesda. Judah stared for a brief moment at the enormous five ton stones of the Temple platform and shook his head at the incredible feat that must have faced Herod's architects in refurbishing the most holy site of the Jewish faith.

They passed under a stone bridge above them and turned down a narrow street leaving the Temple behind. A dog poked its nose from a pile of garbage that had been discarded and a lame man lay upon a mat shaking a small cup for alms. John failed to even look at the poor, grey-haired beggar who watched them pass with sadness as he called out for help. John crossed to the other side of the barren street, fists clenched, his concentration fixed on what he would discuss with Simon.

Judah watched a few Pharisees scurry by as they picked up their robes, trying not to attract attention. The men stole quick glances at the determined Zealots, daring not to say a thing. Judah looked back and saw one of the Pharisees flick a copper coin at the beggar and then carry on to catch up with his fellows who had continued on without him.

Judah was shocked as John had not even bothered taking a guard. Even though a shaky peace ensued between Simon and John, the streets of Jerusalem could be hostile and unpredictable. John, however, had suddenly felt bold in his anger, brushing the thought of personal protection aside, wanting to waste no time.

Shouts and protests arose from somewhere ahead of the men and John abruptly hesitated for a moment. He seemed to realize his predicament and felt slightly vulnerable as he glanced back at Judah. "Are you armed? That is good," he softly said and then patted his own sword strapped to his side. "Just in case one of Simon's thugs should feel bold," John added giving Judah a wink. "Come, we must hurry." John continued onward as he picked up his pace, passing under a high arch connected to the Temple compound above.

A throng of Idumean soldiers suddenly appeared on the street in front of them. They were heavily armed and shouting as some shoved each other with curses. Officers among the rank, screamed back at the men to maintain discipline. Their reaction seemed to cool the clusters of soldiers totting spears and shields. John and Judah tried to look inconspicuous as they passed the troops and John even pulled his cloak over his head to conceal his face. Judah felt vulnerable as he watched numerous Idumeans glare at them, some trying to recognize the identity of the two strange men, while others in their rage sought to strike fear into anyone different. One large officer at the rear of the soldiers, turned and shouting at the two men said, "Who are you?"

"Just men of John taking an important message to your King Simon," John replied slowing his pace and glancing back.

The officer scowled shaking his head and spat upon the street. "Our King Simon has caused many to bleed beyond our walls. Even now if you listen carefully you will hear the hammers of the Romans nailing our brothers to crosses."

John nodded and shrugged. "My heart is saddened by what you say, but regardless we must leave and find your commander."

The officer shoved one of the Idumeans who had stopped to listen and barked at the man to continue on. Then turning he replied, "You know where to find him?" He saw the men shake their heads and said, "He is by the Tower of Psephinus considering another attack to rescue the crucified captives and cut them down."

"You think that is wise?" John asked.

The officer sighed and wiped his forehead from the sweat which glistened from his face. "Simon doesn't seem to have sense at this point. There are many opposed to another attack." He frowned and called out, "You said you're John's men?" The two cloaked men nodded and the officer said, "What does John say? I heard his men were driven back as well?"

"John will have his revenge, for that I am certain. Have you heard of spies?" John asked in a gruff tone.

The officer folded his broad arms across his chest. "I have heard some talk; it would make sense. Simon executed two men this morning he felt were spies, can't say they truly were, if you ask me. One man I knew, hated the Romans with every bone in his body. Simon had the man's throat cut and his body tossed from the wall. However, the one who did the honours did an awful job and used a dull blade. So now the accused spy lays at the foot of the wall paralyzed, but still alive. Simon has guards watching him die slowly and if anyone tries to rescue him or put him out of his misery they will quickly find themselves skewered like boars."

John shook his head and while nodding at Judah shouted back at the officer, "We must be going, shalom."

The officer bowed his head humbly and replied, "And shalom to you, my brothers."

Judah did not say a word as he followed John. They passed by home after home as the streets were vacant of any life. Garbage littered the streets and pools of dank water lifted an unsavoury stench into the air. John gave a sour look towards some human excrement lying near a door and shook his head, uttering how dirty this place had become.

Judah gazed up at the enormous towers of the Antonia seen above the roofs of the homes. He could make out guards stationed upon the battlements with loaded scorpions and ballista as their crews gazed down upon the Bezetha.

Eventually the two men emerged from the twisting streets and beheld a high wall and gate house across the space before them. Soldiers loyal to Simon littered the area as they guarded the Fish Gate and some appeared to be attempting to reform into collected groups at the shouts of officers. Random fires burned within pits that had been dug by prying up flagstones and hurling them aside. The streets were dirty as black smoke belched upward into the air from the fires, while men congregated around, heating caldrons and stirring the contents.

"They boil pitch," John said, acknowledging the putrid, wafting, smell. "Simon is readying his men."

"The Romans are close. Men from the Antonia saw a lot of activity west of the wall." Judah crouched down and studied the fires. He saw a group of about fifty bowmen sitting near the gate inspecting arrows scattered upon the ground. Among them, skilled craftsmen repaired arrows, fixed every fletching with new feathers, and replaced iron tipped heads. "They will come soon."

John glanced at Judah for a moment considering the weight of his words and then exhaled loudly and said, "Let's go."

"What, to the gate? Simon's men will fillet us when they find out who we are," Judah retorted standing.

"They fear me."

"John, here you are but one man. You have left your bodyguard behind you. We will die." Judah suddenly felt anxious and uncomfortable.

John growled under his breath and bit his lower lip for a moment to think. Then he spit upon the ground and said, "We have to talk to Simon. I must know what his next move is. The only way, is through that gate." John pointed across the space and harshly grabbed Judah's shoulder. "You're coming with me." He dragged Judah from the safety of the street and then let him go as the Lion commander had no other choice but to follow. "Just pretend they do not exist," John uttered in a hoarse whisper.

Judah watched the grim faces of the Idumean troops as they patrolled around and checked their weapons. He could hear the bubbling sound of the thick pitch as it was stirred and he could see the stained blackened hands of the men as they attended the sludge with great wooden paddles. He watched as old pieces of rope and timber were piled on the fires beneath the pots as the flames roared at the delight of more things to consume.

John and Judah neared the gate successfully, and for a moment it appeared as though they would slip through completely unnoticed. Everyone seemed to be preoccupied with getting ready for battle that they hardly looked up. It was not until John was passing through the gate that a soldier demanded for them to halt as he approached the two suspicious men with a drawn sword.

"Who are you? I don't know you," asked the man.

"Do you know everyone in the city?" John responded sarcastically feeling anger well up inside of him as he watched the man narrow his eyes.

"What is your business?" the Idumean asked. He pointed the blade of his sword at John and shouted, hurling spittle at the warlord, "I asked you a question!"

"We have urgent business to attend to. I have a word from John of Gischala for your master," John replied facing the Idumean and bracing for attack.

The man halted and shook his head. "Your accent is interesting. You're from the Galilee, aren't you? I think I should teach you manners? A dog of John's must be taught manners!" The Idumean turned and shouted at a group of spearmen to the left of the gate, "Look, my brothers, at the pricks that have come down from their nest!"

Judah stared wide-eyed at the Idumean as a cluster of menacing soldiers gathered behind him. He glanced quickly at John, trying to catch his eye and cursed the man for his stupidity and bullheaded nature. Now they were both on the verge of getting beaten to death by Simon's thugs.

"You would do well not to touch either myself or my brother here," John muttered in a whisper. He lowered his gaze and clenched his fists. Broadening his stance, the warlord from Gischala prepared to fight to the death.

The Idumean laughed tossing his head back and then smiled. "You bleeding dog! You think you can strike fear into me? I hold the sword, not you! You expect me to quiver? Perhaps you came to kill our King of the Sicarii? That would be punishable by a slow and painful death and I will gladly piss down your throat till you drown!"

"Touch him and I will cut off your manhood and feed it to you while you squeal in pain!" sounded a booming voice from inside the gate. Simon approached the Idumeans with a dagger in his hand and a horde of men at his back, and he did so with a grin.

The Idumean soldiers, who had been eagerly jeering at John and Judah with death threats, became like lambs instantaneously. All of the men quickly bowed, shuffled backwards, and held their gaze to the ground. The Idumean ringleader sheathed his sword swiftly and feeling a bout of fear fill his frame offered up a quick apology praising Simon as king.

"You would really kill such men?" Simon honestly asked the Idumean with a pouting expression. "I do declare that before your sword would fall, I have no doubt that John of Gischala would snatch the life out of you before you even knew it." Simon held his gaze upon the trembling Idumean and then turned to the two men. "Isn't that right, John?"

John straightened and maintaining his pride gave a stiff nod. "Simon, we need to talk."

Simon laughed and rubbed his chin. "To what do I owe this pleasure? You bring only your trusted Judah ben Yosef with you, and make it to the Fish Gate? I do thank God you do not hate me more, for then I might fear for my life. However, I thank you for the sake of my men, for if you had made it beyond this gate I would have had no choice but to kill them all for *insolence*." This last word was spoken harshly as Simon glared at his guards. "You useless amusements." The soldiers lowered their downcast faces with shame and Simon suddenly clapped his hands together. "John, follow me."

John and Judah watched Simon's guards scatter as the king turned and strolled calmly back the way he had come. Only a short, fat, ugly man followed at his heels next to a massive warrior whom both John and Judah understood to be Ananus ben Bagdatus, or better known as, Bastard Bagdatus.

Simon led them through the streets of the New City until they came upon the Third Wall. The ominous mountain of stone blocks which rose before them was the first barricade of defence keeping the Romans out of Jerusalem, and Simon knew this. Everywhere Judah looked he witnessed a massive army. Men lined the high ramparts of the walls and congregated below in massed units as they equipped themselves for battle. Even a vast city of tents had been erected near the walls where a heavy guard could be stationed within a short distance in case of sudden attack. Every tower was manned and every gate guarded. Contingents of troops were seen awkwardly hauling up large black caldrons of pitch as torches were fitted to the battlements and wood faggots stacked below.

Simon had prepared his defences as best he could. He had strengthened all the towers along the wall and reinforced the troops upon the battlements that stretched from the Hippicus Tower northward to the Tower of Psephinus then east towards the Kidron Valley. He felt pride in his work, grinning at John as he stared upwards. "I might not have all your ballista, John, but I make my own preparations. The Romans shall not get inside while I rule." Nothing was said between the men as the nasty chuckle of Yehoram was heard snickering behind the Zealot commander.

"Come, we shall talk upon the walls. I want you to see the Romans as I see them." Simon led them towards the Tower of Psephinus, the largest of the city towers standing over thirty metres in height. The roof was capped with red tiles shaped in a pyramidal top and surrounded by massive stones protruding upwards. Ten metres below the roof, large rectangular windows had been constructed giving absolute superiority over any enemy who dared to assault the tower while protecting those within. This was one of Simon's prized towers and he had established a temporary command centre within the heart of the structure.

The men entered the tower and climbed the spiral stairs for what seemed like an eternity until they came to a platform. Instead of ascending further, Simon led them onto the rampart walls to the south. Bagdatus lingered behind as Judah and John followed Simon along a section of the wall where no troops were stationed. Simon extended his hand outward and said, "Behold the Roman army!" He gave a sweep with his hands westward and saw the effects of the startling view upon the faces of John and Judah.

Neither man had seen the ramps from this angle. It was frightfully intimidating and a diabolical masterpiece of professional siege warfare. In a thousand years, the Zealots could never have fashioned such effective ramps. The close attention to detail in which the Romans gave their projects attested to the strength of their ingenuity and resolve to never give up.

The three massive ramps rose from the ground, coming so close to the walls that it felt like a man could reach out and touch them. In fact, the sense of how close they really were caused John to wince. Even now he watched as hundreds of wicker shields stood erect like makeshift walls protecting the workers below as they hauled up loads of earth and rubble. Each ramp had lengths of timber protruding from all sides as these helped keep the shape and strength of the siege platforms. Large oxen groaned as over a hundred carts of lumber made their way along the sides of the ramps, each guided by a driver. The lumber, stripped from the countryside, secured the foundations of the ramps to strengthen them under the sheer weight of the testudo battering rams which were destined to come.

"Brash, they are. Working right under our noses and there is nothing we can do. It is pointless to shoot arrows at them; the wicker shields protect them and they will respond with heavy artillery fire of their own. Believe me, we have tried." Simon pointed beyond the ramps and shook his head as he watched crosses being raised up with screaming men attached to them. "Those are the captives taken in our last attempt, an attempt which the Romans expected." Simon stared at John for a moment and then looked away.

"I thought you were organizing a counterattack?" John asked.

Simon shrugged. "I gave the order to keep the men busy. The truth is that those men out there will die upon the crosses. The Romans have doubled their guard and have archers. It is pointless to proceed; Titus is crafty."

John stared out at the ballista and catapults set up beyond the ramps and shuddered. He leaned out and gazed to the north near Titus' camp and saw monstrous, siege towers twenty-two metres high, their bodies covered in metal plates and resting upon massive wooden wheels. It would only be days now before they would attack. "What if I was to give you some artillery?" John mumbled as if lost in a trance.

"That would do no good at this point. We would have to extend parts of our ramparts to accommodate them. It would take a day to bring them here and nearly a week to get them in place. We have run out of time for that." Simon gestured at the ramps and shook his head. "They are ready to attack; we have no time for such a venture. Besides, the Romans would rip them to pieces sooner or later, and we will need them when they breach these walls." Simon grinned at the puzzled look upon John's face.

"I thought you said the Romans would never get in here?" John asked with a sideways glance.

"I said what my men want to hear, John. Truth is that we all must fight like beasts and kill as many as we can. Maybe we can demoralize their ranks, but they will get in here, especially through this unfit wall." Simon shook his head and patted the stones of the battlements. "The Romans knew which wall to attack; I was hoping they wouldn't notice this weaker section and give your wall a try, and then they would never get in." He gazed over the ramps as his face appeared to be filled with sorrow. "Why did you come here?" he sniffed, turning to face the men.

Judah felt a chill from the conniving stare of Simon. He glanced away, staring at the Romans, yet this did nothing to alleviate the tension. Judah was staring at supreme world power before him stretched out before the walls of Jerusalem. Smoke from cooking fires rose from the camp north of the wall as a cloud of dust drifted up from the horizon by the hooves of a few hundred cavalry.

John leaned forward, placing his hands on the stones. "Your attack today, was it successful?"

Simon smirked and crossed his arms over his chest. "You tell me. I hear your assault was stopped before it even began."

John stared at the arrogant man for a moment, noting his nicely groomed beard and hair. The man lived like a king, pampered and surrounded by wealth and women. John envied him and hated him, but he pushed these thoughts from his mind and licked his dry lips. "Our attack was halted by Roman soldiers disguised as labourers. Then to add to the confrontation, at least two cohorts waiting for us charged out from the Tenth camp. Our assault disintegrated and my forces fell back in disorder."

Simon laughed, glancing back at Yehoram and Bagdatus. "You have a rat problem, John. You know what rats do? They scurry here and there and carry disease that will kill you if you don't watch out."

"Speak plainly and not in riddles. I know we have a problem with spies, Simon. This is not new to me. I think I know where they come from." John stepped closer to the self-made king.

Simon looked shocked. "You accuse me?"

"Someone in your camp is working for the Romans." John leveled his eyes at Simon who up until now had been amused.

"If someone is in my camp working for the Romans, well then, you have someone in your camp passing information to the someone in my camp." Simon chuckled thinking of his word choice and then stroked his beard. "You so easily forget that my attacks were failures too." Simon paused for a moment and then continued, "It would appear we both have a problem."

"How do we solve it?" John asked obviously frustrated. "I have only caught two spies in the past and both are dead."

"Men grow desperate, John, above all you should know this. If you fail to inspire them they will look for another way, and if you fail to lead them they will turn on you." Simon watched a flash of anger in John's eyes and he smiled, provoking him. "I know you hate to hear this from me, but you must look to your inner circle of command. I caught three men, and they are all rotting away in prison without food. I hear their moans and my men hear them, it is to be a reminder of whose side one should be on."

"I do not wish to think of a traitor among my men," John coldly replied.

"You may not wish to think it, but that doesn't mean it is not there. Today I saw two carefully planned attacks by the best of my soldiers completely get foiled. How many assaults of yours have failed?" Simon asked.

"Two, what is your point?" John grumbled.

Simon hummed to himself. "Your men will think you're weak! That is obvious and when they unite against you, they will cast you from the walls." Simon watched a confused look spread across John's face. "Don't think I am actively working against you to steal power, it is out of my control." Simon watched John's face twitch and then he laughed. "You think *it is* me, don't you? Yes, you do! You think I am secretly stealing your plans and passing them to the Romans so you become unpopular and your men kill you, allowing me to take control."

"It does make sense," John retorted icily.

Simon shook his head. "I almost wish it was me, that is a brilliant plan, now is it? Sadly, for this one I cannot take the praise. The truth is someone works us both. You knew of my attacks this morning and you planned your own. Someone in either your command or mine passed this information to the Romans and this someone must be daring." Simon stared at Judah for a moment testing the man's resolve. When Judah glared back at him he simply smiled and looked away. "Will it all matter anyway, John? When the Romans attack these walls no information in the world will be useful from inside. It will be every man for himself."

"A spy can still do damage, Simon. Do not underestimate this one point: a spy can betray a city to its doom." John looked out over the Roman works.

"Then do as I do. Select men you have no doubt in, only those you trust unequivocally, and make this group small. Then double your guards at all your entrances and exits and give them the power to arrest anyone suspicious. Deal dreadfully and terribly with offenders, even suspects of treacherous activity, and your men will fear you more then they love you. Do this and the spy problem will vanish." Simon turned to John and said with a smile, "You see, I make my own law."

*　　*　　*

CHAPTER XXIV

May 2ⁿᵈ, 70 A.D. / 5ᵗʰ of Iyyar, 3830
Northern Roman position
The Base Camp of Titus
Midday

As Yosef walked he stared upwards and squinted. The sun had not a cloud to hide behind as it beat upon the ground like liquid fire raining upon the earth. The land stretching before him was barren of trees. All the valleys and fields surrounding Jerusalem had been stripped bare of all beauty native to the land, a necessity for the Romans erecting the three earthen ramps which lay stretching towards the high city walls on the northwestern side. Dust lingered in the air and Yosef shielded his face from a gust of wind. Sweat ran down the sides of his face and he glanced back at the formation of Roman cavalry arrayed in their finest armour, banners flying from their signi. Titus was at the very center, his breastplate and helmet glistening from the high polish they had received. The Prince gave a firm nod of reassurance to Yosef and the Jewish General looked away, focused on the task set before him.

To Yosef's left and right artillery of all sorts were being dragged by horses and men to placements surrounding the ramps. The lethal weapons were hurriedly unloaded and set up as men loaded the engines with an assortment of projectiles. A variety of scorpions were fitted with stone bullets the size of a man's fist or long iron lances. These deadly machines were fast loading as they could take a man's head clean from his shoulders in one sudden, grisly instant. The bulkier catapults took larger stones, and although they were slower to load, the simple purpose of these was to smash walls apart and clear swaths of enemy troops from ramparts. Yosef had seen such weapons devastate cities and armies in the past. He shuddered to think of what the Jewish soldiers were pondering as one hundred of the death-dealing war engines were positioned for the assault that was coming.

Yosef rubbed his bandaged, aching arm as he walked towards the middle dirt ramp. He was impressed how packed down and level the earthworks were. Over a month ago the ground before the city walls had been unforgiving to any wheeled engine which sought an easy approach under the watch of the walls. The terrain had been rocky and uneven, filled with holes, ruts, ditches, and ravines. When the Romans had arrived they had simply done what they do best: create an even battlefield.

To level the battleground had come at a high cost, but Titus had voiced his opinion over and over again, that no cost was too high in order to achieve victory. Titus would say, *"Our Father Vespasian watches over us all and so does the empire. They will weigh our courage and by the power of the gods they will not find us guilty of cowardice."* It was true and known by all that the Flavians could not succeed in Rome if they could not succeed in Judea.

Yosef passed through the shadow of Psephinus Tower to the middle ramp, then climbed it slowly and halted partway. He drew a white cloth from within his cloak and held it above his head for a moment before letting it drop. He watched the commotion upon the ramparts high above him as soldiers pointed and shouted to their comrades. They all knew who he was and what he had come to say. As Yosef waited, he glanced around him. He had made sure he was safely out of the distance from the bowmen, so not to repeat what had happened earlier. His arm still ached dreadfully from the healing wound, but at least he had cheated death once again.

Wicker hurdles stood all over the sides of the ramps, each one driven into the ground and fixed with wooden spikes. The hurdles closest to the walls had been covered in tarred leather and plated iron so they were virtually waterproof. Throughout the last couple of nights the Romans had kept a close watch on the ramps with hundreds of torches burning, legionaries on patrol, and scorpions set up covering the ramps, loaded with stone missiles. The Romans would not take a single chance of having a Jewish sortie burn the hurdles or destroy their ramps. If such a sortie burst from any of the northern or western gates, they would quickly find themselves engulfed in a volley of killing missiles which would tear them to pieces. The Jews had known this and therefore had passively stayed behind their high walls keeping a sharp eye on everything going on around them.

Finally Yosef saw a large group of soldiers appear on the battlements near Psephinus Tower. The men walked calmly along the wall staring at Yosef, and among them was John of Gischala and Simon ben Giora. Yosef quietly noted the significance of the two warlords.

"What do you want, Yosef? Has Titus' whelp become lonely? You wish for some proper Jewish comfort? I beg you, come, and have some!" John shouted aloud to the resounding chorus of laughter from the soldiers around him. He broadly smiled and leaned upon the stone as he gazed down at the small figure of the man he hated the most. "Has Titus deprived you of your fancy clothes? I know you adore them. Well, I can tell you one thing that will put your mind to ease. Someday soon, I promise you, a Jew like the thousands here will get close enough to kill you, and when they do, you can be buried in your fancy clothes and you will never be separated from them!"

"Are you finished, John?" Yosef called back clearly irritated.

John shook his burly head. "No, I tell you when that day comes and you bleed the ground red, there will be such a cry of joy rising up from the Temple courts that not even the beating feet of Titus' legions will stifle it. The sound of the shofar will not be enough to quench the happiness that will come to every Jewish man, woman, and child at the news of your death! You are a pig and one of them! Why do you waste your time approaching our city and our walls? You are not fit to even stand before this holy place."

"This holy city will be no more with talk such as this!" Yosef shouted back. "Look before you, I beg you, John. Your words may be of hate for me but surely you have pity for the lives of tens of thousands of your people? Look around you," Yosef turned, opened his hands, and gestured at all the artillery and ramps. "This is but a fragment of what comes for you. You have not even seen the beginning! What will you do once the ram touches the wall? It is too late when that happens! Titus offers you a life without slavery, you will be spared and the city not plundered. You can lay your arms down, open the gates, and the Temple will stay standing. The sacrifice will not change, and the priesthood will be left intact. Come and reason! This is the end for you, there is no other way."

"Have you forgotten your God? I see you no longer have faith in the mighty works of His hand! Our God will fight for us and Titus' legions will be driven away like the Seleucids! The legions will be swallowed up like Pharaoh's chariots! We shall sing the songs of Moses and celebrate for weeks. We will see the ancient hand of David raised up and Rome shall be smitten from the field of battle such as the Amalekites or the Philistines." John climbed upon the wall and lifting his hands high he shouted, "You think we fear you? I see four legions brought here with their pomp, gods, priests, plunder, and slaves and we tremble not. We are here, and here we stay! We shall not bend a knee nor offer prayers on behalf of Caesar no more! We are Jews and this is a Jewish city!"

Not a sign of vocal support could be heard from the walls. John had expected a shout of praise and elation with the end of his defence, but none came. He dared not look back as to appear weak but instead glared at Yosef. Pointing to the distant Roman camp John shouted, "Go back! Leave us!"

A pained expression filled the lines of Yosef's face. He thought about calling out again but held his tongue instead. He stared at the hardened men upon the walls, and some, he observed, looked nervous and agitated. They knew what was coming, and once it started, they would all become intimate with Roman policy towards stubborn city defenders. Cities in the past which put up strong resistance against Rome, yet finally yielded, brought with it the sword, rape, and total plunder. Complete devastation was at hand if a city was not victorious and Yosef knew Jerusalem was doomed. How Yosef knew this was simple, the man who led the legions was no ordinary general: it was Titus, son of the Emperor, and he had an impression to make before the entire Roman world, at whatever cost.

* * *

Judah stood in front of the wooden door contemplating whether he should even be here. The streets around him were silent and peaceful, but his mind was the exact opposite. Ever since listening to the argument between John and Yosef he had felt unnerved. Then the orders had been given and he had swallowed hard trying to be brave. As soon as he had found an opportunity, he had known exactly where to go. Yet now he hesitated, and this bothered him. Judah slowly raised his fist as it felt doubled in weight and clumsy. He stared at the quiet door for a moment, almost wishing nobody would be inside. Then it opened suddenly and Hadassah smiled at him.

Right away she noticed his downcast face and her smile vanished. "Is everything fine, Judah?"

His face grew pale and he shrugged stepping into the coolness of the home. Hadassah gently closed the door behind her and bolted it. She watched him cross the room and glance into the bedroom where her sick mother lay asleep. "She has not woken in a day. She speaks in her sleep and tosses and turns. I fear she doesn't have very long."

Judah turned and looked at Hadassah for a long moment memorizing her slender body, hair colour, and eyes. "You have my sympathy." He paused, choosing his next words carefully. "I have been posted to the Third Wall on the western defences, along with my men."

A silence filled the small home and a bird chirped somewhere from the street outside. As if not fully understanding what Judah had meant Hadassah quickly said, "The Third Wall? Isn't that where the Roman ramps are? You guard the Temple, why would you be posted there?"

Judah nodded sickly trying to maintain his courage which was thinning. "They will come soon, and Simon has requested soldiers from the Zealots. He cannot maintain maximum strength on both the west and the north, and so two hundred of John's men have been directed there."

"When do you go?" Hadassah asked bluntly.

"After I leave here, I will sleep on the wall tonight," Judah muttered as he lowered his gaze upon the stone floor.

Hadassah stiffened with shock and remained silent for a moment. The space between her and Judah seemed endless as the two fought back emotion and fear. Then she turned, walked over to a small niche in the wall and said, "Have a seat."

"What?" Judah responded puzzled.

"There," Hadassah pointed to a stool. "Have a seat." She bent down and began moving a few objects aside in the cubby hole. Hadassah scowled, peering in the low light and did not even think of lighting a lamp as she continued to move small bottles and cups aside.

Perplexed, Judah obeyed and quietly took a seat making sure his sword did not scrape the floor. He watched Hadassah for a moment and then looked away as she shook her head in frustration. It felt like an eternity to Judah as he sat upon the old wooden stool thinking about his future, however dim and dreary it appeared. Suddenly he heard a sound of triumph come from Hadassah as she found what she was looking for. When she turned around with a whisk of her gown upon the floor,

Judah saw her holding a beautiful ivory comb inset with small gems. He lifted his eyes to meet hers. She stepped forward and gently touched his chin. "Turn around," Hadassah said softly.

Judah obeyed and waited. He felt the touch as if it were a feather upon silk. Hadassah's hands were like magic, scented in jasmine. Gently taking the edges of his outer robe, she carefully slipped the heavy wool cloak from Judah's shoulders. He brought his arms slowly back to help her. Hadassah removed the cloak and carefully laid it on a table. Then ever so tenderly, she took his tough hair of knots and curls and began to comb. She applied a small amount of oil to the scalp and continued combing, one by one dragging the knots free. Judah felt the gentle tugs and listened to the bristles of the comb against his hair in absolute silence. His heart was suddenly calmed and his spirit seemed to lie down and rest.

It was as if everything in the world had suddenly vanished but them. Judah could picture them safely tucked away somewhere in a world with no Romans, no bureaucracy or masters, nobody who would tell them to do anything. It would just be the two of them, and they would be in love. Judah knew he loved her, he felt it so deeply that it hurt and burned within him, for in this moment Miriam's spirit seemed at peace. The memory of her did not surface. He felt warm and guiltless, almost to the point where he could smile. He wanted to touch Hadassah. He wanted to touch her hand and feel her skin against his fingers. He wanted to stand up, slip his arms around her waist and kiss her deeply, drinking in the beauty and loveliness that surrounded her. He dreamed of taking her away to some place far across the sea so they could start a new life and have a family. All of these things he yearned for, dreamed of, and longed to be a reality. The tragedy of Miriam plagued him, but now, in the stillness of Hadassah's home, the toil and agony melted away.

Suddenly, a loud shofar blast trumpeted somewhere in the city signaling the changing of the guard upon the western ramparts. Judah's fantasy of fleeing with Hadassah dissipated with the reminder of duty. As the horn was cut off, all Judah could do was sit upon the stool, craving Hadassah's affectionate touch, while she combed his hair in tender silence.

*   *   *

May 3rd, 70 A.D. / 6th of Iyyar, 3830
Western defences of Jerusalem
Dawn

With the first hint of sunlight, the drums began to beat and trumpets blared, awakening the Jewish fighters upon the ramparts. Men scrambled desperately for their weapons as shouts from the towers raised the alarm that the Romans were assembling. Amidst an orange haze from the sun splitting through a wispy curtain of cloud, century after century marched from the Fifth's camp and Titus' base. The columns of legionaries, boldly following their signi, appeared like a mighty armoured snake, slithering from their camps to the Jews who watched. Then with expert precision, the columns of each century began fanning outward into their respective rectangular battle formations according to the typical checkered legionary deployment of ten cohorts.

The Twelfth Legion formed to the left of the furthermost ramp and the Fifteenth Legion assembled upon the right side. The Fifth Legion marched further to the south, than wheeling to face the walls, began to form up as they would be stationed as reinforcements. The Jews could see what was happening as a clear path to the ramps lay between the legions.

The last centuries to emerge from the camps made up each legionary First Cohort with six centuries in each. These eighteen centuries from the three legions, burst forth with a new melody that thundered from trumpets accompanied by a rolling beat from animal hide drums. Once deployed in their battle formations, the three larger cohorts stomped the ground in a rhythmic beat as their vexilla were hoisted and their signi shook. A dyad of cornu trumpets sounded, one deeper than the other as a third descant melody wailed above the other drones sounding a battle song which the legionaries began to chant words unbeknownst to the Zealots upon the walls. The three cohorts marched into their usual place upon the right flank of each legion as the sound of thousands of hobnailed sandals beat the ground. Jewish soldiers gripped their spears and fought back fear as the iron studded aprons of the legionaries shook with every step causing a haunting reverberation of jingling to rise up from the ranks.

Centurions, made known by their transverse, blonde plumes, shouted orders at the front of each century. The optiones in the rear, however, kept the formations solid and spaced properly with the help of their long *hastilis*. A chorus of trumpets added to the spectacle as mounted tribunes and officers joined the two legions filling the space before the ramps while artillery crews dragged scorpions and *onager* catapults into position with the help of oxen and horses.

A cheer of praise erupted from over ten thousand vocal chords as Titus appeared riding from his camp wearing a breastplate of gold with the face of his father molded upon the front. A finely crafted gold and silver helm, topped with a bright red plume, sat upon his head with the wings of victory etched into the sides. Titus drew his gladius and waved it high in the air as if he had already conquered Jerusalem to the ovation of his troops. Achilles was arrayed in a vibrant red blanket covering most of his body along with the skin of a leopard. This likeness of Alexander the Great brought forth an explosion of cheers which was the response Titus had hoped for. With a broad smile upon his face, Titus thundered, "Victrix!" They responded unanimously with, "Imperator!" to suit his ego.

Titus was followed closely by Tiberius Alexander, Marcus Octavian, Titus Frigius, Sextus Cerealis, King Agrippa and King Sohaemus as they rode between the legions to the front. A new tune blasted from the trumpets to welcome the generals and suddenly order was restored to the legions as all thirty cohorts stood motionless.

From the right of the legions marched two long columns: one of Palmyrene bowmen led by light cavalry from Agrippa's force and the other Syrian infantry dispatched by King Sohaemus. The Palmyrene's were led to the front of the legions where they began spreading out into a skirmish line. A couple hundred servants dashed out from Titus' camp pushing hand carts filled with arrows and soon these were distributed among the archers to bolster their stocks. As this went on, the Syrians moved in front of the bowmen about five metres so not to block the archers, but to have enough time to join the immediate fray once the rams approached the walls.

With the stationing of over fifteen thousand men before the northwestern walls of Jerusalem, Titus turned to watch as three massive siege *aries* appeared from the camps, each drawn by twenty oxen. Each battering ram was suspended beneath a large testudo of a heavy timber framework and wooden wickers covered by metal plates and uncured animal hides on the sides and roof. Within each engine, was a massive beam with the head of a ram at the front. Each ram had been individually forged and shaped by the Roman engineers who furled the creature's eyebrows, curled the horns, and accentuated the menacing snarl upon each ram's lips. The head of each ram had been made from solid wood and then overlaid with molten iron. Once this was done, the craftsmen had shaped them according to their skill and then fitted each one to the end of a perfectly balanced beam suspended within the testudo by a balance arm supported by cables and a rope in the middle.

With the proper force, the ram could be drawn back and then catapulted forward, appearing to any bystander as an enormous tortoise head projecting out from within the shell-like apparatus. After repeated blows, according to the strength of a wall, the stubborn iron head of the ram and the exhaustingly hard work of the legionaries within had the power to crush stone, which was the desired effect.

The drumming continued as Titus silently watched the rams form up before the three ramps. Another blast from the cornu hailed the arrival of three dominating siege towers slowly approaching the rear of the legions, as they were drawn by twice as many oxen which had dragged the rams. The towers seemed like mountains to the Jewish defenders as they watched the wide, black plated engines approaching like great monsters. The Romans cheered their creations and Titus proudly grinned as they crawled by at a snail's pace.

When the towers were in place, one in the middle and the other two on the extreme left and right of the rams, the trumpets ceased. Following the ensuing silence, a contingent of legionaries from the Zeugma legion trotted up to the three towers and entered the structures where massive beams were spaced out inside to push the great machines forward. The oxen moaned as they were unclasped from the towers and led to the rear where they were hooked up again.

Then, under the cover of hurdles, servants dashed forward with great coils of rope and ran ahead of the towers under the watch of the Jews. The servants dragged the heavy ropes to stakes of wood which had been driven into the ground just under ten metres from the city walls. The Jews were tempted to shoot at them but the servants moved quickly. With much haste, the servants secured the ropes around the stakes, ran back to the towers and hooked the ropes to the harnesses of the oxen so that they might pull the towers forward by walking in the opposite direction, thus using the stakes as a pulley system. The men from the Zeugma would aid the oxen in hauling the towers to the stakes and from there, with all their might, they would push them as close to the walls as permitted.

However, the first movement upon the soon-to-be battlefield was not the towers or the legions, but the three testudo battering rams. After a few moments of frustration on behalf of the oxen, they finally pulled the rams up to the edge of the ramps and halted. Then servants were dispatched to the teams of beasts and they were swiftly unharnessed and led away.

Titus gently nudged Achilles forward with his heels and stopped near one of the mighty rams. He squinted up at the high walls looming before him and resisted the temptation of calling out to them to surrender one last time. Instead, apathetically he shouted, "Once the ram touches the wall, the fury of *Roma* has descended upon your city. There is no hope. *Silent enim leges inter arma!*" He turned in his saddle and shouted, "Jupiter be with us!" Then with a wave of his hand the Syrian infantry suddenly rushed forward and disappeared into the bodies of the three great *testudines*. With a loud grunt the rams began to move up the ramps at a slow menacing speed.

The Palmyrene archers jogged forward and with a single command fitted their bows with arrows and waited. Behind the skirmish line of bowmen, nearly a hundred scorpions were brought forward loaded with stone missiles and heavy iron spears. Following this deployment, the entire front cohorts of the Twelfth and Fifteenth shifted forward with a synchronized step as they approached the rear of the ballista line. Commands were given and larger catapults and *onagri* were loaded with rocks covered in pitch as men stood at the ready with torches waiting to unleash hell as the drums continued to beat.

Titus turned his mount around and trotted back to his legionary generals and kings as they watched the rams crawl up the ramps. Titus gazed over the thousands of men stretched out before him and grinned with pride. He glanced at Octavian, Frigius, Cerealis, and Alexander and gave an abrupt nod. "When the ram strikes, I want a full attack. The Fifth will be held in reserve, so that should keep the Jewish forces spread out."

"What of the Fretensis?" Frigius asked.

"They are assembling to the east, but will not be deployed today." Titus glanced at the generals. "I want the enemy guessing." He pointed at the city and said, "Better for us if they don't see our entire army concentrating on one point. With Antiochus and his cavalry covering the south, we will slowly suffocate them into submission." Titus turned to Agrippa and said, "After the ram has touched the wall, you can have your three contingents of Palmyrenes ascend the towers to provide cover. I don't want the Jews rushing out to try and burn the rams."

*   *   *

Judah stood among his men crammed along the ramparts, watching in silence. Adam and Moshe stood on his left and Caleb on his right. They held their peace with a grim sense of dread as the impregnable battering rams were pushed up the ramps to the sounds of grunting men. Judah could see clouds of dust drifting out from underneath each testudo as the crews struggled up the dirt earthworks under the immense weight of the machines. He could hear men shouting from within and then a single voice counting for the others and encouraging them amidst the stuffy, stifling, cramped space. Still the three siege towers remained motionless.

Judah took a step back and glanced down the long row of fighters. Over three hundred bowmen clustered the ramparts with countless numbers of Zealots and Idumeans clutching spears, shields, and drawn swords. A short, squat, bearded man caught Judah's gaze and stepped out from the ranks, shuffling his way along the narrow space. When he drew close he cursed and shook his head. Judah recognized the man as Yakov, one of John's captains sent with the detachment of two hundred to reinforce Simon's troops. The man looked frustrated and roused into a fury as he fixed the uncomfortable leather breastplate strapped to his chest, then swore shooting a quick glance back out at the legions.

"Judah, what should I do?" Yakov growled.

Judah scowled at the man, looking confused. "What do you mean?"

"Archers are a damned waste against those rams and you know it! And those towers, we'll get slaughtered! Titus is bound to put archers in them and they will be higher than our own walls," Yakov said irritably, gazing back at the looming Psephinus Tower where Simon ben Giora safely watched the brewing Roman forces.

"Are the Palmyrenes out of range? Shoot at them! Yakov, you don't need my advice!" Judah retorted scowling and frustrated at what he perceived as incompetence.

"The Palmyrenes are the least of my worries, we have no artillery! Once those bastards give us a volley there will be nobody left up here." Yakov stared at Judah for a quick moment and sensing he was getting nowhere turned, spit over the side of the ramparts and marched away.

Judah noticed a few men glance nervously back at him from the reckless words Yakov had spoken. "Don't worry, we can outlast them. We hold the wall and defend God's city," Judah said, not really sure if he really believed the first part himself. He glared up at the Psephinus Tower, upset that the 'King of the Sicarii' should cower while they were all exposed spelling certain death. These were the prized warriors of the Jewish forces, the elite veterans who had been fighting for years, and their silence disturbed Judah. He stepped between his Lions and while tightening his face he drew his sword and shouted, "We hold them here! Guard yourselves and kill anything in those towers should they come near! My brothers, today we fight like beasts, like Lions!"

Either because of patriotic fervour or fear, everyman upon the ramparts suddenly shouted with defiance at the observing Romans and shook their weapons in the air. For a moment the Jews felt like champions upon their invincible walls as the Romans did not seem so threatening. However, all voices were quickly cut short as the fighters crowded against the parapets to watch the first testudo halt about a metre from the end of the ramp. Beyond this was a sheer drop as the height from the ramp to the ground was about seven metres. Every Jewish fighter knew this gap was for when the wall collapsed under the pounding rams, thus, creating a natural breach which would spell the capture of the Bezetha.

Judah gripped his sword and gazed over the wall at the middle ramp and the large testudo directly below him. Everything was silent for a moment and he quickly looked to the other engines. The hush had picked up the curiosity of many fighters as they stared down at the peculiar Roman creations, most of them never seeing such weaponry before. It was as if no life existed within the shell-like beasts of the battering rams as the sun reflected from the iron plates upon their roofs. A nervous fighter called out that maybe the Romans had fallen asleep, and this joke drew a light chuckle down the ramparts. Then ever so cautiously, Judah watched as a shield poked out from the rear of the middle testudo. A second and a third shield quickly followed as men cowered behind the only protection between them and hundreds of people who hated them.

"What are they doing?" Caleb asked shaking his head.

Judah gulped. "Securing the rams." He looked at his friend and touched his shoulder. "You are a man of honour. I have never known such a man. Your father would have been proud."

Caleb held Judah's gaze for a second, then looked down at the ram and concentrated on the hammering sound of spiked posts being driven into the packed earth of the ramp by men concealed behind the shields. A few times Caleb caught a glimpse of an iron hammer rising high into the air only to disappear from sight followed by a deep thud. Then there was a moment of eerie silence again as he imagined sweating men in armour, pushing past one another inside the testudo with a thick coil of rope which was firmly bound to the posts securing the engine.

Caleb gently closed his eyes and whispered, "*Elohim*, give me peace and courage."

The tension was great. As all the Jewish fighters spotted the back of the swinging ram appear from the rear of the testudo, a man upon the wall suddenly shouted, "God, no!" Following the man's shriek a loud grunt echoed from within the center testudo as the Syrians swung the beam forward with a mighty heave. The iron ram's head shot out of the front and cracked against the wall with a sickening jerk causing the stone beneath everyone's feet to vibrate. As the Syrians drew the ram back for another thrust, an eerie murmur arose from within the city. The sound began as a groan and with the second strike of the ram against the stone, Jewish soldiers began to turn their attention to the poignant resonance coming from human vocal chords.

Judah noticed some men already facing the haunting sound with ghostly pale faces. He squinted in the sunlight, speechless, as he watched hundreds of people gathered upon their rooftops petitioning to heaven with loud weeping. Some threw their hands up while others lay covering their faces and shouting. He watched an elderly man collapse upon the vacant streets below him and listen to the steady pounding beyond the wall. The repeated thuds were joined a few moments later by a chorus of two more equally steady crashes against the wall from the other testudo engines. A look of trepidation was so deeply ingrained upon the elderly man's face it disturbed Judah to see such utter frailty and he looked away.

"They weep because of a bleak future," a young Jewish soldier said trembling next to Caleb. "They weep, for hope is lost." The man groaned as he inclined his ear towards the sobbing which drifted through the city streets.

"Pray," Caleb softly said. "Find courage, for we battle the enemies of God."

A large crash of shattering rock suddenly exploded into a hailstorm of shrapnel. Three bodies were hurled backwards in a shower of blood from the rampart at Caleb's far left as men shouted with panic. Judah quickly came to life giving orders above thundering impacts that showered down upon them from the barrage of stone missiles.

The Jewish fighters struggled amidst the onslaught as men toppled great rocks down upon the testudines, and threw flaming fire brands upon the iron plated roofs. The Jewish bowmen crowded upon the battlements fired volleys of arrows at the Palmyrene archers who quickly charged forward and took up positions behind wicker hurdles. Suddenly, three large contingents of archers broke away from the hurdles and ran to the towers. Soon clusters of Palmyrene bowmen began to emerge upon the turrets of each tower as they swiftly fixed their bowstrings with arrows. With the crack of whips upon the brute hides of snorting oxen, the great siege towers slowly began to lurch forward.

Despite their cover, the Jews upon the ramparts were enduring hell as their numbers were slowly reduced to bloodied and cleaved piles along the walkways. The stone missiles crashed and shook the walls showering men's heads with shrapnel as they ducked with every incoming volley. Heads were removed from shoulders with sickening precision as fellow comrades recoiled in terror or retched from foul smells. Wounded fighters bleated out in pain, dragging themselves away to escape death.

Judah helped direct the defences as best he could, but he knew they needed to do more against the battering rams which smashed the wall with repeated blows. That was when a message came from Psephinus Tower. A short man, cowering under the missile fire, ran along the ramparts shouting for Judah and protecting his face from flying bits of debris. When he found the Lion commander he was nearly overcome by the bloodied bodies lying about and the desperation upon the men's faces. He shook a dying man's grasp from his cloak and then shouted, "Simon wants teams of men to rope down over the side and try to burn them out!"

Judah stared at the man with wild eyes and shook his head as he instinctively ducked another stone bullet which ricocheted off the battlements and disappeared into the city behind him. He had received a blow from a rock shard that had grazed his cheek bone, and now an open wound gaped from his face, bleeding into his beard and down his neck. He momentarily touched the wound with a grimace and stared at the sticky blood upon his fingers. He gave the man a strange look and shouted over the havoc, "What does Simon want to do? Speak up!"

"He wants you to send men over the side with torches onto the roof of the middle ram. We can sabotage it and try to burn out the men inside!" The man winced as a loud impact from a stone nearby shook the wall. "We have more soldiers organizing assaulting parties for the other testudo engines so you need not worry about them."

"That is madness!" Judah yelled making his point. "Perhaps you wish to be in one of those parties? Those men will get slaughtered!"

The man nodded and held up his hands wanting to hurry this conversation on and return to the safety of Psephinus Tower. "It is daring and foolhardy, yes, but it is all we got at this point. Simon wants to strike back! I think Simon wants to keep them busy and try to damage them where the Romans least expect it. He is working on a two-wave attack against the cohorts and the towers so consider that move more maddening." The man grinned at Judah and then continued, "You're in command here. Pick twenty men and send them over immediately. We must clear the rams and as much artillery as possible for our attack." The man turned and then quickly looked back at Judah. "I hate to be the bearer of bad news, but Simon wants you to lead the first wave." Then he ran back towards the tower.

Judah noticed Caleb slightly bent over as he stared at him. "It's not good if that is what you're thinking!" Judah shouted at his friend and then looked away. Judah gazed over the rampart and down into the Bezetha where reinforcements were clustered below. "Bring up lots of rope and torches now!"

By the time coils of rope and dozens of burning torches had been brought up to the ramparts, dead and wounded men lay strewn about in bloody heaps, some corpses unrecognizable. "Aim for the towers!" Judah shouted at Yakov's bowmen as a melee hailstorm began to rain down upon them from the towers which halted about twenty metres from the wall. Judah witnessed the skill of the Palmyrene bowmen as they constantly seemed to be playing games with the Jews. In an unpredictable dance, a Palmyrene would reveal himself, loose an arrow, and duck down with another instantly appearing to do the same thing. The situation was quickly deteriorating with Jewish fighters getting picked off one by one. Judah hollered at Yakov's bowmen a second time and then received a quick response to the Palmyrene threat as volley after volley of arrows poured into the siege towers.

The feeling upon the ramparts among the surviving Jewish fighters was one of frustration and rage. If one was to risk a glimpse over the wall at the Roman positions they may be able to count the enemy dead on both hands as a majority of the arrows fired by the Jews had ended up embedded into the wicker hurdles or the ground. Against the towers, arrows had little effect. Other than having killed only a handful of Palmyrene archers, Judah was just relieved that the deadly, point blank missile volleys had slackened as the enemy bowmen realized the skill of the Jews who congregated as close as they could get to the towers and shot at anything that moved.

As the Romans concentrated their efforts, they moved their artillery up to be more effective. The pressure upon the northwestern Jewish defences began to escalate as causalities increased and men became fearful, thus minimizing their own ability to retaliate. Judah could see the effect the concentrated Roman artillery was having, as most of his fighters remained crouched down behind the riddled battlements. He looked to his left across the suburbs of the Bezetha and his eyes traced trails of black smoke billowing from scattered homes as the newer streets of Jerusalem suffered from the barrage of missile fire. Judah also noticed a mass of over a thousand Jewish soldiers in tight formation approaching the battered walls. The double wave attack that the messenger from Psephinus Tower had spoken of was clearly brewing. This meant he had to act fast.

Judah gave orders to Caleb and Adam to assemble volunteers for the attack. Out of the men, Moshe, one of Judah's own fighters and one of the last remaining survivors from his Lions, decided to volunteer. The men gathered around Judah under the continued crashing of stones and listened to the instructions as the Lion commander shouted until he was hoarse.

"We will secure ropes to the wall and over you go! Do not hesitate and drop as fast as you can. Yakov will have all of his archers concentrate on the towers and artillery and any Roman bowmen who may spot you. Three men will have shields. Protect each other as best as you can and work swiftly. Pry up the plates with these," Judah held up an iron bar and the men nodded. "Once you have an opening, shove some bitumen inside along with a torch. We will toss down stacks of bitumen which you can use, so keep your heads up. Do not stand or try to climb back up for they will pick you off quickly. Just stay on top of the rams and help will come.

"We are planning a two wave attack of thousands; we hope to destroy much of their artillery and the rams as well. During this attack we will have men who can pull you up, or you can join the fight. Questions?" Judah waited for a moment and then gave a sharp nod as torches and pry bars were handed out.

"Leave anything that would weigh you down!" shouted Adam as he mingled with the group trying to reassure them.

Judah joined Caleb as he watched the ropes getting tied to the walls and men strapping the iron bars to their waists while others secured spears upon their backs for quick access. "How many volunteered?" Judah asked Caleb.

"Twenty-six. We passed the word along and none of Simon's men wanted it. Even though we needed twenty the other six wouldn't hear of it, they refused to stand down. Leave it to the best."

Judah nodded and patted his friend's shoulder. "Are you joining me for the assault?"

Caleb was quiet for a moment, then scowled. "You mean the frontal attack being assembled?" Judah nodded and Caleb looked shocked for a moment. "We're watching things up here. There are a couple thousand of them down there, why do we have to join?"

"Turns out, Simon has ordered me to lead the first wave," Judah said with a blank expression.

"Simon ordered you? Well, to hell with him. We're John's men!" Caleb retorted loudly shaking his head. "It is suicide to lead that attack, Judah."

"You think I don't know that? We're temporarily under Simon's command. I must lead this attack, I don't have a choice," Judah mumbled the words which were barely audible for Caleb to hear above the constant pounding of the Roman artillery machines.

Caleb bit his lower lip and then sighed, giving a pitiful nod. "I will join you in the ranks."

"Judah!" Yakov shouted. "At your word!"

Judah turned and looked over the twenty-six men one last time. Only a few could manage to carry torches as most preferred taking personal weapons and iron pry bars. "We will drop fire brands down for you if needed. God be with you all." He walked over to Moshe and embraced him firmly and while looking into his eyes said, "God give you strength, Moshe. You have been one of my best."

"We will not let you down, Judah," Moshe replied as he tightened the rope firmly in his grasp, turned and climbed over the wall followed by the rest of the men.

Moshe felt the rope burn his strong hands as he descended quickly. He heard a scream above him and then pressed close against the wall as a body, pierced by three arrows, fell past him, crashing down upon the roof of the testudo with a loud thud. Moshe gritted his teeth and loosened his grip upon the rope so he slid even faster. The ropes dangling to his left and right were still absent of men as he knew he had been the first over the wall and the quickest.

The testudo was a large siege engine, and it felt as if he could almost touch the roof with his feet, but it was still another five metres below him. Moshe stared straight ahead and watched as numerous Palmyrene archers, watching the human chain descend by ropes, attempted to warn the Syrians inside the siege engines. However, the Palmyrene's were forced to seek cover behind their hurdles as a mass of arrows from Yakov's bowmen were loosed from the city walls. Moshe spotted a single Palmyrene stumble backwards with a shriek, as the shaft of an arrow protruded from his face, while his desperate hands clawed at the wound. It was like advertising the perfect target for Yakov's bowmen as another three arrows struck the man in the chest and shoulder knocking him to the ground where he screamed for a moment, trying to crawl away, then expired in a bloody heap.

Moshe rolled to his right as he narrowly missed getting skewered by an iron javelin fired from a scorpion. He caught his breath and stared up at the rope nearest him. He saw the figures of six men scrambling down, one even wounded with an arrow in his leg but unwilling to give up. Looking down the wall where another assaulting party descended upon a ram, he watched sickly as they struggled amidst a hail of arrows. Moshe saw three men plunge to their deaths with screams as the archers on the walls above tried their best to give them cover.

The towers were another issue. He could hear shouts from the tops as bowmen tried to shoot at them from the sides, but the Jewish archers furiously worked to prevent this. One was successful as Moshe saw a Palmyrene, caught through the throat by an arrow, topple over the side and scream as he fell to the ground, his body snapping under the weight of the impact.

It had seemed like an eternity for Moshe to reach the testudo, but with a heave away from the wall, he let go of the rope and landed upon the roof. Instantly he reacted to the perilous mission which faced him. He climbed across the stinking, uncured animal hides and immediately went to work tearing at the roof like a mad beast digging a hole to escape a terrifying prey. For all he knew, the Syrians operating the ram inside had no idea of the danger lurking above as they would be unable to hear anything upon the roof due to the noise and chaos within. As Moshe frantically worked, more Jewish fighters joined him as they dropped from the ropes. The men tore at the hurdles, cut through the ropes that bound them and pried apart the iron plates, ignoring the shouts from the Palmyrene archers who attempted to warn the Syrians operating the ram.

"Grab the torches and get those shields up!" Moshe shouted as one of the men dropped dead over the side of the engine, pierced through the heart by an arrow. In another second, three men hefting heavy shields were positioned on the edge of the ram protecting the Jews who fought to dislodge sections of the roof. Torches were dropped down to them along with bundles of dry bitumen and they continued to work frantically with excitement as they saw the possibility of achieving a minor victory.

"Moshe watch out for...!" a fighter began to shout as suddenly a spear point stuck him in the throat from a Syrian infantry man who had emerged from the testudo. The Jewish fighter fought against the force of the jerking spear for a brief second as a fountain of blood soaked his hands and chest. Then his eyes rolled back and his heavy body toppled over onto the Syrian soldier who lost his footing and fell off the side of the ramp with a scream.

"Stop them!" Moshe hollered as he saw five more Syrian spearmen appear. A number of the Jews scurried to the edge of the testudo and thrusting their spears and swords, managed to delay the angry Syrians who called for more aid. "There!" Moshe cheered heroically as he pried up a section of the plating, captivated with a thirst for blood as he watched the leather cords and ropes snap under the force. "Light it, quickly!" he shouted with a grunt from the weight of the plates. Suddenly a spear point came jabbing straight at him through the hole and sliced his exposed right arm. Moshe cringed, nearly releasing his grip on the heavy plates and then shouted for help.

A large Jewish man behind Moshe stepped forward with his iron pry bar gripped in his massive hands and roaring like a lion he struck the spear head, snapping the bronze point clean from the shaft. A bundle of bitumen was shoved desperately into the hole as curses could be heard from within. Then a flaming torch was plunged into the flammable, dry kindling. The fire consumed the bitumen almost immediately as shouting and coughing erupted from within the ram. With this new found energy, Moshe shoved the ignited bitumen deeper into the hole with a kick and then let go of the plating which sealed the trap as he gave an exhausted hoot of joy.

A cheer erupted from the Zealots as dirty, black smoke began to pour from the belly of the siege engine as the ramming abruptly ceased. Within seconds, coughing, cursing, and sputtering Syrians began stumbling out the rear of the testudo followed by jeers from Jewish fighters upon the walls. The Palmyrenes sought to cover the disillusioned Syrian retreat, but the Jewish bowmen reacted quickly and began raining down volleys of arrows upon the frantic, exposed men. As Moshe watched, his eyes beheld a single glorious moment where droves of Syrian soldiers were cut down in a bloody mess while they fled, surrendering the ramps and engines to the Jewish forces.

*　　*　　*

Titus and the legionary generals had sat upon their horses in shock when they saw the desperate Jewish parties repel down upon the testudines and ignite them. For a moment, Titus had not known what to do when he realized the Jews were being successful. He had expected the Zealots dangling upon the ropes to get slaughtered pathetically by a combination of artillery and bowmen, but it had been completely the opposite. The Jewish archers upon the ramparts had provided quick cover fire to their repelling crews with deadly accuracy. Now with smoke billowing out of two battering rams, Titus suddenly shouted for cohorts three and six from the Fulminata to advance swiftly and recover the engines.

"Concentrate all scorpions and onagri on Psephinus and the battlements from the center, and clear the bastards off the walls!" Titus yelled. He glanced to the far left where the third Jewish assaulting party had been annihilated and thanked the gods that at least one of the rams was out of danger.

"My lord, what of Agrippa's men?" Titus Frigius shouted.

Prince Titus threw his arms up angrily and cursed as he replied, "Do you think I care about them? If we don't act now the rams will be lost and those sacks of swine will destroy the ramps or attack the men in the towers!"

A trumpet blast was sounded and orders were speedily sent to the catapult crews. They quickly redirected their deadly machines, aimed, and began pelting the battlements. The Roman crews worked mechanically as they reloaded, cranked the arms of the onagri down, and then yanked the levers to send enormous stone projectiles at incredible speeds.

Where the Fulminata was positioned, a tribune wildly rode to the rear and delivered a message to an optio. The officer then ran to the front and relayed the order to a frustrated *pilus prior* centurion who had just watched the idiotic, acrobatic act the Zealots had just pulled off. With the delivered orders he signaled the other centurions in the centuries of the cohort and then turned and bellowed, "Agrippa's men have failed! Granted, they are not legionaries! But they have disgraced us! The Syrians have given up the rams and fled like virgin women wagging their tits. Now let's reclaim them back! We, the Third Cohors, would never have run!" His cohort gave a deep shout in agreement and the centurion rejoined the front of his century. "Prince Titus watches us lads. Let's remind him we are not the same men who fled with Gallus! Ready!" He waited and stared down the line as the other centurions drew their swords and the signi of each century was raised. "March!"

The Third Cohort stepped forward with shields locked and pila lowered while the Sixth Cohort matched their pace. The two formations swiftly closed the gap between them and the two testudines which belched clouds of black smoke. The legionaries approached silently as they stepped over the bodies of the slain Syrians who fled the peril of fire only to be picked off by archers upon the walls. Shouts rose up from the tight Roman ranks as arrows began to rain down upon them. The legionaries met the Jewish volley by raising their heavy scuta to the sound of thuds as arrows peppered their ranks.

A few soldiers screamed in pain as some darts found exposed legs or thighs. One of the centurions, who quickly recognized the Jewish adjustment of their aim, placed his whistle to his lips and emptied the air in his lungs. Then with a wolf-like bellow, he shouted for the ranks to form a testudo. The optiones leapt into action, assembling the men and keeping them tightly formed as sections of the cohorts split apart, swiftly forming two dense squares under the hailstorm of arrows.

Moshe and the other Jewish fighters upon the rams watched both cohorts form their squares successfully as a few wounded legionaries limped back to the safety of their legions. Undeterred in their mission, the cohorts continued their advance now formed into four impregnable testudo clusters. These new formations worked wonderfully against the arrow storm the Jews sent down upon them as the darts imbedded themselves harmlessly into the shields or grazed off the flat surfaces. Moshe heard a man behind him grunt and fall back with two arrows lodged into his chest.

"Stay down!" Moshe shouted, realizing that despite the covering fire form their comrades, there were still hundreds of Palmyrene bowmen who wanted their heads.

"What do we do? We can't stay here, Moshe!" shouted one of the Zealot's, staying as low to the ram's roof as possible.

Moshe could feel the heat emanate from the roof's iron plates as the fire roared beneath his feet and he quickly covered his eyes from the smoke. "They will come. We can't go anywhere or we're dead. Just wait, our brothers will relieve us!"

As if in prophetic fulfillment at the words just uttered, the large doors of the city gate to the left of the middle ramp opened and a fury of shouting Jewish fighters poured through in the hundreds. Moshe watched them stream endlessly by, their feet shaking the ground. The size of the sudden attack was naturally funneled between the ramps, as the Zealots and Idumeans scaled the dirt earthworks to spread out. The charge shook the ground and the Jews delivered a deafening war cry as they careened towards the surprised Roman formations before them. Ignoring the threat from the walls, the Palmyrenes in the siege towers began to rain death upon the Jews, picking targets and sending arrows speedily into victims who collapsed amidst the charge. The Palmyrene bowmen upon the ground cowering behind the wicker hurdles quickly abandoned them and fled as the Roman testudo formations hurriedly began to reform into their rectangular battle units to face the approaching onslaught.

"Get into rank!" yelled desperate centurions as they ran along their frantic centuries. "Prepare for volley!" The legionaries, fighting against panic from the thousands of charging Jewish warriors, jostled into their positions clumsily and spaced their ranks, drawing back their spears, waiting for the command to hurl destruction upon the thundering enemy. By the time they were ready another two cohorts from the Fulminata had joined the force and swiftly took their positions. Hardly a moment passed before the command was given by tribunes shadowing the ranks, and with a heavy grunt from nearly two thousand legionaries, they hurled their pila in a torrent of sheer terror at the attacking Jews.

Whatever shields the Zealots and Idumeans carried were quickly reduced to splinters as they broke or split with the impact of the spears. These broken shields were quickly discarded to continue the charge, but the attack had faltered momentarily under the horrendous results of the volley as men lay upon the ground bleeding in agony and screaming. The Jewish attack, however, lost not an ounce of momentum as they bravely hurled themselves at the Roman lines with vicious curses, gritted teeth, and blades eager for flesh.

The Romans met the attack as a solid wall, like water breaking upon rock, as a loud crunch and clash of steel echoed above the din. Gladii flashed in and out as legionaries lunged with thrusts at their Jewish enemies, who likewise jabbed spears and blades at the faces and arms of legionaries. Blood sprayed up from the ranks as swords sawed across flesh; men screamed as both sides shoved and heaved one another. Spear shafts that broke upon Roman shields were used as clubs or cast away as men beat with their fists or tried to tackle their opponents. Wounded from both sides could be seen attempting to crawl away from the fighting as they moaned and wailed, some missing limbs, others trying to hold their entrails from falling out, as ghastly wounds dripped blood from hanging muscle and flesh. All around the fighting intensified as another Jewish wave of a thousand burst from the gates charging across the ground. Clusters from this second wave of Zealots broke off in an attempt to finalize the destruction of the rams and these numbers began to dwindle as the Palmyrene archers in the towers turned their attention to these men out of fear of hitting their own troops.

With the second Jewish wave the attack swelled and buckled under the pressure. Prince Titus immediately saw the danger, and rather than commit more cohorts into the action, he demanded that scorpions and onagri attempt at slowing the charge down. This worked only for a few seconds as the onager missiles tore through Jewish ranks sending a splatter of blood, limbs, and bodies into the air. However, as soon as the Jews were under the range of the catapults, Tiberius shouted for the Prince to reinforce the attack or outflank it by sending in a few cohorts from the Fifth Legion. Titus, afraid to use men from the Fifteenth in case of Jewish attacks from the north, sent a rider to urge forces from Sextus' legion to attack the rear of the Jewish sortie which was quickly escalating into a full scale battle. Then sending a runner to the Fulminata with instructions for another cohort to join the attack, Titus rode forward to survey the situation from a close vantage point, despite Tiberius' warnings.

"Get the men back into lines!" Titus shouted as he pointed his gladius at an optio who held his hastile sideways pressed up against the backs of a number of legionaries who were inching away from the fight. The man shot the Prince a worried look and Titus saw the shaft of a broken arrow jutting out from the man's thigh as he limped in pain. Blood oozed down the side of his face from a wound to his forehead and his cheek was swollen. Titus locked eyes with the man for a brief moment and then wildly galloped down the line of struggling troops from the renewed vigour flooding the tide of Jews pressing into their ranks.

A company of mounted guards, armed with lances and oval shields, quickly followed the eager Prince. Titus wheeled Achilles around to face the mounted contingent and stared at them with streaks of sweat glistening upon his face.

"The Boars need to join the fight! The men are lingering!" Titus shouted to no one in particular. "You," Titus shouted pointing to one of the mounted guards with four arrows embedded into his shield. "Ride swiftly and tell Marcus to form up his Boars and flank the dogs! We cannot wait for the Fifth Macedonica!" The trooper gave a sharp nod, swung his horse around, and thundered off with clumps of earth kicking up from the sharp hooves of his stallion. "We have to maintain order," Titus said scanning the battle line. Then he swore as he watched the dark billows of smoke continue to pour out from two of the rams.

*   *   *

Judah parried a sword thrust and then was pushed back by a heavy scutum. He shouted savagely at the legionary, throwing his body into the shield, and saw fear in the man's eyes as he hunkered behind the scutum protecting his face. Judah felt a steady shove behind him as Jewish fighters at his back pressed forward. He narrowly dodged another harrowing attempt from the attacking legionary as the gladius point seared past him, cutting the hand of another Jew who cursed loudly with a shriek. The sword instantly retracted and up came the scutum in another strong heave as Judah fought against the pressure. He stepped back, nearly tripping over a body lying upon the ground caked in dirt and blood, whose face was unrecognizable as it had been pulverized by feet.

A spear head from the second Roman rank suddenly tore past Judah and skewered a man next to him as it ripped through the Zealot's throat. Blood splattered upon Judah's face and stung his eyes. His mind was a swirl of chaos as he reached up and gripped the spear shaft to stable himself from toppling over. With one eye closed from the warm blood upon his face, he tried to yank the spear away from the legionary's grasp.

The stubborn Roman fought trying to reclaim his spear while the dying Jew convulsed and tried to scream as his throat was torn apart with blood soaking his chest. The choking Zealot gave one more violent tug and then with a spasm, as both hands clutched the spear in his throat, he finally collapsed. Judah stumbled back and the spear was yanked from the legionary's grasp.

Judah fell hard to the ground with the spear in one hand and his sword instinctively pointing upward as he expected to be stabbed to death. The body of the dead Zealot behind him broke his fall and he rolled over the man with what little space had opened up around him. Judah watched his opponent, who had narrowly missed skewering him as he had fallen, quickly leap forward with scutum poised for attack and the flash of steel at his side. In that moment Judah thought he would die. The legionary gave a shout of defiance and knocked Judah's sword aside. With a grimness of hatred and beastly rage in the legionary's eyes, Judah watched as the gladius was readied for the killer blow.

Judah had not the strength to scream, but in his mind he cried out to God to save him. However, as the Roman leaned forward to bring his sword down, a spear suddenly thrust overtop of Judah and punctured the man in his shoulder between two plates of his segmented armour. The legionary fell back with a shriek and dropped his sword. The wounded Roman grabbed the spear shaft as a tug of war ensued.

Judah watched as another three legionaries quickly pressed forward to rescue their wounded comrade as he staggered against the agony of the lodged spearhead. The spear suddenly broke free followed by a gush of blood over the Roman's armour and then he was dragged away to safety between the rows of soldiers who filled the gap.

Judah felt hands grab him by his cloak and haul him backwards as he was pulled from the fray. It was then that he realized he was not in a dream but was still alive. Simultaneously he noticed the piles of dead lying amidst the pressing bodies of fighting men. The smell of urine and excrement was nearly overpowering as he suddenly felt like weeping. He still clung to his sword, not knowing what was happening as he continued to be dragged back. Judah became disillusioned, confused of which side he was on, and he suddenly panicked, believing that it was Romans dragging him away to be crucified. With this terrifying thought, Judah tried to twist away violently from the hands clutching his garments and he shouted in alarm kicking at the soiled ground.

"Help me!" Judah called out finding his voice. He heard a muffled response behind him, as if he was immersed under water, and gazing to the heavens above he shrieked without shame, "No! Help me! Ima! Miriam!"

"Judah, Judah!" Adam shouted back as he flipped his friend over and pressed his face near Judah's.

Judah's hand shot up and touched the side of Adam's face, soiled by dirt and blood. He held it firmly and then his mind was restored and he knew he had been rescued. "Adam, what is happening?" Judah pitifully sputtered.

"We have to retreat. We are getting surrounded!" Adam shouted back pulling away from Judah's grasp and looking around as he still clutched his spear.

Judah sat up and realized he had been dragged from the fighting. In most areas the Zealots and Idumeans still fought, but the Romans were slowly gaining the upper hand as they had been reinforced by the Zeugma legionaries who charged out from inside the towers to aid their comrades. With Romans hacking away in the rear and pressing from the front, the Jews would soon be enveloped and risk total annihilation. In large groups, many of the Zealots began fleeing back to the city as bowmen upon the walls showered volleys upon the Romans in an attempt to protect their retreating comrades. The Palmyrene bowmen, unable to have been ejected from the towers, now became a serious problem as they began to butcher the men below as hysteria and panic broke out. Finally, the Jewish attack shuddered and a great bellow went up from the ranks. Like a beast trapped and fighting in its final moments of agony, the Jewish forces turned and fled to the city in chaos.

"Judah, let's go!" Adam shouted pulling his friend to his feet at the sound of horses' hooves pounding the earth as the Boars charged into the right flank of the Jews, trampling men beneath their weight.

"Marcus," Judah said in a daze as he stood and watched his rival charge past him at the head of his cavalry.

"Judah, let's go!" Adam shouted hitting his friend upon the shoulder to snap him out of his state of mind. This worked, and Judah instantly turned and fled back to the Women's Gate with Adam hot on his heels.

*   *   *

"My Prince, they have fled and the rams have been recovered. I think they are salvageable. Only the one on the right seems to be spoiled." Tiberius wiped the sweat from his brow and licked his lips as he watched the cohorts of the Fulminata reinforce their ranks and move out of range from the slackening missile fire from the walls. "The ram can be repaired. I can send men to reclaim it and drag it back, if you wish."

Titus sighed and sheathed his sword as he looked around at the battlefield. "They have a will of steel, my dear Tiberius, one that I have never witnessed before."

"The legionaries fought wonderfully, I couldn't agree more," Tiberius replied.

"No," Titus shook his head. "I meant the Zealots. Sure our men fought well, but the Jews seem to care nothing for their lives. The way they threw themselves at our ranks, even under the threat of arrow and stone, they went all the way. Remarkable, I have never seen that before." Titus stared at the piles of dead, both Roman and Jew, strewn before the cohorts and then watched with weary eyes as well over a hundred bleeding and exhausted legionaries were helped into wooden carts. Some could be seen with gashes and severe cuts upon arms and legs, while a few wailed and moaned from bloody stumps that had once been limbs.

"The surgeons will be busy, no doubt," Titus mumbled. "I want the butcher's bill as soon as it has been recorded." The Prince signaled for Tiberius to follow him as he edged Achilles away from the exhausted cohorts.

The two generals rode back to the center of the field where the rest of his legionary staff awaited. The look upon Titus' face must have been fierce for nobody wished to make eye contact as the frustrated Prince shook his head and asked for a towel to be brought so he could clean his face. "It is simple: continue hammering the wall! I want those rams kept in action. Well done to the Zeugma legionaries and the Fulminata. I will deliver the proper dona to the most deserved." Titus gave Marcus Octavian a firm nod and wearily said, "As for now, relieve your cohorts with fresh ones, Marcus. Your men could use a break." Titus glanced to Sextus and then turned in his saddle and pointed to the ramps. "Your men are too far to the right. Reposition them at the edge of ramp three and keep watch. If anything moves, kill it. Start pounding the battlements at Hippicus and to the right, keep them ducking."

Titus looked to Frigius and then said, "Send contingents to the rams. I will have legionaries operating them from now on. My apologies, King Agrippa, but your Syrians fled too easily. I will have you speak to them later. If they do that again, I will personally flog their captains and decimate the lot of them." Agrippa nodded in embarrassment, seated upon his horse with a gloomy stare.

Titus grunted and spit a stream of saliva upon the ground and rubbed his achy neck. "I don't expect everything to go according to plan, but I do expect my men to have the balls and the courage to fight! Praise be to Jupiter the Palmyrenes held on. Splendid work and my thanks." This compliment helped restore some pride in Agrippa and the client king nodded graciously to the young Prince.

Titus grunted and then took a clean linen towel that was handed to him from a servant standing beside Achilles with a copper basin of water. Titus wiped his face from the dirt and sweat, tossed the towel at the servant, and plunged his grimy hands into the cool, fresh water from the basin. He rubbed them together and then splashed some water upon his face.

Titus sent the servant away with a flick of his hand and turned as Marcus Sulla joined the group with an expression of victorious glee upon his face. "My thanks to your Boars. A number of men will get awards this day; make room upon your cuirass, my dear Marcus. The gods smile upon you and your reputation." Titus looked at the other generals and kings. "Well done to you all. We tested their resolve and faced it head on. Have the artillery crews take a break. Do we have prisoners?"

"Yes, my Prince, there must be at least forty," Sextus replied pointing to a cluster of Jews kneeling upon the ground behind the Fulminata and surrounded by spear tips at their throats from legionaries wishing to use them.

"Good. Clasp irons on their hands and feet. Send half of them to fetch the ram needing repairs. Inform them that if they run, all their remaining comrades shall be crucified. To show them I am not bluffing nail one up at this moment before the walls for everyone to see." Titus smirked at his plan. "Why risk our own men to reclaim the ram; get these bastards to do it."

"An excellent plan, my Prince," replied Sextus as he sent a junior officer to deliver the message.

As Titus watched one of the prisoner's get selected for crucifixion and begin sobbing for mercy, he turned to General Octavian. "Your lads fought well. They are a sturdy bunch and put up a scrap."

"Well, I would ask for nothing less, my Prince. We have a good crop of centurions leading them. I think they all wish to impress you." Marcus bowed his head humbly and smiled.

"You piss in my ear, Marcus. They care to impress Gaius Antony! The man is a god among the ranks, truly. I thought of sending him in, but the other cohorts needed to prove themselves." Titus hesitated for a moment as he observed two long pieces of timber brought over to the prisoners while a hole was quickly dug. "He will be of incredible use once we make a breach in this wall. We will need to clear the walls and the Bezetha. It's a dirty business, but it needs to be done." Titus watched the legionaries steady the two pieces of timber as they crossed them and then fixed them together with long spikes.

"The Fifteenth and Twelfth will be used at the breach, my Prince?" Marcus asked.

Titus nodded. "We will fill the towers with legionaries and push them right up to the walls! At the same time we will send men through the breach. I want you to choose your best and Frigius will choose his!"

The prisoner began screaming and struggling as he was laid upon the cross by seven Romans holding him down. The other Jews looked upon the cruelty with faces of ash as the nails were driven deep causing the helpless victim to shudder, wail, and vomit horridly. Next, his arms were bound by rope and his garments were torn from his body until he was naked. Then the two-and-a-half metre cross was stood up and allowed to drop into the hole as the Romans pushed the earth around the edges of the base, then fixed it with stakes. The man, left to hang with his feet not even nailed, sobbed and gasped for air as his body wiggled. One prisoner started to weep at the horrible sight before he was silenced by a legionary who stepped forward and smacked him across the back of his head. Then thirty prisoners were ordered to stand and after a quick explanation was relayed to them concerning the fate of the other ten if they should run, the prisoners were marched off towards the smouldering testudo.

Titus watched the prisoners climb the ramp as they stepped over bodies and gazed up at the high walls, unsure if they should call out to their fellow comrades to kill them rather than be destined to a life of slavery which awaited them. However, nothing happened. No arrows were fired, and the prisoners slowly pushed the ram back down the ramp under the watchful eyes of the Jewish fighters above who listened to the wailing of the crucified prisoner.

* * *

CHAPTER XXV

May 3rd, 70 A.D. / 6th of Iyyar, 3830
Upper City, Jerusalem
Herod's Palace

"Make way!" shouted an Idumean as tears ran down his blood stained cheeks. "Yohannan has been struck down! We need bandages, please!" The Idumean carried an unconscious man by the arms while two of his comrades each held a leg. The body of the dying commander of Simon's failed assault was covered in blood with a face pale like the white marble of the Temple. Two long black arrows protruded from his chest and his left arm revealed enormous wounds, deep and grisly looking. The Idumean men gazed frantically about with tears welling up in their eyes until they finally set Yohannan upon the ground and watched their captain wheeze in pain for a moment, then grow stiff with death.

"Oh God have mercy, he's dead!" wailed the men as more soldiers gathered around in grief to gaze down upon the corpse.

One of the soldiers collapsed to his knees in shock as his hands trembled. Then with deep sobs he slowly pulled a linen shroud over the body and covered the bruised, pale face. "He is dead, my brothers!" the man called out in grief, falling upon the corpse. More Idumeans gathered around to lament and comfort one another as shrieks, screams, and moans of the wounded filled the halls of Herod's grandiose palace.

Yohannan the Idumean had been loved, respected, and was known as a valiant warrior. He was Simon's best and had led the assault on the Roman cohorts with bravery and ferocity. Yohannan had survived the charge, the brutal fighting, and the retreat. He had retired in frustration back to the battlements to survey the aftermath of the coordinated attack upon the Roman force. As he had talked with a comrade, a single Arab bowmen, unseen and hunkering behind a wicker hurdle, had suddenly sprung out, unleashed two arrows, and had slain the commander.

"What is happening?" Adam asked as Moshe stepped over a man upon the ground who was writhing in pain as he was tended by two women.

"Yohannan the Idumean is dead." Moshe slowly sat leaning against a pillar and stared at Caleb who lay upon a thin straw mat upon the floor with Judah by his side.

Judah slowly turned, gazed at Moshe, than looked away as he held Caleb's firm grasp. "Hadassah will help you; have strength my friend," Judah reassured the panic in Caleb's eyes as he shuddered and struggled to breathe.

Hadassah knelt across from Judah with a vessel of water and strips of white linen. She stared down at the bleeding man with pain glazed over his eyes as he gritted his teeth and clawed at the tiled floor. "Hold him," Hadassah commanded firmly as she took some linen.

Adam quickly moved around Judah, squatting near Caleb as he stroked his forehead and steadied his trembling shoulders. Warm blood flowed upon his fingers from the chest wound that bubbled and oozed with every breath Caleb took. "Calm, my brother, just calm yourself. You're safe here," Adam continued to say, trying to reassure the whimpers escaping Caleb's lips as he bit them so hard they began to bleed.

Hadassah worked fast, but it was difficult. Caleb had been stabbed through the gut once and then slashed across the chest as the skin had peeled back to the ribs. Now she attempted to fold the flesh over, stitch what she could, and then cover it in wrappings. As Adam steadied Caleb's head, Judah gently and ever so carefully rolled his friend onto his right side so Hadassah could get underneath his body with the cloth. Once successful, Judah laid Caleb back down as a tremor rippled through his body, causing him to gasp for breath, arch his back in agony, and then groan.

Judah fought back tears as he handed Hadassah the cloth with bloodied hands. He sniffed and grunted as he stared down at his helpless friend and then looked away as she tightened the cloth in an attempt to clot the bleeding. Caleb shook violently and shrieked with pain. He began to whimper like a child as tears rolled down his cheeks.

"I am sorry," Caleb whispered to Judah. "We should not have been there." A spasm took hold of him and he shook like a rag doll for a moment. Then he was calm.

Judah drew close to Caleb's face and softly replied, "You fought better than all the rest, Caleb. You must live! You have to live." Judah watched his friend try to smile and then tightly close his eyes as another wave of pain shook his body in convulsions. "You are the best of me," Judah said, shaking his head as tears ran into his beard.

"You must pray, Judah. You can't hold on to her forever. Give it away." Caleb swallowed hard and his chest began to heave out of rhythm as he tried to steady himself.

Hadassah finished mending Caleb and sat back with a look of pity at the suffering man. She slowly wiped the blood from her hands and then said with a small voice, "Caleb, are you thirsty?" She watched him jerk and then nod. Hadassah reached into the vessel and drew forth a copper ladle filled with cool water. She brought it to his lips and raised his head from the ground like a mother feeding a small child. Caleb choked on the water and coughed but some managed to go down and this seemed to soothe him as she gently laid his head back upon the blood-stained tiles.

Hadassah met Judah's eyes and softly shook her head. A pained expression filled Judah's face and she whispered, "He may last a day."

Judah sat back upon his heels in shock. Staring down at Caleb, Hadassah's words seemed to ring true at the condition of his friend. Already the blood had soaked through the bandages and trails of red could be seen running out from under the cloth where it dripped upon the ground. Judah stood, his eyes fixed on Caleb and his mind spinning.

"Judah? Where will you go?" Adam asked.

"Do you need something?" Moshe voiced his concern.

Judah did not respond to either man. He lifted his gaze to Hadassah and stared at her with a broken expression. He turned as if in a stupor and said with a stammer, "I need to leave. I will return."

Judah stumbled off through the palace hall as he stepped over bodies and past motionless men covered by blankets. Everywhere there was misery. Men wept, called out in wails, cried for their mothers, and prayed. Judah passed by countless men who he heard in their dying moments reciting the *Shema* above a whisper with trembling lips and peace in their hollow, bloodied frames. Faces everywhere were cast into misery. The halls echoed with suffering and were dank and dark despite the sunlight outside.

When Judah burst out of the palace hall, it was like a gust of fresh air suddenly filled his lungs. The putrid stench of blood, sweat, urine, and feces evaporated as he passed by a calm pool featuring a defaced statue of some nameless god or hero erected in the middle upon a podium of marble. Instead of men lounging upon cushions or drying themselves from a swim, as would have been common during Herod's day, the pool's edge was crowded with exhausted soldiers and the lightly wounded.

Judah's head began to spin and he halted next to one of the pillars surrounding the pool which had a beautiful vine twisting around its marble body. He leaned against the stone and suddenly felt overwhelmed as he bent over and vomited upon the tiles. Not a man around him seemed to care as he spat and groaned, catching his breath as a string of spittle dangled from his bottom lip. If Judah had retched upon these tiles eighty years earlier, Herod the Great would have had his head upon a platter, but the insane architect, obsessed with gaining the love of his people, was only a distant memory compared to the horror Judah had just come from.

"I see you are one of the fortunate ones to live and come out of the fight unscathed," said a voice which caused Judah to look up and wipe his mouth from the bitter vomit. Two men, one dressed as a priest, and the other looking equally as pious with tzitzit hanging from the hems of his shawl and a beautifully knit *kipa* upon his head, stared at the disgruntled Lion captain. Judah recognized the old priest as Zechariah and the other elderly man as John of Gischala's friend, Shimeon ben Gamaliel.

"I haven't seen you since you quoted from Lamentations that day in the Antonia," Judah muttered. "What do you want with me?"

"I have seen your friend," Shimeon said softly, stepping closer. "Zechariah showed him to me." A dreamy look filled the old man's eyes and he sighed. "So much agony; so many dead."

"Have you come to remind me? I just came from there," Judah replied bitterly as he tried to regain his composure.

"Judah, John sent us to see if you lived," Zechariah explained in a gentle grandfather-like tone. "He refuses to leave the East Gate out of fear of a Roman attack."

Judah scowled and leaned against the pillar as another rush of dizziness and nausea came over him. "The Romans have no ramps there, what does he fear?"

"The Tenth Legion has gathered with torches and pry bars and John believes they may try to fire the gates. He has stationed what archers remain and has moved more of his scorpions to the east. He asks, if you are able, to come and take charge," replied Shimeon.

Judah shook his head and pointed to where he had come from. "My friend dies in there; I have no mind to come calling to John's bid at this moment." Judah wiped tears away and stared at the old men with a face so hot that fire could have leapt from his skin. "John has men, let him use them."

Shimeon folded his arms and glanced to the priest for help. Zechariah calmly approached Judah and touched his cheek warmly. "Your friend is not dead yet. Go to the Temple, throw yourself upon the mercy of God and He may turn to you and heal him. There is still hope! I will tell John you are occupied."

With dirt and blood streaked upon his face from the tears, Judah gave an abrupt nod of thanks and stumbled away. He passed the poolside and ignored the faces that watched him as he began running down a long corridor crammed with men sleeping in their armour, still clutching blood-stained weapons.

When Judah burst from the palace, he could hear the crows and vultures feasting upon the battlefield beyond the walls. He saw billows of smoke rising above the enormous silhouettes of the Hippicus, Phasael, and Mariamme towers that dominated the corner where the First Wall ran to the west gate and then connected to the battered Third Wall. Judah stared at the stacks of bodies being gathered inside the gate as they were stripped of weapons and wrapped in cloths in an attempt to preserve the dead and keep the smell down. Yet, he had to wonder where they would end up since there was no place they could bury them. His eyes traced the black smoke trails of destroyed homes from the Roman artillery fire. Somewhere beyond the alleys and streets a woman screamed and a baby wailed loudly.

Judah exhaled loudly, wishing the woman would cease, then turned and began to run. He passed a street which led to the Gennath Gate in the First Wall and continued on until he turned south past Agrippa's Palace and the Horse Gate. He pressed on as he picked up speed and passed a column of soldiers marching somberly near the gymnasium. Some of the men called out to him but Judah paid them no attention as the street began to descend into the valley of the Tyropoeon. He could see the high walls of the Temple Mount appear as if rising from the earth like a great mountain as the colonnades were dotted with guards.

He pushed hard and suddenly found himself at the bottom of the stone steps which reached upward to the plateau of the Temple Mount. Judah stared at it for a moment with thirst gripping his dry, scratchy throat and then he began to climb. He found his mind drift back to that day Simon, John, and Eleazar had met upon the stairs and the tension which had been brought with it. Back then the city had felt impregnable and strong, but what he had seen today had struck a chord of terror in his soul for the first time since his career had begun as a fighter in John's army.

Judah wondered if Jerusalem would survive the legions of Prince Titus Vespasianus. *Did Gaius Cornelius Antony fight today?* Judah thought. *Would the centurion have tried to kill me if we had met in battle?* Judah had not seen the man. In fact, he could not even recall a single, precise memory of the fight other then the mayhem that had ensued. He stopped abruptly at the top of the stairs and gazed back across the valley at the expensive homes of the priests who dwelled nearby. Beyond the mansions he could see the three towers and the smoke filling the sky above them. Sweat beaded off his forehead and he caught his breath.

What was Yosef thinking? Judah thought, remembering the Jewish General's plea for John to surrender. He shook his head and buried his face into his hands. *He called to us, but what did he expect would come of it? That all of us would simply come willingly down from the walls?* Judah angrily cursed the Jewish General. He found his mind wander briefly to the simple truth that Capito was still alive and that he had heard no response from Titus. *But Gaius has sworn to me, he has sworn upon his ancestors! Titus has to honour this pact, Gaius will convince him,* Judah thought. Then he felt anger at his predicament. He felt humiliated by a sense of shame with his obligation to Rome as a collaborator who had caused many to die. Judah cursed under his breath, pushed the guilt away, then charged underneath the porticoes and stumbled into the Outer Court.

Judah crossed the courtyard which was nearly vacant from soldiers as every able bodied man had been called to the colonnades surrounding the Temple plateau. He could see them lining the parapets three-men deep. The soldiers waited nervously staring across the Kidron Valley and up the slopes of the Mount of Olives to where the Fretensis had taken up positions. Judah did not give the thought a second more as he suddenly lurched forward towards the gleaming white Temple. His feet pounded upon the flagstones as he neared the looming structure with its golden spires upon the top. A number of doves flew overhead as they circled around him and then soared effortlessly away across the blue sky.

Judah ran until he stood before a high gate of wood and gold that had been left slightly open on the southern side of the Temple. He looked to his left down the glistening wall of white stone and could see four sets of stairs leading to four more gates. Beyond the gates a white tower stood at the corner with a smaller gate at its bottom and parapets built upon the top. Judah glanced to his right and stared at another white tower which guarded the eastern end. He could see a few men within the tower and one of them gazed back at him as he leaned out a window. Without acknowledging the man, Judah slowly passed through the entrance.

Nothing appeared to move inside the Women's Court as he crossed the stone floor, the plaza feeling larger than he could remember. Perhaps it seemed this way due to its vacant nature, or because the columns could be seen in all their glory encircling the court beneath the marble capitals which held up the heavy roof. Yet, despite this miniscule feeling dominated by the beauty which surrounded him, Judah continued on.

Judah surveyed the court as he came to a brief halt. Each pillar was capped in gold and covered in intricate designs of golden leaves, vines, grapes, or pomegranates which had been decorated into the white marble. The courtyard was magnificent and utterly breathtaking, but not in the least compared to what awaited him at the end of his journey.

Judah stared at the glorious Nicanor Gate. The edifice in itself was intricately beautiful. A large circular staircase of fifteen steps ascended from the courts flagstones, and to each side were doors which led to chambers where the Levites kept musical instruments. At the top of the stairs to the right and left of the bronze Nicanor Gate were two more doors leading into side chambers of significant value. On the right was the Chamber of Pinchas, where priestly vestments were kept, and on the left was the Havitin Chamber, where the meal offerings were prepared.

The Nicanor Gate was handsome and carried a rich appeal. Plated in bronze, they were over six metres high, had stars and vines engraved into the metal, and were so bright from the sun that Judah had to squint. Above the Nicanor Gate was an arch with bronze bars filling the space and on either side of the arch were large windows outlined in a deep red. The face of the stonework around the gate was white marble with grey veins and swirls imbedded into the rock.

The sight of the final gate before the Court of the Priests always captivated the attention of pilgrims. However, on this day Judah merely climbed the stairs and entered into a small space called the Court of the Israelites, where the Jewish men could stand and watch the priests working upon the burnt altar.

Judah could see the massive golden doors of the Sanctuary Gate behind the stone altar and the clusters of solid gold grapes hanging from the beams of the Entrance Hall. Judah stared for a moment at the golden leaves and grapes and thought of how these generous gifts of the Temple would have given him pride and joy growing up. Now, he just looked on, apathetic and angry at what had brought him to this place.

He turned to the left and followed the wall as he passed under a number of pillars. He watched a column of white cloaked priests suddenly appear carrying split logs as they climbed the ramp of the altar to the top and added them to three fires which burned simultaneously, one being much larger than the others. Judah halted abruptly and watched as ten more priests appeared from the Temple with the daily meal offering. The men carried the *tamid* which was to be offered twice a day, morning and afternoon. The priests were barefoot, wearing white cloaks with red sashes tied about their waists and white turbans upon their heads. The line of dedicated men marched with solemn expressions as they quietly approached the altar.

The priest leading the procession carried a laver of silver which was filled with wine and the man immediately behind him held a closed basin with the sacrifice of organs. The other priests carried the rest of the sacrifice, each man holding a part as they proceeded with the daily ritual. Judah carefully watched the priests halt before the ramp and wait patiently. Three more priests then emerged from the Temple and approached the altar, each clutching a golden *mizrak* filled with the blood of the slain animal. They silently passed the column of waiting priests and then one began to fling blood from the mizrak upon the corner of the altar as the other two poured the bright scarlet blood at the base. Once this was done, the priests recited a prayer and then stepped aside, allowing the procession who carried the animal parts to start their ascent.

Judah silently observed as one by one the animal limbs, including the head, were hurled upon the largest of the three fires. The priest with the silver laver approached one of the smaller fires and raising his eyes to the sky began praying as he poured the wine libation upon the burning wood which began to smoke.

Judah followed the funnel of smoke with his eyes as it drifted upwards from the meal offering as the meat burned and the priests continued with their diction of prayers. His eyes filled with tears and he felt his knees grow weak as he slowly slid to the ground with Zechariah's words pounding in his mind. The old priest had told him to pray at the Temple for God to heal Caleb. Aside from the priest's studious command, the sobering words uttered by Judah's dying friend had beckoned him to find peace and let the thought of Miriam go. Judah reached up and grabbed his hair as he pulled it with tears flowing down his face. He bent over until his face touched the stone and his tears wet the ground.

"Adonai, hear me!" Judah lamented, stretching his arms outward and flattening his hands upon the tiles. He could still hear the priests at work upon the altar and the sound of the crackling fire as it devoured the logs, but he kept praying, his voice turning to silent muttering.

Nearly prostrate, Judah lay as if dead. His mind recalled the historical imagery of recent events: the desperate fight against the Romans; a man hanging upon a cross; and stones hurled at the walls as if they barely moved. He could see the siege towers and the archers, and he remembered the first attack upon the Tenth Legion as they fought bitterly upon the Mount of Olives. Judah's mind drifted to the caves north of Jerusalem where the Lions had lived. How they had sought out the Boars and ambushed them. He could still hear the screams of the women and the shouts of the men amidst the smoke filled caverns as they were killed by the Roman troopers. Then they had fled into the cistern.

His mind stretched back further to the Upper Market slaughter and the cohorts that had murdered countless women and children. He could see Capito leading his legionaries forward over the bodies of dead babies and trampled mothers, washed in blood and lapping it up like dogs. Tears flowed as Judah could see Miriam's body in the fountain, how he had pulled her broken form out and recognized the scent of lavender still present upon her wet hair. He had wanted to cry to the heavens in a primal rage. The love of his life, limp and motionless in his arms. He had killed his first man that day, and the taste of blood had excited him, deepening his anger.

Four years had passed and where was he now? He was amidst the suffering of the city and fighting the same people he hated. Surrounded by this, Caleb had instructed him to pray. Judah steadied his breathing and sniffed. He felt his tears dampen his forehead as they ran between the tiles. He could not think of anything else but 'Adonai' and he began to recite this title incessantly as if it would cure him of the misery he felt.

Suddenly, Judah blurted out, "Spare me this broken body, let me die so that I may find peace!" Judah moaned as he pushed himself out further upon the tiles, as if he sought to become like the very stones he laid upon. "Let me die, Adonai! Please let me die. Elohim, do you hear me? Your mighty Temple is kindled with the flames of the menorah; it is scented by the incense and warmed by the sacrifices! Have you not enough blood spilled here that you would demand that of my friend now? Was Miriam an evil woman that you required her life? Why is it that you have allowed this city to be built up and now it awaits destruction? What is the price I must pay? You taunt me and cause me grief and yet no peace can be found. Do not forsake me, Adonai!"

Judah began to weep and cough as he sputtered rubbing his face in the tears. His entire body began to tremble and shake with grief as he clawed at the stone. "Miriam, oh how fair you were. My love. Please, Elohim, just let me die!" Judah's tears slowly ebbed away leaving stains upon his cheeks and a swollen redness in his eyes. He took in deep breaths as he whimpered, and then like a baby in his mother's arms, he fell asleep.

John of Gischala stood in the entrance of Nicanor Gate and stared at Judah's body lying upon the stones. He leaned against the doorpost with his broad arms crossed and dark eyes watching his bereft captain. He had been told Judah was attending to other matters. Then he had caught a glimpse of him crossing the Outer Court and entering into the Women's Court of the Temple. John had left strict orders for his men and then followed Judah wondering what he might discover.

Now he watched his most trusted officer broken upon the ground in grief. Not wishing to embarrass Judah, John slowly entered into the court and stared at the altar for a moment. He watched as a few priests continued their work and then he moved closer to Judah who lay still upon the ground.

John steadied his hand on the hilt of his sword and slowly bent down beside his captain who appeared dead. "Judah," John softly whispered. A groan came from the captain who slightly moved his head. He laid a gentle hand on Judah's head and sighed watching him stir slightly. "Judah, it is a shame about Caleb. I pray he recovers."

"He will die, John," Judah muttered and then pulled himself up, trying to shield his face in shame from his commander. "I did not know you were here."

John stood and shrugged. "I saw you and was worried." He watched Judah try to regain his composure and fix the sword hanging at his side. "The Fretensis have not made a move. I am not sure they will."

Judah nodded and stared with a blank expression at the altar. "I would assume they will do nothing today. It appears Titus' main efforts will be on the weaker wall along the northwestern side."

John was silent as he thought about some of the words he had heard Judah pray. "Can I count on you?" John asked, honestly searching the forlorn look which filled Judah's eyes.

Judah stared with a puzzled expression at the large warlord. "What do you mean?"

"Walk with me, Judah," John responded as he ushered his captain to follow him.

Both men exited the Temple in silence as they strolled out into the Outer Court which remained barren of life. Judah stared at the grandeur of the colonnades and the rows of pillars surrounding the Temple grounds; it truly was an inspiring sight. He looked to the west and could still see the black smoke filling the sky, a reminder of the danger that was never far away.

John was the first to break the silence as he turned and said, "It is only a matter of time until the Romans come through the wall. They did not make much progress today, but we will not be able to do an attack like that again. Simon's stunt was short lived; from now on we will be kept inside. Titus is a quick learner and he is figuring out our methods. They will become more brutal and will use all their resources to destroy our western defences. Expect tomorrow to be worse."

"There is nothing to be done?" Judah asked.

John shook his burly head. "Nothing."

"Would you ever consider surrender?"

John gave him a strange look and then raised his chin. "There is no surrender. We would all be slaughtered or enslaved. Rome sees us as guilty of treason, there would be no quarter. We cannot surrender the city; that is out of the question."

"You know they will slaughter us all. Rome will not be merciful and they will burn the city," Judah bluntly replied.

John slowed his pace and refused to make eye contact with Judah for the heaviness which his words carried. "We must push on. The legions are not endless. I believe if we kill enough and ruin all their attempts, they will have to retire, they must retreat." John felt the dull words roll off his tongue with no satisfaction to the hopelessness which seemed to lie heavily upon him. He yearned to believe those words, but he knew them not to be true. The Romans would never give up so long as a prince led them. So they would fight until the city lay in ruins or they had all starved to death. "I will need all your focus, Judah. You must do what you can and fight well." John stopped and stared at his captain, seeking to reignite the flare in Judah's eyes, and it worked. "You know, that man Capito could be out there. Would you surrender to him?"

"I know he is, and that is my business." Judah looked at John carefully searching his commander's face for any sign that he might know something about his escapades with Gaius and Yosef, yet nothing was betrayed. "I will return to my station," Judah said with an edge of tenacity to his voice.

John watched Judah turn and begin walking away. "Judah," John called out and the Lion captain halted and half turned. "Will you seek death in battle?"

"That is for me only, John," Judah replied and then walked away.

* * *

May 6th, 70 A.D. / 9th of Iyyar, 3830
West side of Jerusalem
North of Hippicus Tower

Clouds of dust clung to the air amidst the tightly packed Roman soldiers crowding the base of the wall. Men with hammers and iron pry bars grunted, shouted, and cursed as they struggled underneath the roof of shields their comrades held aloft for protection. Arrows sailed upwards at the walls from the Palmyrene bowmen amassing behind hurdles as more archers sent volleys of missile fire from the towers which remained at a safe distance from the walls. Loud echoing metallic sounds rang out from the working crews who hammered against iron bars trying to crack the mortar and stone. Men heaved and gritted their teeth as centurions walked among them shouting for them to cluster together and put their backs into the labour.

Gaius Antony bent down and squinted through the dust as he watched his men struggle against the weight of the stone. "Pull together!" he shouted watching one of the partially dislodged stones stop moving under the immense pressure of the wall above it. The soldiers grunted with frustrated and exasperated sounds as they tugged at the stone. When this failed to work, two men with hammers began to strike the stone in an attempt to break it up. Gaius shook his head at the brutal, hard work as he instinctively ducked from a deep thud above his head as another falling stone grazed off the shields. He looked to the right and stared upward at the ramp and the constant noise the ram caused as it shook the wall. Gaius could make out giant cracks and splits in the stone where the ram worked and he knew that soon the wall would begin to undermine itself.

"Oil!" shouted a soldier falling to the side as a wash of sticky sludge fell upon the roof of shields causing a shift in the formation as men knew what would come next. The smell was putrid and incredibly strong as Gaius covered his mouth and encouraged them to keep working. Then a fire brand was hurled down from the wall and soon a raging fire was burning on their left flank. A few men screamed as they rolled on the ground, their bodies ignited by hot flames. A pail of water was hurled on one of the burning victims which did nothing to quench the flames as the soldier thrashed and shrieked some more and then lay still as the stench of roasting flesh wafted through the working ranks.

"Keep focused!" Gaius shouted as he looked away from the smoking corpse. If they were going to survive this day they could not be soft. "The sooner these walls are weakened, the sooner this is over!" Sweat poured down Gaius' face as he felt the dust stick to his skin, clinging to his legs and feet. "Come now, men of the Hydra, wolves of the legions! Don't give the bastards anything to rant about! You're the best soldiers in the world! Give it some muscle! We can prevail over these walls! Remove the foundation and the cursed wall will collapse in on itself! Steady men, push together!"

Gaius looked to his right. He winced at the sight of his optio seated upon the ground, hunched over with blood streaked across his pale face and flecks of red upon the wolf hide which covered his shoulders. The man's breathing was shallow as he held a cloth to his head in agony. Gaius stepped over to him, knelt down and rested his hand on his shoulder.

"Priscus, you will live, don't worry lad." Gaius gently pulled the cloth away, saw the deep gash still pulsing blood and shook his head. "Keep pressure on it. When we retreat the surgeon can stitch you back up!" The optio gave a weak nod without raising his head. "I am jealous, my dear Priscus, you will be out of this damned fighting for a few days. Mars has smiled on you. You will be fine!" Gaius patted him heavily and then strolled across the hard ground as he watched the progress of his legionaries.

The earth around the First Cohort remained red with the blood of men who had fallen as they had approached the walls. Now these men lay to the rear, dragged from the wall in bloody heaps to be removed later. Gaius glanced back at a corpse lying in the dirt. The man's helmet had been crushed into his scalp from a stone hurled from the wall. He remembered the legionary as one of the first men who had dashed from the ranks to the wall holding a hammer and his shield. The man, in his eagerness, had failed to lift his shield in time to deflect the falling piece of granite. Gaius stared at the dead man's face and thought to himself that it resembled the likeness of a crushed grape in a wine press. The legionary's jaw had been shattered, crushing his teeth. His cheek bone gleamed in white bloody strips from the skin which had been torn away and the rest of his face was covered in matted blood as grey dust clung to it. The soldier had been killed instantly. As the rest of the century had clustered to work, Gaius had ordered the young man to be dragged back and left until they would be ready to withdraw later in the day.

Titus had sent orders to the Fulminata in the early morning hours for three cohorts to work at the walls next to the ramps in an attempt to dig under the stones and pry them out. The Prince had elected the First, Fourth, and Eighth Cohorts to do the honours and Gaius had led his Hydra Herculean Century to the middle of the wall with the other four centuries of his cohort stretched out on his right. All of Gaius' fellow Primi Ordines had rehearsed this move hundreds of times in training. Whether on the drill grounds in Rome, Caesarea Maritima, or Alexandria, they all knew it would be the most dangerous in the center, but such a risk and challenge was expected of the First Cohort and so the men never complained. However, Gaius still wondered why Titus would not fully utilize the siege towers which were equipped with rams of their own to destroy the upper parts of the wall, but as a Praefectus Castrorum, he would not question such commands from the Prince. Despite Gaius' obligation to voice his opinion in council to his commanding general, Marcus Octavian, he still tended to keep his mouth shut in matters relating directly to commands from Titus himself.

Finally the stone split from the hammering and the legionaries managed to pry it out from the wall with a sense of victory. A great hole was the only thing they could see and when Gaius pushed through his soldiers and bent down he saw another stone behind the one they had just removed. He shook his head and stood up catching his breath. He swore and moved aside as his crews leapt into action again. "Clear the one out beside it!" Gaius bellowed as another hailstorm of rocks thundered upon the shields which overlapped above him.

*   *   *

"We need more rocks up here. Get the largest you can find!" Judah shouted at a number of men who were running up the steps of the ramparts. "Get going and find as many men who can help you!" Judah watched the Zealots hesitate as they appeared to be confused. "Get moving now! Tear down homes, if you must! Now go!"

The Romans had attacked again at first light as the rams continued to pound upon the walls as they shook and trembled. Volleys of missiles continued to rain down upon Jerusalem. They crashed into the battlements and reduced homes to piles of ruins, all the while as the streets of the Bezetha were choked with clouds of dust, smoke, and fire. Reports had been brought to Judah's attention that indeed parts of the wall were beginning to crack and shatter under the constant onslaught. The Romans had clamped down on their resolve to breach the wall, leaving the Jews unable to retaliate. Forced to cower behind the walls, the Jewish fighters could only resort to hauling up large rocks and hurling them over the battlements upon the legionaries below.

Hezekiah ben Chobari, a Zealot officer who had served under Eleazar ben Simon, now came running up to Judah hunched over, refusing to look up as flaming boulders from Roman catapults hissed by overhead. He halted and caught his breath as lines of dirt and sweat streaked his bearded face. "The wall to the north will collapse soon, I think. I heard it groan and men from below say that they can hear the Romans prying out stones. It can't be long now."

Judah stared at the man for a moment. "Be ready to pull your men back when it does collapse. Orders are to fall back to the Second Wall."

"And surrender the Bezetha?" Hezekiah retorted as he buried his face in his hands.

"Do you have a better idea? We cannot defend the Bezetha properly once a breach is made. We will have to retreat! Anyone who stays behind will be slaughtered," Judah shouted over the sound of an explosion behind him which rocked the city walls. He glanced back and saw a large home implode on itself from a Roman missile as fire leapt from the hole and dust rose from the collapsed walls.

Next to join Judah and Hezekiah was Jacob ben Soras, one of Simon's officers commanding a large division of the Idumean forces. He had left the Psephinus' Tower with orders and looked worried as he cowered next to the men. "Simon sends word: we will fall back when the breach is made! Efforts to take back the Bezetha will have to be made after we can coordinate with John's forces."

"What makes you so sure we can even take back this wall? Once inside the Romans will tear it down, there will be nothing to take back!" Judah said shaking his head.

"It makes no difference, these are the orders!" Jacob replied, annoyed at Judah's tone. "A contingent of my men will cover our retreat! We will leave everything! Expect the breach tomorrow at this rate."

"What of civilians in the Bezetha?" Hezekiah asked.

"Not our concern!" Jacob replied. "They have had plenty of time to get out. We can only concentrate on so many things at once, and right now the Romans are priority." Jacob stood and glared at the men for a moment. "Keep your heads up, and when this wall comes down, run as fast as you can and get as many men to the Second Wall." Jacob turned and left quickly as he navigated his way through the soldiers.

Hezekiah was quiet for a moment and then shrugged. "Maybe we will have more of a chance defending the Second Wall; we do have the Antonia and John's scorpions."

"Judah! Judah!" a man called out in distress from the rampart steps.

Judah turned and glanced over the side. "What is it?"

"I have a message sent by Adam. He says to come swiftly!" the man shouted back.

Judah's heart quickened at the news and his mind suddenly cleared as he thought about Caleb. His friend had been moved from Herod's Palace after the first night to Hadassah's home near the Ophel as they had managed to stop the bleeding. On that day two things had happened for Hadassah, she had prepared a space for Caleb and with much grief had watched as Adam and Judah had carried her dead mother from her bed.

Hadassah had been unaware that her mother had died during the early morning as she had chosen to spend the night at the palace with Caleb who fought for his life. She had only discovered the stiff, cold, rigid form of her mother's body upon returning to the home to settle Caleb in. Judah had comforted her as best as he could. Moshe and Adam had taken much care with the body and had prepared it in silence to the sorrowful rocking of Hadassah's body curled up on the floor with Judah close by. At the sight of the wrapped corpse of her mother, Hadassah had broken into deep sobs and terrible wailing. Judah had instantly moved to her side and turning her away, had gently pulled her into his strong embrace. Moshe and Adam had carried the body from the Ophel to be discarded outside the city walls on the southern side where other bodies had been piled. After this, the two men had returned and Judah had left them with Hadassah to care for Caleb and keep her company in her frail state.

Judah had paid his friend daily visits as fever gripped Caleb's weakened state, but this became less frequent as his presence upon the walls was demanded more as the situation deteriorated. Often during the night Caleb would cry out in pain or whimper, and Hadassah would find herself dabbing his forehead with a damp cloth while Adam or Moshe changed his bandages. As each day passed, the room had begun to stink more of blood and infection. Caleb's skin soon began to yellow and his eye sockets became sunken as sweat covered his body. He constantly battled with feeling cold and hot and then the fever would lapse into violent spasms, shivers, and shallow breathing.

Now hearing this message sent from Adam, Judah braced himself for the worst. Without another word he stood and ran down the rampart steps and out into the Bezetha to the shouts of Hezekiah demanding he return to his duty.

*   *   *

Adam met Judah in the doorway to Hadassah's home. The large man nearly filled the entire entrance, a testament to his strength and size, but his face revealed something else. His eyes were watery and his face was flushed with colour. Adam looked feeble, vulnerable, and overcome with sorrow. He quietly stepped forward and laying a heavy hand on Judah's shoulder whispered, "This is it, Judah. He asked for you, but he has not much time left."

With widened, puzzled eyes, Judah stared into the giant's face as salty tears ran down his cheeks. Adam gave Judah a firm nod and then stepped aside. For a moment Judah hesitated, unsure if he truly wanted to see his friend, but then he found strength and entered. The home was gloomy and hazy as the windows had all been covered and the door was shut. Lamps burned upon a number of tables, their scent of oil mixing with the stench of blood. Moshe stood near Caleb's room and he gave a grieved look to Judah, wiping his face with the sleeve of his cloak.

Judah held his breath as he stared at a closed door to the room where Hadassah's mother had died. The room would remain unclean by law until Hadassah had completed her mourning which would end in two days. For the meantime, a mat was laid upon the floor for her bed, and in the kitchen evidence of where Adam and Moshe slept was visible.

"Judah, come in," Hadassah whispered gently as she stood in the doorway next to her mother's chamber. "He has been reciting the *Shema*."

Judah nodded and stepped into the dark room. Stretched out upon a small bed and covered in a sheet of linen lay Caleb. His face was pale and a dark patch of red could be seen through the sheet from the dried blood. A bucket of water sat near the bed with numerous cloths and bandages immersed in the water while an empty cup lay upon the stone floor next to it. Judah could see the glisten of sweat from Caleb's face and shoulders as he approached his friend, kneeling down next to him. Caleb stirred with a mumble and then opened crusted eyelids. A subtle joy could be seen lifting upon the edges of his mouth.

"You came, Judah. You live," Caleb said weakly. "I thought you were hurt."

Judah shook his head and took Caleb's hand in his. "I am not hurt."

"How are the men?"

"They still fight on."

Caleb nodded and slowly turned his face so he could look closer at his friend. "Did you pray that day I told you to?"

Judah's eyes filled with tears and he squeezed his friend's hand. "I did."

Caleb closed his eyes and smiled. "Do not forget where your strength comes from. God will lead you to find peace. Remember, Judah: still waters and green pastures."

"I remember the Psalm." He watched a tremor tear through Caleb's body and Judah felt him tighten his grip. "But what does it matter if I find peace?" Judah whispered. "She is dead and my parents are as well. I have done evil. I am not a good man."

"No," Caleb said, trembling with another spasm. "No! You are a man of anguish, courage, and principle. Pray, Judah. Offer a sin offering; take this to God, He will hear you. Oh, your words are sad to hear. Miriam is at peace, for that I am sure. She holds nothing against you."

"I failed, my friend," Judah began to weep as he squeezed Caleb's hand. "I can't see her face."

Caleb stared at Judah for a moment. Then grunting and using what little strength he possessed, Caleb pulled himself upright. Judah quickly rose to his feet to stop his friend, but Caleb shook his head and pushed Judah away. Hadassah, Adam, and Moshe watched from the doorway as the stubborn, dying man finally succeeded in sitting up and then collapsed against the wall in exhaustion. "I say to you, Judah," Caleb said with heavy breaths as sweat poured down his chest, soaking the bloodied bandages. "You will see her face again soon. You will." Caleb coughed violently and then trembled again but managed to continue, "You will see her again. Do not, do not forsake HaShem. Do not push Him away. Find your faith, my brother. Whatever scrap you may have left, cling to it. HaShem has not forsaken us. Somehow in all of this, He has not forsaken us."

Judah watched his friend take a deep breath as if he would say something else and then his chin fell upon his chest and he exhaled with a hiss as his hand went limp in Judah's grip. The room was silent for a moment as light from the oil lamps flickered upon Caleb's still body. Then Judah buried his face into the mattress of the bed and wept as Hadassah ran to his side and held him.

*　　*　　*

CHAPTER XXVI

The legionary commanders stood quietly around a table under a burning four-wick, bronze, oil lamp which hung from a chain above them. Sextus glanced upward at the lamp and briefly admired it. Each lamp had the head of a god or goddess engraved into the bronze as they appeared to spring out from the metal. Upon one lamp Dionysus, with his wild hair and wide smile, the god's crooked grin humouring Sextus' gaze. The second lamp, next to the rascal god of revelry, was a serious, dreamlike stare from the youthful face of Helius. Sextus glanced around the table at the quiet group of generals and kings. Nobody said a word as they all waited for Prince Titus. Feeling slightly awkward from the silence, Sextus reached up and gently turned the chandelier to admire the other two faces. First, the head of Hercules was evident with his great beard and stern eyes, and next, the fawn-like face of Venus and her lustful invitation for sexual pleasure.

Coiled around the chain above the oil lamps were the tiny forms of naked nymphs and goddesses with perky breasts and firm buttocks accentuated by the artisan's tools. Taking a closer look, Sextus could see that the point of the nymphs went far beyond the celebration of the body. He could easily make out the likeness of Priapus, tongue out provocatively in a mischievous grin as the god gripped his erect penis. Next to Priapus was the goddess Victoria, with feathered wings protruding from her back, gazing down eagerly at the sexual ploy, as she refused to cover her nudity. Written in a bold Latin script around the base of the lamp Sextus read to himself, "*With a trunk like Priapus I will find her Sea Shell.*" Sextus smirked and looked away.

Artwork such as this littered the room of Titus' personal quarters. It was no secret the Prince enjoyed the craftsmanship of one of Rome's most famous artisans known simply as Quintillus. He was popular throughout the empire for his capture of realism through bronze, copper, and marble, but notorious for his sense of perverse promiscuity. There were, however, some in Rome who deemed such work as '*going too far and fit for pornographers.*' But for a woman charmer like Titus, statues such as these that aided in pointing half-drunk women in the direction of his bed were worth keeping around.

"Prince Titus Vespasianus arrives!" hollered a guard outside the tent. All the generals, kings, and officers turned, parted from the table, and either saluted or bowed as the young Flavian marched inside.

"I do thank you for waiting. There were some issues to clear up with the siege engineers. I have also requested the advice of my Chief Engineer Porcius Marius Gracchus to accompany us in this council." Titus turned as he motioned for an older man dressed in a breastplate of bronze to step forward and be recognized. "Porcius has been running things thus far. He will have some things to say tonight, and you all better pay attention."

Titus gazed around the room nodding at some of the faces. "Ah, I see we are privileged to be in the company of our fearless Praefectus Castrorum. Well done in your deployment of soldiers these last six days." Titus stared straight at Gaius Antony and gave him a firm nod. "Now, I want to acknowledge the client kings and say your assistance never dwindles, and your alae have not let me down yet." Agrippa, Sohaemus, and Antiochus showed their appreciation with quiet bows. "Legate Gallus, although you frequently keep to your quarters, your wit and contribution have added greatly in organizing your artillery units from Syria. I thank you." All eyes watched the plump Cestius Gallus humbly close his eyes and nod. "Now, Gessius Florus, where have your duties taken you this last week? I don't believe I have even heard your name," Titus said sarcastically.

"I have been assisting in any way I can with the victory over this city, my Prince. I can assure you that the alae have been equally distributed on all fronts, and the checkpoints remain tight with all eyes open," Florus replied as he briefly examined a finger nail.

"Pilgrims still come to the city?" Titus asked scowling.

"Every day. Some days more than others, but we search them as my Prince has commanded." Florus smiled as some of the generals turned away with sour looks. He knew many despised him and he reveled in it with delight.

"How many today?" Titus questioned, crossing his arms.

Florus stared up at the ceiling of the tent as he stalled for a moment and then shrugged. "Ninety-three, to be exact! About a dozen turned away, we crucified one who was caught with a hidden sword, and the others we let through to the city."

"And they opened the gates? There are still Jews wanting to go into the city?" Tiberius Alexander asked dumbfounded.

"To get to the Temple for sacrifices," Agrippa replied, interrupting Florus' chance to respond. "Most Jews will stay away, but for some, it does not matter if there is a siege going on. It is incumbent upon them that they make sacrifices; whether personal or not, they will come."

"And they shall be stuck there to die! Do they think we will let them out again?" Titus Frigius retorted. He looked at the Prince and shook his head. "This must stop, my Prince. What if these pilgrims are used to fight against us?"

Titus rubbed his chin as he approached the table with Porcius on his left. "For now, any unarmed pilgrims may pass through. I do not intend to upset their God. Just inform them that nobody leaves the city." Titus leaned forward and stared down at the map spread out before him. "Now to business, so take heed." Titus glanced at Porcius to begin and the elderly man did not hesitate.

"I have besieged over a hundred cities in my lifetime; this by far will be the most brutal. I have experience in towers, rams, ramps, camp defences, mining, catapult positioning, and breach assaults."

Porcius stared at the generals and tapped the western side of the map where wooden counters stood upon the leather representing the legionary deployment. "Our ramps hold firm and the rams work hard. Soon, we will make a breach, I expect by tomorrow."

A hushed silence filled the quarters as the generals and officers digested this fact. The engineer cleared his throat, cracked his knuckles, and continued, "The wall is cracking in five places: here, here, and there." He tapped the leather map along the sketched outline of the wall. "The crews sent in to pry out stones have not been any help." He cleared his throat and continued, "We knew that would be the result. We didn't send them in to topple the wall, but to distract. The rams will soften up the foundation, but it would take at least another week or two to do significant damage and create a breach." He shook his head and in his gruff, shaky voice said, "That is why we will use the towers tomorrow. They are fitted with higher elevated rams and these will help cause the foundation to crumble and will assist in breaking the stone so it falls into the city creating a natural ramp for the legionaries to use.

"However, this will mean all three towers must be in use and all three towers will need to be mounted to the walls so we can fight upon their ramparts. The towers cannot get this close unless we fight back. The Palmyrene bowmen will work from the ground and at least two cohorts per tower will be used with whatever remaining strength massed on the ground below to charge up the breach." Porcius paused for a moment and hefted up the belt about his waist which had slid down below his belly. "My generals, the breach will be in the center and will collapse about five meters on either side. You will, therefore, have about a ten meter breach. Not much, but workable. I leave all infantry tactics to your glorious minds, but this is my profession and my calculations, and now you have heard it." Porcius gave a firm nod and stepped back.

Titus gazed around the table and then stopped where Larcius Lepidus stood. "I will have a vexillatio of one thousand men from your cohortes, Larcius. I want your best. They will operate from the tower on the extreme left. Frigius, you choose the same for the middle tower, and Sextus, you have the right tower nearest Hippicus. I will position scorpions on the right and left to engage Jews in the Psephinus and Hippicus so they can't concentrate on the towers. The Twelfth, Tribune Octavian, will have the honours of charging the breach.

"I am sure the First Cohors would not turn this chance down?" Titus asked glancing over to Gaius who saluted and firmly nodded. "Good. With that said, all units will converge on the breach and the towers will clear the ramparts. As soon as we have the Jews fleeing we can bring up artillery and secure the Bezetha. The rallying point for Simon's soldiers will be the Second Wall here," Titus tapped the map. "We will also have problems with the Antonia which dominates these suburbs, but we will deal with that later. Your orders once inside, are to destroy all homes in the northern corner and establish a camp there. Pile the rocks high and double the guard around this camp. Take all precautions. The Jews will fight like animals to drive us out."

"What about prisoners, my Prince?" Marcus Octavian asked.

Titus picked something from his teeth and flicked it away and then gestured for a servant to bring wine. "Don't make too many examples; slaves could be useful later on. Once the Bezetha is secure, I plan on using Yosef again to deliver terms. For now, we shall give quarter to aristocrats, patricians, and their families. I must be seen as reasonable. Do not slaughter everything that moves, not yet.

"I will have the Boars shadow the walls and gates, to kill anything that flees. Once the New City is ours, the Boars will join us inside and the alae mounted units can take up the task of border patrol." Titus pointed to the ceiling as he made a point and said sternly, "Do not get into a heated engagement at the Antonia. It is far too large and difficult, and any forces to engage it are sure to suffer heavy casualties. Pass the word along that I will execute any centurions who lead their men in an attack against that fortress. We must be prepared for assaulting the Second Wall and the Antonia, and that will take weeks. One step at a time and Mars will give us glory."

Titus nodded and stared back down at the map. "Use the drums and the cornucen to accompany the legionary deployment. I want every legio drawn up in full order before their walls. Have the men remain silent, including the alae, at the other parts of the city. I want a silent approach to the towers with the imagio of my family in the center of each legio. I want every Jew to know who is storming their city." Titus was silent for a moment as he leaned over the map with his fingers clenched into tight fists. His full attention was upon the western side of the map where he stared at the wooden legionary counters with a fixated obsession. "Do the rams continue to operate, Tiberius?"

"All night, my Prince," Tiberius candidly replied. "The wall is so lit by torches we will see if the Jews try anything. We have two hundred artillery units pounding their positions and two thousand men drawn up."

Titus nodded. "Good, you are all dismissed." He watched the relief come over their faces as the tense atmosphere evaporated. The generals whispered quietly amongst each other as they left for a drink of wine and Titus watched as the four legionary Praefectus Castrorum prepared to leave behind the kings. "Gaius Cornelius, stay a moment if you would."

Gaius turned and snapped his heels together as his comrades left. As Marcus Sulla passed by him, the Tribune patted Gaius' shoulder and whispered, "Victrix in the morning my friend, dine well tonight." Gaius nodded at the cavalry officer, but remained silent.

Once the room was clear, Titus signaled Gaius with a jerk to follow him over to a couch. The Centurion obeyed as Titus gave a great sigh and collapsed upon the soft, plush cushions. He watched humorously as Gaius awkwardly sat on the edge and snickered as the Centurion blushed. "Gaius, wherever my home may be, you may always relax and put your feet up."

"My Prince is too kind," Gaius replied.

"Gaius," Titus said as he dove right in, "What do you think of my father?" Titus picked up an ornamental deer horn from a table nearby and played with it in his hands as he stared at the Centurion who was sixteen years his senior.

Gaius looked startled for a moment from the direct question, then shrugged and said, "I think he is proud, wise, courageous, and a good soldier." Gaius rubbed his hands together hoping the answer appeased the Prince.

Titus held Gaius' gaze and then chuckled. "He would like to hear such an answer. He is also plump around the waist and has a sense of humour, you forgot those." Titus teased as he watched Gaius smile. Then the Prince clapped his hands and said, "Wine?"

"Yes, my lord," replied Gaius.

A servant appeared carrying a copper platter which contained two ornate goblets and a silver pitcher with a long-necked spout. The servant carefully filled the goblets and as he lowered the tray the Prince and the Centurion each took one. "The finest of wines they make here. I think I shall bring some back with me when this is all done."

"I have seen the vineyards in the north. Very studious and rich," Gaius added feeling silly in the conversation, but he held his own and the Prince appreciated it.

"Tell me, Gaius, what do you think of me? You have told me of my father, now what traits of me do you see?" Titus shifted his gaze from the goblet in his hands to the silent officer and grinned. "Come now, this is not a trick question. You will not get flogged for your answer. I want to know your mind, be honest."

"Why my opinion, Prince? Surely you have men who know you much better than I," Gaius stammered.

"Because my father trusts you and calls you Cornelius. So please, if you may," Titus motioned him to speak.

Gaius took a drink of wine and said, "I see much of your father's virtue in you, my Prince. You hunger for glory and treat your men well. They trust you."

"Trust?" Titus said slowly, mulling over the word. "Do you trust me, Cornelius?" Gaius nodded and remained silent. "Have you ever met my brother?" Gaius shook his head and Titus tossed his head back and laughed. "A good boy. A schemer, but a good boy. Domitian tries so hard for father's blessing and attention, but I am the eldest. I am to gain the trust of more than this army one day. *Roma* and the lands which she controls will one day look to me as Caesar, and I will have to be trusted."

Titus sighed, finished his wine and then set the cup next to him on the cushion. "I have been thinking about what is to come, and I have found myself recalling a certain

Jewish man I had made a deal with. I have had a mind lately to send this Judah ben Yosef to Hades, along with my promise to him. But I see things different now." He paused, then leaned forward and pointed at Gaius. "I want to use him, keep him on our side. He is a Jew who delivered and maybe his help can still be used. So, Gaius, I want you to meet him tonight."

"Tonight? But how?" Gaius replied shocked.

"However you do it, just do it. Send him a signal, a message something. I cannot send Yosef as it would be an utter disaster if he was to get captured, poor man would be pulled to pieces." Titus cleared his throat and sat back. "You can make this happen. I care not in the style you do it in, just meet with him. Tell him Capito will be delivered once we are in the city. I shall commit a cohors of his to battle and have them withdraw so Judah can make his move. I will arrange it with the cohors optio beforehand, along with a handsome purse filled with coin. I will offer him Capito's office as senior Centurion. Who could turn that down? Money and rank speaks volumes, Gaius."

Titus was quiet for a moment and then burst out with sudden laughter and an animated gesture as he pointed to himself. "You said you trusted me. Now I betray the life of one of my officers to the blade of a Zealot and will pay off another with money and the promise of a better future. Who is there to trust? Oh, we men are wretched things." Gaius awkwardly smiled and Titus wiped the tears away from his eyes as he calmed himself. "Well, it is for the glory of *Roma* and victory. We must sacrifice in the end for greater glory and power. No senator sat in the Forum without sacrifice and my father has bled and given up much. Now it has come time for my turn. That is what Basilides would desire; the eagle must remain strong and never die. Is that not right, my dear Gaius?"

"Yes, my Prince." Gaius replied.

Titus moved to stand but Gaius beat him to it as the Centurion snapped to attention and awaited to be dismissed. The Prince nodded with an expression of gratitude and placed a warm hand upon Gaius' shoulder. "You are good for the army and an excellent soldier. You know, I have figured something out about you." Gaius looked surprised, but Titus quickly continued, "You are honourable to *Roma* and to your wife. You fight valiantly and fear nothing and you are truly trustworthy, even more then I." Titus grinned at the shock on Gaius' face. "I suppose that is why I will one day be an emperor and you will not. You are to honest of a man, Gaius. Never think I would dishonour you. You gave your word to Judah, I remember the token you gave to him. May it be safely placed in your hands soon."

"Thank you, my Prince," Gaius stammered.

"Fight well tomorrow, and may the gods overshadow you," said Titus.

"I am honoured, my Prince."

"Dismissed," Titus replied with a nod. He watched Gaius turn away and then spoke up with amusement. "Gaius, I am thinking about building an amphitheater in

Roma when this siege is finished. It shall be the largest and grandest amphitheater in the world. It will sport gladiators, beasts from Africa, and mass games. The treasury from this city will be enormous if they do not surrender and I will use it for the entire undertaking. I wish to give something back to *Roma*, what do you think?"

"It will be glorious, my Prince, of that I am sure." Gaius saluted and left the tent as Titus rubbed his chin and thought about a name for his amphitheater.

Gaius stepped into the fresh air and took a deep breath. Night had descended upon the land as all around him quietness arose from the rows of legionary tents. Torches burned along the intersecting roads and the sounds of horses stirred somewhere in a dark stable nearby. A dog barked twice followed by a quick rebuke from an unknown soldier and the camp grew silent again. Two legionaries on duty passed by and saluted the Praefectus Castrorum as they continued their routine patrol to the sounds of snoring men. He thought for a moment about how he could make contact with Judah then heard the sharp snap of a twig nearby and saw a centurion standing a few metres away, partially concealed by the shadow of Titus' tent.

"Who are you, centurion? What centuria do you command?" Gaius asked with authority.

The man snickered as he stepped out from the darkness and tossed away the broken branch. "I am a long way from my post."

"What is that supposed to mean?" Gaius questioned.

The man pointed to the east and yawned. "Mount of Olives is my station; I just came by for the council."

"The council ended nearly an hour ago, why do you still linger?" Gaius asked turning to face the man who smiled back with an indifferent gaze.

"Because I like this camp. I accompanied Florus who is still paying Cestius Gallus a visit. Do you want me to barge in there and break up their bond?" the man replied shrugging with a cocky expression.

Gaius glared at the man, hating him instantly and sensing something of a bothersome nature which seemed to follow the centurion like a plague. "What is your name, Centurion?"

"Capito Vorenus Bibalus, Hastatus Prior of the Falcon Cohors, that is the Third, and honoured to serve in the Fretensis." Capito gave a slight bow smiling the entire time and when he straightened he gestured thoughtfully Gaius' way. "I know who you are, Gaius Antony. You are Titus' number one. Congratulations on your recent promotion to Praefectus Castrorum, you must be honoured."

Capito stepped closer into the light. An ugly scar trailed across his face down his neck and his left eye seemed a bit milky due to blindness. Stubble dotted his chin as his jaw was set and teeth gritted with defined cheek bones. His eyes seemed smaller than normal, but they possessed an ill favour which Gaius did not like as Capito raised an eyebrow and chuckled. "I seem to have caught you off guard? It is no secret about your promotion. I merely send my regards, nothing more."

"Is that so, Centurion Capito of the Falcon Cohors? Well, you are too kind then," Gaius replied sarcastically as he felt unclean being in the presence of the man with his obnoxious grin and unsavoury eyes. "I must go. Leave immediately once Florus calls on you."

"Humbly I will," Capito replied with a scowl. He watched Gaius turn to leave and then called out, "So you will lead the First into the breach? Are you ready?"

Gaius halted abruptly and turned staring back at the arrogant man. "What kind of a question is that? If you are so familiar with my record, why don't you tell me?"

"I will be in the vexilliatio to attack from the most northern siege tower, on the left," Capito said ignoring Gaius' sharp response. "Personally, I look forward to it. If there is one thing I learned being stationed out here under the wisdom of Gessius Florus, it's that there is a strange sense of ecstasy one feels watching a Jew die." Capito slowly drew his sword and stared at the blade as if in a trance. "I have killed many; the Jewish women are something else, totally different from a man or a pathetic child. It actually excites me, Gaius, seeing the fear in their eyes and watching them die under my sword. I even think their blood smells different. I tried to force this one woman once, I had my toga up and everything, she could have had a piece of old Capito, but no, she refused to look at me." Capito lowered his voice in almost a whisper as he watched the torchlight reflect from the steel of the blade, "Even when I was killing her she said nothing. It was incredible."

Capito paused as if he had solved the greatest philosophical problem known to the School of Athens and then slowly said with passion, "We wield incredible power, don't we?" He glanced up and grinned at the sickened expression Gaius returned to him. "But surely you must know that there is no greater feeling then commanding a troop of men. They will do whatever you ask in a heartbeat. The thunder of our caligae and the wall of shields, it sometimes unnerves me.

"The last time I truly felt this pride and fear was the day Florus dispatched my cohors into the marketplace, here in Jerusalem. The bastards deserved it, collecting pennies for a Procurator? Utterly a shameful and disgraceful bunch of thieves they are. The dogs wouldn't even give us the names of the criminals; the blood of those we killed rests on their hands."

"You murdered them!"

Capito shook his head and said in defence, "We had orders to slaughter the enemy. We literally trampled over the barbarians as we rid the world of their scum. I have only come now to realize how important that day was as we now stand outside this city, ready to destroy it. We failed years ago under Cestius, but now Titus will lead us all the way." Capito chuckled and shook his head fascinated with his own story. "It is pure ecstasy that the gods have shown me, a sense to see the way of the world, and the right of *Roma* to rule it. 'The glory of war is in the might of our arms and in the reach of our iron hand,' that is what Florus used to say. Now the Jews are finally about to feel it, wouldn't you agree, Primi Ordines?"

Without saying a word Gaius slowly walked towards the Centurion and halting before him, he softly said, "You know, I will pray to the gods and my ancestors, Capito, that a Jew somewhere in that city, is able to look upon you with this ecstasy you claim to know, while his blade spills *your* blood. Then maybe you can finally learn what it is like to live out your fantasy the other way around." Gaius stared directly into Capito's eyes, hoping the Centurion would make a play, than he could drag the sadist out of camp to be food for the jackals. "Stay away from me, Capito, or I will kill you and it will be relief I will feel, not excitement, as I remove your damned carcass from this world." Gaius glared at the Centurion who smiled, gave a respectful nod, turned and sauntered away into the dead of night.

* * *

Chapter XXVII

Adam stared at Judah who lay motionless upon the stone ground. A dying fire crackled nearby, revealing in the darkness of the early morning, the forms of five other men snoring soundly. The large warrior quietly knelt and gently shook Judah. He watched as his friend murmured in his sleep and then rolled over. Adam gave his sleeping friend another shake and whispered, "Judah, it is Adam. Wake, you must wake."

Judah slowly opened his eyes and took a moment until he could make out the familiar features of his bearded friend staring down at him. "What is it?" he asked with alarm as he sat up and looked around.

"A boy calls for you," Adam replied with a shrug as he stood.

"A boy?" Judah rubbed his eyes and yawned. He was silent, not understanding why Adam had woken him, and then relived an itch, glancing back up at the giant man. "Why are you here?"

"A boy calls for you on the other side of the wall, Judah. I thought it strange, but then what do I know, everything has been less than normal."

Judah groaned and stood, trying not to disturb the sleeping soldiers. "Where is he?"

"On the other side of the wall. I can't exactly invite him in, now can I?" Adam responded with a shifty look as he tried to figure Judah out.

"Other side of the wall?" Judah asked sharply and then listened for a moment. "The rams have quit?"

"Hours ago. The sun will not rise for another two hours." Adam leaned upon his spear and sighed. "What is this about? How does this boy know you?"

"The lad must be drunk," Judah said as he refused to make eye contact while he fixed his clothing.

"The lad is younger then my nephew, I suppose too young to be drunk, and he spoke to me in Hebrew," Adam paused. "He is one of us."

Judah shrugged, as if not having a care in the world for Adam's worries. "A drunk slave then," he smirked as he bent down and gathered up his shield and bedding. He faced Adam, stared into his bearded face for a moment and then moved to the side to step around him.

Adam quickly blocked Judah's path with a raised hand, yet gentleness in his deep, calm eyes. "Judah, what are you hiding from me?"

Judah bit his lower lip as he thought about it for a second and then shook his head. "I am sorry, it is better if you don't know. Did this boy say who he was?"

"No, but he said he knew you," Adam replied uneasily.

"Show me where he is." Judah stared at Adam for a brief second and then the giant just growled with frustration and turned as he shook his head.

Adam led Judah through the darkness of the night towards the glow of torches which ran the length of the wall. To Judah in this moment, it felt almost impossible that on the other side of the great stone wall there could be a threat. The walls seemed to offer a false sense of security and hope, as if the mountains of stone would hold forever. However, one look over the wall changed everything as three massive ramps stretched back into the dead of night. Along with the threat of the earthen mounds, enormous siege towers also stood like mystical, sleeping giants waiting to bring death with approaching doom. Upon the walls the sentries could see the lights of the Roman camps and sense the impending dread which would come in the morning.

Judah climbed the stairs in the dark, making sure to watch his step as he followed Adam. At the top, Adam checked to make sure no sentries were close by, then signaled Judah and strolled over to the ledge. "Swear to me you will tell me what is going on. I deserve to know. Before you arrived at the house, Caleb told me to watch over you. He said that you should not die, as long as I lived."

Judah stared at the dark figure of the warrior, contemplating if such a promise validated Adam knowing about his business. Finally Judah gave a hasty nod and replied, "I will tell you soon, but Moshe can never know. He would not understand."

"Fair enough," Adam sighed. "I pray that on a cool night such as this you do not taste death." He stared up at the starry sky for a moment and then pointed over the wall. "Your *drunk* lad is down there waiting."

Judah approached the parapets and carefully leaned over the wall, staring into the darkness until he could make out a faint wisp of white cloth being waved near the ramp. Judah waved at the signal and then said to Adam, "Do you have a rope?"

It was not long until a rope was secured to one of the stone parapets and around Judah's waist as he expertly climbed over the side to scale the wall. Adam warned him to be quiet and that if any guards ventured over he would try to steer them in a new direction. "If this is impossible, you will find the rope tumbling down beside you. Consider this a signal to get as small as you can and don't make a sound. When it is clear I will have to get another rope to let down."

Judah nodded and without another word began to climb down. He felt the cords of the tightly woven rope burn his hands as he gripped them, fighting against the walls slippery stone as he pushed his feet against them to aid his descent. When he was close enough to the ground he let go and landed hard. He lost his balance and fell onto his side with a grunt. He felt something poke him and when he rolled over he discovered a broken arrow lodged into the cool earth.

Judah caught his breath, freed himself from the rope, and gazed around him. A foul stench suddenly filled his nostrils as he gagged and covered his face with the hem of his cloak. He scanned the ground and noticed bodies everywhere. Some lay in piles, while others were partially buried in the dirt. All of the corpses were Jewish as the Romans regularly collected their dead. Judah heard the sounds of ravens pecking at the flesh of men and heard the squealing of mice and rats as they scurried about the great banquet spread out before them.

Almost as strong as the scent of blood was the putrid smell of bodily fluids as men, who had lain cut open for days, began to decompose. Judah continued to cover his face as he picked his way among the bodies, looking for the boy who had strangely disappeared. Faint silver light began to illuminate the ground as shadows were chased away from the moon that began to shine through thin black clouds. With the arrival of the moon, Judah could see the tools of destruction lying before him. The siege towers cast a long shadow upon the ground as he could make out clusters of guards, adorned in great cloaks, surrounding the machines and keeping watch. No fires burned and nothing was said as Judah knew they would be able to see him. He hesitated, unable to decide if he should proceed or not, and that was when he saw a single man step out from the cluster of guards.

Judah glanced back at the unseen wall behind him and the rope he knew that waited there. He turned again and watched the lone man advance across the battlefield of wicker hurdles and corpses as he lifted his garments to step over bodies. Judah squinted, wishing for more light, praying this was not an ambush. Then the clouds in the sky dissipated and the moon shone gloriously as Judah saw Gaius Antony lift his right hand in acknowledgment.

When Gaius lowered his hand the moon hid itself once again and the land became lonely and desolate of the living. A killing field of mutilated flesh, stinking carcasses, and hollow faces surrounded Gaius as he walked across the soiled dirt. This was the work of the cohorts, but at great cost. Three hundred and forty nine pyres had burned from legionaries and alae who had been slaughtered in the last six days under heavy Jewish attacks. This was the very thing that drove a man like Titus to seek the help of a common Jewish Zealot, and Gaius was the one who would work to foster such a relationship.

Gaius had not known if the slave boy would have been able to locate the Jewish fighter, but the boy was good and had his own personal method, as well as motivation from Roman leverage over his family. The power of life and death seemed strange to Gaius on this cool night among the company of hundreds of corpses.

"Gaius, what do you want?" Judah whispered in Greek when the Centurion was close.

"Do you wish to speak here?" Gaius slightly turned and gestured back to the tower. "It is safer over there, my men can light a fire and we can speak privately behind its shelter." Gaius could sense Judah's hesitation as he stepped closer. "Judah, I swear no harm will befall you. Have I not been a man of my word thus far?"

"Will they stay?" Judah asked motioning to the guards.

Gaius looked back and shook his head. "Them? No, they fear ghosts and witches among all this dead more than they fear you. Some of the sentries speak of becoming bewitched and haunted by Jewish spirits. They say your men are so ferocious in life, they fear meeting them in the after world."

Judah nodded as he gave one last stare back to the wall and Adam's shadowed outline behind the parapets. Silently and with no indication of objection, he followed Gaius past the wicker hurdles to the middle siege tower. He watched nervously as legionaries stepped to the side in the dark as he could feel their heated gaze as if it burned right through him. Judah heard murmuring among the soldiers as they clustered together watching him behind their scutum shields and the security of their spears.

Judah watched as one of the men, adorned in a wolf fur which covered his helmet, shake his head and spit upon the ground at the sight of him. Judah looked away, staying close to Gaius with a fear that if the Centurion suddenly vanished, the legionaries would crucify him on the nearest olive tree.

"Start a fire, and remember that you will speak to none of what you see," Gaius growled. "You are all sworn to secrecy and I have your names, as does the Prince." The impatient Centurion waited as a number of soldiers carried faggots of wood over and arranged them on the ground. Some dried grass was used and soon a small fire warmed Judah as it lapped hungrily at the timber. Gaius stared at Judah from under the weight of his and whispered, "Are you comfortable?" Judah nodded, quickly glancing to his left and right at the legionaries who watched him. Gaius crossed his arms as he studied the Jewish fighter for a moment. "Are you hungry?" Judah hesitated and Gaius saw the weakness. "Here," he picked up a cloth bag from the ground and tossed it across the fire at Judah. "There is cheese, bread, and dried fish in there. It is enough for a few days if you keep it close to you." Gaius watched him nod as he accepted the gift. "What is the current situation of food in Jerusalem?"

"I cannot tell you that," Judah replied. "We make do."

Gaius folded his arms and stared at the stubborn man for a second. "I will wager that there are thousands of civilians who have hardly any food to eat, and that hundreds are dying of starvation and bear sickness and boils. I would bet this to be rampant in the Lower City as John and Simon naturally stockpile the food for fighters."

"Have you come to question me about if I eat lamb stew and freshly baked bread? I don't have the time nor will I tell you these things just so you can inform Titus about how we suffer." Judah stared stubbornly at the Centurion and breathed deeply.

Gaius pointed at the food he had given Judah. "This has no strings attached. Titus does not know of it. Consider it a gift, Judah."

"Well, I take no gifts from Rome, but this is for someone else." Judah tucked the cloth bag deep into his cloak and made sure it would not move.

Gaius smiled. "She will enjoy the food; it is from my banquet table."

"So what word do you bring? Will Titus honour my fulfillment of the bargain and give up Capito?"

Gaius nodded. "He will honour the deal. It will be complicated, but he will honour it."

"How complicated?"

Gaius sighed and scratched his chin. "In a few hours, Judah, eight thousand men will wake and form up directly in front of these walls. Even if you tell John and Simon there will be nothing they or anyone can do to stop it. The wall is weak and will crumble. I tell you this because you and anyone you value as a friend should pull back to the Second Wall or the Antonia.

"Titus will mount an attack and crush the wall and everyone left in the Bezetha will die. My cohorts will lead the attack through the breach and soldiers will sweep the ramparts and towers above. By midmorning the New City will be ours and secured. This is inevitable and nothing can stop it." Gaius paused as he watched the effects of his words settle upon the shocked and pale face of Judah. "Capito will be handed over to you in an attack on the Second Wall. It will be covered up so nobody suspects anything; it has been arranged. I will be unable to deliver any messages to you in person and so I will tell you plainly how to spot Capito, so listen closely."

Gaius slowly walked around the fire and lowered his voice, "Capito is a senior Centurion in the Third Cohorts of the Tenth Legion. His centuria emblem is a golden falcon on a red standard with the word *Tertius* in gold letters followed by Centuria III. This is how you can recognize his unit. Like I said, it has been arranged. The centuria will attack and then pull back. You should be ready to strike at Capito quickly. It must look like an accident when the centuria withdraws and Capito is forgotten. You understand? Do not hesitate to kill him. Whatever god watches over you, he has given you a golden egg to have your vengeance and this is it. Fortune favours the bold, Judah. Take hold of Fortune's hand, and she will give you peace."

Judah was quiet, then sighed heavily and nodded. He found this union bizarre and strange. Here he faced a man he was sworn to kill and considered a bitter enemy. At any other time he would not have failed to spring upon the chance to kill Gaius, but here the two men needed each other. It was an odd fate that had knit these two together to share this strange bond, but deep within, Judah knew he respected the Centurion and admired him. Judah reached inside his cloak and slowly removed his hand which was tightly clenched in a fist. Gaius stepped closer and looked down with curiosity. Judah opened his fingers and there lying in his palm was the image of Livia

Gaius had given him that night in the cistern. "I will give this back to you. I fear death with this image in my possession."

"Keep it, Judah. It may keep you safe. It has watched over me all these years." Gaius gave Judah a warm nod.

Judah stared down at the graven image for a moment and then shook his head. "I don't believe in an image protecting one from harm. I am a Jew. I follow the direction of my God and His Torah and not in the carving of a woman baked from clay. It is forbidden in the Torah to make or possess a graven image."

Gaius gently took the image and stared at it for a moment. "My wife had this made for me before I left on campaign," he mumbled and when he looked up Judah was still. "That was six years ago when everything began to boil over." Judah stood shocked and transfixed from the intimate detail the Centurion had confided in him. "My Livia is the love of my life. I thank the gods for her and for the children we have had together, all gems from a place of bliss I shall never come to fully understand." Gaius firmly wrapped his fingers around the image and nodded at Judah. "I would kill anyone who would threaten her. I would take my time against any man who would take her from me. Judah, I spoke with Capito. I saw his eyes. He deserves to die."

Judah felt a swell of burning tears well up inside of him as they clung to the rim of his eyelids. His face felt flushed and skin hot as sweat beaded upon his forehead. He stared at Gaius feeling both jealousy and a longing to find peace. The conviction with which Gaius had spoken swirled inside Judah's mind as he contemplated, in a confused state, at what exactly his relationship with this Roman was.

On one side Judah felt obligated as a Jew to hate such a man, as Gaius symbolized the very oppressive power which slaughtered his people and spat in the face of their sacred faith. However, the other side of the paradoxical coin was that Judah recognized a man of honour, courage, and trustworthiness that appealed to him. Judah considered these traits to be part of his own personal makeup. Yet, Gaius had one thing he did not have, that was a family and Judah longed to have such an identity.

"Thank you and shalom," Judah managed to say amidst the conflicted emotions.

Gaius watched Judah turn to leave and quickly called out, "Judah, if you meet me in battle tomorrow, would you try and kill me?"

"Wouldn't you do the same?" Judah replied, as he quietly stepped away from the light of the fire and disappeared into the darkness of the morning as a blue haze began to light the horizon.

* * *

CHAPTER XXVIII

May 7th, 70 A.D. / 11th of Iyyar, 3830
Two hours after first light
Western side of Jerusalem

"Climb those ladders, you perky virgins! And give them hell!" a Centurion bellowed inside the tower as legionaries pushed past him to climb the ladders to the top level of the siege tower. "Wait for contact and then blood and iron on my word! Unleash hell and send the dogs into the flames!" He patted the shoulders of men as they passed by while some of the younger ones gave him nervous looks. "Fight together, you Fifth bastards, and push them from the walls! This is where your training has taken you, either to Elysium or glory! Come on, up you go!"

The Centurion felt the tower begin to lurch forward as grunts sounded from below as men pushed the siege engine towards the wall. The Centurion stepped forward, tipped his helmet slightly back and pressed his sweaty face against the iron plating as he closed one eye to get a better look. He peered between two interlocking plates and held his breath as he concentrated. A thunderous crash sounded as an explosion hurled stone shrapnel everywhere. At his back he could hear the catapult and scorpion crews shouting the common command, 'Loose!' Suddenly a hailstorm of objects began striking Jerusalem's walls and careening overhead to disappear into the city.

He could only see a handful of Jews crowding the parapets directly in front of him as they clutched spears and swords, anticipating the approaching fight. The Centurion noticed fear on their faces and smiled as he thumped the sides of the tower shouting, "Cheer up lad! They're afraid! Let's skin 'em alive!" He stepped away and turned around as he stared back out the open rear of the siege tower.

Drawn up like a game of sticks, the cohorts of the Fulminata waited silently as they faced the middle ramp. All that had to happen was someone with a gambling nature needed to toss the dice, give the trumpet blast, and send them forward through the breach once it had been made. He shook his head, glad he was not leading the first wave as he watched the eight hundred men of the First Cohort. The Centurion lifted a hand in salute to his General who watched below, then turned away, and thanked the gods he was not standing where Primus Pilus Gaius Antony now stood.

*   *   *

Gaius clutched the grip of his heavy scutum with white knuckles slick from sweat as he hefted it off the ground. From his position he possessed the best view of the battlefield as he studied the action unfolding before his eyes. He watched the three siege towers approach the walls like great mythical giants. Teams of men on the third level of each tower readied the great rams as they stared through the hole in front of them where the ram would catapult through. Above the ram on the fourth level, Gaius could make out the turrets of each tower crammed to capacity with legionaries and bristling by iron spear points. The cluster of soldiers resembled a sleeping, segmented scaled beast as they waited, hunkered down behind their scuta and the low iron-plated parapets which surrounded them. Gaius stared at the middle tower's turret and could make out a blonde transverse plume from a centurion who knelt at the head of his men, bracing himself for the spiked ramps to be dropped. All the while soldiers pushed the towers forward, shouting out in unison to the steady beat of drums and the chorus of the cornu.

At the base of each siege tower which was crammed with soldiers, stood huddled masses of legionaries from the vexilliatio as they crept forward with every metre the towers gained, waiting to board once the ramps dropped. Gaius saw a soldier from the far left tower stumble with a look of pain plastered upon his face as a black arrow protruded from his leg. He collapsed upon the ground and a comrade quickly pulled him inside the protection of the engine.

"This will be over quickly, I assure you," Titus said as he gave Gaius a nod. Since the Prince had given the order to renew the assault at first light, he had joined the Twelfth Legion in the center and had desired to remain near Gaius. Only Tiberius Alexander accompanied the Prince as the other generals and kings remained a few metres back as they watched the fight. "The gods have smiled upon us; there is little resistance from the walls. The Jews are beaten!" Titus declared as he gave Tiberius a smile.

"There are still men crowding those ramparts, my Prince. They will put up a stiff fight, I wager," replied Tiberius as he dampened the Prince's mood. "The slice and dice of the gladius should work like a charm on those close confinements." Tiberius chuckled and shook his head. "Crawl or fall, those are the only options left for anyone who will fight." Tiberius arched his back slightly and groaned as it cracked.

"Bed stiff?" Titus asked.

"Not exactly. I had trouble sleeping last night. Damned waste. The pillows are stuffed with feathers, so I should have slept like a baby." Tiberius yawned and then scratched his leg. He pointed at the three testudo battering rams stationed to the left of each ramp and said, "You sure the walls are weak enough?"

"Porcius said they were," responded Titus.

"And you trust your Chief Engineer, my Prince?" Tiberius asked with a clever smile.

Gaius heard the Prince chuckle lightly and then the two men quieted down as the towers halted before the walls. It was like a blurry dream for Gaius. It seemed like it had taken all of eternity to get to this point, as if the months of training and preparation would never offer satisfactory results. Now, before his eyes, the ramps of each tower dropped, the spikes below the heavy platforms shattering stone as if claw-like fingers now gripped the walls and refused to let go. Like a flood of iron, the legionaries sprung to life and charged the ramparts with such force that high pitched screams could be heard as Jewish fighters toppled over the side, plunging to their death. Even with the distance, Gaius could hear the sounds of sword blades biting into flesh and shields thumping men as they fell, only to be trampled.

Whistles blasted from centurions as the legionaries on the ground quickly entered the towers, climbing the wooden ladders up to the fourth level and onto glory. Amidst the bitter fighting on the ramparts, Gaius caught a glimpse of a tall Zealot who suddenly picked up a legionary single handidly and held him thrashing in the air, poised above his head. Titus gasped in shock and Gaius watched as the Jewish Hercules hurled the man over the side of the wall who shrieked all the way down until he drove into the ground with a sickening thud. The Zealot hardly had a time to admire his work as six spear heads were driven through his chest causing the man to spew blood and fight for a few final moments against the shafts of pila which tore his insides to pieces. Gaius heard a roar from the dying man, like a great wounded lion, and then the Zealot disappeared amidst the fighting.

With the sixth strike upon the wall from the middle ram, nicknamed *Nikon*, the stones began to crumble and groan. With a deep grind of crushed stone the wall seemed to ripple, shake, buckle inward, and then come to life as it suddenly pitched back with the screams of men who fell with it. A dense cloud of smoke rose into the sky as the fighting nearest the breach came to an abrupt halt. What few Zealots remained, stared into the great chasm of rubble where the wall had once stood. Then Jews began to shout as order and determination began to give way to confusion and fear.

"Here we go!" shouted Quintus Cassius Aemilius from the Wolf Cohors as he looked past the ranks of men to his left where Gaius stood, watching the destruction of the city walls.

Gaius drew his sword with intensity as he stared at the breach. Some of the rubble had filled the gap between the ramp and the wall but most had poured backwards into the city crushing men and buildings. Now the way into Jerusalem had been carved out by brute strength. Gaius would lead his men directly into the lion's den as he could see Zealots clamoring awkwardly over the rubble as they attempted to form a battle line.

Gaius took a deep breath and tightened his face as he rallied courage. He narrowed his eyes and gripped a small whistle which hung around his neck, placing it between his lips. Gaius nodded to his signifer who hoisted the signum proudly, causing all the shields of the century to rise. A second later the other centuries did the same as spears were lowered.

"Successfully take the breach, Gaius, and you and your officers will each get dona," Titus ordered as he lifted the reins and nudged Achilles forward. "Mars will give you victory! *Roma Victa!*" Titus shouted to the First Cohort as he drew his sword and pointed it to the city.

"*Roma Victa!*" shouted eight hundred legionaries as they suddenly stepped forward to the blast from Gaius' whistle. The cohort broke into a jog as a trumpet sounded and all five centuries maintained a perfect cohesiveness as the wall of shields approached the city rapidly. The ground shook under their hobnailed sandals as the jingling from every soldier's iron-studded cingulum rang in their ears.

Not a shout or war cry was heard from the advancing First Cohort as they neared the ramp. They had been ordered to approach the enemy in the regular Roman fashion, and that was in silence. As they came to the ramp, the centuries rearranged themselves without difficulty into battle columns with the Hydra Herculean leading the formation as the Fortis, Lion, Wolf, and Serpent centuries followed closely behind.

It felt as if Gaius' armour had tripled in weight as suddenly his legs felt encumbered and shoulders heavy. He pushed the daunting thought aside, which he interpreted as fear, and surged onward climbing the ramp with the heavy breathing of men at his back. He glanced down for a moment as chalk white dust plastered his sweaty feet and bronze greaves from the collapsed wall. Giant chunks of rock could be seen lying at the bottom of the ramp as he continued to climb. He gazed up for a moment and noticed the broken, jagged edges of stone, either side of the breach, stained red with blood as limbs from bodies hung over the side. He could hear the sounds of battle raging upon the ramparts and the shouts of men as they struggled. It was in this moment that all thoughts suddenly vanished as over two hundred Zealots, who had formed in the breach upon the rubble, quickly appeared, lunging forward with a wild cry.

"Shields ready!" Gaius bellowed as he broke into a charge up the ramp. He gripped his gladius and held his scutum in front of him as he peered over his shield at the mass of Jews climbing across the rubble and running towards them with an uncontrollable rage.

The first Zealot Gaius met was a bear-of-a man as the Jewish warrior tried to skewer him with a heavy spear. Like a choreographed dance, Gaius blocked the spear, knocking the thrust to his left side, then lunged with the flash of his blade and buried it deep into the man's lower abdomen. The Zealot grunted, closed his eyes, then gasped as he collapsed to his knees, shuddering from the flow of blood that suddenly drenched his cloak. Gaius lifted his foot, braced it upon the man's shoulder and pushed him back as his sword slid clean from the body with a ribbon of scarlet.

"Forward!" Gaius shouted, as if the kill had not even fazed him. With a sudden thunder from the century they drove forward with locked shields. Jews fell from the sides of the ramp, were trampled underfoot, or slaughtered by the jabbing pila which tore them to pieces. Gaius lunged with hacks and thrusts into the Jewish formation which struggled against the Roman tide. Shields shattered and blood began to soak the ramp as the fighting intensified. Gaius could see more Jewish fighters pouring down from the breach in an effort to push the legionaries back. Slowly the Roman battle column gained ground despite the surge in Jewish fighters, as the legionaries barred their teeth, cursed, and heaved upon the Zealots who flung themselves at the solid wall of scuta.

Gaius watched two legionaries fall over the side as they lost their balance on the edge of the ramp. They shouted in desperation as their heavy armour impeded their ability to recover. Instantly leaping on their vulnerability, four Zealots descended with eager blades. The Romans shrieked as they were stabbed to death. Then the Zealots turned to face six more legionaries who charged down at them with spears. As the small fight ensued upon the side of the ramp, one of the Jews was instantly killed while a legionary pitched back clutching his leg as blood poured over his fingers from a sword wound. Another legionary and a Zealot grabbed one another, grappled for a split second, than began to throw punches as they struggled, finally falling into the dust next to their broken weapons. The Roman shouted for help as the Jew tried to strangle him, but the other legionaries were too busy dispatching the other Zealots. The suffocating Roman managed to shriek once more, causing one of his comrades to leap to his aid with his spear and drive the iron point through the back of the Jew. The Zealot cocked his head back screaming in pain. Then in an instant, he revealed a curved dagger and plunged the blade into the side of the legionary's neck he had been strangling. Gaius saw the Roman's eyes grow large, a torrent of blood flowing out from his neck as the Jew collapsed dead upon his chest.

A gladius shot out from the front Roman rank past Gaius, and a Jewish corpse toppled back headless as blood washed upon Gaius' cuirass. Another Zealot quickly surged forward with a blade of his own and slashed it across the exposed arm of the Roman, cutting through skin, muscle, in a grisly scene. The Roman's arm went limp, as the sword fell to the ground, and the legionary howled in pain as he fell backwards. Gaius charged the Zealot with his shield and ploughed into the man. The Jew had seen the attack coming and braced himself as he tried to push back. Gaius gritted his teeth as he heaved, leaning into the Zealot. Then like a great eruption from a volcano, a volley of spears were hurled from the third and fourth ranks of the century and a gap suddenly opened in the Jewish line as men called out to God in agony as they bled to death. This was all the time Gaius required and he jumped at the opportunity as he thrust with his sword. The Jewish man stepped back to avoid the blade and found himself alone. Panic filled his eyes and he tried to flee. Gaius struck with his blade and slashed the edged steel across the man's exposed back. The Jew grunted and stumbled. Gaius charged forward, knocking the bleeding man upon the ground, and his century followed.

The breach was empty of Zealot fighters and feeling courage swell within him, Gaius ran as he pumped his legs. "Quickly now! Hold the breach!" he shouted and began to climb over the rubble. The legionaries at his back howled like excited dogs as they followed their fearless leader around boulders and half buried bodies. Gaius felt victory at his fingertips. He gazed up at the walls above him and could still hear fighting although it had slackened. Then he was on top of the breach. Gaius took a moment to stare into Jerusalem for the first time.

Piles of bodies littered the breach, and below the wall hundreds of bloodstained wounded called out for mercy or tried to drag their ruinous selves away. Stretched out like a vast ocean of activity, thousands of Jewish fighters, women, and children fled. Gaius watched them as they pushed their way through packed streets carrying weapons, personal belongings and wounded comrades. The entire Bezetha was being emptied before Gaius' eyes and even men on sections of the ramparts turned and ran. He could hear the sounds of crying children and screaming babies. He heard women calling out for their lost husbands in frantic wails as the roar of people echoed and vibrated from the buildings. Dust still clung to the air from the collapsed wall but Gaius could make out numerous homes engulfed by flames as black smoke poured into the sky. Other homes were simply piles of rubble, completely unrecognizable from the beautiful dwellings they had once been.

Gaius turned and faced his men. The four ranks behind him were smeared in dust, blood, and sweat as their chests heaved from the desperate climb. Gaius raised his sword and shouted, "No plundering! We are to secure the Bezetha and drive the enemy away! Forward!" Gaius ran down the rubble and led his men into the streets of the suburbs.

It was a wholesale slaughter. The ruthless legionaries, frustrated and enraged, cut down swathes of fleeing men, women, and children. They pressed forward with shields locked as they plowed through the streets stabbing with their spears and slashing with their swords. Sheets of blood stained the walls of homes and the ground as screams echoed loudly above the cruelty of the soldiers. Doors were broken down as torches were hurled in and soon entire neighbourhoods were burning.

Gaius watched as the rest of the Fulminata cohorts plunged through the breach and filled the Bezetha. Orders were instantly given by centurions as units broke off from the main body to begin construction on a new camp in the northwestern corner of the city under the shadow of Psephinus Tower. Titus had named the new base "The Camp of the Assyrians" after the dreaded enemy of the Jews and he had chuckled at the idea, thinking it brilliant. Supplies for the new camp were easily gathered from destroyed dwellings or homes that needed to be torn down. A number of soldiers began to fetch stone from the rubble in the breach but were quickly scolded by engineers who had just arrived. The breach was to be covered with packed earth to create a mobile ramp inside the city to make way for the rams and siege towers for the next round of fighting.

"Splendid job!" Marcus Sulla exclaimed as he stood at the top of the breach admiring the slaughter around him.

Gaius wearily gazed up at the Tribune, wiping a streak of sweat and dirt from his forehead. "If you say so, Marcus."

"Gaius, your face," Marcus said out of concern, pointing to his own cheek. He watched his friend touch his face and then wince from the cut above his jaw he had been oblivious to. "Your men fought well; the Bezetha is ours." Marcus listened to the continued screams and shouts rising up from the New City mixed with the common clapping sound from the legionaires caligae upon the stone streets. "A great victory. Finally something is going right," Marcus muttered as he briefly shook his head and climbed down the rubble. He cringed for a moment at a dismembered corpse protruding between two large stones spattered in blood and then passed by.

"Why have you come? You could get hurt," Gaius said revealing a smile.

Marcus returned the smile and patted his friend on the shoulder with a heavy hand. "Titus sent me ahead to get an account, probably so I wouldn't be bored." Marcus rubbed his face, and gave a heavy exhale. "How many men do you think you lost?"

Gaius shrugged and shook his head. He licked his dry lips yearning for water to quench his parched throat, but instead just sighed. "It is too early to tell. Maybe thirty? I don't know."

"I counted twelve wounded being carried back in the carts. The Jews fought like demons on those walls, I couldn't believe it. The fighting has only just stopped and our lads are too exhausted to chase them." Marcus turned and pointed up at the ramparts. They could see lines of blood running down the sides of the wall. Limbs and bodies hung off the side as the walkways were packed by Roman soldiers. Some sat with their heads between their legs while others leaned against the parapets with blank faces covered in specks of blood.

Gaius nodded, cleared his throat, and spit on the ground. "This was a hard brawl. We can only expect it to get worse when we fight that." Gaius pointed beyond the clouds of smoke and dust which filled the city to the enormous citadel of the Antonia. Even from where he stood he could see Jewish fighters crowding the towers as they waited with loaded scorpions. "Excuse me, Tribune, but I need to make sure my men don't stray too far. Titus' orders."

Marcus nodded. "Once the camp is up and the Bezetha is ours, we will make a palisade at the Second Wall near the Corner Gate. There is a tower we think will topple by smashing the foundation, so one of the rams will be put into action as soon as this breach can be made passable."

Gaius scowled and then rolled his eyes. "A palisade? Casualties will be high, and if the Jews are pushed into a corner too quickly it could be bad for us."

Marcus shrugged. "That is what I offered the Prince, but he thinks differently, as always. The man sees fortune right in front of him and desires to grab it. Tiberius actually supports him on this. To push the Jews harder could benefit us. If they flee the Second Wall, the Mishneh is opened to us to make a direct attack on the Antonia, Temple, and First Wall. It will give us more leverage. The more we look at the strength of the Antonia, the worse everything gets. We need multiple access points to attack it, and we cannot gain any advantage without the capture of the Mishneh. I suppose a contingent of the Fifth Legion will attack by palisade while the rest of the attack will concentrate on the other points and the Antonia. It will be mayhem either way we go." Marcus crossed his arms and stared into the city at the distant Second Wall rising above the Bezetha. "At least that wall is not as tall as the one we just came through."

"But it is stronger," replied Gaius. "Is the Prince coming in?"

"Later. I assume new ramps will undergo construction soon. There is ground to build up against the northern side of the Antonia, and we cannot tarry. You will have to get new orders. I don't know what is in store for the Fulminata or any of the other legions. I just heard about the Macedonica and a palisade. I saw the ladders being brought from the base camp. Well, that is all for now, I will leave you as I have matters to attend to. You did a good job here." Marcus nodded at Gaius and then marched back up the breach.

Gaius watched the Tribune disappear over the crest of rubble, then turned and saw his optio and signifer walking over to him. "What is it?"

Both men halted, saluted by striking their chests, and then the Optio said, "Most of the enemy has fled and nearly all homes have been searched, Primus Pilus! So far the centuriae are staying clear of the Antonia as I have word the Jews operate their own scorpions. We have many slaves though, and they are being gathered now."

"How many?" asked Gaius.

The Optio shrugged and replied, "Maybe three hundred, mostly women, children, and older men. We captured some Zealots and other fighters that we think hail from Idumea."

"Those would be Simon's men." Gaius thought to himself for a moment and then asked, "Any news of Simon?"

The Optio shook his head. "Escaped, most likely, I would say. I spoke with a centurion from the Fifth who said he thought he saw Simon flee the tower." The junior officer pointed to Psephinus and then squinted in the sunlight.

"How did he know it was Simon?" Gaius responded, inspecting his gladius for any chips or dents in the metal.

"The centurion said he saw a man fleeing the tower wearing a purple cloak and surrounded by large armed men. I guess he supposed it was Simon." The optio glanced at the signifer who remained silent and then stared back at his commanding officer.

Gaius nodded and replied, "Have the captives escorted from the city back to camp, and pass the word along." He looked at the signifer and said in a hoarse voice,

"You come with me. We must rally the centuriae and pray to the gods that the Jews don't hit us."

*   *   *

"John, Simon is here!" shouted one of the guards at the door.

John stood on the ramparts of the Antonia staring out at the destruction going on in the distant streets of the Bezetha as the Roman standards entered the city. He turned and watched Simon emerge onto the wall followed by an entourage of officers and spearmen. Parts of his royal clothes were blackened by soot and spattered in blood. His face was smeared with streaks of ash, his eyes were red from smoke, while his lips were cracked and caked in dirt. The proud man looked infuriated as he halted before John and glared at the warlord. He shot a hateful gaze towards Judah, Adam, and Moshe who stood behind John, then shook his head and spit over the wall as he attempted to fix his hair.

"You made it out," John said indifferently as he stared at the man.

"Many didn't, and their blood stains the streets and walls they fought from." Again Simon glared at Judah and then vehemently accused him saying, "Why weren't you on the wall? You obviously didn't fight today! Why did you leave?"

"Do not question his loyalty or his motives, Simon," John responded harshly in Judah's defence. "I have allowed him to stay. He is under my command, not yours."

Simon cackled with laughter and shook his head as he turned, gazing out over the parts of the city that burned. He listened for a moment to the sounds of collapsing rubble, hammers, and iron pry bars working steadily and then shook his head again as he clenched his fingers into tight fists. "We were slaughtered, John! Nearly everyone on the ramparts where the towers attacked were killed. Hezekiah ben Chobari is buried somewhere under the stone." He pointed to the rubble. "I saw the miserable man tumble down with the rock, followed by half of the archers on the platform, all crushed. You remember the son of Cathas?" John nodded gravely, and Simon looked away with bitter tears in his eyes. "He was decapitated by a legionary who jumped from a parapet as that poor lad hauled away a wounded brother." Simon stared up into the sky with a daze and mumbled something inaudible as if he were praying.

"Then what would you say is the condition of your men? Your officers?" replied John with a serious tone.

Simon shrugged. "Most of us escaped. I can elect new officers to fill the sandals of those killed. We have reformed on the other wall and I have stationed a horde of Idumeans inside the Mishneh. These are pike men and they are stubborn. They will fight to the last if they have to and would walk through the Hinnom if it burned again. I have even pulled troops back to the First Wall. I have men in the towers and we still hold out. The Romans have the Bezetha, but we still hold the high ground." Simon was silent for a moment as he could see Roman crews filling the breach as they poured bags of earth upon the rubble and worked aggressively to clear obstacles. "You know what they're doing down there?" Simon glanced at John cynically and the large man did not speak. "They are smoothing out the breach so they can bring in their damned rams and towers. I am sure of it."

"They have to build ramps to reach these ramparts with their towers, Simon. This will take weeks if they are even successful at all, and we will be fighting them the entire time." John watched the Sicarii King shake his head and close his eyes.

"The walls are lower which surround the Mishneh and the gates are harder to defend. They won't need ramps against these. They will get through and once they do you will find your impregnable fortress surrounded." Simon watched John rub his chin as he mulled it over. "We should attack them now," Simon hissed.

John scowled. "The Romans are too many, and they are no doubt elated by their tiny victory. We would be foolish to assault them now, Simon." John stepped closer to the filthy man and placed a hand on his shoulder. "Listen, if the Romans should get into the Mishneh, we can hit them there. We should be prepared. The Mishneh is packed with many homes and the streets are narrower than the Bezetha. It is a perfect breeding ground for an ambush. We could slaughter hundreds of Romans." Simon nodded, seeming to stare at nothing in particular. "What we should do," John continued, "Is have men formed up behind gates from the Upper City and the Temple. I can commit to you a thousand men. How many could you organize in the Upper City?"

"Well, they are bound to attack us along the outer wall near Herod's Palace, but the walls are higher and I don't think they would be very successful. Messengers say the Fifth Legion is strung out along the wall with artillery but no towers. I could give maybe another thousand to this scheme of yours. If they were ready near Agrippa's Palace, they could have access into the Mishneh should the Romans take the bait." Simon thought to himself for a moment and then nodded. "A combined attack could work, like a pincer we could suffocate any attack the legions make."

"We know these streets; the legionaries would be lost and incapable of making a stand suitable to their liking. We could have men in homes and on the roofs. We could slaughter them like we did at Jotapata and Gamla." A flare of hope ignited in John's eyes as he thought the plan through and gave a firm nod. "I will dispatch a few of my captains to you. I can have Yeshua ben Sapphias, Zacharias ben Phalek, and John ben Dorcas lead my thousand. They are good and ruthless, especially Yeshua."

"Was not he the one from Tarichaeae?" Simon asked.

John nodded. "Men say he slaughtered six Romans at one time with a dagger. They say he was covered in their blood and screamed so much like a wild man that he chased another twenty Romans away!"

"I will have Jacob ben Soras lead my men; they can coordinate together. If it weren't for the rams, my Idumeans could keep the legionaries at bay, but the tower's foundations are weak past the Corner Gate and Bread Wall. The Romans will know this, especially with men like Yosef ben Matityahu and Marcus Agrippa. We can hold out, but not for long. Those rams will bring down our towers and walls soon."

John cursed under his breath. "I would very much like to snatch the life from Yosef with the edge of my dagger. I pray for such a chance. That man has betrayed us and blasphemed God with his treason."

"There may still be a chance, John," replied Simon.

"With my scorpions and onagri I can make it hell for the Romans attacking this fortress! They will have never experienced such brutal precision as what my men can give them. They will pay for their labour in blood, I swear it." John walked a few steps along the rampart and gazed down at the flagstones below where he believed the Romans would set up their earthworks. "These walls and towers are the strongest in the city, next to the colonnades of the Temple." John faced Simon and outstretched his arms. "The Antonia is the key to the city; we must defend this with our lives."

Simon rubbed his hands together. "Hopefully our little spy problem died in the rubble." He stared back at the Roman work lines and swore at their progress.

"Let us pray we are that fortunate," John muttered. "However, I feel it is not complete. We must keep our eyes and ears open. Spies may still be around us."

"I will personally gut anyone I find," Simon said looking back. "I have Bagdatus and his men on it day and night. They search homes all over and I have agents working from the Sicarii with knives eager to disembowel." Simon nodded and grinned. "Yes, that is my punishment on those I catch. We slit their throats and rip out their intestines, a gruesome enough sacrifice to the obliteration of their pathetic treasonous pleas."

"You have found more?"

Simon shrugged. "No, but we remind people of who still holds the power as they see the hanging corpses nailed to doorposts." He turned as one of his men brought him a clean towel and a basin of water. Simon dipped his hands into the cool water and rubbed them together. Then he immersed the towel, pulled it out, and watched it drip for a moment. He buried his face into the cloth, wiping away the grime, then draped it over the arm of the soldier and sent him away. "Ah, that feels much better. You know, John, we have squads of men dumping bodies from the walls in the south of the city."

"I have heard," John said through partially gritted teeth.

"They are dying quickly as there is hardly any food left in the Lower City. I hear of murders and suicides daily. We just dispose of the bodies we find in the streets. My men can't even clean themselves according to the law because of the impurity that exists in the stinking and dirty streets. The *mikvot* haven't even been cleaned and some have been emptied by the poor who sneak into them during the night looking for water. I tell you, the city has never been worse. Have you been down there?"

"No."

Simon smiled. "You will know you are close by the smell. It never goes away. You know, decaying humans smell so strange compared to everything else. It used to make me feel ill, but now I am used to it. Did you hear that I had bottles of perfume brought into my palace so I can't smell the death? On a day when the wind picks up it is the worst, but there is nothing we can do since there is nowhere to bury them. The Romans watch as we wheel out cart loads of corpses to dump into the ravines, and that is the only time they don't hassle us. I think they are terrified of Jewish spirits haunting them."

John shifted uneasily and said in an attempt to change the subject, "I have no answer for that. We all suffer together. Now, we must look to our defences and I will dispatch a thousand men to camp near the gate of the stone arch from the Temple. They will be able to get into the Mishneh quickly once the Romans are inside. I bid you shalom." John turned to walk away as Judah and the others followed.

Simon called out with a raspy voice, "Shalom to you, John. Worry not, my friend, for we shall kill the Romans in the Mishneh without haste." Then he departed, instructing his men to search for a place where he could bathe and fetch new clothes. The day was still young and he would look his best as the Romans continued to attack Jerusalem.

* * *

Cicero Vindacian and Quintus Cassius shook their heads as they watched cohorts of the Fifth Legion forming up for a palisade assault against the Second Wall. The two Primi Ordines gave thanks to Jupiter that orders for such an attack had not been given to them as they watched legionaries of the Macedonica pick up the heavy ladders and wait for the trumpet blast to advance. The cohorts stood among destroyed homes and piles of rubble as they faced the high walls with silent and exhausted gazes. These were the men who had survived the rampart fight on the Third Wall, and now they had been regrouped inside the Bezetha, given a new death warrant.

Cicero and Quintus, with their regrouped centuries, had formed up under the shadow of the smouldering Third Wall as they waited for orders to move against the Antonia to the east. Their orders were to wait until the entire First Cohort had regrouped and then they would move out. Already columns of legionaries began to appear from the other centuries and Cicero waved to Marius Junias Livianus who emerged from a smoke-filled alley with his optio, signifer, and thirty soldiers.

"Mighty Fortis!" Cicero exclaimed, raising his sword, and Marius returned the gesture with a grin upon his blood stained face. Cicero glanced behind him at his century and nodded to his men. They looked tired and their faces remained caked with grey dust from their charge through the breach. He looked to his right to the sound of creaking and saw a small cart pulled by a donkey as it wobbled over to Cicero's Lion Century. Inside the cart were vats of cool water and Cicero shouted, "Refresh yourselves on the double! Then form up and prepare to move out!" A second cart appeared in the breach carrying water and Quintus dispatched his Wolf Century for a drink as he joined Cicero.

"The men talk about doom and massacre, they think they are going to end up like the Fifth over there," Quintus gestured to the cohorts standing motionless with their ladders.

"The Antonia's walls are too high, and it would be a massacre if we were to try. I heard a tribune say that we will be put to work building ramps. Once the breach is passable, our onagri and scorpions will be brought in." Cicero continued to watch as more legionaries emerged from the smouldering ruins of the Bezetha. He crossed his arms, turning to the sound of hatchets and hammers pounding upon wood and stone. The new camp was being constructed and the amount of legionaries pulled from the Fulminata and Macedonica appeared like ants scurrying about as men in the hundreds piled up stone walls, erected towers, and set up their tents. "I wonder who will be staying in this new camp?"

"Most likely us," Quintus replied.

"How do you come to that conclusion?" Cicero responded.

"Since we are the legio attacking the Antonia, Titus will have all the cohorts involved in the work. It will be different from the other ramps; here the enemy has their own catapults for us to contend with." Quintus coughed and spat on the ground. He turned as Marius approached them and ordered one of his soldiers to fetch him a cloth so he could clean his face. "My, do you look frightful!" Quintus said with a smile.

"Been a day of dirty work, I dare say. My men deserve feather pillows on plush beds for their duty in those damned streets." Marius rubbed his eyes and sighed.

"What happened?" asked Cicero.

"I lost eighteen men back there, that's what happened. We gave chase to a group of armed Zealots and lost ourselves in the smoke and fire, but we kept charging straight through. A number of the bastards must have dodged into some of the homes because soon we found them at our backs. I called the charge to a halt, and we fought the whelps in the choking damned smoke! We could hardly breathe but we slaughtered the bunch and captured at least forty. There, look," Marius pointed as a line of Jewish captives paraded past them with an escort of twenty legionaries.

The Jews were bound together in misery as the look of defeat and shame could be seen upon the faces of once proud men. Many of the prisoners bore light wounds from the fighting as blood soaked their garments and dirt plastered their faces. A number of them looked ready to collapse as they coughed and hacked from the dust and smoke still in their lungs.

Near the front of the prisoner column, a large man shouted out a Hebrew curse to the legionaries by the water carts, gaining their attention. A short Roman soldier, to the delight of his comrades, ran over to the prisoner with a mouth filled with water and spit it in his face followed by a punch to the captive's gut. The defiant Jew doubled over as he collapsed to his knees and another prisoner behind him spit into the mocking Roman's face. The Roman reeled back in disgust as he wiped the spittle away. Then in a rage he drew his sword and moved swiftly to strike, but an optio among the Roman guard stepped forward and called him down.

Cicero shook his head at the sight of the optio as the Roman soldier complained and argued relentlessly. "Those are Zealots you captured, Marius, ruthless and brave. I would wager that those men would be the toughest I have ever encountered."

"Which is why I don't expect much of that," Marius replied as he gestured over to the twin cohorts of the Fifth Legion waiting to assault the Second Wall. "Who leads them?"

"I have no idea," Quintus said as he scanned the ranks of the cohorts, failing to identify any centurions as only two optiones and a signifer were present.

"It is not our concern," Cicero responded as he turned and instructed his optio to call the men to form up.

"What will happen to them?" Quintus asked Marius as he pointed to the Zealot prisoners being led up the breach by shouting legionaries.

"Most likely sold to the mines in Corinth or used as gladiators," Marius shrugged. "Either way, I make money. I had my men mark the bastards. I swear to you that by nightfall you can count on a throng of merchants slithering around the slave pens looking for the best fit and the most strong to be bought."

"Pepi will be happy," Cicero said as he stared for a moment at the new camp being erected. "That Arab always enjoys the best, and he pays handsomely for it." He glanced over to the Fifth Macedonica cohort as a cluster of centurions finally arrived and took their positions in front of their centuries. "They are ready," Cicero dryly mentioned as he shook his head, trying to push from his mind the thought of how many soldiers would be dead by the end of the assault.

Marius shrugged. "Futile, but Titus wants to keep up the pressure. We must keep the Jews behind those walls until we can secure the Bezetha."

"At the expense of more lives?" replied Cicero as he rolled his eyes. "Poor bastards. Look, the Jews await them eagerly, like carrion for the vultures." Cicero watched the battlements of the Second Wall quickly fill as Zealots and Idumeans awaited the Roman advance.

A tall *princeps prior*, with a multicoloured plume of white and black, stepped away from his Fifth century and glared up at the enemy. He wore an elaborate bronze breastplate with the face of a fiery sun upon it, while greaves matching the finery were strapped to his shins. He raised a clenched fist into the air, drew his sword and then gave a hoarse shout for courage, honour, and victory. Four hundred and eighty scuta instantly followed his command as they lifted from the ground followed by the distinct metallic sound of swords being drawn from their scabbards. The ladders were readied in the second and third ranks of each century as the legionaries braced themselves for the charge. A moment of eerie silence invaded the five-men-deep ranks of the cohort and then like a sudden clap of thunder the centurion shouted for the Macedonica to advance.

The cohort dashed across the flagstones and met the hailstorm of spears and rocks hurled from above. The ladders were brought up to the wall with haste while a contingent of Syrian bowmen, formed up behind the Romans, began to pepper the Jewish attackers on the battlements. The Zealots and Idumeans responded just as suddenly with archers of their own, and within moments, Syrian bowmen could be seen writhing upon the ground in pain with streaks of blood smeared upon the stones as the Jewish darts ripped through their ranks.

One Syrian alae of high rank, screamed at his helpless bowmen as they died in the open with no cover. Suddenly the officer's shouts were silenced as he took an arrow in the eye which projected a stream of blood like a fountain from his face. The discipline of the Syrian troops cracked and a spirit of panic filtered into their ranks. With the officer prostrate and dead upon the ground, the Syrians turned and fled leaving behind dozens of dead as their wounded wailed in agony meanwhile trying to crawl for cover.

With the loss of the Syrian bowmen, the situation deteriorated quickly for the Macedonica as they ascended the ladders with shields raised in an effort to protect themselves. The ladders that could not be pushed away were left alone as the Zealots chose to wait for the legionaries to appear upon the last rung where they would be dispatched with screams. Nearly twenty ladders were pushed against the wall as columns of legionaries climbed upwards. Zealots above began to roll boulders over the side which crushed men and shattered shields. Some legionaries, in an attempt to avoid the deadly stones, leapt from the ladders, most breaking their ankles on the hard street below. Only a handful of Romans managed to fend off sword blows and spear jabs for a few moments at the top of ladders as they were seen fighting for their lives. However, the concentration of Jewish attackers on the wall failed to relinquish any space for the legionaries to push forward and one by one the Romans were killed.

Marius buried his face into his hands and groaned. Cicero shook his head and said, "That was over before it even began." A sick expression filled his face as he surveyed the dead archers strewn upon the ground and then watched the bitter struggle at the wall as shouts rose above the screams of the wounded. Finally a whistle was blown and the Macedonica turned and fled in disorder as they took most of the ladders with them. The Jews cheered in victory with raised weapons as they spit over the wall at the piles of dead men and shattered ladders below.

Quintus grunted as he cleared his throat and watched the exhausted legionaries of the Fifth walk past him in shame from the failed attack. He turned to the sound of a soldier striking his chest in salute and was handed a wax tablet inscribed in Latin. Quintus took the tablet and mumbled, "What is this?"

"Dispatched orders from Tiberius Alexander! Your cohors is to assemble and move to the right and take up position to face the fortress of the Antonia." The soldier waited while Quintus read the orders and then saluted again when Quintus gave him a nod.

Quintus passed the order to Marius and scratched his chin. "So, we move out. Where are Rufus and Gaius' men?"

"Should be here soon. They were in the streets with us when we were fighting." Marius read the orders a second time and handed them to Cicero with a sigh. He looked around for a moment and then pointed to their right where two columns of soldiers marched, one slightly more rugged and dirtier than the other. "The Hydra and Serpent have arrived," Marius said as he watched Rufus and Gaius lead the pack of legionaries across the debris covered streets. He raised a hand in greeting and saw Rufus reply with a smile as Gaius kept his head down, seeming to be uninterested.

When the final remnants of the First Cohort were organized, the orders were given to Gaius who read them with a stern expression. He stared at the tablet as if he could not believe what he read and then looked up with a weary expression. Gaius rolled his eyes at his fellow centurions and slipped the tablet under his arm. "Anything else?"

"Like what, Primus Pilus?" replied Quintus.

"There are no further orders? Tiberius just wants us to form up before the Antonia and guard it?" Gaius asked with a suspicious tone.

The other centurions shifted uneasily and stared at one another with blank expressions until Marius replied, breaking the silence among the men, "That is it, Gaius. There was nothing about earthworks or artillery, although they will come. Shall I send a runner?"

Gaius shook his head. "What difference will it make?" He glanced over at the Second Wall and the Roman bodies lying at the base. "The palisade failed?"

"Was an utter, bloody disaster," Cicero retorted, following it up with a curse.

Gaius gazed at the men. "Expect much more bloody disasters such as that. We are in Jerusalem, if you haven't noticed, and we're fighting under the shadow of their Temple. Remember, many of these men we fought against in the north, have been soaked in our blood before. They will gladly sell their lives." The centurions looked at one another with the validity of Gaius' words resounding in their ears. "Form up your ranks, keep a tight order, and let's move in column." He rested his hand on the pommel of his gladius and took a deep breath.

Gaius turned and squinted up at the four cornered towers of the Antonia and shuddered. Unnoticed by the other centurions, Gaius wondered about the outcome of attacking such an impregnable looking mountain of stone with spiked battlements crammed by Zealots and scorpions. He contemplated this, as if a struggle for the Antonia had already occurred, with ramps of stone and earth built up high and thrust against the fortresses walls, yet covered in hundreds of cleaved Roman bodies. Gaius thought of Livia, and wondered if this would be the place where he would finally meet a gruesome death under the silhouette of the Antonia's walls.

*   *   *

CHAPTER XXIX

"They've broken through!" went up the cry from the Mishneh as Zealots flooded through the streets towards the ramparts. Soldiers with pikes and swords moved like a great tide of water towards the western corner of the Second Wall as dust rose from the tumbling stones. A number of bodies littered the ground at the wall's base as Idumeans and Zealots drew up in thick ranks with lowered spears. They stared straight ahead at the gaping hole, but still no Romans appeared with drawn gladii and golden coloured scuta emblazed with the image of the white bull of the Macedonica Legion.

All the Jewish fighters held their breath. Deep thuds from the rams continued to hammer against the wall while stones and iron missiles sailed overhead crashing into homes and bringing them down in heaps of dust and crushed rubble.

Word spread quickly that the breach had to be wider before the legionaries would try and break through. The Zealots instantly set to work piling up the stone in an attempt to create a second inner wall while soldiers from the ramparts continued to fight off the palisade from three cohorts of the Macedonica who threatened their defences. Messages came swiftly from where the First Wall joined the Hippicus Tower that two more cohorts of the Fifth Legion were attempting an assault. So far Simon's men had held out against the onslaught, but the news was bore by the grim appearance of messengers splattered with the blood of their comrades who had been slaughtered by iron spikes launched by Roman scorpions.

Men were on the verge of panic as they crowded the streets of the Mishneh, some crying out to God while others took the time to sharpen their blades with grinding stones. Archers crammed the alleyways with full quivers as they were led up to the ramparts strewn with bodies and slick with blood. As they climbed the stone steps everything shook and vibrated with the deafening sound of rock splitting. Once on top, the archers took cover behind the parapets, and with fixed bows, delivered numerous volleys into the mass of Romans beneath.

John of Gischala marched through the alleys of the Mishneh accompanied by his most trusted officers. Judah tried to keep up with the warlord's pace as Adam walked silently at his side with a spear held firmly in his hands. Moshe followed behind Judah and said nothing, as he winced with every crash reverberating throughout the city, half expecting the next catapult stone to find him and crush him to pieces.

Judah stared at the back of Yeshua ben Sapphias' head and then glanced at Adam. He could not believe the mad-man from Tarichaeae had been elected as one of the commanders to lead a thousand Zealots of John's force in an ambush, once the Romans widened the breach and attacked the Mishneh. Judah knew Yeshua was a valiant warrior and greatly feared, but he was also madly insane and unpredictable. Adam said this was why Judah was among the attack as well as Zacharias ben Phalek, so they could keep Yeshua in check. Judah still could not trust the man and this deeply worried him. Neither Adam nor Judah knew John ben Dorcas personally, but Zechariah the elderly priest had sworn that the son of Dorcas was honourable and had the intentions of God in mind as a defender of Jerusalem.

When John found Simon he looked worried as he refused to take his attention off the breach being created in the wall. The Sicarii King stood atop a house, under the range of catapults and ballista. Simon just bit his nails and wondered what to do. However, John's temper flared up and he shouted at Simon to make better preparations for he knew they had to fully commit everyone to the Mishneh.

"And what would you have me do? Storm their new camp? We can't even piss without getting crushed by stone!" Simon lashed back angrily. "Don't worry about my men, Gischala. When the Romans come, we will do as you said earlier: two assaults of a thousand each. With the proper force we can recover the Bezetha."

"The Bezetha is now indefensible." John looked worried as he turned and stared out towards the Antonia and the catapults which hurled stone at its walls. John's men could retaliate with their own artillery, the response being swift and hard for the Romans, but it also meant more Romans and more defences. By midday the ground before the Antonia had been overtaken as the Romans pried up flagstones, smashed homes, and brought in cartloads of earth. John knew the Romans would erect earthworks and ramps which would eventually set the stage for rams and siege towers.

"We have to slaughter them. We need to let as many into the Mishneh at the right time and surround them. It must be perfect. They need to think we have all fled and retreated." John crossed his arms, looking at Judah and Yeshua. "My men will attack from the western side of the Temple Mount, and you have your army ready to the south. With God's strength, we will sweep them out."

Simon rubbed his neck and then ran a hand over his mouth as sweat beaded his forehead. "Let's pray we do this soon. I won't have an army left if this keeps up." Simon paused. "Have you seen the Bezetha?" John nodded and Simon continued, "A messenger says they can fit an entire legion in that new camp of theirs. And Jewish cowards of the citizenry keep trying to flee. My guards say they saw nearly a hundred of the aristocracy flee this morning and the Romans practically gave them their virginity with open arms!" Simon scoffed as he began to laugh. He drew his sword and pointed the blade towards the breach. "I want to see this point buried in a centurion's belly by nightfall."

John looked at Judah and then stepped close to Simon. "I have a crop of engineers. These men are miners and skilled with stone. I intend to use them against the earthworks prepared at the Antonia. They say that it will be at least a few days before that breach in the Second Wall is wide enough for a proper Roman assault. We still have some time, Simon, but I need your help."

Simon held his breath for a moment and turned as Yehoram snickered behind him. He gave the fat, ugly man a glare and Yehoram quickly shuffled away. Simon then looked at John and with a sullen, motionless gaze he said, "What would you have me do?"

"Have your men continue to rebuild the inner wall, but not too high or strong. I want to bait the Romans," John said.

"To make them overconfident?" Simon replied.

"Exactly. When those dogs come through the breach, I want them to fully believe they have triumphed yet again over the weak Jew." John pointed to the breach and gestured with a nod. "Then when they are massing in the streets and plundering the homes, we strike. Have your men pack numerous homes that surround the inner wall with dried faggots and bitumen. Then have men hide in the homes and wait. When the legionaries come through the breach and begin to search the quarter, we attack! At the same time fire the homes so that the rear of the Roman position consists of a wall of fire, smoke, and death. We can descend upon them from rooftops, through streets, and from doorways. We will kill thousands."

"You are so sure they will just come pouring through?" Simon asked.

"I have fought against the Romans far too long to forget about their insufferable arrogance. They think they are the masters of the world. That only they have the right to enslave and take life, that every knee must bow to Rome and worship their gods and Caesar." John rested a heavy hand on Simon's shoulder and stared directly into his face with fierce eyes set ablaze. "But I swear to you, that when those centurions, who envision glory and Roman prosperity, see our wall crumble, they will lead cohort after cohort into the gap to fill the quarter. Then we who know this city best, can descend upon the sheep like a pack of wolves and rip them to pieces. The slaughter will be so great that the dead will be mourned in Rome for centuries!"

Simon was quiet for a moment and then smiled. "It will work," he replied simply. "I told you before that I will have your thousand, but your plan is brilliant. We shall stock the homes like a tinder box and fire them when the legionaries fill our streets." Simon turned to Yehoram and said, "Send word to Jacob to put together one hundred men immediately to fill all homes with anything that will burn."

Yehoram scowled slightly as he wanted to remain with Simon, then turned slowly and trotted off. Simon watched him go and then said, "Pathetic fool, and hopeless, ugly twit. But, he will do whatever I say and follow me around everywhere I go. An honest and stupid dog Yehoram is."

Judah watched Bagdatus chuckle behind Simon, then catch his glare and give a slight bow in defiance to the Lion warrior. Judah looked away but tightened his grip on the hilt of his sword as another explosion of dust, smoke, and fire erupted from a home some ways in the city behind them.

Judah could not believe he was living in such a time as this. He had spent over an hour of the morning from one of the towers of the Antonia gaping like a fool at the vast workings of the Roman army as they deployed into the Bezetha with even more force than the previous day. With huge sections of the Third Wall pulled down, all eyes could see the siege towers like great, bored giants with nothing else to do. Along with the towers, also sat three more testudo rams as another two hammered at the Second Wall where the breach had been made. Judah stared beyond the rubble at what had once been an area of Jerusalem for the rich and noble. Now he could see a landscape devastated by Roman abuse stretching into the horizon. It was truly like a dream.

All the gardens, orchards, groves, and pastures had been tilled, burned, dug up, and plowed. Every tree had been cut, save for twisted useless ones for crucifixes. Now all that could be seen were dark Roman camps of stone walls, wooden towers, ditches with stakes covering the ground, and the fires of patrols burning all around. The land had been slashed and burned.

In his dreams Judah saw himself wandering relentlessly around a deserted city. He would shout and growl for Capito to come out so he could kill him, but then everything would vanish and Judah would hear Miriam's voice and listen to her laughter. Only once in the last week he had seen her standing before him in the darkest part of his dreams, but always faceless and afraid. Judah had tried to speak with Zechariah about his woes and the meaning of the dreams, but the aging priest had sighed, desiring to speak of something else. Judah felt alone in his thoughts, haunted by the suffering of his dead betrothed.

Judah watched John and Simon leave the rooftop as the two men carried on in deep discussion. Most of the officers followed the two warlords, but Judah, Adam, and Moshe remained, along with Ananus ben Bagdatus who stared at them with a harrowing grin and dark eyes. Adam scowled at Bagdatus and then turned his back on him, whispering privately to Judah, "My mother has taken ill and father cares for her. My two sisters sent word this morning. They have only food for today and that is it." Adam furrowed his eyebrows and winced at the thought of his suffering family.

Judah gazed for a moment at his friend and then said, "What will you do? There is no food."

"In the Temple stores there is," replied Adam with boldness. He glanced at Bagdatus for a moment and then whispered, "I shall beg John."

"That won't work. He won't listen," Judah said shaking his head with sorrow at his friend's desperation.

"He must listen. If I do it privately and remind him of my loyalty, he has to relinquish some of the bread, anything. The sacrifices continue and we all starve. There has to be something that can be done." Adam's eyes filled with tears and he wiped them away discretely so Bagdatus could not see.

Judah was silent as he mulled over his friend's words and then he shrugged. "Do it privately, and John may have mercy. But tell no one, Adam. If anyone was to find out, John will never give you food."

Adam nodded and shuddered as the anguish seemed to flush from his body. All the Zealot fighters were allotted food from the stores of the Temple, but it was closely monitored and strictly forbidden to leave the Temple grounds at those times. This was so John could make sure his men were getting the food they needed to keep fighting and that it was not going into the poor, suffering parts of the Lower City to feed families and friends. It was a cruel mandate, but viewed as imperative to fighting off the Romans and defending the city.

"Still bedding that woman, Judah?" Bagdatus said with a grin and then licked his lips. "That young whore of yours could bend over any day and accept my graciousness; it would be better than what you give her."

Adam turned and glared at Bagdatus as Judah's face remained expressionless. "Close that forsaken hole in your face, Bagdatus, or my spear shall close it for you."

Bagdatus laughed and shook his head. "Was I talking to you, you Nazarene prick? Your Messiah ain't coming, because the Romans killed him and they will do the same to you. I would oblige them to allow me to do the honours, but Simon says to leave you alone for later."

"Why wait?" Adam responded as he faced Bagdatus and held his spear.

Bagdatus smiled again, then looked past Adam at Judah and pointed. "You think I don't know? I know it was you who killed Ephraim the Idumean. You may have the others fooled, but not me! Your Hadassah was going to be food for the wolves and you rescued her." Bagdatus paused, then motioned to Adam and Moshe. "You probably had some help too, I would imagine."

"You speak of things you do not know, Bagdatus. Run to Simon and nip his heels for attention. Your master awaits and should not find it difficult to get you a wet nurse to suckle!" Judah calmly said seeing a flash of anger fill Bagdatus' face. Judah smiled and turned to leave.

"You would walk away? You coward!" Bagdatus shouted partially drawing his sword.

Judah halted and stared up at the clear blue sky for a second and watched a few doves flap by with gentle coos. He bit his lower lip, glanced over to Bagdatus and said, "I know who you are, Ananus, and what you have done. I know how people have suffered under your wrath and how you have plundered that which is not yours. I know how you have raped women, killed husbands, and served Simon by doing every cruel and wicked thing. This you will be judged by and this you will pay for with your blood. But the suffering you have caused will be turned to laughter and joy at the sight of the torture that awaits you someday. I say, you will be all alone, and none will beckon to your side despite your crying out. The sun will be squelched and all life will ebb away into blackness, save for your tormented soul."

The three Lion warriors left the rooftop while Ananus stood in a frozen state of rage. His eyes burned with anger at Judah and his voice seemed to be snatched from his throat as he could think of nothing to say.

*   *   *

May 9th, 70 A.D. / 12th of Iyyar, 3830
Camp of the Assyrians
One hour after dusk

"Your men have been fighting with exceptional skill since the day the Jews tried to fire the rams and charged from the city. We have been able to push them back and crush all resistance." Titus scanned the faces of his legionary generals around the table as they listened. He drank some wine and then set the goblet near the map as he took the time to give it another glance. "We have eradicated all resistance in the Bezetha and have reduced their "New City" to a waste dump. I applaud your men and the skill of our engineers who have speedily constructed this new camp, smoothed out the breach to ease the entrance into the city for our engines, and successfully destroyed much of the Jews' Third Wall. Times are hard and our nerves our tested, but all goes in our favour, wouldn't you say so, Tiberius?"

"Yes, my Prince," Tiberius stoutly replied with a bow.

Titus smiled and tapped the map where the line was drawn of the Second Wall separating the Mishneh from the Bezetha. "My engineers tell me that in three days' time they will have widened the breach large enough for a full storm of the Mishneh. Along with the breach we will collapse two towers on the wall which has been weakened. The towers protect either side of the breach. We have had one ram work relentlessly on destroying the foundation of the tower to the left of the breach, while crews with pry bars, picks, and shovels have undermined and weakened the other.

"I will again offer terms to the Jews, but if this is refused then I will order an all out sacking of the Second Quarter. I want the Mishneh leveled. All who resist are to be slaughtered, and everyone captured are to be bound and taken away as slaves regardless of age. Until this breach is wide enough, I will have cohorts of the Fretensis and Apollinaris take over from the Macedonica with palisade attacks to continue along the Second and First Wall. Troops of the Fulminata will continue with raising earthworks against the Antonia and cohorts of the Macedonica will move in to support."

"My Prince, what about a threat from miners against our positions around the Antonia?" Tribune Marcus Octavian asked as he rubbed his chin and stared at the map.

Titus glanced to Tiberius for help and the older General gave Marcus a nod as he replied, "We have never seen the Jews use miners. We have no reason to believe they even have the capability to mine let alone the organized manpower. The ground here is rocky and incredibly tough. Anyone trying to mine would be doing so blind against where our earthworks are being built up and would have to dig under the deep fortifications of the Antonia. It would take months and I doubt the Jews are up to the task. I would not worry about miners from the Jewish ranks. If they do try and dig, I would expect their mines to collapse due to poor construction rather than pose as a threat to us."

"Well, despite your lack of concern about miners, I still would humbly request engineers to be dispatched to the task of trying to detect any heinous activity," Octavian said glancing from Tiberius back to Titus.

The Prince grinned and then shrugged. "I can do as you wish, Marcus. We just can't spare a lot of time and effort into such philandering. If Tiberius sees the possibility of mining unlikely, then I am inclined to agree with him."

"My Prince, although we may agree the Jews do not possess the means or knowledge to tunnel, we do not know who all is in the city," Marcus pushed as he gestured at the map to make a point. "John may have made preparations beforehand to pay for men who can tunnel. We should not risk the chance."

Titus again looked at Tiberius and the General just shook his head and sighed. "It could be possible, unlikely, but possible."

Titus, uncomfortable with the answer, turned and invited Chief Engineer Porcius Gracchus to join the group. "What is your mind, Gracchus? Can we detect such a threat?"

Porcius stood among the ring of generals and stared at the map for a moment. He glanced up quickly at Marcus and said, "You're worried about mining by the Antonia?" Porcius watched the General give a nod and the engineer hummed silently to himself as he examined the map. Then he gave an exhaustive sigh and shook his head. "It will be almost impossible to detect if they are mining."

"Why?" Titus replied with a scowl.

Porcius pointed to the map and said, "If they go beneath the Antonia or where the wall foundations meet it, they will go so deep we won't hear them. If they tunnel, they will have experienced men. I can see nobody undertaking a task such as that if they do not have the men for the job. Thus, if they have miners, they will do so in silence. Besides, against all the noise from above, that will drown out any possibility of hearing them."

"But we have no proof or reason to believe they have such men?" Titus asked Porcius.

The Chief Engineer sighed and scratched his arm to relieve an itch. "Some of the best miners come from places like Ephesus, Corinth, and Thessaloniki. Parthia is a possibility, but we have no reason to believe any miners from that region have joined the Jewish rebellion.

"This land is not known for its abundance in miners. Most miners in the area would have left for employment in the north; I see no reason to believe any would have stayed." Porcius paused for a moment and then shook his head. "We have been at war nearly four years; I can't see why any men would have stayed behind possessing this craft. It is such as Tiberius said, most likely they will get desperate enough to try, but without the experience, they are doomed to fail. Mining in this region is incredibly hard, and mining under this city, impossible."

Although, Marcus Octavian did not look totally convinced, Titus interjected and added, "We have none qualified who can detect a mine to spare, as they have all been fully committed to the erecting of earthworks, additional siege engines, and monitoring the condition of walls and structures. So, let us move on now.

"I want all cohorts not engaged in fighting or siege construction to remain on high alert working with the alae. I want patrols to increase and for cavalry to continue to make a show of force around the city. Double the guard at all access points of the city. People are still getting in and out of this city and I will not tolerate it. Scouts report the signs of starvation in the lower parts of the city and with that, disease will become rampant. Civilians will become desperate and I will not have scavengers and forgers darting through our lines looking for food. Either chase them away or kill them. I also wish no units to approach the city from the south, due to the piles of rotting corpses. I will not have disease break out in our camps. We must offer constant sacrifices and pray to the gods that no plague will decimate our ranks."

"I have four men in quarantine, my Prince. Already I have lost twelve men among patrols in the south," King Sohaemus added. "The bodies are blackened with spots and the stench can be smelled from the Hinnom and the southern end of the Kidron."

Titus nodded thanks and added, "They cart them out and dump them in piles, but stay away and keep a leash on company dogs. I heard of one dog the other day found eating a corpse." A wave of silence filtered around the table momentarily and then the Prince said, "We will not give relief for the Jews, our artillery crews must bombard them day and night. Generals Larcius and General Frigius, have two cohorts prepare to assault the breach in the Second Wall, and another two as reinforcements. The Mishneh will be totally destroyed as was the Bezetha. Understood?" Heads nodded and Titus finished his wine. "You are all dismissed from my presence, except you, Centurion Antony."

Gaius looked startled at Titus' brashness, but he quickly stiffened and saluted. He watched the generals and kings exit the tent and ignored a grin by Marcus Sulla who had been standing near him as the Tribune wondered what the Prince of Rome had in store for the Praefectus Castrorum. When the tent was emptied, Gaius watched Titus return to the map and gaze at it obsessively again.

The silence which filled the quarters grew awkward as the sounds of many sandaled feet stamped past. Gaius watched the Prince concentrate on the map, as if he had totally forgotten he had just asked the Centurion to stay behind. Another few moments slowly went by and then the Prince straightened and gazed at Gaius with resolve in his eyes.

"Once the breach has been widened and the towers brought down I will be sending in four cohorts of troops to cleanse the Mishneh of all life. Blood will flow like rivers, Gaius, and the golden eagles will triumph once again. I tell you this, not because you will be leading any of the attacks, but because I have given orders to General Larcius to place Capito in the front ranks as senior centurion." Titus watched Gaius stiffen, as his jaw tightened at the sound of the despised centurion's name.

"I expect this will be when Capito shall be handed over," Gaius simply replied.

Titus nodded gravely and glanced down at the map one last time. "Capito will be sacrificed as arranged. I feel no remorse for what he did to Judah's family and woman, but I do this to complete a promise made and a promise delivered. You will make contact one last time to Judah and tell him of this. Then inform him that *Roma* will continue to call on him and values his cooperation."

Gaius bit his tongue. He knew where Judah's allegiance truly lay, and it was not with Rome. Capito was his means to seek vengeance and nothing else. Gaius respected the restless Jew, for in the depths of his soul, the coldest and most apathetic part, he understood why it was important for Judah to have his revenge.

"Tell Judah that Capito will be delivered in three days' time and will be sent through the Mishneh to the south western side." Titus paused as he collected his thoughts. "It has been arranged for Capito to be abandoned and then Judah can make the kill. In no way will this lead to anyone and it will look like a simple result of war." The Prince briefly stared up at the ceiling and then placed his hands upon his hips. "Find a slave in one of the pens outside, make sure he has a family, and then force him to deliver this news to Judah or we kill his family. Have the slave take a quill and parchment and tell him Judah must write his name if he has understood the message. If the slave boy returns without the name on the parchment, we crucify them all. This message must get to Judah for this arrangement to be closed." Titus yawned and then walked over to a small table where a vessel of wine stood. He brought the wine over and refilled his goblet and then drank deeply. He licked his lips and complimented the sweet taste with a smile.

Gaius waited for Titus to say something else, but when the Prince remained quiet, he struck his breastplate in salute and bowed his head, "I will do as you wish, my Prince."

"Gaius," Titus spoke up as he faced the Centurion. "You and I are a lot alike. We believe in courage, strength, honour, and will do whatever it takes to survive. I feel

Judah will aid us in even greater ways than before. It is helpful to have such a man in Gischala's ranks and he has proven his worth, I dare say. The gods have honoured him and we honour the gods. I will be writing to my father soon. I hope to add that the Mishneh has been burned and scuttled, that the Antonia is breathing its last gulp of air, and that the Temple lays before us bare and naked for our legions to trample should the Jews resist.

"My father longs to offer a sacrifice in the Temple of Jupiter in *Roma*, and Alexandria needs him no longer. *Roma* calls him home to a throne that Basilides, our guardian, long ago prophesied. The Son of the Monarch watches over the Flavians; he has shown us an eagle bursting from the mouth of Jerusalem into victory. Go now and do as you have been ordered." Titus then turned and left for his private chamber.

*   *   *

Gaius left Titus' quarters in the newly erected Camp of the Assyrians and stared for a moment across the scattered piles of rubble which still covered the broken flagstones of the Bezetha. The light from torches danced upon the golden stones causing shadows to flicker as darkness descended upon the city, ending the third day since the Romans had broken into Jerusalem. Flames would be kindled in Jewish homes as erev Shabbat descended upon the city. Wives and mothers everywhere would light oil lamps, cover their eyes, and recite the blessings while family members would stand nearby in reverence.

Despite the Roman threat, life seemed to crawl onward throughout Jerusalem. Shabbat continued to be observed, feasts were celebrated according to the Hebrew lunar calendar, and sacrifices burned daily as columns of smoke drifted upward from the inner sanctuary of the Temple for all eyes to see.

Gaius cleared his mind from the thought of Shabbat and gave a quick glance at two guards who stood like statues. He marched past them out into the cool night as he pondered his new orders. He watched a patrol of thirty legionaries quietly pass, followed by two tribunes leading their horses. Both men were engrossed in a deep conversation which soon erupted into laughter as one shook his head and slapped the other on the shoulder. Otherwise, the camp seemed lifeless as the men from the Fulminata slept while the rest were on active patrol, stationed under the dark looming mass of the Antonia.

Gaius gently slipped his helmet on and headed down one of the narrow streets between the canvassed tents. Somewhere behind him he heard the hammering of steel from the smithy and a snort from a horse in the stables. He turned east down a wider street of the camp and passed an officer's barrack and then a small hospital. He halted before the surgeon's tent and quietly crept up and poked his head through the flap. Gaius took only a minute to stare at the rows of cots which contained the wounded. Soft groans filled the air mixed with snores from exhausted men as the smell of blood and sweat wafted into Gaius' nostrils. He cringed from the unsavoury scent and shook his head as he let the flap fall back.

Gaius passed a few cooking fires surrounded by men who were mesmerized by the flames. A few signum were driven into the ground nearby one of the fires accompanied by a cluster of javelins and shields stacked upon one another. The soldiers had stripped themselves of their armour as they enjoyed the liberating sensation, free of the weight, as they stretched out sore legs before the open flame wearing only their togas. Gaius smiled to himself and continued on. He finally emerged from the tent city and found himself before a stone wall over a metre high with guards silently patrolling on the top.

One of the legionaries nearby gave Gaius a firm nod, saluted quietly, and then continued on. Gaius gazed up at an enormous wooden guard tower that dominated the eastern corner of the camp. Access to the tower was by a wooden ladder through the center. The tower was topped by a sturdy platform and surrounded by a spiked wooden turret. The Camp of the Assyrians had only four such towers at the corners, but each tower was guarded by six sentries and a ballista.

Gaius took a deep breath and passed through the eastern entrance. He heard a sudden crash somewhere in the city followed by sounds of recoiling mechanized groans of wood, iron, and rope. Gaius held his breath as he heard shouts and calls mix with the crushing and shattering rock. He stared off into the darkness where the continued thuds and crashes echoed. He could see flashes of light from ignited catapult missiles hurled upwards against the dark fortress of the Antonia only to suddenly dissolve into thousands of flaming pieces of shrapnel as the missiles exploded against the wall. Gaius could make out a glow above the distant ramparts, which no doubt would be crammed with Jewish defenders, crouched low and praying for the endless volleys to end. High up on the towers of the Antonia Gaius could see a few lights from torches and hear the faint shouts from Zealot fighters as they responded back with missiles of their own.

Gaius cleared his throat with a grunt and marched away towards the breach, marked by large fires burning upon the ground. Small clusters of cloaked legionaries mingled around as Gaius passed them by, finally spotting the slave pens. He marched up to the wooden cages and stared inside with an ill gaze at the pathetic forms of sleeping men, women, and children strewn upon the ground in heaps. Gaius scanned the slaves unsure of whom he should elect for the task of carrying Titus' message into the city for Judah. His gaze went from a young girl to a small boy curled up in a ball nearest the cage door.

A short, squat legionary, who stood guard by the pen's gate with a ring of keys about his belt, saw Gaius' interest and said, "Can I help you, Centurion?"

Gaius shook his head, ignoring the guard, and stared at the slaves. His mind drifted to the miserable, pointless future that was in store for them.

"The old ones will die and be discarded before they reach the seaport," sounded the familiar voice of Marcus Sulla. "The others will be scattered abroad, no doubt bound to hack it out at the games, mines, brothels, homes of the rich, or as prostitutes in the temples. None of these would last long in the games or mines."

Gaius turned and gave a solemn shrug in agreement. "You are awake?"

"Not tired," Marcus replied as he walked up to Gaius and stopped to peer inside the pen.

"And no doubt can't find anything more interesting then to follow me?" Gaius teased with a gesture of amusement.

Marcus laughed with his usual boisterous roar and a few slaves stirred with moans inside the cage. "I can think of so many other things to do than follow you around, Antony. But alas I am here, and you are here." Marcus scowled at the slaves and then gave a questionable glance at Gaius. "Why are you here staring at slaves on this night of nights?"

"A mission of Titus. You know of Judah ben Yosef?" Gaius asked and Marcus nodded. "Well, I have to choose a runt from this crop to deliver a message and make it back before dawn."

"And whatever message it may be, Titus obviously trusts Judah to continue assisting us?" asked Marcus with humour edging the corners of his mouth.

"Something like that."

Marcus hummed to himself as he looked into the pen. "Allow me, much easier this way." He turned to the guard and said in a gruff tone, "Open the door!" The guard instantly obeyed as he fumbled with the keys, snapped open the lock, removed the chain, and then stepped aside. Marcus looked at the door for a moment and then back at the guard who suddenly uttered and apology and opened it for the Tribune.

Marcus shook his head as he grumbled under his breath and stepped into the pen. He kicked the nearest sleeping form inside the cage and within seconds women whimpered for mercy, children cried, and men glared at Marcus with hatred. All the slaves stood quickly as they watched Marcus peer at them with fierce eyes. "Who understands Greek?" Marcus roared at the slaves in Koine. He waited for a moment and then drew his pugio and pointed it at their faces. "By the balls of the gods, if you do not answer me I will fillet you all!"

A few of the slaves quickly began to nod and Marcus' eyes darted among the group. He picked one woman and approached her. "You smell nice," he said as he touched her hair. "You lived in the Bezetha?" She nodded. "That's how you know Greek. That your son?" Marcus pointed the dagger at a boy wrapped in her arms. The woman began to cry and tightened her grip on the boy. "Yes, that's your son. You know Greek, then he will know Greek! Don't worry, I won't hurt him. We just need him for a bit!" Marcus quickly reached out and grabbed the young boy by the arm and yanked him to his feet. The boy's face went pale but he did not resist. The woman screamed at Marcus, trying to grab her boy, but Marcus growled at her to shut-up and get back. The woman wailed, crumpling to the ground as she watched Marcus sheathe his dagger and drag her son from the cage.

Marcus tossed the boy on the ground in front of Gaius and then crouched down next to him. "You understand Greek?" The boy nodded. Marcus grinned and stood. "This is the one you want, Gaius. He will do anything you want him to do. Am I right?" Marcus stared down at the boy and smiled when he nodded. "That's what you got to do, Gaius. They are servus these ones, and if you're tough, they will spill the truth. No need to beat them like some do. Just show them a little steel and they will obey." Marcus tapped the dagger at his side.

Gaius gave Marcus a brief glance, then knelt beside the boy and pulled out a small piece of bread. The boy stared at Gaius for a moment and then with a quick snatch he grabbed the food and devoured it under the watchful stares of hunger from the other slaves. Gaius then pulled out a piece of parchment, turned his back on the slave pen and whispered, "I have something for you to do, and if you do it, no harm will come to you or your mother. Do you understand?" The boy nodded slowly and Gaius told him everything he was to do. By dawn the boy had slipped back into the Bezetha carrying the parchment with the name "Judah ben Yosef" printed upon it in Hebrew.

*　　*　　*

Chapter XXX

May 12th, 70 A.D. / 15th of Iyyar, 3830
Second Wall of the Mishneh Quarter
Three hours past dawn

Jerusalem was like a woman in child birth. With arched back, eyes wide open, and shuddering from pain, she had lost hope, as if she knew the child she so painfully wished to birth was already dead. For the Jewish defenders it was like something out of a stark, cold dream where colour ebbs away and a ferocious wind builds up leaving one helpless, destitute, and consumed by fear. The vibration was felt in the chests of every man near the wall. Eyes widened in terror as the northern tower and cornerstone collapsed in a heap of dust, rubble, and screaming men who disappeared amidst the loud crash. The very heart and soul of the city seemed to shake. A tremor was felt through the streets as a tidal wave of trepidation rippled from the Mishneh to the Lower City. Then an eerie moment of silence followed the prelude of dust which clung to the air. Suddenly, a flash of fury and steel appeared. Harrowing war cries thundered from the wide breach as battle columns of legionaries poured through the gap.

The Apollianaris legio was unstoppable and terrifying. In one bloody moment, they toppled the inner makeshift wall of stone, which the Zealots had used in an attempt to close the breach, and began to slaughter everyone in their path. Jewish fighters fled the ramparts of the Second Wall as everyone knew what the outcome would be for those who stayed behind. The Roman columns pushed through the streets, hacking their way through as a futile front of Zealots attempted to stem the never ending tide of golden eagles carried into the Mishneh. Shouts and screams became constant as blood splattered the streets and stained the Roman caligae as the legionaries marched onward.

Nobody was spared. The fury and anger of the Roman soldiers became constant as they lunged at the backs of fleeing Jews and killed them, shouting out the names of their comrades who had died during the palisade days before. What Zealots remained to fight were soon eradicated. Clusters of Jews tried to barricade streets with tables and furniture taken from homes, but the cohorts soon trampled these and tore them apart like hungry, starved lions craving meat. Heavy stones and spears were hurled from Zealots at the tightly formed legionaries who filled the alleyways, but the stout scutum shields, made to deflect such objects, easily cushioned the blows.

After nearly thirty minutes of bitter fighting, with bodies lining the streets to attest to the carnage, shofar'ot began to sound and the surviving Zealots fled in a stampede to evade the eager Roman blades.

Word of the Jewish retreat and surrender of the Mishneh came quickly to Titus who waited near the breach of the Second Wall. A smile of victory spread across the Prince's face and he congratulated Tiberius with a firm slap on the back in jubilation. Cautiously, Titus climbed the rubble to the top of the breach and peered through, meanwhile surrounded by a legionary guard of twenty men with raised shields. He gazed around at the wreckage, and bodies stretched out everywhere. He only spotted three dead legionaries and this meant a wholesale victory to the Prince.

Titus grinned. "A handsome sum shall be paid to the leading centurions and first men through the breach! Well done!" He raised his fist in the air as the three cohorts of Apollianaris troops at his back beat their shields with their swords.

Tiberius climbed the breach and stared inside the city as the sounds of fighting began to dwindle. He could make out a few hundred legionaries still formed up inside as they tried to see through the dust and smoke. The sound of doors splintering as they were kicked open began to thud throughout the Mishneh as homes were searched. Tiberius scratched his head. "It was too easy."

Titus looked at his second-in-command and frowned. "The victory was ours, Tiberius. Our men have triumphed once again. The Jews cannot stand up against the modern tactics of the empire. The evidence lies before you. Basilides has been faithful to our plight and has welcomed our generous sacrifice. Mars looks on us and smiles; the bull gave a good omen this morning. You know what the Chief Priest told me when I arose from my bed?" Tiberius shook his head with a sigh and the young Prince responded undeterred, "He saw an eagle flying high with a broken stick in its talons. A smaller bird flew behind it and screeched with respect every time the eagle called. He said the broken twig was Jerusalem, and the smaller bird was this land finally subdued under the eagle of *Roma*. A good omen along with the signs found in the bull's liver: the spots were acceptable and the nostrils of Mars breathed in the burnt meat with a smile. It was a good omen." Titus surveyed the grim scene with a chuckle and shook his head as he looked up at the sky, saying a prayer of thanks to Mars and Jupiter.

"That is a good report indeed, my Prince. I too was put to ease with the signs found in the bull, but regardless, we must not turn our back on John of Gischala. He is too crafty of a man. We need more men in there as the Jews could counter attack!" Tiberius quickly said as he lifted his gaze to the high walls of the distant Antonia and Temple colonnades. "They are watching us right now, my Prince. We need to secure the streets and wall!"

"You're expecting something?" Titus asked as his eyes darted from the ramparts to the hundreds of tightly packed homes amidst the maze of streets.

"If I know the Zealots, they will most definitely be planning another attack! They cannot give up the Mishneh. Their pitiful wall was a ruse," Tiberius replied, pointing to the row of toppled rocks. "That pathetic pile of rubble was the best resistance they put up against us." Tiberius was quiet for a moment, his suspicious eyes scanning the battlefield. "The Zealots dissolved against our attack, almost intentionally to the sounds of their horns. Why not put up more of a resistance? They could have doubled their attack and tried to pile us up inside the breach."

"Speak plainly, Tiberius. What is on your mind? You obviously suspect something," Titus asked agitated and annoyed at his second-in-command who stifled his sense of achievement.

The older General paused as he scratched his chin and fixed his gaze on the high walls of the Temple colonnades. "We should flatten the homes! Utterly destroy the city and then secure it, like we did with the Bezetha. That will crush their will."

Titus shook his head. "Not now. I want to send in Yosef to speak with them again. We can destroy the homes later if need be. I want to crush the resistance, but if possible, stand as a conqueror over an intact city and not ashes! This must not be like Carthage of old, with Scipio watching the grand city razed to the ground. If we can, we spare Jerusalem."

"My Prince, rebels could hide behind the homes or in them. It will be difficult to conduct anything in this neighbourhood. We need to be in control and continue to display a show of force to these rebels. The Mishneh must be razed."

"Your point is duly noted, my dear Tiberius. However, I also must be seen as a man of mercy." Titus pointed out over the death laying everywhere and exclaimed, "Where are they? We have just slaughtered hundreds and sacked the quarter! The Jews have felt our wrath once more and for now they cower in fear. I will not rally them by smashing their homes down, not yet anyway. I will offer them a pardon and if they shall refuse then we will clear the quarter."

"I do not like it, my Prince," Tiberius said. "They are clever."

"And so am I," Titus responded, staring coldly at Tiberius. "They are desperate men, prone to abandon reason. The walls of the Antonia and Temple are the highest we have yet to face. The Jews will feel safe behind them. Deploy more troops into the quarter and search the homes. I will send Yosef in immediately. John and Simon will be too perplexed to rally an attack force and strike us when they see Yosef." Titus crossed his arms and glared into the sacked city as legionaries within continued to search homes and dispatch the wounded with merciful strikes from their swords. "I still believe they have to see their fate and surrender."

"Yes, my Prince," Tiberius uttered with disapproval.

Titus turned to the elder General and stared at him for a moment. "Tiberius, do you trust my father?"

Tiberius quickly bowed his head and gave a firm nod. "With my life, my Prince."

"I thought so. He appointed you from Egypt to be my second-in-command. Emperor Vespasian watches us in this moment, and when the eyes of the emperor have closed in years to come, I will be father of this empire and will not forget those faithful to me when I was yet a prince. Do you understand?"

Tiberius straightened and struck his chest in salute and gave a heavy nod. "Forgive me, my Prince."

Titus approached the General and rested a hand on his shoulder and said tenderly, "My father chose you because of your quality. I do not despise your council and I recognize what admirable qualities you possess and bring with this posting. My father chose a man of war to lead the legions, but this man of war is still under authority. Granted, I accept your council, but my word still remains final." Tiberius closed his eyes and bowed his head humbly. "Very well, you may continue, Tiberius Alexander."

Tiberius nodded once more from the reprimand, turned slightly, and shouted, "Cohors Five, Six, and Seven! On the double! Look lively!" The senior centurions of each cohort, and a number of tribunes attached to the attacking units, quickly ran over to the breach and saluted. "I want cohors Five on the ramparts to secure the towers, and parapets. Get some scorpions up there if you can. You will restrain yourselves unless engaged! The rest of you will reinforce cohors One, Two, and Eight in the Mishneh! I want the homes searched now! Kill anyone found!"

Tiberius could not help but look sourly as he and the Prince stepped to the side and watched as fresh units poured through the breach to reinforce the legionaries inside. Within moments the Fifth cohort filled the ramparts above Tiberius on the Second Wall and cheered as they planted their vexillum upon the battlements, raising their signi from each century as they basked in the glory of the sweet taste of victory. Swords and spears were waved to the cries of "*Roma victa*" as the legionaries sought to encourage their fellows below and jeer at the Jewish fighters who watched from the towers of the Antonia. As Tiberius listened to the elation, he looked at Titus and gave a firm nod as he began to think that perhaps the Jews, feeling beaten, humiliated, and afraid, would not be making a move to attack the dense streets of the Mishneh crammed with legionaries.

Prince Titus left Tiberius upon the top of the rubble and carefully made his way down to where Yosef waited alongside General Titus Frigius. "Frigius, your men have performed exceptionally well this morning. I know the cost has been high, but they have done well."

Frigius snapped to attention as he extended his arm outward to acknowledge the Prince's gracious remarks. "Their swords were eager for revenge, my Prince. I heard them talking this morning. It would take more than a palisade to dampen their spirits."

"No matter, I want the names of those centurions who lead this morning's assault, and those who showed bravery by vote of their peers. They will be rewarded." Titus stepped past the legionary General, clasped his hands behind his back, and gave Yosef a simple nod.

Yosef bowed low in the presence of the Roman Prince and lowered his gaze. Although a cool morning wind nipped at the hems of his garments, he felt a trickle of sweat cling to the back of his neck. He tried to hide the sorrow which lined the edges of his face from the report by Titus that the Mishneh had fallen. In his deepest thoughts, Yosef could see the faces of his countrymen dead and bleeding upon the streets of the city he loved. He wrestled with the accusation of treason which was constantly shouted from the mouths of his brothers, who even now plotted against him and lurked overhead with resentful eyes of malice.

In his personal writings he viewed himself as a patriot, a man who had surrendered in an attempt to save his people by convincing them of the folly of resistance. He had seen the devastating outcome the legions had left behind from places like Gamla and Jotapata. The piles of bodies turned over into mass graves or pulled from the sea had left him feeling hopeless and empty. He could still remember seeing the blood lining the banks of the Galilee weeks after the sea battle. Everything had been in vain, even his own commission to arm the northern forces and prepare them for invasion.

John had thought he could have done better. He had tried to arrange Yosef's murder to topple him from power, but John had been unsuccessful because of friends who had trusted in Yosef. Perhaps John may have done a better job, perhaps more Romans would have died under the warlord of Gischala, but the end would have remained the same. The endless lines of chained prisoners and the wailing of raped women would always convince Yosef that this rebellion had been one of bitter seeds of hatred, which had been so blind they could never have conceived of this outcome. Yet in his mind, Yosef remained the only man who had perceived this outcome all along, and because of that he wept bitterly. However, despite this inner turmoil that raged within him, Yosef's histories continued to lengthen as he recorded and penned all he saw and interpreted before him.

"Yosef, are you ill?" Titus asked, seeing a streak of paleness underline the Jew's face and grip his hollowed cheeks.

Yosef grunted and smoothed his beard upon his chest as he straightened. He then shook his head and cleared his throat. "I am fine, my Prince." He swallowed his pride. "Congratulations on the victory."

Titus gave a brief smile. "I am sending you in once more. The Jews have seen another quarter of their city taken and destroyed by overwhelming force. The bodies of their soldiers cover the ground; their blood is bright and is a reminder of their destiny should they refuse my good graces.

"I want you to deliver a message to John. Speak to him and promise a pardon to all who lay their weapons down. I will spare their city and exile the leadership to Perea, along with their families. *Roma* will provide homes for them and a living if they surrender. However, all ranked officers, their families, along with John and Simon, can never again return to this land. The rest of their soldiers can rebuild and populate Jerusalem again, but *Roma* will continue to rule and impose law." Titus paused for a moment making sure Yosef understood all that was asked of him. "Tell them to open the gates of the Antonia and Temple and surrender. I will have the legions stand down and march from the city."

Yosef slowly bowed and nodded. "I understand, my lord."

Titus watched the Jewish General pick up the corners of his outer cloak as he passed him to climb up the breach. "Yosef," Titus suddenly called out as he watched him stop and turn. "Do you think the leniency I am prepared to offer them will be enough to strike a truce?"

The wind picked up and blew Yosef's long hair across his face. He brushed it aside and then tightened the belt about his waist to keep his cloak closed. "I cannot be sure, my Prince." Yosef glanced from Titus to General Frigius and then looked beyond them at the Camp of the Assyrians and the destruction of what had once been the Bezetha. He could see columns of mounted cavalry organized beyond where the Third Wall had once proudly stood. Near the cavalry troopers, a thousand soldiers from the Fretensis suddenly appeared, marching in road formation as they emerged from the outermost eastern foundations of what remained of the Third Wall where the Corner Tower stood. When he turned, he humbly bowed his head at the heated glare from Tiberius, as the aging chief consultant to Prince Titus stared with misgiving at the defeatist façade of Yosef ben Matityahu.

"My Prince, he is here as you requested," said a tribune, striking his breastplate with a firm salute. A legionary from the Fretensis stood next to the tribune wearing his sagum which had been pulled around his chest and pinned to his shoulder so that whatever was underneath it was concealed.

Titus, who had been watching Yosef slowly climb the breach, turned to the tribune and flicked his hand at him. "That will be all," he said to the officer. The tribune awkwardly took a step back and then gave a jerk of a nod and departed without a word. Titus glanced over his shoulder and waited until Tiberius had turned away to watch Yosef descend into the Mishneh. Titus had made careful steps to make certain that the circle of people who knew about this was small, and he wished to keep it that way. When he was certain Tiberius' attention was somberly distracted, he quickly turned back to the man with apathy, retrieved a tightly rolled up parchment, and handed it to him. "Make sure this gets to the optio of the Falcon Cohors. He will know what to do."

The man discreetly took the orders and not wasting a second, slipped it underneath his sagum. "Orders for the Mishneh?"

Titus gave a firm nod. "Orders that involve Hastatus Prior Capito; it has been arranged. Make sure this order gets to his optio. It must not fall into the hands of Centurion Capito. The Third is on standby and waits in reserve. They are to be a shock troop assault to guard the south eastern end of the Mishneh Quarter." The man struck his chest in salute and Titus held up a finger for him to wait. The Prince did not lack scruples; he had learned in the years that in secret dealings, the best way to insure absolute secrecy and trustworthiness was to pay for it. He produced a small leather coin purse and tossed it to the soldier.

"What am I to do with this coin, my Prince?" the soldier asked with a slight grin as he took the hint.

"It is a year's pay for a decurion. I am sure you shall find a resourceful way to spend it." Titus watched the man test the weight of the coin in his hand, give a smile with a low bow, then turn and hurry away.

*   *   *

Yosef descended the rubble of the breach and hurried past the ranks of Roman cohorts neatly filling the northern space of the Mishneh. He stepped over bodies and tried not to gag from the putrid smell of bile fluids that reeked heavily in the air. Dust and blood clung to his sandals as he continued on. As he passed by the columns of red scutum, the stares from legionaries and centurions was like a hot furnace of white flame and glowing embers.

A blast from a horn sounded followed by a booming voice which shouted, "Falcon Cohors forward!" Yosef glanced back as another cohort emerged into the Mishneh. He squinted at the vexillum carried by the cohort and saw a falcon embroidered upon the dark red cloth with gold tassels and fringes. A large numeral 'X' was emblazoned beneath the falcon and Yosef scowled wondering why a cohort of the Fretensis had been sent into the quarter. The unit thundered past him at a jog and he watched as the columns of Apollinaris troops moved out of the way as the leading centurion from the Falcon Cohort shouted at them with drawn sword.

Yosef shuddered and lifted his gaze to the ramparts above the breach. Legionaries lined the parapets in tightly formed ranks as they gripped spears. Clusters of men could be heard grunting and shouting as two parties struggled and fought to hoist up scorpions to the ramparts with large ropes.

A grim looking Centurion swiftly approached Yosef. Tipping back his helmet, he glared at the former Jewish General and asked, "What are you doing here?"

"Prince Titus has ordered me to speak to the rebels. Can you provide me with a place to do that?" Yosef quietly said as he hoped not to offend the Roman with his direct response.

The Centurion sneered and shook his head. He spit a stream of saliva upon the street and then rolled his eyes. "Titus sent you?" Yosef nodded and the centurion shook his head again. He sheathed his sword and taking a step to the side, hollered at a nearby legionary to come quickly. "I should be able to find you a place." The Centurion handed his shield to the young soldier who jogged over and then licked his dry lips caked in dust. "Some of the homes have been fired, most have been searched, and some have collapsed." The Centurion crossed his arms and swore to himself. "How about a roof to speak from?"

"That would do," Yosef meekly replied.

"Very well, come with me." The Centurion turned and marched down an alley, shouting for a cluster of soldiers to follow as a guard. "Optio, do you know of any homes closest to the Temple walls that would provide a decent roof to speak from?"

The Optio, who had joined the guard, ran to the Centurion's side as they marched along and nodded. "Yes, Centurion, it is not far from the First Wall, and it is a two level home with an open roof. It should do just well."

The Centurion glanced back at Yosef and shrugged. "We go there."

Yosef and the armed party continued as they passed burning homes and debris scattered in the streets. The further they went, the fewer bodies they encountered. However, the piles of broken pottery and furniture attested to the plundering that had taken place. Yosef noticed many of the homes had broken doors as they had been smashed from their hinges and thrown into the alleys. A number of times, soldiers from the guard were sent ahead to clear the streets to the shouts of the Centurion who would wait until the way was clear. Yosef could sense the Centurion growing more agitated and nervous as they continued on. The officer soon began glancing around him, calling out to soldiers from the alleys to reinforce his guard.

By the time Yosef and the legionary escort arrived at the home the Optio had specified, their numbers had swelled to sixty soldiers who were dispatched right away to secure the perimeter with drawn swords. The Centurion gazed at the front entrance of the home, taking a moment to study the broken door which lay on the ground. An eerie silence filled the home apart from a haunting wind which blew through its lifeless corridors. From where he stood, the Centurion could see broken crockery, dirt, and overturned furniture inside the large front room of the home. He stared up at the side of the dwelling to where wooden blinds had been torn from windows and smashed. Not a sound came from the home and the Centurion slowly drew his sword.

The Optio detected an uneasiness which came over his commanding officer and he whispered reassuringly, "Centurion, my men and I personally raided this home. We encountered a family. What appeared to be one of the sons attacked us with a knife; all were killed. There is nobody here."

The Centurion looked back at the junior officer for a moment and then sighed, dropping his gaze to dozens of broken clay tiles lying in the street outside of the home. He listened to the Optio's report concerning the broken tiles, that during the raid they had ransacked the roof and destroyed parts of it to make sure no one was hiding.

"You two with me," the Centurion said as he pointed to Yosef and the Optio. "And you six as well." He motioned to a number of soldiers standing nearby. "Come. Let's get this over with."

Yosef watched the Centurion enter the home. When he felt a nudge in his back from the Optio, Yosef stepped forward with trembling hands. He stopped in the doorway, gently closing his eyes for a moment as he reached up and touched the cracked stone mezuzah, then he kissed his two fingers. When he opened his eyes he beheld the destruction of the home. Yosef bit his bottom lip as he followed the Centurion across the floor. He looked to the left at where a dining area had been set up. The low table had been broken, pillows torn apart, and stools damaged from being flung aside. Yosef noticed some smashed plates and cups, and other vessels made from clay scattering the floor, but the interior of the home spoke of wealth which had naturally been ransacked of all finery.

The place had been looted. What had been impossible to take or thought worthless, such as drapery, table cloths, and empty chests, had been ruined. Yosef accidentally kicked something and stared down at the tiled floor. He halted and slowly bent over. He took hold of a bowl, carved from stone and richly smoothed by hours of pain-staking labour. He held the vessel in his hands and followed his gaze across the floor to more bowls and plates like it that were scattered about.

"What are you looking at? They are worthless, leave them," the Optio growled with annoyance.

Yosef slowly stood and handing the bowl to the junior officer he said fighting back tears, "This was the home of a priest." He turned and followed the Centurion to a stairwell going up to the second level. Upon the steps was a body of a young boy. One arm was outstretched, as if he had meant to grab someone or something, as his other arm dangled over the side of the staircase. His face was turned to the side and blood stained the steps running down to the floor. Yosef grimaced at the body and the Centurion frowned, glaring back at the Optio.

"This boy attacked my men," the Optio replied defensively.

"I am sure," retorted the Centurion. "He looks no more than fourteen." He gave a disgusted groan as he tried to step over the body to avoid the foul smell it gave off.

Yosef followed the Centurion quietly, desiring nothing more than to turn on the Optio and strike him dead. He muttered a prayer under his breath for the dead boy, wishing to treat him with respect and avoid stepping on him. He heard the Centurion curse vilely and saw him shake his head as he came to the top of the staircase and gaze out at the slaughter before his eyes.

At the end of the room an old man with a white beard lay propped up against a wall. His glassy eyes remained stretched open and dilated as the pupils were like gazing into a haunted mirror from the terror the man had witnessed before dying. His white garments he wore were red with blood and a pool of crimson ran out from where he lay. His chest had been savagely torn apart from repeated sword strikes and his exposed white ribs could be seen as the man had been pinned against the wall and butchered. At his side, still in the sheltering grip of his right arm, lay a dead woman against his chest. She was not mutilated like the man, but revealed wounds in her chest from multiple spear strikes.

Yosef could not help himself as tears streaked down his cheeks. He gazed to his left, past the woman, and saw a young girl lying face down, the back of her head soiled in blood from the ghastly blow that had killed her. He turned to the Optio and said with a face flushed with anger, "You bastard! You slaughtered a priestly family!"

The Optio took a startled step backwards and then raised his gladius with the other soldiers behind him lowering their blades. "You dare curse me, you damn Jew? I will cut your heart out and…"

"Optio you will silence yourself!" shouted the Centurion. "This man is under orders and the protection of the Prince of *Roma*. If you speak further, I will have you up on charges! If you harm him, I will have you flogged raw! Now shut your mouth!" The Centurion's eyes were ablaze as he glared at the junior officer. "Go back down and get a contingent of soldiers to help clear these bodies from here. They are to be treated with respect. Wrap them and take them from the city and bury them! Then you are relieved to go back to camp!"

"But, Centurion…" the optio stammered.

"Now, or I will remove your balls with my pugio! You will obey me. That's an order!" the Centurion bellowed. The Optio glared for a moment at Yosef and then stubbornly saluted and backed away leaving the other soldiers in the room. "Now, if you six have the sense to say nothing, you will follow us to the rooftop!"

The Centurion, Yosef, and the six legionaries crossed the room and found a small, narrow staircase jutting out from the wall next to where the bodies laid. They climbed the steps in silence and finally emerged into the fresh air. The rooftop of the home revealed the damage which the Optio had spoken of. The floor was covered in broken tiles, shingles, and overturned vessels once containing plants and small trees as soil had been scattered about. The centurion glared at one of the large vessels which had been pushed over, smashed, and then dug through. He moved some of the dirt around with his foot and then grunted. "They were looking for hidden wealth contained in these pots."

Yosef said nothing behind the Centurion and tried to regain his composure. He wiped away the tears and took a deep breath to steady his thinking. He gazed up at the high walls of the Temple Mount's West Colonnade which loomed not far from where he stood. Yosef could see Jewish fighters, who had spotted the Romans, clustering on the ramparts with the enormous white-marbled Temple in the background.

"You can speak from here," the Centurion said, interrupting Yosef's thoughts. "We will protect you."

Yosef gave a nod of thanks and cleared his throat. He slowly walked to the edge of the rooftop and heard a ripple of distasteful shouting erupt from the ramparts as the Zealots recognized who he was.

* * *

CHAPTER XXXI

Second Wall of the Mishneh Quarter
Two hours past dawn

A large bearded man, named Shmuel, quietly opened a door and peered through. He held his breath and tightened his jaw. A bandage of linen was tied to his left arm, failing to conceal a spot of dried blood that had seeped through. He felt someone slightly push him from behind. He glared back, raising an open hand. Then with a grim stare, he turned and scanned the quiet homes of the Mishneh.

Judah pressed his way through the fighters, accompanied by Adam, as they found John ben Dorcas near the front. "Why are we not moving?"

John shook his head and gazed back. "Shmuel is making sure we are clear."

"Well, tell him to hurry. The other group will be moving out next to Phasael Tower soon. We cannot waste time." Judah gripped his sword with sweaty fingers and gave Adam a frustrated look. When John refused to say anything more, Judah angrily swore, stepped past the commander and ignored the plight of Yeshua ben Sapphias who cursed him nearby. "Shmuel," Judah whispered, crouching low behind the large man. "Do you see Romans?"

The beast-like warrior stepped back and gently closed the door so that only a splinter of light could be seen. He squatted next to Judah, whom he respected, and shrugged in the shadow under the West Colonnade. "No Romans, Judah, but that doesn't mean they are not on the other side of the homes closest to us. We could walk right into a trap! We're blind."

Judah glanced back at the hundreds of fighters and then turned to the burly man. "Jacob ben Soras leads his army near Phasael. We must coordinate together. That is the plan. There are enough homes to shadow our movements, right?"

Shmuel nodded. "Where we are located is deep in the Mishneh, most likely no Romans have made it this far." Suddenly a muffled voice could be heard on the other side of the door. Shmuel quickly turned and listened intently.

"Who is that?" Judah replied concentrating on the voice but unable to make anything of it.

Shmuel cautiously crept forward, gently opened the door, and stuck his head out. He was motionless for a moment, then stepped back in and closed the door. "That's Yosef ben Matityahu speaking."

Judah scowled for a moment. "What? Where?"

Shmuel shook his head. "I can't see him, but he isn't far away. I think he calls out to our soldiers on the colonnades." Shmuel thought to himself for a second and then sighed. "He must be on a rooftop."

"Judah, that is perfect," Adam said from behind. "If Yosef is speaking, that means the Romans are distracted."

Judah briefly was silent, then gave a heavy nod and signaled John and Yeshua to his side. He watched the two officers press through the fighters. When they were close, Judah said in a raspy voice, "Yosef ben Matityahu is calling for Gischala to surrender. Shmuel thinks he calls out from a rooftop although we cannot see where."

"That will mean the Roman dogs will be unaware, we should move now," Yeshua responded eagerly as he rubbed his hands together with excitement.

John nodded at both commanders and replied, "We move as ordered, two groups circling from the north and the west along the cover of houses. Once in position we wait until Yosef finishes his speech. That should give Soras' group enough time."

"I will go north," Judah volunteered.

"Right," said John. "Yeshua and I will move west. We fight to the breach, retake it, and barricade it. We will have more reinforcements from Simon and Gischala as soon as we have secured the Mishneh. The report is that our men in the homes nearest the Roman breach have not been discovered. They will fire those homes as soon as the battle begins."

"Fight like wolves," Judah replied with a nervous edge to his voice as Yeshua grinned at him. Judah turned away and nodding at Shmuel said, "Open the door."

The great man extended a heavy hand to Judah and patted the Lion warrior upon the shoulder. "May God let his face shine upon you, Judah. I will see you after." Then he turned and took hold of the door. With prudence he opened the door, took up his spear, and lunged through with speed.

Judah followed Shmuel and turned right as he kept low and ran along the base of the colonnade walls for nearly twenty-five metres. He halted next to an abandoned merchant shop and watched as a steady stream of fighters continued to pour from the doorway, splitting off into two long columns which resembled a centipede with thousands of legs. The only sound was the soft clapping of their sandals upon the flagstones as they moved in haste.

Shmuel and Adam quickly reached Judah as the column of Zealots stretched all the way back to the open door. Judah gave the two men a sharp nod and then set off again at a fast jog to the nearest home along the looming walls of the western side of the Temple Mount. When he reached the home, he listened above the sound of men's feet beating against the stones. He heard jeers and shouts rise up from the ramparts beyond as Jewish soldiers shouted profanity at Yosef. Judah slowly edged along the wall as the sunlight warmed his body. He felt the cool stone with his fingers as he reached the edge of the building and slowly peered around the corner to inspect a vacant alley. Somewhere, beyond his vision, he could hear the sound of trumpets, the jingling of Roman cingulum and the distinct noise of hundreds of caligae.

"What should we do?" Adam asked as he responded to the deafening Roman trumpet blasts. "I think Yosef speaks from that direction," he said pointing to the north.

Judah nodded and tried to steady his breathing. His heart pounded so loudly in his chest he was afraid the noise would beckon the Romans right to their position. "Forget about Yosef," Judah said and then signaled to Shmuel. "The Romans are down this alley." Judah held his breath as he heard more shouts and curses from the ramparts followed by Yosef's voice pleading with them to surrender. "Shmuel, you lead half of the men down this alley and I will lead the other half a little further behind these homes. Then turn inward where we can strike." Shmuel nodded, wiping the sweat from his eyes. Judah leaned out from the wall of the home and gazed down the ranks of crouched fighters who used the buildings and merchant booths as shelter along the colonnade walls. No more Zealots emerged from the door and Judah looked back to the burly man. "Get men up on the rooftops when you get closer to the Romans. These homes are so packed together they should be able to leap from roof to roof."

"Judah," Adam said as he moved closer to his friend. "It has been an honour. If this is the last day we shall live, it has been a privilege to serve with you."

Judah bit his lower lip and breathed heavily. He patted the side of Adam's face and smiled. "If I die, you shall take care of Hadassah and get her out of the city at all cost. Promise me this!"

"I promise," Adam said and then paused, wrestling with his own mortality. "You will tell my parents if I should fall. Take my body to them, Judah. Do not leave me to rot."

Judah embraced his friend. "I shall fight to the last."

"Judah, tell me one thing," Adam said with a whisper, taking up his spear. "That night on the wall where that boy called for you, what was that about? You said you would tell me, but alas I have forgotten to remind you with all that has taken place."

Judah smiled and shook his head. "I have a feeling you shall find out today, Adam. May the God of Abraham, Isaac, and Jacob be with you, my friend." Judah stepped away from the wall and raised his sword in the air to signal the fighters. Then he turned and moved to the north with two hundred and fifty men.

Judah led them quickly, pausing only to send a couple dozen men at a time onto the rooftops, instructing them to lay low and remain quiet until the fighting began. The Zealots moved swiftly. Like a tide of army ants, they covered the homes and streets, fanning out in all directions, yet remaining invisible, like an army of phantoms. The voices of Romans began to be heard more audibly as the stealthy Jewish Zealots infiltrated the Mishneh with every passing minute. Their shadows danced upon the homes they passed, like a great predator closing in on its unsuspecting prey. In the streets furthest from the Bezetha, five lone legionaries were discovered and dispatched swiftly with sharp knives across the throats, as hands covered the mouths of the thrashing victims. Soon the Mishneh was filled by Jewish warriors from both factions, as Idumeans led by Soras, slipped through gates and doorways near the Phasael Tower, entrenching themselves among the winding suburbs.

The Romans, despite their strength in the Mishneh, remained completely unaware of the daunting threat encircling them. Seven cohorts had been committed into the quarter, with one fortifying the ramparts of the Second Wall and another, the Falcon Third Cohort of the Fretensis, moving deeply into the Mishneh to the southeast where Judah's men lurked. The remaining five cohorts had been recalled just inside the breach and now were drawn up in their usual rectangular ranks. As the Jews listened passively to Yosef ben Matityahu's pointless pleas to John and Simon on the West Colonnades, the warlord from Gischala braced himself with delight. With the closing vice grips of the trap slowly tightening below, two thousand Jewish warriors moved swiftly to strangle their victim and slaughter him.

"Check those homes now!" thundered a voice from around the corner of a house Judah hid behind. Judah stared at the mass of fighters accompanying him and held up his hand for them to be completely silent. Slowly, ever so carefully, Judah crept to the side of the house and slid to his knees as he peered around the corner.

A narrow street separated the houses on either side, littered with debris from the ransacking of the Mishneh nearly an hour ago. Marching down the street in force was a Roman cohort tightly packed together, spears lowered and scutum locked as one. A Centurion led the formation and was ordering units of legionaries into homes as doors began to be kicked in. An Optio followed close to the Centurion with a blonde, black-haired plume as he carried his hastile which he used to spread out the soldiers and direct them. However, what caught Judah's attention was the banner hoisted above the cohort which bore the image of a golden falcon, the Roman numeral 'III' and the word 'COHORS' below. A signum carried closest to the Centurion, also showed the numeral 'LEG X FR.' underneath the open palm of a hand enwreathed upon the top.

Judah turned back and collected his thoughts, remembering the message he had been given the other night by the Jewish boy. He had heard the instructions carefully, forcing the boy to repeat them before signing the parchment. Gaius had been trustworthy after all. On the other hand, the Prince of Rome was convinced Judah was a sympathizer of the people that slaughtered his countrymen and burned his cities. Judah moved again to the edge and watched the Centurion. He narrowed his gaze as he stared at him. His eyes became watery and his cheeks became flushed. His heart steadied itself and his adrenaline was like sheer power as it raced through his veins.

"This is for you, Miriam, my love," Judah quietly whispered. He gently closed his eyes for a moment and turned back from the corner of the home. For a second he could smell Miriam's perfume and hear her laughter. Then his eyes snapped open. He stepped out from the wall and raised his sword to his men. Judah gave a firm nod, and gaining their attention he realized he could no longer hear voices. Yosef ben Matityahu's terms had ceased and the only thing audible was the racket from the cohort of legionaries down the street. Judah locked eyes with Adam and said, "It ends here." Then he turned and dashed around the corner of the house with two hundred men at his back howling like demons.

Judah tightened his grip upon the hilt of his sword as he screamed his war cry and charged down the street. The ranks behind him swelled into a dense pack of men with spears lowered as they were gripped by the rush of war. The Roman centuries which filled the street before them reacted quickly, almost in a panic, as optiones shoved men into line. The front ranks lowered their pila and braced themselves behind their wide shields. Legionaries were still emerging from searching homes when the Jewish charge hammered into the Roman formation packed between the homes and fumbling around as they tried to form a battle column in the narrow alley. The Jews slammed into the shields with the force of a crunching avalanche as spears snapped, shields shattered, and men howled with rage. Sword blades flashed out from the ranks as blood was spilled. Both sides heaved and pushed, as each attempted to gain ground. Men in the Jewish ranks closest to the front began to strike at the Romans feet as they shattered ankles and sliced their calves with swords and spears. Legionaries screamed as they toppled backwards trying to escape the horrendous wounds being inflicted upon them and at this time a hail of spears descended upon the centuries from above.

Judah cheered till he was hoarse as Jewish fighters from the rooftops unleashed another volley into the ambushed cohort. Like birds of prey descending upon a helpless, wounded beast, dozens of Zealots began leaping into the Roman units as they scattered their ranks, plunging swords into chests and throats. The Romans tried to retaliate and reform but the damage had been done. With their ranks splitting in disorder, the Jewish onslaught pressed into them striking down legionaries in droves. A Centurion in the rear, sensing the defeat and seeing his men butchered before his eyes, blasted on his whistle and screamed for them to retreat. This command only sought to ignite more passion in the Zealots, who like suicidal, insane men, charged the Romans making it impossible for them to maintain order and withdraw.

Judah stepped over the bodies of legionaries, hearing the wails of mercy behind him as the wounded Romans were quickly killed. He swung his sword wildly at an Optio who blocked it with his hastile. The Optio gritted his teeth and glared at Judah as the jackal fur head cresting his helmet, seemed to stare at the Jewish warrior with its eyeless face. The Optio growled like a beast, dropped his staff, then drew his gladius and lunged with the blade. Judah darted to the left, escaping the intended strike as it seared past him. With deadly speed, Judah rammed the junior officer with his shoulder and brought the hilt of his sword up, ramming it into the Roman's face, causing cartilage of the man's nose to explode under the pressure, spurting up a fountain of blood. The Optio shrieked and then was suddenly grabbed by his chest armour and pulled back into the protection of his century which enclosed around him.

"They are breaking!" Adam shouted at Judah as he plunged his spear through the chest of a legionary. He tugged on his spear as the dying Roman screamed and thrashed on the ground. Adam yanked back on the shaft and when it would not come free, he moved forward, planted a firm foot on the Roman's chest, drew his sword, and plunged it into the man's throat killing him.

Judah acknowledged Adam with a nod and signaled to press on as Zealots poured past him. The Roman ranks finally managed to close their gaps, but the officers knew the danger and needed a way out. The Jews, on the other hand, could sense their enemy's fear like a lion stalking a wounded deer. Jews who held shields began to beat them incessantly while others stomped the ground calling the Romans cowards. Each time the Jews made a feint charge the nervous legionaries would halt, and collapse back into their rigid, compact formations. When the charge would not come, the legionaries would continue to shuffle back down the alley followed closely by the Jewish assault party, looking for a weakness exploit.

Suddenly the Romans halted and drew up their tight stubborn ranks as if to make a stand. Judah watched Capito make his way to the front as he shouted to his men, encouraging them not to back down. He pushed between his legionaries, calling on the Jews to attack him as he spit upon the ground. Bodies of Jews and Romans lay at Capito's feet as he grinned with a face speckled in blood. He took a step forward and howled at the Jews like a dog.

"Come on, you virgins! You whores! Let's get this over with!" Capito removed his helmet and hurled it at the Zealots who became infuriated and threw it back. A few Zealots hurled spears at Capito and the cocky Centurion simply just stood aside and laughed. "Is that all you've got!" Capito turned as his optio with the broken nose stepped out from the ranks and whispered something in his ear. Capito shook his head, pointed at the Jews and said, "We are not retreating! I don't care what you say, we are going nowhere." At that moment, the Optio completely caught Capito by surprise, as he swiftly brought the hilt of his sword up and smashed it into his Centurion's face, knocking him to the flagstones. Complete silence filtered through the Jewish ranks as everyone watched the blithering Centurion spit a stream of blood onto the stones then fall to his side in a daze. The Optio stared at his men for a moment, then turned once more to his Centurion. With all his might, the Optio drove his foot into his senior commander's chest and then kicked Capito's sword away.

Capito flailed upon the ground choking and swearing as he gasped for air, blood flowing from the gash in his face. He tried to recover from the blow, but all he could do was shake his head and shudder. The Optio stared for a moment at Judah as the distant sounds of battle began to erupt all around him from other parts of the city. He looked over his shoulder, startled by a deep echo that boomed throughout the streets. He saw a rush of fire and huge billows of black smoke suddenly fill the sky.

Then the Optio shouted for the centuries to retreat and ever so cautiously they fell back.

Judah watched Capito claw the ground, shrieking with anger as he watched his legionaries abandon him. "Come back, you traitors! Marius, you would leave me here? Brother?" he screamed with rage as blood and broken teeth spewed from his mouth. The Optio turned, saluted his Centurion with a grin and then signaled the centuries into a full retreat as the Romans fled. "Curse you, Marius! I curse your very bones!" Capito screamed as the blood began to pulse even stronger and flow down his face.

Judah hardly had to say a thing. With the sight of Capito sprawled upon the ground and the fleeing Romans, the Zealots instantly sprang into action as they burst into a charge. Judah watched Capito stare with wild eyes, mouth agape and his body transfixed by shock as the Jews bore down on him. Then Capito mustered whatever strength still remained and managed to scramble to his feet, fleeing desperately down a side street. "Drive them from the Mishneh!" Judah hollered as he stopped at the mouth of the alley and watched Capito hobble away.

"Where are you going, Judah?" Adam shouted as the Zealots stampeded past him in pursuit of the broken centuries.

"I am going to kill the Centurion, you push on! I will join you soon!" Judah yelled back as Adam pressed through the Zealots.

Adam glanced down the alley as he spotted the Centurion arrive at a corner of an intersecting street, cautiously glance around and then draw his pugio. "Who is that?" Adam said, scowling at Judah.

"What does it matter?" Judah angrily turned to give chase.

Adam caught Judah's arm and said, "Is this what you wanted to tell me? Is this why you left the wall that night? Judah, you better talk fast. Do you know that optio?"

"Don't be ridiculous, Adam. Let me go and return to the fight, that is an order," Judah said raising his voice as he pulled away.

"It looked planned! Why would that Optio strike his Centurion and then leave him to die? The colour of his plume and the medals on his chest prove he's a senior Centurion!" Adam watched Judah halt and glare back at him. "Why would the optio do such a thing and then retreat?" Adam stepped forward and stared at Judah with heated eyes. "Why is a cohort from the Fretensis even in this part of the city when the Fifth Legion has been attacking? Who is he, Judah?" Adam glanced past his friend and watched the Centurion stumble around the distant corner and disappear. "Is it Capito? Have you been working with the Romans to get Capito? What have you told them?" By now a dark and foreboding look infiltrated Adam's eyes as he stared at his friend. Adam shook his head at Judah's silence and then raised his chin and bit his lower lip. "Are you a spy? The one John seeks?"

Judah's face was flushed with anger. His breathing became heavy and shaken. "It is Capito, you are right. I will kill him and gain my vengeance, Adam. I have hunted the man, and have sought to take his life for many years. For Miriam's sake he has now been delivered to me. Yes, I should have told you. I only didn't tell you to protect you and the others. But alas, Caleb is dead, and everything has changed."

Adam glared at Judah. "You are foolish! Revenge? You would put this city's fate on the line for this man? Does your hatred know no bounds? Your anger is blind!"

With exhausted eyes Judah gazed for a moment at the dozens of bodies strewn along the street in piles with streaks of blood upon the stones. "I am not a spy!" Judah declared looking back at Adam. "I have never forsaken this city or its people! I will fight till I die. You must believe me. I will tell you later, but I must do this. God has turned his back on me. He has looked away. I have sought peace, but it evades me. You must understand; I have to do this." Judah stared at his friend and then whispered, "You have followed me for years, and you know me better than anyone. Surely you cannot think I have betrayed this city and become a spy for Rome? The very people who slaughtered my parents and the love of my life? You think that? Surely you cannot!" Tears welled up in Judah's eyes as he grabbed Adam's arms and squeezed them like a clamp. "I lost everything! I am hollow and broken with anguish. Now let me take back my honour, I beg of you!"

Adam's face grew pale and he slowly stepped back. "He turned left at the end of the alley." Adam was silent, then shook his head. "I trust no one more then you. I will rejoin the attack. Be careful, Judah. He has a weapon and he is desperate."

Judah nodded, then turned and ran down the alley. He held his sword at waist level as he slowed his pace, keeping close to the homes on his right. When he came to the end of the street he listened intensely. Nothing. Nothing could be heard but the distant sounds of battle at the other end of the Mishneh. Judah slowly peeked around the corner and noticed droplets of blood upon the flagstones. He was close. Calmly, Judah followed the blood droplets as he moved from street to street.

Judah stared up at the sky as his eyes traced the black smoke and his nostrils smelled the charred wood. He moved further along the quiet, vacant streets with an intensity that seized his body and sharpened his senses. Suddenly he saw Capito ahead of him, crouched near the corner of a home as he held his chest with one hand, wheezing and gasping for breath. Judah stepped out from the shadow of the house allowing himself to be seen, and faced off with the Centurion.

*　　*　　*

Capito hunched over and winced in pain as he struggled to breathe. He reached up and wiped blood away from his mouth with the back of his hand. He swore again and grinned, fantasizing about the cruel end his Optio would face once he returned to camp. *The bastard wants a promotion? I will see his flesh peeled from his body for this,* Capito thought to himself. *I will flog him till he dies and then strangle all of his comrades who were involved in this.*

Capito's body ached. He felt inside his mouth using his tongue and then swore, as he counted three missing teeth. He groaned as he knew a number of his ribs had been broken when his Optio had kicked him. "Prickly shit," Capito swore as he slowly stood using the wall of the home to steady himself. He slowed his breathing and spit a red stream of bloody saliva upon the ground. His eyes still watered and he rubbed them. He suddenly paused and squinted in the sunlight at the blurry image of a man facing him nearly thirty metres away. "What in the…" Capito muttered as he raised a hand above his eyes. "You want to come here?" Capito moaned. "I will fillet you." A line of blood trickled from his nose and mouth as he narrowed his gaze, yet the man did not respond or move. "Who are you?" Capito shouted, sensing an edge of fear grip him. He raised his dagger and pointed it at the man as he leaned against the wall, feeling sweat run down his neck. Capito turned as he smelled smoke as the wind picked up. He watched as black smoke filled a street next to him and right away he knew that would be his getaway. "I will see you in Hades," Capito shouted at the man who still did not move. Then hunched over in pain, Capito stumbled away into the thick smoke to escape.

Capito pushed on as he began to choke and cough from the thick, grayish-black, soot which began to blow in his face. The smoke was suffocating and tasted awful. He kept his head down, scrunching up his face as the smell burned his nostrils and throat. Capito finally noticed the smoke beginning to dissipate before him and he smiled, sensing victory. He stopped to catch his breath, naturally relived at being alone. Capito gazed back and listened for any sign of someone following him. Nothing unusual could be heard and he felt safe. A broken, bloodied smile spread across his face. He shook his head and listened to the fighting which intensified as he neared the battle. It would be simple, he would join the fight, aiding one of the Fifth cohors, then after they had beaten the Jews and secured the Mishneh he would request an audience with Titus and turn over the perpetrators. Except in this case, he would beg Titus for permission to enact the punishment on the rogue optio and legionaries himself.

"Capito," called out a sudden, phantom-like voice from the smoke.

Capito's heart pounded in his chest. With a flash he swung around and raised the dagger in his trembling hands as he stared through the blindness of the smoke. His mind swirled in desperation. He had heard his name spoken clearly as the haunting envelopment of the smoke struck him with fear. "Who are you?" Capito pleaded as he pushed away from the edge of the street and hobbled to the centre. He stared through the smoke and saw nothing. "You have come to kill me? Please try," he taunted as he tried to bolster his courage.

"I have searched for you for many years," replied the voice again.

"Do I know you?" Capito replied. "You speak in Latin, you're Roman then?" Capito heard the voice reply but he did not understand the words and he scowled. "Was that Hebrew? Aramaic? Are you a shit Jew? An educated one at that, but still a shit Jew! Show yourself, you bleeding whelp!" Suddenly, before Capito could react, a blade shot through the smoke and sliced into the muscle of his arm which held the dagger. The wound was deep and instantly caused him to drop the knife as his arm went limp with a spill of blood. Capito shrieked in pain and fell backwards. He grabbed the wound, in an attempt to stop the bleeding and slowly dragged himself backwards with a whimper.

Slowly, Judah stepped from the smoke and walked up to Capito who lay helpless upon the ground gasping. Judah kicked away the dagger and then unwrapped his face covering and glared indifferently at the man. Capito cringed, as if the man unveiling his face should give him recollection, but nothing stirred in his mind. He winced and briefly looked at the wound, cursing the Jew with a mutter.

"Who are you? You obviously know me," Capito said as he gasped and tightened his grip on the wound, trying not to lose consciousness.

"I am one who has dreamed of this moment for years." Judah watched the puzzled Roman scowl at him. Judah knelt down and looked him in the eye. "Four years ago you took something from me. You were given an order. You slaughtered thousands in the market place of this city."

Capito's eyes widened with fear at the tone of calm revenge. "It was just an order, you Jews had angered Florus. It is his fault! Why do you come after me? He was the one who gave the order."

"But it was your sword that spilled innocent blood. It was your feet that trampled upon women and children. Do you not remember? Once you had killed everyone there was one who stood and faced you next to that great fountain. That man challenged you and you turned your back on him." Judah glared and watched the Centurion cock his head slightly to the side.

"Ah, yes. I remember you." Capito smiled and shook his head. "Old enemies, right? You have returned to kill me? A man consumed by hate. That is good. Well, my work was accomplished."

"What do you mean?"

Capito nodded and closed his eyes to collect his thoughts. "It was Florus' will to spread hatred to you people. He wanted your cities burned, your women raped, and your children enslaved. He always hated your kind. He paid well, and I came on board. He told me to try and leave survivors, which I did. These survivors would make it impossible for Agrippa to find peace and put an end to rebellious inclinations. Florus said many times that the hatred would spread and soon Nero would have no choice but to dispatch the legions to wipe your country out. We have done well so far, would you not agree? It was men like you, who fueled that rage among your people and put a halt to the emperor's sacrifice in the Temple. It is because of you, and not me, that this city will burn."

Judah suddenly lunged in rage at Capito and punched him twice in the face as he smashed his knuckles into Capito's eyes with a howl of anger. Capito's head smacked against the stone behind him and he groaned as blood gushed from a cut under his blackened eyes. "You are a wicked man, Capito, and I will snatch your life from you today. I will avenge the murder of many. You killed those I love and now you will suffer." Judah stood and lowered his blade.

"You can kill me, Jew. But we will still burn your city. More loved ones will die. Look at me, what have I to live for now? I have obviously been betrayed." Capito coughed and then licked his split bleeding lips as he stared up with swollen eyes. "You will kill me, and still my face you will see."

"I shall not kill you as quickly as you would prefer." Judah said and with a sudden motion hacked his blade into Capito's left foot, severing it from the leg. Capito shrieked as he retched and thrashed. Judah took a step back and watched the Centurion scream as he let his wounded arm go and tried to reach for the mutilated foot. Judah wasted no time. He took Capito by the hair, yanked his head back, and with a sawing motion he cut his right ear off. "You will enter Hades as a deaf man." Judah said calmly and then stepped back as the Centurion helplessly wailed as Judah tossed the bloodied ear to the side.

"Please, please! No more!" Capito shrieked and then vomited upon the ground as he trembled. "You have done enough! I am forever ruined!"

"Your Prince has given you to me, Capito! You have been sold as a slave! You are a slave with a destiny, and that destiny is my sword." Judah lowered the blade to the horrified look upon Capito's face. "I will cut your head off and thrust it onto a pike! Then I shall attach it to one of the towers of the fortress Antonia for your Prince to see."

Capito shook his head as his body convulsed with shock. "Impossible," he stuttered. "There is no way Titus would give me to you."

"Why do you think that optio struck you as he did? He will be the new senior centurion by nightfall and will thank whatever gods he worships for the swiftness of my sword." Again, Judah grabbed Capito by the hair, turned, and then dragged him to the centre of the street. "You know how I learned your name?" Capito began to whimper and sob as Judah continued, "After I fled the market place I found two of your men. I killed one and dragged the other into an alley, like I drag you now. I cut him to pieces, and removed his balls. The last thing he uttered to me was your name." Judah turned and wrenched Capito's head back, exposing his neck. "You were right, Capito, I have become a man of hatred." He paused for a moment and then drew close to the agonizing man and whispered, "This is for Miriam."

With a complete look of apathy, Judah stepped back. Then a surge of bitter anger came over him as he swung his sword and watched the blade, without hindrance, cut through the flesh, jugular, and spine of Capito before bursting out the other side of his severed neck. The head fell to the ground as Judah planted his foot upon the body and pushed it over. He stared at the corpse for a moment, then closed his eyes and wept.

* * *

"Hold the ramparts! That is an order!" shouted Tiberius as he paced up and down the Roman cohorts who were slowly getting torn apart from the massive Jewish assault. He swore and spit upon the ground as he clutched his gladius and shook his head. "Keep it up, cut the bastards to pieces!" he shouted and thumped the shoulders of legionaries as he passed by to encourage them. Tiberius strained to see if the Jewish waves had an end in sight, but all he could make out was densely packed formations of screaming Zealots stretching back throughout the streets as they howled like demons from the abyss.

Tiberius swore again. How could they have been so foolish and haughty? He glanced back at Titus standing atop of the breach watching intensely and not moving a muscle. Beside the Prince stood legionary generals Titus Frigius and Larcius Lepidus, along with Yosef ben Matityahu who had barely made it out alive. Tiberius shook his head again as he remembered how the panic-stricken Jewish General had bolted from an alley of the Mishneh closely followed by a Centurion and two wounded soldiers.

The Centurion had reported an ambush in the streets and that all of his soldiers had been slaughtered. As the Centurion had gasped for air, he told of how Jews had leapt from doorways, jumped from rooftops, and charged down the streets. Tiberius' worst nightmare had come true. At that instant, the proud Roman General, who had mustered a lifetime of experience on the battlefield and in politics, turned utterly dumbfounded with a horrified expression to the sound of rampaging thunder. Hundreds of Zealots, infused with a maddening rage, appeared in a double-pronged attack from the east and west neighbourhoods of the Mishneh, stampeding towards the Roman ranks like a massive tidal wave.

Tiberius had leapt into action. He left the side of his Prince, ignoring Titus' pleas and hysteric shouts at the aging man with his grey hair and balding crown. Tiberius had hurried to the bottom of the breach, bellowing like the great Cyclops himself, for the cohorts to draw together and hurl their pila. The suddenness of the Jewish attack had caught the centuries so off guard that by the time they had tightened their ranks and spread out to deliver their volley, the Jews were ramming into them with spears and swords.

Upon the ramparts, Roman archers tried to help in any way possible as three scorpion crews fired their deadly bolts, but soon these came under heavy fire from the fortress Antonia as its towers sprung to life with bowmen and artillery hurling missiles of their own. Within moments the ramparts had become a bloody mess with broken men wailing and screaming in agony.

General Lepidus had instantly taken the initiative seeing the dire circumstances of the cohort upon the ramparts as they huddled behind their shields, trying to retaliate. Running down the breach and into the Bezetha, Larcius had shouted at two cohorts of his own to bring up ladders and lean them against the outside of the Second Wall where the Apollinaris cohort was getting crushed. It was a rescue mission, and Larcius sent up soldiers to the parapets who shouted over the side to their comrades to abandon their futile stand and flee. Prince Titus, on the other hand, saw retreat as a sign of disgrace and shouted for Larcius to send up more troops and bowmen. This quickly resulted in chaos as Larcius argued that until they could secure the Mishneh it would only spell death to attempt to hold the ramparts.

Both men's hotly debate only ended, however, when all remaining soldiers upon the ramparts fled in sheer terror. What legionaries could not access the ladders or the stone steps of the battlements took other desperate measures. Titus and Larcius watched as men leapt from the walls only to shatter bones, snap their backs, or be silenced by death from the fall. The soldiers, who hesitated from the grisly scene of their comrades leaping onto the stones below, were simply cut down by arrows which protruded from their exposed legs, necks, arms, and faces, abandoned to die painfully as they attempted to crawl away.

Tiberius watched the entire cohort on the ramparts scatter, many to their demise, and he swore as loud as his vocal chords would carry until his face was suddenly speckled in blood. He staggered backwards and winced as droplets of crimson stung his eyes. Tiberius shook off a soldier who grabbed him to see if he was okay, and after rubbing his eyes he stared at a young legionary on the ground, skewered through the throat by an arrow. "To the breach!" Tiberius finally shouted in frustration. He filled his lungs with air again and bellowed, "Back up to the breach! Slow and with order!" He wildly looked to an Optio and yelled, "Pull them back through the breach! We cannot stay here like this!"

"My General, there are still men fighting beyond our ranks!"

"What in the name of all the gods? By the balls of Jupiter, where?" Tiberius threw both hands up in the air as he felt as if his chest would burst with frustration. *The Mishneh had surrendered too easily. I smelled the trap and we walked right into it,* Tiberius thought to himself.

"The men are near the alleys, at least a hundred or more. Too hard to tell from here, General Tiberius," replied the Optio.

"We move back to the breach in order! Sound whistles and trumpets. Bang anything you bloody well have and get their attention! We will stand and fight in the breach until they are all out!" The Optio gave a sharp nod and the frustrated general turned and wearily marched back towards the piles of debris.

"Tiberius, why aren't the cohorts pushing forward?" Titus shouted as he appeared distraught on the rubble plateau of the breach. Sudden blasts of trumpets and whistles began to blow throughout the cohort ranks and the columns of legionaries started to backup ever so carefully.

"We cannot win like this, my Prince! We have men scattered everywhere, perhaps hundreds dead and wounded, and the Jews are only reinforcing themselves." Tiberius climbed the breach and gazed out over the dismal situation. "You see that! They know they are beating us!" Tiberius pointed to the long streets that stretched beyond the Romans as they were packed with Jews who had begun to cheer. He turned and looked at the humiliated Prince. "We have to give up the Mishneh today, there is no other way!"

"We can commit more men into battle. We can drive them from the streets," Titus stubbornly replied as he shook his head and clenched his fists.

"And risk more lives? The Fifth Cohors were massacred on the ramparts, my Prince. I dare to think if they will recover. The Jews surprised us. They know these neighbourhoods, and we cannot deploy a strong enough force in order to push them back, at least not like this. The Jews have closed the fighting field into a small space, and therefore have the upper hand," Tiberius angrily replied at Titus as he now began to see the damage done as countless bodies of legionaries could be seen cleaved and bloodied upon the ground.

"So then, what do we do? Just leave Jerusalem?" Titus responded sarcastically as he cursed under his breath.

"No, my Prince." Tiberius shook his head and stared at Titus with a sudden coolness about him. "We regroup, repair what we lost today, and hit them tomorrow! We widen the breach, tear down the towers and retake what is left of the ramparts to add some height to our defences. Then we fortify the Mishneh and pull down the homes."

Titus was silent for a moment. He stared with a blank look at the burning homes encircling the inside of the Second Wall and then sighed. "You are right, you think clearer than me at times, Tiberius." Titus smiled candidly, then scratched his head and turned to leave. "Pull the men back through the breach. Bring up artillery to kill anything that comes through and we attack tomorrow at first light."

Tiberius watched Titus march down the rubble. The proud Prince tried to appear undefeated as he held his head high and demanded his horse be brought to him. "Frigius, Lepidus!" Tiberius shouted as he turned his attention from the sour Prince to the two legionary generals. "Have your men pull out of the Mishneh and reform out here. Send runners to have artillery brought up and point them all at this gap."

The generals saluted and departed without a word as they passed the orders to junior officers and runners. Soon onagri, catapults and scorpions were dragged up. The distance was measured, every engine loaded, and positioned in the Bezetha as they pointed to the breach. Tiberius descended the rubble, along with the higher ranking generals, and took up a position to the rear of the artillery under a veranda surrounded by guards.

After a few moments, legionaries began to pour over the summit of the breach and flee down the rocky slopes into the Bezetha to escape the slaughter. Most were stained with dust and sweat, but many revealed wounds to the legs and arms as they called out with pitiful cries for surgeons to come to their aid.

The confusion seemed endless on the other side of the Second Wall as soldiers flowed into the Bezetha scattering about with shouts and panic. However, soon officers and sergeants began to regroup contingents of men to form up as they faced the breach in grim silence, watching the wounded flood past. Long lines of carts, dispatched to collect the wounded, constantly cycled through the breach as men by the dozens were loaded into them with painful wails. Some legionaries, who reached the bottom of the rubble, collapsed and had to be dragged or carried away as exhaustion and thirst threatened to kill them.

A lone soldier jogged slowly over to the veranda from a filthy, sparsely thinned rank of clustered centuries that milled about at the bottom of the breach. Titus Frigius, who had been observing the damage to his cohorts, descended the steps of the veranda as Larcius and Tiberius looked on. "What have you to report?" Frigius asked as he stared at the damaged plates of the soldier's *lorica segmentata* armour where it had clearly deflected massive blows.

"General, I beg to report that the Sixth Cohors has lost many. I have been sent by the pilus posterior of the cohors to request retirement to the rear, my General." The soldier stood with a pulverized face and arms that trembled. The sword he held was stained in blood and his shield was hacked nearly to splinters.

"Do you have numbers?" Titus asked patiently.

The soldier shook his head and shrugged. "There were piles of dead at my feet, General. The wounded cried in misery and were slain by the Zealots. I am a soldier in the third rank of my centuria, General. The front two ranks were cut down in droves. My hastatus prior and optio were both killed. The Zealots even killed our signifer and broke our standard in pieces."

Frigius was motionless for a moment as he looked stunned. His eyes gazed past the broken and miserable soldier to the remnants of the Sixth Cohort. He bowed his head, lowered his voice and said, "Send word that the Sixth may retire to the Camp of the Assyrians. You will be replaced for now."

The soldier gave a weak salute and stumbled away in a daze. Titus slowly turned and stared up at Tiberius as he grumbled, "We must respond quickly! This is a dastard failure! We are dishonoured."

"We will see to our wounded this day and secure the breach," Tiberius replied as his face was flushed with anger. "Make no mistake, tomorrow we shall raze the Mishneh and snatch any spirit of victory from the Jews. They will wish they had never been born."

*   *   *

Camp of the Assyrians
Private quarters of Prince Titus
An hour before midnight

With his hands clasped behind his back, Prince Titus slowly turned. He stared at his scribe as the man waited calmly, a sharpened quill in his hand and a small bottle of black ink next to him. A single piece of parchment glowed in the fire light as the oil lamps burned warmly inside the vast princely quarters. "Are you ready, Albinus?" The fat man nodded. If it had been another night, Titus might have chuckled at the fatty jowls of the man, but a dark brooding nature was about him, soured by the horrible losses of the day. "Let us continue then, shall we," Titus muttered as he strolled over to an end table next to his bed and picked up a goblet of wine. He sipped the rich drink as he concentrated on the succulent, divine taste and then cleared his throat. "We shall make the introduction brief, and to the point.

"Salutations and warm greetings to Emperor Titus Flavius Vespasianus, ruler of the provinces of *Roma*, protector of her peoples, and the guardian of the earth, indwelled by the power of Jupiter. May the gods preserve and guide you! Blessings in the name of Jupiter, Mars, and Minerva, as they watch over you. May eternal praise be given, the blood of war rewarded, and the wisdom below the earth, on the earth, and above the earth, always be a delight to your ears." Titus paused as he watched Albinus delicately write each Latin letter with a fine tuned eye for every detail. "May the comfort of Alexandria and the power of our patron Basilides find you in good health. I pray Isis will shine upon you and grant you favour before you depart for *Roma*.

"I report to you that we have surrounded Jerusalem in its entirety and have destroyed the Bezetha which has been reduced to rubble. We have sacked the Second Quarter, which is called the Mishneh, and have fought the enemy hard. However, the resolve of the enemy remains intact and a battle for control of this quarter currently ensues. I swear upon the gods of our family and upon the names of our ancestors that the Second Quarter will be razed by the morning as we prepare an assault on the fortress Antonia.

"So far, we have continued to keep the Zealot element of John of Gischala's forces at bay by concentrated volleys from our artillery, but John and the Idumean leader, Simon, continue to coordinate assaults on our cohortes. I swear, though, on the black flesh of the Apis bull, that when this city has surrendered, I shall sacrifice greatly unto its honour. Once the Second Quarter falls, all efforts for John and Simon to communicate will be silenced. Like a slave strangled by his master, the grip of these legions which I lead, will ever tighten until the Jewish resistance is crushed." Titus watched Albinus continue to write as the well-fed man dipped the quill into the ink every couple of words.

"My desire to see the efforts of Yosef ben Matityahu produce results is still to be decided as the Jews scoff him and seem to have no faith in his words anymore. I will continue to use Yosef, however, at my disposal as I do believe he has done some good. Although he has failed to convince the Zealots to surrender, we have seen high numbers of the aristocracy flee the city.

"I have continued to question every prisoner and have ordered necessary crucifixions when deemed fit. All access to the city from pilgrims has been cut off. My surgeons believe disease and starvation are already setting in, especially in the Lower City. However, spies continue to feed us information and they say that resistance is still strong within the Jewish ranks, despite all the victories we have had." Titus paused for a moment as he finished his wine.

"As always, the advice, leadership, and military knowledge that General Tiberius Julius Alexander brings to this post continues to be of an invaluable fortune for which I am grateful. I have committed all available troops to bringing this siege to a conclusion and I will expect the matter to be decided before the winter as the fortress Antonia and the Temple will be our most difficult obstacles to overcome. I will not concede ground and will capture or kill the rebel leadership unless they parlay for surrender. I remain ever your eldest son, and commanding general of the Judean legions, Titus Flavius Vespasianus the Younger. Send my love to Domitian when you see him, as well as to mother and my sisters...that will be all Albinus."

Albinus finished writing, then sprinkled some sand on the parchment and gently shook it off. He nodded at Titus, reached across the table, and picked up the smouldering tip of a wax stick. He dripped the contents onto the parchment and held it to the Prince. Titus firmly pressed his signet ring into the wax and pulled it away to reveal the imprint of his seal.

"Prepare it for a courier. It goes out tonight," Titus mumbled as he took a step back. He turned as he heard some commotion outside and marched to the front of the tent, drawing back the flap. A number of legionaries and a centurion were clustered nearby as they spoke with the sentries of the Prince's quarters. The whispering men suddenly halted their discussion and snapped to attention as they struck their breastplates in salute. Titus noticed they were all armed and the numerals upon their scuta revealed they were from the Fulminata. As he stepped out from under the canvassed veranda and into the torchlight, he recognized the Centurion right away as Gaius Antony.

Titus scowled as he crossed his arms. "What is the meaning of this? You men were on duty. Cornelius, what is happening?" Titus instantly regretted the slip of using Gaius' clan name in front of the other soldiers but he had no time to backtrack.

Gaius seemed to not even notice the tender use of his clan name by the Roman Prince and stepped forward. "My Prince, we have just come from our position by the Antonia. You must come with us; I think you will want to see this."

Titus looked puzzled for a moment as he hesitated and looked back at the warm confinements of his quarters. "Centurion Antony," he replied with more formality. "Are the Jews rallying to attack us?"

Gaius shook his head and whispered, "It concerns Judah ben Yosef, my Prince."

Titus took a deep breath and gave a nod. "I shall call for my escort."

"No need," Gaius interjected. "We have enough men here, we can escort you, and besides there are another six hundred men on guard between here and the northwest tower of the fortress."

"That is where you are taking me?" asked the Prince furrowing his brow.

Gaius nodded with a grave, serious look about him. "This will only take a moment."

The Prince sighed and acknowledging Gaius he began to walk as the legionaries rallied around him, marching in silence with only the jingling of their studded aprons filling the dead space.

Gaius led Titus under the shadow of the deserted Second Wall, as no Jews had tried to reclaim it. They could hear few voices on the other side as they spoke either in Hebrew or Aramaic, but apart from that nothing stirred. From what the Romans had been able to gather during the afternoon, the Jews had simply rebuilt the barricade inside the breach and had fortified the streets of the Mishneh, no doubt in an effort to defend it with their lives the next morning for the expected Roman assault. As morning was still hours away, both sides had time to gather their forces, strengthen their resolve and fill their stomachs.

The escort party cautiously widened their space between them and the wall, then headed toward a long column of torches and entrenchments where Roman sentries patrolled. Gaius halted the party, slowly extended his hand, and pointed upwards without uttering a single word. Titus stared at the pale face of the Antonia as it rose into the night like a great mountain. The height of the towers was vast as they dwarfed the ramparts of the walls below them. Upon the battlements of the northwestern tower, Titus found himself staring at a cluster of torches burning together, lighting up something hanging from below. The Prince gasped slightly as he caught his breath and then he clenched his fists. Dangling against the side of the tower from a long rope was a bloodied head still wearing a Roman helmet. By the colour of the plume, it left Titus with no doubt in his mind that it belonged to a centurion. A streak of blood ran down the side of the tower from the shredded stump and the tongue could be seen hanging from the parted mouth of the mutilated face.

Titus glared at Gaius and pointed up at the head as he whispered, "That is Capito, isn't it?"

Gaius nodded. "He was unaccounted for in the casualties today. His body was not claimed but the Optio sent me word that Capito had been abandoned. Now we know Judah killed him. The head was hung not even an hour ago."

"And he sends us this message? Bastard!" Titus swore as he spit upon the ground. "Judah was never going to work with us, was he? He wanted that pig's head to hang as a trophy!" Titus gazed up at the head and crossed his arms. "I thought by honouring his wish, we would gain Judah's undying trust and the man would continue to help us." Titus shook his head. "It was all for nothing." He paused for a moment and then bitterly whispered, "It was vengeance."

"I fear you are right, my Prince," was all that Gaius could say. Yet, for some strange reason he hoped that Judah had finally found a sense of satisfaction.

"Curses!" Titus suddenly shouted. "Curse them all!" He stared up at the tower with a face flushed with anger and then snapped his attention to the ground as he tried to calm himself. "Very well, it is done." Titus glanced up at Gaius, shook his head and then gave a frustrated smile. "My mercy has limits, Gaius, and I am running out of goodwill and charity. We shall regroup, and tomorrow, by the hand of Mars, we shall crush the Mishneh and slaughter everyone within her walls." The Prince gave Gaius a wild look and said through gritted teeth, "You are never to speak to Judah ben Yosef again! He is an enemy, just as guilty as everyone else in there.

"I therefore, condemn him to death for treason, either by sword, spear, or crucifix. I swear this and pray to the gods for his blood. He has made a mockery of me, Gaius, a mockery, and I will not stand for it. *Roma* will have the glory, the oracle of Basilides proclaimed it, and there is nothing their Jewish God can do. Send word to Marcus Octavian. I am convening my military council in four hours. We will destroy the Mishneh at dawn and the Fulminata will lead the way. The Hydra Herculean will strike, my dear Cornelius. You will strike with the speed of a viper and send the Jews reeling for mercy."

*　*　*

CHAPTER XXXII

May 13th, 70 A.D. / 16th of Iyyar, 3830
Ophel Quarter, Jerusalem
Two hours before noon

Judah gently knocked on the door again and waited. He heard nothing from within and glanced down the street as his suspicion was aroused. Then a soft rustling sound came from within the home and the scraping of a wooden bolt was slid to the side. The door partially opened and Hadassah stood peering through the crack at Judah. "You're alive?"

Judah took a step back and lowered his gaze. "I am alive," he softly replied.

Hadassah was motionless for a moment as she stared at Judah, then she slowly reached up and wiped her eyes. "I heard you led one of the attacking forces into the Mishneh. I thought you had been killed. Word around this neighbourhood has been ill and spreads quickly. Many say the Romans will take back the quarter today."

"We still hold it, Hadassah," Judah responded trying to sound audacious, as if telling himself this over and over convinced him that they still stood a chance. "We have closed the breach, and now over two thousand men have been stationed inside."

"You have stung the pride of the Romans; they will not back down, Judah." Hadassah sighed and brushed her hair back over her ears.

"Are you going to invite me in or make me stand in the street?" Judah replied.

A smile lifted the edges of her lips and she closed her eyes and shook her head. She took a step back and opened the door. Judah stepped into the quiet home, empty of her mother who had died weeks earlier. Judah had not bothered Hadassah since her time of *sheva*. A few widows in the Ophel had extended their kindness in grieving with her, and he had always made sure that food was sent to give her strength, even if food was growing dangerously scarce. Hadassah had become lonely and her despair was evident, for Judah could see it in all her mannerisms. She had lost everything, and the knowledge that her mother had not even received a proper burial continued to press upon her, stirring up grief.

"I have brought you more food." Judah unwrapped a small piece of bread and set it on the counter near the window.

"Have you eaten any of it?" she replied staring at the small loaf.

Judah shook his head and shrugged. "That is not important; I ate this morning. We fighters are taken care of, believe me. Nobody will notice I have brought you this. Besides, I am becoming used to not eating as much." Judah walked over to a rickety, wooden chair and sat down. He undid his belt, removing the weight of his sword as he laid it on the floor.

"What happens now?" Hadassah asked bleakly. She saw Judah scowl in question and she continued, "Is it true the Romans will attack today?"

"That is not confirmed," Judah mumbled.

"Don't lie to me to make me feel better," Hadassah retorted, raising her voice as tears filled her eyes. "People live in the Ophel who have seen the Mishneh. They speak of it as smoke, fire, rubble, and dead everywhere. They say that your ambush worked, but it will just embolden the Romans to commit more to its destruction. Once they are in, what is there to stop them from attacking the Temple?"

Judah gave a heavy nod. "It is true the Romans will come today or tomorrow, we all expect it. But please take courage. Titus has yet to face his greatest obstacles. He cannot assault the West Colonnade with the Antonia standing; we have prepared an excellent defence."

"And you will fight from there?"

"Yes!"

Hadassah shook her head and crossed the room in an instant, falling at Judah's feet. She reached up and took his hand and gazed into his startled eyes. "There is another way."

"What are you talking about?" Judah asked, leaning close to her as he searched her eyes.

"You do not have to fight. You and I can leave this place. There is no sense in fighting any longer. The Romans are destroying Jerusalem. They will kill us both or enslave us, and I could never live as a slave."

"No," Judah stood backing up as he knocked the chair over. "No, I could never run. I have a duty."

"Yes, a duty to live, Judah! You and I have lost everything. All the people we have ever loved have died. We should be together, please. Do not fight!" Hadassah begged him as she gazed up at his stiff face.

"I must fight, that is all I am!" Judah retorted.

"And how many more must you kill? I know about Capito!" She saw Judah's frame tighten and his jaw clench. "Men everywhere claim that Judah ben Yosef has slain a senior centurion and cut off his head, which even now hangs from the Antonia! Men say you cut out his eyes and cut off his ears! Will your hands ever be clean of blood? Will the killing ever cease?"

"No, Hadassah, not while the Romans are here," Judah replied ardently, defending himself. "Do not judge what you do not know."

"Am I made to be a judge because of what I see? I have seen your hatred for Capito consume you, and even now that he is dead, it's as if you are becoming him!"

Judah suddenly stared at her with hot eyes and a face flushed red with colour. His stomach twisted and his soul writhed in agony. He glared at her beauty which reminded him of Miriam. He wanted to curse out loud for his tortured mind, but no words came to his tongue. Judah held his gaze for a single moment, then swallowing his pride he said upon numb lips, "God has left me. The God of our fathers does not look upon me. I have prayed in the Temple, and not a sacrifice or *mitzvah* can undo what has been done. Alas, I am left with the only thing I know: to defend this city and protect the Temple." Judah turned slowly and mumbled, "Perhaps if I can do something great, God will forgive me."

Hadassah stood with trembling hands and wiped away her tears. "Judah, I love you."

Judah caught his breath and stared at the floor pondering this. He licked his dry lips and exhaled loudly. His throat was parched and felt raw. He could feel sweat bead upon his neck and his muscles ached. Judah slowly turned and took in her frail, delicate form. "I do care for you, Hadassah, but you should not love me. It is impossible for love to be between us with the misery which has befallen this city. I cannot leave my post. Men, who were like brothers to me, have died here and so shall I if that is the destiny God has for me. I shall not be known as a coward, and I shall seek peace, whether in this life or the next, but I cannot leave."

Judah saw the sting of hurt his words had on her and his heart shattered into a million pieces. "Please understand, I cannot come here anymore, nor should you look for me. The fighting is getting worse and men are growing more desperate. I do not wish for you to be harmed trying to find me." He paused as she covered her mouth with a gasp.

"I came here," Judah softly said, "To tell you to throw yourself at the feet of Mordechai ben Levi; he is a wealthy and upright man in the Ophel. I have told him of you and he is one I trust. It has been arranged and he can use your services. You are to become his servant, and therefore will fall under his hand of protection. He has sworn to me that he will flee the city the first moment he gets. The Romans will spare him and his household, of that I am sure. You can still live, Hadassah, perhaps marry, but you do not have to perish here."

"Judah, no," she protested through tears.

Judah shook his head and stepped close to her, holding her firmly. "This is my final wish for you. If you ever loved me, do this for my sake, I beg you." He gently pulled away, kissed her forehead, gave her one last gaze, then took up his sword and left the home without looking back.

Nearly overcome by grief, Judah pressed on as he walked down the narrow street away from Hadassah's home. He raised his chin, fighting to regain composure and a sense of balance, but he could not remove from his mind the look she had given him. He had spoken with Mordechai earlier and had paid the man handsomely to look after Hadassah. Mordechai had pledged his word and Judah had given the elderly man specific instructions to send over a few servants to collect her so she would not try and run. He kept telling himself that there was no other way, but his mind continued to plague him with pessimism that somehow he was making a mistake.

Further down the street ahead of Judah, a robed figure suddenly stepped out and faced him. Judah halted abruptly, naturally going for his sword, but then froze with his fingers wrapped around the hilt as he recognized the old man as the Priest Zechariah. Zechariah slowly raised a withered, pale hand and gave him a greeting with a smile. Judah relaxed and stole a glance behind him at the deserted street.

"Come, Judah, you feel threatened from an old man as I?" Zechariah spoke plainly as he chuckled and took a few steps forward. "I have seen too many years to get the better of you, and for what profit?"

Convinced by his word, Judah approached the old priest and gave a sharp nod. He stared at Zechariah's leathery skin, sunken eyes, and thin lips surrounded by his silk-like white beard which hung past his belly. "What is it? Did you follow me here?"

"Nonsense, you speak nonsense like you always have," smiled the warm, familiar face. "I have better things to do, young ben Yosef, than to slither through the streets, trying to understand your philandering. No, I have a few old friends you should meet, my son." Zechariah did not even give Judah the time of day to reply or consider his offer as the priest slowly turned and hobbled away expecting the young Gischalan fighter to accompany him. With the element of secrecy brought about by the priest's demeanour, Judah followed reluctantly, puzzled as to the identity of Zechariah's 'old friends.'

The meeting was not to be as secretive as Judah had expected it to be. No dark home, or bleak, damp alley. Instead the old priest led Judah from the familiar street around a corner to be greeted by three men, two of them familiar and the other a stranger.

Zechariah gestured to the men and said, "Judah, you know, Shimeon ben Gamaliel and Matthias ben Theophilus?" Judah nodded, caught off guard to see the former Chief Priest Theophilus among the group. Zechariah noticed Judah's stare and perceived his thoughts, but continued, "This is Rabbi Benyamin ben Asher, a *Nasi* and a Pharisee. He is a close friend of ours and yours." Zechariah watched the expression of curiosity and shock cover Judah's stunned face as he fumbled for words. The old priest chuckled and gesturing to the rabbi he said, "Tell him, Benyamin, tell him what you know."

Rabbi Benyamin gave a slight bow and fixed the knitted skull cap in his curly black hair. He smoothed his great beard for a moment and stared at Judah with lively eyes. The rabbi contemplated where to begin as he watched Judah hold his breath, as if the rabbi were about to say something profound and life altering. However, Benyamin just cleared his throat and said, "I knew your abba." Judah was still for a moment, his eyes glued on the rabbi as if Zechariah, Matthias, and Shimeon had all vanished in a flash of smoke. The rabbi saw the effects of his words and smiled. "I studied alongside a certain man named Amos ben Zakkai, of no relation to the great sage, Yohanan, but I think you should recognize the name."

Judah nodded as he stared with a puzzled expression at the rabbi who was over thirty years his senior. "He was a rabbi in Jerusalem. My father wanted me to study under him when I lived in Beit Lechem, but it never worked out."

"Yes, I know. Amos was a great admirer of your abba. He said he was a bright man, upright, one who adhered to the law, the *mitzvot*, and always gave to the poor. It broke my heart to hear of his death on that fateful day in the Upper Market." Rabbi Benyamin paused and stepped closer to Judah. "I met your abba weekly in synagogue and grew to love him. We would pour over Scripture, discuss everything, and grapple together. He was not a rabbi, but he could have been. Until this day, I do not know of a single time when your abba did not keep our customs, offer the proper sacrifices, attend the feasts, nor raise his children to love and honour Adonai. Am I wrong to assume this?" Judah shook his head slowly and Rabbi Benyamin continued, "I have supported the cause of John of Gischala, more favourably then Simon, but times are dire, and we still await a sign from the Almighty."

"How does this involve me?" Judah asked, suspiciously looking at the other three men.

"It directly involves you," said Benyamin. "You see, your abba always talked about how proud he was of you. He said that if you wanted, you could be a great rabbi, a sage like Hillel. He bragged about your memory for Scripture and that you would make a great *talmid chacham*. Yet, one thing grieved him, and that was how you seemed to drift away from study as you aged.

"Your abba often would discuss this with Amos and me. After Amos past, your abba and I would discuss how you had turned away from religious studies, but he never gave up. He continued to give to the poor and kept praying for you on your behalf to the Almighty. I have never seen such love for a child as he had for you. I only met you once, but I swore to myself I would never forget your features for I knew the Almighty still had a plan for you.

"After he and your mother died in the massacre, I could only assume you had too. The Romans had dragged the bodies from the market and had dumped them into the Hinnom where they were collected by grieving families. I searched for you for two days in the Hinnom, neglecting study and my students. I looked at every dead boy's face lying in that valley. Every young man I stooped and wiped the blood away, until my robes were red, to see if I should finally find the son of Yosef. Alas, I did not find you and many said that the Romans had slaughtered so many that some were burned. I did not want to believe it, but I could only conclude you had been one of those burned. I recovered the bodies of both your abba and ima, and had them buried together in a purchased tomb in the Kidron, but you were lost, never to be found." Rabbi Benyamin's eyes sparkled with a new ray of hope as he smiled and said with mirth, "Now, I see you living, and I speak to you, HaShem be praised."

Judah was motionless, unable to blink. After the massacre, he had fled in a rage with the sword of a Roman he had killed. He had fled Jerusalem and the panic, leaving it all behind. He had lived for days in the wilderness, then over the weeks and months he had built up the Lion band to seek revenge and slaughter every Roman they should come across. He had led them with a gruesome precision to wreak havoc in the Judean hills, yet had never considered returning to Jerusalem. He could not even remember thinking about returning. He thought often of his parents and Miriam, but the horror which had faced him within the Holy City always haunted his memories. To him, Jerusalem had become a memory of tears.

Judah glanced at the other men and finally focused on Matthias ben Theophilus saying, "You have all come with this rabbi to reunite me to him? Why?"

"It is more than that, my son," Shimeon ben Gamaliel replied. He reached out and took hold of Judah's arm and held it firmly despite his frail, boney fingers. "There is much work to do and no Roman shall interfere."

"What is it?" Judah demanded feeling agitated by the very presence of Rabbi Benyamin who reminded him of a past he had sought to forget for four years.

Matthias looked at the others and then spoke softly, with power in his words, "The Romans are tightening their grip and the city is suffering. Disease and starvation are rampant in the lower parts of the city. Men take their own lives and babies die because their mothers cannot feed. The city is divided and death lies everywhere. We seek to serve the people. We have all supported the rebellion and have sacrificed much. The Temple has been polluted by the Zealots and Phanni ben Samuel struts around like a priest by the puppet strings of Gischala. He blasphemes God and constantly gets the rituals wrong. He is a man not worthy of his role, and we are unable to do anything."

"Yes, but why come to me? You are thinking of an uprising, but I am not your man. I will defend this city with my sword, but I will not be your spy." Judah gazed at the men who were silenced by his words and Matthias looked to the others for help.

"We are not asking you to spy, neither are we spies ourselves nor do we wish to form an uprising. We merely speak the truth," Rabbi Benyamin replied. "We serve the people, and they suffer. We would like to call on you to help us get as many out of this city as we can. We have to choose only those the Romans will spare. Both John and Simon will kill anyone they see attempting to flee so we must be careful. But soon this madness will drag us all into it and none will survive."

"Did you not expect this when the Romans marched on these walls?" Judah sarcastically responded.

"They were never supposed to get here; the northern defences were believed to be strong enough to hold back Vespasian. Alas, they crumbled. Then we did not foresee Simon's arrogance and the divisions that have existed. John, Eleazar, and Simon burnt precious food stores and through their fighting have reduced our chances to survive." Rabbi Benyamin rested a hand on Judah's shoulder and said, "Your abba gave everything to the betterment of people. He loved God and served Him always.

"Now, do this for your people. I am sure more than ever that your survival on that day, when so many died, was meant for a reason. As God rose up Gideon against the many throngs of Midianites, so too has He given you strength like Samson, to destroy the foes of Israel. But, you can also help your people by saving them. We ask you not to stay your sword, but to help us in this endeavour to liberate as many Jews as possible from the clutches of death. To save one soul is as if you have saved an entire world."

Judah wanted to walk away, he knew he should leave, but he hesitated. The pleading look in Rabbi Benyamin's eyes drove to his very soul. "How do you know the Romans will spare those who surrender?"

"Titus wants peace, we believe that," Matthias replied, interjecting. "The government, had it survived, would have sought to parlay a peace upon fair negotiations. We would never have sold our people or this city to the dogs as the Zealots came to believe. Titus wants to end this rebellion in favour of his father, no doubt, but already the casualties he suffers are mounting. He cannot take delight in this war. I have heard word he is sending those who surrender to Gophna, but he is selective of who goes."

"Selective? How?" Judah asked rhetorically as if he was finding this out for the first time.

"Only aristocracy and citizens are being spared with no reprisals and taken to Gophna. The rest are taken as slaves or crucified. We seek to save all those possible for a rebuilding of the future." Matthias watched the effects of his words run deep in the eyes of Judah and he quickly added, "Surely you understand, as your abba was moderately wealthy. Men like you and the citizens are our best chance to rebuild. Titus will not spare the common people; they will face a grueling death or deportation."

"So you want me to put my life on the line for the rich? So they can escape this hell to live another day?" Judah replied with a look of disgust.

"Not just them," Rabbi Benyamin said stealing a glance at Matthias. "We will not turn anyone away who wishes to leave the city, rich or poor. We just can't promise that Titus will spare them. We only speak about things we already have seen."

Judah was silent as he stared at the men. He mulled over their words and considered everything. "I am in John's most trusted circle and an officer. I cannot give much time to something such as this. I will be suspected and arrested."

"We have power and influence among the people, Judah. But your power lies with the army. They will listen to you. All we ask for is that when the time comes, Zechariah will give you word, and you give certain orders to see this happen. That is all." Rabbi Benyamin nodded at Judah and patted his shoulder with assurance.

"You may be running out of time. The Romans will destroy the Mishneh soon and drive deeper into the city. Then there will be one more defensible wall between them and the entire Upper City. If that falls, so does the Lower City with it," Judah replied gazing at the men. "Your possible methods of getting people out are shrinking as is the size of this city."

"We know that, but we have to try. We cannot give up hope that the Almighty will come at the last minute and destroy the pagans and cleanse this city." The look of fervour was entrenched so deeply in Rabbi Benyamin's eyes that Judah could not resist its beckon as he continued, "However, none of us can be sure of this destiny. So we pray, study, teach, and act. None of us can wield a sword anymore, but there are other things we can still do. So we look to the remaining gates under our control in order to free a population that is slowly dying."

"You will think about this and consider our proposal?" Zechariah asked. "You would be safe from John; he would never find out."

Judah wanted to tell them about the many squads John had already dispatched in search for spies, and about the men he had personally executed, but he said nothing. He wanted to tell them of the fear that had constantly plagued him when he had been sending information to Titus, but Judah held his silence. He just gave a somber nod and replied to their relief, "I will consider this."

* * *

CHAPTER XXXIII

May 14th, 70 A.D. / 17th of Iyyar, 3830
The Bezetha
One hour past dawn

Gaius could see a few trails of smoke curling upwards above the walls of the Mishneh as he waited patiently. He covered his mouth as he yawned and then checked his helmet strap beneath his chin for the second time. Gaius glanced over his shoulder at the entire First Cohort drawn up in rank as they waited. Titus had given orders for the Fulminata to capture the outer wall of the Mishneh and destroy the clogged breach. That was exactly what they would do. Gaius gave Marcus Octavian a brief look, then picked up his shield and held it firmly. He drew his sword and stared at the blade with intensity in the coolness of the morning. A hint of light danced from the steel as he narrowed his gaze along the razor edge to the sharpened point. He raised the gladius and with two practice swoops, sliced it through the air feeling his muscles loosen to the pounding of his heart as he thought of what was to come.

The sun had barely peaked over the Mount of Olives and was just beginning to light up the golden stones of the city as Jews everywhere soon begin to say their morning prayers. From where the cohorts stood they could hear the distant prayers from the Temple and see the coil of grey smoke rising up from the high plateau. Within the Inner Court the priests continued their duties as if they were clueless that an invading army resided within the walls of their city. The deep groan of a shofar wailed from the Temple compound and a chorus of voices began singing. It was the beginning of a new week, as the Shabbat for the Jews had ended the evening before.

"Are your men ready?" Marcus mumbled, taking a step closer to Gaius as he refused to take his eyes from the empty breach.

"Yes, General, they are," Gaius somberly replied.

"Are they asleep?" Marcus asked and shook his head towards the quiet breach. "I don't like it, but what is there to like? Let's get this over with." Marcus turned to the men and gazed up and down the long ranks. "I want a full charge into the breach, Gaius. Kill the defenders, break down their wall and secure the ramparts and towers. You are not to enter the city streets. Titus wants this secured first. Understood?"

Gaius nodded and sighed. "You should fall back to the rear, General."

"Right, I will. May the gods be with you, Praefectus Castrorum, and fight like a demon." Marcus rested his hand on the pommel of his sword and while lifting his rod of office towards the cohort said, "Gaius, you have the best men in the legion on a fetter. Turn them loose and spill the enemy's blood! You are wolves now, not men!"

Gaius watched his General march away past the ranks of legionaries who had been given specific instructions to remain silent. When Marcus Octavian reached the rear, Gaius turned and faced his men. He slowly raised his gladius and like a rehearsed drama, nearly eight hundred men drew their swords at the ready. Behind the cohort lay stacks of pila as the soldiers had abandoned them, expecting a vicious fight in the tight confinements of the breach.

The centuries were drawn up in regular order with ranks four-men deep. To the extreme left was the Serpent Century commanded by Rufus Garus, who stood out from his men with his signifer at his side. Next to Garus' men stood the Wolf Century commanded by Quintus Cassius Aemilius. In the middle, the Lion Century was positioned with its vexillum held high among the ranks as Princeps Posterior Cicero Vindacian stood at the front like a statue atop the Acropolis in Athens. To Cicero's left was the Fortis Century. The beast-like centurion, Marius Junius Livianus, planted himself three metres in front of them with a look of steel upon his face as his legionary tattoo was proudly revealed upon his right arm. Marius grinned at Gaius, then spit, and broadened his smile as he was eager to get this over with. To Marius' left was the final century, Gaius' own Hydra Herculean. They looked as grim as ever, each man in rank staring outward with cold, menacing eyes, waiting for the moment when Gaius would signal the charge.

In the middle of the cohort stood a number of men who held long brass cornu instruments with the furs of jackals and wolves covering their helmets. They readied themselves by placing the mouth pieces to their lips with all eyes upon their commanding senior of the cohort.

Gaius gently closed his eyes as he whispered, "Jupiter, watch over my dear Livia Drusilla, and our children. If I should fall, may they never taste the pang of war. Spare them the misery they shall feel upon knowing of my death. I pray to thee, O Mars. If I shall indeed fall, may my blood cause you to smile and my courage always be a delight, for I have served you without falter and cessation." When Gaius opened his eyes he felt infused with strength. He took a deep breath, feeling his heart pound within his chest, and without hesitating he narrowed his gaze at the high breach, raised his sword, and began to run.

The cohort had anticipated this moment even before the musicians had time to react. As the blast of notes echoed from the ruins behind them, the legionaries thundered across the flagstones like a great earthquake splitting the ground and charged up the fallen debris of the breach. Within an instant Gaius was surrounded as legionaries pressed at his back in an attempt to make sure that their senior officer would not face Jewish swords alone. Near the top of the breach a great shout rose up like a horrible monster as the Romans opened their mouths and let loose all the rage pent up in their souls.

Upon reaching the top of the breach, the Romans began to flood into the city as they overran a crude wall that had been built up in an attempt to close the gap. Jewish attackers sprang down from the pile of rubble which had been their inner defence, and within seconds men were screaming as the elite Roman veterans wasted no time in dispatching them. Spears and javelins were hurled into the thick Roman ranks as they continued filling the breach, pushing past the outer exteriors of the inner wall to the shouts of Jewish commanders trying to rally their men. A number of Zealots quickly climbed the crude wall and began pushing stones down upon the legionaries which succeeded in crushing three men under the weight. However soon, enough legionaries had circumvented the wall and soon the Jewish Zealots were hauled down and stabbed to death.

The attack was precise and deadly. The Roman centuries continued to storm into the city and past the inner wall, which was now completely abandoned by the Jewish defenders. Units were deployed to the ramparts to halt the hail of arrows and spears that reigned down upon them from a hundred Idumeans that had taken to the parapets. Gaius continued to press inward, spreading out the centuries into a great fan formation as they surged forward into the waning Jewish ranks that began to crumble within minutes. Only a scattered number of legionaries had fallen and the droves of Jewish dead strung out along the stones seemed to give a supernatural elation to the Romans as the centuries began cheering amidst the battle, dashing out in clusters to terrify their enemy.

As the Jewish fighters turned and ran, the Romans showed restraint as their centurions bellowed orders to hold their ground and not give chase. Once the Zealots began to notice the stubborn will of the Romans, they began hurling insults at them and mocking their colours. One such Jew, who had decapitated a legionary and now held his head, finally threw it back in frustration, laughing when it thumped off of a soldier's shield, spraying a bloody ribbon into the air. Yet the Romans just formed their ranks and planted their shields upon the stones as they glared at the Jewish fighters who eventually withdrew to an unseen neighbourhood in the Mishneh.

Gaius' cohort had taken the Second Quarter, but he did not like it. His men had killed over eighty Zealots and had only incurred six losses, but that was not what aggravated him. It was simple: he was unsure of what awaited his men deeper in the Mishneh and he was worried his men could suddenly be faced with a Jewish attack of thousands, leading to a repeat of how the Romans had been driven out to begin with.

Gaius immediately sent messengers to report to Marcus Octavian and then had no choice but to wait. His signifer offered him water, which he gladly accepted. He splashed some on his sweaty face with a sigh as it soaked his neck and cooled his stifling chest. He gazed behind him up at the ramparts and watched as a handful of soldiers picked through the Jewish dead and then heaved them over the side, laughing as how the bodies struck the stones below with sickening thuds.

Marius strolled over to Gaius, his blood-stained sword at his side. He gave him a nod as he extended a hand of gratitude. The two men clasped wrists and Marius said, "Quickly resolved, I would say. What do you think now?"

"We need to secure this ground, and our cohort cannot see it done alone." Gaius glanced at Marius' sword and gestured. "You killed one?"

"Just one, most fled at the sight of my men. I see you weren't so lucky," Marius teased pointing to Gaius' clean blade.

"The battle was decided in no time."

"And yet you are worried?" Marius replied.

"At a counter attack, yes." Gaius sheathed his sword and wiped his eyes free of the sweat which stung them. "The breach must be widened, men placed in those towers, catapults brought in, and reinforced by at least another two or three cohorts." Gaius looked to his left and right at the large empty spaces on either side of the cohort which remained vulnerable. It was true that some of the Mishneh remained destroyed from the assault two days earlier, but the Jews had been clever in piling up stone and leaving it intact. Gaius felt like his men were in the middle of a maze, and that reality was dangerous.

"Well, you have sent messengers. There is not much we can do but wait," Marius replied stating the obvious. "Come now, the Jews wouldn't dare test the steel of the First Cohors twice in one day. Look at their dead to ours; it is obvious who has the upper hand."

Gaius sighed and ignored his friend, as a high ranking individual, accompanied by his staff, entered the Mishneh on foot calling out his name. Gaius and Marius approached the man who saluted and then gave a humble bow, smiling with perfectly white, straight teeth and bright gums. The man was of a darker complexion, well groomed and wearing expensive-looking armour. He was scented with a fragrance that neither Gaius nor Marius had ever smelled before, and was at least a head taller. He extended a gracious hand of trimmed, filed fingernails and soft skin to Gaius who took the man's wrist and shook it with an awkward smile. To Gaius, the man looked as though he had never fought a single battle in his life, but the stranger carried the rod of Titus' office and so he kept his mouth shut, recalling his manners.

"Excellent job, Praefectus Castrorum, indeed an excellent clean up." This second part had been said as the aristocrat stared at the dead with a pale look. He shook the discomfort from his face with a jerk, swallowed his pride, and tried to appear bold, portraying himself as the soldier that he was not. "Once again you have excelled and crushed the enemy. I am commander of the Nabatean horse troops of his highness Antiochus. We have been dispatched from Mount Scopus to assist you in defending the Mishneh. My name is Jason."

Gaius stared at the strange man of Arab descent who held a Greek name and spoke with the authority of Antiochus, one of the client kings. Gaius' interest was drawn upon Jason's staff of twelve men, each one sprouting a black beard, a white turban, a purple cape hanging from their shoulders, and rich appearing multi-coloured garments of silk. "Where are your men?"

"We are under your command, Gaius Cornelius Antony. I have deliberately left them on the other side of the breach until you tell where you would like them positioned." Jason smiled humbly at Gaius and pointed to the breach with his rod of office as he seemed to flaunt his power.

"How many men do you have?" Gaius asked, annoyed at how Jason held back information.

"Three hundred bows and five hundred spears. I have also given orders for another three hundred to begin widening the gap." The sound of thuds and cracks began to echo beyond the wall as Jason's men worked.

"Is General Octavian coming here?" Gaius asked.

Jason shook his head. "He has been called away to other business. But another cohort of your legion has been called up and has begun to assemble, along with an artillery contingent."

"That is good news," Marius replied behind Gaius. "We should expect them in the next hour then."

"Well, Jason," Gaius replied awkwardly, not knowing how far he could go with this high ranking captain under Antiochus. "Position your men to the left of the First Cohort and give them specific instructions not to advance. They can search homes closest to them, but I do not want them upsetting the line by scouting any further."

Jason scowled. "You are to address me as '*Your Highness*', Centurion Gaius."

Gaius slightly stammered with annoyance and then muttered, "As you wish, your Highness."

Jason smiled, turned and muttered to a member of his staff, then he faced the Roman centurions while two of his men jogged away to relay the orders. "We will hold the left and not fail you. Would you like my bowmen in the towers?"

Gaius scowled at the pompous grin on Jason's face then reluctantly said, "Yes, you may dispatch a hundred of them to the wall, your Highness."

Jason gave a brief bow and left with his staff following closely on his heels. Gaius glared at Marius and shook his head, "Who in the name of all the gods was that?"

Marius chuckled and shrugged. "That, my dear friend, is the son of Antiochus. Men say Antiochus is as wild as a maddened centaur, but his son is like a damn lily! The man has never had to draw his sword to defend his life." Marius leaned over and whispered, "And he enjoys male company at that. Some say his father has killed three of his lovers, but dares not lift a hand against his son because he is his only heir."

Gaius stared at Marius for a moment and then glanced back at Jason as he disappeared over the breach. "Then in the name of Flora, what is he doing here?" Gaius groaned. "How can Marcus Octavian even allow such a man inside and expect him to secure the Mishneh?"

Marius shook his head. "My guess is that Marcus didn't have any say in the matter. This must come straight from the top. Titus probably wants to shut the boy up by making him feel as if he is of some importance to the siege. If you ask me, I would wager the bastard Jason has whined to his father for far too long about gaining battle experience and has driven the man half mad. Jason is a man who has an eager prick for his mate and is a brainless shit. Keep an eye on him. He cannot be depended upon." Marius watched as a flood of Nabateans began to file through the breach and march to the left. "They are good fighters, but I worry about such a leader. You should discuss this with Marcus Sulla when you get the chance. Marcus could be a strong voice to Titus to have this Jason removed."

Gaius nodded and watched as Jason appeared at the top of the breach. He stood with his arms crossed, looking valiant, as if he and his men had just conquered the Mishneh instead of the Romans. Gaius swore to himself and turned to Marius. "I will see what we can do, but for now we are stuck with him."

*　　*　　*

Fortress of the Antonia

Judah stood listening to the sounds of picks and hammers as they pounded at sections of the Mishneh wall from down below. In the northwestern tower of the Antonia he had a fantastic vantage point over all the activity, but nevertheless, whenever he wished to take a peek he had to make it quick since Roman archers and scorpions were on the towers at all times, shooting at anything that moved.

Judah had not even bothered to watch the fight in the early morning, although from the Outer Court of the Temple, Adam, Moshe, and he had heard the screams and clashing of swords. Nearly two thousand Zealots had crammed the mouth of the breach behind their inner, makeshift wall during the night, but the Roman tide had washed over them as if they were twigs stacked upright. John's faith had not been optimistic concerning the security of the inner wall as he had given strict orders, prior to the battle, for the Zealots to fall back into the streets of the Mishneh and secure the neighbourhoods. He was convinced that the Romans would not make the same mistake twice by pursuing them and thus he made plans for his men to hunker down and hold the Mishneh.

It was imperative to hold the alleys and homes of the quarter which would provide them a staging area to launch more attacks in the future. So without delay, the Jewish fighters had seen to careful preparations. They barricaded streets, stocked homes with food and spare weapons, and drove out any remaining citizens.

Nearly a hundred Zealots had fallen in the initial blow from the Roman attack and the remainder fled to their fallback positions, leaving their dead behind as they vanished among the homes like ghosts. John had been right about the Roman outcome. The victorious cohorts, instead of charging after the Zealots, had secured the breach, cautiously drawing up in their regimented order as they became masters of the ramparts and towers of the walls.

Now the Antonia tower was deserted and Judah remained alone, caring not for what was happening below him or in other parts of the city, but focused on a tethered rope hung over the edge between the parapets of stone. He took a deep breath and glanced behind him. Nothing moved and silence was all that came from the dark winding staircase that led up to the tower's fighting platform. Judah slowly walked over to the rope and touched it. Even now he could still feel the tension in the braided cords as a weight hung upon the other end against the tower's face. Judah shuddered and leaned against the wall as he closed his eyes and wondered why he was even up here. Yesterday the excited sounds of competing ravens had been loud on this side of the tower, but now all that drifted on the wind was an eerie silence.

Judah raised his gaze upwards as his eyes watered and he stared at the wispy clouds stretched across the vast, blue sky. He fought against the glare of the sun and winced as it stung his vision. "Adonai," Judah softly said and then felt tears dampen his cheeks, running into his curly beard. "Adonai, of Abraham, Adonai of Isaac, and Adonai of Jacob, hear my prayer." His mind swirled and searched for something more to say but all he could do was mumble, "I am so alone and in despair." Judah sniffed, his mind recalling the *Shema*, as he placed his hand upon the rope.

He stared down at the rough cord, as if desiring to glean some understanding from the inanimate object, but instead he suddenly heaved upon the rope and began to pull. He could feel the dangling object, secured to the cord, bump against the wall, but he refused to stop. He only slowed down when he knew he was nearly at the end. Then he halted and took a deep breath. Judah stared down at the rope bunched up and tangled at his feet, then he traced it through his hands to the edge of the battlements. He tugged it once more and saw some hair upon the end. He swallowed, his throat feeling raw and parched, then gave one more pull and watched the head of Capito slip over the hewn stone. Judah took a step back and raised it up.

He watched the head spin and grimaced at the state of rotting flesh, empty eye sockets, and mouth stripped of its lips, gums, and tongue from the birds. With the other hand, Judah slowly removed a small sack from his belt and opened it. He lowered the head into the sack, untied the rope, and closed the top, tying a knot. Judah backed up and slowly set the sack upon the coiled rope. He stared at it for a moment, then slowly bent over and knelt. Judah reached out with a trembling hand and gently touched the sack. It was in that moment that a flood of emotion washed over him. To his inner dismay and puzzlement, he bitterly wept.

Adam watched his broken friend sob pathetically as he hunched over the sack which contained Capito's head. He had searched for Judah in the courts of the Temple and the halls of the Antonia, and now he found him reduced to a crumpled, defeated man. When all other men would have mocked Judah for his behaviour, Adam felt only pity. He slowly removed a water skin from his belt and crossed the platform.

Adam had never seen Judah in such a state and it clearly bothered him as he approached his friend, not knowing what he should say. However, Judah was the first to speak as he noticed Adam's shadow. "Why are you here?"

"I did not know where you were, so I came here to check." Adam humbly extended the water skin, looking away to give Judah a moment to clean his face.

With wet cheeks and red eyes, Judah took the water skin, softening to Adam's kindness. He eagerly drank the cool liquid and splashed some onto his face. "I had to take care of this. I don't know why, but I shall dispose of it in the Kidron." Judah handed the skin back to Adam, then sat down next to the rope and stared at the sack.

"So that was the man who led the massacre?" asked Adam with a curious glance. He had hardly spoken with Judah since that day he watched his captain stumble off through the smoke to pursue the wounded Centurion. Since then, Judah had taken to isolating himself from everyone, praying in solitude within the Temple courts. Adam had never said a thing, until now. "Many of the fighters speak of countless pigeons and lambs you have brought to the Temple priests for sacrifice. What has your heart been praying so much for?"

"Forgiveness, peace, and relief," Judah slowly listed in a dull tone. "I have done many terrible things, but only a few haunt me. This brother, who I hated and slew, has brought only anguish to my soul. It is beyond words." Judah patted the sack trying to regain inner strength. "You know what he said to me before I killed him?" Adam quietly shook his head and Judah sighed heavily. "He said that it was because of people like me that the city would burn. He spoke of my hatred for Rome and that even by killing him I would still see his face. He never lied about that; he spoke the truth. I still see this man, whom I hated with every fiber of my being, when I close my eyes." Judah sorrowfully stared up at Adam with a grief stricken face, riddled from a lack of sleep. "Alas, I am to take this bitterness to the very end. I feel forsaken."

Adam watched the broken expression upon Judah's face deepen as his friend bowed his head in misery. "Once I heard Rabbi Yacov of the Jerusalem Nazarene Council say in a sermon that the Teacher Yeshua, whom I believe to be Meshiach, once said that those who live by the sword shall die by the sword." Adam paused and then continued as Judah gave him a baffled look, "The master said this after his Talmid Chacham, Cephus, cut off Malchus' ear, the servant to the High Priest, when they came to arrest Yeshua in Gethsemane."

"It sounds like either your murdered rabbi speaks in riddles or else he would not have supported our fight here? To let the enemy trample us rather than fight back? Is that what he spoke of? Perhaps that is why your type fled to Perea and left us here to die," Judah said with scorn.

Adam was hurt, but he let the vulgar words slide away as he bent down and stared Judah in the eye, calmly saying, "I think it means that those who live for vengeance shall die by vengeance. Vengeance only knows one master, and that is death. It will soon swallow everyone alive who lives by her. Rather, we should live as God wants us to live and seek His Kingdom and righteous living. That is what I live by. Yes, they fled to Perea, for they knew of this day and they believe the end is near, but I have stayed."

Judah instantly regretted his earlier words. "Yes, you have been faithful and have served by my side. What you say is wise, yet I shall not know how to serve any other master. It is as if I have already been consumed and shall pay for it." Judah sighed. "I have gone so far. I cannot turn back now for I can only do what I see right."

With a furrowed brow Adam softly said, "Judah, what do you speak of?"

Judah sighed and gave a shrug as he could not believe what he was about to say. The secret that had been dormant within him for so long, was about to finally stir and be given life outside of its tormented soul. "I swore to you that day I killed Capito that you would soon hear of everything. So let me tell you and I pray to God you will understand." Judah then told Adam about Gaius Cornelius Antony and Yosef ben Matityahu.

*   *   *

CHAPTER XXXIV

May 16th, 70 A.D. / 19th of Iyyar, 3830
Jerusalem
The Mishneh

"We're getting slaughtered!" shouted a number of Idumeans as they recoiled in fear from the violent clash of swords as the Roman cohort smashed into their flanks. The men held up their shields in desperation as arrows thumped into the wood testing their nerves. Suddenly a great chorus of agony rippled through the Jewish ranks as resilience ebbed away, replaced by screams and hollers of pain from the throats of men as the effects of the Palmyrene volley rained down upon them like iron tipped hail. Men shouted, cursing the Roman bowmen's fortified positions entrenched upon what had once been their ramparts, walls, and towers. Idumean and Zealot alike ducked for cover or flattened themselves behind the bodies of men as arrows continued to tear holes in the Jewish ranks. They bellowed loudly with no other choice but to stand and fight as the legionary cohort slowly murdered them.

The piles of dead became an awful, bloody mess. Men slipped upon the flagstones, streaked in gore and filth, cluttered with moaning, wailing men, who were cleaved and bleeding as they shouted in pain from the feet that trampled them. Jewish officers in the rear had to constantly shove men back into the fight as the butchery intensified, yet the main Jewish attack still held its ground.

Judah watched the stalled attack safely from the nearest streets of the Mishneh. So far the city streets and homes had not come under direct catapult fire as the Romans were still preoccupied with keeping an aggressive artillery assault upon the heavily defended Antonia. Judah watched as a cluster of Gischalan fighters appeared between the parapets of the southwestern tower and unleashed a scorpion missile that slammed into the ramparts of the Second Wall, sending four Palmyrene bowmen flailing threw the air in bloody ribbons of scarlet and torn limbs. Just as suddenly as the Jewish scorpion crew had managed to get off a shot, a large Roman onager responded. Judah traced the boulder as it streaked through the air, smashing into the parapets as it exploded into a thousand pieces of stone shrapnel that severed the heads clean off of three Jewish fighters. The sound of the impact was deafening. Even where Judah stood he could tell that it would be awhile until another Jewish scorpion crew worked up the courage to try for another shot. The southwestern tower of the Antonia seemed deserted as the Roman engineers cheered from below.

Judah turned and stared at Adam, Moshe, and the four hundred other reserves. John and Simon were of the same mind when it came to the importance of the

Mishneh. In a war council the night before, each man had proclaimed the importance of defending the Second Quarter and trying to drive the Romans from the breach like they had done days earlier. Simon had wanted to set a trap in the homes of the Mishneh again, but John had held a different opinion. The large man from Gischala had driven his fist into an open palm and declared that it was time the Romans saw how real Jews fought.

Whenever John spoke with passion and fervour, his men would love him all the more. The Idumean officers, who had been ordered by Simon to hate John, now began to admire his tenacity and vote in favour of his ideas. However, this did not sit well with Simon, and he clearly showed it with occasional outbursts and forced declarations of loyalty from his own staff who feared him.

"Judah, Judah!" a man shouted, pushing through the ranks of men. "I bring word, Judah!"

Judah turned around, his hand on the pommel of his sword, and watched as a man pressed between his soldiers. "Let him through," Judah shouted. "What news do you bring from John?"

The messenger was panting by the time he reached Judah and he spit upon the street as he cleared his throat, wiping his forehead. "John has sent me. He says the Romans continue to build ramps against the north face of the Antonia and they are rising quickly. Even I could see rams waiting among the remains of the Bezetha.

"The legionaries have also filled the Struthion Pool so they can pass across it, and they are unencumbered in their approach. They have heavy catapults, and concentrated volleys from the Syrians make it almost impossible to return fire. We have suffered heavily in the towers. Many are dead."

The man strained to speak and Judah motioned to Moshe to give him water. Once the man had relieved his parched throat, a pale fear seemed to sink into his face as he continued, "Roman engineers have also been working hard at clearing the ground on the northwestern side of the Temple platform; it looks as if they are softening it up for future use."

Judah shook his head, cursed quietly, and said, "They need to prepare for an attack on the Temple itself. They will go for the fortress first, I would wager everything on that."

The man nodded quickly. "That is John's mind, but he worries. Defending the Antonia seems impossible right now with the heavy Roman attacks through the Mishneh. John has had his men fill the outer gates with piles of rubble so the Romans can't get in and the outside is heavily damaged."

"Tell me what I don't already know! Why have you come here?" Judah asked, his face flushed with anger at the feeling of suffocation that was coming over him.

The man stammered to speak as his nerves griped him and he swallowed hard saying, "John wants to tunnel. He is making preparations to tunnel under the Roman earthworks that are rising up as we speak. He has men who can do it, and he wants to entrust the duty to you and your Lions to supervise."

Judah looked shocked. "But there are only three of us left! What do we know about tunneling?"

"He gave me the order and I am just delivering it. Ask him about it. He told me your men are to wait by Kiponus while *you* go to the fortress steps. He knows the Antonia is the key to the Temple and I think he sees the dwindling hope we have in this accursed place." The man glanced over his shoulder at the glares he received from the other warriors as the screams and shouts of war continued in the distance. "You are to pull out, leave this reserve in charge with another, and report to the steps of the Antonia. Those are your orders."

Judah was perplexed as he gave Adam and Moshe a puzzled glance. Then he heard chanting behind him and turned as voices hollered in Latin, "Longinus, Longinus, Longinus!"

Judah watched the distant mass of the Jewish ranks begin to shift backwards as men tumbled and tripped over their dead. From where he stood he could still make out bitter fighting going on in the front, but a strange, eerie silence was beginning to swell within the columns of nervous Zealots.

Exhausted men, covered in sweat and weary from fighting, began to cautiously back away as they took shelter behind their shields. Soon, both sides had pulled back, leaving a graveyard of tangled dead and pools of blood in the middle. It was like a great mangled spider's web of human bodies as men lay cut apart, pierced, crushed, and torn. Ghost-like faces smeared in dirt, sweat, and blood stared up at the blue sky with frozen expressions ripe with fear and horror by the savagery which had killed them. Many of the wounded, lying among the dead, stirred in misery which gave the scene a crawling effect. Neither side renewed the attack, and only a handful of men attempted to drag their wounded comrades from the dead as every man watched each other with glares and blood splattered faces.

Judah could hear Roman trumpets calling the cohorts to hold their positions as centurions and tribunes inspected the ranks and shouted for water for the weary soldiers. Likewise, hundreds of Jewish fighters could be seen bent over and gasping for air. Some had collapsed to their knees, while others vomited upon the ground. Men overcome by exhaustion on both sides were quickly replaced by fresh units as they braced for another blow.

Judah stared for a moment in disdain at a cluster of legionaries who continued to chant upon the distant breach, "Longinus!" The mob of jubilant Romans soon appeared to be congratulating a fellow cavalry trooper, patting him upon his mailed shoulders. The cavalry soldier turned, lifted his oval shield and blood stained sword in the air and gave a loud hoot of victory at the withdrawing Zealots.

Judah grumbled under his breath and turned to the messenger. "This is not over. We cannot abandon the Mishneh." He angrily called for Moshe and Adam to follow him and then pushed past the startled messenger. "We go to the Antonia!"

*   *   *

"Have them pull back slightly and reform!" Titus ordered as he pointed to the space between the two opposing sides that was littered with bodies. He stood like a tyrant atop of the breach, wearing fine armour and holding a brass baton in his left hand with an engraved eagle upon the end. "We have given them a match, but the cohort tires."

"Shall I bring in reserves, my Prince?" asked Marcus Octavian, straining to look down the line of legionaries as he squinted in the sun and attempted to shield his eyes with his hand. He glanced back with annoyance and the slave behind him moved quickly to readjust the angle of the umbrella. Marcus sighed with relief from the shade and wiped the sweat away from his brow. He gave Titus a glance and noticed the Prince pondering his question while staring down the ranks to the far right. Marcus redirected his gaze and said, "Is that not Jason and the Nabateans?"

Titus nodded and shook his head. "Fool, see how that worthless man arranges his men. They are in loose rank and disorderly! A pathetic sight and embarrassment to the men of steel at their left! This would never hold favour in *Roma*."

Marcus shrugged and shook his head as he said candidly, "Did not my Prince order them to the right flank?"

Titus shot Marcus an annoyed glare. "Antiochus came and begged on behalf of his boy! The whelp is inexperienced and wants glory! I entertained it and thought it wouldn't hurt once we had established a firm presence in the Mishneh. Better his soldiers die than mine, by the way!"

Marcus chuckled and gave the Prince a grin. "Better a Nabatean grave then a Roman one I suppose, my lord." Marcus scratched the side of his head and whistled as he watched the Nabatean line slowly advance with the shrieking excitement of Jason to the rear. "Prick will get himself killed."

"Like I said, he craves glory!"

"Yes, granted so, don't we all? But not like that!" as quickly as Marcus had spoken, a renewed surge of energy entered nearly a hundred Jewish fighters who faced the Nabateans and they rushed forward with howls. Even before his men had a chance to react, Jason scampered back shouting for retreat as the two sides clashed in a mangled, confused confrontation. "The bastard will get all his men slaughtered!" Marcus said in disbelief as he watched the inexperienced, poorly formed Nabatean line get mulled and torn apart in droves.

Titus swore loudly and turned. He searched the breach, spotted a Tribune, pointed to the man and gestured for him to approach. "Send word to Jason that he is to fall back in an orderly fashion before all his men die. I want him to retire once nightfall approaches! He is done here!" The Tribune saluted and marched away. Titus glanced at Marcus and said, "Once the Nabateans are gone, send in your Fifth Cohors and position them on the right."

"Yes, my Prince," Marcus responded dryly watching the Nabateans turn and retreat, leaving behind their bloodied dead. He watched, almost humorously, as the Tribune shouted at Jason, trying to get his attention. From Marcus' vantage point he saw the Arab Prince throw his hands up in the air in a fit of blind rage, glance over at the breach, and then quickly run towards them as he held the hems of his long robe so they did not drag upon the bloody stones.

"My Prince! My Prince Titus." Jason climbed the breach, nearly tripping over the stones as he panted for air. "I was told by that Tribune, in a most indignant tone, that you wish for my men to retire? That we are to leave once it is night? But we have only begun to attack the Jewish rebels. Why is it that my Prince makes such an order?"

"To save your men from annihilation by your hand, Prince Jason," Titus retorted with a growl, clearly irritated by the groveling, sniveling, pompous, arrogant man. "Your father asked me to give you experience in battle and you have proven ill of yourself. Please, retire your force now and you may still carry yourself with honour, telling all those who dine at your side that you fought in Jerusalem. Now, leave this matter to me and retire your men at the agreed time."

Jason quibbled and looked startled by the harsh words of the Roman Prince. His face reddened and his eyes narrowed as he fought to reply, but he only stammered instead, then humbly bowed with a frail and awkward pose. "I shall obey your order and retire as you're most gracious and humble servant." Jason took a step back, his eyes lowered to the ground in shame and then he softly said, "If I have indeed gained some honour by fighting at your side, I ask you merely to remember me and if there is anything further..."

"Please," Titus interrupted with a wave of his baton. "You have done enough. That is all." He watched Jason turn away with a pale expression, and then he walked back to his men allowing the hem of his robes to drag in the blood.

Titus looked over his shoulder and gave a simple nod to Marcus Sulla Maximus who sat upon a stone with his back against the broken wall of the breach. "I trust your brother Gaius Antony and his fellow centurions of the Primi Ordines have you to thank," Titus said pointing to the recuperating centuries of the First Cohort.

Marcus Sulla tipped the brim of his helmet gently back and bowed his head. "It was my lord and Prince who gave the order, I just whispered in his ear."

Titus gave the cavalier Tribune a smile. "It is better this way. Antiochus wanted to shut his son up, now the snobby idiot can crawl under a rock and die for all I care." The Prince gave a huge sigh and turned to glance at his legionary General of the Fulminata. "Your men have yet again fought valiantly today, General Octavian. There is much reward to be given, and dona to be hung from the chests of the victorious.

I heard the First Cohort chant a man's name earlier, who was it again that they spoke of?"

"That would be the trooper, Longinus, my Prince," Marcus Octavian quickly replied.

Titus gave a nod and hummed lightly to himself. Then he cleared his throat and licked his dry lips. "A cavalry soldier, most excellent," Titus said and stared back at Marcus Sulla. "Longinus, do you know him? Is he one of yours, Sulla?"

"Longinus, Longinus," the Boars Tribune whispered to himself and then shook his head. "None of my men should be in this action, my Prince. Most likely from one of the other units! A centuria of troopers joined the Fulminata earlier. I think they are piled up on the left." Marcus Sulla pointed down the ranks of centuries to where over a hundred men stood suited in mail coats and carrying the typical oval Roman cavalry shields.

"Indeed, the man did something great. He will be rewarded." Titus stared up at the towers of the Antonia as they appeared deserted. "Seems they have lost the will to fight this afternoon." He scanned the blood stained parapets as they showed major signs of damage. "The ramps will go up quickly, and soon we shall be tearing down those confounded towers," Titus said, speaking to nobody in particular. "Once that is complete, the Western Colonnades of the Temple will be opened wide, like the legs of a woman, for us to thoroughly enjoy the prize." He snickered at his own distasteful joke and gave Marcus Octavian a crude grin as the legionary General gestured to Titus as someone approached.

Gaius Antony trudged up to the base of the breach, stepping over bodies and avoiding men who passed him by to collect the wounded. His face was stained with streaks of sweat and splattered in blood as a number of plates upon his chest armour showed signs that he had received heavy blows from the enemy. He rubbed his neck briefly and then slipped his hand under his armour to inspect his shoulder.

Titus saw the discomfort and called out to Gaius, "Cornelius, my brother, are you wounded?"

Gaius gazed up at the concerned Prince and shook his weary head. "Not at all, my Prince, I just received a nasty blow." He struck his chest in salute and rested his shield upon the ground. His feet were a strange reddish-brown colour from the blood and dirt smeared across the stones. A trail of crimson could be seen streaked upon the skin of his exposed legs and the corners of his tunic. "I have come to report."

Titus was filled with compassion at the sight of his most respected Centurion. Acting quickly, he took a clean towel from his servant and descended the breach of dirt and stone. Gaius was moved and surprised as the Prince extended the towel to him and smiled warmly when he took it. As Gaius cleaned his face, the voice of Marcus Octavian barked orders for a contingent of legionaries upon the breach to protect the Prince with all haste. Slightly embarrassed, Titus held up a hand to Marcus Octavian, who seemed beside himself with worry, as legionaries quickly ran down the ramp with raised shields and pilum to surround the Prince from the threat of Antonia's towers.

"So, what have you to report?" Titus asked cheerfully as he held out his hand, accepting the bloodied, sweat-stained towel.

Gaius swallowed. His throat felt like a barren desert, but he found his voice and raised his chin. "The butcher's bill is nearly two hundred, which includes our wounded. About half are Nabateans." Gaius gazed to his left as Prince Jason of Commagene, sulking and pouting, watched him with suspicion. "My Prince has called the Nabateans to stand down?" Gaius watched Titus nod in reply and the Centurion did not respond, yet his expression was one of thanks. "I estimate the Jewish losses are about the same number, maybe less. They fought well, but their resilience and strength dwindles. They are exhausted; morale must be low."

"That is good to hear. They do have reserves, we could see them from the top of the ramp, yet they do not move." Titus watched Gaius take this into consideration. "Who is Longinus?"

"A trooper attached to the Macedonica. About one hundred and fifty of them were sent over by General Sextus this morning to support our left and take pressure off of the center. I would say they did their part. I saw Trooper Longinus leap out of formation into the Jewish rank and strike down two rebels with quick thrusts of his sword. It was expert swordsmanship and I would say both rebels were dead before they knew it. Anyway, the Jewish attack was stalled as many of them reeled back in shock, and Longinus, ever so cleverly, rejoined his comrades and raised up a cheer." Gaius rubbed his nose and unstrapped the water skin that was tied to his belt. He took a swig of the stale water, swished it around in his mouth for a moment, then swallowed, feeling it moisten his throat and cool his chest.

Titus patted Gaius upon his shoulder. "You will be honoured tomorrow and this Longinus duly rewarded. Your men have fought well today."

"May I ask what is tomorrow?" Gaius replied puzzled.

"We have been fighting for six days straight, a rest is in order. I have decided to parade a portion of the legions to receive their pay. Orders will be passed out by nightfall but the legions are to be in full regalia with trumpets, drums, and banners. We will do this on the Mount of Olives in plain sight of the enemy. I expect those who are rewarded to be recognized before their comrades, peers, and officers. Longinus and you shall be two of many. As for now, hold the line and maintain your foothold. When I write to my father, the Emperor, he will hear of your courageous deeds, Cornelius." Titus patted Gaius once again upon his shoulder, then turned and marched back up the breach.

Gaius heard the Prince ask if anyone knew where Tiberius Alexander was and then he disappeared over the breach, making his way down into the rubble of the Bezetha. Gaius turned, spit a stream of salty saliva upon the soiled ground and sighed.

He inspected the loose ranks of his century for a moment. Then he hollered at them to tighten up and look lively. Before rejoining his Hydra Herculean, Gaius caught a look of surprise upon Marius Livianus' face as he stood out from his Fortis Century, pointing to the Nabateans who were picking through their dead. Gaius gave a nod in Prince Jason's direction, drew a finger across his throat, and Marius' face lit up like gold as he started to sing in a boisterous roar of delight.

*   *   *

By the time Judah had arrived at the southern steps of the Antonia fortress, the sun was beginning to set and the sounds of battle had been left behind. Scattered upon the steps were fist-sized chunks of debris that had fallen from the high towers above. Judah stared at the open doorway before him which was filled with wounded men either lying upon the cool stones or leaning against the heavy cedar doors. A number of women inspected them, walking between the bleeding men with jugs of water and rags. Someone sobbed near the back and Judah watched one of the women straighten, stare into the hall of the fortress, and call out in the direction of the distress. When there came no response she continued bandaging a soldier with a chest wound who lay unconscious.

Judah turned his back to the misery and stared down the long rampart which reached the extreme north-western corner of the Temple Mount. He could see trails of black smoke rising up into the sky, but not a single arrow or catapult stone was fired and this told him that both sides were probably retiring for the day. The Gischalan Zealots had struggled for the past six days in the Mishneh and still they held, although in Judah's mind their strength was waning. He had offered his humble opinion again and again at the nightly war councils, pleading for Simon to strengthen their forces with another thousand men, but the Idumean King was hard pressed along his defences and would counter Judah with frantic pleas for more troops from the Temple Mount to reinforce his own positions. John would end the protests with frustrated shouts and often would pound the table trying to bring a sense of reason to the council of officers.

Judah ran his fingers through his beard and then scratched his chin. He reached up and fixed his kipa, then stared with a look of depression at the wall of black smoke which hung over the southern part of the city where Simon's forces were stationed. The smoke could be seen daily as homes burned from the Roman attacks. In his mind, he could still hear Simon's frantic voice shouting in the war council the night before about the hopelessness concerning the destruction. *"The Fifteenth and Tenth legions are destroying the Upper City and they are doing a splendid job of it!"* Simon would complain, tossing up his hands with curses. *"My men cower all day in fear as many are buried alive by collapsing debris or are lit up like human torches from the fire!"* The bombardment of the First Wall had been a twelve hour Roman sojourn. All day the Roman artillery crews loaded and fired while ranks of cohorts made assaults against the Hippicus and Gennath Gate. Simon's paranoia and fear had finally reached an all-time high when, on the previous day, he had ordered the gate to be completely shut up and buried with rock, timber, and earth, out of fear that the legions would tear down the wood, stones and pillars of the gate and come pouring through.

What was known as the Towers Pool also had been filled with debris, but not by Simon. His Idumeans had watched as the water had been drained dry, the marble broken and torn apart by the legionaries, then filled with debris. Long mounds of dirt had also begun to rise, revealing new ramps, appearing like great giants having been buried beneath the flagstones of the streets, attempting to push up from the ground as they cracked the stones with their mighty backs.

Fire burned almost continuously from the residential quarters of the Upper City as flaming missiles and stones from the Roman arsenal had been launched into the suburbs with no regard for human life. Both women and children were killed as thousands could be seen packing up their belongings and moving into the southern parts of the city where they camped, slept, and lived in filthy, infested streets.

"Judah, I see you received my orders," John gave a quick nod at the startled Lion Captain who quickly turned with a surprised look. "Are you alright?"

Judah wiped his forehead, exhaustion gripping the edges of his face. "You just gave me a start that is all." He watched John slowly walk out from the doorway and descend the steps as if the entire world was upon his shoulders. "You probably are wondering why I pulled you out from the Mishneh?" Judah nodded and John gave a heavy sigh. "I send men there to keep the Romans busy and buy us time, but you and I know it will fall unless God does something. I need you here by my side, not dead somewhere in the Mishneh. It will fall any day now."

Judah did not say anything but instead gave a worried look in the direction of the Mishneh. John stared at Judah with a far off, poetic expression and then said, "I will not leave them to die, do not worry. But the walls have been captured, the suburbs burned, and the Romans grow stronger as we grow weaker. Come, walk with me."

The two men strolled along the portico ramparts in silence. Both men seemed fixated upon the columns of grey smoke rising up from the Fretensis camp upon the sloping mountain as the heavens above appeared cold and indifferent. Finally, John gave a light sigh and shook his head as he seemed disturbed by something in his spirit. "I miss looking out at a mountain of olive groves and gardens; they are all gone now."

"We will replant them again, and this land will flourish," Judah said offering up a hopeful future that seemed bleak. "So, you will tunnel?" he added, steering the warlord away from impossible fantasies.

John slipped his burly, strong arm around Judah's shoulders as the two men continued to walk and he said with great focus, "I have found men who once lived in Parthia. One came here from Babylon years ago. He said he learned from the

Parthians how to tunnel and with a crew of men he could burrow under the Roman ramps rising upon the northern face of the Antonia."

"To collapse them?"

"Exactly," John said with a dark grin as he entered into his wild world of military strategy. "We go deep through the granite and limestone. We dump the earth inside the court, reinforce the walls and ceiling with timber, then pack the end tightly with bitumen and dried faggots. Then we pour pitch all over the timber, ignite it, and-" John made a gesture with his hand and smiled. "It will cave in bringing down the ramps, men, siege towers, and anything on it."

"We should wait until the Romans have built up at least two weeks of work. Destroy that and you crush their spirit," Judah responded seeing the ray of hope in John's plan.

John breathed deeply. "It will devastate them and be a much needed victory for us."

"Do you think Simon can hold the wall?"

"He has to," John said passionately. "When the Mishneh becomes impossible I will give Simon four hundred of my men to help him. The First Wall cannot fall. If it does, the Romans will take the Lower City as well and will then cut off our water supply. With that, they will be able to come at the Temple from all sides."

John rubbed his chin while pondering something and then said, "I wanted to tunnel when I was in the north holding Gischala. It would have been perfect. Even better than Gamla before it fell and thousands of our brothers perished, bless their memory. But nobody knew how to tunnel. I heard they tried in Gamla, whether it was to escape or bring down Roman earthworks, the tunnel collapsed and buried forty men inside, all died." John paused and was quiet for a moment. "I want you, Adam, and Moshe to run the operations. You are all trustworthy men and when the time comes, I want you, Judah, to light it! I will give you this satisfaction against the Roman dogs who murdered Miriam and your parents."

Judah thought it strange for John to bring up the painful memory, but he gave a humble nod of thanks nonetheless. "Have you considered an all out attack once we collapse the ramps?"

John shifted his gaze back to the Antonia and halted. He could see the ends of the ramps and hear the working picks, hammers, and shovels from the exhausted legionaries. John watched a column of cavalry ride by as they kept their distance, many of the troopers gazing up at them as they passed. "When we bring down the ramps, it will be too chaotic! The ground will be so unstable and uneven it would be impossible to lead a well executed assault." He glanced at Judah and drove a clenched fist into his open palm as he said, "But we will give them a taste of steel. I plan to send out at least two hundred fighters."

"When will you take this to the council? When do you plan to start digging?" asked Judah.

"Soon, very soon. It must be done right. Our ranks are still infected with spies. We will have to tunnel under the walls of the northwestern edge of the portico. The miners will have to go deep, and it will take days, if not weeks. We must start soon, but it must be kept a secret. Only a few trusted men and workers shall be allowed to enter."

Judah nodded and fumbled to fix the belt about his waist. "I will do my best to ensure the tunnel remains a secret." Judah watched the tall warlord turn thoughtfully and clasp both hands behind his back as he strolled on. "Is that all, John?"

"There is one more thing, Judah, and I believe you are the man for the job," John replied with a stern tone. "At the beginning of the war I was named one of the war chiefs of the north. I obeyed the new government that was put in place and humbled myself beneath the generals chosen by popular vote in the Temple courts that day. Although I did not particularly favour the vote to make Yosef ben Matityahu a general of the northern forces, I served him nonetheless, yet I serve our cause more.

"The Jewish forces in the north were in a terrible state that only a military tactician could change. They were disorderly and lacked experience as most of them were farmers, fishermen, town folk, or wanderers. Early on I put together a force comprised of Zealots who had been fighting the Romans for years, and our base became Gischala. I had one purpose and one purpose only, and that was to be God's hand on earth and smite the enemies wherever they resided. I believe now, Yosef had other motives.

"True, Yosef, strengthened many of the towns and raised the defences of places such as Gamla and Jotapata, but he also allowed the Greeks to run Sepphoris and Tiberias. Men such as those should have been given a simple choice: stand with us or die. The land could not be properly defended with anarchists and rebels amidst our own cities and villages. I saw this from the beginning and voiced my opposition, but Yosef was careless and greedy for power. He cast shame on my men, and sought to do things his way. I complained to the governing council in Jerusalem, and an envoy was arranged, but by that time the Romans had gathered for invasion. I pleaded with Yosef to give me a command, but he thought I hungered for his power. He trumped up claims that I had tried to have him murdered in Tiberias and he mocked my experience.

"I believe it when I say that Yosef had it in his heart from the beginning to betray us. He came from a wealthy, priestly family of much influence and had friends on the governing council in Jerusalem. His arm outstretched into the Sanhedrin and could turn the hearts of men in the north. He was a patrician and a lover of Rome." John paused and fiercely stared at Judah. "He never had the mind of his people close to his heart." John gestured for Judah to follow him back to the Antonia and the two men turned, strolling along the rampart as John continued.

"When Vespasian's forces swept into the north, they slaughtered us. True, we put up a fight and beat them back many times, but we were unable to defeat them as my brothers fell by the sword. Vespasian was not like Cestius Gallus. Vespasian had been commissioned with a larger army and he bore the image of Nero to seal the fate of those they deemed as treasonous."

John's face was flushed with anger as he vented. "Not once in my life did I swear allegiance to a madman such as Nero, but they called it treason. We were all sentenced to death and slavery because of the insane wiles of Florus that pushed us to desperation. No more would Zealots hide in the caves of Arbel or sweep through the valleys of the heights. Now we would occupy towns, fight from high walls, and clash with the legions.

"Yosef saw the end, we all did, but he had played his dice most efficiently in his favour. Where I saw the destruction of the north and realized the seriousness of fleeing to Jerusalem to defend her from unclean pagan hands, Yosef wished to bed the whore that is Rome, and fatten off of the milk from her breasts." John glared at Judah hotly, infuriated by the memory of his greatest adversary. "Yosef fled like a dog from the gates of Tiberias into the defences of Jotapata and from there, I believe, he hid in his cave and waited for the end as he cooked up a fable to entice the superstitious mind of Vespasian, purporting himself as a prophet.

"As soon as I heard about the fall of Jotapata, I dreamed with a smile of Yosef hanging from a cross, the vengeance of God having been justly fulfilled on that treacherous dog. However, we soon heard of Yosef's capture and my heart sank. Men said they were rumours, they said that there was no way the Romans would have taken prisoners, but I knew these rumours to be true. Yosef had given himself up and had gone over to the enemy's camp. I have prayed, since then, on every Shabbat, that Yosef and Vespasian, who is known as the spirit of *Amalek*, would be cursed and meet their end. I have prayed that their bodies would be given to raw, festering sores, and that hounds would lick them open every time they scabbed. I have hoped that they would die from horrible discharges as their flesh would rot and their minds would wane." John stopped near the steps of the Antonia and faced his silent Captain. "I want you to kill Yosef."

Judah stared at eyes of fire that seemed to blaze inside the sockets of John's face. "You want me to kill him? How?"

"The next time he approaches the Antonia to call up to us, that will be your chance." John pointed across the portico ramparts, slightly to the left where the colonnades met at the corner. "There is a passageway under this platform that Herod built long ago. It is a passageway that leads under the wall and comes to a small spring. This passageway was disguised to appear as a cistern for fresh water leading to a pool not far from the paved street parallel to the Western Colonnades.

"Now, the pool is dried up and empty. If you take the passageway you will come to the inner wall of the pool where there is a hidden door made of cement. You will know it is the door because there is a Herodian coin which was set into the cement from the inside. You will need to unhinge the door and pull it back and then you can crawl into the pool. The pool is not deep at all and rises above the flagstones of the street. You should be able to have a perfect view of the ground between the pool and the Antonia. Yosef will be there. Take with you a bow and quiver and strike the coward down."

Judah had never heard of such a passageway before. Although he had passed by the small pool many times he had never thought of how it was filled or if an alternate passage had been dug which could be accessed. "Why me? Why is it that you want me to kill Yosef? Should it not be you, John?"

John was still as he mulled over these words. Then he shook his head and slipped his arm around Judah's shoulders. "It cannot be me, for I will have to be upon the Antonia speaking with Yosef so he is not alarmed to danger. He is a crafty man, and cannot be allowed to suspect anything. Strike him down, Judah, and I promise you glory. When the Romans have been defeated, and Simon has been either pacified or removed, we will set up this country as it once was before the Romans came here. The High Priest will be both king and judge as it should be, God will be honoured and worshipped for all time, and the country will be governed from Jerusalem. We will open up trade with Parthia, Rome's enemy. We will grow strong and influential and Rome will be unable to threaten us ever again.

"In that day, Judah, Jerusalem will need princes and commanders of our armies to defeat Agrippa, Sohaemus, or anyone else who challenges our right to rule. I will make you my second and give you wealth, men, and power. You will stand alongside me and rededicate the Temple back to God as we cleanse it from the blood that has been spilled. You shall always be known as Judah the Lion."

*　　*　　*

CHAPTER XXXV

May 17th, 70 A.D. / 20th of Iyyar, 3830
Mount of Olives
Jerusalem

Just after dawn, the drums began to roll and trumpets sounded as the Fulminata legion assembled upon the Mount of Olives in full regalia. Elements of the alae were present as the mountain top, stripped of all vegetation and foliage, was amassed with armoured men, horses, colours, and flags. It was as if the mountain side had come to life, rippling with the movement of centuries filing into columns as they marched past Titus who calmly sat atop his horse, Achilles. The Roman Prince acknowledged the jubilation of the legionaries as they passed him and formed long lines at collection tables manned by clerks. All efficiency was given as centurions and optiones kept the men in check, as the clerks jotted down every soldier's name, century, age, and place of birth, before finally passing out the required pay.

The rolling percussion of cymbals, trumpets, and drums continued as the entire landscape appeared as one large parade. Each cavalry unit formed up accordingly to their designated unit number and name. The proud troopers rode their mounts up to their Prince, saluted, called out blessings upon him, than dismounted to receive recognition and pay. The troopers were indeed a noble sight which spoke of the wealth of the empire.

Each trooper wore his finest armour and a parade helmet which had been polished by servants through many painstaking hours the night before. Their mail glistened in the sun, and their riding boots had been cleaned of all dust as they completed the rich ensemble. The manes of the great warhorses had been combed, their tails braided, and ostrich feathers fixed to the heads of the larger destriers. Each stallion held its head back for show and lifted their front legs like they would in Rome upon the grounds of the *Campus Martius*.

Titus nodded at the shouts and hails of his men as they passed by. He spotted Tiberius Alexander and grinned. "The men are in high spirits."

"Well, they should be. They are getting paid," Tiberius grumbled. He gazed back at the quiet city of Jerusalem as he could see the distant ramparts, facing the Kidron Valley, clustered with Jewish fighters as they watched the spectacle. "So you plan to do this for four days, my Prince?"

Titus gave a cheerful nod and shifted in his saddle. "Indeed, I do, Tiberius. It is a morale booster for the men, a mockery for the Jews, and it gives the army a chance to rest. The defences are held well; the remaining three legions and alae are more than capable of holding ground."

"I could not agree more with you, my Prince. I just fear the time we may be losing." Tiberius saw the smile vanish from Titus' face as the young Prince grew serious. "John of Gischala will have time to reform and prepare counter measures. I fear the pressure we have put on him for the past six days may dissolve by the time we have paid the four legions."

"I have considered that as well, but the men grumble and have fought very hard. I seek to reward them, Tiberius. Sometimes a little charm does not hurt. We need to pay attention to other needs as well, not just the war in which we fight." Titus scratched his thigh and relaxed as he smiled at a column of soldiers who raised their spears to him.

"But what of the bombardment? Surely that should at least continue?" Tiberius added, pressing his opinion on the stubborn Prince.

"I ordered a rest for all catapult crews on this day, Tiberius. The men need to know I care about them. I cannot have them think we just simply intend to work them to death. They have built ramps, earthworks, scaled walls, toppled towers, and fought among maddening streets filled with howling Zealots." Titus raised a single finger in the air and continued, "Today they rest." The Prince caught a look of frustration etched into Tiberius' eyes, and to smooth it over, Titus quickly added, "You need not worry, my friend. I will order them into action again tomorrow."

Tiberius was silent for a moment as he watched the vexillum of the Fulminata flap in the wind above the First Cohort that was forming up to wait its turn for the money tables. A large banner of the Emperor's imagio fluttered slightly higher above the legionary standard as the face of Vespasian looked sullen. "When will you reward the brave and honourable?"

"After this matter is put to rest we will recognize those worthy of praise." Titus glanced back over his shoulder as the cavalry, who had finished receiving their pay, mounted and circled back beyond the infantry to form up in a three ranked column. The young Prince turned and faced his aging second-in-command with a short pause and eyes which searched for truth. "How do you think our progress is going in the Mishneh?"

Tiberius shrugged and rubbed his hands together. "I think with a strong push we can drive them from the residential quarter. John and Simon have to understand their power has withered and become pathetic. It is a matter of time."

Titus gave a sharp nod and turned Achilles to face Marcus Octavian who was a few metres away, watching with a wearisome look from atop his horse as the First Cohort marched into place. "General Octavian, a word, if you please." The startled General snapped his head up, nudged his horse forward and humbly bowed his head. "What is your opinion of our fighting in the Second Quarter?"

Marcus tipped his helmet back slightly and scratched his forehead. He flicked the hairs of an elaborate, ivory handled fly-whisk upon his legs to shoo away the insect pests, then swished it again with a curse. "Well, my humble opinion, which I hope Tiberius can appreciate, is to bring in the thunder and roll over the dogs with half a legion's worth. Then we flatten the entire quarter, haul down the towers and wall, and wait to see what happens."

Tiberius swung his mount around and cleared his throat. "We will never be able to get that many men into the Mishneh with any hope of organization, Marcus. Although I do appreciate your passion, it could fail and we would have heavy casualties." Tiberius glanced at the Prince and then whispered, "This is humble advice from a humble man, my Prince."

Titus rubbed his chin as he candidly replied, "Whatever we do, one thing is certain, we cannot unite the Jews or give them hope. I believe we should close this matter with pay for the legions, then press our attack and make it unbearable for the enemy."

"I agree, my Prince, a wrong move could be dire. We must be calculated. Until we move against the Temple itself, we need to keep these assaults to a controllable amount of soldiers." Tiberius paused as he coughed and then watched the First Cohort pass through the money tables as each man was handed a small leather sack of coins.

"Perhaps we need more vexilliatio among our attacks," Marcus said, receiving nods of approval from both Titus and Tiberius. "My First Cohors is the best I can offer, but they are few if they're pitted against a thousand angry Zealots. Units of such high caliber taken from other centuries among the legions and formed into assaulting ranks of shock troops may be ideal to capture the Mishneh completely."

"If that is what it takes, we can assemble such shock troops. Your Gaius Antony is a legend on the front. Was he not wounded in Cestius' retreat?" Titus asked with a quizzical interest.

Marcus bobbed his head in agreement and flicked the fly-whisk again, obviously annoyed at the pests buzzing around his legs. "He was indeed. He would have succumbed to his wounds if I had not dispatched my most skilled physician to his aid. Gaius most assuredly stood in the gap of a breach and blocked it against a wave of Zealots. He did so to protect his men and paid in blood. It would have been a great loss for Roma for such a man to have fallen that day."

"What has Cestius even been up to?" Tiberius suddenly exclaimed as though the previous governor of Antioch had somehow evaded his memory. "Does Gessius Florus, that worm, still lurk nearby picking up the scraps from Gallus' table?"

Titus nodded. "The man is uncontrollable and self-seeking. I will not allow such a man to participate in leading soldiers into battle. I fear he would be even more senseless than Jason of Commagene. He is here on Cestius' bidding and because I needed Cestius' siege equipment. Plus, the man gave tribute and support to my father. I could not say no to Gessius, but I can restrict the man to a tent."

"I heard that Florus was quite upset about the display of his senior centurion's head upon the Antonia tower," Marcus added to the gossip as he flicked the fly-whisk once again and gave a sour look as a fly buzzed out of reach above his head. "I have good eyes and ears in the legion and men report to me the rants and rumours which float around. I kind of like the gossip," Marcus mused with a grin. "Fornicators, thieves, slanderers, and cheaters are what I enjoy the most to hear of, and Florus' ass is not any more clean then the next man's."

"What did you hear?" Titus asked, his curiosity captivated.

"Just that the man nearly destroyed his quarters in a fit of rage and then lamented that his most loyal servant Capito, had been killed and mutilated by the dogs. He vowed to crucify women, rape them upon the crosses before they were even erected, and then cut their children in half before their eyes." Marcus chuckled and shook his head. "The man is mad! Prince Jason may have fancied a boy over a girl, but at least he is not stark-raving mad like that bastard, Florus!"

Titus looked down the mountainside where a line of crosses stood next to the Fretensis camp with skeletons hanging upon them. His mind drifted from the many crucifixions he had ordered to the civilians he had spared. Titus remembered the old man with the women and children who had cried out to him, repeating the name of Judah ben Yosef. The Roman Prince had shown mercy that night under the flickering torchlight and menacing glares of the legionaries as they had itched to raise up more crosses. Titus had spared the poor peasants, and even more, he had sent them to Gophna with the rest of the refugees. He had been worried that his men may have thought of him as weak, moved by the emotional plight of the oppressed, but he had truly thought Judah had been a sympathizer and one who believed in the glory that was Rome.

Now, hearing of Florus and seeing the crosses, Titus wished he had chosen differently. Perhaps he should have broken his word with the Jew, ordering his capture in a mock meeting arranged by Gaius so he could nail him up for the whole city to see. He could have done that, along with the old man, the women, and the children, but something had stayed his hand, and that troubled him.

"My Prince, are you well?" Marcus asked, noticing a look of perplexity upon the young Roman commander's face.

Titus lifted his gaze, then shrugged and said, "Let us reward the brave and retire."

Titus leaned forward, touched his heels to Achilles' flanks, and rode along the mountain side past the clerk tables to where each cohort had formed up in a checkered pattern as they waited silently. Tiberius and Marcus followed the young Prince, along with a mounted standard bearer and a signifer carrying the imagio upon a great spear. A number of servants in white tunics followed on foot as they guided a cart behind the Prince which contained a number of finely crafted wooden boxes.

"Men of the Fulminata, wolves of the legion," Titus bellowed in a thunderous voice hoping the Jewish fighters would be able to hear across the valley. "Today, you have received your pay for services rendered thus far, and you have paid for your duty by the sweat of your brow and the blood which you have shed for *Roma*, our Emperor, and myself! You have been diligent and have fought like beasts from the underworld! We have taken and destroyed nearly half of the city, and the rest will be yours! You have taught the Zealots to fear you and have not backed down! Stories will be told of you for thousands of years and you will become legends to be remembered! Your names shall be carved upon monuments around the world and everywhere men shall remember you as the Legion of Judea.

"You are the men who shall cast her down low into the dirt! The gods have strengthened our arms and the steel of our swords. We shall prevail! We will carry wealth to the ends of the world and fill the Temple of Jupiter with gold! Men of the Fulminata, you honour me with your presence!" Titus gave a nod to his servants and one of the boxes was opened and the Prince was handed a piece of red cloth, rolled and bound by gold cords. Titus drew his pugio and with a flick of his wrist he cut the fetters. Sheathing his dagger, he suddenly unfurled the banner and shouted, "Men of the First Cohors, be recognized for glory, honour, and valour!"

Nearly five thousand men broke the silence with an explosive cheer as they thumped their shields, raised spears in the air, and beat the ground with their feet. Upon the Cohort's legionary banner were emblazoned gold numerals declaring 'XII', and below, 'I Cohors'. Underneath the designated numeral of the cohort, between jagged lightning bolts, was the embroidered name, '*Victrix Judea*'. The entire mountainside quaked from the jubilation as the banner was attached to a pole and presented to Gaius Cornelius Antony and the company signifer. Both men saluted Titus as the banner was then raised valiantly and paraded in front of each cohort with pride.

Soon, a blast of trumpets silenced the thousands of men as Titus again prepared to speak. He held up his hands, waiting for the ranks to quiet and then shouted, "Now, I wish to recognize men who have fought in the service of the empire and for the glory of our Emperor Vespasian, whose eyes are upon us now. May the gods grant him good fortune and a long reign!" A brief cheer erupted as men called out the name of Vespasian before quieting down. "Today we recognize a man for valour and courage, one who has defied the enemy in his face, and who in the midst of battle, rushed forth to strike many of the Jewish rebels down. Trooper Longinus of Thrace serving in the alae, come forward and be recognized by your peers and comrades for your dona! May the fury of Mars in war go ahead of you and give you fortune."

Longinus, who waited in rank with the other cavalry troops, lifted his hand into the air as he smiled. Then with a stern and proud face, he handed the reins of his mount to a fellow comrade nearby and approached the Prince, passing between the legionary ranks. Longinus struck his mailed chest in salute and went rigid as the Prince dismounted, took an engraved bronze medallion with the face of Mars upon it, and hung it around the trooper's neck. A small pouch of gold was given to him and then Titus gestured for him to face the legion to receive his due glory and recognition.

When Longinus turned, the legion began beating their spear butts upon the ground as each man raised up such a loud cheer that Longinus felt it vibrate within his chest. He raised his hands as the victor and then held the medallion high as the sun reflected off of the image of the god's youthful face etched into the metal.

Then a double blast of trumpets sounded and Longinus took his place among the legion. Next, Titus made ready to call Gaius Cornelius Antony forward to receive a silver disc for his cuirass. It was crafted with the utmost intricacy as palm fronds lined the edges and the face of Vespasian dominated the centre. It was to be awarded to a man of great respect, emulating true leadership in the face of great danger, and who had never let down the name of the Emperor.

As Titus called Gaius forward, the mountainside shook with such ferocity even Titus wondered if it would be possible to break it in half. Gaius marched forward to receive his glory and Titus raised the medal high to honour his most experienced, senior of the Primi Ordines.

Gaius bowed his head humbly to accept the medal and Titus grinned warmly as he said, "You honour *Roma*, Gaius, and more importantly, the good name of the Flavians whom you have given your loyalty to." Then as Titus slipped the dona around his head, he whispered close to the Centurion's ear, "You wear the divine face of my father, your Emperor. I fear the road ahead of you may be the most difficult and dangerous of all the days you have faced. Many of the men who stand in your ranks will not be with you in the weeks ahead. Will you sacrifice their lives willingly to see victory, for *Roma*?"

Gaius stared with a grave and sorrowful look into the Prince's steady eyes, flaring with intensity and war. Then he gave a heavy nod and replied, "If the cost of victory is to be written with their blood, and if this should be the payment requested of Mars to achieve victory, then so shall it be, my Prince."

*   *   *

May 21st, 70 A.D. / 24th of Iyyar, 3830
Temple Mount
Northern end of Solomon's Colonnades
Afternoon

"You know, watching the Macedonica get paid is not going to make you feel any better," Adam said as the corners of his lips curled into a smile. Judah gave him a heavy nod, clearly exasperated by the Roman pomp. "It is designed for one thing, my friend, and that is to create within our hearts the curse of envy. Of all the days Titus has to pay his troops, he chooses such a time as this, out of desperation I think."

Judah raised his eyebrows and stepped away from the stone parapet of the rampart. "You think the Prince is really feeling the cost of this siege of his?"

Adam shrugged. "I don't think it is because he cares about his legionaries getting paid. He is trying to show off Roman power, wealth, and that they feel no fear. I would guess the truth is the exact opposite. The Roman's delay in the Mishneh tells me they are being prudent and weary."

"The Romans face an enemy who has nothing to lose and everything to gain: liberty and freedom." Judah whispered the last word as if it tasted a bitter sweet flavour in his mouth while he contemplated the meaning of true freedom. "The Romans are arrogant and foolish! They blaspheme God, profane this land, and purport their own rulers as divine." Judah gave a sarcastic chuckle and shook his head as he approached the parapet once more and rested his hands upon the stone. "Now they stand in plain view, out in the open, and collect their wages. Wages earned by the blood of women and children!

"For the last four days, Titus has paraded legion after legion before our walls, as if it were a parade of victory and triumph for his people, but he forgets that we, proud Jews of the one true God, stand behind unconquered walls and are ready to die to defend this city!" He swore under his breath and scanned the distant shapes of erect crosses scattered over the mountainside with half decomposed bodies hanging from them. "What man Titus may have been once, has now been traded for the heart of an animal and the mind of an evil spirit. What I would give to have an army of ten thousand at my finger tips right now," Judah muttered with a dazed and far off expression chiseled into his worn face.

"But if you were to have such an army, Judah, would Rome ever go away?" Adam said softly as he turned from the Mount of Olives and leaned against the parapets, slouching upon his spear. He watched Judah give him a startled expression for a moment and then exhaled loudly. "We drove Cestius from this city, and now an army nearly eight times larger stands before us today."

"It took them four years to get here, Adam, that has been four years of freedom from Roman rule," Judah whispered not fully believing what he said.

"Has it? People starve and die of sickness within our walls, our brothers have fought and killed one another, the priesthood has been replaced with a mockery, and the rich have fled to preserve their lives." Adam paused for a moment as he stared at the stone walkway of the rampart and then said, "I fear that even if we were to obliterate the Romans today, and they were to never come back, Simon and John would not waste a moment to turn on one another and more blood would flow in Jerusalem's streets. Even the Romans do not kill their own as we do."

Judah's eyes watered for a moment as salty tears clung to the lids of his sunken sockets. He gently closed his eyes for a moment and rubbed them, feeling a sense of grief as he shuddered at the raw truth which he knew to be real. When he opened them he stared motionless at Adam for a few seconds until he slowly replied, "Then why don't you leave like the rich Jews did?"

Adam gave a warm and tender smile as he laid a hand of friendship upon Judah's tired shoulder. "I have sworn an oath to myself, never to abandon this city while it stands as a Jewish city, and to never forsake my service to you, Judah. Until my dying breath I will never leave your side. I shall be like the fervent loyalty of Prince Jonathan to God's servant David. Even under the threat of King Saul, Jonathan's friendship never waned."

Judah cleared his throat and touched the side of Adam's face and gave a firm nod. "A better friend, there is none. I have only known two men of the highest honour in my life: Caleb and you." Judah stared back at the slithering columns of Roman troops passing through the clerk tables upon the mountainside and shook his head again. "I feel as if there is something you wish to ask of me."

Adam hesitated and then humbly agreed with a grunt. "Judah, I have never asked anything of you before, and I have always served you with my spear, sword, and my life."

"I already know of you as a man of honour, you mustn't prove your loyalty to me, Adam. Speak plainly and if it is in my power I will grant it."

"I humbly ask of you to help me save the lives of my parents and sisters by helping me smuggle them from the city," Adam said plainly as he saw a look of surprise cover Judah's face. He quickly continued with urgency, "There is almost nothing to eat and my sisters fear rape from the Idumeans crawling around the streets. Many of the neighbours are sick with plague and my father grows weaker every day. They must be given a chance or they will all die, I fear, if they cannot leave. I shall never ask of you another thing for as long as I live, if you would just do me this one wish."

Judah was silent as he stared into the pleading eyes of his friend, the look of desperation from a man who was nearly at the end of himself. Judah thought of his commitment to Rabbi Asher, Zechariah, Shimeon and Matthias and knew he was already way in over his head. Although none of the aging, influential men had approached him since their meeting that day in the alley, Judah knew he had joined their league, and if caught, John would surely kill him. Judah also understood that having accepted this charge meant that he was in more danger of being discovered then he had ever been for he would be operating within the walls. However, knowing that Adam knew of his dealings with Gaius Antony and Yosef ben Matityahu and still pledged loyalty to him, somehow gave Judah a comfort that perhaps God would still forgive him for his past deeds.

"There is something I must tell you, Adam. Eight days ago I was confronted by four men, three of whom you know, Matthias ben Theophilus, Simeon ben Gamaliel, and Zechariah. The fourth was a rabbi who had known my father. I was unaware of this rabbi's knowledge of me, but he is a prominent man of the nasi; his name is Benyamin ben Asher."

Adam scowled. "I have heard of this rabbi."

"Anyway," Judah continued. "They have formed a plan to try and help people who wish to leave the city. They do not believe in Simon's effort and they question John, but more importantly they believe the innocent should not perish due to this war. I agree with them, and although I have continued to pledge my sword to this cause against Rome, I will help these men. I saw Zechariah yesterday and gave him my pledge that I would help."

Adam leaned back in puzzlement and slowly shook his head. "Judah, do you understand the danger? This is nothing like when you met with Gaius. Simon and John have men everywhere. How could you even possibly get people out of the city without being discovered?"

"You want me to help your parents escape yet you condemn me for aiding others?" Judah asked surprised.

"Helping my parents would be simpler then aiding many, even you have to understand this." Adam was silent for a moment and then asked, "What do they want you to do?"

"To use my authority as a captain under John to make sure certain gates are unguarded so that people can slip out."

"That can only be successful once or twice, Judah, before someone sees you. The punishment would be worse than anything John has ever done, for you would cut him the deepest out of all his enemies. You are the closest to him." Adam watched Judah flinch from the known consequences should he and the league be discovered.

"I am aware of that. I will just have to believe that John is capable of reason," Judah replied in a controlled tone.

"He has never shown reason in cases such as these, Judah," Adam responded stating the obvious.

"I do see your point," Judah said with edge to his voice. He turned and glared back out at the Mount of Olives and then relaxed slightly. "I feel in my soul that I must do this. I must do something righteous and good. From all the blood and all the death, the pain never leaves."

Judah turned and gazed at Adam with a distant yearning for something that he craved, yet still seemed far beyond his grasp. "I need to believe that I can do a great mitzvah in all this. If some Jews can be safe, that is good enough for me. Rabbi Benyamin told me my abba loved God and always served his brothers. He said that this would be the greatest thing that I could do to honour his memory. I have thought it through, and see truth in the rabbi's words. I will not stay my sword, but perhaps I can save some lives. I must take the chance, and pray to HaShem that any unfavourable eyes are cast aside when I receive my instructions on what to do from Zechariah."

Adam scratched his neck as he thought about Judah's words. "This is a dangerous game you play, Judah, but if I can help then call on me and I will serve. This I pledge to do."

"I cannot get you involved, Adam, but I can use this to help your family. The problem is, and Zechariah and the others are aware, that the Romans have been selective with their prisoners. Anyone they deem weak, feeble, and poor they crucify and the rich and aristocratic they send to Gophna to live in freedom," Judah replied, his eyes dropping to the rampart stones as he searched his mind for an alternative solution.

"In God's name then, what is there that can be done? Speak, please, of what hope I see upon your face!" Adam resounded with a pained groan.

"First, Zechariah is the one we must bring this to. These men are willing to help anyone, they just believe it is suicide for those poor and destitute to flee, and they would be right. However, we must convince Zechariah that your family is willing to take this chance…then we give them the choice between trusting Zechariah or trusting me. It is only fair that they be given the choice to decide; when it means life or death, it is only right."

"What do you mean trusting you? I trust you, Judah, with my life," Adam retorted firmly.

"No, hear me out," Judah replied softly shaking his head. "If your family chooses the aid of Zechariah he will want to meet them, so your abba better be prepared to have an ear for reason. Yesterday, Zechariah said to me that they are currently putting together a list of people who will be smuggled out as soon as it is feasible. We shall add your family to that list, if your abba chooses, it is his decision and we must then convince Zechariah that they will depart on the chosen night. You must understand, Zechariah along with the others believe it a hopeless situation for the poor, like your family, but this is his terms and if your abba convinces him, your family can leave with the other people."

Adam nodded, "And what is your method of getting them out?"

Judah took a heavy breath as he gathered his thoughts. "If your abba does not accept Zechariah's proposal, and they seek to accept mine, they must still pretend to comply, for the priest cannot know of my plan." Judah stepped closer to Adam. "You have to believe me when I say, beyond the walls your family would be easy pickings for the Romans. Surely your sisters would be raped and killed and your parents crucified."

Judah lowered his voice as a number of guards passed by and then when it was safe he continued, "What you do is hide in your home with your family and wait till I come for you on the night chosen by Zechariah for the people to be smuggled out. I shall convince him that your family is among those leaving, but they will not be. Instead, once it is dark, I will come for you and take your family through the streets and sneak them into the Mishneh."

Adam's eyes widened. He shook his head and whispered, "Are you mad, Judah? My family will be slaughtered by Roman sentries before they can do a thing. At least in the Kidron or Hinnom they would stand a chance!"

"They shall not be harmed, not if they cry out the name of Gaius Cornelius Antony!" Judah stated and saw the effect on his friend's face. "Yes, that is their only way to live. The sentries may mistreat them, but they cannot kill them if they but throw themselves onto the mercy of Gaius."

"And you believe this Centurion will be merciful? You really think he would spare a family of sickly Jews who have no gold or silver or any status whatsoever?" Adam pleaded in a broken tone.

Judah nodded. "I believe Gaius to be a man of honour. He may be a Roman and the enemy, but his word means something to him and I have seen him deliver."

"Judah, I have to have more assurance than that. I could never live with myself if my parents did such a thing and suffered terribly from it. What if Gaius has become a changed man in how he views you ever since you hung Capito's head from the Antonia?"

"He gave me an image once," Judah replied with distaste but he knew this to be the only reason he had been able to fully trust the Roman. "He gave me an image that he prayed to which represented his wife and children back in Italy. He pledged his word to my face and had not a look of betrayal in his eyes. He cares about his word, and that is why we can trust him." Judah paused, feeling a tinge of envy for the life Gaius had awaiting him back in his home country. "He is our only chance if your parents are to live longer than the three days it will take for them to die painfully upon the cross. If your family is to survive outside the walls, we must appeal to Gaius."

Adam stared down at the stone rampart, overcome, as if a great burden hung, strapped to his back. Then without looking up, Adam muttered, "I trust you, Judah, but for this, I cannot give you my word on their behalf. My abba will decide." Adam shuddered as if a cool wind tugged at his garments and he looked up into the eyes of his commander. "Send word to Zechariah to come and visit my family. I want you to be there as well. I want you to tell my abba your plan from your own lips."

*   *   *

Chapter XXXVI

The sounds of homes collapsing and catapult missiles thudding into the First Wall came as distant thuds where Yosef and Titus stood. The sun had climbed high into the sky as midday approached as the heat baked the rocks causing the former Jewish General to perspire as he looked at the Roman Prince and cringed with the thought of approaching the looming fortification. Titus turned, glanced behind him, then gave a sudden wave of his hand for a party of six legionaries to come forward and surround Yosef who acted as the Prince's emissary.

"Remember my terms, speak eloquently, and we shall see what happens," Titus said as Yosef sighed and squinted at the high walls clustered with Zealots. "Offer them the four day truce and a pardon for any fighters who may surrender."

Yosef bowed humbly and cleared his throat. "I pray they listen." He glanced around at the leveled sections of the Mishneh stretching out before him as he stood atop the breach. Once a bustling neighbourhood of priestly housing and merchant shops, had now become piles of rubble and charred remains as enormous earthworks, rising up against the side of the Antonia, were in the process of becoming newly erected ramps.

"These men will protect you." Titus took a moment to inspect the Jewish General's fine garments and then nodded. "You are ready."

Without saying another word Yosef began to descend the breach with the guard party as he took gulps of hot air and wondered why he was so nervous. One of the legionaries marching beside him noticed the awkwardness in Yosef's step and the pale streaks ingrained upon his face. "What is the matter?"

Yosef glanced at the soldier wondering why this legionary would even care of his mental state, for few did, but he saw the concerned look in the man's eyes and so Yosef shrugged. "I don't enjoy this."

The legionary did not reply but gave an understanding nod, returning to his duty as he scanned the high walls and raised his shield.

Yosef reached the bottom of the nearest western ramp and struggled to control his composure as he began to climb the packed earth which the engineers had spent days leveling. The ramp was far from finished, but it would provide Yosef the platform he would need to clearly speak. The Roman scuta, held firmly by the guard, would protect him from any sudden missiles or rocks that may be fired. He could sense the glares from above as vehement hatred seemed to pour down upon him from the towers. Yosef scanned the high parapets and the men upon them as he felt the back of his neck moisten from sweat as his nerves begin to race and his heart quickened within his chest. He convinced himself again in his mind that what he was doing was out of honour and concern for his people, as Yosef did not wish to see Jerusalem burned or vanquished.

The Jewish General halted abruptly when he reached the middle of the ramp. His trust for the Zealots had limits and he did not wish to test them. The Roman Centurion leading the guard whispered to Yosef that he should not step out from their tightly formed circle, and the Jewish spokesman complied, as a number of Zealots above could be seen with raised spears and fixed bows.

"Do not hesitate a moment longer, Yosef! Say something!" muttered the Centurion with worried glances and a sense of vulnerability.

"Men of the Antonia," Yosef suddenly blurted out in Hebrew and watched as the spears and bows were lowered causing the Roman guard to breathe a sigh of relief. "I come before you once again as a brother, amidst the suffering of this place. If you look beyond your walls you will see much of your city in ruins, and though it pains me to say this, the legions will not cease so long as there is rebellion and opposition to Rome. Please, take heed of my words! I say them as a common man and as a man who has experienced the generosity of Rome.

"Nay, they have not made me worship their gods or bow to their statues. I live in comfort and pray to the God of Abraham, Isaac, and Jacob. I bind my left arm with tefillin and place the box upon my head to recite prayers and read Scripture. Rome has even been gracious to provide me with the scrolls of Moses so that I may even now, continue to study diligently as you continue to do so from your place of refuge.

"I am a man who is torn apart daily by the sight of my city being attacked. I am a priest and I once served within these walls. I was chosen by a government long since destroyed, to serve faithfully in the north. I was captured in Jotapata, and spared because of a divine word that was given to me. Am I to be judged by what God has spoken to me? Should I be condemned because I live? You wish for liberty and freedom, but you do not know what you seek after. You believe that freedom will come by the edge of your sword and the point of your spear, yet HaShem has made the Romans our masters for this age and you defy the purpose of the Great Almighty. Look, even now in your defiance your city is being ruined. How much longer until you see reason?

"I call you to surrender and save your country and spare our Temple! Do not display greater indifference for your own people than the foreigners! They have come here by charge of their Emperor and to keep peace and stability in their empire; you, on the other hand, fought and killed each other for power and control! Who is guiltier? We were servants of Rome and we rebelled, but in our rebellion we lost sight of our brothers and drew blood from their bodies. Now, does not the blood of your brother cry out from the soil? Does not the blood of your brother weep and gnash his teeth by the wiles of your constant fighting? I say, this war has driven us all mad and in doing so we have sacrificed righteousness and holiness for a burden of strife."

Yosef stared up at the men on the wall and searched for anyone who may have been moved by his words, but nothing changed. He shook his head and outstretched his arm to them and pointing upward shouted, "Where is John of Gischala? Does he still command you into silence?" "I am here, Yosef. What do you want with me?" The familiar voice of John surfaced as he climbed on top of the parapet and stared down at his enemy surrounded by the Roman guard. "I see you have brought your allies to give you comfort and peace; well, I dare say to you that once again you have chosen the path of tyranny." John crossed his mighty arms and glared boldly at the frustrated emissary below.

*   *   *

Judah pushed through the narrow passage below the Temple platform. The tunnel was cool and moist as a layer of soft clay covered the floor so that it squished over his sandals, soiling his feet. He panted for air as it was stifled. Judah pushed forward as his cloak snagged upon the rock walls which seemed to narrow the deeper and further he went. Across his back was strapped a black bow and clutched in his left hand was a quiver of arrows, which he sought to keep out of the clay. In his right hand he held a torch that dropped burning sparks of oil upon the floor of the cistern channel. Judah paused for a moment as he caught his breath and listened. From where he stood all he could hear was the distant sound of dripping water. Judah knew he was close to the pool door.

Nearly thirty minutes ago, Judah had been standing on top of the western wall of the Antonia, between the towers, guarding the parapet and wondering if the Romans would continue the day with raising the ramps. However, all that had changed when Yosef and Titus had appeared on the distant breach. John had taken Judah below the platform, deep into the western tunnels below the colonnades until they had come to the entrance to a narrow passage. John had handed Judah a bow and a quiver of arrows, then had rehearsed once again with his Captain what to look for in the tunnel: a cement door with a Herodian coin sealed into the stone. The last Judah had seen of the ferocious, wild Gischalan warlord was when John slapped him on the shoulder, told him to strike down Yosef like David had done so to Goliath, and then quickly ran back through the tunnel to the Antonia so Yosef would not suspect anything.

Judah listened once more to the sound of the dripping water and sighed. Was he ready to kill Yosef if he got a clear shot? Could he kill Yosef? To murder Yosef would be the killing of a priest and a man Judah had conspired with in order to seek his own revenge against Capito. In his meetings in the old cistern outside the city walls, Yosef had not struck Judah as the warlike type, but rather a man of education, purpose, and political backing. Yosef was working for the Romans, but had he any other choice? John always spoke of Yosef as if he had willingly gone over to the Romans, but was that true? Would a man truly align himself with the killer of his own people and then stick around while his holy city was destroyed? True, Yosef proclaimed himself to be a seeker of peace and one who cared about the innocent Jewish civilians of the city, but could that all be a masquerade for what really lay beneath? Could Yosef truly be working for the Romans for his own greedy purposes, having forsaken his people, faith, and country to be accepted by the Rome?

To Judah, the truth seemed stretched from the possibility that Yosef had become so corrupt and evil in the sight of John. It was war, and unthinkable decisions happened daily. Judah knew this all too well as he thought of the Jewish farmer he had killed in anger, the Roman he had tortured that day Miriam had been murdered, or the look of pity, shame, and fear in the eyes of Capito before he had cut his head off.

Judah had become a man of war, a savage, and one whose hands had been immersed in blood. He felt haunted by the memories of the men he had tortured and killed in the past, and their faces never left him. Judah would see them in his dreams, during the day, and in the men he met. Overshadowing him constantly was the thought that he had sinned against God, and not an offering in the world could make atonement. Not the blood of a ram, goat, sheep, or even a red heifer would take away the sense of filth he felt covering him. It did not matter how much Judah studied and worshiped in the synagogue each Shabbat, or even when he broke fast upon *Yom Kippur*, he would always walk away feeling empty and alone.

Often, Judah would find himself wishing he had been of priestly descent. Perhaps then he could enter the Temple, throw himself upon the floor at the foot of the veil, and plead with God while raising his gaze. But what would he even expect to see if he had such an opportunity? First, Judah would pass the golden incense altar, barefoot, as it sent up a waft of fragrant smoke that would draw attention as it filled his nostrils. However, naturally he would seek to get closer to the holiness and power of HaShem, right to the great veil before the Holy of Holies. Thus, to do so he would pass eleven golden *menor'ot*, and eleven golden showbread tables, each stacked with twelve loaves to add a scent of warm sweetness to the air. Yet still this would not be good enough for him.

He had no doubt in his mind that next he would throw himself to the floor, as was customary for priests to do so, and call out for God to speak with him. Would this be enough? Would a sign enter his mind or appear above the massive golden cherubim woven into the fine, red silk of the twenty-five-metre high Babylonian tapestry? His eyes would be filled with all the colours of the panoramic heavens embroidered upon the veil in purple, blue, and scarlet. Then he would beg HaShem to relieve him of such mental anguish. But would relief even come? He had done despicable things and would no doubt feel as if his very skin was soiled against the white priestly garments as he wallowed in misery.

Apart from Judah's priestly vision, he had stomached much suffering. Caleb, who was Judah's one sense of foundation and reason, was dead. He had also sent Hadassah, a woman he loved, into the care of Mordechai ben Levi and now would arrange for Zechariah to smuggle them from the city. Judah had been an orphan now for four years, bereft of his betrothed, thrown into violence, and headed to a grisly and painful death at the hands of the Romans. Yet daily he tried to fix his reason on the chance that God would use him to vanquish the enemy, and thus, had risen up men like John of Gischala to do so.

When Judah reached the end of the passage, his body was sore from bending over and his hair was caked in dirt and mud. He held the torch in front of him and inspected a wall of what appeared to be stone. Near the bottom, where the floor of clay and dank water lay, he saw a cement door bolted by rusted hinges. Judah bent low and squinted in the fire light as he saw the faint image of a copper coin pressed into the cement. The coin reflected off the dancing flame for only a second until Judah straightened and found an iron bracket in the wall to hang the torch. He took a deep breath of the humid air and slipped the quiver under his arm. Judah ran his hands along the edge of the cement door, then found an iron latch and lifted it. He gripped the door with his strong hands and while heaving with his might, opened it with a clang as reddish-brown dust fell from the hinges.

A waft of cool air blasted Judah in the face as he sighed and gazed through the narrow opening into a dried, empty pool. With a sickening expression, Judah slowly crouched down and peered through the doorway at large pieces of rubble laying in the pool. The once beautiful blue tiles which had shone brilliantly upon the floor and sides of the pool, were now smashed, chipped and covered in dust. Without giving the pool a second thought, Judah awkwardly crawled through the door and into the sunlight.

As he stood, the sounds of shouting and jeers could be heard coming from beyond Judah's position. He cautiously gazed out over the piles of rubble and the charred remains of buildings towards the giant, snake-like ramps that rose from the ground. Judah could barely see Yosef upon the ramp which ran up to the north face of the Antonia. Yosef's concealment was only possible because the Romans had built the western ramp at a slight angle and he had not proceeded any further.

Yosef stood stiff, poised like a statue, as he gazed upward at the high walls. His chest was slightly pushed out and his chin jutted up to the sky as he shook his head at John's speech upon the parapet. Yosef shook his fist in the air and gestured at the destroyed blocks of housing as he hollered at the Zealots. Judah could see the former Jewish General's face flushed with frustration as he tried to reason against the jeers and curses from above. Judah glanced from Yosef and the legionary guard, towards the breach where a cluster of Roman officers waited. There was no doubt in Judah's mind that the Prince of Rome was among them.

Judah ducked back down into the pool and scanned the fletching's of each arrow to find the choicest one. He would only have one opportunity and then would have to duck back into the passageway quickly, lest the Romans locate him. Judah found an arrow with dark, speckled feathers and slowly drew it from the quiver only to find a wicked looking, barbed head on the end. He touched the cold steel and inspected his finger as a droplet of blood appeared. Judah took the arrow ever so delicately, as if it were a sleeping baby, and set the quiver on the ground. He then un-slung the black bow and fixed the arrow fletching into the cord as he cautiously rose up again, peering over the edge.

From Judah's vantage point he could not get a clean shot as Yosef was nestled safely among the Roman guard, yet he watched patiently as the Jewish General's anger was roused more and more as the shouting intensified. Then, suddenly to Judah's surprise, Yosef moved forward between two of the legionaries and stepped into the open. Yosef shouted up at the walls with a clenched fist as his voice boomed throughout the devastated Mishneh and Judah saw his chance. He calculated the distance at around thirty metres and knew he could not miss with Yosef towering upon the ramp like a colossal orator, standing apart from the Roman guard.

Judah's muscles tightened while his vision narrowed as he slowly raised the bow and drew back the heavy cord. An aching pain seared through his forearm against the resistance of the bow string, but he drew the cord back until it reached his ear. Judah steadied his breathing as he leaned forward and closed his left eye staring down the shaft of the arrow with the barbed head aimed at Yosef's chest. He watched the Jewish General shake his head and shout up at the Zealots upon the wall who patronized him. Judah could picture the goliath-like form of John upon the parapet, hands resting on his hips, clearly undeterred from Yosef's logic and the dizzying point from which he stood elevated upon. John's body would be stiff with rage as he fumed from his stance, refuting Yosef with angry jeers at what he deemed to be impossible pleas from a man sold to *Ba'al Zebub*.

Judah looked away from the high walls of the Antonia and focused again on Yosef who now bowed his head and shook it with frustration as he covered his face. Judah watched Yosef glance back at the Roman guard, give them a gesture of faith, then renew his defiance at the high walls and the crowd that had gathered to hear him.

Judah swallowed, feeling nervous, as if a great lump of stone was caught in his throat. He felt sweat trickle down the sides of his face and his fingers became moist with perspiration as he held the great instrument of war. Could he truly let the arrow fly and strike Yosef? Judah tried to brush aside the fact that it had been Yosef who had aided in his revenge over Capito as he began to reason within himself if he really should kill the man. Strict orders had been given from John to commit this murder, but a part of Judah was angry that such an order had even been thrust on him to begin with. Could not John have had Simon speak with Yosef in his place? Why could John not have crept through the passageway, with bow in hand, to crawl into the pool and cast down his enemy? Could he even live with himself were he to slay another fellow Jew? Judah slightly lowered the bow with an exasperated pause, yet he kept the arrow drawn as he toiled inside between duty, honour, and the state of his soul.

John had never spoken a decent word about Yosef, but did that make him evil? Was it God's will that such a man must die? Judah had grown to respect the bureaucratic, conniving, Jewish priest and patrician. True, John and Simon along with most of the Jewish fighters might have dreamed of nothing better than to shove the blade of a sword into Yosef's chest, but Judah saw something else in the Roman prisoner and emissary. It was obvious Yosef worked for the Romans, but what plagued Judah's mind were two unanswered questions.

First, what really had happened with Yosef's capture? In war, men were often driven to acts of desperation. Perhaps in Jotapata, Yosef really had been captured and offered either the position of a Roman spokesman or the way of crucifixion. This possibility, naturally was at odds with the story John had spread saying Yosef had merely walked over to the Roman side and had begged them to spare his life so he could join their cause. If Yosef had truly been captured, and offered such choices as assisting the Romans or dying upon the cross, it would have been a decision that no man could ever judge another for making.

To be crucified was by all means considered the worst possible way for a man to die, and often Jewish fighters would speak of how they would rather kill themselves than fall victim to such a fate. Judah had seen only a handful of men hung upon crucifixes before the war, and they had all be convicted criminals, but now it had become the norm.

The Romans were masters in the art of death. With the outbreak of the war, Judah had now become accustomed to seeing hillsides and fields littered with the dead and dying, all hung upon trees like twisted ornamental trophies to the delight of the legionaries who were always willing to crucify more. It was as if the screams, even of children and women, was not enough to slake Rome's thirst for blood and the unquenchable lust for torture.

The second question that plagued Judah's mind laid in the essence of Yosef's continued service to Rome and what the real underlying reasons were for him to switch to their side. Could it not be, that Yosef may have actually bartered a deal with Titus, not out of treacherous actions, but because he cared about his people and the city? Thus, there could be a real legitimate reason for Yosef's allegiance with Rome, and that was to spare the city and its inhabitants. If this was truly the reason for Yosef doing the bidding of the Romans as an orator, then Judah knew he was not so different. Had not he himself given his word to Rabbi Benyamin ben Asher that he would assist in helping people escape the ravages of war? Like Yosef, this too would be viewed as treason by John of Gischala, and thus, Judah himself risked execution.

In, Judah's opinion, both Yosef and John saw themselves as men attempting to represent the people they claimed to fight for, whether with physical arms or the mastery of words. John and his Zealots boasted that they alone fought for the true ideals and freedoms of the people, and they did so by provoking the legions to war. Yet, at the same time, Judah thought, they had also submitted under a government, led by Ananus ben Ananus, which they had eventually allowed to be overthrown. However, now they were rebels against their own cause which had started at the birth of the rebellion with Rome. Yet, the Zealot belief was that God had ordained and appointed them as guardians of the Holy City, the Temple, and a future Israel unhindered by Gentile hands and glorified, like the Maccabees, to set up the High Priest as king, priest, and judge.

The complete antithesis against the Zealot movement was Yosef, who voiced that he alone had the true cares of the people and city in mind. For the Jews of Jerusalem, including Judah, they all knew that if Yosef's wish were to come about it would mean total surrender, a restoration of Roman occupation, and continued existence under the tyranny of Rome. Slavery and execution for the ringleaders and all who supported the rebellion would be a number one Roman concern, even despite Yosef's denial that this would happen. Occupation, therefore, would remain as a threat against the Jewish way of life. However, the city, its people, and the Temple would be spared, and the land given a rest from years of ravaging war.

In the minds of the Zealots and Idumeans, to conceive of such a notion as surrender was utter blasphemy and treason. It spat in the face of their faith and everything they had fought so long and hard for. In their minds there was only one thing they could all agree on, Jerusalem was not a city to be bartered or sold. Nor would they bow before the vilest of men who represented the complete opposite of their faith. They would be seen as weak. The Romans would stamp their coins with victory emblems, building arches and temples in honour of overthrowing the people of the one true God. This was simply impossible, and it would have meant that for the past four-year struggle against the greatest power the world had ever seen, everything in the end had amounted to nothing. Judah knew he could never live with himself should an outcome such as this pan out in the annals of history. Yet, was not this what Yosef represented? Would not a man who parlayed surrender speak with the authority of the Prince of Rome?

Judah held the bow tight, wrestling in his mind as he stared at Yosef beyond the point of the arrow. He could hear the boom of John's voice rail down from the high walls of the Antonia as the Jewish General folded his arms and shouted back. Then, Judah watched Yosef's gaze fall to the packed earth of the ramp, as if a heavy thought seemed to cloud his mind. Judah could hear the pounding of his voice within him, ordering him to let the arrow go, watch it sail to its target, and smile with victory as it struck down the traitor. But he could not do it. It was not that he lacked the strength or the fortitude to kill Yosef, for he knew if he convinced himself enough he could take the shot. Rather it was to Judah's dismay that he observed Yosef raise his head, stare across the broken rubble of the Mishneh, and stare directly at him in the empty pool.

Yosef locked eyes with Judah and gave the stunned, proud fighter a friendly nod. Taken back, Judah slowly lowered the bow, fearful he would be seen by either the Romans or the Zealots. However, the Roman guard remained unaware of Yosef's subtle communication. Judah hunched over seeking shelter in the pool as he watched Yosef turn, and signal to the legionary guard that he wished to leave. Judah ducked down into the pool, as his mind raced with a sudden jolt of panic that Yosef's signal to him and his failure not to carry out the assassination may have been noticed by the Zealots on the walls. He held his breath, carefully pushing his body up against the broken tiles as he peered up at the high walls, quickly scanning the ramparts. Judah saw nothing out of the ordinary, as what Zealots he could make out, continued to jeer at the retreating Yosef and the Roman contingent. Judah wiped the sweat from his forehead with the back of his arm. He snatched up his bow and quiver, darted back into the hidden passage, and made for the Outer Court of the Temple.

*   *   *

Yehoram stood upon the ramparts, slightly crouched over with his fat belly pressed against the parapets. His warmongering gaze peered down into the Mishneh with a dark expression ingrained upon his ugly, blotched face. Yehoram rubbed his stubby, coarse beard and then relived an itch beneath his eye patch. His skin was weathered and his nose was swollen and red, but despite his hideous features, a smile lightened his complexion as he softly chuckled to himself. He ducked down for a moment and watched as Judah scanned the walls from his hiding place within the empty pool. Yehoram rubbed his hands together as his dark, sadistic mind searched out every possible scheme to ruin the reputation and sentence the Lion Captain to certain death.

It had been two weeks since Simon had assigned Yehoram to watch Judah for any possible leak of activity on behalf of the Romans. Simon had bragged to the ugly fat Yehoram that he did not trust the renegade Judah or his men, and that if someone was passing information to the Romans it had to be a man such as Judah. Yet, even Yehoram had begun to doubt that possibility as day after day had turned up nothing against Judah. But now, like a gift from heaven in a cataclysmic instant, things had changed. Yehoram had seen everything. First, Yosef had spotted Judah, than acknowledged him with a nod. Following this, Judah who could easily have made the shot, had cowardly stood down and checked to make sure he had not been seen. Yehoram felt the dark elation of a conniving victory arise within him and with excitement he suddenly dashed to the other side of the ramparts and gazed down into the Outer Court.

He waited anxiously, growing concerned that he might have missed Judah, but then he saw the Captain emerge from underneath the pillared roof, cautious and careful, as he scanned the area for any suspicious activity. Then, to Yehoram's delight, the emboldened Captain casually strolled a few metres into the court and halted. Moments later, Yehoram watched John of Gischala approach from the direction of the Antonia. When both men were close enough, Yehoram watched them with the eyes of a hawk as they spoke with one another in low voices. He saw John cover his face with his hands and give a brief nod as he accepted the bow and quiver. John stared at the bow for a moment, then patted Judah reassuringly upon the shoulder before he turned and marched away.

"Finally the Roman snitch has been found," Yehoram whispered to himself as he licked his lips and smiled exposing four yellow teeth in calloused gums. "Now to destroy you and watch you squirm for mercy." Yehoram then ran to tell Simon all he had discovered.

*   *   *

Fortress Antonia
An hour after sunset

All faces were grim and set into looks of steel, as if the expressions of the men had been forged through fire, plunged into water, and hammered until every edge and line resembled that of tempered iron. The council chamber was tense and quiet as the Zealot and Idumean officers contemplated as one accord. They knew the Mishneh did not have long until it would fall into the same misery as the Bezetha before it.

John of Gischala stood hunkered over a long table of olive wood and stared fiercely at a map, as if his eyes would burn a hole through the animal hide. Every once in a while he would clear his throat, and anticipation would rise within the hall as men waited for the warlord to speak. But only silence stole the great oak of a man's voice as a strained stillness, ripe with unknown days ahead, settled upon him.

Simon, on the other hand, seemed less pessimistic, with little interest in the map, and more taken by the succulent, delicious wine which he drank and cooed over. The large shadow of Bagdatus stood behind the Sicarii King and at his side, like a faithful dog, was Yehoram with a look of utter malevolence about him. Only once did John give the fat, ugly Yehoram a hateful glare, yet Simon did not seem to mind. It was as if the irritating man had grown wings, like a cherub, for his sense of humour would lift and become decorated with light gestures and jokes. Whenever Simon adorned this aura of benevolence, he would take delight in stealing gawking, sarcastic glances John's way. This sadistic visual dance of Simon's only sought to entice the large man to frustration as he tried to strategize. Sometimes he would get a reaction out of Gischala, and other times John would simply ignore him, but when John lashed out with annoyance it would closely follow the chorus of giddy laughter from the Sicarii King.

John finally let out a heavy breath and crossed his arms as he scanned the room, giving Judah a firm nod of reassurance before beginning. "Comrades, men, the keys to victory lay under ground. We shall mine and the Romans will never suspect a thing!" John let this thought sink in as a number of hushed whispers floated about the council hall. "We have men in Jerusalem, men in our ranks, who have experience with mining, and this must be our main point of focus if victory is to be achieved. We have tested the Romans, and their steel is true and their fighting disciplined. We cannot face them head on, but we shall face them where it hurts: their pride.

"We all know how great builders these Roman foes are who face our walls. We have seen their ramps rise up, erected from the ground. Their earthworks are stout, solid, and true. Their camp defences are nearly impenetrable and they build with such a tenacity I have yet to see among mortal men. So, we shall strike their pride and destroy their morale." John extended a single finger and touched the map where the sketch of the Antonia lay with its black lines of towers and walls set deeply into the hide by the ink made from pomegranate dye and black charcoal. "Our men hail from the far east: the Kingdom of Parthia. They are Jews from the shores of the Euphrates and they come with a great skill. I have had them scour along the walls, the foundation stones of the Antonia, and into passageways beneath the Temple, where even I have never trod. Men, they have an interesting report, hear them."

John stepped back and two dark skinned men with black beards and flowing robes approached the table. "I am Eliyahu, and this is my brother Amos," one of the men said with a foreign accent. "We worked in the mines of Parthia, near the border with Scinites of the Arabians. There we received contracts for the constructing of city walls in such places as Ecbatana and as far as Susa in Elam. We have lived many years along the Euphrates and have learned the ways of the Parthian as well as we speak their tongue. This can be done and we are ready to do it, all we need are the labourers, which will not be a problem.

"First," continued Eliyahu, "The only way to be successful and not risk a cave in, which usually kills everyone inside, will be to dig off of one of the coexisting tunnels under the Temple works. There is one which runs very close to the foundations of this fortress and we should be able to chip through rock and dirt and excavate under their own ramparts as they erect them." Eliyahu gave the silent crowd of officers a stern look. "Tunneling, if done right, can be a devastating blow to the enemy. The Romans, I would have to presume, will not expect it as John has said."

"What if they do, and they dig counter tunnels to close ours off or break through?" said a concerned burly officer pushing between two men to get a closer look at the map.

Eliyahu shook his head. "We can avoid such catastrophes. We will have to dig quickly, we must not cease. We dig both day and night and constantly change out work crews. Amos will listen for any vibrations or noise coming through the stone. If the Romans are digging, we should hear them. Our only chance is to go deep underneath the walls, so we do not risk a cave in from above, and then try our best to match it with the ramps being built above. We will need men with a keen eye to keep watch on the parapets so we can correct ourselves, should we stray off course."

"We dump the rubble and earth inside the court, under the porticos, pack the tunnel with flammable wood, and then light it up," Amos added. "The heat will cause the ground to shift and give way, causing a cave in and bringing down anything above. Legionaries will be buried alive, mark my words."

The chamber was motionless as everyone digested this hopeful information and watched as Eliyahu and his brother stepped back and glanced at John who, without flinching said, "We will have shifts of fifty men at a time, removing dirt, bringing in supplies, and strengthening the tunnel for its destruction. I have nominated this charge to be placed in the hands of Judah ben Yosef, who will work with our miners in finishing the tunnel with all possible speed and collapsing it with deadly precision.

"I have spoken with Simon, and we shall follow the collapse of their ramps with an attack by his spear infantry as they will sweep down into the startled Roman ranks. That will be the time to cause them to *quake with fear*," John said these last words as he drove his fist into an open palm and then leaned upon the table. "Digging will commence right away in the morning and all effort will be made to finish the tunnel as quickly as possible. If we fail, the Mishneh will fall and that will be catastrophic to our positioning, especially if they break into the Upper City."

"I wish to add to the voice of the council, something far dangerous to our effort, and that concerns traitorous brothers," Yehoram suddenly interrupted, causing a look of fury to suddenly boil upon John's face as he stared at Simon's puppet.

"I shall not waste a moment listening to your words of hypocrisy and filth, Yehoram. Not in this council shall your words be uttered," John replied with a growl as his hands turned into tightly clenched fists.

"Oh, John, I do not think you have a choice," Yehoram shot back, lifting his voice in thunder. "Men of rank, Zealots and Idumeans, lend me your ears. We have all tolerated calculated planning only to see them unravel again and again by the works of spies among us. John and Simon have caught men in the act, and have quickly sent them to their deaths to discourage any more such actions of treachery, but still they continue." Yehoram began to strut among the clusters of officers and captains as a dark hush came over the council hall.

"I have seen it with my own eyes, and it pains me to give this report," Yehoram craftily said, outstretching his arms and cocking his head to the side as if overcome by grief. Then the flash of a smile appeared as his crooked teeth were exposed. "I saw it today, and the man stands among you, even now. He has been like a symbol of honour and loyalty, but in secret, he is covered in the shit of betrayal which bears such an overpowering stench it must be revealed. He must be dealt with harshly and you men shall be his judge." Yehoram halted, and shot a clever glance across the table at Judah who stood, arms crossed and jaw set with tension as his eyes narrowed at the despicable man.

Judah felt his entire body grow stiff with Yehoram's stare. Had the puppet of Simon seen him earlier when he had decided not to kill Yosef? Sweat began to dampen his neck as a flush of heat filled his chest and face. His fingers felt clammy and cold as he tightened them, trying not to appear guilty while his mind raced in alarm. Judah could feel a gaze of panic at his back, as Adam stood behind him wondering what to do. Slowly the giant warrior, always faithful to Judah, slipped his hand unnoticed by the officers, upon the hilt of his sword.

"Who do you speak of, Yehoram? Who is this man?" Simon chattered loudly with a grin knowing full well what Yehoram's report had been hours earlier.

Yehoram stared at John for a moment. The Zealot warlord from Gischala looked as if he would lunge over the table and kill him. John held his stance, unable to react as the inquisition unfurled before his eyes. Yehoram swung his gaze to Simon, who gave a simple nod. Then the ugly, fat man, with the black patch, despised by all, hungrily pointed a bony finger across the table and shouted with delight as his voice cracked, "The spy is Judah ben Yosef, my officers, captains, and lords! He is the one!"

John exploded into a fit of hysteric rage as he slammed both fists upon the table with such a thunderous force that many of the men standing around him reeled back in shock. "That is absurd!" John shouted. "Your poison has gone too far! You lie!"

"It is true! I saw him with my own eyes!" Yehoram screamed, sending a string of spittle upon the map as his face reddened, the blotch upon his cheek glistening with swelled anger.

With a loud scrape of steel, Adam drew his sword, pushed Judah aside, and pointed the blade across the table at Yehoram and shouted, "I stand with Judah and give him my allegiance! These are lies and slander from a man so filled with evil he cannot be held as a reliable witness. He is corrupted by selfish desires that would see Judah's good name ruined!" A number of the men around Adam quickly stepped back giving the giant with the sword room. Adam's chest heaved as his steady hand held the blade at Yehoram. "I vouch for Judah. He is a man of honour and has fought bravely for years against our enemy which is Rome, and he has served John faithfully."

"I agree!" John boomed, drawing his own sword. "Judah has fought with his life to bring victory, he is my most trusted! You accuse *him*, then you accuse *me*! You accuse us all, for he is brother to us!" A dozen men standing behind John also drew their swords and shouted for men to get away from Judah or else test their wrath.

With eyes wide with anger and shock, Simon quickly said, "What is this? You would accuse us of lies and defend a man who could be a spy?"

"His loyalty runs deeper then you could ever know, Simon. Judah has served me faithfully, there is no fault in him," John shouted back sternly. "If your man, Yehoram, wants to test his allegiance, let him come to me, stand in my company, and proclaim it."

Yehoram's face twitched as he suddenly saw the impossible situation before him. His blood boiled and his heart pounded in his chest as he shook his head and spit on the floor. "Should not your man be judged to test his guilt? I have just accused him for having seen him with my own eyes! And you protect him? He could have killed Yosef ben Matityahu and he did not. I saw Yosef look at him and give him a signal, and Judah backed down! That is proof he has worked with the enemy, let alone in the least did he fail to see your orders carried out! He should be tried and if found guilty put to death!"

"I do not know what you think you saw, Yehoram," Judah said in defence. "But I can assure you your accusation is ludicrous and mad!"

Like a charging bull John suddenly plowed through the officers, sword in hand, followed by his elite captains. John caught Yehoram by the cloak before the fat man could flee and swung him violently around as Yehoram yelped. Bagdatus, who stood a few feet behind Yehoram, half drew his own blade with a quick action, but then had second thoughts as the enormous assassin stayed his hand and watched with piercing eyes as John took Yehoram by the throat.

"I said, Judah is innocent, he will not be tried, humiliated, nor accused. Do you understand?" Yehoram gasped for air as John's large hand tightened around his throat. "I have strangled whelps like you before and they have all pissed themselves before turning blue with death," John whispered. "Do you understand? Judah ben Yosef will not be judged and his honour shall be restored!" Yehoram gave a sharp and frantic nod and John loosened his grip. "Proclaim it to them all, you dog!"

Yehoram rubbed his bruised throat and gasped for air as he stumbled back, wincing in pain. "What?"

"Proclaim his innocence, Yehoram, and that you were wrong, or I shall take your head right here." The passion and savage edge to John's voice rattled even Simon's nerve as the Sicarii King shrunk back behind the shadow of Bagdatus and said nothing to aid of Yehoram.

Humiliated and branded a coward, Yehoram gave a heavy nod and said in a scratchy voice, "I did not see anything to condemn Judah ben Yosef. He serves God, the Temple, the city, and our cause faithfully. He is a Zealot with honour." Yehoram gave Judah a malicious, yet defeated look and then grunted. "Judah ben Yosef is no spy. I was gravely wrong!"

John glanced over at Judah, gave him a nod and sheathed his sword. "It is done. Judah ben Yosef is no spy, and his honour is intact. You will say nothing of this to anybody. It ends here." John looked to Yehoram and said through gritted teeth, "Remove yourself from this council at once. You are disgraced and neither fit to be among brothers."

Yehoram turned, looked sheepishly at Simon and then with his head hung in shame quietly shuffled out of the chamber. Simon crossed his arms and stared at John with a heated gaze. The warlord from Gischala had embarrassed him and discredited evidence that he himself had believed. Yehoram's information had always been reliable. Even if the man was scum and a malevolent bully, his reports to Simon always bore truth. However, John had snatched that away in an instant, taking charge of the situation as he was backed by his own officers. There had been nothing Simon could have done, and for that, hate for John filled his heart.

Simon's eyes turned from the son of Levi to the Lion Captain who had garnered such trust. He stared at him for an instant, studying his face and then gazed at his faithful compatriot, Adam, who was Bagdatus' equal. Simon's face tightened with indignation as Adam sheathed his sword and laid a hand of reassurance on Judah's shoulder. Simon cringed at the men and felt the humiliation well up inside him as he fought to contain it from pouring out upon his face like a great flood. He watched Judah spot him and the Sicarii King gave him a graceful nod and forced a grim smile as he saw the effects filter out upon Judah's tense frame.

Simon knew he would continue to invoke the cooperation of Yehoram's efforts, even if the ugly man was banished from future councils. He would not stop until Judah had been brought low and left for dead in the street. The Romans may be knocking at their walls with rams but Simon knew there was still much to do, especially once they had defeated the legions, and it had all started within the council hall of the Antonia.

* * *

CHAPTER XXXVII

Rocks and missiles sailed through the air slamming into homes and sections of the First Wall, its ramparts crammed with spearmen from Simon's army. Each impact shook the city as men ducked from fragments of stone, iron, and fire which soared overhead threatening to kill anyone not quick enough to escape its lethal path. Below the ramparts of the First Wall, Idumeans flooded the streets of the Mishneh in force. They poured onward like a rushing wave of water between the homes toward three cohorts of Roman infantry pressing at their flanks and threatening the suburbs in a massive offensive.

Beyond the fighting in the Mishneh, which had erupted at dawn, were the continuous sounds of the Roman engineering projects. Like in a chorus of crude instruments, the many sounds of picks, hammers, shovels, and labourers echoed throughout the corridors as hundreds of men moved like a great host of ants upon the ramps which rose up against the walls of the Antonia. A hail of catapult fire was nearly constant, as placements of onagri engines unleashed a fury of missiles that soared overhead the working Romans, slamming into the turrets and parapets of the Antonia's defences. At the base of the ramps, a safe distance out of the range from Jewish bowmen, stood Roman Chief Engineer Porcius Gracchus and his staff, under a covered veranda as they compared the work before them according to their plans. Every so often, Porcius would dash out from the veranda, inspect the ramps by squatting and closing one eye, and then retreat back to compare notes. He would insist this be done only by him, as his pride would not trust any of his other engineers, despite them all being capable men. "It must be done right or not at all!" Porcius would insist. "If not, the whole damn thing will collapse and I will find myself disgraced and in exile with the whole lot of you."

Positioned before Porcius was the greatest fortification he had ever faced. The magnitude of the Antonia and its massive towers and walls was immense. The stone was strong, the foundation deep and thick, its battlements armed to the teeth, all the while strengthened by Jewish batteries of scorpions. Two of the three ramps had been deployed against the northern face of the Antonia, which threatened the taller and largest of the towers. Porcius had little choice, for to attack from another angle would then condemn the rams and siege towers to cross-fire from the Temple colonnades. The third ramp had begun to rise up along the northern walls of the Temple Mount, not far from what the Jews called the Sheep's Pool, next to the grander Pool of Bethsaida. Both of these pools had long been drained by the Romans in an effort to conserve water and therefore had been abandoned as the toils of war spoiled them.

Porcius had been instructed to see two more ramps raised near the First Wall: one to the left of the Tower's Pool and the other inside the Second Wall, the latter which would begin once the Mishneh had fallen. However, Titus' instructions had been clear. The Antonia was the key to the city and all possible resources were to be used in seeing it destroyed.

"My lord, at this rate these ramps shall be finished shortly," said one of Porcius' stewards after nearly ten minutes of examining charts, maps, and a number of scale models that had been crafted from wood. "As long as there are no interruptions, we appear to be on schedule."

"A man's schedule is a relative matter, Albinus. In war, there is no schedule. Nothing goes perfectly to plan." Porcius gazed upward at the man and then stared behind him at the growing ramps. "But you are correct, we shall be done soon." Porcius sighed. "The ramps need to be perfectly strengthened on all sides. If the ground is packed and sealed as it should be, the towers should not have a problem with their approach." He grumbled something under his breath and straightened as he shook his head. "The stones are strong and well set; the Antonia was well built."

"It was well built because the hand of Rome had it built," commented the steward. "The Jews should have never taken it over."

"It was only guarded by a garrison, my dear Albinus. Do not fret about trivial things. The garrison was slaughtered years ago. There is nothing to be done now but to avenge them and take it back." Porcius picked up a sharpened quill and tapped it against one of his charts as he furrowed his eyebrows and studied it.

"A magnificent building, fit to be a fortress in Rome, no doubt, and now plagued by treasonous dogs." Albinus said flatly crossing his arms.

Porcius rolled his eyes and gave an exasperated sigh as his concentration was broken. "Are you going to plod along like a mournful woman or are you actually seeking to assist this effort?"

Albinus sensed the strain in Porcius' voice and embarrassingly grunted and returned to the charts with a look of awkwardness. "Forgive me, my lord."

"I waste no time on forgiveness, you impotent man, just focus on your duties and let me not reprimand you a second time. I have neither the taste nor the heart to do it again, you hear me?" Porcius said, annoyed that he even had to have this conversation. The steward gave him a sheepish nod and Porcius growled in the back of his throat, while his brown, conspicuous eyes glared out of the pale mask of his face. He tried to ignore the sounds of battle happening not far away in the alleys and streets of the partially destroyed quarter, but the noise was a reminder that danger lurked close by.

The loud sound of jingling from the cingulum of an approaching cohort warred with Porcius' inner desire to concentrate on the work at hand. As his irritation piqued from the battle formation which passed the veranda, he began to whisper aloud his calculations for the ramps in an effort to remain glued to his duty. However, the centurions and optiones of the marching centuries soon began to shout out orders followed by a blast from trumpets and a roll of the drums. Porcius jolted his head up and snapped the quill between his fingers. He gave Albinus and the other six staff members of his engineering team a foreboding stare, before strolling to the edge of the veranda to watch the cohort. His eyes beheld the troop vexillum for a brief moment and then identified them as men of the Fifteenth by the large golden palm branch of victrix, upon the red dyed leather surface of the elongated, convex shields. A Tribune followed closely behind as he called out to one of the centurions. Porcius gave a huge sigh and rubbed his neck to relieve an aching muscle. The cohort carried on past the veranda and Porcius observed the Tribune turn his mount and ride back towards the widened breach in the Second Wall.

At the base of the breach, Porcius could see a shelter set up, much like his own command, but larger. The legionary flags of the Tenth and Fifteenth stood outside of the shelter where the Generals Larcius Lepidus and Titus Frigius coordinated the assaults in the Mishneh. The presence of the legionary echelon and the constant attacks being carried out proved that the situation required a steady hand over troop movements within the confinements of the narrow quarter.

Porcius now watched another cohort emerge from the breach in a column formation as the legionaries stomped their feet upon the ground and held their bright red scuta before them. Whistles rang out in various pitches as the soldiers filed through and called out in response. Drums rolled from the percussion musicians at the rear and a number of trumpeters upon the ruined Second Wall blasted their instruments with a great breath of air as the sound sailed throughout the quarter. The banners of the cohort fluttered, and the symbols of a falcon with the numeral "III" were embroidered upon the vexillum that waved in the breeze as the senior centurion led the march. Accompanied next to the centurion were two of the cohort's signifer as they carried the battle standards proudly. Porcius clearly noted a bronze eagle gripping two broken arrows above a wreath upon the top of one signum. On the top of the other signum was the legionary symbol of the wild boar standing upon a tasseled curtain above a turreted gate of an unknown city. Upon each standard Porcius could see the Latin inscriptions of "LEG X FR" on bronze discs fixed to the poles. Both signifer were cloaked in the furs of wolves and bears as the hides covered their helmets.

Porcius turned to Albinus and said broodingly, "How many cohors have been committed today?"

Albinus shrugged and counted to himself, with the use of his fingers, then replied, "That would be the fifth, my lord."

"Five cohors? They seem optimistic today." Porcius turned and watched the trumpeting cohort begin to form its battle formation once it had cleared the breach.

"There is Lepidus," Porcius said to himself as he watched the General ride out from his command post to the men of his Third Cohors as they arranged themselves. "Looks like they are to be sent in," Porcius muttered to nobody as he listened to the intense sound of fighting which came from the distant streets.

Porcius watched Lepidus ride down the line of five hundred legionaries and shout a few words at the formation which were inaudible from where the Chief Engineer stood. He wondered what the General had said to them, for the entire rank of men lifted their pila and gave a single shout in salute as Larcius returned to his post. The centurions stepped out from their centuries, drew their blades, and signaled them to advance. The drums kept a steady beat as the cohort shifted forward like a great wall of metal and flesh as if it consumed the very ground it marched on.

Porcius turned away and slowly stared down at the broken quill, still in his fingers. Albinus noticed the disconcerted look come over his commander and he gave an uncomfortable glance at the other staff members as he cleared his throat and softly said, "My lord, are you well?"

"Nonsense that you should ask such a question, Albinus. You need not worry about my condition. It is hot and miserable here, and we have a job to do." Porcius scratched the side of his head and wearily sighed. "Retirement would suit me well," he muttered to himself and then straightened to the sound of approaching horses clattering upon the flagstones of the streets.

"Tribune Maximus and his Boars approach, my lord," Albinus nervously said as he moved around the table to distance himself.

Porcius did not move a muscle. He watched as the column of horses approached like a long serpent from around the northern face of the fortress. The famous unit's signum led the column of horses as the head of a boar could be seen with clenched teeth, flared nostrils, and razor sharp tusks. The faces of the most notorious troopers were like molten steel as not a single man seemed to possess emotion. Their eyes were cold and piercing as the column approached the veranda, their oval shields of black held tightly against their bodies.

Porcius walked to the edge of the platform and rested both hands on his hips. He licked his dry lips and squinted in the sunlight as the two leading horsemen veered to the left and right as Marcus Sulla appeared in full battle armour with a red horsehair plume atop his helmet. He pulled back on the reins and slowed to a light cantor before halting a few metres from the engineer's post. "To what do I owe this pleasure, Tribune Maximus?" Porcius drily asked.

Marcus shrugged and gave a smile as he bowed his head, with lines of sweat gleaming from the sides of his cleanly shaven face. "My boars are ordered to patrol the outskirts of the city and I thought to myself, how is the Chief Engineer doing this fine morning?" Marcus struck his breastplate in salute and leaned forward in his saddle. "I trust your building is satisfactory this day."

Porcius nodded and stepped off the veranda as he strolled over to the wild-looking Tribune sitting upon his black mount. "The word satisfactory is for men who know no better and are given to wine, my dear Tribune." Porcius smiled. "It is good to see you." He held up a hand and the two men clasped each other's wrists in friendship.

"It is dirty work, my lord, but someone's got to do it and you have staked yourself a notable reputation for getting things done, even the impossible." Marcus paused and glanced up at the Antonia and watched a half dozen catapult missiles slam into the parapets causing the defenders to duck and leap out of the way. Marcus shook his head as he heard the artillery captains some distance behind him give orders to reload. "They're valiant and bullheaded," Marcus said, acknowledging the Jewish defenders with a nod.

"You admire them?"

"Sure I do, they fight tooth and nail! John is a formidable opponent. I sometimes wonder what it would be like to face off with such a man." Marcus loosened the chin strap on his helmet for comfort and then scratched his groin.

"Men say that he is a clever fighter," Porcius added.

Marcus nodded. "Truly, the man outwitted Prince Titus, although his royal highness hates people talking about it. John of Gischala truly burned him." Marcus shook his head and gave a dry chuckle. "Honour the Sabbath, he told our Prince, and then fled in the night."

Porcius was still for a moment as he turned and stared up at the high walls. "Sometimes I look at such stones and wonder to myself, is it ever possible to overcome such an obstacle?"

"Yes, when you are the builder and architect, Porcius. Herod may have been an excellent master builder, but even those stones paid in gold will topple. From the looks of it, your ramps are nearing completion, yes?"

Porcius shrugged and glanced down at the broken quill still in his weathered hands. "Maybe ten days, or slightly more. I have over six hundred men working throughout a fourteen hour day."

"Titus' orders? He is in a rush to complete the job," Marcus stated, reaching for a water skin.

"It comes from the Emperor, I believe. I try and slow things down. One must do it right so the whole bloody thing doesn't collapse, and then we have an awful, damn mess on our hands." Porcius shook his head and bit his upper lip. "I push the men and they push me. This ground is awful. It is like digging in hell. The ground is hard and packed and the stones of the fortress, well, some weigh an enormous amount and the rams would never pound through those. So, I have to raise the platform even higher. It will be an awful mess, Marcus, simply hell."

"That is why you were brought on as Chief Engineer. Prince Titus knows what he is doing. Your illustrious record stands as a dona for the whole empire to see. Men like you are gods; you can hammer through anything. Just think, without your ramps and works, this would be impossible and thousands would die. No legion could do it. You are the beating heart of this siege and Titus knows it." Marcus struck his chest twice with his last statement and smiled.

"You must join me in my quarters tonight for wine. Albinus, my steward, has been able to purchase some wonderful aged wine from the merchants."

"Ah, Pepi is still in the wine business. Less whores and more wine, is it?" Marcus chuckled.

"The Arab still has whores, practically a legion of them, but I fear disease, so I stay away. You are familiar with Pepi?" asked Porcius.

Marcus nodded thinking back to Drusus and Varro, the two decurion he had caught ages ago in Pepi's tent with the prostitutes. He scratched his chin and leaned over. "I am all too familiar with that sly dog! That man makes a fortune off of the legions."

"Good business for him. That's why they do it, and it keeps morale up." Porcius glanced back at the veranda and glared at Albinus as the steward ducked back down and pretended to focus on the charts. "The Arab set up his vendors and tents to the north of the Bezetha. I may go there tonight and buy a piece of jewelry. I have a mistress back in Rome I think I shall send it to. She is obsessed with the east, although she has never been here herself."

Marcus laughed. "Perhaps you should have brought her here if she desires a holiday. Look for something of jasper or onyx maybe. A string of pearls perhaps would suit her fancy. I saw a necklace of Persian coins once with orange beads, but the bastard charges too much."

"It is well crafted, my dear Tribune, and worth every sesterces." Porcius muttered to himself as he did some calculations and then raised a finger. "He offers good sales sometimes if you buy two. Do you have someone back home who may profit from such a purchase?"

"My dear, Porcius, do you infer that I have a lover?"

The engineer shrugged, slightly embarrassed. "Maybe a wife?"

"I shall disappoint you then. The only *someone* I might have is one of Pepi's girls. Yet, if you are interested in squaring a deal with someone, then might I suggest the Praefectus Castrorum Antony of the Fulminata. Now that man would be interested." Marcus glanced up again at the walls of the Antonia and said, lost in thought as he scanned the parapets, "He has a wife and children. Perhaps he would purchase something with you."

"I know of the man in which you speak of. He is the Primi Ordines who attends the war councils. I heard he is greatly admired by the Emperor." Porcius glanced back at the silent Tribune, taking note of the sudden intensity that had befallen his face. "Tribune Maximus? What is it?"

Marcus' dark eyes glanced at the vacant turrets of the towers and the quiet ramparts below as the Roman artillery fire began to slacken. A stone missile, launched from a kicking onager, slammed into the parapets along the ramparts bursting into a thousand pieces of rock shrapnel, but that was not what Marcus cared about. He instinctively moved his hand to the pommel of his gladius and gripped it with sweaty, tense fingers.

Porcius noticed the change in the Tribune's demeanour and grew worried as he turned, trying to see what had seized Marcus' attention. It was useless as his eyes darted from tower to tower and then surveyed the high parapets beyond the veranda. "Marcus, what do you see?" cracked Porcius' voice as he suddenly felt uncomfortable with the ghostly sight of the deserted enemy ramparts. Another volley of iron bolts was fired from a dozen scorpions as they careened into the stone defences cracking and breaking up a number of the parapets, yet, still not a soul could be seen. "Marcus?" Porcius said sternly as he turned and stared up at the Tribune.

"There's nobody on the walls," Marcus said, his voice far off and distant. He slowly dismounted, and his signifer followed suit. The Tribune drew his sword and walked a couple metres past his horse. Marcus gazed down the paved street below the southern walls of the Temple Mount colonnades. He stared at a lonely looking gate not far from the high arched bridge. He looked above the colossal walkway at more empty ramparts and felt his pulse quicken. Marcus looked to his right as the third cohort of Roman infantry from the Fretensis had long since disappeared as the sound of battle could be heard ringing out in the distant streets of the ruined neighbourhoods. He turned back to Porcius and said, "Are your labourers armed?"

"Most of them are alae, but yes, they can be armed. What is it?" Porcius asked with an edge of fear in his voice.

Marcus ignored the question and glanced back up at the deserted walls. "Have the alae take up arms and get here on the double!"

Without hesitating, Porcius turned and shouted at Albinus to alert the captains of the work detail to move around to the west side on the double. As the awkward steward scampered off the platform running as fast as his little legs could carry him, Marcus turned, hollering for his Boars to dismount and form a battle line two men deep.

"Should we not fight mounted, Tribune?" asked one of his new decurion in a concerned tone.

Marcus shook his head. "We will not have the advantage on this uneven ground!"

"Should we call for the cohorts to move back?"

"There is no time, there is nobody else." Marcus glanced at Porcius, "Have your staff pull back immediately, clear out now!"

"Tribune!" shouted the decurion staring past Marcus as he quickly fumbled for his sword.

Marcus swung around as a horde of Zealot spearmen emerged from the gate in front of the merchant's square. They charged down the stairs like a flood of raging water and poured across the paved road, fanning out to widen their attack among the destroyed remnants of the quarter.

"Porcius, get out of here now!" screamed Marcus as the Chief Engineer turned and fled with his staff. "Quick men, form up!" thundered the Tribune as he jogged ahead a few metres and widened his stance.

"By the mercy of Jupiter," whispered signifer Publius, who stood behind Marcus gazing out at the massive attack converging on them. "We're dead men."

"We are Boars!" Marcus said, spitting upon the ground and looking over his shoulder at the frightened man. "No retreat! We hold them here!" Marcus shouted as his men abandoned their mounts and ran to his side. "Form up and fight as one! Remember your training!" He cringed at the horrid arrangement of his men as they stumbled over rubble and tried to pull themselves into a tight formation. Marcus had assembled only two hundred and fifty men for his patrol and now he faced over five hundred of the enemy. "Hurry! Wait for the signal!" Marcus gave a wild look at the trumpeter behind him and held up his hand.

The cavalry troopers locked their shields before them as best as they could and with hardly any spears, they knew this would be up close and personal work. Each man hunched over in an attempt for the shield to protect more of the body as they held the blades of their swords at waist level and prepared to engage. A silence took over them as they stared out at the superior enemy quickly closing in around them. Nearly everyone prayed silently to whatever god they could think of.

"Sound the charge, now!" Marcus shouted at the trumpeter and then grinned at his nervous signifer and said, "You will find glory today, Publius, that I am sure of!"

With the double blast of the trumpet, and the Zealots about ten metres away, the Boars bolted into a frantic charge as they let loose a great war cry. The Jewish attack slowed in time to hurl a fury of spears into the Roman ranks. Shields splintered and shattered from the heavy javelins as dead and wounded troopers collapsed in bloodied, mangled droves, tripping up men behind them. Desperation was felt by everyone as the Roman shields met the shattering impact of the Jewish momentum. Screams and shouts became constant, as sweat mixed with blood and the drone of grunting could be heard as men shoved each other, slashed and thrust with their blades. The light weight cavalry shields had done their part to stall the Zealot force and rally the vulnerable Boars, but quickly the odds were turning against them as the Zealots began to hack them to pieces.

Marcus felt like a madman. He cut, slashed and thrust, his hand washed in blood and his breastplate splattered with crimson. Sweat poured down the sides of his face as he lunged, cutting open the chest of a large Zealot which caused the man to jerk, gasp, cock his head back, and let loose a terrible cry of pain before tumbling back in a wash of gore. Marcus saw a spear butt come at his face and he only had an instant as he attempted to duck. He felt as if his head had exploded as a thousand stars appeared in his blurred vision. He stumbled to the side, knocking into one of his men.

Suddenly hands caught him under the armpit as Publius steadied him and at the same time slashed with his sword to protect his Tribune from the onslaught.

Marcus heard Publius grunt in pain as a sword sliced open the muscle of his thigh, but the large signifer reacted quickly, ploughing into the Zealot and knocking him down. At the same time a Jewish fighter, with fiery eyes and a thick brown beard, leapt at Publius with a short pike and drove it into his shoulder, the barbed head tearing through the links of mail. Publius was silent as he fell back, as if he was dead. Marcus felt the body crumple against him, and he watched as the Zealot with the spear, tried to free it, as it was caught in Publius' muscle. Marcus roared like a lion and stepped over his wounded signifier. He had the Zealot's attention for a split second as he swung his gladius at the man's neck. Marcus screamed like a barbaric savage as the head separated from the shoulders, sending up a torrent of blood as the decapitated corpse rolled back into the Jewish ranks.

"Come get me!" Marcus screamed with widened eyes of insanity as streaks of blood covered his face and soaked his armour. He did not have time to stare at the piles of dead comrades around him as their crushed, pulverized bodies lay in heaps mixed with the torn and mutilated bodies of the Zealots. "You bastards!" Marcus shouted as he tasted blood in his mouth. He swung his sword at them which sliced the air, and shouted, "Forward! Give no ground!" At the same time he could hear a new cry going up from the rear and Marcus glanced back as his wounded, bloodied troopers stumbled around him with raised shields to protect their Tribune. A surge of hope suddenly raced through his veins, charging him with an invincible power, as he watched hundreds of alae pour from the north corner of the Antonia. The Zealots also noticed the threat and with weapons lowered, they cautiously began to distance themselves from the Romans as their ranks in the rear fell back.

Marcus' chest heaved as he gasped, stepping over the bodies which lay strewn before him. He squinted, as a look of surprise came over him, and then suddenly called out, "I know you!" He raised his sword and pointed the blade at a prominently dressed Jewish fighter with a bristling beard and deep eyes. He was one of the few Zealots who wore a breastplate, and the way men gathered around him showed that he was a man of rank. "I know you, I have seen you before!" Marcus shouted again with a sore, parched throat. He watched as a large, giant of a man with a leveled spear, stepped in front to protect the Jewish captain.

Marcus lowered his gladius, staring with sullen, cold eyes across the bloodied streets as the Zealots backed further and further away. He wished the Jew would call out but not a word was said and Marcus wondered if he even understood him.

"Tribune Maximus!" called the decurion. "The alae have arrived!"

Marcus turned and watched as hundreds of Syrians and Thracians poured past the battered cavalry troopers and charged the Zealots who suddenly turned and fled back the way they had come. Marcus shook his head and gave a sigh of relief. "Send for doctors immediately. Collect the wounded and get them attention now!" He wiped the sweat and blood from his face, then approached Publius' body. "That man saved my life," Marcus muttered as he stared down at the lifeless body of his signifer, lying in a pool of dark blood with the spear still driven into his shoulder.

"He bled to death, there was nothing we could do," replied a soldier in a choked, broken voice. Publius' head lay in the soldier's lap as he knelt before Marcus with a wad of bloody bandages in his hand.

Marcus gave a heavy nod, reached forward and closed the eyelids of the corpse. "You fought well." He stood slowly and with weary eyes, stared at the dead before him. Marcus swore under his breath and grunted as he longed for a drink. "Decurion!"

The junior officer waded through the bodies and saluted Marcus as he snapped to attention. "Tribune?"

"Have surgeons collect the dead and wounded. Have the men pull back to the Camp of the Assyrians. There will be no patrol today," Marcus replied in a soft and distant voice.

*   *   *

CHAPTER XXXVIII

Later that day
Tunnels below the Temple Mount
Afternoon

Judah's muscles still ached from the bitter fight of the morning. He had washed the blood from his arms and legs, sharpened his sword, and changed into a clean garment. Zechariah had praised Judah for his bravery and had recited a blessing of thanks from the *Tehillim* at his preservation from the battle which had claimed so many lives. However, Zechariah never dwelt on the loss of life, he would only tend to the wounded and bless them with kindness as he would sing the songs of David to restore peace. Now, Zechariah sat silently, in a deep state of pondering, at the mouth of the large tunnel beneath the Temple platform where the miners had begun their excavations.

The aging priest watched silently as a column of men entered the mine followed by small, handheld push carts that would come rolling out every couple of minutes piled with earth and stone. Zechariah listened to the constant thuds of the picks and chisels working away deep within the mine as voices were hushed and men laboured in the stuffy, arid space. As the mine deepened and dipped further beneath the Antonia, men fixed small torches to the walls inside to give light.

Judah was in charge of the work detail, and he took his duties seriously as he learned from the Jewish mining team and directed traffic among the workers to clear the rubble and strengthen the roof of the mine with beams of timber. Enormous amounts of dried faggots began to be piled at the entrance next to where Zechariah sat, so much that eventually the priest had to move out of the way as pots of pitch were also stacked for future use. Every so often Judah would appear at the mouth of the tunnel and say a few words to Zechariah who seemed most interested in the project. Each time, Judah would invite the priest down to inspect their work, but the priest would just shake his head and rub his thin beard. Zechariah would state that prayer was more important than his opinion on something he knew nothing of.

"Where is Judah?"

Zechariah looked up and gave a thin smile at the hulking form of John of Gischala who stood before him with a group of six men. The old priest reached out a frail hand and John helped him up. "He is deep in the mine. He says they have begun to tunnel under the foundation stones of the Antonia."

"That is good. They have been at it for three days now; the Antonia will be the hardest part," John said glancing down the tunnel.

"That is what Judah says," Zechariah remarked with a light chuckle.

John scowled slightly at the old man and touched his shoulder tenderly. "Why are you down here? The air is not good. You should be above ground, Zechariah. You could get hurt down here."

"Nonsense, a man must pray, shouldn't he?" Zechariah stepped back and touched one of the stacks of dried faggots. "You go on down, I shall be okay here."

John eyed the priest one last time, then giving a nod, signaled for his men to follow and they trotted off down the dank tunnel. John traced the cool stone walls with his fingers as he squinted from every torch he passed. The main tunnel they entered would lead to a clothing chamber for priestly vestments, but that is not where he would be going. This was the tunnel the miners had discovered which was the best place to dig from as it was nearest the Antonia.

John stepped aside and called for his men to do the same as a cart rolled past pushed by four men, their bodies streaked in sweat and dirt. John patted the shoulder of the man nearest him and received a bright smile upon a filthy face, then the cart plodded onward. Silently, John signaled his men forward and soon they reached a large hole in the wall of the tunnel, barely wide enough for a man to enter. John crouched down and peered through the adjacent shaft as he could hear the chipping of stone from clanging hammers upon chisels.

"This is supposed to bring down the ramps?" whispered one of John's men causing the warlord to glance over his shoulder.

"Don't worry, they will widen it. It is unwise to make it so wide to begin with, especially working off a pre-existing tunnel and then digging under the weight of the Antonia. We don't want to collapse it." John paused for a moment and then waved them forward. He ducked into the narrow tunnel, feeling as if the walls would close in and crush him. He soon found himself panting for air amidst the space as fewer and fewer torches lined the walls. Finally he began to pass men with beams of timber who were fixing them against the walls and roof, reinforcing areas deemed weak. John squeezed past the men, walked a few more metres and then found the shaft beginning to widen.

Soon he found himself walking through a mine at least two metres wide with a ceiling of three metres in height. The marks of chisels and picks could be seen upon the walls and roof of the mine as he continued on nearly in the dark. One of John's men coughed and complained about the smell to which he just replied, "We can't burn too many torches down here. We will lose the air."

The men continued on until they finally reached a part of the mine that was even wider, as enormous hewn stones were revealed upon the ceiling. John halted and stared upward as he panted for air. "That is the outer wall of the Antonia." The Zealots said nothing and John continued steadying his pace until he finally found the workers.

A cluster of eight carts stood waiting to be removed as they were filled with rubble and earth. A group of men sat upon the floor resting and when they noticed John, they scrambled to their feet, humbly nodded and began rolling the carts out. John walked around for a moment watching twenty men at work with iron tools as they dug into the earth and pulled out boulders, which they rolled to the side to be split later. Judah spotted John standing among the workers, and strolled over to the Zealot warlord.

"You are making great progress. This is looking good," John said as he stared up at the ceiling.

"It was a slow start, but we are finally coming to easier ground to dig through. The hardest part was around the Antonia, we didn't want to widen the mine too much." Judah peered at John through the dim light and saw the inquisitive commander rub his beard.

"Where are you now in relation to the ramps?" John asked.

Judah shrugged. "They should be right on top of us, that is what Eliyahu reports. I don't understand fully how he does it above ground, but he manages. Twice, I have heard activity above. We are moving as quietly as possible. Amos says nobody is to call out and we have to chip at the stone with lighter taps." Judah paused for a moment and pointed straight ahead of where he stood. "We have to dig much further and widen it more as we try and encompass as much of the ramps as possible. Then when we light the fire, the heat will cause the ceiling to give way and crumble the earthworks above."

"Excellent. When will you be ready?" queried John.

Judah shook his head. "We have had men digging nearly all day and night for the last three days, but work has been progressively slower as we push deeper under the Roman ramps. There is no way to fully tell when we will be done, we can only guess."

John scowled in the dark. "What is Eliyahu's guess then?"

Judah left John for a moment, then returned with the short miner whose hair was matted in dirt and hands were black, but the crack of a grin could be seen upon his face as it was clear the man was proud of his work. "At this rate, maybe a week or more," Eliyahu said, getting right to the point. "We cover more ground during the day when everything is noisier above, but the night is slow." He shrugged and rubbed his hands together. "We might get three to four metres in total; it's just too slow at night."

"Can't we have men on the walls at night to see if their sentries get close to the ramps?" John asked, searching for a solution to complete the mine sooner.

Eliyahu shook his burly head and stepped closer to John. "It's the vibrations I am worried about. With the type of stone above us, and the street, vibrations can be felt for quite some distance if we have too much activity going on down here. We cannot risk that. John, if you want this to work, and for the Romans to suspect nothing, we can't move much faster."

"I see," John replied as he took a step away from Eliyahu and Judah to observe the workers.

"John, I can try and commit more workers if you want, but we risk being heard. Plus the air can be a problem with too many bodies," Eliyahu stated bluntly as he gave Judah a glance for help.

"We will finish the mine and it will work, John," Judah added.

John was silent for a moment and then turned. "What worries me is the rate the earthworks are rising daily and the distance we still have to go in order to destroy them both. Preservation of the Antonia, is key. The ramp to the east against the Temple Mount is not important. Do you not notice that Titus has directed most of the workers to the ramps against the Antonia? We must complete the mine and bring down the ramps. I estimate the Romans will be done in ten days or less." John paused for a second and glanced at the front of the mine. "How long will it take to ready it to burn?"

"At least a day," Eliyahu replied. "We will begin covering the ceiling in supporting beams that will be held up by pillars of wood within. Then we will fill the entire space with faggots and bitumen soaked in pitch, then light it."

"It will burn very fast and very hot. Nobody should be in the mine but the man to light it." Judah looked at Eliyahu. "Plus, the entire mine under the ramps will collapse. We will never be able to dig here again."

John gave a heavy nod, then squatted and picked up a few shards of stone from the floor. He had mentioned to Judah the night before his desire to try and leave a possibility for another mine to be dug later on, in the case that the Romans attempted to rebuild. But he knew and understood, that the possibility of a second mine after the cave in was extremely unlikely for everywhere around it, including the ground that did not collapse, would be very unstable.

"Thank you, Eliyahu, and keep up the work," John mumbled half-heartedly.

The miner bowed graciously and returned to his supervision over a number of men who were digging near the ceiling. John watched the little man climb up to where the diggers were and touch the rock as he stared at the floor in deep concentration. Then he signaled to Amos and after a brief discussion, Eliyahu's brother trotted past John, disappearing down the tunnel.

"You fought well today, Judah," John said, cutting the silence between the two. Judah gave a weary nod but remained quiet. John walked over to him and whispered, "You led a precise attack that was high risk, but you did it well. Your men nearly destroyed the Boars. I thought you may like that opportunity to strike at your old foe."

"They fought well for the odds not being in their favour," Judah replied as he rubbed his aching arms. "It was under the command of Marcus Sulla where my Lions were betrayed and slaughtered." Judah sighed as he thought back to the treachery of the Roman he had spared, Quintus. "I remember that day all too well, the choking smoke and the terrible butchery as Marcus' men came down into the caves."

"Well, that day has been avenged, unless you are intent on killing Marcus Sulla. You must have wiped out close to half his men. The Boars are finished as a unit, at least for now," John replied. "Your honour has been restored, Judah. What Yehoram accused you of does not hold weight in my eyes. You fought bravely, like a patriot of Israel. Your strike was swift and the edge of your sword lethal; the Romans cannot forget you. Marcus knows you and will report to Titus about how deadly your attack was. Titus will quake with fear as he knows that more relentless strikes await him and his men. The legions will be destroyed before our walls, for that I vow to you."

"I thank you, John. I have only ever had the city's defence in my best interest. Yehoram speaks of what he does not know." Judah stepped close to John and whispered, "I fear that if we are victorious over Titus, and the Romans leave, that Simon will renew his struggle against you."

A look of understanding came upon John's face. "You speak the truth, I am afraid you are right. Simon's heart is corrupt and filled with jealousy. I never once have thought his alliance is a genuine bid for peace. This pact we have has only been a necessary step to defeating the Romans.

"Once this is complete, Simon will become my enemy. We can only hope that the people of this city will realize the same and will unite around us to drive him and his Idumeans from the city by the points of our spears." John watched three carts filled with dirt and rubble roll slowly past him followed by the strained grunts of the men pushing them. "Judah, we have so much to focus on at this moment, and the ramps are essential. I firmly believe that if the Antonia falls, the Temple will be exposed. Titus knows this, no doubt. He is well informed by his councilmen, particularly Agrippa and Yosef." John suddenly swore as he stared at the foul, mire which covered the dirt floor of the tunnel. "I should have killed Yosef when I had the chance years ago. There is so much I regret, you know." John looked up with moist eyes and stared at Judah.

"Like what?" Judah quietly asked.

John shrugged. "I should never have left Gischala like I did, especially abandoning the women and children of my men." Judah was quiet as John confessed soberly. He brushed his hands across the sides of his great bear-of-a-face and then wiped his damp forehead with the edge of his cloak. "We were surrounded, Judah. Titus had over a thousand horses and rumour was that half a legion of troops were on the move to seal us in. It was only a matter of time. We had seen what had happened at Jotapata and Gamla, and we did not want to share in their fate. I wanted to stand and fight, but the men had wives and children in the city. There were not enough of us, maybe five hundred. Gischala had walls and a few towers, but the reality was we would not be able to man them all. The defences were nothing in comparison to other cities and we knew that once the Romans breached them, we would all be slaughtered and our families crucified.

"So, I brokered a treaty with Titus and sent him word that we would surrender after the Shabbat, for it was only erev." John looked up at Judah and although a dark shadow was upon the warlord's face, Judah could sense the grief in his broken voice. "Titus agreed to the terms," John continued. "During the night we fled. It only took us an hour to assemble and we slipped through the sentry line, killed three of Titus' guards, and made our escape for Jerusalem."

John sniffed; his voice shuddered as he spoke. "Titus wouldn't have even discovered we had left for at least six hours. I heard later, that at dawn the next morning it was an elderly Jew who opened the gates and called out to Titus informing him we had left. While we had been in the city, much of the townsfolk opposed us, believing our presence there would be the end of them. That is partially why we left, but I knew the moment we were gone, and light split the horizon, we would be given up by our own brothers." John sounded bitter as he spit upon the floor. "They could have given us another day, or at least hours more until the Romans discovered the dead guards. We could have all made it, Judah." This last statement was made as John rested a heavy hand upon Judah's shoulder and stared at him with pleading eyes.

"I heard later that Titus entered the town, searched the homes as it must have quickly become apparent that the Jew spoke the truth. What happened next I will carry for the rest of my life," John said as he gave a heavy sigh, his arm becoming like dead weight upon Judah's shoulder. "I had given the order for us to leave Gischala in the first place, but my men had pleaded with me not to separate them from their families. I gave in and allowed the women and children to accompany us, but they could not keep up and they slowed us down." A glisten of tears could be seen in the dim light as they streamed down John's face. He grunted and quickly wiped them away with shame. "I knew we had lost valuable time and so did my men. With the unthinkable before us all, I gave the order to leave them. I ordered my men to leave their wives and children in the wilderness, the very flesh and blood of their bodies. The cries of the children and the wailing of the women haunt me, Judah. I will never be free of the guilt and the innocent blood that follows me."

John was still for a moment and then said, "I gave my men only minutes to say their farewell. Men hugged their wives, kissed them, stroked the heads of their children, and wept. It was clear, by surveying the land around us that there would be no place they could hide. Duty was before us. We had to continue to fight. My men knew this to be true, but the pain of separation and the knowledge that they would all likely be killed was an incredible torment for my men to bear, for me to bear." John's voice sounded empty and far off as he mumbled, "We left them! Only one of my men refused and he stayed behind, he was the better of us all. None of the other men even objected to my face, but the look of pain and agony could be read in their eyes, and I knew they would never forgive me. They all knew we had no other choice."

John paused. "We reached Jerusalem and our trick against Titus worked, but I heard reports from peasants that Titus caught up with the women and children and killed them all. He found them heading west, Judah. Even though we had abandoned them for death, the wives of my men had led their little children across the lonely hills to the west so that Titus would be cast off course and never find us. Even in betrayal our loved ones never forsook us, as we forsook them. Their blood has soaked the earth and cries out for their husbands and fathers. It was something I can never ask of my men ever again, they sacrificed so much."

"John, you did not sentence them to death," Judah uttered. "This war has brought suffering upon us all, and that is owed to Rome, and Rome only. Titus could have spared them; their blood is upon his hands, not yours."

John gave a bitter chuckle. "You really believe that? You should learn from your own words, Judah. What of your Miriam then? You still blame yourself, I know you do, yet it was Gessius Florus who gave the order that killed her. Why not let go of that, Judah? We men are wretched things. We fail the ones we should protect and sell our lives dearly. We always have a choice, it is just what we truly wish to sacrifice that matters. I chose to fight again and come to the aid of Jerusalem to defend her, which was our highest priority, and in so choosing, we had to give up the fate of all those women and children. You had a choice as well, Judah, you also chose the path of war," John replied in a grim voice as he wiped tears away from his moist cheeks.

"You are wrong, John. My choice to fight was forced upon me. It was out of my hands. The war had not even started and Miriam was separated from me when the cohort attacked. She was struck down and killed in the midst of the chaos, and I could do nothing," Judah said with a choked up voice, terrified to admit the possibility that he may have been able to prevent it.

John grinned at Judah through the darkness of the tunnel as men continued to work around them. "True, you could not have done anything, but you should have seen it coming. Only a few of us did. But you are wrong about one thing, Judah. The war didn't just begin when Gessius Florus dispatched his murderous cohort. It had begun much earlier, but you just chose to ignore it. Rome had oppressed our people since the days of Herod when the Zealots rose up and threw off the shackles of pagan Rome and said 'No!' It was no mistake that Zealots based themselves in the Galilee and hid in the caves of Arbel, choosing when and how to strike at the Romans. The Romans and the Hellenists branded us as treacherous thieves and murderers and crucified us whenever they could. But, we grew in strength and number and continued to take the fight to them." John shook his head, "The war had been happening for fifty years before Miriam died that day. Judah, your desire to lead a quiet and comfortable life by taking over what your abba had built was nothing more than a dream. It was wishful thinking and grounded in illogic. The legions were destined to arrive here one day; you just chose not to accept it, not to see it."

"Many of us did not want this, John. Many of the Pharisees even claimed that God had sent the Romans because of our disobedience."

John shook his head in defence and scowled at Judah. "Then they too were misguided. How could a Jew in his right mind, not bought by Roman indulgence, even claim such a thing? We Zealots fought for God's kingdom on earth, for all filthy rags to be stripped clean and cast aside. How could such men urge us to bow down and continue to serve Rome by our very blood? In the time of the Maccabees, things of that nature were shouted from the roof tops from Jews loyal to the Syrian-Greeks, and in the village of Modi'in, Matityahu cast them down by the blade of his sword at the foot of Zeus' altar, declaring, 'Whoever has zeal for the Torah and the commandments follow me!' Judgment and punishment will befall anyone who deems they know the heart of God and yet oppose us. We stand here today in opposition to Rome because we know this is God's city and His Holy Temple."

"John, you mustn't preach to me! I talk not of opposing Rome, but the method. You lecture me of the idolatry of Rome and I agree with you. What I merely seek to tell you is that we too cannot know the mind of God. What if Rome was ordained by HaShem to rule over us because we have turned away? It happened in the past with Assyria and Babylon…even the prophets proclaimed judgment from the walls and dungeons."

John placed his hands upon his hips and stared at Judah as a glow of orange danced upon his face from a flickering torch nearby. "I do not question your loyalty, Judah. I know where your allegiance lies. What worries me is if your heart has wandered from our cause."

Judah firmly gazed at his commander and gathered his thoughts. "My allegiance lies with defending this city and fighting by your side. I want to believe that we are doing the will of God, there are priests and teachers who preach such things from the Temple courts and synagogues, but I am afraid they might be wrong."

"You must trust in the anointment upon their lips and from the success we will have when these tunnels bring down the ramps." John raised his hands in the air and stared at the roof. "I understand things look bleak, I have felt them before, truly I have, but we must stand firm and not question our role in this war. God will intervene, this city cannot come to ruin. We fight for the name of God in this land. The men of Israel and Judah in the old days were overthrown because their hearts were corrupt and given to idols. We seek to smash those idols! God will not abandon us to ruin, but He is using us to purify this land like King Josiah did, and turn things back to ancient days before the divided kingdom. Men will turn their hearts back to Torah, and all influence, whether Roman or Greek, shall fade away with the blood of the Gentiles which we spill." John rested both hands on Judah's shoulders and stared into the eyes of his Captain. "You and Adam are instruments of war, and your swords have been guided by angels to win battles! This is not over, Judah, the legions will be ruined and we shall see victory soon! I promise you!"

*   *   *

CHAPTER XXXIX

Everyone had been assembled. All legionary generals and commanders stood among the war council, as did the client kings of the alae. Chief Engineer Porcius Gracchus had also been summoned, along with Syrian Governor Cestius Gallus. The conniving Gessius Florus lurked in the background behind Gallus, and every Praefectus Castrorum from the army was present, notably Gaius Antony. Titus had called the meeting to discuss the days ahead, even opening up the council to the men of the *aquilifer* and tribunes, which simply meant he desired the opinion of Marcus Sulla Maximus, who stood casually behind Gaius staring up at the roof as if the whole meeting was a waste of time.

"I have called you here to discuss the first of my orders," Titus began as he scanned the faces of the men. "The ramps are nearing completion and soon I intend to unleash the fury of the legions upon this city. Up until now we have been fighting with one arm tied behind our back. I have offered truce after truce to the Jews, but soon that will come to an end. I fully intend to crush this rebellion and the doorway to do this is through the Antonia.

"Attacks will continue against the First Wall; with Simon's forces kept at bay, this will give us the chance to concentrate efforts on breaching the Antonia walls by collapsing them. Three ramps are nearly finished, and I will deploy siege towers and engineering crews to weaken the wall and dislodge stones. I have discussed this course of action with Tiberius and we are of one accord. To support the attack, every *scorpio* and onager available will be used as cover fire against the Antonia defences. We shall also use heavy artillery fire from our *ballistarii* along with Palmyrene and Syrian archers. We must clear their ramparts and wipe out any resistance that can get between us and completing our task. Archers will be stationed on the ground and upon what remains of the Second Wall." Titus paused and pointed at the Antonia on the map and made a cutting slice with his finger across the layout of the fortress to the west colonnades of the Temple Mount. "Once we have taken the Antonia's walls, the entire fortress will crumble and the Temple will be open before us. I plan to have a couple dozen scorpio engines stationed upon its towers and then raze the western colonnades and torch the gates for a clear passage in. The other option is to construct

a ramp along the western colonnade that will be accessible to the Temple's defences."
Titus smiled, "It shall be over soon, I assure you."

"My Prince," Larcius Lepidus interjected, clearing his throat. "The rebels are bound to fight to the last to control the Antonia, and use whatever means to do so. We should count on a secondary wall within their own defences, as well as heighten our siege towers to clear their ramparts; we may need to breach their walls by way of the legionaries storming the Jewish parapets."

Titus glanced at Tiberius and gestured for him to answer. The seasoned commander did so with a steady voice as he eyed Lepidus and pointed to the map. "The Prince and I *expect* the Jews to build a counter defence, this is likely. However, the second wall will not be as strong and should not be a problem for us to extend the ramp and smash that down. Besides, if we are able to undermine the Antonia's walls or the tower at the western corner, we may very well destroy any second wall they have built. The fortress' stones are massive and heavy. If they topple they will crush anything in its path as well as provide us with a natural breach. Either way, Porcius' ramps will provide us with an elevated, tactical advantage in which the rams in the towers will be able to effectively bring down the walls, we estimate in four days. The Jews will be powerless to put a stop to it.

"The siege towers will also be used against the First Wall, and should be able to do considerable damage on those defences which are incomparable to the Antonia. Using the towers on the Antonia, however, will most definitely bring about higher casualties as we attempt to force our way onto their ramparts, but the essential purpose must be to breach their walls. That is our only way to effectively take the Antonia."

"General Alexander," Tribune Octavian said raising his voice. "I do believe we could breach their walls with our towers if we muster a vexilliatio of our best and storm the enemy parapets. We have trained for this, and if we can clear the walls and gain control, we should be able to drive the Zealots away and open the gates for the army. This will be swifter than depending on the rams to smash through the thick stone, and if I am not mistaken, will take a great effort to do any considerable damage, let alone bring down the wall."

"I have considered that and for the time being it is out of the question," interrupted Titus. "Not only would the butcher's bill be high putting all of our focus on storming the fortress, but you would be facing the best of John's men. He has catapults along with scorpio engines and could shoot them directly into our men coming from the towers, which would be devastating. There would be no way for us to clear such machines from the Antonia's turrets and your men would be struck down in droves. The towers will be able to weaken the walls enough to undermine them and are fortified enough to withstand scorpio fire, but a direct attack from the towers upon their ramparts would be too costly." Titus watched Octavian back down with a nod. "Everyone will be committed to this effort, even the *equites legionis* from each legion will take part. We will commence as soon as the ramps are complete and will focus all our effort on these two points: the Antonia and the First Wall." Titus stared across the table at his chief engineer and calmly asked, "Porcius, do you have anything to add?"

The older man pressed his chin against his chest causing his jowls to crease with wrinkles of flabby skin as he concentrated on the map. Then he gave a hoarse grunt and nodded. "Certainly, I do have something to say, my Prince. If you would allow me for a moment," Porcius sputtered as he moved around the table for a closer look and then produced a tiny measuring tool which he leaned over the map and did some calculations to the amusement of the generals. Then the squat, paunchy engineer slipped his measuring tool away and glanced around the table. "We have three ramps, with a space of ten metres between each earthwork. This is done so that the towers are not too close, and for crews to work between them where they can attempt to loosen the foundation. I have built siege works against many forts and cities in my life, and this is by far the largest project I have undertaken.

"The size of the stones, which General Alexander speaks of, is the truth. They are large and cumbersome bastards which will be near impossible to see them moved! Crews with picks, hammers, and crowbars will be needed. They can work on them all day and I am not sure how successful they will even be."

"The only way to find out is to try," grumbled Sextus Cerealis who stood next to Larcius.

"Truly, you are correct," spoke the engineer fluently and not wasting a moment. Porcius gazed at the Prince and slowly said, "This task will demand everything from the men, I merely wish the Prince to understand this."

"The legionaries of the Fulminata will be deployed, I only ask of the highest service from these troops, they will not fail," Marcus Octavian quickly said in their defence.

"With the strength of Heracles, I do believe you," replied Porcius as he crossed his arms.

Titus gazed between his engineer and Octavian, then sighed. "I will have Legio Fulminata in charge of the Antonia deploying such crews to the ramps. The Macedonica will share the struggle and advance with the towers and assault the walls. I want six cohorts deployed throughout the day and a double guard at night. I will not risk another devastating sally from these rebels.

"In the meantime, I want the Mishneh captured with lethal force and reduced to rubble. That duty shall fall upon the Fretensis. Do not fail me, Larcius. I will draw up orders soon for the assault. I want a complete envelopment of the entire quarter. Spare no one. Phalerae of great worth will be rewarded to officers who are complicit and use the necessary force to see this done. I intend to continue to use Yosef ben Matityahu. Even if he is unsuccessful, his words demoralize them.

"I want to increase pressure on these rebels, have them begging for mercy and wishing they would accept my gratitude. On the first day we attack the walls of the

Antonia, I want thirty prisoners crucified before their walls. I want their eyes put out, ears cut off, and their tongues removed. Let this be a sign of things to come when they reject my mercy. Remember this saying of the great orator Cicero, *'Silent enim leges inter arma,'* and it shall be good for you. Tell this to your men, for we are to become beasts before this work is to be done.

"The Fulminata and Macedonica will concentrate on the Antonia, and the Fretensis and Apollinaris will occupy the front of the First Wall and take the Mishneh. I will not play their games any longer. Be vigilant and aware of renewed sallies from the Jews. Today, we were caught asleep and if it hadn't been for Marcus Sulla's Boars, the ramps could have been overtaken." Titus gave the group a sudden heated stare and then pointed firmly at the map. "I will not be made a mockery of! One hundred and thirty of Marcus' troops were slaughtered, yet they fought valiantly and did not retreat." Titus paused and then calmly said, "If it hadn't been for the quick assault by King Agrippa's spear troops, I fear the Boars would have been ruined. Protect the ramps like you would your own family!"

The tent was silent as everyone considered Titus' words. It seemed the Prince had brought the fight to a new level as everyone began to sense the true bitterness of the fight that awaited them. Up until this point, the assaults had been cautious to preserve conquered ground, and prudent against the sudden Jewish attacks. Many of the men wondered where this sudden vigour came from, and then they got their answer as Titus produced a rolled manuscript bound by a purple ribbon.

Titus held the letter aloft for a moment, saying nothing. Then he cut the ribbon, broke the wax seal and unfurled it saying, "This letter was dispatched to me from Alexandria. It bears the seal of our Lord Emperor Vespasian, and reads, *'To my son Titus, who commands the legions of Judea, encamped in siege around Jerusalem. Greetings from the divine seat of Roma in Alexandria. May the fortune of the gods go before you and guide each cohort and century. May the name of Jupiter and Mars be bathed in the glory that guards Roma. I do write you with confidence that this great war in which we are so decisively entrenched in, will no doubt see victory and our eagles and standards paraded through the city. Jerusalem will be a city of the past, never to rise again to greatness, and the gods of the east have proclaimed this to be true in their wisdom.*

However, upon the eve of my setting sail for Roma, I must implore you to make great haste in seeing this matter closed. It is imperative for the empire that you not lack in any hesitation to crush this rebellion, nor can I let its existence wane in the minds of those seated in power throughout the provinces. As Pontifex Maximus and Emperor, I do swear to you that fortune and glory awaits you in Roma and a triumph through the city as you carry your trophies and spoils before the crowds. This war will be accounted for in the annals of history and you will be remembered forever. Yet, to achieve this, all resources must be spent and all pressure poured upon the Jewish rebels to bring a swift close to this matter before the winter months. I know you will not fail this oath which you have taken, nor bring disaster and shame upon the glory that is Roma. Resolve this and restore the Pax Romana as

I wish. I demand victory and so do the senatus populusque romanus. I have all faith in you, Titus, that you will crush the rebellion and return to Roma with honour.'"

Titus lowered the letter to the silence of his commanders. He stared around the tent and gently tossed the manuscript upon the table for all to see. The golden emperor seal caught the light from the hanging chandelier of burning oil lamps above as all eyes fell upon it for an instant to verify its authenticity. "We need to become ruthless. I do not state that we have been lax, but I will make this point clear. The Emperor has ordered us to close this matter, and the only way is straight through the Antonia to the Temple. To achieve this goal is a simple task; we must bring down the walls and slaughter anyone in our way, thereby giving us the glory my father demands! You are dismissed!"

Gessius Florus gently pushed past the generals, tribunes, and camp prefects as they exited the quarters. Florus could hear many of the men discussing among themselves in hushed whispers how Vespasian's letter might alter the siege, but that was not his care as he made his way to the Prince.

"I would like my quarters cleared, Florus. I require to be left alone," Titus said, glaring at the former procurator of Judea.

"Certainly, my Prince. I simply wished to extend my sincere congratulations on the war against the rebels thus far and wanted to say that I am sure your command here has far exceeded the expectations of the Emperor." Gessius bowed humbly and turned to leave.

"What do you want?" Titus asked, caught off guard by the sudden charm in the procurator's voice. He watched Gessius turn and play with the rings on his plump fingers as a sly grin broke his somber face.

"To have a chance at command, my Prince," Gessius replied, getting straight to the point. "I merely watch this siege from the doorway of my tent. Cestius Gallus commissioned me to accompany him when we arrived here in the early days of spring, but under what need, I am unsure of. I would formally request a command to regain my honour and assist you in this great campaign."

"Why would I grant such a request unto you? Your role in this whole rebellion has a stench of anarchy to it. The Third Gallica was nearly wiped out, and you left a cohort behind to get slaughtered at Herod's Palace, just so you could live. Then the garrison at Cypros, near Jericho, was wiped out by the rebels. Blood spilled and for what purpose? It could have been avoided, stopped, but you pushed the Jews too far." Titus watched the proud Florus clasp both hands behind his back and raise his chin as darkness seemed to creep into the edges of his eyes. Florus said nothing, yet his stiff, tense frame betrayed otherwise, as his jaw tightened and his breathing became rife with anger. Titus sighed and shook his head. "I have read the letters and manuscripts sent by delegations of the Sanhedrin at the time of Nero. Yosef has even told me firsthand of the things you have done." Titus raised his chin and stared at the groveling man. "You pushed them, Gessius, you pushed them into an impossible corner."

Gessius shook his head against this accusation. "For the glory of the empire, my Prince, that is all I cared about. The Jews were up to rebellion long before I was given this post. Judea needed to be cleaned of rebels; Nero commissioned me to do that. I united the Greeks in the land. Sepphoris and Caesarea Maritima are evidence of my good graces. The Jews had dark thoughts of this government. They despised Roma and I brought it out into the light. They seek to have no such alliance, my Prince, they never have."

"We have good relations with Jews in Alexandria, Roma, and Ephesus, as well as other cities. Why not here?" Titus retorted.

"Yet, in Alexandria, as in other cities of the empire, the Jews have been attacked and killed for their scheming. They cannot be trusted," Gessius stated raising an eyebrow.

"There is no conspiracy, Florus. Those attacks were not perpetuated by my command nor did I sanction such atrocities. The Jews, for the most part, are good citizens of the empire." Titus paused for a moment and then sighed. "I have read the edicts you passed while you were procurator, and I can see very well how they would be construed as offensive. You gave these people nothing but an arrogant voice and you cared not to understand them."

"All a façade, my Prince. In my defence, hear the truth. I have ruled over the Jews for a long time, and they seek not a will of goodness. I brought to them the end of my consular rod, nothing else. I evoked the full measure of Roman law here and saw it spit upon. Nero defended me and so will your father once this is over." Gessius watched Titus' face twitch with this last comment and he bowed again. "Your family is rich and illustrious. You come from a proud line that looks to the future, my Prince. The Flavians will thank me for what I did here. My actions helped make your father an Emperor!"

"Careful what you say, Gessius. You seem to desire to take the place of what the gods have willed. The omens have been favourable and your ruckus in this land has been ill favoured, like Governor Pilate during the time of Agrippa's father. He dealt harshly with the Jews and nearly pushed them into rebellion. It wasn't until a stern word from Caesar Augustus himself that Pilate finally surrendered. Now, you seek to turn it around as if you have done the Flavian line a favour? You are mistaken and forget yourself.

"My father ascended through strength and swift action. He was chosen by Basilides and not by your whims as procurator. Now I, one who is destined to be Emperor one day, must clean up your wretched mess in this land. Do I thank you? You only provided a step from whence to walk from, nothing more. This was ordained in the heavens, Gessius, long before you ever sacked the market place and killed those thousands. You had no part in my father becoming emperor, nor shall a favour be bestowed upon you." Titus paused as he walked over to a small table and plucked a few figs from a bowl. "Get out, now," he said coldly and Gessius left.

*   *   *

May 28th, 70 A.D. / 2nd of Sivan, 3830
Lower City of Jerusalem
Evening

Follow me and do not hesitate, were the words Adam had spoken which kept coming back to Judah as he followed the giant man. Behind him walking at a brisk pace, was Zechariah, who had covered his head with the edge of his long garment so he was not noticed. Adam did not slow his pace as he pressed onward, leading the two men down the narrow, dirty streets of the Lower City.

Beggars littered the alleys and street corners calling out for mercy as the men passed by. Many of the poor were crippled or blind and they laid on mats of straw in the filth and muck piled up on the sides. Insects filled the air as garbage sat in piles covered in maggots, while waste gathered in pools from men and women who had no other place to defecate. Sounds of misery were clear as they would pass homes where mourners gathered, their sobs and wails echoing down the winding streets. People would hobble by with downcast, hopeless stares plastered upon their faces, as Adam, Judah, and Zechariah plunged deeper into the labyrinth of crammed housing.

Judah guessed Zechariah must have noticed the look of disgust upon his face after seeing another beggar with festering sores, for the aging priest said in a calming voice, "The work before you is of degradation. There is no food and nowhere for these people to go. They will starve here, Judah."

Judah gave a shocked look behind him, as if he wished for the old priest to be silenced, but he had not the strength to mutter anything. He watched the priest hesitate to recite a prayer from the *Tehillim* for a peddler who looked near death, and he winced as the sick man whispered something in return. Judah could see the dying man's chest, racked by hunger with ribs which looked as if they would suddenly snap forth and open the thin cavity. The man's face was retched with sores as they oozed with green pus upon blotched skin. Sunken eyes gazed without reason from sockets set deep into the skull. Yet, Zechariah blessed the man as a sputtering whimper fell from the beggar's split, bleeding lips. Then the priest apologized for having nothing to give and moved on leaving behind the helpless old man to die alone.

"There is nothing to be done," Zechariah spoke, anticipating Judah's demand, which won the priest another look of perplexity and shock from the young Captain. "This is the price we must all pay, Judah. The lives of these men, women, and children are upon our heads. There is no turning back. There is just the little good we can do, that is all. Put it from your mind, my son."

Judah ambled along as if in a drunken stupor with the priest's advice ringing in his ears. He had never experienced such grief before in his life. Judah had heard all the stories about what happened in the Lower City, but had never ventured to have a look for himself. Now he saw the tone in Adam's panic concerning his family, as he saw the horrid conditions with his own eyes, hating Simon ben Giora even more. The Lower City was under Simon's control, and the people had been neglected, abandoned to suffer in silence, reminded only of their torment when the wind would change direction.

Adam halted and quickly signaled Judah and Zechariah to the side of a home as he stared around the corner. "Two of Simon's men! We will wait until they are gone," Adam said with disdain as he clenched his fists and entertained the desire of drawing his sword and killing both of them.

"Those would be the first I have seen," Judah whispered.

Adam nodded. "Simon's men don't come down here too often anymore. There are lepers in the Lower City, and they are greatly feared." Adam turned and gazed at Judah and Zechariah. "The Idumeans keep to the ramparts on the First Wall and the Upper City."

"Where are we?" Judah replied, covering his nose from an unidentifiable stench that suddenly wafted around them.

"If we were to turn this corner and head east you would soon come to the paved street over the sewer which would lead you straight to the Siloam Pool." Adam sniffed and wiped the sweat from his forehead. "If we were to head west, you would find the aqueduct that runs out near the Gate of the Essenes."

Judah looked around as he got his bearings straight and then nodded. "Adam, you must forgive me if there was something I could have done much earlier to relieve your family of this suffering."

Adam looked deeply into Judah's eyes. "There was nothing you could have done."

The three men continued south, winding through the streets and passing the quiet, deathly sounds of the starving quarter. Children, matted with dirt and tormented by fleas, watched the men pass from the small windows of their homes. Despite the brilliance of the sun shining above in the blue sky, a suffering, close to that of *Gehenna,* surrounded them as the men traced the streets along the Tyropoeon Valley.

Adam finally halted before a small, crudely shaped door and gestured to the home. "This is where my family lives. My abba is Elisha and my ima is Ruth. My sisters, Hannah and Tamar do not know of you, Zechariah. Please say nothing until I have spoken to them. There are not many they trust and they will be suspicious."

"I will hold my voice, Adam. But when called upon, I will tell them everything, the risk they take, everything," Zechariah said in a whisper outside the door.

"I would expect nothing less of you, Zechariah." Adam glanced at Judah and laid a hand of friendship upon his shoulder. "I owe you my life, everything I have. How can I ever repay you, Judah?"

"I do this not for a price, my friend. You have served me well," Judah replied as Adam gently rapped on the door and made himself known in a whisper. The sound of a latch being lifted could be heard as the door creaked open and an elderly woman stood adorned in garments that reeked of sweat and mildew.

Judah saw the great heart of Adam break as the giant man stepped into the doorway and tenderly embraced his mother in love as he kissed both her cheeks. A thin smile escaped the sorrow upon her face as her eyes glittered with the sight of her son. Judah remained where he was, covering his sword with his outer garment, as he watched Adam present his mother with a gift tightly wrapped in cloth. Judah heard him whisper to her and saw a flutter of hope ignite upon the worn lines of her face as she realized Adam had smuggled them food.

"Ima," Adam said with a tinge of hesitancy as he gently stepped aside. "This is Judah ben Yosef, a man I owe my life to, and Zechariah the Priest."

"Adam, you bring a priest into the squalor of these streets?" Ruth asked in shock as she brushed a strand of hair away from her face. "You will be defiled, kind sir."

"I am on business with the favour of God, kind woman. I am here to help. Any defilement I touch is between God and me," Zechariah replied with a light tone.

Ruth gave Adam a puzzled look, then stepped forward, took Judah's hands in hers, and kissed them. "You have led my Adam through fire and he has served you faithfully. Whatever home we have left is yours, Judah ben Yosef."

Clearly moved, Judah's eyes watered as he searched the gentle face of Ruth. "I have no better man under my command," was all he could think of saying, but the affects of his words greatly emanated from her face as she held back tears.

"Hurry, we cannot tarry out here, come in." Ruth stepped aside and the men entered the home.

The door shut and Judah stared around the small dwelling, which reminded him a lot of the home Hadassah had lived in before he had placed her in the care of Mordechai ben Levi. The main room was dark, except for one burning oil lamp, and the rest of the house appeared gloomy and dirty. A number of straw mats covered the floor where Adam's father, Elisha, lay propped up by a couple of cushions. Next to him sat two young girls, their thin, pale faces staring at the strange men who entered with their brother.

"Adam, who have you brought to my house?" Elisha said weakly as he coughed.

"Abba, this is Judah ben Yosef, I have told you of him before," Adam quickly went to his father's side, crouched down, embraced him and kissed his face. Adam gave his sisters a smile and then continued, "He is the man I serve, Abba. He is a captain for John of Gischala and one I have fought under for years."

A smile spread across the weathered father's face as he peered up through the dim light at Judah. He repeated his name twice, then shook his head and smiled even further as he outstretched his hand to Judah. "Judah ben Yosef," Elisha's eyes brightened as Judah took the old man's wrinkly hand and squeezed it. "I have heard much of you and how my son respects your name. My house is open to you." Elisha continued to smile up at Judah, then gazed at Zechariah and said as his voice cracked, "You bring this Priest into my house? Adam, is this man blind? Does he not see such filth around?"

The hem of Zechariah's garments swished gently upon the floor as he knelt down next to Elisha and humbly nodded his grey head. "I have come at your son's beckoning and have come willingly."

"Abba, you must listen to what he has to say," Adam said as he motioned for his mother to sit. "He is an important man who seeks to help people like us."

"Very well, let the man speak," Elisha responded as he watched the priest sit and make himself comfortable.

"I am Zechariah, and I am here to offer you safe passage from the city, if you so choose. The future of this city is in God's hands, but we seek only to bring relief to those such as yourselves and the only way we can do that is by getting you outside of the walls. I will state right away that I will not give up the names of the men I am working with, in case you are captured by those loyal to Simon, for the price we would pay would be with our lives. But first, before I go further, do you wish to hear what I have to offer?" Zechariah gave Elisha a blank look as he waited for a response and finally the weak, old man gave a heavy nod.

"The men I am collaborating with are assembling fifty people of all classes that we seek to smuggle from the city in the early hours of morning two days from now. The city is suffering more and more, for that we cannot help. Any food stores and provisions are being used by John and Simon for soldiers, there is no use fighting it. Thus, any chance of survival must be thrown upon the Romans for mercy. It is true Titus has been merciful to those escaping the city, especially the innocent, and he has spared their lives."

"Where is he sending them?" Elisha asked seriously.

"Gophna."

"As slaves?"

Zechariah shook his head. "As freed men and women to rebuild the lives which they have lost. However, there is a great risk of death and for that I would strongly ask you to reconsider. I have instructed Adam about this and it is clear before me, you are poor and have no wealth. Many of those Jews with no wealth or status are simply sold as slaves or crucified. The legionaries are more likely to kill you than let you speak, and the chance of them having mercy is very unlikely. However, your son pressed me and so I have consented to offer this chance to you and your family. If anything ill is to happen upon your lives, I will not be held responsible. That is it, those are my terms." Zechariah stood. "I will need to know your answer now. I must leave soon."

Elisha gazed at Adam; he knew his son had gambled with his life by bringing this Priest and his Captain here. Elisha was familiar with the Idumean soldiers who regularly patrolled the foul streets. The Idumeans did not have a care in the world for the innocent people. They were wicked in his sight, unlike the dignity of their brethren who had left the city over a year ago after realizing they had been mislead. Elisha had been a stronger man then, and he had watched the endless columns of spearmen march away at dusk, as Simon ben Giora and his force bitterly jeered at them from the walls above Herod's Palace. That had been so long ago. The city had changed, and men had changed, but Elisha knew the time had come to put all that behind him and guard his family, even if the odds of survival were minimal.

Elisha reached out a hand and grunted. "Help me up, Adam."

"Abba?" Adam whispered with little protest as he quickly moved to his father's side and pulled him to his feet.

Elisha stood with trembling legs as he fought for strength. His arms were thin and body stricken with hunger, but he tightened his face and gritted his teeth as a flare of resolve flickered in his eyes. "Zechariah, you honour me with your presence. We will accept your offer. As head of this home I accept all responsibility; it is no longer on your head. My wife and I and two daughters will be among the people who wish to leave. May HaShem give you a steadfast mind and wisdom in executing the plan."

Zechariah was motionless as he stared at Elisha's condition, fighting the desire to intervene and refuse, but something inside cast him into silence. The Priest just nodded, turned and walked to the door. "I know my way back," he said. "You need not come, Judah," Zechariah held up his hand and pushed the latch down. "Be at the Gate of the Essenes at dawn two days from now. I will wait for you. Go in the shalom of HaShem, the Master of All, and the Timeless, Infinite One."

Elisha watched the Priest quietly leave the home and close the door behind him. He looked up at his son and sighed, "A priest in my home and I have nothing to offer, no bread, cheese, or wine."

"I brought bread, Abba," Adam quickly said as he gestured to his mother.

Despite his obvious hunger, Elisha turned and glanced at Judah. "So, my only son tells me you have another plan, and that I should hear you out. He says if I think Zechariah's plan is too dangerous then we can rely on yours. Well, I think Zechariah's plan *is* dangerous, dangerous for us." Elisha coughed as he sat back down and covered himself in his cloak. His breathing was raspy and he licked his thin lips, but finally he extended his arms outward for a moment and said nonchalantly, "You keep me waiting?"

"Abba, remember I trust this man. No matter what he says, he has reason," Adam interjected before Judah had a chance to begin. Elisha returned a puzzled look to his son and then nodded graciously.

Judah gave a warm smile and sat down upon the floor across from Elisha. Ruth, Hannah, and Tamar gathered around, all eyes upon the Jewish captain as he tried to weigh in his mind what their response might be once he told them. "To tell you plainly, I have a single man I trust of high stature who can ensure your survival should you get to him." Judah let his first statement sink in as he began to see a shroud of mystery unfold upon the desperate family. "Your presence with him would not be questioned, nor would any harm come to you. He would make sure you reached Gophna to start a new life together."

"Who is this man, you speak of, Judah? Come, no more riddles, tell us plainly of whom you speak of?" Elisha gently pressed.

"He is a Roman." Judah's voice may as well have echoed in the small household for not a word was said as the looks of shock upon each face were as evident as storm clouds.

A few moments went by until Elisha managed to close his gaping mouth. Ruth took a breath to speak and the old man held up a hand and stopped her. "Who is this Roman?"

Judah felt a tinge of guilt, but he knew he had no other choice. There was a chance that, by doing such a mitzvah as helping those seated before him, it might restore his inner peace. "He is a Praefectus Castrorum of the Twelfth Legion which is encamped in the Bezetha. He is also a senior Primi Ordines of the First Cohort attacking the Antonia. His name is Gaius Cornelius Antony. I trust him, his *word* can be trusted, and he knows me." Judah blinked twice, suddenly feeling uncomfortable, but he plodded on and continued, "On the morning you are to leave, at dawn, it will still be dark out. I will have convinced Zechariah you are at the Gate of the Essenes with the others, but you will hide here. I will come and get you, take you to the Mishneh and you will be on your own, I can go no further.

"Keep your daughters close, Elisha, and your wife near; make your way through the streets stopping for nothing. You will quickly be discovered by the Roman sentries and taken captive. You must not waste a moment in silence, you hear me? You are to call to them in Latin, or else your lives shall be forfeit. Shout to them in their tongue and call out, 'Fulminata, Primi Ordines Gaius Cornelius Antony!' Say this over and over until you are certain they will not kill you. They might mistreat you, but if they understand what you say, you shall live, for that, you have my word." Judah was still as he saw the reality of what lay before them sink upon their faces. "Remember what I said, repeat in Latin, you are to use no Hebrew, it will only infuriate them. Speak in Latin!"

"But once we are taken to Gaius then what?" appealed Elisha still unable to believe what he was hearing from the lips of Judah. "We speak only Hebrew, he will not understand us."

Judah sighed. "If you let my name be the first thing to fall from your tongue when you are taken before him, I am confident Gaius will fetch a man who can speak with you, his name is Yosef ben Matityahu." He saw the affect his words had as question and doubt was plastered to their faces like the very skin which covered their bodies. "Remember, this is the only way to live, this is the only chance you will have." Judah saw Elisha wince at his son and exhale loudly. "I swear to you, half of the people who will flee from the Gate of the Essenes will be crucified within the first hour of leaving, I can promise you that. Titus will have very little mercy for Jews such as yourselves, but with Gaius, he will spare your lives."

With his large arms folded and a look of deep brooding in his eyes, Adam stared at his father for a moment longer, then said just above a whisper, "Abba, what do you wish to do? Will you choose Zechariah's plan or Judah's?"

"We will trust Judah," Elisha responded abruptly looking up at his son. Then, hesitating not a second longer, he mustered up his courage and said lovingly to his wife, "Go, break some of the bread, Ruth. Let us eat together."

* * *

CHAPTER XL

The sun burned upon the dry earth as Titus rode Achilles at the head of his personal guard. Tiberius Julius Alexander followed a ways behind, as the Prince was fixed on the view before him. Titus edged his black mount past the quiet ramps and surveyed the grisly aftermath of yet another Jewish sally. Bodies were strewn everywhere. Some upon the ramps or in ditches, while others lay along the street in pools of blood as flies swirled around in thick clouds. At the base of the Antonia's walls, were numerous bodies in contorted positions, some impaled by arrows with bones shattered and broken after falling from the high parapets which were now vacant of life.

A number of legionaries lay among the dead, some with their segmented armour streaked with blood while others had their heads smashed open like melons, their faces caved in from the sickening impact of rocks hurled from above. Limbs and intestines also lay among the dead where the most brutal of the fighting had unfolded near the furthest western ramp. The Romans had driven the Jews away with two densely formed testudo squares as they had marched directly into the attack, pushing them back and cutting them down. No matter what arrows were shot or spears hurled, all the missiles had glanced off the overlapping scutum roof of the legionary formation as they had plowed forward, turning back the Jewish ranks in waves.

Titus navigated Achilles around the piles of dead. The stench of blood and bodily fluids was so foul that he grimaced as he stared at dozens of slashed open corpses, some so pulverized from the mayhem of battle they were beyond recognition. The loud cawing of crows could be heard as Titus glanced up, watching the black birds congregating in the air or resting upon the parapets of the silent fortress. He shook his head at the sight and steered Achilles away from the stench of death.

Titus turned and watched as a line of carts crossed the stones from the distant breach as a detail of soldiers had been sent to collect their dead. The faces of the men were sullen and expressionless as they separated and began to pick through the bodies to retrieve the lifeless legionaries. Keeping watch over the work detail stood two fresh cohorts guarding the ramps in battle formation. The air was tense, yet eerily silent, as the soldiers waited with brandished swords and readied pila. Titus drew back on the reins and squinted as he examined the intact ramps.

They were near completion, Porcius Gracchus had said earlier in the morning. The Chief Engineer had assured the Prince that he only sought to raise the ramps another metre or two if possible, and then reinforce the base of each earthwork to insure maximum strength. Already huge wooden posts with great pulleys dangling from them had been driven into the top of each ramp. The pulleys were to handle the majority of the weight from each attacking battering ram, as ropes would be attached to each testudo engine to pull them up. A grand picture now stood before Titus of Roman dominion over the earth as the gods had blessed the empire, and this thought gave the Prince a smug grin.

Titus turned in his saddle and gestured with a wave for Tiberius Alexander to accompany him. The older General gave a nod and tapped his horse's flanks with the heels of his riding boots as he rode up to the Prince with ease. Tiberius had more of a somber disposition than Titus. Clearly, he was more worn from years of campaign and politics, seen upon the edges of his face, the calluses of his hands, and the scars on his body. Tiberius had been Vespasian's first choice as Chief Advising General to his son, for the man commanded the field of battle with complete control and was held in high respect among the legions.

"Tiberius, are you well today?" Titus asked, pointing to the red faced man who squinted beneath the weight of his helmet.

"As well as I can be, my Prince. It is but the sun, that is all," replied the General as he rubbed the sweat from his eyes.

"We are nearly ready," Titus said pointing to the ramps. He stared up somberly at the deserted Jewish defences and then sighed. "They do not understand what power faces them here."

Tiberius nodded with an exasperated pant and shouted for his signifer to bring him water. "My apologies, my Prince, I am feeling the heat today."

Titus ignored the older man as a skin of water was brought for Tiberius, who then proceeded to pour it upon his face, before taking a long drink. "Refreshing, yes?" Titus quipped.

Tiberius agreed with a sigh, smiled and then handed the skin back to his standard bearer. "The ramps are Porcius' masterpiece, truly."

"They shall do just fine. The iron heads of the rams should be able to crack and split the rock. It will be hard work, but I am confident the Fifth will get the job done." Titus waved a fly away and then shook his head as he glanced down at a dead Jew, impaled by a pilum, head turned back with gaping eyes. A trail of blood ran from the corpse's mouth, now changed to a pink hue as it had soaked into the earth and dried. Titus coughed loudly and glanced at Tiberius. "They fight with such tenacity and fearlessness. They charged right into our ranks like mad demons. I do pray to Mars they surrender once the Antonia is breached." Titus edged Achilles close to his General. "Ride with me awhile."

"Where will we go?"

"To inspect the works of the Fretensis and Apollinaris," Titus said simply. He watched Tiberius turn awkwardly in his saddle to call to the rest of the mounted guard and Titus quickly interjected, "Leave them, my dear General. We will ride it alone."

Tiberius followed Titus into the Mishneh, deserted from all civilian life as the Roman legions had gained complete control, yet the threat of Jewish attacks was always a sobering reality to the working legions before the First Wall. Danger was ever present, and armed cohorts were placed on guard constantly as the Jews continued to seek ways to threaten their siege operations. However, during the last few days, Simon's men had become accustomed to hiding behind the First Wall as they witnessed an impossible situation become more impossible as the legions entrenched themselves deeper and stronger in the captured second quarter.

Tiberius found it haunting as he walked his horse behind Titus through the ghost-like suburbs of the quarter. Everywhere around him homes could be seen bearing great damage from the Roman attacks as roofs had caved in, buildings toppled, and dwellings ransacked. Entire blocks of housing appeared to have been burned by fire, and the stains of blood still covered the streets as it had not rained in nearly three months. Somewhere in front of him a dog barked, and a window shutter creaked. He gazed around at the destruction and devastation from the captured city, feeling a tinge of sorrow for the sight that he knew all too well as a man who had vanquished many cities in his past.

Echoes of caligae beating upon the stones ahead of the men restored the conversation as Titus spoke up cheerfully and said, "Tell me of Alexandria, Tiberius. How was it being the *Praefectus Praetorio* among so many of your people? Especially on the eve of the rebellion, Nero must have seen something of notable character in you." Titus glanced back at his General and uttered, "You are Jewish are you not?"

Tiberius nodded. "Yes, I was born into a wealthy Jewish family in Alexandria."

"But that life did not suit you?"

Tiberius shrugged. "It is complicated, my Prince."

"Keep your mystery to yourself then. But tell me how it was like to govern such people?"

"I was born there, and I am one of them, so naturally I know how Jews think. Between them, the local Egyptians, Romans, Greeks, Arabs, and black Numidians it was not so bad. Under Emperor Claudius, I was given the role as procurator of Judea, replacing Cuspius Fadus, about twenty four years ago. I held my post for two years and retired to military matters later under Gnaeus Domitius Corbulo in Parthia. However, it was during my post as procurator that I learned how to govern the Jews.

"They are a very opinionated people, my Prince. If you understand their religion, you can avoid a mess. Not like Florus did," Tiberius responded harshly with a growl. "The Jews of Alexandria are not like those here, in Judea. They are more understanding and open minded, however, you still get your fanatics and pious men who would riot if you were to bring anything that resembled a graven image through their streets. I dictated to all soldiers within my ruling, to respect these laws, and not to push them. I even took great lengths to advise visiting senators and consuls of these cultural and religious expressions. I never wanted a revolt or riot in my borders, never."

"Yet, you dealt with the uprising in Alexandria with a heavy hand, Tiberius," Titus commented.

A downcast look shadowed Tiberius' face as he sighed and shook his head. "It should never have happened. The Jews had rioted upon hearing about their brothers to the east and that a number of Greeks in the city had taken Jewish prisoners. The Greeks then held an assembly. I was not aware of it, but needless to say the Jews arrived, strong in number and brazen for a fight. The Jews surrounded the Greeks and threatened to burn them alive if they would not give up their prisoners. I was made aware of the situation; a solution seemed distant, but I was intent on squelching it. I would not stand for insurrection, nor allow the Jews to take to the streets in an uproar like what had spilled out in the east. Jerusalem had been sacked and the garrison slaughtered. I was not about to let that happen in Alexandria."

Tiberius furrowed his brow, replaying all that had happened during that desperate time. Then he exhaled loudly, finding no solution and continued, "I sent mediators and emissaries to the Jews to broker a deal, but they would not come to their senses. To them, they saw us suddenly as oppressors, even though they had lived comfortably under my rule. Alexandria was not Jerusalem, and I was no Gessius Florus. I appealed to them throughout the day and threatened to use the legions at my disposal. I had over two thousand soldiers arrive from Libya earlier that week, and they were mustered and ready. When the Jews refused to give heed and violence began to escalate, I had no other choice." Tiberius paused and then slowly said, "I enacted a brutal punishment on them for not listening to my words. It was their fault for their rebellion and I had to act. My hand had been forced and innocent Greeks had been killed and battered. I sent the legion in and gave them freewill to crush the dissenters, to plunder their properties, and to burn their dwellings.

"The Jews faced the legion off in a place of the city called 'The Delta' and inflicted casualties upon my legionaries. Finally, the cohorts pushed through and slaughtered them all. It was horrific, truly. I did not take pleasure in such measures, but reckless barbarism must be dealt with. I invoked the full measure of the law upon them, and they fought back. I only relented once they begged me to show mercy, and only then. If I had not intervened there would be no Jews in Alexandria living today. The legions hotly pursued them and through drudgery, spared none."

Titus stared at the regret woven into his General's eyes like a web. "How many did your legion kill that day, Tiberius?"

Tiberius tried to look proud for his duty and life to Rome, but the deadened sense, that he had lost something within him that day, was all to prominent. "Fifty thousand, my Prince," he said with a grunt, as if the very figure tasted bitter in his mouth. "I have regretted that day ever since, but they pushed me to it. I had no choice." Tiberius turned away from the surprised look upon the Prince's face at the high death toll. It was then, in Tiberius' mind, as if he could look back in time and see the blood flowing down the streets and hear the savage toils of slaughter above the pounding caligae on that fateful day.

"Well," Titus said, interrupting Tiberius' dark thoughts. "You served Nero, Galba, Otho, and then declared loyalty to my father. I see no fault in your actions, Tiberius. You have served this empire with steadfast loyalty, you cannot truly regret that? You placed the needs of the empire above that of which was dearest to you. Is not sacrifice the greatest act of vigilance a man can make in order that the empire continues to breathe?"

"Yes, my Prince," Tiberius dryly responded.

"Good, you have used much of that since being deployed here with me. I want you to know, Tiberius, that I could never have done all of this without your eye for detail and your hand of leadership. You are a man of considerable quality; the gods have blessed you, Tiberius. You possess the mind of Minerva, I might say, and it is prevalent in your administration." Titus smiled at the shocked General and bowed his head.

"You flatter me, my Prince."

"It is alright to flatter a man worthy of such deeds," spoke Titus as they emerged from the quiet streets into the full view of the siege works spread out before them. "I shall see you duly rewarded for your efforts and allegiance to my father and the Flavian right to rule. The gods appointed us, and you are of their mind, my dear Tiberius."

"I remain a faithful servant of the Emperor, my Prince," Tiberius replied, feeling courage restored and pushing the dark memory of the massacre in Alexandria far from his mind. He had done what was needed at the time, and had been praised by Nero, that was all the justification he needed to put the matter to rest.

"There is Larcius," Titus pointed at the General who was speaking to one of his officers near the lines of onager catapults. "Come, Tiberius, we shall see to matters here."

Both men rode along the earthen trenches as flagstones had been pried from the ground and broken for rubble used in the ramps. The crevices of trenches and dykes, which ran parallel to the Jewish occupied walls, resembled that of great claw marks gouged from the earth, which posed as a formidable defence for the Romans should they be caught off guard by a sudden enemy sortie.

The Tenth and Fifteenth Legions had taken every precaution against the Jewish defences of the First Wall, to insure the protection of the ramps. They had fixed the bottoms of the trenches with hundreds of long, jagged, wooden spikes, built towers, and had dug pits for scorpions and catapults. The block of housing nearest to the Roman earthworks had been torn down and dragged away so that the fighting ground before the wall was flat, even, and wide. Unlike the dangerous working conditions near the Antonia, the Roman labourers piling up rubble and earth upon the ramps at the First Wall could do so freely without threat of catapult fire or sudden attacks.

General Lepidus glanced up to the sound of approaching hoof beats and straightened in his saddle as he saluted Titus and Tiberius who had slowed to a cantor. "My Prince Titus and General Alexander, to what do I owe this pleasure?"

"What news on this day, General Lepidus?" Titus asked, drawing on the reins and halting Achilles.

"The morning was uneventful, unlike the scrap at the Antonia I heard about. A swift victory I trust, my Prince?" Larcius asked, receiving a nod of confirmation from Titus. "Our defences are strong, and the ramp against the wall nearest the Hippicus is nearing completion." Larcius turned and pointed across the Roman defensive lines to the foundations of another ramp rising from the ground. "That will be our second ramp and it is still in its early stages. The ground has been nothing more than a wearisome project as we have had to pry up the streets and collapse vacant homes. However, we have finally begun on the second ramp, and it will go directly up to their wall. We do expect resistance once we get closer. I was about to order an afternoon of volleys to give Simon and his dogs a chance to duck and run for cover."

Titus gave a nod and stared for a moment at the working crews hustling about at the base of the developing ramp. "Where is General Frigius?"

"Retired for the afternoon, my Prince. He is vexed and suffers from an ailment of the head. He informed me that it aches and I insisted he see my personal surgeon, who is much more equipped with these types of symptoms than the sad, unfortunate fellow Frigius brought with him." Larcius glanced at Tiberius and smiled. "I pray you are keeping well, General?"

"Charmed, Larcius." Tiberius paused for a moment and then rubbed his chin with a satisfactory appeal. "I like what I see and I do say it is coming along well. Still, our real threat before us is the continued existence of the rebels in the Antonia. We should be fit to launch an attack very soon, within days."

"Well, with foresight from Mars, we should be able to see this through. I have faith in the men of the Fulminata and Macedonica; they are brutes and always ready for a brawl. They will no doubt take care of the whims of Gischala. Meanwhile, I shall carry our standards through these defences once we create a breach. Venus shall look down from the heavens and see us carry the image of the bull straight through, and I mean to plant a signum on their parapets once I have done so. The boar and the ship of Neptune will be the wrath the Fretensis will bring once I unleash them upon Jerusalem's streets. Great victrix will be for all and the Idumeans will be hacked to pieces, for that I swear to you, my Prince."

* * *

North Western side of the Outer Court
Temple Mount
Two hours before dusk

"Have the next detail begin, Eliyahu, we need to move faster," Judah said wearily with bloodshot eyes and dirt smeared upon his face.

"Amos is taking them through the tunnel now, Judah, you need not worry." Eliyahu stared at the exhausted Captain as he stood hunched over a large, empty copper basin, taken from the underground priestly chambers. He watched Judah lift up a clay jug with a trefoil spout and a narrow neck and then pour cool water upon his hands. The ragged and worn commander sighed with satisfaction, then inhaled loudly with shock as he splashed some of the cold water onto his face. "Take some rest, Judah, we can work without you."

Judah splashed some more water onto his face and set the jug down. He stared at Eliyahu for a moment, water dripping from his beard and eyes begging for sleep. "I will return in an hour. I shall find a spot on the eastern side of the courtyard. Come and get me should my services be needed."

Eliyahu graciously bowed and patted Judah's shoulder warmly. "Take two hours, Judah, you need your strength."

Judah watched as the tiny man returned into the black corridor and disappeared like a phantom as the sounds of digging echoed from within. Being tired and sore from fourteen hours of constant work and supervision was still not enough to dampen his spirits as a slight smile cracked upon Judah's face from the kindness of the miner. It was a gloomy and dreary place to labour, incredibly volatile and dangerous. However, the little man and his brother worked in the tunnel as if their true home was below the earth. Pondering about the necessity of the ramps caused Judah to feel elated.

When the mines collapsed, thus caving in the ramps, there was no doubt in his mind the Roman Prince would question his role in the entire siege, which would be to the benefit of the Zealots. *There could be a chance at victory,* Judah thought to himself. *And it might just lie within the terrible sight of the destruction of everything the Romans have worked so hard for. The shaming of their arrogance will be the new enemy of Rome. Titus will not be able to quell the outrage that will grip the legions like an infectious disease.* Judah stared into the haunting tunnel for a moment and then turned to walk out into the sunlight as a thought crossed his mind. *"Desertion and mutiny will be the new order of the day, to replace the staunch discipline of the legionaries. The age of Titus is over."*

Judah strolled out and squinted as he raised his hand against the sudden penetrating light that made his eyes water. Once his eyes began to adjust, he glanced around the Outer Court at the quaint stillness about him. Most of the soldiers had been dispatched to the western ramparts of the colonnades or to the Antonia as the threat of Titus was still very real with the ramps nearing completion.

Judah recalled the conversation he had with John that morning. Judah had been hard at work, bent over and clearing rubble like a mole, when the warlord had approached him and demanded an audience. Judah had listened to John, clearly unnerved with paranoia, as he vented a deep grievance, threatening to arrest a man at the Eastern Gate whom he feared would open the doors for the Tenth Legion encamped on the Mount of Olives. John had stated again and again that it appeared the Roman sentries had moved closer throughout the night, and he was convinced they did so at the behest of Jewish assurances that the gates would be opened. Once John said that he was of the mind to demand that Simon send troops from the First Wall, Judah had intervened. It had taken an argument of great length to convince the warlord that no conspiracy existed, and it had not pleased John until Judah had recommended four Zealots to be posted to watch the guard in concern. The great warrior from Gischala had shaken his head, held up both hands in defence, and without a word, had retreated back the way he had come.

Now, Judah followed the high columns of the porticos past the Antonia to the east as he gazed up at the thinned ranks of guards patrolling above. That told him one thing, John had abandoned the insane fixation that there was a spy at the East Gate willing to open it up to the legionaries.

Judah shed his outer garment from the heat of day and slung it over his arm as he let his sword hang freely at his side. He listened to the light cooing of doves around him, despite the echoes and crashes from Roman missiles landing in parts of the city and the thudding against the Antonia's walls. Judah looked up and observed as a white dove flapped its wings vigorously as it sailed from one of the many Corinthian capitals amongst the hundreds of pillars which encircled the Outer Court. He watched the bird fly towards the northern side of the Temple, and for a moment the bird looked as if it were suspended in mid air. Then suddenly the dove cooed again, careened upward into the heavens, and Judah lost sigh of it by the shimmer of the golden parapets on the edifice's roof.

Judah heard a shuffle near him and glanced to his left, seeing nothing out of the ordinary. His curiosity heightened as he heard the sound again and suspicion took hold of him as he slowly drew his gladius. Judah halted and could sense someone behind the pillar he faced. He paused, for a moment, took a deep breath and then said in a cold voice of steel, "Who goes there? I know someone is there!"

"It is I, Judah, stay your hand," replied a female voice as an old woman leaned out from behind the pillar with a frailty Judah had seen before.

"Ruth?" Judah said in shock. He quickly sheathed his sword and darted under the shelter of the portico roof, taking her firmly by the elbow. "Why have *you* come here? You risk too much!" Judah scolded her in a gruff whisper. He pulled her gently behind the pillar and gazed into her eyes. "You *shouldn't* have come. It looks suspicious having you here." Judah glanced back around the pillar and scanned what ramparts he could see in the distance. He hoped nobody had seen them. "I should not have given Adam such blind trust, now I see I was a fool to do so."

"This has nothing to do with my son, Judah, do not think less of him."

A look of worry filled Ruth's eyes and Judah sensed the change in her demeanour. "Is everything alright? Has something happened?"

Ruth shook her head and gathered her thoughts. "We fear this plan of yours, Judah. We have much to lose."

"I told you as long as you reach Gaius, you would come under no harm. I gave you my word. Now you question it?" Judah was confused and stared at her, still perplexed she had even made it this far.

"Elisha and I are to put the lives of our daughters into the hands of this Roman centurion, and you pledge your word? I need more than that, Judah!" Ruth stared into the eyes of the hardened Captain as she pleaded with him. It was as if a wall of mortar and stone had been built up against his eyes, for even the window of his soul seemed impossible to penetrate. She searched for a place of vulnerability, desperate to trust a man who had taken league with the enemy. "Do you know what the Romans do to Jewish women they capture, Judah? Should I remind you, or have you too heard their screams and moans of pain."

"I do not need to be reminded of such grief, I know of it," Judah said, eyes suddenly ablaze, anger seething from within as he felt accused of being involved in the brutal treatment committed daily by many of the legionaries.

"Yet you trust one of them? You have given allegiance to them?" Ruth paused, then wrapped her arms around herself and stared down at the flagstones. "You have friends in the Roman camp and you wish us to trust you?"

"Why did you come here?" Judah replied in a dark and beleaguered tone. "If you seek to not leave this city then you must only tell me and I will inform Zechariah. It is that simple."

"Have you always been this arrogant and foolhardy to think of nobody but yourself in a time such as this?" Ruth suddenly said with vehemence. She watched Judah's face tighten with shock from her response and she pressed again, "My son trusts you, he has said so. Adam says he would die for you and he owes you his life. If Adam trusts you so, please convince me to feel the same. The lives of our daughters hang in the balance, Judah, and I see a man who has a Roman friend, at a time like this, and I am afraid."

Judah was frozen with shock and conviction. He stared into the aging eyes of the woman and saw both pity and warmth. It disturbed his soul. Judah felt discomfort, but the gaze from Ruth also stirred within him a sorrow and regret for everything that had happened. Judah looked at her and then slowly took a step back. "Ruth, for reasons I do not know, God has caused me to wallow in the mire of misery and pain. I pray, study Torah, recite *Tehillim*, and offer sacrifices in the Temple, but He hears me not. I feel like King Saul, for I fear Adonai has turned His face from me for the things I have done.

"I cry out to HaShem, but I am taken by silence. I cannot tell you of the pain that torments me. I hear a thousand different reasons uttered from the lips of men as to the nature of my agony, yet an answer evades me. I once had a love, a woman, I was to wed. I had given a dowry, and then she was taken from me by the point of a spear. It is a long story, one that has taken me through the low places of Sheol and back, but the Roman I speak of helped me and stayed true to his word so that I could have my vengeance."

"And that vengeance, Judah, where has it left you?" asked Ruth in a whisper. She saw the stunned look of pain wash over Judah's face like a torrent of rain and she softly added, "It has consumed you, my son. I see it in your eyes and in the anger that burns from you like a great furnace."

"You speak of what you do not know," Judah said with a shudder.

"If you follow this path, Judah, it will be the end of you." Ruth stepped forward and laid a gentle hand on Judah's shoulder. "Please do not take my son with you to meet such an end, for if you ask of him, he will follow. He is a loyal man, and will walk with you into death's camp. I wish not upon my son the agonizing death he shall meet, should the Romans capture him, Judah. I could not bear the thought, and it would kill Elisha to know Adam suffered so."

Judah tightened his jaw and raised a defiant chin as he fought against the shame and sorrow which split his heart. "I swear to you, that you will be safe in the hands of the Roman. I do not work for Rome, and I will fight to the end to protect this city, but this man is a good man. I swear to you nothing of ill tidings shall touch your daughters, for that you can only trust my word."

*　　*　　*

Synagogue of the Cyrenians
The Ophel
After dark

Yeshua ben Sapphias stayed in the shadows as he kept an eye on the door of the synagogue. The streets were dark and deserted, and the sounds of the artillery barrage had long since subsided. For now, the city appeared to sleep, despite the evident signs of destruction and the tens of thousands of Romans encamped around the walls. At this point, however, Yeshua did not care for the impending doom which lurked outside the city. For now, his eyes were fixated upon the door of the synagogue and his ears were tuned to the singing recantations of the pious men inside. There was a brief pause in the prayers, brought forth by the riveting passion of Rabbi Benyamin ben Asher as he read from the weekly portion and then raised his voice long and hard in a wavy melody as a chorus of men said together, *Amen*. Yet, Yeshua was not there to take part in the worship. He only cared to wait for one man, John of Gischala.

Finally the service ended and the doors opened cascading light across the street as men, wrapped in their long *tallit'ot*, exited in clusters engaged in deep theological discussions. Yeshua pulled his cloak across his face so he would not be noticed and narrowed his gaze as he watched the bearded men walk down the paved street. He suddenly spotted a large man appear in the doorway and halt. The man's muscular form blocked much of the light as he stood motionless and surveyed the empty street.

Yeshua knew it was John, and he watched as the warlord took a single step into the street and rubbed his hands together. A number of equally large men followed closely behind, wearing long outer cloaks and wrapped in head coverings. Each man wore a heavy sword that hung from their belt and they stooped to pick up their shields that had been discarded upon the ground near the doorway.

Yeshua cautiously crept forward to the edge of the shadow and cleared his throat. He saw the warriors react suddenly as they shot a startled, blind gaze into the darkness and reached for their swords. John did not move, even when his men begged him to retreat behind them out of fear that Simon may have sent assassins. Upon hearing this, the big man just scoffed and peered into the shadows.

"John, I need to speak with you, it is important. It is I, Yeshua ben Sapphias." Yeshua watched as John gave his men a cautious glance. "I give you my word that I have not come to harm you."

"Then why do you hide yourself?" John asked, carefully resting his hand on the pommel of his sword.

"To wait for you, of course. There are unfavourable eyes in this city. I am alone," Yeshua replied as he hesitated to reveal himself.

"If you are alone, step out and come to me! There is nobody here but myself and these men," John implored with a slow gesture. "Come here!" Yeshua emerged from the shadows and dropped his cloak from his face. John scowled and shook his head. "You even concealed yourself? You are not one of the Sicarii, are you? Come to assassinate me for Simon's sake, is it?"

"I am unarmed," Yeshua cried.

"Nobody walks through these streets without a blade, I don't believe you," John shouted. "Come closer! Search him!" He called to his men and they rushed forward as Yeshua raised both arms high in the air and let the Zealots pat him down, checking for weapons.

"He is unarmed, John, he speaks the truth," said one of the Zealots.

John approached Yeshua and stopped only inches from his face. He stared at the unpredictable man who had a thin, sickly face, and scraggily beard. "You either are mad, or up to something, and I think it might be both," John softly said in a low, menacing tone.

Yeshua grinned and stepped back, giving the warlord a disappointed look. "Like I said, I had something to tell you that is a pressing matter. You will want to hear what I have to say."

"Stand watch," John said to his men, glancing over his shoulder.

"I am alone, John. Nobody has come to kill you," Yeshua commented with a sneer.

John gave him a despondent look and then a wave of impatience washed over him like water upon a rocky coast. "Do not mock me, Yeshua. I don't trust you, if you must know. You are a man of lawlessness and posses a thief's heart." John watched the devious sneer disappear from the wild man of Taricheae and then he said, "Speak, Yeshua, if you have something to say."

"You will learn to value my opinion, John. You will soon want to trust me." Yeshua let that sink in as he watched John's face twitch slightly. He smiled as he struck a nerve in the big Gischalan commander and then bluntly said, "I saw Judah ben Yosef consorting with an elderly woman in the Outer Court today."

John was silent for a moment as he watched Yeshua instinctively take another step backwards, expecting a punch that would shatter a tree trunk, but John did not move. "What did you say?"

Yeshua hesitated and then slowly said, "I said, I saw Judah ben..."

"Who was the woman?" John interrupted, clearly angered.

"She is the mother of one of his Lions, Adam, I believe his name is." Yeshua saw a look of utter contempt appear upon John's face at the news and he quickly added, "I had her followed to her home in the Lower City, which is how I found out who she was. It is all true what I tell you."

John gazed at the man, irritated at his very existence, but behooved in his heart at the accusation against Judah and the chance it might be treasonous. Suddenly the large warlord shook his bushy head and closed his eyes for a moment. "I understand your reasoning. Great jealousy riddles the ranks of my men against the profound success and bravery of such a man as Judah ben Yosef. He has been accused before by that worm, Yehoram. Judah is a man of *honour*. I demanded it from the lips of that swine, Yehoram, and you accuse him still? There must be an explanation for this! Adam is Judah's man, and he is just as loyal and brave. Perhaps his mother possesses a mind of worry for her son, that can be common, and a justifiable reason she would approach Judah as Adam's Captain. Granted, it is strange for an elderly woman to speak to such a man as Judah, but if she felt there was no other way, it is not enough to accuse and condemn the man." John turned to leave as his blood boiled and it took all of his strength to resist the urge from snapping the man in half.

"But John, I heard them speak!"

John halted and gave Yeshua a heated glare that could melt metal. "You heard what they said? I am listening." John could not believe he had given the scoundrel a platform to entertain his lunacy, but he had to, his own soldiers had heard every word of the conversation and could easily tell others.

"She confronted Judah about a Roman that Judah was like brother to, she was afraid to trust Judah about something concerning this man and Judah became angry. When she pushed him to make assurances, he only looked conceited and distant. I did not hear everything but there is a plot of conspiring and deceit that is among your ranks, John. You must say something." Yeshua watched a sudden calm overcome John like a layer of fresh dew upon a grassy plain in the morning. John looked appeased and thankful as Yeshua tried to relax his tense nerves.

"You swear this is true?" John mumbled softly and Yeshua nodded eagerly. John slowly approached him and opened his hands, as if welcoming the relief of solving the spy issue that he had feared for months. However, with a ferocious speed and agility, John lunged, caught Yeshua by the neck with both his hands and squeezed as the man gagged, trying to scream as he fought back helplessly.

"I could crush the very life from you, and I could do so with a clear conscience. I could murder you right here, squeeze your throat until it looked like pulp and your eyes burst from your skull. I could do so and then turn around, walk back into the synagogue, and read from the portion. God would welcome such justice that I could wrought upon this city to wipe out the miserable name of Yeshua ben Sapphias. What do you think?" John squeezed some more, feeling in his great hands the pulsing of Yeshua's veins in his neck as he closed them slowly. Yeshua's face was turning a shade of blue and John let go as the man's eyes had just begun to roll back into his head.

Yeshua fell back choking and coughing as he gagged lying on the ground in a ball. The tall warlord stared at him for a moment, considering shedding his blood on the stone street, and then finally turned, gesturing to his men to leave with him. Yeshua continued to gasp for air as he propped himself up and watched the proud man of Gischala saunter off. He slowly stood, looking disheveled as a line of saliva was streaked upon his face and mixed into his beard.

"John!" Yeshua shouted aloud and watched as the warlord turned suddenly. "If you say nothing I will tell Simon and everyone I meet, that you let the spy of Jerusalem get away without punishment." Yeshua then turned and ran away into the night.

* * *

CHAPTER XLI

May 30th, 70 A.D. / 4th of Sivan, 3830
Southern Jerusalem
Lower City
One hour before dawn

Light dew dampened the streets as Judah hurried along. His face was wrapped in his head covering and he steadied the sword which hung at his waist. Judah stopped against the side of a dark home and listened. The city was still asleep and nothing stirred. He picked up his pace as he followed the narrow alleys of the Lower City and passed by the sleeping forms of beggars lying in the gutters. Judah heard the gentle tapping of a staff upon the paved street. He caught the glimpse of a blind man sitting upon the cold ground between two homes with a filthy rag tied around his head, covering his eyes. The blind man sensed a person nearby and held out his tin cup as he bobbed it up and down. Judah hesitated for a moment, staring at the sick man, but dared not say a word, then he picked up his pace and left the beggar alone in the darkness.

Judah saw the shadow of a man ahead, standing alone and motionless near the doorway of a small home. The dwelling had long been abandoned as the door was torn off its hinges with the shutters upon the windows broken and uncared for. He watched the man notice his approach and then step away from the ruined home with suspicion. Judah silently raised his hand and saw the figure relax as he stepped back into the shadow which was his sanctuary and protection against unwanted eyes.

"Zechariah, all is ready?" Judah asked in a whisper once he drew closer.

The Priest nodded and looked past Judah. "You weren't followed?"

"I was careful and nobody suspected anything when I left the court. The gate will be clear for another hour before the next guard. We cannot tarry." Judah glimpsed around the edge of the house at the Gate of the Essenes which stood boldly, built into the high wall, with a magnificent arch and parapets of pointed, decorated stone. The great doors of the gate were made of thick cedar and were sealed by two large beams which lay resting in iron latches. Two torches burned upon either side of the massive doors and above on the vacant ramparts.

"I will get them now!" Judah whispered with an edge of panic.

"Is something wrong?" Zechariah uttered.

Judah shrugged. "I see no sense in drawing this out any longer then need be. Anyone could give us up, Zechariah. People are desperate. We need to act fast."

"All has been accounted for, Judah. Rabbi Asher prepared things well, there is nothing to fear." Zechariah rested an assuring hand on Judah's shoulder. "Trust in HaShem, this will work for good."

Judah gave a partial nod as he quenched fear and panic in his soul. He had gone to great lengths to make sure no guards would be posted at this hour. The gate now stood empty, and he did not wish to test the good fortune that had blessed them thus far. Judah noticed a flicker of grievance in the old man's face as he watched the Priest stroke his beard. "Zechariah, does something disturb you?"

"I keep thinking about the ones who will surely die once they are outside the walls. The Romans shall not spare many. I wonder if I have erred in this matter, perhaps they would stand a better chance staying." The Priest stared into Judah's covered face with only his eyes peering out between the folds of cloth. "Adam shall lose his family. Will it not tear him apart to see them die?"

Judah sensed doubt in his friend's voice and feared he might intervene if he did not speak. "There is nothing to be done now, Zechariah. They have chosen their destiny. They are in the hands of HaShem. What you do, will be remembered forever! We are giving them hope and a chance at life, the price to pay will be by their blood, but even if one were to live, it would be as if you have saved the entire world. You mustn't consider turning them away. They have given everything and pledged their lives to this. They are brave, Zechariah. This maybe the only time they have ever been able to muster such courage, do not take that from them by refusing their given right for freedom."

The Priest's eyes misted over as he stared warmly into the face of the fierce warrior. "Judah," Zechariah said with the smile of a grandfather. "You would have made a great rabbi. Hear the word of HaShem from the lips of the prophet Ezekiel, *Thus says the Lord God to these bones: 'Surely I will cause breath to enter into you, and you shall live. I will put sinews on you and bring flesh upon you, cover you with skin and put breath in you; and you shall live. Then you shall know that I am HaShem.'*" A look of despondency and dejection fell upon his face but he refused to draw his gaze away. "*'I will put My Spirit in you, and you shall live, and I will place you in your own land. Then you shall know that I, HaShem, have spoken it and performed it,' says HaShem.*"

Zechariah paused for a moment and then softly whispered, "Judah, we men of bones shall live. Although we suffer, our people shall one day be given life in this land again, no matter what tomorrow brings, we will have breath once again." He nodded and a look of fierce passion and duty suddenly flared in his eyes. "Get them ready and send them out."

Without saying another word Judah turned and ran out into the open as he moved quickly to the gate. He reached up and removed one of the torches from its iron bracket and raised it in the air, waving it twice to the unseen eyes of Rabbi Benyamin ben Asher who led a huddled crowd of frightened Jews from the dark streets. Judah lowered the torch and watched them emerge quietly, yet with confidence amidst fear of the unknown. Wives clung to their husbands and children were kept close. A number of them carried small bundles of their belongings, while others had nothing but what they wore.

Judah watched Rabbi Asher and two of the men among the group approach him for instructions. Judah directed them to the large beams that locked the doors and two men each took an end. With all their strength they heaved upon the timber and lifted it out of the iron brackets. They carried the beam to the side and carefully set it on the stone street and then ran to lift the second one. The group of fifty Jewish men, women, and children watched silently as the doors to their freedom stood before them. A few spoke in hushed voices, but most remained quiet as they contemplated what they would face beyond the walls.

Then, in a mechanical-like response, with steadfast determination, Judah and the rabbi tugged upon a large iron latch and partially opened one of the great doors. Standing in the gap of the door, Rabbi Asher looked at Judah, and outstretched his arms in friendship as he smiled. The reluctant Zealot embraced the Rabbi as he heard Benyamin whisper, "Shalom to you, Judah, upon this dark night." Rabbi Asher let Judah go, gave him a simple nod, turned away, and approached the cluster of nervous Jews in order to have a few last words with them.

Judah stepped to the side and pulled his face-covering away. Suddenly, he caught a set of frightened eyes among the people that he recognized and his body jerked wanting to dash forward, but he held his ground. Judah could only stare at Hadassah with an empty look as he pleading eyes seemed to beg him to reconsider. Mordechai ben Levi, the wealthy Jewish tradesmen whom Judah had arranged to care for Hadassah, stood next to her with his wife and Judah knew Hadassah would be safe. A part of him wished to take her in his arms, kiss her, fill his nostrils with the scent of her delicate skin, and gaze into her eyes as he would tell her he loved her. But Judah knew this was the only way that she could live and have the life she deserved. With this reality, he prayed silently that God would spare her from the clutches of the Roman sentries once they discovered the Jewish refugees.

"They are ready, Judah. They should leave," Rabbi Asher said.

Judah nodded. "I must go now, so no one suspects anything. You will have the men help you lock the doors?"

"Yes, and then I shall lower them from the top of the gate by rope." Rabbi Asher briefly glanced at the men who had lifted the beams, then smiled Judah's way. "Go in peace, my brother."

Judah returned an empty nod to the Rabbi. Despite how he was helping these people flee the suffering of the city, he remained stricken with a sense of solitude and seclusion in his mind that constantly plagued him with doubt. Judah stared at Hadassah among the group and suddenly felt the need to express the sorrow which clung to the tip of his tongue, but he held his composure and quickly said, "Get them out of here."

He took a couple of steps backwards and watched as Rabbi Asher directed the group to the gate with words of encouragement as he beckoned them to hurry. Hadassah stared longingly at Judah, as she was hurried along by the hand of Mordechai's wife. She shook her head at Judah as tears streamed down her cheeks, and only once reached out to him. With a look of utter helplessness, Hadassah was pulled through the gate and into the darkness of the valley which surrounded Jerusalem. Judah felt a sudden panic well up within him. He wanted to scream her name, run to her side and whisk her away from all of this. But instead, he stood there, eyes red, body stricken with grief, and legs feeling numb and weak. Judah shook himself from the trance, turned, and hurried away through the dark streets towards the home of Elisha and Ruth.

*   *   *

"Get away from the window, Elisha, you may be seen," Ruth demanded from the darkness of her home.

Elisha turned with a look of annoyance and stepped back. "I watch for Judah. Keep your voice low, wife."

Ruth looked to her son and shook her head. She touched his hand softly and whispered, "Your Abba need not be there. Tell him to come back to us. Judah will come, he swore to me."

Adam reassured his mother with a smile and slowly stood as he moved between his sisters. He crossed the room to where his father had taken up his station next to the window and said, "Abba, let me watch for Judah."

"What if something has happened?" Elisha rattled to himself as he strained to see down the dark street.

"It is still an hour till dawn. Judah had business at the gate, remember? He will be here, I am sure of it." Adam laid a calm, but strong hand upon his father's shoulder. "Abba, go wait over there." Elisha turned to his son, stared out from his pale face, then heeded his word and hobbled from the window to the straw mats where his family waited tensely. Adam sighed, clutched the shaft of his spear, and prayed as he stared out into the haunting street.

Like a dream shrouded in mystery, Adam saw a silhouette moving slowly down the street towards the house. The figure was wrapped in a dark outer garment and seemed to shield his face against a wind which did not blow. A dog barked somewhere in the city. The silhouette abruptly halted and looked up at the dark sky as a sliver of the moon shone forth cascading the street in silver highlights. Time seemed suspended as the mysterious person continued to listen, without moving a muscle. Adam saw the flash of a sword blade as the man stood motionless, alarmed from a sense of impending danger.

Adam opened the door a crack and whispered across the dark street, "Judah! Is something wrong?" He watched Judah hold up a hand to silence him.

Adam clutched his spear and slowly raised it so the jagged point protruded from the open doorway. He stared into the early morning as he could see a splinter of light splitting the lower horizon, projecting a light blue and orange aura up into the blackened sky. Morning was not far off, and Adam felt a layer of cold sweat suddenly dampen his chest as he held his breath, considering moving out into the street. However, before he could make up his mind, Judah sheathed his sword and trotted over to the doorway in a pant.

"Get your family now!"

Adam scowled and straightened. "What is wrong?"

"I fear I have been followed; we only have this one chance. Tell them to hurry." Judah gave Adam a wild look and then turned as he edged along the side of the home, squatting down in the shadows, readying his hand upon the hilt of his gladius.

Adam failed to waste not a single second. He darted back into the home, closed the door and with an excited tone said, "Quick, to your feet, we must leave now!"

"What is the matter?" Elisha replied, rising to his feet with the help of his daughters. "Is not Judah here?"

Adam nodded and took the arm of his mother. "He fears someone may lurk nearby. We cannot waste time. Come, follow me!"

Leading the way Adam opened the door and stepped into the cool morning air. He glanced back up at the sky, afraid that the night would suddenly melt away spilling the light of day over the city. He saw Judah rise in the shadow with drawn sword and Adam turned to his mother. "Take Abba and follow me!" He stepped forward, with spear in hand, taking the lead with Judah as they darted around the house and moved through the streets in silence.

Judah continued to glance over his shoulders into the blackness behind them and this unnerved Adam who furrowed his brow, feeling his hands becoming slick with sweat upon the shaft of his spear. "What is it?"

Judah shook his head. "I passed an ill looking man earlier whom I took for a beggar. The man would not have known my identity. But such a man soon began to follow me. I wound through a number of streets and then doubled back through an alley before I reached your home, but I fear he is still looking for me."

"One of Simon's men?" Adam asked with dread.

"I do not know," Judah honestly replied.

"He employs the Sicarii. They can mask their movements and stay concealed well. If he is following us we must hurry." Adam glanced behind him as his family stayed close by. He thought of asking them to hasten but held his tongue. "Should I double back and see if I can find this man?"

"No, the man could be an agent of Simon's. He must not know who we are." Judah looked to his friend. "We must be swift."

It felt like they had been moving through the narrow streets for hours when suddenly Judah halted. Adam instinctively raised his spear expecting a confrontation, but then found himself standing before the First Wall. He stepped forward and laid a hand on the cool stone and shook his head as he looked to his friend for help.

"The gymnasium is just to our right. You know where we are, Adam?" Judah asked as he removed the covering from his face exposing a dark grin. "We will get them out." He strolled a bit to the left and then wrapped his knuckles against a small wooden door which was bolted from the inside. Judah glanced up at the quiet ramparts above, then slid the iron bolt back and cracked the door open. "This is as far as we can go!" Judah watched Adam hesitate and he quickly said, "We cannot be sure this door will stay open if we go through. We can go no further. You must say your farewell now."

Judah watched his burly friend slowly walk to his family and embrace each one as he kissed them, weeping quietly. The frail hands of Elisha clutched the sides of Adam's face as he drew his son close so he could whisper words of love amidst the flowing tears from his two daughters.

Judah stepped close to Elisha and gently cleared his throat. "Remember to speak in Latin. Remember the words, Fulminata, Primi Ordines Gaius Cornelius Antony. Repeat those words and live."

"We are forever indebted to you, Judah son of Yosef. I shall never forget this mercy which you have shown us," Elisha said with choked emotion. He looked to his wife and reassuringly nodded. "Come, Ruth, take our daughters."

Judah and Adam watched them approach the door and before they ducked through Elisha calmly said to his son, "You are strong, Adam. I love you. Shalom."

Judah saw pain wash over Adam's face as the great man breathed deeply in the night. He gave Judah a grief stricken look and then turned away, unable to bear the soft sounds of the departing footsteps of his family as they fled into the silent, streets of the Mishneh. As Judah slowly shut the door and bolted it, Adam covered his face, for he knew he would never again see his family.

*　　*　　*

Elisha kept his family moving. The stench of death and smouldering homes was all around them as fires cracked and hissed throughout the destroyed quarter. They passed the decomposing bodies of Idumeans which lay along the streets in piles from the days of fighting. Everywhere debris was scattered: broken furniture, clay bricks, shingles, glass, pottery, and torn fabric. A haze of smoke still hung in the unfavourable streets as light could be seen above as darkness ebbed away from the vast sky. The smell of blood was everywhere and Elisha could see it smeared upon the streets, and lining the edges of the flagstones as his daughters whimpered to themselves, stepping over rotting bodies.

"Elisha, who is that man?" Ruth muttered pulling on her husband's sleeve as she gazed back.

Elisha turned and saw the shadow of a man coming towards them in the smoke with the flash of a dagger in his hands. The stranger was wrapped in black garments and the sound of his sandals striking the paved street began to echo above the ruins of homes on either side of him. "Quick! Run!" Elisha called out sensing panic and remembering the whisper of Judah earlier concerning a man who had followed him.

Elisha jolted forward as he limped, gritting his teeth in pain. His heart pounded within his chest and he let his daughters go as they ran ahead. Ruth clutched her husband's hand firmly as she gazed back with terror-struck eyes at the swiftly approaching man. She heard the rasp of Elisha's breath and felt his fingers tighten around hers. The shadowed form of the man raised his dagger, plunging through the smoke as he closed the gap with such speed she knew they would be overtaken within moments. But suddenly Ruth heard her daughters cry out in surprise as a glow of flame warmed the walls of the dwellings upon either side of the street with shouts erupting ahead of her.

Ruth watched as six legionaries, with grim faces of iron, restrained her two girls as a number of other Roman sentries stood with drawn blades behind raised shields. Ruth only had another moment before capture and she took it by gazing back down the smoke-filled street at the image of the mysterious man who turned and fled, his dark cloak flapping behind him.

"Hold them!" shouted one of the soldiers clutching a torch. "You two, search them now!"

Elisha was exhausted as he collapsed to his knees to the sound of his crying daughters being searched by the legionaries who began to joke and jester at their beauty, one even clawing at Hannah's breasts like a hungry dog.

"No!" Ruth shouted letting go of her husband and reaching out to protect her daughter's purity.

"Silence!" bellowed a guard who stepped forward and struck the older woman in the face sending her reeling back to the screams of the young girls. "Try that again, Jewish whore, and I will introduce you to my pilum!"

Ruth gasped for air as the flow of warm blood oozed from her nose and split lip. She felt the tip of a spear touch her neck and gazed fearfully into the man's face. He gave her a devilish smile, staring down at her as light from the torches flickered across his squared jaw. She mumbled something and held up a hand, barely conscious from the blow and the man pressed the spear point further so she could not move lest it puncture. "You wanted to say something, whore?" the soldier asked with a dark chuckle. "Or else you must be uncomfortable? Jewish whores like you always wear too much!"

The Roman sentry raised his spear and planted a firm foot on Ruth, the iron studs of his caligae bruising her shoulder with his weight. He handed his spear to one of his fellow soldiers nearby and bent down as he drew his pugio, grabbing her cloak with his other hand. "You will like this!" he whispered as he clawed at her with stubby, filthy hands. The soldiers around him chuckled as he cut her garments and peeled them back exposing the wrinkles of her tanned skin and sagging breasts.

Ruth sobbed as she tried to cover herself and roll over. The Roman straightened, pressing down with his foot so that she moaned in pain as he laughed aloud. "What?" he called out to one of his comrades who had commented. "Should I finish her or introduce her to my prick? Strip the other two!"

"Fulminata, Primi Ordines Gaius Cornelius Antony!" shouted Elisha suddenly, not knowing where his strength came from. He had been so weak the legionaries had ignored him, as if he had not even existed. They had been too distracted from the women, but now Elisha stood with trembling legs, staring down at the shame of his wife, bellowing out in Latin to the surprise of the soldiers. "Fulminata, Primi Ordines Gaius Cornelius Antony!" Elisha stumbled over to the soldier who had his foot on his wife and collapsed next to her as he continued to shout the words. Reaching forward, he took hold of the man's foot, pushed it off, and then covered Ruth with her torn garments.

The legionary took a step back from the old woman, still holding his pugio as he stared for a moment at the man who continued shouting his Centurion's name. "I will take care of him." The soldier stepped forward with his dagger and grabbed the Jewish man by the back of his head. "I will cut your throat and cover your wife's nakedness in your blood, you dog!" he whispered into the man's ear and then brought the blade against his neck with a grim chuckle. "Then we shall have fun! I will cause her to moan like you never could, then all these men shall have their turn."

"Sheath your pugio this instant!" shouted a commanding voice that startled the sentries. An Optio, holding his hastile, stood near a cluster of scuta that leaned upright against each other. "Are you all stricken with deafness, you bunch of dogs? Does this not seem odd to you that such a Jew calls out the name of our Centurion? And you seek to murder him? For the love of the gods, stand down and let those two girls go! Priscus, Demetrius, gather these people and accompany me at once!"

The Optio watched with annoyance as the men ambled around, clearly upset that their commanding officer had spoiled their fun. "In the name of the blessed gods and my ancestors, move on the double, you lumbering bastards!" thundered the officer shaking the men into action. "Priscus, give the older woman your sagum for the sake of all that is holy! You would rape her here? A woman of that age? Jew or no Jew, you are truly from the maggot hole of *Hades* if you think that is honourable. Come men, should we not be wretched beasts?" The young Optio growled under his breath as he watched the scolded men give him dark looks, but nevertheless they complied with his orders.

The older woman was helped up, wrapped in the dark, red, outer cloak of Priscus, the man who had sought to rape her, and led over to the Optio along with the two young girls and the old man. The officer leaned upon his hastile and stared at the elderly man who had been silenced from his rants.

"You understand Latin?" the Optio said to the family, which only brought looks of puzzlement and question. "You spoke Latin, did you not? Do you understand me?" questioned the Optio with signs of impatience filling his chiseled face. "Do you speak our tongue? Greek, then perhaps?" The Optio shook his head from the embarrassment of rescuing such people who were now proving to be difficult and make him look incompetent.

Some of the legionaries chuckled and the soldier named Demetrius said, "Perhaps it is all a ruse, sir."

"I know I heard what I heard. They know of Gaius Antony, I am not deaf." The Optio watched the old man nod quickly at the sound of the name. "They didn't just guess such a name, they were told to say this."

"Are you saying there is someone beyond the wall who knows, Centurion Antony?" Priscus scoffed.

"You will not say another word, Priscus. The mere fact I will not have you scourged should be warning enough to keep your opinions to yourself. If you ever pull out your prick again while on guard duty, I shall summarily relieve you of it." The Optio glared at him and watched the soldier back down and bow his head in submission. "You hear me?"

"Yes, Optio," Priscus replied, striking his chest in salute.

"Good." The officer stared at the family again, particularly at the old man and cleared his throat. "Do you know Praefectus Castrorum Gaius Cornelius Antony?" The Jewish man nodded frantically and uttered again the Latin he had memorized. "We will get nowhere like this. Demetrius, run ahead to the quarters of the Praefectus Castrorum and give word to his servant that I will bring these fugitives to him. Go now!"

*　　*　　*

Gaius held up his arms slightly as his servant approached him carrying folds of white linen. The servant humbly bowed and then began to wrap the garment around his master, taking every care that it hung as if it was to be adorned upon a magistrate of the highest calibre. When he was nearly finished, he held the corner of the rich cloth upon Gaius' left shoulder, and then taking a brass ring, he passed the fabric through, folded the linen, and then sealed it with a long pin. The servant moved around to Gaius' right, stooped down, gathered up a length of the garment, and folded it neatly over Gaius' arm in a dignified fashion. Gaius gave the servant a nod and then held out his hand as the servant retrieved three golden rings, one with a large ruby set into the crafted gilded metal.

"I will wear my sash," Gaius softly said as he stared down at the signet ring.

"Yes, master," replied the servant giving a quick bow as he scurried around the high ranking officer and produced a beautiful, red silk sash edged in gold the entire length. The servant carefully slipped the decorative title of office over Gaius' head and then rested it on his shoulder, making sure to fix any folds or creases.

"Am I ready?" Gaius asked nonchalantly.

"Yes, master," responded the servant, stepping back and bowing low.

Gaius took a deep breath and then crossed his personal quarters, brushing aside a heavy tent flap which led to another chamber. Two legionaries stood guard behind a wooden, throne-like chair planted upon a striped tiger hide with a red carpet flowing out underneath.

Gaius slowly took a seat, brushing his garments to the side, as he let the folds fall across the arms of the chair. Gaius straightened his back, raised his chin, and tightened his face into an emotionless, stern look of judgment. A serious tone entered his eyes as he levelled his gaze at the front entrance to the chamber, staring at the shadowed presence lining the bottom of the canvassed flap as another guard stood outside. The light of dawn had just split across the sky, and he had been awoken by an urgent message that a Jewish family had surrendered and knew his name.

Gaius half turned his head to one of the guards and nodded. He watched as the soldier crossed the rug, the iron studded straps from his cingulum lightly jingling with each step. The legionary brushed the tent flap aside, spoke a few hushed words, and then stepped back as the entrance was opened revealing a small company of troops standing outside accompanied by an Optio who entered with the bound hostages. The officer struck his chest in salute and snapped his heels together simultaneously, his body stiffening to attention.

Gaius nodded and raised a single hand as he leaned back. "What have you brought to me?"

"Praefectus Castrorum Antony, I have a number of Jewish prisoners in my charge that were caught in the Mishneh. They crossed into our sentry line and my men apprehended them." The optio turned and gave a jerk as he said in a commanding voice, "Bring them forward!"

Gaius watched as an elderly couple and two young women were led across the red carpet and thrown to their knees by two guards who held lengths of rope tethered to the captives. The Jews looked filthy as a smell arose from their lack of hygiene. With a long brooding gaze, Gaius scanned their faces slowly, not recognizing them or seeing any connection to why they would have been brought here in the first place.

The Optio saw the puzzlement in the eyes of the Camp Prefect and stepped forward. He extended his hastile under the chin of the elderly man and lifted his head up. "My lord, this man here stated your name when we captured him. He said the name of our legion and knew of you."

Gaius scowled and narrowed his eyes at the helpless Jew. "So he speaks Latin?"

The Optio shook his head abruptly and shrugged. "Unfortunately, that is all he said. I fear he does not understand what we say to him. However, he does know your name and for that I thought it my duty to secure him and bring him before you."

Gaius nodded his thanks and stared down at the pathetic man whose head was turned up by the butt end of the hastile. Gaius pointed to himself and said, "I am Gaius Cornelius Antony." He watched the man nod frantically with fear filling his eyes. "What do you want with *Roma*?" Gaius switched from Latin to Greek and frowned as he continued, "Why did you beckon to have council with me? Are you not a Jew? Should I have mercy on you?"

"Fulminata, Primi Ordines Gaius Cornelius Antony," ranted the old man as he held the hand of the older woman next to him.

Gaius extended his hand and pointed to his servant who stood across the room. "Is this man Gaius Cornelius Antony?"

Gaius watched the prisoner nod again as he repeated the Latin words with a flutter of hope filling his eyes. Gaius gazed from the prisoners to the optio and then shook his head. "The man clearly knows my title, but not my face. He thought my servant was me. It is obvious they are an uneducated rabble as well as pitiful and nearly worthless."

"It looks that way, Praefectus Castrorum." The Optio looked at the soldiers who restrained the captives and said, "Hold them, Priscus." He glanced back at Gaius, who was slightly hunched over in his seat of office, rubbing his chin with his hand. "Should we send them to the crosses? Or have them penned? What would you have us do, my lord?"

Gaius shook his head and gestured to the guards. "Bring Yosef ben Matityahu here, he will be able to speak with them. If there is anything to know, it will be with his help."

*   *   *

It only took moments for the former Jewish General to be awakened and brought before Gaius. The look upon Yosef's face bore a thousand questions. However, when he saw the Jewish captives kneeling upon the floor in shame, his expression changed as he stepped past them in surprise and humbly bowed before Gaius.

"The reason I have called you here, Yosef is kneeling before my seat of office. These Jews were captured. Now I can see the status of their life is of dire poverty, and Titus has been clear, people of this state are not worth saving. These would not be spared, not even as slaves, especially the elderly couple. They cannot be servus, and thus would simply be crucified." Gaius paused as he reconsidered something. "The girls are pretty enough, and seem somewhat healthy, so there could only be hope for them, but the other two, would be worthless. Do you understand me?"

Yosef nodded and glanced at the captives. A sense of shame was clearly woven into his eyes from the verdict laid out before him in the presence of such people who did not understand that their fate lay in Gaius' hands. "Then why have you called me here?" Yosef softly asked as he turned to face the Camp Prefect.

Gaius looked from Yosef, to the Optio, and then finally to the soldiers. "You men are relieved, wait outside." Gaius understood their reluctance at leaving the prisoners alone in the quarters with only their Praefectus Castrorum and Yosef, but he needed privacy. Gaius raised his hands and stood up. "I want this chamber cleared now. You are to wait outside for my word, understood?"

The Optio slowly nodded and struck his chest in salute. "Yes, Praefectus Castrorum. You four with me!"

Gaius watched the soldiers leave quietly and then glared at his servant and the man dashed away. When he was sure nobody was listening, Gaius looked at Yosef and said lowering his voice, "Now, I want you to speak to them. They know my title and name. Somebody sent them through the Mishneh, gave them this information and trusted that I would spare them." As soon as the words had left Gaius' tongue he realized he had answered his own question. It was obvious to him that the only Jew in Jerusalem who could possibly know of him was Judah.

Gaius watched Yosef speak quickly with the elderly Jewish man, and then listened intensely as the story unfolded. The elderly man made gestures to the women he was with and only once glanced at Gaius and pointed to him. Eventually, Yosef nodded and patted the man on the shoulder with assurance. He stood and softly walked across the carpeted floor, briefly glancing over to the veil of cloth that separated them from Gaius' sleeping quarters.

Gaius caught the hint and whispered, "My servant would not say a thing. What news do you bring me? Who are these people?"

"Well, these prisoners are the family of one of Judah ben Yosef's compatriots. The father is named Elisha and that is his wife and two daughters. He tells me they are from the Lower City and were starving to death as there is nothing to eat down there. Elisha said that his son was desperate and went to Judah who arranged for them to be smuggled out of a gate in the First Wall. Elisha says it was Judah who told them about you and told them to recite your name and office." Yosef was silent as he noticed the look of shock upon the face of the Centurion.

"And, Judah believes I can save them? Judah sends me the scraps of his people, with nothing to gain and expects me to uphold this deal? That I should be some shepherd of the Jews? I risk too much with this, Yosef." Gaius shook his head and turned as he vented to himself, hating the position he had been put in.

"Elisha says that Judah trusts you, and that your word is a word of honour." Yosef watched Gaius stiffen at the last word.

Gaius gave a great sigh. "Judah got his revenge. He was faithful to his word, but any arrangement now has been broken. We are closing in upon the city and the Prince will not allow charity."

"Is not the Prince wanting to extend mercy?"

Gaius bit his lower lip and folded his arms. "Not to these unfortunate ones, Yosef. The people he sends to Gophna are the wealthy and influential. The ones he sends to the mines and ports he wants to be strong and able to work." Gaius glared at the Jewish captives for a moment seeing their future pan out before him. "The elderly would be crucified right away, the two girls might be pawned off to Pepi as whores, but none are fit for Gophna or the mines." Gaius swore as he closed his eyes, rose from his chair and took a few steps away.

"May I speak freely, Prime Ordines?" Yosef watched Gaius turn and jerk his head in agreement. "I believe you respect Judah and you do not wish to see these people suffer. This is a personal request from Judah, which no one would need to know about."

"Careful what you say, Yosef," Gaius said through clenched teeth. "What do you propose?"

"Clean them up, clothe them in some new garments, adorn them in a little inexpensive jewellery, and send them with an escort to Gophna. You could order such a thing, Primi Ordines, and no questions would be asked." Yosef watched the demeanour of Gaius change as the senior Centurion thought to himself while pacing about the chamber. He glanced back at the prisoners, raised a gentle hand for them to keep silent, then looked back to Gaius who was deep in thought with his brow furrowed.

"These would cost me a small fortune to dress like royalty," he groaned considering the expense. Finally he gave an exasperated growl. "You have two hours, Yosef. Get them to your quarters, clean them up, cut their hair, and scent their bodies. Purchase what you must for them to appear as moderately well off. I will place the Optio and guards into your care, they can escort the captives to the Mount of Olives where Jews are being transported to Gophna." Gaius watched Yosef nod and relay the instructions to the Jewish family as relief suddenly came over them as tears flowed. Elisha, outstretched his bound hands, said a few words as he wept and then pressed his hands to his lips and kissed them.

"He says that God will bless you and grant you favour for what you have done," Yosef translated as he went to calm them down.

"I am merely upholding the wishes of Judah, a man I trust. I feel nothing else for these people. Yosef, silence them now." Gaius shouted for the Optio and guards to return, which they did so immediately with curious expressions at the joy upon the faces of the prisoners.

"I have orders for you Optio, which I will have you carry out with all speed." Gaius watched the officer stiffen. "There has been a mistake here, these people are of no threat and are of high status in Jerusalem. They have suffered under the tyranny of the Zealots and escaped certain death. These are the types which Prince Titus seeks to spare to rebuild this war torn province. You are to take the prisoners to Yosef's quarters where they are to be cleaned up. Then you shall escort them to the Mount of Olives where they shall be sent to Gophna."

"Gophna? My lord? They are only poor folk, miscreants of the Lower City. What mistake has been made?" mumbled the optio in surprise as he looked over at the bound hostages.

"A mistake which has now been rectified and cleared by my authority and seal. This proves their status and my word is final. Divide it among yourselves and do my wishes," Gaius replied tossing the officer a leather sack of gold coins. "Now, take them and leave."

The Optio balanced the weight of gold in his hand, looked at Priscus and Demetrius who eyed the small fortune, then tucked it into his belt and saluted with a grin. "We shall do your bidding and see to it, Praefectus Castrorum."

*   *   *

CHAPTER XLII

May 30th, 70 A.D. / 4th of Sivan, 3830
The Fortress Antonia
Morning

Dawn was broken by a chorus of trumpets and drums as the ramparts and towers of the Antonia became alive. Men scrambled to their posts as every scorpion was loaded. Archers fitted their bows and spearmen crammed the parapets, three-men deep, along the entire length of the walls.

The deep drones of shofar'ot echoed from the great fortress to the colonnades below as thousands of Jewish fighters manned the porticoes of the Temple Mount and the First Wall. Frantic shouts and orders became constant as ranks of troops moved into position at the behest of officers who rallied them with drawn swords. Columns of smoke trailed from the high windows of the Antonia's towers as they coiled upward and streaked across the sky. Archers regrouped upon the four turrets readying missiles and collecting firebrands to shoot into the impending approach of the enemy gathering below.

Beyond the high defenses of the fortress, the destroyed blocks of the Bezetha had become overrun by swarms of Roman legionaries. Six cohorts from each of the two legions stationed at the Antonia had been mobilized for attack. Before the thick blocks of legionary cohorts, shone two golden eagles with their fixed, sideways gaze and spread wings. The eagles were held high and the men looked to the coveted, sacred icons that bound their allegiance to the service of Jupiter as legionaries of the empire. The steady crescendo of drums was relentless as they rolled and it was as if the earth seemed to move, as it came alive to the marching of the deployed battle formations.

Each cohort moved into its place in unison with terrifying professionalism to the stamping of feet and jingling cingulum as they took the appearance of a great scaled monster. Tribunes directed the ranks into place as centurions blasted on whistles and shouted orders. Optiones in the rear of each century kept the men in place with their hastile staffs and every unit's standard was hoisted with flags unfurled. The fury of Rome had been unleashed.

The ground shook with a tremor as thousands of men marched before the two massive snake ramps of earth, rubble, and timber which rose against the northern face of the Antonia. The legionaries maintained discipline, tightened their ranks, and braced for the attack to come. Hundreds of scuta were locked together in long lines of gold blazoned walls of wood and metal bosses, as pila were lowered along the fronts of every century like the quills of a porcupine. The red, blonde, and white plumes of officers' conical helmets bristled upward from the steel of the soldiers as if small flowers bloomed from the war machine.

A delegation of generals, engineers, and tribunes gathered at the rear of the advancing cohorts, as the Prince of Rome sat upon his black stallion wearing a *paludamentum* scarlet cloak, with a red sash tied in a bow across the front of his molded, leather chest armour. The sun reflected with a glare from the expensive armour as the face of Mars, enwreathed in olive branches and arrows, glared out with dead eyes from the front of his breastplate. Titus watched an array of red flags flutter in the wind from a wing of cavalry that had been stationed on the right of the attack. He watched with determination as the imagio of the Emperor was gloriously unfurled from the front ranking signifer, who sat boldly at the front of the horse troops, staring up at the high ramparts with a defiant, complex gaze.

"The legions are in position, my Prince," Tiberius said calmly as he faced the fortress next to Titus.

The Prince nodded and paused, as he considered using Yosef again, but then he just cleared his throat and said, "Carry on! Bring the towers first and get them into position to cover the assault."

"Yes, my Prince," Tiberius replied as he passed on the orders to a *tessera*, who scrawled them furiously upon a wax tablet.

"Tiberius," Titus said, turning to the seasoned general. "For the glory of *Roma*."

"For the glory of the empire, sire! Your father would be proud to see you at the helm of such strength! This is what we have all fought so dearly for. We shall vanquish the enemy and cast him down." Tiberius rode forward and then swung his mount around to face the Prince with fierce passion in his eyes. "I shall lead them forward, my Prince." He raised his arm in salute and then, as if transformed into the young, spirited soldier he once had been, he called for Marcus Octavian and Sextus Cerealis to accompany him to the rear.

Titus watched the men gallop to the rectangular formations of the twelve cohorts stretched out in front of the Antonia. There was little doubt in his mind that the fortress could prevail. Even as he squinted up at the three, twenty-eight metre high towers facing his legions and the taller southeastern corner tower at forty metres high, there was no doubt in his mind that this could fail. A resilience of tenacity and sheer power was on his side. Not even the God of the Jews could come to His people's aid. Jerusalem was doomed, and the proof was laid out before him at the command of nearly six thousand men.

Upon the ramparts of the Antonia the Zealots were ordered to hold their position. John of Gischala, Judah, Adam and many other officers, surveyed the developing scene with clear minds and steady hands. All the men were silent as they contemplated their future and the Roman trap which was set. Orders had been strictly passed out, men deployed, and all catapults readied. All that needed to be done now was to wait and anticipate the move of the proud, arrogant Roman Prince, then unleash hell. The plan was to lure the cohorts to fully commit and then dissolve their ramps in one horrendous instant that would shock the pride from the legions below.

John saw two enormous siege towers emerge from the Camp of the Assyrians and he gripped the parapets with great anticipation. The twenty-metre high, armour-plated, siege machines moved towards them, pulled by rows of bellowing oxen as the engines great wheels creaked and groaned across the paved streets. The towers moved at a menacing, dreary pace as they lurched forward, their massive wooden wheels creaking with every rotation as slaves pulled and pushed.

The engines were the muscle of Roman siege warfare, and many of the Zealots felt unnerved by the sight. However, John and Judah were both of the same mind. They hoped Titus would order the towers to make the climb upon the ramps, instead of sending the smaller testudo rams. Then the devastation would be far greater than they had even dreamed of, for when the ramps crumbled and imploded they would destroy the towers, taking with them every living soul from within.

John could make out ram heads protruding from each of the giant iron, timber bodies of the towers, and saw the parapet castles filled with Palmyrene archers. The great machines approached the rear ranks of the cohorts and a hush fell upon both sides. The towers passed by like staggering giants as they loomed over the dwarfed legionaries below, now spread across the fighting ground in tight ranks. An eerie silence ensued, which allowed the creaking and groaning from the towers wheels to echo chillingly off of the stone walls of the fortress.

The groaning teams of black oxen were led in their long lines towards the ramps as they squared off with the high parapets of the Antonia's defenses. Commands rang out as quartermasters shouted for the beasts to halt. A host of slaves dashed out from beneath the towers, unhitched the lumbering oxen, and led them to the rear of each tower where they were secured again. Both John and Judah watched silently, bracing their hands against the stone wall as the towers remained in their positions near the approach of the two earthen ramps.

A whistle blast sounded as two columns of legionaries sprang into action and ran to the towers to gather up lengths of thick coiled rope. Then with haste, they trotted up the two ramps with raised shields and secured the ropes to great wooden pulleys firmly entrenched in the packed earth. Once this was done, the men retreated to rejoin their ranks. The ropes were wound through iron rings, secured to the sides of each tower and then clasped to the teams of oxen stationed behind. Once ready, the oxen were led away from the towers with the cracking of whips so that the long ropes were now tight. With a mournful blast from a brass cornu, the legionaries raised their spears in the air and bellowed in unison, "*Roma Victa, Roma Victa, Roma Victa!*" John scowled as he felt the chill of the words run down his spine. He stepped away from the wall and shook his head, feeling uneasy.

"They will use the towers, John. Look!" Judah pointed as nearly a hundred legionaries ran beneath the towers and waited to advance. "They will mount these on the ramps and try to scatter us. See, the oxen are ready and will pull much of the weight to get the towers up to the walls." Another blast from both the cornu and buccina horns bellowed, and the towers began to roll forward.

John watched tensely as silence over took the cohorts as the towers drew closer, passing between the lined formations. He held his breath and narrowed his gaze, clenching his fists. Slowly, the towers of iron, wood, and cured animal hides approached the two ramps as the great wheels turned and rolled across the flagstones. John crossed his broad arms, lowered his chin, and stroked his beard. Once both siege towers were at the ramps, he turned to Judah and gave a silent nod.

Judah briskly walked along the rampart as he passed the double ranks of soldiers covering the length of wall. Many of them gave him nervous stares as he sought to reassure them by patting their shoulders and telling them to have courage. Adam followed hot on his heels as the two men entered into the northwestern tower and then descended a long winding flight of stairs in the coolness of the structure.

Archers and spearmen passed them in long ranks of file as they pressed upward with grunts and heavy breathing. Judah led Adam through a side door which opened onto an upper balcony that wrapped around the entire second level within the heart of the Antonia. Judah leaned out and gazed upward past the red tiled awning above the balcony at the open sky, then shook his head. He gazed out over a large courtyard, one of three that the Jerusalem Roman garrison had used to drill in years past.

"Where do we go from here?" Adam asked leaning against a wooden rail and looking down at the quiet courtyard, neglected by the Zealots. Above him, he could hear the sounds of men shouting and the blasts of trumpets. "Let's hope this works."

"Follow me," Judah replied as he led him along the open portico to a set of wooden stairs that took them to the hard packed dirt of the drill grounds. They quickly crossed the vacant space and found a door locked with a sliding latch. Judah unlocked the door and opened it as sunlight streamed in causing him to squint. "Quick, this way!"

Judah led Adam onto the colonnade roof of the northern end of the Temple Mount until they found a wide staircase leading to the plateau below. The two men rapidly descended the stairs as they steadied the swords which hung upon their waists. "To the tunnels," Judah called out as they crossed the empty court, void of soldiers and priests.

The two men plunged beneath the high columned porticos and found the tunnel which led to the mine. Taking a torch, Judah and Adam followed the deep, winding cool passage until they came to the mouth of the mine. Dipping their heads, they trotted along, picking up their pace as they could hear the pounding of their hearts in their chests, and the sounds of their feet pattering upon the dirt floor. It felt like they would never reach the end. The strong scent of the burning oil from the torch stung

Judah's nostrils as he pressed further into the mine. He suddenly felt himself growing anxious with every step as he began to doubt if this would work, although Eliahu and Amos had assured him the mine could not fail.

"Here it is!" Judah halted before the enormous stacks of dried faggots and bitumen as the stench of pitch reeked. Judah raised the torch, being careful not to get too close, and followed the towering piles of wood straight up to the roof of the mine as the ambush had been cleverly set. He traced the faggots jammed around the roof's supporting beams and then stared at the black tar substance that had been hurled over the stacks of kindling.

"My God, this is going to burn hot! Judah, you need to be quick! The heat could kill you if you do not get out soon enough." Adam shook his head in amazement.

"We don't have much time." Judah gazed up from the vibrations he felt in the floor. He saw trails of dust leaking from the ceiling between the wood and felt the ground shake. "The towers are advancing! Adam, run to the end and call for John! I must know when he wants this ignited!"

Adam did not hesitate and dashed from Judah's side down the dark mine. Judah listened to the sound of his friend's heavy steps fading quickly away. Then all was silent except for the tremors. Judah stood, alone and deep in thought. He looked at the torch in his hand, recognizing that this simple tool would be used to engulf the chamber in such heat that the roof would cave in, sending at least a hundred men to their deaths and destroying both towers. Nobody could survive the cave in. The dry, caked earth would suffocate and the flames would roar upward, burning men alive as it devoured everything.

"Judah!" Adam called out as his voice trailed through the dark tunnel. "John says light it now! Now!"

Judah's eyes widened and he found his hand begin to shake. He stepped forward and lowered the torch. He watched, almost mesmerized, as the flame touched the first dried kindling immersed in pitch and suddenly caught, hissing as it built up and howled. With a ferocious, vicious roar the faggots exploded into a hot white, orange inferno that raced up through the gaps in the wood like a drowning man fighting to get air. Judah leapt back from the intense heat, and looked up as the supporting timbers caught fire. Then he turned and ran for his life.

The huge battering towers had passed the midway point of the ramps and were moving quickly as the men inside heaved them forward. John moved to the edge and peered between two parapets, his eyes searching the ramps for any sign of the fire that should be burning underneath. He swallowed hard. What if the wood had not lit? What if something had gone wrong? John gripped the stone with his hands and held his breath. He could hear the men within the bellies of the towers as they counted aloud and timed their momentum. Already the tower on the left had reached its position and was being secured to the dirt mound by large wooden stakes. John stared with a wild look in his eyes at the silent cohorts as they watched, assured in their faith from the iron heads of the rams, and for a split second John wondered if the end was actually upon them as arrows started to fly.

Then a deep and tumultuous groan was heard, followed by a strange knocking sound that reverberated up from the ramps, causing many of the Zealots to pause and gaze over the walls at the towers. In a shocking instant, a fountain of fire suddenly spewed upward from the ramps, sending a shower of sparks high into the air. Then a heavy crash gave way as the Roman earthworks imploded and collapsed in a massive cloud of dust, fire, and screaming men. The Zealots watched in jubilation as the towers were swallowed up into a pit of burning timber and bitter vapours of black belching smoke. Men fell with horrific shouts and screams as the roar of the flames and the chasm snatched them away in an instant, drowning their cries from the choking cloud of ash that jutted above the ruins.

A ripple of horror spread across the formations of cohorts as shock turned to chaos. Nearly two hundred men dashed from their ranks to the edge of the crater, now a pile of smoking wreckage. All order was momentarily broken as curses and protest rose from the legions as men shook their spears and fists at the Jews. Centurions ran to rally the hundreds of legionaries who now stood along the edge of the destruction, calling up to the Jews to come out and fight, but the Zealots broke into a deafening cheer as they raised their weapons, howling with delight. The enraged Romans could only stand in powerless disbelief over the weeks of work wasted and ruined in only seconds.

"Get the men back! Reform them now!" shouted Titus in hysteria, throwing his helmet upon the ground. "How, in the name of the gods, did this happen? Curse them! Bastards! They are shit upon the walls and they mock us like this? Oh, Jupiter, strike them down!" Titus cursed loudly as he covered his face in shock. He watched as numerous legionaries attempted to pull dozens of badly wounded Palmyrenes from the rubble, and he shot a glare at his Chief Engineer.

Tiberius, equally shocked, quickly rode back to the Prince and yanked hard on the reins of his horse. "My, Prince, this is a damned disgrace!"

"What happened, Tiberius? Tell me now!"

"It appears they dug a mine and collapsed it. That is the only explanation! This is preposterous!" Tiberius bellowed, clearly shaken from the cruel consumption of the men who had operated the towers.

"What can you see?" Titus demanded, straining to gaze through the massive dust cloud which covered the northern face of the Antonia.

"Our towers are in hell, my Prince, so is everyone inside, I would wager. Damn them!" Tiberius shook his head. "We must reform. Those bastards could attack us at any moment."

Titus glanced down the line of shock upon the faces of his generals and staff, spotting Porcius Gracchus who dabbed his sweaty, pale face with a cloth. "Porcius, can you explain that!" Titus said sharply as he pointed at the fire and smoke. Titus watched his Chief Engineer give him a sheepish look and the Prince slapped his thigh. "Where are my ramps? Have they just vanished? What the bloody happened?"

"I would presume General Alexander is correct, my Prince. It appears the Zealots used a mine." Porcius swallowed sickly as he watched the Prince's eyes ignite like the fountain of fire which had erupted from the mine.

"You would presume? My ramps have been swallowed up and shitted upon, Porcius! And by who? The *Jews*, that's who! *The Jews*!" Titus swore again, his face flushed red. "They were not supposed to be able to have the wits to tunnel!" Titus swung Achilles around as Porcius babbled and stammered, not knowing what to say. "Tiberius, send crews to clean up and check for survivors! Maintain your position!"

Tiberius saluted, striking his breastplate. "Yes, my Prince. Where do you go?"

"Back to my quarters! Have the cohorts retire once this mess is sorted!" Titus looked at his Chief Engineer and yelled above the continuous cheers from the Jewish defenses, "Porcius, ride with me now! We have much to discuss."

* * *

Night

Simon stared at John from the doorway of the vacant council hall as the great man was hunched over a table, consumed by the maps he stared at. He watched the Gischalan warlord turn one of the maps slightly and then draw his face close to the leather as he peered at the etched diagrams, making calculations in his head.

"Your victory is complete, John." Simon watched him jolt upright.

The chamber had been emptied of officers long ago and the warlord had seen it as his duty to stay behind, wishing to examine the maps one more time with a keen eye. John stared at Simon for a brief moment and then looked away. A long, naked dagger lay upon the table next to a goblet of wine, and John made it obvious to Simon that he was always vigilant, as he turned the blade in a semicircle.

A grin spread across Simon's face as he rubbed his hands together and approached the burly man who was on edge by his lingering presence. "Can you not revel in your superiority over the enemy for just one moment?" Simon gestured to the maps and charts as he halted near the table and gazed down, squinting from the dingy light given off by the lamps which burned throughout the chamber.

"We triumphed over the enemy today, Simon, but they will come back. We must be ready. The mines were a success and the Romans have been set back weeks in their effort." John glanced up at his political rival and scowled as he wondered what the real reason could be as to why Simon stood before him appearing interested. "Titus will come at us like a lone wolf stalking a wounded deer in a forest. We have used up our only successful resort to stop him, from now on it will be by power from the Almighty and the edge of our steel."

"Surely your cunning knows further bounds, John." Simon studied the warlord for a moment as he watched his face twitch and then he gave a brooding look towards the maps. "My God, do you regret your move?"

John shrugged and shook his head. "My only regret was that the ramps didn't contain more of the enemy that is all. We killed only one hundred; compared to thousands, that is nothing. We only stung the enemy, Simon, yet we failed to deliver the killer blow we sought. To finish Titus off before our walls, we must pray for a better outcome. I would dare say our greatest victory yet was when my army stormed the Fretensis camp on the Mount of Olives and scattered them in droves. It was bitter sweet and the hillside was strewn with the bloodied corpses of legionaries. Titus may have won the day, but his mood was soured and his men were terrified of our sheer boldness. They thought we would quake beneath their boot heel, yet I say, we have fought like a caged beast, released from captivity and thirsty for the blood of its oppressor."

"You miss the triumph, John. Today's act was detrimental to morale. The victory was in the destruction of the earthworks, surely that was worth it?" Simon felt like reeling backward in the presence of John's pitiful remorse and loathsome drawn face as the lines of worry were etched into the large man's forehead.

Simon felt a surge of energy race through him from war, which was like the sweet taste of aged wine, fermented and savoury as it clung to one's palette, soothing the throat. The sight of blood and the command of troops was power Simon had never known until in the last years. Ever since his conquests in Idumea, he had thirsted for it constantly, like a wandering man would yearn for water in a desert. Simon saw doubt and weakness in John's eyes and this delighted him as he cleared his throat gazing down at the map for a moment before he whispered, "It was worth it, John."

"I fear it was premature. The Romans may have brought up more troops if we had waited." John tapped the leather hide and pointed to the dark sketch of the Antonia. "Titus will raise his ramps again, much quicker for he knows the time he has lost seeing them collapse and crumble.

"We only destroyed one of the towers, but they fetched the other before we could do anything more." John looked at Simon with a pondering expression. "When they raise new earthworks, I cannot dig anymore, my miners have warned me. The shafts and tunnels are too weak; we can only look to other means, a counter wall maybe."

"But you can dig further back and extend new mines, John. Surely what is above new tunnels will not falter? There may be another chance. If Titus is to raise more ramps this will be your only option lest he bring down your walls. The Antonia cannot hold forever." Simon crossed his arms. "If he succeeds in raising new ramps, you are finished." John gave Simon a furious gaze, but the Sicarii King calmly repeated himself in a whisper, "You will be finished, John. It is a matter of time. No stone wall, no matter how strong, can live up to the repeated heavy blows of the ram. They will find a breach, and when they do, God help you."

John glared at Simon in an instant, but maintained his composure. "Your wall is being tested too, Simon. The Fretensis will come through as well, perhaps you have other things to worry about rather than taunt and mock me."

Simon chuckled tossing his head back and then calmly smoothed his hair with his hands. "I do not mean to mock your wisdom, John. The First Wall will hold for now. They have one ramp against it and a second one still under construction by the Hippicus, not far from the Almond Pool near Herod's Palace. I do not fret from their sight. It is clear that Titus is directing all his concentration against your positions. Mine will hold for the time being." Simon noticed a smudge on one of his rings and steamed it with his breath before rubbing the corner of his silk garment furiously upon the gem. "I have a plan for the Fretensis that will most assuredly exploit a breach," he replied candidly as if bored.

"What is that?" John asked, clearly annoyed at his cryptic reference.

"A diversion that will work to my favour. The Romans are stretched thin and the Apollinaris are busy like bees at a hive on the second ramp to know what will be coming. But, the trap has been planned, and at dawn, the second day from now, hell will be brought to the doorstep of the Tenth." Simon clasped his hands behind his back and smiled at John, as if he baited the warlord into inquiring upon his genius.

John sensed the arrogance too, and it drove deep under his skin as he stared at the irritating man. "What do you have in mind? What trap?"

As if he was already the king of Jerusalem, Simon strolled over to a window and stared out into the night. "They stopped an hour ago, John. They have been hammering at our wall all day with their bloody ram. I believe it was when your mine collapsed that we were spared a moment's break. The First Wall is not the Second Wall, or thick and sturdy like the Third Wall. It is in disrepair and weak. When my Idumeans retreated behind it weeks ago, I feared getting trapped with no room to breathe. Herod's Palace is a good fortress to fall back to, but if they come through our wall, the Upper City will lie in ruins by nightfall, I swear this to you."

Simon glanced over his shoulder at the motionless commander from Gischala who listened intently as he continued, "Those siege towers cannot be penetrated from above or the sides as they are far too strong. My men hurled stones, spears, and anything they could get their hands on, but they just bounce off the sides like pebbles. While the ram was in action, I counted three cohorts standing guard near the base of the ramp, just waiting to foil any sortie I foolishly would commit.

"The cohorts make it impossible, John. While that great tortoise smashes at my wall, the legionaries just stand there watching with delight. A dastardly and hopeless end for our city, should it be that those walls come crashing down." Simon smiled and casually leaned against the window sill.

"Delay no longer, Simon. What have you planned?" John suddenly asked, splitting the silence that had fallen upon the chamber.

"Three men, John, my plan rests in the brave hands of three men who came forward to do the bidding of heroic deeds which will be remembered for generations, it is true. Their bravery will be sung beside every man's warm hearth and retold in Jewish homes throughout the empire and they will be honoured." Simon turned and crossed his arms. "Before I came to you, three men from my ranks came to me. They have chosen to rush out from the wall and set fire to the Roman earthworks and towers. With there being only three of them, I doubt they will be noticed in time, long enough for them to ignite the whole siege ramp."

"They will most assuredly be killed, they do know this?" John queried taking a step away from the table.

"They have accepted this fate. But it is vital, for as the earthworks burn, I will commit a large force to smash through the Roman sentries and storm their positions." Simon drove his closed fist into his palm, satisfaction upon his face.

"Who are these men?"

Simon raised a finger to make a point. "I know only their first names, which was all they would give me. They are, Tephthaeus, who is a Galilean by birth, Megassarus, a member of the royal servant hood of Agrippa, and Ceagiras, who is a disabled man in his left arm who hails from the village of Adiabene and who pledged his loyalty to me long ago. Ceagiras, has been with me the longest. He fought against the hordes of Idumeans in the deserts of the south; he has given much. These three I trust and these three I will honour with their sacrifice."

John considered Simon's words as he mulled them over and then looked up and saw a tall Zealot standing in the doorway to the entrance of the chamber. The man had large, square shoulders and a stout chest as he stood with his arms crossed and his jaw tightly set. John did not recognize the man and instantly felt an alarm of danger creep into his being. He knew the man was not of Simon's force and he slowly strolled over to where he had left his goblet.

"What do you want?" John said as he took the glass of wine and drank it.

"Yeshua ben Sapphias demands to speak with you, John," the man said mechanically as he refused to budge.

John noticed the look of surprise in Simon's eyes from the Zealot's tone but John showed no care as he set the goblet down and leaned against the table, the dagger next to his left hand. "Demands to speak to me, you say?"

"I think it would be unfortunate if you declined him." The powerful looking Zealot stepped into the room and planted both feet firmly like tree trunks as the light danced off of the long Persian blade that hung at his side. A great scar trailed across the man's face as a brown head covering hung upon his back down to his waist.

"You think such a thing?" John said facing the man, cleverly slipping the blade inside his sleeve. "Where does Yeshua get such courage to demand anything of me?"

The Zealot looked from Simon back to John with a menacing gaze and then smiled, exposing raw gaps of missing teeth. "You would not wish to make such a mistake."

"Where is he?"

"He waits for you near the parapet, John. I will escort you there." The Zealot took a step to the side and gestured at the doorway.

"Am I to follow you blindly? To throw my life into the hands of an assassin?" John asked shaking his head.

"The turret is well lit, and Yeshua is accompanied by only one other. He only wishes to speak with you. There is no ill nature in this. You have no choice, John. Trust the word of Sapphias, it is all you have."

"I would never trust that dog," John muttered as he looked over at Simon.

John crossed the chamber, glared at the brute man, and then passed through the open doorway and took a burning torch from the wall. The Zealot pointed up the cool staircase and said nothing, just his presence alone was haunting as John ascended, feeling the handle of the dagger clenched tightly in his hand. The steps of the Zealot were heavy and slow as the giant man followed closely behind. Knowing that a trap awaited him above, John tried to clear his mind, recalling the weight and balance of the dagger as he concentrated on every detail.

"Continue to the top!" the Zealot growled as John hesitated next to a wooden door upon a landing. He turned slightly, looked back at the warrior and shook his head as he obeyed, climbing higher.

"Now open it slowly," the Zealot said in a deep guttural tone as they reached the top level which led to the open turret of the fighting platform. The Zealot half drew his blade as he noticed John considering this option. He shoved John fiercely and barked, "Open it! And give me the torch…slowly!"

John complied, gently sliding the latch back and pushing the door. It opened with a creak and he stepped into the cool night air with the Zealot close at his back. John moved to the side as the Zealot circled around him, holding the torch like a weapon, his other hand on the hilt of his sword. John could make out the silhouetted shapes of six scorpions, armed and loaded, as they were positioned near the edge of the tower. Dust still clung to the air, the stench of charred timber burning his nostrils, but all of that did not matter as Yeshua and another man emerged from the shadows.

"So you accepted my invitation," Yeshua said with a grin.

"Did I have a choice?"

Yeshua shrugged. "You could have refused."

"And fought your man, unarmed?" John stood with his arms comfortably at his side as he peered at the mischievous Yeshua ben Sapphias.

"Well, we have much to talk about." Yeshua gestured to John sarcastically. "I told you we would speak again! I have news of *the spy* in your camp and still *he* fights by your side. I take it you have not told Simon?"

"That is not your concern, Yeshua. You talk of what you do not know. You are a man who possesses the tongue of a coward and a fool, nothing more." John watched Yeshua stiffen and raise his chin from the insult. The two Zealots at his side stood ready to attack at any moment.

"No, John! I am a man who will have honour, even if it is at your expense! I will have a seat at your table, and a title, or I shall tell Simon and he will break any truce that remains. Even if he cannot afford to renew his struggle against your Zealots, he can sit idly by and watch you and your men burn from the Antonia as the Romans storm this shit hole. Simon doesn't have to send you reinforcements and that will be the result if I talk. You know that and you can't hide behind it anymore."

"You're mad!" John said his eyes ablaze and nostrils flared.

"You are the traitor so long as you keep your mouth shut from what the fighters of this city should know, and that is that Judah ben Yosef is a betrayer and shall die for his treason. He has bedded with the enemy far too long, and I have a mind to think your allegiance has swayed too. Are you in it with Judah?" Yeshua retorted, as he took a step forward and pointed at the warlord.

"Your accusations are preposterous, Yeshua, you simple-minded fool!"

"We shall see! Search him for weapons!" A grin split across Yeshua's tense face as the two Zealots slowly approached John with raised hands and steady eyes.

John took a step back and swore as he outstretched his arms, shaking his head. "You are making a mistake, Yeshua. My men will never follow you nor listen to your voice in council. They know you for who you are. I should have never let you in the company of my men."

Yeshua watched with delightful eyes as John appeared to surrender and he called back in a scoffing tone, "You are finished, John! I have a mind to spare you, throw you in a dark dungeon and forget you ever existed, but not before you watch Judah die. I shall cut out his eyes, remove his ears, and then throw him from the walls screaming! I will make sure the fall doesn't kill him, and then the crows can eat his paralyzed body."

As Yeshua let loose a cackle of laughter, John moved swiftly. The large Zealot, who had ushered him from the chamber hall, was the closest to him and had not a moment to react. In a flash, John revealed the dagger, curving the blade inward, as he struck it across the man's throat, peeling back folds of flesh and sending an eruption of blood upon the Zealot's chest as he choked and dropped to his knees. The second man lunged at John, seeing the grisly slaughter of his comrade, but not before John was able to bring the lethal dagger back around in recovery and hurl into his chest.

Yeshua stood gaping in shock as he watched the other guard collapse with a desperate wheeze as he clawed at the blade protruding from his chest. John leapt to the dying man, wrenched back on the hilt, and tore it out with a sickening sound, before advancing to Yeshua with the agility of a predator. Yeshua panicked, seeing no way out. He yelped in fear as the strong hand of John grabbed the collar of his outer garment and pulled him viciously forward as the blade was raised, ready to be plunged into his throat.

"No, no!" Yeshua wailed. "I will do anything! Wait!"

John glared at him with fierce eyes, as if a storm was brewing within his narrowed pupils as thunder and lightning crashed around the white edges. "Why should I even hesitate a moment?" John breathed hot air into Yeshua's terror stricken face as he suddenly cast his dagger aside and took hold of the man in his great arms. "Be gone from my presence!" John shouted as he dragged Yeshua to the edge of the parapet, picked up the squealing, thrashing man, and then hurled him over the side, listening to him scream until it was silenced by a grotesque thud below.

John's chest heaved with rage. He slowly leaned out and stared down at the mangled shape lying among the wreckage of the destroyed ramps. He watched the poor, wretched, broken Yeshua squirm a bit and then lay still as a pitiful moan ascended up to John's ears. John stepped back, dusted himself off, glanced at the two bodies which lay in pools of blood, then calmly walked to the open door, leaving behind his grisly work.

*   *   *

Chapter XLIII

June 1st, 70 A.D. / 6th of Sivan, 3830
North of the ruined Bezetha
Jerusalem
Two hours past dawn

Gaius walked with his head bowed and his hands clasped firmly behind his back. He moved across the rocky ground in the coolness of the morning which bit his warm skin and filled his nostrils in a satisfying way. Gaius' heavy sagum hung from his shoulders and was tucked under his left arm as he strolled on, his mind adrift with thought.

Yesterday had shaken the legions. Up until the collapse of the mines, the entire army of Judea had been soaring upon the wings of victory, despite past mishaps. Gaius had sensed the final hours of the Antonia approaching fast as he had assembled his cohort only to watch the massive ramps come crashing down in a torrent of fire, dust, and smoke. The screams of the men being crushed had been short lived as the twelve cohorts had been left reeling in shock.

Gaius kicked a pebble with his caligae. He readjusted the strap under his chin and then slipped two fingers under his helmet to relieve an itch upon his temple. He knew that it had been a battle in itself to wake up this morning with a sense of duty and propriety such as he had possessed in past days. The memory of the wreckage just beyond his quarters had soured his mood as his servant had dressed him quietly. Gaius had eaten some stale bread, drank a cup of water, and had left for a brisk walk beyond the Bezetha.

He halted, staring up at the clear sky and the rising sun. It would be another hot day. Gaius rested his hand on the pommel of his sword and felt the rough whiskers on his chin. He turned and stared for a moment at Mount Scopus. Then he scanned the rolling mountain as it dipped into the saddle before rising with the heights of the Mount of Olives. Gaius dropped his gaze to the great city of Jerusalem, with its once proud outer walls, now reduced to piles of rubble. From where he stood he could look right into the leveled Bezetha and see the cooking fires rising up from the Camp of the Assyrians which was sprawled in the shadow of the tower of Psephinus. In the distance, against the backdrop of Psephinus, Gaius could make out the other notorious towers: Hippicus, Mariamme and Phasael. Herod's three illustrious defenses, careening like great pillars upward from the city skyline. Trails of smoke and dust caught Gaius' eye, drifting across the view of the three towers from the renewed efforts of the Fretensis and Apollinaris against the First Wall.

Gaius noticed a dark shape approaching his way from the city and squinted, wondering who it could be. A few moments crept by until he could make out long, flowing robes and a turban-like head covering. Gaius knew it was Yosef ben Matityahu. He watched Yosef raise a distant hand in greeting and the Centurion exhaled loudly, crossing his arms.

"Why are you here?" Gaius called out once the former Jewish General had come close enough.

"I have news from the Antonia, and I think you should hear of it." Yosef drew closer and gave a humble bow to the Centurion. His beard was beginning to grey and his skin appeared worn, like leather, from exposure of the sun day after day. He was adorned in expensive looking garments of dyed linen, wore a beautiful pair of boots crafted in Parthia, and his fingers glistened with gold rings. Yosef's narrow eyes gazed at the Centurion with a look of purpose and perplexity as he ran ink-stained fingers through the curls of his beard. "Your sentries found a man this morning."

Gaius stared at Yosef's calm demeanour, his interest aroused by the report. "Who was this man, and where did they find him?"

"Have you heard of Yeshua ben Sapphias?" Gaius shook his head and Yosef continued, "He is a ruthless, rogue of a man, conniving and not to be trusted. He is a Zealot who escaped the fires of the Galilee and fought in many battles around the sea. I knew of him when I was posted in the north, and met him on more than one occasion. Yeshua was a paranoid, delusional man given to erratic behaviour and bouts of pure madness. Yet, he led men into heavy skirmishes against the legions under your father, and fought bravely. He was neither afraid to suffer or scared of death. A wild man, he was."

"So this is the man they found? How can such a wild man give himself up to the sentries?"

"He didn't give himself up, Gaius. He was discovered lying amidst the wreckage of the ramps, moaning and wailing to himself, his body crushed and bones broken. He was paralyzed and bleeding, yet still alive." Yosef saw a puzzling look flash upon the face of the Centurion. He gave a nod and shrugged. "Your sentries collected Yeshua's body and carried him to their lines where an optio, the same man in your tent the night before with the Jewish prisoners, questioned him. He told me that he gave Yeshua an easy choice to make. It was simple, tell him everything and the optio would have his men dispatch Yeshua quickly with their spears, or keep silent and they would dump him back into the rubble to suffer and bleed out slowly. It appears Yeshua said quite a bit."

Gaius took a step closer to Yosef, now very interested in the account. "What report did my optio gather from the prisoner?"

"Yeshua said he was hurled from the tower of the Antonia by John of Gischala." Yosef saw the affect his sudden words had on Gaius as he mulled over the barbarity of the incident. "Yeshua said he was planning on arresting John, he said that he knew of a spy in his ranks and was going to bring it to the council, but John murdered his two guards and threw him over the side."

"Judah, he has to mean Judah!" Gaius quickly responded in an anxious tone. "But Yeshua was unsuccessful? It appears John was able to dispatch them before anything leaked out."

"It would appear that way. But John still might be suspicious of Judah. He will watch him closely. Judah should be safe as there is no further need for him to reach out to your graces anymore." Yosef watched the Centurion lower his gaze as he pondered for a moment and then shook his head.

"Was anything else taken from this man?"

"The Zealot camp is divided and stretched thin, as is Simon's rabble. He said that the Zealots are desperate, food is low, but they still believe God will save them from the legions."

Gaius scowled. "Ridiculous! They had good fortune yesterday, but Titus shall not give them another chance. I am amazed at their stubborn, unrelenting adherence to a God who has abandoned them and their cause."

"Their will is not so easily broken, nor their undying faith in God. They believe they are being tested, nothing more, and that with faithful service, God will annihilate their enemies at the gravest hour." Yosef paused, seeking to change the subject. "The transports to Gophna leave in five days. You will be satisfied to know that the Jews you spared will safely depart with it."

Gaius nodded. "Good, my pact with Judah is over. I have kept my word and he cannot hold me to it anymore. I have to be careful, Yosef, as do you." Gaius scratched his chin for a brief second. "What came of Yeshua ben Sapphias?"

Yosef gently closed his eyes, remembering the wild man and seeing the look in his glassy eyes after he had been dispatched by the heads of two pila. Then, without hesitating Yosef replied, "The optio had him killed. Two men stabbed him through the throat with their spears. Yeshua ben Sapphias is no more. He is dead."

*   *   *

June 2nd, 70 A.D. / 7th of Sivan, 3830
The First Wall of the Upper City
Jerusalem
Dawn

Tephthaeus gently cracked the door open and slowly peered out as he held a burning torch. He stared through the fog at the distant shapes of weary Roman sentries patrolling the far edge of the nearest ditch line. Tephthaeus counted eight soldiers as he scanned the defences of the Tenth Legion and recognized the hulking, dark shape of the siege tower, as if it were asleep, positioned at the bottom of the ramp. The earthworks were abandoned and a whisper of silence seemed to float in the air from the dreary Roman positions. Tephthaeus ducked back inside and gave a hasty nod to Megassarus and Ceagiras who were crouched nearby with drawn swords and lit torches.

"Is it clear to the ramp?" Ceagiras muttered as he held the blazing firebrand next to his face.

Tephthaeus nodded, wincing as he moved over to them with a quick hustle before squatting. "The fog still has not lifted, but I can see a few lights from the Roman side and count eight guards. They do not suspect anything."

Megassarus glanced nervously at Ceagiras. "We need to be certain the way is clear."

"I did not see anybody next to the earthworks or the tower," Tephthaeus replied. "Remember, two for the ram and one at the earthworks. Ceagiras, you are with me and we will burn their ram. Sheath your swords. You won't be able to carry both the faggots and your blades. Pile the wood as deep as you can and light it quickly, as you won't have much time until the sentries rush you!"

"I am ready to die," Ceagiras responded with bitter confidence. "I trust you both have accepted that as well." He awkwardly sheathed his sword with his poor arm, then stood up, taking hold of a stack of thin shanks of wood bound together.

"We would not have volunteered if we feared the cost," Tephthaeus said as he steadied his nerves and retrieved his pile of faggots, darkened in pitch.

"Simon will watch us from the wall, let us not disappoint him. We will be forever remembered, my brothers." Megassarus raised his chin in pride, gave the two men a firm nod, and then bent low to scoop up his bound wood.

Tephthaeus did not utter another word as he crept back to the door and opened it. The flame of the torch rushed next to his face, heating his skin as he gazed out across the sleepy ground. He counted seven guards this time and only took another instant to search for the eighth before giving up and stepping through. Tephthaeus only delayed a moment as Ceagiras hobbled up next to him, and then they dashed through the fog, bending over and keeping low as the third raced for the earthworks. The morning was crisp and refreshing as both men breathed heavily, hastening for the great monstrosity which lay before them and the iron head of the ram which jutted out.

The tower sat upon layers of planks that spanned a deep dyke, channelled out of the ground by Roman workers, and both men used caution as they scaled down the side of the four metre ditch. Once at the bottom, they took a second to collect themselves, then scrambled up the other side, digging their fingers into the moist clay and dirt as they struggled with the stacks of wood they carried. Tephthaeus made it to the top first and gave a desperate look back to see the shape of Megassarus shoving his faggots into the side of the earthworks before plunging the burning point of his torch into the dried wood.

"Are we clear?" Ceagiras tensely whispered as he pressed against the cool earthen side of the ditch.

Tephthaeus ignored Ceagiras for a moment, suddenly spotting the shape of the eighth Roman sentry with his back against the tower, armed with a spear and shield. The guard seemed to be resting, and had not yet noticed them nor smelled the smoke that was beginning to rise from Megassarus' work. Tephthaeus peered down at Ceagiras, and said anxiously, "There is one guard at the tower. I will take care of him. We must hurry. Megassarus has already lit the earthworks."

"Then go now!"

Tephthaeus felt a slight shove from Ceagiras as he pushed himself up and crested the edge of the dyke, caked in soil soaked by morning dew. He quietly laid his stack of dried timber on the ground and drew his sword as he crept toward the ram. His eyes were intensely fixated upon the lone soldier who stood silently, unaware of the impending danger. With blade raised and neck moist from sweat, Tephthaeus reached the plated body of the siege tower and readied his sword for the strike. He silently made his way along the cool edge of the machine, steadying his hand as his body was pressed against the damp iron plating of the tower. When he had gone as far as he could, Tephthaeus took a number of quick breaths, to summon courage, then sprang around the corner with a flash of steel, gritted teeth, and pulsing eyes.

Tephthaeus wasted not an ounce on mercy. Like the stealth and speed of the Sicarii, he plunged his sword under the legionary's right arm where he was most vulnerable, feeling the point drive deep as it punctured through muscle, rib, and lung. Immediately with his other hand, Tephthaeus wrapped it tightly around the man's face, covering his mouth and sealing off the sudden rush of breath to muffle any scream. The legionary struggled for only a second, his eyes seeming like they would explode from the panic and terror-stricken face. Then, as life drained from the soldier, he finally crumpled back into Tephthaeus' strong arms with a groan while warm blood ran down the side of his body and collected at his feet. Tephthaeus laid the body upon the ground, drew his blade from the corpse, and hastily cleaned it off with the dead man's woollen garment.

Ceagiras watched the kill from the edge of the dyke. As Tephthaeus dragged the body under the cover of the tower, Ceagiras scrambled to the top and raced over to join his comrade. He stared at the dead Roman for an instant and watched as a trickle of blood bubbled around the corpse's lips, running down the cheek to mix with the chalky earth. "Clean kill, my friend."

"Get to work. We must hurry." Tephthaeus pushed past Ceagiras as the man, with his disabled left arm, dragged his stack of timber inside the tower and attempted to jam it up into a section of the roof where there was a gap. Meanwhile, Tephthaeus poked his head out from the sanctuary of the battering tower and stared at his lone pile of bound faggots lying near the ditch. He licked his dry lips and caught his breath. The surge of adrenaline that had led to the slaying of the legionary, had consumed his very being. Now that it had past, he felt exhausted and weak. Yet, Tephthaeus knew he had to retrieve the bundle of wood or risk being discovered by the other sentries who patrolled the lone rim of the long dyke.

"I will be back, don't light yours yet, we need more fuel." Tephthaeus stared up at Ceagiras' work and gave him a rewarding nod as he handed him his torch. "Wait and be patient." Then he dashed out into the open, crouching as low as he possibly could.

Tephthaeus reached the bundle of faggots swiftly and bent down to pick them up by the strong cord which bound them. He heard the faint sound of a jingle and snapped his head up as he sensed a threat, yet nothing could be seen through the blanket of fog. He cringed wondering if he should attempt at lying upon the ground behind the bundle of sticks, and then realized he did not have a choice. He watched the shadow of a Roman sentry halt about ten metres away and rest his scutum upon the ground. Tephthaeus could hear the man let loose a loud yawn and gaze towards the dark walls of the Jewish defences. It would only be a matter of time before the guard noticed the obscure shape of the faggots and Tephthaeus' body sprawled behind it.

"Is that you, Vorenius?" the sentry called out above a whisper. Tephthaeus lay like a dead man, holding his breath, praying the man would walk away, but the cautious guard only lowered his pilum. "Who goes there?" Tephthaeus watched the soldier take another step closer and then hesitate as he strained to make out the shape.

When the soldier turned his head, Tephthaeus knew the guard was about to call for help. In that instant, he knew his only chance to get ahead of the weighted down Roman soldier had presented itself to him. Leaping to his feet and grabbing the bundle of sticks, Tephthaeus made a mad dash for the looming tower as if pursued by a dozen ravaging hounds. He heard a shout of alarm from the sentry, but ran on, refusing to look back.

"Light it now! Make ready!" Tephthaeus bellowed, knowing they had been discovered. He saw a look of panic in Ceagiras' eyes before the brute man limped over to the mass of kindling fixed into the roof and shoved his fire brand into the faggots. Immediately smoke began to fill the body of the tower as Ceagiras stumbled to the front coughing loudly as he passed Tephthaeus who dragged his own bundle of timber into the heart of the giant tower.

"Leave it, the roof has already caught!" Ceagiras shouted. Then his eyes bugged out and a gasp escaped his lips as the point of a pilum tore through the mist, driving through his chest. "Tephth..." was all he mumbled as he tried to breathe, dropping to his knees with a grunt. Ceagiras only had another second to live, for when he looked up he saw a single Roman soldier step out of the fog with a menacing glare.

Without hesitation, the soldier slashed his gladius across Ceagiras' throat. The Roman watched the body of the Jew shudder, chest heaving upward with desperation to breathe, followed by a red wave of blood that streamed down the man's chest.

"Piece of shit," the Roman said, shaking his head as he took a step back from the billowing smoke. He raised a hand to shield him from the burst of heat and shouted for help. He saw jagged flames begin to lick at the unprotected wood inside and swore. The sentry shouted again and took another step back. "Damn them all," he muttered as a dense cloud of smoke trailed out from the distant earthworks on the other side of the dyke. He looked back at the dead Jew, then noticed a pair of blood stained caligae poking out from beneath the smoke which swirled about and he knew he had found Vorenius.

"How did this happen?" hollered numerous sentries as they trotted up to the smouldering tower and suffocating smoke.

"How did they get by us? We are better than this!" exclaimed a guard as a wave of vulgar profanity filled the air. The tense legionaries covered their faces in shame and spit upon the ground as their minds filled with the fear of what could possibly await them as punishment once Larcius Lepidus was made aware of this disaster. Then all fear of legionary reprisal melted away as two of the guards called out in alarm, pointing their pila across the dyke as a horde of wild Idumeans poured towards them in a solid wake of fury.

"They will burn the earthworks!" shouted one of the guards frantically as the rest called for reinforcements. Within a few seconds at least thirty more sentries were at their side as they clustered together with lowered spears and raised shields.

The Roman who had slain the Jew at the mouth of the tower, now stood at the front with his blood stained gladius, clutched with tense fingers as he roared, "Brothers, we must avenge our honour. We cannot let them destroy both the ramp and our tower! We cannot abandon our post! If we run, we seek capital punishment, and if we stand, glory! Together, now, with me!" He stepped out from the frightened Roman guards like a mythical god that sensed no fear, as if flesh and blood had been transformed into the being of an immortal warlord of air and legend. His courage filtered through the depleted ranks, as men considered their reality, that if they fled, scourging and execution would surely await them back at camp.

"Meet them at the dyke! We'll have the advantage!" shouted another one of the sentries as they ran to the edge of the steep ditch. In an instant, a formation of sixty locked scuta and bristling spear points bore down on the Idumeans who charged into the ditch swelling it with men who attempted to scramble up the steep side.

The legionaries thrust their spears into the Idumean mass with deadly precision as they piled up at the base of the ditch, attempting to breach the crest. The sudden, lethal Roman strikes quickly reduced the maddening Idumean attack into a wild frenzy of screaming men who reeled backward in bloody ribbons as more pressed forward to fill their place. Anyone who attempted to scramble up the side of the ditch, or slash his sword at the exposed Roman feet, would get three or four pila thrust at him with blinding speed. A cluster of Idumeans began to hurl their spears at the compacted Roman formation as the legionaries braced themselves against the flexibility of the scuta. The pulse of each soldier raced, yet they continued to bellow with rage as the volley of heavy spears struck their shields and deflected with hard thuds.

Then the tight ranks of stubborn legionaries began to shift back against the immense weight of the attack. Trails of blood could be seen, streaked upon the ground from deep flesh wounds inflicted on soldier's thighs, ankles, and arms, but still the sentries fought bitterly. Spears began to snap and bend and men quickly resorted to drawing their gladii as they lunged forward with each strike.

A legionary shouted in alarm as Idumeans began to crest the ditches on all sides, surrounding them with howls and bellows. Now they were encircled, and the grisly scene became impossible as legionaries collapsed in bloody heaps, their bodies continuing to be stabbed as if the Idumeans feared they would come back to life. The Romans closed their gaps and tried to drag wounded men back, but it was fruitless. With a torrent of spears and the hacking of sword blades, the Idumeans attacked their flanks, leaping at them like wolves finishing off a wounded beast. The Romans called out in panic as they stood and fought, every man now displaying multiple wounds upon their bodies as the corpses piled up. Then with a sudden roar like a mighty tempest, three hundred Idumeans bolstered up their courage, and charged with a great cry into the dwindling Roman ranks.

The scene was like a farmer harrowing lengths of wheat with a great scythe. In one moment, the Romans stood valiantly against their peril and bleak future, then the Idumean tidal wave pushed into them, knocking them over. No more was the sound of sword against sword heard, or the thud of spears striking shields; now that familiar clamour of battle was replaced with slaughter. The sound of cutting flesh, wailing men and screams echoed from the blood soaked ground as men were stabbed, pierced, struck, and strangled. The legionaries fought with every ounce of their fading will. They reached up and dragged Idumeans to the ground as they slit their throats, gouged their eyes, or choked them with bloodstained hands. The wild cackle of misery and sheer agony rippled through the piles of struggling men who wrestled each other with fists and daggers, dying among piles of strewn bodies. Finally, the last Roman sentry was slain and the Idumeans rallied their disgruntled, broken force. Twenty men were dispatched to walk through the piles of Roman dead and silence any wounded by the points of their spears, while the main horde was reinforced by another three hundred warriors, eager to join in the killing spree.

By the time the ranks of Idumeans had been organized a call alerted the men that a cohort of legionaries approached. A blast of horns sounded as men raised spears and called their brothers into solid ranks. The mist had lifted and now the Idumeans were presented with a daunting force which suddenly bore down on them. In a stretched out rectangular battle formation of centuries, four-men deep, the Fourth Cohors of the Fretensis came at the Idumeans at a quick jog, their caligae echoing upon the flagstones. Another row of defensive ditches, fixed with thousands of wooden stakes upon the bottom, lay before the Idumeans and they knew the Romans would be more than fine with occupying the northern side, thereby holding them in a stalemate position until more cohorts could be brought up. For the Idumeans, this was not acceptable as they doubled the Romans in force, yet the danger of getting trapped and slaughtered in the ditch was intimidating enough for the Idumeans to send back a runner to give word to Simon.

A few tense moments slowly crept by as the two sides glared at each other. The Idumeans hollered insults across the ditch at the long rows of legionaries who stood behind their red scuta, as each shield bore the white images of a bull, two dolphins coiled around a double-headed spear, and an oared warship with a square sail. The Romans watched, under strict orders from their centurions to hold their ground, as the Idumeans mutilated the Roman corpses of the dead sentries, cutting off their heads and fixing them on the ends of their spears as trophies. Despite this display, the Romans retained their position and composure, yet filled their hearts with hate and revenge.

When the centurions of the Fourth saw two gates open along the First Wall and another long stream of Idumeans dash out to reinforce the sprawling horde which stood before them, they began to grow nervous. Whistles blasted down the ranks as officers screamed at the legionaries to hold their positions and prepare for a frontal assault, while optiones in the rear hollered back across the vacant ground behind them for more help.

A Centurion, who patrolled in front of his century, began to shout loudly to his men, testing the strength of their armour by grabbing it or knocking his fist against their shields. He cried out that his century was made up of gods, not men, and that they had become lions to devour the pathetic Jews. A long scar trailed across both his cheeks which held all the signs that it had been crudely stitched together by a surgeon long ago. However, the ferocity and violence in his voice was contagious as men began to nod, feeling courage fill their veins like warm drink.

He turned as he heard a rise in the Idumeans begin to build like a tumult and said with thunder in his voice, "Watching! Keep watching! We must avenge our fallen brethren! Look where they lay! Look at the shame of our friends! Simon would have their heads for his table! Their blood cries from the earth, 'Avenge us brothers! Avenge us brothers!' No matter what comes at you, you will hold the line and stand your ground. You are legionaries, never forget that. Keep your ranks! Hurl your spears on my command and make it count! Drive them back and fill the ditch with their dead! Reclaim the honour of the Fretensis! You men are the gods of war, shall you back down? No!" he screamed, sending spittle from his mouth as his eyes burned and cheeks flushed with rage.

He watched as the Idumeans surged forward, pouring into the ditch as they tried to avoid the wooden stakes which slowed their charge. The Centurion observed the Jewish horde stretched out on either side. Knowing that soon, like the sentries, they too would be threatened with envelopment, he bellowed for his men to throw their pila and draw swords.

With a taste for revenge, the ranks of the Fourth Cohors let loose a terrible volley which filled the air with dread as hundreds of pila sailed down into the thick Idumean mass. The effect was devastating. Men pressed tightly together pushing through the bottom of the dyke, took care to avoid the jagged stakes but were unable to move, let alone raise their shields, against the hail storm of iron-headed missiles.

In a great shudder of horror and collapsing bodies, the Idumeans were reduced to withering, bloody screams as the pila struck them down in droves. Men who were wounded, fell upon the wooden stakes only to be impaled with awful guttural shrills that rose above the din. Blood poured everywhere, so that the bottom of the dyke became a river of waste and crimson. The immense host of men were halted for a moment, chaos gripping their souls. The front ranks hid behind what shields they carried, as men cared not for their brothers strewn in heaps as their eyes remained fixated upon the waiting cohort that now stood poised and ready. The cries of helpless men among the Idumean ranks grew louder and louder as they were trampled, suffocating in the bloody, moist clay by the weight of scrambling soldiers above them, only to drown in misery.

Then a great shout went up, and with a volley of their own, the Idumeans hurled their spears, drew their swords and lunged forward as they tried to climb the ditch. The Romans sensed the dire situation immediately begin to rise. The threat of the enemy seemed to grow and take on a life of its own as they cried out like jackals and swung their swords at the exposed feet of the legionaries. Leaving piles of dead and wounded men behind them, Simon's army filled the ditch and began to stream out on all sides of the cohort. The legionaries were soon forced to cower behind their scuta, as they created a temporary wall against the onslaught. The Idumeans soon became enraged at their lack of being able to strike out at the Romans as many tried to grab their shields and yank them away.

"Square! Form square now!" shouted the centurions on the flanks as the stalled Idumean attack crested the ditch on either side of them and charged like howling demons. Within moments, nearly four hundred legionaries became surrounded as they were forced to defend their lives, until their shields began to shatter and splinter. The Idumeans charged again and again, each time wearing the legionaries down as the bodies piled up between the two forces in a space of death. Soon, the flagstones surrounding the cohort were no longer visible as corpses lay entangled with discarded weapons. Exhaustion gripped men as muscles felt consumed in flames, yet every time the Idumeans charged the Romans would meet them with menacing glares and angry shouts.

"Hoist the signum!" cried a Centurion, weak from multiple wounds and pale with exhaustion. He stood in the centre of the desperate Roman formation, among twenty men who lay upon the ground dying from horrible wounds. The Centurion stared at the backs of his frantic men, trying to hold their ground as they were constantly bombarded and attacked. Beyond the frail ranks of legionaries, the Centurion could hear the bellows of the Idumeans as they could smell the fear and see the last moments of their hated enemy.

"Someone hoist that signum!" the Centurion shouted, pointing at a dying standard bearer who leaned upon the teetering company icon, his face a horrid mess where he had been slashed across his mouth, his left arm severed at the elbow, revealing scraps of broken bone and torn flesh. The Centurion watched as a young legionary moved to the side of the signifer and took the standard. With exhausted eyes of pity and trepidation, the young legionary helped the dying signifer lie down, then left him and raised the signum above the dwindling Roman square.

From where the Centurion stood, he could see the backs of men, as they recoiled from another ensued attack, then lunged forward with their swords and shields to strike. He heard his men call out the names of comrades as legionaries collapsed, and soon the screams became constant as they were ravaged by the emboldened Idumean forces.

Finally, the sides of the cohort began to buckle as legionaries tripped and fell backward. A few Romans had retained their pila and now thrust these out at the leaping forms of Idumeans who now began to infiltrate and hack their way into the crumbling square. No more were the Idumeans retiring to regroup. Now the fighting was constant as exhaustion made it impossible for the Romans to fight back effectively, as they felt the end drawing near.

The Centurion knew it was simple: either the entire cohort would be wiped out, or they could smash their way through and retreat back towards the Mishneh, pushing for the breach in the Second Wall. At least at the breach they had a chance, as archers and scorpions could retaliate, thus ending the supernatural power that seemed to race through the veins of the Idumean assault. He knew it meant leaving the wounded, but they had no choice. The Centurion surveyed the ground around him for a brief instant, then bent down and grabbed two men who had light flesh wounds on their legs and arms. "We are going to get out of here, I don't think you want to stay!" he shouted into their shallow, blood-speckled faces. They nodded at him with bleak, distant looks and he let them go as he winced in pain from a wound he had received on his upper right thigh. If he was going to live through this day, he had to ignore the agonizing pain and fight like the crazed savages he had faced in northern Germania.

"Men! Retreat back to the breach! With me now! Save yourselves and fallback together!" he bellowed, his throat parched and burning. He raised his sword and led the way. He pushed fiercely between two legionaries, then took a head clean off an Idumean in one fell swoop as he roared with a sudden frenzied instinct to live.

The Centurion paved the road to freedom for any legionaries who followed, as he thrust his blade forward and slashed it across any Idumean who stood in his way. With the deep cry of a beast, he ploughed over anyone in his way as if he tilled living bodies from the ground with the edge of his gladius. The spear points of the legionaries who followed the Centurion, struck more Idumeans down until they dripped with blood, having been bent from the driving impact of piercing mail, cloaks and bodies. Soon the spears were left quivering in the corpses of men as the legionaries used their swords, hacking out from the sides of the retreating cohort as they fended off lunging strikes.

After an exhausting effort, the column of weary legionaries managed to break through. Following their fearless Centurion, they plunged into the streets of the surviving neighbourhoods of the Mishneh. The pursuit was a terrifying one as the hostile Idumeans charged behind them, striking down stragglers and hurling spears at the rear ranks of the withdrawing cohort.

Nearly a hundred Idumeans hung back from the main attack as they began to scour for spoils, collect weapons and armour from the dead, and slay the Roman wounded. Men knelt next to bodies, pulled rings from their fingers, found money purses, and discarded useless objects. They slit the throats of legionaries who resisted, and removed their caligae either for themselves or for a fellow comrade. The plunder was sufficient, and the Idumeans laughed with delight, holding up trophies for their friends to see. Another forty men were sent by Simon to collect their wounded, and they walked up and down the dykes as they checked the bodies.

The wails of the wounded were terrible, and one that would not cease. Men were collected missing limbs, having their entrails spilled upon the ground, or appearing without eyes and ears. For many, death was imminent. In some cases a fellow Idumean would just sit with a wounded man and recite a prayer or attempt to make him comfortable, but for most, the luxury of friends or comfort evaded them and they were left to bleed to death in agony.

Smoke continued to billow from the earthworks as it had been completely forgotten in the midst of the Idumean victory over the two Roman assaults. The ground spoke of their triumph as the corpses of legionaries lay everywhere, and the Idumeans who mingled around the killing field, gave off whoops of jubilant praise. The sound of battle continued to be heard deep within the Mishneh, but for the men who saw to the dead and wounded, nothing could appear to be better. The tower had been destroyed, and the clever plan of Simon had been successful, yet still at great cost.

A file of women, carrying lengths of bandages and water, walked through the open gates, spreading out as they tended to the wounded with care. Men groaned and limped back to the First Wall as some were carried or dragged. There were too many bodies piled in the ditches and strewn across the flagstones to get to everyone in time, for soon, echoes of pounding feet and shouts could be heard rolling back steadily towards them.

The look of panic was in the eyes of the retreating Idumeans who hurried back to the First Wall. Their bodies were covered in sweat and blood as many had abandoned their weapons in haste. Hundreds could be seen stretched back through the long streets while at their rear, a host of cohorts and mounted Roman cavalry surged forward, slaughtering everyone they encountered.

Simon, who had been watching from the walls since Tephthaeus, Megassarus, and Ceagiras had charged from the gates into the morning mist, now gripped the edge of the stone parapet and screamed in anger at what he saw. He cried down to the men, who picked through the dead and wounded, to reinforce the tide of fleeing Idumeans, but it was hopeless. Simon watched as the Idumeans poured from the streets and fled across the ground where the cohort had been defeated. The Roman cavalry was on their heels as they chopped down at them with long swords and struck them with their spears. Dozens of Idumeans who tripped over bodies, had only moments to thrash and scream as they were trampled by the horses and pulverized by their hooves. The fresh Roman cohorts who followed behind the troopers, fanned out as they assaulted the frantic Idumeans and chased them down into the ditches, swallowing up their flanks.

The once glorious feeling of Idumean elation had now been reduced to a stampede of panicked men as Simon watched in fury as survivors fled through the open gates. Simon shouted for archers to cover the maddening retreat, and soon the ramparts were thick with ranks of bowmen who began to rain down a storm of black darts upon the Roman enemy. His victory had been stolen. The chance to regain the Mishneh and uproot the Fretensis had failed. He had hoped to drive the enemy back through the breach to the Camp of the Assyrians, and had committed over a thousand men to do so. Yet, now hundreds lay dead, and he feared that any chance to disrupt the Roman aggression to capture the First Wall had been lost. Now he was hemmed in.

A dark frown covered Simon's face as he watched the Romans halt their pursuit. He cursed under his breath and wondered if he should have committed more soldiers, as he watched in silence, his demoralized army retreating back into the Upper City. For the moment, they were safe.

*   *   *

Camp of the Assyrians
Two hours before midnight

"In three days the rebels have managed to destroy over two weeks of work, kill three hundred and sixty two of my legionaries, kill twenty alae, wound two hundred and ninety, completely destroy two towers, damage another, collapse two of my ramps, and set fire to a third. Have I missed anything, my studious legates and tribunes?" Titus glared across the table at his ashamed legionary commanders and his Chief Engineer who wore a sullen look of embarrassment. "My desire to capture the

Antonia has been set back, and our lines in the Mishneh were overrun. If it had not been for a combined effort by Frigius and Lepidus to rally four cohorts, along with the assistance of the recovering Boars, those damned Idumeans would have chased us from the breach with our damned tail between our legs!" Titus struck the table in anger. Tiberius Alexander stood behind him but dared not say a thing as the young Prince vented.

Titus jabbed a finger into the air and shook it furiously as he raised his voice, "Shall the army recover? This turnaround has cast our efforts to see this war brought to an end into such perilous depths that I am afraid to even venture into the camp of the legions at what I might hear. They are demoralized! Morale is crucial for seeing a siege of this scale effectively to the end. Failure is not an option for the Judean Legions and I will grind whatever the mill requires for victory! These men are damned legionaries! I expect them to perform as such! We represent not ourselves, my Generals, but our Father and Lord over this entire vast empire; the eye of Vespasian watches everything."

"My Prince, the men have seen hard times such as this before. They will bear it with hate and anger, but bear it they must," Tiberius said, finally breaking the tense lecture the Prince had drilled them with. "Jotapata and Gamla were giants to overcome, and many fell in the weeks it took to take those cities. Jerusalem will be vanquished, and the men can sense it. John and Simon have thrown everything they have at us, and we endured it all with gritted teeth. The Zealots can't have much more to sacrifice."

"That is where you are wrong, Tiberius. It was said they did not have the faculties to mine, yet still they brought both ramps down like a bedded whore! Now they rush out in daylight and sack our lines? How do they do this if they have little to sacrifice? They have everything to sacrifice, their lives they sacrifice, and they do so with gladness! Lepidus had an entire guard of sentries slaughtered and the Fourth Cohort was all but nearly wiped out. About half of their force now rots the ground and awaits the pyre. It is unacceptable. I want all guard positions doubled and always have two cohorts ready for anything." Silence filled the quarters of Marcus Tullius Octavian, and they all waited for the Prince to speak again.

"Now," Titus said, taking a deep breath. "We have a problem, and that is what seems to be a precious commodity of this hot, damned region…wood. Your reports say that we are dangerously low on timber. How are we to repair the earthworks and rebuild our towers if we lack wood?"

"I will dispatch Marcus Sulla on a foraging expedition, my Prince. We will give him as many carts as he can take, as well as a detail of troops to hastily gather it." Marcus Octavian watched the face of the young Prince twitch but he held his composure. "Give them four or five days to strip the land of trees and we should have enough wood to rebuild the earthworks."

Titus watched the Generals nod in agreement and he relaxed, finding the suggestion satisfactory. "Fine, have the Boars depart at first light."

"My Prince, if I may state a point." Frigius piped up, receiving an unobtrusive bob of the head from Titus. "Why not take other measures instead of delaying another five days, or however long it shall take to collect the wood. The land is already bare and Sulla's Boars will have to venture far. If I may be so bold, why not simply starve the despicable Zealots and the whole lot of them? All we would have to do is camp around the city, tighten our positions and wait it out."

"Not possible. It would take far too long and these legions need to be dispatched elsewhere once this matter is closed." Titus leaned against the table. "No doubt one legio will be stationed here to maintain peace and order, but the Judean Legions will be disbanded and sent to other parts of the empire where they are needed. The time it would take to starve the Jews into submission is not permissible."

"I would agree with the Prince," Tiberius added. "We do not know exactly how much food stores remain. It could take months, or even a year."

"What about a full attack from all the legions, including the alae?" Sextus piped up.

"Way too bloody and not guaranteed it would even work. The casualties would be enormous, like in the days of Hannibal," Tiberius quickly responded, shaking his head. "With the walls intact we would have to attempt a palisade and that would still require much wood to build ladders high enough for the walls. How we would even take the Antonia and Temple plateau would remain near impossible with a palisade."

"Torch the gates and storm them. Cover the troop advance with all the ballista and scorpions we have. The Jews would give way; they would not stand," Sextus pushed vigorously, wanting to see the affair closed without more delay. Already they had been there for nearly two months and it was wearing on his legionaries, and his own patience.

"Still, a massive loss to the legions would be inevitable," Titus said. "I want to return back to my father intact legions, not sorely depleted ones. We have to be prudent in our actions, but aggressive when we must. The best course of action still lies in reconstructing the ramps and smashing their walls to create a breach, and we must do this with haste. My father has cared to remind me that this war needs to be decided soon. So long as we tarry, his seat of power in *Roma*, and his place in the senate, will continue to exist with holes of doubt in the minds of men who have supported my father and now question his competency in crushing this rebellion. Allegiance from the praetorian is essential and must not wane. A flex of Roman muscle has to be given and the Jewish resistance removed to remind the empire that Emperor Vespasian is the only man who can restore a sense of normality.

"Furthermore, we will conduct this siege in a more brutal effort. I have given clemency to deserters and refugees from the city, and have sent Yosef to them many times to deliver my merciful terms to have them spared as well as their city, but this will now change." Titus paused as he let his words sink into their minds. Then he gestured for Tiberius to deliver the plan they had been working on in the hours prior to the war council.

The elderly General rubbed his chin and took a swig of wine from a goblet upon the edge of the table. "After careful planning, the Prince and I have devised the formation of a plan to tighten the strangle hold upon Jerusalem. Beginning tomorrow, we will begin to construct a wall of circumvallation around the whole course of the city. It will begin and end on the hill in the Bezetha, which to our estimate will be around five miles in length. Porcius Gracchus will be overseeing construction and four thousand alae and legionaries will be committed to the effort. It will stand three metres in height and will possess thirteen forts along its perimeter to be manned constantly by troops taken from King Agrippa and King Sohaemus' forces.

"This should prevent the Jews from penetrating deep into our lines, should they seek to launch a sortie. This will also halt the night foraging that has been constantly happening which we have been unable to prevent. The wall will be lit along its entire length and will also serve to remind all rebel forces that their days are numbered."

"These are your orders and they provide details on the layout of such a defensive wall," Titus said as he waved a servant over who held a silver tray with four tightly rolled scrolls upon it. Each scroll was sealed in wax and bore the signet impression of Titus himself. The Prince watched his Generals take the orders, as they considered the effect a perimeter wall surrounding the city would have upon the rebel cause.

"My Prince, I believe this wall can possess the spirit needed to crush resilience in their audacious hearts," Larcius said with a firm nod. "It may well be the very thing needed to tighten our grip on this city and to the eye, it will be demoralizing. With any fortune, the common people may just rise up and revolt against their cruel taskmasters as they grow desperate."

"Fortune, my dear Lepidus, would be for a frustrated Zealot to shove a knife into the back of John of Gischala and then open the gates of the Temple to our legions," Titus said with a smirk. "But the sense of dread the city will feel, once they see that their path to freedom has been shut off by our enveloping siege wall, will do just fine."

*   *   *

CHAPTER XLIV

June 4th, 70 A.D. / 9th of Sivan, 3830
The Fortress Antonia
Midday

John stared at the thousands of Roman workers in the ruins of the Bezetha as he began to piece together in his mind what they were up to. It was a wall of enclosure with a purpose of painting a dismal picture for anyone in the city who retained the hope that victory could be in sight. It also posed as a reminder that the Romans would not back down and were here to stay. He watched as files of men, as far as the eye could see, carried crudely hewn stones upon their backs to numerous piles of rocks that sprang up at the base of the long, winding wall that rose from the earth. John could see individual stones from the piles being passed up to men on top of the thick wall, where they were positioned and set into mortar. As time passed, the wall grew higher and higher, as if a great snake of rock was furiously battling to emerge from the broken earth.

John fought against the nerve to shout at the workers and curse them, but he worried that if he did so they would interpret it as fear and therefore delight in his obscenity. He felt an edge of cold prickle the back of his neck, as if a horde of ants crawled across his skin, and he instinctively scratched, despite knowing it was all in his imagination. John stared up into the clear blue sky and shuddered. His stomach felt uneasy, his chest heavy, and his shoulders weighted down as if chains hung from them.

He redirected his gaze back to the long, snake-like wall and stared at the finished sections that stood three metres high. It was wide enough to patrol upon, and already he counted forty strangely dressed soldiers with tall spears and oval shields strolling upon it in the heat of day. John guessed the men to be allied auxiliaries of the legions and he studied their movements for a few moments. To the far left, nearly out of view, John could make out a twelve metre high tower of stone and timber with a thatched roof above a wide turret. He spotted more soldiers inside the tower, but at this distance he failed to count their numbers, although he guessed that the turret could hold at least eight men. John gave a low growl in the back of his throat and spit between the parapets as he leaned forward and shook his head. All he could do was watch helplessly and curse them.

"Their wall will surround the city, John."

The warlord from Gischala turned to the familiar voice that disturbed him from his sour, bitter pondering. He stared at Simon, his mind a wallowing hole filled with grief, anger, and frustration. Then he took a step away from the parapet and nodded. "I guessed as much. What have your men seen to the south?"

"The same thing you see before you, a thousand Romans and allied troops building a wall fixed with towers. It would seem they wish to convey a stern message."

"And what would that be?"

Simon grinned and gave a shrug. "That rebellion is futile."

"And would you agree with them?"

"The last week has proven to be a dagger through the heart of these arrogant Romans. We hurt the pride of Titus, and he will never forget that. So, I would say that so far our rebellion has been effective. The north may have been a disaster, but taking Jerusalem has proven to be much more difficult than they anticipated. I would say that dog-of-a-man who calls himself primped royalty does not know what to do, and so he keeps his men busy constructing a useless wall." Simon strolled across the platform and gazed out at the Bezetha.

"You really think Titus has been foiled?" John responded as he exhaled loudly. "For everything we have thrown at the man, he has met us head on."

"What are you trying to say?"

John stared directly at Simon. "He cares not for the lives of his men. It would appear he is willing to sacrifice anything to see this city destroyed." He looked back at the distant workers, appearing to him more like an army of ants than a legion of Romans. "Pressure must be coming from Rome."

"Do we even know if Vespasian is there yet?" Simon asked. "It doesn't matter. A thousand filthy senators who care more that their beds are warmed by boys and girls could never make a difference here, even with an emperor whispering sweet honey into their ears. It is us and Titus, nothing else." Simon made a grand gesture at the impressive wall dividing the remains of the flattened Bezetha and scoffed loudly, "If the Prince of Rome wishes for us to slay his men by the thousands, we should thank God. Perhaps this is how the Almighty shall use us to crush the legions encamped around us."

John was silent. His faint heart wanted to believe what Simon said was true, he wanted to feel the surge of pride and confidence that had once gripped his soul. Yet, as he considered the ruinous end the Romans had met, here they were back again, building a defensive wall to surround the city, carrying on as if nothing had ever happened.

The destruction of their ramps and the casualties in the hundreds seemed to mean nothing. The determined spirit of the legionaries was something he had never seen in his Zealots. He had stood bravely arm to arm with his men against wave after wave of cohorts that had smashed against the walls of forts and cities in the north. They had fought with pride and a tenacity the legions had rarely seen in an enemy. But still, at the end of such a long and tumultuous struggle, he knew that when the situation had become dismal, he had fled Gischala and left the bodies of hundreds of women and children to rot in the wilderness. They were different, and something inside told him that the Romans would never leave, no matter how many they killed. It was as if the legions had taken on the manifestation of a dark spirit to haunt the Jews forever. The spirit of Amalek, as it was called, was encamped around them, hailing from the malevolent city of Rome, and it desired to swallow the chosen people of God, binding them in slavery and tyranny forever.

"What occupies your mind, John?" Simon asked watching the burly, tall man bow his head and close his eyes.

John shook the dark thoughts from his mind. "We need to assemble the war council tonight. We have much to discuss."

"What else could there be to discuss, John?" Simon replied sarcastically as he shook his head towards the Roman wall which cut through the New City. "We need to pray, not discuss," he said with the nervous cackle of a man seeing all hope diminish.

John stared at the man he had hated for so long. A grimace covered his face as he scowled at the pathetic madman, loathing the very fact he had to speak to Simon, as if the man was his equal, deserving of respect. All Simon had ever done was intervene in the matters of the Zealots, disrupt the populace of Jerusalem, and put to waste much of the resources they needed in order to survive such a siege.

John blamed Simon for everything. The man had descended upon the Zealots like a warmongering, senseless wind of evil and had swept the city into turmoil, divided men, and now made light of future preparations to insure the city would not fall. John hated Simon, and for an instant he considered tipping him over the side of the tower as he had done to Yeshua ben Sapphias. John knew he would likely smile, watching Simon plummet to his death with screams and pointless thrashing, his body breaking upon the rocks below with a sickening thud. Yet, John knew that such an act would risk civil war.

John knew that another bloody uprising would occur if he was to murder the bastard who was now leaning between the parapets and staring downward at the activity below as legionaries worked at cleaning the mess of the devastated ramps. John was familiar with the insurgent mentality even within Simon's own camp, and if Simon was to be thrown to his death by the strong arms of the warlord from Gischala, another incompetent madman would rise up from the ashes to declare war on the Zealots, even with the Romans knocking at their front gates.

"Just assemble your officers for council. Bring everyone, Simon." John watched a twisted smile break upon the smooth face of the self-proclaimed king and he suddenly wanted to drive a clenched fist into the annoying expression. But instead, John nodded Simon's way and calmly added in a gruff tone, "I will expect you there to add your voice to the council."

*　　*　　*

When night had fallen upon the city with the streets vacant and quiet, the officers of John and Simon's forces met. Everyone was present, and the great hall within the Antonia was packed to capacity as men whispered away and spoke of the ill tidings that were being erected around the city. Ananus ben Bagdatus stood like a massive pillar near the great council table, as he stared down at scattered maps and documents with a stern gaze about his face. Men loyal to Bagdatus stood around the malevolent killer, enjoying the fear and attention they received from many of the Zealots who eyed them suspiciously with deep seeds of hate in their hearts. A few comments and insults passed over the table, as the Zealots clustered on one side and those loyal to Simon stood on the other. A few fingers jutted out in accusations as tension rose, while the minds of men swirled to and fro like a great sea tossing a helpless ship about. It had been ages since the officers of each contested side had gathered for council, and with the aided pressure of the suffocating Roman stranglehold, they were all on edge.

Judah, Adam, and Moshe stood at the far end of the table, not far from John and his bodyguards as they looked on. Judah listened to the racket of hurled insults and watched as Bagdatus joined in, shouting profanity and then tossing his head back as he roared with laughter at what he perceived as lowly, pitiful replies from the Zealots. The air was ripe with frustration and it was deteriorating swiftly as Judah gave John a worried look. The warlord understood it all too well as he finally rapped the table with his fist and cleared his throat.

"Silence yourselves. We have much to discuss!" John bellowed as men quieted down, yet still maintained deep glares at one another. "The time to set aside old hatreds has come. Bury them now, my brothers, for we face a dire threat." He waited for a moment as faces began to turn his way with an assortment of expressions. John furrowed his great eyebrows and scrunched up his chin as he lowered his gaze. He watched with a foreboding irritation as Simon fixed his hair and then studied the jewelry he wore on his fingers, as if the whole charade was a waste of time. "The first order of business affects us all, and that is the issue of food, so pay heed.

"The city is dangerously low on food and fresh water, this is no secret. The pilgrims who arrived during the past feasts, have refused to leave out of fear from the Romans encamped around our walls. Anyone who has fled has ended up on a cross. Every mouth desires to eat, and we do not have this luxury. The Lower City has become a dump and a waste of starving people and rotting bodies. They are hurled from our walls into the valley because there is nowhere to bury them. Even we go with little food." John paused and softly said, "Should it be that starvation becomes our bitter enemy and not the Romans?"

"If your Zealots had not burnt the food stores when we arrived here, we would not be in this place!" shouted a man standing among Simon's commanders.

A host of Zealot voices rose up in opposition as they yelled back and threw up their hands in outrage. Judah thanked God that it had become a standard rule to leave weapons outside, for if even a number of them had held swords there was no doubt in Judah's mind they would have slaughtered each other. Moshe shouted at the Idumeans next to Judah and thumped the table with his fists. Then the young man, with his short temper, shoved a large Idumean, shouting at him wildly as he jabbed the air with his finger near the man's nose. Soon the chamber was filled with the clamour of accusations, curses, and threats as order melted away into pandemonium.

Judah glanced at Adam, who held his composure, and his friend simply offered a shrug. Adam took a step back, as if sensing that soon everyone would resort to murdering each other with their fists or anything they could get their hands on. Finally, the hulking Lion warrior just turned to Judah and said above the din that he would rather leave than stay. Judah just shook his head helplessly.

Then Judah noticed something leaning against one of the columns near the back of the council hall. Judah took a step past Adam, and for a moment his friend misinterpreted the move, believing that Judah wanted to leave as well. But when Adam saw him dart over to a pillar and pick up a shofar, he knew what awaited the chamber. Judah raised the ram's horn to his lips and gave a loud blast.

The stark sound jolted the men of the chamber into a stunned silence as he pushed the high pitched note further, straining his cheek muscles and closing his eyes as he let the sound sail and reverberate off the walls. When he lowered the shofar, over a hundred flushed faces stared back at him with beady eyes and agitation lining their tense figures.

Judah strolled over to John's side and tossed the ram's horn onto the table. "You all sicken me! We see doom with our very eyes as the Romans build up their walls and seek to erect new ramps and you choose division amongst yourselves? It does no good to accuse and blame. What has occurred in the past cannot be undone. This city is on the brink of a renewed effort by Titus to see it pounded into dust, and you swear at one another? Your own people starve and die of disease, yet you would rather banish them and purge their suffering in order to scrap like two dogs over a bone absent of meat?" Judah watched many of the men lower their faces in shame, while others, like Bagdatus, stood prouder than ever, glaring at Judah as if his voice had become a filthy substance wafting in the air.

John stared at Judah for a moment and then said, "We have limited food stores that remain. Beneath the Temple are vast warehouses and chambers that contain offerings from the First Fruits and tithes which have been preserved. That alone can sustain many men for weeks. There are also grain stocks which were assembled and hidden away before the siege, and those should be portioned equally so we can make it last as long as possible. These are our two main sources of food to feed our men and maintain our hold against the Romans."

"But if this shall be consumed, where can we go for supplies? Without food, our armies will be too weak to fight back and the city will collapse," John ben Dorcas called out.

"There are always private supplies of grain from the populace to consider," Bagdatus suddenly spoke up, shifting the gaze from John onto himself. "Search all homes of the aristocracy, merchants, anyone who would have ample enough. Dispatch squads to scour the streets and knock down people's doors. Conduct a search on this scale and you might be surprised what turns up."

"Anarchy on this level should not be considered," James ben Soras replied as he stared at Bagdatus, then looked from Simon to John. "We need the city on our side. When we defeat the Romans, how will we restore order if they hate us?"

"They already hate us. Just look at how they live in the south. They despise us because they do not understand what we represent and seek to do," Simon replied in challenge. "We desire to bring them liberty and they blame us for their suffering."

"Because our concept of liberty comes at their expense, which is the root of their suffering," Judah said sharply. "If we would not have held them hostage, the situation might have been different."

"Is this a matter of point, Judah, or does it come from somewhere else?" Simon shot back angrily.

"You...I...we all have seen the bodies and had our nostrils filled with the stench of their suffering. We cannot pretend any longer that we have not committed an injustice upon these people, our people, in order to lash back at the Romans. It always will come at the expense of the innocent. Our mandate has brought death upon the civilians of Jerusalem, and we are forced to stand firm, not look back, and face the Romans, as the people die for our cause." Judah stared through the crowded chamber at the quiet form of Matthias ben Theophilus standing in the back. The old priest seemed to detect his stare and looked up as he gave Judah a firm nod, maintaining his silence and composure.

Simon stiffened at a loss for words. He raised his hand in the air and shook a fist at Judah as he suddenly shouted with anger burning in his voice, "We are liberators and patriots! God has ordained our struggle! How dare you question that!"

John held up his hands and called for silence. He gave Judah a glare, which clearly warned him to hold his tongue, and then glanced at Simon saying diplomatically, "We all have differences how we perceive the terrible things that have happened. Alas, let us resolve the most difficult of problems set before us, and that is storing food." John paused as he gathered his thoughts. "The fact is simple, we are already despised and there is nothing to be done that can reverse that. Right now, we need to consider how to survive, and searching homes and streets for food may be our only way. With the Roman wall being built to surround our city, I fear that foraging outside the walls, as many have done, will not be possible anymore." John studied their faces for any objections, but nothing was betrayed.

"And what of desertion?" came the shaky voice of Matthias as he pushed through the men and stood at the table. His white beard almost glowed in the torchlight which burned throughout the chamber as his eyebrows curled upward above his small, weary eyes. "Much of the wealthy and influential have fled. Many of the poor, out of desperation, flee as well. It is those people we see hanging upon fresh crosses every morning, hearing the sounds of the legionaries pounding nails. With those people who desert us, they take with them valuables and food, which only falls into the hands of eager Roman sentries on guard."

"There is nothing to be done for those who escape cowardly in the night. Their fate is not our concern," James ben Soras said.

The chamber was silent. All remembered the break of morning light cascading over the Mount of Olives as three women had lain unconscious upon the ground, bound to rocks and naked from being raped during the night. The bright flesh of the women, burning in the sun, revealed lacerations and deep cuts as streaks of blood shone from the pale rocks they had been grappled to. Death would be slow, their bodies soon to be a feast for the vultures.

Finally, Simon broke the silence as he vowed to all raising a finger, "Do not worry about the desertion problem. I will tighten the patrols I send into the Lower City. We will have all the gates guarded and secured. Nobody will escape."

John nodded in agreement and driving his fist into his open palm stated, "Anyone caught attempting to flee, will be thrown into the dungeons to rot. If it is one of our men, he will be put to death immediately without trial."

"Agreed!" Simon responded boldly as he raised his chin in defiance. The reign of terror had begun.

* * *

June 6th, 70 A.D. / 11th of Sivan, 3830
Mount of Olives
Noon

Titus gently dug his heels into the muscular flanks of his great warhorse, Achilles, as he galloped along the side of the Mount of Olives. The ground was more even now with the weeks of hard, intensive labour which had been dedicated to leveling the slopes and removing obstacles. It had been totally transformed into a barren hillside, its many olive groves now replaced with a forest of crosses. He stared up at the mountainous peak and counted the twisted looking crucifixes lining the summit. Some were empty, having the corpses pulled down days ago, while others revealed gruesome skeletal remains of victims torn to pieces by the flocks of carrion which circled above. He stared for a moment at the quiet city and the clouds of dust which drifted from the northern side of the Antonia where hundreds of labourers had been dispatched to begin the task of erecting new ramps, higher and wider than before. Titus would not be outwitted by the Jewish rebels again, and he loathed the very memory of that humiliating day which occupied his mind almost constantly.

Titus felt as if he was flirting with a desire for personal revenge. He had decreed that any prisoner, not showing a sign of wealth, was to be scourged and then nailed to a cross. To start his edict of terror, he had ordered one hundred prisoners to be marched down into the Kidron from their holding pens outside the Fretensis camp, and crucified upon the withering remaining olive trees that stood in the valley. Some of the larger and wider of the trees were able to support two or three of the thrashing victims, while others had barely enough room for one.

When the trees had run out, the centurions and legionaries had drawn from their more creative, sadistic side. Prisoners were to be bound to the burning faces of stones with ropes tied to their ankles and wrists, with their limbs spread out and secured by iron stakes driven into the tough soil. The dozens of crosses and screams which lifted up from the valley's floor that day had its desired effect on the Jewish soldiers who peered down with horrified expressions at the misery of their people. Yet, still the city's force refused to capitulate.

The Prince spurred Achilles down the side of the mountain towards the valley where another line of thin, sickly looking prisoners were being prepared for crucifixion. With utter apathy, Titus rode past the doomed lines of men, women, and children who had pale, fear-ridden faces. One man unexpectedly leapt out in front of Achilles rattling his chains, causing the people secured at either end to lose their balance and topple into the dust. The man clasped his hands together and raised them in mercy to the stout, defiant Prince who stared down at him as if he were inhuman.

"Please, your majesty and Prince," the prisoner pleaded in Greek. "I beg of you, cast aside your wrath and spare us! We will be your servants!"

Titus drew back on the reins and gave a dark foreboding glare at the pathetic prisoner as three legionaries rushed the captive with lowered spears. Titus raised his hand to the guards who were poised to skewer the captive where he stood and the legionaries backed down as they tightly secured the man's chains so he could move no further. "You are a Zealot? You look like one of John's men?"

"No! I escaped merely to live with my family. We were oppressed in the Lower City, there is no food there. I beg you, my Prince, I am no Zealot! They are evil!"

"Yet you look like a man who has eaten much more than everyone else you are chained to. How many soldiers does John have? What does he plan to do next?"

"I don't know," the man squealed anxiously.

"Piece of shit, you do know!" Titus roared back.

"I will help you get into the city, I know a way!"

A sly smile spread across the usually charming face of the Prince and he shook his head. "You are a Zealot, and a coward! You would do anything and say anything to be spared your fate! You think I need you? I hate your kind the most. You would weep like a whore to be saved, but would not hesitate a moment to kill me if you had the chance." Titus looked at the two guards holding the captives chains and said in hollow sounding tone, "Move this one to the front. Put his eyes out and then crucify him!"

The prisoner gave Titus a shocked, open-mouthed gaze and then started to cry out as the legionaries kicked the back of his legs, until he collapsed, then dragged him away.

Titus stared at the line of demoralized captives, focusing on four children who were shackled to the line as they whimpered. He felt his chest burn with anger and wished he had a quart of wine to calm his nerves. It was their fault he even had to do this sort of business. The Jews had started it all and had forced his hand. If they wanted it to stop, all they had to do was open the gates and surrender.

Titus stared up at the high walls of the Temple Mount and shouted, "I am not the one who sentences these young ones to death!" He pointed a bony finger at the shackled children to single them out and continued, "You are the guilty ones! It is you who crucifies them! You hear me! For every strike that the nail is driven, it is your hand which holds the hammer! May their blood be upon you all!" Titus watched the men upon the high ramparts stare down at him, but nobody said a word. Titus grumbled something under his breath, turned in his saddle and shouted for the centurion to make haste and be sure the work was completed in the hour. Then he swung Achilles around and galloped up the mountainside.

Titus felt the wind cool his back and the sides of his face as the sweat dried and his eyes watered. He was happy to leave the misery of wailing prisoners behind him, and he cursed their stubborn souls silently in his mind.

He rode along the outside of the stone walls of the Fretensis camp and heard the sound of legionaries calling out to him in salute, but he ignored them. Titus made his way around the camp to a large tent erected near the top which bore a legionary flag fluttering from a pole next to it. It was the station for Jewish deserters bound for Gophna. Titus had delivered strict orders to his generals for only the aristocracy to be spared; captives made from the class of money. They were merchants, patricians, priests, or wealthy land owners, anyone deemed fit to be of an intellectual caliber, sympathetic to Rome, and eager to please.

Titus neared the tent and relaxed as he let himself be soothed from the motion of the great, warhorse's powerful body. He noticed a number of Jews standing solemnly outside the quarters and they briskly moved away as he approached. One of the men, familiar to Titus, remained and lifted a hand in greeting to the Prince as he warmly stepped forward.

"My Prince, it is good to see you healthy and riding about," Yosef ben Matityahu said with a cheerful smile, despite the sense of melancholy that hung around the aristocratic company of Jewish hostages.

"Yosef, what are you doing here?"

"Interviewing captives for my histories. I must have as much information as I can get from what is happening behind those walls. It is incredible some of the hardships these men and their families have gone through, and for what the Zealots did to them it is most dreadful." Yosef saw a flicker of interest in the Prince's cavalier eye. "Most have lost everything to the greedy hands of John's men. Some managed to bury their fortunes and escape with them, but only some."

"They will continue to be allies to *Roma?*"

Yosef nodded without hesitation. "Their allegiance is binding. They completely reject the Zealot cause, and find them loathsome, barbaric savages. The Zealots and Simon's forces have stripped the wealth of the city, everything they have touched dies. However, many of the merchants and tradesmen I have interviewed are confident in the security of invested assets through their businesses that they will be able to regain their status and influence in these lands once the rebellion has been crushed."

"Leave that up to me, Yosef. I will ensure they are compensated for lost dues. The Emperor will not forget them. They will be essential men in the rebuilding of this forsaken land." Titus leaned forward in his saddle as he pondered and then his face brightened. "You will join me for dinner tonight? I am hosting a feast with the generals to instill morale and I would be delighted if you would recline at my right."

Yosef bowed low to the ground, feeling great satisfaction at the compliment. "I would not miss it, my Prince. Once again your kindness runs deep."

"You have been an invaluable asset to me, Yosef. Keep serving with diligence and courage. You will be rewarded justly once this matter is put to rest." Titus heard a number of gasps escape the lips from a huddle of wealthy Jewish men arrayed in vibrant colours and he scowled at their gawking expressions which gazed across the valley.

The Prince turned, his eyes scanning the stone walls of Jerusalem and the pinnacles of the Temple. It only took a split second for him to realize what had shocked the merchants. Upon the ramparts of the Lower City's eastern walls, Titus could see men clustered upon the top, dumping over the sides what appeared to be garbage. He narrowed his steady gaze as he attempted to make out the shapes much clearer. Then it dawned on Titus and he suddenly realized that the falling objects, which twisted and contorted in the air, were dead bodies.

"War is a terrible duty for a Roman who seeks to bring the world into the light. But it is necessary to see her glory spread as it has." Titus watched the bodies tumble some more and then glanced down at Yosef. "It is why one must always keep his camp clear of the dead. Starvation and sickness can easily set in and devastate a troop. My father saw it many times, both in the camp of the enemy and his own. Men grow desperate and will do almost anything, even devour one another when there is nothing left. An absence of hope. Jerusalem has chosen its fate," Titus said softly, as if the stunned historian needed an explanation as to what transpired across the Kidron Valley. "This is out of my hands Yosef, surely you understand?" The Prince watched the Jewish General soberly nod and Titus grinned down at him. "I will expect you at my table tonight; I trust you will enjoy the food."

*   *   *

621

CHAPTER XLV

June 9th, 70 A.D. / 14th of Sivan, 3830
Lower City
Morning

Judah led a small detail of ten men through the narrow, filthy streets. Adam was among their ranks, as they finished searching the block of houses and moved on to the next suburb, leaving behind the sound of wailing women and cursing men. The detail was among a hundred others like it that had been dispatched by John and Simon's command. Their mission was simple, yet in many ways shameful, as each man pushed the degrading guilt as far from their mind as possible. They were on a foraging expedition among their own people, ordered to collect any food they discovered, leaving only a week's ration in each house, which was a slow death sentence for any family it happened to fall upon.

However, Judah was more merciful. Where other details were seizing nearly all food stores, Judah was more lenient, taking only a meager amount while instructing the occupants on how to better conceal it. He had bound his men to silence, using every sort of oath he could think of, and since the men were honourable, he knew any decision of his would be kept secret.

Judah's detail had all the trappings of the other bullying squads who chose only to knock once and then break down the door. Yet he could never bring himself to treating fellow Jews so poorly, and for those who did, he despised them. Yet, Judah also knew he could not return to John empty-handed. Thus, he was forced to take from families what little they had, and brush aside their pleas and venomous curses which they heaped upon his head.

His men would shove people aside, overturn beds, tables, and floor tiles in their maddening search for food. When the precious food was found, they would take a portion, return the house back to normal, and hide what remained, where they knew no Idumean or Zealot would ever consider looking. Judah always tried to deliver an impotent apology upon leaving, usually to the man of the house, who would spit in his face or attempt to strike him. He knew if the roles had been reversed he would have done far worse than spit in some bearded Zealot's face. He knew he would have tried to kill the whole lot of them.

Judah halted, pointed his spear down a narrow street and shouted at his men to divide up to search the homes in pairs. He turned to Adam and signaled to his friend to accompany him further down the street to where the first doors were being forced open by his men, their angry shouts ringing out as they demanded admittance.

Judah watched as a number of helpless people, wrapped in dirty garments, scrambled from the street and ran away. He loathed his very presence in such a place. Before the rebellion, he was known as a delightful, soft spoken man of action. When Judah had seen something that needed to be done or said, he would do so. He could never have perceived of a time when he would be an officer for a Zealot warlord, terrifying people in the streets of Jerusalem.

"Do you smell that?" Adam quickly said as he suddenly stopped in the middle of the street. His chin jutted upward and he sniffed, his stomach beginning to churn as his eyes darted back and forth.

"What is it?" Judah asked, feeling uneasy.

Adam shook his head. "It smells…it…smells like roasting meat?" He turned and gave a bewildered look at Judah. "You don't smell that?"

Judah watched Adam walk a couple of steps further, halt, swirl around, and shake his head with a perplexed look, as if somewhere a feast was happening and he had not been invited. Judah slowly moved forward and then his nostrils were filled with a salivating, familiar aroma. It took him a moment to identify it, for roasted meat at a meal was a thing of the past, hardly even smelled other than the sacrifices which continued to burn throughout the day and night.

"I smell it," Judah said, as if not knowing what to do. His mind raced with a sense of guilt, as if he was the one sitting by a fire roasting a shank of lamb. Then he felt anxious. What should he do with such a person caught with such valuable food? A barrage of questions ran through his mind faster than he could count. Where did they get meat? Who gave it to them? Where did it come from? Should he arrest the culprits? Should he join in on the meal?

Adam ignored Judah's confused predicament and silently moved along, straining his senses as he followed the rich smell. Finally, he stood outside a small, damaged home, and pressing his ear to the door he listened intensely. For a second it seemed like Adam had stopped at the wrong house, then he quickly waved at Judah with excitement and moved back from the door.

"It's in here…whoever is roasting meat is in here!"

Judah scowled as he trotted over to the door and lowered his spear. The sweet smell accompanied by the sound of crackling meat over a fire filled his being and whet his appetite. Judah gave a haggard look to Adam, with craved-filled eyes. "We need to go in quietly. Can you open the door without much noise?"

"That is if it is not bolted, then we need to kick it down."

"Agreed. Try it first."

Judah widened his stance as he leveled his spear point at the wooden door. Adam crept up and gently laid his hand on the weathered timber planks of the flimsy door. He gently pushed and the door opened, as if nobody was home. Adam shot a steady look at Judah as a thin wisp of grey smoke drifted out.

Judah slowly edged past Adam, piercing the smoke veil with the point of his spear. The room was vacant of any furniture or life, but was strong with the scent of meat. He waved his hand in front of his face from the smoke and scowled back at Adam. The house was very tiny, maybe two or three small rooms, but both men knew one of those chambers would contain the roasting meal and its foolish occupants.

For Judah, it was obvious where the meal was being cooked. He could see a thin trail of lingering smoke rising up from a partially closed door. Both men moved cautiously across the dusty floor, stepping carefully, eyes focused on the target as a sharp crack sounded from the popping sparks of a wood fire. Judah and Adam froze in mid stride, hearing a haunting, eerie hum arise from the smoke filled room. With a crisp woman's voice, came a torrent of words rambling one after another.

"Oh, must make sure it is cooked through, yes I must. Only meat which is good is that which is cooked, right? Oh, Eleazar, you would thank me, you would understand. I will provide like the virtuous woman in the Proverbs of Solomon, that is right. I have it memorized, you would be glad to know, as you recited it aloud to the children every Shabbat with your loving hand resting on my shoulder, and with you wrapped in your tallit. Hear me now; I will recite it, even if it is not Shabbat." The woman cleared her throat and continued to the bafflement of the armed men beyond the chamber. "*Who can find a virtuous wife? For her worth is far above rubies. The heart of her husband safely trusts her; so he will have no lack of gain. She does him good and not evil all the days of her life. She seeks wool and flax, and willingly works with her hands.*"

Judah listened to the perfect recitation of the Scriptural passage of wisdom that Israel's third king, Solomon, had written hundreds of years earlier. Words that were considered sacred and beautiful were now spoken in a hysteric rant that made Judah's skin crawl. There was a moment of silence, then he heard the woman continue quoting from the passage, "*She also rises while it is yet night, and provides food for her household, and a portion for her maidservants.*" She paused and then said, sniffing back tears, "I would never let you go hungry in a place where food lingers not. Do you think I am incapable of love? You I wed, and you I care for. Our children were born from my body and will grow to be strong men. Maybe they shall be a rabbi, builder, carpenter, merchant, or farmer?

"Remember, meat needs to be fully cooked, and this will taste like the meat from a king's table. I turn it just right and you can try some in a bit. No bread to go with it, but meat is just fine. Wait, Eleazar, please do not speak, it is nearly ready. You should wash up and come lay at your table. Rest yourself, for you look tired. The meat is almost ready."

Judah and Adam stared utterly dumbfounded at one another as they listened to the one sided discussion, convinced that an entire family must be reclining around a small table as the wife of the house cooked the food. Then they heard a soft weeping sound drift from the room and it steadily grew as it filled the house. The soft tears from the woman soon turned to a beating breast and a deep wail of anguish as she gasped for air, sobbing horribly.

"She's all alone," Adam whispered as it dawned on him. "There is nobody with her; we should go in now."

Both men catapulted through the mask of smoke confidently behind their quivering spear points as they burst into the chamber. A woman, squatting in the centre of the room by a small fire, suddenly screamed and fell back. In a panic she crawled away with tears streaming down her cheeks as she held her stomach and wept. What roasted above the fire froze both men in their tracks. Neither uttered a single syllable as their eyes fell upon the form of a dead, mutilated baby which lay near the burning embers and jagged flames of the cooking fire. A crudely shaped knife lay upon the ground, and skewered onto its blade was one of the small, plump, baby's legs, the flesh partially roasted. Beside the knife lay the other leg, but this one already devoured to the bone.

"My God!" Judah said with parted lips and widened eyes. Adam stood beside him equally speechless with a grotesque expression plastered upon his face at what was before him.

Blood streaked the woman's clothing as she chewed nervously on one of her fingernails, before slowly shuffling towards them on all fours like an animal. "Please, kind men, there is plenty left. I did not mean to have it all for myself. Eleazar would not want that. Please, you are my humble guests."

"Get back woman!" Judah shouted as if awakened from a terrible nightmare. He lowered the spear point at her tear-streaked face and she scampered back in fear. "Blasphemy! Utter wickedness!" was all that tumbled off his lips as he still could not comprehend what he actually was witnessing.

Suddenly the woman, as if a demon clutched her soul, stood up and pointed an accusing finger at the men, shouting in a shrill voice, "The only wickedness is that there is no food! All food has been taken from us! The meat is good, I have cooked you a meal! But if you do not wish it, leave me now! Get away from me! Eleazar will be home soon and will hate to see you! Get away now!"

Judah and Adam stumbled backwards from the insane woman, nearly tripping each other up as they fled the home, pouring onto the street. Adam kicked the door shut behind him and shook his head as he stared at Judah with a face of ash. Soon, the other men from the detail heard the commotion and jogging towards them they demanded to know what had happened. Yet, all Judah could say was that the house was cursed and none should enter.

"Judah," Adam rasped as he tried to recover from the horror he had just witnessed. Judah stared at him wild-eyed as Adam blurted out, "The words are true, they have come true before our eyes."

"What words?"

"Remember the words of Moses, as it states in the Scriptures," Adam paused as he took a moment, then slowly recited, *"The tender and delicate woman among you, who would not venture to set the sole of her foot on the ground because of her delicateness and sensitivity, will refuse to the husband of her bosom, and to her son and her daughter, her placenta which comes out from between her feet and her children whom she bears; for she will eat them secretly for lack of everything in the siege and desperate straits in which your enemy shall distress you at all your gates."*

Judah was still. He vaguely remembered the Torah passage. Judah had hardly attended services in any synagogue since the war had begun, but the lightning edge curse that had rang out from the lips of the prophet Moses long ago to the children of Israel, was ever clear in his mind. The ranting and sacrilege of the woman attested to the curse, and at their gates the enemy of the world had come to distress them and destroy the ancient City of God.

All the men kept deafly silent, as if a ghost had passed between them and stricken their vocal chords. They all stood motionless in the street, as the sweet scent of roasting meat drifted from the home and lingered in their nostrils. The ruin of war upon the innocent was what haunted Judah's mind as he looked to Adam for an answer he knew could never be given.

"Let's return to the Antonia," Judah finally said, turning from the profaned home. "We should report this to John."

The men filed in behind Judah and marched silently through the streets as they left everything behind. They moved quickly, with no desire to halt for anything. Beggars held out bandaged hands and called for mercy, but the men swiftly passed them by without hesitation. The streets cleared before the detail of soldiers, like Moses parting the Red Sea for the children of Israel to escape the armies of Pharaoh.

Judah kept his silence, and listened to the somber treading of the men behind him upon the dirty flagstones of the Lower City. The stench of human waste and dank water clung to the air, so much that Judah eventually wrapped his head covering over top of his mouth so that the heat of his breath became moist against the spun wool cloth. His eyes darted to and fro, watching the empty gazes of peasants who huddled at the corners of homes or hobbled along the edge of the street, having no care to step from the gutters. Depression and sorrow gripped his soul, but Judah felt anxious. He could not help them; he had nothing.

Adam fell into step alongside Judah as they came upon a wider paved street that led them uphill towards the southern corner of the Temple Mount, where the Royal Porticos towered above the squalor of homes further south. "Will you really tell John?" Adam said in a reserved tone.

Judah shook his head followed by an apathetic shrug. "What difference would it make?"

"He might call off the search details, if he knew the extent of the suffering."

"You really think he would?" Judah replied sarcastically. "Pressure from Simon is strong, and John knows that his fighters need food. The stores under the Temple are depleting, and he will have the priests to contend with if he wishes to seize that food. No, it is easier for him to send out soldiers, like us, to rob our own people of any chance to survive this hell."

Adam nodded gravely, his mind empty of anything further to say. He watched as the homes around them slowly began to change in size, style, and appearance. Less and less filth covered the streets, the beggars all seemed to disappear, and people looked a touch healthier and less afraid. Narrow alleys were replaced by wider thoroughfares and plant life, as small gardens grew up around two-level homes.

More soldiers began to appear from other food details as they carried sacks of grain, baskets of bread, and vessels of dates, olives, figs, and other fruit that had been gathered in the Upper and Lower City. Some of the soldiers laughed at the lack of food that Judah's detail had collected, but most just trudged up toward the southern steps of the Temple Mount in silence, heads hung low.

Suddenly, loud, angry voices began to rise like thunder. Judah looked up to the stone steps which led to the Hulda Gates as a crowd surged through and descended rapidly. He glanced quickly at Adam with a puzzled expression and without a word he began to jog towards the growing storm of men flowing down the steps. Adam shouted Judah's name, scrunched up his face in frustration, then ran after his Captain.

The crowd had grown nearly double in size as Adam pushed through shouting men who tossed up their hands in the air and cursed. He searched for Judah, his eyes darting back and forth as he pressed through the mob, asking many as to what was happening, but never getting a straight answer. Adam noticed that most of the men were Idumeans, and they yelled like barking dogs, frothing at the mouth for a meal that was beyond their reach. The deeper he pushed his way into the mob, the tighter he could feel men pressing back. Finally he saw a flash of Judah's face in the crowd, standing with a repulsive gaze upon his face. Adam shouted Judah's name and then fought to push through the men around him as he felt cramped and suffocated. Insults were hurled at him, but he did not care. Adam lashed back in rage and shoved his way through, knocking a few swearing Idumeans over, until he reached Judah and laid a heavy hand on his shoulder.

Adam bit his tongue. He did not utter a single word as everything melted away into stunned silence in his mind. With eyes filled with bewilderment and desperation, he found himself staring into the centre of the mob, which had fanned out into a circle, surrounding four men who were forced to kneel. A frantic prayer raced through his mind as he recognized one of the men as Simon's adviser, Matthias ben Theophilus. Even at this distance Adam recognized the former High Priest who had been deposed by the Zealots long ago. The bruises and shattered nose, which revealed a flow of blood, were not enough to conceal the tender face of Matthias. A man of service, respect, honour, and wisdom, now tethered by a rope tied around his shredded, swollen neck and held tightly by the strong hands of Bagdatus.

"What is this?" Adam said with disgust. "This is an outrage!"

An ugly Idumean, whose face was streaked with crude scars, stood next to Adam and looked at him with a grin as he shouted above the racket, "Matthias and his sons have conspired against us! They are Roman whelps!"

"I don't believe it!" Adam retorted in anger.

The man gave a toothless smile and wiped his running nose. "It doesn't matter what you think. They were caught giving information to the bloody Romans. Simon had them all collected and dragged through the Temple court. They will pay."

"What do you mean?"

The Idumean raised his chin, dragged his finger across his throat and laughed. "They will die a traitor's death! Filthy dogs!"

Adam was shocked and looked at Judah. He knew Judah had heard everything the man said, yet he had not moved a muscle. An expression of terror filled the face of Matthias who stared helplessly across the empty circle at his bound sons who had been scourged and beaten. The three sons knelt upon the stones, their hands tied behind their backs. Each son was hunched over with torn garments as droplets of blood speckled the ground around them. Their faces were a wreck. Their ears were fractured, noses shattered into a bloody mess, lips split, eyes black, faces bruised, and hair strewn with spittle and mucus. They watched the mob with pleading eyes and frantic calls for mercy, but this only enticed Simon's men all the more as the crowd continued to shout, jeer, and swear at them.

"Judah, you have to do something," Adam said quickly.

"How can I? They have condemned Matthias and his sons to death, there is nothing to be done," Judah replied apathetically, however, his face betrayed the inner turmoil of his mind. How could Simon stand at the helm of such an accusation against Matthias of all people? Judah could not think straight and he locked eyes with the helpless Priest. He stared at Matthias and winced when the old man humbly nodded his way, closing his eyes against a stream of saliva which splattered against his face. Judah stared furiously at the shouting Idumeans. *You bastards,* he thought. *You are unfit to even call yourselves Jews! Don't you know who you condemn? If it wasn't for Matthias you would have never risen to greatness!* No matter what Judah screamed inside his head, he saw no way out for the captives as the blood-thirsty, swelling mob began to chant for the execution of the traitorous spies.

"Judah, I see John!" Adam shouted, pointing to the warlord who stood higher than all the other men around him. "Go speak with him! If there is anyone who could spare Matthias and his sons, it is John!"

In a dream-like state, Judah saw the beaten elderly Priest open his eyes as he struggled to kneel upon the stones, his body raked with pain. Matthias' hands trembled at his side, and Judah could see his bruised chest through the torn rags that used to be garments of office and status. Matthias kept looking to his sons, and above the raging mob, Judah heard him shout as blood dripped from his swollen lips, "My sons, I love you all. Do not fear."

"Judah! Did you hear me?" Adam shouted clamping both hands down on his friend's shoulders and shaking him out of his daze. Judah swung around and started to wrestle with Adam as he frantically heaved against the large warrior. Adam would have been knocked off balance from the surprise assault had it not been for the piles of bodies pressing in behind him. Like a bear, Adam took Judah in his arms and managed to restrain him. It worked, and Judah suddenly snapped his gaze up as he stared into the bearded face of Adam. "Judah! It is I!"

Judah immediately stopped struggling and Adam let him go cautiously. "I... don't...I...what is happening?"

Adam stepped forward and brought his mouth close to the startled Captain's ear and said cupping his hand, "Simon is going to execute Matthias and his sons! You have to get to John and tell him to cease this at once. He is over there! You see him?"

Judah nodded, turned, and began to press through the throng of shouting men. He gritted his teeth as he was shoved from every angle as irritated men yelled back at him and raised their hands as if to strike. Judah ignored their threats as he bellowed John's name over and over again. When he noticed the warlord glance his direction, Judah raised his hand and jumped up to be seen. He saw John give a firm nod and a wave in return, his eyes barred like iron with a deep frown conquering the better half of his face.

"What is it Judah? This day is shamefully bleak."

"John, what is this? Has Simon gone mad?"

John snickered briefly and then his frown was restored. "Of course Simon is mad, but this is different. They found letters in Matthias' personal quarters, Judah. There is no going back now."

"Who found the letters?"

"Who do you think?"

"Bagdatus?" Judah replied appalled as he stared across the widened circle at the violent, unruly thug who held the rope bound around Matthias' neck. "You can't be serious?" Judah gasped, astounded at the ridiculous nature of Bagdatus' validation record. When John said nothing, Judah shouted, "Matthias is innocent! This is preposterous! You can't allow them to commit murder, John!"

John suddenly turned on Judah with vehement eyes and drew his face close so he stared directly into the Lion Captain's face. "And what am I to do? You have eyes, look around!"

"But you are John ben Levi. There are men of honour who will support you and oppose, Simon! There are men even in Giora's camp who hate him and would fight for you."

"You ask me to cause division while Rome knocks at the front door? We would gain nothing to act now, but only condemn the city."

Judah shook his head. "So you would just let Simon and his dogs murder a former High Priest and all of his sons?"

"Don't make this out to be my fault, Judah!" John crossed his broad arms as he hated the very thought of what was unfolding before his eyes. "The letters were addressed to Titus and bear Matthias' seal. Simon's commanders, mine, and half the city has heard of this now. There is no going back."

"So Matthias will be thrown to the dogs? Like scraps of wasted meat from the table? All to quench Simon's madness for blood," Judah replied bitterly. John was silent and Judah slowly slipped his hand upon the hilt of his gladius.

"Don't even bother. They would skewer you before you could even do a thing," muttered John in a sullen voice.

Judah clenched his fingers so tightly around the hilt of the sword that he thought it would shatter into a thousand pieces. Then he turned to the voice of Simon, demanding for silence as he strolled to the middle of the circle.

All voices died away as the crowd pressed in and Simon ben Giora stood triumphantly before the humiliated, beaten captives like a tyrant king who had finally vanquished an age old rival. Except this time his rival had been a High Priest and he stood at the base of the southern steps with the massive walls of the Royal Portico rising above in the background.

"The charges against Matthias ben Theophilus have been considered and a sentence has been decided upon. Let the verdict be known to all witnesses against Matthias and his three sons. They sought to conspire with the enemy and dictate letters, which are in my possession, to parlay the city to Titus. I elected Matthias as my chief of council because I trusted him, yet he used that trust to whore himself into the bed of Rome at the expense of our beloved city and Temple." An uproar of curses and shouts rose up violently as Simon pointed his finger at the humiliated priest. "He would have you all killed, your women raped, and your children enslaved!" While everyone yelled at the top of their lungs, Simon grinned as the victor, finally able to depose of the man who stood in the way of his freedom to rule.

Judah wanted to dash out with his sword and in one smooth motion cut Simon's head clean off his filthy shoulders, but instead he felt the strong grasp of John upon the back of his arm.

Simon raised both arms in the air and as loud as his voice would carry he shouted, "What should their penalty be?"

"Death!" chanted the crowd.

"And what do we do to traitors?"

"Kill them!" chanted the crowd like a bunch of jackals fighting over a carcass.

Simon signaled to a number of his Idumeans to hold any unruly people back and they complied, pushing against the crowd with the shafts of their spears. "Now then, a verdict has been given. The accused have been condemned." Simon turned so he faced Matthias. "You leave me no choice. You and all your sons are condemned to death!" He stared into the bruised face of the old man and smiled. "What are you thinking?" Simon asked sadistically.

Matthias straightened as his breathing was broken into quick, weak gasps. He stared straight into Simon's wild, crazed eyes and softly said, "You have won...Simon. You are...and... will be...the king of Jerusalem...one day. But please...I beg of you...slay me first...so that a father...needn't see...the deaths...of those...from his seed. I...have served you...faithfully...and sought to give...you godly council... during...these days. Please...I beg you...honour my word...just this once."

Simon took a step back. He appeared shocked and perplexed from the sorrowful words. Then he smiled, and kneeling at Matthias' side, he rested a hand on the beaten man's shoulder. "You expect me to honour the request of a traitor, Matthias?"

Matthias slowly turned his head and stared with bloodshot eyes into the depths of pure evil that wallowed within the dilated pupils of Simon. He felt a sudden surge of fear creep into his being as tears ran down his cheeks. "What...is it that I...did to fail you?"

"You are pathetic, you always were," Simon lashed back as he stood.

"I let you into the city...I opened the gates for...your army! Please...I beg you!" Matthias said as he struggled helplessly against the strong grasp of Bagdatus who was enjoying every moment. Matthias watched Simon stroll calmly over to his bound sons and then snap his fingers. He felt the rope about his throat slacken and then grow tight again as the muscular thighs of Bagdatus brushed past him.

"No...wait!" Matthias pleaded as Bagdatus drew a razor sharp dagger from his belt. "HaShem! Please...no...don't do this, Simon! Take me!" Matthias wailed with hysteria as his sons began to struggle. "I love you, Aaron, my son!" Matthias shrieked and then he let loose a primal, agonizing scream as Bagdatus grabbed the scalp of his first son, pulled his head back and slashed his throat.

A hush struck the crowd, both from the horrible cry Matthias had given and the gruesome scene as the son bled to death, a jet of crimson from the lethal cut soaking his chest. The young man's eyes rolled back as he struggled to breathe. The other two condemned brothers wept as the body collapsed in a bloodied mess. A red pool slowly formed around the head and trailed out between the cracks of the flagstones. A few men cheered and shouted slogans against the traitors, but most maintained their silence as the executions proceeded.

Judah watched miserably as colour drained from his face. Calmly, Simon snapped his fingers a second time. Bagdatus stepped over the motionless body of the first son, and in the same manner slit the next one's throat. A few murmurs of disgust trailed from the crowd as the second body fell over, convulsing upon the ground for a few seconds. Matthias had not even seen the death of his second son. He now lay prostrate, heaving upon the stones and covering his face as tears wet his hands. Judah looked at the priest and felt his pulse quicken as Simon snapped his fingers for the third time, and Bagdatus obeyed like an obedient dog for its master.

The third son died slower. Bagdatus was clumsy with the dagger as he slashed it across the poor man's throat and then realized he had not cut deep enough as the son began to gasp and shake, his eyes tightly closed. A horrible shudder escaped the wounded man's lips as blood ran down his neck from his partially severed windpipe. Bagdatus moved quickly to cut the rest of the way and peel back the beating jugular. He did this by pushing the son onto the ground, putting his knee between the bleeding man's shoulder blades, turning his head to the side, and slashing the exposed neck. Judah reeled, his body instantly filled with the desire of a predator to tear his foe to pieces. Bagdatus had cut the man like a bull to be sacrificed, and hate beyond recognition filled Judah's soul. The son lay on the ground, wriggling slightly and trying to push himself forward before he let out a final gasp and died.

"*Shema, Yisrael, Adonai elohenu, Adonai Echad! Baruch shem K'vod mal'Chuto La'Olam va'ed.*" Matthias wailed as he lifted himself to his feet and began to rock back and forth in prayer. He quickly began to rattle off passages from the *Tehillim* and Judah saw an enraged look fill Simon's face. The calm display he had put on throughout the executions was quickly replaced by clenched fists and pulsing eyes that seemed as if they would burst. Simon shouted for Matthias to be silent, slightly worried if killing a man while he prayed would be something unforgivable in Temple offerings. Simon looked to Bagdatus for assistance and the large man picked up on the visual command as he crossed the circle and planted a heavy, bloodied fist into the old man's gut.

Matthias staggered, gasping for air and then dropped to his knees as he sobbed. As if his head was under water, Judah heard Simon give the order and felt himself tighten as if all his muscles and nerves had been clenched by some supernatural force. Judah's lips parted but nothing came out as he watched Bagdatus smile grimly, slip the dagger under Matthias' beard, and then jerk it suddenly across the flesh as a bright stream of blood flowed. The old priest struggled, moving his lips, gaping at Simon with strained, panic filled eyes. He twisted his body slightly, as if to try and clutch his throat with his bound hands, but then he let out a murmur before falling upon the stones, dead.

"Throw their bodies from the wall! No honour for traitors," Simon ordered.

Judah heard Adam say something in a mortified tone, but it was drowned out by a deafening roar from the crowd as they sprang to life at the sight of the corpses. Judah shook his head and backed up in a daze as men pressed in around him for a closer look at the bodies. Simon jubilantly declared that justice had been served. Finally, Judah turned and bellowed angrily at anyone in his way as he charged through the crowd to escape the madness.

He pumped his legs as he fled the noise of the jeering crowd and headed down into the Ophel. Judah's eyes burned with hot tears as he pressed on, his lungs aching and mind spinning. He felt tainted, as if it had been he who had held the dagger and not Bastard Bagdatus. The sword knocked against his left leg as Judah ran, but he refused to steady it. Instead he moved his arms back and forth for momentum as he passed shocked men and women who leapt out of his way.

The league was over. His pact with Matthias and the others, to safeguard the helpless and rescue them from the suffering of the city, had died with Matthias' execution. As Judah plunged down the streets of the Ophel he could not focus on anything else but the crime that had been displayed to everyone, as none had objected. Yet, had he not objected? Adam was against it to. And John had opposed it, knowing that its trumped up charges were false and that Simon had forged the letters, planting them in Matthias' home, but even John had refused to act. They had all just stood there, including Judah, watching as innocent men were slain under the evil hand of the tyrant Sicarii King, as if Simon were God and the city *his* holy city.

Judah stopped and gasped for air as he bent over and spit upon the ground. When he looked up, he stared at the front of a synagogue and then jogged forward, kicking the door open as if it were one of the homes his detail had searched earlier. Judah stared at the shocked expressions upon the faces of pious Jews wrapped in their tefillin, diligently at study.

Rabbi Benyamin ben Asher stood rigid, taken aback from the loud thud of the door. He stared at Judah over an unfurled scroll before him which rested upon a stone podium. Benyamin slowly pulled his tallit from his head, taking care that the black, wooden box of tefillin did not fall from his forehead. He let the prayer shawl rest comfortably upon his shoulders as he kept his silence and watched Judah enter the synagogue, not even paying heed to the mezuzah on the right side of the doorframe.

"Judah?" Benyamin whispered with surprise as many of the other worshippers grumbled. "Are you alright? What has happened?"

He watched Judah abruptly halt as he stood rigid, with men seated upon two tiers of stone benches to his left and right which wrapped around the inner walls of the synagogue. He seemed to stare past the Rabbi, as if his eyes wandered, and Benyamin turned slowly as he knew Judah had locked his gaze upon the veil at the back, which covered the ark of scrolls.

"Judah?" Benyamin stepped around the podium and signaled to two other men who stood near the scroll to continue with the recitation. When he saw the flow of tears, he took Judah tenderly by the elbow and ushered him outside.

"He had him killed! And his sons!" Judah said burying his face into his hands.

Rabbi Benyamin swallowed the lump in his throat and gravely nodded. "Matthias has been executed?"

"Along with his three sons." Judah stared at the Rabbi and then scowled. "You knew?"

Benyamin nodded again. "I heard the voices of men passing by."

"Yet you did nothing to prevent it?"

"Matthias has told me many times of his fear that Simon would someday have his family and he put to death. He said that Simon would often threaten him with this fate when he would oppose the madness of the courts. When I heard, I prayed for Matthias. That was all I could do. I prayed that God would take him quickly and without pain."

Judah's face was flushed with anger and he stepped close to the Rabbi. "He was taken alright, gasping for air, his blood soaking his chest, and fear in his eyes. I saw terror in his face after his sons were brutally murdered and now he too is dead. Is that what you prayed for, Rabbi?"

"Judah, don't confound my intentions or the purpose of prayer. I pray for *Tikkun Olam*, you should know this. We pray for Meshiach to come and make this world better. To purge all evil is what we strive for and it breaks my heart for the wickedness that has befallen my people. But there are still those of us who are righteous, Judah, those of us who would die to bring sense and goodness to this world. *Hakol L'Tovah.*"

Judah shook his head and stepped back. "You think I am righteous? It is why HaShem has turned from me. I am filthy from what I have done. Now, I stood aside and let this happen."

"The wrath of God is about to pour out on this people, as it was written by the very hand of Moses, this people have profaned the Shabbat which God blessed and commanded. Israel has failed to be a holy people; these men and this land will incur the wrath of God that has been promised to be poured out like waste upon this nation. The Romans are not here because of coincidence, Judah. A city with no justice will not stand!

"The city is crumbling. Those who cannot fight die in the streets or flee." He paused. "Shimeon ben Gamiliel fled the city early this morning. He has been spared." Benyamin nodded at the stark look of shock upon Judah's face. "He goes to Yavneh, to repair what has been lost and what will be lost." Benyamin furrowed his brow and pulled his tallit back over his head. He peered at Judah and then whispered, "But God's favour will be extended to Jacob again one day. The holy prophets of our sacred Scriptures proclaim it! Zion shall return."

Judah watched the Rabbi slowly turn and walk quietly back into the synagogue, as he took note to carefully close the door behind him. Without hesitating, Judah turned and dashed across the street to the nearest corner of a house, and there he wept bitterly.

* * *

CHAPTER XLVI

June 11th, 70 A.D. / 16th of Sivan, 3830
Camp of the Assyrians
Morning

Marcus Sulla let the legionary take the reins of his horse and dismounted with a frown upon his chiseled face. He could hear the distant sound of work resuming upon the destroyed ramps and watched as a line of legionaries marched past him in silence to the steady rhythm of their feet upon the flagstones. Each legionary in the column carried an assortment of tools; the most common in the legionary's kit was the long iron *dolabra* pick and the scythe. The men rested the weight of these implements upon their shoulders as they trudged onward; destined for the Antonia to relieve the exhausted work details slaving away on the new earthworks and ramps.

Marcus made his way into the camp through the main gate, passing two sentries who saluted him dutifully. He ignored their respect as he entered the uniform grid of alleys stretched out on either side, safely secured behind a four-metre wall of stone and looming towers which surrounded the city of tents. He passed row after row of perfectly lined, canvassed tents set along streets of paved stone, all leveled by the careful eyes of the camp engineers and road-building parties.

The signi of each particular century lined the street before the tents of standard bearers as Marcus passed, and he took only fleeting moments to glance at their icons as he plodded along. An officer's quarters stood on his left, the entrance sprouting a number of spears stuck in the hard clay as the shaft of a wooden pole with a purple flag gently fluttered in the breeze. Beyond the officer's tent stood a granary and then a small temporary bathhouse for the officer rank. Marcus noticed its entrance occupied by a number of off-duty optiones wearing nothing but towels around their waists as they chatted to one another, waiting for the water inside the hot room to be heated. Not all camps surrounding Jerusalem had such luxury, in fact the Camp of the Assyrians was the only one. As Titus stayed in the camp, he had requested the legionaries to dig out a number of pits, line them with tile and stone, and fill them with water. The only complicated part had been the clay piping for the caldarium, which had soon been figured out.

Marcus received a warm reception from a contubernium of eight soldiers who squatted around a fire, and they stood up and saluted him with praise to his distinguished name. Marcus revealed a slight grin towards the men, and nothing else, but it seemed to lighten their hearts as they sat back down and talked excitedly.

The loud clang of a hammer against metal rang out from a smithy within the camp as he continued on with purpose in his step. He moved to the side as a stretcher was carried by bearing an unconscious man with his face partially covered in bloody bandages. Marcus grunted, pushing the image of the wounded man from his mind, and began to slow his pace as he neared the heart of the camp. He did not want to miss the turn. Marcus spotted the smithy on his left down the street. He gazed up on his right and squinted at Psephinus Tower which loomed in the background against what was left of the Third Wall. Even from that distance, Marcus could make out a number of Roman observers high up in the octagonal turret staring out across the city at the work crews near the Antonia.

Marcus passed a street that led to one of the camp's praetorium, erected on the western side as the tents of the Fulminata surrounded it. A lone white flag stood outside the quarters of Tribune Marcus Tullius Octavian, along with his personal signum which leaned against one of the tent's supporting posts. A number of horses were being fed outside of the tent by four servants, and Marcus recognized one to be Titus' destrier. He wondered what the ingathering of generals could be discussing on such a bland morning as this, but kept his curiosity to himself as he continued on until he saw the fluttering red banner of the Praefectus Castrorum.

A young clerk exited the tent and bowed his head at the sight of the approaching Tribune who shed his elaborate sagum and nonchalantly handed it to the man. The clerk graciously took the garment, then darted back into the tent while Marcus leaned against a post and rested his hand on the pommel of his gladius. Soon, the tent flap was drawn back and instead of the clerk, Gaius Antony stood with a warm smile. He extended his hand and both men clasped each other's wrists in friendship.

"It does me good to see you, Marcus. It seems like all sense and order is amuck, but you being here gives me pause and a reminder that there are some of us who know what is going on," Gaius said cheerfully, stepping aside and ushering the Tribune in.

"You give me far too much credit, Gaius. If there is anyone who cares little for order, it is me." Marcus grinned and helped himself to the comfort of a reclining couch. He sat down heavily and felt the piece of furniture shift with a groan as he reclined, propping his head up with a firm hand. "You look worn."

"I have barely slept in two nights. I dare say it is due to all the endless councils, letters I have written, orders given, logs and ledgers examined, and on and on. The life of a statesman, I would say. It can grow tedious. Sometimes I miss the simple life of a centurion."

"But you have retained your title as Primi Ordines, what more could you wish for? Titus still sees a benefit in you leading your centuria. With the pay, I would think you would welcome such a promotion," Marcus replied teasingly. "You're not a boring, old, fat politician, Gaius, Titus knows that. A man with your ample quality will always see the front of an attack, you can count on that."

Gaius shrugged. "It is not the fighting I am talking about, just the responsibility. Not that I can't handle it, it just wears on me. Wine?" Marcus nodded and Gaius flicked his hand at his servant. Soon a silver jug and two goblets were brought. "Have you seen the progress of the ramps?" Marcus shook his head and Gaius continued, "They are rising again. This time Porcius has widened them even more. They should take maybe another week or more. He is also adding another level to his siege towers."

"I am all too familiar with that new development, my dear Gaius," Marcus said as he shook his head and removed his helmet. "I depart tomorrow at dawn to gather wood like a damned peasant. It seems Porcius managed to convince the Prince that what we gathered days ago is still not enough for his little plans. So I leave again for another week to scour this damned, dry and barren countryside already stripped of life. To have my Boars become damned woodsmen instead of warriors is almost more than I can bear. To see my men with axe in hand chopping at damned trees is a disgrace; I detest it."

Gaius watched the Tribune down his entire goblet and helped himself to another cup. "Surely, it will be the last venture? You filled over a dozen carts with wood, heaped so high it looked as if your cavalry towed a column of rams yourselves. One more expedition should be the last, I would presume."

"Let's hope so. I have a mind to fight my way through the Antonia, leap down into the Outer Court and seize the wood from their very Temple!" Marcus roared with laughter spilling some of his wine. "Wouldn't that be a sight! Would the Jewish God strike me down?" He continued to chuckle while he drank his wine and some of the dark fluid leaked out from the edges of his mouth, staining his tunic.

"Titus has ordered the legions to focus on rebuilding the ramps and earthworks," Gaius said as he changed the subject. "He has halted all further aggressive action until we can regain our foothold in these areas. The Antonia is still the key. The Fretensis and Apollinaris are digging deeper and spreading their front further to the east, but all this extra timber you are foraging for is going to the earthworks and towers at the Antonia.

"Since the siege wall has been completed, the Jews have been unable to move around or threaten our flanks. We can finally work with very little threat to our positions." Marcus listened intensely to Gaius as he looked over the brim of his goblet, slowly sipping his wine. "Titus had one hundred and thirty people crucified in the Kidron, and nearly every day more bodies are being dumped over the walls from the Lower City. They have to be coming to the end of themselves. There cannot be enough food to support such a population."

"Yet still Titus chooses to save some of them from their doom, like that one rabbi the other day," Marcus chided.

"An influential man, who had Yosef on his side petitioning to the Prince," Gaius pointed out raising his brow. "He was a good choice to spare. He was not a Zealot nor aided them in their revolt."

Marcus shook his head. "I know these Zealots all too well. Your Judah ben Yosef nearly took my head at one time. His little band of thieves and cutthroats ambushed a patrol of mine which I led. I lost many men and we had to retreat. I have seen their resolve. You can cut the head clean from a man, skewer another with a spear or hack him to pieces, all in the sight of their fellow comrades, and still they will face you. As other enemies would tremble with fear, this only enrages them further.

"They will hold out in this city even if they all starve. I have seen the disease-ridden corpses, covered in black spots and boils. Their skin was yellow with faces bony and full of blisters. The mere sight of such suffering would cause nearly every other city to capitulate, open their gates and beg for mercy, except this one." Marcus was silent and then shrugged. "Most cities would have surrendered at the very sight of our legions, Gaius. When was the last time *Roma* drew such a force against a rebellious people? Not in my lifetime. Maybe the wars between Augustus and Marcus Antonius would compare to our numbers."

"Titus still has hope," Gaius added. "He is not convinced they will bring the city to ruin. He believes with more pressure…"

"Do you truly believe that?" Marcus interrupted. "You have seen and heard John of Gischala shout to Yosef from the walls, have you not? You have heard and seen Judah's resolve. Do you believe they will ever lay down their arms?"

Gaius felt uncomfortable from the question, like there was not an ounce of hope to be found, as if the whole land would be consumed in fire as well as all of them with it. He stared at Marcus, taking a brief pause and then somberly nodded. "I know of their zeal."

The quarters were silent as both men took more wine and listened to the comforting sound of the camp that surrounded them. Gaius called for bread, cheese, olives, and some fruit and it was brought within moments. Gaius bit into a juicy fig, savouring the taste in his mouth as he wanted to close his eyes and wish everything would just vanish into thin air. Marcus studied an olive with an inquisitive, philosophical gaze, then popped it into his mouth and removed the pit with his fingers.

"Have you heard what Titus aims to do with some of our food stores today?" Gaius asked, gaining the Tribune's interest. "Display it to the city in baskets."

Marcus bobbed his head up and down as he chewed on a date. "That will get a rumble of thunder from the Zealots."

"The Prince wishes to make it unbearable for them."

"That will certainly do it. The sight of food will drive them mad. There is always the small hope the city will mutiny against the Zealots and overpower them. It would be a massacre but it could give us a chance to seize an opportunity." Marcus nodded in delight from the date and took another. He licked his fingers from the sticky substance left behind and then raised his hand to make a point as he swallowed, but instead, frowned and sought out another comfortable position by moving aside a number of cushions.

"Are you alright?" Gaius asked seeing the trivial frown remain upon the Tribune's face.

"My mind is occupied, that is all." Marcus lifted his gaze to his friend and said above a whisper, "Before we set out to gather timber days ago, one of my troopers was grazing his horse close to the walls where a patch of dried grass remained. The man was a fool to do so, for the Zealots could have captured him or struck him down with a dart, but neither of these fates occurred. But what did occur, was the man saw a great host of Idumeans suddenly appear on the ramparts just south of the colonnade walls where they dumped four bodies over the side. The corpses were drenched with blood, and it appeared they had all been executed. He said one of them was an elderly man."

Gaius was still as he held his goblet by the stem, turning the glass in his hands. "Executed?"

"Their throats had been cut. Obviously an execution, and the way they were handled tells me the Idumeans and Zealots perceived whoever these men were to be enemies." Marcus finished his second cup of wine and smacked his lips together, enjoying the soothing sensation upon his palate. "It does tell me the Zealots are afraid. They may have great resolve to hold out against everything we hurl at them, but they still are overcome by fear within their own ranks."

A voice could be heard outside the tent and Gaius' servant moved briskly to see who it was. Within an instant he reappeared, bowed before the Praefectus Castrorum and politely said, "My master, a centurion from the Macedonica and your optio await outside. Shall I usher them in?"

Marcus rose to leave and Gaius cleared his throat, inviting the Tribune to stay and enjoy more food and wine. Gaius then glanced at the servant and nodded silently. He reached for another fig as the tent flap was pulled aside, letting in a flood of light that cast shadows upon the canvas walls of the quarters, as the centurion and optio entered. Gaius rose to greet his guests and smiled at the two officers as they snapped to attention. Marcus also stood with goblet in hand and another half-eaten date clutched between his fingers.

"Tribune Marcus Sulla, this is Julianus. He is a Centurion from the Fifth in command of a centuria in the Fourth Cohors." Julianus saluted the Tribune and gave a gracious bow. "And this is…Fortunatis, my Optio. He has been by my side leading my centuria since this campaign began. The Hydra Herculean would not be the dogs they are without him."

Fortunatis struck his breastplate with a fist and bowed graciously. In his left hand he clutched his hastile and resorted to leaning on it as he gazed from the Tribune to Gaius with charming eyes and a smooth, handsome face.

"Julianus' centuria lost a dozen men when the ramps collapsed. They would like nothing better than revenge to fill their appetite," Gaius said as he ushered the officers to sit. "Wine?" Both Julianus and Fortunatis graciously declined as Gaius had his servant refill his goblet.

Marcus gave both men a nod and then retook his seat upon the plush couch as he finished his date while the servant refilled his cup. "Glad to see fighting men; always a delight."

"Primi Ordines, we come to report that the Prince has requested a contingent of your centuria and mine, to organize baskets of food to be displayed before the city," Julianus spoke up as he removed his helmet and scratched his head. He was at least ten years younger than Gaius, but still had the makings of an excellent centurion.

Gaius glanced to Marcus and the Tribune laughed, accidentally spitting a piece of fig onto the ground as he jabbed a finger into the air and called out, "I told you didn't I! You shall drive them all damned mad with the sight of food!" A hiccup escaped from the lips of the teetering Tribune as he finished his goblet and asked for another. "It appears as though I shall drink all of your wine, Gaius. It was ill favoured of you to have ever offered me some in the first place."

Gaius grinned and shook his head casually at the sight of the tipsy commander, seeming to be drunk upon his couch. But Gaius knew him better than that. He had seen Marcus, on more than one occasion, consume enormous amounts of alcohol beyond which any normal, sensible man should, and at all times of the day. During these sorts of feasts and bouts of revelry, Gaius could have sworn upon the name of every god he knew that he would have to carry the stumbling Tribune back to his quarters. However, Marcus would just stand up and strut away with a wild looking composure and eyes of metal, as if he was preparing to charge into battle. Where most men would slip into a deep sleep or vomit from the erroneous amounts of drink, Marcus remained a wine prodigy. It was in those moments that the mood of wine would wear off and he would become fierce and lively with concentration.

"When does the Prince expect this?" Gaius asked as he watched the Tribune, in his peripheral, refill his cup and consume it like it was only water.

Julianus obviously disliked the attitude of the Tribune, interpreting him to be reckless, but he kept his composure and answered Gaius saying, "In the hour."

"Should I select a contingent, Centurion?" Fortunatis asked eagerly, battling not to appear shocked at the consumption of wine the Tribune was filling himself with. Since they had arrived he had drank two cups of wine and seemed to be attempting to have a third as he shooed the servant away with the flick of his hand and took the wine jug.

Gaius nodded at his Optio, annoyed at the officers' distraction. "Rally half of the men. I will join you shortly. I could stretch my legs and do something apart from ledgers." Gaius stood and turned to his servant. "Bring my armour."

"My contingent is assembling as we speak. We can meet at the main gate of the camp," Julianus replied.

"I will collect my Boars and perhaps keep you company. I should like to see Porcius' progress on these new ramps," Marcus suddenly interjected with a clear voice as he stood. He grinned at the startled expressions upon the faces of Julianus and Fortunatis who now stared at a man who appeared to have transformed from a drunk into a sober, battle-hardened Tribune.

Gaius detected the amazement in his two impressed officer's and wanted to smile, but instead reinforced his stern expression of discipline as he said to Marcus, "You will accompany our work detail?"

Marcus nodded and crossed his broad arms. "I must lead a patrol around the city, then prepare for our departure at dawn. We have miles to ride and much to prepare. We also need to collect those damned carts again." He smiled graciously at Gaius. "I thank you for the company, food and wine." Then in five long strides, Marcus left the tent in haste and closed the flap behind him.

* * *

The Fortress Antonia
Noon

Adam found Judah sharpening his sword on the edge of the western drill ground inside the Antonia. He held a small stone in his hand and slid it along the blade's edge in quick, rhythmic motions as the grate of metal echoed in the empty yard. Judah took note of Adam and then returned to his expert honing. The city had grown eerily silent since the execution of Matthias and his sons, and the quietness had given him much time to reflect.

Adam sat down next to Judah and watched him restore the sharp edge to the sword, then polish it clean with his outer garment. He stared for a moment at the gladius as a hint of light reflected from the blade. Then Judah lowered it upon his lap and carefully ran his finger along the double-edged weapon, testing for any divots or dull spots along the full tang of steel. When he was done, Judah picked up the wooden scabbard, wrapped in a thin layer of stretched leather, and then slid the sword home.

"Is something wrong?" Judah finally said to his silent friend.

"I don't know if it is possible to end such violence among each other," Adam replied in an empty voice.

Judah rubbed his forehead, then looked at Adam with bitter eyes, having been reminded of the daily executions which had been going on for the past three days. Simon had unleashed Bagdatus upon the Upper and Lower City as John did nothing but sit back and watch as droves of people were hauled before Simon's throne to await a quick verdict, a death sentence nearly every time.

"Two priests were executed today, known as Ananias and Aristeus. With them, fifteen men of the aristocracy, who had been thrown into prison, were also put to death as traitors. I was not there, but I heard the mob calling for their end. A Zealot who was there, said every last one of them pleaded with Simon, begging for their lives, but they were soon dragged outside Herod's Palace and slain upon the street. They lie there still. I mean, to execute priests one has lost all honour! It is madness." Adam watched Judah lower his head, a flicker of rage tightening his face and blazing within his eyes.

"What were they accused of?"

"Does it matter? Simon is judge and jury. He condemns them at will and scoffs when they plead for mercy. Bagdatus rounds up anyone of wealth and influence who remains in the city. Rumour is, people have resorted to hiding in the sewers to escape his warpath. Some even gamble with their fates and flee the city. People are hung upon crosses daily."

Judah set his sword down and leaned forward as he rested his weary face upon his palms. "They have no hope, no chance. Simon has become king, Adam."

Adam was silent as his mind replayed Judah's sorrowful words. "Simon sent a herald through the streets at the head of eleven men in shackles this morning, announcing to everyone their crimes. You did not hear them?" Judah shook his head. "These men were of Simon's army, soldiers and one officer. They were accused of trying to defect to the Romans. They were guarding one of the towers near where the Fretensis is digging, and were planning on surrendering, but they were caught. They were all executed before I came and found you here. Simon had them all beheaded."

"God has left this city."

"What did you say, Judah?"

"That is what Rabbi Benyamin ben Asher said to me after Matthias had been murdered. I fled to the Ophel and found him praying in the synagogue. I told him about Matthias and what Simon had done and he said that a city with no justice will fall, it will be destroyed." Judah's face paled and he slowly looked into Adam's eyes. "Is that what your Rabbi Yeshua meant when he said not one stone would remain upon another? Was he speaking of Jerusalem's destruction because it had become a lawless city?"

Adam shrugged. "He always spoke truth. I think that He looked into a future time, such as this, and saw the horror, suffering, and jealousy we have for one another. Yeshua wept for this city, Judah. He saw her depart from being a city of righteousness, only to descend into the pit of despair." Adam laid a gentle hand upon Judah's shoulder and softly said, "You need to go to John and beg him to stop this madness. I believe he alone can put an end to Simon's anarchy."

"John has let this all happen, Adam. He did nothing to put a stop to Matthias' execution. A part of me wants to think John believes he is powerless and that to confront Simon risks the breakdown of any sense of order. Perhaps it is the common knowledge that Simon's army is too vast, that stays his hand. But, I dare say, I also believe that John allows this to happen because he still feels spies have infiltrated the city and that people work against him." Judah shook his head. "There is nothing I can say or do which will sway his thinking. John is a stubborn man. He will not order Simon to stand down. John knows that outside the Antonia and the Temple plateau, Simon truly is king. He has an army of nearly twelve thousand and John has a quarter of that number. There is nothing that can be done."

"Yes, but John trusts you, and only you. If there was ever a time that he would take advice from you it would be now. I believe you are the only man who can get through to him. Simon may have a vast supply of men willing to do his bidding, but they fear John and his Zealots. The Zealots have a reputation and Simon will stand down if John applies enough force.

"Simon may delight in causing pain and suffering, but he also wants to rule more than anything, and to do that he needs John on his side. The only thing keeping the Romans truly at bay is that they face Zealots. Simon knows that, and so he will not wish to provoke John into all out war. He can't risk it and he knows that, no matter what petty threats he makes."

Judah rubbed his eyes. "Maybe, I could try."

The sounds of feet moving quickly upon the balcony above attracted the gaze of both men as they stared upward. They heard the rustle of feet suddenly stop and then a frantic whisper came down to them from a familiar voice.

"Moshe, we are down here!" Adam called back up.

"Quick, you both need to come to the eastern colonnades now!"

"What is it?" Judah replied standing and moving out into the courtyard as he looked up at the anxious Lion warrior gripping the edges of the balcony.

"I can't explain, better to see for yourself."

Judah grabbed his sword and Adam followed as the two men exited the courtyard through a wooden door that led out onto the top of the northern colonnade.

Judah and Adam trotted along the ramparts which had once been clustered with Roman patrols of the Third Gallica. Judah slowed his pace as both men saw a massive host of Zealots and Idumeans gathered along the eastern side and staring across the valley at the Mount of Olives. The ramparts exploded into shouts as men raised their arms, shaking fists and spears.

Moshe joined Judah and Adam within seconds as the men reached the crowd of angry soldiers who were cursing. They pressed through the tight ranks as they made their way to the stone parapets above the Eastern Gate. When they reached it, Judah became speechless. Adam started to say something but caught himself and covered his face in shock.

Moshe on the other hand, began to swear and hurl insults across the valley as he shook his drawn sword in the air, calling on the legions to test their resolve. Then he began to plead with HaShem, begging Him to send a pillar of fire from heaven, like in the time of Elijah, to consume the camp of the Fretensis and all the legionaries he could see covering the Mount of Olives like sand upon the seashore.

Beyond the Kidron Valley and part way up the mountain, were over a hundred baskets heaped with bread, figs, dried meats, corn, wheat, olives, dates and grapes. Besides these were massive vessels clustered together in tight groups with their tops uncovered. The angry Zealots could see legionaries standing next to the earthen vessels as they dipped bread or their fingers into the great containers, only to show their appalled spectators the dripping oil and honey before devouring it in their sight. Others, lifted cups into the air and then plunged them into large jugs before drawing them out and drinking all kinds of rich wines. The soldiers raised such a ruckus consuming the wine that when they begin to belch and laugh, the chorus of curses rose even higher from the walls.

"When did they set this up?" Judah shouted in Moshe's ear.

"Not long ago. They brought them in wagons. We didn't know what they were doing until they began to unload them and set them out upon the hillside." Moshe shook his head, a pained expression deeply set into his face as he pointed helplessly. "Enough to feed an army and it is right in front of us while we starve behind these walls."

"This is what they want us to think. This is how they want us to react!" Judah said suddenly lifting his voice. "Listen to me! Hear me!" Judah scrambled on top of the wide parapet and waved his hands at the angry mob. "This is what they want, don't give it to them!" Judah screamed as the crowd of Zealots began to silence. "They wish to drive us mad with hunger! Let us not be tempted. Hate them in your hearts, but do not show it now!"

It was as if a sense of normalcy was restored to the mob as men began to nod their heads and retire rather than be tortured by the temptation of the endless piles of food before them. Judah lowered his arms, gave a firm nod to Adam, and hopped down.

"The Romans should not have the luxury of regaling themselves with today's events. I do not wish for them to sleep soundly knowing they have torn down our resolve and plagued our minds with doubt." Judah turned, stared at the distant piles of food and spit over the wall. He noticed that some of the legionaries, who had been taunting them, now stood gawking back in shock from the silence that had overcome the Jewish defences. Judah smirked at the thought of some poor sod reporting to Titus that the Jews had hollered at them for five minutes and then had left quietly, while their food spoiled in the heat of day.

"Judah! Look!"

Judah turned quickly to the alarm in Adam's voice who stared down into the outer courtyard of the Temple. Amidst all the Zealots descending the ramparts and scattering across the vast plaza was a woman wrapped in long garments gazing up at him. Judah peered at her for a moment, sensing that there was something peculiar about this woman. He raised his hand to his eyes from the glare of the white stone from the Temple and held his breath. His heart quickened and his blood raced through his veins as he suddenly recognized the woman. It was as if someone had seized his throat for not a word was said, nor could he even think of any response for this impossible situation which now held his attention. Leaving Adam and Moshe, he slowly descended the stairs, one step at a time feeling as if his weight had doubled from the heaviness that flooded his being.

When Judah reached the bottom he gently raised his hand, partially covering his mouth in shock, as he uttered, "Hadassah?"

Hadassah unveiled her face covering and stared at the surprise which seemed to come in waves upon Judah's face. She said nothing, but her eyes said everything. She took a single step toward Judah, her hands trembling at her sides, but still she kept her silence, as he remained frozen in disbelief to the steps of the ramparts, not believing what he truly saw.

Judah had no recollection of stepping forward, but finally found himself standing before Hadassah. His mind raced, yet still the woman he loved remained silent, waiting for him to speak. Then he felt a surge of anger and frustration boil up within him. It was as if his sense of reasoning had poured from his soul, dragging away every scrap of understanding, to be hurled into an abyss where the door was locked and the keys destroyed.

"Why are you here?"

Hadassah lowered her gaze, knowing that the anger in Judah's voice was on the verge of becoming ungovernable. She wanted to fall into his arms, to hear him say that she was lovely, to stroke her hair and kiss her forehead, but she also understood that she had disobeyed his will for her. She knew Judah had put his life on the line to keep her from danger, and she had defied that risk by slipping from the refugees and hiding.

"Why are you here?" Judah repeated himself.

"You will not understand."

Judah suddenly grabbed her arms and forcefully pulled her close, glaring into her eyes as if he loathed the very sight of her. Then like a flash, the anger fluttered away and he just stared at her, his hot breath blasting against her face like a desert storm. "I will not understand?" Judah snapped through gritted teeth. He looked past her at the Zealots in the Outer Court and felt vulnerable. He gave a wild glance behind him at Adam and Moshe, who looked down on him from the rampart above, and then he pulled Hadassah underneath the colonnade, behind the safety of a pillar. "Why are you here? You fled the city! I helped you flee the city!" He pushed her against the pillar and placed both of his strong arms on either side of her against the granite column so she could not escape.

Hadassah winced from the heated gaze of Judah. "I couldn't leave, Judah. I couldn't."

"How did you escape? I did not see you."

"You hardly waited. You sent me away and then left almost immediately after. Rabbi Benyamin didn't even see me. He was too busy figuring out how to lock the gates and lower the men from the wall. I just slipped away into the darkness and hid in my house."

Judah's eyes widened and he shook his head. "If you had been caught, you would have condemned us all! You risked everything, and for what?"

"For you, Judah!" Hadassah pleaded as she began to cry. "I love you."

Judah felt his knees suddenly weaken, his eyes soften, and he took a step back lowering his arms. He could no longer look at her in anger. His heart ached, his mind spun, and his fingers felt numb. He stared at Hadassah, screaming in his mind to regain the strength needed to keep her at a distance, but he felt powerless. He wanted to harden his expression and scowl at her, to insult her and cast her out, but her tears were too much.

"Hadassah, you should never have stayed. I can't protect you here. You would have lived. Mordechai ben Levi would have been good to you. He was spared you know, he and his whole house. They were never crucified. You would have lived."

"Judah, I could never live without you. Please, I would have been an empty shell if I had gone with Mordechai. I would have watched my life melt away into nothingness. I would have never forgiven myself for leaving you."

"That decision was not for you to make!"

"And it was for you to make? As if I was simply a slave of yours sold to another master? Do you not feel the same for me as I for you?" Hadassah stepped away from the pillar and stared straight into his eyes.

Judah held the gaze for a moment, then looked away. "I did what I thought was best. It is the only way. I am a soldier, Hadassah. The Romans will soon break through our walls and we will all die. Titus will never spare a man like me, not after the things I have done. He knows me, he knows who I am."

"You are not a Zealot, and we could hide and outlast the Romans. Then we would be together," Hadassah replied, not understanding what Judah had spoken of. She watched him hang his head in despair and she touched the side of his face tenderly. "I know what I did was wrong, that it put you and the others at risk, and I thank God it did not come to that. But please understand, Judah. I could never have lived with myself to watch Jerusalem burn and know you were within her walls."

"That is the life I have chosen, Hadassah, there is no turning back. I cannot abandon this city to the legions."

"No, that life was forced upon you. That is not who you truly are."

"Please, Hadassah," Judah whispered. "You do not know who I really am. You do not know of the things I have done, the things I have seen and welcomed."

She reached up with the other hand and lifted his face gently. "Judah, do not cast me away, my love. If you will stay and fight, I shall stay with you. If you shall die, I shall die too." She took his hand and tenderly kissed it, feeling his heart quicken within him and his body melt.

Suddenly, Judah jolted back, panting like he was out of breath as he shook his head. "No," he groaned, staring up at the high portico roofs. "No, you cannot stay. I cannot accept your fate as part of my own. You are not supposed to die here, Hadassah, not like this. I will not allow you to die, like Miriam did." Hot tears of anguish poured from Judah's eyes and rolled down his cheeks. "You will not die like she did. I will not have that on my conscience. I cannot lose you, not like that." Judah quickly wiped away the tears with the back of his hand. "You have to leave. At the first opportunity, I will get you out of Jerusalem." Judah watched her tighten up as she slowly shook her head. "Hadassah, I plead with you and beg you. If you ever loved me, you will not stay."

*　　*　　*

CHAPTER XLVII

June 16th, 70 A.D. / 21st of Sivan, 3830
Eastern side of Jerusalem
Mount of Olives
Noon

Marcus turned in his saddle and stared for a moment at the high dust cloud which had collected behind the train of bellowing oxen and wooden carts. The dust had risen against the sky like a thin veil, separating a perfectly blue sky with a sheet of filth. Marcus shifted in his saddle, thanking the gods that the sight of Jerusalem and the Roman camps had finally come into view, yearning for the heat and moisture of the caldarium in the Camp of Assyrians. The crack of whips and shouts from men driving the carts echoed between the valley of Mount Scopus and the desolate hillside that had once been the Mount of Olives as the long line of wagons slowly rolled on.

Since leaving on his foraging expedition, they had travelled nonstop for five days, cutting down every tree in sight. They had hacked off useless branches, and piled the timber beams high. Each wagon load had been secured by rope and was drawn by a pair of lumbering oxen which never seemed to cease their moaning as they plodded along, heads dipped low and secured by great yokes of wood and iron straps.

Marcus glanced to his left and right, taking note of his single file, cavalry formation that had protected the caravan. At the rear, Marcus had ordered a vanguard of eighty Boars drawn up in column, riding three abreast, in case anybody had sought to harry their journey. But, like he had expected, the countryside was barren as what few impoverished farmers they had seen, had possessed enough sense to flee into their homes and watch the column pass behind the safety of locked doors.

A young trooper named Helvius, who had replaced the deceased Publius as Marcus' signifer, touched his heels to the flanks of his mount and galloped to his Tribune's side, steadying the famous signum with the boar's head fixed upon the top. He saw Marcus tilt his head slightly back at the approach of hoof beats and Helvius smiled cheerfully, giving him a sharp nod.

Helvius had been proud to fill the place of the heroic Publius, who had received honours by Marcus for saving the Tribune's life in battle. Publius had been burned upon a pyre, prayers recited, and his name enshrined within the minds of all the Boars as another faithful brother struck down by the horrid enemy. Now, Helvius was eager to prove himself as a man worthy to carry such a relic into battle and to be the one man who would be the closest to the Tribune than anyone else.

"Tribune, may I offer you water?"

"Enough wine awaits me back in my quarters to forget all of this, Helvius. Save the water for my horse." Marcus did not even glance at the handsome standard-bearer as he shifted in his saddle thinking about how nice it would be to have a dip in the baths.

"Shall I ride ahead and bring the news of our return to Prince Titus?" Helvius replied, nudging his horse into step alongside the Tribune.

Marcus glared annoyingly at Helvius out of the corner of his eye and watched as the young man caught the look and quickly diverted his gaze. "Helvius, you are not a messenger that I would send you like a dog wagging its tail to the Prince. He can see our approach just as well. If it suits him he will ride to us." Marcus jerked his head back. "No need to be hasty. We guard the caravan right to the gates of the camp and then we are through with this. If I need someone to ride to let the Prince know anything, I would ask for someone else. You are meant to signal the troop at my behest and to aid in rallying the men, not skirting off."

"Yes, Tribune," Helvius responded with a tinge of embarrassment.

"You are still getting used to your new office, have faith. The gods have increased your pay and your status among men. That should be better than the life you have left behind, is it not?"

Helvius bobbed his head and then fixed the chin strap on his helmet. "Yes, Tribune!" He rattled off the rehearsed response that he had grown so used to saying now that he rode at the head of the cavalry in his new designated spot. Helvius had been with the Boars for nearly four years, and his service had been impeccable, so much so that when Publius had died, his name had been given as the most reliable man for the job. With that, the newly elected office of signifer had also made his money purse a little heavier, earning him an extra two hundred drachma a year which was a handsome raise from his regular trooper pay. But, what gave Helvius the most pride was the fact that wherever Marcus would be seen, there he would also be. As Publius had done so faithfully, Helvius to would fight by the Tribune's side and lead the troopers valiantly. This also meant that with steadfast service, Helvius could one day be promoted to a decurion and then maybe a Tribune if he went far enough.

"Sound company to halt!" Marcus barked.

"Trumpeter, sound company to halt!" Helvius shouted, wasting not a moment to relay the order. Within seconds a blast echoed above the moaning oxen and the line came to an abrupt stop with horses snorting and stamping the ground as troopers strained to see what caused the delay.

Marcus gave a sharp nod for Helvius to follow him and they rode out to meet the cluster of horses and fluttering flags that swiftly approached along the slopes of the Mount of Olives. Helvius clutched the wooden shaft of the signum firmly in his left hand and gripped the leather reins in his right as he moved with the thundering motion of his horse pounding upon the dusty ground. The wind felt good upon his face. Even if he could not push his mount to its maximum speed, because of the angle of the mountainside, the cool rush was still a relief as it dried the sweat around his arms and gushed underneath the mail he wore over his chest.

Helvius could make out the standard of Prince Titus, and knew that the company which surrounded him had to be of the highest echelon. So he reminded himself to act natural, remain silent unless addressed, and to appear as if he knew what he was doing. He saw the Prince draw his warhorse to a slow walk and then he halted, raising a hand in greeting. Helvius scanned the other men with the Prince and identified them as: Tiberius Alexander, Sextus Cerealis, Marcus Octavian, as well as accompanied by their personal signifers.

"Tribune Maximus, the sight of your wagon train and the colours of your company are a delight to my eyes," Titus said in a friendly tone as the other generals stared at the halted caravan of carts, wood, oxen, and troopers.

"We pressed as hard as we could, my Prince. It is good to see you in such spirits."

"Truly. Once again your service to *Roma* is shown to be nothing short of successful. Your efforts will see this siege through to victory and glory for the empire. When it is done we shall all echo the words of Caesar when he said, '*veni, vidi, vici.*' The gods have smiled upon you and watch you now." Marcus graciously bowed his head to the high spirited Prince, while Helvius remained stiff at attention slightly behind him. "Now, what is your report?"

"Thirty carts filled, my Prince. We cut over two thousand trees. We had to cover a span of fifteen miles and rode for thirty. The land has been laid to waste behind us, not a tree stands unless we are to venture further." Marcus sighed and made a wide gesture with his hand. "There is nothing left."

"With Porcius' estimates, that should be enough. We need to rebuild two towers, repair another one and build three new ramps." Titus stared up at the sky as he seemed to make some calculations in his head and then nodded. "That should do. Otherwise, any trouble?"

"None, the countryside is quiet. The only inhabitants we saw were peasants; it is truly desolate. They have no spirit, and no will to even stand in our way like they used to."

Titus shook his head with a grin. "The Jews follow a God unable to defend his people. They have preached from their walls that their God shall overcome us and lay our camps and legions to waste, but this God seems to take a better liking to the Roman deities. I think we should not be surprised: one God is but a dry leaf blowing in the wind against the countless gods who honour us because of our strength. Jupiter has given us the spirit to conquer all, and Mars blesses us with the courage and power to do so. The army of *Roma* is the true power in this world, only gods with sense and a desire to be worshipped and sought after will pay any heed to us." Titus pointed at the city. "The edge of the sword always speaks the final words. The days of Jerusalem and the Jewish God are numbered."

"As it appears, my Prince," Marcus dutifully replied as he stared down at the small forest of crosses in the valley, revealing the hanging forms of bodies upon them.

Helvius stared nervously at the clear blue sky. He muttered a quick prayer to any god who might happen to be listening, for a fear had crept within him because of the boastful words of the Prince against the Jewish God. Helvius knew that if the Jewish God was anything like the Roman gods he faithfully served, then He would surely strike the whole lot of them with boils and plagues, but nothing seemed to happen and so Helvius relaxed.

A fierce expression filled the Prince's eyes as he pointed down the mountainside into the Kidron Valley below. "Tribune, before you retire, you are to lead the wagon train down into the valley and follow the bottom in clear sight of the rebels. I want them to see that we have the means to rebuild, and that they will not have such fortune a second time. Then you may rest your troop and turn this over to the engineers who will have this piled safely behind the Camp of the Assyrians."

"Yes, my Prince."

Titus exhaled loudly and glanced to his other generals. "Between the carts of wood and Yosef speaking at the Antonia, I believe this shall give them something to ponder."

*　　*　　*

The Fortress of the Antonia
Afternoon

"John, Yosef approaches the walls!" shouted a sentry as he peered between the stone parapet holding a spear and round shield.

John grumbled under his breath as he strolled across the wide turret and gazed over the edge just in time to see Yosef dismount from a finely groomed horse. John crossed his arms and furrowed his brow as a slight breeze lapped at his outer cloak. He saw Yosef, timid in nature, begin to climb the partially finished ramp on the left as he squinted up trying to make out the dark figures gathered upon the towers.

As John observed, Yosef seemed to pick up his pace. Numerous legionaries continued to work around him as they carried rocks, timber, bags of earth, and various tools, all with a mission to finish the two massive snake-like ramps. Yosef ascended with confidence, his chest slightly pushed out, and a stern look of theatrical intensity upon his face, as if the ramp had suddenly transformed into a theater stage and all the sweating, cursing Romans were actors.

John watched his enemy with indifferent eyes and felt his body begin to tighten as anger boiled within. He observed Yosef halt on the ramp, pick up a fold of his garment, tuck it neatly over his arm, and then continue the climb. By now fifty Zealots had assembled to John's right and left and they all watched the Jewish General halt before the steep drop-off of the unfinished earthworks and examine his speaking platform.

Lengths of timber beams could be seen protruding from the end of the carefully packed earthen ramp, as the Roman workers had buried them in a crisscross pattern inside to strength the incline as it rose to nearly ten metres above the ground where the hated orator stood. Yosef boldly gazed up, shielding his eyes from the sun as the breeze cooled his body. He could see both towers and the ramparts along the Antonia's wall now filled with Zealots and he knew they all waited for him to speak. He glanced with annoyance behind him as the sound of a hammer pounding a spike echoed with a dull thud. The legionary looked up carelessly, scowled at him, and then strolled away with the hammer dangling from his loose grip. Yosef had to concentrate and remember every detail, for the Prince could be listening and he did not wish to falter with a single word.

Yosef had rehearsed his speech during the morning, standing in front of a glass mirror to gauge his posture as he used a slave boy as a listener. He had strategized his skill of oratory, and would try not to sound defeated at the beginning. True he was speaking to vile, distasteful scoundrels, but even scoundrels had weaknesses and fears. Even men such as the Zealots would rather live then die. Yosef knew he had to penetrate soul and mind if he would ever seek to convince them to open the gates and surrender.

Yosef had to be clever. He would strive to carry his voice to all the other soldiers, not just John. Yosef hoped that his volume would even reach the civilians deep within the city, but he was really not sure of how much good that would even do given their plight and circumstance. The city was held hostage, and his duties had been specific from the Prince.

Titus had said, *'Speak well, deliver my terms, and pray to whatever god you worship that they capitulate.'* Yosef was not sure if he could resonate with such a statement, but two things were clear: the sight of the ramps rising up from the ground were demoralizing, and the dark menacing reality that the rebels would soon face newly constructed siege towers had to be a reminder that the end was near.

"Men of the Antonia!" Yosef began as he filled his diaphragm with a gust of air and belted the words out in Hebrew, loud and true. "Heed my voice! Your victory is short-lived if you think Rome shall not rebuild its ramps that you destroyed. Rome also knows you can no longer tunnel and so these ramps *will* rise and they *will* be thrust against your walls! Then, I do not have to remind you what is to come. Surely you know?"

John of Gischala gripped the edges of the rough parapet, his eyes piercing and back arched like he was suddenly going to pounce from the wall at Yosef. His stance was menacing and his jaw clenched as he listened to Yosef deliver his speech like an actor who was in love with his own voice in order to impress a crowd. He thought about ordering a volley of arrows at the fool, wondering what the accuracy would be like from this distance, but then he shook the thought from his mind. He had a better idea. John's face eased with a devious glimmer in his eyes as he turned and nodded at a burly officer standing near the open doorway which led onto the wide platform of the tower.

"Send them out, strong and fast. The cohort standing guard is far enough away and they don't seem lively. I think the men should be able to get the torches into the earthworks and make a mess of the legionary workers scattered about."

"How many should I send?"

"At least a hundred should be good. Any more men and they become inviting targets for the Roman scorpions and archers. Send them out the side gate. By the time any sentries spot them it will be too late."

The officer grinned and left quietly. John had ceased caring to listen to Yosef, but turned anyway and pretended to be interested. His mind conjured up all kinds of delightful images, like the sight of Yosef's body slashed apart from swords and then burning with the rest of the ramps. John scoured the grounds beyond where Yosef stood and began to formulate in his mind the response time that would take the legionaries once they saw the Zealots burst around the corner of the Antonia. He looked to the far left at the distant trails of smoke coming from the Camp of the Assyrians and then strained further to the southwest, where a thin cloud of dust rose from the Romans who toiled and laboured by the First Wall.

Somewhere within his mind Yosef's voice sounded more like a muffle, as if his head was under water. John's mind raced with so many thoughts and angles that he hardly cared what the Jewish traitor hollered from the ramps. Even when he stared down at Yosef, all he could see was the man's lips moving and his finger jabbing the air, as a deafening silence pounded within his ears. John thought about the wagon train of carts that had eerily rolled along the eastern side of the city over three hours ago, and the sight of the Roman cavalry escorting the column of oxen with the towering piles of wood.

He knew what Titus attempted to do, beyond just proving that he had the resources to rebuild the ramps and towers. John knew that the Prince was attempting to use an allocated, clever plan to war with their minds. If the future could be made to look as bleak as possible, then maybe John would call for his Zealots to lay down their arms and walk from the city in a long column of defeated men. But, John knew this was only a Roman fantasy. He would make sure that these barren landscapes, which the Romans had worked so hard to level, would be filled with their graves by the time the legions were obliterated, and this thought gave him comfort. Even with all the ramps rebuilt and the siege towers hammering at their walls, John would still feel safe, as he could not see any real threat while he was behind the thick, stone walls of the Temple colonnades and the fortress Antonia.

A sudden shout went up and John snapped back to reality as he watched the wave of Zealots, like a pack of wild dogs, rush towards the shocked Roman workers who were frozen amidst their duties. Even before any of the legionary labourers had a chance to react, Yosef was already running at full tilt back down the ramp, weaving in and out of the wicker hurdles as he fled to a chorus of jeers from the walls. The workers then broke and fled. The fortunate ones on the ramps were able to escape easy enough, but nearly thirty were caught spread out along the steep embankments of the ramp and slaughtered. Some attempted to fight back with their scythes and picks, however they were easy targets as they were thoroughly routed and hacked to pieces.

Nearly half of the Zealot attack rushed the ramp while the other wing peeled off and chased the workers from the scene, leaving behind swathes of bleeding dead and wounded legionaries. As torches began to be buried into stacks of timber, using hurdles as fuel, the cohorts standing guard sprang into action as they converged on the Jews. A pathetic volley was fired at the swarming Zealots, but they were so spaced apart that the damage was minimal as John could only make out two dead fighters and one hobbling back with an arrow driven into his upper thigh.

Now it was the Roman's turn to swing the fury of the skirmish back in their favour. The pitiful resistance of the Zealot contingent floundered and then seemed to evaporate as they fled like scattered deer. A trumpet blasted from the attacking cohort, causing it to slow, as John watched, as the middle Roman century, to the double blast of a trumpet, took off in a full charge to pursue the retreating Zealots, leaving behind the other five centuries to get control of the smouldering fires.

A number of fighters next to John groaned as they watched their comrades flee the hungry, devouring tide of Roman metal. John listened as a number of them cursed the Romans and then commented with amazement on how quickly the disciplined legionary cohort had met the attack. The talk soon became divided as men argued and disagreed, as many said that if a larger attack had been ordered, the cohort would have been smashed to pieces.

"We tested their resolve!" John called out with vehemence, bringing a halt to the heated discussion. "As long as they fear us, we continue to win. HaShem has struck our enemies with fear and trembling. They know not what tomorrow holds."

"Fear and trembling, John?" retorted a large man with a patchy beard. "They regrouped right away and chased our men away. We merely slapped a fly on a donkey's back, and only irritated the donkey, nothing more. They have plenty of more wood. What they showed to us was how confident they are in the siege wall at their backs. Look, they only defended the ramp with five hundred men, rather than the many cohorts we saw weeks ago. They fear nothing! We are trapped men!"

"HaShem fights for us. Should you be the one to doubt at this time?" John watched the man shrug and move to another part of the turret shaking his head.

"John, you should come to the First Wall! Something is happening," called a man who stood in the doorway of the battlement nearly out of breath.

"What is it?"

"One of your fighters called Yonatan, has taken a place on a pile of rubble opposite the Tomb of the High Priest, and is jeering at the Roman workers. I think he is getting to them." The man spit upon the ground and wiped the sweat from his forehead. "Either way, you should come, I think something will happen."

* * *

Centurion Priscus, senior officer of the work detail at the western earthworks under the shadow of the Hippicus tower, shouted at his men to ignore the belligerent rambling Zealot who had been harassing them for the past twenty minutes. He still held his sword at his side, having drawn the steel when the cursing Jewish fighter had shown up with his roar of laughter, shameless expressions, and foreign curses that thundered around them all. The Zealot had been intent on introductions to the working legionaries and had shouted his name, Yonatan, above all other guttural slurs and mocking colour that decorated his speech.

"Eyes on your picks!" Priscus bellowed above the rants and din of Yonatan, as the bristling bearded man began to throw small stones at the legionaries closest to him as they shuffled away, protecting their exposed faces.

"Someone should kill the bastard, Centurion," one of the workers said with vengeance. "I don't know what he is saying, but no doubt he will bolster the courage of his companions."

Priscus stared at the laughing Jewish fighters lining the tops of the wall and then shook his head. "We don't have time to push them into a scrap, legionary. The Prince has ordered us to erect these ramps with as much speed possible and we will do just that. Your hate for the man is considered, now back to work." Priscus moved on as the legionary grumbled, yet continued to drive his *dolabra* into the hot dirt.

"Keep working, men!" Priscus shouted again seeing numerous legionaries halt their digging and stare back at the Zealot who was clearly getting on their nerves. "Come on. The sooner we get this finished, the sooner we can stick a spear in that dog's brain!"

"I will fill your helmets with shit!" Yonatan suddenly shouted in Greek and all heads of the legionaries turned his way in surprise. "I shit on Jupiter, I shit on Mars! Those gods are gods of the ignorant and the weak hearted! Vespasian must be desperate to send his little boy Prince to this side of the world to introduce himself to us. Is he bored? You play in the sand and try to impress us, you dogs! You are like the shit of cattle, to be tilled in the ground for our crops! I see a bunch of women adorned in twigs for armour! You think Rome is glorious? Rome is the waste of everything that washes up on your shores of blood. You are a people of harlots and whelps! Apollonaris is a legion of children and diseased lepers! You wish to make us slaves? It is you who dig in the ground like a slave with your boy-loving centurions watching your backsides all day! Go to the baths, you smooth-skinned eunuchs! You dogs, jackals, and damned idiots!"

Priscus listened to the vulgar spew of profanity drip off the lips of Yonatan like a salivating dog staring at a shank bone dropped from the table. The sound of digging had been silenced and the faces of the legionaries were red with rage and humiliation from the continuous verbal abuse.

"You cowards and imbeciles! I dare you to become men! Even think about it and you might just lift your togas and run away with your yellow-pissed tails between your legs, you skinned maggots! I call to you, anyone who be man enough, come to me now and I will teach you what it is like to beg for your life! Come! Who dare defy me? Show your peers you are worth something more than the pathetic duties which you have been given. Win yourself gold from your commanders! Come, kill me, I dare you!" Yonatan descended the pile of rubble part way and now was egging them on with gestures as he drew a long sword and began to wave it before them in broad strokes while a cruel smile was plastered upon his face.

"Keep working! A man who cares not for his own life is not worth fighting. He has no honour!" Priscus shouted, but before he could react, one of the alae dashed out in a fury with drawn sword as he accepted the challenge of the Zealot. Some of his fellow comrades shouted after him and Priscus heard his name called as Pudeus, but the man was intent on silencing the confounded Zealot who danced with delight like a dog at the sight of his first meal in a week.

Pudeus was quick and agile. He drowned out all the shouting behind him from the Romans and his fellow Thracians, and focused on the prize, killing the defiant Zealot. As he neared the rubble, he noticed how large of a man Yonatan really was. Yonatan had time to shed his outer garment and now his arms rippled with massive muscles as he flexed them and roared with laughter. The Jews above Yonatan cheered like he was their own personal gladiator as Pudeus bolted forward to the thunder of jeers and curses railing down upon the Roman company insignias of the Apollonaris.

Pudeus skirted around some boulders as he approached the base of the debris pile, refusing to take his eyes off the beast-like man whose face was now set with a menacing grin. He began to climb, steadying himself as he repeated over in his head that it would be swift action that would defeat this giant. Yonatan, on the other hand, did not seem to consider anything as the great man stood like a mythical god-warrior atop his rubble fortress, ready to smite anyone who might disturb him. But, Pudeus had noticed one flaw in the Zealot's stance and it was there that he lunged.

Yonatan stepped back, feeling his heels strike against stone as he searched for a ledge above to step upon. The soldier of the alae moved quickly, and Yonatan noticed this right away as he swung his sword to fend off the man's advance in a desperate move and then cringed as he suddenly realized this is what his opponent had wanted all along. Yonatan watched as his blade cut through thin air as the soldier ducked. The giant Zealot felt a prickle of fear penetrate the back of his neck, rippling down his spine as he expected the flash of the gladius to pierce his chest in a bloody mess, but then the unexpected happened.

With delight, Yonatan watched as the soldier stumbled and then slipped, his eyes wide with terror as he perceived the swift dread of the oncoming wrath which was about to fall upon his helpless tumbling body. Yonatan let loose a loud howl of jubilation as he sprung forward, his blade biting through the air and pure hatred filling his eyes.

Priscus watched Yonatan drive his sword into Pudeus with such fierce power that the body of the helpless soldier convulsed horribly with the impact. Then a river of blood soaked the stones all around where Pudeus lay twitching as Yonatan drove the blade deeper until it stuck out his back and scraped the rock underneath. The Jews suddenly let loose a cheer for their man and the Romans raised their hands in the air and shouted curses upon Yonatan for being dishonourable. Yonatan stood next to his fresh kill, leaving his sword in the dead Thracian, laughing as he planted a foot of victory on the corpse. He raised his arms in triumph and bellowed for the next contestant.

Priscus wasted not a moment. It only took him ten seconds to move through the screen of workers, who blocked his view from the exuberant Yonatan, and snatch up a black bow that had been carefully laid upon the inside bowl of a shield. In another second he chose an arrow with an iron, jagged tip and white feathers from the quiver. Fitting it perfectly onto the cord of the bow, he drew it back to his ear, aimed, and let it sail with a muffled twang.

Most of the Roman and alae workers did not even know where the arrow had come from. One moment, there was Yonatan with his foot on Pudeus' corpse like a Germanic champion, and then the next instant, a long arrow was skewered through his neck with him clawing frantically at the wound as blood flowed from his jugular, pouring from his mouth. Silence struck both the Jewish defences and the Roman workers as Yonatan collapsed next to Pudeus, gasping for air and eyes tightly shut from the pain that riddled his body. Then, he died, propped up against a large stone with his head drooped upon his crimson chest, a strange look about his face, as if he was staring at something hilarious about the way Pudeus lay.

Priscus tossed the bow upon the ground and all the Romans surrounding him began to cheer as they believed Pudeus' life had been avenged. As far as they cared, the Zealot beast had been killed and put in his rightful place. Priscus glanced up at the high ramparts of the First Wall and listened to the Jewish fighters as they booed him and pointed angrily in the air at what they saw as cowardly action. Among them was John of Gischala, and he just stared at the Centurion with a loathing gaze and then glanced over at Yonatan's bloodied corpse upon the rubble, hunched over the dead Thracian as the Romans resumed their work.

*　　*　　*

Chapter XLVIII

June 20th, 70 A.D. / 25th of Sivan, 3830
Fortress of the Antonia
Morning

Simon stood silently in the doorway and watched the hive of activity within the inner courtyard of the Antonia. Where the space had once been open, flat, and covered in soft sand for training, it was now taken up by piles of hewn stones and sweaty men scattered everywhere with hammers and chisels. Even the military observation points encircling above them, like a three-tiered spire of balconies, were quickly vanishing as the railings were being dismantled and the roof reinforced with great beams of timber.

The Sicarii King seemed to stare at nothing in particular, as his eyelids were nearly closed with a melancholy expression upon his furrowed eyebrows. He flicked a long strand of hair from his face and crossed his arms as his sight narrowed upon John of Gischala who was hacking away at the rough edge of a stone with a large iron hammer and well-used chisel.

Simon stared upward as he took in the full view of the incomplete inner wall which rose from the courtyard. Men were clustered on top as they heaved upon ropes that fed through pulleys in order to pull the stones up and slide them into place. The wall ran the entire length of the courtyard and connected with another wall inside the Antonia that had been originally built to separate one drilling field from the next. Only a small door at the base of the divisional wall had provided access in the past to legionaries wanting to move between one field and the next. However, now this door had been removed and the entrance crudely widened for easier access.

Simon squatted down and peered through the newly renovated gateway as rubble lay all around with dust smeared everywhere. He could see the continuation of the Zealot's wall running along through the next courtyard on the other side of the barrier and just shook his head as he tried to consider all the strenuous, blistering work.

John felt a tap on his shoulder and ceased working with his hammer suspended high in the air, clutched tightly in his massive hands which were covered in a fine white dust. He glanced at the man next to him who pointed casually beyond and muttered something John could not hear over the hammering, but he turned anyway and saw Simon descend into the muddled courtyard with a grimace upon his face. John carelessly dropped his tools upon the ground and wiped the sweat from his brow which smeared a chalky streak of sweat and dust upon his face. Then he marched over to Simon.

"What in the name of God is going on here?" Simon said as he rubbed his chin.

"We make ready for the worst possible outcome once the Romans bring their towers up the ramps," John replied as he attempted to clean his hands upon his outer garment.

"By building an inner wall?"

"Exactly."

"You do not fear this might be a waste of time?"

John shook his head. "If the Romans come through our wall, they will have this to greet them. Granted it won't be as high or as strong as the outer wall, but it will do just fine if we must fall back to it. The Romans do not even know it is being built; they will not suspect it." John stared proudly at his creation and then pointed through the widened entrance they had smashed through. "The inner wall will run the entire length of the Antonia, so long as we have time. It will be thick enough to buy us another day or two if they are to use their rams against it. But, that would mean extending their earthworks to reach it and that would be very dangerous, especially if we still occupy the towers and ramparts."

"When I was told four days ago you were raising the defences within the Antonia to meet a frontal assault, this is not what I had in mind."

John shrugged. "What did you expect? This will serve us well and its wise preparation. I have heard of this being done many times in the past."

"There is a rumour you have your men digging again?" Simon cautiously stared at John out of the corner of his eye as he tilted his head forward in a prudent and dictating gaze.

John's pride flickered with a twitch across his face as he scowled and slightly pushed out his bottom jaw. "There is no other way. The ramps will be finished this time. Their siege wall encircling this city has been a strangle hold. With its towers and ramparts they are able to position scorpions upon it and archers. It has given them security and elevation. They no longer need such large forces to guard their ramps, and we cannot rush them and try to pull them down. We would get slaughtered.

"They are building higher towers, Simon, and wider ramps. They have extended their earthworks an extra five metres width. They will be able to smash at our walls with their rams, and bring up crews to pry out stones, or even a testudo to pound at the base. We can't just wait for them to finish, and then it will be a bloody struggle once they attack.

"I spoke with Eliyahu and Amos a few days ago. They assured me it could be possible to extend the mine further to the north, and tunnel under the new ramps. If we can do that, and manage to collapse them again, the Romans shall not recover, I swear to you."

"What of the ground we stand on? The wall you built? Is not the foundation weak if there are more tunnels winding beneath us?" Simon lifted his left foot slightly off the ground as if afraid the earth would suddenly open up and swallow him into oblivion.

John shook his head. "Eliyahu says the ground is stable beneath us, for they can still work off a section of the previous tunnel. If it were to be weak, that would be over there." He pointed to the northwestern corner and shook his head. "Directly below that is where the old mines collapsed, we could go no further, but the ground is still uneven and unsettled. The Romans stay away from that corner. I think they fear a cave in. Nevertheless, the new mines are being dug as we speak, and to save time we are working off of the old tunnels. We have no other choice."

Simon walked a few steps past John and placed both hands on his hips as he gazed around. "The Fretensis and Apollonaris continue to dig in and widen their dykes, trenches, and build up the barriers. Two fixed wooden towers upon the siege wall covered in animal hides and iron plates face us. The sentries inside watch us all day." Simon turned, trying to muster up his confidence. "The furthest ramp, the one near the Hippicus, is nearly finished. That was the ramp we were unable to get to when we razed the other one."

"The Antonia is still the key, Simon. Titus will throw everything at us, for that you can count on. He will keep you occupied, maybe even use one tower, but I know he will bring everything here to these walls." John gestured around him and shook his head. "I wish there was another way, I do. If he takes the Antonia, that pagan dog will be looking down upon the Outer Court of the Temple. To even think of what his wicked mind might conjure up in a moment such as that is like the sight of maggots upon rotten meat. He could stock the towers of this fortress with archers and catapults and fire missiles into the Temple." John spit upon the ground and stroked his beard. "We cannot let that happen. If he takes the Antonia, the entire city is in jeopardy. Your entire position at the First Wall will be in danger."

"We have Herod's Palace if we must fallback."

"But if they can breach these walls, he will find a way to deal with you. It is a gamble to tunnel now, I know the cost, but it is one that is forced upon us," John lamented. "We must pray, and ask God to foil their attempts, cast confusion into their camp, and send the Angel of the Lord to smite them in their sleep. If they arise one morning with the ramps complete and move the towers up against our walls, God save us."

"If you need men, all you must do is request it and my graces will be extended to you," Simon said, cutting the dreary, morbid talk. "When you request these reinforcements, I can take them from all the gates of the Lower City; that should give you two hundred more spears to defend your fortress with. I will only leave light patrols to keep order in the streets; everyone else is to be pulled to the First Wall and the Antonia. When the Romans come at us they will strike at full force, like a viper. Cut the head off and the poisonous vermin is useless and quickly dies. I shall pray your tunnels are a success and that we show the Romans once again whose city they have come to."

A couple metres away, Judah ben Yosef observed Simon turn and walk away from John with a determination in his stride. He glanced back to see the burdensome shoulders of the Gischalan warrior shrug his way over to a large stone, then stoop for his hammer and chisel. Judah had heard every word the vain Sicarii King had uttered, and what had immediately lodged in his head was the simple declaration that when the Romans came, Simon had pledged to pull all his troops from the gates of the Lower City. The thought of unmanned gates quickly lifted his spirits as he thought about getting one person safely out of the city, Hadassah.

* * *

July 1st, 70 A.D. / 6th of Tamuz, 3830
Northern Colonnade of the Temple Mount
Just after dawn

"Hadassah, wake up!" Judah knelt by her side and shook her gently. He watched her eyes snap open with alarm and she sat up pushing her hair back from covering half her face. "The Romans are attacking, I must go! Take shelter and don't come out until I return."

Hadassah looked confused for a moment. She stared at the empty mats lying around the portico from the many men who had gone to defend the walls of the Antonia. She glanced up at Judah and watched him adjust the leather breastplate he wore, then tighten his belt as he shifted it comfortably to the side upon his left hip so his sword hung freely. He reached down and touched her face as he locked eyes with her, wanting to remind her to remain calm until his return. But Hadassah did not seem convinced and stared back with longing, fearful eyes.

She had desired him next to her side during the night. To feel the warmth of his body, breathe in the scent of his neck and feel his strong arms around her, pulling her into his body in a powerful, tender embrace. But all he had done was whisper to her for awhile, touch her chin and then depart to sleep somewhere else as a small cooking fire burned into embers.

A number of women had collected around her throughout the night, many being the wives of Zealots who were standing guard somewhere. The women had settled down quickly, not having many words to say to one another, and only one had chatted with Hadassah until she could barely stay awake. The young woman had noticed the exhaustion upon Hadassah's face, and told her that whatever man she was with, he was a fortunate husband to have her as such a beautiful wife. However, before Hadassah had a chance to object, the woman had hustled away to her bed mat to sleep, leaving Hadassah alone with eyes so heavy they could shut forever.

Yet, despite the aching of her bones and the weariness that overtook her, her night had been one of restlessness and fear. She had found the sleep deep and troublesome, remembering the times during the night she had tried to wake, but had been forbidden by some unknown force, as if her eyelids had been secured by chains.

Now, only a wisp of smoke trailed up from the warm coals. Hadassah watched the peace of dawn shatter, as the sound of pounding feet, shouting men, and the scrape of swords from scabbards echoed from a vast company of armed Zealots that dashed by. Drums could be heard rolling in a steady percussion from the direction of the Antonia as dozens of shofar'ot mixed with the high brass calls of Roman trumpets.

The sky above was grey, with the swollen sight of a deep glow set behind the layers of cloud as the sun struggled to penetrate. It was a strange morning for the month of Tamuz, and she sensed it through her entire being. Hadassah watched a flock of doves flap furiously away from the capitals of the pillars around her, as the pounding of drums and the chorus of trumpets startled them from their perch. Then she heard shouts rise up and she knew something terrible was about to happen. She looked into Judah's eyes sensing that he wished to tell her something as he hesitated to leave, but all did was pick up his shield and depart across the flagstones with regret in his heavy steps.

*　　*　　*

"Judah, they approach the walls! Two siege towers!" John shouted as he saw his Captain emerge onto the ramparts. Already the scorpions from the Antonia were firing their iron bolts and stone bullets into the looming monstrosities that slowly climbed the ramps with rows of oxen pulling them up from behind. Judah froze as he watched the scorpion missiles slam into the bodies of the towers with loud crashes, doing very little, as they either got lodged between the iron plating or ricocheted leaving a massive gash in the structures. Judah saw the worry in John's eyes as he shook his head and then he cautiously peered between the parapets at the thousands of Roman legionaries gathering behind the siege towers at the base of the two ramps. For the first time since knowing John ben Levi, Judah thought he was considering surrender.

The cohorts were stretched out in thick ranks, readied for battle, and they stomped the butts of their spears upon the ground as the towers lumbered forward. They were stretched out within the Bezetha like a sea of steel with row upon row of bristling, iron-tipped pila and walls of red scuta. The two legions held their position as the towers dominated the scene. The great wooden wheels of the engines groaned and creaked with every rotation as they were held together by forged straps of iron, nailed and secured. Judah stared at the iron plated giants that were eyelevel to where he stood. He instinctively drew his gladius, knowing that soon the Romans, crammed into the top levels of each tower, would be dropping the heavy, spiked bridges upon the Antonia's walls to cross over and storm the ramparts.

"Archers, ready!" John shouted, as a hail of darts began to pepper the parapets of the Antonia as Palmyrene bowmen appeared in the open battlements of the siege engines. John dashed along the ramparts shouting and calling his archers to respond as dozens of Zealot spearmen collapsed with screams from the lethal volley. The hail storm of darts continued to devastate the Jewish ranks as the soldiers on the crowded ramparts scattered and sought cover. Judah, who was crouched behind the parapet, watched as a Zealot next to him stiffened and gagged on the bloodied shaft of an arrow that pierced his throat as he stumbled back and plunged headfirst off of the rampart between the Antonia's outer wall and the newly constructed inner fortification below.

When the Jewish bowmen managed to respond, the ramparts appeared a bloodied mess of tangled bodies and writhing wounded who clawed the ground. However, as the siege towers neared, the Jews soon had their revenge by the tips of their arrows, for the Antonia's high turrets subjugated the Roman engines by over twenty metres. As the Jewish bowmen sent volley after volley of iron tipped missiles into the turrets of the siege towers, their deadly accuracy soon became apparent.

The Palmyrenes struggled to respond as their ranks turned into a mass of dead and dying men strewn about and crammed into the small space of the battlements upon each siege tower. Yet, they were fierce, for they took everything sent their way with barred teeth and armour smeared in the blood of their comrades as they fired in quick successions.

The heavy exchange of arrows whistled and soared through the air. They struck rock, iron, and got snagged in the animal hides of the engines. Others buried deep into their victims who let out horrific shrills and screams as many fell from the parapets of the high stone towers to their deaths below upon the rocky ground. Trails of smoke lifted and spiraled in the air from the Antonia's four massive turrets as the Jews began to fire concentrated volleys of flaming tipped arrows into the sides of the towers as they hissed and struggled in vain to burn the thick animal hides.

Finally, one of the scorpions in the Antonia's northwestern tower managed to get a deadly shot off at the nearest siege engine. In one sudden moment, the iron bolt blasted into the top of the turret, shattered the structure, sending eight Palmyrenes flailing through the air with severed limbs. A victorious shout rose up from the Jewish defences as the fighting platform of the siege tower consisted of smeared blood, intestines, and mangled bowmen who howled in pain, trying to drag themselves from the top.

A captain, commanding one of the scorpion crews in the northwestern tower, shouted valiantly for his archers to respond over the dazed enemy and soon the remaining Palmyrenes began to get picked off. The entrenched Roman artillery, which covered the rear of the siege towers, swiftly pummeled the Antonia with a concentration of stone missiles as they peppered the northern tower. Within moments, a single shot hurled from an onager, took off the heads of two archers and split a third in two which covered the scorpion crew in a sheet of crimson.

The Jewish captain, who had been knocked to the side, groaned from a fragment of stone lodged in his right shoulder and then shouted at his scorpion crew to respond. However, before anything could be done, the entire turret was torn apart as onager fire from the Roman positions upon the Second Wall zeroed in on the tower by firing wave after wave of projectiles. In a cataclysmic instant of dust, debris, blood, and torn bodies, the turret was reduced to a state of complete carnage and destruction.

Judah only had an instant to gaze up as rocks and debris started cracking and toppling upon the ramparts behind him as men desperately pushed passed him to flee. He saw full sized stones from the tower fall with a resounding crash upon the rampart, engulfing three men whose screams were instantly silenced. Judah leapt to his feet, arrows soaring and whizzing by his head as he ran from the pounding debris joining the panicked wave of escaping men. He tripped over a corpse and tumbled into a cluster of fighters as they crouched as close to the parapets as possible against the deafening storm of artillery fire. John helped Judah up, his face speckled with droplets of blood, and then joined the sheltering men as they stared in horror at the destroyed turret, now smoking and covered by a cloud of dust.

"They will cease once the siege engines get closer out of fear they will hit their own men," John shouted trying to bolster the courage of the frightened soldiers.

"They have never hit us like this before," cried a Zealot as another catapult stone smacked into the wall and shook the ramparts.

"Sure they have, just not this lucky!" John replied, striking the man across the shoulder to be quiet.

Judah tried to count the dead and stopped at forty-eight. He sat up, and winced as he examined a number of deep cuts on his left arm from the debris. He still held his gladius as tight as ever and stared at John with baffled eyes.

"No one survived up there," Judah said as he pointed at the turret.

John just shook his head and slowly pushed his back up against the parapet and then cautiously leaned out and stared at the nearest tower. It was so large and grisly looking as its crude shape leaned back and forth with movement as it creaked endlessly while the oxen drew it up the ramp by the long ropes coiled through the pulleys below. John could hear the sounds of the legionaries within the belly of the great monster shouting out and grunting as they toiled against the weight of the tower, steadying it, and digging their feet into the packed earth.

"They are bringing up two testudo rams!" John suddenly shouted with surprise. "They are coming up alongside the towers." He watched as the tortoise-like battering rams, one on each ramp with their pyramidal roofs of overlapping plates, rolled up under the force of the men pushing from within.

Judah stood as the catapult fire slackened. He felt the first vibration under his feet as the testudo engines began to do their heavy work. On the tenth strike from the rams, Judah braced himself, for the siege towers had arrived and the bridges were about to be dropped.

*   *   *

Gaius led his century at a quick trot as they dashed out from the ranks of the First Cohort to the Antonia. The siege towers would reach their targets in minutes, the rams had already begun to pound at the lower foundations, and he and his men had been given the task of dislodging stones. It was an exhausting and dangerous job, but that was why Tribune Marcus Octavian had given it to him. The Tribune had said that if there was anyone who could succeed, it was Gaius, and the Centurion had believed him. But as they neared the Antonia and fell under its captivating shadow, he began to doubt if it would ever be possible to bring down such a mountain of stone.

"Move it! Get to the walls, lads! Work together!" Gaius bellowed, as they rushed up the ramp as a single unit next to the thundering testudo that delivered one massive crunch after another against the stone. "Shields!" Gaius shouted, as arrows glanced off their helmets or struck the ground around them. The legionaries formed their own makeshift testudo as they kept moving.

"Picks and hammers! Let's get this done, lads!" Gaius hollered, as the men spread out in a double rank, the rear protecting the men in front with their scutum raised to deflect rocks or arrows.

The legionaries worked furiously. They rammed the picks and crowbars as deep as they could between the stone as sweat poured down their faces and dust gathered upon their lips. They spit and swore as loud as they could as the testudo rammed the wall at their side. As the crowbars were held in place, two men would take turns in quick successions to strike the heads of each bar with hammers that chipped the stone from the force.

Gaius walked up and down the tightly packed rows of men as they worked and struggled. It seemed like the endless charade of a madman. Slam the crowbar, strike it two dozen times before adjusting the iron bar, and then repeat the whole process once more. A legionary's shield shattered from a dropped boulder on the right and two men collapsed, one cradling a broken arm with the bone splitting through the skin, and the other lying unconscious with a smashed helmet. Gaius moved to the men, and knelt by the unconscious fellow, whose face revealed thick lines of blood streaming from the forehead. He silently rose, knowing the legionary would not survive the day, and then dragged the other wounded man under the roof of shields as he winced in pain and grunted.

"You'll live, legionary! You're useless to me now, you do know that!" Gaius shouted in the man's ear above the racket. "You can either try to make it back or hide out in the siege tower and wait till we retire for the day. You will only get in the way."

"What about him?"

"Does he look like he will make it? Now, decide, I can spare no one to help you if you stay!" Gaius stood and helped the man to his feet. "Decide! I can do no more for you!"

"Yes, Centurion." The man grunted, and then turned and ran back to the lines.

Oddly calm, Gaius watched as two more centuries of legionaries from the Macedonica dashed out from their respective cohorts to work on the other ramp. He saw Julianus take the lead and gave him an unseen nod as he turned and pressed through his men to where twenty of them were tackling a large stone they had managed to partially dislodge and split. He watched as six men began striking the stone with repeated blows from long, iron chisels. The ground at their feet was damp with their sweat as it dripped from their faces under the weight of their brass helmets. They worked steadily at the stone, men changing out when they became too tired so they could be replaced by fresh soldiers. A water skin was passed around as the legionaries took drinks of the cool liquid, sighing with pleasure before resuming the hot, toiling, and grueling work. Finally, the great stone gave way and split into six pieces as it crumbled. The men fetched the stone out, piece by piece, carrying each one to the edge of the ramp and hurling them off.

Gaius bent down and peered into the hole at the smooth face of another stone inside. "Common, there's more! Put your backs into it and let's remove these damned behemoths!" He glanced straight up the wall as the siege tower halted next to his century. He watched the bridge drop with a grinding thud as feet suddenly trampled upon it followed by a clash of swords and knocking shields. "Let's get this business done with! Hurry!" Gaius shouted while the men began to curse as they fought a battle of their own at the Antonia, against stone and mortar.

*   *   *

Camp of the Assyrians
Quarters of Prince Titus
Dusk

"Four stones dislodged. We will do better tomorrow, Gaius." Titus stared at the Centurion who was streaked in dust and sweat. "You did well. You dislodged three stones and the Macedonica managed one. That is why my father trusts you. You produce results, Gaius, I like that." Titus called for wine and then glanced at the Centurion with a smirk. "I can live with four."

"Yes, my Prince," Gaius replied drily.

"What were your losses?" Titus asked as he watched his servant fill two cups.

"Our casualties were low, only two, not that I can say as much for the Palmyrenes or the Macedonica lads who attacked the ramparts."

Titus sighed under his breath. He accepted one of the goblets and watched Gaius take the other. "Men will die in war. It is a natural fact of life." He took a long drink of the dark, rich liquid. "I just always expect more of *them* to die than ours."

"Yes, my Prince."

"Agrippa's bowmen do justice, as do Gallus', that old tyrant." Titus smiled as he plopped his weary body upon a couch then downed the rest of his cup. "That is good, now isn't it?"

"Yes, my Prince," Gaius replied after taking his first drink.

A look of confidence mixed with a glimpse of hope and relief flooded the Prince's face. He had been happy to see stable ramps supporting the towers and battering rams, not collapsed ruins. He was convinced the Jews had exhausted all resources to foil the earthworks, and now he knew it was only a matter of time. Porcius Gracchus' services had paid off for he had constructed excellent ramps that would see the Antonia crumble into a heap of rubble within days.

"Did you think it would be easier at the wall, Cornelius?" Titus said, using Gaius' clan name in a friendly manner. "You look defeated, my faithful steward of *Roma*. Why the long face?" he asked with pomp, as if Jerusalem already lay in smouldering destruction.

"My Prince, I just thought we would see more results from the testudines and it looks as if they have hardly done a thing."

"Give them time, Cornelius. The walls will soon weaken and undermine themselves." Titus turned the silver goblet in his hands while Gaius remained standing, wondering the nature of his beckoning. "You will try again tomorrow. I will order the same centuria forward so make sure your men rest well tonight.

"You know more than any man, Gaius, that once the breach is made, we will storm the Antonia. We will throw everything we have at them. That fortress must be taken. Once that is complete, I will see every stone dislodged and thrown into the valley of the Kidron. We shall pull the entire thing down into a mountain of rubble. We shall need to raze the fortress to breach the Temple colonnades. What is your opinion, Gaius, how would you attack the Temple plateau?"

Gaius humbly said, "The colonnades are a fortress unto themselves, if I am not mistaken. I have never been within their walls but they seem impregnable from the outside and very thick. Most likely, in my opinion, my Prince, a proper stage for assault would be to create one large ramp out of the Antonia's rubble and set it against the northwestern corner of the plateau. If we are successful we should be able to directly attack them head on."

A look of complete concentration seemed to have frozen every facial muscle of the Prince as he took a moment to consider this. "That is what Tiberius suggested as well. Either launch a charge up a sloping ramp, or fire the colonnades first and see what happens. Whatever we do, it will come at great loss. I swear that to you. The Temple will be our hardest and most bitter fight yet. If Yosef is correct, the Jews will sell their lives dearly to protect that shrine."

"You seek to destroy it?"

"The Temple? I have not decided. If they push my hand, I shall have no other choice, but that will be up to them."

A legionary rapped his fist upon a tent post outside to announce himself, and then entered Titus' quarters. He had the appearance of a hardened veteran and carried the scutum of the Fulminata as he saluted Titus with a calm discipline. "I beg to report, my Prince."

"Speak."

"Our forces have successfully retired for the night and the towers and testudines have been pulled back and are safely guarded."

"Very well, you are dismissed." Titus watched the man linger as he hesitated and the Prince scowled at the soldier and stood. "There is something else?" "Yes, my Prince. Thought you would like to know that we caught four Zealots examining the walls from today's action. They had taken great care not to be noticed, but we spotted them and a chase ensued. We killed three and captured a fourth. What are your orders for the prisoner? Should he be questioned?"

Titus glanced at Gaius for a moment feeling all worries in the world melt away at their success during the day. Then he looked at the legionary with an apathetic smirk and replied, "Nail him up, legionary. Crucify him before the Antonia. Be sure he is conscious and wails all night long. Then spear him in the morning when we resume our assault."

The legionary struck his chest in salute and bowed. "Yes, my Prince."

"You are dismissed!" Titus responded, feeling good about his decision. He was tired of extending mercy to the miserable rebels and thought that the sight of a wriggling, pinned up Zealot upon a cross might do the legions some good in boasting morale. He saw a flicker of distaste upon Gaius' face and smiled. "You disagree with my judgment?"

"Your judgment is final, my Prince, I have nothing to disagree with."

"But you think I should handle this captured Jew differently? You can speak plainly."

"I just think he should be questioned first; we may learn something valuable from the prisoner…like if they are digging again." Gaius saw a flash of irritation cover the Prince's face momentarily and then it was replaced with the charming, dignified look that was customary of Titus the Younger.

"If he knew anything important, he would not have been sent to inspect the wall. John of Gischala is cleverer than that, I dare say. Porcius also is assured that the Jews cannot tunnel any more for the ground would be far too unstable. If they have men who know the craft of mining, they must know that to dig further would condemn their own defences should there be a cave-in. They would have to channel the mine from a completely new place and that would take far too long, especially digging through the layers of bedrock.

"Gaius, our ramps are safe and the Jews shall count their final days on one hand. The breach in the Antonia will be open soon and when it is, you will lead the First Cohors into the mouth and capture the fortress. By the gods, you shall plant the imagio of the Emperor upon the highest turret in victory and Mars shall gain the glory. I shall offer to him as a sacrifice the greatest prize of all: the fortress of the Antonia."

*   *   *

Lower City of Jerusalem
An hour till midnight

Judah and Adam were careful not to be noticed as they moved along the paved street, descending further into the poverty and misery of the Lower City. When they reached the stepped street, they halted and listened for anything throughout the silent residential suburbs of the tightly packed homes. A few shouts could be heard in the distance, but nothing caused them to take heed or consider abandoning their mission. The night was peaceful and wrought no misdeeds as the silver moon hung in the sky and cast shadows upon every home.

They hurried along as the road began to bend and dip slightly to the east. It was this paved street, with its many steps, that priests and pilgrims in the thousands during the feasts would journey up to the Temple, rejoicing in the God of Israel after purifying their bodies in the waters of the Pool of Siloam. It was a sacred street and one which held the truths of the children of Israel as a people set apart from the violent, pagan nations which surrounded them. Yet on this night, the city felt smothered as the most powerful pagan nation the world had ever seen, had come to their doorstep.

Finally, the street opened up and there before the men, laid a great rectangular pool with long, wide steps of stone descending into the waters on the northern end. A huge dam of stone had been constructed at the southeastern side, and it rose upward as a large battlement joined the outer part of the First Wall. Great bulkheads of stone had been thrust up against the wall on the outside as a supporting base, which fought back against the pressure of the vast pool, as open channels flooded into the water, churning its body so it would not be stagnant.

On the pool's northern face ran another wall which separated the ancient City of David along the ledge of the Tyropoeon Valley. Here, the Palaces of the Kings of Adiabene stood within the upper quarter near the Ophel. There were two gates, this far south of the Temple, that could be accessed, yet they were always under guard by Simon's forces. One was on the far side of the barrier wall beyond the dam, which was known as the Sheep Gate. This humble gate was slightly to the northeast of the Pool of Siloam. The other gate lay further to the south of the pool, and faced the vast graveyard of tombs within the dark Hinnom Valley.

Judah and Adam stared at the dark pool for a few minutes, counting twelve Idumeans toting spears and shields as they quietly patrolled the full extent of the water. The shadows of another eight guards could be seen upon the walls above the dam and their whispers and laughter trailed lightly over the water where Judah watched them.

"Can we get past them?" Adam whispered.

Judah strained to see further down the paved street, but it was swallowed up in the darkness with only a sliver of moonlight cast upon the narrow road. "We have to check the other gate."

"Wait till the guard turns to patrol to the north." Adam crouched down, his eyes narrowing in the dark night.

When they were sure it was safe, they dashed out and kept to the shadows. The moment they moved beyond the guards at the Pool of Siloam, they relaxed and continued down the dark street. Soon they reached another opening where the residential housing ended abruptly and the First Wall stood, bathed in torchlight, its great stones rising up into the night. The two men took cover behind the nearest available home and counted ten guards above the sealed gate. All of the guards except one stared outward into the lonely blackness of night, while the tenth stirred the embers of a small fire upon the wall as he cooked something over it.

"That is the gate we will get Hadassah through," Judah muttered. "When the guards are taken away, we can make our move."

"You are sure of this?"

Judah nodded. "I heard Simon speak of this with my own ears. He will send John reinforcements from all the gates of the Lower City, at least two hundred men is what he said."

"You have not told her? She will not wish to leave, Judah. If she slipped away last time she will try it again."

"I will not take my eyes off of her this time. She will have no choice; she cannot stay in the city."

"But is that your choice to make?"

Judah glared at Adam, not understanding why he would ask such a question. "She proclaims love to me, Adam. It is my duty to guard and protect her. If I cannot do this from inside the city I shall do so by sending her forth."

"And you think she will be safer outside? The Romans crucify everyone these days."

"Your parents were spared, were they not? What makes you think Hadassah will not share in the same divine providence?"

"Because of the siege wall, that is why. She cannot get to the sentry lines like my parents could when the Mishneh was still open. They will kill her, Judah. Those guards in the towers and patrolling the wall will not hesitate to strike her down. Unless you know something I do not, I see no other outcome."

Judah squatted down and picked up a twig that lay on the street next to him. "Your parents were spared because Centurion Gaius Antony had pity on them. I knew him to be a man of his word and a man of honour. He proved it that night and I pray that God blesses him." Judah glanced into the dark eyes of Adam. "Hadassah will be saved when she calls on the name of Tribune Maximus."

"What? The man is your enemy, not your friend. Marcus' men slaughtered our band, have you so easily forgotten?"

"Don't be foolish, Adam."

"You think I am foolish? Judah, Marcus is the commanding officer of the Boars, our enemy and a cavalry wing we fought, ambushed, and struggled against for over a year in the Judean hills. It was personal when he sent Quintus Fabius to our ranks as a deserter, and it was revenge when Quintus told Marcus where our camp was. You cannot trust him! He is not Gaius; you have never spoken with him! You don't know how he feels about you to trust Hadassah into his keeping. He is a violent, godless, and unruly man."

"Nevertheless, he is a man of honour, I know it. He might be our old enemy, but I know it in my bones, Adam. He will spare Hadassah."

"He is more inclined to rape her than to spare her mistreatment!"

Judah furiously shook his head. "No. Twice he has seen me on the battlefield and acknowledged me as a worthy adversary. He will have mercy."

"What are you saying?"

"Remember when Titus rode before our walls that day he crested the plateau of Scopus? Well, when we rushed out and caught him by surprise, it was a contingent of Boars we fought. I saw Marcus recognize me and the man saluted me. Then, when I led the ambush weeks ago where we nearly slaughtered them all, I saw Marcus again as we retreated, and the man still held the same respect, even in the face of annihilation." Judah nodded to himself and mumbled, "He will have mercy if he knows from whom Hadassah is sent by."

"Judah, you could be sending her to a miserable death. It would be far better for her to die here or for you to run her through with your blade, than to send her to be crucified." Adam saw the flash of anger ignite in Judah's eyes for an instant and then his friend bowed his head.

"Marcus has to be friends with Gaius, so he would know about me."

"How do you know that?"

"The night the slave boy came to me with a message about Capito. Remember, I had to sign my name proving I had heard the message and we sent the boy back."

"I remember not wishing to let the poor lad go."

Judah glanced at the gate as he made sure all the Idumean guards were accounted for and then said, "That boy told us the orders had come from the Prince, and a centurion. Remember what he said when we pressed him not to depart? He had great fear and told us that a large Tribune had been with the Centurion, and had forced him to deliver the message and if he did not return his mother would be killed. Marcus must have been that Tribune from the boy's description, and if that is so, then it means Gaius has no doubt spoken of me. Besides, Quintus Fabius knew my name and who we were, surely Marcus does to."

Adam growled under his breath. "I trust you know what you are doing, Judah. I will help you once again, my loyalty wanes not, but I do know that since Miriam's death you have never forgiven yourself. If Hadassah should be crucified, I know you shall never be able to continue living."

Judah scowled. "What do you mean?"

"You love her, Judah. I know you do."

Judah was still. His face was hidden by a shadow, but his breathing betrayed his feelings and the impossible struggle he was faced with. He thought about Adam's words, knowing them to be true, knowing that if he was ever to wake in the morning to see Hadassah's bloodied body hanging from a cross, he was likely to be so filled with bloodlust that he would charge from the walls in a mad rage and be killed. Anything would be better than to live with himself knowing she suffered, but what choice did he have. Death was imminent if she stayed in the city, and he knew in his heart that if she could get to Marcus, the hardened Tribune would be stilled by her beauty and connection to Judah. It was a gamble, but it was all he had.

"We must go," Judah whispered.

"What do you ponder?" Adam quickly replied, not budging.

"I do love her, Adam. But I must do this, for my sake and for Hadassah's. I have to know she is safe. Her only chance is outside the walls. If she can live, there is hope for me; if she dies, I have failed in life. Do you understand?" Judah watched Adam slowly nod and then the two men hurried back up the street towards the Pool of Siloam.

"Halt! Who goes there?" boomed a voice in the night.

Judah and Adam obeyed, knowing they had been spotted and to run would only result in a chase. The Pool of Siloam stood off to their right as a cluster of Idumeans approached with lowered spears and silently Judah cursed their eagerness as he spit upon a paved step in front of him.

"Who are you two?" came the same voice as the Idumeans picked up their pace and surrounded Judah and Adam with menacing looks. A number of them drew their swords and pointed the blades at them as their piercing eyes gazed out from partially concealed faces.

"My name is Judah ben Yosef. I am a Captain under John ben Levi. This is my man, Adam ben Elisha." The Idumeans relaxed their tense stances but kept the points of their spears and swords trained on them. "What is the meaning of this? Lower your weapons! I have identified myself! Why do you mistrust my word?"

One of the Idumeans peeled away his face covering and stared at Judah with a braided beard and dark eyes. "Simon's orders are to watch for deserters." He cocked his head slightly to the side and planted his spear butt on the street so he could lean on it. "You two wouldn't be looking for a way out, would you?"

"You are a fool to ask such a thing and to use such a tone against me," Judah vehemently spoke with confidence. "If you even knew who I was and how I have faithfully served John and this city, you would grovel and beg for forgiveness." Judah slid his hand to the hilt of his sword showing all he intended to defend his honour if necessary.

The Idumean saw the action and smiled as he humbly bowed. "Judah ben Yosef, the Captain of the Zealots, hey?" He signaled to his other comrades and the spears were lowered and swords sheathed. "What were you two doing this far south? Surely you didn't come for a swim?"

"If you were not so blind, Idumean, you would have noticed we have come up from the south, beyond Siloam."

"That thought had crossed my mind, being that your roost is at the Temple and Antonia."

"Is not Jerusalem for all Jews?"

"Is it? Truly during these days do you still think that?" the Idumean replied with a gruff voice.

"Regardless what you think, Adam and myself have been inspecting your positions, making sure you are all alert and on guard. You have proven it to us most grandly, that is all." Judah gazed around him at the other hardened faces and held his ground, ready for anything. In his mind he knew that if these men intended to jump him, he would take at least four with him, not to mention the speed and strength of Adam which would spew forth.

"Why would you be inspecting *our* positions? Why would Simon send such men he neither knows nor trusts?"

"You are wrong on three accounts, you dog!" Judah suddenly said with fervour. "Simon knows my name, you can ask him, Simon knows I am trusted, for that he will tell you, and third, your finite mind must be able to grasp the understanding of the word, *truce*. Since this has happened between you Idumeans and us Zealots, surely you know that forces have crossed over and supported one another. If you can understand that, you insolent man, then you might be able to grasp why we could be here in the first place. If we actually were intending to desert, we could've come up from the shadows, slit all your filthy throats and open the Sheep Gate ourselves. Is that convincing enough for you, you pathetic whelp?"

Adam braced himself, taking hold of his sword with his right hand and grasping the hilt of his dagger with the other. He widened his stance as his hulking mass towered above the other men. Judah's challenging words hung in the air like a suspended ballista stone ready to take the head off a man, then suddenly the tension dissolved as the Idumean officer chuckled lightly and stepped back with a forgiving gesture.

"Right you are. You may go in peace."

Judah eased his grip upon his sword. He bowed his head, uttered thanks, and confidently turned, walking away as Adam followed close on his heels.

The Idumeans stared at the two retreating men. The officer grimaced, then cursed under his breath and turned to one of his spearmen. "Follow them at a safe distance to the Ophel, and make sure they do not turn from the street. Then fly to Simon and tell him of this confrontation, let him decide if there is something further to be said." He mulled over a barrage of thoughts which filled his mind, then angrily grumbled, "They are up to something they sought to conceal. Simon will find out what it is, or Bagdatus will strangle it from them."

"I know of Judah ben Yosef. Bagdatus could never do such a thing in a hundred years. He is John's most trusted man," the soldier replied.

"I don't care what you think of this Judah. The man is arrogant and will get killed for it. He was up to something, he must be found out. Go now before you lose them!"

*   *   *

"By the power of the Almighty, Judah, I thought you would get us killed back there," Adam said with great relief as he glanced back at the cluster of Idumeans who watched them.

"We will be safe once we reach the Ophel."

"Would you really have fought them?"

Judah glanced at Adam with a grin in the silver moonlight. "What do you think?"

"We would have been killed. There was fourteen of them," Adam retorted, as he exhaled loudly, trying to remove the thought of how close they had been to getting cut down by men who were supposed to be on their own side.

"I had faith you and I would have killed half of them, and the survivors would never have forgotten us. Even they would have limped away with bloodied wounds. I have carried this gladius for four years, Adam. I took it off the first man I ever killed, a legionary who had been a part of the cohort that attacked the Upper Marketplace. I killed Capito with it and have slain countless other legionaries, as well as despicable Idumeans such as them."

"But you have also shed innocent blood upon its blade, Judah. No one man's hands are clean in this war."

Judah was silent as they walked and then he softly replied, thinking of that day he murdered the Jewish farmer, "You speak of cleanliness? You need not remind me of such judgment that surely awaits me for what I have done. I have sought God, but He turns His face from me. I pray that God will be merciful, and see what I have done and how I have served Him, our people, and this city. When it comes to such a day as that, I pray my life may be weighed accordingly. But that is between Him and me, Adam, nobody else."

* * *

CHAPTER XLIX

July 2nd, 70 A.D. / 3rd of Tamuz, 3830
Fortress of the Antonia
Midmorning

The avalanche of rocks crashed into the overlapping roof of Roman shields with a shuddering cacophony that terrified the soldiers beneath the thin shelter as stones careened away in every direction. The legionaries shouted and cursed at the explosions against the walls from hurled catapult stones and the thundering of the pounding of the rams. Everything resounded in their ears as they struggled at the base, slamming the long iron crowbars between the chipped edges of stone and hammering furiously to dislodge them.

Screams and jeers echoed from above as the legionaries of the Macedonica charged across the gangplanks of the siege towers and fought against the Zealots who crowded the ramparts. Bloodied, smashed corpses lay strewn along the base of the wall, some lying upon the ramps in crumpled piles while others were on the rooftops of the testudines, arrows or spears protruding from their chests.

Every time the onagri fired its stone missiles, the air would be filled with a sudden crack from the discharge. This was followed instantly by a flicker of shadows, soaring above the heads of the legionaries, as the projectiles found their mark, shattering into a million pieces against the walls, parapets and towers, which sent Zealots flying backwards in bloody sprays of torn flesh and severed limbs.

Gaius pushed his way along his men, steadying any legionary who stumbled or tripped. He patted their shoulders and told them they were beasts, wolves, lions, and a whole host of other ravenous creatures. Gaius glanced back down the ramp as the testudo next to him shifted and two men dashed out to secure it with ropes and wooden pegs. He saw three dead legionaries lying face down upon the ramp, one of them curled up in a ball as if he was a sleeping child. Pools of blood soaked the soil and drizzled down from where they lay, and Gaius shook his head.

Their approach had not been as fortunate as the day before. The Jews had managed to place some skilled marksmen between the parapets of the wall, and they had struck the men down before Gaius even had the chance to order a testudo formation. The men had been in the front rank of the century and had collapsed instantly without a cry.

The two centuries of the Macedonica had been hit even harder. Upon their approach, a scorpion bolt and a catapult missile, fired simultaneously from the northeastern tower, had murderously ploughed a hole right through the leading century. Gaius had even heard the impact thirty metres away over the pounding of his men's caligae. Twelve legionaries had flown through the air like dried leaves blown by the wind as their blood had sprayed upward, soaking the shields of those in the rear. The bodies, scattered upon the ground in a grisly scene of chaos, had halted the entire century while panic and shock gripped their souls. The century had shuddered, like a tremor passing through the body of a man dying of fever, and the wounded had wailed with high-pitched shrieks as they lay about in all sorts of horrid contortions.

The centurion of the Macedonica had recalculated the situation within seconds, realizing the danger they were suddenly in by being out in the open. The centurion had cringed, watching his Optio scream as he dragged himself along the ground with a long streak of blood soiling the light coloured sand from his partially severed leg. The century had regrouped at the blast of a trumpet, formed up with locked shields, and had chosen to charge the wall to get under the intense fire from above that peppered their ranks. Julianus had followed behind at a quick pace as well, especially seeing the dreadful effects upon the century before him, and thus reached the walls unscathed.

Gaius halted at the edge of the ramp and gazed down the steep, ten metre embankment. Two dead legionaries lay alongside six Zealots among a pile of debris. Next to them was a large piece of one of the siege towers which had broken off and now burned with intensity as Gaius could feel its heat. An awful scent drifted up and filled his nostrils as he took a moment and stared at one of the corpses lying among the fiery wreckage, scorched and charred black. He winced with disgust and saw Julianus across the expanse looking into the testudo as he shouted at the men. When he glanced up, he caught Gaius' gaze and ironically sent him a wave with a cheerful smile, turning as he resumed command.

A holler echoed behind Gaius and he swung around to see a torrent of hot oil slam into the roof of the testudo, spraying a number of his men who leapt back from the boiling, sticky sludge that burned their skin.

"Move back!" Gaius yelled, as a fiery brand drove into the plated shell of the testudo, sending up a roaring pillar of fire and suffocating, black smoke. Gaius ran along the row of legionaries, then dashed over to the testudo, darting inside as a number of arrows thumped into the roof above him. The belly of the great siege machine was stifling hot, and dust clung to the air as it reeked of sweat. The great suspended beam was swung forward with a deep, groaning thud as it crunched into the stone wall and was drawn back again by the forty men. Gaius tapped one legionary on the shoulder and brought his face close to the man's ear as he shouted that the roof was on fire.

A grin broke out on the legionary's dirty face as sweat streaked the dust upon his cheeks in long lines down to the nape of his neck. "We feel the heat, Centurion, but the ram will hold. Those plates are overlapping in three layers, and not a droplet of oil has seeped through. We should be fine; the fire will soon expire."

"You're all Macedonica troops, are you not? What is your state?" Gaius replied, trying to peer through the dust at the cracked stones that the iron-headed ram slammed into.

The legionary glanced back at Gaius and shrugged, "The wall is thick and these stones are enormous, but they won't stand forever. We have shifted the ram today, and we cracked two stones at the base yesterday and so far a third. When the debris is scraped out, we shall be able to adjust the beam to get further distance, eventually this wall will come down and a breach will open." The legionary let go for a moment and stepped back near the rear entrance of the testudo. "What news of the towers?"

"Fighting upon the ramparts, for the most part. A bloody mess, but the ram in the tower has managed to weaken the walls as well. Pray that Mars will give us victory soon. It's a damned, filthy mess what we do, but it can't last forever."

The legionaries gave a great heave driving the beam forward at lightning speed and another crunch echoed as the ram shuddered. A deafening crash thundered upon the roof that shook the frame of the battering ram, causing some of the men inside to stare up at the ceiling momentarily in hopes that it would hold.

"Your relief will come soon!" Gaius shouted to the legionary as he turned and stepped to the edge of the testudo, waiting for the next barrage of arrows to pass.

He looked down the long ramp at the hordes of legionaries who were drawn up in orderly ranks as they observed the struggle. Gaius could see onagri and scorpions, too many to count, elevated on mounds of packed earth and surrounded by wicker hurdles as they launched their projectiles in deadly volleys. It was inspiring to see the Roman war machine at work as the artillery and ballistae crews immediately jumped to reload, following each recoil, once the engines shot their payload at the walls with lethal speed. Gaius could not imagine storming a city without the assistance of the catapults and he felt comfort in knowing that such veterans and experienced marksmen were on his side.

Gaius took a deep breath as he built up his courage and fought the temptation of staying within the security and safety of the testudo. He knew he had to rejoin his men and that they still had hours of strenuous work ahead of them. With two short gulps of air, he ran out feeling an arrow sing overhead.

"Give a report!" Gaius shouted at the nearest legionary who was swinging a hammer with fury in his eyes.

The soldier struck the hammer once more upon the head of the crowbar and then wiped the sweat from his face as he turned and gazed at his Centurion. His chest heaved in and out as the tired legionary stared down at the hammer, then shook his head. "Still as strong as ever, Centurion. These rocks were quarried by a master craftsman that is for sure. They are perfectly placed and most of the time the crowbars and picks bounce off of them when we strike, as if every ounce of force we send into the bastards doesn't do anything."

"Any fortune along the line?"

The soldier was about to reply, then quickly lowered his gaze, staring oddly at his feet as he furrowed his brow with a scowl. He lifted up his left foot slowly, as if he had just stepped into something detestable and then planted it down again, confusion plastered upon his sweat-stained face. Gaius frowned, as he considered restating his question before he felt a tremor beneath his feet. He could not believe his eyes as the packed earth began to separate and shake, as if a great earthquake was about to strike. Suddenly he felt himself drop half a metre with a violent jolt, as the ground peeled away. A vapour of hot air blasted him, burning his nostrils from the stench and putrid fumes. Gaius only had but an instant to lift his gaze to his men, as half of them were dragged down, tumbling into one another in piles of flailing bodies.

Gaius felt as if time slowed. He opened his mouth and tried to shout, but felt his firm foothold disappear. It was accompanied by a great, sickening crash mixed with shouts and screams as the ramp disintegrated. A cloud of choking blackness stung his eyes as his body slid downward and then became wedged into something that felt as if it would crush his legs into pulp. In terror, he saw the testudo at his right vanish with an enormous groan and a jet of flame. The men within the tortoise shell only had an instant to scream before being consumed. In a daze, Gaius swung his blurred vision to his left and looked upward as the siege tower sunk, then appeared as if it would topple as it titled and shifted, pulled downward from the rising cloud of thick smoke and ash. Suddenly the lumbering giant jarred to an abrupt halt as five bowmen toppled out of the turret and fell headfirst. With flailing arms and legs they screamed horribly the whole way down, disappearing into the crumbled ramp below with sickening thuds.

Then a loud and roaring wave of cracking stone pounded in Gaius' ears, like the mightiest of tempests hammering a helpless ship against the rocks in an attempt to shatter it into splinters. Gaius watched in a fixated, helpless stare as the entire northern wall of the Antonia came crashing down as it swallowed up the ramparts with its gluttonous appetite, sending men to their deaths as they were devoured by the debris and buried like mortar between stone. Gaius could see the helpless bodies of the Zealots disappear with high pitched shrills as a cloud of dust shot upward into the sky, dwarfing the towers of the great fortress.

For a few eerie moments, a haunting silence filled the expanse as the roar of fire stabbed into the sky from the burning earthworks and devastated sections of the Antonia. The ghastly sounds of shrieking men trapped in the rubble and slowly suffocating, began to resonate with a trembling chorus of dither as Gaius snapped out of his foggy daze, attempting to free himself. His left arm protruded from the debris of what used to be the ramp and he tried to move it. He could see bubbles of blood running from wounds along his forearm and the pain caused him to wince and let out a groan. Gaius tried to turn, but his body would not let him. His ears rung loudly as he tried to wriggle and move his other arm, but it was impossible. He twisted his head to the side, fighting frantically to see what condition he was in. Then it dawned on him; he was buried up to his neck in stone and earth.

The condition of his century came to his attention and Gaius called out as loud as he could, his chest struggling to expand with air. Instead, his voice was weak and feeble. He wheezed as his vision began to blur and his head throbbed. Gaius spotted a number of scattered helmets, shields, and tools lying about. He saw the shape of what looked like a legionary beside him, motionless with a massive stone upon his caved in and broken chest. Gaius slowly moved his bloodied and cleaved arm closer to his face and studied it. Six wooden splinters jutted out from the cut flesh as the blood ran. He cursed loudly, praying he would not lose it.

How could the Jews have built another tunnel and succeeded in collapsing a second ramp? Gaius thought. His mind raced with every possible explanation at what had happened, and he quickly began to calculate a damage report. There was no doubt that the testudo had been destroyed and everyone inside killed as Gaius strained to see the flames rising and falling from the cavernous hole where the battering ram had fell into. The siege tower was damaged but not ruined. From the looks of it, all that would be needed to salvage the engine was to drag it from the rubble and make minor repairs.

His century, on the other hand, had been working on the edge of where the greatest damage of the collapsed ramp had occurred. The Jews must have worked furiously in an attempt to redirect the new mine under their ramp, and thus had only managed to tunnel under a section of the right side. Nevertheless, Gaius' men, for the most part, should have been able to escape, except for a few who, like him, had been closer to the ram.

The Jewish wall had been weakened and now had been dragged down by the imploding mine. Gaius knew that the devastation for the Jews far outweighed what had stricken the Romans. If the Antonia's ramparts had not collapsed, the morale of the legions would have been shattered a second time, possibly leading to a mutiny. But now the door seemed wide open for the legions to storm the fortress, despite the pathetic inner wall that Gaius was beginning to see through the haze of dust. The newly constructed wall could be surmounted by a palisade, and no doubt Titus would order such an attack as soon as the ruins had been cleaned up and the survivors found.

His ears were still ringing as Gaius began to hear muffled calls and shouts. He could not tell from which direction they were coming from, but he prayed it was a rescue party. He saw a legionary stumble in a daze from the back of the siege tower and collapse upon the ground. Gaius tried to call out but his throat burned as dust caked the inside. He saw the man slowly stand, tear his helmet off and toss it. The legionary's armour was filthy and some of the segmented plating was bent or twisted. The legionary walked a few metres from the tower and gazed at the pile of rubble from the collapsed northern rampart. The man stood with both hands upon his hips, as if no Jews were left and the entire city of Jerusalem had been swallowed up. He shook his head and Gaius heard him chuckle to himself.

The legionary must have seen Gaius' helpless state for he trotted over to him and collapsed to his knees with a smirk. His face and hair were plastered in dust and a bloodied gash could be seen on his forehead, but the man seemed not to care as a knobby grin froze his face into a timeless gaze.

"That is one way to bring down a wall!" he said as he began to dig around Gaius. "Don't worry. I shall have you out of here before too long."

"What happened?"

"The bastards collapsed the ramp and brought down their own wall," the legionary replied, as he scraped the earth away and dragged a rock free which had been wedged up against Gaius' back. "If you ask me, it is an ill omen of bad tidings for the dogs. What centuria are you apart of?"

Gaius winced as the legionary accidentally knocked his injured arm and then gave an apologetic look. "Hydra Herculean...I am the Praefectus...."

"I will get you out of here, my lord," he said as he continued to dig. "You are right buried, if you ask me. Did you fall straight down?"

Gaius nodded faintly and the man kept digging. Suddenly a pounding of feet could be heard and the sound of arrows soaring overhead. The legionary anxiously glanced up and then waved both arms in the air. Gaius watched as at least twenty legionaries appeared with raised shields against the storm of arrows. The men were dusty with faces like metal as they clustered around Gaius, sheltering him from the volley of darts that were sailing down from the Antonia's northeastern tower.

"Primus Pilus, can you hear me?" shouted Gaius' Optio.

"He is buried. Help me dig him out!" yelled the legionary who had found Gaius. Ten of the legionaries formed a protective wall with their shields as the others assisted in pulling Gaius from the rubble.

"Centurion, can you hear me?" said the Optio, straining close to Gaius' ear. He saw his commander faintly nod and was filled with relief. "Most of the centuria escaped. We came back when we realized you were not with us. We have maybe a dozen missing."

"Will Titus attack the wall?" Gaius groaned softly.

"I know of no orders at this moment, but everyone was just as surprised as us this happened. It seems the Jews have another wall, much smaller and weaker of course, but something we should be able to get over." The Optio brought a skin of water to Gaius' lips and poured some of it down his throat as they dislodged his other arm and cleared out the stones and earth from around his chest. "Can you move?"

Gaius said nothing. He was surprised he could actually move. Apart from being covered in dust and bruised, he was virtually unscathed. A legionary steadied his wounded arm, covering it in linen to protect it, as he was finally dragged from the rubble leaving one of his greaves behind as two soldiers dug to retrieve it.

"Stay together and watch the flanks," pointed the Optio to the wings of the small formation. "Move together! You two help the Primus Pilus, now!"

The cluster of legionaries slowly descended the remains of the destroyed ramps as they helped Gaius, two men on either side of him supporting his weight.

"Go slowly lads, don't rush. We're covered!" the Optio said, as Palmyrene bowmen on the ground began to fire up at the Antonia's remaining towers in an effort to shelter the retreating Roman survivors.

The Optio led the party safely to the lines of the Fulminata as a doctor appeared with three servants who rushed to Gaius' side, their arms full of fresh bandages and jugs of water. A stool was brought and Gaius collapsed wearily upon it as the servants undid his breastplate, removing it with his cuirass and torques that were taken back to his quarters. Another servant appeared with an umbrella which he held over the Centurion as the doctor knelt down with a number of small instruments that he unfolded from a linen cloth. As the doctor inspected Gaius' body, the servant offered a bowl of cool water to the exhausted Centurion and a fresh towel to clean his face. Gaius did so with some assistance, and nearly melted at the feeling of the water upon his hot, worn skin.

"You are a fortunate man, Praefectus Castrorum. The gods smile upon you indeed. It didn't penetrate the bone," the doctor said as he carefully removed the splinters from Gaius' arm.

Gaius tightened his face from the sting of pain, as a wave of dizziness washed over him. "That is good news." Then he swung his gaze to the servants and said, "I would like wine."

One of the servants trotted away leaving the bowl of water behind, and Gaius stared down at the doctor. "Wrap it tightly. I must return to my rank." Gaius turned on the stool and waved the man away who held the umbrella. "Bring my armour and my sword, right this instant."

"Praefectus Castrorum, I would recommend you rest for at least two days. You do not wish for these wounds to fester. I have some herbs I can supply you with. Have your personal servant grind them into a paste and rub them over the wounds twice daily."

"Nonsense, I cannot be bedridden for two days, not now," Gaius replied, looking over at his men.

"Gaius, good to see that you were spared from dining in the underworld tonight," came a familiar voice.

"Tribune Marcus, it does me good to see you," Gaius wearily said.

Marcus grinned as he dismounted and handed the reins of his horse to a legionary. He stared for a moment as the doctor mended Gaius' wounds and then smiled. "You are damned lucky. The ground sought to swallow you up for dinner. The poor lads in the testudo didn't have a chance." He crossed his arms and stared out at the dust cloud. "The Prince cursed the Jews when the ramp collapsed and then praised the gods when the walls fell. It seems like this might actually play to our benefit."

"And the inner wall?"

Marcus shrugged. "It is a wall built by whores and children, Gaius. A palisade will see it breached. How is your arm?"

Gaius stared down as he winced from the last splinter that was pried from his flesh. He watched the blood run until the doctor dabbed it, and then proceeded to pour water over the wound. "It shall not keep me from my duty."

"I do implore you not to exert yourself. You must rest," the doctor interjected.

Before Gaius could object a second time, a number of horses swiftly approached with the Prince and Tiberius riding at the front. Gaius stood up with shaky legs and bowed his head as the beating of hooves ceased and Titus leapt from the saddle of Achilles.

"Gaius, you are alive!" Titus strolled right up to the weak Centurion and planted both hands on his shoulders as he stared at the Camp Prefect. "It would appear the Jews would have to send more your way to see you crushed. I thought all hope was lost and that perhaps Mars slumbered somewhere in the heavens, failing to hear our prayers and cries, but alas, Fortuna has smiled her face upon us again. The Antonia is undone. The end of Jerusalem approaches." A glimmer of passion reflected in the Prince's eyes and he touched the side of Gaius' face. "It was regrettable. The legionaries that died will be remembered and mourned when their bodies are reclaimed for proper funerary rites, but now we must seize this opportunity."

"Yes, my Prince." Gaius looked down at his bandaged arm and back into the fiery eyes of the Prince. "What would you have me do?"

Titus warmly smiled and took a step back. "You will rest, my great warrior. The glory of *Roma* radiates from you, Gaius. You have served her well, but I will need your arm healed when you trounce upon the enemy and snatch victory."

General Octavian gave Gaius a firm nod from atop his horse as Generals Sextus and Tiberius whispered quietly between each other. Titus turned and surveyed the damage as he gazed out at the dust cloud which was finally thinning. The towers of the Antonia remained, but the majority of the northern wall had fallen. Only a handful of Zealots could be seen in the towers and upon the new heights of the inner wall, but they failed to make the Prince bat an eye. The looming shape of the siege tower could be clearly seen as a number of legionaries remained within it to guard against any Zealots who might seek to rush out and set it alight.

All eyes were on the Prince as he walked past his horse surveying the final breaths of a dying enemy. Unlike the centuries at his back, not a hint of dirt could be seen upon him as his armour and helmet shone brilliantly in the glare of the sun. He now stood on the verge of capturing the fortress Antonia, the key to Jerusalem, and he took it all in with a satisfied grin.

Titus had never expected such an outcome. Not in a thousand years could he have dreamed for such fortune to befall him. When the testudo had vanished and the ramps crumbled, he had sworn to have Porcius stripped of his rank and thrown into a dungeon, but then the wall had crashed into a ruinous heap to the jubilant burst of praise from the Prince's lips. Titus' thoughts were interrupted by the sound of one of his commanders dismounting heavily and approaching him. The young, energetic Prince turned to see Tiberius, and flashed the aging General a smile. "Tiberius, this is what victory feels like. The Antonia will finally come to ruin and the Temple will be wide open for our legions to undermine."

Tiberius was silent as he pondered the reality of the Prince's words. He too felt relief at the sight of the crumbled Jewish defences, and he also knew that the inner wall could easily be conquered. "I would respectfully ask to send an attacking party immediately to the wall, my Prince."

"Test their resolve?"

"Yes, the Jews have suffered a heavy toll. I would have to presume over a hundred dead and their defences shaken. They could not have counted on this. If we move quickly, we may be able to push them here and now from the Antonia."

Titus glanced at the senior General and nodded. "What do you have in mind?"

"A palisade, my Prince. Send a small volunteer party, promise reward, cover them with every onager and scorpion in position, and have them mount the wall. If they can hold the wall for even a little while, we can bring up a full cohort and push our way in. The Antonia could be ours. The Jews have to be shaken. They will flee if they see their wall captured."

Titus rubbed his hands together with excitement and then swung around as he faced the Fulminata. He signalled to the legionary who held Achilles and the man led the black warhorse to the Prince's side. Achilles knelt on the ground with his front legs as Titus swung his leg over the saddle and then took the reins.

"You men have been the best of me! You have redeemed your name from years ago! Your honour has been restored and you have fought the Jewish rebels valiantly with courage and determination. Even now, you do not back down! You stand strong, like your brothers of the Macedonica, Fretensis, and Apollonaris. You are gods of war! Even the alae have shown to be men of valour who fight like fierce wolves! Mars has blessed the legions which crush this city. Jupiter has hailed us as blessed among the living of this land. We are men of iron who shall carry his mighty name to the Far East!

"Many of you crossed the Middle Sea years ago, or journeyed from the sands of Syria into this region. You hail from Italy, Egypt, Spain, Nabatea, Perea, Emesa, Commagene, Asia, Greece, and many other parts of the empire. Some of you even bless the cities of the Decapolis and the Greek colonies in Sardinia, Sicily, Corsica, Cyprus, and Rhodes. We have men from Ephesus, Thessaloniki, Antioch, Alexandria, and as far as Cordova in Spain."

Men cheered at the names of their provinces and cities as Titus continued with a raised fist, "You hail from the lands of Gaul, and posts as far as Londinium in Britannia, the mountains of *Cisalpine Gaul* to the hills of Capua. You have gathered to this army from the waters near Pontus and Moesia, to the lands of Macedonia,

Thrace, Dalmatia, Numidia, Galatia, Cappadocia, and the dunes of Arabia. You were chosen by the gods and elected as legionaries of this army by our Emperor Vespasian to see this rebellion through and the banners of your cohortes planted on these smouldering city walls. I promise you a triumph in *Roma* when this is done. You shall march with glory, carry spoils of plunder upon your backs, and be men of legend before the crowds of citizens and the gates of Jupiter's Temple.

"A senator shall listen with delight to your stories and deem you honourable. A governor shall host a party for you and embrace you as a brother. A priest shall anoint you as a worthy man and sacrifice a bullock to your name as one beget of the gods and blessed by their hands. An emperor shall thank you with great reward to your service, with title, land, and money so you may settle and bear children in peace with wives as beautiful as the sun, and a prince shall never forget you and he will speak of you all the days of his life.

"Monuments and games, never before seen, shall reach the ends of the empire, the furthest realms, in honour of your blood, sweat, and tears shed these past years. Everything I say is because you have served with me here this day!" An explosion of cheers rose up from the legions as men thumped their shields and raised their pila to Titus who acknowledged them with grace, riding up and down the front of the formed cohorts.

Gaius watched the Prince shout something to their praises as the legion chanted his name over and over. Marcus gave Gaius a shrug, then grinned as he walked over to him and whispered loudly in his ear, "The Jewish wall collapses and they shall make him a god. I wonder what the young soothsayer shall do now!"

"I need twelve volunteers!" Titus shouted, as the cheering died down. "I need twelve men, the bravest of my soldiers. I call them to take up a ladder, rush the Antonia, and scale the inner wall! I promise a mural crown to the man first upon the wall and an *amulae* of gold to the others as a reward to wear proudly, they shall forever be known as *Titus' Men!*" A ripple of cheering filtered through the ranks and for a moment nobody moved.

Finally, a large man stepped out from the side of one of the centuries and held up a thick spear, declaring his allegiance. The man was not a regular legionary, and bore all the signs of the alae as he wore a long tunic with a leather breastplate overtop, and a pointed helmet. He was a massive man with a braided beard, thick, muscular arms and broad shoulders as he towered over many of the legionaries next to him. Titus hailed him with an outstretched arm and asked for his name.

"Sabinus, my lord!" the soldier replied in a bear-like voice. His eyes were dark and his skin nearly black. He drove the head of his spear into the soil, and drawing a curved sword, saluted Titus by striking his chest with a clenched fist. "I swear to you that it shall be I who will earn the mural crown!"

At this proclamation, a loud applause of shouts and foot stamping echoed. Soon eleven legionaries joined Sabinus to make up the attacking party. Two long ladders were brought forward as Porcius Gracchus examined the inner wall from afar, deeming it possible to breach from the piles of rubble. Soon, the towers of the Antonia began to crawl again with activity as Zealots could be seen gathering upon the turrets, reloading their scorpions and catapults. Upon the inner wall and at its base, a host of Jewish fighters had begun to assemble, while thirty Zealots picked through the rubble.

Titus sent orders for all artillery crews to be ready to cover the advance of Sabinus and the attacking party as soon as they departed. Then commands were given to Marcus Octavian to select a cohort from his standing army to be deployed to the Antonia the moment Sabinus and his men reached the inner wall. Marcus chose Cohors Six and had them repositioned at the front in battle column, ready to approach upon the twin blast from a cornu.

Two groups of three men from Sabinus' force were selected from the twelve to carry the ladders and the remaining six were given one extra pilum to use once they reached the wall. The men shed any excess weight and formed their attacking party into two columns with the ladders carried in the inside so they could be sheltered by the legionaries hefting their scuta on their right. The aquilifer of the Hydra Herculean stepped forward carrying the legionary eagle in one hand and a bear hide cape in the other. He held out the bear fur to Sabinus, who took it and stared at the man with grim eyes.

"This was from our signifer who was swallowed up and crushed when the ramp collapsed. Wear this and avenge his name, Sabinus," said the Aquilifer as he held the legionary standard firmly in his hands.

Sabinus inspected the menacing fur with the revealing empty holes where the eyes had once been and the embalmed snout and row of white fangs. He smiled at the ominous teeth, then he flipped it around and pulled it over his helmet so that the sharp fangs hung down near his forehead. Sabinus tied the bear cape's small cord around his neck, then picked up his pila and shield, than joined the party as they broke into a trot, leaving the legion behind them.

Sabinus led the way, feeling a surge of power through his massive legs as they pounded upon the ground. A sudden crack from behind him revealed a sky streaked with soaring missiles and arrows that seemed to crash into every square inch of the Antonia. Despite the daunting Roman volley, a hail of arrows began to flicker past the charging Romans, fired from the towers and ramparts of the crudely built inner wall. Sabinus heard a scream behind him and took only an instant to gaze back at the crumpled form of a legionary from his party sprawled in the dirt with two arrows protruding from his chest. *That means eleven,* Sabinus considered, as he suddenly let loose a roar as if it came from the lifeless bear cape he wore. He charged up the steep ramp, dodging arrows that tore past him as he climbed further and further. A handful of Zealots remained among the rubble below the wall, and now rushed to meet the attack. Sabinus screamed at them and hesitated only for a moment as he hurled his first spear into the nearest Jew who pitched back with a shrill. Another Zealot soon crumpled upon the ground, struck down by a legionary who hurled his pilum next to Sabinus. The Jewish warrior lay among the piled debris writhing with horrific, choked gasps as he clutched the bloodied spear shaft with agonizing, trembling hands as he bled out upon the stones.

That was all it took. With the sight of the two dead Zealots, the other Jewish soldiers scrambled away under the fury of the mad Roman charge who shouted together and chased them to the base of the wall. A legionary opposite Sabinus, dropped his shield and spears with his eyes closed tightly and face pointed to the sky as a flow of blood ran from his throat, chest, and thigh with quivering arrows infused into his torn flesh. The man stumbled along for three more steps, then dropped to his knees and rolled onto his side. *Ten more*, Sabinus thought. Yet, he kept his eyes fixed on the prize, and the thought of the mural crown placed upon his head by Prince Titus only pushed him further as he struck down another Zealot with his last spear and drew his sword.

"The cohors are approaching!" shouted a legionary who paused to throw his spear. The pilum slammed into the stone wall, narrowly missing a Zealot as that was the final pressure needed to cause the remaining fighters to flee the base of the wall completely.

"It's ours! Hurry, together with me!" bellowed Sabinus, as an arrow ripped past him, grazing his right arm and causing a sudden flow of blood, which he ignored, baring his teeth like a wild animal. Both ladders were thrust against the wall and a legionary, standing back a couple metres, hurled his spear upward at a Zealot who attempted to push one of the ladders away. The pilum skewered the man through the belly and sent him barrelling backward over the rampart.

"Waste not a moment, brothers!" Sabinus screamed, as the legionary who had just made his kill dropped dead with two arrows in his chest. *Nine more.* The thought pounded within Sabinus' mind but he refused to tarry for only the courageous and most brave would earn the mural crown.

With sword drawn and shield raised, Sabinus leapt onto the rungs of the ladder and began to climb, followed by his legionaries below him while two more scaled the other ladder on his left. Sabinus felt his head get knocked to the side as an arrow grazed off his bear cape. He screamed, his eyes a burning inferno, as he climbed higher, keeping his weight balanced properly against the ladder and protecting his left side with his shield. Sabinus heard a scream near him as a legionary fell from the ladder with an arrow buried deep into his thigh. *Eight more.* Sabinus' fate would not be like the shattered legionary upon the ground, and he felt his blood boil with rage as he neared the top.

A Zealot, who dodged a hurled pilum from one of the legionaries below, crouched upon the wall and grabbed the ladder with both hands to heave it aside. However, just as suddenly as the Jewish fighter was about to dislodge the heavy ladder, the flash of a sword blade shot upward and cut open his jaw, burying itself into his face. The

Zealot fought against the blade for a desperate moment, cutting his fingers upon the steel as blood soaked his hands. Sabinus rammed the blade further and turned his face slightly as blood poured down his arm from the Zealot. Sabinus pushed up another rung, driving the blade through the man's skull and into his brain, then shouted with triumph as the Zealot's eyes rolled back. Sabinus pressed himself past the last rung, and using his weight, managed to turn the corpse to the side and free his blade. He stood like a wild victor, drenched in blood, stricken with rage, and now dominating the rampart wall. He had reached the top first, and the sight of the mural crown was as real as ever before him.

The next legionary to crest the wall did not last long as an arrow caught him in the face and sent him reeling backward in a half flip as he crashed upon the rubble below. The following soldier made it, as well as a second legionary from the other ladder. *Seven more.* Sabinus gazed at the vacant rampart and raised his shield against three Jewish bowmen who let loose a volley from one of the towers. The arrows thumped into his shield loudly and he roared in triumph as the archers notched their bows a second time.

"Where are the cohorts?" Sabinus screamed, as he deflected the second wave of darts, shuddering under the impact.

"Their approach is too slow. We won't be able to..."

Sabinus swung his gaze to the silenced voice as the legionary lay upon the rampart next to him, blood flowing from his mouth and an arrow lodged through his eye socket. *Six more.* He saw sudden fear in the eyes of the other soldier on top of the wall, who was not sure what to do as they were exposed to the shooting gallery above. A long, iron tipped arrow suddenly drove into Sabinus' thigh and he howled in pain. Grinding his teeth he reached down, managing to spare two large fingers from the hilt of his sword, as he wrapped them around the arrow's shaft and snapped it. A ripple of agony shot through his body as he cursed and recovered his stance, trying desperately to guard himself with his scutum.

"They're not going to get here in time!" yelled the legionary as an arrow found its mark between the layers of lorica segmentata at his shoulder. He groaned as he dropped to one knee from the blow, then shouted in panic, "Hurry! For the sake of the gods hurry!"

Out of the corner of his eye Sabinus saw two arrows drive into the exposed back of the legionary and his other knee gave out as both shield and sword fell from his weak hands. A third arrow glanced off his helmet, then a fourth penetrated his spine causing the man to gasp and then fall upon his face. Sabinus swung around, a trail of blood running down his leg and soaking his feet as he felt the wind get knocked from him. He tried to breathe and felt his body shudder as he stared down at the vibrating arrow protruding from his leather breastplate. His chest suddenly felt warm and sticky with blood as he battled to stay conscious.

Sabinus felt abandoned, lost, alone, and forgotten. The image of the mural crown faded and he lifted his gaze, wanting to bellow and show himself as a ferocious man, unafraid of anything before him, but soon found he had no wind to do so. Another arrow struck him in the shoulder and he grimaced in pain as he grunted through barred teeth. He felt his body weaken. He slowly peered back over his shoulder and watched as the approaching cohort slowed, then halted, knowing their chance to capture the wall had evaporated like a light rainfall in the desert. Sabinus tried to speak, his lips moved but nothing came out. He turned as he watched over a dozen archers in the nearest tower draw back their bow strings and let go.

*　　*　　*

Camp of the Assyrians
Personal quarters of Prince Titus
Two hours after dusk

Titus stood staring down at the scale model of the fortress Antonia, constructed by Porcius Gracchus and his staff. The wooden walls stood a third of a metre high, and the towers were slightly taller, giving a real depiction of the fortress. With expert hands the rampart wall of the model had been collapsed in the same fashion as it lay beyond the camp, and not a detail had been ignored as the ramps were raised against the model's wall, and the sunken tower positioned correctly. Blocks of wood coloured in red and gold signified the legions as markers had been inscribed upon them so that they could be identified. Artillery placements had been aligned and Jewish defences marked as the model beheld the perfect strategizing tool for the occupants of the Prince's quarters as dozens of tensely drawn generals, kings, and officers examined it, as if the model was the true obstacle to conquer.

A servant whispered in Titus' ear that Marcus Sulla and Gaius Antony had arrived and the Prince lifted his gaze to search for the two men. He saw Gaius move past King Agrippa and then he turned to the other delegates, picking his opening words carefully as he felt the moment of elation coming swiftly like approaching hoof beats.

"My generals, kings, tribunes, centurions, and optiones, pay heed. We stand at the crux. When the ramp crumbled I was vexed. We all saw fortune cheat us once again, but then, like the gods do so many times when they test us, the power of Mars became like a great hammer that brought down their wall." Titus was handed a long pointer, stepped towards the model and rapped it upon the wooden pile of makeshift rubble that represented the collapsed wall. "Here is the key to capturing the fortress. John has had his men build a second wall, an inner structure that spans the entire breadth of the fortress, dividing what used to be drill grounds.

"The towers still dominate the wall, but the northwestern turret has been damaged and no longer gives them much cover. With concentrated volleys from King Agrippa's bowmen, we can clear away any threat. The approach will be straight up the middle. Every onager, scorpion, and catapult at our disposal will pummel them into dust, but this will be to cover the main assault. What I plan to use first is a night attack." Titus watched the expressions of the officers change as they considered this. It was no secret Roman generals of the past loathed the very thought of night offenses, for the simple reason that chaos could easily ensue. But, the Prince saw little chance of failure and his eyes lit with zeal as he crouched down and tapped the inner wall of the Antonia model.

"I will have a selective vexillatio chosen from the Fulminata to do this." Titus stared straight at Gaius as he continued, "Twenty men will be chosen, including a signifer, carrying a legionary emblem and a trumpeter to signal to the main attack that the wall has been captured. Once the wall is secured, I will send a full attack that will clear out the Antonia and see it finished." Titus drove the pointer stick straight through the fragile wooden wall and smiled when it crumbled and splintered. The Prince stood and leaned on the stick as he glanced around the chamber. "Will your arm heal, Gaius?"

Gaius cleared his throat as he stepped past Larcius Lepidus and bowed. "Yes, my Prince. There was no major damage done."

"It does me good to hear such news. The Fulminata chafes at the bit, I dare say, to conquer the city single-handedly. It is the fury of the gods that drives your men to erase the stain of the past. It is what truly makes a Roman a Roman. Glory is only given to those who honour the gods, and take life when needed without hesitating.

"The gods play a game with us, men. They ignore the weak and scoff at their feeble attempts to greatness." Titus shook a finger in the air. "The gods do not care for petty qualms. If there be one lesson to learn, my esteemed sirs, then let that be in the understanding that the gods only lust after the mortal strength of men who shall honour them and bestow power upon this world worth paying attention to.

"It is true, the gods we serve would never admit such things, and dismiss it as folly, but mark my words, it was the gods of cloud, storm, fire, and sun that watched *Roma* at her beginning. Romulus knew of this, and that is why he killed his brother Remus. For the gods had decided on that day to choose the ground by the Tiber to plant their feet upon. The birth of *Roma* would flow so sure through the veins of its future citizens that they knew the world would quake and shudder. *Roma* is the blood which gives life to those who seek it." Titus paused and locked eyes with Gaius. "You shall lead the vexillatio, so choose your men carefully. Where Sabinus failed, you shall overcome, I am confident of that."

Gaius stepped back in shock. He felt his heart pound within his chest and the image of Sabinus sprawled upon the wall with six arrows in his back flooded his memory. Would he die in the same way? Would he even make it up the ladder? Most of the men with Sabinus had never even made it up the wall, and those that did had died horribly. Gaius could still see them desperate, transfixed in terror as they watched the cohort that was supposed to rescue them, halt and retire.

"Silence is the key. We will hit them the evening of the fifth, just before dawn when the Zealot guards will be most tired. You have three days, Gaius. Train them well and be prepared." Titus began to pace before the commanders as a look of deep gravity and triviality fell upon the lines of his profile. He rubbed his hands together furiously, as if trying to stay warm and then jabbed a finger into the air with a sullen expression. "The rebels have sought to mock us many times, but throughout this siege it has been the tenacity of the legions who have always had the last word. I have been more then merciful with these incompetent rebels, willing to parlay, and sparing those deemed worthy. John of Gischala and Simon ben Giora were long ago deemed enemies of the empire, guilty of treason, barbarism, and murder. They have awoken the wrath of our gods, stirred our legions into action, and have thus brought upon themselves desolation and destruction.

"We have laid their lands to waste, razed their cities, enslaved their people, and recognized those worthy to honour our rightful claim to rule. I speak to the kings who stand before me, your allegiance has never swayed nor have I ever questioned your loyalty. You serve the empire and have taken part in building its glorious future.

"To legionary consuls and tribunes: your service to *Roma* is the pulse that makes her mighty and favourable by the gods. You serve the might of Jupiter, and Mars blesses you with quick action and strength.

"To centurions and optiones: your leadership and command of each centuria has been impeccable. Many have fallen through these bloody months, yet the heart of the men remains intact, and their obedience as legionaries is their true metal. I salute you all and hail you as gods of war in this long journey. As your Prince and future emperor, after my father, I shall not hesitate to ask more of you, that this war and siege be determined swiftly and only with a victory for *Roma*. May the gods be blessed and forever adored.

"In the morning I shall have four bullocks sacrificed in the sight of the Antonia as a thanksgiving offering to Mars for preserving each of the four legions. The men will be assembled at daybreak and all shall watch as the blood of the sacrifice is shed to give us strength."

* * *

Fortress of the Antonia
Near midnight

Judah moved the torch along at the base of the newly erected inner wall as he inspected the unimaginable damage. *The outer wall had crumbled like it had been made of twigs*, he thought. He held his sword tightly in his other hand and swung the torch around to stare out at the dark night. Nothing moved and so he continued. The sounds of sixty other men moving awkwardly over the rubble reminded Judah that he was not alone as they searched for survivors. It was unknown how many had actually died. It had all happened so fast. Nobody had taken any account of how many had been on the ramparts when they melted away in the trembling thick cloud of dust and fire.

The fighting had been desperate and bloody. Men hacking each other to pieces as the ramparts had been crammed with Jewish fighters, determined to make sure that not a single legionary remained alive upon the walls. The ramparts had appeared more like a bloodied brawl then two sides fighting in organized ranks. Men had been thrown from the heights of the wall, had their skulls crushed by stones, were impaled by spears, hacked in two by swords, pulverized by fists, or strangled to death. The last Judah had seen of the ramparts, they had been drenched in blood, as long lines of crimson had trailed off the stones and ran down the inside of the wall. Then the ramparts collapsed, as Judah watched everyone vanish from the tower he had been commanding from.

Judah could still recall the look of absolute shock ingrained upon John's face when he had recovered from being thrown back by a stone missile. The warlord from Gischala had stood, watching the enormous dust cloud rise, and had run to the parapet shaking his head, nearly pulling the hair from his scalp. When the Roman towers had first dropped their gangplanks to the thundering chorus of charging legionaries, John had given the orders to ignite the fuel-laden tunnel like they had done before. Except this time, Amos the miner had insisted on doing it. When a shout of praise had risen at the sight of the destroyed testudo and sinking siege tower, John had felt his spirits soar as Zealots danced upon the ramparts. Then the catapult ball had sent him flying through the air followed by the sickening crash of the crumbling wall.

Judah knelt next to a dead legionary and rolled the corpse over, staring down at the arrow wounds. Blood soaked the man's chest and Judah could see his head had been partially caved in from the fall. He stared up at the height of the new wall, guessing the legionary had most likely been a part of the charge that had scattered the Jewish fighters at the base and attempted to scale the wall before being killed. The legionary looked strangely at peace and Judah shook his head feeling a wash of anger flush through him. He stood and sighed. *There is nobody left alive*, he thought, *as they're all buried and crushed*. Judah turned as he saw John approach from behind and gesture at the dark looming shadow of the tower.

"That is not going anywhere. Some think I should send men to burn it, but the Romans are keeping an eye on it quite closely if you ask me." John pointed over to the fires burning from a horde of legionaries clustered twenty metres from the siege wall, with the shadows of a dozen loaded scorpions dancing upon the stones at their backs.

"We could try and turn it over."

"It is of no use, Judah. The Romans will pound what remains of the Antonia until it looks like this," he bent down, picked up a jagged rock and tossed it. "I should not have ordered the second tunnel to be dug."

"You could never have known. You did what was only possible."

"We could have waited it out, continued to sally forth and fight them, use boulders or oil." John exhaled loudly and lowered his torch to the dead legionary's face. "Twelve men, that's all it took. Twelve men and they scattered us like we were school children. That does not look hopeful, Judah, when men stand upon our ramparts unopposed."

"We had not yet recovered, John. We shall not let it happen again."

John chuckled in the dark. "They will not stop, Judah. It will happen again and it will be bloodier than today."

"How many died?"

John shrugged. "Maybe one hundred and fifty, it is too early to tell. We shall know soon enough. They are shut in below us, in the very tombs that killed them, Judah. Poor wretched men buried by the very thing that sought to liberate us." John looked up at Judah and shook his head. "Amos died in the tunnel, his brother grieves his loss. His mind is ruined. We shall not tunnel again."

"What will we do, John?"

The gruff warlord pressed his bearded chin against his chest, staring long and hard at the dead legionary. "We have no choice. We will try to hold the Antonia and kill as many as we can. The Temple will stop the Romans for awhile with the strength of the colonnades and porticos. They will attack from the north, without doubt. Titus will have his eyes set on the western portico. I shall require every single fighter that Simon can send and I will require them in the morning. Simon must heed the urgency which is upon us all. This city shudders, and once the Antonia is out of our hands, we have only the Temple, Judah. The sacred Temple Mount is all Jerusalem is to us. Nothing else matters. We must defend it at all cost.

"The Zealots will fight like the Maccabees of old, Judah. They shall never let the Romans profane the sanctity of the Temple, not while there is air in their lungs and blood pumping through their hearts. We shall look to that as our last stand, and pray that the God of Abraham, Isaac, and Jacob comes to us to annihilate this brutal, pagan enemy that defies Him. That is all we can do right now, Judah. I fear, my friend, the Antonia is lost."

Judah was disturbed by John's sorrowful words as he watched the great warrior leave his side to continue to scour amidst the rubble, hopelessly searching for any Zealots who may still be breathing. The air was cool and dawn was hours away, but nothing more would happen tonight. The Romans would be in their tents celebrating and toasting their gods for fortune, and the Jews would be thinking about their fate which was sure to face them in the coming days.

But Judah could not tarry, there was still one mitzvah he was required to do. Now that John had confirmed that the time had come to put pressure on Simon to spare every soldier possible, Judah also knew that his plan to get Hadassah from the city would likewise have to be soon, for only God knew what tomorrow would bring.

* * *

Chapter L

July 3rd, 70 A.D. / 4th of Tamuz, 3830
Lower City, Jerusalem
Night

Judah instructed Hadassah to keep to the shadows, then he stepped out from the dark corner of the home and stared at the quiet, vacant gate. A number of torches burned upon the parapets above the great doors which had been sealed by a large wooden beam, than shackled with chains. His senses heightened as he knew the probable danger that lurked at night through the tight alleys and black streets of the Lower City.

Idumean patrols loyal to Simon were irregular and often spontaneous. No longer would they be regimented and disciplined as they once had been. Everything had changed since Simon had redeployed most of his soldiers, who guarded the gates and battlements along the First Wall, to reinforce John's desperate hold on the Antonia. Even with the absence of Simon's troops in force, danger was never far away, seen in the eyes of the people throughout the slums who continued to hide, as if nothing would ever change.

After he scanned the gate for the second time and examined the battlements above, Judah trotted off to inspect the dark alleys. He drew his sword and crept along carefully, straining his ears to pick up the slightest bit of sound that might come from one of Simon's men who had followed him. He searched around homes, examined the sleeping bodies of beggars, peered down alleys and streets, taking time to check numerous doors from silent, empty dwellings. When he was confident nobody had followed him, Judah sheathed his gladius and quickly made his way back to where he had left Hadassah.

Judah took both of her hands in his and stared into her soft eyes. His mind was empty of any words to say as he felt her hands tremble and Judah gently rubbed them trying to restore courage. Hadassah faintly smiled among the comfort of the shadows around her, and a glisten reflected from her eyes as tears built up.

"I pray you can understand," Judah softly said, touching the side of her face. "I could never let harm come to you while I still breathe. Knowing you are safe will be an answer to all I ask for."

Hadassah sniffed, trying to rally strength. "Judah, I am afraid."

For a moment Judah just stared at her, as he warred within himself against giving up everything and escaping with her. The scent of her hair and skin was intoxicating, seeming to speak to his soul with a luring purr as he ached inside. He exhaled deeply as he reached within his outer cloak and produced two gold coins. "Take these. It is all I have."

"Where did you get them?" Hadassah asked, as she examined the luster of the precious metal in the moonlight.

"John gave them to me when he elected me Captain. He said I was a man of integrity, and that a man of integrity should have some kind of fortune for he deserved it." Judah gave a distant smile that lingered. "I never knew what use the gold would do for me trapped in a city with nothing to buy. They are worth much. Where they are useless to me, they may save your life." The smile vanished and Judah drew himself close to her with a flash of intensity in his eyes. "If you are captured and Marcus Sulla Maximus is not nearby, align yourself with the oldest looking legionary. Pick a man who appears kind and unsure of how he should treat you. They usually have older legionaries mixed with the younger ones standing duty. The more seasoned ones won't be as brash as the younger soldiers. Cast yourself upon him in mercy and give him the coins, he will feel obligated to protect you from the others. He will make sure you are taken to the Tribune."

"And what if no man exists, Judah?"

Judah straightened with a glimpse of pain in his eyes as he fought back emotion. "Take this and hide it within your garments." He drew a dagger and handed it to Hadassah. "If no man exists as the one I have told you about, be brave, know that I love you, and drive this through your heart." A look of horror washed over her face as she stared down at the knife in her hands. "I will avenge you, if it should come to that. I swear I will kill them for what they made you do."

"No...Judah...no. If it shall come to that I will not hesitate to do such a thing, for dying quietly upon the ground is far better than to be raped and crucified, but do not seek vengeance on my part." She saw him draw back, puzzled at her words, and she touched his hand. "Vengeance has swallowed your soul, Judah. It is what keeps you here. Hate has deprived you of a life worth living, a life of joy and happiness, a life where God has blessed you and you see purpose. Bitterness has rooted itself into your soul and mind at the cost of revenge."

"You are wrong, Hadassah, it has kept me alive to meet you," Judah replied, trying to reassure her.

She shook her head as tears ran down her cheeks. "Do not make me such a thing in your eyes, Judah. I would like to depart knowing it was hope that kept you alive and not hate. You are like no man I have ever met, a man of quality, pride, honour, and loyalty, but a man driven by pain. Please, hate is no master to embrace; you will die, Judah. This master which refuses to surrender you will drive you to ruin. If I am to die, then so be it. I understand why you wish me to leave, and I don't seek to rest blame on your shoulders.

"But I beg you with my heart, Judah, abandon the memory of Miriam which drives you to hate men and kill them. It will be such a memory that will only pull you further from life and further from me. You have killed men for years, Judah. Your soul has become black, and your eyes feel no pain. It is Rome you try to hate, but you will not find peace through war. Rome will destroy you, Judah, and Simon along with it if you should harbour such sentiment."

Judah felt uncomfortable and scowled. "Justice can only be served one way, and Rome can only be driven away by the point of a sword. That kind of power is all they understand. You mix hate and revenge into one, as if you can understand how war stirs within a man and the higher purpose of which he sees."

"And what is that purpose? I have seen many men of war, Judah. The men I have seen have killed each other and hated one another as much as they despised Rome. Has this city become like scraps of meat that little dogs should fight over, while a larger and more ferocious dog awaits beyond the walls? You follow men who kill, steal, and delight from their wicked deeds. You are not like them, Judah, but you war within yourself against shame, hate, and revenge. Blood is so thick upon your hands you cannot see flesh. My love, should I leave you like this? You will be swallowed up forever in this twisting fate that has wrapped itself around the men of this city. You shall be lost, only to become Capito!"

Judah was stunned, feeling a sting of anger which soon dissipated into remorse. He let her go and slowly stood, his body feeling weak and feeble. "Your words penetrate flesh and spirit, Hadassah. You speak of what you cannot understand. But one thing is true, I have embraced the master of hate; I know no other master. I am empty and have journeyed too far. It has kept me alive. Miriam's fate, Caleb's death, Capito, they all drove me to this point in life where I must weigh evil from good. I have tried to keep my honour and serve God faithfully, Hadassah, but the road seems too narrow and stretches forever before me."

Judah steadied himself against the wall of the home and raised his eyes to the vacant gate. A look of weariness was upon his drawn face, as if the Romans, Simon, John, and all the suffering around him melted away. It was as if he was transported to a place where the spear had missed Miriam, and they had escaped together. Where danger had never plagued Hadassah. It was an impossible place to where he found himself now, so much pain, so much loss, never to go back, unable to change a thing of the past. Judah sighed and glancing down at Hadassah's beauty, he softly said, "To save a life is as if one has saved the entire world. Do not fear for me, Hadassah, I can still find favour and peace."

Judah stooped low, helped Hadassah to her feet, and then picked up a coiled rope which he had brought. Adam had advised him to lower her over the wall rather than attempt at opening the gates, and it seemed like the most logical way. Judah rushed over to the left side of the gate, as he clutched Hadassah's hand and tried to keep to the shadows. They quickly found a narrow staircase ascending up against the inside of the wall to the ramparts above and Judah paused, only for an instant, to draw his sword as he led the way. Once they reached the summit, Judah carefully glanced down the long, quiet battlements, then sheathed his sword silently and nodded to Hadassah who was crouched down beside him.

Judah hurriedly tied the rope into a firm loop and tested the strength to make sure it would not tighten any further. Once he was sure, he slipped it over Hadassah's head and showed her where to keep it fixed against her back. He briefly glanced between the parapets, staring down into the valley below the high wall. A raven cawed somewhere in the night and he was pleased with the stillness around the city. Judah could see the shadows of legionaries patrolling in the distant towers and along the ramparts of their siege wall, but he knew they would be unable to make out anything substantial throughout the thick blackness of night. Judah extinguished two torches above the gate and then gave Hadassah a nod that he was ready.

"As I lower you, just lean back, keep your feet planted upon the wall, and grip the rope. All you will have to do is walk down as I give you more slack. Whatever you do, don't say a word. I will take it slow and you will be fine." Judah studied her features, detecting fear upon the edges of her tense face, but she nodded nonetheless and stepped over to the parapet.

Judah held the rope firmly in his hands as he stared at her, wondering if he should change his mind and refuse to let her leave. They were two people who had lost everything in life, yet had met one another in the most miserable of times, and now, when they needed each other the most, he was letting her go, never to see her again.

When they separated, Judah's eyelids felt heavy and his lips craved to taste Hadassah's, like a starving animal seeing a plate of food set before it. Judah watched her, wanting to proclaim his undying love, to declare they would never be separated and that he would wed her, raise children, and take her far away from all of this. But, she just smiled softly, lifted his strong hand to her lips, kissed his skin tenderly, and then stepped to the wall and crawled between the parapets, disappearing over the side.

*   *   *

A pair of unseen eyes watched the man above the gate lower the woman over the side and then steady himself as he continued to feed the rope between the stone parapets. The man, who hid in the shadows watching, knew it was Judah ben Yosef, and a smile cracked upon his face as he knew what he witnessed would be the one thing that would sentence Judah to death. He had been careful not to be spotted, knowing that a man of Judah's experience would thoroughly check the area before acting on impulse. That is why he had crawled up on one of the dwellings rooftop and flattened his body in the shadows, just enough to watch everything before him but remain concealed. Now he was certain that Judah helped people desert the city, and it was equally possible he worked with the Romans.

He had followed Judah once before, where his great burly friend Adam had tagged along on that lonely, dark night so long ago. They had rushed a family into the

Mishneh, and if he had not lost them temporarily throughout the maze of residential housing and streets in the ensuing blackness, he would have been able to end it then. He had eventually found the gate in the wall that the family had slipped through, but Judah and Adam had left. Knowing that capturing the family could equally help his chances in seeing Judah sentenced as a traitor, the man had pursued the family through the dangerous streets of the Mishneh, where he would have fell upon them if it had not been for the Roman sentries. But he was paid to be clever, and so had remained hidden close enough to hear the Jewish father of the family cry out a Roman centurion's name. Up until then, he had thought Judah had just helped a poor family escape certain starvation, but at that instant he had become convinced the Lion Captain worked with Rome. Of course, at the time, he had nothing solid to go on. He had cursed that night and everything he could think of, yet still he would need to let the Sicarii King know of his information.

Simon had reminded him that only capturing Judah in the act would ever produce the results they wanted and the man had understood this very clearly. If Simon ever wanted to encourage men to defect from John's camp and join his own, they would need to expose Judah as the traitor he was and then watch everything unravel. However, nothing substantial had presented itself, until two nights ago when an Idumean soldier reported that Judah and the brute, Adam, had been caught wandering near the Pool of Siloam. Simon's interest had piqued and he had dispatched his best man to see to it. Now that man lay concealed in the shadows watching everything unfold.

Once Judah had finished lowering the woman from the wall, the unseen man watched the Lion Captain gaze over for a long moment, then quickly coil up the rope and descend from the ramparts. The man knew better then to confront Judah. Even if he managed to kill him, he was sure to leave with a number of deadly wounds himself. Besides, he knew the sweet taste of shame and the horrible execution that would await Judah once the trap was sprung was worth the wait. Then, after Judah had been tried, sentenced, and his throat slit, the man lying in the shadows could roar with laughter and drink to Judah's bones. The city would be ripe for the picking and Simon's influence would be unstoppable; the unity of the Zealots would be shattered.

Judah disappeared as he headed up the street towards the Ophel and the man chuckled to himself. He wondered, half amused at the thought, if the woman had been the Hadassah he had heard about. She had just shown up one day in the Outer Court and never left Judah's side. Had she not a home in the Ophel? The man smiled and pushed himself up when he was sure Judah had vanished. Judah ben Yosef had finally been caught, and would pay for his treason with a slow, painful death. John might refuse to believe such an accusation, or delay such a penalty to save face, but the pressure Simon would be able to push upon him would be terribly heavy. John's hand would be forced, and when that happened it would be clear to all who had finally won the struggle of Jerusalem. Simon would reign for years to come, his throne uncontested.

Once that occurred, Ananus ben Bagdatus knew he would be given a seat of honour and would have the office of Captain of all of Simon's forces. His wealth would be amassed as women and wine would endlessly fill his appetite. Everything had been set, and now Bagdatus slipped down from the rooftop to run to Simon with news that would sing like sweet music in the ears of the Sicarii King.

*   *   *

Hadassah shuffled blindly through the dark. The last she had seen of Judah was a wave from up above as she stood on the ground below. Now, it was a different world. Fear was never far away as she moved along, not knowing what direction she was going or who she would suddenly run into. Her imagination seemed to taunt her, casting a shadow of terror upon her heart as if every sound throughout the night would bring death.

She tripped upon a stone and fell onto the ground as her foot throbbed from the instant pain. Hadassah winced from the bruise and moaned as she struggled to her feet. Staring through the thick darkness of night, as the moon lay concealed behind a blanket of clouds, she could see multiple orange glows ahead of her. She knew it was the siege wall, but where else did she expect to end up? The siege wall circumvented the city keeping her penned in like a frantic animal and there was nowhere to go. Did she actually expect to forever wander aimlessly?

Hadassah knew if she was caught outside the walls once the light broke up the dark sky, she would be exposed to both the eyes of the Jews and those of the Romans. Judah had felt it best for her to surrender to the Roman sentries and she quickly felt within her garments for the gold coins, then relaxed once they were tightly in her grasp. Hadassah touched the cold steel of the knife and remembered Judah's instructions, although she did not know if she even possessed such will power to take her own life. Perhaps if the idea of crucifixion became a reality she would find such strength in herself.

She moved toward the glowing shapes of the orange torchlight cascading toward her from the siege wall. She found herself reciting prayers as she rattled Scripture from the *Tehillim* in a torrent of desperate whispers while she clutched the gold coins so tightly that she began to perspire as the lights from the siege wall grew nearer. Hadassah watched a shadow on the wall pass by one of the torches and a wave of terror suddenly filled her mind from the danger she walked willingly into. Vulnerability, like Hadassah had never felt before, plagued her being as she saw rows of crosses in her mind's eye, hanging with flogged victims nailed to the trees. Hadassah abruptly halted as the shadow of the legionary passed by the torchlight a second time and she felt like curling up into a ball and crying.

Hadassah could not recall what gave her away, but soon a voice coming from the direction of the siege wall shouted at her in a language she failed to understand, yet it sounded terribly frightening. Panic filled her face as she instinctively held up her hands, to the pounding of approaching feet as she fought against the urge to hide or flee back to the city. It was as if Hadassah could already feel the blast of hot air upon her face from the shouting legionaries as they descended upon her like vultures in the night. In her mind she saw her end come in a cruel vision, like a torrential downpour.

First, she would feel a sensation of excruciating pain ripple through her body as a whip shred her back into strips as she knelt, tied to a post, to the amusement of laughing soldiers. Second, she would be dragged half unconscious to the foot of a tree where they would strip her naked, outstretch her arms, and drive long iron spikes through her soft flesh. It was only a horrid dream that dominated her mind, yet it seemed to take on a contorted form of life as the unseen legionaries swarmed in upon her from the blackness with shouts and the jingling of their cingulum.

Hadassah did not know what to do. She had never rehearsed for anything such as this before, or had ever considered it possible until now. All she felt was a weakness strike her legs as she dropped to her knees in sheer terror at the sight of twenty legionaries emerging through the night carrying torches, shields, spears, and drawn swords. Before Hadassah had time to react, the legionaries surrounded her as a few scattered about in the dark looking for anyone else. She held up her hands, begging for her life with gasps and widened eyes. Soon, the legionaries began to grin her way, like starved wolves in the orange flash of firelight, as they gawked at her from beneath the brims of their iron helmets.

Once the soldiers realized it was only a lone girl, they started to laugh and joke with each other as they stared at her helpless state. Hadassah listened to their foreign words and worry struck her as she could only imagine what they discussed, while spotting one man lean his shield up against his thigh and openly grab his groin in her direction which received a chorus of laughter from the other legionaries. For an instant, Hadassah realized she had forgotten the name Judah had instructed her to say, and she whimpered as two soldiers handed their shields and spears to their comrades, then began to cautiously approach her with hungry, lustful expressions.

Suddenly the Tribune's name echoed within her mind. Hadassah frantically shuffled back a metre from the two men, felt the point of a spear suddenly poke her in the back, and completely terrified, she shouted, "Marcus Sulla Maximus!" The laughter instantly died and the legionaries stared at her with gaping mouths. "Please," she pleaded in Hebrew. "Take me to Marcus Sulla Maximus! Please help me! It is just only me!" Hadassah saw a few grins appear on the faces of a number of the soldiers and she knew they could not understand her. But, they knew the Tribune's name, so Hadassah shouted again, "Marcus Sulla Maximus!" She watched the two legionaries, who had halted at the sight of the shouting girl, glance back at their comrades as if to ask what they should do next.

Hadassah spotted an older legionary standing at her right. The man had a weathered face full of whiskers and thick grey eyebrows set over narrowed eyes. He stood quietly poised, his demeanour soft-like, with his shield thrust in front of him and spear lowered. Not a smile split his face nor had he even laughed at her since arriving. In fact, in Hadassah's eyes, the man looked outright annoyed at the other soldiers scattered about. She also had a moment to notice that his shield was different than the rest. It's curved, elongated face was gold with the image of an emblazoned black bull upon it. The other shields were gold set by bolts of lightning jutting upward into the four corners with a coiled, two-headed vertical spike between them and a thick, white, horizontal stripe splitting the centre.

Hadassah reacted quickly and scurried on all fours over to the legionary, while clutching the golden coins in her right hand. A few of the legionaries reacted in anger as they shouted at her, but Hadassah refused to stop and gazed up at the older man with the bull upon his shield as she collapsed at his feet. With tears streaming down her face she hastily reached up and clutched his leg with one hand and slowly opened the other, showing him the gold coins. Hadassah saw his face lighten with warmth in his eyes as he raised his spear and supported it against his shoulder. He reached down, touched the side of her face, gave her a smile, then slowly and ever so delicately, he closed her hand over the coins. Hadassah's spirit soared with hope at this kindness and she remained clinging to his leg as he suddenly yelled at the other legionaries not to touch her.

"You are a pretty girl," he said with a grin, knowing she had not the slightest idea what he even spoke. He watched her nod and then a faint smile shone up at him. "I will protect you, don't worry. These varmints will not touch a hair on your head," he added raising his voice for the others to hear. "You can call me, Atticus."

"You can't keep her, Atticus!" shouted one of the legionaries with an irate voice. "I spotted her first from the wall, old man!"

"You wish to test an old man, Burrus? I dare you! I shall call all the curses of the gods upon your head if you such as defy me." Atticus glared at the young legionary who backed down and he pulled Hadassah closer to him as he planted his shield in front of her, sheltering the girl from unwanted eyes. Atticus felt her cling to him with both arms wrapped around his legs as she pressed her head against his thigh and remained still. "Now, I will take her to see the Tribune. She obviously has something to say and will get her chance to say it."

"And then what, Atticus, you will bed the whore?" called out another legionary with a mocking tone.

"What business is it of yours what I do?" he barked back angrily. A number of the legionaries departed with laughter and an optio from the Fulminata approached him. Atticus gave a frustrated sigh and slightly moved his scutum so he could look down at her again.

"Atticus, I don't know if you can take her as a slave. The men might be jealous. If anyone should own her, it should be Marcus Sulla," the Optio softly said to the veteran of the Macedonica.

Atticus shrugged glancing at the officer, then crouched next to the girl and brushed her hair back. "She is beautiful, Caius. I could offer to buy her from the Tribune."

"What would you do with a slave, Atticus?"

"I would take her as a wife. I saved her life, Caius, she could bear me sons."

"That will be for the Tribune to decide. Alright, I will place her in your care for now. Even though you are with the Macedonica you can take her to Marcus, but take her there now."

Atticus looked up at Caius sheepishly. "Is it not too late?"

"You can't bed the girl tonight, Atticus, not till the Tribune decides what she knows and what to do with her," the Optio retorted. "Be careful too, if word gets back to Titus she might get crucified. She looks poor. You could sell her to Pepi if the Tribune lets you keep her. I would imagine a girl like that would fetch a handsome price."

"I would never do such a thing, Caius. I will take her to the Tribune and then request to buy her from his will."

"With what money, Atticus? She would fetch more than the thirty sesterces you could offer," Caius replied with a chuckle.

Atticus ignored the remark and soon Caius trotted off, giving another stern reminder to immediately escort her to Marcus. Atticus grumbled to himself as he helped the girl to her feet, then he stood back and stared at her for a moment in the dim light. "I wouldn't do you any harm. You have nothing to worry from an old sod like me. You are as beautiful as Venus. What is your name?" Atticus continued to smile and pointed out in the darkness towards Jerusalem. "What were you doing wandering out here? The gods are with you, girl. You are fortunate I came along. Those wolves would have eaten you alive. Their pricks were standing at the very sight of you. But you shall not worry, old Atticus shall protect you."

"Marcus Sulla Maximus."

"Yes, I know who Marcus Sulla Maximus is." Atticus grinned again when she showed him the coins. "You keep those, girly, you may need them later."

"Marcus Sulla..."

"Yes, I will take you to him," Atticus interrupted. "What is your name?" he asked as he began to walk with her by his side. She was silent and Atticus noticed her face was pale and uneasy. "Look, old Atticus here won't harm you. You will be safe, I will convince the Tribune, and buy you with those gold coins if I have to. You will be safe. After this is over I will bring you back to *Italia*, this is my last year and then I am mustered out of these ranks. I will have land to look forward to, and you know that land and a house will need a woman. I have always dreamed of farming. You could raise me sons and live out your days in the green countryside. Would you like that?" Atticus saw the girl nod at him with a nervous smile and he laughed. "You have no idea what I am saying do you?"

Hadassah was happy to listen to the kind man ramble on with words she did not understand, rather than be surrounded by malicious legionaries. She had quickly gathered that his name was, Atticus, and she liked the soft, comforting tone of his voice. Hadassah was still unsure why he had refused the gold coins, but was confident enough in following him, trusting that there was some other purpose for the gold.

"Hadassah, Hadassah," she said to Atticus, finally pointing to herself with a nervous smile.

"Pretty name," the old legionary replied, bobbing his head. "You are safe with me. No harm shall come to you." As the words fell from his lips the deep sound of hooves beating the earth rose up behind Atticus and he turned, holding out his hand to steady Hadassah who trembled with fear.

Torches burning in the blackness approached swiftly with a hint of steel that flashed from the approaching cavalry. Deep, beast-like sounds drifted through the dark as the cantering formation of horses slowed to a brisk walk and stamped their hooves wanting to charge forth. The flash of fire from one of the torches blazed across the head of a boar for only an instant and Atticus grinned as he glanced at Hadassah.

"Here come the shepherds of the sheep," Atticus said with a whisper, as the outlines of the large destriers could be seen with troopers seated comfortably in their saddles gripping long spears and oval shields. The cavalry was brought to an abrupt halt, as most of them remained unseen through the piercing night. All Atticus was able to make out was the light from their firebrands, the moonlight from their helmets, and the sound of heavy breathing from the warhorses. He wondered if he should announce himself, weighing the terrible possibility that if they had not seen him he could spook them and end up dead. However, before he could muster such confidence, movement stirred within the closest ranks of the horse troops as a single mount broke from the rank and trotted in his direction.

The company's signifer held a grim look upon his face when he saw the legionary and girl and it was as if he would ride his mount right over them, but then he drew hard on the reins at the last possible moment. The dark, grey horse, with fiery eyes, jolted its head with a snort, than stepped uneasily to the side as it dug its shod hoof into the packed soil. The horse snorted again, nostrils flared, than let loose a high pitched whinny before lowering its head and searching the ground for any shrubs, weeds, or thistles. The signifer peered strangely at the couple, as if he had never before seen a legionary in the company of a girl, then he gave an exasperated growl, shook his head, and frowned.

"What in the name of the gods are you doing out here, legionary?" asked the signifer coldly. "Are you trying to desert? And who is the woman?"

Before Atticus could reply, another horse drew up alongside the signifer. In the faint light its body revealed powerful, muscular flanks, eyes burning like embers, flared nostrils, a braided black mane, and a hide like silk, as dark as Atticus could imagine the pit of Hades to be. For a single moment, the horse seemed to hover over the earth with an empty saddle, but then a rider appeared, back straight, the glowing face of a god moulded upon his breastplate, and a chiselled stern expression upon his sharp features. The crimson red plume that crested his helmet gave him the appearance of being at least three metres tall, but with his falcon-like grey eyes staring down from his perch, Atticus recognized him as Tribune Marcus Maximus.

"What is this, Helvius?" Marcus said in a low, sobering tone.

"I had just asked the legionary the same question, Tribune," replied Helvius, respectfully moving his horse to the side.

Atticus wasted not a moment, stiffening to attention as he struck his chest in salute. "Tribune, my name is Atticus. I am a legionary with the Macedonica, Second Cohors. My centurion attached me to the guard detail this night upon the siege wall to the south. Just after my post had begun, we spotted this girl wandering in the dark. The sentries I was with sought to bring harm to her, but she cried out your name. Optio Caius can verify my account. I was not intending to desert to the enemy. My orders were to bring her to your quarters, which is where I was going when you came."

Marcus leaned forward in the saddle and watched as Atticus slowly stepped to the side and presented the girl who had been hiding behind him. His lips cracked into a grin and he pointed to her. "She is from the city?"

"Yes, Tribune."

Marcus sighed and then hummed softly to himself as he pondered over the sight of her and nudged his horse forward to get a better view of the Jewish girl. She was beautiful indeed, a delight to his eyes. He stared at her narrow waistline, the impression of her breasts, her long dark hair, and finally her enchanting eyes. "You pick your captives well, Atticus of the Second Cohors. Are you sure you didn't just steal her from the high paying quarters of Pepi's Charm Tents? She could be a working girl!" The Tribune laughed as Atticus kept his silence. Marcus dismounted with a groan, then tossed his reins to Helvius. "Let's take a closer look."

Marcus clasped both his hands behind his back and approached the girl who stiffened at the sight of him. He intended not to hurt her, but strangely enjoyed the sight of a woman nervous at his commanding presence. "Do you have a name?" he asked, watching her face twitch with fear.

"Hadassah, that is what she said, Tribune," Atticus replied in her stead.

"Does she speak their tongue?"

"Yes, Tribune, it appears that is all she knows."

Marcus walked around her as Hadassah moved in a semi-circle to keep an eye on him. He smiled at her, touched her shoulder gently, then felt her hair and frowned. "Definitely of the poor, I would say. Even Pepi's girls have softer hair and scent their bodies with spice. This one is filthy." Marcus took a step back and sighed. "With a bath, makeup, and ointment this one could be a princess. Put a string of pearls around her neck, a wristlet and ring about her hand, and nobody would know the difference. They would think she was a maiden from Lesbos." He snickered and heard Helvius chuckle behind him. "So...she just said my name?" Atticus nodded and Marcus frowned. "Anything else?"

"No, Tribune. We caught her very quickly and surrounded her; she had nowhere to run. Before two men could restrain her, she just shouted out your name a couple of times and then scurried over to me."

Marcus was silent for a long while as he stared at the girl, stunned by how beautiful she really was, especially up close. A thought swept across his mind as he considered taking her to his bedchamber as a mistress and he liked the idea. He imagined himself falling in love with such a young woman who would bear him sons and take on his name. He could take her back to Rome and give her a world of beauty. She would be the envy of all senators and weakling generals who littered the forum as they drooled over her goddess features. Marcus' gorgeous new wife would be the gossip of all the snobbery he hated so very much. He would take great delight in knowing he had something they could never afford, nor gain with all their pomp and influence. Their jealousy would never go anywhere beyond their perverted wishes and he would drink to the memory of their madness every night in the sight of his beautiful, scantily clad wife, lying upon a couch of leopard skins, dressed in white trails of silk upon her soft skin, scented by the fragrance of flowers.

"Tribune, are you well?" Atticus awkwardly asked for the second time glancing over to the signifer who appeared worried.

"Yes," Marcus replied with a grunt. "Now, where was I. Ah...yes," he stammered, slightly embarrassed he had been caught in a dreamy daze. Marcus peered at her and cleared his throat as he flatly said, "I am Marcus Sulla Maximus, and you are Hadassah?" He watched the girl nod with a ray of hope and he gently bowed his head in the manner of a proper Roman man in the presence of a lady. He felt nervous all of a sudden and crossed his broad arms as he tried not to show it. He was a man of war, trained and tested, having survived the wretched fate which so many of his men had fallen to before him. However, now he felt a tinge of softness fill his hardened form, a sense he had not felt in years, and it both disturbed him as well as gave him an exhilarating thrill that puzzled his faculties as a commander and legionary Tribune.

Marcus turned and gestured to Helvius to give him privacy. When his signifer hesitated, Marcus raised his chin, glaring until the trooper submitted and swung his horse away to rejoin the rest of the waiting troop. When Marcus glanced back at Atticus, a staid complexion was cast upon his face like a shadow and he whispered through gritted teeth, "I will speak with her now. She does not trust me, so you can stay. But I shall swear an oath upon your head, Atticus of the Second Cohors. If you so much as utter a word to anyone of what transgresses here between us this night, I will fillet you wherever you are found, whether it be in your tent, asleep on the ground, or in the damned line of battle. I will do so and then shove your head upon a pike and drink to ruin and chaos. Questions?"

Shock flooded the eyes of the legionary. He stood like a statue, mouth open, unable to speak for a brief moment until his voice cracked and he gave a sharp, disjointed shake of the head. Marcus grinned, handed him a small leather purse of coin, and said, "There is enough in there to buy you your own future wife, whore, or whatever you want. This girl is mine." Marcus frowned at Atticus, who was about to object, but then he kept his calm. "Before the Boars, I was attached to the Gallica. When they were decimated by the rebels, I was later reassigned by Vespasian, to the broken remnant of the Fulminata that was brought up to strength. It seemed as if they needed men with the balls of a war-god to wipe their piss stained crotches after they lost their eagle. Make no mistake, Atticus, I speak not of Gaius Antony, who is more man than all the fat, boy-loving senators you shall ever care to meet in your life. Anyway, I have been in this region for four years, in Syria before that for two years, and Alexandria for another five. What I am saying, Atticus, if your seasoned years as a legionary can comprehend anything, is that I speak their damned language."

"You speak...*Hebrew?*"

"Not as well as her but she will understand me. You see, a man of my tastes would be frowned upon if they knew I had studied such a language from a rabbi in Egypt. It would not be thought of as a nice venture during this time, if you know what I speak of. I have many enemies, Atticus, some have already had their bloody skeletons striped from the feast of Prometheus' raven, while others would still like to gut me and seize my office. I am sure you understand the complexity of what I have just told you. Keep your silence, and fortune will follow."

Atticus nodded hastily and stared down at the money then cleared his throat. "I shall keep my silence, Tribune."

"Good, I would hate for the Second Cohors to find one of their legionaries missing at dawn. They would assume a damned rebel had got him in the night, but now such a story shall never be told around cooking fires." Marcus locked eyes with Atticus for another moment and then turned away to stare at the girl.

Marcus chose his words carefully. Then, with flawless Hebrew, he softly said, "Your name is Hadassah and so you know mine. I am a Tribune, a ranking officer attached to the Thundering Twelfth Legion." He smiled at her look of stunned perplexity, as if her voice had been snatched from her throat. Marcus continued fluently, enjoying every moment. "I will protect you, and this man, Atticus, has turned you over to me. No danger shall befall you. What I first require, is how did you know my name and why were you wandering from the city? Surely you know of the danger you were in should you have been captured by far less kindly people?"

Hadassah watched Marcus usher her gently with another gracious nod and she relaxed. She was completely baffled that such a hardened, Roman might know her language and be transformed into an elegant, soft spoken man. The image in her mind of how Marcus would look and act had been completely undone. Now she stood before a man of great stature and honour. "I live in Jerusalem. My parents are dead as well as my husband. All have died in this war.

"I had come to know a man, Judah ben Yosef." Hadassah watched Marcus stiffen at the name as his face tightened, but he let her speak and she talked quickly with an edge of panic in her voice. "Judah protected me, a widow, from being raped by Simon's Idumeans and so has guarded me for months. He believes that the city will fall, and wanted me safe and so he cast me out from Jerusalem, afraid for my life, and told me to call out your name. He told me that you were a man who would know his name and that long since you have been enemies. Judah said, however, that you are a man of honour. He believed that you would spare me and at least take me as your slave if I but threw myself upon your mercy and begged."

"What if I was not the man Judah believes me to be? What would you do?"

Hadassah fought to retain her courage and slowly withdrew the dagger and showed the Tribune. "Judah said that I should plunge this into my heart rather than be crucified."

Marcus eyed her carefully, with a still gaze as he watched Hadassah lower the blade against her chest and look back at him with beautiful eyes that seemed to sing to his soul. In a whisper he said, "You need not think I would do such a thing. Judah is right, I am a man of honour, even though some of my own men might not think it, I am. Throw away the blade. You will not be brought to harm."

Hadassah hesitated for a moment and then saw the sincerity in Marcus' worn face. "You will spare me?" She watched the Tribune nod pleasantly and bristling with courage Hadassah dropped the dagger upon the ground.

"Do you love this Judah ben Yosef?" Marcus asked as he watched a worried expression strike her brow and fill her cheeks as she glanced back down at the knife. He smiled. "You need not worry, you can answer me."

She lowered her gaze. "Yes, I do. But I know I shall never see him again, for he will die within Jerusalem."

"You are brave and answer boldly with virtue. Your love for him is strong, but will change in time. Death finds us all, Hadassah. We are born as wretched men destined to die. It is entwined within a cruel fate that should grip the souls of men and lead them to a death worthy of much glory, which is what every man craves. Those who know not of the sense I speak of, are weak and fade away with the annals of time.

"Know this, Hadassah. Judah is an adversary worthy of glory. I have never faced a man such as Judah upon the field of battle. Judah ben Yosef is the warrior I think that I shall never have the privilege to kill. He has eluded me these four years and he shall elude me again, even though he is now before me." Marcus smiled. "He would have made an excellent tribune, as fierce as I ever was."

"You have fought many wars?"

"Many."

"You are Roman?"

"Every part of me."

"Yet you speak a tongue your people say is for barbarians?"

"It is a long tale, but I shall tell it to you soon enough."

"Then I am to be your slave?" Hadassah said with hope in her eyes, glancing over at Atticus.

Marcus shook his head and stepped forward. He reached out and touched her arm. "Hadassah, I am a man twice your age that has traversed this empire with the legions of Rome, squelching any resistance found. I have killed your people with my sword on the field of battle, for those who resisted and sought to slay me. I might like to think that a time of rebirth awaits me in the future. I have prayed to Venus and Minerva about my future. I know they are deities your people do not believe in, but I tell you that they have real power in this earth and the hearts of those who worship them. They have looked upon me with favour. An oracle long ago told me that I would find comfort in the east. The oracle came after the death of a woman I had loved. A priestess of Venus gave such a prediction and I have come to yearn for something real.

"You love Judah ben Yosef, but that will change. There is nothing that can be done to cease the fate of Jerusalem, as it speedily approaches. Judah will die within the city, and I know you understand that, for I can read it in your eyes.

"Hadassah, I do not seek such a woman as you to be a slave. That would not inherit me the life I so crave. I want you to know that I sacrificed a bullock in the desert three nights ago. I lifted my hands to the sky and prayed to my ancestors that they would give me the intuition to know when I had found such a rebirth of joy, and now I know it can truly be something." Marcus paused as he rallied his thoughts. "I would like not to force such a woman such as you, or sway your mind to believe there was no other option. I shall speak plainly and let you decide, Hadassah. I would like you to be my wife, and when I depart for Rome, I want you to live with me and I shall love you in my fashion." He saw the surprise in her eyes as a meek and naive uncertainty stared back at him.

Marcus glanced down at the ground, caught off guard with what he was saying, but the more he considered it, the more he knew he craved it. "What I have spoken must weigh heavy upon you, but I do know you will learn to feel the same. My hands have been drenched in the blood of too many men. I shall muster out of the legions when this campaign is done, and I would like to take you away from all of this, not as a slave, but as a woman with title, honour, and a life of comfort. I shall request it of Titus, and he will reward it to me. I have served Rome faithfully for fifteen years. I can give you a home, not a grand villa, but a life of ease. Will you give me that? By the love of Venus, can you give yourself to me?"

Hadassah was quiet, like a wind that suddenly dies upon a vacant desert of stretched, barren land. Then, like a stir of the faintest breeze that plucks at a person's hair and chills their neck, Hadassah whispered, "I will do that, Tribune."

"It would do me a greater tribute, Hadassah, than all the beauty of the bulbs which Flora could paint throughout the fields of Elysium, if you would call me Marcus."

*   *   *

CHAPTER LI

July 4th, 70 A.D. / 5th of Tamuz, 3830
Fortress of the Antonia
Dusk

Simon left his guard standing at the entrance of the dimly lit council hall and sauntered in with malicious intent within his dark eyes. Only three small oil lamps burned, wrapping the back of the long chamber in a shroud of blackness and stirring shadows, yet it was just enough to outline the shape of the hulking warlord from Gischala, who stood near one of the windows, staring upon the courtyard below. John heard the shuffle of metres behind him and turned to see Simon halt next to the long, wooden council table. He smiled grimly at John. The warlord scowled, looked away with hands clasped behind him, and raised his proud chin.

"Your defences have been shattered," Simon said in a low, menacing voice which trailed like sweet venom throughout the hall. "You cannot hold for too much longer. What shall you do when Titus smashes your wall? Where shall you retreat to? The Temple? You know he will come for you, don't you? John, what does your mind ponder?" A conniving smile broke upon Simon's sober face as he cocked his head to the side and continued to slowly walk around the table as he ran his bony index finger along the smooth, finished wood. "What shall you do?" Simon wanted to laugh when he noticed John's body stiffen as he pretended not to care, staring out the window with a bleak face. "I know you hear me." Simon glanced down upon the table with an uninterested gaze at the scattered maps. He picked one up, turned it in his hands, and then dropped it apathetically.

"We will fight them," John finally replied in a choked, gruff tone.

Simon chuckled lightly to himself. "You cannot hold this fortress, even with the men I supplied to you. You have failed, John. You must retreat to the colonnades while your men are still among the living."

John turned with a glare upon his face as his jaw clenched. Even as a wounded beast he was still lethal, and he stared at the despicable man he hated with every beat of his heart. "Your taunts can cease, Simon, and if you have nothing to do but waste my time flaunting whatever it is you seek to amuse me with, you can depart from my sight now."

"Ah...but I have not yet told you what truly amuses me." A playful, dark flicker flashed in the Sicarii King's eyes and he saw John's lips slowly part in puzzlement. Simon laughed and picked at the table edge with his fingernail. "You see, I know things that have the power to strip you of your command, John. Your men would flock to my ranks if they knew you harboured a spy of Rome." Simon saw the look of fear and shock hit John's face like a hammer smacking the head of a spike. "I could ruin you," Simon whispered, as if ice clung to the breath of his words.

John bit his upper lip and crossed his broad arms in defiance. "You speak more lies, Simon. First, your dog Yehoram, now you?"

"Quit pretending, this game has ended. The last die has been cast and turned in my favour, John. You can do no more." Simon smiled, gestured to the door and Bagdatus appeared. "He means no harm, just here to make sure you do nothing you might regret."

"What would I regret?" John asked, refusing to take his eyes from the threatening stance of Simon's right-hand man.

"Judah ben Yosef is a traitor. He has helped people escape the city and works with the Romans. Ananus saw him last night help a woman from the south gate in the Lower City. Judah lowered her from the wall with a rope, defying my orders and yours. He also sent a family out of the city, into the Mishneh many days ago, and Ananus would have caught them if Roman sentries hadn't got them first. Well, Ananus is clever, and he hung back to listen. He heard the poor captives crying out the name of a Roman, and soon they were taken to him. Shall I continue, John?"

John was in shock. His body was rigid and he suddenly felt very warm as sweat wet the back of his neck. His pulse pounded within him and his mind swam. A thousand questions raced in the deep confines of his memory, yet not an answer surfaced. His gaze fell to the floor, betrayal was upon his tongue like a foul taste, and the lines upon his forehead became like deep crevasses. John felt his breathing burn against his nostrils like hot vapours and he shook his head and uttered distastefully, "Impossible."

The smile returned to Simon's face as his eyes mellowed with surprise. "Impossible?" he scoffed. "I will tell you what is possible, John. I would give the Antonia a day or two, and then the Romans shall storm this place, kill everyone, and pull down every stone. Once they have that, their eyes will look to the Temple and its courts. Like a man would harvest his wheat with a scythe, so shall the cohorts of Titus cut you down. They will trample you, crush you, and then cast your Zealots to the wind like chaff. That is possible.

"However, before your end, I shall announce, with heralds through all the streets of this city, that Judah ben Yosef is a Roman spy and you knew about it. I would enjoy watching how many of your men would seek to give homage to me and join my spears."

"I did not know about his treachery!" John suddenly roared shaking the room as he half drew his sword, feeling cornered and desperate. He felt trapped, and if this was how Simon would seek to overthrow him, he would kill as many men as he could.

A look of false pity took over Simon's being as he nodded and gave a bow. "Of course you didn't know. How were you to know that your most trusted captain, a man you have sworn upon, forced men to honour, and who you yourself deemed innocent, was plotting behind your back. John, you know how it shall play out. Your men will slit Judah's throat and hang him from the wall. Then, if they don't drag you through the streets by your ankles until you're dead, they shall swear allegiance to me, the one man who would never tolerate such a thing."

John was gravely silent, so much so that the breeze stirring outside the window could be heard. "Then why have you not done so?"

Simon shrugged. "That is not how I seek to conduct this affair. I have a vast army, nearly twelve thousand spears at my command; you have maybe four thousand. If I was to announce such a thing, your men would divide, like I stated, many would come to fight for me, yet still, not all. You would hold a host of bandits, John, and the Temple would fall swiftly once the legions moved in on you. Either that or your men would all kill each other as they chose sides between you and me, and sought to drive each other from the Temple plateau. We both know that we need as many swords as we can in order to defeat Titus, and a couple thousand dead Zealots would do this city no good deed. So, I offer you this," Simon strolled over to John with a smug look. "You allow me to arrest Judah, conduct a trial, and then execute him swiftly."

John scowled. "That is all?"

"Of course not, John, I am a man of reputable majesty and power. Judah dead and gone would still not give me what I want, and you know what that is better than any man. I want you to swear you will turn over all your men-at-arms into my fold once the Romans are done. Your life shall be spared if you do this and then you must leave Jerusalem, never to return."

"You think you can destroy the legions? Even if you do they will come back; remember who you are fighting."

"I know exactly who I fight, John. I shall have the glory when this matter is concluded." Simon stared at John and whispered, "Do we have terms?"

"We have terms, under the condition that I conduct the trial of Judah ben Yosef, otherwise I shall chance it with my Zealots against your pathetic word."

Simon's face tightened and then he reluctantly nodded. "Fine, I shall honour you in the seat of judgment over Judah. But there can only be one verdict for Judah as he is a traitor, and that is death."

* * *

Judah stood within the Inner Court of the Israelites listening to the prayers and watching as the evening sacrifice and libation finished. A pillar of smoke trailed up from the burnt altar as a line of white-robed priests filed back into the Temple. Two bearded priests with red sashes bound upon their waists silently walked up the stone incline of the altar, as one carried a long three-pronged fork made from copper and the other a silver shovel. Judah watched the silhouettes of the two priests closely as he studied their shadows against the massive open sanctuary doors which towered behind the altar. He slowly knelt upon the tiled stones as he recited a prayer and moved his lips inaudibly. The priest with the fork turned over the offering which sizzled and crackled among the stack of burning logs, while the other priest scooped up a heap of ashes in the silver shovel and descended the altar's ramp. Both rites were conducted in silence, with the utmost reverence and respect.

Near the west side of the burnt altar, Judah could see two more priests working dutifully before two tables, one of marble and the other of intricately moulded silver. The priest who stood before the marble table, worked with the expert hands of a butcher as he cut the body of a goat open and began to skin the animal using a razor sharp blade. At the silver table, the priest was positioning different Temple vessels and utensils of copper and silver, which included great spouted pitchers and bowls of various shapes.

Judah breathed in the aroma of the burning sacrifice and bowed his head as he placed both hands on his thighs to support his posture. He prayed as he began to rock forward and backward, as if in a trance, as he whispered to God for a sign that Hadassah still lived. At dawn Judah had scoured the landscape around the eastern side of Jerusalem and had gazed from the towers of the Antonia, but nowhere was the gruelling sight of Hadassah hanging from a cross. Had God spared her? Had she been taken to Marcus? *Surely she still lives,* Judah thought as he continued to pray, wanting to discover a sense of peace in his heart about what he had done.

"Judah, Judah!" Adam and Moshe shouted as they ran over to their praying friend, startling the priests at the ritual tables who glanced up with annoyed looks.

Judah stood quickly seeing panic and worry in their eyes as they clutched the hilts of their swords. "What is it, Adam? What is wrong?" Judah said, feeling a sensation of alarm and fear consume him like an invisible cloak.

"Simon is after you!" Adam said as sorrow filled his great face and his eyes reddened. "It is over! Somehow he suspects you, but it is over! They are coming to arrest you!"

"Who approaches?" Judah ranted, not believing what he was hearing.

Adam covered his face in grief as he moaned. "Bagdatus leads a contingent of twelve men. They have orders for your arrest! They are proclaiming it now!"

"They say you are an agent for the Romans!" Moshe exclaimed in disbelief as he turned to the thundering of approaching voices.

A commotion suddenly broke the wondrous feeling of worship before the looming Temple as a host of men entered shouting, with Bagdatus at the front marching in long strides with a grin upon his face. When he spotted Judah, Bagdatus did not hesitate a second, but cut the air with his finger as he jabbed it at Judah and shouted for the armed men accompanying him to make the arrest.

"Do not fight them!" Judah said to Adam and Moshe raising his voice as they stepped to the side and drew their swords. "They will surely kill you! Stand down!"

"And they shall surely execute you," Adam retorted in anger. "They call treason upon your head, Judah."

It took a moment for Judah to even believe what Adam was saying as the guards rushed him and grabbed his arms. Judah allowed himself to be taken willingly, without a fight as his sword was seized and his arms bound with coarse rope.

"If I find out that you had a hand in his treachery I shall be after you as well, Adam!" Bagdatus boomed. "Sleep in fear tonight, Lions!"

"You know where to find me, and I will snatch your life should you come," Adam roared back above the crowd as Bagdatus laughed.

"Judah ben Yosef," Bagdatus said as he turned his large, bearded face upon the bound, shackled prisoner. "You are arrested by order of King Simon ben Giora and by the authority of John of Gischala. You will be tried and condemned for your treachery."

"You son of a dog!" Judah shouted back. "Bagdatus, your hands are soaked with innocent blood! If anyone should be condemned, it is you!"

"But I have not shared secrets with Rome!" Bagdatus replied with a grin. He stepped forward and with all his weight, planted a heavy fist into Judah's gut with a delightful grimace. Judah gasped from the impact as he stumbled back and then was forced to stand by the guards who held him. "You are stripped of your rank and deemed a criminal. Take him away! Take him to Simon and John in the Chamber of Hewn Stone!" Bagdatus barked at his soldiers who dragged Judah across the Temple stones.

Adam and Moshe followed closely behind the mob that surrounded Judah as they headed across the western plaza of the Court of the Israelites. Their shouts and jeers echoed in the empty court as they passed the massive oaked doors of the Nicanor Gate on their left and the burnt altar to their right. They moved with great haste towards the Chamber of Hewn Stone which was nestled between the Water Gate to the north and the Chamber of the House of Oil to the south which occupied a space within the Court of the Women. Adam and Moshe watched as the great veiled curtains of red were drawn aside leading into the hall of the Sanhedrin's seat of judgment beneath the portico roof and they knew it was in there that Judah would be declared guilty.

Six menacing guards clutching shields and spears confronted Adam and Moshe, blocking the entrance to the chamber as they glared at them beneath pointed helmets. The message was clear to both Lions. Anyone loyal, or a friend to Judah, was not permitted access to such a trial, which spelt a swift conviction and verdict with no hope for the Lion Captain. Adam growled under his breath at the guards and turned from the threat of barbed spears as he shook his head. He glanced at Moshe, who was now reduced to a look of defeat and failure.

"Moshe come! Let us wait near the gate." Adam pointed weakly to the Nicanor Gate, then wiped tears from his eyes. Everything had suddenly become so hopeless and he prayed to God that Judah would be given courage to stand up against the men who sat in the seat of mockers.

"We have journeyed this far with him, only to fail him, Adam," Moshe said in a hollow, stunned voice with moist eyes. "He believes more in what we do here than anyone else. I know that to be true, you can see it in his eyes. Now they seek to cast judgment upon him as a traitor? Judah hates the Romans. They killed his parents and Miriam. It is wicked that they could even contrive of such a falsity. And John, of all people. How can a man as noble as he even stand for this?"

"I have no words, Moshe that shall bring comfort." Adam swallowed, feeling the lump in his throat ache and he covered his face in shame. He should have refused to help Judah. He should have threatened to report him, done anything to stop him from aiding Hadassah. He must have been seen; someone must have followed him. Adam knew that Judah had been convinced that not a soul had been aware of such dealings, but that was all irrelevant now as he stared at the closed veil of the Chamber of Hewn Stone. He knew Judah would stand judgment for his capture and Adam braced himself for the coming execution that would soon follow.

If Judah was to be executed, Adam knew he would surely die as well. He knew he could not continue living knowing he had failed his Captain, having pledged an oath to protect the man he had served and followed so faithfully for four years. He had vowed to guard Judah and fight for him, and his oath could not wane, not even in the face of acclaimed judicial execution.

Adam walked over to the open Nicanor Gates and Moshe followed reluctantly. Adam knew he could say nothing to Moshe about Judah's involvement with Gaius Antony, for if the young man was to find out the truth, he might very well join the mob that sought Judah's death. He would honour Judah's memory in one of the minds of his last surviving Lions and he would do so by not uttering a word of truth. Yet, in Adam's conscious, he knew he faced the end of his life which was wrapped up in Judah's fate. So, Adam slumped against the wall and began to formulate a plan in his mind to kill Simon ben Giora before they had a chance to murder Judah.

*　　*　　*

The Chamber of the Hewn Stone was a large square hall. Its walls were covered in heavy red veils, its lamps were of gold, and its ceiling was beautifully crafted in wood, inlaid with gold, exquisite to the eye. The flagstones upon the floor were marble as they reflected the light of the lamps that burned. Surrounding the hall, a host of men were seated, some in flowing robes and head coverings, while others wore armour.

At the far western end sat two priests seated before wooden tables with quill in hand, an ink bottle next to them and a clean sheet of parchment stretched over the top to write upon. The chamber was silent as the men waited, all with deep frowns, as if the verdict had already been drawn up and the trial considered a waste of time.

Along the northern wall sat John and Simon upon large council chairs of crafted wood, with one of the hall's other entrances at their back and a gold tiered mantle above.

Judah stood in the center of the hall, his hands bound tightly behind him and the heavy grasp of Bagdatus upon his shoulder. Next to Bagdatus stood two guards with shields and drawn swords as if ready to commit the sentence upon that very spot. Judah felt the air rife with anger and burning hatred against him. However, there was one who remained indifferent.

"Judah ben Yosef, this Sanhedrin of judges has been convened upon your arrest, to try you of the crimes for which you stand charged," Simon said, as he propped his elbows upon the arm rests of his chair and rested his chin in his hands.

"What Sanhedrin is this?" Judah mockingly said. "I only notice a few men left, men worthy to be called such members of the council you speak of. Where are all the rest?"

"Don't speak of such insolence, filth. This is the Chamber of the Hewn Stone; you stand in judgment. Our laws need not to be explained to a traitor, nor do we have to reason with you of our role in this matter. This is the elected Sanhedrin and you are a criminal," Simon raised his voice and a murmur spread around the room.

"You proclaim judgment over me, Simon? The reason this hall has so many new faces is because the ones absent lie rotting in the Hinnom! You, and the murderer at my back along with half of your men who call themselves officers worthy of rank, should be standing on trial, not I!"

"Silence! You insolent swine, be quiet!" Simon shouted in a rage slamming both fists down upon the chair as his face became red and his eyes pulsed.

"I have served this city and fought Rome for many..." Judah began to roar valiantly and then felt a heavy blow to the back of his head and collapsed to his knees with a grunt. Before he had a moment to recover, another blow crunched into his ribs which sent him reeling upon the floor, his face driving into the tiles, unable to help himself from his bound hands. He winced from the sharp pain, feeling a trickle of blood warm the back of his scalp and soak his hair while Bagdatus chuckled next to him.

"Now the prisoner is quiet, your majesty," Bagdatus spoke politely, raising his voice.

Judah lay in a battered daze for a moment and then moved his head outward as he strained to see John. He watched John, dishevelled and sullen, look upon him with shame ingrained within his eyes, as if the mere fact of him sitting next to Simon, participating in this jester court, aggravated him beyond measure. Judah tried to catch his eye but watched as John lowered his gaze in disgrace and sighed. At that moment, Judah knew he would die because Simon was in charge.

"Stand him up!" barked Simon.

Judah felt a pair of strong hands grab him and pull him to his feet as he swayed from the dizzying blow to his head. He felt the back of his neck become wet and knew it was blood running down from the gash in his scalp. Judah's vision blurred slightly and the faces watching him seemed to spin and grow hazy as he struggled to remain conscious. He found himself wishing he had a blade to ram through the snickering face of Bagdatus and then shuddered as a riveting bolt of pain shot through his forehead and down his spine.

"Now, let this council commence with the charges!" Simon relaxed upon his chair and smiled at Judah, enjoying every minute of his role as judge and executioner. "We shall hear from our witness and you will all see that this man's corruption knows no bounds. It will be made clear to you all who sit in judgment, that Judah's desire is to see this city destroyed by the Romans and their pagan, gentile hands to be wiped upon the Temple. Scribes, you will proceed to record everything."

Voices echoed around the assembled council as Bagdatus left Judah in the care of the two armed guards, strolling boldly towards Simon and John as if he was to be rewarded for some great feat. Then he halted and scanned the room. His gaze animated like hot fire being fanned, contorted with a smug glare, which riveted them to their seats as his massive hands became clenched fists.

Bagdatus grinned at the prisoner, mentally drawing a finger across his throat in the presence of the doomed man, and then bit his lower lip with delight as he pointed at Judah. "Judah ben Yosef has helped people desert this city. He has helped enemies of our cause flee to the side of the Romans so that they may maintain their status and wealth. These deserters are filth, they are scum who praise Titus and support him in his effort to ruin Jerusalem. They are not worthy to be called Jews. They follow Hellas ways and are perverted dogs that suckle the tits of a godless empire. Judah has crawled into the bed of such people by helping them flee. His declared love, loyalty, and honour to defend this city has only been that of an actor strutting before a laughing stock!

"I followed Judah one night where I saw him help a family escape into the Mishneh. I was unable to catch Judah, and he outwitted me even then, for the wicked presence which seeks to destroy this city must have been a part of him, confusing me from his trail." A short burst of angry shouts filled the chamber as men pointed at Judah and laid curses upon his head. Bagdatus beamed in the glory of the stage he was given.

Bagdatus raised both hands in the air as Simon rapped upon the wooden arm rests for silence, and then the large warrior continued with a spiteful colour to his dark voice. "But, I was able to smell the stench of betrayal, and found the door in the First Wall where he had helped the people through. I gave chase, and was nearly upon them when Roman sentries seized them first. I lingered back, even though to be captured would bring the fate of crucifixion upon my life, but it was worth it to know of Judah's wicked intentions. I heard one of the Jewish captives cry out the name of a Roman, for they spoke in Latin, and I knew then, that Judah ben Yosef was a spy, an agent for Rome working against us." Another chorus of jeers split the air as men shook their fists at the bound prisoner. "Hear me brothers," Bagdatus shouted. "Judah ben Yosef has earned the trust of everyone; we thought him a man of honour! Even John ben Levi made Judah a captain above captains, yet was tricked by this soothsayer and magician of words and acts."

Bagdatus strutted slowly over to Judah and spit in his face. "Yet, Judah has forgotten one thing: treason is like shit, it always stinks. The other night I caught him smuggling yet another whelp from the city, this time the southernmost gate in the Lower City." Bagdatus smiled at the sight of his spittle running down the side of Judah's face and then laughed at the hateful look he received. "Even now, the truth is too much for Judah, that if we cut his fetters he would seek to kill me! He is a man of deceit who has aligned himself with Titus!

"Who can know of why he has committed such treason?" Bagdatus paused savouring the moment. "Maybe they are lovers, Judah and Titus, the Prince leads Judah around by his prick to show him who is the master!" Bagdatus gave a roar of laughter along with many in the crowd and then sent another stream of spittle into Judah's eyes.

Simon smiled and then raised a hand to silence the screaming mob. "What say you to that accusation, Judah?" The smile vanished as a frown set in and Simon leaned forward, irritated at Judah's silence. "Did you hear me? A witness has brought forth evidence that you are a Roman spy, what say you to that?"

"Answer him, damn you!" Bagdatus yelled, stepping in front of Judah and driving his fist into his stomach. Judah grunted and collapsed to the ground with a heavy gasp for air. "Only the guilty keep silent! You will answer your king!" Bagdatus sent another clenched fist against the side of Judah's face and the pulverizing smack echoed loudly in the chamber as a stream of blood sprayed out the side of Judah's mouth.

"Stop this at once!" John suddenly burst out leaping to his feet. "Bagdatus you strike him one more time and I will sever your head and use it as my wine goblet!"

Bagdatus swung around like an angry bull as a horde of Zealots in the chamber drew their swords. His chest heaved with anger as he glared at John and then looked to Simon, but the Sicarii King was frozen to his seat, shocked by John's unpredictable explosion. "He is a criminal!" Bagdatus weakly hollered, trying to rally the jeers from the council again.

"That has not been proven!" John bellowed, his nostrils flared like a beast. "He is still my man! He will not be beaten by you, nor questioned in this manner!"

"John, what are you doing?" Simon asked, slowly rising from the throne. "You agreed to this."

John wildly turned upon Simon, fire in his eyes and a face black with rage. "We agreed that I would oversee such a trial! Remember, you are but a guest here! My Zealots hold the Temple and law is given by my voice alone! I will deem what is said and is not said! You wish to challenge that?" John swung his gaze around the room and shouted at the men once more, "Who wishes to challenge me here? Come, I will slaughter you with my own hands now!"

Simon tensed with anger as he stared at John with loathing eyes of abhorrence. He felt maligned and disrespected as his voice melted away. The chamber was full of Zealots now, all appearing with eager blades and Simon was powerless. How could John have shamed him so? He felt as if his robes of royalty and power had been soiled upon, spit on, and dragged through the streets. His mind swirled with the possibility that John would double-cross him, break his word, and set Judah free. If he was to do so, he would surely put all his efforts to ruin John and destroy his army.

"Everyone out now!" John screamed at the baffled looks from the council. "Get out!"

Simon shook his head with a sulky downcast look of defiance and picked up the long trails of his robes, swearing under his breath. "If you let him go, I will pull down every stone on top of you, John! You cannot survive long should you oppose me!"

"Is that a threat, you vile bastard?" John shot back.

"Consider it a warning. You do not wish to cross me, John! You do so, and you put this city at risk! Your men will desert you."

John scrunched up his top lip into a snarl and shook his head as he whispered to the angry Sicarii King, "He will not go free, but I will judge him myself, not you, Simon."

Simon's narrow face grew pale as he gritted his teeth and wiped his hooked nose. Then with a spiteful glower, he walked away followed by a number of his personal staff. John instructed his guards to wait outside as he watched the Chamber of the Hewn Stone empty with shuffling men as an awkward silence soon clung to the air. Finally, the main veil was closed and Judah was left kneeling upon the floor staring weakly at John who had not moved a muscle.

John sat back down upon his judgment seat and thoughtfully stroked his curly beard as his piercing, grey eyes studied Judah, as well as the puddle of blood and spittle upon the marble tiles next to him. The silence was almost haunting as the distant sounds of hammers and shouting men could be heard beyond the Temple porticoes. The coolness of the chamber was a relief, yet the stench of body odour still wafted in the air. Eventually, after what seemed like an eternity, John sat forward, raised both hands in the air with question and said, "This is your time to speak, Judah. Tell me everything."

Judah spit a stream of blood and saliva upon the floor, than raised his head. A splitting ache pounded within his forehead and he groaned silently. His eyes burned and the imprint of a deep bruise covered the better half of his face. "What Ananus says is true...I have helped the destitute escape the city."

John's face tightened with a wave of anger as he fought to control his nerves. "Who did you work with?"

Judah shook his head. "Alone...I was alone."

"I don't believe you, Judah! That would have been impossible! Give me names and I shall let you live! You will spend years in the dungeon but you shall live."

"Do you really think we have years left, John?" Judah replied with sorrow.

John froze, then slammed his fist so hard upon the wooden arm of the chair that it splintered and shattered. "Why, Judah? You have brought dishonour to your name, our cause, and my name! I gave you trust, spoke for you, defended you, *praised* you! To think all this time it was *you* who was the betrayer! I swore upon your name that you were a man of honour! You made a mockery of my trust." John's face beat red with a spasm of irate rage and he looked up at the ceiling as he bellowed like a wounded beast. Finally he glared at Judah and then shook his head, overcome with emotion. "Have you really sided with Rome?"

"No, my allegiance was always to this city and to you."

John scratched his chin and then rubbed his face vigorously with his hands, as if trying to awake from a terrible dream. "How did the people that you helped escape into the Mishneh know this Roman's name then if not by you?"

"The people I helped, John, were starving and dying. I never intended to dishonour your name, nor have it like this, but I thought that with such an act, God would give me my soul back."

"What did you seek after, Judah?"

"Peace from HaShem. The burden I have carried, John, grows ever so heavy. This war has taken everything from me, and I thought that if I helped a few people survive this misery, that such a mitzvah would earn me peace to die well." Judah struggled to stand and then hung his head. "God has turned his face from me. I have filled my heart with hate against Rome, so much that I have lost everything I once cherished."

"And the Roman name those people knew that you smuggled out? From where did you get such a name if you are not a Roman spy?"

Judah lifted his gaze to John. "All you must know is that I never betrayed the city."

John was struck motionless from the answer. He stood, towering over Judah like a cedar of Lebanon as wrath filled his posture contorting it with frustration as he seethed within. "You will answer me! How did you know the Roman's name? You deny your allegiance with Rome, yet you hide from me certain information, which is treason! Has anything you said to me been the truth? How did you know the Roman's name for the deserters to announce? If the sentries spared them, you obviously have someone in Titus's camp you know of! Tell me!"

Judah defiantly shook his head. "John, may HaShem forgive me if I have done any evil to you or our people. I have prayed this every day. Guard yourself, for Simon will try to kill you."

John's eyes widened. "You seek to protect me, you scoundrel? Tell me about the Romans! Answer me, damn it! Do not seek mercy from me, you dog!" John suddenly ran over to Judah and wrapped both hands around his throat as he squeezed, watching the colour drain from Judah's face. "You will tell me! Have you sold out the city? What was the Roman's name? Answer me or I shall snatch the life right out of you!"

"It is true, John it is true," Judah wheezed as his face began to turn purple and eyes fluttered. "All our hands are stained with blood...no one...is innocent...John...we have failed. Oh, God...weep for Jerusalem."

Shock took all fleshly colour and hue from John's face as he let go of Judah's throat and watched his body slump back upon the marble floor, gasping for breath and choking. John's hands trembled at Judah's words and he gazed down, as if he would find his hands stained crimson as Judah had proclaimed. Tears wet his cheeks and he silently crouched down near the man he had trusted for nearly a year, watching as life rushed back into Judah's face.

"You know I will have no choice but to see you put to death, Judah. Such a fate I would have never wished upon you, but I am left with nothing." John reached out and touched Judah's shoulder. "Simon seeks your life, and I have to give it to him upon a platter." John groaned, seeing no way out of this predicament. "What made you turn to Rome against your own people? Have they not suffered enough from one pagan tyrant to another? HaShem is not with you, Judah, because you have forsaken your people, Torah, and everything you have ever known." John slowly stood and stared at his helpless Captain sprawled upon the floor. "This peace which you seek, shall never be found, Judah. You have betrayed us for godless company. Your transgressions will separate you forever from us. You are no longer of your people."

Judah watched as John crossed the floor of the chamber in long strides and pulled back the heavy red veil, revealing a number of Zealot guards who stood nearby. Then, before Judah slipped into the watery, chaotic, dream world of unconsciousness, he heard John give orders for them to drag him down into the vaults beneath the Temple and keep him there under locked guard.

*   *   *

July 5th, 70 A.D. / 6th of Tamuz, 3830
Camp of the Assyrians
Three in the morning

Gaius Antony led twenty men of the Hydra Herculean Century from the southern entrance of the camp, across the flagstones of the destroyed Bezetha, towards the dark towers of the Antonia. Each man had smeared ash upon his face, scabbard, and shield. All had shed their armour so that they moved with agility and swiftness as they carried two long wooden ladders. Victory lay upon the fragile element of complete surprise, and Gaius had made his preparations well. He had handpicked the best men he could think of, looking for experience, strength, and speed. They moved like shifting shadows among the rubble as they approached the fortress from the west.

Their eyes constantly darted upward to scan the battlements of the towers and the base of the collapsed outer wall, but nothing seemed to stir in the blackness before the dawn.

Only six torches burned upon the rampart walls of the newly erected inner defence, and the stench of rotting corpses still lingered in their nostrils as they began to quietly climb the piles of rubble. The giant shape of the sunken siege tower lay ruined before them. All that was heard was the whirring breeze and the soft scraping sounds of their hobnailed caligae upon the stones.

Once they reached the rubble summit, Gaius sent one team of ten men past him as they steadied the ladder and cautiously crept along, daring not to give their position away. He watched with fierce eyes as both ladders were raised and gently set against the high wall, then they regrouped. Without a word Gaius gestured to the men who stood in their tunics, some wearing helmets darkened in pitch or ash, while others had wrapped their bodies in their heavy sagum cloaks. Orders had been delivered in detail before their departure from the camp, and every man knew his duty. They separated into two groups, gathering at the base of each ladder as they waited and listened.

Gaius made sure that the third man behind him was the trumpeter. He sent the standard bearer over to join the other party as he gripped the side of the ladder and placed his foot upon the first rung. His heart pounded inside his chest and he took a deep breath, as if afraid the sound of his own beating heart might raise the alarm among the Jewish ramparts above. He stared blindly up, following every rung till the ladder's height ended about a half a metre below the wall. If Jewish fighters waited with eager blades, Gaius knew they would all suffer the same fate as Sabinus and his attacking party, but if they slept, than the glory would be given to the Fulminata on this night.

Gaius glanced back through the dark as he wondered if the cohorts would be gathered in time, to reach the wall swiftly and reinforce their attack. *They should already be assembled with no torches, no calls, or trumpet blasts*, Gaius thought. Three cohorts would have orders to form up near where the Third Wall had stood. Over a thousand men would rush forward once the sentries atop of the inner wall of the Antonia had been killed. The plan depended on conquering the Antonia with the larger force, but Gaius' assaulting party would clear the way, being the first to secure the approach. If the Antonia was to be captured on this darkest of nights, then everything had to be perfect.

Gaius gave a nod to his men, then with hand in front of hand, he began to scale the ladder. He pushed himself further and higher as he climbed, feeling his heart beat faster with every rung he overcame. He dared not look down, not out of a fear of heights, but from a sense that if he was not totally committed then everything would collapse. Gaius felt his pulse throb in his neck and his blood race as sweat soaked his body. His mouth felt dry and face flushed with colour, but still he climbed watching the crest of the Jewish wall get closer and closer. Gaius looked to the ladder on his left and counted five men scaling upward, one after the other, and grinned with pride at their unshaken nerves.

He reached the last rung, gripped it tightly, and held his breath. Nothing stirred above and not a sound could be heard. Gaius rattled off a prayer in his mind, asking for Mars to guide his sword, and then he slowly scraped his gladius from its scabbard. Filling his lungs with a rush of air, Gaius thrust himself upward, balancing for a single instant upon the top rung, before scrambling between the crude parapets on the rampart wall. Gaius could make out the dark shapes of at least a dozen Zealots fast asleep, yet his excitement did not overtake him as he stepped to the side and let the next legionary behind him climb over. Within moments, six legionaries stood on the ramparts like phantoms cast upon a veil of jet black cloth as their haunting silhouettes stared down at the vulnerable, sleeping Jewish guards. In that moment, Gaius knew that the gods had delivered the Antonia into their hands, and it had come, for the Jews, at the cost of exhausted, slumbering men.

With a flash of sword blades in the night, the legionaries spared not a soul. Every Jewish sentry had their throats slit and chests stabbed multiple times by the hounding edge of the gladii as the legionaries worked swiftly. Mouths were covered as blades plunged into each Zealot's chest, giving off a sickening sound as the Jewish guards had but moments to struggle and thrash about with the surprise that quickly snuffed out their lives. Soon, trails of fresh blood soaked the length of the rampart wall and twenty grim legionaries stood like conquerors. Gaius scanned the silent turrets of each tower and then gazed over the edge into the inner courtyards of the fortress below. He could see the forms of more sleeping Zealots covering the ground, but knew they posed no threat to him or his men. At his signal, the cohorts would come charging through the night and the Jews would scatter to the Temple, their souls gripped with the chilling breath of fear.

The standard bearer planted his signum firmly upon the wall as the trumpeter raised his lituus to his lips and sounded the high pitched blast across the quiet space of the Bezetha. In an instant, pandemonium filled the Antonia as dread became absolute among the panic-stricken Zealots. At the second blast, the shimmer of metal could be seen in force, rapidly approaching the fortress through the dark to the stampede of feet that rumbled like the rise of a great earthquake.

To Gaius, it appeared as if the entire Bezetha had come to life at the sight of the thundering cohorts that appeared like a rolling tide of water, surging forward to break upon the walls and towers. Suddenly a hundred torches lit in the darkness amidst the legion ranks, illuminating the steel of their blades and the walls of scuta. Frantic shouts and calls rose up from the Antonia's turrets as awakened men beheld the sight before them. As the cohorts delivered a deafening roar of victory and charged up the rubble with dozens of ladders to scale the wall before them, Prince Titus followed closely behind shouting his praises to consolidate the victory he knew was certain.

The Zealots sensed the end of the Antonia and none stood to fight as legionaries filled the ramparts and descended into the courtyards below. Within moments the towers had emptied. Whatever Zealots had wrestled to load the scorpions were soon overwhelmed and slain as the Romans took all four towers, slaughtering everyone they found. Soon, the courtyards of the Antonia had become a chaotic entanglement of dead men and ranks of legionaries who gave chase to the horde of Zealots attempting to flee. Trumpets began to blast from the towers and walls mixed with the deep drones of the shofar'ot as centurions led their men into Jewish ranks and massacred them in the darkness.

John of Gischala, who had been woken in the southeastern tower after the first trumpet blast, now bellowed for his surviving men to flee to the west and northern colonnades as he led over two hundred terrified fighters into the narrow tunnel circuit below the fortress which was their only escape to the Temple Mount. Any Zealot who sought another way was eventually pinned and cornered, only to be cut down by the droves of legionaries who scattered about to hunt them. Screams and wails echoed throughout the fortress constantly as the cohorts worked effortlessly with a grim determination for revenge, and soon walls, stairs, and flagstones were streaked in blood.

Gaius pushed forward through the tunnel system below the fortress, the stifling heat causing lines of sweat to run down the sides of his face as the legionaries pursued the Zealots. Dozens of bodies covered the floor as legionaries stepped over them, struggling with the thick ranks of Jewish fighters slashing back at them to cover their retreat. The tunnel was only wide enough for four men to fight side by side, and the Roman ranks did so by locking their shields together and thrusting out with their blades against any Zealot who tried to attack.

The tunnel soon became crammed, end to end, with the Romans pouring into the system which fed below the floors of the Antonia and the Zealots defending the exit which gave way to the Temple. In the middle of the tunnel it widened, and here the Jewish ranks formed row after row of men jammed shoulder to shoulder as they pressed into the oncoming Roman attack with a hedge of lowered spear points.

"They have formed a phalanx, Centurion!" shouted a wounded legionary who hobbled back through the tight ranks. A gush of blood flowed from his left leg and he winced in pain as he leaned weakly upon Gaius.

A cloud of dust filled the tunnel, as it stung Gaius' eyes and burned his nostrils. He helped the soldier over to the wall and let the man lean against it. Gaius brought his mouth close to the soldier's ear, and shouted over the loud clash of fighting. "Can it be broken?"

The legionary reached down as he inspected the wound and then shook his head. "We are holding. Our shields are stronger and we're better armed. The Jews can't stand against us! But neither side can really move!" A loud jeer echoed, followed by a crunch of shields and clang of swords as another cloud of dust drifted overtop the helmets of the legionaries. "We're a mixed group. Nobody is leading this attack. I passed an optio who was giving orders with a centurion stuck helplessly behind. There are men from the Twelfth mixed with the Macedonica. None of the centuria is intact. Everyone is separated and spread out in this damned space. I could hardly see. I tried to deflect a spear thrust and suddenly I find myself bleeding like this." The legionary gave Gaius a baffled look and then shrugged as he clamped his hands around the wound. "But we hold them. We figure the problem is that the Jews are reinforcing themselves from the outside...that is, from the Temple."

"Only the gods know how many men they have up there," Gaius retorted, not appreciating the confusion. "We only mounted this attack with twelve hundred men. It is not enough to force the Jews out."

"They won't surrender the ground, Centurion. They fight for their bleeding Temple!"

Gaius looked at the man's scutum and then rested his hand upon the legionary's shoulder. "You're from the Fifth Macedonica?

"Yes, Centurion, Fourth Cohors. My Centurion is Julianus."

Gaius snapped his attention to the thick mayhem before him and the sounds of fighting. "Where is he?"

"He commands from the front, Centurion," replied the legionary.

Gaius glanced at the pale faced soldier a moment longer and then ordered him to seek help for his wound. He watched the legionary hobble away as he fought to push between the ranks of soldiers. Gaius heard another roar of angry shouting, followed by blood curdling screams as the legion ranks in front of him managed to surge forward a couple of meters before coming to a standstill. He strained to see what was happening, but the tunnel was so tightly packed he could only stare between the heads of the men in front. But somewhere down the long, dust filled tunnel, Gaius heard a renewed roar of voices and the grunts of men heaving as repeated thuds reverberated back to his ears.

Then a sudden bellow arose and Gaius spotted some men making their way back. He could see files of legionaries moving out of the way to let the men pass, only to reform again to close any gap. When the soldiers in front of Gaius stepped to the side, he saw the bloodied body of Julianus being carried by weeping legionaries who shouted with cracked, hoarse voices to make way.

Gaius held up his hands to stop the men and when they recognized him to be a senior Centurion, they set the body down with grief upon their horrid, bloody, dirt-covered faces. Julianus lay upon the ground, a ghastly sight. His entire body looked as though it had been trampled by the hooves of one hundred horses, and then thrown upon a dozen spear points to be torn apart. Parts of his face had been slashed away leaving but one eye in the grisly mess. His chest had the appearance of a fountain of blood as his armour was soiled with filth and crimson. His left arm had been severed and now was black with dirt, with fragments of dangling flesh clinging to the stump, and his legs appeared mulled as if partially eaten by lions as they revealed strands of muscle and horrible puncture wounds as if fanged teeth had gnawed upon them.

One of the legionaries saw the devastated look upon Gaius' face and wiping away tears he said, "He refused to surrender ground, Centurion. Julianus was braver than any man I have ever known. He leapt into the Jewish ranks from the hole a pilum had made, and he struck down three of them before he slipped." The legionary began to sob as his chest shuddered and he buried his miserable face into his hands. "We just couldn't pull him out in time. The poor man screamed helplessly under their spear points as they slew him. We tried, but nothing could be done. We were able to push them back to reclaim his body. We dragged him out of the fray, but he was already dead."

Gaius stared at the gruesome sight of the dead Centurion as soldiers continued to file past the body to join the fight deep inside the tunnel. It was hell within the confinements and the stench of blood was strong in the humid, dank air. Gaius squatted down next to Julianus and then slowly removed the sagum he wore and draped it over the body. The Antonia had been taken, and soon they would retire from the desperate fight in the tunnels. The Jews would no doubt barricade the tunnel with stone the first chance they got, and Titus would level the entire fortress, thus casting his eyes on the next prize, the Temple. Yet, in this moment, Gaius also felt like weeping. He knew the list of dead would only lengthen with time, and the glory of Rome, so sought after and avidly talked about, would be like a sour taste upon his tongue once Jerusalem had finally fallen. No mural crown awarded to him, for being the first man over the wall, could ever shed any light of victory or hope upon a future that seemed already so dark and bleak.

* * *

CHAPTER LII

July 5th, 70 A.D. / 6th of Tamuz, 3830
Mount Scopus
Two hours after dark

Gaius watched the fifty pyres glow as a tambourine rattled somewhere in the night. He could see two cohorts of the Macedonica standing still as they watched the funerary, sarcophagi towers of wood burn the corpses lying stiffly upon them. The great rush of fire roared in the blackness as the light danced upon the motionless troops, solemnly keeping in rank, with their centurions and officers bowing their heads. To Gaius, it seemed that the entire summit of Mount Scopus burned with the dead. He squinted from the bright light and felt the warmth of the flames beat upon his face, despite his distance from the fire. The mood was sullen, yet honourable, as the legionaries paid their respects to the dead and hailed them as heroes through silent grief.

Gaius' eyes fell upon a certain pyre that was taller than all the rest as it was silhouetted against the burning fires that encircled it. He could see the form of a body lying upon a bed of wood in full armour as a century of legionaries assembled at the base of the pyre and marched around it in circles while gazing up at the corpse above. Afterward, the century formed a wide circle around the pyre, locking their shields and lowering their spears as if they would attack it. Gaius watched as a single legionary approached the pyre with a torch, then slowly climbed a ladder against the tower of wood and stone. When he reached the top, the soldier waited and listened as a priest began a benediction, crying out to the gods with a mournful voice as a junior servant beat incessantly upon a drum. As the prayers were recited, bread and wine were passed out among the legionaries. Then they began to eat and drink as they rested their shields upon the ground, raising their cups in honour of the deceased.

"Will Julianus be given a *mausoleum*? He was a great centurion of the Fourth," Marcus Sulla said as he halted next to Gaius and watched the legionary upon the ladder shove the torch deep into the dried wood.

"He was not a wealthy man, but he has relatives in *Roma*. I believe they will collect his ashes and send them back when the army retires after the siege," Gaius uttered softly.

Marcus nodded as the pyre caught fire and sent a pillar of smoke up into the starry sky. "He was a good man. No doubt all the proper care was given for his body. He is at peace now, Gaius. What's done is done; there must be no regrets. Julianus was a man who understood the danger. He died bravely, a servant of *Roma* and with honour."

"He spoke often about his ancestors. He wanted to prove to his father that he was a man of Roman morale and character. A man of virtue, what all men of valour strive to be." Gaius watched the soldiers finish their funerary meal and then depart in groups as they made their way down the dark slopes of Scopus back to camp. "I don't even know if he had a wife and children."

"They will see him again," Marcus replied. "His effects will be returned to them. That will be the duty of his optio and steward. It will be taken care of."

"Do you often wonder what men will say of us when we die, Marcus?" Gaius' his eyes followed the dance of orange flames as they consumed Julianus' body.

"I do not pay much heed to death. It distracts me from sending others that way." Marcus gave a playful grin trying to cheer his friend up but received a scowl. "Well, when I die my men shall drink to my memory, and officers, senators, and governors throughout the empire will throw parties that have never been seen before. They will drink to the fact that, I shall trouble them no more."

"But what your men think of you is what is truly honourable, Marcus. What the snobbery thinks of a man is but worthless refuse. To have your legionaries drink to your journey into the next life and weep for you shows true Roman virtue. I dare say that few men did so for Galba or Vitellius."

"Well, maybe they did, but they're all dead now." Marcus smiled warmly. "I thank you for your kind words, Gaius. You spoke them like a philosopher-war-poet." Marcus watched Gaius return the smile and then stare with uncertainty at the pyre. "Do you worry about death and glory, Gaius? You need not be worried as you have earned a glory bestowed upon you by the gods. For sweet Mars' sake, the Emperor calls you Cornelius."

Gaius chuckled. "I worry about what would become of Livia and my daughters should I fall. If she received an urn with my ashes, I dare say it would destroy her."

Marcus planted a hand of reassurance upon Gaius' shoulder and pointed to the pyre. "If you should die, I will make sure all honour is given to you. Then I will personally offer my services to your family and take them in as my own. I will make sure Livia is well looked after and suffers not."

"I thank you, Marcus. You are a man of esteemed integrity."

Marcus laughed. "Then you must have me confused with someone else."

"How did you know to look for me here?"

"Because I knew these dead men would be up here, and you would not hesitate to pay respects to the memory of Julianus."

Gaius nodded and exhaled loudly as he glanced back at Jerusalem. "Now that the Antonia is ours, I fear the worst of the fighting stands before us. I hear some of the men celebrating as if Jerusalem has fallen, but we have only cornered an angry wolf, and that wolf, which still has teeth, will fight with everything it has."

"You may be right, Gaius, but let me remind you that although we have cornered a wolf, think more of it as being muzzled, and us standing over it with spear in hand ready to strike. It shall be over soon."

Gaius stared at Marcus, noticing something different about the Tribune and scratched his whiskery chin. When Marcus caught Gaius' interest, he lifted his eyebrows with a dubious expression and a smirk appeared at the corners of Centurion's lips. "Have you done something?"

"What do you mean?"

Gaius crossed his arms and raised his chin. "I mean there is something different about you."

Marcus grunted, gave a firm nod as he furrowed his brow, then rubbed the back of his neck. "Well, there is something I do wish to tell you, Gaius. I was unable to do so earlier, as you know why. But, you will find out sooner than later, so I might as well come out with it. Last night, soldiers east of the city captured a young Jewish woman wandering beyond the walls. Apparently she knew my name. She was spared any mistreatment and brought before me. I questioned her, her name is Hadassah and I found that she was in love with a man you know all too well," Marcus lowered his voice as some soldiers passed by. "Judah ben Yosef."

"Judah ben..." was all that escaped Gaius' lips as the thought lingered in his mind.

"I should tell you that I have decided to spare her from death and slavery, and seek to take her as my...wife." Marcus watched Gaius' reaction grip the muscles of his face as they tightened.

"She will be your wife?"

"She has agreed to it, and I am a Tribune, it should not be a problem. I will report this to Titus and be given clemency. In fifteen years of service I have never asked for benefit or status. But, I do feel fortune has played a part in this, and Venus has been gracious. I am up in my years and should like to feel the warmth of a body next to mine at night." Marcus fought back a joyous grin as he whispered, "I have earned this, Gaius. I want sons to carry on my name."

"What part of Jerusalem is she from?"

"South."

"Then she is of poor stock? How were you able to question her? Does she understand what you want of her?"

"Gaius, I am not stupid."

"I did not intend to give you such an impression, but if she is not to be your slave and rather your wife, she should be able to grasp what that means for her. She will be a freewoman, Marcus, not property. You will take her back with you? How will she respond to that? She has loved Judah as you say, and Judah is a man who hates *Roma*. What will this woman even think of you?" Gaius shook his head. "She is more liable to slit your throat then to warm your bed."

Marcus gave a frustrated sigh and stared at the ground for a moment. He cleared his throat with a grunt and then said above the sound of the burning pyres, "I speak their bloody tongue, Gaius. She knows exactly what she has agreed to."

Gaius was stunned for a moment. He tried not to show the surprise upon his face but knew it was too late. Marcus scowled at him and Gaius reached out and touched his arm before the angry Tribune could march off. "Alright, you know their language and she has agreed to this, only the gods know. You deserve joy and love, and if this is what you want, I would not seek to stand in your way or refute it, Marcus. But, you must open your eyes and consider what lies before you.

"She is Jewish and from Jerusalem. You are an enemy of her people I do not have to tell you what you already know. But, you do know that what we have done and what we will do, will follow her forever. When you have taken her far from this place, back to your villa outside of *Roma*, she will look at you as a man who was part of destroying her old life. It is not your failing, Marcus, it is the way of the world and what the gods have called us Romans to do. But, should such a reality as this stand in the way of love? If she loves Judah, she will forever know he died in Jerusalem, for Judah will not survive. Do you think such love will fade away, Marcus? What if it is you who kills, Judah? What if the Temple is burned to the ground?

"You and I both know Titus will hold a triumph in *Roma* when Jerusalem is ruined. Will your wife, who is a Jew, look favourably upon such a victory parade? You, Marcus, will be honoured in such a triumph, called upon by the Emperor and Prince to be praised. Your wife would be by your side, can you tell me that she would smile and bow? All of *Roma* will celebrate the sight of plunder and Jewish captives as they are led to the Forum, and your wife, who is one of them, will be expected to attend such feasts that praise the destruction of her city. Do you think she will be truly happy?"

A dark look came upon Marcus' face like a shadow as his mind turned over each question Gaius laid out. Whenever he thought of Hadassah, he smiled, but now a grim reality clung to his shoulders and screamed in his ear that any sense of joy he felt was all but fleeting desires. He had never pondered such questions, he had only saw the instant gratification before him embodying a beautiful woman as his wife and he had leapt for it. Now, a barrage of questions had been hurled his way, each one with weight and validity and suddenly he felt cold and abandoned. Marcus did not blame Gaius, he knew the man's loyalty was undying and true, but he feared that he would lose such a woman as Hadassah, and that made him nervous.

Marcus had only known her for a day. He had not taken her into his bed yet, for he wanted to be viewed as someone who truly cared, seeking only to love her in such a way when she was ready. He interpreted her reluctance as nervous fears which would naturally slip away with time once she began to trust him. Since he had questioned her, Marcus had only seen Hadassah once, and on that occasion she had been asleep, curled upon his bed with the scent of her freshly bathed, fragmented skin wafting in the air. Marcus had ordered his personal servant to set up a second bed in another chamber to give Hadassah privacy, and he knew she had appreciated the gesture. Marcus could remember how worried and tense she had looked when he had first brought her back to his quarters, as if she had expected him to throw out the formalities and tear the clothes from her body. However, the Tribune had graciously directed her to the bed, brought her food to eat and water to clean the filth from her skin. Then he had departed, to sleep somewhere else. Marcus fervently wanted to love her and for her to love him back with every gaze and touch, but what Gaius had said did nothing less then spread a wave of doubt into the recesses of his mind and he grimaced at the thought of losing her.

"Marcus, you have not said a word," Gaius whispered feeling guilty for being too abrupt. "I did not intend to offend you, my friend, merely to raise honest questions."

Marcus gave a heavy nod and finally looked up at the Centurion. "I will find time to speak with her. I want to believe there is hope. There is an estate I own that I would wish to leave her, should I die. It is not a grand villa, but it is worth enough for her to pursue a comfortable life. However, she would have to be my wife for me to do so." Marcus paused. "Yet, I will not force her to be the bearer of my children, nor take her as a slave, Gaius. I could not do that to her. Well then, if she feels differently for me as I do for her, then I shall set her free and send her to Gophna. I bid you a goodnight, Gaius. May the gods watch over you, and may Julianus dine with Charon the ferryman and Aeacus the key holder of Hades." Marcus gave Gaius a firm nod, then walked quietly away into the night as the mountaintop continued to burn with pyres of the dead.

*   *   *

July 7th, 70 A.D. / 8th of Tamuz, 3830
Vaults beneath the Temple Mount
Morning

"Leave me with this man," echoed the growl of John's voice down the tunnel as Judah sat up from the filth on the damp, straw floor. He peered through the iron bars and heard the sound of the retreating guards as they left, closing a door behind them with a thud. Silence filled the musky dungeon as the shadow of a man grew upon the wall from the torchlight. Judah watched the dark shape get larger and larger as if a great beast approached him with heavy feet and drool clinging to its fangs. However, he knew it was only John, and Judah wondered if the time had finally arrived where he would be dragged out to be executed.

John's large frame came into view as the warlord slowed his pace, passing the empty dungeon cells on his left and right. Judah watched him halt in the middle of the tunnel and stare at the cell which had become the dwelling of a man he had respected, yet now despised. Judah had not seen a single person other than the prison guards for the last three days. He had nearly come to believe that John's intention was for Judah to just rot in prison and die alone with some terrible disease eating away at his flesh. Yet, as the prison guards delivered food to him once a day, it seemed that John's wish was to keep Judah alive, but weak, destined for a future which seemed bleak and hopeless.

John glared at Judah who settled back down behind the filthy bars as he sat with his knees raised against his chest. John felt his anger begin to rise, as if his blood boiled within his veins, yet he refused to show it as he slowly approached the cell. "The Romans attacked the Antonia," he began in a harsh whisper as he stood like a dark giant before the cell door, blocking the torchlight with his trunk-like frame. "They thought that with the outer wall collapsed they could easily scale the inner defence, but they were wrong. Shall I tell you, Judah?" John watched his Captain gaze at him with silence and the warlord grinned. "They sent two cohorts against us, a night attack. We killed many with our scorpions and catapults, and then as they sought to mount a palisade, my Zealots cut them down upon the ramparts. Their bodies still cover the ground.

"The ravens peck at their flesh." John smiled and crouched near the barred door as he stared up at the stone ceiling and took a deep breath of musty air. "The ravens eat the eyes first, must be a delicacy for them, but they always eat the eyes. Then they rip apart the nose, ears, and lips. Once that is done, the black winged beasts strip the rest of the flesh from the skulls with razor sharp beaks. It is a gruesome sight, but that is the only skin they can get at, apart from the hands. Once they abandon the bodies, the corpses rot." John scratched his bearded chin. "We killed two hundred Romans, Judah. They fled with terror in their hearts. Your Roman friends are not coming for you. You are alone; they have abandoned you."

John eyed the prisoner with a grim look, then grabbed the bars of the door and drew his beast-like face near as he spit at Judah. "Why won't you just tell me? I can still save your worthless skin. You have betrayed everything and everyone. You are a disgrace." A rush of anger swept by as John remained frustrated. Then sorrow suddenly filled his eyes. He sat back and shook his head as he stared at the floor. "Why did you do it? Was it really to find peace?"

Judah stood, his face worn and haggard. He paced around the cell for a few moments as John watched, and then Judah halted with his back to the warlord. There was a lingering pause as Judah concentrated on formulating his thoughts, and after he chose a place to begin, he cleared his throat.

"When I came to Jerusalem, I was a man filled with rage and hate. I thought that if I continued to fight valiantly for God, this city, and for our people, I would be cleansed of guilt." Judah half turned and stared past the dark prison bars into the large warrior face of John. "I never thought of myself as a soldier.

"When I was young, my abba wanted me to study Torah, the writings of the Sages, and follow a teacher. When I showed no interest in such pursuits I began to work with him. He had a trade business. We imported goods from the Middle Sea and sold them to merchants and caravans that traveled to all parts of the further east. I never thought I would pick up a sword to kill men." Judah's gaze fell to the floor. "When Miriam died, I was consumed with hatred." Judah was still for a few seconds. "Hadassah said I was given to the master of hate. That it had swallowed me up, even to the extent that I had become like the very people I hated. To reach that cliff's edge is a sobering, horrifying thought. I had been utterly devoured by the rage within my soul, and it soon controlled me. That is you and I, John. That is you and I."

"No, that is duty, Judah. We fight to live as free men from the yolk of bondage that is Rome. Without freedom there is no life worth living. Your mind has been plagued, and you have sided with the enemy. The peace that you have striven for has misguided you to the camp of the devil. You are lost, Judah. You trusted in godless men, rather than God."

"God is the only one I have ever trusted in! You speak untruth, John. I have sought God for four years since the day Miriam was killed, and He has turned from me because of what I have done."

"What have you done then to earn such a standing before the Almighty? What have you done more of, then what any of us have ever committed? We have all hated, lost loved ones, and seen our brothers killed and treated with cruelty. You seek to justify your anger and it has led you down the path of treason! You have failed to see that all men have regrets, we all have done terrible deeds and seen terrible things. But, we still seek to preserve the law of our people and what God has ordained for us as Jews. We uphold what the commandments from Sinai represent, and the Romans spit upon that. So we oppose them. Yes, we have all done evil which begs the question, would God leave us? But, I tell you, Judah, that as long as we defend this Holy City and God's Holy Temple, He will never leave us! We are *shomreem* upon these walls, fighting for our way of life against pagans who blaspheme our God, the one true God. You have turned from all of this, from everything you know and ever believed in. Judah, you are a cursed man."

"Because I defied your orders and sought to help starving fellow Jews escape this mad city you and Simon have created? You speak of liberty and honouring God, yet you imprison thousands, watch them starve and become like wretched animals in their appearance. They eat of their own flesh, John. Is this a task which is given to the shomreem? You, Simon and Eleazar drenched these streets with the blood of your own people! Who are the real traitors? Who will God look upon? What Temple sacrifice can even remove such a stain, such a blotch on the soul?" Judah watched the warlord from Gischala glare at him, as if the heat from his stare would melt the bars. "You are as cursed as me, and you can tell yourself otherwise, but you know I speak the truth. There is no hope for us."

"You speak of what you do not know. How could you know? You were never here when it all began. You do not know how Simon forced his way into the city. You are nothing but a dog, Judah. Filth flows from your mouth and soils the floor. I shall not see you live down here very long." John writhed with anger as he stood clenching both of his hands into tight fists.

"And why have you not executed me? Why do you tarry?" Judah asked, surprised that he actually taunted the warlord about his own execution. "Simon must not like it that you have locked me up down here. Why not now?" Judah outstretched his arms and shouted, "Does it look like I have anything to live for?"

John stared back with a scowl. "Do not tempt me, Judah. I have the power to snatch your life. Tell me who you were in league with and, I swear to you, I will let you live. What is the name of the Roman that you told to the family you helped escape?"

"I told you I could not give you such information."

"Then maybe Adam or Moshe would?"

"They know nothing. I acted alone and never said a thing."

"And when you and Adam were caught sneaking around the Pool of Siloam, what did he think it was?"

"Exactly what I told to the Idumean guards, that we were patrolling the gates to the south and making sure they were defended and on alert."

John crossed his broad arms and peered at Judah. "What if I had you tortured? Would you give it up then? I have means at my disposal, Judah. Do not think I will not do whatever it takes to get you to speak. The reason you are not a corpse, as of this very moment, is because I have convinced Simon you still have valuable information for us. If we were to find this not to be true, then all I need do is give the order."

Judah stepped to the bars and glared through. "Then give the order, John, give the order. You may burn me, cut me, beat me, but I have nothing more to tell you." He heard John inhale deeply and saw his cheeks flush with colour as his dark eyes plotted, considering Judah's words. When he turned to leave, Judah shouted, "I shall tell you one thing Adam told me once long ago." John halted and stole a glance back at the cell. "He said that a rabbi he followed once mourned over Jerusalem. This rabbi spoke of the Temple, and said that there would come a day when not a single stone would remain on top of another. Death shall come to us all, John, even if you still hold the Antonia, it will come swiftly."

*   *   *

July 9th, 70 A.D. / 10th of Tamuz, 3830
Camp of the Assyrians
Quarters of Prince Titus
Dusk

Consul Sextus Cerealis gestured graciously for Marcus Octavian to enter first and the commanding Tribune of the Fulminata smiled and pushed past the tent flap. A young slave, with dark Nubian skin, bowed low as Sextus followed closely behind Marcus, handing his helmet over to the waiting slave with a raised eyebrow at the new addition to the Prince's property. The slave handled the beautifully crafted helmet with care as he offered wine. Sextus frowned at the black slave, then gave a hasty nod.

Sextus seemed mysteriously drawn in by the Nubian's presence, almost with suspicion, as he watched the slave quietly pour him a goblet of red wine from a long, narrow, silver pitcher. The Nubian was not a tall man, but had thick arms, a bald scalp, and muscular thighs which were revealed from his high cut tunic. Sextus observed the slave wipe the rim of the goblet clean of any drips and then pick the cup up with both hands, cradling it as if it was the most expensive Roman glass in the empire. Sextus smirked and took the glass with a carefree attitude as the slave returned to his post near the main entrance in the dark shadows. Sextus gave the man a quirky stare, drained the wine goblet, smacked his lips together and tossed the empty cup at the Nubian, chuckling as the slave leapt in panic to catch it.

"Where did you get that one, my Prince? His skin is as dark as night and his eyes are troubling. I don't trust it!" Sextus let his cheerful voice trail off as he glanced at the silent slave.

Titus looked up from the scale model of the Antonia and then strolled over to the council table as he laughed heartily. "He is from the west of Africa. Brute he is, and arms like an ox!" Titus smiled at Sextus. "Man would make a superb gladiator! A wrestler of lions, jackals, and hyenas! Can't you see him smiting a *murmillo*? I would set him in the armour of a *thraex*, or maybe a *hoplomachus*."

Marcus laughed with the Prince and shook his head, glancing to Sextus as he candidly joined in. "The Nubian beast with a *sica* and *parmula* shield would be a delight to the crowd. Picture him in the layers of Thracian style, oh my, he would be a frightful and terrible champion. An eye pleaser for the crowd, yes."

"More like the mob, Marcus," Sextus commented.

"Mob, rowdy swine, crowd, gallery, I mean...truly Sextus, whatever you wish to call them, spare me your dribble. The Nubian would no doubt be a victor of victors over the sands of combat and send any fool with a trident or net toppling into the dirt like a fat senator's wife with tits larger then Vesuvius!"

Titus howled in high spirits at Marcus' jest and Sextus sent an icy glare over to the slave. "Whatever you say, Marcus, obviously your grand history as a gladiatorial *lanista* is far beyond this world," Sextus growled as Marcus smiled and playfully made a pretend sword stroke in the air with his hand. "I worry of the slave's ability to perform magic of the dark arts. I have heard rumours that African slaves curse their masters. I would be careful, my Prince, watch him closely."

"If he curses me I have priests to counteract such petty evils. Besides that, if the Nubian would dare, I most certainly will have him branded with the *stigma* and ship him to the sands of the nearest arena." Titus cackled from the table as he stared at the maps and then raised a finger to make a point. "I am a man of endless possibilities for such a man as a Nubian who would dare curse me. He would find his black skin fighting the talons of tigers, lions, and bears if he cursed me so, and he knows it." Titus shook a scolding finger at the passive slave who remained in the shadows and then he looked back at his maps. "I still have my scribes and stewards, they watch over me. The Nubian doesn't touch my food and the wine is already checked before he serves it. He doesn't even sleep near my tent."

"Just a suspicious muse, my Prince, that is all I meant by such a warning," Sextus replied, graciously bowing his head. He glared back at the slave, as if to seal the Nubian's fate with his heated gaze, hoping to discourage any thoughts of hexes or curses should the African have already considered them.

"Let us gather for why you are present, my Generals." Titus gestured to the maps as Sextus and Marcus peered at the detailed charts. "You had called this council?"

"Yes, my Prince," Sextus responded.

"It is a plan to storm the Temple Colonnades? Let's hear it. Inspire me, Generals."

Marcus gave a nod to Sextus and the commander of the Macedonica sniffed once, outstretched his hand, and tapped the leather canvas of the map where the lines of the northwestern edges of the Temple plateau had been sketched in black ink. "Any attempt upon the colonnades will, with no doubt, need a vast and superior fighting force. The Temple is a fortress in itself, much more complicated then the Antonia and poses a far greater loss of life when we attack it. There is no time to construct full earthen ramps, they would have to be massive undertakings and rise up from the lower Mishneh."

"Not only would constructing ramps against the western colonnade near the arched bridge take too long, but we still have no guarantee that when the Temple falls the Zealots will surrender," Marcus added. "We would still need to deal with the Upper City and the Lower City, which could take another month or two."

Sextus crossed his arms and spoke with fervour, "I don't believe we would be able to undertake such a task as building fresh earthworks with winter nearly four months away. The scale would be too much to decide the siege by then. We would need at least four ramps, more towers, and to build a second legion camp to the south to efficiently secure the Mishneh against Jewish sorties. Both Marcus and I have consulted Porcius and he is of one accord on this matter. To go to such an undertaking as ramps and towers could be folly with wood being so scarce. We would have to fetch resources from Alexandria and Antioch, and with winter, our work would slow. We would have to sit on our backsides until spring before we could be back in action. However, all of this is nullified since the Emperor Vespasian has demanded Jerusalem be grounded into fine powder and razed before winter. Thus, we have no choice but a frontal assault.

"Employ thirty of the best men from each centuria, a vexillatio, my Prince. Take them and gather them into cohorts of a thousand. These are to be the best trained, veteran men who will be deadly and disciplined; an army of elite shock troops. Assemble these into seven cohorts from the legions into a fighting force of seven thousand. With the Antonia destroyed and in ruins, the piles of debris are high, and they are high enough to reach the colonnades by palisade. With a blanket of missile fire from every onager, scorpion, and catapult at our disposal, we should be able to breach the walls, and with fire from the gods, destroy them."

Titus was silent as he brooded over the plan. His eyes stared at the map until the images dulled in his vision. Then he blinked and gave a grunt. "How long would such a strategy need until we could unleash it?"

"Give me a week, my Prince. I will have the assembled units train and drill behind Mount Scopus so they can properly move together," Sextus beamed with pride as he saw the pleased look in Titus' eyes.

"Well done. Begin the selection immediately in the morning and push them in your drills. I want this force to bear such wrath as the world has never seen." Titus gave a firm nod. "Send out orders by *tesserarius*, to all officers, especially to all of the *centurionate* and each legion's aquilifer. The attack shall commence at first light in seven days. You will take charge of the attack, Sextus. I will watch from behind in the remaining southeastern tower of the Antonia accompanied by Marcus and the other legionary generals. I pray that the gods, and your ancestors, shall deliver fury through your sword as you lead them."

Titus grinned as his mind raced over the battle plans. Glancing down upon the map, at the position they now retained, it was as if he could finally see the golden eagles planted firmly upon the colonnades as the entire porticos burned and hissed from spilled blood. It would all be resolved soon as a triumph awaited him upon his return to Rome. Glory would be bestowed upon mortal men who would climb as high as the gods upon that day, and the Flavian name would forever be deified into the annals of history, never to be erased. With that, Prince Titus Flavius Vespasianus looked up, raised his goblet to his Generals and cheerfully said, "To glory and ruin! May the gods bless us and may Venus send us nymphs to warm our beds. You may both retire."

* * *

CHAPTER LIII

July 16ᵗʰ, 70 A.D. / 17ᵗʰ of Tamuz, 3830
Northwestern Colonnades of the Temple Plateau
An hour before midnight

John kicked the sleeping sentry in the shin causing the dozing man to yelp loudly as he scrambled to his feet embarrassed. "You wish ruin upon us, you damned fool? Do you know what the bleeding Romans do to their own soldiers when they catch a guard sleeping? They beat him to death with clubs! Should I do the same to you who keep guard upon the wall?"

"Forgive me, John," the Zealot stammered quickly, his eyes gaping wide with panic. "I am put to shame."

"That is how we lost the damned Antonia! To sleeping guards!" John shouted to all the other sentries patrolling the rampart. He pointed through the night to the ruins of broken rubble. "Look at how busy the Romans have been. They tore down such a mighty fortress in days! *In days!* Now, Titus gawks at you sleeping dogs from his lone tower! Just waiting for you to slumber so he can send his men up here to cut your throats! Keep alert and a clear eye or I shall spare Titus the trouble and cut your own damned throats!" John swore, letting the profanity spew from his lips with a shower of spittle upon the frightened guard's face. He had lost over half of his scorpions and catapults, yet the worst was that a majority of his seasoned artillery crews had perished when the Antonia had been sacked.

He seethed inside, tempted to drive a fist into the terrified guard's face before leaving, but he just stepped forward and shook his head as the heat of his breath blasted the man's pale expression. "Remember my words." He jabbed his finger at the man's face and caused the guard to recoil with a flinch. "If I catch you sleeping again, I won't bother to wake you. I mean it. I will cut your head from your body and shoot it down at the Romans with one of my catapults. This I swear upon the fate of our city."

John slowly stepped away with a menacing glare. "You all defend the Temple of God, the holiest place in this world. We are the gate keepers, the stewards entrusted with the Torah. We stand upon a praecipe, gazing down into the bowels of Sheol and waiting for Meshiach to return to vanquish our dreaded enemy. But until He no longer tarries, we will dip our swords in their blood and send their souls screaming from this world. Be on guard! The enemy does not sleep and he is before you all in the blackness of night! Tomorrow is Shabbat. We will pray together for Meshiach to come with sword and fire to save us."

A young soldier ran up the stone steps to the ramparts above and breathed a sigh of relief when he found John. He winced from the fiery look the warlord gave him, but he cleared his throat and rambled off the message. "John, I bear word. Simon has beckoned you to meet him at the Chamber of the Hewn Stone."

"He is here, at this time?" John replied suspiciously. "Does he have a guard?"

The man nodded and gulped. He felt nervous from the fury which seemed to seep from the warrior's demeanour as John's fists remained clenched and his back slightly arched. "He has six men with him, all Idumeans, and Ananus accompanies his entourage as well."

John broke the tense silence with a roar of laughter as his eyes watered. He rubbed his eyes and sighed at the startled look upon the soldier's face. "Entourage? They are a mob of cutthroats and dogs, but if you shall call them such a thing as an entourage, then be my guest. Did Simon tell you to call his guard that?" The young soldier half nodded and John laughed again. "Spread the word and rally ten men to my side. Wake them up if you have to. I will depart at once to meet Simon."

The young soldier ran along the torch lit ramparts and descended the nearest staircase to the plateau below. John grinned at the stunned guards and then raised another hand in warning but said nothing as he left. The air was oddly cooler then the last few nights, but John enjoyed it. He thought of himself as a beast of a man, infused with passion, like a burning furnace that gave him the warmth he needed. *I would only feel better if I could crush a Roman with my bare hands*, he thought to himself. Within moments a small company of ten men rallied around him clutching spears and toting shields. John lingered not as he led them through the quiet Outer Court towards the Water Gate of the Inner Court.

"If even *one* of Simon's men moves for his weapon, we kill them all," John muttered to his pensive soldiers as they passed through the open doors of the gate and turned right. He gave an apathetic glance to the burnt altar and wondered for a second if High Priest Phanni ben Samuel was attending to his priestly duties. This really meant that he was either asleep or being straddled by his naked mistress while he panted and grunted like the pathetic little impotent man that he was. John grinned in the night at the crude thought and found comfort in knowing he had power over the High Priest, who had been elected by the Zealots when they had banished Matthias ben Theophilus from the Temple.

"There they are, John," growled one of the Zealots behind the warlord as a cluster of shadows came into view.

"Remember what I said; watch their hands and be ready." John felt in complete control as his men fanned out on either side of him to face off with Simon's brutes. An Idumean, standing behind the Sicarii King, held a torch. As the fire lit the smug smile upon Simon's face, John gave a distasteful grimace. "Well, why are you here?"

"You always bring so many men, John. Is there something you are afraid of?" Simon replied.

"I could ask you the same, just don't tempt me, Simon. So, why did you send one of my men to drag me down here? What do you want?"

"I shall get straight to the point. Why is Judah ben Yosef living? He sits in a dungeon, does he not? He still breathes the air and sleeps in comfort, and he does so because you are weak." Simon smiled at the flicker of rage upon John's bearded face and gently massaged his hand as he peered at the commander from Gischala.

"Weakness has nothing to do with it, Simon. I have interrogated Judah, and when he has nothing left to offer he will die. What do you fear? He is in a prison; he is going nowhere."

"You know what I demanded of you before, John. Do you remember? Shall I remind you that it was before the Antonia was a pile of rubble."

John clenched his giant fists as his body tightened. "You dare blame me for the loss of the Antonia? Your men were of those sleeping upon the ramparts, you damned imbecile."

The insult seemed to deflect from Simon as if it had never been said, and he smiled. Bagdatus, who stood behind Simon, grinned at John with confidence as he stood like an oak with his massive arms crossed. Simon took a step towards John and began to speak as he concentrated on every word, "Judah ben Yosef will die tomorrow and you will do the honours. Then, you will send parties of your men into the Lower City and continue to hunt for spies; they are amongst your army and will be rooted out."

"Again, you are mistaken if you believe me to be your whelp, Simon! I will do this my way or fight you now, you decide."

Simon chuckled lightly. "Recall what I told you, John. I will destroy you if you do not pay heed to sense."

John gave a wave of disgust. "You want to be master of the ground you stand on? Come, now is your chance, you bastard! Come, you drunken whore, I will feed you to the dogs." John watched Simon and his men for a moment as they did not budge. He smiled, taunting them, and then shouted at his men and walked away leaving the Sicarii King with a deep frown.

* * *

July 17th, 70 A.D. / 18th of Tamuz, 3830
Beyond the ruins of the Fortress Antonia
Dawn

The sound of feet was like thunder rolling across the sky with such power that it sought to split the earth in two. Gaius clutched the grip of his scutum and set the pace to a jog at the head of one thousand shock troops. They moved in a long column as they descended Mount Scopus and headed north of the Third Wall where they would form up. The refrain of the men's cingulum filled Gaius' ears as he gritted his teeth and followed a legionary in front of him who carried a torch. He had hoped the dawn would bring light, but the sky revealed not a single splinter of morning. Sextus' orders had been simple: do not draw attention from the Jewish defences until they were upon them. As a result, wax tablets had been delivered by tesserarius messengers which ordered all centurions to use only one torch per cohort, that meant seven measly lights to dot the steep slopes as seven thousand men descended in full armour.

It was supposed to be a quiet approach, and Gaius was worried the pounding feet would be heard for miles throughout the still night. Yet, they were committed. Sextus had selected from the Primi Ordines of each legion to command the cohorts of veteran troops, and they had been given a week to deploy them into a disciplined fighting force that operated as one cohesive unit. It had been a grueling week as the men had slaved for hours on end: with marching, wheeling, charging, drawing up into battle columns, testudines, volley formations, and a dozen other manoeuvres, all safely screened by Mount Scopus.

Sextus had been convinced that a single, head-on attack was what needed to be prescribed to break the enemy's back. Every commander was to know his duty and thus pass instructions down to local optiones of every contingent. They would move like a viper which slithers under thick brush to snatch the life of its prey. The blanket of night served their approach well, but Gaius also feared the fragility of chaos breaking out if any of the cohorts were to get confused.

Gaius raised his gaze to the golden eagle of the Fulminata held in the firm grasp by his aquilifer who trotted at his side. The legionary's bear cape looked menacing enough in the dark night, for the torchlight seemed to make the bear's white fangs glow. The soldier gave Gaius a nervous look who returned it with a steady nod as his hands felt slick upon the hilt of his gladius and the handle of his elongated shield. Gaius quietly steered the jogging column of legionaries from the base of the mountain as the ground swept past them with the dim glowing light of Jerusalem in the blackness.

He pushed himself harder, feeling his heart pound underneath his breastplate. Gaius wore a heavy sagum secured neatly to brass rings upon his shoulders and cringed as the chin strap of his helmet chaffed upon his rough, calloused skin. A breeze suddenly picked up which cooled Gaius' legs and he sighed to himself as he pushed on.

The column moved swiftly with the remains of the Bezetha on their left as they continued on in rows six- men deep, their formation stretching far into the night. Another two cohorts followed the Fulminata with their ranks still descending the mountain as banners and eagles led the way. Sextus rode past with a number of tribunes and Gaius watched them disappear as he prssed on, feeling his lungs ache and chest tighten. Sweat ran down the sides of his face and the taste of salt was upon his lips. Finally he slowed as he raised his sword and stepped to the side. It was a cumbersome duty to lead so many men at once, and the other centurions attached to his cohort did their best to rally the men and draw them into a battle formation as the air was filled with panting, anxious men.

Gaius wanted to bend over, to ease his strenuous breathing, but he pushed the thought from his mind. Right now his men needed to see a centurion who was in control and ready for a brawl, even if it was in pitch black. As he stood watching the clustered ranks form, Gaius felt trails of sweat begin to trickle down his legs from underneath his woolen tunic and stick to his skin beneath the brass greaves upon his legs. He shuddered in the cool morning, feeling the back of his neck prickle with the edge of racing nerves. Gaius turned and stared, nearly blind, at the few torches that burned upon the Jewish colonnades beyond the piles of ruined stones that had once stood proudly as the fortress Antonia.

An Optio shouted behind Gaius and he turned to see the long, unending ranks of legionaries drawn up like a wall of steel as every man rested his scutum upon the ground. He scanned the line and began to pace before them as he inspected their formation and depth. Faces were grim, like stone before him, although he heard a few men gasp and wretch somewhere deep in the ranks. Gaius saw the eagles of the Fretensis and Apollonaris shuffle behind the Fulminata, as their cohorts became lost by the great host of soldiers which stood before him. Upon the left flank of the Twelfth, the Macedonica drew into formation and stretched out into the darkness as they anxiously waited for the order to advance.

Approaching hoof beats pounded the ground and Gaius turned as Sextus appeared, pulling hard on the reins while he gazed at the assembled legionary cohorts. He nudged his horse into a walk and then halted next to Gaius as he stared down at the Primi Ordines and veteran of the Thundering Legion. Sextus returned a polite nod when the Centurion saluted and then lifted his gaze to scan the city before him. His face was stoic and chiseled, as if he posed for the steady hands of a sculptor about to create his personal bust. Then he calmly said, breaking the silence, "You lead the eagles of *Roma*. You will march in battle column under complete silence. No calls, drums, or trumpets. Advance through the ruins of the Antonia and scale the colonnades. How many ladders does your cohors possess?"

"Fifty, which is what each cohors should have, General."

Sextus bobbed his head with appreciation. "The heights of the rubble to their ramparts must be around three or four metres, it should be easy to breach the wall. The rubble is thrust right up against the Temple walls so it is possible to mount the palisade. Move swiftly and be aggressive. Prince Titus, along with the other generals, will observe the battle from the standing tower of the Antonia. I shall follow up in the rear and advance with the force.

"Orders are clear Gaius. As you are the front cohors, you will storm the colonnades, drive the Jews back and make room for the rest. Tonight, by the grace of the gods, we shall end this siege once and for all. Watch your flanks and do not wheel too much, especially on your left. You do not want men stumbling around in the ruins or bunching up. Pray we're as fortunate as when you took the Antonia's ramparts. If the Jewish sentries sleep, the city is ours. Move swiftly and may Helius grant us some light on this damned morning! It seems like blackness from the pit of Hades, does it not, Centurion?"

"It does indeed, General. Is there anything else?"

Sextus sighed and rubbed his eyes with both hands. He shook his head and whispered, "End this, Gaius. You lead the army tonight."

"It is your force, General, and your plan."

Sextus smiled. "But it will take valiant gods to crush through the colonnades, and those days are far behind me now. Mars go with you; advance when ready." Sextus swung his horse around, dug his heels into the mount's muscular flanks, and bolted through the night.

Princeps Marius Junius strolled over to Gaius' side as he listened to the retreating hoof beats of Sextus' departure. "I don't care much for this. Helius has not graced our advance with light. Something is amiss either above the earth or below it. I don't like it."

"Helius will give light when it is needed, right now Mars has instructed him that the best advance is under cover of darkness."

"Coming from you, Gaius, that is a surprise. You despise night attacks."

Gaius raised his eyebrows. "Don't we all? But these are our orders and we will advance. Don't fret about the gods; the omens were favourable this morning."

"And the bullock that bled at midday had a maggot in its liver. What do you make of that?" Marius countered stubbornly. "Besides, they're myths," he added nonchalantly with a grin.

"And we worship the myths. There is truth within them and they serve us. The gods will repay us for our service. I try not to confound them. I keep my head above water and they smile down at me."

Marius shrugged. "The last thing I remember that smiled down at me was one of Pepi's girls last night." He saw a skinny dog suddenly dart out from behind some rocks and skirt away, but not before noticing a stain of blood upon its furry face in the torchlight. "That is not a favourable sign," he muttered with a sideways glance and then pushed a pebble aside with his foot.

"Very well then," Gaius said and extended his hand. Both men clasped one another's wrists firmly, their eyes meeting as a gaze of encouragement passed between them. "Go with the power of Mars and the favour of your ancestors."

"Strength and honour go before you, Gaius. For the glory of *Roma*, my old friend."

"For the glory of *Roma*, Marius. I will see you after." He watched Marius strut away with confidence and wished he possessed such courage. All that seemed to plague his mind was an uncomfortable doubt, but Rome had never been built on doubt. It had been forged in the smelting pot of war, politics, and the refusal to ever give in or settle for less.

Gaius hailed his aquilifer to his side and with a bold voice said, "Raise the eagle! Signal the cohort. We advance now!" Gaius turned and gestured to his optio who ran over to him to receive his orders. "Shock troops swing to the outer flanks, advance with pilia guard in the centre."

"Yes, Centurion!" replied the optio striking his chest and running back to his legionaries.

Gaius rotated his neck to either side, listening to the internal crack of the joints as he loosened up. He licked his dry lips and took a couple of deep breaths to calm his nerves. Then he silently raised his gladius and held it there for a moment as his aquilifer stabbed the sky with the golden eagle next to him. His hands felt clammy, but his breathing was low and eyes piercing as his forehead burned. Gaius began to march and he listened to the even strides of feet behind him which sent tremors splitting through the earth. He counted to thirty and then broke into a jog as his caligae beat the packed soil, and within moments, echoed upon flagstones.

The cohort advanced swiftly like a tide of rising water rushing to a helpless shoreline to engulf all life within its towering shadow. Soon, the ruins of the Third Wall were behind them as seven cohorts poured through the Bezetha. Its silent advance slowed as it drew up along the siege wall that circumvented the city. The troops hurriedly began to pass freely over top with the help of dozens of wooden ramps that had been set up on both sides. As each cohort breached the siege wall, they reformed with few problems, and then continued their advance into the darkest sections of the destroyed city.

Gaius slowed to a walk. He could hear the breathing of the thick ranks of legionaries as they followed with caution and lowered spears. It seemed like a mountain of stone was before them as they neared the ruins of the Antonia, and looming above, against the dark sky, was the remaining tower of Herod's fortress from where the Prince of Rome would watch the battle. To each legionary, knowing that the eyes of the Prince watched from above was like the taste of sweet honey upon their lips. Yet, with the eyes of royalty upon them, the pressure to succeed was all the greater as they fought an internal battle against the blackness of the morning which sought to swallow them up. As the thousands of legionaries neared the base of the Antonia, each man prayed to their horde of gods that the Jewish sentries would be sound asleep.

* * *

The Zealot sentry stood gazing out into the night with a scowl. His comrade had asked him three times what the trouble was, and every time he had told him to shut his mouth. Since John had humiliated him, threatening to kill him if he was ever caught sleeping again, he had been in a sour mood. He gazed at the man next to him and shook his head. "Do not ask me again what the damn trouble is, just watch like you're supposed to."

The man, clearly annoyed at his friend's rude behaviour, scowled back and replied, "What, you mean fall asleep again?"

The Zealot sentry glared at his sarcastic friend, desiring to return an equally ravaged remark, but held his tongue for he had seen something. He stepped forward, staring off into the night and furrowed his brow as he rested his hand upon the parapet. The intensity in his eyes caught his friend's attention and soon he too was straining to search for anything that might have unsettled his comrade's nerves.

"What did you see?"

"Shhhh you! Be quiet!" growled the Zealot. He held his breath and then his eyes caught another dull flash in the darkness below. The sentry's form stiffened and he quickly whispered with a rasp in his voice, "Hand me the torch now!"

The other sentry leapt to the command and scrambled for the nearest burning flame that rested in an iron bracket upon the wall. He quickly handed it over and watched as his comrade clutched the torch firmly, gazing into the darkness below. Then with a great hurl, the Zealot threw the torch between the parapets. He watched the flame spiral and turn in the air before it suddenly illuminated a legionary's scutum as the torch exploded into the shield with a hail of sparks. In an instant over a dozen other legionaries were revealed for a few precious seconds as they abruptly halted in shock before the fire was extinguished, thereby cloaking the ruins of the Antonia in blackness once again.

"Alarm! To arms! For God's sake! Sound the alarm!" screamed the Zealot with all the fury and passion he could muster. What followed next was haunting as dozens of shofar'ot blasted from the ramparts with their deep moans which carried and echoed through the night as hundreds of Zealots rushed to the rampart defences.

Below in the Outer Court, John rallied a multitude of Zealots as he bellowed until his voice was hoarse. Officers desperately ran throughout the vast court waking everyone and shouting as they formed ranks and sent them to the blocked Temple vaults which led out into the Mishneh. The air was rife with panic as the reports began to flood down into the courtyard that a great host of legionaries were advancing upon the vulnerable northwest defences with ladders. John waved his sword about and clutched a large shield as he called men to his side. He knew he had to raise a large army and depart from the safety of the Temple Mount if he was to stall the oncoming Roman assault. If the Roman advance was given a clear path, he knew that with such a force in the thousands they would surely take the colonnades.

"How many men are here?" John's voice boomed, echoing off the tall pillars behind him. He needed at least two thousand, maybe more, to stop the Roman front.

"A thousand, John, at least!" replied one of his officers.

"Damn, there is no time! Follow me," he valiantly shouted as he led them like a hungry pack of wolves into the vaults. His heart raced like it had never done before and his mind swirled with every possibility. John tightened his grip on his sword as he ran through the tunnel system followed by the hustling of men pressing in behind. The distance was short but tense as the vaults glowed with the fire from their torches as the feet of hundreds of Jewish fighters scurried along carrying spears and swords.

John finally reached the end of the tunnel and handed his sword and shield to the man behind him as he unbolted the heavy ironclad door then removed the crossbeam. He slowly opened it and peered out into the still night. He could hear muffled sounds of shouts from the colonnades and knew the way was clear.

"Pass the word along. We fan out into the Mishneh and then advance at a run to the ruins of the Antonia. We will face off with the legionaries," John said, as he retrieved his weapons. One of the men behind him stared back with a pale face and then suddenly bent forward and vomited upon the packed soil. John gave the heaving man a wild look, then shouted in the tunnel, "Let us fight Amalek on this day! Do not stand down for the Temple will be exposed! Take torches and move quickly now!"

John dashed out into the cool air as the long line of Jewish fighters followed, stretching out as they formed a massive host of bristling spears. Soon a thousand savage and inexorable faces were arrayed into a vast square lit by over a hundred burning torches. John checked the flanks, passed out last minute orders, and without wasting another moment he rushed forward through the dark at the helm of the Jewish host. They cleared the rubble of the Mishneh swiftly, passing every obstacle with menacing tenacity. John could not believe he was even standing in the Mishneh. It had seemed like forever since Jewish forces had battled the Romans in this quarter and now he felt regenerated with anger at the sight of it.

John gave one last valiant shout as he stabbed the air with his sword and burst around the northern corner of the Temple Mount to begin scaling the rubble. As his soldiers spread out, closely on his heels, John felt himself wishing that he had Judah by his side on a night such as this. He had admired Judah's ability to charge into the most intense and hopeless situations, and each time he had emerged alive, with honour bestowed upon him. John had never known another man to be as brave a warrior as Judah. It angered him at the sting of betrayal he had felt. The sense of shame and humiliation that he faced every time any of Simon's men even looked upon him was a raw wound that would never heal. But there was no time for regrets, not at this moment.

John felt his pulse surge like wildfire as his eyes suddenly beheld hundreds, if not thousands, of Roman legionaries coming into view before him. He could see their scuta and the reflections from the iron bosses in the center of each shield from the torches his army carried. John felt a resurgence of fear, as if it gripped his soul with icy fingers and squeezed. It was the same fear he had felt that day where he had wondered if the mines would work, meanwhile watching the siege towers roll up the ramps. It was also the same terror that had showered over his being when the legionaries had breached the Antonia. Now that mesmerizing dread sought to challenge his warlord soul and destroy any confidence he attempted to grapple for.

Flustered by these unwanted, but powerful nerves, John suddenly delivered a thunderous, almost melodious, war cry that echoed from the colonnade walls at his back. It was as if another person had sprung forth with seeds of rage planted firmly within his mind. He scrambled upon the rubble, climbed the mountain of stone, and gave a deafening cry followed by a maddening scream, announcing to the enemy that it was John of Gischala who they would toil with this morning.

It quickly became apparent to John, in the midst of his charge, that the Romans had lost all sense of what threat actually faced them. He watched as legionaries everywhere scrambled back to reform tighter ranks as they stumbled miserably upon the piles of stone, before finally retreating to even ground. John's eyes widened with the sight of the endless ranks of cohorts as they seemed to drift on for eternity in the darkness, filling the Bezetha and forming walls of shields to face the approaching Jewish attack.

John knew the hopelessness in a frontal attack against solid cohorts and so he halted upon a large, cracked boulder and yelled for his men to rally upon the ruins. As the Zealots milled about, covering the rocky ground, John quickly sent runners to fetch more reinforcements and have the ramparts above bolstered with ranks of archers. For now he was fine with keeping the Romans cautiously at bay, but remained worried as he noticed that the legionary lines stretched beyond the lone tower of the Antonia.

*　　*　　*

"Hold the line! Keep your shields locked and eyes front!" Gaius shouted as he moved between the first and second row of legionaries. He thanked the gods with silent prayers that he could now see clearly from the light that separated the sky, washing away all signs of night. The moon was now just a shimmer of silver cast upon a velvet blanket of blue as thin wisps of morning clouds began to form patches along the horizon. Yet, the bite of crisp air remained, obsessively apparent in the midst of the endless intensity and anticipation that filled the expanse of mountainous rubble, between the defensive formations of the Roman lines and the horde of Jewish warriors gathered at the base of the Temple colonnades.

It had now been over three hours since the chaotic, bloodless confrontation in the pitch black, and Gaius was growing anxious. The legionaries had advanced cautiously over the heaps of stone debris which remained of the Antonia, only to be faced by hundreds of Zealots pouring around the western Temple walls to scale the fortress of rubble. With the enemy ascending like wild dogs, and the sight of archers filling the ramparts, the Romans had retreated back to a defensive position in the shape of a hook, where the extreme right flank began at the western end of the Antonia's ruins, then turned inward to guard the lone tower.

As it quickly become apparent that the standstill would stretch far into the morning between the prudent enemies, Sextus thought it best to consult the Prince and his council of generals. Thus, the legate, whose strategic battle creation had been stalled, now found himself absent for most of the morning, leaving behind seven thousand legionaries with exhausted faces glaring at the hounding ranks of Jews clustered forty metres away.

"It is almost noon," Marius said as he caught Gaius' attention

Gaius peered across the rocky ground at the Zealot ranks, which had taken some time to assemble into a proper battle line, yet now waited silently to see what the legions would do. He shook his head as the stillness seemed to close in around him. Both sides had abandoned the jeers and curses hours ago, now waiting with a sense of dread and hatred which were interwoven as one single rope. "We do nothing until Sextus returns with orders."

"How long can it take? We stand out here like a damned disgrace doing nothing," Marius replied with his usual irritated voice. "We should plough forward and crush them. For the sake of the gods, we outnumber them three to one, and their conduct is shabbier than ours is on our worst day!"

"They are backed into a corner; it will be a bloody mess. They have archers covering the walls above. If indeed we have a pitched battle here it will not be favourable for anyone caught in there."

"Move to the defilade then. It is wide enough to cram in a couple hundred men and even enough ground to hold a line." Marius strained to see over the nearest boulders in front of him to the open area where the Antonia's inner courtyard remained.

Both debris and stone were cleared free from the defilade and Gaius had made note of the promising battle ground as he had moved through it in the dark. Yet, to reach the defilade, the cohorts would have to awkwardly climb and stumble over a sea of wreckage before them, all the while with Zealots pouring down upon them. However, if they could reach the open space, or fight their way to it, it would provide an even field for them to skirmish, with the Zealots piled up on the rocks above.

"We will push for the defilade, Marius, but not until Sextus returns," Gaius reminded the stubborn Centurion who growled inaudibly under his breath. At that moment a call went up as someone shouted his name. Gaius pushed between two legionaries, stepping out of the formation and into the open. He saw relief wash over a legionary's face as the man spotted him and broke into a run as he moved swiftly along the line.

"Centurion Antony, I bring word from General Cerealis! His orders come from Prince Titus. You are to send word to all the cohorts to reform a solid defensive line and advance to engage the enemy and drive them back to the Temple. There, you are to attempt a palisade and clear the ramparts. Great reward will be given to the first man to take the Temple wall." The legionary carried the gold shield of the Macedonica and its iron plated edges showed visible signs of combat as they were dented, revealing a few slash marks upon the shield's face that had been crudely repaired with paste. The young soldier had vigorous blue eyes and a chin spotted with thin groupings of whiskers, which attested to his youthful age. He grinned with pride at the veteran Primi Ordines standing before him and stiffened with a salute. "Centurion, the Prince will give a torque or amulae to the first officer over the parapets. That could be you, sir."

"Return to your cohort immediately," Gaius replied, ignoring the soldier's last remark. He meant no insult, but sought to not waste a moment longer as the heat of day began to bake the stones. Gaius watched the legionary give a startled nod, then trot off as he sent a dozen more soldiers to convey the order to the other cohorts.

With the element of surprise having long since passed, trumpets and drums began to beat as they called the thousands into tight formations, ready to move into the lair of rock heaped upon the flagstones. Every signifer present raised their battle standards and the eagles jutted up into the sky as the sun reflected blindly off their golden bodies. Whistles blasted from the lips of officers and each optiones made sure that the rear ranks were solid and formed perfectly as drummers beat upon the tightened skins, raising a rhythm of anticipation. A bellow echoed from the ranks of the Fulminata and the entire front line of legionaries lowered the points of their pila alongside each scutum which created an impenetrable wall of bristling spears. The Fulminata's vexillum was raised from the crossbar of a lance and a mournful trumpet wailed as the cohort of one thousand shifted forward with a steady approach.

The links and scales of hundreds of suits of chest armour clinked and scraped as the cohort moved slowly over the rubble, paying great care for men not to stumble or trip. The menacing silence in which the massive rectangular formation moved with was haunting as the soldiers hunched slightly over and peered above the iron rims of their shields. When a space of ten metres lay vacant behind their rear ranks, the next cohort advanced, this one with shields emblazoned with the crimson of the Fifteenth Legion bearing the golden palm branch.

Upon the left flank of the Fulminata, the Macedonica now wheeled and swung its formation hard toward the right as they passed the Antonia's tower, swallowing up the cracked, split stones under their marching feet. Next, the Fretensis was on the heels of the Fifth cohort. They awkwardly pushed past the tower, then briefly halted as men slipped and stumbled with curses upon the rocks. A yelp sailed up into the air as the cohort's standard-bearer snapped his ankle and the signum was quickly handed off as the man limped to the flanks, spitting in anger as his comrades pressed on. The air became consumed by the jingling of thousands of cingulum as the menacing

Roman approach neared the defilade while the tense Jewish horde glared down at them hatefully with eager swords.

*   *   *

John's jaw ached. For over an hour he had clenched his teeth so firmly it now gave him a splitting headache. Yet, that was the least of his cares as he observed the cautious Roman advance. He could feel the anxiety of the Zealots surrounding him. As if all eyes were on him, desperate for a command and terrified of the warmongering hedge of locked shields facing them with more helmets of iron then they could count. John tightened his grip upon his sword and raised his shield. His heart pounded rapidly within his chest and he leaned slightly forward, like a great beast ready to pounce.

The Zealot ranks were deafly quiet as everyone watched the disciplined war machine roll towards them, each man with angst and doubt shadowing their minds. It was the very force they hated, fought against, and had lost so many brothers to. It was Titus, the cruel, despotic, tyrannical man that sent them forward. Yet, all the writhing hatred that could be mustered from every Zealot alive would never be enough to satisfy their craving thirst to see the Romans wiped out and destroyed. The eagle was the symbol of everything that had ever terrorized these men. They had all seen the faces of the victims hanging upon crosses while the legionaries always mocked the suffering victims.

John slowly turned and faced the deep ranks of his army. Harshness radiated from his bearded face as his dark eyes bore the fury of a tossing storm. John's mind was raked with a strange sense of calm, despite his nerves of anger that seemed to spew into the chaos reflecting in his eyes. He was the warlord of the Zealots and protector of the Temple. His life would now become an honourable sacrifice to safeguard the city he loved and adored.

"Zealots! Jews!" John boomed with passion as he thrust his sword into the air with all his pent up rage. "You have followed me for years, you have bled for me! Now, the eyes of the Almighty watch you from His throne on high! Fight them, brothers! Fight them in the name of the God of Israel!"

John bolted forward as an explosion shook the ground from the screaming voices of the Jewish warriors as they charged like madmen down the mountain of stone towards the open defilade which filled with legionaries. A weak volley of pila brought down a number of Zealots with screams as they tumbled among the stones, but the pouring momentum of the charge continued with John of Gischala at the head thundering like a wild savage, eyes wide with fury as his beard was covered in spittle. Arrows sailed overhead the Jewish charge as the legionaries raised their shields and then advanced with a shout to meet the Zealots head on.

With a grinding crunch of packed bodies and roaring men, the two sides clashed into each other with the force of a thousand storms that reverberated back to the

Temples colonnades. Sword blades slashed and cut as blood-soaked victims fell back, only to be replaced by fresh fighters. Spears sought out gaps in the formations, jabbing with deadly speed to sever arteries or tear open throats. Men choked as they strangled one another, pleaded miserably as they were trampled, and many called out in agony to their comrades who had abandoned them in the savage, bitter squalor of the battleground.

The shouting and bellows grew louder as the two sides fought in the defilade. Soon, the ground reeked of human waste, blood, and sweat as corpses piled up. Limbs and entrails lay scattered as the wailing wounded lay intertwined among the rubble, weeping and shrieking in pain as blood was shed and more dead was added.

The Zealots hurled themselves into the heavy shields of the Romans, and hacked at them until many were splintered or shattered. They pushed into the legionary ranks and sought to split apart all sense of order. However, the Zealots quickly realized the strength of the solid wall of Roman soldiers as they swarmed upon the Jews like hungry hyenas, meanwhile reinforcing their lines and advancing into the fray by the cutting blades of their gladii.

The hail of arrows continued to fall steadily upon the rear Roman cohorts that piled up behind the Fulminata, and soon officers began to curse aloud and shake their heads. Being deprived of the opportunity to advance, the Apollonaris soon began to hurl their pila blindly over the heads of their comrades in the front, until they had no spears remaining. Then with great urgency, flanking shock troops of the Fifteenth were sent around the right of the Fulminata, in an attempt to penetrate the defilade from above and charge into the Jewish rear. However, their movements were quickly countered by a host of Idumeans who engaged them in a bloody struggle upon the uneven ground as dozens of scattered battles erupted across the rubble.

The Idumeans pressed hard and bore the greater number as their ranks began to overtake the Roman shock troops that lacked the safety of their favoured battle formation. With arrows striking down soldier after soldier, the crags and caverns of the ruins above the defilade began to pile up with dead legionaries. Seeing the urgency, commanders of the Apollonaris sent another wave, double in number than the last attack. Soon the Idumeans began to feel the edge of their blades as the shock troops pushed them back, rolling up their flanks like a great carpet and scattering the Jews into a full retreat.

In the defilade, there was not a stone or patch of ground that was not crimson. Corpses lay in contorted positions everywhere, in some places as deep as a metre, as the mountains of dead began to rise like barriers, preventing men from killing each other. Neither side gave ground or refused to back down. It was as if Hades, the place of torment and suffering, had descended up from the earth to spill its ugliness among the ruins and wreckage of the Antonia.

Men shrieked as their eyes watched themselves commit atrocious acts. They strangled their enemies, gouged their eyes, and thrust knives into their stomachs, groins, faces, and necks. Soldiers on both sides staggered, as if in a drunken stupor, as ghastly wounds sent riveting bolts of pain and torture through their bodies. The grisly scene was hell as the heat of day began to rise and the flow of blood trickled between rocks, running down to the flagstones below the Antonia. Legionaries grimaced as they stared down at the rivers of blood, and saw the horrific, frozen gasps of death upon terror-stricken faces. The throes of battle rose and dipped like a lyric, tragic poem, spelling a prolonged agony, caught within the net of the bloody mortality of the killing horde of warriors.

A legionary with a blood-stained face and filthy armour pushed along behind the front line of soldiers. He winced from the repeated heavy blows upon the shields of his comrades who feigned off the slashes and heaving of the Zealots who screamed at them with wild eyes and enraged faces. He picked up his pace, slipping and stumbling along as the second rank of legionaries moved past him. A sour look covered his face as the stench of vomit and urine filled his nostrils and he tried not to gag. He bore an important message given to him by Sextus, and he had to locate Gaius Antony who was somewhere among the killing grounds.

Finally, the legionary saw the transverse, blond helmet crest above the men in front of him and he steadied himself against the locked shields on his right from the second cohort rank which waited to relieve the exhausted men from the front.

"Centurion!" he cried above the din, pushing closer when Gaius did not turn. He watched the famed Gaius Antony wrestle against the spear of a Zealot who seemed equally stubborn not to let go until he was yanked forward and another legionary nearby hacked off the man's left arm at the elbow. The last the soldier saw of the Zealot, the man was reeling back in a high pitched shriek followed by the spurting blood from the wretched looking stump. "Centurion Antony!" The soldier shouted again and Gaius returned a startled look with a face speckled in grimy blood.

"What message do you bear?" Gaius shouted, as he stepped back from the front line and let an eager legionary take his place. The messenger saluted, striking his chest, and Gaius wearily sighed as he stared at the ground with a troubled gaze. "We have been slogging this out for nearly an hour. My men are exhausted and too many are dead." He gestured to the thinned front ranks and the many corpses wearing lorica segmentata upon the ground.

"General Sextus sends his regards, sir. He says that the Prince believes the cohorts line is too narrow and that the defilade is not a strong enough position to capitalize on."

"His majesty has not to say such things. It's bloody obvious that this hell hole is a poor position!" Gaius shook his head and pointed to the legionaries. "Our own men wish not to retreat because they have a Prince watching their asses, and the Jews refuse to leave because that would spell doom for their Temple. This is a damned draw, legionary. What does Sextus want to do about it?"

The man ducked as a burly Jew roared and hurled himself into the legionaries nearest him before being shoved back with jabbing swords. The soldier recovered his wits, pushed his helmet up and awkwardly fixed his chin strap. "General Sextus says that with the missile fire from the colonnades and this defilade jammed up, the Fulminata will not be able to gain the superior advantage. You would be fighting uphill, and it's already a mess!"

"Once again you state the bleeding obvious," Gaius shouted back annoyed. "What do we do?"

"General Sextus orders you to withdraw!"

"You could have told me that right away when you found me!" The soldier apologetically shrugged and backed away as Gaius turned, raised his whistle to his bleeding, cracked lips and blew twice. He watched as a number of legionaries from the front ranks gave desperate glances back and Gaius bellowed, "Fall back in order! Keep together! Watch your step, lads. Give the Zealot bastards space and they will leave you alone."

It was true. As soon as the legionaries began to step back, cautiously deflecting whatever blows came their way, the aggressive ranks of the Zealots and Idumeans ceased to harass them. At the sight of the retreating cohorts, the Jewish forces slowly regrouped and watched with exhaustion as the enemy departed. Men collapsed to their knees, unable to stand as they were too tired and weak. With the awareness of self preservation washing over them, they knew that momentarily the danger had subsided. They had survived another battle, the most vicious any of them could ever remember, and in dwindling groups, they left for the sanctuary of the Temple courts.

John had not received a single wound, as he was drenched in blood, as if he had bathed in it. He now sat upon a large rock, not knowing how to feel. *Had victory been achieved? When would the Romans return?* John had been surprised at the tenacity and stubbornness of the legionaries, but inside he beamed with pride. His men had fought like true Zealots and had never retreated. He stared down with an empty expression into the bloodied heaps which filled the defilade. He had never seen so many bodies before, and most of them lay dead despite the weak cries of the wounded. To him, the defilade looked like the top of an enormous altar, covered with the mutilated bodies of hundreds of human sacrifices. Almost fourteen hundred men had been killed in the narrow space and among the ruins. The air was rife with the reeking stench of blood and vomit, yet for now, the Romans had retired and the Temple had been saved. John closed his eyes as he muttered a silent prayer of thanks. He arose with aching muscles and shouted for his soldiers to return to the colonnades. His next move would have to be planned carefully if he sought to prevent the next lethal Roman attack, and he knew just what to do.

*   *   *

CHAPTER LIV

July 17th, 70 A.D. / 18th of Tamuz, 3830
Quarters of Tribune Marcus Sulla Maximus
Afternoon

Marcus handed the reins of his warhorse to his slave and instructed the man to thoroughly wash the mount down and brush the tangles from its mane and tail. He inspected a spear wound upon the large animal's flanks and opened the gash to see how deep it was. The horse whinnied from the pain, tossed its head into the air, and pawed the ground with its massive hooves. Marcus patted his horse, tenderly speaking a few soothing words to it, and then glanced back at the bloody wound as the destrier flared its nostrils, trying to pull away from the slave's firm hold upon the leather reins.

"Burn a length of rope and let her breathe in the smoke and say a prayer to Epona," Marcus said as he stroked his horse's muscular flanks. "Clean the wound with fresh linen and then wipe it with a cloth soaked in wine. Make sure nothing obtrusive remains in the wound, then stitch it up."

"Yes, master. Shall I fetch a basin of water and fresh towels for you?"

Marcus shook his head as he removed his helmet. "That will not be necessary. See to it that I am not disturbed. Now be off!" The slave bowed and led the horse away to the private stables behind the Tribune's quarters. Marcus turned with a heavy sigh and pushed passed the tents heavy flap.

He stood in the doorway, gripping the cheek plate of his helmet at his side while he gazed longingly at his chamber bed. Next to him on a small table stood the chiseled statue of the double-faced god, Janus, who Marcus revered as a deity who stood for beginnings and endings. Janus was also a doorkeeper god, and paying respects to the bearded deity with its long, curly locks was thought to bring fortune. Marcus approached the god and as he touched each forehead upon both faces, he mumbled a prayer.

Something stirred in the shadowed corner of the tent and Marcus glanced up as he saw Hadassah quickly rise from the floor and smooth the folds of her cloak. Marcus smiled and softly said, "How many times must I tell you, Hadassah that you need not sleep upon the floor like a dog. You have my bed when I am away."

She busied herself as she scurried over to a small table next to a reclining couch and lit one of the oil lamps to provide light. "You must tell me only one more time, my lord."

"Call me Marcus. I am to be no lord over you."

"Yes my…" Hadassah caught herself, and then softly whispered, "I mean, Marcus." She stared at the floor with her hands clasped in front of her like a servant, sensing his powerful gaze as he remained at the entrance of the tent. Hadassah slowly looked up in the dim light and noticed the blood splattered upon his armour and the exhaustion in his eyes. "You were in a battle?"

"Yes, please bring me water and a towel." Marcus made his way slowly over to a stool and dropped his helmet upon the ground. He unstrapped the heavy war-belt at his waist then carefully wrapped it around the scabbard of his gladius and pugio with the dangling straps of the iron cingulum.

Hadassah set a copper basin of water upon the ground next to him with a linen cloth and silently watched as he concentrated on the dust-covered war-belt. Marcus moved to set the belt down but Hadassah intervened, taking the heavy, leather, bronze belt and setting it carefully upon the wooden table next to the burning oil lamp. Marcus stared at her complexion and traced the curves of her body with his eyes. She was lovely and pure, like no woman he had ever known in his life.

Hadassah stepped behind the weary Tribune as she unbuckled the leather straps at his shoulders and left side before helping him out of the awkward, moulded muscle armour. She held her breath from the stench of sweat and blood that clung to the breastplate, yet was not careless in setting it upon the floor next to the wooden table.

"You will not clean that," Marcus said stubbornly as Hadassah squatted next to the breastplate and inspected it for a moment. "That is what slaves are for. They will see to it that it is washed and polished."

Hadassah quietly rose and watched the Tribune plant a foot upon the stool and undo the leather straps of his bronze greave. Marcus let the piece of armour fall upon the ground with a clang and then saw to the other greave as he drew back heavy, exhausted breaths. When the final greave was removed, he exhaled, slumped upon the stool and closed his eyes. His body reeked of a sour odour and his legionary tattoo glistened upon his sweaty forearm.

Hadassah moved to his side and stooped next to the basin. She dipped the cloth into the warm water and stared at the scented flowers and spices which floated upon the top. When she drew forth the cloth Hadassah touched it to Marcus' arm and with a single stroke wiped the grime and dirt away. She watched him look at her with a sleepy gaze in his eyes and he gave her a smile. Hadassah's eyes darted away from the Tribune's kind glance and she plunged the cloth back into the water, then rung it out as she rose to wipe the back of his neck.

"That feels good," he groaned. "Your touch is soft."

"So, where were you fighting?"

Marcus raised an eyebrow to the question, but did not turn as she washed under his arms and then underneath his toga upon his back. "Sextus led an army of seven thousand against the northern face of the Temple colonnades, but it came to nothing. The legionaries fought valiantly, not wanting to disappoint Titus, but your people were just as stubborn and would not retreat." Marcus sighed. "Titus called off the attack about two hours ago. I was in the Kidron at that time, with my Boars watching the eastern defences. Well, nothing happened for so long that I allowed some of the troopers to graze their horses. There were two hundred of us and only a handful of Zealot guards watching from above.

"Yet suddenly out from the Eastern Gate charged a vast party of fighters, none of us expected this. The Zealots have not ventured from the walls for some time now." Marcus turned slightly as Hadassah continued to bathe him, but the intensity of her eyes showed she was enveloped by the story. "We were on the far side of the siege wall, and I sent a rider to send word to Titus, I knew reinforcements would be needed. The howling pack of Zealots were at least three times our number and poured over our siege wall killing all the guards except the ones in the towers above.

"I formed up my Boars and we fought them in the valley bottom, among the rocks, crags, and ravines. Many of my troopers were killed and their horses slaughtered." Marcus sighed again and closed his eyes from Hadassah's tender touch. "They were everywhere. But they were more intent on charging past us to raid the Fretensis camp above which was mostly emptied of soldiers due to the morning attack. Maybe a hundred legionaries from the camp were able to assemble and charge down to our aid, but the situation was dire.

"Seeing the success of the first attack, more Jews came from the Eastern Gate and they flooded down to us. It was a bloody mess, but another contingent of cavalry joined and we were able to regroup and drive the Jews back to the city. That is what happened. I came here as soon as order was restored." Marcus gazed into the basin as the water had become a pink hue from the blood staining his arms and legs.

Hadassah remained silent after hearing the battle account. She dipped the cloth back into the water and then knelt down and washed Marcus' leg clean. She listened to the soothing sound of his relaxed breathing and knew he was watching her every move. She was thankful he had never tried to force her into his bed or make harsh demands.

To her, Marcus was an honourable man who had shed a deep burden of hurt that he had carried for so long when he met her. He had the look of a man who had seen the most grotesque of things in his life as a soldier, yet his eyes told a different story when they stared at her. She always blushed when he would look at her with such eyes, and she would quickly turn away so he could not catch her embarrassment, but somewhere within her, she craved that look.

Hadassah had been in his care for two weeks now, and yet it felt longer. The memory of Judah ben Yosef seemed to fade and dim with each passing day, and now she felt as if the comfort of Marcus' quarters had become her new home. It was not that she never found herself thinking of Judah, but the time to herself had given her ample opportunity to reflect on everything that had come to pass in the last year. The more she thought about Judah, the more she became frustrated and hurt that he had sent her away. Yet, her life had completely changed. Hadassah had gone from staring death in the face to living within the tent of a Tribune who respected her and desired to take her as his wife. Marcus had never pushed her, or forced her to comply, and she had begun to feel that he was giving her all the time in the world to make up her mind.

Every day, she would stay within the safety of the tent, afraid to venture out into the light where she would be seen by unfriendly legionaries. Marcus' quarters stood among the large camp called the Assyrian Camp, and it was surrounded by endless rows of tents from his Boars. He had assured her that she would be safe. Marcus had spoken highly of his men as he declared them to be the most trustworthy of all Romans and that they would treat her like a queen, making sure no harm came upon her head. However, she had remained hiding within the tent, and each day the Tribune's slave, known simply as Burrus, would bring her food and leave without saying a word.

One man she did not like however, was Marcus' signifer Helvius, who had disapproved of Hadassah being spared and destined to be Marcus' wife. He had stated to the Tribune, in the privacy of his chamber, that the only use for Hadassah was either as a slave or a mistress, but he abhorred the idea of his commander taking a poor Jewess for his wife. Hadassah had been hiding behind a thick veil in Marcus' quarters when she had heard Helvius, and the only reason she had found out what he said to begin with, was Marcus had told her, instructing her to stay clear of such a man. Marcus had reassured Hadassah that a couple of threats to silence the signifer had worked, and Helvius would never disturb her, but she remained leery, always keeping a watch out for the scowling, young man.

"Hadassah, can I speak with you," Marcus said in Hebrew, splitting the silence. He felt the cloth lift from his skin with a sense of tension and he chuckled. "It is nothing to worry about. I wish to hear your thoughts." With Gaius' advice echoing loudly in his mind, Marcus rose, gently took her by the hand, and led her over to the edge of his bed where he took a seat. Hadassah slowly seated herself next to him, her eyes watching his demeanour. "I do not know how to say this so you will understand, but I feel I must." Marcus smiled at her for a fleeting moment, then shyly looked down at the floor as he hunched over and clasped his hands together.

"In my desire to take you as a wife, I believe I may have left you feeling like you had no choice, that I would be like any other Roman man and force you to concede. Well, most men may do such things, but I am not most men." Marcus straightened and gazed into Hadassah's soft eyes. "I do wish to wed you and take you from here back to *Roma*, but I will not do so if that is what *you* do not wish. I don't want to pretend that you would be happy, and squelch all joy from your heart as a Jewess.

"The truth is…that once this campaign is over, Titus will hold a triumph in *Roma* where he will parade captured Zealots and plunder which shall be carried upon the backs of legionaries and carts through the streets. I am a Tribune and a Roman. I would be expected to attend feasts and parties, perhaps even participate in the triumphal march. If you were my wife you would be expected to attend such festivities. There would be feasts where we would drink to our victory over your people." He paused as he watched her close her eyes and hang her head. "I could not refuse such invitations to take part in these feasts, especially not if Emperor Vespasian invited me.

"I promise you I would spare you from anything I could, and I would never expect you to adopt the gods and ancestors I pray to. There are many Jews in *Roma* and they worship your God and attend synagogues where they study and pray. They are protected by the law. Vespasian will not put them to harm as Nero did. I swear to you that I can give you a good life, a life of comfort, far away from this suffering which dies before you. If you desire me as I you, I will give you all of this, but the choice must be yours." Marcus was still and Hadassah opened her eyes.

She had lost everyone who she had ever loved in Jerusalem, and had been abandoned by the one man she once desired. She pitied Judah, but was angry with him. He had lowered her from the wall that dark night and had given her only a dagger with the terrible reality that if she was to be raped and crucified she was to kill herself. It now seemed like a dream, a nightmare, but the gold coins, still in her possession, were a reminder of how Judah had pushed her away and turned his back on her. She knew he had said it was for her own good, but the small voice inside had instructed her otherwise.

Judah had never stopped obsessing over the memory of his dead betrothed. That obsession had blossomed into a life of hate and guilt that had eventually neglected Hadassah, casting her overboard into the churning waves of war. Now that she was in the safe keeping of a man who wanted her as a lover and wife, all she could do was look back upon the memory of Judah, knowing that he would perish in the maddening blood bath that soaked the sacred walls of Jerusalem.

Hadassah gently touched Marcus' hand and whispered, "I choose to wed and accept you as a husband that will care for my every need and seek no other."

Tears formed around the edges of Marcus' eyes as a lightning of nerves raced through his body at her warm touch. He felt his fingers cling to hers and slowly moving forward, he kissed her sweet lips as he drew forth a delicious taste that soothed his bones. He could sense her breathing quicken as he kissed her again and then felt her body melt into his as he gently slid his free hand underneath her garment and felt the delicate touch of her skin, as if it were silk. She moved closer to him with a slight moan of surprise from his wandering hand. Then kissing Marcus more passionately, her heart began to race. Excitement gathered between her thighs as his hands cupped her breasts and massaged them, and reality seemed to blur like a dream that pulled them down into a labyrinth of passion and desire.

* * *

July 19th, 70 A.D. / 21st of Tamuz, 3830
Northwestern Colonnades of the Temple Mount
Morning

"Keep moving, men. We mustn't tarry; the Romans watch us!" shouted John as he surveyed the destruction from the colonnades. Ever since the bloody battle that had been fought before the walls, John had felt the vulnerability of their position as the Antonia's rubble lay piled against their rampart walls. Only four metres now stood between the top of the heap of ruined fortress stone and the parapets where his men guarded, and John knew this would not suffice. Eventually the Romans would come back and when they did they would simply force their way to the colonnades, scale them with ladders, and conquer the ramparts. If that happened, the days of the Temple Mount would be numbered.

After John had consulted his officers, it had been agreed that the best possible solution to delay the Roman approach was to dismantle the piles of rubble and hurl them into the valley. This dangerous ploy would mean cracking and splitting each stone, then moving them, a chore liable to take a vast amount of manpower and time. But, if successful, it would mean a wide gap between the colonnade porticoes and the Roman positions. It would destroy any hope for the Romans to breach their walls with a palisade, ensuring the Jews more time and an elevated fighting platform. It was a desperate plight, but one that was necessary should the Jews continue to occupy their strong foothold on the Temple plateau.

John had set a thousand men to work at once, caring not to waste even a single messenger to send word to Simon about what was being done. John hated Simon, and despised him all the more due to the pressure that continued to bombard him for Judah to be put to death. John had brushed the measly threats away offering excuse after excuse, and willing for the time being, to let Judah rot away in the dungeon.

John strolled along what remained of the ramparts as the echoes of hammers, chisels, and picks from the working Zealots reverberated off the wall below. Archers everywhere had been stationed to cover the working parties as the remaining scorpion ballista engines had been loaded and readied. Yet, for the last few hours since setting upon the rubble, it seemed as if the Romans were comfortable to just watch the heightened activity of the Zealots as they busied themselves. John wondered if it was typical Roman pride and arrogance that kept them at bay, as if they simply desired something more difficult to overcome so they could gloat. But he did not wish to test them, so he thanked God for the relief they had been given to see to these preparations, and ordered his men to hurry so Titus would not change his mind.

John stared out across the blood-stained ruins of the Antonia at the dozen legionary sentries who watched quietly from the wooden towers of the siege wall. John strained to see beyond the Roman defences, but the lack of movement in the ruins of the Bezetha failed to betray anything out of the ordinary. Only a company of allied cavalry rode near the siege wall, opposite the wooden guard towers, destined for the Kidron Valley. John lowered his gaze and scanned the killing fields of stone where his men toiled. Much of the dead had been collected from the battlefield over the last couple of nights, so the only corpses that remained were those left to decompose within the rock defilade under the heat of the sun.

John observed a number of black ravens as they hopped among the bodies, searching for eyes or any scraps of flesh to tear for their meals. The loud caws of the birds echoed across the mountain of stone. John leaned forward between the parapets and watched his weary, sweaty men below hacking at the stone and piling them up into packs which were carried away to be dumped. John licked his lips, tempted to shout at them to hurry, but knew it was in vain. He could only push them so hard and expect so much before they would collapse. John knew now more than ever before that it was imperative to retain their loyalty and be loved, especially if Simon wished to confront him so publically about Judah.

Well, to hell with the man, John thought to himself as he grimaced at the idea of Simon ben Giora threatening him. *Am I a dog that he would simply believe he can throw a stick at me and I shall run to get it? He does not know what I am capable of and does not know who he truly threatens. I have an army of seasoned fighters; each one of my men could kill six of his. Simon's insanity must have limits with his own soldiers. Should he test me and push me, surely his Idumeans will feel shame and come to my side, especially when it is I who defend the Temple and not their precious boy king.* John snickered to himself and shook his head as his mind tumbled over one thought after the next. *If it wasn't for my Zealots, this city would have been lost ages ago! HaShem has called me to defend these stones, to sacrifice life, so to ensure that it is spared the molestation of pagan hands which would defile it should our armies fail.*

And who does Simon think he is? A bloody king? The man is mad, like Florus and Nero combined, and has divided the city. If it wasn't for him, I would have unified the people and we would have driven Titus away months ago like Cestius' bastard soldiers. John's mind quickly remembered Yosef ben Matityahu and he silently cursed under his breath. "I pray I have the chance to crush that man under the heel of my foot."

A shout called up to John and he snapped out of the spiralling thoughts which plagued his mind as he glanced between the parapets. A burly Zealot stood below clutching a pick and gestured at the ruins around him that had shrunk drastically since they had begun working.

"John, if we widen it as far as you ordered, that should give us at least a ten metre gap," the man said with a weary grin. "That will mean they will have to build another ramp if they seek to breach our walls."

"That is good. Let's make the Romans toil in pain for daring to set a foot against this holy mountain."

The man shrugged and raised his pick in the air as he brought it down with a heavy thud against a stone, splitting it in two. John stepped away from the parapet as a murmur of voices rose up from the ramparts and he turned to see a delegation of priests approach him with High Priest Phanni ben Samuel at the forefront. A number of Zealot officers stood among the cluster of men and John gave them an uneasy nod as he frowned at the priests wondering what they were doing so far from their duties. Instinctively, he gazed towards the Temple's Inner Sanctuary and his mouth parted with shock at the absence of a smoke cloud drifting up from the concealed burnt altar.

The priests halted before John, and Phanni gave the warlord a rigid, awkward bow of his head. He clasped his hands in front of him, and silently stared at John with an expression of shame lining his face, sunken deep into his eye sockets. The priestly ephod and breastplate glistened upon Phanni's chest, and his blue turban, with the golden band enwrapped around his forehead, sparkled in the sunlight with the Hebrew words, *Kadosh L'Adonai* boldly inscribed upon the front. The turban was pulled down low upon Phanni's forehead, so that the gold band nearly touched his thick, black, brows which darkened his piercing eyes. Phanni looked weathered and his skin had lost the glow that John remembered upon his groomed, bearded face.

The delegation of priests and officers waited as Phanni seemed content to just stare at John, as if begging him to inquire why the High Priest would even venture beyond the premises of the Temple courts. John folded his arms, feeling uncomfortable, as he dreaded to speak, while many of the archers and some of the labouring Zealots noticed the priests and gathered nearby.

"The time for Zion to crumble has come. She has been a blossoming flower, yet now has withered and died," Phanni said with a growl. He gripped the edges of his ephod, where the rings of gold secured it to his shoulders, and for a moment considered tearing it from his chest with the sense of humiliation and impending dread that had overtaken him. Instead, Phanni slid both hands miserably from the ephod and covered his face as he wept. "The lambs have run out; the daily sacrifice has ceased. Oh, Jerusalem, where is thy master? Oh, Jerusalem, if I forget thee!" He suddenly wailed and collapsed to his knees. Two priests behind Phanni quickly ran to his aid, weeping with him, as they lay upon the rampart at John's feet.

The silence was haunting. People everywhere looked upon with shock and dismay while some stared back at the dead-looking Temple with watery eyes. John's hands felt numb and cold, as if the sun had suddenly been squelched and winter had settled upon the land. He listened to Phanni, not having an ounce of strength in his body to shut the High Priest up or make the situation appear better and less ugly than it already was.

John stepped passed Phanni and firmly took hold of one of his officers. "What is the meaning of this? What has happened?"

The man stared at his commander with red eyes and glistening cheeks. He shook his head and replied in a broken voice, "It is as he says it is. There are no more lambs. They have nothing to continue the daily sacrifices or libations. Phanni believes God has cursed us."

John scowled at the man and shook his head vigorously. "God has not cursed us, we fight for Him. We fight for His glorious name!"

"There is more, John," the man said wiping his nose. "Food is dangerously low. Some of the men haven't eaten since yesterday this time. One soldier took sick last night and died this morning. He was only a boy, yet thin and diseased. Hunger killed him, and there is hardly anything to be found."

John's breathing intensified and he stared back at Phanni. "Plunder the Temple stores, take anything, bread or meat. Take the..." John paused as he cut himself short. He had considered telling the man to seize the showbread within the Temple but stopped there. Many already believed God had cursed them, and instructing them to steal the sacred loaves of bread would only send a declining situation into the depths of Sheol.

The man must have understood what John implied, for he groaned and partially covered his sorrowful face. "We must leave enough yeast and flour for the priests to make showbread, John. It is commanded for them to do so. We should not anger God even more."

"You're right," John muttered with an empty, hallow voice. "Leave the showbread and enough yeast and flour to continue to do so for a month. Take everything else and make sure it is distributed. Any man caught eating more than his equal share will be put to death."

The officer nodded and signalled to the other men of rank to follow him. John gestured to one of the priests. "Take Phanni back to the Temple and you are to do exactly what I say. Close all the gates leading to the Court of the Israelites and do not let a soul inside, even to pray, unless it is I who wants to enter. Then, I want you to continue with your duties as if nothing has changed, you hear me?" John watched a confused look of bafflement cover the priests face as he shook his head.

"But we have no lamb. If we have no lambs to slaughter and sacrifice we cannot do any of the libations, meal offerings, ash removal..."

"Burn timber," John interrupted, keeping his voice low and close to the priest's ear. "Sprinkle it in blood and burn whatever dead carcasses you may have left, just cover up so that all of these men putting their lives on the line will see a funnel cloud and believe in their hearts that God is continuing to accept our sacrifices."

The priest stammered in horror at the suggestion as he tried to speak, but only succeeded in a few babbled words as his eyes were wide with shock. Finally he said, "That is blasphemy! We cannot pretend. This is the Temple ritual, commanded by God through our prophet Moses, and you wish for me to spit upon these commandments by pretending?"

John brought his finger to his lips for the man to keep his voice low, then slipped one of his giant hands around the priest's shoulders and squeezed the little man into his massive bear-like body. John brought his face next to the priest's ear and whispered, "Listen to me carefully. God will understand, that is why we call Him the Almighty!

If it is a lamb God requires, He will provide it as He did so for Abraham and Isaac. Where is your faith? But, as God's soldier, I am to defend His Holy Tabernacle, His Holy Temple! I will shed my blood for this city if I must.

"Open your eyes. For the past month it has not been solely the lamb that has been sacrificed, but Jewish men, women, and children. I will not let their memories of death be in vain because of your fears of offending God. He tests us now, so do not disappoint your greatest hour where your faith will be judged.

"Listen to me carefully," John said. "You will do all I have instructed you to do! You will collect Phanni's miserable body, take him back and burn timber as if it is a lamb. Nothing will change as you will do your duties before man and God. You will declare to all that the priesthood is appealing to God with great petition and must not be disturbed. Then you will close the gates. You will do this or I will slit your throat and burn you myself! Do you understand what I say?" John stepped back with a calm, yet frightful stare and the priest nodded sheepishly. Then the terrified priest rushed to help Phanni to his feet and announced to all the men gathered around that a special group of spotless lambs had been reserved. Therefore, the priesthood should not be disturbed, for they had to prostrate themselves before God and beg Him to save them all.

*   *   *

The guard closed the wooden door and then peered through the barred window as he watched the tired soldiers walk down the long tunnel of the vaults beneath the Temple Mount. His watch was the fourth rotation of the day and he turned, strolling quietly past the empty cells on his left and right while a glow of torchlight lit the dank conditions. The eyes of the other two guards watched him with suspicion as he passed them, and he gave a glance of annoyance, which caused the men to roll their eyes and grumble. He pulled up a stool next to the last cell near the back of the chamber and tapped upon the iron bars to wake the prisoner who lay on the floor.

"Judah, are you awake? It is Aaron here," called the guard as his eyes adjusted to the dim light. He saw the body stir within the reeking straw, then heard a slight groan as Judah sat up and rubbed his eyes.

"I'm awake now, Aaron. What time of day is it?"

"Middle of the afternoon, I would guess. It has been days since I last saw you." He grimaced at Judah's condition, then licked his dry lips and said trying to cheer up the prisoner, "You have my company for the next four hours." Aaron smiled briefly then stared down at the floor. He yawned loudly, stretched his legs out and leaned his spear against the wall beside him.

"You shouldn't be speaking with the prisoner, Aaron," warned one of the other guards with a low tone. "If John found out you would be flogged."

"And who would tell him such a thing, Asher, you? If I were judge, Judah would go free. This man has done more for our cause and the defence of this city then any two men combined." The guard returned an exasperated look, and then turned away to lean against the bolted main door with boredom as he counted the minutes in his mind, wishing he was somewhere else. Aaron glanced back at Judah and smiled.

"You are going to get yourself beaten on my account, Aaron. He is right. You shouldn't be wasting your time talking with me," Judah quietly whispered.

"And how else would I pass the time? Making friends with Asher?" Aaron retorted. "It is a pity you were arrested and have been treated like a common criminal."

"I am a criminal, at least in the eyes of John and Simon."

Aaron shook his head and batted his hand sarcastically in the air. "You're a fool then if you think so. In the eyes of Simon, unless you are a blood-thirsty madman who rapes women and worships the very throne he sits upon, then you are a criminal and to be viewed with suspicion." Aaron lowered his voice and whispered, "To tell you the truth, I don't know why John even calls him an ally. Simon can't be trusted, and at the first moment he gets he will stick a knife in old John. Ha! Then where will the city be?"

Judah was quiet as he picked straw from his tangled, unkept beard. He shuffled across the damp floor of the cell and leaned against the cool stone wall near the bars so he could talk privately with Aaron. "Have you seen my men?"

"Adam and Moshe? They keep to the porticoes in the south, not far from you. John questioned them two days ago. He asked them if they would be up to anything with you locked down here. He threatened them and walked away. I have not said one word to either man. I suppose if John saw me he would suspect me of ill deeds, since I am your guard." Aaron shifted upon the stool and sighed pleasantly.

"Thank you," Judah mumbled. "So what is really going on up there? Nobody says a thing to me and John tells me lies."

"He may tell you lies, but John is keeping you alive. What for, I do not know, but Simon hounds him constantly to see you put to death." Aaron snickered to himself, glanced at Judah and saw an eye brow raise. "Alright, but you didn't hear it from me. The Antonia is in ruins, as I told you the same day it fell. Two days ago at dawn Titus launched the largest attack I have seen. There were thousands of legionaries and they came at dawn. They must have mustered in the dark for we never saw them. Anyway, they advanced right under our watch and if it wasn't for one of the guards who remained vigilant they would have slaughtered us. It was only a four metre drop from the parapets of our walls to the ruins of the Antonia and they brought hundreds of ladders.

"However, one of our sentries spotted them. John led a thousand soldiers to cut the legions off and it worked, except neither us, nor them, had the courage to engage. It was not until nearly two hours after first light that the Romans advanced." Aaron sighed as he shook his head at the account. "It was a struggle, the most blood and bodies I have seen. We couldn't retreat, not with the Temple open as it was at our backs. We fought the legions until the bodies were piled so high they created walls of their own and cut us off. The Romans broke off the fight at midday. It took us all afternoon and evening to collect our dead. A frightful time that was, Judah."

Judah listened intensely, his eyes fixed upon the guard as the story unfolded. He knew nobody else would tell him of the news from above, but he could trust Aaron. "How many dead?"

"Five hundred," Aaron replied not missing a beat. "Six hundred were wounded in the fight and at least half of that will die before Shabbat. John was reinforced, you see, another thousand came to help fight, and at least three hundred of Simon's spears. There must have been three times that number of Romans who advanced to attack, maybe four times. They seemed to stretch forever across the ruins of the Antonia and into the Bezetha."

"Titus wants the city," Judah muttered.

"And John takes more chances. He ran at them like a savage. I have never seen him like that before. When he returned, it was as if he had been bathed in blood. The battle ground was a wretched sight to see afterward." Aaron sniffed loudly and spit upon the floor. "Sure you helped some people escape, what man wouldn't do such a mitzvah if he had the chance. This war is not for helpless old men, women, and children. The way I see it, you would be far more useful above ground then below it." Aaron lowered his voice and said, "John needs you alive more than he needs you dead. I know that is his mind."

"Then why does he leave me here to rot? John does not see clearly. He hates the Romans and is terrified of people leaking information to them. He has surrendered and betrayed the people who are most loyal to him."

"Spies have been caught before, so you're not the first to be accused."

"And neither will I be the last, I dare say."

A curtain of silence descended between the two men who sat collecting their thoughts. Outside a muffled trumpet blasted and silence again was restored to the vault. Finally, Aaron shifted close to the bars. "John had over a thousand men working this morning."

"Doing what?"

"Surviving. He had them lowering the pile of rubble and clearing it to make a gap. I would say at least ten metres span the distance now from the edge of the rubble to the colonnade walls, not like before where the Romans would have been able to stroll up and send greetings." Aaron coughed once and scratched his bearded chin. "Now Titus will have to build another ramp if he wishes to send his regards."

"He will do just that, Aaron. The legionaries can have a ramp built in a week if they want to. They have levelled the Third Wall, Second Wall, flattened the Bezetha, destroyed the Mishneh, and reduced the Antonia to a pile of stones. They will build another ramp, mark my words. Unless Meshiach arrives and smites the legions, they will return." Judah stared up at the dark ceiling. "God, hear our plea. Why do you turn from me and refuse to answer?"

Aaron leaned back, listening to Judah's short prayer and cleared his throat. "God may have turned away from all of us, Judah, not just you." He watched Judah glance at him in question and Aaron gave a great sigh. "Word is that Phanni reported to John that the lamb had run out for the daily sacrifice."

"What?"

Aaron hurriedly nodded. "The High Priest was so grieved he threw himself upon the stones and wailed. I don't know all the details, but shortly after that the priesthood officially announced that there remained but a short supply of spotless lambs, they closed all the gates and nobody is allowed access. They said they are appealing to God with fasting and nobody is to break their service."

Judah furrowed his brow in suspicion. "Is there still a cloud of smoke from the burnt altar?"

"Within the hour after the High Priest returned, yes, there was a cloud of smoke and it was still there when I came down here for my shift."

"Does it smell like an offering? Or burnt wood?"

Aaron leaned back with shock, as if he had never even considered such a preposterous possibility. "You think the priesthood would profane the altar with such a charade?"

"This priesthood was put in place by a despotic ruler, if you haven't forgotten, Aaron. Simon murdered the last official High Priest. I think it is possible to believe that this priesthood would rather live then feel the edge of John's sword."

Aaron covered his gaping mouth with surprise. "You think he would threaten the High Priest with death?"

"He allowed Matthias to die, did he not? And Phanni was chosen by John and Eleazar. Yes, I think that Phanni will play to whatever tune John drums out for him. Everyone is afraid at this moment, but everyone still wants to live." Judah picked up a handful of straw and threw it up in the air. "Matthias would have rather died, though."

"Matthias let Simon into the city. He is not without fault."

"Did he have a choice? What would you have done? The Zealots shamed him, stripped him of his title, and threw him out of the Temple service. He had nothing left, and must have thought Simon would liberate the city."

Aaron scowled in the dim light. "You knew him?"

Judah nodded soberly, a wash of guilt upon his face. He saw the image of Matthias in his mind, kneeling upon the ground, helpless, as his sons lay sprawled out with their throats cut and blood everywhere. Aaron saw the regret in Judah's eyes and slowly stood, taking his spear. He looked into the cell at the broken man with his hands clasped tightly around his knees which were drawn against his chest. "There is nothing you could've done, Judah. In the next life, Simon will be judged by HaShem for such wickedness." Aaron quietly walked away, leaving Judah wondering what *his* judgment would be like when he stood before God, and the thought sent a chill down his spine.

* * *

CHAPTER LV

July 21st, 70 A.D. / 23rd of Tamuz, 3830
Southern Royal Porticoes
Dusk

The pot of goulash diminished rapidly as the men scooped out what little stew remained with light, fluffy, bread that had been distributed. The goulash had been a pathetic sight from the start, with hardly enough vegetables and meat to even call it a proper goulash, yet the men had kept their comments to themselves, each tearing off a scrap of bread as it was passed around. The exhausted men sat quietly before a burning fire, savouring what little food remained while they were mesmerized by the flames. Guards had been stationed in double ranks upon the northern colonnades, while the rest of the Zealots had taken the opportunity to rest and eat, not knowing what the next day would hold.

John sat among the group with his head drooped low as he chewed upon the soft bread and sighed at the lingering taste of stew which ignited his taste buds. The sky above was already darkening as rays of orange and pink hues split across the sky with the faint, ghostly shape of the grey moon hanging in the sky by invisible chords. A few stars sparkled above and a gentle breeze tugged at the long garments of the soldiers. The mood was sullen and little talk entertained the cluster of Zealots as the sun sunk upon the horizon and darkened the vast Temple courtyard.

John watched an older woman approach the group with a single slab of flatbread and hand it to one of the Zealots. "I found some more flour. Enjoy what HaShem gives us, for He has blessed us with the bread of the earth." She waddled off and John glanced hungrily at the flatbread. The man who had been handed the bread, gazed down at it as if it were the most precious thing in the world, and then tore off a piece when the warlord nodded his way.

"If He is the Almighty, why must we eat like the poor? We are his fighters. Why does HaShem not grant us more reward if He blesses us with the bread of the earth? We hardly have enough bread to eat," grumbled one of the Zealots as he tore off a scrap and passed on the depleting remains of the flatbread.

"HaShem tests us. It is not our place to cast judgment or question His will," retorted another soldier who gladly received the last piece of bread. All the soldiers silently watched the man close his eyes as he uttered a prayer, devoured the precious food, and finished it off by licking his fingers from the olive oil.

The community of men drifted again into a bout of silence as they sat motionless around the fire with no more food left to eat. One man inspected the empty pot which had contained the goulash and wiped the inside with a finger, then licked what sauce remained. He offered the pot to the man next to him and the Zealot nodded graciously and scooped up what he could with two curled fingers, then stuffed the dripping, gravy-covered appendages into his eager mouth. John quietly watched the pot get passed around until the man sitting next to him embarrassingly glanced down at the small cauldron wiped clean of any residue and muttered an apology. John laid a gentle hand on the Zealot's shoulder and smiled. Then he stretched his legs before the warmth of the fire, the desire of sleep hanging off his shoulders like a massive burden.

A conversation began between two Zealots across from John, and he listened intensely, trying to distract his mind from the worrisome reality that the Romans had begun to construct a ramp against the northwestern colonnade. The conversation flowed in a usual Jewish flavour as the men debated and argued the meaning of certain Scripture and how the Sages interpreted such teachings. The talk swayed from the schools of Shammi to that of Hillel and then branched off into questions of conversion for Gentiles who showed an interest in the Jewish faith. Finally, the whole group of Zealots were captivated by the discussion, and others started to voice their own opinions as the subject veered towards the question of Gentiles and whether a proselyte was indeed to be considered a righteous Jew.

"Caleb was a proselyte, as was Ruth," one of the Zealots stated, pleading his case. "It is possible for such Gentiles to see the light of truth through the Torah and be brought into the fold of Israel."

"Ruth was a woman, who adopted the faith, yet cleaved to a righteous man, Boaz. I think she accepted our faith as a part of role and necessity. Boaz was a true Jew, yet she had been an idolater," piped up another soldier.

"Yet, Abram was an idolater before HaShem called him. Surely, all men were such things before God chose Israel. Ruth was faithful and gained favour in the eyes of Boaz who saw her zeal and heart. She was a woman of virtue, yet in the beginning a Gentile," spoke a Zealot named Eli as he raised a finger into the air.

"So, should we preach to the Gentiles?" asked a man, raising the controversial subject. "What of the Samaritans?"

"They profane the name of God with their idol house on Mount Gerizim," John cut in, shaking his head. "They are half-breeds and care nothing for Jewish *Halakah*. Look what the Romans did to them? God has punished them. The Gentiles are lost and do not care for the light of truth. They worship countless gods."

"Yet, we are to be a light to the world for all men. What do you make of that, John?" Eli replied with a scholarly passion in his eyes. "Did not the prophet Moses utter such things?"

"But he did smite the pagans, and Joshua ben Nun was a man sent to cleanse the land of such filth. The light of Torah can only penetrate the darkness when the hearts of men allow it to. That is why we Jews must keep to our righteous law, worship the true God, and in time the Gentiles will crawl to our feet, begging us to show them the truth of HaShem. The Prophet Zechariah even spoke of such a day when he stated that ten men from ten nations would take the hem of a Jew and declare to be ushered into the presence of HaShem. Until that day, we should stay separate and far away from them. They are a filth which can only corrupt us.

"Look at the Hellenized ones that we used to call brothers. They lived around us in their pomp and cared nothing for their fellow Jews. They are the worshippers of the golden calf." John pointed across the fire at Eli and said, raising his voice, "Why do you think signs in stone in the Temple bear the message in Koine, *No foreigner shall enter into the balustrade of the Temple, or within the precinct, and whoever is caught doing this will be responsible for his death that will follow as a consequence.*"

John paused as he glanced around the circle of men. "It says that because they are unclean pagans. A Gentile who crawls towards a rabbi and cries out, 'Save me,' is only worthy to be saved into the fold of Israel if his heart is honest and that rabbi wishes to take the time. If you ask me, there are no genuine Gentiles in this world that would seek to worship our God. Their hearts are corrupt and they worship pleasure, idols, and gods. They defile their flesh and strut it around with pride. We Jews are called to be righteous and separate; the Gentiles can waste their years until the day Meshiach comes and wakes the nations."

A few men nodded with murmurs as some remained divided and sought to argue, reciting numerous scriptures and Jewish laws that pertained to the matter. However, the debate quickly died down when they noticed a small cluster of soldiers approaching and at the head was Simon ben Giora. John stood with a groan from his sore muscles and fixed the sword which hung at his waist. Six other Zealots closest to him also stood. Their eyes scanned the faces of Simon's party and picked out the hulking form of Bagdatus, the fat and ugly Yehoram, and the elegant James ben Soras. Heated glares of suspicion passed between the two parties as they surveyed each other with hands upon the hilts of their swords.

"I am glad for you, John, that you still find time to grapple with the meaning of Torah, but we have other grave matters to attend to." Simon crossed his arms and gave a thin smile as the firelight danced upon his elaborate garments.

"What matters could I ever have to discuss with you? The last time we spoke you threatened me," John retorted, at ease from the greater number of men at his back.

Simon shook his head and gave a low, dark chuckle. "You always neglect the question. You know who I speak of. Well, I shall get straight to the point for the sake of your men so they know where your allegiances truly lie. Why do you still hold Judah ben Yosef? He is a treasonous criminal, yet you do not evoke punishment upon this man, as you have done to so many in the past."

"At my time, Simon, not yours."

"I have heard that before." Simon outstretched his arms and bowed. "You are weak, John, and incapable of defending this Temple. You have lied to your men. You want to release Judah, a traitor and a dog! You have punished Zealots in the past for such crimes and have executed them yourself, yet this man is close to your heart and was the only one who tricked you for so long. Yet, when he is finally caught like a rat, you spare him." Simon stepped close to John. "You are a man of few qualities. Your lies and secret alliance with Rome will be revealed should you not execute Judah, for that I am sure of it."

Simon smiled at the glare upon John's face and skirted out of the way with a tinge of fear from the unpredictable warlord. "John is powerless! You Zealots follow a despondent fool! He is a coward who keeps a traitor locked up. You call yourselves soldiers of God and guardians of the Temple, yet you allow your commander to spare a man who is an agent for Rome, in a vault beneath our Temple. You men bring shame to this city! You abhorrent cowards! God will never forget this dastard stain upon His name! You defile the ground you stand on! You are all cursed and will perish for not putting an end to this! John ben Levi, the man from Gischala, is a wretch and a weak leader. Should you continue to fight for him? He is a man who condemned hundreds of women and children to the swords of Titus who cast their bodies upon the rocks of the wilderness! I would *never* have left them! I would never have made you choose!" Simon turned and faced John who had lowered his gaze to the stones. A twisted grin spread across Simon's face and with a soft voice, as if he cared for the warlord's reputation, he said, "But, when you all stand before HaShem with the memory of the Temple smouldering within your minds, you can tell the Almighty that you chose to follow such a weak, feeble man in the hour you were needed most to defend this *Holy City*." Simon said the last words as he jabbed a bony finger of seething rage at the shocked Zealots.

An awkward silence fell upon the soldiers as the fire crackled and blazed. John slowly raised his burly head and glanced humbly at his men. Most of his Zealots looked at him in sympathy, but a few stared into the glowing embers with shame. "Simon," John whispered as he looked at the Sicarii King. "You are a guest here, and yet you come with words from the blackness of Sheol to accuse me with lies from your forked tongue. It is my forces which keep the Romans at bay and this city protected, not yours."

Simon laughed. "Spoken from a man who may be closer to the Romans then we all believe, am I right, John? Are not the Romans building another ramp as we speak? What deal have you bartered with them? What promise of land and money have they promised you?"

The impossible situation that surrounded John was like the very darkness of night. He saw the power of Simon's words and their influence upon his men, and he moaned inwardly at the thought of such accusations going to the thousands of warriors that made up his army. If he was not equally clever, he knew that in the least his army might divide and split, therefore, dooming the future of the Temple and casting it upon the mercies of the Romans eager blades. Then again, a civil war among his men was equally possible. Each dreary outcome that lined up in his mind one after another looked dismal and revealed the strangle hold that existed upon his command as he knew Simon would stop at nothing to destroy him.

"Eli, bring Judah to me at once," John suddenly snapped, startling everyone. He glowered at Simon until the pompous, self-proclaimed Jewish king raised his eyebrows mockingly, amused at what might transpire as a result of John's order.

Soon the dragging of chains grated across the flagstones as everyone turned to see Eli and two prison guards leading Judah towards them in shackles upon his feet and wrists. Simon stepped to the side with a grin at the sight of pride which still beamed from the condemned man. Bagdatus snickered behind him and Simon playfully raised his finger to his lips, then chuckled with the large warrior as the other Idumeans observed the scene.

John stared at Judah, seeing a flicker of fear in his eyes as he believed the end had finally come. Eli kicked Judah in the back of the legs and forced him to his knees while the chains were firmly held. Judah raised his chin and clenched his jaw as his breathing rapidly increased and he stared up at the warlord defiantly. A hush fell among the Zealots and Idumeans. John loathed the very fact that Simon now observed him, as if testing his loyalty and allegiance, all the while a distasteful, sadistic grin of violent pleasure upon his face.

"You have been tried before a council, Judah ben Yosef, and found to be guilty," John exclaimed loudly to the company of witnesses. "Therefore, I sentence the penalty of death upon your soul, to be carried out when the Almighty grants us the strength to defeat the Romans and drive them from our lands."

"What?" Simon shouted with shock as he threw his hands up in the air. Bagdatus swore with disgust and the Sicarii King swiftly moved to the shackled prisoner. "You profane the decree of law that sentenced Judah as guilty in the Chamber of the Hewn Stone. You must execute him!"

"And I will when the Romans are driven from our lands by the Almighty!"

"That is absurd!" Simon scoffed.

"So you doubt that HaShem has the power to do so? Do you believe that God can destroy the Romans? Do you question this?" John challenged. "I dare you to say to any of my men that they should follow you and abandon their ideals that God will spare us and defeat the Romans! That Meshiach will not come to restore His kingdom! Proclaim this, Simon, and see how far you get!"

Simon bit his tongue with a sour glare and then stared down at Judah with distaste, sensing the trap John had pushed upon him. When it all came down to the root, the Zealots would stand loyal to a man who believed God would liberate them and fight for their cause. Simon glared with hate at John, and knew the warlord had seized any control Simon might have possessed before. "But he is a traitor! You have to put him to death," he whined with a pitiful growl.

John stepped close to Simon so that their faces nearly touched and he looked straight into his enemy's eyes. "The verdict has been given. He is my prisoner and he will be punished for his crime, but on my terms. When God delivers us from the legions, I will have Judah summarily executed. Until then...to show my men justice, I will have Judah's men banished from the Temple Mount and cast into the streets of the Lower City."

Simon was powerless, and this was evident as he shrunk away cursing and called for his men to follow. Bagdatus dragged a thick finger across his throat towards John's Zealots and two men quickly obliged him by drawing their swords, shouting threats of their own before John silenced them with a bellow. Bagdatus laughed heartily at what appeared to him as pathetic, weak men, and then stalked away through the darkness.

John had Adam and Moshe brought before him by the points of half a dozen spears and they glared at him with anger. Yet, when Adam saw Judah, his eyes gaped wide with horror and he pleadingly stared at John as his lips parted, then he jerked forward to run to Judah's side. Three Zealots wrestled Adam to the ground and held the roaring man, as if they were attempting to tame a great lion. John watched silently as Adam fought, struggling against their grips and shouting with a voice like thunder. Moshe did not move, but watched Adam with a sorrowful expression, believing that Judah was about to be executed before his eyes. Two more guards were sent to restrain Adam and finally the great man ceased his struggle as he was held to the ground with strings of spittle throughout his beard and sweat beading upon his enraged face.

"I have not called you here to witness Judah's execution, not yet. He will be executed for his treason, but only once the Romans have been chased away by the righteous remnant." John watched Adam quickly stop fighting and gaze up at him with shock as if it was a trick. Moshe also stared at John with suspicion, then glanced down at Judah who remained kneeling upon the stones in shame. "I have decreed this, and Simon ben Giora has no ruling here. Judah ben Yosef is my prisoner." John walked over to Adam and looked down at him. "But you and Moshe are faithful, loyal soldiers to Judah. You would do anything to save him and spare him what is to come."

"So you would kill us as well?" Adam shouted up at the warlord as he renewed his struggle.

"I seek not to bring either of you to harm. I will if you try and set Judah free. I have decreed that you both be banished from the Temple Mount as of this moment, for you are company that I can no longer trust."

Moshe gasped. "You banish us from the city? You may as well kill us now for we will hang upon crosses before dawn!"

John shook his head. "You will be driven into the Lower City to survive with Simon's dogs. You are fortunate I do not have a mind to execute you both as well, for I have no doubt that you were involved somehow with Judah in his treacherous exploits."

"Believe what you want, John. We never betrayed the city!" Moshe stated as he seethed from the shame cast upon his name. "We followed you as faithful soldiers, fought for you, and you know that Judah..."

"Moshe, do not argue for my sake!" Judah suddenly interrupted. "Depart from me now, brothers." He stared at his two Lions and then softly nodded at Adam who pushed the men off of him and stood with a painful look etched upon his bearded face.

"Take them away!" John ordered. "If you even think of approaching the southern colonnades, my men will slay you both! Get them from my sight!" John watched his guards shove the backs of Moshe and Adam at the threat of prodding spears as they were driven towards the Hulda Gates.

"They were good soldiers, John," Eli whispered softly, and shrugged to himself when the warlord glared harshly at him.

John sighed with a cavalier, haughty last glance at Moshe and Adam as they disappeared down the stairs with the guards, then he turned and signalled to a few of his Zealots. "You two, return the prisoner to his cell." He looked at his remaining men and drearily said, "Come, let us patrol the ramparts to the north." He did not wait for his men to gather their weapons, and strolled away through the night as they rushed to follow him.

As John passed the edifice of the Temple, he stared up at the funnel cloud of smoke that rose from within the Court of the Priests. His eyes fell upon the closed, barred gates of the colonnade walls of the Inner Court and he shook his head at the noticeable smell of burning wood hanging in the air.

John studied the hundreds of men crowded around fires throughout the plaza. Some sang while others rocked back and forth with prayer. Sleeping bodies littered the ground everywhere, some curled up next to women, while others were wrapped tightly in their cloaks as they snored. The shadows cast from the cooking fires danced upon the high columns of the porticos surrounding him and he gazed upward at the ranks of Zealots standing guard above as they patrolled. The sound of steps from the soldiers accompanying him soon fell in sync with his as they moved across the courtyard and ascended a staircase near the ramparts of the northwestern colonnades.

A few Zealots acknowledged John with dutiful nods as he passed them by. He took only a fleeting moment to gaze between the parapets at the gap the Zealot labourers had created between them and the distant rubble of the Antonia, which was now slowly being overtaken by the foundations of another Roman set of earthworks. He could clearly make out that the ramp was protected by wicker hurdles as working Roman crews hauled up loads of earth and packed it down in the moonlight. The very sight of the Roman progress angered him, and he swore in the cool night air as he stood back with a discouraging somber stare.

John squinted in the darkness at a distant row of torches beyond the ramp and lost count at fifty earthen mounds with catapults mounted on top. Beyond the Roman artillery, he could see a vast array of engines and a company of archers drawn up silently to protect the labouring work parties. To the left and right of the ramp stood two cohorts of legionaries like stationary walls, observing every move the Jewish sentries made upon the high ramparts.

"They will work for at least three more hours, John," stated one of the guards with a shrug. "They have done so the last two nights. It seems like they will complete the ramp soon at this rate."

John ignored the comment and quietly examined sections of the broken colonnades that had been pounded by artillery fire throughout the entire day. He studied the condition of the partially burned wall which had split in places, showing gouges in the stone that had been peeled away by the force of hurling projectiles. John tried to do the calculations in his head, comparing the distance between the colonnades defences and where the Romans worked, then sorting out the progress the legionaries were making on a daily basis. The result was staggeringly depressing and he moaned as he rested his weary hands between the parapets.

"Maybe we should let the Romans breach the colonnades and fill it," continued the guard as if John cared. "Then with them packed upon the ramparts we could charge their ranks and fight them. At least it would keep the cursed Roman missiles down."

John suddenly swung his attention onto the guard and grabbed him fiercely which stunned the man. Yet it was the look of an epiphany rather than anger that filled John's eyes. "Did you say we should just let the Romans onto the ramparts?"

"Yes, John...I meant no dishonour..." the guard stammered with surprise.

"No," John shook his head as an idea grew. "You see, you may be right." John turned and without another word fled the ramparts as he descended the stairs and called for his officers to gather. The weary men trickled to his side and he shouted louder for them to hurry as he turned, facing the enormous pillars of the colonnades before him, seeing his plan come to life in his mind. When nearly forty of the Zealot officers had gathered John pointed to the capitals of the columns and said, "I want each man here to choose ten soldiers. Scatter wherever you can, bring me as much pitch, dry timber, and anything that will burn and have it here at dawn."

"What do you plan to do, John?" asked an officer nearest him.

"I plan to lure as many Romans onto our ramparts as possible and fire it. We will withdraw from the walls, making it seem as though we have fled. The Romans will be tempted, they will see our deserted walls, and rush forward with ladders." John turned eagerly with a flash in his eyes as he saw the reality of the trap. "It will work. The legionaries will flood upon the ramparts. The ramp is high enough and they will be able to reach the parapets. When the wall is full of Romans, we ignite the trap! You see," John said pointing underneath the high portico roof. "Fill and pack the wood tightly between the pillars then thrust it against the stone and soak it in pitch. Stack the timber underneath the beams of the roof and make sure everything is set. The fire will consume every living soul upon the rampart and survivors will have to leap to their deaths. We can kill hundreds of them!"

"And lose our own colonnades! We could ruin them for good," replied another officer.

"No, it will devastate the legions. We can kill so many they will hate Titus even more. We can take the pride out of their victory over the Antonia, sting them back. They failed to breach our walls when we held them days ago. Now they are forced to toil in the heat of day and build more ramps. Their patience must grow thin. I am confident that at the sight of hundreds of men engulfed in flames and screaming to their deaths, the legions will be so demoralized they will hang Titus themselves." A fury of passion filled John's stance and flickered within his eyes as he stared at the officers before him.

"Where do we find that much timber?" asked one Zealot.

"Dismantle abandoned homes in the Lower City; take them from the Ophel! The beams in the roofs of most homes should do, as well as bring hundreds of stacks of straw and kindling. We will light the colonnades up like a great beacon of death for Titus. He will see the power of our God when he beholds the sight of his cohorts burning, and for the Prince of Rome, that will be the end of his days of glory."

* * *

Chapter LVI

July 26th, 70 A.D. / 2nd of Av, 3830
Ruins of the Fortress Antonia
Three hours after dawn

The legionary wiped the sleep from his eyes and yawned as he made his way throughout the rubble of the Antonia next to the earthen ramp. It was a quiet morning and everything was still except for the exhausted sentries standing guard. He halted next to the earthworks and traced it to the walls of the northwestern colonnades with his eyes. The legionary sighed and leaned upon his spear as he rested his scutum on the ground.

The ramp was not yet complete. There were still days of work to do, but with great determination the labouring soldiers had managed to fill in the gap that the Jewish rebels had made. It had taken tons of dirt and stone to complete the task. Each load had been painstakingly hauled upon the backs of the legionaries who had formed long lines which had stretched to the top of the ramp. To the direction of engineers, the soldiers had dumped their loads into the steep ravine to span the distance to the partially ruined Temple walls.

Porcius Gracchus had sent hundreds of soldiers to the task which had been a grueling week as the sun had cooked the men in their armour as they toiled. Ten men had died from heat stroke and exhaustion, but their deaths had done nothing to slacken the demands for the ramp to be finished. Titus was determined to breach the Temple colonnades and so he instructed Porcius to raise the ramps at the highest possible speed. Thus, work parties of three hundred men at a time had been dispatched in four hour shifts, working from dawn until long into the night as they slaved away, leveling the ground and building up the massive ramp that would usher in the legions of Rome to attack the Jewish Temple.

The legionary licked his dry lips and found himself wishing time to speed up for the next call to relieve the guards and send him back to the comforts of his tent. His muscles were sore and bones ached as he rotated his neck to each side, feeling the discs in his spine crack with a sense of relief. He cleared his throat and breathed in the moist, crisp air as he slightly tipped back his helmet.

The soldier stared up at the parapets of the colonnade walls and scanned them. He scowled, picked up his shield, and walked a few strides forward, his eyes fixated upon the ramparts. Not a single Jewish sentry could be seen. He held his breath and listened, but only a gentle breeze seemed to flutter around him. He glanced to his left and strained to see as far as he could and felt a tug of urgency grip his stomach as not a single Zealot moved upon the long rampart wall.

The legionary took two steps back and glanced to his right at the vacant, ghost-like walls before him, devoid of life. He hefted his shield and spear as his heart quickened. He turned, raised his spear towards another guard who stood ten metres away, and whistled to get his attention. When he saw the legionary acknowledge him, he signalled with his pilum and the man trotted to his side with a puzzled expression.

"What is it, Corvinus?" the legionary asked as he scanned the walls.

"Does anything strike you as odd?"

"It's quiet."

Corvinus shook his head and pointed up at the ramparts. "There's nobody up there! Look, its empty."

The legionary mauled over the predicament as he stared at the wall with a bleak, neural, and uneasy expression. "Where are they?"

Corvinus spit upon the ground and grimaced as he pondered what to do. He shifted, stared up at the lone tower of all that remained of the Antonia, then turned to the sound of a muffled, low, trumpet blast. Both sentries watched as a long, double-ranked column of legionaries marched sleepily towards them from the Bezetha.

"That will be the first work detail from the Macedonica. Run and bring this news to the centurion in command." Corvinus gave a grunt and began to jog towards the tower.

"Where are you going?" the sentry called out.

"To the tower to see if the ramparts are indeed empty! Watch for my signal!" Corvinus shouted back as he moved quickly across the rubble.

The sentry stared at Corvinus for a moment longer, then felt his heart leap and pound within his chest as he picked up his shield and ran towards the approaching work detail. He moved swiftly, panting for air as his chest burned. He felt a tinge of nervousness race through him as he glanced towards the tower for a brief second, spotting Corvinus as he disappeared into the spire of stone. The work detail drew closer with every stride he made and the wind rushed against his face as he pumped his legs harder and faster. He noticed the Centurion, who led the cohort, halt as he watched the approaching sentry, then take two steps from the column of soldiers and wait.

"What is it, guard?" called the Centurion, sensing the urgency in the sentry's behaviour as he slowed down, sweat glistening upon the sides of his face.

"Centurion, I have news! The ramparts are clear of the enemy! There is nobody standing guard; they are empty." The sentry watched the Centurion's eyes narrow as his brows furrowed and he jolted his gaze past the recovering guard to the vacant, quiet ramparts beyond. "Corvinus, one of the sentries, has gone to the tower to get a better look."

The Centurion was still, as if he was adhered to the stones he stood upon. His hand instinctively gripped the hilt of his sword and he nodded to himself as his eyes filled with zeal. "You have a man in the tower you say?"

"He will signal to you if the ramparts are clear!"

"By the power of Mars," muttered the Centurion to himself as he turned to his optio. "Great fortune and glory stands before us. Have all the men dispatch their tools on the ground at this instant. Send word to anyone nearby to arm themselves and meet us at the ramps. Tell them to bring ladders, as many as they can find. We will wait for the signal and if there is no one on the ramparts we will breach them."

"Should we not send this news to the Prince, Centurion Paulus?" the optio stammered.

"There is no time, now go!" Paulus tightened the chin strap from his helmet then turned as the legionaries behind him dropped their tools upon the ground and drew their swords. "You will stay with me!" he said to the sentry as he signalled to the cohort to tighten their ranks.

"Are we really going to attack?" the sentry asked with a nervous stutter as he glanced back at the high walls.

"If they are clear of enemy rebels, this may be our chance to capture the Temple. We cannot waste time here!" Centurion Paulus waited for another moment as the column of soldiers reformed and prepared to advance. Once they were ready, he set a light jog as the column of three hundred soldiers followed their fearless officer up the earthen ramp. Tension clung to the air around them as all eyes watched the quiet ramparts above for any movement. The soldiers clustered together in tight ranks, each man gripping his shield with numb, sweaty fingers as they approached the golden walls of stone.

Paulus gritted his teeth as sweat dripped from his nose upon the dusty ground at his feet. Hardly a sound came from the hundreds of men at his back as they stalked up the ramp like a snake eyeing its prey. He raised his sword and the column froze to a halt as golden shields were raised and every man braced himself. Paulus swallowed, his throat feeling dry and parched as his tongue felt like it would cleave to the roof of his mouth from the nerves that raced through his tightened frame. He glanced back at the tower, squinting in the morning sun, and saw a single legionary lean out of one of the high turret windows and deliver a frantic wave.

"That's his signal," the sentry said as he stood next to the Centurion.

"If you should die, you will live again, legionary," Paulus said with a wild look upon his primal face. He grinned as the sentry closed his eyes, gave a fearful nod, licked his lips, and fumbled with his spear.

"Centurion," whispered a soldier behind the officer. "Reinforcements approach with ladders."

Paulus glanced back without turning and watched as another hundred men dashed across the Bezetha towards them with a dozen ladders. "Wait for my signal, pass it along," he whispered to the men behind him. "Make way for the ladders."

The soldiers upon the ramp shuffled to the side as the ladders were brought forth to the walls while the reinforcements swelled their ranks. Marius Junius Livianus pushed past the men with a menacing, grim expression that lined the edges of his scarred face. He gave a casual nod when he approached Paulus and held out a hand of greeting as the two men clasped each other's wrists firmly. "What have we here, Centurion Paulus? I was told an attack was to commence to breach the walls."

"The walls are empty, Marius. I have a man in the tower and he signalled to us that it is clear," Paulus replied. "We cannot tarry. We need to bring the ladders forward. I will lead the attack and you can follow from behind with your men."

Marius took a moment to stare up at the walls. "You're sure it is not a trap?"

"Legionary Corvinus is in the tower. He should be able to see the full extent of the ramparts, and he says they are empty," Paulus countered as he glanced at the ladders held by Marius' men. "We need to move now!"

"Your men will have to move quickly once on top. I will follow and have a runner return to assemble more legionaries. We will need a larger force." Marius grunted and dislodged a scrap of food between his teeth using his tongue, than he spit it out. "This doesn't make much sense, Paulus. When have the Jews ever pulled their sentries off guard?"

"The gods have confounded them, Marius. Helios has blinded their eyes and they have been struck dumb. We will prevail for Mars will guide our swords."

Marius glanced at the eager Centurion. "Alright, but I don't take much gain in believing the gods plan our attacks for us. They have a way of humbling the mighty at times. You cannot fully trust them, Paulus. The gods will lead you astray if you place such faith in myths. They only honour the strong. The man who respects and worships them, yet stands alone and fights his own battles, will seek utter greatness, higher then Mount Olympus ever did for the Greeks."

"Then what do you trust in, Marius, if not in the gods to bring you victory?"

"My reason is what I trust, that is all I have."

"I saw a falcon kill a small bird this morning; it is an omen from Jupiter and we will end this today. You have your reason, Marius, and I have the gods of sun, moon, storm, earth, and water fighting amidst the ranks of my shields. The black bull of the Fifth will end this! Make ready your Thundering Troops!" Paulus raised his sword and whispered loudly, "Bring the ladders!"

The ladders were pushed through the ranks which gave way as they were firmly planted upon the ground and raised against the stone of the five metre high walls. Paulus gave Marius a firm nod, than began to ascend the nearest ladder as he moved up the rungs swiftly followed by soldiers below and at his left and right. He moved smoothly, pacing himself as he neared the parapets. When he reached the last rung, he paused and waited for all the ladders to become full. When there were three men to a ladder, Paulus drew forth a deep gust of air, than jolted forward with a heave as he scrambled between the parapet, planting his foot upon the rampart. He felt an exhilarating sensation fill his soul, and the realization dawned on him as he was the first Roman, since the Jewish war had begun, that now stood unopposed upon the colonnades of the Temple, and it was enough to make him feel like a god.

Paulus watched as legionaries began to pour upon the ramparts on either side. The sensation that they too were upon the brink of ending the siege seemed to fill them as they hurriedly fanned out and bolstered their ranks, locking their scuta together with the blades of their gladii resting comfortably upon the iron edge of each shield. Paulus waited till nearly a hundred men had formed into rank before he dared to move.

Paulus could see the vast, monolithic Temple court stretching beyond, as if it had no end. The massive edifice of the Temple filled the center of the Outer Court as it towered over fifty metres above the ground, its beauty incomparable to anything made by the hands of man. His eyes followed the column of smoke which ascended up from within the Temple's Inner Court and he wondered for a fleeting moment what was being burned. Then Paulus began to shuffle towards the edge of the rampart as he strained to see into the enormous courtyard below. As he moved, he noticed hundreds of tiny spirals of smoke drifting upward from cooking fires and his eyes beheld thousands of dark shapes strewn everywhere throughout the vast Temple plaza.

"Jupiter be praised," he softly whispered, tilting his face to the sky as he realized that the enemy slept. Courage, as he had never known it before, surged through his veins and he spotted the nearest staircase which led from the ramparts to the court below. Lifting his gladius for all his men to see, Paulus began to run towards the stairs as his entire cohort now stood upon the Jewish defences.

However, as Paulus pushed forward, seeing glory before his eyes, his career filled with honour and praise, he heard sudden gasps and calls ring out behind him from his men. Paulus halted and as he gazed down into the courtyard, he could not believe what he saw. It was as if the entire Temple plaza had sprung to life as Zealots everywhere began to stand and gaze up at them. He watched as many rushed for their weapons while others, closest to the northern colonnades stared up with dark grins. Paulus' eyes widened as he sensed the impending dread before him. He heard a number of panic stricken shouts rise up from his legionaries as some of the men began to back away while a few fled to the ladders which were filled with soldiers climbing up. Like a frightful, terrifying dream, Paulus saw an enormous, savage-looking, bearded man step out from the nearest cluster of Zealots. Shouting up at them with words Paulus did not understand, the warrior raised his arm and slashed it through the air in a cutting motion.

For a second nothing happened. Then a whirling murmur was felt beneath the feet of the legionaries. In a cataclysmic instant, a curling, jagged wall of fire erupted around them hissing and howling as it spiraled and tore, blasting through their ranks with incredible force. Hysteric screams pulsed above the roar of fire that engulfed the colonnades. Legionaries were burned alive as they flailed with shrieks, colliding into one another while their flesh melted and peeled. Men, desperate to flee the inferno, leapt from the parapets as they fell with screams to the rocks below. Others, driven by sheer madness as the intense fire burned their flesh, turned and jumped from the colonnades into the Outer Court below, only to snap their legs upon the flagstones.

Paulus watched in horror from the edge of the burning colonnade, as many of his men lay in contorted positions upon the flagstones wailing in agony, while Zealots rushed them like a pack of hungry, starved dogs only to fall upon each legionary with spears and swords. The wounded soldiers tried to crawl or limp away as they called for mercy and screamed, but the Zealots spared none. With the roar of fire heating his back, Paulus watched helplessly as the Jewish rebels hacked his soldiers to pieces, sending their blood spraying and upon the stones.

"Centurion Paulus!" cried a voice above the roar of fire, but the burning colonnades only cracked, shattered, and blazed as the flames spread.

Paulus turned and stared through the inferno as his escape route was completely cut off. He backed up, and for an instant he saw the hazy image of Marius rippling in the heat of the fire, as he stood upon the parapets trying to locate the trapped Centurion. Paulus wanted to shout for help, but his throat was painfully dry and his face flushed with heat that struck his body. He shielded his burning skin as the fire suddenly spewed out with a rush of wind, as if it possessed fingers hoping to grab him. Paulus took a step back as he cringed and felt his woolen garments weighed down by the sweat that soaked his body. He stared at the dozens of corpses he could see lying among the flames, which fed the endless appetite of the fire that was breaking apart the colonnade roof and ramparts. His throat seemed to scream for water, yet Paulus was frozen in shock as he watched a legionary near the parapet, drop to his knees, his body completely consumed in fire. The soldier's dark shape seemed to teeter for a moment and then crashed into a heap upon the rampart with his flesh black and helmet melted to his scalp.

Marius had disappeared and Paulus knew he had no choice left. He could not make it to the ladders and had been forced back so far it was apparent that if he was to leap from the wall he would plunge to his death. The fire continued to spread quickly, as it devoured the very stones he stood upon. Paulus hurried out of its way, attempting to keep ahead of the heat. When he had gone as far as he could, he turned frantically and watched as a host of Zealots ascended up to the ramparts.

All Paulus had to defend himself with was his gladius and he held it firmly, knowing that death was approaching swiftly. He quickly recited a torrent of prayers in his mind as he took another step from the flames and widened his stance to meet the Zealots. He had no shield and so nothing would cast him off balance, yet he knew if he remained as close as he could to the burning fires the Zealots would be unable to encircle him. That way he could fight them one by one and hopefully kill a few. Paulus took a deep breath as he watched the Zealot host reach the top of the ramparts and pause to stare at him. Their faces were expressionless, yet their eager hands that clutched the swords at their sides betrayed their real intentions.

"What are you waiting for?" Paulus suddenly shouted at his enemy, as fear poured out upon his face and tightened his muscles. He felt tears well up within his eyes as he readied himself, keeping the blade low so he could thrust it easily at his attacker.

The Zealots did not move and stood with amusement, content to watch the terrified Roman consider his fate, with the burning dead at his back. A flicker of a grin finally exposed itself upon one particular Jewish warrior's face, John of Gischala, and he chuckled at the Centurion's grim possibilities and the terror captured in his eyes. John pushed past the Zealots, holding the shaft of a spear, and slowly approached the Roman while pointing the iron head at his enemy's chest.

Paulus recognized the great warrior as the man who had signalled to those below the portico roofs to ignite the fire trap, and he felt a sudden intense hatred for the man. He also knew the fighter was someone of great importance at how the other Zealots reacted around him, and he prayed to Mars to grant him the courage to slay him. He knew he would not escape with his life, but he continued to pray that Jupiter would see his courage, with the words of Marius echoing loudly in his mind that the gods revered a man who stood alone and fought till the bitter end. But then Paulus watched the giant man abruptly halt, spread his stance and extend the spear straight back so that the iron tipped weapon was nearly at his ear. Then with an enormous heave, like a scorpion projecting its deadly missile, the spear was hurled with a powerful, loud grunt from the Jewish warlord. It sliced through the air with blinding speed and drove straight through Paulus' chest, bending his torso nearly in half, and sending him pitching back near the eager flames.

Paulus clawed at the shaft of the spear as his body trembled. Blood spurted from the wound and filled his mouth as it ran from the cracks of his parted lips and down his chin. His body shook with a revolting spasm and he cringed with a horrified moan. He felt the intensity of the fire behind him, yet was helpless as his strength waned and his body weakened. Sticky, warm blood now soaked his breastplate and tunic, flowing onto the stones of the rampart as he tried to drag himself to the parapets. He groaned and struggled as salty tears streaked his face. Then he felt a hand tighten around his ankle and pull him away from the parapets. Ignoring the strength of the hand, Paulus grappled again upon the stones with his clawing hands as he tried to pull away from the hold, but it was too powerful. When he finally looked up, his vision was blurred and he could feel his pulse sinking. His breathing was raspy and uneven. All he could do was watch as a large, beast-like hand tore his helmet from his head and wrenched him up by his scalp.

John watched the pathetic Roman close his eyes as colour drained from his face. The warlord had seen this look many times upon helpless men, knowing death was but seconds away, and he greeted it with a smile, feeling a rush of victory fill his strong beating heart. He forced the man to his knees, drew his sword, and took a step back, poised and ready. Then with a deep, booming war cry, John brought the blade down in a swift motion, cutting with such speed that the steel edge easily sliced through the Centurion's exposed neck. The head spiraled through the air with a bloody ribbon from the severed stump, and John watched it roll upon the ground until it bumped into the parapets.

A crimson trail flowed from the decapitated body across the stones to where the head lay. Without hesitating, John took three strides, stooped down, and picked it up. He held it high, gripping the hair with his fierce fingers as he inspected the sunken eyelids and the last expression frozen upon the face. He savoured the moment of triumph and gazed down to where three cohorts, shocked and perplexed, watched him from their battle ranks at the base of the ramp.

The legionaries did not move a muscle and silently took in the sight of the burning colonnades as the fires jutted upward into the sky with billows of smoke, black as night. John stared at the Romans and then threw the head over the side. John watched the head twist, as though suspended in midair, until it suddenly fell and bounced off the stones below with a sickening hollow thud as it split apart. John caught the glimpse of a black, war horse appear as it galloped to the rear of the cohorts. At the sight of Titus' arrival, John bellowed terribly across the rubble and raised both hands in the air as he waved his blood stained sword in circular motions above his head.

*   *   *

Camp of the Assyrians
Quarters of Prince Titus Flavius Vespasianus
Afternoon

Porcius watched patiently as the Nubian slave poured him a goblet of wine and then he accepted it with a subtle acknowledgement. He inspected the craftsmanship of the silver cup and hummed to himself at the intricate inlay of tiny red jewels making up the flowing hair upon the face of a god in the centre. Porcius ran his finger overtop of the god's face and traced the beard with his nail, then gave an impressed nod as he faced the Prince. "What god does this represent?"

"Neptune. It was made in Sicily, although my mind is at a loss for the artisan's name. He is skilled in silver and gold work and I had the jewels specially commissioned to be added. The man is the best in his trade. There is nobody within the whole island who is supposed to be able to match his skill." Titus finished his wine and set his empty goblet on the table as he watched Porcius inspect the silver cup again with satisfaction. "If you like it so much, I shall give it to you as a gift when the Temple is captured."

"My Prince, I am honoured," Porcius replied with a joyous bow as a smile spread across his face. "It would so honour me if you had the goblet inscribed with your wishes."

"Very well, I will have it sent to Joppa once this engagement is decided. There are silversmiths within the port that should be able to do such a thing. Now, let us begin," Titus said as he ushered Porcius over to a comfortable couch with plush cushions. "I shall call Albinus my scribe to record anything we deem necessary." Titus flicked his wrist at the Nubian slave and the man quietly left as the Prince seated himself upon a chaise across from his Chief Engineer. "The Zealots have been emboldened since this morning. Reports say they continue to jeer at our soldiers working upon the platform, even while the colonnades still smoulder."

"It is as you say, my Prince. It was a tragedy that befell the Fifth, but a harsh lesson learned." Porcius nodded firmly, scrunching up his face as his hand rubbed his scalp to relieve an itch.

The fat Albinus entered the quarters quietly carrying a small wooden tray, a few scraps of parchment, a bottle of ink, and a sharpened quill. He awkwardly sat down upon a stool and there he remained, back straight and eyes focused upon the Prince, should he give a signal to begin to record.

"One hundred and thirty men burned to death," Titus said softly, absorbed in his thoughts. "Fifteen fell to their death, and another sixty wounded have been recovered." Titus sighed. "The wounded consist of mostly broken bones or fractured ankles. A tragedy as you say, Porcius, but indeed a cruel lesson of the gods. Romans cannot be too eager. Failure and victory hang in the balance and are in the will of the gods," Titus stated, shaking a finger. "What was the Centurion's name who led the attack?"

"Paulus Tatianus of the Third Cohors. He was a seven year veteran and a hastatus posterior of his centuria. His entire centuria perished in the fires. All others that died were scattered soldiers from the other centuria of the Third and ten men from the Fortis Centuria of the Fulminata First Cohors."

"Who commanded the detachment of the Twelfth?"

"Marius Junius Livianus, but he escaped harm. It appears the Jews who set the trap, must have used some sort of flammable stock which they would have filled the portico ceiling with. Survivors said the Jews appeared to have been asleep, then suddenly came to life and ignited the trap." Porcius soberly shook his head. "It was a terrible blow to the Macedonica."

"Truly," Titus replied with a grunt. He nodded at Albinus as he began to dictate with a tumble of elegant words. "To General Sextus Cerealis, commander of the Macedonica Legio with regards to the Third Cohors of the Fifth. Recovery of the centuria that has been crippled is of utmost importance. News of the death of Paulus

Tatianus has come to me with the sorrow from which must be felt by the entire Third at the death of such a respectable centurion. No doubt Paulus has paid the ferry toll and has crossed into the next world. May his memory be prayed for and glory given to his ancestors.

"Thus, as is accustomed in times of war, you will elect a new hastatus posterior immediately, and fill in any gaps that may remain. As well, my orders are direct and to the point. The Third Cohors is to be replenished and their numbers strengthened with all possible speed and care. As the days ahead of us will test the resolve of this army which we have gathered, I do implore you to use whatever tools at your disposal to see such a thing come to fruition.

"As for now, my orders are that you visit King Marcus Julius Agrippa on this day and request a contingent of his most seasoned spear troops to support the Third. Take one hundred in number, and begin training them immediately to function with your remaining centuria of the Third. May glory and honour be forever bestowed upon you by the gods that safe keep our grand empire. Titus Flavius Vespasianus." Titus shook his head and grumbled under his breath as he watched Albinus finish the last sentence. He glanced at Porcius, a sense of duty sinking deep within his cold eyes. "I know they are eager, but we need absolute discipline on the line. The Jews will try anything; we have them penned in and pushed into a corner." He cleared his throat and stamped his sealed ring into a small tablet of wax that was to be sent with the message and then handed it back to Albinus and motioned for him to leave. "What is to be done now?"

"Well, the rams should be brought out of the Bezetha. The ramp has been built to support both testudines which should be able to work side by side, along with engineering crews with crowbars and picks. The stones are twice the size of those we toiled against at the Antonia, my Prince. I do believe we will not get very far."

"Nevertheless, Porcius, I do implore you to try. What happened today has vexed me. The enemy needs to see our power upon the ramps and we must do whatever is necessary for victory."

"What about ordering a palisade?"

"I wish to explore all other options before such an order is given. A palisade will be bloody and is unpredictable. One can never judge the outcome of a palisade. The ramparts are wide and the Zealots can get many men upon them."

Porcius wiped his nose and set his empty goblet down. "Yet, we could attempt to clear them with our artillery. The Temple colonnades are partially in ruins, especially with the fires, and there may be an opportunity. The legionaries are furious about what happened today, and the Jews cannot spring such a trap a second time. The legions will want to spill Jewish blood like never before. I urge you to act on this anger while you can."

"My orders will remain, Gracchus. Bring up the rams as soon as the ramp is complete and we shall see what progress can be made. A palisade will follow if the rams are not successful. Have the Fulminata operate the engines and working crews once the attack is to commence. I want Gaius Antony overseeing the testudines."

Porcius stood and struck his chest in salute. "I will dispatch your orders, my Prince. Jupiter be with you." Then he strolled out of the tent and into the air which still hung with the sour smell of burnt corpses and smouldering wood soaked in pitch.

* * *

CHAPTER LVII

July 27th, 70 A.D. / 3rd of Av, 3830
Mount of Olives
Quarters of Jewish prisoners bound for Gophna
Morning

Gaius shook his head as he marched up the steep slopes of the mountain. He had just been approached by a jubilant Marcus Sulla who proclaimed to him that Hadassah had agreed to be his wife and that she would accompany him back to Rome when the siege was over. Gaius had been shocked to hear the news, but had offered his congratulations accepting the invitation to join in the wedding feast that would eventually be held at the Tribune's villa. Marcus had shared to his friend in a torrent of emotion and soothing words that Hadassah was more than a lover and was a delicate individual who would be an honourable wife and mother to his future children. The Tribune had professed such feelings for Hadassah faster than Gaius could keep up with him and the love stricken man had thanked Gaius with a bear hug and a pledge to faithfully repay him someday. When Gaius had asked what he had even helped with, Marcus had laughed.

Gaius was genuinely happy for the brute man, and believed that what he saw was a real expression of love that had been deprived from the Tribune for so long. However, he still believed that Hadassah really had no idea about the new life that awaited her upon her arrival in Rome. Yet, Gaius hoped that Venus would shadow them both and preserve their new passions together, as he had been granted such a blessed life with his Livia for all these years.

Gaius climbed higher as he passed the stone walls of the Fretensis camp, feeling the sweat run down his chest and soak his tunic. He headed for a cluster of tents above the legionary camp where the flags of the Tenth fluttered in the wind. A cloud of dust spiraled and tore past him as he squinted and screened his face from the biting particles of sand. The earth beneath his sandaled feet was already baking in the sun, and he glanced down at his tanned legs as they were streaked in dust and sweat. Gaius glanced out and surveyed the slopes for a moment, then shook his head.

The mountain was no longer as it had appeared the day the legions had arrived back in the spring. At that time it truly had adopted every meaning of its name, Mount of Olives. The mountainside had been covered in olive groves, gardens, and vineyards. Although the wind regularly blew along the slopes, there had not been such shifting dust and sand in those days which existed now. The landscape had changed, from the olive mountain to Scopus, than down into the rocky valleys stretching to the rising city of Jerusalem and the Temple Mount.

Gaius recalled marching here with Cestius Gallus' army in the late summer of the first year of the war. It had been presumed that they would trounce the enemy, drag down the walls, and destroy the rebellion. The war had sure started that way, as Gaius could remember. Gallus had sent the legionaries to the city and they had breached the walls, driving the Zealots away. They had destroyed whole neighbourhoods and settled down to make the next move against the Mishneh and the Temple itself. No matter what the Zealots attempted to do, Gallus' strategic positioning had driven them back. It was early in the war and the Jewish forces had not had time to mobilize and form cohesive armies. When Gallus marched to Jerusalem, not even six months had passed since the Jews had cancelled the daily sacrifice to the emperor. It had seemed as if the Romans would crush the rebellion into pieces before it had any time to grow. Then, Cestius Gallus had ordered the withdrawal of all forces from the city, and Gaius had nearly been killed in the desperate fighting.

The reason of their retreat had always baffled Gaius. It had been a time of immense shame and embarrassment for the Twelfth for they had lost their legionary eagle. He could remember the sight of the helpless, panic-stricken aquilifer, separated from the bloody remnants of the First Cohort as they fled and abandoned him. Gaius had done all he could to try and reclaim the precious eagle, yet in the end he had been saved by his comrades and dragged away. Still, he could remember watching the lone aquilifer being hacked to pieces by the blades of eight swords as the Zealots had swarmed in around him. The Jewish rebels had then lifted the standard high into the air, with the fingers from the severed hand of the aquilifer still wrapped tightly around the shaft of the pole, the sacred eagle now a trophy, to be carried away to its new home in Jerusalem. The sight had caused Gaius to weep, and utter shame had been washed over the legionaries that had abandoned their eagle. It had been that very shame that had driven many soldiers to volunteer for Cestius' planned suicidal shock troop of six hundred who would cover the retreat of the Fulminata. They had volunteered out of bravery and glory, desperately trying to regain the honour of their stained image in the face of their commanding General. However, nearly all of the shock troops would never be seen again, as thousands upon thousands of Jewish rebels chased the fleeing army all the way past the borders of Judea, swallowing up the brave six hundred.

Gaius shook his head and spit onto the ground as he remembered the immense humiliation that had befallen the crippled army as it had limped back into Antioch. They had been scattered, smashed, undermined, chased, driven, and slaughtered. When Titus had sent word to Cestius Gallus that the legion was to be reformed and strengthened for the siege of Jerusalem, all the men had known that finally their time had come for revenge. No Roman general wished to take command of such a legion that had lost its eagle, yet finally the commission had been given to Tribune Marcus

Tullius Octavian and the men had rallied around him as the one who could help them restore the stain of the past. To regain the honour of their legion was their highest priority, and they had done so by spreading carnage wherever they fought.

Gaius approached one particular tent, rapped upon a wooden pole, and poked his head in. A Jewish man sat quietly upon a stool at a table covered in parchment as Yosef ben Matityahu furiously finished writing out his thoughts. The Jewish man noticed the Roman officer and leaned back with a sense of trepidation as Yosef looked up and smiled at Gaius. "It is good to see you, Praefectus Castrorum. To what do I owe this honour?"

"I have come to speak with you," Gaius muttered weary eyed as he gave a suspicious sideways glance at the humble Jewish man sitting across from Yosef. "What is this?"

"I am interviewing a merchant who escaped from Jerusalem three weeks ago and is still awaiting transport to Gophna."

"Must be a wealthy merchant."

"He is a silk merchant. He sold cloth from the Orient and was trapped here when the Zealots closed off the city. He tried to get out when pilgrims were still venturing in during the feasts, but his accent betrayed him many times and they would not let him go. He was beaten twice by the Zealots. His account is very interesting. It shall help me immensely in compiling my histories of what has happened." Yosef grinned as he gestured to the stack of parchment scrawled and covered in lines which contained neat rows of elegant Koine letters.

"Did you record yesterday's ambush?" Gaius asked as he stepped into the tent and stared down at the transcript.

"I try not to leave anything out. It is a great task. I interview prisoners, generals, soldiers, and anyone who will heed my voice and give me reliable information." Yosef drank from a simple wooden cup that sat near his stack of papers.

"Surely the eye of the Prince shall read your work?"

Yosef bobbed his head in agreement. "He is commissioning it. It is to be published after this is all resolved. There are still fortresses to the south to be conquered. I shall write about those battles."

"Will you travel south with the army?"

Yosef chuckled lightly and shook his head. "The desert does not appeal to me. I may make excursions to collect what I need in due time. We shall see, Gaius, the Prince would first need to release me."

"Hmm," Gaius relented. "Walk with me, Yosef."

Yosef hastily nodded, said something to the Jewish silk merchant, then stood and left the tent with Gaius. They walked along the summit of the mountain, tracing the rocks before them with every step as they slowed to a casual pace. Yosef kept the folds of his cloak tightly against his body as he strolled with his bearded chin pressed firmly against his chest from the wind and dust. Gaius, on the other hand, faced the stinging breeze with a sense of melancholy as he pondered what he would say.

"Yosef, the platforms have been finished and the rams are in place. We will mount the attack tomorrow against the Temple colonnades." Gaius paused and saw the somber effects of his words upon the Jewish General's face. "I will be on the front lines tomorrow until we have captured the Temple. My cohors is to be one of the main fighting units. The Tenth and Fifteenth will maintain their hold on the First Wall and attack them simultaneously as we launch our offensive, but the pressure and resources will be given to our assault. The Fifth will be in support tomorrow. We start at dawn."

Yosef gave a heavy nod, feeling a weight descend upon his shoulders and he gazed towards the Temple with pleading eyes. There was no going back; the Temple would fall. "So, you have come to tell me this?"

Gaius halted and faced Yosef as he rubbed his chin. "Yes, and more. I will be leading the frontal attack when we breach the colonnade ramparts. They are in disrepair and weakened by the fire, so it is only a matter of time. However, when we storm the Outer Court it will be a bloody fight, as you most probably know. The Zealots have not relinquished one section of ground without a fight, and now we have pushed their backs up against the most holy place in your people's religion. I know that before this is over the courtyard of the Temple will run with blood. My purpose in coming here to meet you is one that pertains to Judah ben Yosef." Gaius paused for a moment choosing his next words carefully. "I will look for him, and if possible, I plan to capture him and send him to Gophna alive. If I do so, I shall call on you to speak on behalf of me."

"You would spare Judah?"

Gaius nodded. "I have surveyed the colonnades for many days now and even gazed down upon the Temple plaza from the Antonia's tower, but I have not been able to spot him. I wonder if something troubling has happened. I shall only know, however, when we storm the Temple. Can I count on your trust to conceal what has been spoken of, and given the chance that I find him, that you would personally escort him to Gophna? You understand the Prince can never know."

Yosef stared at the crippled city of Jerusalem that stood before him. It had changed so much and the scars of war could be seen upon the destroyed walls and razed quarters. He could make out the long earthen ramp rising up from the rubble where the Antonia had stood, as it had been thrust against the northwestern colonnades. A thin trail of black smoke rose from the Jewish ramparts as the fires still smouldered from a day ago, and Yosef could make out Zealots crammed upon the walls watching the Romans below.

When Yosef finally turned to face Gaius he saw a tinge of nervousness in the Centurion's eyes and a sense of sympathy. Yosef slowly nodded his head as he swallowed the bitter taste in his mouth. "I am your humble and faithful servant."

* * *

July 28th, 70 A.D. / 4th of Av, 3830
Temple Mount
Northwestern colonnades
Midmorning

"John! John, you must wake up!" shouted a short, squat man from the doorway of the vestments chamber.

It was one of the few rooms below the Temple that John could sleep undisturbed and he groaned as he rolled onto his side and blinked a few times waiting for his vision to clear. "What is it?" he asked as a jolt of pain burned his throat.

"The Romans are bringing two rams to the walls!" The soldier watched John slowly sit up as he planted his bare feet upon the cold stone floor and rested his weary head upon his open palms. "John, did you hear me? The Romans advance."

"I heard you," he groaned again as he wiped the sleep from his eyes. "The stones will hold, the walls are thicker than the Antonia and the rams will be useless." He stared up at the ceiling in the hazy light as the flames of three burning oil lamps flickered and cast shadows upon the walls. A sudden wave of annoyance washed over him. He lowered his gaze with a scowl and stared at the man who had not budged from the doorway. "I will come when I am ready. Have guards stationed at all the gates of the west colonnades, and send an envoy to that bastard, Simon." John rubbed his temples and hung his head as his breath was sour. "We need more men. Have Simon send more men." He felt like plunging back down upon his straw mat but lifted a weary, blurred gaze and stared at the empty doorway. The man was gone.

John sent a long stream of saliva splattering upon the dusty stone floor and shook his head. With despair flooding his soul at the reality that the Romans would come at first light, John had seen to it the night before that he would not be disturbed, having plenty of rich Temple wine at his disposal. His mind was hazy from the heavy drinking and his body ached in every possible joint as he buried his face into his massive hands. John could remember drinking until his mind blurred and his body had become so numb that the fate of Jerusalem seemed to melt away. He could remember laughter, but was unable to place the source in his mind and so groaned.

John stretched his arms above his head and winced as he gazed down at the lines of five long cuts striped across his sides. He could see the blood had dried and touched the wounds as the scabs broke and fresh blood oozed from the damaged skin. John cringed as he examined the partially healed marks, and then looked at his left side and saw another set of long bloody scratches deeply gored out of his muscular flesh. Who or what had done this was beyond his foggy recollections of the night before. And that was when a soft, delicate touch stroked his back.

John leapt to his feet with clenched fists and his hulking body appeared like a Grecian wrestler. It took him less than a second to realize two things. The first, he was naked, and the second, there was a woman in his chamber. John watched as a bare breasted woman recoiled with a yelp of surprise, then laughed to herself and began to crawl forward like a stalking leopard with enticing eyes. A look of dumbfounded awestruck hit John like a catapult stone at the sight of the woman and he hungrily traced the roundness of her hanging breasts and the curves of her body right to her buttocks. She looked like one of the Greek nudes that his Zealots had toppled and destroyed in the palaces when they had seized Jerusalem so long ago. Her skin appeared like silk, her hair smelled of perfume, and her smile was lustful as she playfully sat upright, her knees bent and legs extended behind her as she rubbed her hands over her breasts and covered her nipples.

"You look so shocked, John! You didn't seem that way last night." She giggled and uncovered her breasts with a smile. "You can take me again. You are so strong!"

In panic and shame, John lunged for the nearest sheet and tore it off the bed to cover his body. His mind swirled about like a storm. "Who are you?"

"Does it matter?"

"Why are you here?"

She laughed. "You don't remember? You have had me visit you often the last couple of nights. You drink until you become wild, like an untamed horse." She pleasurably gritted her teeth and laid down, propping her head upon a pillow. "You don't remember?"

John scowled as his gaze fell. Had his men observed his behaviour? Jerusalem hung in the balance of being destroyed and he was drinking himself into a stupor and bedding prostitutes? A deep riveting thud gently shook the room snapping him out of the plaguing thoughts of regret and remorse. He reached for his garments and began to dress hurriedly, not wishing to gaze at the woman as if she were a vixen capable of cursing him. The woman breathed a sigh of annoyance and sat up exasperated at his startled behaviour.

"I thought you said they couldn't pound down the walls." She watched as John slipped on his outer garment and then began to don his sandals. "Did you like the marks I gave you? They were a gift." She watched him straighten with a tinge of humiliation, then stand to buckle his sword belt about his waist. "I have never been with someone so forceful before. The pleasure was beyond this earth. I'm not sure you can live without me, John." She smiled again at the sense of power she held over him as he gave her a dark, resentful stare. "You liked it, John. You told me so as you spread my legs. You need me. I will be waiting for you to return. Have your men bring more wine for us tonight."

John glared at her with such a venomous gaze that she shifted uncomfortably among the cushions and blankets to conceal her nakedness. "Never come here again or I will kill you," he whispered, and then left the chamber to the thudding din that rose from above the ground.

*　　*　　*

"Together heave!" Gaius shouted with a resonating order, as the heavy ram was drawn back by the grunting men, then thrust forward as it slammed into the stone wall and shook the entire body of the testudo. "Again! Heave!" he bellowed for the tenth time as the ropes that suspended the heavy beam groaned as the iron-headed ram shot forward. Sweat soaked his body so much that he felt like he had just stepped from the steam of the baths. Dust filled the stifling hot, cramped space of the battering ram as rows of men, either side of the crossbeam, drew it back with a grunt and then pushed it forward.

"Halt!" Gaius bellowed as a heavy stone smashed into the plated roof above them. The men steadied the ram as Gaius pushed past three soldiers and stared at the charred walls of the northwestern colonnades. He shook his head. The ram had done nothing so far. The stone appeared not even to bear a single crack. "Continue!" he shouted, as he made his way to the rear of the testudo not wishing to show feelings of discouragement that this whole charade was a waste time.

Gaius cautiously poked his head from the shell of the ram and stared at the other testudo next to his. He caught a glimpse of Marius standing at the rear, shaking his head and cursing in frustration. The sharp musical-like racket echoed loudly with the clang of iron as hammers, picks and crowbars furiously worked around the rams, unseen by Gaius. He pitied those men, knowing how dangerous it was for he had been there before. Now, Rufus Garus of the Serpent Century held the command over the panting, grunting crews. Gaius listened to the Centurion's continual shouts as Rufus cheered the struggling men onward, encouraging them to do the impossible by breaking up and dislodging one ton stones.

"Halt!" Gaius bellowed, shaking himself out of his thoughts. He moved forward to inspect the wall and was greeted with the same familiar sight. The ram was doing nothing. In fact, slamming the ram against the stone had only succeeded in denting the snarling, iron ram's head more than it had pathetically attempted to chip the stone. Gaius cursed, and ordered them to continue, knowing that the Prince was observing everything.

Fine, he thought, *I will just smash at the walls until this ram splits apart and shatters itself.* Gaius spit upon the ground, spewed a number of foul words, than moved to the rear. He understood that Titus was only using up all his options before his generals would push him to order another palisade. However, Gaius knew that when it came time for a palisade, it would be a similar bloody struggle as it had been the morning when the legionaries and Zealots had crammed into the defilade below the walls to slaughter each other like madmen.

"Centurion Antony!"

Gaius turned to see a clean looking legionary standing before him, slightly hunched over from the projectiles that were hurled from above. When an arrow singed close by his helmet, the man instinctively stepped under the covering of the testudo and saluted. "I have orders from Prince Titus! The attack is to be called off at the blast of two trumpets. You are to recover your men and make an orderly withdraw back down the ramps."

"Did he state why?" Gaius shrewdly asked.

"I think it's obvious. Looks like we may attempt a palisade. We haven't got much choice left. But that is for another day and for the generals who shall be far away from harm to decide."

Gaius nodded astutely and patted the legionary upon the shoulder. "We will be ready. Let Marius and the others know."

The soldier cautiously peered out from the safety of the battering ram and then quickly moved to the next. Gaius wiped the sweat from his face and stared down at his wet hand. He knew Marcus Sulla was observing the struggle, and no doubt would hear a chorus of smart remarks and sarcastic comments about how he had been right all along. But for now, his charge was for an orderly withdrawal of one of the most awkward, lumbering siege machines that the Romans built. It was all fine to push the iron plated tortoise up the ramps, but then it was an entirely different challenge to inch backward without losing control and toppling over the side. However, Gaius reminded himself that his men were not fresh out of the ranks of legionary training like a bunch of inexplicably raw recruits. But they were professional, seasoned soldiers, skilled and honed in the craft of war.

"Alright lads, wait for the trumpet blasts and try not to wave your pricks at the enemy like a bunch of bleeding virgins. Withdraw smartly and slowly and we all get back alive!"

* * *

The Ophel
Southern end of the Temple Mount
Two hours before midnight

Adam and Moshe kept to the shadows of buildings as they neared the Olympian-sized walls of the colonnades. Adam could not help but be amazed with their immensity, as he always had been. The Royal Stoa was a monstrosity, as it towered above the walls like the Tower of Babel, held up by the unseen four rows of Herodian portico columns within. These high portico pillars separated the nave with aisles on either side that stretched onward to the ritual bath nestled inside an apse upon the eastern end. The pillars of the far southern row had been cut in half and set into the wall in such a way that on the outside of the colonnades, protruding columns of stone jutted out with Corinthian capitals arranged on top to give the appearance of the pillars which they resembled from within.

The great columns of the Royal Stoa stabilized the breathtaking ceiling that unravelled such splendour and wealth as never seen before. Hundreds of wooden carved square panels, each one plated in gold gilded work, extended under the entire stoa as if heaven had touched earth. Above the middle row of double pillars, the Royal Stoa vaulted high above the lower roofs upon either side, with a second row of columns stacked on top of those below, in order to support the magical golden ceiling.

Every pillar had been hand carved by the greatest artisans in the world. Each marble entablature bore the most intricate designs of flora and fauna. Holding up the incredible weight were the Corinthian capitals, each one identical to the next, chiseled with care and love, almost as if an innate sense fused the sculptor with the stone. However, to complete each pillar, they had to be perfectly balanced in strength, size, shape, and length. Even to the untrained eye that stared in wonderment, it was obvious that with careful precision, each capital had been gently set in place upon the shaped plan shaft, which rested firmly on the strong multi-tiered base stone, all done at the direction of Herod's architects many years ago.

A scattered number of guards could be seen patrolling the walls above the Hulda Gates. The silhouettes of the soldiers were streaked upon the rising red, shingled, stoa's roof as the ramparts enveloped the domineering structure. The Royal Stoa had sixteen windows burning brightly with light pouring from its southern face as the beautiful, elevated tiered structure ran nearly the entire length of the two hundred and seventy-eight metre wall. Adam strained with the utmost care, trying to keep track of the sentries above as he bid his time. Adam watched as a single guard strolled to the southwestern end, near the pinnacle of the Trumpeting Stone, than halted as he stared far off into the city below. Moshe crouched at Adam's side, his face covered by a black scarf and a long head covering draped low past the nape of his neck. The eager young man, ten years Adam's junior, moved to have a closer peek and then prudently held up his surrendered hands when Adam gave him a heated glare.

"It helps to have two pairs of eyes," Moshe complained as he reluctantly moved back into the shadows.

"It also helps not to get caught!" Adam replied with a harsh whisper. He shook his head, knelt down next to Moshe, and stared at the Lion warrior. "The guards won't have time to see us if we move quickly. It is the Hulda Gates I worry about. If they are watched, it will pose quite a dire situation for us." Adam paused as he stared to the right at the large Triple Gates, with the middle doorway being the tallest of the three and topped with an arched lintel. Below the Triple Gates to the left, stood a multi-level public building that contained a study hall for Biblical intellects. To the left of the public hall, a three leveled ritual *mikva'ot* bathhouse had been constructed that was commonly used by worshippers ascending to the Temple through the Hulda Gates above. A long staircase led to each gate, and both were divided by the buildings to accommodate the masses of pilgrims that wanted access to the Temple during the feasts.

The entrances of the Hulda Gates were of equal size, divided by an enormous pier of stones in the center, and stretched underneath the Temple Mount in a long tunnel that led up to the Outer Court. The middle of the tunnel was divided by three stunning pillars which included a wall of stone further down, so that the worshippers ascending to the sanctuary would be herded in an orderly fashion, only to emerge upon the Temple plateau at the other end. The ceilings of the long tunnel vault revealed domes of intricate gold designs. Patterns of twisting vines, diamonds, shells, grape bunches, and decorated squares were interwoven among geometric, floral designs as each dome held its own unique beauty. The Hulda Gates were the widest and most beautiful of the entrances to the Temple Mount from the south. They possessed the rich lustre that would strike awe into the hearts of pilgrims as they neared the Temple through the cool tunnel. Yet, upon this night, access through the Hulda Gates was the goal of both Adam and Moshe as they hid in the shadows, staring through the blackness, contemplating the danger that lay before them.

Adam rehearsed their route in his mind and then glanced at to Moshe. "Remember the last words John said before we were driven away?"

Moshe grumbled softly, "We shall become carrion for the vultures if we get caught trying to slip back in. I am sure that is what he meant."

Adam could not help but grin at the sarcastic comment and Moshe flashed a smile in return. "Right, follow me to the wall and then we will silently approach the Hulda Gates. If they are unguarded, we continue through the vault tunnel as there is no other choice HaShem has set before us. Judah is still alive, and if there is an opportunity to seize honour, even through death, then so be it. I cannot abandon him."

"Nor me," Moshe said as he rested his vigorous hand upon the hilt of his blade.

Since being driven from the Temple plateau they had spent the nights in silence within one of the abandoned homes of the Lower City, counting away the miserable days in the gloom. However, in those darkest of moments, when the dreary lack of positive expectation burdened them with the sounds of war throughout Jerusalem, a spark of hope had seared so bright it seemed as if it would illuminate the night. Adam had first purported the plan to fight their way into the dungeons to save Judah and had masterfully shaken every foggy detail into reality. Moshe had leapt at the idea if it meant it would put his blade closer to the throats of either Simon or Bagdatus.

Adam took a mighty breath and dashed across the black stones as Moshe followed. Neither man dared to breathe, as if the guards above might sense a shift in the air.

They reached the eastern side of the ritual bathhouse and moved up the stairs like ghosts. Soon, both men found themselves with their backs pressed up against the cool stones of the southern colonnade walls, with the massive twin entrances of the Hulda Gates on their right. Adam's chest was heaving as his nerves raced and he fought to maintain control. He took a couple gulps of air, than steadied himself as he signaled Moshe to follow.

Adam moved along the wall until he came to the first doorway of the Hulda Gates. He had been through these gates countless times before on his way up to the Temple, yet he never could have perceived of a day when he would be standing in this very spot with his life in danger, trying to avoid the very people who were supposed to be his comrades. Adam glanced up past the gigantic stones that formed the relieving arch and lintel of the Hulda Gates and listened as he held his breath. Once again the silence of night came flooding back to him with encouragement. He made a sharp gesture to Moshe, then carefully and ever so slowly, he peered around the corner and down the dimly lit vault of the tunnel. Not a single human could be seen and Adam whispered a prayer of thanks to God.

"Is it clear?" Moshe whispered with an edge of fear. He loathed the feeling of being exposed in the open, and at that very moment he wanted nothing better to do than to slip through the gate's entrance and be safely hidden.

Adam gave a hasty nod and held up his hand to steady Moshe. "We move slowly and quietly. Take off your sandals." Adam watched as Moshe scowled before complying. When both men were ready they slipped into the dim light of the Hulda Gates and made their way through the long tunnel.

The flagstones felt cool against Adam's calloused feet as he moved, passing across the shadows which the pillars cast from the torches lighting the way. The vault was eerily silent except for the gentle moan of the wind that stirred across the far openings. Adam took a fleeting moment to gaze up at one of the beautiful domes above him, and if the threat of danger had not lurked so close by, he would have liked to stop and praise the artwork.

The patter of their soft footsteps was light as Adam and Moshe kept to the right side of the vault as it divided and drew towards the mouth of the Hulda Gates. Both men slipped their sandals back on hurriedly and clutched the hilts of their swords as they inched along the wall into the pale moonlight streaked upon the courtyard before them. Flickering flames of torches lined the colonnades as far as the eye could see, and Adam gestured for Moshe to crouch low as he surveyed the plaza.

Adam stared at the dark, sleeping mounds of snoring men scattered around dozens of dying cooking fires and felt a flicker of hope wane within his soul at the scene. He could make out a number of guards patrolling the ramparts above the walls and lights glowing from the inner sanctuary against the Temple which rose up from the vast stone platform like a white mountain capped in gold. A crow cawed somewhere in the darkness and the flames of a cooking fire nearby cracked as they devoured what logs remained, sending up a few floating sparks into the air that sizzled before they touched the stones.

"Do you know where Judah is even held?" Moshe whispered, as he kept to the comfort of the dark shadows.

"Someone is bound to know."

"You plan on asking one of the guards? Are you mad? If we get caught, I don't..."

"I understand all too well," Adam interrupted. "This is the only way. We pretend to be Zealots or soldiers of Simon and keep to the shadows. Besides, none of the guards would expect us to suddenly appear."

"What if they don't know? Once dawn strikes we will be found."

"We stay in the cover of the colonnades and hide. There are places to go where the eyes of men shall not fall upon us, Moshe." Adam synched his belt tighter about his waist and adjusted the scabbard of his sword so it hung comfortably.

"We don't even know when we can set him free. What if we are up here for days?" Moshe groaned as he covered his face. He had not even considered being trapped on the Temple Mount. With few places to hide for long durations of time, they were bound to be discovered and have their throats slit.

Adam laid a heavy hand upon Moshe's shoulder and shook the young man until his eyes met his. "God will preserve us and protect us. We seek a righteous end, Moshe. Judah does not deserve such treatment, and if we do not try, he will die in vain." Adam breathed in the cool air that was scented with the smell of burning wood. He glanced out into the Temple court and shook his head. "The city doesn't have much time left, Moshe. I can feel it."

"What do you mean?"

"The Romans will breach the walls soon, and when they do, the Temple will burn."

A startled and wordless expression gripped Moshe as he considered this horrible fate. The strength he had always known seemed to melt away as emotion stirred and welled within him. He stared blankly at the Temple, wishing it would uproot itself and hide. He could hardly imagine the land without it or what the Jewish people in Judea and the surrounding regions would do.

Without the Temple they could not perform the sacrifices and libations, honour God the way they knew how, send tithes from abroad, or have a functioning priesthood. The Temple was the very centre of their expression of faith, love and worship for God. All Jews revered the holiness of the mountain known as Zion or Moriah, and journeyed from all corners of the empire to celebrate *Purim, Pesach, Shavuot, Rosh Hashanah, Yom Kippur, Sukkot*, and *Hanukah*. The Temple represented the light of Torah which God had given to his people, and for Moshe, he could not see a world without it. The Jews had recovered centuries ago when the First Temple had been destroyed by the Babylonians. Later, Cyrus the King of Persia had allowed it to be rebuilt. But could the Jews survive a second destruction, another displacement and scattering?

"You believe the Romans will burn the Temple?" Moshe finally said in a meek voice.

Adam stared at the man with his great bearded face and gave a silent nod. Then he stood like a giant and jerked his head for Moshe to collect himself and be ready to move out. Adam spotted a guard strolling nearby and desired to question him. Both men set out again, this time at a brisk walk so as not to draw suspicion. They neared the sleepy guard who straightened when he noticed the approaching strangers, and firmly clutched the shaft of his spear.

"*Shalom aleichem*, my brother," Adam called out with a friendly hushed tone to the guard, as not to wake the sleeping men near him.

"*Aleichem shalom*, to you on this dreary night," replied the sentry. He shifted his gaze to Moshe and gave him a firm nod of greeting, than his eyes narrowed with stern duty. "Who are you two? I don't know you."

"We were sent by Simon to inquire about the prisoner," Adam responded without a pause.

"What prisoner?"

"The traitor, Judah ben Yosef, of course. Are there others?"

The guard smiled. "Depends who you talk to, really. We got a number of royal treasonous dogs in dungeons, but they are all in the Ophel and Herod's Palace. Judah is the only one kept up here. Why do you ask?" The guard glanced suspiciously at the two men, then spit upon the ground behind him.

"Simon wants to know of the prisoner's health and if he is up for execution soon." Adam saw the guard's eyes squint as he moved his jaw about with curiosity. "He wants the dog judged and killed for his crimes!" Adam added, watching the sentry's face lighten with a sense of humour.

"Well, even many of John's men wish for such an outcome. The sod sold us out to the Romans…at least that is the word. Anyway, you can't see him. Strict orders by John! There are only a handful of guards sent to keep watch, and you're not one of them! John is the only one allowed to question the traitor. Sorry to disappoint you! Now you can leave! We are through."

"Well, how do we even know you speak the truth?" Adam said quickly as the guard shot him a glare of annoyance. "I mean, Simon says that John is weak and refuses to execute Judah. What word should we give to Simon? How do we know you haven't just released the bastard?"

"He's in a bloody jail!"

Adam stepped closer to the guard and stared in his face. "You expect me to believe your little jest. Simon sends us to see the treasonous spy, and we are barred from our duty? This is madness! John hasn't even told Simon where Judah is even kept! And there is supposed to be a pact of peace between the two? Outrageous! With the Romans at our gates, I have never seen or heard such appalling cowardice in my life. You have to give me something before I return to my master or else I shall bring Bagdatus here. I cannot return empty handed."

"He's in a vestment vault, damn you!" the guard said gritting his teeth and seething with anger. "I cannot show you him, but send word to your Sicarii King that he is in a dungeon below the Temple. There is a passageway that leads to the underground vault through the Chamber of Hewn Stone! He's down there! Now leave me alone, you filth!" The guard swore with a growl, swung around and stomped away causing a few men to stir nearby.

Adam faced Moshe silently, yet the exhilarating grin said it all. He led Moshe quickly back towards the south, and when they were sure the guard had moved on, they turned and scurried to the high porticoes of the eastern colonnades. There they hid quietly behind the pillars and breathed a sigh of relief. Moshe wiped the sweat from his forehead and continued to shake his head at Adam who had made the most daring move he had ever seen.

"So, now that we know where he is, how do we get him out?" Moshe pried, feeling strength restored to his muscles.

Adam ran one of his hands through his hair. "We have to wait as long as we can. How everything has been happening I don't think we have much time. Our best chance will be when chaos breaks out and the Roman pressure is so terrible everyone is called to defend the Temple. God will reveal it to us when that moment has come. We will have to move quickly and be ready for anything. There is a chance that we may meet resistance that will need to be dealt with."

"You mean kill Zealots?"

Adam nodded. "We cannot tarry or hesitate. If we do, we are both dead men and Judah is too. Once we're past the guards we should be able to break Judah free."

"And go where?"

Adam was still for a lingering moment. He leaned back against the pillar nearest to him and slid down to crouch upon the flagstones. He drew his dagger, stared at the blade for a few seconds and then softly said, "We will escape the city through the sewers. The Romans can't know they exist, and if they do, they will have nobody who will know their way around. Once out of the city we can flee to Beit Ani. There will be time to do so for the whole Roman army will be committed to destroy Jerusalem."

"Abandon Jerusalem?"

"It is gone, Moshe. There is no saving Jerusalem now. We can only save ourselves. I will not force you to leave, but if you stay you will die here and be forgotten. Or you can leave with Judah and I and we can all rebuild what is left of our shattered lives."

"What if Judah doesn't want to live, Adam?"

"Then I shall give him a holy kiss, depart this madness, and flee to Pella to rejoin my brothers and sisters in the faith."

Ruins of the Fortress Antonia
One hour before midnight

"You have been silent. You have barely uttered a word. Well, come now, what do you foresee, Praefectus Castrorum?" Marcus asked, glancing at Gaius as he strolled along next to his friend.

Gaius navigated around a large stone, split through the middle, and cast his eyes wayward across the rubble of the destroyed fortress. He shook his head with a blank expression and then stared at the high earthen ramp that stretched up to the burnt colonnades of the northwestern walls. "What is there to foresee? Titus has ordered the palisade." Gaius slipped back into his silent rendition as he shrugged and recalled the lively discussion throughout the war council they had just departed from.

Titus' quarters had been packed by generals, kings, and officers of every rank as final orders were distributed and outlined carefully with precision. The Prince had been filled with hope for what he deemed as the final stroke of the siege, and everyone knew his strategy was direct, yet brutal.

"Surely you have an educated opinion of the matter?" Marcus queried with a testy garble as he scowled in the night and gazed up at the scattered Jewish sentries observing them.

"It will be very bloody and hopeless."

Marcus glanced at his friend with a puzzled, bewildered expression. "Why do you say that? We have stormed cities in such a way before."

"We have never faced such ferocious enemies before, Marcus. We have cornered them against the most precious thing they revere in this life. They will fight like Hercules. True, we have seen victory through palisades, but you know a palisade is *always* a bloody affair."

"So what would you suggest?"

"Either pound the weakened colonnades into ruin and make a wide breach or fire the gates." Gaius halted and took a deep breath of night air. "I can feel it."

"Feel what?"

"It's almost over." Gaius wrapped himself in the comfort of his sagum, as if he was cold, and stood still like an erect statue pondering the future that lay before him.

"When this is over, will you stay with the Twelfth or return to *Roma*?" Marcus asked inquisitively.

A gentle smile appeared on Gaius' face and then he gazed up into the starry sky. "I would like to return, but I have one year left until I can muster out. I will request a leave to see my family. It has been so long since I took in the scent of Livia's hair and felt the warmth of her skin next to mine. And to see my daughters will be a delight to a father's eyes."

"You have never told me their names?"

"Drusilla, Camilla, and Leta. They are granted beauty from Venus, I dare say. Drusilla is old enough to have boys chasing her." Gaius wiped his forehead and sighed. "I have not seen them in nearly five years, Marcus. Should they not know their father when he returns, my heart will break."

"They will know you; your wife will have never let your memory die. You are a good man, Gaius Cornelius Antony. The gods have been merciful to you. When so many others have died, you have been spared thus far."

"Well, it is not over yet, Tribune." Gaius' grin widened when Marcus chuckled. "And will Titus let you retire to your villa with Hadassah?"

"Yes, but with strings attached, my dear Gaius. The Prince told me not to get too comfortable for he may call on me in due time. But yes, if the gods shall keep me from the sword until Jerusalem is dealt with, then I shall return to my villa and have a proper ceremony to wed Hadassah." Marcus' face lit up and he lowered his voice, "She is the most beautiful woman I have ever known, Gaius."

"Truly?"

Marcus hastily nodded. "She will be the queen of my estate."

Both men found peace in silence as they watched the Roman sentries patrol past them while studying the distant Jewish ramparts. The air was rife with tension as every guard's face seemed to betray a sense that the end was approaching.

Finally, Gaius gently bent down and scooped up a handful of dark soil. He held it in his open hand, staring down as he studied its temperature and texture. Then he lightly let some of it trickle through his fingers and he whispered, "For Julianus." A little more fell from his hand and he said, "For Publius." Then he let everything else spill upon the ground with a soft pattering sound and he said, "And for the thousands we have lost since the war. All shall be burned upon pyres and their ashes scattered to the wind."

Marcus bowed his head and humbly added, "Charon the ferryman has been in the best of company upon the river Styx."

Gaius nodded with a distant and sorrowful gaze into the black sky. "While Cerberus guards the gates of the underworld so that none shall escape the watch of Pluto." Gaius paused, then softly muttered, thinking of Judah, "Yet Capito can wallow in the gloom of *Tartarus* in that dungeon of torment and suffering where murderers and thieves dwell."

*   *   *

CHAPTER LVIII

July 29th, 70 A.D. / 5th of Av, 3830
Temple Mount
Near the Northern Colonnades
Morning

The soldier halted and stooped low next to the sleeping giant of John ben Levi, curled up and covered by his thick outer cloak. The soldier's face was flushed with heat as droplets of sweat gathered in his beard. He gently shook John's shoulder and said, "John, you must wake!"

John stirred with a groan and his eyelids cracked open as he collected his thoughts from his blurred, hazy vision. When the soldier's face came clearly into view, John sensed the urgency and bolted upright, casting off his cloak as he instinctively reached for his sword. "What is the matter, Eli?"

"The Romans did not bring up the rams this morning, John." Eli sat back with intense eyes and gripped the shaft of his spear.

"What?"

"Their rams sit at the bottom of the ramp, deserted." Eli glanced back uneasily at the charred colonnades and felt a sudden chill descend upon his spine.

"Is there any movement?"

"We could not see anything, but a fog still clings to the Bezetha. It is a thick haze which has disturbed many of the men."

John scrambled to his feet and tightened his belt. His stomach churned, yet he knew little food existed to calm it. He gathered up his spear and tested the balance of the ash wood shaft in his hand. Then he inspected the iron head and analysed its strength as he felt the edge of the cold steel. His mind raced with possibilities, and for a moment he stilled himself, holding his breath as he listened. Nothing could be heard except the sounds of doves cooing from their perches high up within the porticos surrounding the Temple. "They are so close to us, Eli. We can practically smell their breath when they approach the walls."

"It is true."

John handed the soldier his spear and grabbed his helmet. He pulled it firmly into place as he tied the chin strap. "They have no reason to quit now. How many days have they been pounding at the colonnades?"

"Two."

John scratched his chin hastily and retrieved his spear. "This is not over, Eli. They have not brought up the rams this day because Titus will try something else."

"What?"

"That is for us to find out! Quickly now, have the trumpeter sound the alarm to rally the troops. Have everyone converge on the northwestern colonnades now!" John suddenly bolted into a run as his heart pounded. Everything seemed to focus in his mind. The only logical, sensible reason for the rams not being brought up was that Titus had realised the futility in trying to crumble the walls. Even in their weakened state the colonnades were still incredibly strong and could withstand constant pounding for weeks. It was already the fifth of Av, and John knew that winter would swiftly descend upon the land in three months where Titus would not be able to properly extend the siege.

Winter was a time of dust storms, freezing torrential rains, and bitter cold, unpredictable weather that would make the conditions for the invading legions unbearable. Still, much of the city lay in Jewish hands, and if the Prince of Rome was to ensure its destruction, he would have to act fast. If the Jews could hold out until winter, the legions would be forced to call off the siege and retreat to their winter quarters. This would be a gift from the Almighty, and many pious Jews prayed for such relief. John knew of Titus' desperation, he could sense it, as if it were infused in his very bones. He knew that Titus would resort to anything, no matter how brutal and costly it may be for his own troops. In this understanding, John could only beg God to spare them and wreak havoc upon the legions with so much death that the enemy forces would be kept at bay.

As John reached the northwestern end of the Temple plateau, shouts of panic began to echo from the high walls as guards hollered and cried out. John reached the colonnades and easily cleared the steps up to the ramparts as trumpets and shofar'ot boomed, followed by the sound of trampling feet as thousands of Zealots rushed with weapons to defend the walls. The large warrior from Gischala caught his breath as he moved between clusters of guards and stared with trepidation at the waves of legionaries rushing forward up the steep ramp with ladders.

A sudden discharge of stone and iron missiles from the Roman catapults blasted the Jewish parapets with a deep resonating crescendo that shook the entire colonnade. Men howled in agony as they were flung high up into the air in mangled, bloody contortions while stone shrapnel cut flesh and shattered limbs. As a steady flow of Zealot reinforcements began to flood the ramparts, arrows struck their victims as volley after volley were shot above the advancing legionaries from the hundreds of Palmyrene and Syrian bowmen who were positioned near the Antonia's rubble in a thick line.

Frightened men recoiled as their comrades wailed and moaned from the deadly shower of arrows. Men stumbled to the edge of the ramparts, gripping the shafts of bolts buried deep into their flesh, only to plunge off the high walls into the courtyard below which was littered with bodies. As the legionaries reached the base of the wall, with hundreds of shields overlapping their heads like a tortoise, John finally managed to assemble his own bowmen who began to rain down a steady stream of missiles of their own. The scorpions and catapults, which still remained in Jewish possession, were fired into the ranks of Palmyrene archers as dozens reeled back in bloody swathes.

"They're coming up!" screamed a Zealot as the legionaries slammed ladders against the stone walls and began to scale them quickly.

"Make ready!" John bellowed as a pilum sailed by his face, causing him to flinch and take a step back. A man next to him shrieked horribly as another spear impaled itself through his chest, shattering ribs and causing a jet of blood to spurt from the wound. John moved to the side as the dying man swayed and then gave a choked gurgle as an arrow pierced his throat, spraying blood onto John's face. A Zealot nearby quickly pulled the dead man back and dragged him away as John winced from the warm blood that stained the corners of his eyes. He grunted and gave a furious shout as he snapped his shield up and felt it jar with the sudden impact of an arrow.

"Kill the bastards!" John yelled like a madman, at the sight of the first legionary who appeared above the wall. The Roman had eyes like fire and an expression of rage as John fought against the terror which consumed his being as he pushed himself up, attempting to raise his gladius.

The ranks of the Zealots were bloody and covered in sweat, yet the anger within their souls was like nothing they had ever known. At the sight of the legionary, one Zealot leapt forward, and with a broad stroke, severed the Roman's head clean from his shoulders. Blood erupted like a volcano and the Zealot delivered an array of maddened curses at the sight of the headless corpse as it fell backwards. The entire rampart of Zealots boomed with fury as more legionaries began to struggle upward and breach the parapets. But for every Roman who would emerge, there would be a Zealot who would lunge forward with an eager sword or spear to send the vulnerable legionary hurling from the ladder with screams and blood spraying through the air like a shower upon the thick ranks below.

"Spare no one!" John shouted, knowing the Roman archers could not respond to the slaughter upon the walls out of fear that they would strike their own troops. "Kill them all!"

The Zealots pushed forward to the edge of the parapets with their shields sensing their triumph against the reluctant Romans who began to hesitantly climb the ladders, their courage evaporating at the sight of the legionary corpses that covered the ground.

"Push them over! Push the ladders from the walls!" John ordered as Zealots soon began reaching between the parapets with sturdy beams of wood to lock against the heavy ladders and push them away. Frantic screams rose up in high pitched echoes as legionaries fell upon the overlapped shields of their comrades, crashing through the flimsy roof. Stones were carried to the parapets and hurled from the ramparts into the tangle of legionaries below as shields shattered and men were crushed. The Roman wounded had nowhere to go in the chaos, and soon men could be seen trying to crawl back or slide down the steep sides of the ramp, leaving behind gruesome trails of blood streaked through the soil. The Zealots refused to let up, and to their delight at the sight of the Roman wounded, they began to hurl spears, rocks, and shoot arrows at the men who cried out and horribly died, their battered, mutilated bodies scattered across the edges of the ramp and debris.

John felt emboldened. Had God finally delivered the Romans into their hands? Had God caused Titus to go insane and send his troops to be killed in droves by the thousands? He prayed it was so. Not one legionary had even set foot upon the ramparts, yet the piles of bodies below attested to the great slaughter they had endured. John ordered the scorpions to reload and his archers to begin pelting the distant Roman bowmen. He grinned as he envisioned another victory to be notched upon his war belt. The legion ranks stretched the entire length of the ramp and could be seen mustered into dozens of rectangular formations beyond. He could make out the different insignia of at least three legions upon the thousands of shields facing him, and he stared at the golden eagles which remained hoisted above the endless ranks.

Beyond the rows of legionaries, John watched as a formation of mounted troops assembled and he could make out Titus upon a black warhorse. John cringed at the sight of his greatest enemy and glowered with anger. He imagined himself leaping down upon the roof of shields below and charging forward to kill the arrogant, proud Prince. The bloody fantasy gave him some comfort, and he surveyed the grisly scene of red-streaked parapets with a grin.

"John, we are holding!" shouted Eli, who made his way over to the warlord.

"We could hold them like this until Meshiach comes," John commented. He paused, seeing a wide gap in the Roman horde below. He threw his spear with a mighty grunt and swore when a legionary's scutum took the blow.

"They have to retire soon," Eli said, ducking as an arrow tore past him. "Their archers are good."

"School children, they are. Whelps without their manhood!" John watched with allure as another legionary was killed trying to scramble up between the parapets. "We will smite their cohorts here. Titus can do nothing to harm us."

"John, look! Something is happening!" Eli quickly pointed out as the Palmyrene and Syrian bowmen suddenly dashed forward to the base of the ramp.

"Pull back for cover!" John shouted, but it was pointless above the din as the first volley tore the front Zealot rank to pieces. John watched countless men pitch back in bloody heaps as some fell between the parapets to the stones below. The volley was deadly, and he saw the long archer ranks fit their bows with another wall of barbed steel.

"Get back!" John bellowed as Zealots began to duck and cower following the second volley of iron that reduced bold men into agonizing, pitiful, shrieking boys.

Soon the wounded Zealots were pulled and dragged from the mounds of dead across the stones of the ramparts that were slick with sticky blood.

The air reeked and was foul with death. Everywhere calls and cries from the wounded blended with shouts of anger and orders as Zealots gathered upon the edges of the ramparts in ranks four-men-deep to escape the hellish ordeal from the Roman archers. The Jewish fighters were relieved to be out of sight from the keen eyes of the Palmyrenes and many wept at the amount of dead piled before them along the parapets. However, soon John began to pace up and down the cowering ranks shouting for them to be brave and meet the Roman attack that was sure to come. He knew that once the legionaries began to crest the wall, the eager Roman archers would have to fall back and wait as the battle warred on. John used every descriptive word he could think of to assemble his men and imbue courage and tenacity within their souls. He called on them to be honourable Jews, worthy of defending the Temple, that God was only testing them in this great hour, to see their resolve and dedication.

John rejoined the ranks and gritted his teeth. His body was drenched in sweat and stained with blood. He could not let anything distract him now, not even the horrid sight of the tangled bodies of his fallen brethren lying before him. He knew he must become a savage beast without feeling, emotion, and soul. John listened to the steady boom of voices that rose up towards them from the Romans as they began to shout and jeer. Then he saw the plume of a helmet rise above the stone parapets before him with a menacing face of steel, and John raised his sword, screaming at the top of his lungs, "Men, we defend the Temple! Should you run now when you are needed most?" With a thunderous cry John dashed forward as legionaries began to drop upon the ramparts and form a loose line.

The Zealot soldiers followed John as they collided with a crunch of steel and wood. The bitter sounds of the struggling men reverberated above the clash as blood ran over the edge of the ramparts and bodies fell. The Romans heaved and pushed against the Jewish ranks, but were unable to gain a foothold as they began to thin. The Zealots howled like dogs and thrust their spears in endless motions as legionaries were reduced to forms of shredded flesh upon the walkways. More legionaries ascended the ladders from behind and tried to reinforce the attack, yet their elation and hope for victory was snatched away like a feather fluttering through the air only to get blown by a sudden gust of wind.

At the front, John pressed through the ranks to face off with a centurion who now stood in a pool of blood with four cleaved bodies lying at his feet. The centurion's face was wild, like John's, and he screamed a challenge at the warlord from Gischala as both men closed in upon each other. John roared like a beast and brought down his sword, hoping to crush the centurion's head. But the Roman reacted with a smooth professionalism as he parried the blow and drove a clenched fist into John's jaw which rattled his head with the impact. John stumbled back with a stream of blood and broken teeth and the centurion hollered with victory as he pushed forward with his gladius stained red.

John knew the centurion had bested him and now closed in with speed to make the kill, and for a moment, John felt a sudden rush of vulnerability. But in the last possible instant, a spear thrust out across John's vision and impaled the centurion under his raised arm. The centurion shuddered with bulging eyes, gasped in misery, and crumpled over the shaft of the spear as if defeated. Then, refusing to give up, the Roman grabbed the spear and attempted to wrench it out of the Zealot's grasp, as blood ran from his wound. John straightened, seeing the end of his enemy. He gave a great bellow, gripped his sword with both hands, swung the blade with his massive, flexed muscles, and cut off the centurion's head. John watched apathetically as the corpse convulsed, then fell sideways into the ruinous heap of bodies strewn about.

*   *   *

"You two, come with me!" shouted a burly Zealot officer at two soldiers he spotted keeping out of sight behind the portico columns. "You cowards come with me, now!" The officer glared at the men, his face glistening with sweat and speckled in blood. His eyes were red, cheeks thin, and possessed peeled lips which begged for water. Exhaustion was worn upon the lines and creases of his drooping face as a haggard edge of tense fear gripped him. His skin was weathered and bore two long scars that crossed over one another, intersecting at the bridge of his nose and disappearing under the head covering he wore.

Adam and Moshe looked worriedly at one another as they rose, gathering their weapons under the watchful eye of the officer. "Where are we going?" Adam said, deliberately not making eye contact with the furious man.

"If you didn't know, there is a battle being fought! No need to shrink away and hide. If the Romans come through, there will be no place to run but to the Lower City." The officer swore at the thought and spit upon the flagstones. "Now, get a move on it. There are wounded to see to and dead to be cleared."

Adam and Moshe hesitated for a moment, pondering the possibility of someone recognizing them, then gave in and followed the officer into the morning air as noon approached. The heavy sound of fighting continued as the noise carried throughout the Outer Court. A cluster of forty soldiers stood nearby, assembled into a quiet host as they observed bleeding men scattered throughout the vast plaza, stumbling to the south as they passed by. The officer gave a sharp gesture for Adam and Moshe to join the soldiers as he counted their numbers. Afterward, he gave a pleasing nod, than shifted the heavy belt upon his waist which was being forced down by his bulging gut.

"You men are to clear the ramparts of dead and wounded," barked the officer. "The Romans are still trying to breach our walls and our ranks need space above. The dead are to be stacked below for now and the wounded are to be carried to the Royal Stoa to be tended to."

"What of men who will not live through the day?" asked a timid soldier as a few heads nodded in agreement.

"We don't have time to pick through the wounded," the officer growled. "Everyone with breath in their lungs goes to the Royal Stoa, so do not tarry. It is up to HaShem if they are to live throughout the day. Understood? Now go!"

*   *   *

Below the Northwestern Colonnades
Noon

Titus drew on the reins of Achilles and halted next to the earthen mounds piled on the streets of the Bezetha. He stared coldly at the rows of scorpions and onagri, gave a firm nod to himself, then turned and glanced at Tiberius Alexander. "Use fire missiles. Hurl everything we have. Have artillery commanders concentrate on the colonnades. Move the archers around to fire the western gates. We'll let it burn throughout the night." He hesitated as he watched over a hundred legionaries picking through the dead along the ramp, unmolested from the sparse Jewish defences above. A sense of quaint solitude seemed to collect around the blood stains soaked into the soil of the ramp as bodies were dragged away to be piled into carts.

Titus stared with a pause of emptiness at the sight of the wounded as they were untangled from the corpses that lay over them. Finally, the Prince cleared his throat and his heavy eyes fell upon his second-in-command. "Collect what dead you can. I think I shall retire for the day and hold council tomorrow three hours past dawn."

"Yes, my Prince," Tiberius said, striking his chest in salute.

"Have the army drawn up at dusk and double the guard to keep watch. By the power of Jupiter we shall see this finished." Titus veered away accompanied by his personal guard and Tiberius watched him for a moment with the other legionary generals patiently waiting behind. Once the Prince was out of earshot, Tiberius stared at Larcius and the others. "It was a bloody disaster. The Jews are defiant."

"Wouldn't *you* be if *Roma* was threatened," Larcius replied as he removed his stifling helmet.

"We should respond immediately," Sextus spoke as he walked his mount up to Tiberius. "The Jews cannot have time to celebrate this victory." He glanced back at the exhausted columns of withdrawing legionaries, then grimaced at the bloody landscape and shattered ladders below the colonnades. "Barbarians," Sextus grumbled as he stared at the severed head of a centurion, still wearing his helmet, thrust upon a pike and attached to the parapets.

"Our response will be deadly and sudden," Tiberius vowed.

"There could be thousands of rebels crammed beyond the colonnade walls. Titus wants us to pound them into dust?" Marcus Octavian asked as he approached.

"He wants the gates and colonnades burning. That is what we will concentrate on," Tiberius replied to the hardened officers.

"We should send a few of the larger missiles at their Temple. It may bring about a shift in the wind, if you hear me," Larcius said as he shook his head. "Damned waste of troops attempting that palisade. The Jews slaughtered our lads. Titus can't do that again, the men will never forgive him."

"The Prince ordered it and we do not question his judgment. Let that be a reminder to your tongue the next time you consider speaking. You know as well as any general here that seeing what options we have is important, Larcius. We cannot afford rash decisions," Tiberius firmly replied. "The men are legionaries, not some bloody volunteer army like the legio once was, they are trained and professional and casualties are expected in any conflict."

"Spare me your lectures, Tiberius," Larcius vented in a low growl as his blood-shot eyes and sunken cheeks revealed the extent of his exhaustion.

"You shall hear my lectures, Larcius, and I pray to Minerva that you honour them. It seems your mind has become idle these past months. I am still second-in-command," Tiberius stated as he looked at the other generals. "Maintain your prudence and caution in the presence of high authority, especially these days. Keep your objections to yourselves. Titus is weighed down and we shouldn't seek to set him off."

"Granted, but now I have to see what new optiones and centurions need to be replaced that were killed today." Larcius gestured at the head and gave a sour look.

"Looks like one of yours, Marcus," Sextus added, acknowledging the bloodied and splintered shield that was hung over the side. He swore and shook his head at the sight of a Zealot who stood on the parapet and began to urinate on the scutum.

"When we burn their Temple they will be begging like whores for us to cease!" Marcus Octavian vehemently spewed with anger.

"That has not been decided," Tiberius replied. He tapped his boot heels into the flanks of his mount and rode to the nearest onager positioned upon a mound of packed soil. The generals, still sulking with harsh words about the failed attack, followed Tiberius who surveyed the artillery lines and inspected their armaments.

Each siege-craft had been elevated upon a ballistae platform and surrounded by wicker hurdles dug deep into the ground. Every hurdle was bound and tethered by lengths of rope to ensure maximum strength to provide protection for each machine's ballistarii crew as they loaded and fired their weapons. Behind the furthest row of catapults, Tiberius observed hundreds of wagons and carts aligned in long columns which had been used to bring up ammunitions in great numbers. To the right of the carts stood herds of pack animals tied together in clusters, overseen by a host of servants and slaves.

The onager was the pride of the legions siege-craft. Each machine could be manoeuvred easily into place as its wide body sat upon four wheels, operated by three experienced men: two to load the weapon and crank it back, the third to sight the target. The onager was the smallest of the Roman catapults, and had received its name from the inspiration of a kicking donkey, for when it fired, it would leap up with a sudden thud as the machine's arm smashed into a thick, padded cushion angled at the front to absorb the blow. Once the arm had made contact, the leather sling at the far end would hurl the projectile with incredible speed.

At the rear of the onager was a cross beam with chiseled notches circumventing the width of the beam. In the centre of the beam, a thick coil of rope was attached to the arm, so that when the crew cranked the beam downward, by sliding a pole into each notch, the rope would lower the arm until it was at the preferred setting. Then with a simple jerk of the cord that held the clamped pin in place, the weapon would jolt forward firing its stone missile.

For every fourth onagri stood a scorpion, its body propped up by four wooden legs at the front, and two long beams stretching out behind to stabilize it. Next to the scorpion platforms were orderly piles of small round stones, and long iron javelins that appeared like arrows. The scorpion resembled a large crossbow, and served its deadly purpose of accurately reducing an organized enemy into a bloody mess. Once loaded, the powerful cord of the scorpion's bow could be drawn back by two wooden poled wheels at the rear of the engine and then fired.

Tiberius walked his horse past the second row of engines and halted as he stared at the largest of the Roman catapults. He leaned forward and scratched his chin while scanning the row of engines. A stout artillery officer noticed the staff of weary generals and approached Tiberius. The officer's face was dirty as his chin sprouted at least three day's growth. A signifer accompanied him carrying the standard of the Fretensis and he looked nearly twenty years younger, as his face appeared barely capable of growing anything and his voice cracked when he saluted, announcing his represented legion.

Sweat dripped from the officer's nose as he squinted up at Tiberius. "What does his Prince desire us to do? Shall we pound the colonnades until there is nothing left?"

"He wants them fired! Burn the walls, ensure you miss nothing. I want them blazing with such fury that not a single Jew will be able to approach them from the heat. Also, fire the gates on the west," Tiberius replied in a flat tone.

The officer gave a sharp nod and stared out at the bodies strewn upon the ramp. "We can soak our missiles in pitch and ignite them. We also have earthen vessels that can burn within once fire is set to the fuse. Those will explode into a shower of flaming debris. The pitch sticks and runs, all the while on fire, and it burns very hot. Anything capable of burning will be consumed. The roofs of the colonnades underneath have to be supported by timber as well as pillars; those will burn and the stone will crack and weaken." The officer sighed as sweat streamed down the sides of his face. "The gates will not be a problem. Use archers for those and enough of them so the Jews can't do a thing about it. I can send orders to the Palmyrenes to form up and make ready. Fire-arrows will work well. Shoot them into the gates and watch them burn. It might take six hours or more, but they will become charred timber over night."

"Once you are ready, proceed. Titus wants this resolved by morning and expects it. You are in command now."

"I will serve, General. By morning, I swear unto Mars that the colonnades will be smouldering ruins and the way into the Temple will be before you. For the glory of *Roma* we will end this soon." The officer gave a humble bow, then jogged back to the catapult line and started to bark out orders as crews scrambled to reload the engines.

Tiberius watched the missiles ignite with roaring flames, feeling an odd comfort at the menacing sight and destructive nature of the Roman siege-craft. He observed the quick calculations of the crews as they cranked the catapult arms into place and called out their marks with precision. At the sudden thunder clap felt throughout the flagstones from the catapults firing, Tiberius held his breath and watched the sky become streaked with flaming missiles that trailed with incredible speed at the vulnerable colonnades. As explosions of shrapnel and balls of fire consumed the walls, engulfing them in putrid, black smoke, Tiberius knew that what the officer had said would soon come to pass. According to Tiberius, it was as if Jerusalem teetered upon the edge of a cliff, with a swirling abyss below, and all that needed to be done now was to give it a little push.

*   *   *

CHAPTER LIX

July 30th, 70 A.D. / 6th of Av, 3830
Camp of the Assyrians
Quarters of Prince Titus Flavius Vespasianus
Three hours past dawn

When the light finally divided the sky and chased away all signs of night, a thick blanket of choking grey smoke hung like a haze over Jerusalem. What had once been bustling streets, markets crammed with merchants, or large villas of the city's aristocracy had now been shrouded by a haunting, grey residue which drifted through the dead air, enveloping the ruins of war. The fires upon the northwestern colonnades had burned all day and night. They roared with anger and ate everything in its path, like a gluttonous giant at a vast banquet table. The Jews had been unable to stifle the fires, helplessly watching their defence burn, along with the West Gate of the Temple Mount.

Hundreds of legionaries had been positioned just out of the fires reach to ensure the Zealots could not try anything. The bombardment had been cruel and devastating. Every catapult and onager that could be mustered, had fired volley after volley of flammable projectiles into the colonnades as they had smashed them into pieces and caved in whole sections until the remnants resembled that of a great white furnace.

Nearly two hundred archers had been sent to fire the West Gate, and after the second volley the jagged spikes of flame had risen so high the Zealot defenders on the ramparts above had been forced to vacate. Now, only petty flames continued to burn as smoke billowed up into the air dwarfing the Temple and stinging the eyes of the legionaries on guard. Endless cracks and pops echoed for hours while the walls smouldered. The odd sound of collapsing, charred timbers and split stone could be heard striking the flagstones of the Outer Court, a view concealed from the eager, vengeful Romans.

Yet, for the legions it was as if an oracle had spoken as they watched the mighty colonnades of the Temple burn. Men remembered the visions of Basilides, the oracles of Delphi, Carmel, and the signs of eagles, oxen, and snakes. Rumours of prophetic utterances stirred their hearts as men dreamed of the day when they would return to Rome in triumph, to march through the streets as men who had achieved immortality, even if only for a day. However, through all of this, the blessings of Jupiter, Mars, and Serapis went before them, refusing to dampen their spirits, even as two hundred more pyres were erected upon Scopus to send the souls of the dead past Cerberus into the company of Charon the ferryman.

Ahead of the expectation of victory, Titus assembled his staff of legionary generals, client kings, prefects, and leading officials. The air was tense, yet filled with great anticipation as the men congregated in the Prince's quarters on the eve of what they felt would be Jerusalem's final days. Only King Marcus Agrippa seemed distant among the men who had already begun to congratulate each other and elect themselves worthy of high standing once they returned to Rome.

After letting his officers savour the meal of victory to come, Titus held up a single hand and Tiberius called the men to silence. They instinctively assembled around a table covered with maps and a few faces held smug grins as their minds wandered back in time to when they had first arrived to Jerusalem. The city had been proud and daunting at that time, yet now was open, crippled, and vulnerable, like a beaten, neglected slave, quivering under the master's rod.

Sextus gave Titus' Nubian slave another suspicious glare and then brushed the foolish memory away; he would let go of any misdeeds he felt the black man was capable of. Sextus was a General of the Fifth Legion and in place to receive great reward for supporting the Flavian effort since the beginning. He had been a loyal patriot and servant of the Emperor and knew his reward would be just and full. The Nubian would vanish from his thoughts once the greatest dona ever imaginable was presented to him, and people would know of his name for centuries to come. Sextus Cerealis would be known as a man of Emperor Vespasian and a studious General to a Prince, who had driven his forces willingly into the mouth of Hades to achieve victory.

Titus eyed the proud generals and kings grouped around his table and sipped his wine. He caught the inquisitive glance of Gaius Antony and gave him a kind gesture. Marcus Sulla stood next to Gaius, and Titus gave the sturdy officer a brazen nod, spotting a flicker of pride flash across the Tribune's face. The room became quiet and the sounds of crickets filled their ears as the hidden insects chirped incessantly. Titus finished his wine and set the silver cup calmly upon the table. He noticed the Nubian in his peripheral move to refill the goblet and Titus waved him away with a bored expression. He rubbed his hands together and his eyes suddenly shone like the sun as he stared down at the maps.

"The fires still burn. Porcius tells me the Jews can't even come within thirty metres of the blaze due to the heat. That is good. The colonnades will be so weak they will crumble. We shall let them burn for a few more hours and then have engineers coordinate crews to extinguish what remains smouldering. The ramparts above are so unstable, and parts of the walls have crashed down into ruinous heaps. I want all debris cleared for the final assault on the Temple Mount." The words tasted like the sweetest wine upon his tongue, and Titus saw each man's eyes flicker, beckoning for revenge within their minds.

Once again, the iron might of Roma shall not be lightly tested. They provoked our arm, and we have crushed them and their God. What power upon this earth can even stand before our legions and the gods of Roma? Titus thought to himself. He grinned as he stared down at the map, seeing his conquest unfurl before him. The very thought was enticing and he entertained it for a split moment.

What he saw in his mind's eye were endless lines of Jewish prisoners, an entire city shackled together with chains and rope, their numbers so great that they would fill the Temple courts. Above the hopeless stares of the prisoners, the screams of hundreds of Zealots being crucified would echo from what remained of the colonnades. And he, a Prince of Rome seated upon his black warhorse with the Jewish Temple at his back, would have John of Gischala and Simon ben Giora grovel before him, chained together, and freshly whipped. They would be brought like dogs to beg for their lives to a master who would gaze down at them with disdain. Titus would only see the shells of men he hated and despised; they were neither human, nor deserving of servus.

Titus' mind returned to the order of the council before him and he glanced prudently at Tiberius. "General Alexander, do you have anything to add."

Tiberius gave a hasty nod and then cleared his throat as he clasped his wine goblet in his calloused hands. "Only to report, my Prince, that the entire northern colonnades have burned during the night up to the eastern corner. But the valley's bottom still faces a steep climb and ramparts that can be manned. Our attack will push through the western corner which we have concentrated on. We should be able to penetrate the Temple courts with a two-pronged attack through the western gate and over the crumbled colonnade walls. The Jews cannot defend either approach at the same time and will be forced to face us on even ground where we will prevail. Cohors will be able to spread out in line and file, and then plough the dogs over. The Zealots cannot face off against organized legionaries, thus our lads will get the best of them."

"They still have the Inner Temple itself," Agrippa interjected softly, causing all eyes to stare at him. "The Temple stands within a series of courts, each one with very large, thick gates which will not be easy to smash through. It would take a testudo a day or more. The Temple is also surrounded by high walls itself. These walls are fitted with ramparts and parapets which can be manned."

"A second fortress within a fortress," grumbled King Sohaemus. "Thousands of Jews can cram themselves within the Temple courts; they could resist for some time."

"Burn the Temple!" interrupted Titus Frigius.

"Absolutely not an option," Agrippa quickly said with a glare. He glanced at the Prince with a sympathetic, pleading stare. "This cannot be considered, my Prince. The Temple must be preserved. There are hundreds of thousands of loyal Jews of *Roma* living throughout the empire. What would they think if the Flavians burned their most holy place?"

"If they occupy the Temple and use it as a stronghold, we will have no choice," Gessius Florus spoke up candidly as he stood next to Cestius Gallus.

"Spare us your miserable tactics, Florus, you dog!" Agrippa lashed back angrily.

"They can't be spared because *Roma* fears to destroy their precious Temple," Florus continued as he stepped alongside the table and eyed Titus, ignoring the riled client king. "The Flavians are too proud and strong to care what the Jews of the empire might say. Besides if they are to be loyal subjects, they will shut their mouths and look away. Let them remember it was their kind that started this damned war in the first place. This is not a trivial matter for *Roma*, as she has lost sons in this war, thousands of them. The Flavians must avenge their memory and if so, the Temple, with all of the Zealots cowering within her walls, should be torched. Bury them in it and you have a great Jewish tomb. Saves us from tending to the dead and it spares the crows from getting too fat."

Titus watched Agrippa grimace at the image, then turn from the former procurator and wait for an answer. Titus looked to his other generals for a moment, then cleared his throat, as he chose his words wisely. "Though I do not need a lecture in the faith of my subjects or what the Flavians should or should not do, Gessius, I do see your wisdom in destroying the Temple if the Zealots do not capitulate once we hold the Mount. Those will be your orders you are to pass to all your centurions and optiones. My word is final and must be followed by your officers and passed throughout the cohors and every centuria. The Temple is to be spared any direct attention when we first breach the walls and push into the Outer Court. If the Zealots refuse to surrender and do occupy the Temple and Inner Court, then my hand may be forced. But for now, the Temple is to be spared. I will not incur unwanted wrath from their God on account that we destroy His Temple. Even if He is weaker than Jupiter, we still cannot underestimate His power for we do not know to what extent it stretches."

*   *   *

Marcus Sulla gave a sigh of relief as he stepped from Titus' tent following the war council. He picked up his step to catch up with Gaius, who remained peculiarly silent, as they exited the Camp of the Assyrians and headed east through the Bezetha. They passed rows of siege equipment, marching cohorts, noisy pack animals, and heard the cadence of clopping hooves upon the flagstones as a company of mounted troops rode by.

Smoke still stretched across the sky in layers as the familiar stench of charred timber burned both men's nostrils. Like snow, flakes of ash drifted upon the breeze and covered the ground. It was mesmerizing as both men watched the clumps of ash flutter and spiral towards them, only to rest upon their shoulders, catch in the plume hairs of their helmets, and become like powder under their feet. To their right, the fires continued to burn upon the colonnades and shut out any view of the Temple, as billows of black smoke stained the blue sky. The sight checked both men as they halted and stared at the destruction. A chill was felt in the air and the ground darkened with a shadow as the sun struggled to penetrate the choking haze.

"So, do you think he will order the Temple burned?" Marcus finally spoke up, cutting the silence.

Gaius sighed and flicked some of the ash from his shoulder. "He is the commander of the legions, so he can order what he wants."

"That is not what I asked, Gaius."

"Titus is unpredictable these days. Anything is possible." Gaius partially wrapped himself in his sagum as if it were a protective shield and then slowly resumed his walk.

"The Jews will have nowhere to go so they will have to flee to the Temple. Of course, Zealots in the southern part of the court could retreat, but I wager they will sell their lives dearly if they see legionaries stampeding towards their holy sight." Marcus sniffed and scratched his chin. "This smoke reminds me of a village we burned in the north. The rebels would not relinquish control. They had a poorly built wall of timber and loose stone; shambles is what it was. It wasn't very high and the Zealots were a mere rabble. They were a handful of survivors who escaped the sea battle. Anyway, we rode right at them with ropes and grappling hooks. We literally pulled their wall down. Orders were to spare no one. Another tribune, senior to me, was in charge."

Marcus grinned when Gaius gave him an insightful stare and he continued, "Well, I could not disregard the order, so we rode into the village and torched it. The senior tribune was the only casualty, after that I was to lead the Boars in sole command." Marcus paused and stared up at the smoke. "We spared nobody, Gaius. Everyone was put to the sword: men, women, and children; over three hundred people. We truly lost our souls that day."

"What was the name of the village?"

"Does it even matter? Anyway, I can't remember." A blank expression filled Marcus' face and he stared at the ground. "I wonder, even though I have Hadassah's love, if she will ever understand why I have done what I have done. Will she ever think less of me?"

"Her view of you as a Tribune of *Roma* will change in time, Marcus. It is duty that has driven us here, duty to *Roma*."

"That was not duty, Gaius, what I did in that village. We hunted terrified children, who had watched us murder their parents and tried to flee. We hunted them, boys and girls, into burning homes, into corners, where they were cowering and begging like frightened dogs, not knowing why we hated them, why we desired to harm them. I killed one myself." Marcus swallowed. "He pissed himself first and then screamed before I did it. I don't remember feeling a thing: no remorse, no mercy, and no soul." Tears formed along the rims of Marcus' eyes. "The boy could not have been more than eight years old. That was not duty, or the glory of *Roma*. We murdered them, Gaius. We spilled their blood and burned their village into ashes. Afterward we counted forty Zealots, out of three hundred dead."

Marcus shook his head in a sorrowful perplexed gaze. "We gave the tribune a funeral worthy of a great man. We said prayers, dined over his memory, and burned his pyre. We gathered his bones and placed them in a mausoleum that took four days to build. We hired a craftsman from Sepphoris to chisel the tribune's name and sculpt a picture of him upon a horse. Yet the dead of the village we left to rot in the open as a warning.

"We stuck the forty heads of the Zealots onto pikes on what remained of the walls. Then we rode away in high spirits, as if it had never happened. As if the memory of the murdered dead had ebbed away with the invisible wind. But one thing we could not ignore was the stench of smoke and the burning bodies." Marcus sniffed and his face hardened as a few trails of tears trickled down his cheeks. "We could smell the smoke for miles. For us Boars, I don't think that smell will ever leave us. We are cursed!

"Even years from now, when we sit in the comfort of our homes with our families and loved ones, and our wives stoke a fire and a waft of smoke rises, we will always remember that we are soulless men. I fear there is a realm of Hades waiting for us, a dark circle where we will be greeted by the dead we murdered that day, and they will say to us, "Drink with us, brothers, for we have waited for you for years." Marcus cleared his throat and wiped his eyes. "That is where Publius sits now, at the warm side of a hearth surrounded and comforted by the dead children he killed."

"I have never heard such things before spoken so true and with such regret," Gaius softly replied seeing the vulnerability in his friend's eyes. "Surely you will find peace, my brother. We have all done horrible things and seen such injustice. War never leaves a man innocent. He bears it with the memory and the nightmares his whole life."

"We are cursed, Gaius. I shall never know peace, even after death. The sight of those ghosts in Hades will stay with me forever. Often in my dreams I see them. Their faces are forever before me."

Marcus and Gaius continued to walk with no destination in mind as they passed the ruins of the Antonia and the loan tower that stood like a monument to attest to the devastation piled around it. They made their way slowly into the valley's bottom, following it for nearly a hundred metres until they halted and gazed up at the eastern corner of the colonnades and the Temple that rose above the walls. Jewish guards could be seen manning the ramparts, but none of them moved as they remained content to ignore the two wandering officers.

"It saddened me to hear of Marius. He was a good soldier and an elite leader," Marcus kindly said resting a hand of friendship upon Gaius' shoulder. "I heard from survivors that saw him fall, that he died with his sword in hand, facing off with John of Gischala."

"His death has shaken the Fortis Centuria, yet their resolve has not changed. They have sworn revenge upon the Zealots and John. They wish, during the attack on the colonnades, to reclaim Marius' body and head. A proper funeral will be given once he has been reclaimed."

"Good."

"I knew him when Cestius marched us here."

"Truly?"

Gaius nodded. "Princeps Marius Junius Livianus, a war dog of a man, crude, but a Roman of virtue. I will pray to his memory tonight, and grant him peace in the afterlife. He will join the hall of his ancestors. I know he has a living son whom I shall visit once I return to *Roma*." Gaius followed the great billows of smoke with his eyes, then turned and looked at Marcus with a sense of duty. He gave the Tribune a firm nod, and said, "Let us return to our quarters, my friend, and ready ourselves for the final stroke."

*   *   *

Noon
The Royal Stoa
Southern end of the Temple Mount

John had assembled every known commander among his ranks. One hundred and ninety men gathered with drawn faces and eyes gripped with fear. They tried to shut out the cries of the wounded as they lay in droves further to the east under the canopy of the beautiful roof above them. John paced before the cluster of silent officers, feeling dread upon his shoulders. He gazed at their faces, sensing their uneasiness and the unnerving reality of the danger that was soon to come upon them all.

John looked out from the shadow of the Royal Stoa and stared across the vast stone plaza to the rising smoke set behind the glistening Temple's marble body. The golden pinnacles of the edifice's stunning mantle reflected brilliantly as it always had. John felt his heart droop within his chest and his mind cloud with thoughts of apprehension towards the notion that Jerusalem may not be saved. That thought had always lingered within the recesses of his mind, yet John had never wanted to admit it. God had to come to their aid. They were *His* soldiers and fighting for freedom as Jews to worship and honour their God, unimpeded by Roman dictation. Would God ever allow Jerusalem to be destroyed? Could the purpose of HaShem ever be that the Temple, *His* Temple, be ruined again? Prophets had decreed judgment in the past when Israel waned from the Almighty's required standard of holiness among the nations, yet surely it could not happen a second time?

John pushed all disconcerting thoughts from his mind and cleared his throat with a gust of air. "Men, you have journeyed with me since this war began. Some of you stood by my side in Gischala; others survived the horrors of the cities and towns the Romans left behind, smouldering in ruins. But you have all survived. You have all gathered here in this city to defy the Romans publically and to watch as the armies of darkness rallied about to stamp out truth and light.

"I ask of you to give more. We have all lost so many brothers, seen our families driven out, scattered, and murdered. We have hardened our hearts and stood against an enemy that would have us live like animals unfit for freedom and liberty from their oppressive rule. We have suffered for our cause which has always remained righteous and holy. Our people have been purified through fire and steel, the useless molten cast aside and trampled by men. Our camp has been divided, and the best have emerged as loyal Jews, given the task from heaven to defend this City of Gold.

"I will not lie to you and tell you that you should think differently. Yes, it is true that HaShem has allowed the Romans to burn our colonnades and threaten the Temple. God has allowed the armies of evil to rally and surround us, to cut us off and starve us. But, my brothers, I am convinced these are tests of faith. This is a troubling time, like what the prophets spoke of. Dead religion and self-serving men have polluted our true faith and Torah. It has taken nearly four years for us to see this, to be brought to our knees in repentance and forsake our brethren who would rather lie in bed with the enemy then stand with God.

"You must see this now. The streets are quiet with the faithful who remain, ready to give their lives to protect this city. But, my comrades, officers, Zealots, brothers, and fellow Jews, we are alone. HaShem has finally turned the wicked heart of Simon from us for we are of the light. Simon has sought to shut himself up, like in the ancient city of Jericho in the days of Joshua ben Nun.

"Remember, the men of Jericho mocked and jeered the priests and armies of Israel as they marched around its perimeter carrying the Ark of God. The Israelite armies in formation marched seven times a day for seven days, and on the seventh, that day set apart, they blew the shofar'ot and watched God deliver the city into their hands.

"I tell you, on the day the Romans come upon us we shall stand firmly within this court and blow the trumpets and charge with the fury of Gideon!" John drove a fist into his open palm with a smack and scanned the host of silent Zealots. "Simon locks himself behind thick doors in Herod's Palace, pretending like there are lines drawn, borders made in the sand, between us and he. As if the Romans merely try to destroy us and then will parlay with him like he is some foreign king. Well, I say, let the viper remain coiled in cowardice within its nest of briers and thorns, for we, the Jews of the God of Israel, will prevail!"

Many of the officers voiced their support with shouts and nods while others kept silent, their faces transfixed with gloom. John studied each face, wishing he could shake their courage, yet he had not the will to force them. He paced before the men as they quieted and then jabbed a finger into the air and shouted, "Now, the Romans surely will come. Let us not expect them to offer terms in this moment. Titus will come with fury, but he is a pagan who follows a pantheon of unknown gods in the face of HaShem. What remains of the ramparts of the northern colonnades is of ill nature. Severely burned and damaged, it looks as if we have lost the colonnade's strength and position. Thus, manning the narrow walkways will be of little use as once the fires are stifled there will be little protection provided, and room only for a single line of fighters with nowhere to go, should they be overrun.

"It has been said that we should concentrate the remaining soldiers around the burnt gates and northwestern corner where the legionaries are sure to storm. But there is one flaw in this plan. Once the legionaries burst through, a stampede of panic is likely which would dissolve any hope in occupying this foothold. This would leave the Temple in their possession. Friends and brothers, the Temple is what we have defended and bled for; it is what we shall rally around." John paused as he folded his wide arms across his broad chest. He gazed at the men with piercing eyes, trying to weigh and calculate their morale and sense of courage.

"Some of you have muttered in weeks past that maybe the time has come to parlay and surrender, to spare the Temple." A few heads hung with shame as most of the men shouted against the notion and declared loyalty to the Zealot cause. "Some say," John continued, "That to give the Temple up and lay down our arms will save the city. But I say this: I would rather die gladly than to know that I had abandoned our sacred Temple into the hands of whores and swine! For them to set graven images within her porticos and busts of gods in her sanctuaries would be the same blasphemy as what this land experienced in the cruel days of Antiochus Epiphanes! A man called "God Manifest" sought to destroy our people and faith, setting himself up as a god! Should we think that the Romans would not seek such a thing? We must fight them, brothers, and slay their bodies even if it must be before the Temple and upon these sacred stones!"

"John! John!" shouted a guard who ran up to him as the officers nervously gripped the hilts of their swords. "Roman workers approach the colonnades and West Gate in the hundreds. They have tools and have begun to clear debris and squelch the flames!"

John looked back to his commanders and rubbed his forehead as he pondered the news. "They will come soon; we should expect them in the next day." He gave a heavy nod and whispered for the guard to return to his duty. He watched the sentry trot away and then reluctantly scanned the plaza before him as his breathing slowed. John suddenly felt his mind drift to Judah locked away in the dungeon and how he had banished Adam and Moshe. They were only three men, compared to his three thousand fighters, yet he knew that the Lions were ferocious warriors, capable of setting the enemy to flight. He felt his mind stir with thoughts of pardoning them, justifying to his officers why he would even make such a decision. However, it was an impossible dream. Judah had betrayed them and no matter how much John would like him by his side, he knew it could never be.

John turned back to his men and began to pace. He outstretched his arm to the Outer Court and shouted, "We will extend our line across the middle of the sanctuary to be ready for the final Roman assault. The left of our position will be anchored near the West Gate to meet the attack that will come across the arched bridge. Our right flank shall be drawn to the eastern colonnade of the sanctuary with our middle occupying the Temple itself and Inner Court. We shall have what archers and scorpions remain to be stationed on the rooftops of the Inner Court and Temple. We will have all the gates heavily fortified and ready with chains and beams to lock the gates if we should have to flee.

"We will face the Roman onslaught like men, and cast their bodies upon these stones that they crave to conquer. If we should have to retreat, the call will be two blasts of the shofar and the gates of the Inner Court will remain open only to take what few are nearby, the rest shall flee south through the Hulda Gates and link up with Simon's forces to defend the Upper and Lower City. Those are my orders. I will have all men save themselves in any way possible if the shofar'ot shall sound twice. Yet, I will remain in the Temple with a faithful guard of a thousand Zealots, to fight until we are either victorious or dead."

A murmur rippled through the ranks of commanders as they considered John's words. Some wept at the sorrow the words held, as if they had never perceived that such a day would come, while others held their heads high, refusing to show sadness. Then a stirring silence began to overtake them, as the commanders began to part with surprised utterances.

John beheld Zechariah the priest approaching him slowly as he leaned against a wooden cane, his back bent over with age, and his white beard stained with soot and dust. Tears moistened the old man's cheeks as he hobbled past the officers who parted before him. Zechariah's gaze was fixated upon John. His usual tender, calm, face was tight and strained.

When he was four metres from John, Zechariah extended a boney, trembling finger and jabbed it at the Gischalan warlord, saying in a shaky voice, "John be Levi, I knew your father and held you when you were young. You were a bright boy, yet a rebel against the teaching of *halakah* and the wisdom of the Sages. You always sought glory, and it broke my heart when you joined the rabble."

John scowled at Zechariah, feeling embarrassed by the scolding and moved to take the old man by the elbow to escort him away. But Zechariah yanked his arm free and stepped back pointing his finger up into John's burly face. "You have trodden down the path of sinners and have done little good in the years I have seen you stray. Your hands are soaked in blood, both of the Jew and of the Gentile. You were taught before your *bar-mitzvah* to love and be a steward of God, to always serve Him with honour and do likewise for your neighbour. Yet, I have seen little in you to be proud of."

"Spare me both your antics and your lecture, Zechariah. You are not my father," John angrily retorted, glaring at the elderly man.

"I am all that survives of the government that the people formed nearly four years ago. They have all been murdered from betrayal and ill deeds. Do you remember, it was in this very spot we elected generals over our districts, passed laws and decrees for the citizens of our new kingdom. We ever minted coins declaring that Jerusalem had been freed." A glaze fell over Zechariah's eyes as they sparkled with the brightness of the fond memory. "Those were days of future and possibility, of law and the beginning of holy living. Those were days where God was still with us. But, you have sold yourselves to ill fortune and blood. You have desecrated this place every day that you occupied it and brought war to our gates."

"Brought war to our gates? Zechariah, have you lost your mind? We oppose the fetters that the Romans would seek us to wear and we cast off their shackles of worldly evils. We stand for God and the Torah! We oppose the Hellenists. What you speak of is nonsense!"

"Is it? You burn timber in the Temple. It is so profaned it would take a month of great mourning to consecrate it. Your zeal has been your mask which has prevented you to know what a holy life is truly about. God placed the Romans here as our masters to teach us the letter of the Torah; the Prophet Daniel predicted their rule. It was the net of feudal rivalry of the Hasmonean Kingdom which cost us our freedom, for God would have none of the deception and spilled blood of that time.

"Now, you only repeat that offence and have brought the legions to our gates! Jerusalem is cast open for the prowler's snare." Zechariah coughed horribly, straightened himself and gazed fiercely into John's eyes. "Jerusalem will burn. She will be cast low to the ground into ashes, not to become great again until God deems her to be pure and rid of her filthy garments."

"You speak treason!" John boomed as he lost control and with a great heave, he suddenly sent Zechariah reeling back across the stones. "You are wrong! You are wrong!"

Zechariah groaned in pain and gritted his teeth as he scraped his cane across the stones, trying to steady himself. When he was too weak to stand, he slowly dragged himself over to the nearest pillar and propped himself up as his chest rose and dropped with strained gasps. "John, son of Levi," Zechariah whispered as he raised a weak, fragile hand and waved it at the stubborn warlord. "Come here."

At the sight of the injured man John had known his entire life, his anger melted away and he slowly drew near, bending down to listen. Zechariah took hold of John's outer cloak firmly in his clenched, wrinkled hands and pulled him close so that the warlord's ear was near his lips. "John, you were a lovely boy. I respected your abba very much. I told him...I would never give up on you. But...you have become unruly...a man of war...please...I beg of you...you must save Jerusalem...and...find whatever morality exists in your heart...release Judah ben Yosef...the man reminds me of you when you...

were young. He wishes to find...peace...Hate has taken...over him. Judah is a good man...John. You must do me this last will...before it is..." A haunting exhale escaped Zechariah's parted lips and his glassy eyes stilled as he died quietly, crumpled against the pillar with John looking down on him with apathy.

* * *

CHAPTER LX

August 1st, 70 A.D. / 8th of Av, 3830
Eastern Colonnades
Two hours past dawn

"Wake up and arm yourselves," whispered a Jewish soldier as he shook Adam from his deep slumber. "John has called for all men to gather their weapons and form up near the West Gate."

Adam rubbed his eyes and fought back a yawn. "Are the Romans coming?" he asked with alarm. He gave Moshe a startled look as the young man awakened to the pounding of feet nearby.

The soldier shook his head and straightened. He held a round wooden shield, a tall spear, fierce eyes and a bushy, tangled beard. "The last hours are upon us, and we aren't just going to wait for the Romans to burst in. John is going to lead an offensive charge."

"Is that wise?" Moshe mumbled as he belted his sword to his waist. "If the Romans should push us back, it will be nearly impossible to prevent them from pursuing us into the Outer Court."

"John was clear. All soldiers to the West Gate; I merely spread the word. Here." The guard produced a stale piece of bread and dropped it into Adam's lap. "That is all that's left. Make it last." He grinned at the shocked expression on Adam's face as he handled the bread and felt the hardened edges. "You know, God is testing us to see if we will serve Him at any cost, when all hope seems bleak. Now move along and hurry." The Zealot gave them one last look and then trotted off to stir more men from their sleep.

"Could this really be it?" Moshe asked feeling nervous. His face grew pale with worry as he stood and fixed his outer cloak. Moshe reached for his shield which lay upon the ground, then clenched his hand into a tight ball to stop trembling.

"You will live this day, Moshe, just stay close to me and follow my lead," Adam said in a soft tone of comfort.

Moshe gave a nervous smile. "You think you shall fly over the legionaries, Adam, like a bird?" He picked up his shield and watched as the large man gave him a smirk and shook his head good naturedly.

"If I was a bird, Moshe, I should have flown away from here ages ago." Adam looked up as a Zealot spearmen jogged over to them carrying two simple looking, pointed iron helmets. The Zealot gave Adam and Moshe a nod of encouragement and without a word, handed them the helmets and departed.

Adam glanced down at the dried bloodstains smeared upon the dented iron forehead of the helmet near the rim and grimaced. "Should this really protect us?" He slipped the helmet over his head-covering and tightened the chin strap. Adam touched his chest thoughtfully, feeling almost naked without armour, then looked up at Moshe as the young man's face turned a light hue of yellow.

Before Adam had a chance to comment, Moshe reeled around out of sight and wretched upon the flagstones as he leaned against a pillar. The bile taste was sour upon his tongue and his nostrils burned as he gazed pathetically down at the string of saliva hanging from his gasping mouth. His stomach churned again and he dropped to his knees as he felt another wave of discomfort, yet this time he only gagged with a dry heave before crumpling back onto his heels to stare up at the high ceiling of the portico. Moshe drank in the fresh air with a few gulps and then spit the taste of vomit from his mouth. He wiped his lips, cringing from the awful, putrid taste, then slowly turned, embarrassed and ashamed. "You have never seen me in such state, Adam. I am brought low that you had to see this. I do not know what has overcome me."

Adam's eyebrows furrowed with concern and he gently strolled over to Moshe's side and rested a fatherly hand on the young man's shoulder. "Every man feels fear, you must not hide it. You are a Lion, one of three who survives when all others have died. You are brave, upright, and proud. I do not think less of you. Come." Adam helped Moshe to his feet and steadied his young friend whose colour began to restore itself upon his face.

Moshe swallowed hard and steadied his breathing. A trumpet blasted and his attention swung to the sight of hundreds of Zealots assembling to the left of the Temple. When he looked back at Adam he humbly nodded to the man he respected. "You know, if we shall fall in battle today, Judah will perish alone in the dungeon. Or else John is bound to go down and kill him himself."

"We will not die, Moshe. You and I will join the attack, but keep to the rear. When our forces retreat, head as quickly as you can back to the Temple, but stay clear out of John's sight. He cannot spot us. The first chance we get we will look for Judah." Adam glanced beyond at the formations of Jewish soldiers that were slowly growing into a vast horde. "Come; let's join our brothers one last time."

* * *

John of Gischala paced defiantly before the clustered ranks of Zealots who formed a sea of faces with bristling spears and drawn swords. He made sure that the front four ranks possessed shields and he struck them one after the other with the blade of his gladius as he walked down the line. Men grunted and called out, trying to bolster their courage as they braced themselves for the charge. When he reached the centre of the army, John halted and gave a firm nod to his men. He raised his sword into the air so all eyes were upon him and declared boldly, "Remember, if the legionaries shall best us, wait for the call of two shofar blasts, and then retreat in order. We must hold them at the gate; do not let them overpower you. God fights for us on this day! We have sacrificed everything and given much for victory, glory, and freedom! Today, we are all free men and we shall fight and die as free Jews! Make ready to advance!"

John turned and faced the high doors of the West Gate, smelling the stench of burnt timber, watching as curls of smoke drifted upward from the charred layers of wood. He gave a stern nod at two guards standing near the smouldering doors and they quickly moved to the massive crossbeam that barred the gates, lifting it from its iron brackets. With the weight of the beam gone, the doors gently creaked open a sliver, as smoke continued to swirl and mingle in the air from the blackened wood. The soldiers gritted their teeth under the weight, but managed to balance the beam upon their shoulders as they moved to the side and gently set it upon the ground.

John felt his heart pound within his chest, feeling the reverberating pulse beat in his ears and cause his fingertips to tingle. His hands became clammy and sweat dampened his brow as he stared with fixation at the unlocked, flimsy gates before him, separating his world from a Roman one. John felt anxious, scared, and yet focused. He mumbled the *Shema* with dry, cracked lips, and felt his stomach groan for food. Then a strange calm drew over him.

Not a sound came from his men and John lifted his gaze upward to the sky, pleading for God to go before him. *Help me die well, if I am to fall. May I honour you in my death.* John felt the thought sharpen his focus and tears gathered in his eyes. He slowly turned and stared sentimentally at all the faces of his brave, loyal men. They were willing to die for a noble cause, yet he wished he could promise them each a different destiny than the merciless one which they would face beyond the gates.

"Fight with honour and know I have loved you all. I am proud to lead such wolves of the Jewish race!" John glanced to his right at the trumpeter and felt a sudden surge of intensity pelt him with an unknown sense, like one who might agonize over a dream upon stirring awake.

John knew once the trumpeter placed the shofar to his lips and blew, that it had the power to muster men, sending them forth into battle as if it contained magic from its paralyzing note. Pondering this power contained within the ram's horn nearly made a grin spread across John's face at the melodious sense of irony. The shofar had been used both in Temple worship and as a war instrument for hundreds of years in Jewish history. It was just as much a holy symbol as it was a trumpet to call men to battle. However, he felt a rush of pertinacity as all his muddled thoughts suddenly came together like the tip of a sword at the grim duty that now confronted him. With an unmistakable nod to the trumpeter, John dashed forward, feeling exhilaration swell his form as all fear melted away. He boomed with a mighty shout at the shofar blasting behind him and thrust open the gates as he charged out like a madman across the arched stone bridge with thousands of men howling behind him.

The rush of Zealots filled the stone bridge which spanned the Tyropoeon Valley as they poured forth from the charred West Gate. The bridge shook with fury as voices lifted in a torrent, and within moments the bolstered, snake-like horde crashed into the surprised Roman lines of the Mishneh as the legionaries scrambled into organized cohorts.

The momentum of the front Zealot ranks carried them hard into the legionary wall of locked scuta of the first three cohorts that met the attack, and the sound echoed with a deafening crunch. The lowered Roman pila drove deeply through the Jewish ranks that were hurled into them, as men screamed endlessly as they struggled and fought. Under the immense weight from the Jewish charge, the cohorts began to buckle, desperately hacking with their swords to keep from crumbling into chaos. The enraged Jews slashed and shrieked with wild eyes as they fought bitterly with curses and jeers. They fought savagely against the wall of opposing shields, trying to wrench the elongated scuta from the hands of Romans or drag the legionaries to the ground to cut their throats. The fray soon bore a blood-stained ground beneath it, strewn and tangled with bodies, as the wounded tried to crawl away with sobs.

The Zealots began to envelop the right and left flanks of the legionaries, and soon whistle blasts rang out as centurions tried to counter the threats using men in the rear ranks. In deadly successions, they began to hurl their spears into the enraged Jewish host while pushing them back with the weight and flexibility of the scutum wall. Finally, a renewed shout rose up at the arrival of another two legionary cohorts and the Zealot wings swung to eagerly meet the attack as the fighting intensified with the constant, incessant clash of steel and iron. Wails rose and dipped with the progression of the battle as more Zealots streamed across the arched stone bridge to be fed into the heat of the struggle wherever it slacked or weakened. Legionary runners were sent to the rear with desperate messages to franticly assemble more cohorts from the Camp of the Assyrians to support the fight, lest the Roman wings collapse. Centurions and officers alike called out everywhere as they hastily rallied their men. Soon long columns of legionaries were trotting out of the camp to swiftly come to the aid of the faltering, engaged cohorts.

After killing his third Roman, John pushed back through the host of Zealots who were crammed against the front ranks of the legionary cohorts with shouts and curses. His face was speckled with blood and his muscles ached. He touched the side of his jaw and spit a stream of blood as he explored, with his finger, at the hole in his gums where a tooth used to be. The knock of the heavy scutum boss against the side of his face had managed to stun him for a moment, gash open his bottom lip, and slice his tongue. But he gave a bloody grin knowing that he had retaliated by driving the entire length of his blade through the legionary's throat.

John pressed through his men, knowing that he could direct the attack better from the rear and finally emerged spitting another ghastly stream of blood upon the dusty ground. "Move to the left and hold them!" John shouted at a handful of Zealots nearby and then turned to survey the vicious battle ensuing before him. From what he could see they were holding the Roman line which had entrenched itself firmly upon the stones at the edge of the Mishneh.

It will be another shoving match, John thought to himself. *If we could outflank them and attack their vulnerable sides, we could put them to flight. All we would have to do is send these cohorts reeling back and we would be unstoppable.* He glanced behind him and scowled at the empty bridge and vacant West Gate. John felt an urge to send a runner to have all his archers brought up to shoot volleys from the bridge into the Romans, but knew they were too valuable to pull from the Inner Court of the Temple which they guarded. He looked to the southwest at the rising towers and buildings beyond the shelter of the First Wall and cursed Simon. The Sicarii King had abandoned the Zealots at their most crucial hour, and any treaty or pact that had ever existed had been burned in the fires of betrayal along with the northwestern colonnades. Now the Zealots were left to themselves to defend the Temple and perish.

*　*　*

Judah stood near the rusty bars of his cell and listened to the muffled sounds of fighting above ground. He could hear the faint noise of thousands of men shouting and the thuds of what appeared to be stones crashing upon the ground. Judah stared at Aaron, one of the prison guards, who stood a few metres away rigid and stiff as his nervous face looked up at the ceiling, wondering how the battle was progressing. The other two guards could be seen at the far end sitting upon the floor as they passed the time playing a game with two dice and a cup. Aaron gave a great sigh and leaned slightly upon the shaft of his spear. He watched one of the guards rattle the dice inside the cup before slamming it upon the ground and lifting it to count the numbers. The guard gave a hearty laugh as the other soldier took the dice in his hands and shook them calling out a number.

"Aaron," Judah whispered to get the guard's attention and then gestured his way. "What is happening?"

"I don't know too much. We were just instructed to remain on guard because John was going to charge out and attack the Romans. With the northern colonnades burned and destroyed it doesn't surprise me that this would unfold."

"You know the Romans will eventually push them back, and when they do it will be impossible to stop them. They will pour into the Temple courts; it could all be over today."

Aaron scowled. "What do you mean?"

"The legions will capture the Temple, you know this to be true." Judah watched him groan and cover his eyes in discouragement.

"Simon has abandoned us, Judah. The Idumeans just sit behind their walls and watch this happen."

"The Temple will fall." Judah moved closer to the bars and stared at the guard who he had befriended. "Aaron, if it comes to that, you must set me free. Give me a sword and I can fight."

Aaron raised his head and stared at Judah with an uncomfortable gaze, as if the very mention of the subject made him testy. "I would be punished for that. I couldn't, Judah. John would have me scourged or thrown in prison with you."

"Do you understand that if the legionaries break into the Temple courts we will all be killed? They won't spare a single fighter. John will retreat to the southern part of the city with whatever men he can assemble and you will be left down here standing guard over me while the legionaries plunder the Temple. There will be nowhere for you to go."

"Aaron, quit talking to the prisoner and come join us!" beckoned one of the guards with a laugh.

Aaron looked with annoyance at the guards, and then ignoring them he stared at Judah's haggard, dirty face. "Judah, I can't do it. The other guards would never go along with it. It would be impossible for me to set you free in time before they stopped me. They don't trust me as it is. I am sorry." Aaron passed a dried piece of bread between the bars. "Eat."

*   *   *

John watched as another cohort reached the fray and slammed into the ranks of his men along the right flank, sending them stumbling backwards as the legionaries struck them down with their swords. Men heaved all along the line as both sides struggled to gain ground. Bodies lay everywhere in pools of blood streaked upon the stones, which made them slick as soldiers slipped and swore aloud. John felt an edge of panic grip his soul and he fought against it as he shouted for his men to keep up the pressure. He stalked up and down the rear ranks of his men and continued to bark out orders as the sound of fighting intensified with the calls of men screaming in agony. Finally, after allowing his Zealots to battle for over an hour without reinforcements, he knew that he either needed to sound a retreat or send in fresh troops, for the Romans at the centre were slowly punching holes in his lines, splitting the Zealot formation through the middle.

John grabbed a soldier nearby and screamed in his face over the din of battle, "Rush back to the Temple! Assemble one hundred men and bring them here at once!" The soldier gave a desperate nod and ran across the arched bridge. John swore as loud as he could at the thought of Simon watching from a tower as the Zealot army was slowly butchered, but he knew there was nothing he could do to sway the stubborn man's allegiance. A distinct call rose up from the right flank and John rushed to the sight where a number of his spearman pointed beyond the amassed Romans to the northwestern edge of the burned colonnades.

John shielded his eyes from the sun and watched as over a thousand Romans were busy tearing down weak sections of the wall and clearing debris. He suddenly felt as if a hand had reached inside of him in order to squeeze his lungs in blinding suffocation. The sight of the legionaries at the colonnades could only mean one thing: they were creating a breach upon which to flank his army from within the Temple's Outer Court. If they were to get in, with his army pinned down, they would all be summarily annihilated. As if that was only the beginning of utter chaos, John also watched as a triple column of mounted Roman cavalry appeared in the hundreds moving steadily across the Bezetha where they wheeled to the left and aimed for his exposed flank.

"Sound the trumpet now!" John shouted feeling anxious. Fear suddenly clutched his entire being and he felt his legs grow numb as if they had doubled in weight. The only voice that screamed within his mind told him to retreat, yet he felt powerless. "Sound the trumpet, for God's sake!" John bellowed like a deranged beast at the stunned man next to him holding the ram's horn, with a face of ash and eyes wide with terror. John did not wait a moment longer. He leapt at the man, grabbed the horn from the trumpeter's trembling hands, placed it to his lips and blasted twice upon the shofar.

At the double blast of the shofar, the Roman horse troops ploughed into the Zealot's left flank, collapsing it in seconds as their swords dug into flesh and tore open men's bodies. The horses, trained for war, charged right through the scattered Jewish ranks. The weight of the impact had disintegrated all resistance and the Zealots turned, fleeing in full retreat for the stone bridge.

Dozens of men stumbled and tripped, only to scream in agony as the horses rode over them with their shod hooves. The Roman cavalry pursued the fleeing Jews. Anyone who hesitated to fight back was quickly slaughtered, and soon the mounted troopers had slowed their charge to a steady push as the horses stepped over piles of bodies lying everywhere. With the undoing of the Zealot left flank, the centre fell into disorder as their rear ranks turned and fled, converging on the bridge which would save their lives.

Both legionary and horse trooper alike drove the Jewish retreat, striking them down in the hundreds and leaving the dying wailing miserably upon the ground. Soon the entire Jewish attack had fallen apart and crammed the stone bridge as they edged backward facing off with the eager legionaries who smashed into them with a formed wall of shields. The pressure was incredible as panic and chaos quickly riddled the Jewish army. Men shrieked as they tumbled over the sides of the bridge and fell upon the paved streets below.

Blood soaked everything and mutilated corpses and limbs were strewn about. Soon the bridge itself became crimson as blood ran over the edge and dripped upon the crushed bodies lying upon the stones below. The front Jewish ranks fought until their swords became blunted or broken, then they leapt at the Romans trying to strangle them or gouge their eyes. However, one by one they were slaughtered and hurled over the side to make room as the cohorts marched boldly into them, presenting an impossible wall for the Jews to penetrate. The Roman machine rolled onward with precise thrusts of their swords, and the Zealot dead soon became so congested that the legionaries finally had to halt and clear the bridge before pushing on.

John dashed through the West Gate shouting for archers to man the roofs of the Inner Walls. He hysterically called for all Zealots to retreat to the Temple and watched as men scrambled from the colonnades surrounding the plaza. He stepped to the side as hundreds of his fighters broke into a retreat, pouring through the West Gate without order. John screamed at them to form up and fight the advancing legions, but it was useless. The legion tide rolled strongly towards them across the bridge, scattering the attack and chasing them back into the vulnerable Outer Court.

John turned to a blast of trumpets and desperate shouts from behind him, watching as the northwestern corner of the colonnades finally crumbled into dust as a charging stream of legionaries emerged through the smoke with a thundering war cry. A little over a hundred Zealots were seen trying to halt the second Roman attack, but were quickly overwhelmed and killed as they tried to flee in the midst of the emboldened legionaries who chased them down. Archers upon the roof of the Temple began to shoot arrows down upon the advancing Romans, but with locked scuta the arrows had little effect.

"Full retreat! Back to the Temple!" John bellowed. Turning he ran full tilt for the safety of the Inner Court as he was joined by over a thousand frantic Zealots. As John reached one of the open gates to the Inner Court, he heard endless blasts of trumpets and the roll of drums as the legionaries flowed into the Outer Court, scattering everywhere as they hunted Jews throughout the pillared colonnades as far south as the Royal Stoa. Safely inside the Inner Court, John quickly ascended to the roof over one of the gates and observed, in horror, as the Temple plateau became a tangle of thousands of fighting men.

John could see trapped bands of Zealots, some numbering forty while others were as large as one hundred, fighting against the cohorts in doomed formations as they were slowly cut down and slain. In the middle of the court, the main bulk of the Zealot army was still trying to reach the Temple. They fought bitterly, like a great beast being forced into a cage, as they became surrounded on all sides. The Romans shoved them and charged again and again into their withering flanks trying to put them to flight. The Zealots backed up slowly as their numbers continued to dwindle and in groups of ten they kept breaking off and fleeing through the gates of the Inner Court. John did what he could, desperately trying to alleviate the pressure and save his men, as he dispatched archers to the roofs and spent what missiles remained from his scorpions. But still the Roman leviathan pushed forward, consuming the Zealots in the Outer Court.

"John! We must close the gates!" shouted an officer in panic standing in the Court of the Women below as he watched the legionaries draw nearer. "If the Romans get too close, we won't be able to stop them from getting inside!"

John stared in misery at hundreds of his men who were still trapped within the Outer Court, fighting for their lives as they attempted to get to the Temple. "We can't abandon them!" John shouted back.

The officer hysterically shook his head and pointed through the open gate nearest him. "If you do not shut them now, you will lose both your army and the Temple!"

John turned and felt his heart sink. Tears suddenly filled his eyes and he screamed with a broken voice, "Men! Hurry! Get to the Temple!" Then an eruption of hot tears streamed down his red cheeks and he gave a nod to the pale-faced officer. "Shut them!"

All the gates were hurriedly closed and bolted. Then the haunting sound of men banging with absolute desperation upon the doors echoed like a steady thunder rolling across the land. Once word had spread to the Zealots in the Outer Court that the gates to the Temple had been closed, men turned in panic, abandoning all sense of order, as they fled up the steps of the balustrade to surround the Temple walls. They begged for mercy, pounded upon the gates until their hands became bloodied, wept aloud, and called for their mothers as piles of Zealots were pushed up against the gates. Many suffocated, were crushed or trampled as the legionaries hacked into them, spilling their blood in a tumult of carnage. Meanwhile, the constant pleading and hysteric screams of the doomed Zealots continued to reverberate in a muffled pitch as their voices penetrated the massive Temple gates. John sat behind the parapet, his arms tightly wrapped around his knees as he listened to men beseeching God and sobbing to be saved. The minutes crept by like an eternity and soon the steady pounding began to dwindle as men wailed.

The officer, who had demanded the gates to be closed, sputtered, then broke into heavy sobbing at the sight of blood which ran into the Court of the Women from underneath the closed gates. He heard a final pound upon the door, a pathetic cry for mercy, and then silence. Soon the fighting died down and the calls of the wounded began to evaporate as legionaries scattered throughout the Outer Court and put them out of their misery.

When John rose and stared over the parapet, he beheld the sight of thousands of bodies scattered everywhere in a shallow lake of blood that ran down into the Hulda Gates. The air reeked of death as billows of smoke rose from sections of the western colonnades that had been fired during the slaughter. It had been a blood bath, and the motionless bodies covering the flagstones attested to the gruesome fate of a retreating army.

Now, the court was bustling, as over two legions of Roman soldiers began to take up positions before the Temple. John watched with shame as a column of legionaries ascended to the top of the western colonnades and fixed their legionary standards to the stone parapets in victory. He groaned and covered his face in trepidation as a tremulous fear stung his eyes at the sight. Silently turning away, he descended the rooftop, needing to find out how many of his men had been spared and what his next move would be.

*   *   *

Titus had a field tent set up under the northern portico roof to shelter his officers from the heat of day. It was his new command post and the eager, jubilant Prince briskly dispatched messengers to rally his legionary generals and client kings to assemble them for war council. Two full legions, the Twelfth and the Fifth, were entrenched in the Outer Court as they enveloped the Temple and set up defences. Catapults and scorpions were brought over to the charred remains of the northwestern colonnades, as the gates along the western plateau were torn down and widened for easier access.

Archers and troops of the alae were quickly positioned upon the ramparts of the surrounding colonnades to observe the surviving Jewish soldiers crammed within the Temple's courts. On the other hand, the divided Tenth Legion continued to occupy the eastern side of the city and support the Fifteenth which faced off against the deteriorating remains of the First Wall.

When the generals arrived to Titus' new command post, the air was rife with pride and excitement. They praised each other and chatted lively about the vicious brawl that had turned in their favour so that now they stood upon the stones of the fallen Temple Mount. Discussion quickly led to the question of surrender and the Temple's survival, but was brushed away by the ardent legionary legates as they boasted about Roman strength, agreeing in one accord that the Jews had lost all opportunity for surrender.

Titus raised his hands to quiet the officers and cleared his throat. The sound of marching feet echoed past the closed tent flap from a contingent of legionaries and the Prince could not help but grin at his generals. "It was a hard fight, but once they were put to flight, the soldiers performed admirably. I expected nothing short of the brute, stubborn response we gave the Zealots and you have not failed me. Marcus Tullius, your men were fierce as they took the bridge."

Marcus bowed humbly, feeling overjoyed. "It was Gaius Antony who led the counter charge that seized the bridge."

"Then he will be duly rewarded." Titus glanced at his Nubian slave and flicked his hand at the man. "Bring wine and fruit now. We must celebrate and drink to the gods." The generals smiled with exuberance as the Prince casually sat down upon a cushioned couch. "Tomorrow we shall capture the Temple or burn it if the Jews force our hand. *Roma* will not tolerate despicable resistance until the very end. Somewhere the hand of judgement must be felt if these people are to be governed."

835

"I would urge the Prince to reconsider destroying the Temple," King Agrippa motioned softly.

"It is out of my hands if the Jews should push me to it," Titus replied with a slight apologetic glance. The Nubian soon returned, accompanied by another slave as they poured dark wine into ornate goblets and offered them to the generals. Bowls of figs, dates, olives, and nuts were quietly brought upon silver platters and the victorious generals hungrily helped themselves.

"If the Jews refuse to surrender, destroying the Temple is all we can do," piped up Sextus as he glanced from Agrippa back to Titus. "Too many legionaries have fallen to validate sacrificing more by throwing them against the Temple walls. Burning the Temple may be our only option left."

"But not our first response, Sextus," Titus commented, spitting out an olive pit. "The Jews might be unruly, but they remain to be many of the empire's subjects. These dogs of Jerusalem will be crushed, and if I can show the Jewish servants of the empire that Titus is capable of mercy by sparing their Temple, then so be it. To burn it would only be regrettable, that is all. The order of everything will have to change anyway." Titus looked at Agrippa and bit down hungrily upon a fig. "The Jews of this region have challenged *Roma* for four years and even after Jerusalem lies in utter ruins, I dare say, we still have strongholds of rebels to the south that will have to be crushed.

"The land of Judea will burn and its smoke will be smelt across the Middle Sea. This land must be a warning to those who choose rebellion over loyal service. What greater symbol to be represented for all men than the stamping out of anarchy by the sight of the great Jewish Temple lying in ruins." Titus shrugged and grinned. "But that is for the Zealots to decide. I wash my hands clean of such action should it be forced upon me."

Titus tilted his goblet to his lips, drinking long and deep until the last drop of wine was gone. He smacked his lips together and burped. "I care nothing for their petty whims. The Jews of Judea have had *Roma* suckling at her tits for far too long. *Roma* has appeased them and granted them favour. Now look at their *great* city!" Titus held out his empty goblet as he chuckled and the Nubian slave refilled it. "My generals are the best and have served well. The legions have fought with the strength of gods, and Mars has overflowed the cup of the Jews with blood so that it spills upon the ground in his unslumbering wrath. I waste not an ounce of mercy and pity on such men. Mars has decreed us strong, and the gods look down upon the sons of Mars with favour. Basilides has blessed the Flavians, and my father is Emperor."

"No doubt the God of my people has blessed your family with power over the earth, my Prince," Agrippa cautiously replied and glanced at Tiberius. "Yet, even those that have not rebelled against you have suffered greatly. Greeks in many cities in the east have rose up to kill Jews, and tens of thousands have perished, all loyal servants to *Roma*. Should these people be deprived of their Temple?"

"My mind has not yet been set," Titus murmured as he drank more wine.

"Should the Temple be destroyed, the Jewish community abroad would faithfully appeal to *Roma* for it to be rebuilt in haste. Would your father the Emperor decree such a request?"

"The Jews as a people are not the enemy of *Roma*, my King Agrippa, but the Temple makes your people wild with fanatical religion and dangerous. This is not the first time there has been a problem." Titus paused, snapped his fingers for food and the Nubian obediently brought it over. "I do not know the mind of my father, but I do know that this region will be punished for its insurrection that has killed thousands of Romans. It must be held accountable for what it has done and will stand before the full weight of Roman law. That is my mind, Marcus.

"The Temple to your God will suffer if need be, along with them. The Emperor will have the final say, and I shall support it fervently to make sure rebellion never happens again in this land. The Jews will learn to fear the gods of *Roma* for our gods have humbled them and brought them low."

* * *

CHAPTER LXI

The Temple
Court of the Israelites
Two hours after dusk

Adam and Moshe kept to the shadows of the southern pillars as they silently crept past the dark forms of sleeping men throughout the court near the burnt altar. Adam held up a hand and both men crouched near the base of a column, watching as a file of white cloaked priests silently stirred the ashes with silver shovels at the top of the altar. The remains of charred timber smouldered upward forming a pathetic cloud as one of the priests pushed the remains of a goat's skull around the burnt embers. At the base of the altar a cluster of priests wept and prayed together as there were no lambs to be slaughtered. The two tables usually occupied by the corpses of slain animals, now stood empty and strewn with discarded instruments. The priests rocked back and forth as an elderly man led them in prayer, then they turned to face the sanctuary doors with its mantle of gold and petitioned God to save them.

"Let's move," Adam whispered as he rose and gripped his left hand around the hilt of his sword. His face was wrapped in black cloth, and his mind was focused on what they had to do. Adam led Moshe further until they reached the entrance to the Chamber of Hewn Stone near the wall that separated the Court of the Israelites from the Court of the Women. Adam glanced in the direction of the Nicanor Gate, and when he was pleased with the stillness of the courtyard, he motioned to Moshe to gently open the door. Within a split moment both men were safely concealed from unwanted eyes that might spot them from the crammed court. Moshe shut the door behind him and bolted it. When he turned, he squinted in the dim light of the council hall and reached for a torch that hung on the wall.

Adam unfurled his face covering and tossed it away as he felt a trickle of sweat run down the side of his face. He slowly drew his sword and pointed the blade before him as he scanned the chamber. Moshe stepped past Adam with the torch, scowling at the benches lining the walls and the great council seats. Then his eyes fell upon the sleeping forms of a dozen men, snoring upon benches. Moshe slowly scrapped his sword free of its scabbard and gestured to the slumbering men.

Adam shook his head at the consideration of slaying the men and firmly took hold of Moshe's hand when the young Lion refused to comply. A look of revenge and fury gazed for an instant at Adam, then Moshe reluctantly surrendered and quietly followed Adam over to the northern wall. Ever so silently, the two men moved one of the great council chairs and then pushed past a thick hanging curtain which led to a small antechamber with a spiral staircase of stone leading into blackness.

Moshe took the lead with his torch and both men cautiously descended the stairs, steadying themselves against the cool stone wall, staring at the light in front of them given off by the burning flame of the torch. The staircase brought them deeper and deeper into the underground vaults beneath the Temple Mount as both men paced themselves, taking steady breaths and feeling the air about them grow damp. When they finally reached the bottom, a floor of dirt greeted them with a tunnel. Four torches hung upon the tunnel walls lighting the space and Moshe hung his firebrand in an empty bracket nearby. They moved slowly down the tunnel, not desiring to arouse suspicion as they concealed their blades and pretended to stumble with weariness. When they began to see a wooden door come into view, which barred their path, they noticed a set of eyes staring at them through a small window of iron bars. Moshe acknowledged the guard and covered his mouth as he yawned. When Moshe drew close he stepped aside for Adam to get by and spotted another guard through the barred window appear next to his comrade.

"Who are you two?" asked one of the guards with a gruff, suspicious tone.

"We have come to relieve you!" Adam replied, rubbing his eyes to convince the men he had just woken up. "John wants a shorter rotation. There is going to be hell in the morning and he will need all his men fresh and ready."

The guard stared at Adam and Moshe with a scowl. "I have never seen you before."

"What is that matter to me? We were just woken up to come down here and relieve you both. If you want to take it up with John, then we shall go wake him up and bring him here," Adam angrily replied.

"Well, no need for that, we just never received word." The guards gave each other an uneasy look and then stared back through the barred window. "Are you armed?"

"We have swords," Adam replied patting his side. He could make out a third guard standing further back from the door holding a shield and spear. "Come on now, you want to waste your precious time with questions rather than sleeping? Open the door!"

One of the guards shrugged as the other grumbled, unhooked the iron ring of keys from his belt, then fidgeted with the door lock. "Sleep will be nice. Smells like shit down here," chuckled the guard as the lock finally snapped open and the bolt was dragged loudly back. The hinges creaked and groaned as the two guards pulled the heavy wooden door open, their thoughts savouring the sleep they craved.

Neither guard ever expected the danger that faced them as they stepped back with tired grins to let the men in. Adam moved swiftly through the door, and unsheathing a dagger from his belt, he thrust it into the throat of the guard nearest him as the man's eyes bulged out in shock. The other guard shouted, trying to lower his cumbersome spear in the tight space, but instead dropped it and backed up as he fumbled to draw his sword. Moshe leapt upon him swiftly with his own blade and in a single action drove it through the shrieking man's chest.

Both guards had been killed so quickly that the third sentry had been given no time to save them. Yet, now with terror upon his face and his spear lowered in his trembling hands, he backed up against the cell door, shouting with surprise as a pair of powerful hands reached between the bars and grabbed his throat.

"Do not resist, Aaron. Surrender now!" Judah said harshly to the terrified guard. "Drop your spear or these men will kill you." Aaron complied with a whimper as he shook in fear and stared at the two men standing before him. "Adam, Moshe, it does me good to see you, brothers. Let this one live; he has been good to me."

Adam slowly stepped forward, pointing his blade at the guard, and said grimly, "Unbuckle your belt and cast your sword upon the ground." He watched as the guard hastily complied without a fuss. Then Adam seized the guard's shoulder and pulled him away from the cell as he escorted him through the tunnel. The guard grimaced at the bloodied corpses outstretched upon the dirt floor and had not a single moment to hesitate as he was pushed through the doorway, instructed never to come back. Adam closed the wooden door and bolted it. He watched as the guard stumbled blindly away, as if in a stupor, before disappearing up the stairs.

As soon as Moshe unlocked the cell door Judah stepped through, touched the side of his face and gave him a grin. "It is good to see you."

"It was all Adam's idea," Moshe replied. "Neither of us could leave you down here to die."

"There is none I trust more," Judah said as Adam strolled over and embraced him with his large arms. "It is good to see you both, my brothers. I had no idea what had become of you."

"We were banished to the Lower City, but managed to slip back in by God's grace," Adam responded. "The Temple is doomed, Judah. It will be like my master and teacher Yeshua said so long ago, that not a stone will remain on another, and now as we speak they dismantle the colonnades and are hurling the stones into the paved streets below. They will come for the Temple next and will spare none. The Romans slaughtered thousands of Jews and pursued them into the Temple courtyard. Now they hold the Outer Court and no doubt are ready to destroy this place at dawn."

Judah stared at Adam with heavy, sorrowful eyes. "How did they get in?"

"John led a charge across the bridge with nearly his whole army," Moshe said. "They fought the Romans in the Mishneh for hours until Titus managed to bring up mounted troops and cohorts at least triple our number. We held them off in the narrow gap, but word quickly spread that the legionaries were breaching through the burnt colonnades at the northern end, and so John sounded the retreat. Two legions pursued us. It was impossible to keep them back. John must have lost over half his army."

"What of Simon?"

"He did nothing to come to John's aid. The Romans occupy the bridge and have seized the towers along the First Wall. Simon's Idumeans are powerless to stop them. It will not be long until the legions capture the Upper City," Adam responded. "We had little choice; we had to get to you tonight."

"And what is your plan of escape, my brothers? We are trapped down here. As soon as John hears of what you have done we will soon be cornered."

"That is why we should have killed the third guard," Moshe replied in frustration. "Now he will alert John to what has happened."

"I could not allow you to do that, he has been kind to me and even gave me word about your keeping." Judah picked up the sword belt upon the ground and secured it to his waist. He drew the blade and gave it a quick inspection. "We must block the door."

"It is already locked," Adam replied, as he stared back towards the wooden door. "It is strong, Judah."

"Yes, and if I know John, he is bound to set it on fire."

"You would think he would not waste such time on us while the Temple was surrounded?" Moshe commented.

Judah nodded. "I stung John to his very soul when I was arrested and tried. He thinks of me as a traitor, and it is all the more a wound to his pride that I have been his most trusted. He will come and we will need to resist them till morning. Once the Romans launch their final attack, John will be forced to abandon us and fight."

"Then we can make our escape and slip from the city. The sewers shall serve us well," Moshe eagerly said, then scowled with puzzlement at Judah's downcast face. "What is wrong?"

"I can't leave the city."

Adam and Moshe were stunned into silence as they digested these words. Then finally Adam spoke, "You are staying? What is here for you now, Judah? You have been betrayed by your own people. Come with us to Beit Ani or Pella. You will be safe there and can rebuild your life."

Judah sadly shook his head. "My life is here, you both must understand."

A look of disbelief covered Moshe's face then quickly turned to anger as he stepped close to Judah and pointed at him sharply. "We risked our lives coming here for you so you could live. If you stay here, the Romans will use you for javelin practice. You can't be serious, you have to..."

"That is enough, Moshe," Adam interrupted pulling the young man back. "Drag the bodies into one of the cells and watch the door!" Adam waited until Moshe was out of earshot, then whispered to Judah, "He is young and means no insult. He would follow you anywhere and he risked much to save you."

"I know."

"Then why would you stay, Judah?"

Judah glanced back at his empty cell. "I have had much time to think. All I have ever had and lost was here in this city. It is where Miriam was slain and where I sent Hadassah away." Judah buried his face into his hands and softly groaned. "I never wanted to let her go."

"You did what you knew best," Adam said. "But you shall not honour her memory if you stay here and die. This is not how you find peace."

A smirk turned up the edges of Judah's mouth and then he looked away. "This is the only way I can find peace, Adam. I do not expect you to understand, but I must find Gaius."

"That Centurion? Impossible! Haven't you listened, Judah? Dawn approaches quickly and the legions will come against the Temple in all their fury. How could you ever find Gaius? You will be killed instantly." Adam stared with a perplexed, confused gaze at his dearest friend, a man he had served for years.

"I know the risk, but I have to try. I have to find out if Hadassah lives, Adam. I must know. I just can't flee the city. I lowered her from the wall in the blackness of night, knowing full well the danger that surrounded her. I can never forgive myself if she came to harm." Judah paused for a brief moment. "Gaius will know. He will be able to give me an answer."

Judah turned, as if to walk away, then looked at his friend who did not respond. "I have spent these last years lamenting over what I have lost. I have felt estranged from God, and haunted by what terror I beheld on that day Miriam was killed." Judah scratched his chin as hot tears ran down his cheeks. "I lived my life hating everyone, Adam. I thought that by killing my enemies the pain would dull and fade away.

"When I killed Capito I discovered I had become lost. Hadassah told me that I had become a slave to hate, that it was my master. I lost everything I cherished and loved, and I can't wander this land forever, restless and with shame." Judah stared at the damp walls of the prison and bowed his head. "You know, I envy Gaius. He is a man who possesses everything I ever wanted: honour, respect, love, a family, and a future. I know it sounds preposterous, but it is true. Here I am, a Jew, wishing for the life of a Roman. Most men would curse me to my face, yet you say nothing.

"I have done so much trying to cast off the weight of misery upon my soul, but I descend deeper into its fold. It is the life I have come to know. Now, when the legions come and we flee from this dungeon, you take Moshe from the city, but I must find Gaius. I must know if Hadassah lives. For my soul, I have to know."

"And what if she is dead?"

Judah jerked his attention upon the burly, solemn face of his friend and then looked away and said with a whisper, "Then such despair will not be worth living."

* * *

John exploded into the Chamber of Hewn Stone in a rage as the slumbering men jolted awake in alarm. He had been in the midst of a council when the surviving guard, Aaron, had brought news of Judah being set free and the other guards killed. John's mind was a whirl of dark thoughts as he roared like a caged beast and moved quickly across the marble floor at the head of thirty armed Zealots following closely behind. Like a wild, unruly savage, John hurled the council chair to the floor and drew his sword. He slashed at the great curtain with an angry shout, then burst into the antechamber and headed for the stairs which led to the dungeons below.

How could this have happened? The thought pulsed with rage in John's mind. *Adam and Moshe have killed my men and seek to set Judah free? Are they mad? I will have their heads on platters before this night is out.* John descended quickly and when he reached the bottom he felt his temper rise at the sight of the bolted door down the tunnel.

This was the last thing he needed. The Temple was surrounded, he only had eleven hundred men who remained, Simon had abandoned and betrayed him, now Judah's men had killed his guards and freed a treacherous, cowardly man deserving of death. John grabbed a torch from the wall and approached the door with heavy steps as his heart pounded within his chest. He knew it would be locked, but tested it anyway giving a heave. John tried to stare through the barred window and clenched his fingers tightly around the hilt of his sword as he pounded the pommel against the wooden door.

"Judah ben Yosef! You coward and traitor! Open the door now and I won't have my men break it into splinters and flay you alive! Judah, I know you're in there, don't keep silent, you dog!" He suddenly saw Judah, Adam, and Moshe calmly step out from one of the adjacent cells, standing their ground as they stared at the wild, crazed face glaring back at them. "What have you done? Did you think you could escape?"

"In time we will, John. Do you think that the Romans will tarry?"

John tightened his grip upon his sword and felt his back arch like a great beast waiting to pounce while the heat of his breath blasted upon the bars. "You think you can intimidate me? The Romans face the House of God. It is up to HaShem whether or not the legions will advance, yet you spit in his face with your insolence. What keeps me from tearing you to pieces, you coward?"

"That door," Judah scoffed.

John's face twitched with anger and he thumped the door again with a heavy thud. "You think there is a power on this earth that can save you? You are wrong! I was merciful, Judah, I even considered sparing your miserable life. Simon has broken his word and I could have restored you. Yet, now your men have shed innocent blood."

"You speak as if you are clean of such a condemnation, John. I know you well. I have served you and watched you," Judah lashed back. "You could have saved Matthias and his sons and you could save this city and this Temple to if you wanted." Judah paused. "I know you had Ananus ben Ananus murdered and cast from the walls. How many Jews shall die? How long shall the list of names be which are written in blood? *You* are the traitor to your people! You are a man who cares for nothing but the twisted fantasy of a Roman-free land."

"You dare accuse me?" boomed John with rage. "You cower behind this door, but I shall burn you out! I shall watch you all burn alive!" John turned to his men and shouted, "Bring dried timber, stack it against the door and fire it!"

*   *   *

Gaius walked slowly down the long row of Jewish dead that had been dragged under the western porticos to clear the Outer Court for the morning. He studied every face as he passed the bodies searching for the familiar features of Judah ben Yosef, yet so far the corpse eluded him. Gaius halted and lowered his torch to a bloodied, mangled body, staring at the dead man's bushy beard and gaping eyes. Then he gave a low sigh and moved on. He had already checked the piles of dead under the high roof of the Royal Stoa to no avail. A stirring within his mind seemed to tell him that Judah was alive, but he had to be sure.

Gaius reached the end of the motionless dead Zealots and crouched near the final body. It was a horribly mutilated corpse of a young man, yet his face was unscathed. The beginnings of a beard prickled the dead man's face and Gaius gently reached forward, closing the partially opened eyes. A lone legionary, who stood a few metres away, watched the Centurion lift his gaze and the sentry quickly looked away not wishing to draw any unwanted attention.

"Do you have a count of their dead?" Gaius wearily asked the guard.

"One thousand three hundred and sixty-two, Centurion."

"And what were our numbers?"

The legionary shrugged as he took a moment to think and then muttered, "Around two hundred and thirteen, Centurion."

Gaius glanced at the four bolts of lightning upon the soldier's gold coloured shield. "You're of the Fulminata. Did you fight today?"

"Yes, Centurion."

"What cohors are you from?"

"The Fifth, Centurion." The legionary paused, then added, "Begging your pardon, Centurion, but you are the Praefectus Castrorum Gaius Antony, am I right?" Gaius nodded and the legionary straightened, raising his chin with pride. "It was an honour to follow the First across the bridge and an honour to fight by your side."

Gaius warmly smiled at the soldier and gave a humble nod. "It is men like you that make us great. Maintain your watch, legionary." Gaius strolled past the soldier and headed out into the vastness of the court.

Cooking fires and torches burned with intensity from the thousands of legionaries that stood guard surrounding the Temple. Gaius could make out the shapes of scorpions and onagri with their crews standing watch as night settled upon the city.

Soldiers saluted him as he passed and he acknowledged the men with firm nods of affirmation.

Lights burned upon the Temple roof and the ramparts of the Inner Court as Gaius noticed the shadows of men pacing upon them. He had no idea what to expect once morning arrived, only that the final battle of Jerusalem might be fought over the holiest site of the Jews. Gaius wondered if Titus would send Yosef again to speak to the rebels, but quickly dismissed the thought as a folly notion. Everything about Titus in the final weeks had shown him to be a man with little patience, eager to crush the burning embers of the Jewish rebellion. Titus would show no mercy.

Gaius continued on, passing assembled cohorts of legionaries standing guard in the night, as their shadows danced upon the stones of the plaza from the torchlight. Nearly ten thousand men had been brought into the Outer Court to envelop the Temple and surround the colonnades. Hundreds of fires burned upon the high portico roofs around him as archers and patrolling guards watched the Temple with a dark intensity. Everything was set and it was as if Gaius could hear the final, struggling breath of the Temple as if it moaned and lay dying.

He halted in the glowing light of a fire nearby and stared down at the dried blood that stained his hands. His century had been at the head of the pack, and he had led them in a desperate chase across the stone bridge. It had been Gaius who had first planted his foot through the burnt, charred West Gates to stand upon the ground of the Outer Court, and he had led his century onward, striking down any Zealot who hesitated or tried to fight back. Gaius recalled the rivers of blood that had run between the stones and stained his caligae. The air still reeked of the blood, and even in the closing night he could still see it streaked across the stones.

Gaius stared at the front face of the glorious Jewish Temple and gazed in wonderment at the golden spiked roof, the massive pillars, and the white, glistening marble. It was an enormous structure that dominated the plateau, and it beheld a beauty he had never seen before. A glow of bright firelight rose up from the Inner Court which splashed the face of the Temple as if it were alive. Shadows flickered upward and voices could be heard as he knew the desperate Jews would be making their final preparations for morning. The atmosphere was tense and unpredictable.

Gaius pondered the thought of what would be going through his mind should the roles have been reversed, as if he had been a Jewish commander trapped within the sanctuary of the Temple, surrounded by the enemy. The future would look impossible, bleak, and hopeless, yet if Gaius was to be anything like John of Gischala then he would have to be fierce in his resolve and unwilling to bend the knee to Rome. Gaius entertained this thought for a few minutes and imagined what John would say to his surviving soldiers.

He would have to bolster their courage in the face of failure and the approaching hoof beats of death. Men would be unable to sleep, kept up all night by the fate before them. John, with little doubt in Gaius' mind, would be planning his final strike against his bitter enemy. What other choices would he have? John would know that the only way out was to be slain in battle or marched in chains to be led in a triumph in Rome. What little hope he had clung to, would have been swallowed up into a black abyss once his forces had been put to flight and slaughtered in the Temple courts. John had to know the end was near, like a wounded beast struggling in a pit of mire, watching with panic as its blood soaked the ground. However, the warlord from Gischala was a proud warrior, and with his pride, he would be a man desiring to choose his own fate, dying with honour.

"Are you praying to the gods or hoping the Jews surrender?" Marcus Sulla asked as he approached Gaius with a smile.

"I was considering what John of Gischala would be planning if I was him," Gaius nonchalantly replied.

"And what would you be preparing for if you were in there?"

Gaius was still as he watched the shadows upon the Temple walls. "The final glorious act. I would charge out and try to catch the enemy sleeping."

Marcus bobbed his head in agreement. "That is his only chance. We both know John will not surrender. He could try and fight his way south and flee into the Lower City, but that is all destiny has given to the stubborn man."

"And leave the Temple to us?" Gaius retorted, shaking his head. "I can't see John doing such a thing, not after defending the Temple for so long."

"Yet, in the end man is man, Gaius. John will look into his soul and desire to live before death." Marcus was quiet as he reflected on his philosophical advice. "What are you doing wandering out here?"

Gaius shrugged, a part of him not wanting to have this conversation. "I searched the Zealot dead, Marcus. Judah ben Yosef is not to be found."

"Why would you be searching for him?"

"Do you believe, that men who have fallen from favour, should be granted another chance by the gods?"

"I do not take much stake in the sensitive mercy of the gods, but I do like to think that men worthy of fortune and grace, yet who have lost much, should find peace and chance."

"Like you have?" Gaius whispered and Marcus half nodded. "Ever since I met Judah ben Yosef there was something I sensed from the man. Beyond the hurt, anger, and hatred for *Roma*, there was something that pricked at my conscience and plagued my mind. Perhaps, he is a man worth saving. To spare his life and offer him a new one, a fresh beginning." Gaius glanced at Marcus who was deep in thought. "I would like to know, when I return to *Roma*, that there was one thing that I was able to change for good in this forsaken land. I have the power, Marcus, to give such a token to change a man whose destiny is but death. I would like to give that to Judah. I have searched the faces of the gods and that of my ancestors for answers to such dribble, but I have found nothing. So, alas, I am left only with this one thing that beckons upon my heart."

"It is a noble wish, Gaius, but even if you could find Judah and offer him this freedom, would he take it?"

Gaius looked back at the glowing firelight upon the Temple's face, as if he was mesmerized by the glamour. "I will not know until I ask him to his face."

"A man like Judah has nothing left to live for, Gaius. He is liable to venture south to join up with the Zealots at Herodium or Masada," said Marcus as he laid a heavy hand upon his friend's shoulder.

"Then I will take him as a slave until this war is finished, then set him free."

"He could slit your throat if you did that."

"He is a man of honour." Gaius chuckled and stared down at the ground.

"What is it?"

Gaius looked at Marcus with a baffled grin and sighed. "I have just never said such a thing about a Zealot before, let alone have had a desire to spare a Zealot. It is in the hands of the gods, I suppose. We appease them, offer sacrifice to their names, and then drink the pain away before heading into battle. What do we trust more, the gods or wine?"

"Dionysius never let me down," Marcus replied with a grin. "Come back to my quarters and share in a drink with me. Let us leave the misery of this night and its dark questions for Hades to mull over. We have brighter things to look upon. At dawn, my dear friend Gaius, we shall capture the Temple!"

* * *

CHAPTER LXII

August 2nd, 70 A.D. / 9th of Av, 3830
Temple Mount
Outer Court
Dawn

The morning brought with it a cool air and a thin, eerie veil of fog. Dew soaked the stones and turned stains of dried blood into pink hues. Legionary guards wrapped themselves in their heavy cloaks as they stared with exhausted eyes at the silent Temple walls of the Inner Court. Drums began to beat within the courtyard as cohorts assembled to the shouts of centurions and optiones that rallied the men into large formation blocks of organized centuries. Beyond where the cohorts assembled, the Temple remained surrounded by a large encircling column of troops, four-men deep, who rested their scuta upon the stones and held spears as they faced the bolted gates of the Inner Court and stared at the vacant rooftops.

A sense of determination filled the air as the drums continued to roll and a single blast of trumpets echoed from the high colonnades at the backs of the formed cohorts. Titus appeared from the northern portico riding upon Achilles as Tiberius and the other generals followed. He raised his fist in the air with an exuberant smile and the legionaries praised him with a deafening shout as the crescendo of drums pounded louder.

Twelve cohorts, drawn from the Fulminata and Macedonica, had been assembled, and they stretched from the rubble of the northwestern corner to the high columns of the Royal Stoa. Their checkered formations were impeccable and the lines of men remained drawn up in tight quarter as the Prince rode victoriously down the face of the front ranks. Titus humbly bowed as he passed the First Cohort of the Fulminata on the far right and watched as the eagle bearing the inscription of *SPQR* was raised along with the battle standards.

"Men of *Roma*, legionaries of the Fulminata and Macedonica! Today you stand upon the sacred ground of the Jews, ready to seize honour and glory and to crush this rebellion! You have sojourned with me these months and have fought countless battles throughout this land. The gods have watched over you, kept the dignity of the legions, and restored honour where it is due!" Titus shouted as he dug his heels into Achilles' flanks and rode past the ranks of men who raised their spears to salute their Prince. "You have given everything, yet I ask you to give more!" Titus drew back on his reins and pointed to the Temple. "The great Temple of the Jews stands before you, occupied by an army of trapped, desperate men! You have beaten them before and trounced upon their ranks. You have scattered them into the wind and struck them down in droves.

"Now, I ask you to do this once more and capture this prize of glory! When you return to *Roma* and unfurl your standards, banners and hoist the eagles high in parade, people will worship and applaud you as immortals. Feasting and drinking will last for weeks, women will beg you to lie with them, and you will fatten yourselves on all that is good, as worthy legionaries and warriors of the greatest empire the world has ever known!"

A loud cheer rose up as the men praised Titus, feeling like gods. "When I brought you here, a city of great strength and resolve stood before you. It taunted you and scoffed at your power. Yet, now we have gathered here, from crossing ashes and rubble that were once proud walls, towers, and fortresses. You have conquered the impossible, cast down the enemy, and destroyed the greatest obstacle we have come across in these distant lands from home. The gods of *Roma* will only favour the bold and strong. You men have become immortal on this day, and you men have defied the God of the Jews and will show the enemy the bite of your steel!"

* * *

It had taken the Zealots hours to find enough timber to be used to burn the wooden door to the dungeon where Judah, Adam, and Moshe remained. John had first sent his men to the Wood Chamber to gather timber for the fire. However, when they had returned empty handed, the men had taken to dismantling sections of roofing within the Chamber of Hewn Stone to scrounge up enough timber to fire the door. Once in piles, the Zealots had quickly realized that the beams were too long to get down into the tunnel, mostly due to the spiral stairs. So a number of small hatchets had been found and John had set them to work cutting the wood into pieces.

As the men chopped and hacked at the stout timber, John had paced within the council hall furious and enraged at the predicament that festered within him. He shouted and cursed when the men became tired, and called for more soldiers to help until the long wooden beams were reduced to splintered pieces, each a metre long. Once the wood was carried down into the tunnels, John had them piled before the locked door and called for pitch and fire. However, when no pitch could be found, curses had reverberated throughout the cramped tunnel as John shouted and kicked the door.

Without pitch to ignite the dried wood, John sent men back to the Chamber of Hewn Stone to break apart chairs and benches and bring scraps of kindling. These splinters and shavings were soon piled about the beams of chopped wood as two Zealots worked furiously with a torch to ignite the trap. Smoke swirls collected about and a tiny fire began to crackle, yet the damp ground and lack of air soon squelched it, causing John to roar angrily. Finally, as dawn began to split across the horizon, John sent a group of Zealots back up to tear down the heavy, expensive curtains that hung in the council hall, to be hastily brought down to burn.

As the folds of cloth were cut and torn to be woven throughout the dried wood, John gazed through the barred window and shook his head at the sight of Judah staring back at him. "Give yourself up, Judah! It mustn't end like this!" John shouted as a torch was finally buried into the heavy silk curtains, reduced to strips of shredded, torn, cloth. John glanced down at the fire and then grinned as smoke began to rise. "It is over, you coward!"

The fire hungrily ate at the silk until flames began to rise and catch upon the dried wood. Within moments the kindling glowed and smouldered as the heat increased. Soon choking black smoke was trailing between the iron bars of the door and filling the prison block. John took a step back and smiled. He had never guessed that Judah's verdict would play out such as this, but he felt appeased all the while as he watched the smoke thicken and cover the door separating his world from that of Judah's.

"John, you must come quickly!" called a soldier from the last step of the spiral stairs.

John scowled as he turned away from the smouldering fire and pushed his way through his Zealots. "What is it?"

"The Romans have gathered and Titus is speaking to them." The look upon the soldier's face was that of fear as he squeezed the hilt of his sword with white knuckles.

John's alertness piqued and he angrily turned with a growl. "All of you, with me now!" His eyes scanned the cluster of men and then he pointed at two. "You men stay here and guard the fire." John quickly followed the soldier up the stairs with his Zealots and when they emerged into the Chamber of Hewn Stone he instantly heard the roll of battle drums. Bursting from the chamber he was greeted by hundreds of nervous faces as Zealots armed themselves and scurried around. Many even walked within the Court of the Priests without care, passing clusters of wailing priests who were gathered around the Burnt Altar which was vacant of any sacrifice. High Priest Phanni ben Samuel, who stood next to the Laver, shouted pointlessly at the fearful men to show respect and clear the court, but it was useless.

John gazed up at the rooftops across the court and quickly passed an order for them to be strengthened. He heard a blast of trumpets and the noise of cheering rise. Feeling anxious, John quickly ascended up to the southwestern ramparts above the Kindling Gate accompanied by a group of sixty fighters. The sight was terrifying as Romans in the thousands filled the Outer Court as they boldly faced the rear of the Temple. John counted twelve cohorts and cringed as he did the calculations in his head. He scanned the wall of soldiers that circled around the Temple and watched as they held their locked shields together and lowered their spears. Dozens of artillery engines were loaded and ready, as John gazed at their crews who stood waiting nearby for the command to unleash their deadly projectiles.

John heard a nervous murmur rise from the lips of his frightened Zealots, yet he could not muster the courage to face them. Courage seemed to hang by a thread and John suddenly felt afraid and vulnerable. He clutched the hilt of his sword, his mind swirling with grim scenes of agonizing death and destruction. He watched as Titus rode up and down the columns of formed legionaries, shouting at them and pointing to the Temple wildly. John could only imagine what the proud Roman Prince was saying.

The legions were preparing to assault the Temple, it was obvious. Yet, John knew if his men remained, the Temple would surely be destroyed and burned as the battle would be vicious and bloody. However, if they tried to fight their way to the south, fleeing through the gates beneath the Royal Stoa, they might be able to make it to the Lower City to survive and the Temple would be spared. It would not need to be destroyed. John mulled the thought over in his mind and gazed to the south, surveying the thin line of legionaries that surrounded the Temple. With a great host of men, the Zealots could smash through the defensive line and escape would be possible. Of course many would be killed, but it was possible.

John swallowed the lump in his throat and tried to calm himself. His stomach churned and for a brief moment he felt like he would wretch upon the stones. He cursed under his breath, then turned to his men and led them back down to the Court of the Israelites.

"Gather all the soldiers now! Everyone to me!" John shouted as he passed the Burnt Altar and hurriedly entered the Court of the Women followed by the surviving hordes of his fighters. John moved to the centre of the court and held up his hands as silence gripped anxious faces.

"Men, faithful Jews. There is no time to tarry, nor to pray, for the enemy is upon us. But cast your eyes to heaven, beg Meshiach to come now, and let us go out and meet the enemy. Right now Titus is drawing up his legions and soon there will not be a chance for us. But listen to me, if we dash out in two groups through the Southern Gate and Eastern Gate we can smash through their pathetic defensive line and make our way to the Royal Stoa.

"If we stay here and fight, the Romans will burn the Temple and destroy her, but if we flee to the Lower City, the Temple might be spared and we can regroup and resume the fight. With Simon's forces we can recapture the Temple. But please, you must decide now! There is little time. You have been the most loyal and brave soldiers ever to take up a sword and spear, and now God watches you and tests you. What will you do? Will you fight?" A chorus of voices thundered and shook the Inner Court and John drew his sword and raised it in the air. "Prepare to move out!"

John moved with haste through the crowd towards the Eastern Gate and felt sweat begin to moisten the sides of his head as the air felt stifled. He nodded firmly at the men he passed, as he patted their shoulders, feeling emotion well up inside of him. It had finally come to this, a desperate and disorderly charge for freedom. John knew most of the men would be killed. He had seen the vast amount of legionaries gathered, but he also knew that this was the last thing the Romans expected.

As John reached the Eastern Gate, six men carried away the locking beam and the Zealot army slowly approached the massive doors. With sword drawn and ready, John outstretched his left hand and touched the beautifully crafted wood of the gate directly before him. It felt cold to his touch and a shiver rippled down his spine as he stared up at the blue sky and took a deep breath. He felt guilt overshadow him at the thought of leaving the Temple to the Romans, but he justified the fact that it was better to continue fighting than to perish in a smouldering tomb that was sure to be the Temple.

"John, the priests are staying," whispered a soldier who came alongside the warlord.

"Then they will all die," John replied, as he continued to focus on the beauty of the sky. Tears clung to his eyelids and his face felt the gentle rush of a breeze. He sighed greatly and looked to the man. "Are the men at the Southern Gate ready?" The man nodded and stepped aside as John turned to face his army. Then with a mournful voice, John sang, "*Shema Yisrael, Adonai Elohenu, Adonai E'chad!*"

John's chest felt weighted down and heavy with remorse and he shouted, "Push hard for the south! May HaShem bless you!" Then he picked out one of his officers and said, "Lead them, Eliahu, I will follow behind."

The defensive line of legionaries which surrounded the Temple did not expect what suddenly confronted them. As Titus' speech was drawing to a close two large gates of the Inner Court suddenly swung open and like a maddened surge of fury, hundreds of Zealots quickly descended the stepped terraces of the balustrade with blood curdling screams. The legionary line met the attack with a sudden hurl of their pila followed by the scrapping of swords from their scabbards as the gap was closed within seconds and the two pronged Zealot attack slammed into their thin ranks.

For a single moment the legionaries held the Jews. Then like water exploding upon rocks in every direction, the desperate Zealots pushed their way through, hacking legionaries into pieces, and continuing on as the Jews ran as fast as they could to the south. However, at the sight of the charging Zealots, Titus instantly thrust his cohorts into action and the Fulminata thundered across the flagstones, severing the Jewish assault from the Southern Gate. The Macedonica was slightly slower to react, but soon they completely overwhelmed the Zealot formations determined to reach the Hulda Gates.

Gaius Antony knocked a wild Zealot aside with his shield and plunged his sword into the man's chest before retracting the blade and shoving him over. He quickly blocked a spear thrust with his scutum and leapt forward slashing his gladius at the attacker's face. "Hydra Herculean form up and move with me!" Gaius shouted as his legionaries pressed in around him, pushing the Zealot attack backwards to the southern walls of the Temple. A legionary shrieked beside Gaius, and pitched back with an arrow through his throat. Soon, the century's shields were overlapped into a testudo as they approached the Temple walls steadily killing the Zealot fighters until blood was running between the feet of the legionaries.

"Give them a volley!" Gaius bellowed and the rear ranks of his century hurled their pila up at the Jewish archers upon the rooftops which scattered them. "To the Temple! Push!" Gaius buried his blade into another Zealot and pulled it out as the man crumpled to his knees, gritting his teeth and trying to grab Gaius' shield. He shook himself free from the Zealot's grasp and plunged his blade again into the man, this time severing his spine and puncturing his lung. The dying Zealot screamed and tried to fight against the blade as blood bubbled and spewed from his mouth. Finally a legionary next to Gaius leapt upon the man, stabbing him until he was dead.

The sound of battle echoed loudly about the court as the Fulminata First Cohort drove the Jews back by the weight of their sturdy shields. Behind their ranks, the legionaries left piles of dead and dying men strewn about as the flagstones became slick with blood and bodily fluids. Men shouted and cursed savagely as they fought.

Inside the Temple Courts, the priests began to panic with hysteria as smoke billowed out of the Temple's windows on the southern side, many rushing inside to try and douse the flames. A legionary next to Gaius shouted with excitement at the smoke which poured from the gigantic Temple and for a moment Gaius hesitated, staring with gaping eyes.

"Centurion Gaius! A legionary has hurled a firebrand through the window. The Temple is burning!" yelled Centurion Quintus Cassius Aemilius from the Wolf Century as he moved down the line. "We must get into the Temple and open all the gates for the cohorts. Great plunder is in there and ripe for the picking!"

Gaius stared back at the sight of black spirals as smoke belched out from the edifice like a great monster of the underworld. Then suddenly an enormous flame erupted from the windows and Gaius felt a rush of heat upon his face. The Zealots fighting against his century, soon noticed the Temple, and in panic, they broke and fled in all directions. Gaius led his troops up the terraced steps and it felt like a dream as they poured through the Southern Gate where no Gentile had ever been allowed before. The legionaries quickly spread out like wild jackals as they began to kill everyone they found. Even women and children, who had taken refuge within the Temple, were cornered and slaughtered. Yet, for the priests, it was as if the threat of the blood thirsty legionaries did not exist as they wailed before the burning Temple, trying desperately to squelch the fire, even casting themselves into the burning flames with hysteric shrieks.

Gaius watched through the destroyed Nicanor Gates as a number of priests struggled with a golden table that contained stacks of bread upon it. Some of the men were badly burned as they had rescued it from the fire and they set it down upon the top of the sanctuary's steps, begging for mercy as they dropped to their knees with sobs at the sight of legionaries charging up towards them. Gaius watched as the priests were slain to a man, their corpses stabbed and slashed as they were left to bleed out upon the steps while the legionaries claimed their prize. At the sight of the gold table, other Roman soldiers began to proclaim that the Temple was filled with gold, and dozens rushed forward to save the sacred objects from the devouring flames.

Upon the Burnt Altar, its place of sacrifice had become crammed with priests, Zealots and women desperately trying to escape the slaughter around them. To the delight of the legionaries below, they began to hurl their spears up at the helpless victims atop of the altar, and force their way along the stone ramp, thrusting with their swords until their blades were dripping with blood.

*   *   *

Adam caught a glimpse, through the blanket of thick smoke, at the backs of the two guards fleeing through the tunnel and then he looked at Judah as he coughed. "Hurry, let's open the door. They are gone."

The three men rushed the door through the suffocating haze and slid the bolt back. Judah fumbled with the keys as he coughed and choked, but soon he found the one he wanted and unlocked the door. Then with a heave they opened the door and a pile of smouldering embers slid to the floor sending a whirl of sparks into the air. Adam screened his face from the smoke and spotting a piece of untouched timber, he pulled it from the fire. His eyes stung horribly, but he refused to back down. Using the timber beam, Adam pushed the burning pile of wood and cloth over onto the damp floor. The scattered flame hissed and coughed up a great billow of smoke so that the only danger that now existed was suffocation. With a desire to linger not a moment longer, the three men plunged through the smoke and ran through the tunnel, their lungs burning horribly and desperate for clean air.

When they reached the spiral stairs they took a moment to catch their breath. Judah spit a stream of black saliva upon the ground and rubbed his stinging eyes as he groaned. Next to him, Moshe wretched upon the ground and then wheezed. Adam stumbled up a few of the steps straining to see in the darkness, then raised a hand and called for the men to be quiet. A faint din could be heard, muffled and distant, but familiar. It was the sound of swords clashing and men shouting.

"The Romans have attacked," Judah mumbled, giving the others a despairing look. "We have to move now!" Judah stumbled past Adam and moved swiftly up the cold, damp stairs as he listened to the sounds of battle drawing closer. When they emerged into the small hall, adjacent to the Chamber of Hewn Stone, the sight of four horribly slain bodies lay sprawled upon the stones in pools of blood. Judah drew his sword and cautiously passed the bodies, hardly paying them any attention as he fixed his gaze upon the abandoned, open doorway.

"Oh, God, have mercy," Judah uttered as he stared at the piles of dead before him and the blood dripping down the sides of the Burnt Altar. He lifted his eyes to the mounds of corpses piled upon the top of the altar and the legionary standards that had been fixed upright by driving them into the bodies of the dead. A few legionaries cheered and waved their swords above their heads as they remained upon the altar, while a column of Roman soldiers carried the golden tables of the Showbread across the Court of the Priests, the bread scattered upon the ground and trampled.

"Blasphemy," Moshe gasped in horror as tears streamed down his cheeks. He stepped out in shock, his sword lowered at his side. He gazed up at the burning Temple and collapsed to his knees. "HaShem!" Moshe screamed with a wail as a few legionaries by the altar glanced his way, then ignored him as they tried to pry the copper Laver from the stones. At the sight of the Golden Incense Altar upon the shoulders of cheering legionaries, Moshe gave a grief-stricken glance back at Adam and Judah, then turned his blade inwards and fell upon it.

"Moshe!" Adam screamed, running forward a few steps, before halting at the sight of Moshe's crumpled body with the sword blade protruding from his back. Adam covered his mouth and looked at Judah who still had not budged.

"You should flee while their attention is fixed on gold, Adam," Judah mumbled with a numb voice as his eyes diverted over to the stream of blood forming around Moshe.

"You will stay?" Adam asked as tears wet his face. Judah humbly nodded and Adam approached him, embracing his friend within his great arms. "May you find peace with God, Judah."

"It is as your Rabbi Yeshua said it would be," Judah said, pointing up at the Temple roof as legionaries worked at prying apart stones in search for gold that had melted between them. Judah touched the side of Adam's bearded face and gave him a firm nod. "Go now and I pray the Almighty spares you."

Adam took a step back, his hands trembling and cheeks glistening with tears that flowed from his reddened eyes. "I shall never forget you, my friend."

Judah watched Adam turn and flee from the chamber as the sound of misery was restored to his ears. As if he was in a dream, Judah slowly stepped from the Chamber of Hewn Stone into the Court of the Israelites which was overrun by legionaries fighting the last remaining Zealots and the piles of dead which covered the ground.

Judah heard a sickening thud to his left and stared at the broken form of a priest lying prostrate with blood jetting outward across the stones. The priest's robes were scorched with fire and torn, yet Judah could tell the man had jumped from the Temple roof to his death. Next to where the Laver had finally been dislodged and ruined, lay Phanni ben Samuel, crumpled upon the bottom steps of the sanctuary with three spears lodged in his chest. Judah watched as a legionary bent down next to the High Priest and cut the jeweled breastplate free, holding it up with a shout of triumph to the cheers of a number of soldiers who carried silver trumpets.

Judah swallowed, his throat seeming as if it would close in upon itself from thirst. He gripped the hilt of his sword and made his way carefully under the cover of the pillars. The sound of flames broiling out from the Temple was like a great rush of thousands of tree branches blowing in the wind and Judah glanced behind him to the sound of laughter as legionaries filled the Court of the Priests, singing songs to Jupiter.

It was beyond all comprehension as he continued on with salty tears falling upon the stones. Judah followed the portico until he came to the dividing wall which separated the Court of the Women from the Court of the Israelites. He squatted upon the ground and stared at the ruined doors of the Nicanor Gate as he decided to wait for Gaius rather than venture out into the mayhem. The shields of the soldiers filling the courtyard before him were all of the Fulminata and he knew that due to Gaius' stature and rank, he could not be far behind. Judah did not exactly know what he would say to the Centurion, but he knew that finding out about Hadassah was all he cared about.

*   *   *

Having been driven back into the Temple when his army had charged the Roman lines, John of Gischala continued to fight like a wild man even when the Temple had begun to burn. He had led a cluster of his men against the first legionaries who poured through the Eastern Gate, and they had killed six Romans before they were swarmed. John had fled with only a handful of survivors and had taken to the rooftop above the Gate of the Flame Singers on the northern side of the Temple. From here, John bellowed challenges to the legionaries as he fought them with all the rage he could muster.

John set himself in a strong position before a set of stone steps that led up to the roof. As the legionaries emerged, he attacked them. After killing three, the Romans had become more cautious, jabbing at his legs with their spears so they could gain more room. Only eight Zealots remained with John and two of them were wounded as they were weak from a loss of blood. Finally a spear head slashed across John's upper thigh and he stumbled back with a great shout of anger. The emboldened legionaries surged forward, killing two of the Zealots as they poured upon the rooftop to battle the survivors.

John swung his sword until his muscles ached and burned, yet his scream was deep and guttural like a beast as he shoved, kicked, punched, and slashed. He sent one legionary reeling back with a shriek as he plummeted over the side to the stones below, then he cut another soldier across the left arm, causing the man to fall backwards. John had made up his mind. If he was to die here he would take as many Romans with him as he could. The sight of the burning Temple only fuelled him all the more and John bellowed his savage war cry, charging at three more legionaries emerging upon the roof. At the sight of the crazed Zealot, the soldiers fled and John was left alone. He turned around and gave a dark grin at the last surviving Zealot who lay propped up against the parapet, a dead legionary sprawled over his legs, and a flow of blood pouring from his chest.

John nodded to the man, feeling a rush of exhilaration at the sight of the dead Romans lying upon the roof. He had done this with his hands, this was his work. He had become like Samson to slay the cruel and wicked Philistines. John felt his chest heave up and down as sweat soaked the sides of his face, dripping from his beard. His arms and garments were streaked with blood, and crimson droplets speckled his face. John felt as if he had been bred for war. He had grown up in the north, his family living with great success in the oil trade, yet now he was a warlord, sharpened and refined through years of fighting. He had lost everything in life except for his undying hatred for Rome.

John spotted a blonde transverse plume upon the helmet of a Centurion who led a formation of legionaries through the Nicanor Gate. He focused on the Centurion, seeing the torques and medals hanging from the man's chest, as John felt his heart quicken and pound within his ears. John dropped his sword upon the ground, sensing the kill and craving it. He bent down and took hold of a discarded pilum lying beneath a dead Roman. John tested the strength of the shaft and admired its pointed iron head. He would hurl it with the intent to maim the Centurion, so that the officer would die days later in agony. John knew he had the force to punch the spear straight through the Centurion's breastplate and he smiled at the thought.

Quickly, John ran to the stairs and rapidly descended, carrying the spear firmly in his hand. When he reached the bottom, he stepped over a dead legionary and poked his head around the corner. He was near the Salt Chamber and the way was clear. He watched the Centurion halt for a moment as he began to give orders, directing men with his sword blade. John felt a seed of anger suddenly sprout forth and take over his mind. He glanced down one more time at the spear and then leaping out from his cover, he drew the pilum back and with all his fury hurled it, feeling satisfaction wash over him.

* * *

Judah had not a moment to hesitate when he saw John burst from the cover of the Salt Chamber with the spear extended in his arm and his eyes fixed on Gaius. Judah leapt forth with a shout, abandoning his sword. He charged past the Burnt Altar, ploughing into the back of Gaius which sent him sprawling upon the ground as the hurled pilum soared overhead and tore into Judah's chest. Judah pitched back with a shriek, feeling his body convulse horribly, as he instinctively gripped the shaft of the spear. The pain seared his body and he groaned, trying to sit up, but instead he rolled back clenching his jaw in agony. His body shuddered as a wash of blood rushed over him, spilling upon the stones. For an instant, Judah caught a blurry image of John of Gischala, standing motionless, mouth open, eyes wide with shock, before the warlord turned and fled.

"Judah!" Gaius quickly said as he was helped to his feet by a number of legionaries.

"That Jew saved you, Centurion!" commented one of the soldiers. "Strangest thing I ever saw. None of us saw the Zealot with the spear, forgive us."

Gaius ignored the pitiful apology and rushed to Judah's side as he knelt down and cradled the dying man. Gaius looked over the wound and grimaced as he wiped the blood away from Judah's pale face. Gaius could feel the heat of the Temple upon his back, yet for an instant he ignored it and stared down at the man who saved his life. He watched as Judah's eyes flickered while his lips slowly moved, and Gaius brought his ear close.

"Hadassah…where is Hadassah?" Judah whispered as he stared up at the face of Gaius.

"She lives. Marcus saved her, Judah," Gaius replied. "Don't move. I will send for help."

"No…it's over," Judah moaned cringing from the pain. His body shuddered again and a small fountain of dark blood oozed out from around the spear's shaft. Then a glazed look washed over Judah's face and he mumbled, "*Baruch atta Adonai, baruch atta Adonai.*"

Judah's breathing became raspy and he wheezed as he lifted his weak arm and outstretched it towards the burning Temple. Tears clung to the corners of his eyes as he watched a column of legionaries pass by carrying a golden menorah. Beyond the sight of the candelabra, legionaries worked to dislodge the Temple stones as gold ran like water into the cracks. Then for an instant Judah held his breath as his bloodied lips parted, and rippling in the lapping flames above the Temple, he saw the face of Miriam.

Gaius heard Judah's breath expire as his face softened and his eyes watered. As Gaius knelt upon the stones with the blood of Judah surrounding him, the legionaries cheered in unison, "Hail Imperator! Hail Imperator," at the sight of Titus Flavius Vespasianus entering through the Nicanor Gates upon his black horse. With jollity upon his face, Titus praised and waved triumphantly to his men. In the Prince's mind, Mars the bringer of war, had prevailed once again over the enemy. Titus thanked Jupiter, Basilides, and the Apis Bull, then gave orders for the Temple to be reduced to ruins and its stones to be hurled into the Tyropoeon Valley.

* * *

Now as He drew near, He saw the city and wept over it, saying, "If you had known, even you, especially in this your day, the things that make for your peace! But now they are hidden from your eyes. For days will come upon you when your enemies will build an embankment around you, surround you and close you in on every side, and level you, and your children within you, to the ground; and they will not leave in you one stone upon another..."

The Gospel according to Luke 19:41-44a

"How lonely sits the city that was full of people! How like a widow is she, who was great among the nations! The princess among the provinces has become a slave! She weeps bitterly in the night, her tears are on her cheeks; among all her lovers she has none to comfort her. All her friends have dealt treacherously with her; they have become her enemies. Judah has gone into captivity, under affliction and hard servitude; she dwells among the nations, she finds no rest; all her persecutors overtake her in dire straits. The roads to Zion mourn because no one comes to the set feasts. All her gates are desolate; her priests sigh, her virgins are afflicted, and she is in bitterness. Her adversaries have become the master, her enemies prosper; for the Lord has afflicted her because of the multitude of her transgressions. Her children have gone into captivity before the enemy."

The Book of Lamentations 1:1-5

*　*　*

HISTORICAL EPILOGUE

After the complete burning of the Temple and the destruction of the Lower City, Titus directed his legions against the Upper City and penned in the Jewish rebels on August 16th, 70 A.D. John of Gischala and Simon ben Giora requested a parlay for safe conduct, which was adamantly refused as new earthworks and ramps were constructed to capture Herod's Palace. During a bitter struggle, the Romans were able to breach the walls and the Jews fled abandoning the Hippicus, Phasael, and Mariamme Towers, which Titus spared to commemorate his victory. It was during these moments that many of the Zealots and Idumeans took to the underground sewers where most were trapped and slaughtered. Among the captured prisoners was John of Gischala, who was bound and shackled in chains to be deported to Italy where perpetual detention awaited him.

During the razing of the fortifications and destruction, a great fire spread throughout Jerusalem which consumed huge sections of the Upper City. In this time, Simon ben Giora also took to the sewers and underground vaults in an attempt to escape, yet emerged upon the Temple site and surrendered. By September 2nd, Jerusalem had finally been conquered by the Romans. Titus celebrated the hard-fought siege with a three-day feast praising the gods for the victory that had taken nearly 140 days. Client King Marcus Julius Agrippa had his kingdom extended, with all the other eastern kings paid handsomely and recognized for their efforts.

In this time, Jerusalem's surviving population was accounted for and processed. For this selection, prisoners were herded into the Temple courts, examined and sorted to be sold as slaves, gladiators, captives for the triumph, or those considered expendable. It was in this time that allegedly 11,000 people starved to death, but for the surviving Zealots, the old and the feeble, they were simply crucified or killed. For prisoners over the age of 17, they were sent to Egypt for harsh labour or to provincial arenas. The children were sold and scattered throughout the empire as slaves.

Simon ben Giora was tried and condemned by Titus and destined for Titus' Triumph in Rome, along with 700 impressive-looking captives and the Temple spoils. However, for Simon's fate, it was reserved for the Triumph where he was strangled to death before roaring crowds as a sign of victory and sacrifice to Jupiter Capitoline.

After the destruction of Jerusalem, Yosef ben Matityahu adopted the Roman name of Flavius Josephus, in honour of the Flavian family and Emperor Vespasian.

He settled in Rome and published his *Histories* that were circulated around the Roman Empire and contained Titus' stamp of approval for the exhaustive works. In his records, Josephus totalled the number of those who died in Jerusalem during the siege at 1,100,000 with 97,000 captured. Although likely an exaggerated number of casualties from Josephus, the Roman historian Tacitus placed the death toll of the besieged at 600,000, which is more persuasive.

The Fretensis X Legio remained in Jerusalem as a garrison and was overseen by Legate Sextus Cerealis. The bulk of the army returned to Caesarea Maritima where Titus held celebrations with gladiatorial games featuring the prisoners; he also held such games at Caesarea Philippi. Titus' father, Vespasian, and his brother, Domitian, had their birthdays marked in the same way: Domitian's on October 24th at Caesarea Maritima, and Vespasian's on November 17th at Berytus, Lebanon. For the victory, Titus also received a tribute at Zeugma as the Parthian king offered him a golden crown.

Following this, Titus marched south to Alexandria and organized the dispatch to Pannonia of his remaining legions: Macedonica V Legio and Apollinaris XV Legio. The Fulminata XII Legio made its way back to Antioch, Syria, and Titus finally returned to Rome in the spring of 71 A.D.

As for the final remaining Jewish strongholds, Herodium, Machaerus, and Masada, they would be dealt with swiftly. Legate Sextus Cerealis of the Fretensis dispatched his newly arrived subordinate, Sextus Lucilius Bassus, to eradicate the remaining Jewish defiance against Rome. Bassus captured both Herodium and Machaerus, but died in late 72 A.D. so that his command was turned over to Flavius Silva. General Silva marched the Tenth Legion through the desert of the Negev to Masada, which was a stronghold located upon the top of a mountain near the Dead Sea.

Masada stood as a formidable Zealot outpost which was occupied by 967 Sicarii under the command of Eleazar ben Yair. Silva faced unimaginable difficulties in taking Masada, and eventually had to construct a massive earthen ramp against the side of the mountain in order to breach the walls, using a twenty-five metre high siege tower. However, Silva was cheated from his victory as the Jews, rather than be taken as slaves, committed mass suicide except for two women and three children who hid in a water cistern under the northen palace.

Emperor Vespasian decreed the full measure of the *Pax Romana* upon the defeated Jewish people of the land. It instituted the following: no rebuilding of the Temple, no High Priesthood or ruling Sanhedrin, and the Temple tax, as paid prior to the war, would be paid directly to the Capitoline Jupiter, the Roman treasury, to cover monetary losses during the war. Through his harsh edicts declared upon the land by Vespasian, most Jewish land became Roman property and tenants of the Emperor. Yet, the seed of Roman hatred was not extinguished among the Jewish people, and therefore would continue to burn for years to come.

Vespasian ruled the Roman Empire until his death on June 23rd, 79 A.D. at the age of 69. He was succeeded by his eldest son, Titus. It was the young charmer, Titus, who commissioned public works throughout Rome, such as bathhouses and victory arches. Yet, the grandest project of all was the Flavian Amphitheater, or famously known today as the Colosseum, that began construction during Vespasian's seat of power and finished in the year 80 A.D. of Titus' reign. This huge building, capable of holding 50,000 spectators, was a shrine of victory commemorating the triumph of the Jewish Wars. It was inaugurated by 100 days of games which included: mock sea battles where the Colosseum was flooded, gladiatorial combat, fights between wild animals, and chariot races. However, Titus's reign was shortened when he died on September 13th, 81 A.D. at the age of 41, the cause suspected to be from poisoning by his younger brother, Domitian. It was Domitian who ushered in a terrible persecution for Christians throughout the empire as he ruled until his death at age 44, on September 18th, 96 A.D.

Despite the destruction of Jerusalem, Judaism continued to survive, sprouting forth upon the eastern shore of Judea in the town called Yavneh. It was here that Rabbi Yohanan ben Zakkai, along with Rabbi Shimeon ben Gamiliel, established a council of sages, similar to a Sanhedrin, where they restructured Judaism without a Temple. The salvation of Judaism was credited to these men, as Zakkai had gained favour in the eyes of Vespasian by making a prophecy concerning his emperorship. The Jewish faith would continue to survive as the synagogue took the forefront of the religious centre.

Always having a Jewish presence in the land, it was nearly 2,000 years later until the Jewish people once again would return en masse, and flourish in their native land. The land of *Eretz Yisrael* welcomed back hundreds of thousands of immigrants from all cultural backgrounds, to rebuild cities, till the land, and prosper. On May 14th, 1948 A.D. the State of Israel was reborn. In echoing the voice of the Bible's prophets, Jews from all across the globe have returned to make Jerusalem, once again, their eternal capital.

"It shall come to pass in that day that the Lord shall set His hand again the second time to recover the remnant of His people who are left, from Assyria and Egypt, from Pathros and Cush, from Elam and Shinar, from Hamath and the islands of the sea. He will set up a banner for the nations, and will assemble the outcasts of Israel, and gather together the dispersed of Judah from the four corners of the earth."

The Book of Isaiah 11:11-12

"The sound of noise from the city! A voice from the temple! The voice of the Lord, who fully repays His enemies! Before she was in labour, she gave birth; before her pain came, she delivered a male child. Who has heard such a thing? Who has seen such things? Shall the earth be made to give birth in one day? Or shall a nation be born at once? For as soon as Zion was in labour, she gave birth to her children. Shall I bring to the time of birth, and not cause delivery?' says the Lord. 'Shall I who cause delivery shut up the womb?' says your God. 'Rejoice with Jerusalem, and be glad with her, all you who love her; rejoice for joy with her, all you who mourn for her; that you may feed and be satisfied with the consolation of her bosom, that you may drink deeply and be delighted with the abundance of her glory.'"

The Book of Isaiah 66:6-11

AFTERWORD

The inspiration to write an epic account of the war over Jerusalem between the might of Rome and the undying will of the Jews has been a long, arduous journey. The mere size of the war and the complexity of the players always seized my attention as a youngster.

The ancient past brings with it a lure and a sense of mystery. Its appearance is majestic and incredible when one examines how people lived, fought, struggled, built, and worshipped. My desire to express this reality upon the pages of a book in the 21st Century is the challenge I undertook four and a half years ago. It is with dedication and solidarity to the Jewish people that I wish to tell their story. It is a story which enshrines indifferent cruelties with feats of human courage, almost stretching to the brink of immortality. I truly feel I have wiped away the sands of time by bringing to life one of the most intense struggles of the ancient world, the first Jewish war with Rome.

The extent of my research began by visiting the primary sources revolving around the First Century A.D. Right away I chose to give the book a traditional feel by using the Gregorian term "A.D." rather than the modern historical term "C.E.". At first glimpse, I had a desire to tell the *entire* narrative of the Jewish rebellion against Rome, which started in the year A.D. 66. However, I quickly discovered this to be too exhaustive to compile into a single book. So, I decided to begin with the latter half of the year 69, when Vespasian was declared '*Imperator*' by his troops, and end with the fall of the Temple.

As for the primary sources, Yosef ben Matityahu, or commonly known as Titus Flavius Josephus (as his name was Romanized in 71 A.D.), is by far the most sought after historian from this time period. This is due to the fact that he witnessed the events of the siege of Jerusalem and saw its destruction. However, one must keep in mind that Josephus' histories were published and commissioned by Titus, later to become the emperor after his father, and so Josephus' approach is biased, careful never to present Titus in a poor light. Titus is seen as the hero who constantly rides in to save his troops and is pictured as lamenting about what to do about the Jewish Temple, whether to save it or condemn it to destruction. I naturally have torn through this bias and attempt to paint Titus for who he was according to other sources, largely aided by the Roman historian Suetonius and his work, *The Twelve Caesars*.

Titus was known as a charmer and a womanizer. He was a young man when he arrived upon Mount Scopus and gazed down upon the city of Jerusalem in the spring of A.D. 70. It was to be his first real command and he wanted to prove himself. As the son of the emperor, he had a lot of favour, yet his will was to be loved by the troops and appear as a valiant general. We know that he did take part in some of the skirmishes against the Jews, yet his appearance as a merciful man in Josephus' writings would have had its limits as I have clearly drawn out in the novel. Titus was interested in destroying Jerusalem and crushing the resistance, and he hurled his legions against the city which resulted in enormous casualties. He was also prone to fits of anger and sheer brutality against impoverished Jewish refugees that either fled or were captured.

Titus was a Roman who believed in many gods, although I have chosen to present him as a little wary and cautious at first against the God of the Jews. However, in all reality he would have cared very little for the Jewish God believing his own deities to be stronger. Thus, my argument in the novel is that he really did not care about the future of the Jewish Temple and might very well have order it to be razed. Josephus presents the Temple's destruction as an accident from an unnamed trooper, but more than likely Titus may have done it anyway had the Jews surrendered. However, absolute proof of this may never be known as it is still a debate among historians concerning whether or not Titus ordered its destruction beforehand.

Studying sources such as Caesar, Cicero, Livy, Polybius, and Tacitus have helped me in shaping the complexity of the Roman military system, their pantheon of deities, lifestyle, campaigns, and interaction with the world around them. As well as a host of secondary sources, I dove into the Roman world in order to bring it to life and present the reader with an accurate picture of the Roman army on campaign. I have interwoven into the novel, not only the planning and strategy of Roman siege warfare and tactics, but the political sphere in the unstable year of the four emperors.

For a brief coverage of the pagan system of Rome, it is simple yet complex. It is simple in the basic idea that they had a god or goddess for everything in life: love, victory, war, bad dreams, deception, valour, farming, drinking, storms, sunshine, underworld, misery, joy, peace, flowers, water, food, etc. Their belief in the favour from these deities was also simple, in that since they ruled the world their gods must be stronger and mightier than those of their neighbours. This idea that the gods only blessed the strong was embedded in their myths, philosophy, and cult practices. Rome had a priesthood that centred around the Jupiter Capitoline (comparative to Zeus) in Rome, and honoured their deities in both times of war and peace. Since belief in their gods and goddesses was woven into the fabric of life, it is expected that this would be expressed vividly in how they conducted war. In the novel we see numerous times where deities are consulted through prayer, music, charms, images, burning of incense, and animal sacrifices. It was common for the Roman priests to play music, chant, and decorate the animal destined for sacrifice as it was a gesture to gain the god's attention and bring favour upon the legions.

For Vespasian, history shows us that he was a mystical man, who possessed a dedication to the deities of Rome, but also the pantheons of the Orient, particularly Egypt. Vespasian, as mentioned in the book, was honoured in Egypt and attended ceremonies in their temples and made inquiries to Egypt's priests. Suetonius narrates a number of stories, which are made to declare in a prophetic light, that Vespasian was destined to become emperor. This is colourfully declared by an oracle on Carmel, a lumbering ox at a party, and prophecies made by a rabbi and Josephus himself.

Moreover, there is a bizarre encounter told of Vespasian visiting the pagan temple to Serapis in Egypt and having a visitation by a spirit named Basilides, or Son of the Monarch. Basilides hints at Vespasian becoming the future emperor and it is from this I created his benevolent and dutiful following of the spirit, including the visions and dreams he has which would not be out of custom with that time period, nor Vespasian's nature as a superstitious man.

To complete my thoughts on the Roman side of the novel, many of the characters were real flesh and blood people. The entire Roman high command in the novel are all based on real people, save for Marcus Tullius Octavian, who is the general of the Twelfth Legion which I had to create because he is unknown in the history books. Apart from that, Gaius Cornelius Antony and the Boars are completely fictitious, along with the decurion trio and their steadfast, warrior tribune, Marcus Sulla Maximus. I created Marcus and his Boars to give credence to the effectiveness of the Roman cavalry in wiping out much Jewish resistance in the interim period prior to Emperor Nero's death in 69 A.D.

For my research of the Jews of Judea, Samaria, Galilee, and Idumea, it was not so easy. First of all, the three years of revolt prior to the beginning of the novel were essential in laying the foundation for where we find the Zealots and fictional characters at the beginning of this novel. When I began my early stages of research to formulate the story there were just too many facets to cover in relation to what was happening. I had to go from a broad perspective and zero in on what I wanted to capture. Thus, my main task was to add flashbacks with characters recalling what had happened, either from the Jewish or Roman point of view, in order to fit together all the pieces of the past so the reader could understand the background.

Unlike the Roman story, which is quite orderly, understanding the Jewish developments and involvements in the rebellion against Rome was complex and chaotic at times. As I researched the early roots of the rebellion, it was easier to lay out the folds with the appointment of the United Provisional Government, the choosing of generals, and the Jewish preparations for the arrival of the legions. I mainly cover this with personal moments of reflection for Yosef ben Matityahu (Josephus), or reminiscing between warlords and soldiers. The recollections of Yosef ben Matityahu with his capture at Jotapata, and his hideout in the cave where he convinces the other Jews to commit suicide rather than be taken captive, is true according to his own histories and retelling of the event. Other points in the novel where I have him interviewing prisoners or his prophetic claim that Vespasian would be emperor are also true in as much as they are recorded by the real Josephus.

In covering the Jewish factions, the historicity is as exact as I can present it. Our best source remains to be the histories of Josephus. Whether in Josephus' accounts or other Jewish and Roman sources, by the time the legions under Titus arrived at Jerusalem the Jews were divided into three armies commanded by different competing warlords: Simon ben Giora, Eleazar ben Simon, and John ben Levi, otherwise known as "John of Gischala." This novel presents the complexities of this inner civil war in a very descriptive and detailed manner, with many obvious fictional elements interwoven to give it more colour and life. Josephus provides record that all three were engaged in bitter fighting and skirmishes prior to the Roman arrival and even at sporadic times during the siege, with John having the upper hand as he held command of the Temple Mount. My descriptions of John's men capturing the Temple sanctuary from Eleazar and the method in which it was done is based on historical research, however the hurling of stones to crush men in the underground chambers was invented. Along with this, all of the skirmishes between John and Simon and much of their meetings are also loosely based on fact, although I still had to invent the places of engagements, names of soldiers, and much of the dialogue.

I found laying out the story of Jerusalem the most challenging. Introducing Judah ben Yosef into the mix was not as complicated compared to describing the relationships between the three warlords and their armies in such a way to keep the reader on edge by creating a sense of tension, suspicion, and reality which I wanted to exist. Josephus' descriptions of the civil war are detailed, and his telling of the horrible sufferings of many of the civilians is stated over and over as thousands of people lacked food, water, and other basic surviving needs. The points in the book where bodies are being dumped over the walls, my descriptions of the terrible conditions of the Lower City, and even the woman who devours her roasted infant child are all based on historical telling of Josephus.

All my descriptions and research concerning the Temple and its courts and colonnades are based directly from personal research compiled from: the Temple

Institute of Jerusalem, Second Temple Scale Model at the Israel Museum of Jerusalem, the Shrine of the Book Museum, the Israel Museum, the Davidson Archaeological Center of Jerusalem, the Bible Lands Museum of Jerusalem, the Burnt House Museum, Herodium Park, and personal notes and tours through the Western Wall Tunnels and many visits to the Temple Mount itself. Descriptions of Temple tools, implements, and sacrifices are based on rabbinic research and other primary sources that I have been able to describe and bring to life within the novel. As well, I have consulted over one hundred secondary sources to create and reshape the world of the First Century to bring it to life for the reader.

All geographical descriptions of Second Temple Jerusalem and the land of Israel during the First Century are based on extensive research with firsthand visits and hikes through the valleys of Jerusalem, upon Mount Scopus and the Mount of Olives, as well as extensive trips into northern Israel and the Negev desert to the south. Further research was conducted by visiting Roman archaeological ruins in Israel such as Beit She'an, Masada, and Jerusalem. I also traveled to Italy on two occasions to tour such sites as Pompeii, Firenze, the forum in Roma, *Castel Sant'Angelo*, Arch of Titus (*Arco di Tito*), *Circus Maximus*, Colosseum, Palatine Hill, *Musei Capitolini*, *Musei Vaticani*, *Museo Archeologico Nazionale di Napoli*, the *Galleria degli Uffizi*, and the Archaeological Museum in Syracuse. I was also fortunate to travel to Malta where I conducted additional research on ancient Rome by visiting the National Musuem of Archaeology in Valletta, the Gozo Museum of Archaoelogy, as well as the National Museum of Natural History in Mdina.

In closing, my desire has been to resurrect one of the darkest periods in Jewish history and tell it as historically accurate as possible. This novel is written as an epic chronology of history and I have infused it with characters that experience the dirt, blood, sweat, and horrific sights of war nearly two thousand years ago. I hope this novel will bring the reader closer to understanding not only the time period, but also what Jews and Romans sought to overcome, and what both sides were fighting for. I try to present people as three dimensional and I trust their lives and experiences are read with the same life I have sought to give them.

Peter J. Fast

GLOSSARY OF TERMS

Latin: Terms are given in singular and plural forms where necessary (i.e. *scutum/scuta*) followed by its definition. Latin terms appear, in some cases, as author's pronunciation/spelling. *Latin phrases are translated by author.

Hebrew: Terms are written phonetically and appear, in some cases, as author's pronunciation/spelling. Hebrew words have been organized in singular and plural formats (i.e. *Shofar/Shofar'ot*) and are followed by its definition. *Hebrew phrases are translated by author.

Latin

Alae: Term used to denote allied auxiliary contingents, both mounted and foot.
Alea iacta est: Latin translation "The die is cast."
Amulae: Latin term for a battle decoration for bravery.
Anno domini: Medieval Latin devised in the year 525 A.D. but not used consistently until 800 A.D. meaning, "In the year of the/our Lord."
Aquilifer: The Roman term to denote the man who carried the golden eagle of a legion.
Aries: Latin term for the structure of a battering ram.
Auctoritatem/auctoritas: Latin for "authority."
Ballista/ballistae: An ancient missile weapon that could launch projectiles at a distant target.
Ballistarii: The Latin term to describe the artillerymen that operate the heavy catapult weapon known as the ballista.
Buccina: Is a Roman horn which is in the shape of a 'C.'
Caldarium: Was a room of extremely high temperature with a hot plunge bath and steam room.
Caligae: These were heavy-soled, hob-nailed military boots worn by both Roman legionaries and auxiliary troops throughout Roman history.
Campus Martius: Latin for the "Field of Mars" which was the military conscription, drill and parade grounds for the city of Roma.
Centuria/centuriae: Latin word for "tribe or company." One of six smaller detachments of soldiers (80 men in each century) that make up a cohors (cohort). There are ten cohors in a legion and all but the First Cohors have six centuria. The First Cohors has five centuria of 160 men in each.
Centurion: The senior ranking officer in charge of a centuria.

Centurionate: Latin for a group of centurions.

Cingulum: Four to six leather or metal straps that hung from a Roman soldier's belt and were studded with iron rivets. This was both for show and also a psychological weapon for when a detachment of legionaries advanced the straps would jingle together creating an intimidating sound.

Cisalpine Gaul: Literally translated from Latin as "Gaul on this side of the Alps."

Cohors/cohortes: A Roman military formation "cohort" consisting of 480 men of six centuria to a regular cohort (cohorts 2-10) and five centuria in the First Cohort of 800 men. There are ten cohorts in a legion.

Colei: Latin word for, "testicles" and used in profanity.

Consul: The highest elected office during the Roman Republic and came to signify a general's rank during the Imperial period and held very little power as they once had.

Contubernium: Roman term which denotes eight men who live together, eat together and fight together.

Cornu: A large horn which curves around the horn blowers body and is held by a cross piece.

Cornucen: Is the name given to the horn blower of the instrument called a cornu.

Decurion/decurianes: A junior rank of a cavalry officer who commanded over thirty mounted troops.

Denarius/denarii: Latin term for "containing ten" which was a Roman currency system of small silver coins and was worth more than a sesterces.

Dolabra: Latin for a long iron pick tool that was used by Roman legionaries as a standard working tool for digging and breaking rock.

Dona: Latin translation for medals or awards won in battle.

Equites legionis: The Roman term for the cavalry wings of the legion.

Felicitatem: Latin for "good luck."

Fortis: Latin for, "strong, sturdy, brave, manly and resolute."

Fulminata: The name given to the Twelfth Legion which means "armed with lightning" or "Thundering/Thunderbolt."

Gladius/gladii: The customary Roman infantry sword with Spanish origins. It was a short sword with a blade two feet (24 inches) in length.

Hastatus: The Roman rank designated to the centurion elite of the Primi Ordines who commands the centuria second from the left of the First Cohort.

Hastatus posterior: The Roman rank designated to the centurion elite of the Primi Ordines who commands the centuria stationed on the extreme left flank of the First Cohort.

Hastatus prior: The Roman rank designated to the centurion commanding the century stationed second in from the far left of Cohorts II-X.

Hastile: The staff of office which is carried by an optio junior officer.

Hoplomachus: The Latin derivative of the Greek word (όπλομάχος) which takes its root from the Greek term (hoplon) which means "shield" and represents a type of Roman gladiator armed to resemble a Greek hoplite soldier. The hoplomachus would wear a bronze helmet, a manica (armour) on his right arm, loincloth, heavy padding on his legs, and a pair of high greaves. His weapons were the spear and a short sword and were often pitted against the murmillo to emulate the Roman wars in Greece and the Hellenist East.

Idem in me: Latin for, "the same for me," which is the closing recitation for witnesses to respond with after the sacred sacramentum is finished.

Ides: Latin meaning for, "day of the full moon."

Imaginifer: The Latin word designated to the soldier who carried the image/imagio of the emperor upon a standard.

Imagio: Latin word for "image".

Imperator: Latin translation meaning, emperor or king. Under the Roman Republic imperator took on the meaning of a commander or general.

Imperium maius: Latin for "degree of higher power/highest power."

Junius: Latin equivalent for the Roman month of June.

Jupiter Optimus Maximus: Latin translation relates to the god, Jupiter being, "all good, and all powerful."

Lanista: The Latin word for an owner (sometimes trainer) of gladiators.

Lanisticius: Latin term for the trainers of gladiators in official schools.

Legatus: Roman term for a general in the army.

Legio: Latin term (legion) ascribed to the Roman military army of ten cohorts, cavalry wings, and all ranked officers totalling between 5,000-5,500 men when completely up to strength.

Lituus: Is a Roman trumpet made from wood and covered in leather.

Lorica segmentata: Roman chest armour that consisted of plated scales overlapping one another for maximum protection and flexibility.

Mausoleum: Term used to describe an honorary tomb to enshrine the dead.

Merda: Latin word for, "excrement" and used in profanity.

Murmillo: Latin for a type of gladiator who wore a large, fish-shaped helmet, a loincloth, belt, greaves, arm-guards made from linen, and fought with a gladius and carried a scutum. Most often, the murmillo would face off with a thraex or hoplomachus in a death match as the strengths and weaknesses of the three warriors would all come into play.

Nonae: Latin meaning for, "day of the half moon."

Obol: Small silver or bronze Roman coin of a low value.

Onager/onagri: Roman middle-sized siege catapult capable of hurling up to 100kg stone projectiles.

Optio/optiones: A junior infantry officer that was stationed usually at the rear of a century and held a long staff called a hastile. It was the role of the optio to keep men in check, the lines straight, and orderly, and the ranks disciplined. In many cases if a centurion was to fall in battle, his rank and title may be passed to an optio of his company.

Orcus: Roman name for Pluto or Hades.

Paludamentum: The cloak that a general or aristocrat might wear which symbolizes their office and title.

Parmula: A small, round shield used by thraex gladiators.

Patrician: A rank of high nobility. A person would have to be a Roman citizen and someone of noble birth to gain this title.

Pax Romana: Latin translation "the peace of Rome/Romans."

Phalerae: A large metal-like bronze or silver disc worn upon the cuirass of an officer as a medal for distinguished conduct.

Picti: Translation being "Painted ones" which was a term the Romans branded to describe the Britons or Celts living in Roman Britannia.

Pilum/pila: The common Roman spear to be hurled at short distance. The pilum has a four foot triangular shaft of ash wood onto which is riveted a soft iron shaft 2.5 feet with a small, sharp point. The object is that the iron (softer then steel) will bend and contort when thrown into a victim or a shield making it impossible to retract the spear. This generally causes an enemy soldier to discard his shield.

Pilus posterior: The Roman rank designated to the centurion commanding the century second from the far right of Cohorts II-X.

Pilus prior: The Roman rank designated to the centurion commanding the century on the far right of Cohorts II-X.

Pontifex: Latin for "bridge builder" and is associated with and was a title for an individual who placates the gods and spirits of the Tiber River. This would later be assigned to the Emperor as Pontifex Maximus or translated as "the most powerful bridge builder."

Praefectus castrorum: Latin translation for Camp Prefect which is the third highest command in a legion.

Praefectus praetorio: Is the Latin title for a high ranking administrative and legal office in the Roman Empire. A man bearing this title would act like a Governor who would directly report to the Emperor on the ruling of a province as a chief aide.

Praetorian: The elite Roman guard to the emperor and police force of Rome.

Praetorium: A Roman commanders tent or magistrates/governors quarters in an occupied city or fortress.

Prefect: A magisterial title of high military command.

Primi ordines: A Roman term for a high ranking order of senior centurions of the First Cohort.

Primus pilus: Roman rank used for centurion of the First Cohors who commanded the centuria on the far right. Literal translation is, "First File."

Princeps: The Roman rank designated to the centurion commanding the century stationed second from the right of the First Cohort.

Princeps posterior: The Roman rank designated to the centurion elite of the Primi Ordines who commands the middle centuria of the First Cohort.

Principia: Latin term for the headquarters of a Roman fort or camp.

Procurator: Latin word for "governor."

Pugio: A short dagger carried by a legionary soldier upon his belt.

Rex: Latin word for "king."

Roma: Latin for the city of Rome, the capital of the Roman Empire.

Roma victa: Translated as "Roman Victory", or, "Victory for Rome."

Sacramentum: The Roman military oath among soldiers.

Sagum: A heavy Roman cloak usually dyed red.

Scientam rei militaries: Latin for "military knowledge."

Scutum/scuta: A large elongated shield, standard issue for all legionaries in the Roman military. A scutum generally stood four feet (48 inches) in height and was just under three feet (36 inches) in width. The shield was made to be flexible upon the edges and contained an iron boss in the center to both protect the hand on the opposite side and to be used to knock into opposing enemy soldiers.

Servus: Latin translation "to be spared" and most likely was a word attributed to taking prisoners as slaves which was seen, in Roman eyes, as someone losing their place in society as a 'person'.

Sesterces/sestertius: Latin term for "2 ½" and was a large brass coin common during the Roman Empire and used as payment in the legions for soldiers monthly pay.

Sica: The sica was a short sword, or long dagger that had a curved blade and was traditionally used by the Thracians and Dacians.

Signifer: The term to denote a standard bearer who carried the signum (standard) of a centuria.

Signum/signi: A Roman standard displaying regalia and symbols of either a personal nature or for a centuria of soldiers. The standard can either bear symbols of family history or inscriptions of battles fought, the names of gods honoured, or medals awarded.

Silent enim leges inter arma: Latin translation as "Laws are silent in times of war" which was penned by Marcus Tullius Cicero the great Roman orator (106-43 B.C.).

Spatha: A longer sword introduced in the first century by Celtic allies of Rome and generally used by the cavalry at its inception.

SPQR: Latin acronym for *"Senatus Populusque Romanus"* which means "The Senate and the People of Rome."

Stigma: A tattoo given to slaves or gladiators which deems them as property.

Tertius: The Underworld where Pluto resides.

Tessera: Is Latin for a messenger who would deliver orders between legions or units preparing for battle.

Tesserarius: A small tile or block of wood (could be inset with wax or a clay tablet) to inscribe orders/watchwords upon it.

Testudo/testudines: Latin term for "tortoise" which could describe either an armoured battering ram with plated roof (like a tortoise shell) or the infantry formation of overlapping shields above the soldiers heads to protect from spears, arrows, or falling rocks.

Thraex: Latin for "Thracian" was a type of gladiator armed with a small rectangular shield called a parmula and a short, curved sword known as a sica. The purpose of the sica was to maim the unarmoured back of an opponent. The thraex would also wear greaves, a protector for the sword arm and his shoulder, a protective belt, loincloth, and a helmet with a side plume, visor and crest. The thraex and the hoplomachus were usually paired against a murmillo which naturally mimicked a legionary fighting against foreign enemies.

Tribune: A high military rank (men of this status would also be of equestrian rank) often being attached to cavalry units or as commanders of cohorts.

Tubas: Roman military brass, long trumpet.

Tubicen: The Roman military term for a, "trumpeter."

Veni, vidi, vici: Latin for, "I came, I saw, I conquered."

Vexilliatio: Is the Latin term to describe a detachment of troops who are drawn from different units to fulfill a specific military purpose.

Vexillum/vexilla: Latin word for a military standard of cloth that is carried and hung from a cross bar attached to a lance.

Victrix: Latin word meaning "victorious."

Virtutem: Latin for "courage."

Hebrew

Abba: Hebrew word for "father."

Adonai: Hebrew word for "Lord."

Ba'al Zebub: Hebrew term for "Lord/Master of the Flies" which is a term given to the devil or Satan.

Bar-mitzvah: Hebrew for the age of a Jewish boy when he comes of age (13 years old) and is considered an adult and member of the community.

Baruch atta Adonai, Elohenu Melech ha'olam, boray pree hageffen, Omen: Hebrew prayer over the wine, "Blessed art thou oh Lord, King of the Universe who gives us the fruit of the vine. Amen."

Bat-mitzvah: Hebrew term for a celebration for the Jewish girl who turns thirteen and is considered of marriageable age in society.

Beit El: Hebrew for "House of God" and the name of a town which is also anglicised as Bethel.

Bezetha: Also called the "New City" in the writings of Flavius Josephus and to denote the northern area of Jerusalem beyond the Temple Mount.

Chametz: Hebrew word for "Leaven" which relates to the story of the Exodus were the Hebrews had to leave Egypt so quickly the bread was unable to rise and they were to clean their homes of leaven in Exodus 12:15.

Eretz Yisrael: Hebrew word for "Land of Israel."

Hakol L'Tovah: Hebrew means, "It's all for the best" or a form of hoping for good cheer.

Halakah: Hebrew for the collective body of Jewish law.

Hallel: Hebrew word for "praise" which is also a Jewish prayer that recites verbatim Psalms 113-118.

Hannukah: Hebrew term for Festival of Lights or Feast of Dedication.

HaShem: Hebrew descriptive of reverence for God simply meaning "The Name."

Ima: Hebrew word for "mother."

Kadosh L'Adonai: Hebrew for "Holiness unto the Lord".

Kinneret: Hebrew word for the body of fresh water in northern Israel also known as the Galilee or Sea of Tiberias.

Kipa: Hebrew word for a knitted skullcap worn upon the head by Jewish men as a symbol of reverence to God.

Ma nishtana: Hebrew word to signify the four questions ("Why is this night so different…") a Jewish boy asks this to his father during the Pesach Seder. This is usually sung.

Maror: Hebrew word for the "Bitter Herbs" the Jewish people eat during the Pesach Seder to remember the bitter tears of slavery in Egypt (Exodus 12:8) and passing through the Red Sea on dry land.

Menorah/menor'ot: Hebrew for "light" is also the seven branched lamp stand of gold found in the Jewish Temple and a universal symbol of Judaism.

Meshiach: Hebrew word for "messiah" or "anointed one."

Mezuzah: Hebrew word for "doorpost" which is to signify the small box/case that is attached to the doorpost, or built into the doorpost, that contains a small rolled up piece of parchment with the Bible passage from Deuteronomy 6:4-9, 11:13-21 which are inscribed upon it. Customarily it is secured on the right side pointing into the dwelling and as one would enter or exit they kiss their hand and touch it to the box or they may kiss the box directly.

Mikveh/mikva'ot: Hebrew term for ritual immersion in Judaism and means "collection" as in a collection of water.

Mishneh: Hebrew name for the "Second Quarter" in the ancient city of Jerusalem.

Mitznefet: Hebrew word for the turban, headdress or priestly mitre that the Jewish High Priest wore during Temple ceremonies.

Mitzvah: Hebrew word for "commandment" and associated with doing a good deed.

Mitzvoth: Hebrew word which refers to the precepts and commandments as commanded by God in the Torah which are 613 laws and rules.

Mizrak: A sacred cup on the end of a long handel used for Temple ritual.

Moriah: Hebrew form written as *"Moriyya"* which means "ordained/considered by the Lord" and was the name attached to the mountain in Jerusalem (Mount Moriah) where the Temple was built upon.

Nasi: Hebrew word which means "prince" and is associated with a member of the Sanhedrin.

Pesach: Hebrew word for "Passover" which is the feast that commemorates the story of the Exodus from Egypt in which the ancient Israelites were freed from slavery. It is one of the holiest of holidays for Jews and celebrated worldwide.

Purim: Hebrew term for the Feast of Esther or Feast of Lots.

Rabbi/rebbe: Hebrew term for "teacher" or "master."

Rosh Hashanah: Hebrew term for Jewish New Year, literally meaning, Head of the Year.

Seder: Hebrew word for "Order" and prescribed to Pesach as the meal has set order of symbols which are seen to before the partaking of the meal.

Shabbat: Hebrew word for "rest," or anglicised as "Sabbath" which is sundown on sixth day till evening on the seventh day of the week in the Jewish calendar. This is prescribed in the Bible as a holy day of rest and a commandment by God. This would fall on Saturday of the Gregorian calendar as the work week for Jews would begin on Sunday.

Shalom: Hebrew word for "peace" and was also used as a greeting and farewell.

Shalom Aleichem: Hebrew for "Peace unto you" and was used as a friendly greeting and prayer. The normal response of the recipient to which this was said to, was to reverse the words in response and say, *"Aleichem shalom."*

Shavuot: Hebrew term for the Feast of Weeks.

Sheen: The second last letter in the Hebrew alphabet (ש) and which also appears on the mezuzah which is attached to the doorpost of a Jewish home. In this case the *sheen* on the mezuzah represents the Hebrew word, El Shaddai which means, "God with us."

Shema: Hebrew for "Hear," which is short for the Jewish prayer, *"Shema Yisrael,"* which is, "Hear of Israel." This is taken from the Bible, Deuteronomy 6:4 and is considered the most observant prayer in the Jewish faith. It is part of morning and evening Jewish prayer services and is a declaration of what Jews believe.

Shema Yisrael Adonai Elihenu, Adonai Echad: Hebrew translation for "Hear, O Israel: the LORD our God, the LORD is one!" taken from Deuteronomy 6:4.

Sheol: Hebrew derivative for grave, pit, or abyss which is the earliest conception for the afterlife in the Bible.

Sheva: Hebrew word for seven. Also associated with someone who mourns over the death of a loved one for seven days (sitting sheva).

Shofar/ shofar'ot: Hebrew word for "horn" which was usually a ram's horn or during Temple ceremony could be a silver trumpet.

Shomreem: Hebrew for "watchman".

Shulchan aruch: Hebrew word for the covenant meal of Pesach (Passover) which literally means, "Set Table" but signifies the, "Covenant Meal of Reconciliation."

Sicarii: The name given to a Jewish splinter group from the zealots which meant "dagger-men." Sicarii is anglicised from Hebrew phonetic term, "sicric'im" (plural). Most likely came from the word, "sicae" which was a small dagger that could be easily concealed. These men were famous for political assassinations and to be very brutal against the Romans.

Sukkot: Hebrew term for Feast of Booths. Also called, Feast of Tabernacles or Feast of Ingathering.

Tallit/ tallit'ot: Hebrew word for a "prayer shawl" used traditionally by Jewish men in prayer (morning) on weekdays and worship on Shabbat and holidays.

Talmid Chacham: Hebrew term for "religious/wise student who follows a teacher."

Tamid: Hebrew word used for the chosen lamb for the daily ritual sacrifice.

Tefillin: Hebrew for the black prayer boxes (phylacteries) which a Jewish man secures to his left arm and upon his forehead. Attached to the box upon his arm is a long, black leather strap which is wrapped seven times around his arm and then secured in a special wrapping around his fingers. Inside the prayer boxes are five small slots which represent the senses. The box on the arm has one slot, and the box upon the forehead has four slots. The command to wrap tefillin comes from the Bible Deuteronomy 6:8.

Tehillim: Hebrew word for "praises" and is the word which is used to identify the Book of Psalms in the Bible.

Tikkun Olam: Hebrew word for, "repairing the world" which is the belief that every good deed and action has the ability to change the world for good.

Torah: Hebrew term for "law/instruction" or synonymous with "revelation" and given as a title for the first five books of Moses, which are contained in the Bible: Genesis, Exodus, Leviticus, Numbers and Deuteronomy. Torah can also mean "teaching" and represent the entire Hebrew Scriptures (Tanach) or Old Testament.

Tzitzit: Hebrew word for the "four stringed ritual tassels/fringes" which hang from a prayer shawl (tallit) and represent the 613 laws of the Torah. This is a command in accordance with what the Torah says in Numbers 15:38.

Yerushalyim: Hebrew word for "Jerusalem."

Yeshiva/ yeshiv'ot: Hebrew term for "religious school."

Yom Kippur: Hebrew for Day of Atonement.

Koine Greek

Elysium: Greek word for the afterlife which was a place men were sent to if they were chosen by the gods to live a happy and blissful life indulging in whatever employment they had enjoyed while alive on earth.

Eros: Greek word for "Desire" which was bound in erotic love. Also the equivalent of the Roman god, Cupid.

Gehenna: Greek word of the place derived from outside the ancient city of Jerusalem which is known in Hebrew as Gehinnom or "The Valley of the Son of Hinnom" where in the Bible (1st Chr. 28:3, 33:6; Jer. 7:31, 19:2-6) apostate Jews sacrificed their children into fires in the Hinnom Valley to various Ba'al gods of the Canaanites (Moloch). This term was to express a destination for the wicked as a place of burning, unquenchable fire.

Koine: Term for the Greek language type that was spoken in the time of the first century as the lingua franca (language of trade and commerce heavily influenced by Alexander the Great's conquests).

Hebrew Calendar

וְסִינָ: Nisan
רִיָּא: Iyyar
וְוָיִס: Sivan
זוּמַת: Tammuz
בָּא: Av
לוּלֵא: Elul
יְרְשָׁת: Tishri
וְוָשְׁחֶרְמַ: Marcheshvan
וּלֵסְכ: Kislev
תבֵט: Tevet
טבָשׁ: Shvat
רדָא: Adar

Edwards Brothers Malloy
Oxnard, CA USA
March 31, 2015